MARY
QUEEN OF SCOTLAND AND THE ISLES

A Novel

MARGARET GEORGE

St. Martin's Griffin
New York

With thanks to: my daughter, Alison Kaufman, and my husband, Paul Kaufman, for living with Mary for four years; my sister, Rosemary George, for historical tidbits and oddities; my mother, Dean George, for humour; my grandparents Charles and Lois Crain for being my Mme. Rallay; my medievalist friend, Lynn Courtenay, for source material; my writer friend Dick Huff for creative inspiration. And finally, to my editor, Hope Dellon, who was "present at the creation" of both Henry VIII and Mary, and has helped mightily at every stage; and my agent, Jacques de Spoelberch, who believed in me from the beginning.

Acknowledgments

Poem, "Nature and art . . ." by Joachim du Bellay, on page 63, translated from the French, as it appears in *The Queen of Scots* by Stefan Zweig, translated from the German by Cedar and Eden Paul. London: Cassell, 1935.

Poem, "The tongue of Hercules . . ." by Joachim du Bellay, on page 63, translated from the French and quoted in *The Love Affairs of Mary Queen of Scots: A Political History*, by Martin Hume. London: Eveleigh Nash & Grayson Limited.

Poem attributed to Mary Queen of Scots, on page 105, translated from the French and quoted in *Lives of the Queens of Scotland and English Princesses*, by Agnes Strickland, Vol. III. Edinburgh and London: William Blackwood and Sons, 1861.

Elegie à Marie Stuart by Pierre de Ronsard, on page 112, translated from the French by Helen Smailes in *The Queen's Image*, by Helen Smailes and Duncan Thomson, for the Scottish National Portrait Gallery, copyright © 1987 by The Trustees of the National Galleries of Scotland.

"Four stages of prayer" on pages 702–704, by Father Albert Haase, Madison, Wisconsin, 1989.

Poem on page 801 and prayer on pages 842, both attributed to Mary Queen of Scots; translations from the French and Latin respectively copyright © 1974 and 1976 by Caroline Bingham, as quoted in *Royal Stuart Papers X: The Poems of Mary Queen of Scots*, by Caroline Bingham, the Royal Stuart Society, 1976.

"Meditation on the Two Thieves" on pages 856–857, by Scott George, Oslo, Norway, 1963.

Scottish ballads, from the collection of Francis James Child.

Cover portrait: *Mary Stuart*, Anonymous; courtesy The Victoria and Albert Museum, London/Art Resource. Cover design by Doris Straus.

Library of Congress Cataloging-in-Publication Data
George, Margaret.
    Mary Queen of Scotland and the Isles : a novel / Margaret George.
        p.   cm.
    ISBN 0-312-15585-9
    1. Mary, Queen of Scots, 1542–1587—Fiction.   2. Scotland—History—Mary Stuart, 1542–1567—Fiction.   3. Great Britain—History—Elizabeth, 1558–1603—Fiction.   I. Title.
    PS3557.E49M37   1992
    813'.54—dc20
                                                            92-20975
                                                            CIP

20 19 18 17 16 15 14

To Scott George

1920–1989

Beloved father, friend, and teacher

The Royal Succession in England and Scotland

Henry VII
1457 – 1509
(REIGNED 1485 – 1509)

Henry VIII
1491 – 1547
(REIGNED 1509 – 1547)

James IV
King of Scots
1473 – 1513
(REIGNED 1488 – 1513)

M. 1st **Margaret Tudor** M. 2nd **Archibald Douglas**
1489 – 1541
6th Earl of Angus
c. 1489 – 1557

Marie de Guise M. **James V**
1515 – 1560
King of Scots
1512 – 1542
(REIGNED 1513 – 1542)

Lady Margaret M. **Matthew Stuart**
Douglas
1515 – 1578
4th Earl of Lennox
1516 – 1571

Mary Tudor
"Bloody Mary"
1516 – 1558
(REIGNED 1553 – 1558)

Edward VI
1537 – 1553
(REIGNED 1547 – 1553)

Elizabeth I
1533 – 1603
(REIGNED 1558 – 1603)

François II M. 1st **MARY QUEEN** M. 2nd **Henry Lord Darnley**
King of France
1544 – 1560
OF SCOTS
1542 – 1587
1545 – 1567
(REIGNED 1559 – 1560)

M. 3rd

James Hepburn
4th Earl of Bothwell
1535 – 1578

James I of England
(James VI of Scotland)
1566 – 1625
(REIGNED 1603 – 1625)

CONTENTS

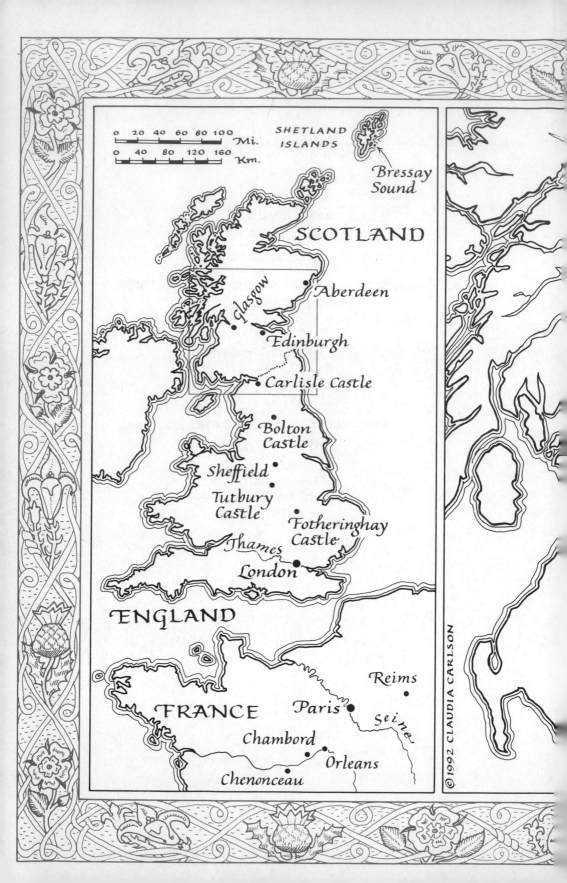

SHETLAND
ISLANDS

Bressay
Sound

0 20 40 60 80 100
Mi.
0 40 80 120 160
Km.

SCOTLAND

Glasgow
Aberdeen

Edinburgh

Carlisle Castle

Bolton
Castle

Sheffield

Tutbury
Castle

Fotheringhay
Castle

Thames

London

ENGLAND

FRANCE

Reims

Paris
Seine

Chambord

Orleans

Chenonceau

© 1992 CLAUDIA CARLSON

The Realms of
MARY QUEEN of SCOTS

Battle of Corrichie

Aberdeen

Lake Menteith
(Priory of
Inchmahome)

Perth

St. Andrews

Stirling
Castle

Loch
Leven

Wemyss Castle

Dumbarton
Castle

Glasgow

Linlithgow

Edinburgh

Dunbar Castle

Battle of
Langside

Battle of
Carberry Hill

Borthwick Castle

Traquair House

SCOTLAND

Jedburgh

N

Hermitage
Castle

Dundrennan

Carlisle Castle

Workington

Mi.   0   10   20   30

Km.   0 10 20 30 40 50

To see the eclipses of Sun and Moon; to see the capture of wild elephants and snakes; and to see the poverty of the wise, is to see that the power of fate is always supreme.

—Hindu proverb

In My End Is My Beginning
England, 1587

In the deepest part of the night, when all the candles save one had been put out and everyone lay quiet, the woman crossed silently to her desk and sat down. She put that one candle at her right hand, and spread out a piece of paper as slowly as possible across the desktop, so as to make no noise. She held its left side down with her hand—a white hand with long, slender fingers, which the French poet Ronsard had once described as "a tree with uneven branches." The hand looked young, as if it belonged to a virgin of fifteen. From across the room, with only one candle for illumination, the woman's face looked as young as the hand. But up closer, although the outlines of the beauty were still there, within the frame of the old loveliness there were lines and bumps and sags. The skin no longer stretched taut against the high cheekbones, the long, imperious nose, the almond-shaped eyes. It lay softly against them, tracing and revealing every hollow.

She rubbed her eyes, which were heavy-lidded and had traces of exhaustion under them, with that incongruously slender-fingered, elegantly ringed hand. Sighing, she dipped her pen in ink and began to write.

To Henri III, the Most Christian King of France.
8 February 1587.
Monsieur mon beau frère, estant par la permission de Dieu—
Royal brother, having by God's will, for my sins I think, thrown myself into the power of the Queen my cousin, at whose hands I have suffered much for almost twenty years, I have finally been condemned to death by her and her Estates. I have asked for my papers, which they have taken away, in order that I might make my will, but I have been unable to recover anything of use to me, or even get leave either to make my will freely or to have my body conveyed after my death, as I would wish, to your kingdom where I had the honour to be queen, your sister and old ally.

Tonight, after dinner, I have been advised of my sentence: I am to be executed like a criminal at eight in the morning. I have not had time to give you a full account of everything that has happened, but if you will listen to my doctor and my other unfortunate servants, you will

1

learn the truth, and how, thanks be to God, I scorn death and vow that I meet it innocent of any crime, even if I were their subject. The Catholic faith and the assertion of my God-given right to the English throne are the two issues on which I am condemned.

She stopped and stared ahead, as if her mind had suddenly ceased to form words, or she had run out of them. The French language was soothing, lulling. Even terrible things did not sound so heinous in French. Her mind could not, dared not, form them in Scots.

"Ce porteur & sa compaignie la pluspart de vos subiectz . . ."

The bearer of this letter and his companions, most of them your subjects, will testify to my conduct at my last hour. It remains for me to beg Your Most Christian Majesty, my brother-in-law and old ally, who have always protested your love for me, to give proof now of your goodness on all these points: firstly by charity, in paying my unfortunate servants the wages due them—this is a burden on my conscience that only you can relieve: further, by having prayers offered to God for a queen who has borne the title Most Christian Queen of France, and who dies a Catholic, stripped of all her possessions.

I have taken the liberty of sending you two precious stones, talismans against illness, trusting you will enjoy good health and a long and happy life. Accept them from your loving sister-in-law, who, as she dies, bears witness of her warm feelings for you. Give instructions, if it please you, that for my soul's sake part of what you owe me should be paid, and that for the sake of Jesus Christ, to whom I shall pray for you tomorrow as I die, I be left enough to found a memorial mass and give the customary alms.

Wednesday, at two in the morning.

Your most loving and most true sister,

Marie R

Queen of Scotland

She put down the pen, blinked once. Then she carefully put two small books on the paper to hold it down. Each movement was delicate, but weary. The fine, slender fingers stretched out once, then rested. She blew out the candle.

Walking slowly toward the bed on the other side of the room, she reached it and then lay down upon it, full length, in her clothes. She closed her eyes.

It is done, she thought. The life that began at the lowest point in Scotland's fortunes has followed that fortune, and now is finished.

A small curve of a smile played about her lips. No. *I* am finished. Or, rather, I would be finished. O Jesu, let me not fail now!

2

BOOK ONE

Queen of Scotland, Queen of France

1542-1560

I

In the smoky blue mist it was impossible to see anything except more mist. The sun, shrouded and muffled, wore a fuzzy circle of light around itself and was the one thing the men could sight on as they attempted to fight. If they could not see the enemy, how could they defend themselves?

The mist blew and swirled, passing low over the green bogs and mushy ground, hugging the soaked terrain, teasing the men as they tried to extricate themselves from the treacherous mire. It was cold and clammy, as unsympathetic as the hand of death, with which it kept close company.

Above the bog there were a few lone trees, their branches already stripped bare in the autumn gales, standing naked and forlorn above the battlefield. Men struggled toward their grey and wrinkled trunks, hoping to climb to safety. Thousands of feet had trampled the ground around the trees into an oozing field. The fog blanketed it all.

When the fog cleared the next day, sweeping out to sea and carrying the last vestige of confusion with it, the whole of Solway Moss revealed itself to be a sorry site for a battle. The mud, reeds, and slippery grass surrounding the meandering River Esk showed the Moss to be aptly named. There, in the southwest corner where England and Scotland met, the two ancient enemies had grappled like stags, floundering in the muck. But the English stag had triumphed over its adversary, and the swamp was dotted with leather shields, dropped there by the trapped Scots. There they would rot, as the sun would never dry them there.

One of the English soldiers, herding away his captives, turned to look back at the site, greenly tranquil in the slanting autumn light. "God have mercy on Scotland," he said quietly. "No one else will."

&

Outside it began to snow—gently at first, like little sighs, and then harder and harder, as if someone had ripped open a huge pillow. The sky was perfectly white, and soon the ground was, too; the wind blew the snow almost horizontal, and it coated the sides of trees and buildings, so that the whole world turned pale in less than an hour. At Falkland Palace, the big round towers reared up like giant snowmen guarding the entrance.

Inside, the King looked, unseeing, out the window.

"Your Majesty?" asked an anxious servant. "Pray, what is your wish?"

"Heat. Heat. Too cold here," he mumbled, shaking his head from side to side, closing his eyes.

The servant put more logs on the fire, and fanned it to tease the flames up around the fresh new logs. It was indeed cold, the coldest weather so early in the season that anyone could remember. Ships were already frozen in harbours, and the barren fields were as hard as metal.

Just then some of the King's field soldiers appeared, peering cautiously into the room. He seemed to see them even through his closed eyes.

"The battle?" he said. "Have you news of the battle?"

They came in, tattered, and knelt before him. Finally the highest-ranking one said, "Aye. We were attacked and soundly beaten. Many were drowned in the Esk in the retreat. Many more have been taken as prisoners—twelve thousand prisoners in the custody of the English commander."

"Ransom?" The King's voice was a whisper.

"No word of that. They say . . . they may all be sent to England as captives."

Suddenly the King lurched from his seat and stood up, rigid. He clasped and unclasped his fists, and a low sound of utter pain escaped him. He looked around wildly at the soldiers. "We are defeated?" he asked again. When they nodded, he cried, "All is lost!"

He turned his back on them and stumbled across the room to the door; when he reached the door frame he sagged against it, as if a spear had pinioned him. Then, clutching his side, he reeled away into his private quarters where they could not follow. His valet followed, running after him.

The King sought his bed; he dived into it and lay moaning and clutching his side. "All is lost!" he kept muttering.

One of the chamber servants sent for the physician; another went out to speak to the field soldiers.

"Is it truly as bad as you reported?" asked the chamber servant.

"Aye—worse," said one of the soldiers. "We are not only beaten, as at Flodden, but disgraced as well. Our King was not with us; our King had left us to mope and droop by himself far from the battlefield—like a maiden filled with vapours!"

"Sssh!" The servant looked around to see if anyone might hear. When he was assured that was impossible, he said, "The King is ill. He was ill before the news; the sorrow of the loss of his heirs, the little princes, has devastated him."

"It is the duty of a king to shoulder such losses."

"The loss of both his heirs within a few days of each other has convinced him that luck has turned against him. Once a man is convinced of that, it is hard for him to lead with authority."

"Like a fainting priest, or a boy with the falling sickness!" cried one of the soldiers. "We need a warrior, not a woman, leading us!"

"Aye, aye. He'll recover. He'll come to himself. After the shock wears off." The servant shrugged. "The King most like by now has another heir. His Queen was expecting to be brought to childbed at any moment."

The soldier shook his head. " 'Tis a pity he has so many bastards, and none of them of any use to him as a successor."

The King refused to rise from his bed, but lay there limply, as if in a trance. Some of his nobles came to him, and stood round his bed. The Earl of Arran, the burly head of the House of Hamilton and hereditary heir to the throne after any of the King's own children, looked on solicitously. Cardinal Beaton, the secretary of state, hovered as if he wished to hear a last confession. The Stewart cousins, all powerful clans in their own right, stood discreetly about the chamber. All wore heavy wool under their ceremonially bright garments; the weather remained bitter cold. In other chambers the King's mistresses, past and present, lingered, concerned about their children. Would the King see fit to remember them?

The King looked at them, shimmering and reappearing, sometimes seeming to dissolve, under his gaze. These faces . . . but none of them dear to him, no, not one.

Scotland had been beaten, he would remember, with stabs of pain.

"The Queen," someone was whispering. "Remember your Queen. Her hour is near. Think of your prince."

But the princes were dead, the sweet little boys, dead within a few hours of each other, one of them at Stirling, one at St. Andrews. Places of death. No hope. All gone. No hope. No point to another; it was doomed, too.

Then, a new face near his. Someone was staring intently into his eyes, trying to read them. A new person, someone brisk and detached.

"Sire, your Queen has been safely delivered."

The King struggled to get the words out. Strange, how difficult it was to speak. Where earlier he had been reticent, now it was his body holding back, even when his mind wished to communicate. The throat would not work. "Is it a man-child or woman?" he finally managed to command his tongue and lips to say.

"A fair daughter, Sire."

Daughter! The last battle lost, then.

"Is it even so? The devil take it! Adieu, farewell! The Stewarts came with a lass, and they shall pass with a lass," he murmured.

Those were the last words he spoke, although, as the physician saw that he was sinking, he exhorted him, "Give her your blessing! Give your daughter your blessing, for God's own sweet sake! Do not pass away without that charity and safeguard to your heir!"

But the King just gave a little laugh and smile, kissed his hand and offered it to all his lords round about him; soon thereafter he turned his head away from his attendants, toward the wall, and died.

"What meant he by his words?" one of the attendant lords whispered.

"The crown of Scotland," replied another. "It came to the Stewarts through Marjorie Bruce, and he fears it will pass away through—what is the Princess's name?"

"Princess Mary."

"No," said his companion, as he watched the physicians slowly turning the dead King, and folding his hands preparatory to having the priest anoint him. "Queen Mary. Mary Queen of Scots."

His widow, the Queen Dowager, struggled to regain her strength after childbirth as quickly as possible. Not for her the lingering recovery of days abed, receiving visitors and gifts and, as her reward for their well-wishes, presenting the infant for their inspection, all swathed in white lace and taffeta and' wrapped in yards of softest velvet in the gilded royal crib.

No, Marie de Guise, the relict—quaint phrase, that, she thought—of His Majesty James V of Scotland must right herself and be poised to defend her infant, like any wolf-mother in a harsh winter. And it was a very harsh winter, not only in terms of the flying snow and icy roads, but for Scotland itself.

She could almost fancy that, in the ruddy flames of the fires she kept continually burning, the teeth of the nobles looked more like animal fangs than human dog-teeth. One by one they made their way to Linlithgow Palace, the golden palace lying on a long, thin loch just west of Edinburgh, to offer their respects to the infant—their new Queen. They came clad in heavy furs, their feet booted and wrapped round with animal skins, and it was hard to tell their ice-streaked beards from the furs surrounding their faces. They would kneel and murmur something about their loyalty, but their eyes were preternaturally bright.

There were all the clans who came to make sure that they would not be barred from power by any other clan. For this was the greatest of all opportunities, the equivalent of a stag-kill that attracted all the carrion-eaters of the forest. An infant was their monarch, a helpless infant, with no one but a foreign mother to protect her: a Frenchwoman who was ignorant of their ways here and far from home.

The Earl of Arran, James Hamilton, was there; had not this baby been born, he would now be king. He smiled benevolently at the infant. "I wish her a long life," he said.

The Earl of Lennox, Matthew Stuart, who claimed to be the true heir rather than Arran, came shortly and stood looking longingly down at the baby. "May she have all the gifts of grace and beauty," he said.

Patrick Hepburn, the "Fair Earl" of Bothwell, stepped forward and kissed the Queen Mother's hand lingeringly. "May she have power to make all who gaze upon her love her," he said, raising his eyes to Marie's.

The red-faced, stout northern Earl of Huntly strutted past the cradle and bowed. "May she always rest among friends and never fall into the hands of her enemies," he said.

"My lord!" Marie de Guise objected. "Why mention enemies? Why even think of them now? You tie your well-wishes to something sinister. I pray you, amend your words."

"I can amend them, but never erase them. Once spoken, they have flown into another realm. Very well: let her enemies be confounded and come to confusion."

"I like not the *word*."

"I cannot promise that there will be no enemies," he said stubbornly. "Nor would it be a good wish. 'Tis enemies that make a man and shape him. Only a no-thing has no enemies."

After the lords had departed, Marie de Guise sat by the cradle and rocked it gently. The baby was sleeping. The firelight painted the side of her face rosy, and the infant curled and uncurled her fat, dimpled little fingers.

My first daughter, thought Marie, and she does look different. Is it my imagination? No, I think she's truly feminine. The Scots would say a lass is always different from a lad, even from the beginning. This daughter has skin like almond-milk. And her hair—she gently pushed back the baby's cap—of what colour will it be, to go with that skin? It is too early to tell; the fuzz is the same colour as that of all babes.

Mary. I have named her after myself, and also after the Virgin; after all, she was born on the Virgin's day, the Immaculate Conception, and perhaps the Virgin will protect her, guard over her as a special charge.

Mary Queen of Scots. My daughter is a queen already; six days old, and then she became a queen.

At that thought, a brief flutter of guilt rose in her.

The King my lord and husband died, and that is how my daughter came to be Queen before her time. I should feel tearing grief. I should be mourning the King, lamenting my fate, instead of gazing in wonder at my daughter, a baby queen.

The child *will* be fair, she thought, studying her features. Her complexion and features all promise it. Already I can see that she has her father's eyes, those Stewart eyes that are slanted and heavy-lidded. It was his eyes that promised so much, that were so reassuring and yet so private, hiding their own depths.

"My dear Queen." Behind her she heard a familiar voice: Cardinal Beaton's. He had not left with the others; but then, he felt at home here, and never more so than now, with the King gone forever. "Gazing upon your handiwork? Be careful, lest you fall in love with your own creation."

9

She straightened and turned to him. "It is difficult not to be in awe of her. She is lovely; and she *is* a queen. My family in France will be beside themselves. The Guises finally have a monarch to their credit!"

"Her last name is not Guise, but Stewart," the bulky churchman reminded her. "It is not her French blood that puts her on this throne, but her Scottish." He allowed himself to bend down and stroke the baby's cheek. "Well, what are you to do?"

"Hold the throne for her as best I can," answered Marie.

"Then you will have to remain in Scotland." He straightened up, and made his way over to a plate of sweetmeats and nuts in a silver bowl. He picked one up and popped it into his mouth.

"I know that!" She was indignant.

"No plans to run back to France?" He was laughing, teasing her. "Made from Seville oranges," he commented about the sweetmeat he was still sucking. "Lately I tasted a coated rind from India. Much sweeter."

"No. If this child had not come, if I were a childless widow, then of course I certainly would not linger here! But now I have a task, and one I cannot shirk." She shivered. "If I do not die of cold here, or take consumption."

It was snowing outside again. She walked across the chamber to the arched stone fireplace, where a huge fire was blazing, by her orders. The baby's chamber must be kept warm, in spite of the wildly bitter weather raging all over Scotland. The Cardinal, who lived luxuriously himself, doubtless approved.

"Oh, David," she said, her smile suddenly fading. "What will become of Scotland? The battle—"

"If the English have their way, it will become part of England. They will seek to grab it one way or another, most likely through marriage. As the victors of Solway Moss, with their thousand high-ranking prisoners in hand, they will dictate the terms. They will probably force Mary to marry their Prince Edward."

"Never! I will not permit that!" cried Marie.

"She must needs marry someone," the Cardinal reminded her. "That is what the King meant when he said, 'It will pass with a lass.' When she marries, the crown goes to her husband. And there is no eligible French prince. The marriage of King François's heirs, Henri de Valois and Catherine de Médicis, is barren. If little Mary tries to marry a Scot, one of her own subjects, the rest will rise up in jealousy. So who else but the English?"

"Not an English prince!" Marie kept repeating. "Not an English prince! They are all heretics down there!"

"And what do you plan to do about the King's bastards?" the Cardinal whispered.

"I shall bring them all together and rear them here, in the palace."

"You are mad! Better bring them all together and dispose of them, rather."

"Like a sultan?" Marie could not help laughing. "Nay, that is not a Christian response. I will offer them charity, and a home."

"And rear them with your own daughter, the lawful Queen? That is not Christian, but negligent. You may see your daughter reap the evil harvest of that misguided kindness. Beware that you do not nurture serpents to sting her later, when you are gone." The Cardinal's fat, unlined face registered true alarm. "How many are there?"

"Oh, nine or so, I think." She laughed, then felt guilty about that, too.

I should feel bad about the King's infidelities, she thought. But I do not. Why not? I must not have loved him. Otherwise I would have attacked the women and torn out their eyes.

"They are all boys, except one girl, Jean. His favourite bastard was the one who carried his name, James Stewart. He's nine years old now, and lives with his mother in the castle at Lochleven. They say he's clever," said Marie.

"I don't doubt it. There's no one more clever than a royal bastard. They have inordinate hopes. Force him into the Church and tie him up there, if you value the little Queen's safety."

"No, the best way is to allow him into the palace and let him learn to love his sister."

"His half-sister."

"My, you are stubborn. I appreciate your warnings, but I will keep a close watch."

"And what of the nobles? You cannot trust any of them, can you?"

"Yes, I trust the ones who have married the girls I brought with me from France. Lord George Seton, who married my maid of honour, Marie Pieris; Lord Robert Beaton, who married Joan de la Reynveille; Lord Alexander Livingston, who married Jeanne de Pedefer."

"But the greater nobles are not on that list."

"No."

Just then the little Queen let out a wail, and her mother bent down and picked her up. The tiny mouth was puckered and quivering, and the big eyes were brimming with tears.

"Hungry again," said Marie. "I shall call the wet nurse."

"She is a beauty," said the Cardinal. "It is hard to imagine that anyone would wish her harm." He tickled the baby's chin. "Greetings, Your Majesty."

❧

"All men lamented that the realm was left without a male to succeed," a young priest named John Knox wrote, slowly and thoughtfully. He looked up at his crucifix, hanging above his desk, as he dipped his pen in the inkwell.

Why have You not provided? he beseeched the cross silently. Why have You abandoned Scotland?

II

The September weather had played peekaboo all day. First there had been a rainstorm, with high, gusty winds that were even stronger up on the two-hundred-fifty-foot heights of Stirling Castle. Then the clouds had blown away, going east in the direction of Edinburgh, bringing piercingly blue skies and an astringent sense of cleanness. Now black clouds were coming in again, but Marie de Guise still stood in the sunshine and could see a distant rainbow over the retreating storm clouds, which trailed a skirt of mist all the way to the ground.

Was it an omen? The Queen Mother could be forgiven if she was anxious this day; it was her daughter's coronation day.

The ceremony had been hastily arranged in an act of reckless defiance of England; it was, nonetheless, supported by all Scotsmen. Almost to a man, they found the bullying and patronizing of Henry VIII intolerable and unswallowable. His smug demands and his schoolboyish threats; his lack of any grasp of the idea that Scotland was a nation, not a sack of grain to be bought and sold; his cool assumption that he held all the power and therefore must prevail—all these convinced the Scots that they must, and would, resist to the utmost.

The first thing to do was to break the forced betrothal of Mary to Edward, a betrothal that had as a condition the sending of Mary to England to be raised. Balked in that, King Henry had wanted to place her in the care of an English household in Scotland and ban her own mother from her presence. He was determined that she be in English hands at all times; in other words, she must be kept from her own people and brought up English, not Scottish—the better to betray their interests later, so his thinking went.

Henry's "assured lords," the captives from the battle of Solway Moss, had turned coat and repudiated the English policy as soon as it was possible, and now the second act of defiance was being hurried forward: Mary would be crowned Queen of Scotland this afternoon, to hammer home the fact that Scotland was an independent nation with its own sovereign, even if she was only nine months old.

The date chosen was most unfortunate, thought the Queen Mother: September ninth, the anniversary of the dreadful battle of Flodden Field, where exactly thirty years before, Mary's grandfather had met his end, hacked to death by the English.

Yet there was a certain stirring defiance in it, as if not only Henry VIII were being challenged, but fate itself.

She looked up once more at the darkening sky, then hurried across the courtyard to the palace. There was no time now to admire the French work that her late husband had lavished on decorating the grey stone palace, down to the whimsical statues he had installed all along the façade. There was even one of her, now looking down at the living model that walked quickly toward the entrance of the palace.

Her daughter was ready, wearing heavy regal robes in miniature. A crimson velvet mantle, with a train furred with ermine, was fastened around her tiny neck, and a jeweled satin gown, with long hanging sleeves, enveloped the infant, who could sit up but not walk. Her mother smoothed her head—soon to wear the crown—prayed silently for her, and then handed her solemnly to Lord Alexander Livingston, her Lord Keeper, who would carry her across the courtyard in solemn procession to the Chapel Royal. As they passed outside, the Queen Mother saw that the sunshine had fled and the sky was black. But no rain had yet fallen, and the baby passed dry in her ceremonial robes into the chapel, followed by her officers of state in procession.

Inside, there were not many. The English ambassador, Sir Ralph Sadler, who saw in this the ruin of all his master's plans, stood gloomily wishing ill on the ceremony and all its participants. D'Oysell, the French ambassador, hated to be there at all, for his presence would seem to condone it. But King François would have to be informed of all the details, or he would punish his ambassador mightily for his ignorance. The other Lord Keepers of the baby Queen constituted an entire row of onlookers. Cardinal Beaton stood ready to conduct the ceremony, hovering over the throne.

The coronation itself was not lavish, or even intricate, as would have been its counterpart in England. The Scotsmen were ready to get on with it, and so, in the simplest manner, the Lord Keeper Livingston brought Mary forward to the altar and put her gently in the throne set up there. Then he stood by, holding her to keep her from rolling off.

Quickly, Cardinal Beaton put the Coronation Oath to her, which her keeper, as her sponsor, answered for her; in his voice she vowed to guard and guide Scotland and act as its true Queen, in the name of God Almighty, who had chosen her. Immediately then the Cardinal unfastened her heavy robes and began anointing her with the holy oil on her back, breast, and the palms of her hands. When the chill air struck her, she began to cry, with long, wailing sobs.

The Cardinal stopped. True, this was only a baby, crying as all babies cried, unexpectedly and distressingly. But in the silence of the stone chapel, where nerves were already taut with the whole clandestine, rebellious nature of the ceremony, the sounds were shattering. The child cried as at the fall of Man, as if in horror of damnation.

"Sssh, ssh," he murmured. But the little Queen would not be quieted; she wailed on, until the Earl of Lennox brought forward the sceptre, a long rod of gilded silver, surmounted by crystal and Scottish pearl. He placed it in her baby hand, and she grasped the heavy shaft with her fat fingers. Her crying died away. Then the ornate gilded sword of state was presented by the Earl of Argyll, and the Cardinal performed the ceremony of girding the three-foot sword to the tiny round body.

Later, the Earl of Arran carried the crown, a heavy fantasy of gold and jewels that enclosed within it the circlet of gold worn by Robert the Bruce on his helmet at the Battle of Bannockburn, not far from Stirling. Holding it gently, the Cardinal lowered it onto the child's head, where it rested on a circlet of velvet. From underneath the crown, heavy with the dolour of her ancestors, Mary's eyes looked out. The Cardinal steadied the crown and Lord Livingston held her body straight as the Earls Lennox and Arran kissed her cheek in fealty, followed by the rest of the prelates and peers who knelt before her and, placing their hands on her crown, swore allegiance to her.

III

Henry VIII unleashed the full force of his fury against the Scots. An army was sent to storm Stirling Castle, capture Mary, and sack and burn everything in the surroundings. Men, women, and children were to be put to the sword; Edinburgh destroyed, Holyrood razed, the Border abbeys demolished, and the harvest, already gathered in, to be set on fire.

The English soldiers slashed and murdered their way into Edinburgh. They came down the Canongate and up to the doors of Holyrood Abbey, and entered into the sanctuary. Seeking the Stewart tombs, they found the great enclosed monument on the right side of the Abbey, near the altar, and broke into it, desecrating the royal burial places. The tomb of Mary's father was opened and his coffin dragged out into the daylight, mocked, and then abandoned, to lie forlorn in the aisle.

Scotland wept and lamented. Scotland was wounded and cried out, but there was none to heed or help her. The dead stank to heaven, the children went to bed hungry, in the care of whatever relative survived, and the razed streets of Edinburgh smouldered. The Scottish people looked at the ruined abbeys and the deserted churches and sought the only help left, the Divine, in a new way. Despite the ban on all Protestant literature, there were smuggled Protestant translations of the Scriptures—William Tyndale's version, and even copies of the English Great Bible of 1539—now coming into Scotland. But where the heretical preachers could not hide, a Bible could be secreted; where God seemed silent in speaking through his erstwhile Church, the Church of Rome, he began speaking directly through His Word as revealed in the Scriptures. Preachers were abroad throughout the land, having been trained in Geneva, Holland, Germany. People listened to their sermons and found solace in God's reaching out to them. He offered His hand and they grasped it.

In Stirling Castle the Queen Mother and her daughter were safe. The ancient castle on its high rock, rising out of the plain, held fast and was beyond the power of the English to capture. Inside the palace walls, Marie de Guise fashioned a home for her daughter, with playmates, tutors, and pets. It was a world in itself, high above the Forth valley, looking down on Stirling Bridge and the gateway to the Highlands, where a person could vanish in safety from any foreign foes that threatened. There were rare excursions to hawk and hunt and see the countryside, before scurrying back to the safety of the rock fortress.

There were mists. And howling winds and ice-covered hills that sometimes the children went sledding on, using a cow's skull to ride down the hill behind the castle. There were little furry ponies that she and her playmates—all also named Mary, which was such fun—learned to ride on. There were fogs and heather, green glens, and an enormous sky with clouds that raced across it like bandits.

Up in the castle, there was a room in the King's apartments—empty now—that had round medallions on its ceiling. Little Mary would wander into the room and stare at the carved wooden heads in the dim light from the shuttered windows. One of the figures had hands that clutched the rim of the roundel, as if he would escape and leap out into the real world. But he never moved; he remained forever on the brink of a new world which he could not enter, gazing down at her from the ceiling.

Her mother did not like her to be there. Usually she would come looking for Mary and bring her back into the Queen's apartments, where she lived and had her lessons; where there were cushions and a fireplace and a swirl of people.

❧

Sometime in that mist of early childhood she came to know her half-siblings. Her mother, with odd charity—or was it political astuteness?—had gathered four of her late husband's illegitimate offspring and brought them to Stirling Castle. Mary loved them all, loved being part of a large family; and, as her mother did not seem to find it offensive that they were bastards, neither did she.

James Stewart was stern and grave, but as the oldest, his judgement seemed the wisest and they deferred to it. If he said they should not sled down the hill once more before the light faded, Mary learned that he had always gauged it correctly and that if she disobeyed she would find herself in the dark by the time she reached the bottom.

Before Marie had brought Mary's half-siblings to spend some time at Stirling, she had assembled another little family for her daughter as well: the four daughters of friends, all named Mary, and all the same age: Mary Fleming, Mary Beaton, Mary Livingston, and Mary Seton.

Mary Fleming was entirely Scots, and also had Stewart blood, but from further back on the wrong side of the blanket: she was the granddaughter of James IV. Mary Fleming's mother, Janet, shared the Stewart family traits of beauty and high spirits, and served as governess to the five little Marys. From the earliest days, Mary Fleming—nicknamed *La Flamina*—was the only one who would take Mary's dares and outdo her in mischief.

The other three Marys, although they had proper Scots names and Scots fathers, all had French mothers, ladies-in-waiting who had come over with Marie de Guise. That their daughters should all be friends with her daughter gave the Queen Mother great satisfaction, and a feeling of being at home in this fortress in an alien land. Although the mothers spoke French to each other, their daughters did not seem either interested or able to learn it themselves, although presumably they could understand some words of it. But the mothers, when they wanted to talk secretly of presents and surprises for the girls, could always speak safely in French.

To differentiate between them, Mary Livingston, robust and athletic, was called Lusty by the others; Mary Seton, who was tall and reserved, was called by her stately surname of Seton, and Mary Beaton, who was plump, pretty, and inclined to daydreaming, was called Beaton because it rhymed with Seton to make a pair. Mary Fleming had been nicknamed La Flamina because of her flamboyant personality. Only Mary was always only Mary, *the* Mary.

The eight younger children romped, fought, had secret clubs, cliques, and codes. They kept pets and played at cards, telling fortunes; they tattled on each other and swore eternal friendship the next day. The ninth, James Stewart, presided over their little world with fifteen-year-old solemnity, suspended midway between the world of the adults and that of the children, fully belonging to neither. Both sides turned to him for advice about the other.

Mary was only six months old when she came to live at Stirling, and the whole world was contained in that mountaintop fortress for her. She was crowned there; she took her first tottering steps there; her tutors taught her her earliest lessons there in the antechamber off the Queen's apartments. When she was only three, she was presented with a tiny pony from the islands in the farthest north of Scotland, and so she first learned to ride there. Lusty, of course, took to the ponies as quickly as she, whereas Seton and Beaton preferred quieter, indoor pastimes. Flamina could ride well enough, but she preferred human adventures to animal ones.

Mary looked up to James, and followed him about eagerly. When she was very small, she clung to him and pestered him to play with her. As she grew older, she came to realize that he disliked being handled and touched, and that such behaviour had the very opposite effect on him. If she wished him to pay attention to her, she had to look the other way and talk to others. Then curiosity would draw him.

One day, when she was nearly four, she wandered away from the upper courtyard where the children were playing ball between the Great Hall and the Chapel Royal, and crept into the forbidden King's apartments. They were always shuttered and dark, but they drew her. The great round medallions on the ceiling cast a brooding presence over the room, as if they were guarding a secret. She kept imagining that if she just looked in every corner, and searched hard enough, she would find her father there. He would have been hiding, playing a joke on them. And think how happy her mother would be to have her bring him out!

Heart thumping loudly, she walked swiftly across the huge guard chamber. She already knew that nothing was in here. The room was bare, and there was nowhere for the King to hide. The next connected room, the presence chamber, was likewise bare. But there were several little hidden chambers off the King's bedchamber. She knew they were there; she had seen a map of them. And that was where the King was probably hiding—if he was hiding at all.

But they were the farthest away, and were very dark. She had never dared to go there before. Once, she had got up to the door of the King's bedchamber and seen, opening off it, the dark entrance to the closet. But her courage had failed her, and she had turned back.

Today she would go. She half wished she had brought Flamina with her. But she knew that her father would not appear if anyone else was there. She had to go alone.

At the same time, she knew it was only a game. He was not really there; this was just a test of courage she was setting for herself. She crept forward in the dim room, making for the bedchamber. Her eyes had become accustomed to the dark, and now she could see much better. She reached the doorway of the bedchamber and peered in.

There was still a bed there, and it even retained its hangings. She dared herself to get down on her hands and knees and peek under it. She did, almost fainting with trepidation. But there was nothing under it but dust and silence.

Now she had to do it; she had to go into the attached closet. There was no sound at all except her own breathing. She wanted to turn back; she did not want to turn back. She held her breath and ran, on light feet, into the room.

It was horribly dark. It had in it a sense of some presence, and it was not benevolent. She forced herself to walk around the perimeter of the room, touching the walls, but by the time she was halfway round, she was so frightened she felt almost sick. Her knees started to shake, and she dropped to all fours and crawled toward the door.

But then she found herself in an even darker room. There must have been two doors in the room; maybe there were three. How could she get out? Terror overtook her and all logical thought fled. She huddled on the floor and shook with the feeling of helplessness.

Then she heard a noise. The ghost! The ghost of her father! He was coming to keep his appointment, and suddenly she did not wish to see him. Above all, she did not wish to see a ghost!

"Why, Mary," said a quiet voice. "Are you lost?"

She leapt up. Who was speaking? "Yes. I wish to return to the courtyard," she said, trying to sound dignified. But her knees persisted in shaking.

"Why have you come here?" The voice ignored her request.

"I wished to explore," she said grandly. No need to tell about the ghost, or the possibility of the ghost.

"And now you're lost." The voice held a mocking parody of sympathy. "What a pity." It paused. "Do you know where you are?"

"Not—not exactly."

"I could lead you out."

"Who are you?" She knew the voice; she knew she did.

The figure stepped over to her, and took her hand. "Why, I'm James, your brother," he said.

"Oh! Thank goodness! Let us leave together!"

"I said I could lead you out." His voice had a slight catch to it. "And that I would be most glad to do, but in exchange I'd like you to do something for me."

"What?" This was very odd. Why was he so strange?

"I'd like a reward. I'd like the miniature of our father that you have— that you're wearing this very minute."

She had pinned it onto her bodice that morning, as if it would serve to call him forth. She loved it; it was one of the very tangible reminders of him that she had. She liked to study his face, the long oval, the thin nose and shapely lips. Secretly she wondered if she looked like him, or would grow to look like him. She knew she did not resemble her mother in anything save height.

"No," she said. "Choose something else."

"There's nothing else I want."

"I cannot give it to you. I treasure it."

"Then I cannot help you. Find your own way out." Quickly he pulled his hand away and ran for the door.

She heard his footsteps disappearing, and she was left alone in the dark.

"James!" she called. "James, come back here!"

He laughed from the outer chamber.

"James, I command you!" she screamed. "Come here at once! I am the Queen!"

His laughter stopped, and in a moment he was standing beside her once again.

"You can command me to return," he said sulkily. "But you cannot command me to lead you out if I decide I will stay here with you. I will pretend I was lost as well. So. Give me the miniature and I will lead you

18

out. Otherwise we will sit here and be lost together until a guard finds us."

She waited, her lip quivering. At last she said, "Very well. Take the miniature." She refused to unfasten it herself; let James stick himself in doing it.

Deftly he unpinned it; he must have eyed it for a long time, since he knew how to unfasten it in the dark, she thought. "There," he said. "You forget he is my father too. I wish to have something of his. I promise I will treasure it and never let any harm come to it."

"Pray lead me out," she said. The loss of the pin was so painful that she wanted to get back out into the sun as soon as possible, as if sunlight could restore it in some mysterious way.

She attempted to forget about it; and in days to come she almost managed to convince herself that she had lost the pin in the dark chambers, surrendering it to her father as a gift. She was glad when James went away for several months to be with his mother on Lochleven. By the time he returned, she had no clear memory of the miniature.

IV

The wind was whipping across the empty, snow-dusted fields as the little party trotted on. They were on their way from Longniddry to the larger town of Haddington; there George Wishart would preach as the Spirit called him, in spite of the warning he had received from the lord of the area, Patrick Hepburn, Earl of Bothwell. As they made their way in the dull January afternoon, they kept alert for any suspicious movement. It might be the friendly lords who had promised to meet them here—or it might be their enemies.

Out in front of the party was a slim, straight-backed figure whose eyes swept the road and whose hands clutched a two-handed sword. He was a young man about thirty years old, who acted as tutor to the two young sons of Sir Hugh Douglas of Longniddry and who also served as a public notary in the district. His name was John Knox and he no longer knelt in front of crucifixes or begged God to reveal why He had abandoned Scotland. The answer had come, by way of George Wishart: it was Scotland who had abandoned God, led astray by the "puddle of papistry." Knox had in turn abandoned his priestly calling and embraced the Reformed Faith. It was a dangerous decision.

Outside the walls of the self-contained castle on Stirling Rock where the

Queen resided, and beyond the equally self-contained castle at St. Andrews where Cardinal Beaton presided, reformers slipped from house to house, carrying their smuggled Bibles and their outlawed messages. Safe from the vigilant eyes and ears of the Queen and Cardinal, they made their converts in a population that, if it did not actually "hunger and thirst after righteousness," at least was eager to try to find new pathways to God. The feeling was abroad in the air, in all Christendom, like an undercurrent, a siren song: Come drink at the waters of this well. People came to drink for all the reasons people come to forbidden waters—some out of genuine thirst, others out of curiosity, still others out of daring and rebellion. Henry VIII's Trojan horse was not the bribed and bullied nobles he had sent north, but the reformers who followed in their wake on missions of their own.

George Wishart, steeped in the new brew of Protestant theology from Europe, taught and preached loudly enough that the Cardinal's ears pricked up, and like a hunting dog spotting an otter, he tried to track him down. Wishart continued his bold preaching to large congregations, eluding the Cardinal for a time. Now he was headed for an area very near Edinburgh, in spite of warnings from the faithful that the Queen and her henchman, the Earl of Bothwell, were prepared to capture him.

At the very least, his partisans begged him, do not appear so publicly.

"What, shall I lurk like a gentleman ashamed of his business?" the missionary had answered. "I will dare to preach if others will dare to hear!"

Now, across the fields of Lothian, they were making their way in expectation of meeting their supporters from the western part of Scotland. For this they had left the safety of Fife, where the largest numbers of converts were.

John Knox drew up the coarse wool collar of his mantle and peered out across the landscape. By God, let any enemies appear and he'd mow them down! He clenched the sword.

Men of the cloth were not supposed to carry weapons, that he knew. But am I still a man of the cloth? he asked himself. No, by the blood of Christ! That mockery of a ceremony I went through in my ignorance, creating me a priest, was nothing, was worse than nothing! No, unless I hear a clear call, direct from God, I'm not a man of the cloth.

Wishart preached twice in Haddington, in the church that was the largest in the area. Only a very few showed up to hear him—after the thousands who had thronged to attend all his sermons elsewhere.

"It's the Earl of Bothwell," said Wishart afterwards, as they took a small evening meal at the home of John Cockburn of Ormiston. "He's the lord of this area; he must have warned people to stay away." He chewed his brown bread carefully. He had blessed it and thanked the Lord for it, and now it tasted different. "What is he like, this Bothwell?" He looked up and down the table to the men gathered there: Douglas of Longniddry, Cockburn of Ormiston, the laird of Brunstane, Sandilands of Calder. Wishart was not well acquainted with Scottish magnates in the Lothian region.

20

"A blackguard," said Cockburn. "A man who betrays everyone. His word means nothing. And ambitious. He'd sell his soul or his mother to advance himself."

"He's already sold his wife!" said Brunstane. "He just divorced her, a fine lady, born a Sinclair, because he had hopes of ingratiating himself to the Queen Mother."

"He hoped to get into her bed," said Cockburn bluntly. "Legally, that is."

"You mean he presumed to try to marry the French Queen?" Wishart was shocked.

"Yes. And he has not abandoned his suit."

John Knox wondered if he should speak up. He ate a few more mouthfuls of his mutton stew before saying, "My family has known the Hepburns for generations. We've fought under their banner in many wars. They are a brave lot, and usually loyal. This 'Fair Earl' is an anomaly; but we should not stain the rest of the family by association. One of his castles is only a few miles downriver, Hailes Castle on the Tyne. He is probably there right now."

"Is he . . . devout?" asked Wishart.

Knox laughed in spite of himself. "The only altar he worships at is his mirror."

Darkness had fallen outside, and the wind picked up. The men grew uneasy, although they tried to hide it. Ordinarily, had each been with other company, they would have pasted over their anxiety with extra glasses of wine. But now they just blinked at each other and waited. Finally Wishart rose and said, "Let us read Scripture and pray."

They gathered at the other end of the small room, where a meagre fire burned in the stone fireplace. Wishart pulled out his worn Bible and let the pages fall open in obedience to a small gesture of his hands. He read from the eighth chapter of Romans, and then led them in prayer.

Immediately after saying the amens, Douglas informed him that he would be returning to Longniddry that evening.

Wishart smiled; he had known this would happen, and that it was for the good of all. He turned to Knox and said, "Then you must accompany your master."

Knox protested. "Nay, I must be here to protect you! I will slash as Peter did in the Garden of Gethsemane, and I will glory in cutting off the chief priest's servant's ear!"

"Return the sword to me, John," said Wishart.

Reluctantly, but with complete obedience, Knox handed it over.

"Now you must return to your bairns, and God bless you. One is enough for a sacrifice."

Later that night, as the true night came on and most people slept, Wishart sat up, waiting. Cockburn sat with him; it would have been derelict of him to go to bed and leave his guest alone.

Cockburn was solicitous in adding more logs to the fire and in bringing the preacher heated ale. But Wishart kept staring at the fire, as if in a trance. Finally he spoke.

"Poor Scotland," he finally said. "It will be a difficult birth, bringing the Reformed Faith out in the open. But only the Faith can save her."

"They have had faith of some sort for a thousand years."

"But obviously it cannot sustain them. Look at Scotland! She is about to lose her independence! The English batter her from the outside, and the French run her from the inside. The Queen Mother and her ally the Cardinal have set up Frenchmen everywhere in positions of authority. And the little Queen is only four years old, just a puppet."

Cockburn drew his blanket round his shoulders. "I fail to see how the Reformed Faith will change any of that."

"Oh, it gives people hope—hope that they have been chosen by God. And once someone feels that, he's no one's slave—not the English, nor the French, nor the Queen's. Then the Scotsmen will rise up and drive their own destiny."

There was a loud knock on the door. Cockburn jumped, but Wishart did not. Cockburn shuffled over to answer it, and found himself staring into the face of the "Fair Earl" of Bothwell himself.

"Ah, there's Wishart!" said the Earl, nodding toward him. "Well met, sir!"

Outside, behind the Earl, Cockburn could hear and see a large company of men. There was also a youth, somewhere in age between childhood and manhood.

"You must surrender to me," said the Earl. "Come along." When Wishart rose but did not come toward him, the Earl said, "There is no escape. The house is surrounded, and Cardinal Beaton himself is only a mile away at Elphinstone Tower with a company of soldiers. But I promise I will keep you safely myself and never surrender you to the Cardinal." He looked to one side, where the youth had pushed in to stare into the room. "My son, James. He's just eleven and wanted a glimpse of the renowned Wishart. Well, sir. Are you prepared to come peacefully?"

Wishart looked at him long and sorrowfully. Then he turned his eyes on the boy, who was staring at him with rapt attention. "I am honoured that you came to see me," he said. Then he looked back at the Earl. "Have I your word of honour that you will not deliver me to the Cardinal?"

"Word of honour," said the Earl.

The Earl took Wishart back to Hailes Castle, and the next day he turned him over to Cardinal Beaton.

The gentle preacher was duly tried and condemned to death. He was strangled and then burnt before the Cardinal, who looked on from a cushioned seat on the ramparts of St. Andrews Castle.

The strangler asked for the traditional forgiveness from his victim; Wishart leaned forward and kissed him on the cheek. Knox, hidden in the

22

crowd, watched as the Cardinal sat, unmoved, a small smile playing on his lips.

At a signal from the elegant Cardinal, the officers of the execution lit the faggots under the slumped body of Wishart, bound upright by ropes to his post. As the flames caught and crackled, the executioners scrambled to jump free of the platform. Knox could see the rising column of flames engulf the body of Wishart; the image seemed to waver and shimmer in the fumes and heat. The skin blackened and peeled; the eyes burst open and dribbled fluid. The hair and beard caught in an aureole of fire, like a halo, so it seemed to his disciple. Then a pungent and inherently repulsive acrid smell wafted on the breeze. It was the stench of scorched and roasting raw human flesh.

Knox saw the Cardinal bring a lace handkerchief up to his nose. But he, Knox, breathed in the ashes of his friend, taking deep lungfuls of the smoky air, as if he honoured and incorporated his spirit in so doing. He had now received the call from God.

V

The Cardinal rolled over and stretched on his silken sheets. It was a glorious May morning, and in the dancing reflections of the ocean playing on his bedroom ceiling, he could read the mood of the sea. It was mischievous and inviting. Rather like his mistress, Marion Ogilvy, sleeping beside him, her thick dark hair like clouds of oblivion. Oblivion: that was what he had found with her last night. But this morning, ah, he was restored to the world of men and had no need of oblivion.

A knock on the door startled him. How late was it? By the sun he had assumed it was yet early. Could he have overslept?

"A moment, please," he said, reaching for his satin gown. Marion murmured and stirred, opening her eyes. The Cardinal rose from his bed and went across to the door, where the knocking continued.

"I hear you well enough!" he warned them. Whoever it was was rude and disrespectful.

He opened the door to find a crowd of workmen facing him—workmen with daggers. Or rather, assassins in workmen's costumes. They surged forward. He tried to shut the door on them, but they flung it back open on its hinges and rushed in. Marion screamed as one of the men grabbed the Cardinal by the neck and another raised his knife.

"Repent of your former wicked life!" the man with the knife hissed. "We are sent from God to punish you! I hearby swear that neither hatred of your filthy person, nor desire for your riches, nor fear of persecution moves me to strike you. I do so only because you have been an obstinate enemy to Christ Jesus and his True Gospel!"

"I am a priest!" he cried. "I am a priest! You will not slay a priest!"

The knives thudded into him, with nothing between them and his soft white flesh but the thin layer of satin in the robe.

"Repent of the murder of George Wishart!" were the last words he heard.

The sun was still only midway to its noon zenith when the people gathered outside St. Andrews Castle saw the sight: the naked Cardinal, his severed genitals stuffed into his mouth, was hanging by an arm and a leg from the very spot where he had watched Wishart's burning two months earlier.

❧

In the May sunshine, Mary and two of the other Marys—Livingston and Fleming—were waiting for their grooms to bring out the ponies. Today they were to ride the little animals all round the pleasure garden beneath the walls of Stirling Castle, called the King's Knot. The Knot had raised geometric terraces, all planted with ornamental shrubs, with roses and fruit trees, like an artificial mountain. But at its base it made a fine riding-path, and the royal gardeners, fertilizing and pruning, did not mind, as they had not begun to work there yet.

Mary had decided that they should have a race. She loved to ride, and to ride fast; clinging to the miniature horse from Shetland, she felt as though she were flying. All too seldom did she have the opportunity to ride as fast as she liked, especially on her favorite pony, Juno. Sometimes she was allowed to ride Juno out beyond the castle grounds; that was when her mother and the Cardinal took her hawking with her own falcon, Ruffles. She always loved these excursions to the woodlands.

Waiting in the warm sun, she announced to Mary Livingston that they would race. Lusty, with a toss of her hair, said that was fine with her, but she did not intend to lose. It would have to be a *true* race, not a pretend one.

The ponies were brought round the corner of the castle ramparts, and all three of the girls rushed to mount their own pets. They were cuddly animals, only about a yard high, their fur thick and coarse, with broad little faces. They had been captured in the northern isles and then sent down by ship. Taming them was a long process, lovingly undertaken by the stableboys. But by now they had all but forgotten they had ever been wild, and were gentle with their young riders.

Mary was first in the saddle and the first to trot away, but Lusty came close behind her.

"Hurry, hurry," urged Mary in Juno's ear, leaning forward over her neck. The pony went from a choppy trot to a gentle canter.

Overhead the sky was bright blue and almost cloudless. A sharp, clean smell of spring permeated the air, brought by winds down from the Highlands in the distance. It was a smell of melting snow and warming earth, and the faint perfume of a thousand wildflowers, just springing up on the carpet of new grass in the glens.

"Move, make way!" cried Lusty, passing Mary on her black pony, Cinders.

"Faster!" Mary ordered Juno. Juno was faster than Cinders, but not so easily persuaded to run. She obeyed now; and Mary saw herself gaining on Lusty.

A horn sounded, its note oddly out of place where no hunters were. A groom, riding on a big horse, was coming toward them from the castle grounds. "Stop!" he said, and blew the horn again.

"By the orders of Her Highness, the Queen Mother, you are to return to the palace," he said, motioning to the girls.

Mary was angry, and Lusty more so. Their race was being ruined. They looked at each other and thought of disobeying and running off. But they knew they could not outrun the groom on his large horse, and so they followed him back to the castle. Flamina had already dismounted and was waiting for them to walk back up the steep castle steps with her.

The three girls trudged up the seemingly endless flight of steps to reach the castle gateway.

The Queen Mother was pacing anxiously, and she could barely keep her hands from trembling.

Do not show them your fear, she told herself. If they are safe in here, do not alarm them. Are they coming? Oh, thank God! she sighed as she saw them enter into the gateway.

"My treasure, my sweet!" She fell on Mary and embraced her hysterically, weeping on her hair.

Mary, caught fast in her grip, could hardly breathe. Her mother continued, and her words were puzzling to the little girl. "They stop at nothing . . . worse than beasts . . . against God and the True Church . . . evil men . . ."

Lady Fleming, who was Flamina's mother and the children's governess, came over to soothe the Queen and take charge of the little girls. "There are some gowns from the time of James IV in a trunk I have just opened," she said. "Headdresses, too, with gold braid. They are in the little chamber off the Queen's bedchamber. Try them on and see who can look most like her own grandmother." She waved cheerfully, and the girls scampered off.

"Now," she said, taking the Queen's hand, "at least we know they are safe."

Marie de Guise stood shivering in the warm sunshine. "Poor little Beaton—it is her own relative, the Cardinal, that they have killed! Oh, how can I ever tell her? Yet if I do not, others will. Oh, Janet!" She turned back to Lady Fleming. "They killed him, hung him up like an animal—I am afraid!" The words came tumbling out. "Next they will come for us!"

25

"Nay, nay," said Lady Fleming. "They will not, they cannot. Stirling is the safest fortress in all Scotland. That is why you chose it!"

"But St. Andrews was supposed to be safe. The Cardinal was fortifying it; day and night the workmen were building it up. And yet—and yet—*they* got through!" She shuddered.

Lady Fleming raised her head proudly. "Yes, but it was the *English* he was fortifying it against. He did not suspect his own countrymen. They came disguised as workmen. Who were they?"

"The Protestants—radical heretics, revenging the burning of their leader, George Wishart."

"Oh, him!" Fleming waved her hand.

"I am frightened, Janet, frightened. Who would have thought they could exact such revenge?"

"Then call in outside help. Call on your mighty kinsmen in France. Your brother Duc François is a mighty soldier and can persuade the King to send ships and arms."

Marie smiled nervously. "Not so, not so. The King in France is very ill; all he cares about is fleeing from his disease. It is not easy to get his ear."

Together they walked over to the ramparts and stared down at the valley below. They could see the beckoning hills leading up into the Highlands, a place where cool breezes swept down all summer. The river lay in its bed like a silver chain in a velvet box. There was no movement of troops, nothing threatening. But then these fanatics did not come in the guise of troops.

Standing on the windy ramparts, Marie realized, suddenly and profoundly, how completely alone she was. Her ally and adviser was gone. There was no one to guide her in her policy, to protect her. She tried not to see in her mind's eye the Cardinal, swinging on the castle wall, hanging by his bedsheets. Or to picture him the way they said he was now, salted like a side of beef and lying in a barrel in the castle's dungeon.

They had let Marion Ogilvy go, after forcing her to witness his murder and mutilation. They did not sport with her themselves; they were much too holy for that, these reforming lairds from Fife, who had come into the castle in the early morning on a cart, diguised as workmen.

"Who are these lairds?" Janet wondered out loud.

"The report is that the assassins themselves numbered some sixteen or so," said Marie, who had questioned the messenger more closely than had the shocked governess. "But others are preparing to join them. They mean to hold the castle for themselves."

"What? For themselves? What for?"

"They are calling themselves the Castilians and sending to England for help."

"Ah." Now it was clearer than ever. "This is all part of the attack on Scotland that never ceases from England. They are determined to swallow us up! Ever since the Scots repudiated the marriage contract, the English have been trying to force a new one upon us by military means," Lady Fleming said.

At the same time, Marie realized with a sickening feeling, that meant they would never stop. And Scotland had no power to withstand them for much longer, if they were that determined.

That night, as Marie de Guise made ready for sleep—a sleep she knew would not come—she allowed her attendant of the bedchamber to brush her hair, which had grown long.

Brush, brush . . . the rhythm was soothing, as it began at her scalp and drew itself all the way to the ends, making her scalp tingle. The fire and the candles cast long, jumping shadows on the wall, shadows that obliterated the pretty coloured pictures of gods and goddesses, knights and ladies, on the tapestries imported from a safe, ordered place like Flanders.

Just as the darkness and shadows of Scotland obliterate all that's sustaining, she thought, her mind set free and drifting by the *brush* . . . *brush* . . . *brush* caresses. It is a land at the end of the earth, where men turn into something else. All of Scotland is like this castle of Stirling—ancient and stained with blood, with just a light cover of diverting statues, decorations, and distractions like the white peacocks walking the palace grounds around the artificial fishponds. They don't mean anything, they just take one's eyes off those misty mountains in the distance, or the enemies creeping up the Forth valley.

Half the nobility seem to dabble in withcraft, she mused. They say Lord James's mother, Lady Douglas, is a witch, and used her spells to bind the King to her, and Patrick, third Lord Ruthven, one of Mary's own guardians appointed by Parliament, is said to be a warlock himself. The dark powers seem so close here.

"That is enough, Meg," said Marie. Her scalp was beginning to hurt from the brushing. "I will take my rest now."

"As you wish, Madam." Meg brought out the lace bed-cap the Queen Mother always wore. She fastened it on her head and then pulled back the bed curtains.

But there is witchcraft in France, too, Marie thought, as she lay in bed. The Italian Woman, Catherine de Médicis—my brothers tell me she consults with wizards and necromancers, with anyone who can cure her barrenness. She would even deal with Satan himself—perhaps even *has*, for at long last, after ten years, she and Henri Valois have a son, François. He was born a year after my own Mary, most inauspiciously, during an eclipse of the sun. Any fool knows this is a bad omen, the worst possible—for what does an eclipse portend but just that, an eclipse of the person?—but they attempted to cover it up by designing an heraldic badge for the child, showing a sun and moon and the bold motto: "Between these I issued." Since then the Italian Woman has had a daughter, Elisabeth, and is pregnant again. The devil keeps his bargain. In his own way he is a being of integrity, so those who deal with him say.

Marie turned over and settled herself more comfortably. She was warmer now; she removed the heavy top cover.

27

They said little François was sickly, but he seemed to be growing stronger. Perhaps he was "eclipsed" most at his birth—perhaps that is all the omen meant, she thought. Perhaps he will live to be an answer to my Mary. . . . Oh, if only the Cardinal could help me! Oh, David!

With no one to hear, she wept for her only friend, her only adviser.

VI

Scarcely half a year later, Henry VIII died, and was succeeded on the throne of England by nine-year-old Edward, but in reality by the boy's uncle and Protector, the Duke of Somerset. The death of Henry VIII did nothing to lessen the ferocious "rough wooing," as the Scots sarcastically called the English military attempts to force the marriage of little Mary to now-King Edward by burning, killing, and looting all over the Scottish countryside.

As winter turned to spring, the French King François I followed Henry VIII to the grave. His son, the weak, ineffectual Henri II, now ruled France and was much more anxious to please the powerful Guise family than old François I had ever been; pleasing them meant, of course, championing the Scots against the English.

The rebels and assassins of Cardinal Beaton had held out in St. Andrews Castle for months, vainly hoping for English succour. Inside the stout castle walls, with the salted body of the dead Cardinal stored in his own dungeon, the murderers alternated between riotous living and deep penitence. Hungry for entertainment and company, certain fathers ordered the tutor of their children to bring the boys to the castle. John Knox, the tutor, obeyed, and came in at Easter.

After some initial hesitation, he took on the mantle of his vocation: he began to preach, minister, and debate with his "congregation," a congregation in exile. The thirty-three-year-old schoolmaster took to the pulpit like a John the Baptist, thundering of the great punishment to come if they did not reject the Synagogue of Satan, the Whore of Babylon, the Roman Church with its Pope, the Man of Sin. He whipped them into a frenzy of religious ecstasy.

The French sent a military force, and by the end of July 1547 the castle was forced to surrender. Knox, captured by the enemy, joined his fellow rebel-prisoners as a convict-rower in the galleys of the French fleet.

Stunned by the French action and hold on Scotland, the English now acted. The Protector himself led an invasion of Scotland, coming up through

Northumberland and passing through on the Berwick side of the coast.

He had an army of about eighteen thousand men, of which a third were cavalry. The foot soldiers were armed with muskets; heavy artillery was present, there were a thousand wagons of supply, and the might of the English fleet hovered just offshore.

Scots from all over had flocked to defend their country, and the Earl of Arran had twice as many men as the enemy—some thirty-six thousand. But they had no guns, only Highland archers; they had no artillery, only spears; and they had no horses. They marched under a white banner proclaiming *Afflicte sponse ne obliviscaris*—"The Holy Church Supplicating Christ."

At Pinkie Clough, beside the town of Musselburgh, some six miles east of Edinburgh, the Earl of Arran dug in to fight. He formed a battle line of four divisions on a piece of high ground, and their glittering spears were like four great fields of ripe barley. Or, as an English eyewitness described them, their ranks and spears were as thick as the spikes of a hedgehog. The black-robed clergy, standing together, were clearly visible, their tonsured heads looking like rows of helmets.

Both sides knew full well what they were fighting for. Somerset himself stepped forward and offered to withdraw if only the Scots would agree to let Mary choose her own husband when she was old enough, and not to make a marriage for her.

The Scots answered by hurling themselves on their foes, heedlessly abandoning their strong position. The English ships fired on them, scattering their archers; the cavalry cut them down. Most of the dead were wounded in the head, because the mounted soldiers could reach no lower with their swords, lopping off heads and hacking necks. Ten thousand Scots were slain, and the dead lay so thick that from a distance they looked like herds of grazing cattle in the green meadow. The white banner with its slogan was pulled out from under a mound of dead clergymen. The mud-stained trophy was sent south to be presented to King Edward VI in token of his victory.

Now even the thick walls of Stirling Castle could not protect its inmates from the horror outside. Amongst the dead, lying somewhere in the slippery mounds of rotting bodies, was Malcolm, Lord Fleming—Mary Fleming's father, Lady Janet Fleming's husband.

A swift messenger brought the news to Stirling, and the high-spirited Lady Fleming slumped and leaned against the wall in the courtyard. Over her, statues of the planetary gods in their niches—Mercury, Jupiter, Saturn—looked on benevolently. French sculptors had put them up, as though order and beauty could have taken root here, thought Marie de Guise, watching her attendant and friend fighting off tears and shock. They put them up on the order of my husband, also dead before his time, dead in a mysterious way.

"Courage," was all Marie could murmur. "Courage."

Lady Fleming stood up, bracing herself against the wall. "I must tell my daughter, I must tell my daughter," she kept repeating, and stumbled toward the children's quarters.

Mary Fleming wept bitterly that night in the bedchamber she shared with her namesakes. They attempted to comfort her, but only by reciting their own losses, losses all too Scottish in nature.

"My father died after Solway Moss," said Mary. "And my grandfather was killed at Flodden Field."

"Both my grandfathers were killed at Flodden," sobbed Fleming. "All my family has now been killed in battle against the English."

"My grandfather died at Flodden as well," said Mary Seton, in her quiet, sad way.

"And mine, too," said Mary Livingston, whose cheerful soul hated the thought of killing and blood.

"We are all sisters in sorrow," said Mary, who until that moment had never considered the matter. She knew of her grandfather's and father's deaths, but not of the subsequent desecration of their tombs and bodies. Thus far her life had been confusing but happy, and her nature was to seek sunshine rather than shadows; to flee the shadows that seemed to pursue her so restlessly. But her friends' sorrows—ah, that was something else. Then there could be no running away from it.

In the darkest part of the night a few days later, Mary was awakened when a candle was quietly lit in her room. Jean Sinclair, her personal attendant, was moving about, fully dressed. Mary could see her gathering clothes up in her arms, lifting the candle to look in shadowy corners. For what was she searching?

Jean came over to her, sat on the bed, and shook her gently. "You must dress, Your Highness, and warmly. You are going on a secret journey."

Mary sat up. Truly, this was a dream. She knew not to ask where, when she had been told that it was secret.

"Are we going alone?" she whispered, starting to climb out of bed. Mistress Sinclair already had her clothes warming on a stand before the fireplace.

"No. Your mother is coming, and the four Marys, and master Scott, the schoolmaster, and your guardians, Lords Erskine and Livingston. But that is all."

"Are we running away?" Mary began to pull on her heavy wool clothes, the ones she used when she rode or played on the ice.

"Yes. We are! No one shall ever be able to find us!"

"Will we stay there forever, and never come back?"

"Perhaps."

"And we will never see this castle again?"

"Perhaps."

Mary dashed about, getting ready, her heart racing.

Outside in the courtyard the travelling party met by torchlight. They wore hooded cloaks and sturdy boots and carried only the smallest travelling pouches. The adults talked together in low voices that did not carry over to the children, who were huddling together. Flamina and Lusty were excited about the midnight ride, Seton resigned to her fate, and Beaton placid and calm. But Mary felt her spirits take wing as the adventure began. There was danger in it, and rather than being afraid, she felt reborn, created in it.

Down the long castle steps the party descended in darkness—they dared not risk flaring torches, not with the English reported only six miles away that afternoon. At the base of the stairs, horses awaited them, and the girls were settled behind the adults; no Shetland pony could go as fast as this party intended to race through the night.

Then they were away, galloping into the darkness, with the head groom from the castle stable as a guide on this moonless night.

The air was chilly, and the ground was covered in mist, which swirled and made eddies as they passed through it. Mary clung tightly to the back of Lord John Erskine; Mary Livingston was riding behind her own father, Alexander.

In the night Mary could hear sounds of animals in the thickets: herds of wild cattle and deer and the beating wings of startled waterfowl. Weasels and stoats scrambled in the underbrush and once—her hair prickled as she heard it—a pack of wolves howled in the darkness.

It all seemed a dream, the darkness and the jouncing and the alien smells and sounds; and so it was not less a dream when they pulled up by the side of a lake and were met by a boatman. As the sky grew milky, and mists were rising from the lake with its reeds standing like yellow sentinels, they were rowed toward a green island with white buildings, glowing in the pearly radiance of the dawn. Mary stepped off the boat onto a carpet of spongy green grass and was met by a tall cowled figure.

"Welcome, my child," he said, bending on one knee. "Welcome to Inchmahome."

His outer robes were black and his cowl so deep she could not clarly see his face. But the voice, soothing and gentle, seemed as much a dream as everything else that magic night and dawn. Sighing, she collapsed in the Prior's arms, carried away by peace.

She slept three-quarters of the day, and when she finally awoke it was late afternoon. Long, honey-coloured beams of light were coming through a row of windows in what seemed to be a large but very plain room. The walls were plastered but not decorated or adorned in any way; the floor was bare stone. The bed she lay on was not soft, but firm, and the sheets were coarse. They had an astringent smell, like clean air and things bleached by the sun. And the faint, lingering odour of sweet woodruff clung to them.

From somewhere she heard the distant sound of chanting. She got up—
she had slept fully dressed—and walked slowly over to the open window.
Outside she could see trees, very green grass, water, and, next door, a small
church. The chanting was rising from there. It was faint, and sounded like
the far shore of Heaven. She leaned out over the windowsill and let the
soft air stir her hair, and lay, drowsing, in the beauty of the sun and the
floating voices. Never had she felt such peace.

It was thus that the Prior found her when he returned to his room after
the service of None. The little girl was draped over the windowsill, sleeping
with a smile on her fair oval face.

The puir wee bairn, he thought. I had never thought to see my own
Queen here in my monastery. She's a faerie-creature that we have all heard
of but no one has ever seen, since they keep her locked up at Stirling.

The Prior, Brother Thomas, was doing penance for "rejoicing in iniquity"
as forbidden in I Corinthians 13:5: *Charity seeketh not her own, thinketh no
evil, rejoiceth not in iniquity.* For Brother Thomas had been, if not actually
joyful at the death of Robert Erskine, the layman who had been handed
the priorship of Inchmahome as a royal present, at least rejoicing at regaining
temporary control of his monastery. Pinkie Clough had claimed young
Robert; his father, the little Queen's guardian, had arrived with the royal
visitors and would doubtless appoint his second son, John, to take over in
Robert's place. But in the meantime, Brother Thomas ruled again—and
quite rightly so, he thought. The ruler of a priory *should* be a monk, not
a royal appointee who did not even know the names of the Divine Services!
Oh, I must do more penance, he thought wearily, as he entertained these
thoughts and even welcomed them.

He gently touched the little girl's shoulder and she opened her eyes—
delicately coloured amber ones with flecks of gold.

"Good afternoon, Your Majesty," he said.

She stretched unself-consciously. "I fell asleep hearing the most wonderful
music. It was like angels."

"It was the monks who live here," he said. "See them walking about,
across the cloister?" He pointed down at the bright green lawn surrounded
on all sides by an arcade with graceful arches. Indeed, black-and-white-
robed figures were moving in all directions, their paths crisscrossing. There
were only three colours to be seen anywhere: black, white, and green,
making an exquisite pattern of stillness against movement. Even the stones
of the monastery were the same hues—black, white, grey, with touches of
green moss.

"They were praying to God," Prior Thomas explained. "We all gather
in that church to do so eight times a day."

"Eight times!" she exclaimed.

"Indeed. The first time is in the middle of the night. That is our vigil
service."

"Why?"

"Why what?"

"Why do you get up in the middle of the night to pray?"

"Because we feel closer to God then, when all the world is asleep and we wait for the dawn."

Mary yawned. "You must love God very much—more than sleep, anyway!"

"Not always. But there is obedience, which is a very high form of love. It just does not feel so pretty at the time as the other kinds."

Like mystical union, and even suffering, he thought, feeling the welts from "the discipline" under his coarse wool habit. Obedience is a dry, dull sort of love; not a *lover's* love. But God seems to prefer it—not the least of His peculiarities.

"You have missed our main meal," he said. "You must be very hungry. I can have some food sent up straightway. Bread, soup, eggs—"

"Can I not eat with the monks?"

"Yes, but—that is later, and I fear the last meal is sparse—scarcely more than a bite or two."

"I should like to eat with the monks," she insisted.

At her age such things are a game, a novelty, he thought. Monks, and a "fasting supper"—only after years does it become both natural and a sacrifice.

"As you wish," he said.

That night, at the long refectory table, Mary took her place, along with her mother and the other Marys. She watched the robed figures of the monks as they silently broke their bread and spooned their soup in slow, rhythmic motions. Beside them, the outsiders' movements seemed jerky and awkward as they brought the food to their mouths and drank from their wooden cups.

Mary found herself embarrassed by her fellow guests, and longed to eat as the monks did instead. She looked over at her mother, who was chewing a piece of bread with gusto. What was she thinking of? Mary tried to catch her eye, but the Queen Mother was completely absorbed in her own thoughts.

We are safe here on this island, thought Marie de Guise. The English will never find us in this place. But now I know Scotland cannot stand alone any longer. The Battle of Pinkie Clough has proved it. This was the end for Scotland as a true independent fighting force. The English will devour her. We must offer ourselves to France, throw ourselves on her mercy.

The thought of such abject crawling was a bitter one. But if she wished to hold Scotland for her daughter . . .

She looked over at Mary, seated with the other Marys. The little girl was watching the monks intently, and hardly eating anything. Her eyes followed every movement the monks made as they broke their bread and bowed their heads over their soup.

To her this is all an adventure, thought her mother. The gallop in the night, coming to an island, hiding here with monks . . . but it is no game for me. It is deadly serious; what I decide today will determine whether my daughter has a future as Queen of Scotland, and whether Scotland itself has a future.

But I *have* decided: We will sell ourselves to France. Pity the Cardinal is not here to catch me saying "we" and "ourselves"—am I become Scots at last? He would find that amusing. But if I must choose between England and France as our master, I will choose France; it is my native land; it is Catholic; it is congenial in all the ways that matter. My daughter is half French herself. . . . All will be well.

She picked up her wooden cup and drank deeply from it. The wine therein was French. All good things came from France, so it seemed.

France . . . Her face grew dreamy in remembering: the sweet autumn days in the family estate at Joinville; the mellow colour of the leaves still on the trees, with the low-hanging sun slanting through them; the spicy crackle when she stepped on the leaves which had already fallen; the fresh cider from the apple orchards; the mists in the early morning, rising in the woods during the wild boar hunts. . . .

The decision felt right, right all the way through. Odd how when a decision was absolutely right it presented itself so easily, and slipped through all the sluice-gates of the mind without impediment, whereas when it was not right, it was such a struggle to force it through, and then there were the nagging points where it caught, clung, and irritated, she thought.

The Queen Mother was suddenly debilitatingly tired. It is over, she thought. It is over, it is done. I have decided.

There remained only notifying France. But that would be simple.

I am ready for rest, she thought. I have earned it.

Mother and daughter were sharing the Prior's room in the upper floor of the west range of the cloister. Brother Thomas had brought out the finest bedding for his royal guests and laid down carpets during the afternoon; the Augustine Canons, less austere than some orders, had such items on hand for honourable visitors.

In the deepest part of the night, Mary came suddenly to a full waking that was preternatural. She lay stiff and still, holding her breath, and it seemed her mother was holding her breath, too, and that the whole room was a stone creature that had sense and feeling and was awake, but silent. Outside she could hear the trees on the island, their leaves rustling and sighing in the wind, not in a lonely way, but in a deeply comforting companionship.

Then she heard a stirring from somewhere, a soft swish: the sound of padded footsteps and the brushing of robes. It was the monks, going to their prayers.

Outside it was completely dark. She crept out of bed and went to the window. There was no moon, but the stars were bright. Against the dark, shiny surface of the lake she could see the moving leaves of the giant trees; and from within the church there glowed a faint light.

The monks were gathering for their prayers in the secret time of the night. She longed with all her heart to join them, and suddenly she knew this was why she had been called awake. Groping for her shoes, she pulled them on, and felt for her wool mantle. Taking care not to stumble, and feeling her way painfully slowly toward the door, she managed to edge past her mother's bed without awakening her. She lifted the wooden latch of the door very carefully, and pulled the door open. It did not creak; the monks kept everything in the most perfect working order, as part of their service to God.

It was cold on the stairway leading down to the ground, and Mary pulled her cloak tightly against her chest. She descended the steps and then ran across the wet grass to the side entrance of the church. Again, there was a perfect latch on the door and she was able to let herself into the church soundlessly. She crept into the recess of a side altar and hid there in the shadows. The monks were already gathered; they must not see her!

They were seated all along the stone benches on each side of the glittering high altar, flanked by two tall candles. Their cowled heads were bowed, and the mumble of rosaries being recited surrounded them like the buzz of bees around a hive.

> Ave Maria
> Gratia plena
> Dominus tecum:
> Benedicta tu in mulieribus. . . .

She did not dare to move, hunched there in her stone recess that was cold and covered in a light film of condensation. Time seemed suspended, not to be passing at all. But then, gradually, she saw the five tall windows behind the high altar in the east begin to separate themselves from the night. At first they were barely noticeable, a smudge of opalescence in the dark; but slowly each hue in them began to glow and become more distinct, until at last there were garnet red and marigold yellow and sapphire blue and twilight violet and sea green, slender long panels of jewels forming exquisite pictures in the dawn.

The monks stirred, and there was a metallic clanking as the incense was lit in its censer. The rich, perfumed smoke rose in soft clouds around the altar and then the chanting began: the Office of Matins.

Te de-um laude-mus. . . .

The deep, measured cadences rolled upward with the incense. The sun sent a first tiny ray through a purple spear of glass in the window. The Virgin Mary, in her niche near the high altar, seemed to glow as the first light caressed her alabaster face.

Mary nearly swooned with the beauty of it all, with the cold, with her excitement, with the forbiddenness of her own presence. She had been to mass at the Chapel Royal in Stirling Castle, but it was a lacklustre, daytime thing: this was magic, a door to another world, a world that overwhelmed her and drew her so powerfully that she felt she could vanish straightway into it.

The incandescent colours, the mystic smell, the deep, beckoning, otherworldly voices, and the glowing face of the Virgin swirled in her aroused soul. Clutching at the wall, she felt herself in the grip of an ecstasy, and, closing her eyes, she let herself be carried away.

So this is God, she thought, as she slid forward soundlessly, and gave herself up to Him.

The monks later discovered her sprawled out on the floor of the nave, near a side altar. She was so deeply asleep they feared she was unconscious; but as she was picked up, she opened her eyes and smiled, a beatific smile.

"Is it time for the next singing?" she asked, and the monks laughed, relieved.

"The Queen of Scots should perhaps become a nun, Your Highness," they said, in returning her to her mother. "Like the blessed Queen, Saint Margaret. She seems to have a vocation for it."

"She has a different destiny," replied Marie. The night's sleep had confirmed her resolution of the night before. "She must marry, and live in this world."

"It is dangerous to ignore a call from God," said Brother Thomas, in a seemingly playful manner. "God is a possessive lover, and He does not suffer rejection lightly. In fact, if He has marked you for His own, He does not suffer rejection at all."

"Perhaps at the end of her life, when her earthly duty is over," said Marie. She found this conversation annoying and pointless.

"God does not want our leavings, but our first fruits," persisted Brother Thomas. "However," he said with an irritating smugness, "he has been known to turn our leavings into a sacrifice of the highest order."

VII

Inside the bowels of the French galley, it was stiflingly hot and reeked of unwashed human skin. The rowers had been at their oars for hours, and now that it was growing dark they knew their torture would soon be over—for a little while. Only ten or twelve of them had been lashed today, for everyone had worked hard, and their master was kindhearted—for an overseer.

"They've sighted the shoreline near Dumbarton," announced the master. "Tomorrow we put in. Rest for a few days—then back to France."

"Here we take on board the Queen?" muttered a tall, sinewy rower. His shoulders bore the fading marks of a not-so-recent lashing.

"Yes, and all her train," replied the master. "Some fifty or sixty young people and their preceptors."

"Bah!" said the rower. "So it is to come about, is it? The little Queen is to go to France, there to drink of that liquor that should remain with her all her lifetime, for a plague to this realm, and for her final destruction."

"What do you care, Knox?" said a fellow rower. "It means a rest for us, that's all it means. I should think you'd welcome it. Who's up on deck— does it matter? We never see them."

"We can *feel* them," pronounced Knox. "Their presence pollutes the air!"

"Do you speak of the Queen in such terms, man?"

"The Queen is a child who is half French and now to be wholly indoctrinated with that unhealthy, twisted manner of thinking. No, she's not *my* Queen!"

He stretched his cramped arms. It had been over a year since he was captured by the French when St. Andrews Castle fell; he had been rowing in the galleys ever since. There had been the ship of Rouen, and even a fairly pleasant stint on the Loire River, although he had never been allowed up on deck to see the fabled châteaux. Now, for the past few months, he had been serving in the fleet of more than a hundred ships that the French King sent out to do a double duty: to land troops on the eastern coast of Scotland, at Leith, to man the garrisons and rout the English; and then to sail around the northern tip of Scotland—what miserable sailing that had been, no galleys before had ever attempted such a voyage—and land on the western coast of Scotland. There, at the stronghold of Dumbarton Castle, perched on its rocky heights above the Firth of Clyde, was the little Scots Queen, waiting to be conveyed to France.

John Knox had almost wept when he saw his native country from the tiny portholes of the rowing deck earlier on the voyage. The spires of St. Andrews had swum tantalizingly at a distance.

"I shall preach again there someday," he said solemnly.

"O' course you will," muttered the man next to him, a murderer and cutpurse whom Knox had attempted, with singular unsuccess, to convert to the True Gospel.

And now he could see the great boulder—for so it looked from a distance—of Dumbarton from out of the porthole frame. A tiny castle was visible, clinging to the top.

She's waiting up there, he thought. That misguided little child, steeped in the abominations of Popery. And next to be dipped, like Achilles in the River Styx, in the river of frivolity and falsehood that is France: to the ruin of her character and the misdirection of her education.

Scotland must not be served so. No, she must not, he thought.

The moment of parting had come. In all the excitement—in the hasty French lessons, and the selection of Shetland ponies as gifts for the French royal children, in the clothes-fittings and farewell banquets—five-year-old Mary had not realized that her mother would not be coming with her.

They had never before been separated. And now, with the wind whipping and snapping the pennants on the ships, with the waters of the Firth jumping in the sunlight, with the large number of lords and ladies assembled for the boarding, she suddenly felt sick. She clung to her mother.

"I cannot leave you," she said, her eyes filling with tears. "I cannot, I cannot!"

Marie de Guise, tears choking her own throat, begged the Virgin for the strength to hide her distress. "My dearest child, do not cry. I will follow as soon as I may," she said. "There is yet business to attend to here. When I have secured your kingdom, when I have made sure no one will ever take Scotland from you, my darling, then I will come to France."

"Will it be soon?"

"It depends how much of a fight the English put up!" She attempted to joke. "Now, *ma chérie*, dry your eyes." She handed Mary a lace handkerchief. "That's my fine girl."

She looked into her daughter's eyes, trying to memorize them, to hold that look in some part of her mind where she could see it forever. "You go to those who love you," she said. "The little Dauphin—he is younger than you, and not so strong. He longs for a playmate. You will seem the answer to his prayers. And you will learn, my angel, that fulfilling someone else's prayers is the same as having your own fulfilled." She hugged her. "God keep you—the Blessed Virgin hold you."

Mary hugged her back, pressing up against her and shutting her eyes.

The onlookers cheered, and began to tease.

"*La Reinette* must come aboard her humble galley," said the nobleman who represented Henri II. "France is eager to embrace you!"

Knox, peeping out of the porthole, could just see the small figure of Mary in her blue velvet gown and its matching hat with a curling feather. The fat cow of a Queen Mother was there also, he thought. And all the grinning Frenchmen, like apes in satin. And the red-haired brood of children—half of them Stewart bastards—going along as well.

Pfah! I hope they will all be seasick and soil their fancy selves all the way to France! he thought, just as the overseer flicked him with the lash to make him take his place at his station.

❧

John Knox got his wish. All the members of the little Queen's entourage were deathly ill with seasickness, for the winds were tempestuous and the waters stormy almost all the way to France. Indeed, Lady Fleming was so ill she begged the captain to put in at Cornwall and let her go ashore; at which the Frenchman, Monsieur de Villegaignon, made the ungallant response that she could go to France by sea or drown on the way.

Only one member of the party was not sick: Mary herself. She seemed to delight in the excitement of the gales, and in the crisis of the broken rudder off the coast of Cornwall. Eagerly she clung to the ship's railing—without Lady Fleming there to supervise her—and watched the sailors straining to fit a replacement. Her brother James Stewart, determined as usual to know everything that was going on, struggled up on deck to watch for a few minutes. But the heaving decks soon made him nauseated again and he staggered back to his cabin.

For several days the captain was unable to land along the western coast of France, in Brittany. When finally he could put in, it was near the little town of Roscoff, at a rocky spot in the heart of smugglers' and pirates' territory.

Mary was eager to go ashore and the rowboats were readied; she was in the first group to land. Fishermen and townsfolk, drawn by the sight of the huge, battered galleys, had gathered on the shore and now stood by to welcome them. Mary was helped out of the boat to take her first step on French soil by a muscular Breton whose hands smelled of fish. It was August thirteenth, 1548.

At first she thought it looked no different from Dumbarton. It was the same landscape of deep blue, vexed sea, and harsh rocks along the coast.

But as the royal party went inland—conducted ceremoniously by the Lord of Rohan and the nobility of the district, who had hurried to meet them—the land suddenly began to look foreign, and Mary knew she had come to a new and strange place.

As they passed through Normandy, the country became flat, green, and well-watered, with many thatch-roofed farmhouses. There were apple orchards and cows everywhere, and at dinners hosted by the local lords en route, they were proudly served delicious, rich dishes made with apples, butter, and cream: pancakes with Calvados; apple flans and caramels. Even the omelets seemed magical, and not to have come from the humble egg at all, they were so fluffy and light.

At length they reached the Seine, where a decorated barge awaited them, sent by the King. They were to take it upriver to the Château of St.-Germain-en-Laye, where the French royal children—*les enfants de France*—would receive them.

The barge was wide and comfortably appointed with luxurious touches: a fully staffed kitchen, a dining room with goblets and gold plates, beds with gold leaf on the headboards, privy stool-closets hung with crimson velvet and perfumed with fresh irises in a silver vase fastened to the wall.

It was at this point that the Scots children began to feel uncomfortable, being surrounded by a silvery-soft language they could not understand, and realizing that in only a few days they would come face to face with the French children in the royal nursery. What if they were horrid little things—crying, whining brats who cheated at games, tattled, and teased? Until that moment "the French children," "the Dauphin," and "the princesses" had had no real significance to them.

And if the Dauphin and Mary did not like each other, what then? Would the alliance be abandoned, or would they be forced to marry, regardless?

Slowly the royal barge made its way up the Seine and its wide green valley, past Rouen, past Les Andelys, past Vernon, past Meulan, and then finally to the landing stage for St.-Germain-en-Laye. A large pier, its posts painted in gold, red, and blue, flew the royal standard of Valois from its staff.

An attendant hurriedly sent his assistant ahead to the château, and arranged for horses to transport the guests, although the distance was not great—the château lay on the upper banks of the river. Big, sleek beasts with heavy leather saddles were led forward, and the Scots stared at them. They were so rounded and gleaming they did not seem the same animals called "horses" in Scotland.

The gravelled path to the château was planted on both sides with tall, slender trees, like a sacred grove in ancient Greece. And then, looming before them, on a ridge above the river, was the grey building of the château.

Servants and attendants now appeared to accompany them up the path and into the courtyard. Their horses were taken and they were escorted into the Salle des Fêtes, a richly decorated hall on the west side of the courtyard.

Mary looked all around her at the high ceiling and the light colours of the wall decoration: pinks, pale aquas, yellows the shade of meadow wildflowers. The men and women in the paintings were wearing thin, transparent clothes that allowed her to see through them as if they were naked. She was studying this when suddenly a deep voice announced something in French, and everyone was still.

The farthest door of the hall opened, and out came three children, two girls and a boy. Only two could walk properly; the third swayed back and forth on her baby feet and had to be helped by the others. They came toward the Scots, and instinctively Mary went forward to meet them.

Across the wide floor of the Salle des Fêtes, the children approached each other, with everyone watching.

So this little boy must be François, the Dauphin, thought Mary. He had a fat little face and slanted eyes, and his tight, curvaceous mouth was clamped shut. The pale eyes were wary. He was very small, but pudgy.

Immediately, Mary felt protective of him, as she did of the small wounded animals that she had insisted on nursing back to health at Stirling whenever she had found them lying injured on the heath or limping about in the palace courtyard.

"*Bonjour. Bienvenue à St.-Germain-en-Laye. Je suis Prince François, et ces sont mes soeurs, les Princesses Elisabeth et Claude.*" The little boy bowed stiffly.

"*Je suis Marie, votre amie et cousine et—fiancée,*" responded Mary, using almost all the French she knew.

40

Then, to the delight of all the onlookers, the two children smiled at each other, laughed, and joined hands.

It was the first time many of the French courtiers had ever seen François smile.

Although the King and Queen were not at St.-Germain at the time, they had assured Mary, *la Reinette d'Ecosse,* of a proper welcome in the person of Diane de Poitiers, the King's mistress. Indeed, when Mary first beheld her coming into the *salle,* she assumed she was looking at the Queen, so beautiful was the Moon Mistress. Her hair was silver, her skin pale, and her satins were a shimmery white and black. She seemed to glide across the floor, like a faerie creature, and François and Elisabeth greeted her as warmly as if she were their own mother. Mary immediately gave the proper, prescribed respect to the woman as Queen, only to have her smile and say, "No, no . . ." and then a string of the unintelligible French followed.

Patrick Scott, a member of the company of Scottish archers at court, hastily came to Mary and bowed. "May I offer my services as a translator, Your Highness? The Duchesse de Valentinois, Madame de Poitiers, thanks you for your kind greetings, and wishes you to know that, as the honoured friend of the King, and in his name, she welcomes you to France. The King hopes you will find all happiness here, as the wife of his son, and among his people as their future queen. He longs to see you, and will be coming soon from Italy, where he is campaigning."

At this delightful game where one person spoke for another, Mary giggled. Then François did, also, for it was the first time he had ever heard the Scots language. The rest of the parties on both sides joined in the laughter.

The Duchesse gestured, and palace servants took their stations and stood by to show the Scottish guests to their quarters. She spoke, in her pretty voice, and then Patrick Scott explained.

"Queen Mary, you are to share a room with the Princesse Elisabeth. It is the King's wish that you should live like sisters. I myself have chosen the furnishings, and I hope they are to your liking. Shall you come and see them now? Perhaps you wish to rest after your journey?"

Used to the debilitation and lassitude of François, the Duchesse was surprised when Mary exclaimed. "Oh, no, I am not tired!" and almost jumped up and down. But then she added politely, "But I should very much like to see the furnishings which you have chosen for me, Madame."

The Duchesse then led them back, through a long, vaulted gallery and up the main staircase, until at last they reached a suite of apartments above the second storey that overlooked the long slope down to the Seine, which shone like a little ribbon in the afternoon sun. It seemed to Mary that she had never been in such a huge building; the rooms went on and on, an endless series of doors and entrances disappearing behind the rustling gown of the Duchesse, which scattered light like the surface of a liquid, and quivered at each movement.

She showed them into a large, sunny room that was panelled in a tawny wood.

"Here it is, Your Highness. Your quarters. The royal nursery."

The little beds, one on each side of the room, their frames carved with birds, leaves, and flowers, were bright with blue and gold hangings. There were child-sized tables and chairs; mirrors that hung at their eye level; wool rugs that made the floor as soft as moss. And in one corner, on a stand, was a wooden model château—it opened up on hinges to reveal miniature rooms and furniture inside. Mary rushed over to it and peeked in its tiny windows. Inside was a magical world, like a dream.

"Oh, Madame," she said. She could not think of any words to express her wonder.

"It is yours to play with, and furnish, as you will. Look—here are the dolls that live in it." Diane pointed to a group of figures in the model courtyard. To Mary's amazement, she recognized herself there. She picked up the doll, staring at it.

It had real hair, exactly her colour. It wore a hawking costume in green velvet, exactly like her own. And to the doll's wrist was attached a *faux* hawk, made with real feathers, identical in shade to the one she owned.

"Is it like Ruffles?" The Duchesse was smiling, looking at Mary, and suddenly Mary felt transported to Heaven, where she was cherished, safe, and shown wonder after wonder. She did not feel at home, but in some place infinitely better and more tender. She flung her arms around the Duchesse's neck and began to cry with excitement and joy.

"Hush, hush, *ma petite*." The Duchesse smoothed Mary's hair. "No need to cry." Over Mary's shoulder she motioned to the chamber attendants. Clearly the little Queen of Scots was overtired from the excitement and strain of the long journey, and needed to rest, regardless of what she said. And it was time for the Princesse Elisabeth's nap as well. It would be good for them to take their rest together.

"How did you know my f-falcon's name?" Mary asked, wondering how that miracle had come about.

"Why, we know a great deal about you, because everyone in France is curious about the brave little Queen who had to flee and take refuge from the English. Here you are already a romantic figure, and we are all in love with you."

"But Ruffles—how did you *know*?" Mary persisted.

"From your relatives here, child. Your grandmother Antoinette de Bourbon, and your mother's brothers, the great François and Charles, Cardinal of Lorraine. They feel as if they *know* you, as your mother writes and tells them everything. Soon you will meet them and they will see you in person."

Mary's own nurse, Jean Sinclair, came forward to help her over to her bed. "The Princesse Elisabeth needs to rest now, and it would be polite if you would lie down as well," she said, and Mary, for once, acquiesced. She was curious to try out the French bed. It had a gilded stepstool beside it— what other wonders did it have?

When all the attendants except her Scottish ones had left, and Mary lay in the soft bed, with its feather mattress and huge feather pillows, covered with a white wool blanket, the Duchesse came to draw the bedcurtains. "Welcome to France," she whispered, and kissed Mary's forehead gently. "This is for you." She handed her a satin pillow stuffed with fragrant herbs. "Put this under your neck and pretend you are lying down in a spring meadow, watching the clouds drift by, falling asleep. . . ."

Mary sighed, clutched the scented pillow, and did as the Duchesse said, giving herself up to a sensual, indulgent sleep.

The next morning Mary awakened to sunlight. She remembered immediately where she was: in this foreign nursery where everything was miraculously child-sized. Then she heard murmurs in that new language that sounded as sweet as the herb-pillow smelled.

"*Bonjour, Mesdemoiselles.* It is a beautiful day. Come, there is a surprise for you. The Queen of Scotland's little horses are here! Dress quickly, and see them!"

Mary's clothes had all been aired, pressed, unpacked, and put away while she slept. Now Jean Sinclair—or Jehan St. Claire, as she was to be called in France—had laid them out for her already.

She and Elisabeth were taken to another room, where breakfast—*le petit déjeuner*—was being served to the Dauphin as well as the four Marys and the three Stewarts. The table was heaped with baskets of fruit, shiny loaves of bread with braided designs, and several large round things on platters, with wedges cut out of them.

François was already seated, in a special chair with high legs, and had helped himself to very little. He was staring at the plate sullenly, but looked up when Mary came in, and smiled.

The Stewart brothers, James, Robert, and John, eyed the spread suspiciously.

"What is that?" asked Robert, pointing to the wheel-shaped thing of pallid color.

"*C'est fromage, de Normandie.*"

"What is that in French?" asked Mary, pointing at a bowl of peaches.

"*Pêches,*" said François.

"*Pêches,*" repeated Mary.

The French laughed at her pronunciation.

"*Pêches,*" she repeated, correcting herself. "And this?" She indicated a jar of fruit jam.

"*La confiture,*" said François. He looked pleased with himself; he felt quite knowledgeable.

"*La confiture,*" she repeated, mimicking the accent well. "And this?" She picked up a loaf of bread.

"*Du pain! Du pain!*" chorused the French children.

Taking a sample of everything she named, Mary had soon eaten so much her stomach felt uncomfortable. But the children had enjoyed the meal, and getting to know one another. Now they were anxious to go outside and see what the Queen of Scotland—*la Reine d'Ecosse*—had brought: a gift of miniature horses.

Out in the courtyard the shaggy little beasts were waiting, saddled and ready. Mary's own pony, Juno, was there, as well as Lusty's Cinders. There were a dozen others, all from the isles so far north of the Scottish mainland, most of them dark brown and all of them with thick, rough coats.

"You may choose your favourite, my dear François," said Mary, gesturing toward the ponies.

He smiled, not understanding the Scots language, but comprehending the gesture.

He walked directly to one of the smallest animals, which had a white star on the forehead.

"I would like that one, *s'il vous plaît!*" he exclaimed. "And I will call her—Marie! In honour of my bride and guest!"

Everyone laughed.

The next few days were spent exploring the Château of St.-Germain-en-Laye in the warm days of August. The flat roof of the palace had been transformed with trees in tubs and flowers in planters, with little benches and awnings to make a pleasant place for people to stroll about and view the countryside and the Seine valley below. The King planned to build an adjacent palace just on the edge of the slope, with terraces farther down, which could be reached either directly from the palace or by long flights of stairs on either side at a lower level. Construction would begin soon.

The King, though kept away by affairs of state—he was inspecting coveted regions of Italy—sent a steady stream of letters north and assured the new arrivals that he and the Queen would be coming as soon as events permitted. In the meantime, they were to consider that Madame the Duchesse de Valentinois was acting entirely on His Majesty's behalf.

The Duchesse arranged for Mary's relatives, the Guises, to come to meet her. She also found a Scotsman who was fluent in French to serve as a permanent translator. It must needs be a Scotsman, as no one but natives spoke either English or Scots; even the ambassadors posted to London from France, Spain, and Italy did not speak English. It was a minor language, utterly insular and useless, and shunned by the diplomatic community. But some Scotsmen sought service abroad, and here in France there were bi-lingual men to be found.

The three most formidable Guises—mother and eldest sons—came to St.-Germain in splendour, riding from their Hôtel de Guise in Paris. The old Duchesse Antoinette, mother of twelve children, straight-backed and straight-natured (she kept her coffin in the gallery outside her room, so she must see it as she passed to mass every morning), the idol and loving support of her daughter, Marie de Guise, was dressed, as always, in black. Her formidable warrior-son, François, called "le Balafre" from a battle-wound on his cheek, now thirty and the same age as the King, rode up on a huge chestnut charger. And his younger brother, Charles, who had crowned Henri II and become a cardinal only five days later at the age of twenty-three, rode on a silver-bedecked, crimson-satined mule. Together they were coming, like the Magi, to view this child in whom they had great hopes—this Princess and Queen who had appeared, like a star in the north, to guide the Guises to final glory. For, married to the Dauphin, yet knowing her family loyalty and instructions, must not Mary of Scotland prove to be their patron saint? And any child she had would be a quarter part Guise and they would be elevated to the ranks of royalty at last.

True, they claimed descent from Charlemagne, but that was in the mythical, misty past, and this reputedly clever, pretty little girl was both the present and future for them, a much more solid thing. . . .

So they took their journey eagerly and made their way up the steep slope to the château, thankful that the usual Guise luck held and they could meet her before the King and Queen did. Of course there was the troublesome Madame de Poitiers already installed there and living with the children, but she was only a reflection, in political terms, of the King—just as her symbol, the moon, emitted no warm light of its own, and Diana the huntress must always give way to Apollo.

Not that Henri II, that sad, timid, unimaginative man, was any Apollo. Yet he liked to think himself so, and the court flatterers obliged him.

At St.-Germain, they were shown into the grandest room, the Salle des Audiences. If this was intended to overawe them, it failed. As a ploy, it was too transparent. Their own château of Meudon had equally impressive rooms. Now the Italian Woman, the Queen, she was more subtle . . . one never knew exactly where one stood with the Italian Woman, or what her secret designs were.

Madame de Poitiers brought little Mary Stewart—or Marie Stuart, as she was to be known in France—into the hall. The little girl, dressed beautifully in a russet gown that matched her long, curly hair and reflected the blush of colour on her cheeks, came forward shyly.

The adults all made obeisance to her, as an anointed and reigning Queen. She stared at the tops of their hats and then gave them leave to stand up. They all looked at one another for a long moment until the Duchesse de Guise commanded through the translator, "Come here, child, and let me look at you!"

Mary walked slowly over to her grandmother. Was this truly her mother's mother? She did not look like her. Was this the mother who had held Marie de Guise, taught her, and written long letters to her in Scotland? She had seen her mother wait for them and read them eagerly.

Mary presented herself to this stern-looking woman. Then the lady smiled, held out her arms, and enfolded Mary in them.

"Thank you for coming to us," she murmured, but of course Mary could not understand her, and the words were too soft and personal for a translator to interpret them. She understood the intent, though, and hugged the old woman back.

"Now you must meet your uncles," said her grandmother, pulling back and indicating them.

"Your mother is my firstborn, my oldest child. My favourite, I think! And my next-born is François here, Duc de Guise, who is a great soldier of France, champion of the King, and eager to do service for you whenever you require it. They call him fearless—and truly he is well known for his courage, which he has proved over and over."

Duc François came forward and kissed her hand.

"My next son, Charles—oh, he is altogether different. He is a scholar and a churchman, although there are those"—she put her arms affectionately around the shoulders of her two tall sons—"who think he is more handsome than his brother here."

This was dutifully translated.

"I am sure His Majesty the King would be well pleased to see Cardinal Charles direct his niece *la Reinette d'Ecosse* in her education," said Madame de Poitiers. "Certainly there is no one better qualified."

The Guises all smiled. So the King had already decided that. So much the better.

"Do you know Latin, Marie?" asked the Cardinal.

"Not yet."

"Ah, yes, soon enough. First there must be French!"

"I believe His Majesty will arrange that as soon as he comes. She makes good progress in learning it every day on her own, and has no accent at all, but it may be necessary to send the other Scots children away, lest she talk to them and impede her development in French. We shall see."

"Indeed." The grandmother nodded. "Soon all things will become clear."

"I think you will find her almost entirely French already," said Madame de Poitiers. "It must be in her blood."

❧

A month passed before the King arrived at St.-Germain, a month in which Mary and her playmates were free to roam the château and its grounds, to ride and walk along the riverbanks and see the autumnal countryside sunk in mists and morning chill. Mary and François genuinely liked one another; if François's timidity and frailty brought out all her gentle feelings, her vitality and happy disposition seemed like sunshine to him, warming and cheering his bleak and lonely nature. He was a year and a month younger than she, and looked up to her in the way a child does to whom a year is a very grand thing.

When Mary and the King did meet, it came about in a very informal way, to the disappointment of foreign ambassadors lurking about hoping to catch the historic moment. The King had just entered the courtyard of the château, with his entourage, when Mary and her four Marys and François rode out from the stables on their ponies. Dressed in bright velvets, they looked like a procession of dolls, little feathers waving on their hats.

Enchanted, the King dismounted and walked over to the trotting party, holding up his hands.

"Are these faerie folk, riding out into a magic forest?" he said, smiling. He took off his riding hat and looked for François. To his surprise and delight, he was there, sitting jauntily in the saddle.

"*Papa!*" he cried. Then he turned to Mary and said, "This is my father, the King! He has come at last!"

Mary stared at him, seeing a man with a long, thin face and slanted eyes. The mouth was smiling, but the eyes were unreadable.

"*Bonjour*, Your Majesty," she said quickly, and smiled back at him.

What a pleasing voice she had, the King thought. And that smile! It was radiant.

"Good morning, *Your* Majesty," he replied, and then, to his surprise, Mary came over to him.

"I am so happy to be here," she said simply. "I love France! And I love François, the Dauphin!"

The King was relieved; so relieved he felt as though some mysterious benefactor had suddenly paid all the outstanding debts of the Crown. (It was a scene he often wistfully envisioned, so he knew full well how he would feel.) The girl was normal! Well-formed, well-spoken, pretty, sprightly! In exchange for taking on the burden of Scotland—a burden that grew greater every day—he had received a treasure after all. His François would be cherished, and would respond in kind, and if anything could promise him health. . . .

"Postpone your ride for a few moments," he said, "and come inside with me—all of you!" he ordered.

His heart was singing, or as close to singing as it ever got.

The next day was rainy, with a cold, penetrating, intermittent rain that stripped the golden leaves off the trees and turned their limbs into black skeletons. There would be no riding that day; but the children, with the first excitement of staying indoors—before it had grown stale and confining—looked forward to playing *rois et reines*: kings and queens. They had decided to act out the story of Charlemagne and have him meet an evil queen of the forest who was holding four princesses captive (after first feeding them poisoned mushrooms to put them to sleep), and rescue them, with the help of his knights. François, of course, got to be Charlemagne; the four Marys were the victims of Mary, who got the best role as the evil queen, and the three Stewart boys were Charlemagne's knights. They built a castle of stools and boards, and created a forest by ordering the servitors to bring in the tubbed greenery from the terrace. The *valets de chambre* were displeased about the mess, but François ordered them most imperiously to hold their tongues and do as they were told.

The game was well under way when François had to seek out the garderobe in a corner chamber. The greengage pears he had eaten for *petit déjeuner* had upset his digestion, so the Great and Mighty Charlemagne had to go relieve himself in the midst of a charge against the castle.

"Look your last upon your victims, villainess!" he cried to Mary. "Prepare to die! I shall return!"

When a few moments later the door opened, the last scene of the drama recommenced: the maidens lay back down stiffly like marzipan dolls, the knights flourished their daggers, and Mary drew herself up for the final battle. But instead of the great Charlemagne in his breastplate—made by strapping two meat platters together—in stepped a squat little woman.

"What is this?" she demanded. "What is this mess?" She looked with distaste at the tub-forest, the stool-fortress, and the soldiers' tents made of bed hangings. "Where is the Dauphin?"

When no one answered her, she ordered, "Remove these things! Clean up this mess! Who gave you permission? Servants' children, having the free run of the nursery—your parents will answer for this!"

Still no one obeyed—partly because they could not understand the exact words, although they understood the intent well enough—and the woman became enraged.

"I tell you, do as I command! Are you deaf, you little urchins?"

Mary left the bulwark of the pillows making up the ramparts of her castle and stepped forward. Looking the woman directly in the eyes, she said, in halting French, "Are you aware, Madame, that you are speaking to, and in the presence of, the Queen of Scotland?" She lifted up her chin bravely.

"And are *you* aware," said the woman nastily, "that you are in the presence of, and speaking disrespectfully to, the Queen of France?" She watched smugly for chagrin and embarrassment to flood the little girl's face. But Mary's expression only changed to puzzlement and confusion. Clearly she did not think this woman looked very queenly.

"No, Madame," she said slowly, but with gravity and courtesy.

The two stared at one another, until François came in and shrieked, *"Maman!"* and ran to her. *"Maman,* here is my own dear Marie, come from Scotland!" and buried himself in her arms.

"Well," said Catherine de Médicis. "We have all been curious about you, and so anxiously awaiting your arrival." She looked down at François. "Does she please you, darling?"

"Oh, yes!"

"Then she pleases me as well. Welcome, little Marie."

48

VIII

As Mary passed her days in the palace suite with the French royal children, France itself came to seem a rainbow swirl of colours to her, and Scotland resolved itself into a dark mist that receded farther and farther with each year, until she remembered almost nothing of it, the way she remembered only shreds of dreams upon awaking.

The light in France was clear, soft, and merry, especially the light in the Loire Valley, where the court travelled from one magical château to another, following the seasons and the hunt. There was Amboise, with its huge circular tower that had a spiral ramp that horsemen could ride up, five abreast, and its geometrical gardens with arabesques of boxwood and sculptures of naked men and women set in groves of evergreen. Uncle the Cardinal said this was quite all right because they were from ancient Rome—and anyway he had a number of them in his own villa, where he had built an artificial grotto as well.

There was Blois, with its grand staircase in an octagonal tower, where Mary liked to look out over the courtyard and wave to the people far below. Its gardens had elaborate fountains that could be operated to put on a water display, or to squirt passersby, and a magical house called an *orangerie*, where orange trees could grow their fruit far from their native land.

There was Chaumont, with its astronomical observatory and the study where Ruggieri, the Queen's astronomer—some said necromancer—kept his instruments. Mary was not supposed to go up there, but once she climbed the steep steps to the tower room and surprised Ruggieri, who was polishing a large flat mirror. He jumped like a guilty man, but then, like everyone else, smiled when he saw who it was.

"Oh, Monsieur *Astrologue*, what are you doing?" she asked, approaching him.

"I am shining up my magic mirror," he said simply.

"Can you tell my fortune?" she asked.

"Yes. I could." He turned the mirror toward her. Her straight, slim form became even more elongated in it. "But I won't. I am sure your future is an enviable one."

"Then whose fortunes do you tell?"

"Those who have reason to be worried about them."

"Do you always tell the truth? What if you see bad things?"

"Then I must tell them. But gently." He put away the mirror. "It can be difficult." He sighed.

* * *

There was the huge white Chambord, sitting in the midst of a great hunting forest, with its enormous kennels with royal packs of hounds, and more than three hundred falcons in the mews for hawking. The massive château— it had four hundred forty rooms—boasted a gigantic central staircase with double intertwining ramps, made so that the people going up could never see the people going down. Mary and François and the other children delighted in playing on it, taking off their shoes and trying to make the ones on the lower ramps guess where they were.

The roof bristled with a forest of chimneys, spires, and capitals, where the children could play and hide—often startling adults who were playing quite another sort of hiding game. The children thought it was screamingly funny to catch a courtier with his hose down and his breeches unbuttoned, wheezing and panting. Once they even saw a bare bottom and recognized it as that of the fat count from Angers, because of the red ribbons on his shoes. As a result of their pestering, court lovers were forced to retreat to their rooms for assignations and abandon the roof.

More sedate activities at Chambord also took place on the roof, when the King, Queen, and Diane, surrounded by all the court, would watch the start and return of hunts, military reviews, and tournaments. The flaring torches, the fireworks, and the brassy blare of trumpets in the rich air made a tapestry of sound and colour in the little girl's mind.

Then there were Diane's châteaux: Anet, which was a white classical palace dedicated to her widowhood and presided over by Diana the goddess, and Chenonceau, a faerie palace spanning the Cher River, rising gracefully on arches over the lazy, shallow river. Here there was nothing masculine, nothing military or commanding. Instead, everything whispered of delicate, chosen pleasures, of appetites stimulated only to be satisfied, as the water flowed slowly beneath.

Always there were the pale blue skies, stretching huge and open under the deeper blue Loire River, bounded by its golden sandbanks and bathed in a serene clear light.

Little by little the strangeness had worn off for Mary, and France and French ways had come to seem entirely natural. Each year there was a new addition to the royal nursery, so that François ruled over his little group quite naturally. She envied him that. Her own older siblings had proved a nuisance in France. They refused to adapt themselves and insisted on disrupting the language lessons, riding only the Scottish way, and carrying child-sized daggers about at court. Mary was relieved when they returned to Scotland after the first year. The Marys, however, had been eager to please and had not even protested when the King had sent them off to a convent at Poissy for a few months to immerse themselves in the language.

As for James, the oldest of all, he had hurried back to Scotland at the earliest opportunity, claiming he needed to look after his mother, widowed at Pinkie Clough. (There was also the rich monastery of St. Andrews, which the late King had left to him, to be attended to.)

That left Mary alone at court for a time, where the King, the Queen, and all the courtiers could pet and pamper her, and where—more important—she could be enveloped by them and taught their ways with no interference.

From the very beginning, all of France had fallen in love with "the gentle dove rescued from the pursuit of ravenous vultures"—as one poetic courtier described *notre petite Reinette d'Ecosse*.

The court, all the more romantic for its surface coating of weary cynicism, fastened with fervour onto little Marie Stuart, as they delighted to call her, that fugitive princess from a barbarous, misty land, destined someday to be their queen. It had been so long since they had had a hero or heroine to extol: François I had been too jaded and jaunty, Henri II was too mournful and plodding. Catherine de Médicis, "the Italian Woman," was to be feared, not fêted. (Had her servant really poisoned the late Dauphin, clearing the way for shy Henri to become King? The servant had confessed, but only Catherine knew the truth of it.) Diane de Poitiers was beautiful in an otherworldly sort of way, remote, ethereal, like the goddess Diana she emulated. She struck awe in the beholder's eye, but not devotion. Besides, she had an earthly side: she was a bit too acquisitive of land and manors to be considered a goddess all the way through.

But Marie Stuart, with her pretty face, pleasing manners, and troubled heritage, appealed strongly to the imagination of the people.

No aspect of her education was neglected. She studied the classics, learning to read and write Latin. She spoke Italian and Spanish. She was taught music, and played the lute, harpsichord, and cithern, as well as having a sweet singing voice. She studied history with de Pasquier, and wrote poetry from an early age. She danced gracefully and especially loved to perform in masques and ballets. She laboured over her needlework and enjoyed designing her own patterns for embroidery.

At the same time, she loved the outdoors, and was skilled at riding, archery, hawking, the hunt. She liked nothing better than to sneak off and practise with her scaled-down bows and arrows with the youngest members of the Scottish Archers, who served as an honour guard to the King.

One day in particular, in early spring when she was just past seven, she had scrambled out past the ever-alert Lady Fleming and managed to get outside at Fontainebleau, where she knew the archers liked to practise in the woods. She had a particular favourite, Rob MacDonald, who was only eighteen and a little homesick himself, and always glad to see her. She had made friends with him, and yet she hoped the day would someday come when she would be able to shoot better than he, at least once in a while.

Sure enough, he was on the outskirts of the woods, practising with his fellows.

"Your Majesty!" he said when he saw her. "So you got away again!"

"Yes!" she said breathlessly. She did not know why she was compelled to do it, or why the other children never seemed to want to. She loved the Marys, and François, but there was a side to her they could not understand, and she felt she had to keep it secret. "And I have brought my bow." She proffered the beautifully tempered and seasoned instrument, with its quiver of arrows all inlaid with her royal crest.

"Good," he said. He nodded toward his companions. "We were just practising at this target. Would you like to start there?"

She nodded. She liked hearing him speak Scots. She did not want to forget it, but she had little opportunity to hear it and speak it for any length of time. She drew out an arrow and fitted it to her bowstring, pulled back as hard as she could, and let fly. The arrow hit at the very edge of the target.

"Achh!" said Rob, almost as disappointed as she was.

"I'll try again!" She pulled out a second arrow, and it did a little better, hitting closer to the centre.

For an hour they alternated shooting, Rob instructing her on the fine points of the sport.

"If you wish to be a good shot, this is the way." He was very patient.

Tired at the end, she said, "But for you it is not a sport. For you it is a livelihood. Why is it that Scotsmen fight for the French King? And how did you come here?"

He put down his big bow; his was almost six feet in height, and could shoot an arrow a hundred yards or more. "The French and the Scots have been friends a long time," he said. "They had the same enemy, England, and those who have the same enemy can be fast friends indeed. They call it the "Auld Alliance," and it is old; it goes back two hundred years at least. As to why there's a Scots Archer Guard—why, everyone knows Scotsmen are the best soldiers in the world!"

"But you aren't answering my question! Not all of it, anyway. Why are *you* here?"

"I had a desire to see something besides my own shores, if only to be content to return to them someday. If I wish to live in my native land and love her, it should not be out of ignorance. There are many other Scots here; hordes of them come over to study in Paris. Have you met any of them?"

She laughed. "No! How would I? I cannot roam the streets of Paris as I can the forest of Fontainebleau."

His captain was sounding a horn. "You'd best be going," Rob said. "I am called to regular duties." He looked at her and smiled. "I will never betray your secret, Most Imperial Royal Huntress. Here." He handed her back a fistful of her arrows. "It's best you not leave these in the woods."

By the time she carefully made her way back into the children's quarters of the palace, the younger ones were just waking up from their naps. Dinner would be served soon, and Mary had worked up a fierce appetite.

Usually the children ate by themselves, watched over by all their nurses and governesses. Today, however, the Queen gave orders that they were to eat with her, in her own quarters. Dutifully they trooped to her privy chamber, where a table was set with crystal goblets and golden plates for the children who were able to comport themselves with such finery: Mary herself, Lusty, Flamina, Beaton, and Seton, François and Elisabeth. Mary felt vaguely sorry for François, surrounded as he was entirely by girls; Rob was better off in the forest.

"Pray, dine with me," the Queen was saying, her oddly expressionless eyes counting them off one by one as they filed into the room. The Queen was pregnant again; soon there would be another child in the nursery.

She fussed over François and insisted on draping his napkin herself. Then she settled down, with a great sigh of her skirts, and began watching them eat. Mary felt her appetite draining away under the scrutiny.

"My dear children," Catherine de Médicis was saying, "we will soon be moving to Chambord for the summer. Now you know that means you will have to leave the pet bear here, where his keeper is. Nonetheless, you may select a hound for yourselves from the kennels at Chambord."

François slammed his fist down on the table. "Want the bear!" he muttered. He was especially fond of the bear, a recent gift, and had named him Old Julius.

Catherine de Médicis's eye fell on him like a black cloud. He fell silent.

"And we must prepare ourselves to entertain a most marvelous embassy from abroad. The Queen Mother of Scotland is coming." She slid her eye over to Mary. "Yes, my dear, your mother is coming to France!"

❦

For the next few months Mary prepared for the visit. To see her dear mother again! It seemed as if the seven-year-old's prayers had been answered, for every night since she had arrived in France she had added a wistful request that her mother come and see her.

She worked extra hard on her Latin; memorized French poetry and studied history as much as she could. She pestered her guardian, John Erskine, who had remained in France with her, to tell her all about what was happening in Scotland. He tried to explain about the continuing problems with the English, but Mary could not really grasp any of it. She understood only that her mother was coming.

Marie de Guise landed in France during the summer of 1550, and she brought a number of Scottish lords with her. King Henri II and Queen Catherine prepared a royal reception in Rouen, and Mary's tutor made her memorize a long, formal greeting to her mother. But when Mary, trembling with excitement, was brought into the *salle* where her mother was waiting, she forgot her speech and flew into her mother's arms.

She hugged her so fiercely her arms crushed the Queen Mother's stiff

53

petticoats and made them crackle. It was not until then that she knew she had not really hugged anyone without restraint since she had come to France.

"Oh, *Maman!*" she cried, and to her embarrassment tears flooded her eyes.

Her mother was stroking her hair, clasping her to herself. Mary's head came up to her mother's bosom, and her tears were staining the jewelled bodice.

"My dearest, beloved daughter!" Marie de Guise took Mary's face in her hands and lifted it up. "Look how you have grown! Soon we cannot call you *petite Reinette* at all." She looked around at the entire court and said, "Soon she will be old enough to have her own royal household, and appoint her own officials!"

Mary could not imagine why her mother would say that; she was not even old enough yet to insist that François could take his pet bear with him when they changed palaces. But she squeezed her mother's hand and looked up at her adoringly. Just to hear that almost-forgotten voice was heaven.

Marie de Guise joyfully met with her brothers, and the three of them would sit down with little Mary and discuss their plans for her. Her education, under the direction of the Cardinal, seemed to be progressing well; her mother was pleased.

"I believe you can start studying Greek next year," Uncle Cardinal said. "Your Latin is quite sound. Do you not think so?" he asked his sister.

"Mine is not sound enough to judge!" she said. "But certainly, add Greek if you feel she is ready. And my dear le Balafre—what is your assessment of the household situation?"

The muscular Duke stirred on his seat; clearly, sitting for a long time was hard for him. "I think we must propose a separate household as soon as it is feasible. But I warn you, the King and Queen prefer to have her as part of their own establishment."

"But I don't want a separate household!" cried Mary, suddenly. "I would rather live with the royal children, and especially François."

Marie's eyes widened. "Oh, so you like François?"

"Yes." Why were they all asking these questions?

"That's good, that's very good," said Uncle le Balafre. "But remember, you have the rest of your life to live with him. As you bcome a little older, it will be better for you to have your own establishment."

"But why? And better for whom?"

"For you, child, for you," said Uncle Cardinal. "If François can see you every day, as if you were a sister, why, then, he may come to think of you that way rather than as a wife."

"But I will miss him!" She did not want to be sent to a separate household, where there would undoubtedly be too many adults.

"Well, we shall see," said her mother soothingly. "It may not come to pass at all."

* * *

When they were alone, her mother took pleasure in inspecting her quarters. She had Mary show her all the chests of beautiful clothes, the bags and shelves of toys, the carved furniture that was scaled to child's size. At length she sat down on one of the little chairs, overhanging it. She took Mary's hands and looked deep into her eyes.

"Now for the truly important things," she said solemnly, and Mary wondered what these could be.

"Yes, *Maman*?"

"Your faith. Have you been preparing that as well as your school lessons? For it is much more important."

"Yes, *Maman*. We have a chaplain here, he's a very kind and learned man—"

"It is time you had a confessor! I will see to it that a suitable one is assigned to you, to you alone. Do you understand?"

Mary started to answer when she saw how tired her mother looked. There were little lines around her eyes, and her mouth did not smile naturally or easily. "You are troubled," she finally said, instead of answering. "What is it that troubles you so?"

"The hardness of the world," the Queen Mother finally said. She thought of the scant thanks she had gotten for her pains in arranging for the Scots prisoners to be freed from the French galleys. No sooner were they free than Knox and his fellows began to pour venom on her, attacking her religion and her government. "Yet I would still tell you—and I wish you to remember this always—that kindness and goodness are the paramount virtues, no matter what the world is like."

"I will always try to be kind and good, *Maman*," said Mary. "I will remember that you told me so."

❧

Mary was both happy and sad. Happy because there was to be a grand fête, three days of them in fact, with archery, tennis, dancing, and hunting. Sad because it was in farewell to her mother, who was returning to Scotland. Still, it had been a year. She was so fortunate to have had her mother with her for a year that the time had seemed compressed, with each day only a half-day's length.

"My dear daughter," said Marie, "tonight you will be allowed to stay up almost until dawn. After all, you are now eight years old, and there's to be torchlight hunting after the midnight banquet set up in the fields. If you become too sleepy, you can just lie down in one of the tents."

"Like a soldier!" she said. "I have always wanted to play at soldiers."

Her mother gave her an amused look. "I pray you haven't already done so. People will talk!"

"But why? Isabella of Castile led her troops, and she was a great Catholic queen."

Marie smiled at Mary. "And is that your desire, my love, to be a great Catholic queen?"

"Oh, yes. It is my dream. But I shan't burn heretics. I hate killing."

Marie was pleased with the way Mary had always shown interest in her faith. The addition of her own private confessor had definitely speeded her spiritual progress in the last year. "Everyone does," she said. "It is a pity that it is sometimes necessary." She turned to look around the quarters. Now was the time to tell her. Surely Mary had noticed the absence of Lady Fleming. "I have a wonderful surprise for you," she began. "There is to be another addition to your household, someone I have chosen for you—Madame Renée Rallay will replace Lady Fleming as your governess. She is a very astute, clever woman from the region of Touraine."

"Is she young? And where is Lady Fleming?" Mary's questions were open and happy.

"No, she's not young—in fact, I think she's in her middle forties."

"Oh!" Mary's face fell. "That's old!"

"But she is full of joy *and* wisdom. You will come to love both sides of her."

"Is her hair grey? Does she *look* old?"

"No, I don't believe so. You'll like her, I promise."

"But where is Lady Fleming?"

Should she just tell her? Was the child old enough to know? If she did not, others would. "Lady Fleming has proven herself . . . unsuited for her position."

Flamina's mother, unfit? "How? How?"

"She has . . . she is . . . with child by King Henri II!" The shame of it! And now both the King's wife and the King's true mistress had turned on the Scottish woman and demanded her ouster. Kings would be kings, but foreign governesses must pay the price.

"What?" Mary's mouth fell open. Lady Fleming, taking off her clothes and getting into bed with the King? Mary had seen paintings of naked women—all allegorical, of course—in Diane's apartments, but that was different. "Oh!" Now she, too, was flooded with shame. Then she immediately thought of poor Flamina. Her mother would be sent away, and then she would have a bastard sibling as well.

"I am taking her back to Scotland with me," said her mother. "There she can bear the child in privacy. Let this be a lesson to you. Women often serve as men's pastimes, and there is nothing more past than a spent pastime. The King and Queen will go on as before, and so will Madame de Poitiers, but Lady Fleming is ruined."

"Oh!" Mary started to cry, thinking of her playmate and her mother.

Marie put her arm around her. How tall the child was growing! She would have the height of the Guises, then. "Not ruined, truly. I am sure King Henri will be generous with her. Now, then, let us think of today's festivities. First the archery. The Scots Guards will be demonstrating their skill, and then the rest of us. You like shooting, do you not?"

* * *

The afternoon's archery contest had been thrilling. The court was presently at Blois, and the butts were set up in the surrounding fields near a hunting park and orchard. In the just-harvested fields, rows of golden stubble stretched away toward the Loire, giving off a warm sleepy scent. Overhead the sky scattered hazy light that was gentle and friendly. The Scots Guards, of course, stunned the courtiers and their guests with an exhibition of their prowess, and Mary was duly impressed with Rob MacDonald's ability to hit his mark from a hundred and fifty yards. She insisted on being the one to present his reward, and as he received it on bended knee in the field, he winked at her. She almost giggled, but managed not to.

Gathered around were King Henri II, who then languidly took his turn at shooting, and Mary's Guise uncles: not only the eldest, le Balafre (who of course was a superb shot) but his three younger brothers, Claud, François, and René, whom she rarely saw. Claud, the Duc d'Aumale, was twenty-five, François was seventeen and already named Grand Prior of the Galleys, and René, the Marquis d'Elboef, was sixteen. D'Aumale and d'Elboef wore skintight hose and drank too much wine, and smiled at her as if they truly liked her.

They are so different from my Scottish relatives, she thought. All the Guises—and there are so many of them!—seem to be either soldiers or churchmen. I know there are four more, and they are all either priests or nuns.

Then ladies of the court took their turns shooting. Diane de Poitiers came forward, wearing her customary black and white—this gown was in the Grecian fashion, loose and flowing, but fastened with black straps. Even her bow and arrows were ebony inlaid with ivory. She stepped up to the shooting line and shot easily, coming close to the target. The King and Catherine de Médicis both congratulated her warmly.

Lusty did well, Beaton less well (but did not care), Seton even less well, and then Flamina stepped boldly up, daring everyone to look at her. Her chin was held high, and she performed strongly. The congratulations that she reaped were not for her shooting but for her bravery.

Mary then took her place and, to everyone's astonishment, hit all her targets dead on. The audience burst into cheers. But all Mary cared about was seeing the pride in Rob's eyes. She turned and bowed, then let the contest continue.

Marie de Guise had brought some Scotsmen with her, and Mary now watched as they took their turns at the butts. There was the barrel-shaped Earl of Huntly, who basked in public attention. She knew he was a great Catholic noble of the north who held great power, but it seemed to her he was vainglorious and even somewhat comical as he strutted and postured.

They call him "the Cock o' the North," she thought, and he does remind me of a rooster. His face is red and he crows. And his bottom sticks out as if it should sport a feathered tail.

She began to giggle, and Lusty, standing beside her, said, "What is so amusing?"

"The Earl of Huntly looks like a rooster," she answered, and then Lusty began to laugh, and soon the whole row of children was laughing.

Next came a man with a stately bearing, who looked to be a true noble. But he was not. It was Richard Maitland of Lethington, one of Marie de Guise's privy councillors and advisers. He was just a laird, a lawyer and a poet for his own amusement. Alongside him was a young man, rather good-looking, whom he introduced as his son, William.

"He is studying here in France, and I must take this opportunity to present him to you," he said to Marie de Guise. "When he returns to his native land, I believe he will prove to be of service to you."

Marie de Guise just gave a perfunctory nod, but Flamina whispered to Mary, "He's handsome!"

Mary wondered if Flamina was only pretending to be interested in such things to prove she was not bothered by her mother's situation. Actually, William Maitland was no more handsome than some of the other men there. But she nodded in agreement.

Some distant relatives of Mary's, the Lennox Stuarts, were also there: John, Seigneur d'Aubigny, and some cousins had come to pay their respects. These Stuarts had had a Scottish ancestor who came to France a hundred and fifty years earlier and were now almost entirely French, even using the French spelling of the name. She rememered Rob saying that the connection between France and Scotland went back a long way.

There were refreshments for the men, and the children took their rest under big shade trees with blankets spread out beneath them. Some of the men—the younger ones, including the King—then went to play tennis until the light faded.

When Mary awakened, she saw that servants were busy setting up formal dining tables under the trees. They were unrolling fine linen tablecloths and, in addition to the candles placed every five feet or so, were stringing lanterns between tree branches. Twilight had come, and the sky was a tender deep bluish purple. Shadows were forming little blue pools around the trees, distant haystacks, and fences. A soft warm breeze was blowing across the fields, right up to the very edge of the forest; where the air met the branches, the leaves rustled and murmured. Fireflies were just coming out, a twinkle here, a brief pulse of light there, when Mary saw a line of people coming to the banquet tables in procession across the fields. Their gowns glowed with sunset colours, and they were bearing tapers and laughing. Before them walked musicians playing recorders and lutes. They looked like figures from a faded tapestry, and even the music was faded and distant.

They approached, and became real, noisy people. The King, freshly attired in velvet, glowed after his tennis game. His Queen flashed with jewels, and rather than seeming odd in the outdoor setting, they graced it. Diane had changed once again to a glistening gossamer gown. Mary's own mother was now dressed in a fashionably embroidered green satin gown, and was carrying an ornate, silver-studded velvet box.

Everyone was seated in the sylvan dining room, and the musicians kept playing. Overhead the sky darkened, and now the only light came from the candles, lanterns, and fireflies. It bathed the gathering in a soft, dreamy light, these people of France and Scotland, Mary's relatives and friends, and she loved them all with a fierce, surging love. She felt so safe, so loved, so protected—secure in the arms of France and all the company gathered under the trees on this balmy summer night.

At the end of the dinner, when Marie de Guise had to make her formal speeches in farewell, she opened the velvet box and held it aloft. Mary could see something gleam red inside.

"This is the treasure that I leave in the keeping of the King and Queen, who also have the keeping of my other treasure, my daughter. This is the jewel that belonged to her grandmother, Margaret Tudor. It was presented to her upon her marriage to James IV, and it is my deepest wish that it be presented to Queen Mary upon her marriage to the Dauphin François. Keep it in trust for me, I beg you." Ceremoniously she handed it to Henri II.

He peered at it, and his normally unresponsive eyes registered an emotion. "*Mon Dieu!* It is huge!" Impressed, he lifted out the jewel and held it up for all to see. It was a brooch in the shape of an *H*, fashioned of rubies and diamonds.

"That is why it is called the 'Great Harry,' " said Marie de Guise. "Guard it well!"

After the dinner, it was indeed midnight. But the party was eager to hunt by torchlight, and the horses and pack of hounds were brought out to seek red deer on the adjacent heath. The children did not go, but stood watching as the flares and noise were swallowed up in the darkness. Still later, as one by one they fell asleep in the tents, they could hear the cries of the dogs from somewhere far away, carried on the summer air into the palace windows. They slept soundly and did not hear the hunters return.

❧

When Marie de Guise took her leave later that month, she clasped Mary to her and promised to return soon.

"Come back quickly," Mary said, trying not to cry. It would be unseemly in front of all these people.

"As soon as I may," said her mother. "And my thoughts are with you every moment."

"I love you, dear *Maman*," she whispered. But her mother was interrupted by King Henri's approach, and did not hear the murmured words.

59

IX

ooking back on it years later, although it was not true, it seemed
to Mary that it was always summer in France as she was growing
up. The air was always rich and caressing, full of the smells of
flowering meadows and ripening plums and apricots. Dusks were milky and
warm and lingering; the stones of the châteaux took on a luminosity as the
light faded and lanterns were lit. Huge, pale, feathery-winged moths would
come to the open windows and light on the lanterns and fly around the
pure white wax candles burning in sconces.

White was the colour of France: the white swans dotting the moat water;
the peculiar Loire stone used to build the châteaux, which whitened as it
aged; the great white fireplaces with their gilded royal emblems of sala-
manders and crowned porcupines; the milk from the she-asses the court
ladies used for their complexions and which Mary began to use as she grew
up; the white lilies of France, the royal flower.

Her first communion was a blaze of white in her white taffeta gown at
Easter. She wore a coronet of lily-of-the-valley in her red-brown hair, and
carried an ivory rosary, a gift from her grandmother de Guise. By her twelfth
year, after lengthy preparation by her confessor, Father Mamerot, she had
longed to make this first communion, and at last her uncle the Cardinal
had pronounced her ready to do so.

"The happiest day of my life," she wrote in her little private journal that
night. And to her mother in Scotland: "Dearest Mother, At last I am come
to be a true daughter of the Church. . . ." She closed her eyes and saw
once again the Madonna lilies around the altar opening their smooth ivory
throats as if they were about to sing Alleluia; saw the thick, immaculate
Easter candle flickering, saw the gentle smile on the alabaster Virgin's face.
"Today I glimpsed Paradise."

But on earth here in France, every sense was bathed in luxury, luxury of
which she became more and more aware as she grew older. The palate was
indulged with strawberries from Saumur and melons planted in the Loire
by a Neapolitan gardener long ago, with trout pâté, Tours pastries, and vin
d'Annonville, with its delicate bouquet. The nostrils were pampered by
the happy work of Catherine de Médicis's Italian perfumers working with
the flowers from the fields of Provence, producing heady fragrances to be
worn on throats and wrists and to scent gloves and capes. Hyacinth, jasmine,
lilac—all wafted through the rooms and from the bathwaters of the châteaux.

The skin was caressed with unguents and the feel of silk, velvet, fur, leather gloves of softest deerskin; goosedown pillows cupped weary bodies at the day's end; and in winter, newly installed Germanic tile stoves at Fontainebleau provided central heating.

Eyes were continually presented with beauty in ordinary objects rendered more opulently pleasing: a crystal mirror decorated with velvet and silk ribbons; buttons with jewels affixed. There were fireworks reflected in the river; paintings by Leonardo; and black-and-white chequered marble paving in the long palace gallery over the Cher that spanned the rippling water outside.

Pleasing sounds were everywhere: in the chirping of the pet canaries and more exotic birds in the garden aviaries; in the baying of the hounds in the matchless royal hunting packs; in the splash and gurgle of the fountains and elaborate water displays in the formal gardens. And above all that, the sound of melodious French, exquisitely spoken; witty conversations, and the poets of the court reciting verses composed to celebrate the aristocratic dreamworld they inhabited, with a haunting melancholy that it would all pass away.

But to Mary and her companions it all seemed eternal, given, unchanging, and the poets' laments purest literary convention. Of course there were small changes: the royal family continued to grow, with more babies swelling the nursery. Catherine de Médicis began to grow stout and her waist disappeared, even when she was not pregnant. Diane de Poitiers, that lady who was immune to time, did not alter in looks, but even she began planning her tomb. It was to be of—what else?—white marble.

One afternoon as Mary was keeping the Duchesse company in her chambers, she watched as Diane sat before her dressing table and arranged, then rearranged, her perfumes and silver-backed brushes. Diane's back was as straight as ever, her silvery hair still thick and swept up, held with a diamond pin. But her face, in repose, was streaked with sadness. Suddenly she turned around to Mary and said, "You will be more beautiful than I." Mary started to demur, but the Duchesse cut her off. "Please. I speak but the truth. Do not flinch from it. I do not. I am proud that you succeed me; I am glad to pass that duty on."

Mary laughed. This made her uneasy. Did Diane have a deadly disease? Was she making her will?

"I am fifty-five now. Is it not time? I have reigned a good long while in the realm of beauty, but it is a hard burden. You are welcome to it!" She gestured at a painting of herself in which her bosom was bare. "You are shocked? You would never pose that way?"

"No, Madame," she said quietly. But then she could not help asking, "When was this painted?"

"Only a few years ago. Now you *are* shocked! You needn't be. Painters are kind; it is not only God who can create something out of nothing! Our court painters are equally adept at it."

Mary had always loved watching the Duchesse as she moved and spoke.

"You will reign in beauty forever," she said. "I fear it is not an office you can resign, like being Keeper of the King's Seal or Royal Treasurer."

"Alas, that is so. Hurry and grow up, then, so you can relieve me of it. Time will push you on and push me off."

Mary's two oldest uncles gained in power and stature. Uncle Cardinal acquired a larger sphere of influence, and Uncle le Balafre shone as a battle hero in taking Metz from the Holy Roman Emperor Charles V, who was fighting France. In Scotland, Mary had achieved the formal appointment of her mother as Regent, and they continued to try to oust the English. In England itself, Edward VI had died and been succeeded on the throne by his half-sister Mary Tudor, who was devoutly Catholic. In a matter of months she had made England Catholic again, and taken as a husband Philip II of Spain. This was a disaster for France, for now England and Spain would team up against France and try to conquer her. That meant that Scotland was suddenly a very important ally for France because of her location.

At the age of eleven, Mary had received her separate household; and when the time came, she was glad to leave the royal nursery after all, because it had become so crowded. There were now six Valois children sharing quarters with her. Mary had become increasingly aware of the intense scrutiny that Catherine de Médicis turned on all the children, and was relieved to escape it.

The Queen had become increasingly dependent on her fortune-tellers and astronomers, especially one called Nostradamus. She insisted on bringing him in to make pronouncements on the children, and when he had seen Mary he had intoned, "I see blood around that fair head!" which had both annoyed and upset Mary—annoyed her by its rudeness, and upset her in case it might be true. Her annoyance at the astrologer (who was, after all, performing his duty) transferred itself to Catherine, who should have had more tact.

Within her household remained the four Marys, John Erskine, Father Mamerot, Madame Rallay, and her physician, Bourgoing. She liked Bourgoing; he was very young and had just completed his studies at Padua. She still had her band of Scots musicians, for she liked to listen to the music of her native land, even though the French teased her about it. Among themselves the Scots continued to speak their native language occasionally as a novelty.

When she was alone, Mary would look at herself in the mirror, wondering if what Diane said was true. Was she beautiful? How much taller would she grow? When she developed a woman's body, would it be graceful and pleasing? Girls changed when they turned into women, that she knew. Plain ones could shine, pretty ones turn out coarse and dull. She hoped—if it did not betray too much vanity, about which Father Mamerot had warned her—that she would not be plain.

By the time she was fourteen, the poets had discovered her. They hailed her in verse after verse, calling her the equal of any beauty since time began. Mary tried to remember Diane's warning about beauty being a burden, but she could not help enjoying the words, since they answered her secret fear.

The court historian Brantôme wrote, "In her fifteenth year her beauty began to radiate from her like the sun in a noonday sky." He praised her hands, "so finely fashioned that those of Aurora herself could not surpass them."

Pierre de Ronsard, the leading poet of the group that called itself the Pléiad, after the constellation of seven stars, gushed: *"O belle et plus que belle et agréable Aurore."*

His fellow Pléiad poet Joachim du Bellay wrote, *"Nature et art ont en votre beauté / Mis tout le beau dont la beauté s'assemble":*

> *Nature and art have combined to make your beauty*
> *The quintessence of all that is beautiful.*

He also proclaimed:

> *The tongue of Hercules, so fables tell,*
> *All people drew by triple chains of steel.*
> *Her simple glance where'er its magic fell,*
> *Made men her slaves, though none the shackles feel.*

The painter François Clouet sketched her and painted her, lamenting that as she was a butterfly or a wild creature, she could not sit still for him, and so he was unable to capture her charm. He did one jewellike miniature of her, with a sapphire blue background and a rose-coloured dress, but she looked stiff and mannered in it, he thought—something she was not in life. It could not speak in her *voix très douce et très bonne,* as a true work of art should. Nor could he get her delicate colouring right; in attempting to capture its translucence he merely made her look wan.

Only the bronze bust sculpted by Jacquio Ponzio captured her posture and bearing, as it could show her exquisitely turned slender neck, and the way she carried her head. She had posed for it daydreaming, her eyes focused on a faraway internal landscape, and in it the artist caught the careless largesse of youth, which thinks it has a thousand tomorrows and does not disdain to dream away today. Her hair was upswept in curls, her almond-shaped eyes serene, her mouth almost melancholy. Only the merest whisper of a smile touched her small mouth; otherwise the statue looked out in Olympian detachment.

X

For all that, the young Queen hailed as *une vrai Déesse*—a veritable goddess—loved to romp and run and ride and often lamented that she was not born a man, to wear a sword and armour. Her uncle the Duc de Guise, the hero-general of France, who had just wrested Calais from the English, compared the girl's courage to his own.

"Yes, my niece, there is one trait in which, above all others, I recognize my own blood in you—you are as brave as my bravest men-at-arms. If women went into battle now, as they did in ancient times, I think you would know how to die well. And I, my dear, should know," he said. "For I have seen enough of both kinds—cowards and brave men. Bravery is a Guise trait; look at your mother's courage in holding Scotland for you against the heretic rebels. Ah, that is true courage!"

"Truly she is beset," said Mary, hurt by the thought. Her uncle was needed to fight against the English who had invaded France, else he could go directly to her mother's aid in Scotland. He was so wonderful, he could do anything. . . .

"Yet, as I said, she holds out bravely." The Duc looked around the room approvingly. It had been an altogether satisfactory arrangement to set Mary up with her own household at court after her eleventh birthday. Of course, the stingy Scots had not wanted to foot the extra bills for it. As if the French should be obliged to, after all they were already spending to keep troops in Scotland! In the end the Scots had coughed up the money, and the furnishings in the royal rooms were quite passable. A few more rugs would be appreciated, but—he shrugged—one could not squeeze milk from a dried-up udder. Or extra money from a Scottish oatcake, those odd, fodder-tasting cakes they fancied.

He looked at Mary, in her establishment four years now. It had all worked out so well, as if Fate herself had arranged all the details. That the girl should grow up to be beautiful but trusting, ready to believe that people were what they seemed to be. That she should have such a love for her mother—a mother so seldom seen that now, in truth, it was a love that existed for an imaginary person, shaped by her own longings—that she would do anything for her, and, by extension, for her mother's brothers. All of them worked together, with one goal: to control both France and Scotland. Mary, this tall, spirited girl, was the central point in the turning wheel around which all their ambitions revolved.

The first step had been taken when the French Parliament had been persuaded to proclaim that it was Mary's desire that she now be granted the right to name her own regent in Scotland; the Scots had to agree, or lose French support. Mary promptly named her mother to be Regent. Out went the erstwhile Regent, the Earl of Arran, head of the House of Hamilton, and all his men. He was pacified with the French dukedom of Chatelherault. In came the French administrators.

Marie then did her part and appointed her brothers to be Mary's keepers and ministers in France: Duc François was to guide her in earthly things, Cardinal Charles in spiritual ones. Mary was an apt and loyal pupil under their tutelage. She would be their perfect queen and perfect creature when the time came for her to mount the throne. Now that Calais had been won, the French people could deny the Duc nothing; so the time had come to press for the wedding of Mary to the Dauphin, to secure it once and for all.

In Scotland things had not gone so smoothly. It seemed that the Scots had a fervent dislike of "foreigners." For centuries they had hated the English, the "auld enemy." But now that the French were close at hand, they decided they hated them worse. They seemed to have forgotten why the French had come there—and at great expense, too!—in the first place: to get rid of the English for them. Now they had started to rebel against the French.

"From what you tell me, dear Uncle, soon more troops will be needed."

"We will send whatever is necessary," he said coldly. "The country will never fall from your hands. France will not permit it."

"Oh! If I were a man! I'd fight them myself!" she cried.

The Duc smiled. "Like your ancestor Charlemagne! Like your other ancestor Saint Louis, on the Crusade against the infidel. Yes, I believe you would!" He looked at her slim tall form, her shining face—like a young knight's. "How tall you are!" he suddenly said, realizing she was his own height—about six feet. "Again, like a true Guise!" He put his arm around her shoulders; her bones were delicate, for all her height.

"Is there no Scots in me at all?" she asked, and he could not tell what she wished the answer to be. Odd, as he could usually read her mind. "No trace of Stewart?"

"When you dress à la sauvage, in the furs and plaids," he said cautiously. She was a pretty sight in that barbaric costume she affected once in a while.

"That is something I put on from the outside. I meant from the inside," she insisted.

"Well, you like your Scots musicians—you've kept your own band all this while to play you that . . . unusual music."

"I enjoy it," she insisted.

"Yes, well, that proves you're Scots," he said. "To any other ears, it's an odd sound."

The gilded table-clock began to strike the hour of eleven, each chime a separate bell.

"Do you like it?" asked Mary.

"Very much." The Duc examined its painted face, black numerals on ivory. It had little gold feet, and a moon dial showing a dreamy-faced disk.

"I gave it to myself," she confessed. "I do not know why I am so taken with clocks and watches."

"Yes, I remember the striking watch with a death's head you gave your—what do you call her?—your Marie?"

"Oh. That." Mary looked embarrassed. "It caught my fancy, with its bell ringing inside the tiny silver skull, and its engravings of time and symbols of eternity. And Mary Seton is—tends to be—so absorbed in religious devotions. It is small enough to be carried into chapel. It seemed the sort of thing a monk would have coveted."

"Monks aren't supposed to covet." He smiled, and the great battle scar on his cheek—the one people called *le Balafre*—buckled along its seam.

"But others covet the things of the monks," said Mary. "Like old Harry of England—he just turned the monks out and took their things."

"If I may say so, Your Grace, at least he was forthright about it—unlike your father, who made his nobles and bastards 'lay abbots' of the rich monasteries, so they could take whatever they wanted. Even your brother, James Stewart, is helping himself to the spoils of—what is his monastery?—St. Andrews. And he is so staid and sanctimonious!" The Duc had little use for the hypocritical prude. He had met him twice and disliked him both times.

"In fact," he continued, "your father made all his bastards 'priors,' didn't he? Providing for them at church expense. John Stewart is Prior of Coldingham, and Robert Stewart, Prior of Holyrood, and another James, Prior of Melrose and Kelso, and another Robert, Prior of Whithorn, and Adam Stewart, Prior of Charterhouse at Perth. A veritable family of holy men!"

Mary felt anger rise in her at hearing her father attacked. "Are things so much more noble in France? How is it that three of your brothers are princes of the church? Two cardinals, and one Grand Prior of the fighting order of St. John of Jerusalem? Why, good uncle Charles was made cardinal when he was but twenty-three! And by the King. Was it because of his upstanding, devout life?"

Le Balafre was caught by surprise. She has a temper, he thought. That's not good. She would be perfect if only she were more docile. Lately she has been too questioning.

"I will let him answer for himself," said the Duc smoothly, as he saw the *valet de chambre* opening the doors for the belated guest. He had been due at half past ten.

"Pardon, pardon!" the Cardinal exclaimed. "I am so sorry to be late!"

A smile lit his delicate features as he came toward Mary and the Duc. He had eyes the pale blue of the March skies arching over the Loire, and his ivory colouring would have made him parchment-pretty, but his chin was weak and made even weaker by a bifurcated whispy beard hanging from it. Its straggly hairs got caught in his impeccably ironed and starched collar-ruff. Why did he wear such a face-spoiler? Mary wondered, not for the first time. She always hoped that he would come in without it the next time, and was always disappointed.

"But I have brought much news, both good and bad!" He patted his velvet dispatch bag.

"Shall we eat first?" said the Duc. "News of any sort digests better on a full stomach." He was starving. During the recent campaign at Calais, he had permitted himself only the rations of his soldiers, which were scant, it being winter. Yet that had won the battle for them, attacking unexpectedly in January. . . . Now he needed to feed well before returning to the field and its deprivations.

"Indeed," said Mary, leading them to the private dining table set at one end of her chamber. With complete naturalness she took her place of honour under her cloth of estate; she was, after all, a reigning sovereign. Eating elsewhere, out from under the royal canopy, would have felt as naked as dining with no clothes.

She nodded to her servitors, and they began to bring in the dishes—some thirty of them. Although most were the usual fare—stuffed eel and bream, chicken in vinegar sauce, goose and duck—she had tried to provide a delicacy or two, difficult in this drear time of year when nothing fresh was available. Spring seemed a long time away.

The servitors were presenting caramelized apple turnovers, and the Cardinal seemed genuinely impressed. Mary was pleased, as the Cardinal was known for his finicky palate and constant searching for novelties at table. He popped a good bit of it in his mouth with the gold-handled fork, and his beard bobbed up and down.

"Exquisite, my dear. Truly." He smiled and took a sip of the sweet, heady wine from Anjou in the Venetian crystal goblet. Sensual pleasure shone in his eyes.

As the last of the sweets was being cleared away, Mary could wait no longer. "What is your news?" she begged. "Please, withhold it no longer!"

"It is this." He smiled and brushed a crumb from his velvet sleeve. "The war goes so well for us that it seems God Himself is on our side. Philip and his English toadies are turning tail." He paused. "But that is news for my brother. For you, *ma mignonne*, I have this: I have just heard from Scotland. The terms of the marriage are approved, and nine commissioners—including your brother James and some of the highest nobles in the land—set sail next week to come here, draw up the legal documents, and . . . attend your wedding to the Dauphin François!"

"Oh! When?"

"In some three months' time. April. You will wed at the height of spring. Can you bear to wait till then?"

"I have waited for ten years. And I will need at least that long to have my dress made—it will be white, I love white—like a blooming pear tree—"

"White is the colour of solemnity, of mourning," said the ever-fashionable Cardinal quickly. "It would be bad luck."

"I don't believe in such things. White is my colour, my chosen colour," she said stubbornly. "I look the best in white; Brantôme says so. He said, *'La blancheur de son visage contendoit avec la blancheur de son voile a qui l'emporteroit'*—'the whiteness of her face rivaled the whiteness of her veil.' "

"You said there was other news," said the Duc, impatient with all this dress talk.

The Cardinal clearly preferred to stay in the land of veils and satins. He sighed. "Yes. At almost the same time as the nine commissioners agreed to the marriage, several of them signed a covenant."

"What sort of a covenant?" The Duc's voice was sharp. "Covenant" sounded like a Geneva, Protestant word.

"Calling themselves 'the First Band of the Congregation,' they have pledged to—to work for the cause of the Reformed religion in Scotland."

"Protestants!" gasped Mary, in the same shock as if she had heard a bat flying overhead.

"Protestants!" growled the Duc. "I knew it! I knew that filthy preacher, Knox, would make more converts there!"

"Oh, and that he has. Made converts everywhere." The Cardinal reached in his pouch and drew out a tract. "This is his latest utterance."

The Duc took it. "The bleating fool must be silenced."

Mary reached out and took it from him in turn. *"The First Blast of the Trumpet Against the Monstrous Regiment of Women.* What is he saying?" she asked. " 'To promote a woman to bear rule, superiority, dominion, or empire above any realm, nation, or city is repugnant to nature, contumely to God. . . . " She read silently on, then burst out, " 'For their sight in civil regiment is but blindness, their counsel foolishness, and judgement frenzy. Nature, I say, doth paint them forth to be weak, frail, impatient, feeble, and foolish, and experience hath declared them to be unconstant, variable, cruel, and lacking the spirit of counsel and regiment. . . .' "

"It goes on for many pages, Your Grace," said the Cardinal. "Lots of Old Testament references, typically Protestant, quite tedious. He writes it against the 'three Marys'—you, your mother, but most against Mary Tudor, because of her true Catholicism. Listen to this, it is quite amusing." The Cardinal thumbed through the manuscript.

> "Cursed Jezebel of England, with the pestilent and detestable generation of papists . . . man and woman, learned and unlearned . . . have tasted of their tyranny. So that now not only the blood of Father Latimer, of the mild man of God, the Bishop of Canterbury, of learned and discreet Ridley, of innocent Lady Jane Dudley . . . doth call for vengeance in the ears of the Lord God of hosts; but also the sobs and tears of the oppressed, the groanings of the angels, the watchmen of the Lord, yea, and every earthly creature abused by their tyranny, do continually cry and call for the hasty execution of the same."

The Cardinal laughed with a laugh as thin as his beard.

"His curses are terrible," Mary said. Was he wishing such evil on her mother? And on her, simply because she was Catholic?

"But not original. They are lifted intact from the Old Testament. The prophets—Jeremiah, Ezekiel, Nahum—*really* knew how to curse in the name of Yahweh. This fellow is a pale shadow of them."

"But a shadow that darkens Scotland. This Knox continually refers to himself as a prophet," said the Duc. "Someone ought to do to him what Herod did to John the Baptist. Where is he now?"

"In hiding, somewhere in Geneva. He was actually in France for two months last year, from October to December. I am ashamed to tell you that he wrote *The First Blast* on our soil."

"I notice he did not stay here for its publication," said the Duc. "That was wise of him."

"Oh, he's clever. He hides his cowardice under the instruction that Christ gave to his disciples: 'But when they persecute you in this city, flee ye into another.' He leaves others to do his fighting for him, and fulfill his curses."

"Words to frighten children in the nursery," scoffed the Duc.

"Somewhere in the Old Testament someone is cursed with 'emerods,' " said the Cardinal. "Now *that's* something to fear!" He laughed depreciatively. "Perhaps I should wish them on master Knox? I must practise my cursing. All I know is the formula for excommunication." Again, the tinkling laughter.

Mary took back the document and continued reading it, slowly. It took her a long time. But at length she reached the ending:

> I fear not to say that the day of vengeance, which shall apprehend that horrible monster Jezebel of England and such as maintain her monstrous cruelty, is already appointed . . . when God shall declare Himself to be her enemy, when He shall pour forth contempt upon her according to her cruelty, and shall kindle the hearts of such as sometimes did favour her with deadly hatred against her, that they may execute His judgements.
> For assuredly her empire and reign is a wall without foundation; I mean the same of the authority of all women.
> But the fire of God's word is already laid to those rotten props (I include the Pope's law with the rest), and presently they burn. . . . When they are consumed, that rotten wall—the usurped and unjust empire of women—shall fall by itself in despite of all man, to the destruction of so many as shall labour to uphold it. And therefore let all men be advertised, for the trumpet hath once blown.
> Praise God, ye that fear Him.

"He rejects the authority of royal blood," she finally said.

"No, he rejects women as rulers," the Cardinal corrected. "You see here." He took the manuscript and read, " 'For assuredly her empire and reign is a wall without foundation; I mean the same of the authority of all women.' You have misunderstood."

"No, good Uncle, *you* have misunderstood," she said in a quiet, clear voice. "Or else you are trying to shield me. When Master Knox harangues the people and says they *should* not have taken Mary for their Queen, then the hidden message is that they *need* not have taken her, if they so chose. And it follows from that that the people have the freedom to choose their ruler—that it is not royal blood that determines who has the right to rule,

69

but the people's will. If they have the power to reject royal blood, then what power does royal blood possess? None, if Knox has his way. He says here"— she snatched the manuscript back—"that 'the insolent joy, the bonfires, and the banqueting which were in London and elsewhere in England when that cursed Jezebel was proclaimed Queen did witness to my heart that men were . . . rejoiced at their own confusion and certain destruction. . . . And yet can they not consider that where a woman reigneth and papists bear authority, that there must needs Satan be president of the council?' "

"Satan in skirts. I like that," said the Cardinal.

Mary refused to laugh. " 'I say that the erecting of a woman to that honour is not only to invert the order which God hath established, but also is to defile, pollute, and profane the throne and seat of God.' The people are the ones with the duty to discern God's will and choice, that is what he is saying."

The Cardinal sighed grievously. "Yes, I admit that is one interpretation, at least by implication. You have a searching wit, my child."

"Then Knox is my enemy!" said Mary.

"Indeed he is!" the Duc burst out. "For above all things, your royal blood makes you special and entitles you to rule."

"Shall we leave the table?" Mary suddenly rose, and the servitors descended on the leavings like crows.

She ushered the two men into her privy chamber, and then dismissed the *valets de chambre* and her attendants.

"There are too many ears out there," she said. "Now we may speak more freely."

The Duc and the Cardinal raised their eyebrows—the Duc's, thick and dark, and the Cardinal's, light and perfectly arched—simultaneously.

"You have gotten quite adept at politics," the Cardinal said. "You must have a natural talent for it. Someone should have warned us." He gave his brother a knowing look.

"I have learned much from the Queen," said Mary. "For example, always to use a cipher in my correspondence. I have some sixty codes I employ in my letters." She smiled brightly.

"How laborious," said the Cardinal. "Remember, a code is only as ingenious as its holders are at hiding the key to it. And there are many agents who are geniuses at breaking codes." He enjoyed the look of disappointment on her face. She had felt wise, secure, adult. Time to educate her further. How much did she know about the Queen?

"What else have you learned from her?" he continued. "Do you keep an expert carpenter in your employ?" Seeing the blank look on her face, he answered her unasked question.

"Why, to make secret drawers for all your silly ciphers and magic potions, like the room at Blois where she has over two hundred of them, some of them dummies. She thinks no one knows how to open them by pressing a panel at the baseboard. But of course everyone knows. Or perhaps to drill secret holes in the floor of your bedroom, like the ones she has at St.-

Germain-en-Laye, where she watches the King making love to Diane on the floor directly below her."

Mary gasped, then giggled. "She *does?*"

"Indeed." The Cardinal laughed, and the Duc began to guffaw.

"What would Master Knox say?" The Duc roared with laughter.

"He would say it was their royal blood that compelled them to act so!"

The Cardinal had to sit down, he was laughing so hard. Tears flowed from his eyes, and he dabbed at them with a lace handkerchief. "Catherine is insanely jealous," he gasped between laughs. "But instead of poisoning Diane, as a good Medici should do, she just resorts to magic spells. Evidently they don't work! The King still takes to Diane's elderly bed, with Catherine watching. What a *ménage à trois!*"

"I think I would kill her," said Mary, who was not laughing. "I could not stand to share my husband. It is a mockery. Or, perhaps, I would kill *him*. It would depend . . . on the circumstances."

As if François, that lily-livered, timorous thing, would ever be capable of taking any woman to his bed, except in trembling duty, thought the Cardinal. Mary need fear no rivals. But he said, "No, you would not. If you were jealous, then that would mean you loved him. And if you loved, love would stay your hand from evil."

"Much evil is done in the name of love," said Mary.

"Which brings us back to Master Knox," said the Duc. "True enough he's safe in Geneva, hiding under Calvin's coattails, but the moment he steps out—I'll see to it he's silenced. Permanently. Odd that Calvin shelters him; Calvin and his men advocate obedience to rulers."

"All that means is that he's wily enough to let others do his fighting for him. Those wretched Calvinists have infiltrated France; they are all over. They slink away to their heretical meetings under the cover of night. 'Night spectres,' we call them—*Huguenots*. Calvin sends them books and preachers; he just won't buy them muskets and cannon. Not *yet*."

"I'll blast them to their Kingdom come," said the Duc. "They won't take root here."

"They already have, but their roots are not very deep," said the Cardinal. "We must uproot them, pull them out."

"After the English are vanquished," said the Duc.

"Knox will not stay in Geneva," said Mary suddenly. "He will return to Scotland, and there trouble my dear mother."

" 'Tis true, he has written her a most hateful letter," the Cardinal agreed. "I happen to have a copy. Master Knox does not use a cipher; he *publishes* everything he writes." He handed her a printed copy, its title, *Letter to the Regent of Scotland*, in bold type.

Mary read it, her face growing more and more angry as she went along.

" 'I do consider that your power is but borrowed, extraordinary, and unstable, for ye have it but by permission of others.' " She shook her head angrily. "He means *me*! He means she has it from *me*!"

She continued.

71

"Impute not to fortune that first, your two sons were suddenly taken from you within the space of six hours, and after, your husband reft, as it were, by violence from life and honour, the memorial of his name, succession, and royal dignity perishing with himself.

"For albeit the usurped abuse, or rather tyranny, of some realms have permitted women to succeed to the honour of their fathers, yet must their glory be transferred to the house of a stranger. And so I say that with himself was buried his name, succession, and royal dignity; and in this, if ye espy not the anger and hot displeasure of God, threatening you and the rest of your house with the same plague, ye are more obstinate than I would wish you to be.

"Ye may, perchance, doubt what crimes should have been in your husband, you, or the realm for the which God should so grievously have punished you. I answer: the maintenance and defence of most horrible idolatry."

"Yes, he compares us to Ahab and all the evildoers in Israel," said the Cardinal. "You need not read it all; it is quite redundant. He never makes a point but he feels he may reiterate it twenty-eight times."

Mary kept reading, captive to all the venom and invective. "But the fearful, and unbelieving, and the abominable, and murderers, and whoremongers, and sorcerers, and idolaters, and all liars'—"

"That is us, my dear," said the Cardinal, in a light, mocking tone.

"—'shall have their part in the lake which burneth with fire and brimstone, which is the second death.' " She shuddered.

"I should be the one to tell you this," said the Cardinal. His face grew serious for almost the first time that day. "I do not want you to hear it from anyone besides your family. Your *French* family," he emphasized. Shaking his ginger-coloured little beard, he said, "Your brother James, who is coming here to attend your wedding, has joined them. He has become a Protestant. He follows Knox now." He ground out the words one by one like a man turning a crank. "He is one of *them*."

XI

Mary lay awake, listening to the faint sounds of birds stirring. It was yet too early for birdsong; the sky was still night-dark. But she could not sleep.

This is the last night I pass unmarried, she thought. This is my last night as a maiden.

But what did that mean? she wondered. Did it mean that she and François would lie together as a man and wife tomorrow night? They would lie in bed together, that she knew. That was part of the ceremony. But when they were alone?

François has kissed me, she thought. But only in the same way as Uncle le Balafre and Uncle the Cardinal; or as the Marys and I kiss one another to say *bonjour* or *au revoir*. It is exactly the same. Indeed, how can it be any different tomorrow? I know there is special knowledge that comes to men, but François is not yet a man.

She sighed and rolled over. The light covers felt comforting in the chilly April air of predawn. François had remained small; he barely reached her shoulder. Moreover, he had never been well; he suffered from coughs and colds and fevers, and had the puffy, pale face of an invalid. And the whining, cantankerous nature of one as well, more was the pity. The only person he seemed to regard as a friend and not an enemy was Mary, his designated partisan and protector. For her alone he managed a smile and an attempt at fetching his own toys. The rest he ordered about languidly.

Poor François, thought Mary. How I wish his body would grow strong!

But her thoughts did not follow where that would inevitably lead. If François had been a normal fourteen-year-old, with widening shoulders and deepening voice, with eyes that followed women, the promise of her forthcoming marriage would be altogether changed.

A chorus of birdsong now sprang up outside the windows, which began to reveal their outline against the fading purple sky. The pale stones, the pointed arches, looked like a church window; and indeed, this was an old cloister, now the palace of the Archbishop of Paris. Outside the windows were blooming branches, trees just getting their April leaves. The birds sat chittering in them, ever more shrilly.

She drifted partly to sleep, the birdsong drowning her senses. She dreamed, or pictured, a man in the branches outside, crouching there, balancing on the limb as easily as a monkey. His face was dark—or was it merely begrimed? He smiled, slowly, making an ivory slot in the shadowy visage. Then he moved, and with such grace and power he seemed more than a mortal man, or perhaps less—perhaps an animal.

He was beckoning her, wordlessly. Or rather, she felt compelled to rise and follow him, to leave the safety of the stone floor and protective windows and come out onto the swaying branch with him. She approached, and felt the chill wind blowing in the open window, and saw the lightening green haze outside, a haze made of the rising sun shining through a hundred thousand baby leaves, translucent and tender. The sun, behind him, made an aureole around his head, and she could not see to whom she was going.

She blinked awake. The covers had fallen away, and the chill breeze in her dream was merely the loss of a blanket. The sun was just rising, but it shone through empty branches. Mary left her bed and looked out at the black limb directly beneath her window, strong enough to support a person, but there was no one there.

73

She was left feeling both uneasy and perplexed. *I should go back to bed, dream again, and then wake up,* she thought. *But it is late already. It will not be long until they come in to dress me.*

Her bridal gown and mantle were draped over a wooden stand at the far end of the chamber, where she had slept alone by her own insistence this night.

Now she made her way to the bridal dress, and stood looking at it as it fell in liquid folds over the wooden form. It was dazzling white; she had had her way absolutely. When she had summoned the court tailor, Balthazzar, and described the dress she wanted, he too had argued. "No, no, Your Royal Highness, here in France white is the colour of mourning. It will not do for a wedding gown!" Balthazzar prided himself on his knowledge of materials, how they draped, and even the history of each fabric and colour. "May I suggest blue, the blue of the skies of the Loire in May—"

"You may *suggest*," she had said with a smile, "but I *insist* on white." So together they had selected a fine white silk the shade of snowdrops and lily-of-the-valley, and he had made the bodice to gleam with pearls like morning dew.

Draped to one side was the mantle and enormously long train, blue-grey velvet embroidered with white silk and more pearls. It weighed many pounds, it was so covered with precious stones. It would take two people to bear it after her.

On a table of inlaid mother-of-pearl lay the crown-royal, made especially for her of the finest gold and set with emeralds, diamonds, rubies, and pearls. Next to it, in an ivory box, lay the Great Harry, her inheritance from her grandmother, Margaret Tudor. She had not been allowed to possess it until now.

She took it from the box and held it up to the light. The sunlight penetrated the blood-red mystery of the stone's inner fire and flashed it on the stone wall of the room. It winked and throbbed in bursts of colour. Its beauty stunned her.

My grandmother was given this as a wedding gift from her father, she thought. *When she was even a year younger—fourteen!—than I am now. And she was going to a husband she had never seen, a man much older than she. Did the stone protect her in any way at all?*

How lucky I am, she thought, *that I am not being sent away to some foreign country to marry a man I've never seen. I can stay in France and marry my friend.*

Marry a friend.

There are those who marry for love, she suddenly thought. *My grandmother, Margaret Tudor, she married once for politics and once for love. And my great-great-grandfather, Edward IV of England, married a commoner secretly. She was older than he, and a widow besides. And then there was my great uncle, Henry VIII, who married for love—not once, but three times! And made a mess, leaving those disinherited daughters.*

She smiled at the thought of the English lover-King. *No, her way was* the normal way—an arranged, political marriage, as soon as the bride was old enough. So it had been with Katherine of Aragon, with Catherine de Médicis, with Margaret Tudor, with Margaret Beaufort, with Madeleine of France, her father's first, frail wife. . . .

Yet all the love matches, scandalous in their time, had been made by her blood relatives, and she found the idea curious. She could not imagine it.

The sun was bright and the sky empty of clouds, piercingly blue over the huge crowds of merchants, shopkeepers, apprentices, and workmen thronging the Paris streets. The fates had granted Mary Stuart a perfect, clear wedding day in notoriously fickle April. Much of the ceremony was to be held outdoors, on a specially constructed pavilion in front of Notre-Dame, called a *ciel-royal,* hung with blue cypress silk embroidered with gold fleurs de lys and emblazoned with the arms of Scotland. A velvet carpet repeated the same colours and patterns beneath their feet. Not for two hundred years had the people of Paris been able to witness the wedding of a dauphin, and the city was in a fervour of anticipation—of the costumes, the music, the ceremony, and the traditional largesse to be thrown to the crowds. They were hungry to be dazzled.

Since dawn, they had been hearing the flourishes of trumpets, fifes, and drums coming from within the monastic courts of the Archbishop's palace, whispering like a promise, "Wait . . . it is coming." So they milled, and ate the bread and cheese they had brought, and felt the sun beginning to chase away the lingering chill that was in the air as it rose slowly over the city.

At midmorning the procession began: the Swiss guards and band appeared, escorting the noble guests into Notre Dame. Then followed the Scottish musicians and minstrels, wearing the red and yellow livery of Scotland, piping and drumming their native melodies; then a hundred gentlemen of the King's household, marching solemnly in step; then the princes of the blood, sumptuously dressed, wearing their family fortunes in jewels which glittered as they moved in slow, swaying motion.

It took half an hour for all these to pass; next came the princes of the church, the abbots and bishops, bearing great ceremonial crosses of precious metal, wearing jewelled mitres and gold-threaded copes, and the four cardinals of France—the brothers Guise, and a Bourbon, and du Bellay, the papal representative.

Then the Dauphin, flanked by his two younger brothers, eight-year-old Charles and seven-year-old Henri. François moved mechanically, his eyes set straight ahead, as if something unpleasant awaited him under that billowing silken canopy—a dose of medicine or a lecture.

A pause. The Dauphin and the little princes passed by, the backs of their velvet mantles puffing out behind them.

Then, a spot of glowing white. The people gasped. Mourning? For a wedding? The tall, proud figure, draped in a dove-coloured mantle, with her slender, elegant neck rising out of the collar, walked on in celestial detachment. A crown rested on her head, and her hair was flowing long and free, to denote her virginity. Her train stretched on and on, in a graceful arc almost forty feet long, held up by two beautiful attendants. Even from a distance the red spot of the famous Great Harry ruby was visible on her bodice.

The rest of the procession, colourful and opulent as it was, did not excite. There were only the squat Queen, the little princesses, other noble ladies and damsels—all secondary to the faerie creature who had already passed by, now taking her place beside her bridegroom, surrounded by acolytes holding lighted tapers. The people strained their ears to hear the vows being exchanged on the open-air pavilion, but the whispers were lost. They glimpsed rings exchanged as the Cardinal de Bourbon married them. They saw the nine Scots commissioners, ruddy and stern, step forward to pay homage to François as their new King.

The Duc de Guise smiled as he heard Mary—safely married, God be praised, nothing could now undo it, *what God hath joined* and so on—salute her husband as Francis of Scotland, which he had just legally become.

It had been easy to persuade her to sign, before the wedding, the three secret documents bequeathing Scotland to France, should she die without a child. François was therefore King of Scotland in fact as well as title, even if the Scots did not realize it. *Ignorance is bliss,* he thought, *for those who are not ignorant.* She had been so alarmed about the growing power of the Lords of the Congregation that she believed it was her duty to ensure that Scotland would become a French protectorate forever rather than drift into outright heresy. The conversion of her brother James had shocked her and she had welcomed him but coolly.

The Duc looked at her, standing so strong and young beside him. She seemed the antithesis of death, glistening with beauty and health before her marriage altar. The paper and all its provisions had seemed preposterous, unnecessary, a macabre joke. She had laughed as she signed them. The Scots, on the contrary, had not laughed as they ponderously insisted on provisions being made for Mary's widowhood; she was to draw a pension from the Duchy of Touraine, regardless of whether she chose to remain in France afterward.

Both sets of guardians were assuming the death of the other one's child.

And that, thought the Duc, is as good a definition of adult cynicism as any.

A cheer was sounding; it was time to scatter the first of the largesse. The Duc snapped to attention, and motioned to his men to begin throwing the ducats, pistolets, half-crowns, testons and douzains—all gold and silver coins. The crowd roared and scrambled as the shower fell on them like April rain.

There were two banquets, followed by two balls—the first in the Archbishop's palace, the second in the old Palais de la Cité, with a procession through the streets of Paris in between. The Dauphin rode on a charger caparisoned with cloth-of-gold and silver. Mary was in an open litter, covered with the same material. The crowd pressed in upon her, shoving to examine her face and gown; she betrayed no emotion other than sweet curiosity to see her subjects.

After the second banquet, served on the same black marble table upon which Henry VI of England had had his coronation banquet long ago, after the dancing, after the masques and pageants—with horses of gold and silver drawing jewelled coaches, and magic boats with billowing silver sails floating on the ballroom floor—the torches finally burned down, their flames ceasing to reflect in the thousands of jewels decorating bosoms, ears, necks, and hair. Night had come, and one by one the guests departed, stealing away in the dark, crossing the bridge over the lapping Seine. They trailed perfume and laughter and music, singing as they went. The moon shone on the white flowering branches of the palace orchard and the little side streets.

Mary and the Dauphin were escorted to the royal bedchamber where they would spend the night. The bed was high and deep, the pillows made of new goosedown and encased in satin.

The Marys dressed Mary in her bridal nightgown and helped her to mount the steps into the bed. Behind the carved screen, François's attendants were doing the same for him. He emerged in a gown of royal blue trimmed with fur, and came forward with slow deliberation. Shaking off their helping hands, he clambered into the bed himself and slid under the covers.

"We dismiss you," he said grandly, waving his hand. "You, too, Uncle." He stopped the Cardinal of Lorraine from blessing the bed. The Cardinal had no choice but to obey.

The door clicked shut, although they both knew full well eavesdroppers would remain outside listening all night.

François put his arms around her and kissed her on the mouth, his childish plump lips sweet and delicate.

"Now you are mine, and no one can take you away," he said solemnly. "Like they took away my lapdog and my pet bear."

"The bear caused so much damage," said Mary with a laugh. "Do you remember when it escaped at Blois? And ran into the house of Madame Pillonne?"

"Dear Old Julius. I hated it when they took him away," said François. He put his head on her shoulder and cuddled up against her. "He had such a sweet way about him, such a soft muzzle. . . ." He drifted off to sleep.

Mary lay for a few moments looking at the moonlight on the floor of the chamber, before she too fell asleep.

The next morning the Cardinal of Lorraine and the Duc de Guise gave out the news that the marriage night had been passed "as all expected, all decently and in order." They went off to their private chambers in glee, where they clanked goblets and proceeded to get decorously drunk.

XII

Mary found herself waking up each morning for the next month saying to herself, *I am married,* and wondering why she did not feel different. She had expected to—had thought that some deep inner change would have taken place. But no—she was the same as always. And François—he was the same, too. When she called him her husband, it felt like one of the games they had played when they were younger and would proclaim themselves pirates, warriors, dragons. Just so it seemed when she would now refer to "François, my *husband.*"

Their lessons continued, but now they had their own household together. Mary had simply brought all her people with her—Madame Rallay, the Marys, Father Mamerot, Bourgoing—and now they lived and worked with François's people, which had already led to a few romances. The larger household meant they had more privileges and bigger expenses, but it was a household made up almost entirely of young people, and it had the effect of being a playhouse in itself.

There was only picnicking, hunting, and riding during the daylight hours; playacting, dancing, poetry reading, music, and card playing in the evenings. The only adult incursions into their glowing world of leisure and youth were the Guises. Mary's uncles visited regularly and insisted on drawing her aside to question her carefully about her studies and report on what was happening beyond her golden household.

It was gloomy, unpleasant news, most of it. Wars, killing, plots, sickness, death. The only happy item they came with was the announcement that, thanks to the marriage, Scotsmen and Frenchmen now had dual citizenship.

"Which means that François is now, by courtesy, a Scotsman," said Uncle Cardinal.

Mary had laughed outright. A sudden picture of François standing in the windy courtyard of a Scottish castle had come to her. It was surprising, this picture; she had not known she remembered such a castle, and was unsure whether it really existed at all. It was high up, on a crag. . . .

"And that means you are also a Frenchwoman," he continued.

"I feel like a Frenchwoman, completely," she said.

"Now citizens of each country can pass freely back and forth; no permission or passports are required. It is the first step in uniting them permanently."

Mary sighed. "I wonder if that will ever truly come to pass. The rebels in Scotland seem to grow fiercer and fiercer. . . ." At the thought of their harassment of her dear mother, her chest ached. Her mother was holding out bravely, trying to fight them off. But Scotland was a long way away, and seemed to have nothing to do with her life here, in the joyous round of days where cares were unknown or never more than a passing annoyance, easily solved.

"The day will come, my dear," the Cardinal assured her.

Christmas was coming, and Mary was deeply proud to be able to arrange for all the festivities in her own household. This year, she and François would have their own Christmas, and invite others to join them. Perhaps this was really what marriage meant: having your own home, your own Christmas, rather than being a guest at someone else's.

A French Christmas!—setting out a crèche, lighting the *bûche de Noël* in a huge fireplace, midnight mass in the royal chapel illuminated with a thousand candles, programs of sacred music—Mary tingled with excitement in planning it.

And for François, a special present; she had ordered an Arab horse for him from Spain. He had so longed for one, had eagerly recounted for her the extraordinary features of Arabians: their intelligence, fire, speed; their delicate bones and large eyes. Oh, he would be so surprised—and beside himself with delight! If the breeder there could deliver . . . if the horse could be brought north safely. . . . Still, just planning it excited her, thrilled her with her own thoughtfulness and competence.

It was just before Advent began that Mary received an unexpected summons to Paris, where Henri II wished to see her.

Why could not the King come here? she wondered. But she obeyed and left immediately.

When she arrived at the Louvre, still chilled and tired from the journey, she was summoned to see the King right away. She barely had time to remove her thick travelling mantle and comb her hair before she was conducted into his presence.

"Mary Tudor is dead," said Henri II solemnly, crossing himself. "I stand now in the presence of the new Queen of England." He nodded in acknowledgment to Mary. "Yes, my child, my daughter. Your good cousin Mary Tudor has been called to her reward, and she leaves her crown to you."

How unexpected! How peculiar! And for an instant, Mary hoped it was not true. If it was, it changed everything, and she did not want things changed. She was so happy as she was. "Did she name me so?" asked Mary. Everyone knew that Mary had refused to name her half sister Elizabeth, both because she distrusted her and because of the uncertainty about her legitimacy.

"She did not have to," said King Henri. "Blood names you. You inherit by right of descent."

"Did she name Elizabeth?" Mary persisted.

"The heretics pretend she did. No one heard her—no one whose witness we can trust. Her only confidant, the only one who knew her heart, Cardinal

79

Pole, died a mere twelve hours later. Only Cardinal Pole knew that truth—that she could not, would not, have named Elizabeth. No, they hope to make a *fait accompli* before anyone can act to prevent them."

"And do *you* plan to prevent them?" Not a war! Not another war!

Her voice was cool and her questions cooler. Ever since her marriage, she had been bolder and less deferential. The King blamed her uncles for that.

"I plan to protest, and see how it is to be received," he replied.

"A protest without troops means little. And I have heard good things about Elizabeth, and that the people like her."

"Bah! They like any new ruler. They cheered and lit bonfires for Mary, too. That's the English for you. Within a year they turn against their sovereign. 'The English vice is treachery'—"

" 'And the French vice is lechery,' " she finished the old saw.

This new self-possession was not at all pleasing, thought the King. I will break her of it.

"You will go into mourning for Queen Mary, and you will quarter the arms of England on your royal plate, on your cloth of estate, and on your insignia. Tomorrow there will be a banquet, and I will have the heralds formally proclaim you Queen of England."

"No."

"Yes. You will obey. I am your King."

"I am an anointed queen in my own right, a fellow sovereign. I am your equal, not your subject."

The King was infuriated. So this was what her uncles were filling her head with. As if Scotland were a real country, the equal of France! The fools!

"You will do as I command you," he said, his already narrow eyes turning into slits.

"The only command I recognize is the fourth commandment: Honour your father and mother. I will honour and obey you as my father, which you are, in law. Not as my superior."

Insolent child! thought the King. She needs to be deflated. But who will do it? The uncles will prevent it.

"Do as I say, and soon you will be a real queen, queen of a real country," he said. She was—must be!—ambitious, and would agree on that basis. "Just think—Queen of England!"

Instead she looked sulky. "I hate falsity," she said. "This is all founded on falsity and empty gestures."

"But to be a ruler, one must know how to make those gestures," he insisted. "They are as important as etiquette and law and even battle. They can sometimes carry as much weight as all three!"

XIII

His Holiness Pope Paul IV shuffled and sniffled his way to his writing table at the Vatican. His thin frame shook with what to him was bone-chilling cold. That was because, at the age of eighty-two, the ascetic pontiff's bones were very close to his skin. This winter was not particularly cold, and indeed there were people strolling about in the great square of St. Peter's with no mantles on. But within the Papal apartments, no amount of gilding on the paintings or depictions of desert sands could make him feel warm.

Elizabeth Tudor had chosen January fifteenth for her Coronation, so he had been informed. It was a very northern thing to do. He supposed they were used to bitter weather, and even to staging outdoor ceremonies in it. The letter must reach her before the ceremony; she must not be anointed and crowned in ignorance of his wishes. No!

He seated himself, and motioned to one of his guards to bring the brazier closer. He did not need to reread her letter; he knew it by heart. She was asking for his recognition; that was simple. It was the *answer* that had eluded him until now. But now he had it. There could be, must be, no compromise. A heretic might be on the throne, but the throne of England was still, officially, Catholic. Thus it must remain, and she must submit to his arbitration and make obeisance before he would consider recognizing her.

His spidery fingers grasped his silver-inlaid pen and began writing in equally spidery calligraphy:

> We are unable to comprehend the hereditary right of one not born in wedlock. The Queen of Scots claims the crown, as the nearest legitimate descendant of Henry VII. However, my daughter, if you show yourself willing to submit the controversy to our arbitration, we will show every indulgence to your ladyship which justice would permit.

He sprinkled sand across the wet ink, feeling as mighty as Saint George.

Shortly thereafter, he found himself obliged to issue a bull directly to the daughter of darkness in England. Sitting at the same desk, puzzled over her prompt reply—which was not even directly to him, but to her ambassador at the Vatican, recalling him—the former head of the Italian Inquisition did what needed to be done.

> January 12, 1559.
> We hereby decree that heretical sovereigns are incapable of reigning and must not be recognized as legitimate sovereigns by any members of

the True Church. Neither allegiance nor obedience is to be shown them, under pain of mortal sin.

There. The battle lines had been drawn. There must be no accommodation. The bull, *Cum Ex Apostolatus*, would be published all over Europe.

☙

Elizabeth had her coronation on January 15, 1559, and it was, from all reports, a glittering diamond of a winter day. Mary eagerly read all the descriptions of it, of the long procession through London, the solemn ceremony in Westminster Abbey, followed by the resounding "God save the Queen!" bellowed out by the people.

I wish I could remember my own coronation, she thought. I must ask my mother to write me a long description of it, for I would cherish knowing all the details.

If my mother has time, she had to add.

For Marie de Guise's time was increasingly spent in trying to govern the ever-more-unruly kingdom of Scotland. The Protestants had issued a "Beggars' Summons" ordering all friars to surrender their properties to the poor by May twelfth. Marie had in turn ordered all heretical preachers to return to Catholicism by Easter. The battle lines were being drawn in Scotland, as well as everywhere else.

In the meantime, Mary dutifully followed her father-in-law's orders, wearing mourning for Queen Mary Tudor at a banquet, where her entrance was announced by a herald proclaiming, "*Place! Place! Pour la Reine d'Angleterre.*" And as she entered the dining hall, the whole company chorused, "*Vive la Reine d'Angleterre!*" Upon being seated, she was served off freshly engraved plates showing the arms of England quartered with those of France and Scotland.

She hoped her cousin Elizabeth would overlook this. Or, she assured herself, if it was true that these empty gestures were the expected thing to do, then such an astute politician as the new Queen of England would surely understand.

XIV

he noise was deafening, and the glass shrieked as it crashed on the stone floor of the church—almost like a living thing, thought John Knox. A living thing that hated to yield up its spirit.

But the spirit was evil, and had to die. It was the spirit of idolatry, the demon that had plagued God's people since first He had made a covenant with them in Moses' time—nay, in Abraham's. It was written in the First and Second Commandments, spelled out explicitly:

> Thou shalt have no other gods before me. Thou shalt not make unto thee any graven image, or any likeness of anything that is in heaven above, or that is in the earth beneath, or that is in the water under the earth: Thou shalt not bow down thyself to them, nor serve them.

How much plainer could it be? But the response of the Israelites had been the Golden Calf—and our response has been *this*! he thought, as he kicked the broken head of a Virgin statue that lay a few feet away from her torso. We made graven images and worshipped them: virgins and saints and pretty coloured pictures in glass to entertain people, to set them to day-dreaming and amusing themselves in God's house, as at a holiday pageant.

The mob had thrown a rope around the stone shoulders of a Saint Peter in his niche, and were yanking him down. They yelled and laughed as the statue hit the floor and exploded in fragments. Saint Andrew in the neighbouring niche followed, and a cheer went up. Dust motes filled the air.

"Careful of the glass splinters!" Knox cried, and they turned to him like obedient children. The shards were everywhere, and could easily slice open a foot or cut a face. He would feel responsible if anyone was hurt.

But the mob was growing, taking on a character of its own, almost feeding on the fallen statues and ruined church. How literally they had taken his words in the sermon about idolatry two days ago here in Perth! How hungry they were for reform, and action! Would Calvin have been proud of him?

At the thought of Calvin and Geneva, a wave of affectionate homesickness swept through him. It would have been so easy to remain there, learning from Calvin, exulting in the experience of actually living in a city dedicated to God, totally purged of idolatry and filled with living saints. I was the least among them, he thought. Only a pupil of Calvin's and Farel's, only a disciple. It was like that first Pentecost in Jerusalem, when the flames of the Holy Spirit came down and enveloped the disciples. To be there, to be partaking of it! *That* was almost heaven.

But even that—there's a danger of making an idol even of Geneva, he thought with despair. The devil turns even our best things against us, uses them on our weak spots. Uses my hunger for righteousness and order and freedom to try to ensnare me. For had I remained in Geneva, I would have been turning my back on my own country, instead of helping to liberate her from the bondage of strangers.

"Master Knox! Master Knox!" They were motioning to him.

He crossed over the nave, picking his steps with care through the rubble. The mob, armed with mallets and iron bars, stood at the ready before the intricately carved rood screen, which separated the high altar from the rest of the church.

"Bless our first stroke!" they demanded.

He did not like the Papist sound of that.

"Am I a bishop?" he argued. "To sprinkle things with holy water or smoke them with incense or mumble spells over them? Nay, either a thing is of God or it is not."

Now they fell silent. He had them under his control, and could direct their actions as he pleased.

"And I say this altar is not of God!" he roared. "It is an abomination, an adornment to grace a pagan ritual . . . the mass! For what is the mass but a superstitious magic rite, so secret and blasphemous that the people cannot even be allowed to look upon it whilst it is being enacted?"

He swept his arms out. "Down with it! Destroy it! Let not one stone remain standing upon the other!"

The leaders began swinging their clubs and stakes, opening holes in the delicate lacy carving, knocking down struts.

"Let the daylight into that dark cavern of evil and superstition! Open it up for the people!" he screamed, and his words rose above the hammering and destruction.

That night he had a sore throat from his preaching and from inhaling the stone-dust, and had to submit to the ministrations of his wife, Marjory. She concocted a drink of chamomile and honey and insisted on his sipping it slowly. He liked the taste of it, but Calvin had taught him to guard against that particular snare; even eating and drinking should yield no pleasure beyond the natural satisfying of hunger and thirst. So, to combat the pleasure of the sweet, warm posset—and the nearness of his young wife—he forced himself to listen to a report by Patrick, Lord Ruthven, one of the Lords of the Congregation. The man himself was unpleasant enough to act as an effective counterweight to both Marjory and the drink—he was rough, wild, and reported to be a warlock—even if his news had been more palatable.

"The Queen Regent has vowed to bring French troops to crush us," he said. "That's the word from Edinburgh." He shook his bushy head, and stroked his claymore—the five-foot-long, two-handed sword he carried everywhere. "We'll give her such a breakfast, she and her froggies—we'll split them, and spit them, and serve 'em for dinner like they do in her beloved France."

"Please." Knox winced. He found the idea of eating frogs' legs repulsive. "How many troops?" he whispered.

"Two thousand or so. Don't worry, we will stand. 'If God be for us, who can be against us?' Romans eight, thirty-one," he said proudly.

Knox smiled. That this uncouth fighting lord, who could barely read, should have memorized Scripture! Ah, Calvin, if only you could share this moment! he thought.

"That is true," he said softly. "But even the Lord is helped by good equipment. Remember the conquest of Canaan? 'And the Lord was with

Judah, and he took possession of the hill country, but he could not drive out the inhabitants of the plain, because they had chariots of iron.' Judges one, nineteen."

Immediately he was sorry he had said it, because Ruthven's face fell. Was I using my knowledge wrongly? Knox wondered. Intimidating my brother, instead of acting in love? It is all so difficult to know! Every action can lead to sin. Pride lurks everywhere.

"The Old Testament has not been widely spoken of here," Knox assured him. "We studied it much in Geneva. And you will see, soon there will be a translated Bible in every church, available and"—his throat stung—"preached freely." He stopped and coughed. "But back to the matter at hand. We will need weapons to combat the Queen and her foreign troops."

"I command and can supply many," said Ruthven. He smiled, a jagged one that showed large teeth lurking just the other side of his thick, furlike beard. "I'll warrant help will come from south of the border, good master. From the English Queen, good Protestant that she is."

"Have you word of this?" In his excitement, Knox raised his voice. Immediately he regretted it.

"Rumours, and something stronger than rumour. 'Tis done; the Parliament has repealed the Catholicism of Bloody Mary; England is Protestant once again. Officially, as of five days ago. You've a sure ally in England now, instead of an enemy."

"The Reformed Church has an ally," Knox corrected him. "The English Queen has never forgiven me for writing *The First Blast of the Trumpet*. She took it so personally"—this genuinely puzzled him—"she even refused to let me set foot in England on my way back here. Ah, well. As long as she supports the Faith."

"That she does. Waved away the monks waiting in procession to escort her to Parliament with their ceremonial torches. 'Away with these torches, for we see well enough!' " Ruthven laughed.

"Good." Knox hated monks. Tonsured, interfering fools.

So Elizabeth was on the Reformers' side. Let her join them, then, in ousting the French and the Catholic Church from Scotland.

The Queen Mother, old Marie de Guise—the French cow, as Knox thought of her—had ordered all the Reformed preachers to return to Catholicism by Easter; when they refused, she commanded them to appear before her on May tenth.

The answer, thought Knox, was my sermon the next day, the sermon that started the rioting here in Perth. Now let her face our army, if she can wade through the rubble of her late Popish ruins! He laughed loudly, not caring that it strained his throat.

And God has spared us the prospect of her daughter ever returning to Scotland and the throne, he thought. She will be tied up for her lifetime in France, in that land of satin and foppery, whilst we go about our business unhindered.

Thank You, Lord, he thought. Thank You. Now lead us on to final victory!

XV

arly summer in Paris, when the city was tender and in its first spreading ripeness, should have been a pleasurable time for the French court. Indeed, high festivities were in hand: King Philip of Spain, that well-rehearsed bridegroom, had been accepted in matrimony by Elisabeth Valois, after abandoning his hopeless pursuit of the new English Queen. The wedding would take place at the end of June, along with the nuptials of her spinster aunt, Marguerite Valois, to the Duke of Savoy—another hapless suitor of Queen Elizabeth, who was discarding them left and right like a housewife sorting rags.

But in spite of the expensive preparations—the commotion in the kitchens, the armour-fitting, the tournament practices—within the Hôtel des Tournelles there was an anxiety, a high hum in the air, although no one acknowledged it. Catherine de Médicis was in a perpetual frown and heaviness, her dark eyes looking to something within herself; Elisabeth, only fourteen, was apprehensive about leaving France and becoming the third wife of a man whose other wives had been so short-lived. And Mary was unhappy: unhappy to be losing her almost-sister Elisabeth, unhappy that François was once again ill, and most of all unhappy with the news from Scotland. Her mother was ill and beleaguered by John Knox's rabid Reformers. Actual war had broken out, with killings on both sides. Led by the Lords of the Congregation, and whipped up by John Knox's preaching, the Scottish people had gone on a rampage of destruction, while their army had attacked the government's forces.

And in back of it was English help. Queen Elizabeth must be secretly sending money to help the rebels. Without English support, the rebels would have been beaten by now.

O my mother! thought Mary to herself as she dressed for the tournament that was to be part of the festivities that afternoon. My mother, my mother—if only I could see you, be with you . . . it has been so long since I have seen you, eight years since your wonderful visit here in France, eight long years . . . I must find a way for us to see each other again, there must *be* a way . . . perhaps I can come to you. . . . The longing was so acute it was like a physical pain, a yearning that tore at her in hidden places.

Riding in her carriage with its gilded wheels to the adjoining tournament grounds on the rue St.-Antoine, being preceded by heralds running ahead, crying, "Make way, make way, for Her Majesty the Queen of Scotland and England," seemed something she was doing for her mother's sake, striking a blow against her mother's enemy, Elizabeth. Her earlier admiration of Elizabeth's cleverness had soured now that it was directed against her own mother. She smiled and waved as the people acknowledged her, and Nicholas Throckmorton, the English ambassador, noted everything and would report it back to London.

She took her place in the viewing balcony on the rue St.-Antoine, next to her uncle the Cardinal, who looked bored already.

"I wish I had a livre for every official joust I have had to attend," said the Cardinal, twitching at his robes. "I should have amassed more than Luther claimed the Church made on indulgences. Ah, well. One cannot have a marriage or a birth or a coronation without them. Spectacle is an investment. If wisely used, that is. Now, this . . . " He gave a dismissive gesture. "Waste. Who sees it? Who is impressed by it? Not Philip. He is not here. He does not reckon this important enough to leave Spain for!"

The thought had been in Mary's mind as well. It was hurtful that Philip did not care enough for his new bride to claim her in person.

"That is a great pity," said Mary. "For Elisabeth's heart is not his yet. He will have to win her, and this is no way to begin."

The Cardinal sighed expansively. "Love and arranged marriages—they are seldom found together." He seemed not to care if Elisabeth was happy or not; it was her lot as a princess to endure. "Your cousin Elizabeth declines the hand of the Spanish bridegroom," he said. "Of course, there is some feeling that perhaps she is not the true Queen. Philip is well out of it. Especially since the Pope has issued his statement recognizing *you* as rightful Queen." He had not exactly "issued" the statement, but the Cardinal's spies had found out about it anyway.

Mary looked out beyond the tournament grounds, which lay between the Bastille and the river, to the buildings of Paris, shimmering in the June sun, and beyond them to the bright green fields. She had seen the same vista in a Book of Hours: brilliant and jewellike.

She sighed. "My heart is too heavy with my mother's troubles in Scotland to concern myself with the romances of my cousin in England, who causes them." She refused to discuss the formal "claim" Henri II had forced her to make.

"She does not exactly *cause* them," corrected the Cardinal. "The English Queen *causes* nothing, she merely takes advantage of what naturally occurs."

"How clever of her." Mary was still looking at the perfect June landscape, so like a miniature. She wished she could enter into it, walk along the winding country road that, from here, looked like a brown thread. . . .

The contenders were milling at either end of the field, banners fluttering.

The Cardinal suddenly took off his hat and began fanning himself with it. "When will they start? This is torture!"

"Soon," she assured him.

He heaved a sigh of resignation, and turned to talk to the Queen, seated on his other side. Catherine de Médicis, dressed in a rich green silk dress, looked sour; her brows were drawn up in a straight line, and she kept twisting a handkerchief in her stubby fingers. Mary heard the Cardinal attempting to entertain her. But she grew ever more agitated.

Tournaments were such pretty things, thought Mary. All the colours, and the ritual—rather like high mass. Perhaps it was a mass, a secular one, of strength and worldliness. . . .

The trumpets sounded. The jousts in honour of the marriage of the King's sister, Princess Marguerite, and his daughter, Princess Elisabeth, to the Duke of Savoy and the King of Spain, respectively, would now commence. Glittering contenders—including the King, wearing the black and white colours of Diane—came onto the field. The first contest began.

For an hour or so everyone watched avidly, but then the too-familiar spectacle wore thin and thoughts began to wander and tongues to chatter amongst the onlookers.

Mary smoothed her blue gown and thought of François. He sat close to his mother, his face pinched with pain from his ever-present ear infection. How did he bear it, never feeling well? Yet he persisted with his lessons, and kept hunting.

Farther down on the balcony sat the Duc de Guise, back from the wars for good. An agreement had ended the wars: the Treaty of Cateau-Cambrésis, which stopped all the fighting. France had had to return all her conquests from the last eighty years in Italy. How futile war was, she thought. All the banners and horses and ordnance, but in the end it was as insubstantial as a joust.

"How is marriage treating you, my dear?" The Cardinal's voice was warm and close to her ear.

"I enjoy being married," she answered.

"In what sense do you enjoy it?" he persisted.

"As a wife should." She would not betray François's capabilities—or lack of them—to him.

"Then we can expect a prince soon?" He was relentless.

"That is in the hands of God."

"God helps those who help themselves."

Should she listen to this? "In what way?" She yielded to the temptation.

"For the good of France, it may be necessary to make personal sacrifices. To set aside certain commandments."

"Such as the sixth?" She paused. "The one commanding fidelity?"

"How perceptive you are. Naturally, the Lord would reward such a sacrifice with minor compensations—such as pleasure." Surely she wanted to taste pleasure! She was fashioned for it.

"My pleasure is in being faithful to the one ordained to me by God."

Oh, dear. What a problem for the succession, he thought.

"But of course," he said smoothly. "I was merely testing you, my dear."

"I know." She pretended to believe him. "That is your job, as Cardinal of the Church and as my—"

A cry rose from the spectators on the balcony. Mary looked out onto the field, and saw the King pitching forward, a splintered lance sticking out of his open visor. Blood spurted out between the golden bars of the cagelike visor, drenching the horse's neck.

Catherine screamed. Diane sat as if cast in stone.

"Christ on His throne!" breathed the Cardinal, rising and clutching the balustrade.

The King was being taken down from his horse, as stiff as a scarecrow, except for a convulsive twitch every few seconds. They laid him on a stretcher and bore him away, before the Queen or any of the royal family could move from the stands or go to him.

"No!" screamed Catherine. "I warned him! I told him! I begged him!" She rushed down to the field and threw herself, weeping, on the horse's bloody neck.

"Come," said the Cardinal. He held Mary's elbow and raised her up. "To your carriage. They will have taken him back to the Hôtel des Tournelles. Go to him."

Mary obeyed and entered her ceremonial car, emblazoned with all her titles. Her coachman started up the horses, and the heralds ran ahead, announcing loudly, "Make way, make way, for Her Majesty the Queen of Scotland and England." Their voices were swallowed up in the yells of the crowd, jostling and excited.

In the Hôtel des Tournelles—the Cardinal had guessed correctly—the King lay on a narrow bed, attended by his physicians. The lance had entered his right eye, and blinded it. Splinters of the wood, it was feared, had penetrated his brain.

For ten days the King lingered, as the splinters from the lance festered in his brain and infection spread. Sometimes he was lucid, sometimes not. But the puzzling thing to Mary was that she sensed he was neither surprised nor reluctant to go to his death at only forty-one. It was as if he were greeting death as a not unwelcome, or unexpected, caller.

Catherine had evidently been warned, both by her astrologer Ruggieri and by Nostradamus, by whom she set great store, of a disaster. In addition, she had had a disturbing dream the night before. All these things she had told her husband, and he had ignored them. Or had he? Had he actually welcomed them and embraced them? His actions seemed to belie a wish to live. He had insisted on running the final course, even in the face of Catherine's pleas, and the wish of his opponent to stop. The King had commanded the reluctant opponent to face him, or be punished.

François stood by his father's bed, pale and shaky. He himself was not well; the earache had subsided, but his fever persisted.

"Father!" he cried. "Do not leave me!"

His father sighed and opened his eyes halfway, as if it were too much effort to open them all the way. "My son," he said, in an almost normal voice, "you are about to lose your father, but not his blessing. May God grant you more happiness than ever He has granted me."

François threw himself sobbing on the bed. His father's chest felt solid and warm, and he believed if he just held him tightly enough, he could keep him forever.

Mary embraced François, putting her arms around him from behind. His thin shoulders were shaking.

The King's eyes closed. He looked asleep. But then Ambroise Paré, the physician, took his pulse. In a moment he shook his head.

"Your Majesty, the King is dead," he said. He was speaking to François.

"No!" François clung to his father.

"Your Majesty," said the Cardinal. He motioned to Mary, who drew her husband up for the recognition.

"We pledge you our lives and our loyalty," said the Cardinal. "We will serve you as long as life remains."

François rubbed his eyes. His mother was weeping. "*Maman!*" He held out his arms to her, ignoring the Cardinal. "*Maman!*"

Together they stumbled out to the door of the hôtel, where an anxious crowd was waiting. Let the Cardinal make the announcement; they would leave for the Louvre. A royal coach was drawn up outside, under a linden tree. They made to enter it. Mary stood aside to be the last to enter, out of respect for her mother-in-law. But suddenly, Catherine de Médicis drew back, and looked at her as calmly as if it had been an ordinary day.

"You must enter before me," she said, in her low voice. "The Queen of France takes precedence over a queen dowager."

XVI

Mary found herself unable to eat from noon on, she was so nervous about her upcoming evening—the first where she and François would preside as King and Queen of France. It was to be a simple affair, and planned by Mary herself, which made her all the more nervous, as every aspect of its success or failure could thus be traced to her.

For several years she had had a private garden of her own on the grounds of one of the smaller châteaux. Diane de Poitiers had noticed her love of flowers, and had helped her to plan this entirely white garden just below the terrace, leading up to the tranquil waters of an ornamental pool.

"For you seem to have a special affinity for white," she had told the girl. "And a white garden can be magnificent by moonlight. And did you know there are some flowers that open only in the dark, and give off the most lush perfumes? They come from Persia."

Diane. Banished now from court, sent away by Catherine de Médicis as soon as Henri II was decently buried. But her garden flourished, and over the years Mary had lovingly tended it and added more flowers to it, until now it extended over a large area, embracing the pool tenderly in a scented frame.

The party would take place here. The guests would stroll along the leafy paths, illuminated by lanterns until the full moon rose and made the white flowers glow. Both French and Scottish musicians would be at hand, walking about, mingling with the guests, playing their violas, lutes, pipes and quihissels; Mary hoped the very informality of it would put everyone at ease—herself and François most of all.

"Madam," said a familiar voice behind her, "is it still to be a Party of Youth?"

Mary turned to see Flamina standing nearby. Her Marys were now her ladies-in-waiting, her most trusted inner circle. She had not expected that becoming Queen of France would change anything between them, but the truth was that they now treated her differently—calling her "Madam" reverently, for example. Or perhaps it was the fact that she was now married.

"No," she said with a laugh. "We were prevailed upon to allow some of the older courtiers to come. But it will still be mainly young people."

Originally François had requested that no one over twenty-five be allowed to attend. But when she had reminded him that meant none of the Pléiad—the group of seven classically inspired poets that gave the court its literary lustre—could attend, he had relented about the age rule. "But only those poets," he had insisted. "Not your uncles!"

"Not even little René?" she had begged. "Besides, he's twenty-four."

"I am tired of your uncles," he had complained. "And they will just bring gloomy news, and ruin the party. All their news is gloomy."

"Good," said Flamina. She tossed her head. Her old childhood exuberance and vitality had lost nothing in its transition to womanhood.

"Is there anyone in particular you hope to see? I hope I have invited him!"

"No."

Men were constantly drawn to Flamina, but they seemed never to forget her mother's proclivities and assume the daughter shared them, so she had developed a strong right arm in fending the lovers off.

"Madam!" Now Beaton joined them—honey-sweet, melting, daydreaming. "Will all be right tonight? Is the moon to be full?" Her large brown eyes were eagerly questioning.

"Indeed, unless it goes backward and is less full tonight than it was last night, skipping the full moon entirely this month!" said Flamina, a trifle shortly.

Below them, the gardeners were busy raking the paths, strewing them with petals, and staking the flowers that were nodding, top-heavy with blooms. Their apprentices followed along behind, watering and weeding.

In the back of the garden, a yew hedge had grown to shoulder height since the childish Mary had first set out the knee-high plants. The ornamental pond had become almost overgrown with water lilies, opening their huge, waxy flowers like yearning mouths.

"And you yourself will not wear white, will you?" asked Beaton anxiously. "If it is to be a white theme—"

"No," said Mary quickly. "Mourning is over."

She had worn the mourning veil for the required forty days after the death of Henri II. François had been crowned King at Reims shortly thereafter, and Mary had been determined to get him out of mourning as quickly as possible to help his spirits recover. He clearly wished to remain in seclusion and mourning as long as possible in hopes of postponing assuming the duties of ruling. But the longer he waited, the more dreadful they seemed to him. So Mary gently coaxed him out in the sunshine and back onto his favourite horse (the Arab had arrived as promised), and gradually he began to warm to the task set before him.

This evening's entertainment was just part of her efforts to ease him into his new authority. She knew he would not be intimidated by an event held in one of his smaller palaces, and limited only to young people and friends. François had permitted her to plan it and select his clothes for him.

"And *Maman* is not to be allowed to come?" he had asked gleefully.

"No, she is too old!" Mary had assured him.

There had developed friction between Catherine de Médicis and the Guises, with the former trying to manage domestic policy and the latter foreign policy.

"I hope the sky is completely clear," said Beaton. "It would not do to have a cloud to mar the light!"

Dear, tender-hearted Beaton, always worrying about conditions.

"If there are, we will just claim they are part of the decorations," said Flamina.

Flamina and Beaton made their way over to the lily pond and attempted to pick one of the blossoms. Immediately two of the gardeners—young and handsome, Mary noted—rushed to help them.

"What a charming picture."

The Cardinal! He had stolen in and was now standing only a few feet away on the terrace, the soft air playing with the hem of his churchly robe. He cocked his head at her as he had since she was a child; *his* manner toward her had not changed.

"Now, you know you cannot come!" she chided him.

"Ah! *Cruelle dame!*" He clutched at his bosom. "And here is the most coveted invitation in France just now—the first fête of Their Glorious Majesties François II and Marie. Where have I failed?"

"What is it you wish?" Of late his nosy inquiries and attempts to direct and control her—subtly disguised, or so he thought—were putting her off.

"Only to share with you some intelligence from Scotland." He made as if he were hurt—slightly. "Or are you no longer concerned with that small, troublesome realm?"

Not Scotland again. Yes, she was still concerned with it, deeply concerned. But could the news from there never be pleasant? "Of course I am. What is it?"

She indicated a wooden bench in the shade of an ornamental shrub, and they took their places side by side.

"I hate to be the one to tell you, but the ships you sent to aid your mother . . ."

Eight of them, loaded with three thousand soldiers, she remembered. The pride of France.

". . . were wrecked in violent storms, and all lost."

"Storms! But it is too early for storms!"

The Cardinal coughed gently. "I know. I know. Perhaps Master Knox controls the winds and seas. They seem to obey him, at any rate."

"Knox! And his mobs have overrun the country, looting and burning, worse than the English armies!"

"They've joined forces now," said the Cardinal softly.

"What do you mean?" The bright day seemed ominous, as if Knox might suddenly materialize out of one of the hedges, or the trimmed topiary take on his shape.

"I mean that the rebels—the ones who declared your sweet mother suspended from the Regency—have signed a treaty of alliance with England, and that Queen Elizabeth has formally taken Scotland 'under her protection.' This allows her openly to send an English army in to aid the rebels, which is what she is doing."

"But—upon what grounds?"

"Upon the grounds that she must defend England against a French army."

"My mother's army! The help I send her!"

"Exactly."

The Cardinal had managed to ruin the party without even being there. "I shall send more and more forces!" she said fiercely. "They shan't prevail!"

After the Cardinal left—reluctantly, she knew—Mary sat staring down at her own feet for a few moments. Clearly she and François would need to make a royal visit to Scotland. Surely that would calm the troubles there. Scotland bewildered her in its swift turn against the religion of its forefathers, under the direction of the fiery Knox. No other country had seen such a quick rise of Protestantism, and of such a virulent type. These Lords of the Congregation—who were they? Were they truly devout, or just power-hungry? And this Knox—what sort of a churchman openly carried a two-handed sword and preached revolution? It was a type never seen before.

Yes. She must visit Scotland. After she and François had become accustomed to their demanding positions here in France.

The sun had set, leaving behind red-purple streaks and a little escort of clouds clustered at the horizon, before the party assembled. King François, grown surprisingly taller in the past year, stood awkwardly on the highest step of the terrace, receiving his guests. His new scarlet breeches were gathered fashionably at the thighs, and his long-sleeved doublet was pierced with a hundred little slashes that let the moss-coloured satin lining peep out. Hose of the selfsame colour encased his long, spindly legs; he had disdained to pad his calves as his tailor suggested. His equally long and slender feet wore slashed shoes. The whole effect was like two green beans with shoes. But François was unaware of the effect, and stood proudly with his flat velvet cap and ornamental sword, welcoming his friends and little brothers, Charles and Henri. At nine and eight, they were the youngest present, and ran off to hide in the bushes and jump out at people.

"Welcome, my dear friends," François said as loudly as possible, lifting up his arms. "My Queen and I delight in having you as our guests. Pray, help us enjoy the full moon when she rises." He turned to Pierre de Ronsard, at thirty-five the oldest guest. "And you can recite your 'Hymn to the Moon'—if you will be so kind."

Ronsard bowed and kissed the King's hand. "When she rises, I will salute her." He turned to Mary. "But this glorious sun, this moon, shines on us already!"

Not now! she wanted to say. His extravagant praise could be embarrassing—all the more so since he clearly would have to praise her even if she looked like one of the donkeys that provided milk for the ladies' baths.

Mary looked at the company she had gathered about her. Rushing across the marbled terrace was Mary Livingston, Lusty. She had grown big as well as tall, and would need a strapping husband, Mary thought. Not only strapping but lively and filled with energy. Who would there be for Lusty?

Not the poet Chastelard, Henri d'Amville's secretary, who was languishing beside one of the potted fruit trees. His large, dark eyes, which looked always as if they were about to weep, were casting about for something to fasten on. He watched with some interest as Mary Seton came out, but his interest faded as she passed by. He could sense immediately that she was not the sort to swoon for love; she was the practical, down-to-earth type. His eye went elsewhere.

There was the handsome young Marquis d'Elboeuf, Mary's Guise cousin, an obviously predatory sort. He had made for Flamina, as he always did. She would reject him, as she always did. He would laugh and try his luck elsewhere. Funny little René. Along with him was Henri d'Amville, the younger son of the Constable of France, Montmorency; Mary saw that he was wearing the rose silk handkerchief of hers that he had found once and claimed to treasure above all things. He had pinned it to his doublet, and when he saw her watching, he deliberately kissed his fingers and touched them to the handkerchief.

The servitors passed silver goblets of white wine around to the company, and they all stood on the terrace facing east, waiting for the moon to rise in the clear sky. No one talked; they just waited quietly. A line of trees at the far end of the garden obscured the horizon, but they could make out a pale gleam as the moon emerged and began her nighttime journey across the sky.

"Ah!" said a quiet voice beside her, and Mary recognized it as Ronsard's.

As the moon cleared herself from the treetops, he began reciting his poem, composed for the occasion.

> "The silver web that you throw, O Goddess,
> lies shining over all the land,
> veiling all things ugly, harsh, rough, loud—
> O mistress of beauty, caress me, coat me with your white magic. . . ."

Together the party walked solemnly out along the garden paths to do homage to the white beauty blooming all around them.

Their voices were soft, low, and intimate, and the gentle breeze, scented with the night-blooming flowers, enveloped them in a delicate mantle of perfume.

Mary felt, at that moment, bathed in happiness and love, and surrounded by all the security that earth could offer.

"*Vivez, si m'en croyez, n'attendez à demain; Cueillez dès aujourd'hui les roses de la vie,*" Ronsard was murmuring behind her. "Nay, hear me, love! Wait not tomorrow! Live, and pluck life's roses oh! today, today."

XVII

Mary lay in bed, trying very hard not to move. If she lay perfectly still, the pain was not so severe. The doctors did not know what had caused this sudden sharp gnawing in her stomach; they prescribed rest and blancmanges to alleviate it. So she had taken to her bed this glorious June day, in her inmost bedroom in the royal apartments at Chambord, refusing to let the curtains be drawn or the windows shuttered. The sunlight danced in, and the summer air, as light as down and as pure as white lace, filled the room.

How boring it was to lie still! she thought, when all the world was revelling in outdoor pleasures. François was out riding, and Catherine de Médicis was galloping along with him, exhibiting her famous shapely calves by exposing them over her saddlehorn.

Mary smiled. Her mother-in-law was a strange woman, with her vanity about her legs—her best feature, and visible only when she rode—her fierce, smothering maternal possessiveness and her sinister reputation for poisoning. Since both she and Mary were united in their goal and devotion to François, there were no clashes between them. All was harmony, and François, after the first shock, had put on the mantle of kingship and worn it as well as he was able.

Mary closed her eyes. The pain seemed to be abating somewhat. Now, if she could just sleep, when she awoke it would most likely be gone. She began reciting a poem by Ronsard backward, his "Epitaph to His Soul":

"dors je: repos mon trouble ne
Fortune ta suis: dit j'ai passant
Commune la par enviés tant . . ."

And soon she was unable to put one word before another.

When she awoke, a violet light filled the room, and there were whispers nearby.

"We cannot—"

"We dare not—not yet—"

"We can wait no longer!"

"But the attack . . . her illness . . ."

"I tell you, we can wait no longer, it is negligence, possible treason, not to inform the Queen . . ."

The buzzing was like the drowsy sound of bees on this summer evening of delicate twilight.

"I will not be blamed!" It was the Cardinal's voice.

Mary saw his face backlit in the hazy light.

"Uncle Cardinal," she said, struggling to sit up. The pain had subsided, but she still felt a slight ache in her stomach. Then she saw there were several others grouped round him like a cluster of grapes, and every face was sour.

"Why, what is this?" she said.

"News, Your Majesty, from Scotland," said the Cardinal.

"Most sorrowful news," said a familiar voice, and Mary saw her other uncle, the Duc de Guise. Then she suddenly knew.

"No!" she said.

"It is true," said the Cardinal.

"Our sister and your most beloved mother is—has died," said the Duc.

"No." Mary kept repeating it, rattling the word like a charm. "No. No."

"She died of her dropsy," said the Cardinal. "But she made a most godly end. She called together the warring factions and bade them all be at peace and forgive one another. And to you, she wrote—" He handed her a letter.

Wordlessly she took it, and asked for a light that she might read it.

The words, the handwriting . . . the same as her many other letters, but so chillingly, significantly different. . . .

She let the letter drop. Then she picked it up again. The date on it was June 1, 1560. That was twenty-eight days ago.

"When did this news arrive?" she asked. "How long have you known?"

"Ten days, Your Majesty."

"And you kept it from me?" All those days of walking with me in the garden, smiling, while you knew? she thought. Of eating at my table, discussing poetry, and the increase in the Huguenots, and you knew, and I knew not?

"I sought to spare you," he said.

"Spare me knowledge? Or spare me pain?" she asked. "For if pain can only be spared by ignorance, it avails nothing."

"Thought to make—thought to keep her alive, perhaps," said the Duc suddenly. "For a person still lives if his death is unknown."

"Uncle, you know better than that," she said wearily. "As a commander, you know a soldier is no less dead because his wife is unaware of his death."

"My dear," said the Cardinal, "believe me—"

But her face suddenly crumpled into a paroxysm of weeping, and she collapsed forward on the bed, burying herself in the bedclothes. The men with the Guises glided out of the room, leaving the two brothers alone with their niece. Then they, too, tactfully withdrew, leaving her to the transports of her private grief.

She wept for hours, with the guilt added to her grief that it was the burden of holding Scotland for her that had driven her mother to her death at only forty-four. While I played and passed my days going from château to château, Mary thought, being praised by poets and floating lazily in flat-bottomed boats along the Loire, my mother was struggling in Scotland, even suspecting I would never return there.

But I wanted to see her! And I meant to, I meant to, as soon as—

The remembrance of their last parting, which now turned out to have been the final one, was so painful she screamed aloud.

Outside her door, the Cardinal turned to the Duc. "I told you it would be cruelly received."

Mary remained in bed, grieving, for ten days—unable to eat, talk, or sleep. She swung between abject misery, laced with black hopelessness, and numb nothingness. Her four Marys hovered just in the next room, but she did not seem to recognize them.

Then on the eleventh day she seemed to rally, to gather strength and return to the world of others, as a drunkard will gradually find his altered sense of time correcting itself.

She felt dirty and in need of a refreshing bath, and hungry as well. She asked Mary Livingston, whom she greeted almost penitentially, to order her a bath of asses' milk and to request a bread porridge for her, laced with cinnamon and sugar. By late that afternoon she felt herself again, although still stunned and shaky.

The Cardinal came to her and clapped his hands in approval and joy. "Thanks be to God! You are with us once more!"

"Part of me is, but part of me has died along with my mother," she said quietly. "Now tell me the rest. For with my mother's death much has changed, outside my heart as well as inside it."

The Cardinal looked hesitant. He reached up and rubbed the spot where his beard had recently been—he had shaved it off in a mood of abandon—to gain time to think.

"I am strong enough to hear it, whatever it may prove to be." Her voice was calm and steady.

Still he hesitated, smiling weakly.

"In fact, I command you to tell me."

She was his sovereign, and he could not disobey her. "Very well, then. The news is simple: It is over. The rebels have triumphed, and even now Cecil, as the English representative, is in Edinburgh to negotiate a treaty with the French, on behalf of the rebels. A *withdrawal* treaty." He saw the shock on her face. "The Auld Alliance is no more. There will be no more French in Scotland, and no Catholics. We are finished there."

"We?"

"The French. You are still Queen there, but in name only. In reality your bastard brother James Stewart rules on behalf of the Protestants—and behind him, the English Queen pulls the strings and controls her new vassal Protestant kingdom."

Mary's mouth formed a perfect oval of speechlessness.

Well, she demanded to be told, he thought, with a fierce feeling of vindication.

"A committee of Parliament ratified these changes. And Master Knox was called upon to write a confession of faith for the newly devout Scots. He hammered it out in four days."

XVIII

Mary Stuart sat on a small bench in the newly fashioned garden at Chenonceau, watching the gardeners at work. The tawny autumn day seemed to bathe everything in a golden light and grace that made her heart rise in spite of herself.

She had hardly noticed the past summer—the heavy bouquets of gillyflowers, cornflowers, and daisies, the dancing patterned butterflies, the languorous white twilights that stretched on until ten o'clock. Who could be lifted or touched by them, when all they did was adorn the rocks of existence without altering them? Her mother was dead, her kingdom taken over by heretics. Even her mother's body was not allowed to leave Scotland and return to France for burial, but was being kept like a hostage by the Lords

98

of the Congregation. A hostage for what? Had they no compassion, even on the dead? She shivered in the friendly warm sunshine of France.

I will bring you home, Mother, she promised. You will rest in France.

"*Bonjour,* Your Most Exalted Majesty," said a gardener coming to join his fellows.

She smiled at him and nodded. It was just now beginning to feel natural to her to be hailed as Queen of France. During the first year she had felt awkward in the title, as if she were merely awaiting the arrival of Queen Catherine. And when they called François "Your Majesty" and "King of France," that was even odder. She could not banish the image of Henri II from her mind, and expected him to step forth from behind a pillar when the title was called, laughing at what a joke he had played on them all.

But he would be shocked to ride up to Chenonceau today and find his beloved Diane gone, sent to another château, and to see what Queen Catherine had done here: laid out her own rival gardens on another side of the château. It was these the gardeners were working so hard upon. Although the Catherine gardens did not—could not—have the tall trees or the sculpted shrubs of the older garden, they boasted the latest fashion from Italy: statues and fountains and canals. In time, there would be trees as well; and Catherine, who knew so well how to wait, whose motto was *Odiate et aspetate*—"hate and wait"—did not mind.

In the meantime, there were these elegant *parterres* to enjoy, the elaborate flat geometrical designs combining coloured pebbles and flowers; the reflection of the sky and clouds in the still waters of the canals; and all of it seen against the tranquil whiteness of the gracious château lying athwart the River Cher. Catherine did not need to share it with anyone, save King François. She had given a fête to welcome him and his bride here, with fireworks lacing the sky and reflecting in the Cher.

Mary saw her mother-in-law approaching, her blocky body making its way purposefully along one of the canal paths. She rose to meet her, and they walked together, their shadows falling before them in the midafternoon as they turned their backs to the sun. Mary's was long and thin and Catherine's short and square; her head barely came up to Mary's shoulder. Mary bent slightly, the better to hear her mother-in-law's low monotone as they strolled. All along the path the royal gardeners nodded and stopped their work as the two queens passed. In the geometrical beds, flowers of enamel hues made carefully laid-out patterns: indigo irises, white alyssum, crimson carnations, deep yellow marigolds.

Catherine made innocuous comments about the flower beds and the heraldry before murmuring, "So you and His Majesty"—she liked using the title—"will refuse to ratify the Treaty of Edinburgh?"

"We shall not *refuse*, but merely not sign," Mary said. Her uncles had advised her, but there had been no need of that. She could not, would not, put her signature to a document abjuring her right to the throne of England. It was impossible. How could a signature render null what was true? She *was* descended from Henry VII, and her legitimacy was unimpugned. She was prepared to recognize Elizabeth as *de facto* queen, but her uncles had pointed out that the treaty did not differentiate between *de facto* and *de jure*. And the provision "now and in all times to come" meant that she could not succeed, even if Elizabeth died childless.

The Treaty of Edinburgh had been a sickening defeat in Scotland, and she had literally been made sick over it. John Knox and his rebels had hounded her mother to death, until she had died of a broken heart and left them in complete control. The Treaty of Edinburgh, rejecting France and Catholicism, was the result. No, she would not ratify it!

They were approaching the *fontaine de roche*, a masterpiece of Palissy's, the great garden designer. Catherine smiled as she came within earshot of its gurgling waters.

"The English will press you," she said.

"Let them!" replied Mary, with a toss of her head. "They do not own Scotland, however much they like to think they do."

"They supported the rebels," Catherine said quietly. "They owned *them.*"

"They may think they own them. But rebels are by definition traitors. And if they will not keep faith where it is due—to their own regent—they are not like to keep it where it is not due. To them, Elizabeth is just a money-bag, to be used as it suits them."

"Perhaps soon they will recognize her as Queen of Scotland. I know there has been a secret proposal to marry the Earl of Arran—the young heir of the House of Hamilton—to Elizabeth. The Lords of the Congregation have sent an offer in his name. What could suit them better? A Protestant pair of sovereigns, to rule over their freshly whitewashed country." Her voice, always low, now sounded almost guttural.

Mary had heard this also; her uncles had reported it. "Elizabeth will not marry him," she heard herself saying. Somehow she knew that. "And then they will turn back to us, to me and François. But until then . . ." Until then, there would be chaos in Scotland—the chaos that came from having no captain at the helm.

"I just pray they are not ready to proclaim a—what have they called it in Geneva?—a 'city of God,' " said Catherine. "Perhaps you and the King must needs journey to Scotland to secure their loyalty." I can manage things here well enough, she thought.

"You know François cannot travel," said his wife reproachfully.

"The journey might strengthen him."

"It killed his aunt Madeleine. No, I shall never permit him to endanger his life!"

The sound of the hydraulic fountain engineered by Palissy forced them to raise their voices. A great artificial mountain reared up in the middle of the crossing of two water canals, and from its sides gushed streams of water, which tumbled, foaming, into a collecting basin at its foot.

Catherine never tired of admiring it, and Mary loved the faience reptiles crawling about the basin—shiny green frogs, glistening crocodiles, and striped vipers coiled on dry rocks, waiting to strike.

The sound of the rushing water drowned out François's voice as he called to them. Only the movement of his waving arms finally caught their eyes. He ran in awkward, loping steps down the manicured gravel path, the buckles on his shoes catching the sun. He was an etiolated version of himself a year ago on his accession, for he had shot up like a plant searching for the sun; and like such a plant, he was pale and spindly.

"*Maman!*" he cried. "Marie!" They stopped and waited for him.

"The Huguenots," he gasped. "I have here a report that—that—"

Catherine snatched away the paper. "They are making trouble again. There's only one way to deal with them—stamp them out, like the venomous serpents they are! Pretend to kindness, to conciliation, then destroy them!"

François stood looking forlornly from his mother to his wife. "But if I gave my royal word, how could I betray it?"

"Yes," said Mary. "That would be unspeakable." She looked boldly back at Catherine. "Just what are you suggesting?"

The older woman shrugged. "Nothing in *particular*," she finally said. "But you must not be so dainty and honourable, if you hope to reign well."

But I always believed that a good heart is the best quality for a ruler, Mary thought. Mercy, and honesty—the core that cannot betray or shrink from the truth. To be to all your subjects as you are to yourself.

She reached down and fingered her long rope of black pearls—a wedding gift from Catherine. She saw Catherine looking at her critically. Catherine was slowly becoming more and more bold; she, too, was emerging from the shadow of the late King. And it was no secret that she and the Guises were diametrically opposed to one another in policy.

They all wish to rule France, thought Mary with a cold, nasty jolt of realization. They think François and I are still children, obedient little children, who will follow directions—*their* directions. Just as the Lords of the Congregation in Scotland think they can issue orders to the child sovereigns. . . .

"There has been too much deceit and blind following of Machiavelli's advice," Mary finally said. "I will not go in that way; and by and by, the people will come to trust me and know that the word of a prince is to be honoured, on both sides."

"Dreamer!" said Catherine.

Mary saw the look of distaste on her face, and suddenly she longed to be away, where the eyes of her mother-in-law and her uncles were not continually fastened on her, studying her, judging her. . . . She longed to be away already on the autumn hunting trip with François, François who was entirely her friend and never, never judged, nor wanted her to be anything other than she was.

XIX

In the late autumn the French court had moved to Orleans, where the surrounding Forêt des Loges, of oak, hornbeam, and pinewoods, broken up by heather moors, gave good game and bird hunting. François adored hunting: he had inherited this love directly from his namesake, François I. As with his grandfather, at times the desire for hunting bordered on obsession for him. He would rather hunt than study, than eat, than take any other sort of exercise; more ominously, would rather hunt than attend to business, even though there was pressing business in the kingdom.

Or perhaps *because* there was. The disciples of Calvin had indeed become strong in France; the Huguenots, in their tightly disciplined "cells," provided almost an alternative government to the royal one moving restlessly from château to château in search of game. The Guises—the Duc, who had been appointed Minister of War, and the Cardinal, who was Minister of Finances—encouraged the King to hunt and leave the governing of the realm to them. They knew how to deal with the Huguenots: exterminate them. Blow them up. Massacre them.

The King did not agree, and although Mary became upset and tried to interfere with the plans of her elders, they merely had to wait for François to have yet another attack of his many recurrent illnesses, and she would be diverted into what was becoming her main role: nursemaid to her husband. With the King either on horseback or in sickbed, the Guises did as they pleased.

Now François had tired of the hunting near Orleans and decided he wanted to remove to the dense forest near Chambord. The weather was cold for November, but although François was clearly unwell—red blotches had broken out all over his cheeks, and the rest of his skin was lead-powder white—he was feverishly eager to keep hunting. Just so had François I been, as he had pursued the game with glittering eyes and dying body in the last stages of syphilis.

The furnishings of the hotel in Orleans were sent ahead to Chambord; but on the morning they were to have ridden forth, François had an excruciating pain in one ear, and could not move. He was hastily laid on a pallet on the floor, for the room had been stripped of its furniture and there was no bed. Fever set in, and he lay delirious and with chattering teeth, tossing on the pallet.

Mary took her place by his side, as she had so many times before. François had had this earache frequently, and always it had been soothed with a mixture of egg yolk, oil of roses, and turpentine, heated and poured into the ear canal. She did this, and laid compresses on his brow, and his eyelids fluttered open and he smiled at her.

"The boar will get away," he said. But he said it tenderly, as if to assure her that he was still in command of himself and his senses.

"They but wait for you," she said. "The biggest boar in the forest of Chambord knows that he is doomed to be served at Christmas to the court. His fate is merely postponed. Lucky boar!"

"Unlucky François," he groaned. "Oh, Marie, I feel so . . . dizzy. And weak."

"Soon you will recover. Already the oil is soothing your ear."

"It hurts . . . behind the ear."

The King did not speak intelligibly again. He closed his eyes, and the fever confused him and made his face erupt in sores in the next few days. Mary never left his side, going without sleep, lying down beside him on a pallet, playing her lute for his unhearing, festering ears, holding his hand.

The doctors gave him a compound of rhubarb, making a paste of it and forcing it down his throat. He seemed to rally for a few hours, but a relapse swiftly followed.

Queen Catherine, who had hurried to the scene, called Ambroise Paré, the King's surgeon. "Save him!" she commanded.

"The physicians—"

"It is beyond physicians," she replied.

The surgeon knelt down and examined the King carefully, turning his head and blowing gently in each ear. There was a large swelling behind the infected ear.

"This must be lanced," he said, and the two queens agreed.

But although he successfully lanced the swelling and extracted a great deal of fluid, the King was not relieved. On the contrary, he grew worse in the next few days.

"I am afraid the only remedy is to operate, to remove part of the skull," said Paré. "There is an abscess in the brain, and it will spread, and—"

"Cut open his head?" cried Catherine.

Paré looked at Mary, the King's wife.

"Do whatever is necessary, but save him!" the girl said softly.

"Are you that cruel?" said Catherine. "Would you have his brains exposed? How could he live, then? No one can live with his head open! Do you have some miracle substance with which to patch it, then?" She turned on Paré.

"No, alas," he admitted. "But perhaps something can be found. Ivory, or a sheep's intestine . . . and I can dull the pain with a mixture we use for soldiers on the battlefield, opium and henbane, so he will not feel the cutting."

"A King with a sheep's intestine covering his brain!" shrieked Catherine. "So you propose to offer France such a King, such an abomination! And

103

he—" she looked at her firstborn son lying *in extremis*—"he could never hunt again, would have to live like an old man, shuffling about in cleansed rooms, wearing a wet turban about his head . . . no, he would not want that."

"How do you know what he would want?" said Mary.

"I bore him, I know him, and I know what is consistent with kingly dignity." She turned to Paré. "No operation. But remove his pain, I beg you. Use your battlefield mixture."

Paré looked at her, and saw the anguish in her eyes. No mothers were present at his battlefields; they never had her choices.

"I will mix it straightway, Your Majesty. And there is another device I know, to induce sleep and calmness. The sound of falling rain is soothing. If you will provide a large kettle on the far side of the room, and have a servant pour water from high above it . . ."

"It is done," said Catherine.

François received the mixture of opium and henbane, and fell asleep to the sound of artificial rain in the cold, bare chamber. Mary held his hand, never relinquishing it, as it gradually grew cold in hers. She held it long after he had passed from life to death.

"Our François is gone, my mother," she finally said to Catherine, who was dozing in a chair. Gently Mary let go of his hand and arranged his hands on his breast. She kissed his forehead. The red splotches on his face were fading, and his lips were parted as if he would speak.

"*Adieu*, François, my love, my husband, my friend."

Catherine burst into tears, but Mary had none left. She was beyond tears; she felt that her life had departed with François.

"*Adieu*, François," she whispered. "*Adieu*, Marie."

In Edinburgh, as soon as he heard the news about the death of François II, John Knox wrote, "For as the said King sat at mass, he suddenly perished of a rotten ear—that deaf ear that would never hear the truth of God."

XX

It was Mary's eighteenth birthday, and she was a new widow, keeping mourning in an artificially darkened chamber at Orleans. Once again she was wearing white, and it seemed a cruel mockery. They were right; I should never have worn it on my wedding day, she thought. It is the colour of death and sorrow. I will never wear it again. If I had not worn it then, perhaps François . . .

No, that is foolish. He did not die of a dress colour, she told herself. He died because he had always been weak, because he was born sickly, because his mother took those myrrh pills to help her conceive, because he was born at an eclipse of the sun. Perhaps he would not have lived so long, had I not helped him, nursed him, played with him, loved him.

An ache shot through her. She loved him, her companion, her confidant, her best friend. She could hardly remember a time when she had not known him, and he had loved her utterly.

Now she was completely alone. Her mother and François, both dead within half a year. There was no place for her, suddenly, upon this earth. France was no longer a safe haven. François's little brother, ten-year-old Charles, ruled as Charles IX, but his mother ruled as regent. Meticulous Catherine, who observed every rule . . . just as she had stood aside to give Mary precedence ten minutes after Henri II's death, just so quickly had she demanded that Mary return the crown jewels after François II's death. There were no lingering niceties, no courtesies. Mary, whose mother was French, whose language was French, and who had been brought up in France, was being told—subtly and unsubtly—to forget France and return to Scotland.

But she was not welcome there, either. Her subjects had rebelled and formally deposed her mother, the regent. A council of lords now ruled the land, enacting laws that abolished Catholicism and made attending mass a crime.

She had no country, no welcome anywhere. After these forty days of mourning were over, then what? Where would she go, what would she do?

And yet a pervasive lethargy seized her. She cared, and did not care. Her loss of François was so gripping that in her pain she only sought surcease: to sleep, to weep, to remember. His presence was everywhere, half comforting her, half torturing her. She, who had so often been entertained by the poetry of the court, now sought to alleviate her pain by writing of her loss.

> *Over my life's early spring,*
> *And over its opening bloom,*
> *My deadly sorrows fling*
> *The darkness of the tomb;*
> *My star of hope is set*
> *In yearning and regret.*
>
> *When day's long toil is over,*
> *And dreams steal round my couch,*
> *I hear that voice once more—*
> *I thrill to that dear touch;*
> *In labour and repose,*
> *My soul his presence knows.*

But who would read her poem, who would understand? Only François, and he was gone, in all the ways that mattered . . . except as a gentle, ghostly presence.

They spoke to her of marrying. In the first two weeks of her widowhood, when she was in deepest mourning, with the only light in her white-draped chamber provided by flickering and smoldering candles, the Guises were admitted, as befitted her closest relatives, and immediately began to suggest a remarriage. There was Don Carlos, the heir of Philip of Spain. There was Charles IX, her brother-in-law, who had developed an abnormal, childish passion for her. She must stay in power. These bridegrooms—immature, unbalanced children—would enable her to do so.

She sat, hearing them out. Indeed, what else could she do? She was trapped in the *deuil* chamber. But, although she had loved François, another child-groom did not appeal to her. Instead, what increasingly appealed to her was escape. Escape to Scotland, far away from the suffocating Guises and the watchful Queen Regent.

Would I rather be a dowager queen in France, pensioned off to live in tranquil obscurity on my estates, of no importance to anyone—although comfortably and safely housed—or would I rather be queen in a small, faraway country?

I am too young to be housed in obscurity, she answered herself. I have learned statecraft from my uncles, my grandmother, and Queen Catherine—and to what purpose, if I retire to a country estate in my youth? God gave me a throne in Scotland as my birthright. Am I meant to take this sceptre? It is even more urgent since the country is so lost, so mired in confusion and errors. I know I am very young and unknowledgeable in deeper matters of theology, but my task would only be to set a good living example of my own faith, not to rival Saint Augustine or some other Doctor of the Church. Perhaps that is what God requires of me to help my country.

Cautiously she broached the idea to Father Mamerot, her spiritual guide.

"Do you think this is required of me?" she asked late one afternoon when the night shadows were coming on.

The priest—small but wiry within his robes—waited a long time before answering. "One can say with certainty that the opportunity is there," he finally answered. "Your country has recently left the fold of the Church, but you have been preserved as their monarch, and kept to the original faith. It is true that people tend to see within a monarch the embodiment of a faith. A king who lies, debauches himself, steals, and acts the coward will drive people from whatever faith he claims to practise. I am not sure, however, that the opposite holds true. You will simply have to try, trusting in God's providence. You cannot set out with that as a goal. It is really up to God to move men's hearts."

"Ah, you always warn me to go slowly," said Mary.

"It is the duty of a confessor to help his child overcome her spiritual weaknesses, and yours has always been acting too quickly or expecting too much."

As the long days dragged on, Mary found herself relying on Madame Rallay's gentle wisdom of the worldly sort as well. She asked her how she would feel about going to Scotland. "I would wish to take the good people of my household, like Bourgoing and Balthazzar. I cannot imagine life without them. But most of all, I could not imagine life without you," Mary said.

Madame Rallay smiled. "Nor could I imagine life without you. I will go with you wherever you choose to go. Is it truly your wish to return to your original home?"

"I—I am not sure," Mary answered. "Some days it is, and other days I do not know. But if I knew you would come . . ."

"I will come."

A return to her original home: the idea drew her like a forlorn melody, coming from deep within a wood.

Then, suddenly, she would be overcome with grief for François, and wondered if her longing for her faraway throne was just a disguised wish for escape from her pain.

Every day seemed eternal and unconnected with anything before or after, as it was played out in a chamber that knew neither day nor night, but only artificially measured hours. The waking hours began with mass, celebrated at one end of the chamber. Then came the condolence visits—in reality, the political conferences—then more prayers, then a dinner, served silently. No one could enter the chamber without the prior approval of Queen Catherine and a thorough searching by the guards. The "frivolous" applicants were turned away; only accredited ambassadors and the Guise uncles were permitted access to Mary in those first two weeks.

She braced herself for these visits, wrapping herself in white fur mantles for warmth in the chilly chamber. The dreary December weather and short days outside seemed to steep the chamber itself in cold, dead solitude.

On the twelfth day, a large man stood on the threshold of her chamber, a leather envelope in his gloved hand. His dark mantle had snow in its folds.

"Greetings, my Queen," he said in perfect French. But she had never seen him at court before. How had he persuaded the guards to admit him?

She motioned him to come in. He did so, and knelt before her, removing the hood of his mantle. His crisp, short reddish hair was rumpled, and his smoky green eyes looked directly at her.

"I bring dispatches from the late Queen your mother, and also I offer condolences on the loss of your late lord and husband the King." He held out the leather envelope, and she moved forward and took it.

"From my mother, you say? Wherefore not earlier?"

He shrugged. "These are not official, Your Majesty. These were what was found when servitors were clearing out her papers. Personal. These are the things she kept. They were ready to destroy them. But I thought you might want them."

Mary thumbed through the thick packet. "Why—here's a letter I wrote *her*!" she said.

"When you were eleven," he said.

So he had read them? Natural curiosity, of course. And they had been ready to discard—public property. He had gone to the trouble of rescuing them.

He was shifting on his knees, and then, without leave, he stood up.

"You could have sent them," she said. "You hardly needed to come all this way in person."

"There are few one can trust. And besides, my Queen, I wished to see your person for myself. Few in Scotland have had that privilege."

"Who are you, then?"

"James Hepburn, my Queen."

She did not like the way he kept repeating "my Queen" like a chorus, when he should have been saying "Your Majesty" in true respect.

"James Hepburn of *what*? Of whom?"

"James Hepburn, son of Patrick the Fair Earl. Surely you have heard of him?" He removed his mantle—again without leave—and draped it on a stool.

He was not as tall as Mary, but he was beautifully made and his build was powerful.

"Indeed I have not," she said.

He laughed. "My father, the Fair Earl—for so he was called for his complexion, not his character—divorced my mother so as to marry your mother. She made him a promise, but in the end did not honour it, thereby *dis*honouring him. 'Tis a queen's privilege, evidently."

"So you are Scots?" This strange claim he was making—could it be true?

"That, or nothing," he said in that language.

"I refuse to believe that of my mother," she said, still in French.

"Believe what you like, 'tis of no matter now. My father is gone and so is she; they used one another out of ambition, and 'tis done. I think"—he grinned—"she won. Of course, she had more cards to play with."

"You sound like a gambler."

"I am." He made no blushing apology.

"So am I," she said, startling herself by the admission.

"All queens—all good ones—must be. Certainly your cousin Elizabeth is one of the first order. The bets are still out on her. She has not married yet, in spite of all her offers. 'Tis a privilege of queens, as I said, to dangle suitors."

In spite of herself, she laughed. "But who *are* you?" she asked, in halting Scots. It had been so long since she had used it. It came out "hoo arr yoo?"

"Ah, that's good. Your enemies say you cannot speak the language. You'll show them."

"Come, sir, answer my question."

"I am Earl of Bothwell. I have other titles as well, which I inherited from the Fair Earl: Lord High Admiral of Scotland, Keeper of Hermitage and Edinburgh Castles, Sheriff of East Lothian, Lieutenant of the Southern Borders. If you're so kind as to confirm them, that is."

"That remains to be seen." She adjusted the filmy white veil beneath her chin, which was part of the *deuil* costume.

"Are you coming back to Scotland, or no?" he demanded. "The talk is that you aren't. That you'll be put out to pasture in France like one of those fine cows in Normandy, there to lie down and graze in soft green meadows. 'Twould please your brother James if you stayed. As son of the King and Lord of the Congregation, with Knox's blessing he'd rule Scotland, as he believes he was meant to do. Destiny calls him, he thinks. Ha! Destiny is calling loud all over these days, starting with Master Knox."

"*Oui. Je reviendrai à l'Ecosse.*"

"Then you must needs not speak French. They hate the sound of it."

No mention of pleasure that she had elected to return, and he was the only living soul to whom she had thus far announced it. She was disappointed. "Where did *you* learn French, then?" she asked.

He looked amused at her question. "All educated people speak French," he said. "You'll find many of your subjects speak French, write French, and have spent time in France. But that does not stop them from hating the sound of it, as I said."

"Then they must needs hate *me.*"

"Why, are you a Frenchwoman?" he said, looking directly at her. He asked it in a schoolmasterly fashion, as if he were teacher, and she his student. It was the way her uncles spoke to her, and in them she tolerated it. But she had grown tired of it, and never realized how deeply until now.

"For all purposes, yes," she answered.

"You're wrong." His voice turned rough and hectoring. "They've taught you that, but they lied, for their own purposes. Listen to the speaker, and always ask yourself, 'What has he to gain by convincing me of the thing he champions?' It suited the Guises to convince you of your Frenchness. But you're only half French; the rest is Scots, and royal Scots at that—the Stewarts, who have guided Scotland for almost two hundred years. Look at your reddish hair, your sportsmanship, your love of the wild country . . . and you'll see Scots written bold upon you."

"How do you know of my love of wild country, or of aught else? I also love courtly pageants and refinements of manners. Now what have *you* to gain from convincing me, Lord Bothwell?"

"I gain a queen in her rightful country. Truth to tell, I think Scotland deserves its own monarch on its own throne. With all due respect, your mother was not our own queen; and a bastard son does not a king make. In the past six generations we've had precious few full-grown monarchs. Minorities and regencies . . . poor substitutes."

"And your titles confirmed, of course."

"Aye. As Lord Admiral, I shall naturally provide the fleet to see you safely home."

"What is wrong with your left eye?" she suddenly asked, hoping to put him on the defensive. There was a large scar right above it.

"It was injured in a skirmish with Cockburn o' Ormiston." He paused, then decided not to tease her into asking who this man was. "A Scots traitor, who was coming north with four thousand pounds in bribe money from the English. You'll find English gold all over Scotland, trying to buy the nobles. Of course, it is not *English* gold, but carefully converted into French money to disguise its origins. Anyway, I trounced Ormiston."

"Is everyone for sale?" she cried.

"No, but they all accept money. The English cannot tell who is for sale and who is not, so they are forced to pay everyone." He laughed. "I can tell you this, my lady, my Queen: I am loyal to the crown and do not take the English bribes. I am the *only* one who does not. My life upon it."

"Why are you then so loyal?" She had forgotten, and was back speaking French again.

"It is a family tradition which my father betrayed and which I have restored. I must tell you now, directly, that I am Protestant. George Wishart preached in my area, although my father arrested him and turned him over to Cardinal Beaton to be burnt. But his words and doctrine convinced me. Yes, I am Protestant, but I am your vassal, and my loyalty is firm unto the crown. A man may believe many things and keep loyalty to them all, just as a person may be many things and still be consistent. What is the English Queen's motto: *Semper eadem,* 'be always one'? Yet she is a mosaic, a thousand parts."

"Thank God for you, James Hepburn," she said slowly.

"When may I fetch you, my Queen?" he asked.

"In the summer," she said.

"The fleet will be at the ready." He smiled and bowed. "I will take my leave, if you please," he said. "The country will rejoice."

"You came all the way for this interview? Have you no other business here in France?" she asked.

"Transacted long since," he said. "I am, as I said, a gambler. And a queen is well worth a sea journey."

"How old are you?" she suddenly asked.

"Twenty-five."

"That is young to pronounce yourself incorruptible. Have a care, James Hepburn, lest you tarnish betimes."

He sighed and made a gesture of resignation. "Only extraordinary events prove our composition. And what man would willingly seek that? Our Lord even allows us to ask to be spared it: 'And bring us not to the test.' "

"If I return to Scotland, must I be drowned in a sea of Scripture quotes?" That even this young adventurer should spout it!

"They only float on the surface, my Queen. Like a lot of flotsam and jetsam. You'll find the waters underneath clean and cold."

110

Long after he took his leave, she sat and read through her mother's papers. Strange how little she had understood her through their formal correspondence, which had been guarded and managed by her privy secretary, William Maitland.

Maitland. Did I not meet him when he was here in France? But that was so long ago, Mary thought. But my uncles told me . . . what? That he was the cleverest man in Scotland—"a sort of Scottish Cecil," they said. And that is clever indeed.

She looked tenderly at the pile of her mother's papers. Here were notes and jottings and all the letters she had kept, which were somehow much more revealing of her person.

At length, when she had finished with them, feeling drained and sad and yet oddly comforted, she remembered: she, Mary, had just promised someone to go to Scotland! And yet it was only a verbal promise to this James Hepburn; it carried no weight. She could still change her mind.

The forty days of formal mourning came to a close on January 15, 1561, with a memorial service at the Church of the Greyfriars. The day was ugly and sleety, the church cold and comfortless as the monks chanted, "*Exsultabunt Domino ossa humiliata . . .*" Mary pulled the hood of her black mourning gown more closely about her head to muffle the cruel sound.

François was embalmed now, she knew. His heart had been removed and would be interred in Paris at St.-Denis, to be with his ancestors. Artists had sculpted a magnificent tomb, so she had been told, near Henri II's, and his heart would lie in a reliquary surrounded by sculpted flames. His heart . . . she hated to think of its being taken from his body, even though she knew it was customary.

Then she was free to leave Orleans, that prison of unhappiness, to which she vowed never to return.

Paris, which she had always loved, was scant comfort now. She was forced to inventory all her jewels and belongings and part with many of them, returning them as property of the crown. Nicholas Throckmorton, the English ambassador, called with the official condolences of Queen Elizabeth, but as soon as he decently could, he changed the subject to the Treaty of Edinburgh and hinted at his mistress's extreme displeasure that Mary had not yet ratified it. The Scottish government had done so, and only her signature was lacking. She demurred, saying that the death of François had changed everything.

How so? persisted the ambassador.

"The treaty was formulated on the basis of my husband and my being King and Queen of both Scotland and France. Now there is only a Queen of Scotland," she said. She was weary of it all and tempted to sign just to rid herself of his pestering. But François—it would be betraying his wishes. She must not sign things out of weakness or laziness.

"It changes nothing, as well you know," he said quickly. "The question is of your claim to the English throne—or the succession." He was a friendly enough man, young, genial—quite attractive, in spite of his flaming red hair and Protestantism. Mary actually liked him. "King François had nothing to do with the matter."

She smiled artlessly. "The matter is too deep for me. I must consult with my Scottish council, since I have no husband to advise me."

Throckmorton almost laughed. As if François had ever been capable of political advice! But did this mean that she did *not* wish to consult her French uncles? Was she freeing herself from them?

"Your Majesty, the question *is* a weighty one, and until it is resolved, it hinders your relationship with your most noble cousin, Queen Elizabeth."

"It grieves me that it is so. But I know the Queen would not want anyone to stand by while her hereditary rights were set aside. The Queen did not do so herself in a similar situation."

Throckmorton nodded. But the matter must be resolved. There was Mary's claim, supported by the Pope, that she was actually the true Queen of England at that very moment. Then there was her legal claim to the right of being included in the succession. They were not the same. The first claim must be abjured; the second, however, might be allowed to stand—*if* the first were renounced. The longer the first was insisted upon, the less inclined Elizabeth was to grant the second in compensation.

Queen Elizabeth's patience was wearing thin, Throckmorton knew. Mary's behaviour was confirming her worst suspicions, and she was increasingly agitated about her cousin's motives.

"This cannot go on," said Throckmorton grimly, and was irritated at Mary's lighthearted laughter in response.

But the laughter was false. Her spirit was still mourning, and she took long walks on the terraces of the palaces, wrapped in voluminous white cloaks, pacing alone. The wind would tear through her garments and leave her shivering. In vain, Brantôme and the other court poets tried to walk with her or persuade her to come inside. Her lonely pacing figure appealed to their poetic fancy, and Ronsard recounted the sight of Mary

> swathing your body from head to waist, your long fine mourning veil billows fold upon fold like a sail in the breeze as the wind drives the boat forward. Dressed in these same sad robes, you prepare to leave the fair country of which you have held the crown. The whole gardens are filled with whiteness of your veils like the sails which billow from the mast over the ocean wave. . . .

That Mary was thinking of leaving France was now widely speculated upon. But she awaited some sign, some portent that would direct her.

XXI

hy did it have to be so nasty, tonight of all nights? William Maitland of Lethington kept peering anxiously out his window, watching the sheets of rain pelting the paving stones on the High Street of Edinburgh outside. Not that rain would keep Scotsmen from anything, but it lent such a grim aspect to the proceedings.

Well, where would you hold it? In a pavilion in a flowery mead in southern France? he asked himself. The business at hand would be just as demanding and draining, no matter where it was held.

He sighed, and forced himself to leave the window. Was he nervous? Was that possible? He, who prided himself on his ability to think calmly— an unusual trait in Scotland!—to allow no sentiment to intrude upon hard decisions . . . could he be nervous?

He looked about the room in his spacious town house, readied now for the expected guests. All was in order, and he permitted himself quiet pride in looking over his library, which included a fine collection of poetry from his father's own pen. There were leather chairs made with softest Spanish leather, and his most prized possession: a marble bust of a Roman youth he had hand-carried all the way from Italy. He had been educated in France and had been able to travel in Europe, especially enjoying the art and the politics of Italy.

Ah, Italy! As always, the marble bust recalled for him his time in Florence—too brief!—when he had found himself surrounded entirely by the ferment of art in the making, and the final polishing of the political creed of Machiavelli. He had felt so at *home* there. But then, those who jokingly called him "Michael Wily" here had no idea of what the real thing was.

There I would be regarded as so inept as to be transparent, he thought with amusement. So it is best that I employ my talents here in Scotland, where subtlety is as yet undiscovered.

The one thing a politician must always do is to be sure in his *own* mind what his goal is. He must never confuse himself. So—what is my goal here, and why is it making me so uneasy? he asked himself.

He sat on one of his chairs, settling into its comforting contours, watching the rain dash against the window panes.

To make the changes here in Scotland go smoothly, he thought. Was that it? Yes, the changes had been dizzying, and the past year the erstwhile Secretary of State had felt that he—and the country as well—was being sucked down into a whirlpool. The religious revolt, completed almost before it was begun; the death of the Regent; the repudiation of the Auld Alliance . . .

113

But he had been delighted by the collapse of the ancient French-Scottish alliance. Once Scotland had become Protestant, its future was inevitably tied to England, its near neighbour. Anyone who thought clearly—and not merely with emotion!—could see that. It was so plain! So obvious!

That was it. I am afraid others will not see it, will not understand, will want to obstruct the inevitable. And I—it will be *my* sad lot to have to try to persuade them.

And Mary, the young Queen, the widow of France . . . *she* will have to be persuaded too. But persuaded to what?

Should she come here?

He jumped up out of the chair, so nervous he felt he could not sit still. He hated waiting. Waiting, waiting, for everyone to arrive . . .

Yes, she should come here. She should come home. We need a ruler of mature years on our own soil and she needs useful work to do. She is too young to moulder in dowagerhood when her own country is in turmoil. We'll persuade her—

There was that word again: *persuade.* Persuading was so difficult! Hadn't everyone had the experience of trying to *persuade* a balky mule to budge? And people were so much more—

He heard a knock. Someone had at last arrived! He rushed to the door, and as he did so, he felt himself slowing down, feeling that he was in command of himself now that he had clarified his thoughts. The mud had settled out of them, and he could see to the bottom.

It was John Erskine, a thin man with an even thinner face, who, strangely enough, enjoyed the pleasures of the table immensely, although they did not show on him.

"Ah! The Commendator!" said Maitland with just barely perceptible sarcasm. Erskine's family had possession of the monastery on Inchmahome, but they hardly cared about religious treasures from the past. James V had given this plum into their hands, as he had likewise many other such monasteries to his favourites and bastards.

"Ah, now!" Erskine pulled back his hood; it spilled rain out all over the floor. "There goes my cowl!"

Behind him there was another arrival. Maitland saw the dark bulk of James Douglas, the Earl of Morton, standing dripping in the doorway.

"Come in, come in!" he told him.

Morton shook his cloak outside and then handed it to a waiting servant. He carefully fluffed up his wild red hair, so that it stood out around his head like a halo. Then he shuffled into the room.

The three men stood waiting, a trifle awkwardly. It would not do to begin this meeting until all were present—no, it would not. Maitland still felt calm. All would go well, he knew it.

Another loud, precise knock. Maitland opened the door to see Lord James Stewart standing there.

"Sorry to be delayed," he muttered, handing his dripping cloak to a servant. He then stepped into the room as if it were his own.

"Erskine has accused you of attending the witches' and warlocks' Sabbat tonight," said William Maitland, greeting him. When Stewart looked stony-faced, Maitland said, "You know, it is May Eve, when they hold their revels."

"He should know all about them," Stewart grunted. "They accuse his own sister of being one."

"My sister is also your mother. It's in our blood, then," said John Erskine. "All true Scotsmen are half witch." He laughed easily, and motioned Stewart to take his place at the table, which had been placed precisely in the middle of the room.

"We are all here now?" said William Maitland, a smile on his face. "Good Lords of the Congregation?" It was a very small group, these four who took it upon themselves to direct the Scottish government.

"Aye." Morton, with his great bush of red hair on his head and face, lifted a pudgy hand in affirmation. In his mid-forties, he was the oldest man present.

Maitland nodded to his servant and then took his place at the table. In a moment the servant reappeared with oatcakes and sugarbread, arranged on a silver platter, and set them down. Morton reached out immediately and took two. He fed on them like a hungry bear, leaving crumbs in his beard.

"We must draft the letter," said Maitland. "We can wait no longer. We have no choice. We must decide upon what terms the Queen of Scots should return here, and what enticements and concessions we are prepared to offer her."

To his annoyance, Erskine spoke up, his thin voice emanating from his thin beard. "Pity about Elizabeth." He was examining one of the oatcakes critically.

"She had no interest in Arran, nor in our throne," said James Stewart. "Still, it was wise to ask her."

Maitland allowed himself a rare "if only." He had never expected that the English Queen would accept their offer of marriage with the Earl of Arran, and its implied dislodging of Mary Stuart from the throne, but it would have solved many problems for Scotland. If only . . .

"She has no interest in marriage, so I am told," said Maitland at length.

"No interest in *respectable* marriage," said Morton, eating another cake. He rolled his eyes to indicate need of ale to wash it down.

All the men laughed except James Stewart, who did not find lechery amusing. "So we must make our terms with my sister the Queen," he said, cutting off the guffawing.

"Your *half* sister the Queen," corrected Maitland.

"Aye. My half sister." Lord James nodded. "We must needs set forth our position: she will not interfere in our religion and will be guided by us, the Lords of the Congregation, in all things."

"Do you expect her to become Protestant?" said Morton. "Or to have no opinions of her own?" Morton had a polished English diction, acquired

115

from many years spent there in political exile, totally at variance with his wild looks.

"Or perhaps we plan to substitute ourselves for her Guise uncles as advisers? And what about John Knox? Why is he not here?" Erskine sounded distressed, as though he had been abandoned. He nibbled the oatcake daintily.

"Ah, yes, Master Knox," sighed Maitland. "You and I know, gentlemen, that he *is* here. In fact, he is *everywhere.* He would be king here. And that is why we need a queen."

"A Catholic one?" asked Erskine. His father had once been Mary's guardian, and he had been her childhood playmate, but that did not keep him from coldbloodedly discussing her now.

"Yes, a pretty Catholic one who will not permit the land to be as dull and grey as the Forth on a November day. She'll dance and wear satins and have music and banquets—"

"Knox will explode!"

"Oh, I think not," replied Maitland. "For at heart he's a hardheaded Scotsman, and he will know that a sparkling court will raise Scotland's prestige abroad. A government of sober men, working in committees, does not appeal to the imagination, or even seem like a *real* country. Even if they actually do the running of it."

"If we could do the running of it—" began Lord James.

"While she dances and sings," Maitland finished. "Do you see?"

"No wonder they call you 'Michael Wily,' " said Morton in admiration. "Machiavelli could learn from you. The pupil surpasses the master. But what if she . . . er . . . ?"

"Refuses to submit? But she cannot. She will have no one to support her. She is completely alone here. No relatives, no—"

Lord James laughed. "We're all her relatives," he said. "I'm her brother, you're her first cousin, Morton—"

"Through illegitimate ties, though. All the Stewart kings left passels of bastards," Morton reminded Lord James.

"What about Bothwell?" Erskine asked suddenly. "Even though he's Protestant, he isn't one of *us.* And he supported the Queen Mother against us."

"If young Mary Stuart puts herself in our hands, he'll be no opposition," said Morton. "We can make sure he is always in the saddle chasing brigands in the Borders or on the sea fighting pirates. He's not a court creature, anyway."

"The truth is, she has no legitimate relatives in Scotland," Maitland said, steering the subject back to its original course. "Her nearest legitimate relatives are the Guises in France and Queen Elizabeth in England and Lady Margaret Douglas and her boy, Darnley, also in England. She has no one here." He was still smiling inwardly at the remark about Machiavelli.

"I see you have already thought this out," Lord James said quietly. He was still angry at being included in the "passels of bastards."

"But of course. And I have even composed the first paragraph of our letter to her. May I show it to you?" He opened a folder, took out a piece of paper, and handed it to Lord James.

While James was reading it, Erskine shook his head. "I have known her since childhood, and my family is supposedly her protector."

"Why, so you shall continue to be," said Maitland. "After all, it is your hereditary office, is it not? Keeper of the royal children?" Even though Mary was no longer a child, she would need a protector. She must not be brought here and then left to fend for herself.

"I cannot protect her from Knox," he said. "He seems like a ravening wolf, ready to set upon her."

"I will allow her the mass, if she insists," said Lord James suddenly.

"Then we will need to protect *you* from Knox," said Maitland. "Remember, the mass is now illegal and punishable by death." Parliament had just passed these laws, in the exuberance of the Protestant revolution.

"Queens and kings have never been troubled by laws and never shall be," said Morton. "Adultery was never legal, yet James V was open about it."

"The mass is worse than adultery to Master Knox."

"Then Master Knox is an idiot." Erskine said the shocking words. No one laughed. "I think ultimately he does not want there to be either kings or queens in the land."

"A country without a king cannot exist," said Lord James. "There is no such thing."

"Except in the case of a baby being king. Then someone must rule in his name."

"Regent, king—'tis all the same thing."

"There hasn't been an adult monarch to come directly to the throne of Scotland in six generations. We Scotsmen have much practice in ruling ourselves by now. It's a queen that'll be a novelty for us today."

"One that may be difficult to get used to. Freedom is a habit that's hard to break," said Maitland. He cleared his throat. "Then let us be agreed: the Queen of Scots should return and take up her sceptre. But she must submit herself to our counsel, and honour our religion. She must have no ideas of reintroducing Catholicism, as her cousin Mary Tudor did in England."

"Perhaps she'll go the other way," said Erskine suddenly. "She's young, and has never seen anything but Catholicism. If she comes here, and her eyes are opened to the truth—"

"Perhaps Knox can convert her!" Morton gave a great blast of a laugh.

This was in danger of turning into a joke, Maitland saw with alarm. The men seemed playful and offhanded. "Gentlemen!" he said, rising, and slapping the flat of his hand on the table. "You are talking about your Queen! Remember we need her—we have needed her since the King died and left us leaderless so long ago. We should be thankful that one has been provided us by fate."

117

"Fate?" Morton rolled his eyes again; it made him look like a mastiff. "It was *God*."

Oh, yes. All these Lords of the Congregation laid everything at the feet of the Lord. "Of course," said Maitland smoothly.

"We'll send the letter," said Lord James. "And I'll follow it in person, if we don't hear from her immediately. Time grows short."

XXII

May came like a pagan spirit to France, flowers springing up in her footsteps in the meadows and along the riverbanks. She opened her purse and let floral perfumes escape on the warm breezes. Her white, swirling robes were the foam on the surging spring streams and the clean, hurrying clouds in the bright blue sky.

Through this countryside, alive with Flora's touch, Mary rode, also in white robes. In leaving Paris behind, she felt the full impact of how life had rushed on past the dead François. In the palaces, in closed rooms, time could be made to stand still. But out of doors, it was a different matter. There had been ice on the ground when François died; now there were fresh new grass and violets and lilies-of-the-valley.

She felt completely removed from all these sights of spring, as if her white mourning gown and veil had encased her in a barrier through which nothing could penetrate—no longings, no quickening of spirit. Yet she did what needed to be done, and she was en route to attend the coronation of François's younger brother, Charles, at Reims, in the beautiful cathedral where François had been crowned less than two years earlier.

Twenty-one months between coronations, she thought. Only twenty-one months that he was King, and I Queen of France. Two summers, one winter.

A pain that trailed off into familiar dullness made itself felt in her heart.

Why, I was happy then! she thought. So happy I did not even think about it, did not treasure it, did not reach out and try to make the moment linger. It passed me by like a mist.

Why did I not pay more attention? she thought. Why was I so careless of my joy? Even my memories are only of *things*: marble pillars and gold salters and banners of fleur-de-lys; silver trumpets and attar of roses; sleek white-toothed hounds and flaming torches and silk-hung litters; ambassadors in velvet breeches and vellum proclamations with orange-red wax seals. . . .

She sat, watching Charles being crowned Charles IX in the deep, cool beauty of Reims Cathedral, heard the echoing words of the ceremony. When François had been crowned, the court was in mourning for Henri II's death; Catherine could not stop crying throughout the ceremony. Now it is I who cannot see through my tears, she thought, and she . . .

She glanced over at Catherine de Médicis and observed how alive with excitement she was. She strained to see every detail of the coronation, and her eyes were glittering.

That is because she will rule in France, thought Mary. She is come into her own at last. Henri is gone, Diane is gone, François is gone, I am gone, and my Guise relatives along with me. She need share her power with no one, until Charles marries.

My uncles tried to persuade me to marry Charles. Catherine would never have permitted that; it was the last thing she would ever have wanted, to continue sharing her power. But what no one realized was that it was the last thing I would ever want. I don't like Charles; there is something wrong with him. He alternates between melancholy and fits of temper; he kicks his dogs and his servants. He sucks on a bottle of *eau sucre* and stares at me in a demented manner. No, I'll none of him! Pity the woman he *does* marry.

The trumpets sounded forth to announce that France had a new king, *Christianissimus*, His Most Christian Majesty, Charles IX.

Not very far away, also in Reims, lay the Abbey of St.-Pierre, and it was there that Mary took her lodging that night. Her aunt Renée was abbess there; and her mother's body was going to be interred there within the week. The Protestant lords had finally let Marie de Guise go, to seek her rest at last on her own soil.

The entrance to the abbey lay at the top of a hill, with a road leading to it that was straight and bordered with a row of plane trees on either side. Their leaves were just starting to come out, making a fine green mist on the dark branches overhead.

The great door seemed to draw Mary, beckoning her as forbidden things sometimes did in dreams; yet when she reached it she felt relief and comfort, not danger.

"Welcome, Your Majesty," said a sister, opening the door and bowing low. Then, right behind her was the round figure of Renée de Guise.

"Come, my child," she said, embracing Mary. "Come, and rest."

It was the first time anyone had offered her anything since François had died, without wishing something in return.

Renée led her to the cloister, where yet more things proclaimed spring. Together they sat on a stone bench, facing the well, which was surrounded by blooming quince trees. At their feet, just beside the brick path, was a bed of herbs just coming up: wolfsbane and absinthe and coriander.

"It is over, then?" asked Renée.

Mary nodded.

"And?"

"The rest of the court has gone on to the coronation banquet at the bishop's palace. And I—I am here." She shrugged. She hoped Charles and his mother had not been offended, but no matter. She could not have endured it—the glittering merriment, the noise, the golden platters and cloying food. And the dancing. "I shall never dance again!" she cried.

"Nonsense!"

Had she actually spoken the thought out loud? She had not meant to.

"You are young, and too spirited never to dance again," Renée persisted. "God will restore you to yourself in time." Uninvited, she took Mary's hand and squeezed it.

Oddly, Mary did not find her touch offensive. Ordinarily, no one is allowed to touch me, she thought with surprise. And I am allowed to touch no one. My dogs, yes, but not people. How odd it all is. . . . She felt overwhelmingly weary.

Time passed; she did not know how long they sat in silence, only that the light began to fail and the blooms of the quince took on a luminescence. A bell tolled.

"Vespers," Renée said softly, taking her hand and helping her to her feet.

As she rose, she felt light and more rested than she had in months. She followed the Abbess into the chapel, and, like a sleepwalker, let the words of the service caress her.

> *Deus in adjutorium intende . . .*
> *Domine ad adjuvandum me festina. . . .*

And:

> *Lord, my heart is not haughty, nor mine*
> *Eyes lofty. . . .*

The words felt like milk to her, soothing and full of sustenance.

I am weaned, because my mother is gone, she thought. And all this— she looked around at the bare chapel, with its echoing walls—feels warmer to me than the court. At the altar, here, is where my mother will lie. She will hear these voices forever, will be surrounded by all this love. And I am cast out into the world, to take her place.

The notes of the chanted Psalm quavered upward.

It was so familiar. She had stood here before, had heard voices just like these, had shivered with the beauty of it. . . .

At Inchmahome. The monks . . .

Around her, the sisters were starting to leave, going to supper in the refectory.

At long tables they sat, backs straight on the low benches, a single candle at each end, eating in silence. There were loaves of brown bread and two dishes of cooked vegetables—stewed apples and baked parsnips.

A young nun—perhaps even younger than I, thought Mary—read the day's portion of Saint Benedict's Rule to the company in a clear, precise voice. "What Kind of Man the Abbot Ought to Be" was the reading for May fifteenth.

"The Abbot should always remember what he is and what he is called, and should know that to whom more is committed, from him more is required."

Like a ruler, thought Mary. But if God has called me to be a queen, why does the abbey feel so much more like home?

After supper, the nuns returned to the chapel for the final service of Compline before making their way with lighted tapers to the upstairs dormitory. There they would sleep in a common room until they were awakened in the deep of the night to return to the chapel for the Night Office.

Renée touched Mary's arm and guided her to the private room where she was to sleep. It was on the ground floor and looked out on the garden where they had sat earlier in the day.

The room was quite well furnished: an ample bed, writing table, chairs, chest, and vases of flowers. On the wall was an ivory crucifix and beneath it, a prie-dieu covered in velvet. A room for a queen.

"For our guests," said Renée, as if reading her thoughts. "All guests are honoured, all pilgrims are equal." She lighted the three candles in their silver candelabra. "I received word yesterday regarding the . . . arrival of your dear mother's remains. Travel is slow . . . the interment will not be possible for another few weeks."

The unspoken question.

"Alas, I cannot be present." Though I want to be, though I long to stay here, become one of you . . . "I must go—out in the world. Perhaps to my dower estates in Touraine. Perhaps even to . . . Scotland." There, she had embraced it.

"The Lords enclosed a letter to you," said Renée. She handed it to her. She would not stay while it was read. "Rest well, my dear child." She started to leave the room, then nodded toward the crucifix. "I wish you to have this," she said. "It is an ancient one that seems to have a soul of its own. I sense it wants to go with you."

Mary started to demur, but something in her aunt's face silenced her. Renée came back to Mary's side. She stood on tiptoe to kiss Mary's head, then left the room, closing the door softly behind her.

Mary sat down on a chair before the table and slowly broke open the seals on the letter. She resented their intruding on her even here, these haughty traitors. *My heart is not haughty, nor mine eyes lofty,* did not apply to them, she thought angrily.

The letter was a lengthy one, filled with carefully balanced phrases and equivocations. They were anxious to justify themselves. A great deal of Scripture was quoted. But the message was this: they wanted her back. They invited her to return, and their tone was not only respectful but warmly cordial. If she would come to Scotland and reside there with her people, they, the Lords of the Congregation, would welcome her and support her and recognize her as their own sovereign, and give her all their loyalty.

Nothing was said about her religion or who would actually do the ruling. Was it to be the Lords of the Congregation, or she?

It was signed by her brother, Lord James Stewart, in his own name as Commendator of St. Andrews, and on behalf of the other Lords.

How surprising, she thought, their change of tone. Perhaps the people cry out for their queen, and the Lords are beginning to feel themselves on shaky ground. For whatever reason, they find themselves in need of me.

She felt her heart beating faster, in spite of herself. They needed her. Scotland was calling her home.

She looked out the window, through its stone frame to the little garden, glowing faintly in moonlight outside. But this is where I belong. . . . The convent had felt like a homecoming, and she had realized how deeply she cherished her faith, how sweet it was to be surrounded by others who were further advanced in spirituality and could teach her.

Out in the world, she thought, it is easy to believe yourself spiritual if you have the merest touch of it. But here—here the truth is revealed. I am a novice indeed in the life of the soul.

Rising up inside her was a surge of energy, of worldly challenge to be met. Scotland sounded a call, and the letter lying on the table was like a gauntlet thrown down, flung at her feet. *Take me up, if you be no coward. If you are able.*

The yellow of the paper, shining in the candlelight, was stronger than the delicate light in the garden outside, and it drew her back toward it. She left the window and picked up the letter to read it once again. And then again.

At length she knelt before the crucifix and held up the letter like a child-offering.

"I know not what to do," she whispered. "Direct me."

The room was utterly silent. She fancied she could even hear the sound of the candles burning, the wax dripping. If only God spoke out loud.

But He does not, she thought. All I hear are my own thoughts.

Is it my duty to go to Scotland, the task for which I was created? For what other reason was I born who I was, if not to shoulder this office?

Is it possible—just possible—that I am to be an instrument to save this land, so muddled now in error? For what other reason can it be that I am the last remaining Catholic in both the Tudor and Stewart families? But I have the horrible example of my cousin Mary Tudor in what can go wrong. I cannot fall into her error.

But if I am gentle, merciful, acting always under the guidance of love, might not they be led back to the truth?

There was no answer from God, nothing but the increasing numbness in her knees as she pressed down on them on the cold stone. The silence surrounded her like a held breath.

At length she rose, stumbling from the lack of feeling in her legs. She made her way over to her narrow bed, pulled back the covers, and lay down stiffly. As sleep crept up on her, she had one drifting certainty of thought: If I do not go, then all my mother's sacrifices were in vain.

The next morning she awakened and sat bolt-upright, filled with conviction. She must go to Scotland.

The decision was less a decision than an order from somewhere deep within her, which had gathered strength during the night and now took command. She did not dare to question it; it seemed to have its own authority.

As she bid farewell to the abbey, glancing at it from over her shoulder, she whispered, "Mother, you and I are now changing places."

She took her route slowly back to Paris. This time the small roads at the height of spring looked different to her. The cottages were hung with garlands, and children swung from ropes on trees, crying out with exuberance; orchards were in full bloom; farmers were tilling the fields, and the smell of fresh-turned earth rode on the air. People called to her as she passed, and in spite of herself, she felt her spirits lifting as she responded to the warm air and the bright spring colours. She was only eighteen, after all.

As she threaded her way along, she silenced her small party of attendants, because she did not want to chatter. The calls of the birds, the cries of the playing children, were soothing to her in a way no conversation could ever be. They rode in single file down the well-trodden path, inhaling the heavy aroma of the flowering fruit trees.

Up ahead was another party, approaching from the opposite direction. A group of revellers, no doubt, looking for a spot to stop and have a picnic, or perhaps pilgrims, paying a visit to some obscure saint's well or grave. It was as much a part of springtime as the mating birds, and as noisy and twittering.

But as they came closer, Mary suddenly recognized the lead rider. It was her brother, Lord James Stewart. He appeared in front of her like a vision, a creature wholly out of place in this blooming, merry, pagan countryside.

"James!" she cried, waving to him.

He came forward and saluted her. "Your Majesty!" He dismounted and took off his hat in token of respect.

In spite of her disappointment in him for joining the Lords of the Congregation, she was pleased to see him. He was family, after all, her blood— or half-blood—brother.

"James! How came you here?" she cried.

"Searching for you," he said. "You were not in Paris." His tone hovered between disappointment and accusation.

"Indeed not. I was minded to visit my relatives."

"Did you receive the letter?" he asked bluntly.

Mary looked back at her party—Madame Rallay, Mary Seton, and Father Mamerot—and signalled them to halt. "Let us seek a clearing, where we may rest and I may speak with my dear brother, the Lord James Stewart, so unexpectedly met."

"There is one a mile beyond here," he said. "I passed it and it looked most inviting." Mounted again, he reined his horse and turned around; his party did likewise.

Once at the clearing, the parties dismounted and settled. Mary drew her brother apart.

"You are persistent and resourceful," she commented. "The countryside is full of roads." Her knowledge that he was a leader in Knox's movement made him seem far away from the brother she had played with at Stirling, and she was guarded with him.

"I was lucky." He smiled, and it made his features quite pleasing. He was a stolid-looking man, with a broad nose and wide cheekbones. "Or else the Lord aided me, as my mission was in accordance with His will."

She stiffened. It was begun already, then, the Reformed preaching. "Your mission?" she asked.

"To speak to you in person, after we had dispatched our letter. To bring you home to Scotland. Yes, we want you. We want you to return. To us, your people."

"My 'people,' as you call them, seem to have strayed far from their obedience to their sovereign." She chose her words carefully. "They deposed my mother—"

"She was not the sovereign," he said quickly.

"She was the ruler appointed by me. Then they made laws about the religion of the land and declared them binding, and defined what was treason and what was not. In short, they took all the prerogatives of ruling upon themselves, under the direction of Master John Knox."

He started to say something, but she cut him off. "Nay, make no demurrings!" she said. "Knox bellowed, and you followed! It was he who directed this 'revolution,' and it is to him you yield your allegiance. For what purpose, then, do you entreat me to return?"

James looked startled and taken by surprise by her attack. "Because you need a country, and we need a queen. And if you would see your way clear to considering the merits of the Reformed Faith—"

"Nay, never! Do not delude yourself on that! I will not change my faith like a hat, for political purposes! This is my faith, and I hold it as dear as any Knox does his! And besides"—she looked at him searchingly—"what does it say of a ruler, that she change her faith for expediency? How could her people rely on her for any consistency? She would be nothing, a wave tossed here and there by every wind that blows." She looked carefully at James. There had been a time when he was being groomed for the Church, when it was thought he would content himself there. He had seemed to take seriously his position as Commendator of St. Andrews. "If you would see your way clear to return to the faith of your fathers, I could see you wearing a Cardinal's hat," she said.

"Like your devout uncle?" he replied. His pleasure at rejecting the proposition was obvious.

They both laughed.

"Two statesmen make political offers to one another, and are refused in statesmanlike fashion," James said. "Now we can proceed to business."

"You seem to be misled," she said in a clear voice. "We are not two equal statesmen, but queen and subject."

He did not reply, but inclined his head slightly. "As to your return, we—the Lords of the Congregation—are prepared to offer you every fealty, if you respect our religion."

"I will respect yours if you will respect mine." He started to speak, but she went on. "I am informed that, under the influence of Master Knox, you have made the saying of mass illegal and punishable by death. This is a great sin, to which your consciences must answer at some later date. But I insist on the right to the practice of my own faith in private. I must be able to attend mass and receive the sacraments, which I need in order to live. Do I have your promise, your solemn word, on this?"

"Master Knox—"

"Master Knox is not king! There can be but one anointed ruler in the land. If it be Knox, I shall not come. Make your choice. I ask but little; it is what you would ask, were our positions reversed."

"True enough." He closed his eyes and seemed to be fighting some inner battle. "But the people must not see your priests, or the Popish trappings, or it may incite them to violence. They must remain hidden. Mass must be restricted to you and your household alone; nowhere else in Scotland may it be held!"

"Yes, brother," she said. Were there no Catholics left in Scotland? How could the faithful survive, with no spiritual sustenance?

"When may we expect you in Scotland?" he was saying.

"In the summer," she answered. "I will notify you later of the exact date."

"My heart is gladdened to be able to take this news to my brethren," he said. But he did not look particularly joyful.

And which brethren did he mean?

❧

The moment of parting had come. The court had journeyed with her to the port of Calais. It was a gay festivity for them, a pageant like the ones enacted at weddings and baptisms. Lord Bothwell had arranged for the ships: a white galley for Mary, and a second one with her goods, including her horses, both flying a blue flag with the French royal arms. There was artificial excitement because Elizabeth had refused to grant Mary a passport in the unlikely event that her ship ran aground and she was forced to come ashore in England. Elizabeth was attempting to register her dislike of Mary's refusal to ratify the Treaty of Edinburgh; Mary used the refusal as an exercise in dramatics for Throckmorton's benefit, saying that Elizabeth could slay her if she wished when she fell into her hands.

The Cardinal of Lorraine stood by the dock and embraced her. "You know that my love goes with you," he said. "Do not lose heart among those heretics."

"If my own religion is permitted me, how can I lose heart?" she asked.

He eyed the galleys. "It would be better if you would leave your jewels in my safekeeping rather than trust them on the high seas in these vessels."

"I have already left most of them in France, as I had to surrender them into Queen Catherine's keeping," she said. "I have only what I brought with me from Scotland, and the Great Harry, and the long ropes of black pearls Queen Catherine gave me for a personal wedding gift."

"I wonder she does not demand their return," he said.

"She has hinted at it. But I did not hear. Besides, good uncle, if you trust my person to these vessels—being infinitely more vulnerable and mortal—then the jewels should be safe enough."

He laughed. "Indeed, they should." He looked long into her eyes, and his smile faded. "May God go with you," he said.

The day was dull and misty, unlike the usual August weather. As the rowers prepared to take them out into the open sea so the sails could be hoisted, a fishing boat foundered in the harbour and went down. All hands aboard were drowned.

As the royal galley waited in respect, the passengers silently lining the rails, Mary felt sudden, unsettling fear.

"What a sad augury for a journey," she said. She looked out at the shore and was aware that she was already beyond its help and comfort.

As they cast off and left the harbour, and France dwindled into the distance, she clung to the railing and kept staring at its receding coastline. Tears streaming down her face, she kept repeating, "Farewell, France. Farewell, France. I fear I may never see you again." Her words were muffled in the sound of the oars and the rush of the wind, a melancholy lost cry.

That night, before she retired for bed, she asked the captain if he would awaken her before they passed beyond the last sight of France. He did so in the cold early morning, and she stood on deck and watched the faint outline of France resolve itself into the pearly haze of sunrise.

OOK TWO

❧

Queen of Scotland

1561-1568

I

he great white galley ploughed through the seas, making its way
past the English coast by the traditional, but hazardous, route across
the North Sea toward Scotland's east coast. Unless a safe conduct
were granted—which it had not been—ships were subject to attack off the
straits of Dover, Yarmouth, and Holy Island all the way up to Scotland, and
would have no shelter if rough weather hit them anywhere along the six-
hundred-mile journey.

Up and down, sliding from wave-trough to wave-trough, the galley slipped
away from France and, encountering no difficulties, approached Scotland
after only five days at sea. The mist had never lifted throughout the entire
journey, and Mary, standing at the rail and straining to glimpse the coast,
saw nothing but white fog.

"Scotland!" said Bothwell, striding up to where the party of Frenchmen
accompanying Mary were standing by the rail staring out at nothing.

"*Où?* Where is it?" asked Brantôme, who had insisted on coming to
Scotland to see it for himself.

"Behind the white curtain, waiting for you." He came to Mary and
whispered, "There it is."

She nodded.

"We will be landing at Leith, God willing."

Was it that problematical to find one's way? she wondered.

Seeing the puzzlement on her face, he said, "Your mother's vessels went
so far afield they landed in Fife instead of Leith. But never fear. The French
have learned their way better now." His grim voice was at odds with his
smile.

So thick was the fog that in spite of the voices and noises as the galley
approached the landing, Mary could not even see the wharf. There were
no trumpets, no gladsome shouts of welcome, nothing but the smell of tar,
the thump of ropes, and the raw voices of seamen crying, "Landing! Tie
her!"

For years Mary had imagined landing in Scotland as an adult queen returning to her childhood home. She and François together, of course, standing at the rail, seeing a great company of mounted councilmen awaiting them, silken banners flying, caparisoned horses gleaming, heralds sounding their trumpets, crowds cheering. And at the head of them all, her mother . . . her mother, who now lay encased in a leaden coffin en route to France.

A loud *whap!* as a rough-hewn gangplank was put down.

"Come," said Bothwell, gesturing toward it.

Mary gathered her skirts and, motioning to the Marys, said in a determinedly gay voice, "Let us go ashore."

They descended the gangplank, five slender figures of black-and-white on the slanting board. The blanketlike fog made Mary feel as though she were stepping out into a dream instead of landing in a real country. She stood on the cold dock, drawing her cloak about her. How drear, how chill—and it only August! Was this the Scottish summer?

How can I survive here? was her first fleeting thought.

"Your Majesty!"

The mist swirled, and out stepped James Stewart in a grey cloak almost the same colour as the surrounding mist. "Mary, have you come, then?" he said.

"Yes, brother! I am here at last!"

She went forward to embrace him, but he stepped back and bowed, giving obeisance.

Now two other figures emerged from the fog: a familiar-looking man with a face so long and thin it looked like an icon, and a man whose features were pleasingly nondescript.

"John Erskine, Your Majesty," said the long-faced man.

"From Inchmahome . . . we were playmates there," she remembered. "And for a little while in France . . . you came when your father was there . . ." She was thinking out loud. "It is indeed a homecoming to find you here."

He smiled, a smile that went all the way to the margins of his narrow face. "I no longer go to Inchmahome," he said, sounding regretful. "But you are welcome there, the same as always."

"He left the island behind, along with the rest of the Popish superstitions," said James, his words clipped.

"I see," Mary said.

"William Maitland, Laird of Lethington, Your Majesty," said the third man. He bowed elaborately, as if to cover an awkward moment.

"We are pleased to receive you," she said, acknowledging him. So this was her mother's secretary of state, reputedly the most intelligent man in Scotland.

Now the most intelligent man merely knelt and said, "Welcome, Your Majesty."

"We were not expecting your arrival today," said Lord James. "But it seems the winds favoured your voyage. Alas, there is a problem with the horses"—he paused—"and also with Holyrood Palace." Shrugging, he continued, "It seems that the English intercepted the galley bringing Your Majesty's horses, and . . . er . . . impounded them in England. We are endeavouring to have them returned forthwith. And Holyrood is not quite prepared to receive you."

Not prepared? They had known she was coming for weeks! she thought.

"However, if you will bide a space here, while it is readied, a merchant, a Mr. Andrew Lamb, has graciously consented to feed—uh, *feast* you in his home here in Leith. In the meanwhile I will procure horses for your party of . . . is it sixty?" His eyes fastened upon a small man in a fur-lined robe in her party. "Who is that?" he asked in a low voice. "Your confessor? A priest?"

Mary nodded, and Lord James looked put upon.

In the late afternoon, Lord James reappeared with enough horses for all, although most of them were sorry nags—their coats dull, their bones protruding, and many of them unshod.

So this was how she was to make her first appearance in her native land—so different from her imaginary entrance on her white horse. At least she did not have to walk the two miles in the mud, or ride a donkey. They set out on the wide, potholed, muddy road leading from Leith up to Edinburgh. The fog had not lifted, and so there was nothing to be seen on either side, much to Mary's disappointment—she was longing to see her half-remembered country that now seemed disinclined to show itself to her. The smoke-thick droplets also veiled the damage from the recent siege of Leith by the English.

"I sent word ahead to Edinburgh," said Lord James. "So there soon should be people gathering." He sounded harassed and resigned—his voice was so impersonal, and there was little left of the brother she had gone sledding with at Stirling.

"Thank you, dear brother." She looked around at her party, all mounted now. "Come, my friends!" she said cheerfully. "It is time to go to our new home!" Resolutely she turned her head in the direction she imagined Edinburgh to lie. But in truth, she was completely dependent on James to lead the way.

They moved out in a painfully slow cavalcade through the dreary streets of the town, made all the more dreary by the ruined buildings on either side of the road, burnt by the English just before the recent fighting ended. There seemed to be no colours at all but this pewter-shaded sky, this bluish grey mist, and the black of charred wood. And the chill! It penetrated quickly down to the very skin. Mary felt herself about to start shivering, and willed herself not to.

A few faces peeked out of doorways; they were colourless, too, and had the resigned, dull look of hungry people who were weary of fighting. She saw how different they looked from French townsfolk. Their garments were rougher and seemingly all of that brown-dun-tan shade of undyed wool.

Their faces, too, were different—the look in the light eyes, the paler skin. Here and there she saw a child with fiery red hair.

"The Queen!" she heard one say in a shrill voice. "It has to be, it has to be, look at her fine cloak—"

She turned to wave and smile, but she saw no one in the mist.

The road began to climb upward; she could feel it. More people now began to gather on the road; word had gone out that the Queen had come.

"Welcome! Oh, welcome!" they cried.

"Bless that sweet face!"

"A bonny Stewart is come tae us!"

They ran alongside her horse, calling out, offering her branches of flowers, little cakes, ribbons.

"Thank you fer comin'," said one old man, who came so close he could have grabbed her horse's bridle. "We need ye—we need ye here."

There were heavy middle-aged women, their bodies worn out with child-bearing, their cheeks flushed and lined; thin boys with lank hair and confused smiles; burly men with the bushiest beards she had ever seen, often streaked with that reddish tint. Their faces were friendly, welcoming.

She reined in her horse, which seemed glad to stop. "Thank you, my good people. It is with great joy that I have returned here, to Scotland, to my own land!"

In front of her Lord James and Maitland had plodded on, unheeding. Just at that moment a swarm of men appeared out the mist and began crying, "Justice! Justice!" They rushed right at Mary's horse, and Bothwell quickly rode up beside her and unsheathed his sword so quickly Mary did not even see the movement; it just seemed to appear, by magic, in his hand.

"Stay back!" he barked. "Do not approach so heedlessly!"

The men stopped, but cried out, "Now the Queen is here, she can hear our grievance!"

"Not now!" said Bothwell. "You can present your petitions at the proper time. Her Majesty has not even been formally received. After that ceremony—"

"No," Mary said quickly. "Let me hear them now, as they have sought me out."

Bothwell looked at her as if she were either stupid or ill-informed. He kept his sword poised, holding it up like a great stave.

"We are poor clerks, who have just saved some companions who were being unjustly jailed! Here they are, Your Majesty!" They pushed forward some young men as their exhibit.

They looked perfectly ordinary, like any village youths anywhere; certainly they did not look criminal. "Why, what had you done?" Mary asked.

"We played 'Robin Hood' on Sunday," said one of them. "We put on a show, for the village. And for that we were arrested, and thrown into jail—by the Reformers!" They indicated one of their number, and said, "And he, as our leader, was condemned to death."

"By what right—" Mary began.

"By every right," said Bothwell, close by her. "The Reformed Kirk now rules the land. Did you not understand that? Did the Lords not spell it all out in their letter? The Kirk makes the laws, and it is now against the law to sport on Sunday. The Lord's Day must not be profaned."

The way he said it—was he in earnest? He had said he was Protestant. Did that mean he believed in these prohibitions? And no, the Lords had *not* spelled it out in their letter. It would have been too ugly to put in writing.

"I pardon you," she said. "I forbid this sentence to be carried out. You are all free."

The men let out wild whoops of relief, and began dancing in the road.

"Come, let us go on," said Bothwell. But Lord James had turned back in time to hear the exchange. He was glowering.

"Your Majesty," he said sourly, "even the Queen must obey the laws of the land."

"What laws?" she said. "How can binding laws have been passed without my consent?"

"Parliament," said Lord James, in that clipped tone.

"All parliamentary laws need the royal signature to be adopted as law," she said. "You sent nothing to me in France to sign—although I understand you passed a multitude of laws recently."

"They await your signature at Holyrood," said Lord James. "Naturally we did not send them to France, knowing you would soon be here."

The men had now started shouting and throwing flowers.

"Oh, the bonny Queen!" they cried. "Will you be our Maid Marian?"

"Aye!" she said.

"Sister!" said Lord James, catching his breath. "The royal dignity!" He urged his horse forward and the party set out again, with the freed youths dancing behind them.

Now the ground began to climb more steeply, as they approached Edinburgh. The city lay on a long, bony spine of land, with a dark, ancient castle at its head and Holyrood Palace at its feet. Part of the city had a stout wall around it to keep out the English, but Holyrood lay in the part that was unprotected.

More people now lined the road, and Mary could see points of light where small bonfires had been lit to welcome her. They glowed through the mist like lanterns.

The road widened as it approached the crest of a hill, and suddenly there was a wall before the royal party. They entered through the fortified gate, and emerged onto a broad street paved with square boulder stones, bordered on both sides by narrow, many-storeyed houses. Lord James reined in his horse and pointed to the bottom of the hill. Mary could see nothing but mist.

"Down there is Holyrood, Your Majesty," he said.

Mary strained her eyes but could see nothing more than the smokelike fog. Sometimes a shape seemed to shimmer within it, but she could not be sure.

"You are upon the High Street, the fair road leading down the hill toward the palace," he said. He turned in the saddle and swept his arm back in the opposite direction. "Up the hill—it's a slow, steady climb—the street continues all the way to Edinburgh Castle upon its great high rock."

She wished she could see it, it was so maddening to be able to see only some ten feet in any direction. "I long to see it all," she said.

"You will see it soon enough," he assured her.

Now there were larger crowds, and next they passed through the Netherbow gate in the city wall and continued down the same street, now called Canongate, where the houses were less crowded together and more gracious.

"The noblemen have their houses here, near Holyrood and outside the city walls. There is more room, so they can have their gardens and orchards," said Maitland, who had ridden up alongside her.

The sight of so many people welcoming her, and being near Holyrood at last, excited her. Gone were the exhaustion and debilitation that had clung to her for months, and the nagging sense of having made a wrong decision, of having left something more important behind.

"I have never seen Holyrood!" she said. "It was never safe for me to be there, when I was a child."

"Peace has come to Scotland at last," Maitland replied. His eyes swept up and down the street, but in the dense fog did not discern any of Knox's loudmouthed followers. That they were evidently indoors, he gave thanks. He felt sorry for the Queen and wished he could spare her what he knew was inevitably coming. Peace? As long as you were of Mr. Knox and the Congregation, yes.

II

John Knox hitched up his breeches as he settled himself at his work desk. Although it was only Tuesday, he was inspired to begin his Sunday sermon. He was now pastor of St. Giles, the High Kirk of Edinburgh, the foremost church of Scotland, and his two-hour-long sermons were heard by hundreds of people and repeated to hundreds more within just a few hours. He did not see it as a reflection on his own oratory, but rather on the power of the Holy Spirit, which gave him the words. He but spoke what he was directed to speak.

The Queen of Scots had set sail, or was about to, any day; he did not know whether she had left France or not. But all his prayers to keep her away had evidently been refused by God. It was His purpose to let her come and ascend the throne in Scotland. Knox must bow to His wishes.

The theme of the sermon that the Holy Spirit had shown him this week was to be upon the Elect of God, His chosen ones, using Ephesians 1:4–5 as his text:

> According as He hath chosen us in Him before the foundation of the world, that we should be holy and without blame before Him in love:
> Having predestined us unto the adoption of children by Jesus Christ to Himself, according to the good pleasure of His will.

As sometimes happened, Knox had not responded immediately to the nudge of the Holy Spirit when first directed to this text, but waited to see if the call was genuine. Alas, it was, and Knox was constrained to labour on that difficult text and doctrine, which Calvin was always refining.

He sighed and looked out the window, which afforded a view up and down the High Street of Edinburgh from its overhanging vantage point. His desk was positioned so that when he was working, he could see the crownlike spire of St. Giles, farther up the hill. Today he could not see it, even though it was only a short distance away, because a strange, thick mist had descended and was swirling around all the buildings, wrapping them in a blanket of cold, minute drops.

It is so unseasonable, he thought. Such a fog, and in August! He reached for a wool blanket and pulled it about himself, thankful for its thick comfort.

The Elect. The Predestined. It was such a thorny concept. If God had predestined some to be saved, "before the foundation of the world," then of what use was preaching? God's own would presumably come forward of their own accord. And what if someone *not* chosen was moved to come forward as a result of preaching? What a cruel hoax on him! And was God that cruel? Would He tease people with a hope of something they could not have? Only little boys did that to their younger brothers.

But I am called to explain this, he thought. And what of the even more difficult allusion in Revelation 7:4 about only 144,000 people being saved? Was Heaven that limited?

He moved on his cushions. It seems to get more and more difficult, he thought. I am forty-seven years old and the Lord keeps veiling things from me. I keep trying to part the veil, but there are always more veils behind each one. . . . Will I never reach His heart?

Perhaps I should preach on "the veils." One of the things behind the veils, hidden from my understanding, is the fact of the Elect, of Predestination . . . yes, but I must trust and believe nonetheless, until more is revealed to me. . . .

He picked up his pen in excitement, dipped it in the ink. I must preach of my own ignorance, yet place it in trust, he thought. I trust that I am one of the Chosen, but I cannot know—it is all to do with grace. . . .

Exhilarated, he began writing as fast as he could, while the day failed to lighten outside as it should. The mist had stifled the sun.

Three hours later, the Spirit left him. He sagged at his writing desk and felt his inspiration dying away. But he had trapped it on paper, he thought exultantly, looking at the curling leaves of writing paper covering his desk. He had trapped the Spirit as a fisherman trapped fishes in his net. We both labour at our calling, he thought.

As he was gathering up the loose sheets of paper—he would not read them over until the next day, for he never corrected his work under the power of the Spirit, only composed—there was a quick series of raps on his door.

"Pray enter," he said. He was ready for company, ready to descend to the lower room, have a bowl of soup, and commune with other human beings. Enough of the muse and the Spirit. His human instrument was weary and longed to be with its own.

His secretary stepped in, and his cloak was shiny with droplets from the fog. "She's here, sir," he said. "The Queen has landed at Leith."

"What, already?" cried Knox. "I had not even received word that she had left France."

"The winds were favourable. It took only five days," replied the secretary. "They arrived early this morning, to a rather meagre welcome, as they were not expected so soon. The Queen and her party had to borrow horses, for their own were impounded in England. But they are even now on their way to Edinburgh."

Knox stood up. It was come, then. The thing he had been dreading, and had prayed to be spared.

"She . . . she is beautiful, sir," said the secretary. "I saw her as she stopped and talked to the people en route. In Scots. She is very tall, and has a perfect complexion, and moves with such grace, like a—a cat, all supple and with perfection—"

"Enough! Are you bewitched with her?" cried Knox. "Your speech is strange, disjointed!"

"I beg your pardon, sir," he said quietly. "I was only attempting to describe her before you saw her. She will arrive in less than an hour. I thought you would want to be notified."

Knox went to the window. Little beads of water covered all the panes, making them opaque. "How many are there in her party?"

"She brings with her a number of Frenchmen—"

"Naturally!"

"I believe there are three of her Guise uncles—"

"Naturally!"

"A poet who elected to come to Scotland, one Chastelard, I believe—"

"Just what we need! Is he the first of a swarm? Better a plague of locusts than a plague of poets!" He turned and glared at the man.

"Sir, I merely bring the news; I did not select the party. Shall I go on, or will you continue to argue and harass me?"

Knox sighed. "Go on. Forgive me."

"Her brother, the Lord James, went to meet her, along with Maitland of Lethington and Lord Erskine."

Good Protestants all, thought Knox. Pray they be not bewitched or deflected from their purpose—which is to rule her, rather than permit her to rule us.

"Ummm." Out of the corner of his eye he saw a flicker of colour. There was something glimmering in the mist. The first of the bonfires. Bonfires of joy, they called them. "The folly begins," he muttered.

O dear God, do not permit this nation to relapse into idolatry and error, he prayed. Do not bring us this far in the way of truth to abandon us now!

"This fog," he suddenly said. "I know now whereof it comes. The very face of Heaven speaks what comfort she brings into this country with her: to wit, sorrow, dolour, darkness, and all impiety." He felt his voice rising, as if he were speaking to hundreds, and not just in this time, but to all time. "For never in the memory of man this day of the year was seen a more dolorous face of Heaven! The surface wet, the corruption of the air; the mist so thick and dark that scarce might any man espy the length of two pair of butts. . . . That forewarning God gives us . . . heed it!"

"Sir?"

"But they do not." He glanced at the twinkling spark of colour that denoted a bonfire. "They do not. They are blind!"

III

Lord James leaned over and said to Mary, "Holyrood was one of our father's favourite palaces. He built the front tower, and he tried to make the palace seem French, to please your mother."

Was there a pause before "your mother"?

Not until they passed into the actual forecourt could Mary see the palace looming ahead, like a dark echo of a French château. The round tower was there, with its conical cap, like the ones in the Loire; but the stone was mottled instead of white, and the windows were small. Against the woolly mist it looked cold and prisonlike; it was attached to the original part of the abbey, which clung like an appendage.

"Oh," was all she could say. She did not want to go into it; it looked

137

menacing. And it was so small! Was this the grandest palace her country afforded?

Inside the palace it was as cold as the outside; nay, colder.

"Welcome to Holyrood," said James, and his voice sounded hollow in the near-empty guard room.

As she looked around questioningly, James quickly said, "I told you things were not quite ready. We understood that you would be bringing furnishings from France."

He led the party up the large stairway and then to the first cluster of royal apartments. "These are the King's apartments," he announced. "Antechamber, presence chamber, and bedchamber." They were empty, but Mary tried to imagine them filled with people, with life and colour, and failed. Central to the picture there needed to be her father, and she had no moving, living memory of him.

"The Queen's apartments are directly above," he said, leading the way back out through the antechamber to a wide stairway. "There is also a small connecting staircase directly between the two bedrooms, but with a party this large I prefer to use the main staircase."

Had he been French, Mary thought, he would have made some allusion to the staircases between the two bedrooms. As it was, he recited it as an architectural fact and nothing more.

He seemed proud of the Queen's apartments, as he stood at the threshold of the audience chamber and beckoned.

Mary walked into the chamber. It was a fair one, with an oratory and fireplace, and several windows looking out onto the courtyard. Tapestries hung on the walls, and the wooden ceiling had been freshly painted.

She made her way across the length of the chamber and crossed the threshold into the adjoining one. For a moment she stood alone in it. It was smaller than the audience chamber, and an odd shape—not quite square, but not round, either. Two outpocketings bulged from the room, framed by doorways.

She lifted the curtain of one and quickly realized what it was: it contained a velvet-hung device called a "close stool." The other minute chamber had a fireplace and a window, although it was only about eight by ten feet.

"Whatever is this for?" she asked James, who had come into the room. "It is so tiny!"

"You may use it as a supper room," he said.

"For dolls?"

"You will find that in the winter, January especially, a small room with a fireplace is most welcome. A table will fit in here, and your mother the Regent had as many as six guests to dine with her here." He paused. "So I have heard. She never invited *me*."

Before Mary could reply, he continued, "This room is in the tower. Remember the round turret you saw from the courtyard? The rest of the rooms, the public rooms, the ceremonial rooms, are all in the front. There is the Chapel Royal"—he looked at her sternly—"which has been lately stripped of its idols and made pure."

"And this is where I am to have my private masses?" she asked. Seeing him frown, she said, "As you promised." She had meant her remark to sound light, but he chose to answer gravely.

"Aye. I promised. And I stand by my promise. Regardless."

"Regardless of what?"

"Regardless of Master Knox." A wonder that he had not been here yet.

"Master Knox!" she said, letting her anger escape her control. "That man who has stolen my brother from his ancestral faith, and who drove my mother to her grave! I give *you* Master Knox, for I'll none of him!"

It is not you who will have none of him, James started to say, but it is Knox who will determine who will have *you*. Instead he said, "Master Knox has wrought much good in Scotland. You will find he is a good citizen, dedicated to advancing his country."

"He is an insurrectionist who preaches rebellion and destruction!"

"You will find, Your Majesty, that many of the nobles here have become corrupt. Years of disorder have taken their toll. They are venal and to be bought. Master Knox is not for sale, and his only purpose is to better his people, both materially and spiritually."

Voices behind them intruded, and Mary turned to her party and began showing them her rooms.

That night, as she lay in bed, it was eerily quiet.

What a strange place this is, Mary thought. I do not seem to remember anything; nothing feels familiar. My father is entombed here, in the abbey church, and my other ancestors lie near him. Just out this window, just below me . . .

The whiteness of the fog faded gradually into blackness and Mary fell asleep without being aware of it, sliding off into slumber like a child sliding down a grassy bank into cool waters.

She heard a strange noise; at first it played about in her dream as if it belonged there, but then it grew too intrusive and demanded her attention. She blinked awake and shook her head, trying to place herself. Music was wafting into the chamber, rising louder and louder.

She went to one of the windows and looked out. Standing below in the courtyard was a crowd of townspeople, playing wild melodies on instruments she had never heard before—primitive fiddles and hollowed reeds and little drums. When they glimpsed her, they let out a great shout and flourished their torches.

"Welcome, sweet Queen! Welcome!" they cried, and struck up a new tune. She managed to open the window and wave to them.

"Thank you!" she cried. She saw little flickers of colour here and there in the fog; they had made more bonfires to welcome her.

The musicians kept playing, and the people thronging in the courtyard cheered and cried with joy. "Dear Queen—sweet Queen—welcome to Scotland!"

"Your music is lovely!" she called to them. "Please play on, and return to play again for me tomorrow night as well!"

When at last they stopped playing, and the crowd slowly drifted away, the flaming torches winking smaller and smaller like fireflies as they dispersed in the fog, Mary lay back down and closed her eyes. How quiet it suddenly was . . . the chamber seemed to be waiting, listening in the dark.

It is only my imagination, she thought. But I don't like those curtained rooms, they remind me of the places where Nurse Sinclair used to tell me bogeys were hiding. . . .

The half-forgotten stories came back to her, chillingly: the stories of the creatures under the bridges in Scotland, hiding in the wells, taking other shapes; of the monsters in the deep, cold lochs; of the witches walking about, passing as ordinary people. They said that Lord Ruthven, a member of the Lords' Council, was a warlock. . . .

It's nonsense, nonsense, nonsense, she kept repeating to herself. But she kept her face turned away from the little adjoining room.

The next morning, instead of dancing sunshine to make a mockery of her night fears, there was still nothing to be seen but a grey smudge at the windows. The fog had not lifted. An immense disappointment gripped her. She was eager to see Edinburgh, to behold Scotland. Why was it hiding its face from her?

Without waiting to call one of her attendants, she dressed herself as warmly as possible. No fire burned in the fireplace; evidently the Scots did not consider heating a necessity at this time of year.

No French nightgowns here, she thought. Not if I wish to sleep in comfort.

There was a smart rap on the door, and she said, "Enter."

Before they even stepped in, she knew it would be Lord James and Maitland. And she was right.

"I see you have risen early," said Lord James, with faint approval in his voice. "That's good. We heard that at the French court, no one rose before noon. That'll not do here."

His shirt was open at the neck, and he seemed to be wearing no under-linen. Was he not cold? Evidently not. "Good morning, brother," she said. "Good morning, Maitland. I cannot imagine who told you such a blatant falsehood, but I can assure you that people in France rise as any other people." She smiled at him. "I slept well."

"Not so well that the musicians failed to wake you last night," said Maitland. "For that, I apologize."

"I found their music pretty and their welcome touching," said Mary.

"I will be pleased to show you about the grounds," said James, "after you have finished breakfast. I have ordered the food to be sent up." He bowed smartly, and was about to take his leave.

"I would like my Marys to join me," said Mary. "Where are they? In the future, they must sleep near me."

"Of course," said Maitland. "Anything you desire, we will attempt to fulfil."

Flamina, Lusty, Beaton, and Seton were with her in a quarter-hour, and were chattering like monkeys. "The fog . . ." "Strange quarters, to be put so far from *you*." "It's so cold here, how do they stand it?" "What shall we do today?"

When the breakfast was brought in, they examined it critically. A mound of whitish, granular material lay in a covered dish, emitting gentle puffs of steam. It had a rough, nutty odour to it. Another covered platter had rows of russet-coloured smoked fish. Yet another had hard, textured buns, arranged in a tier. Luckily in a moment a servitor appeared with more plates, spoons, and sugar.

"This is oatmeal," he said, spooning it into dishes for them. " 'Tis to be eaten with milk and sugar."

The five women looked at it dubiously. It looked most unappetizing, but it smelled good. Mary took the first bowl and the first bite, and dutifully pronounced it good.

Giggling, the others followed suit.

The servant went on to explain that the smoked fish came from the nearby area and were considered a great delicacy, and the buns should be smeared with butter.

All of them had trouble understanding him. Mary vowed to become proficient in Scots as fast as possible. Her vocabulary was still that of a child. She realized that Lord James, Maitland, and even Bothwell had been speaking French to her, and it had seemed so entirely natural that she had not even been aware of it at the time.

"The Scots people hate the sound of it," Bothwell had said.

After breakfast, Lord James and Maitland reappeared to escort the women around the grounds of Holyrood. As they stepped outside, Mary saw that the fog was still as dense as ever; so dense, in fact, she could not even detect where the sun was.

"Is it—usual to have fog like this?" she asked in Scots, very slowly.

James looked pleased at her attempt. "No," he said. "No, not at all."

"Knox will, of course, say it was caused by your arrival," Maitland said suddenly. "He will use it after his purpose."

"Knox!" said Flamina. "Tell us about this creature!" She tossed her head.

Maitland laughed, and drew her aside. "John Knox," he said, "is the leader of our Kirk. . . ."

Mary did not hear the rest of the conversation. Lusty, Seton, and Beaton had fallen in with Maitland and Flamina, leaving her with James.

The mist was curling and uncurling around their feet as they walked. Mary tried kicking at it, to clear away a yard or two, but it refused to flee.

She laughed. "I am anxious to see Scotland, and yet it veils itself from me! All I have seen so far is that it must be very green, for green glows through this mist."

"Yes. That it is. If you could see, now, you would see the fair front of the palace, and off to the left, the Abbey church, where our royal father lies in his tomb."

Our royal father. How he loved the phrase, she thought.

They stood quietly for a moment. Then James continued, "Stretching out farther to the left—if only you could see!—are the ornamental gardens and the orchard. There are also ornamental gardens on the other side, and a large hunting park behind the palace, not to mention a graveyard as well. The Abbey was an ancient one."

But the way in which he said the last sentence betrayed no sadness or lingering fondness for the old ways.

"I pray no one else saw your priest yesterday," he said quietly.

"I realize that my situation is unique," she said. "There has never before been a ruler whose personal faith was at variance with his subjects'."

"Ah!" Before replying, he turned to see where the others were. "This is a difficult matter. It is best you not antagonize people. There is already enough suspicion that you do not hold your native land in high esteem. It is said you consider yourself French, that you wept upon leaving, that you clung to the rail lamenting the parting."

"You were not there!" How dare he steal her private moments and make them into something silly and pitiable? "And I do care for my people, and my land."

"Not as Master Knox—"

"Master Knox! Master Knox! What does he know of ruling? And what does he know that fits him for this office to which he feels called? He loves Scotland, yes, but there needs to be more than that! I am called by blood to my throne."

"He feels called by God."

"To a throne?" Her voice was sharp. "I am called by God, too. So how can we both be called to the same station by the same God?"

"He does not aspire to your throne," James said gently.

"No, he merely takes it upon himself to prescribe how I sit upon it! 'Pray you, look this way!' 'Move your head so!' "

To her surprise, Lord James burst out laughing. "You have a searching wit," he said.

Just then a large number of Mary's French relatives and guests came bounding up. The young Guises looked eager to go riding, or hunting, or hawking. Mary suddenly remembered, with a sinking feeling, how poorly they tolerated inactivity. But she did not know what could be offered them at this moment.

"How does one amuse oneself here?" asked René, the Marquis d'Elboeuf, his quick dark eyes dancing.

"Yes, indeed, unless one plays blind man's buff, what can one do in this fog?" cried his brother Claud, the Duc d'Aumale.

Joining them, the young Mareschal d'Amville and his secretary, the poet Chastelard, looked perturbed that no sports were in the offing. "What about our horses?" asked d'Amville. "When will the English return them?"

"I have sent a messenger to Cecil," said Lord James, "and soon he will respond."

Brantôme, the courtly historian, came strolling up. "What of the Abbey? Is there anything of interest there?"

"Not to us!" cried the young would-be warriors. "Perhaps we can learn to play the—what is it? The golf. Yes. Can we play it here, in the fog?"

"No," said James, smiling tightly at their breezy ignorance. "Not here. Golf is a game that must be played near the sea, on the links where the grass grows sweet and wild. 'Tis at St. Andrews, near the sandy sea cliffs."

"Ah!" said Mary. "Golf! I do long to learn it! And I will journey to St. Andrews soon, when I set out to see the rest of my kingdom. I'll take a . . . what does Elizabeth call them? A progress." She laughed at the happy thought of it.

"Oh, so you're minded to do that?" Lord James asked. "So soon?"

"Yes, as soon as possible!"

"But there are other things to be attended to first, and you must have your ceremonial entry into Edinburgh, and select your Privy Council—"

"Yes, I know! I know! But soon! I'm longing to see it all!"

"I see we cannot even shoot on a day like this," d'Aumale said morosely. "So we might as well go get drunk!" They turned on their heels and went back inside.

Mary felt embarrassed, but did not want to apologize for them in front of James. He was looking at her quizzically. She straightened her back and said to Brantôme and Chastelard, "Maitland and the Marys have gone up ahead to look at the gardens. We can look at the Abbey along the way. Pray, let us join them."

The gardens were a sorry sight. They were not well laid out, nor had they been maintained. Two broad walks, sparsely gravelled, intersected, and where they met, there was a fountain. But it was dry and it looked as if there had been no water in it all season. There were struggling beds of flowers, but they looked unhealthy to begin with and then had been further neglected. The entire design, borrowed from a monastery garden plan, had been outmoded in France for a good eighty years.

"O! Has the garden of love withered, then?" Chastelard asked mockingly. Everyone tittered—everyone but Lord James.

"We have been most unsettled for a dozen years," said Maitland. "Nonetheless, our gardeners have attempted to preserve the plant stocks so that, when our Queen returned and our country was restored to peace and prosperity, they could also be restored. Look!" He stepped over the border and plucked a stunted flower. "It is not dead, merely waiting. As all of us are.

For our Queen, as I have said, to restore us to peace and prosperity." He presented Mary with the flower; it was a crimson carnation.

She took it solemnly, as if it were a pledge. She longed to nurture this poor, broken country and bring it back to life. "Thank you," she said.

They continued their walk around the palace, finding a greensward there that could be used for archery.

"We can, perhaps, lay out a course of pall-mall here as well," Mary told her Marys, who were dutifully trotting along behind her. Like their mistress, they were finding their native land to be exotic and almost forgotten.

"I wager there is no jousting in the whole of Scotland," said Flamina.

"Probably not," said Mary. "But I shall not miss it." When she thought of jousting, all she would ever see was Henri II clutching at his helmet, tumbling from his horse in spasms. "There will be other things here to amuse us."

After the midday meal—consisting of unidentifiable bits of meat in a barley stew—the people sat around the room forlornly. Mary decided to consult with Mary Seton's brother, whom she was minded to appoint master of her household, about selecting court musicians and poets.

Lord George Seton, whose family had remained staunchly Catholic, could not hide his delight at having both his sister and his Queen back in Scotland. He was several years older than they, but still boyish-looking, with gold hair and searching grey eyes. His family lands lay near Edinburgh, and it was easy for him to travel there on short notice. Mary knew him well, for he had come to France several times over the years.

"Ah, it is so wonderful to see you back here!" he said as he entered the room. "I used to imagine how you would look here, and I must confess, my imagination failed me."

Mary laughed and turned round once, holding her arms out. "So, do I look natural here?"

George Seton nodded gravely. "As natural as heather and hawks."

"I must needs set up my household," she said. "I brought my own physician, my confessor—"

"Thank God!" he said loudly.

"—some French servants especially skilled in embroidery and ceremonies, and my personal attendants. But I would fain bring the Scottish poets and musicians to court."

George Seton looked bewildered. "But there are none."

"None?"

"None of any note, Your Majesty."

"But that is . . . that is impossible! No poets?"

"Some few, perhaps, could be rounded up." He shifted from one foot to the other. "At St. Andrews University, perhaps. The truth is that our only poetry these days comes from the songs in the Borders, all about killing and lamenting and so on." He paused, thinking hard. "There's Alexander Scott," he finally remembered.

"But he's so old!" He had been at court with James V.

"And there are other so-called poets who dare not publish their names, for their verse is lewd, calculated to appeal to the bestial wits of men deep in their cups."

Mary could not help realizing how she had always taken the refined poets thronging the court for granted in France. "And what of painters and sculptors?" she continued gamely.

"None, Your Majesty." When she kept looking at him, he said, "You must remember, we have been at war. These niceties had to go by the board. And what little remained, the Reformers have done away with. Music and dancing are now frowned upon by the Kirk."

Chastelard was looking even more forlorn. "What do you do in the evenings, then?" he asked plaintively.

"Why, we go to sleep," George replied.

The Marys all burst into laughter. Then Mary Seton explained, "We are not laughing at you, just at the answer."

"This must all be remedied," said Mary. "I am sure there must be young people who would welcome the opportunity to write verse and compose music, to paint and draw. We must gather them here!"

"Yes, Your Majesty," said George. "Perhaps you should speak to James Melville about it. He is a courtier of the old school—although he is not very old."

"Then I shall. And if none are to be found here, then I shall have to bring some from France after all," said Mary.

All afternoon, Mary busied herself setting her rooms in order. She ordered all her miniatures to be unwrapped and set out on a shelf, and she had her embroidered bedcovers and valance put on her bed. She set her chiming clock on her mantelpiece, and last of all, she took the ivory cross from the convent out of its protective wrappings and hung it in a small, shrine-like box on the wall near her bed. The morning sun would illuminate it, caressing its smooth planes.

Later in the evening, she sat looking at it. She was exhausted; the exhilaration of the arrival and the exploration was giving way to crushing weariness. The cross reminded her that religion might become her biggest problem here. Her very tiredness made thoughts swirl through her mind, blowing this way and that.

Perhaps if I assured them right at the outset that I mean no harm, that—Christ forgive me!—I come not to bring the sword, as He said, but peace.

Like the decision to come to Scotland at all, this one also rose up and seized her. It was less a thought than a feeling.

She reached over and picked up her little bell, and summoned her secretary.

"I am minded to issue a proclamation," she said.

"What? Now?" He looked out the window into the dark.

"Yes. Now. It can be posed straightway. It is not very long. Write it down."

The little man fetched his writing materials and then waited obediently for her to dictate.

"Say: 'My good subjects, it is the command of the Queen that there shall be no alteration or innovation in the religion of the country as she found it upon her arrival in this land, nor any attempt against the form of public worship in use, upon pain of death.

'At the same time, Her Majesty commands that the French people in her service who wish to practise their own faith in private may do so without molestation. Signed, Marie R.' "

Brantôme, who had overheard her, came and stood by her side. "Perhaps you should not be hasty," he said. "This is noble, but it may cause your Catholic subjects to lose hope. They could take it amiss. And it will not win the Protestants to you. Only your own conversion can do that."

"No, I wish it posted," she said stubbornly.

"I pray you, wait until morning," Brantôme said. "Never do anything on impulse."

Mary yawned. "I will concede and wait an hour. But only an hour!" She looked at him fondly. "Old friend, 'tis true you have seen many courts and years, and have much wisdom."

In an effort to stay awake, she took up her needlework and began stitching. But it seemed to lull her even more toward sleep.

Just as her eyes were closing, there was a knock on the door. Mary Seton answered it and was surprised to see one of the councillors standing there. His eyes were searching the chamber for the Queen. When he saw her, he smiled. "I have just received this from England," he said.

Which one was he? He had been present at the dock, and today . . . those buttonlike eyes. Maitland. Yes, Maitland. She was pleased with herself for remembering. But what was his Christian name?

He was holding up a heavy envelope, which he handed to her. The seal on it was so massive it had partially torn the paper. It showed a woman seated on a throne: Elizabeth of England.

Mary ripped it open.

We hereby do permit and extend our protection to our most dear and loved cousin, Mary Queen of Scotland, should it chance that the Lord Almighty should cast her upon our shores, or necessitate her passing through our realms.

"It is the passport I sought before leaving France," Mary said. "The passport that she refused. Now she issues it, after the fact. To what purpose?" She was thinking out loud, but Maitland replied.

"It seems"—he looked at the date—"she issued it just before your actual departure."

"When she knew I could not possibly receive it in time," said Mary, wonderingly. "Yet perhaps she wished to make a gesture of friendship, and this is what the belated passport means. My dear"—what *was* his name?—

"William, I wish to send you on a mission, to go direct to my sister sovereign."

"What? Tonight?"

"Nay! I am not that impulsive. But after the ceremonial entry to Edinburgh, I would dispatch you to the English Queen, on business of the utmost importance." She looked at him. Her mother had chosen him and trusted him; he must be worthy.

"May I inquire of what this urgent business consists?"

"Certainly. I wish to end all misunderstandings with her, and for us to deal honestly with one another from henceforth. After all, we are nearest kin to one another, both queens, both in one isle—should we not be in loving closeness?"

He bowed, stifling a smile of joy, both at her ultimate mission and at being the one selected to carry it out.

"You will arrange it," she said confidently. She wondered if she ought to show him the proclamation, but decided not to. It did not concern him.

Later that night she gave orders that it should be posted at the Mercat Cross on the High Street in Edinburgh, where all royal proclamations were read. By morning everyone was talking about it.

IV

The fog continued to blanket the city, where the people were busy readying the streets for the ceremony to follow on the morrow. The fountains had to be converted so that they would spout wine, and glasses provided so that the Queen could be saluted; the stages and decorated arches for the pageants and allegories had to be erected. But all the while the people were murmuring and wondering about the proclamation. What could it mean?

At last the fog lifted, on the very day that Mary was to make her ceremonial entrance into her capital city, as if it wished to humour the natural curiosity of both Queen and subjects alike. It fled away in shreds, leaving piercingly blue skies and a sun that made sharp shadows.

Mary, dressed still in grey-black mourning, but wearing the Great Harry on her breast and a diadem of gold and pearls on her head, set out with a splendid company to make the mile-long journey up the hill to Edinburgh

Castle, where she would dine in state, and then return to Holyrood by nightfall.

As she approached the castle, it loomed larger and larger until it filled the whole sky with its sombre outline. It gave an overwhelming impression of darkness, of brutish melancholy. The greenish tint of moss on cracks and crevices reminded her of tombstone growths.

Once inside, she was ushered into the Great Hall, where the tables were set as fair as any in France, much to her surprise. There were places for at least sixty people: the leading men of her realm. Each, before taking his place, knelt before her and murmured his name, title, and promise of allegiance. Some she recognized, others she tried to commit to memory. She studied each face diligently, trying to assign something to link the face and name together.

There was James Douglas, the Earl of Morton, with his bright red hair—the colour Judas' was supposed to be—and his tiny dark eyes. He had inherited the sword of his ancestor Archibald "Bell-the-Cat" Douglas, and was wearing it this day. It was richly ornamented and heavy, bespeaking its history.

There was George Gordon, the Earl of Huntly, a square-jawed man with florid colouring. Mary knew he was the leading Catholic magnate in Scotland, with vast tracts of land in the north. He looked vaguely familiar, and then she remembered: when he had come to France years ago, she and the Marys had thought he looked like a rooster. He still did.

She was having difficulty suppressing a laugh when the rooster said, "That proclamation! How could you have done it?" His voice was rough.

Before she could answer, the next man was kneeling, saying, "Archibald Douglas, Your Majesty."

There are so many Douglases, thought Mary. The Red Douglases and the Black Douglases, and they all marry into the other families, so that the Earl of Morton's wife is sister-in-law to the Hamiltons. I shall never, never remember it all! Yet they know these things so perfectly they conduct their lives according to the exact degree of kinship. I fear I shall always be an outsider in understanding these webs of loyalty—although I myself am kin to half of them!

"James Hepburn, the Earl of Bothwell, Your Majesty." He looked up at her and she took his hand, bidding him rise. "I know this castle must seem hateful to you," he said. "Have you seen it yet?"

She did not understand, and he looked embarrassed.

"I meant the room in which your mother passed her last days," he said. "If you like, I can show you." He paused. "Another time."

Yes. She had known her mother had died here. And she would have to force herself to enter the very room and say farewell.

"I would appreciate that."

His place was taken by Erskine, then by Archibald Campbell, the Earl of Argyll, then another Stewart, the Earl of Atholl. . . .

* * *

After the dinner, they waited, mounted, in the great courtyard that wound around the castle like a snail shell, spiraling down toward the castle gates. As Mary sat her white palfrey, which had finally been returned by the English, she could look out on the countryside in all directions, even as far as the glitter of the waters of the Firth of Forth. Directly below the castle on the north side was a loch, oval-shaped and motionless this windless morning.

" 'Tis a fair city, is it not?" said a voice behind her. She turned to see Lord Bothwell, mounted on a huge charger. "And I see the English have seen fit to return what's rightly yours." He nodded to the pure white horse upon which she sat. His eye appreciated the fine breeding and good configuration of the horse. Surprising that the English had surrendered it. He imagined that Robert Dudley, Elizabeth's Master of the Horse, had seen to it his mistress had had a ride or two on it first.

"Yes. It spreads out before me like a perfect model. So beautifully situated, so neat."

"They say 'tis like an ivory comb, the Royal Mile of High Street, with the center clean, but the teeth on either side stinking and foul. The wynds—the side streets—are beyond description, I fear. At least to a Queen. But the High Street—it's the fairest in the world!" He could not keep the pride from his voice.

Today she would not have wished to be anywhere else; even Paris seemed sprawling and unimaginative compared to this dramatic wedding of hard, dark, natural rock and smooth, polished building-stones, of steep cliffs and equally steep-pitched roofs and gables surmounting them atop tall, thin town houses, all framed by the bright blue sky with its racing clouds.

Behind her were her household, her Marys accompanied by their distinguished fathers and brothers; her French and Scots servants; her household guard. The French servants wore black livery and the Scots, red and yellow.

Then came the leading nobles and officers of the realm, and the royal archers.

"Are you ready, Your Majesty?" Lord James reined up beside her.

"With all my heart!"

With a resounding crack, the cannons of the castle were fired in salute, sounding like thunder.

They set out, riding slowly down through the castle gates and then into the town proper, where it seemed that all thirty thousand inhabitants of Edinburgh were waiting for her, for they burst into cheers as she emerged onto the upper reaches of the Royal Mile.

Sixteen members of the Town Council, dressed in black velvet, came forward to welcome her officially, and then the cavalcade moved slowly past the cheering crowds and beneath the triumphal arch. Along the way, on stages constructed for the purpose, costumed children sang and various allegorical plays were enacted, some more blatantly Protestant than others.

In one, idolatry was condemned, in the form of Old Testament transgressors, like the little-known Korah, Dathan, and Abiram, being burnt.

"They meant it to be a priest at the altar, did you know that?" said a harsh voice.

She turned to see the glaring eyes of the Earl of Huntly.

"But I stopped them!" he said triumphantly. "Can you imagine the insult they intended?" His face was turning red in anger.

"I thank you," she merely said, hoping to damp down his fury.

They reached the Tolbooth—the city prison—where the criminals, still fettered in the stocks for lechery, blasphemy, and vagrancy, cheered the Queen with all the rest. The bankrupts, wearing their yellow hats, called teasingly, "Largesse! Largesse!" until their guards silenced them.

Passing St. Giles Cathedral, they reached the Mercat Cross, where Mary was greeted by three virgins representing Justice, Policy, and Fortune, who welcomed her to the fountain spouting wine. A vast party of people stood, their glasses already filled, and when the Queen took hers and drank, they all lifted theirs simultaneously, drank, and then broke all the glasses at once to signify their loyalty.

"Lest the glasses ever be used for a lesser toast," whispered one of the virgins.

Mary was startled by this spontaneous display of generosity in such a poor country.

They continued down the gently sloping street, with its houses made of dressed fieldstone hedging the Royal Mile like a tall fence. Many of the houses had outside staircases and most had wooden upper storeys that jutted out and abutted their neighbours'. One, a particularly handsome house on the left with a large second storey, actually protruded out into the street like a knuckle.

"John Knox's house, Your Majesty," said Bothwell, who had been riding close behind her.

She looked at it, sticking out into the street, completely out of line with the other houses, making an obstruction and a nuisance of itself. It attracted attention, like a stone in running water.

So the house was like its master. Was he in there? For she was sure he would not be outside to welcome her. Was there a face in one of the windows?

It was impossible to tell. Reflections made dancing images in the glass, and they seemed to move as she moved. She dared not be seen gazing up at the Reformer's window like a disciple, while all around her people were clamouring for a glance or a smile from her. Leaving the house behind, she continued down the High Street toward Holyrood, waving and smiling.

❧

Knox, seated at his desk as he would have been on any ordinary workday, was well able to spy what was going on in the street below. Without even moving his chair, he had easily seen the approach of the cavalcade as it moved slowly down the High Street. There had been tableaux all along the route plain enough for anyone to understand—anyone who was *willing* to understand!—demonstrating the truth of the Protestant religion. Effigies of the sons of Israel who had offered false sacrifices had been burned. The Queen had even been presented with a Bible and Psalter in Scots, and a costumed child had made a speech suggesting outright that she should abandon the mass. But had she heeded it? No, she had merely smiled in that inane way and tucked the Holy Word under her arm, and kept waving and turning her head.

The fountain near the Mercat Cross had spouted wine, to make the people drunk and pacify them. Everything had been arranged, no expense spared in the masques and farces to lull the people and buy their fickle loyalty.

Knox stared at Mary as she passed, her grey mantle open and spread out across her white horse's flanks. The rubies on her breast caught the sunlight upon her grey bodice; her face seemed the very workmanship of all Satan's cunning to make vice alluring.

He dipped his pen in ink and wrote, "In farces, in masquing, and in other prodigalities, fain would the fools have counterfeited France."

On the street below, the people were singing, "Welcome, O Sovereign! Welcome, O native Queen!"

Three days later, on Sunday, Knox took his accustomed place in the pulpit of St. Giles and looked out at the packed congregation. He had had no difficulty with the selection of his topic this Lord's Day: it had been thrust upon him.

"One mass to be said upon this soil is more to be feared than the landing of ten thousand foreign soldiers!" he cried. "Shall we allow it?"

Later that selfsame Sunday, as Mary's priest and his assistants made ready to celebrate mass in the Chapel Royal, a crowd began to gather in the forecourt of Holyrood Palace. The chapel, completely bare in accordance with Calvinistic doctrine, had to be furnished with candles and an altar for a mass to be celebrated in any fashion at all. The assistant, carrying the candlesticks and candles from one side of the courtyard to the main entrance, ran afoul of the crowd.

"Shall that idol the mass be suffered again to take place in this kingdom? We were purged of it! Shall the dog return to its vomit? It shall not!" cried Patrick, Lord Lindsay of the Byres, one of the recently converted nobles.

The deacon halted. The crowd was large. But would not the Lord protect him? He enfolded his candles and candlesticks in his arms and tried to go around them, reciting slowly, "O Lord my God, in Thee do I put my trust: save me from all them that persecute me, and deliver me: Lest he tear my soul like a lion, rending it in pieces . . ."

A burly butcher—still smelling of his trade, although he did not wear his apron—grabbed the deacon by the shoulder. "The idolator priest shall die the death, according to God's law!" he yelled.

"I am no priest!" the deacon cried, twisting free of his hands and running to the door. The crowd pursued him, pushing past the sympathetic guards and rushing up the main staircase and onto the landing leading to the chapel. The terrified deacon ran ahead of them and bolted the door of the chapel, where Mary and her French relatives and members of her household were kneeling in prayer, rosaries clasped between their fingers.

"Die! Die! The idolators must die!"

Mary heard the words being shouted right outside the chapel, and then saw the stout wooden doors straining as the crowd pushed against them.

She rose, her heart pounding. What was this? Had her own palace been invaded? In spite of her conciliation to their religion?

"Stand back!" Lord James was speaking. "Do not touch this door!" From the sound of his voice, her brother was standing with his back pressed against the door. "I say, do not trespass! For within here is wickedness and evil: the mass! No good Scotsman should take it upon himself to expose himself to it, lest he fall once more into the devil's trap!"

There were murmurs, then compliance.

James! she thought. That is not what you promised! You have not defended my right to practise my religion in privacy, you have insulted it and tricked the people . . . Why do you not admit to our agreement?

The priest, shaking in his robes, could hardly perform the ancient and necessary ritual.

But James achieved his purpose, thought Mary, as the mass ended. The crowd has left. My brother is very clever.

V

Mary looked down the long table at the faces turned toward her. They all wore smiles, as if they were the most affable of men, ready to pass a morning of pleasant conversation about trivialities.

But it will not be trivial, Mary vowed, however much they may try to keep it so.

"Good lords and gentlemen, I welcome you to court." Let them know who was doing the welcoming now! "I am pleased to call this first meeting of my Privy Council and officers, whom I have selected according to what

I believe each man can bring to his appointment. Among you there are both Catholics and Protestants, as you can see."

They were still smiling, waiting for her to venture further into the matters at hand.

"I wish to appoint George Gordon, the Earl of Huntly, my chancellor for the realm."

The rooster stirred his rather substantial body in his seat and tried not to grin. "I thank you, Your Majesty," he said.

"For my chief minister, I choose Lord James Stewart." She nodded toward him curtly. She was still angry at him for his behaviour at the riot over the mass.

"As secretary of state, I wish William Maitland of Lethington to continue in that office, which he has discharged so well in the past." Mary saw his genuine pleasure at being named. "For the Privy Seal, Sir William Kirkcaldy of Grange, a man I hear is a most distinguished young soldier." He was a handsome, thin man with muscles that bulged through the arms of his fine velvet doublet.

"And for the rest of you, you are all invested with the responsibility of helping me. I have chosen you because I know you have talent and strength. I wish you to use it in my service, rather than against me."

The men now began to look more alert.

"I thank you for the ceremonial entrance to Edinburgh," she said. "It was carefully and lovingly arranged. But"—she looked carefully from face to face—"the attack on my household for holding the mass is not to be tolerated."

"Your Majesty, I prevented it!" Lord James protested.

"Not until the mob had been allowed to enter the palace. The guards were either disarmed or never attempted to stop the intruders. Why?"

"Perhaps they sided with the mob," said Morton. "They are most likely good Protestants all!"

" 'Good' is not a word that can be applied to mobs," said Mary. "You have promised me the use of my religion in private. And in my proclamation—"

"Issued without our knowledge!" said Lord James indignantly.

"Why, did its contents displease you?" Mary asked.

"No. But it is not right—"

"That I issue a proclamation without informing you? Surely that cannot be so." She glared at them. "But I only did so knowing I was confirming what had already been decided by Parliament." She smiled and her voice grew gentle. "We must not work at cross purposes. You see, I respected your decision to become a Protestant country. Can you not trust me?"

"Is that why you did it, then?" Erskine asked. "So that we would trust you?"

She looked at him in surprise. "Why, you have known me all your life. Do *you* not trust me, John Erskine?"

"I meant in matters of state," he said hastily.

"He raises an important point," said Mary. "We must all trust one another. For we have an important task before us: to restore Scotland to its lost glory. It will take all our effort, working together."

"And how do you plan to do this? Scotland lost her glory on the battlefield of Flodden over fifty years ago," said Maitland.

"First, to have an end to wars—"

"The Treaty of Edinburgh took care of foreign wars," said Morton, "and embracing of the Reformed Kirk took care of fighting amongst ourselves."

"Will you refrain from interrupting me?" asked Mary pointedly. "With peace in our land, we can once again look beyond our shores. Foreign ambassadors will be posted here, we will be included in councils abroad, artists will come, Scots will travel . . ." Her voice trailed off. The men were stony-faced.

"Do you mean that you see greatness only in terms of diplomatic postings and artistic entertainments?" Bothwell asked quietly.

"Scotland has rejected such fripperies!" said Lord James.

"Yes, it smacks of something Henry VIII would have wanted—banquets, singing minstrels, lovelorn poets!" said Morton. "Or the *French*."

"I did not mean that," said Mary. "Clearly we must set our house in order first. That is why I wish you, Lord Bothwell, to take up your duties as Lieutenant of the Borders and depart immediately. There must be peace throughout Scotland; there cannot be one area where thieving and robbery are rampant."

Bothwell looked surprised, but pleased. "Yes, Your Majesty. Straightway."

"And I am sending Maitland to London to confer with Queen Elizabeth," she said. "It is time that our differences were settled."

Lord James looked surprised and confused.

"Then I wish to depart for a small journey around my realm," she said. "It is time I saw more than just Edinburgh and heard more than John Knox. I am anxious to see the countryside. Not all of you need accompany me— just you, Lord James, and you, Huntly. And Morton, you may inform John Knox that I command his presence at Holyrood when I return."

Morton's beard flapped down as his mouth opened.

"My dearest sovereign and sister," said Lord James, "it is now our pleasure to invite you to a special banquet. You may tell us if it is what you have in mind for restoring Scotland's lost glories and customs."

Now it was Mary who was taken unawares. Her brother was full of surprises.

The banquet was to be held in the other wing of Holyrood, where high-ranking courtiers were assigned quarters. Lord James, as acting regent, had appropriated a suite, and now he saw fit to have the banquet served in the large, double-aisled chamber directly beneath his rooms.

Mary remarked as she changed her clothing, "I have never been a guest in my own palace before!"

But Lord George Seton assured her it was quite in order. "It's a custom here," he said.

The Queen and her ladies took their places at the high table, along with Lord James, Maitland, and Huntly, and Mary looked around the room curiously. There was nothing particularly unusual about it, and the goblets and platters seemed very similar to those in France.

Lord James rose and lifted his hands. "Let us give thanks to the Lord for having brought our Sovereign Queen safe to her own shores," he said. All present—except Mary's party—instantly bowed their heads. James rumbled on, "And vouchsafe, O Lord Almighty, that she might rule in wisdom, having a tender care for her people—"

"Amen," everyone mumbled. But no one crossed himself.

So this was what they said instead of a welcoming speech! Mary felt her cheeks flush. Everyone was looking at her. Was she supposed to lead a prayer?

"I thank you," she merely said.

Lord James nodded, and the servitors began to bring in the food. At the same time, a small group of musicians appeared at one end of the hall.

By Mary's side, a lad stood with a silver flagon, ready to pour the wine into her goblet. She nodded, and noticed what a pinkish colour the wine was. It glowed like a flower petal through the glass.

The first course, a steaming pot of soup with a peculiar odour, was presented, and ladled into her personal bowl. There were green filaments in it, and white knotty lumps. When she tried to bite one of the lumps, it was spongy and impossible to cut through. The green threads were slimy. What *was* this? She attempted to swallow the mouthful of round objects whole, and they almost got stuck in her throat.

Lord James, seated next to her, was looking. "Is it not refreshing?" he asked. "It is cockle stew, with seaweed." Another servitor was approaching. "Ah, here's the Dunfermline dumplings!"

A pale, bloated, spherical lump lay with its fellows on a platter, arranged in a pinwheel. Resolutely Mary allowed one to be speared for her and placed on her platter.

"It needs this sauce," said James, and a boy stepped over with a bowl of clotted something.

Mary attempted to cut it, and it slithered around her plate, leaving a watery trail oozing from its innards. She smiled weakly. Just then a dish of baked lampreys was presented, followed by a gritty, grey mound. Both were heaped on her platter, covering up the dumpling. Mary poked at the granular bastion.

"What is this?" she asked James.

" 'Tis made from pig's liver and caul," he said, smiling. "And here comes the powsowdie—it has a sheep's head in it."

Mary half expected to see an eyeless head peering out over the rim of the bowl. She suppressed a shudder.

Just then a blast of screeching music jolted her out of her chair. It rose to a crescendo and then wailed off in a whimper. It sounded like a supernatural scream.

"The bagpipes," said James. "They are played by squeezing a bag and sending the air out through the pipes. It has a different sound than your delicate French *cornemuse*, which looks similar but has no strength at all!"

Then some of the other musicians joined in, playing instruments she was more familiar with, like the shawm, the lute, and the pipe and whistle. But the bagpipe blasted forth again, drowning them out.

Mary took a sip of her wine and was horrified to find it tasted musty. She held up the glass and looked at it.

"Beetroot wine, Your Majesty," said Lord James. "As you know, grapes do not grow here. We must make do."

Suddenly the bagpiper began screeching frantically. A cohort of men had appeared at the entrance to the hall, and they carried a large silver platter reverently. Everyone rose from the table. Mary followed suit. The mysterious object was borne around the room, steam rising from it.

"The haggis," said Lord James. "Something only true Scotsmen can appreciate." He paused, before explaining, "It contains the heart, lungs, and liver of a sheep, boiled in intestine. With suet and oatmeal, of course."

Of course.

Everyone was looking at the haggis in profound admiration, before being reseated and taking a helping. A steaming spoonful was put on Mary's plate, and she took a substantial bite. It was not worse than the cockles. In fact, it was better, for at least it yielded to teeth.

"Ah, now I know you're a true Scot!" said James.

Only then did Mary look around and notice that all the men were eating with their own daggers. Evidently they carried them at all times and used them as they pleased, even at formal banquets. She also noticed how few of the men seemed to have wives present. Was this a nation of bachelors? Lord James himself, of course, was not married. But neither, evidently, was Maitland, or the Earl of Argyll, or Bothwell. Or young Hamilton, the Earl of Arran. How curious. And these were all men in their late twenties or early thirties, certainly well old enough.

After the blood pudding had been passed, it was time for the final course, of sweets. Mary expected that here, at least, she would be on familiar ground. But no: along came something that James assured her was a lard cake—charming name—and a whisky cake.

Then, as the crumbs were being scraped up, the bagpipe screamed again and this time flagons and bottles were borne in and several were placed on each table.

" 'Tis courtesy of the Earl of Atholl, from his estates in the Highlands, and from the Earl of Huntly, who also has lands in the north, that we are privileged to taste this heavenly brew tonight. Whisky!" Lord James held aloft a bottle of deep brown liquid.

Mary had heard of this strong drink. "Is it what they brew out of heather?" she asked.

"No," said Huntly. " 'Tis brewed from the running streams of our Highland water, and good grain, and has the flavour of peat in it. 'Tis unlike anything of this earth."

"What he means is, he plans to drink barrels of it in heaven!" cried Morton.

"His stuff is fit for hell!" said Argyll. "It is *my* whisky they drink in heaven!"

"Compare, then, compare!"

Tiny glasses were filled with a sample of each type. Mary was surprised how small the glasses were—they held so much less than a wine goblet. She raised one to her lips and sipped. It filled her mouth with a burning sweetness, deep and compelling, yet searing. It burned all the way down into her stomach. But the taste it left in the mouth was comforting, calling for another sip. Its flavour was like nothing she had ever tasted, and it was so much stronger than wine it seemed another creature altogether.

She tried the glass of the Earl of Argyll's brew, and immediately discerned that, beneath the fiery taste, the flavour was slightly different, deeper, smokier.

After only the two small samples, her head began to feel different inside. Resolutely she refused any more, partly out of fear. But she saw the men refilling their glasses without hesitation.

The drinking continued for what seemed a very long time, with the noise of conversation rising, until a thin woman with reddish braids took her place at the end of the room. She was holding a harp, but of an unusual size and shape: it was smoothly curved and could be held easily. She plucked the strings like a mother caressing her child's head, and began singing in the clear perfect tones one imagined came only from angels. Immediately the room hushed.

> " 'I'll set my foot in a bottomless ship,
>   Mother lady, mother lady:
> I'll set my foot in a bottomless ship,
>   And ye'll never see mair o' me.'

> " 'What wilt thou leave to thy poor
>   wife,
>   Son Davie, son Davie?'
> 'Grief and sorrow all her life,
>   And she'll never see mair o' me.' "

Some of the Lords were weeping! Was it the whisky had done it? Or the plaintive song? It was disconcerting to see these warriors, still clutching their daggers, moved to tears over a song.

In the meantime, the French were looking embarrassed. The Duc d'Aumale had a smirk on his face, and she was strangely disappointed in him.

"Thank you, Mistress Jean," said Lord James. He turned to the company.

157

"Although the Kirk frowns on frivolous music, on dancing and masquing, good honest songs from our people are to be treasured."

"Aye! Aye!" they all cried resoundingly.

Mary looked around at this company of fierce men—fierce in their joy and their eating and their drinking. She was sober herself, but despite the lack of whisky in her veins, she felt something within her very self that answered them.

VI

The day was fair and green when Mary rode out, with a party of some fifty persons, to visit the scenes of her childhood in Scotland. They left Edinburgh, riding west along the Firth of Forth as it narrowed. The weather was the September tease of sparkling clear skies chased by quickly moving grey clouds; before they had reached Linlithgow, only eighteen miles from Edinburgh, they had been rained on three times, and dried out in between each shower.

The sun was out as they passed through the old market town near the palace, and then, suddenly, they came upon the arched outer gateway with medallions depicting the four orders of knighthood. They rode farther up a slight incline, and then the entire palace revealed itself to them, golden and tall and elegant against the jewel-blue sky.

"Oh!" Mary said, halting her horse. It was beautiful—as beautiful as anything in France.

The palace was five storeys high, and built around an open courtyard. They dismounted and entered, finding themselves in a large open space surrounded by graceful crenellated walls and six-storey towers at each corner. At the very centre of the courtyard stood an ornate, massive fountain of many levels.

"Our royal father brought French workmen to construct it," said Lord James, standing beside her, pointing to the fountain.

"I was born here," she said. "Where is the room?"

"Why, in the Queen's apartments, of course," he said. "They overlook the loch. Come."

He led her up the great staircase in one of the towers, then through the empty and quiet apartments until finally they stood in the very room, a corner one.

She looked about, in the small room with the high windows. There was an oratory, and its windows looked out onto the bright blue loch.

"So . . . this is the place where I was born," she finally said.

"Indeed. And baptized at St. Michael's Church, just inside the grounds," he said.

She wished to see the church, to look at the font where she had been baptized, but not in front of this heretic. She would return later.

"This is a luxurious palace," he said. "Tiles imported from Flanders . . . a great hall that Parliament met in, oak-panelled rooms . . . it is the most fashionable palace Scotland has to offer you."

"I can see that." She hoped the French would be satisfied.

The next day they set out for Stirling, thirty-seven miles west of Edinburgh, still following the Firth of Forth as it narrowed and finally turned from a bay into a river. They were treading on historic ground, where Robert the Bruce, her ancestor nine generations back, had trounced the English at the Battle of Bannockburn and saved Scottish sovereignty at the very base of Stirling. Here was located the only bridge crossing the Forth. Lower than Stirling there were only ferries; higher than Stirling the fords were in the mountainous and dangerous country. Stirling controlled the bridge and hence the entire valley and the glens leading into the Highlands. The key to Scotland, Stirling was called.

From many miles away they could see the great rock that held Stirling Castle two hundred and fifty feet above the plain. Although Mary did not recognize it from a distance, as they began the long, steep climb up its path, and finally reached its courtyard, separate memories began to coalesce and come back to her.

She walked wonderingly across the upper courtyard square and looked at the palace, built with stone as grey as the crags it sat on, and studied all the statues standing in their ornamental niches along the walls.

She remembered the statues! Yes, she did! And there was one, on the other side of the palace, that Lady Fleming had told her was her father. As a child she had stared at it for a long time, trying to make it move and talk. Now she stood before it, examining the dark carved stone. It was not a lifelike image and it told her nothing about her father. Its eyes were large and accusing, its face frowning; it looked condemnatory, like John Knox.

Looking down at the gardens far below, she asked Lusty, "Do you remember our pony races around them, racing around the King's Knot?" She did remember that, and remembered sledding down the steep hill on a cow's skull on winter afternoons.

But as she was guided through the palace, and finally took her rest in the Queen's bedchamber—the King's stood empty, even though it was grander—with her Marys and Madame Rallay, she was distressed that so little of it felt familiar. Her memories were scattered and sparse.

The next morning she wished to see the Chapel Royal and the splendid Great Hall flanking the palace across the courtyard. The Chapel Royal was distressingly bare—the Reformers again!—but the Great Hall was magnificent. It had a high ceiling of hammerbeam timberwork and several fireplaces along its walls, with viewing balconies high above the floor. It was some hundred feet long.

I could celebrate my marriage here, she thought. I could be married in the Chapel Royal, and then have a banquet and masques here. . . . As she thought of it, the empty hall became filled with flaming torches and throngs of people; music sounded sweetly above the din of voices, and she saw herself dancing. . . .

Married! she thought. Married to whom? Not one of my subjects, surely. And were I to marry a prince from Europe, it would never be here!

This time last year, François and I were hunting the wild boar in the forest near Orleans. . . . O François! she cried silently. She felt guilt at having, even for a moment, pictured herself at a second wedding.

They stayed only two days at Stirling, and then, crossing the old stone bridge across the Forth, they set out through the valley leading in a northeast slant toward the town of Perth, which was situated at the very end of the Firth of Tay, where it dwindled into a river, directly above Edinburgh's Firth of Forth.

The Tay was smaller than the Forth, and Perth itself was a small town, although it stood near the old site of Scone, where the sacred Coronation Stone of Scotland had once been. Legend said it had been brought long ago from Ireland; it was no matter now, as the stone had been carried off by Edward I of England and was now in Westminster Abbey. The town of Perth, once the capital of Scotland, had likewise undergone some fundamental changes. It was here, in St. John's Church, that John Knox had preached his inflammatory sermon two years ago that had started the looting and destruction.

John Knox! He would be waiting for her in Edinburgh, doubtless with his Bible in one hand and his sword in the other. She dreaded the moment when she would have to take him on, but she would not allow herself to practise for it.

Her heart was heavy as she rode past the damaged buildings, and in spite of the gracious reception of the townspeople, she could not help wondering if she was truly welcome. A chill had come over the day.

And she could hear Lord James and Huntly arguing about something, although she could not make out their words. James's lips seemed to shrink as they struggled to hold in his anger, while Huntly's face grew redder and redder.

That evening, after supper, she insisted on knowing what it was.

"Huntly keeps muttering about allowing the mass to be said again, in certain shires," said Lord James.

"I said it was not right for it not to be! There are still Catholics in the land; Parliament could not force us to convert!" yelled Huntly.

"Please!" said Mary. "In the future, do not give scandal by openly quarreling in front of the townspeople. Wait until you are safely within private walls."

160

"You yourself give scandal!" blurted out James.

She was genuinely shocked. "How so?"

"It is not meet here in Scotland for you to ride sidesaddle in a manner to show your legs! It is unseemly, and seems lewd!"

Relieved, Mary began to laugh. Was that all it was? But later she thought of his words, and wondered whether she might cause inadvertent offence in other of her actions. As late as it was (possibly another offence?) she sent for James Melville with a special request in mind.

When the courtier arrived in her chamber, she held out her hands to him. He seemed loath to take them. He merely stood back and bowed deeply.

"Ah, Melville! We have known each other too long to be ill at ease with one another," she said. "Is it not so?" James Melville, who was about Lord James's age, had come with her to France and been trained there, although he had also served in German courts and taken his turn at soldiering in Scotland. As a result, he was one of the more sophisticated men in the Scottish court, and she assumed he would be an ally for her.

"What is it you wish, Your Majesty?" he asked.

"It is simple," she said. "I am unfamiliar with customs here and may, with the best of intentions but through simple ignorance, give offence from time to time. For example, obviously you did not wish to take my hands. Not that I think you were offended!" she hurried to assure him. "But other acts, meant innocently, may not be taken so innocently."

He was looking at her curiously, his attractive face open and pleasant. In fact, if one had to choose a word to describe him, she thought, one should say "pleasing."

"I do not understand. I have not been offended."

"I believe I may have given offence today in Perth, but I am not sure. Lord James made a remark. . . . Be that as it may, I would like to ask you to assume the office of my monitor. Good Melville, I ask you to please take it upon yourself to tell me if I am at any time giving offence by my speech, dress, or habits. Lord James said the way I rode sidesaddle was not seemly."

Melville looked embarrassed. "It did seem a bit . . . provocative. To the people here, I mean! You and I know that Catherine de Médicis has shown her legs that way for years," he said knowingly.

"That is precisely what I mean, Melville. Customs vary, and I wish to be correct here in all I do. In minor matters of etiquette, that is! I do not mean in matters of conscience. Now, do you promise always to inform me?" She sounded playful, but she was serious.

"I—I will try."

"And not be bashful about it? Remember, you will be doing me a great service."

"I—yes. Well, I might as well begin now. Here in Scotland, the monarch does not clasp hands with his servants, nor lean on them, nor touch them overmuch." He paused. "It could be taken amiss. Of course, you and I know better. . . ."

* * *

From Perth the party journeyed briefly to Dundee, a town also situated on the Tay, but nearer its mouth, and from there crossed over the Tay into the region of Fife, which lay between the Firths of Tay and Forth, and which from ancient times had been a kingdom unto itself.

All along the journey, Mary had been struck by the clean greenness of Scotland, with its empty, treeless tracts and its hundreds of little lochs. Forests that were cut down here took a long time to grow back. All the colours were soft, often blurred by mists, except for that vibrant green which seemed to shine through everything.

There seemed to be few people to walk these expanses, and few farmers to till around the grey boulders that were strewn everywhere. Overhead the sky was huge and the weather changed from moment to moment. Clouds in the west raced across the sky, rained, and passed on in less than an hour.

Scattered here and there, rearing up over the rugged landscape, Mary saw square towers. They were completely isolated, sticking up like thick fingers.

"Tower-houses," Huntly explained. "Purely defensive."

There had never been anything like them in France, strongholds without a castle. But this land was closer to the struggle for survival.

But it was strangely beautiful, with its odd diffuse light and its muted range of colours, the still lochs reflecting silver and grey from the sky. "What a fair land this is!" she said to Lord James, as they rode along a rutted path. The sea was seldom out of view; she could glimpse it, sparkling and flat, off to her left.

She was struck with the thought that, if white was the colour of France, green, grey, silver, and brown were the colours of Scotland. The rocks, the very base of the land itself, were grey in all its variations: from the palest speckled pebbles to the almost-black jagged rocks singing in the sea. These stones were the only building materials, so that the castles were grey, the little cottages were grey, and the paved streets were grey. But so many shades of it! Grey itself began to look rich and mysterious.

And the browns! There were brown sheep, and a deep ashen-hued wool that came from them, woven in the people's garments. The hills were dun-brown with bare patches, and the fierce little terriers were drab brown. Cottages were topped by pale brown thatch, bogs were greenish-brown, and the bracken and reeds were brown. Even the whisky had been a lively brown!

Lying like a patina over the browns and greys was the silver, for both these colours could shade off into a misty translucent version of itself, so that the sedge could have a pearly sheen to it, and the walls of a castle be wreathed in a luminescence. The lochs, reflecting a tranquil sky, looked like oddly shaped mirrors lying on the land where some careless lady had left them.

Swirling around these plain, honest colours was the ever-present, transcendent green that seemed to appear in such unexpected places, such as in

162

the cracks between the stones of any building, and which lay like a mist over all the land.

In the autumn, another colour briefly held sway, coating the hills with soft purple: the blooming heather. And there were the tiny touches of orange—wildflowers, autumnal brush, fresh-cooked salmon, the flaming hair of one person in a crowd—to catch the eye.

The people lived, for the most part, in sad little stone cottages without even fences around them. They would emerge from their doorways to gape at Mary and her party, to wave shyly at them. They were a sturdy people, and Mary was struck by how often she saw reddish hair and freckled faces among them.

"They don't usually own their land or cottages," Lord James explained, "and so they've no reason to put up fences or make improvements. Pity!"

Yes, it was. Was this what it meant to be a poor country? Mary wondered what could be done to improve their circumstances. But how could a country, such a small one, cease to be poor? Scotland had only about one-twentieth the population of France, and it was so far north. Unless gold were discovered, how could Scotland ever improve its lot?

After they crossed over into Fife, the landscape became gentler and lusher.

"This is the soft, friendly side of Scotland," said Lord James. "Over on the western side, with the isles, it's cold and bleak. Farther north, too, beyond the glens and in the Highlands, the people are different. They live in their mountain fastnesses and keep to their own clans, free from interference. They are for the most part still Catholic. Or so they call themselves. But the truth is, they're still pagan."

"Has a king ever visited them?" she asked.

"Our father made a sea-journey up to the Orkneys and then down along the western coast. But no, no ruler has ever gone into their mountains. They speak a separate tongue and they probably would have no idea who he was. They only know their own clan chiefs."

Seeing St. Andrews made Mary sad, for it was in the cathedral—completely ruined by the Reformers—where her mother and father had had their marriage blessed. Just across the way lay the castle where the murdered Cardinal Beaton had been displayed. St. Andrews was now a shrine to the Protestant revolution.

The town would have been pleasing otherwise, for it was situated dramatically on cliffs overlooking the restless, noisy sea, and the sound of the waves and gulls flooded the bracing air. But Mary was glad to put it behind her and strike out for Falkland Palace.

They rode through quiet forests—here in Fife were royal hunting preserves—until at last they saw the walls and towers of the palace. It lay basking and golden in the late afternoon sun, stretched out in the hollow like a dozing lion. Behind it was a dense forest.

"Look! Look!" Mary called to Mary Beaton. The golden-haired Beaton rode up to her mistress and looked eagerly where the Queen was pointing.

" 'Tis your home from long ago," said Mary.

Mary Beaton stared at it, trying to remember ever having seen it before. Her father was hereditary Keeper of Falkland Palace, and she had been born there. But since the age of four she had been with her namesake and Queen.

"How odd it feels to come home to a place one cannot remember," she finally said.

VII

William Maitland stood waiting. But not anxiously! he assured himself. No, not anxiously.

It will be gratifying to see Cecil again, he said to himself in his calmest tones. I enjoyed our previous meetings, and his wife was most gracious. After all, it is not as if this were my first diplomatic mission to London.

But it was his first for a face-to-face meeting with the English Queen. And he was curious about her, she who had excited so many tongues and sparked so many debates, not the least of which was whether she was entitled to sit on the throne of England at all. There *was* the matter of that charge of bastardy. . . .

Maitland was neatly attired in a sombre blackish brown velvet suit that he had had made by Edinburgh's finest tailor. He called it his "diplomatic suit," because it was sedate enough to please those of a joyless religious persuasion and yet sophisticated enough to meet the approval of a Parisian. The stitching and the material were the finest, enough to deflect all critical eyes that might seek to discern Scotland's financial woes in the costume of its chief secretary.

His mission had been made clear to him: to come to an understanding with Elizabeth and arrange for a meeting between the two Queens. It sounded simple but was not.

He caught himself pacing. This would not do. He forced himself to look at the linenfold panelling on the walls, to examine the catch on the windows, to stare with intent interest at the Thames rolling by, its surface covered with small boats and its banks lined with people fishing. It was a glorious September day, one of those days that seemed more like summer than summer itself, and up here at Richmond, the rhythm of the countryside was more apparent than in London. He could even see fields stretching away in the distance and, on another side, the royal hunting forest that

164

was still deep green, as if it had no intention of dropping its leaves for winter.

"Her Majesty will see you now."

Maitland turned around with a start. The door had been opened and a guard was holding it back, while a secretary was peering out. He made his way into the beckoning chamber, remembering all that he had to achieve.

Elizabeth was there, standing, her hands clasped before her. His first thought was how small she was; he had become used to Mary's height.

"Your Majesty." He bowed low. "Most glorious Queen, I bring you sisterly greetings from my sovereign Queen of Scotland."

"I am pleased."

From his vantage point he could see her long, white fingers—very like Mary's—motioning him to rise. He did so quickly, and saw her smiling at him.

He tried to keep the scrutiny out of his manner, but he noted everything about her.

"These are my most trusted councillors, William Cecil"—Cecil nodded—"and Robert Dudley." Dudley also inclined his head.

"I have had the privilege of working with Mr. Secretary Cecil before," said Maitland.

"Indeed, yes, during the Regent's time of office. It is a pleasure." Cecil acted as though it were true. Perhaps it was. Cecil himself was agreeable to work with, being very well organized and coming quickly to the point, and he was a shrewd judge of character as well. As for Dudley, Maitland was eager to behold this lover who seemed to offer women something of which he, Maitland, was ignorant.

"I am curious about my famous cousin the Queen of Scotland," Elizabeth said bluntly. "To be frank, ever since she was born she has been an object of interest to me."

Maitland looked at her admiringly. The thin, red-haired woman knew well how to put others on the defensive, and to come directly to the point.

"I believe she is curious about you, as well," he said. "She would welcome a meeting, so you could behold one another face to face. But in the meantime, she wishes to exchange portraits."

He had meant to present his mistress's gift at a more opportune time, not at the very beginning of the interview. But it seemed appropriate now, and so he was forced to give Elizabeth the miniature he had carried with him.

She unwrapped it, folding back the bright blue French silk enclosing it. The miniature showed an oval face with guarded eyes, lips with the merest hint of a smile, a bit of reddish brown hair peeking out beneath a white headdress. She looked like a very young nun, a girl who had taken the veil in the throes of promised religious ecstasy.

"Is this a true likeness?" she asked Maitland.

He took it back and looked at it carefully, his intelligent brown eyes narrowed.

"Yes, and no," he finally said. "It was painted when my Queen was in mourning for both her mother and her father-in-law. The white veil is the French *deuil*. She was weighted with sorrow, and that shows upon her countenance. She is much more beautiful than that, for her beauty is joined with motion and spirit."

"These deaths made her doubly a queen, did they not?" asked Elizabeth. "Therefore her sorrow must have been ameliorated somewhat."

"She mourned them greatly," Maitland replied. "And within a few months more, she had to mourn her husband's death. Three blows within eighteen months—"

"These blows brought her back to Scotland." Elizabeth motioned for him to seat himself. He did, gratefully. Standing for long periods of time hurt his knees. Cecil and Dudley took seats also. "For which the people must surely rejoice."

Was that a question? Only if he cared to treat it as such, he decided. "Indeed they do. It has been long since we have had a sovereign with us. A regent," he said, "is not the same."

"So it would appear." Elizabeth sat back and folded her hands. She stared at him with her black, birdlike eyes.

Cecil leaned forward. "Dear Mr. Secretary," he began, "when last I wrote to you, in Scotland, you assured me that your Queen would approve the treaty we so laboriously contrived, regarding the French, the English, and the Scots. We have abided by our word; we have withdrawn from Scotland. The French likewise. But your Queen has never ratified it, giving, quite frankly, vague and flimsy reasons. As you know, she was to renounce her pretensions to the throne of our glorious Queen here present."

Maitland welcomed the opening. He smoothed his sleek beard, so evenly trimmed; he was quite proud of it. "That is because, as the treaty was written, my dear Queen was obliged to surrender not only any present claim to the throne of England, but also any rights to the succession, even if you—God forbid!—died without leaving heirs. That she cannot do, in good conscience. For that would mean renouncing the rights of her successors—which, God be willing, she will be granted—regardless of how they might be needed should the occasion require."

"What occasion?" Dudley asked suddenly. His voice was loud, and bordered on the blustering. This was attractive to women?

"Neither of these fair Queens is wed," replied Maitland, in his smoothest, most soothing tone. "In the next generation, who will rule, failing an heir on either side? It is only prudent that each could step in to save the throne of the other in such straits."

"Prudent!" snorted Elizabeth. "Dangerous temptation! Not that *I* am tempted by Scotland, mind you!"

"But your son might be," said Dudley. "And if Mary were childless—"

"Exactly. Or vice versa," said Maitland. "You should choose each other's kin before all others. You do not want to resort to strangers."

"Mary Stuart is a stranger," Elizabeth said stubbornly.

"Not by blood," Maitland persisted. "And if you would agree to a meeting, that would end such concerns."

"Oh, I agree to a meeting," said Elizabeth airily.

"When?" Maitland pressed.

"Not until after the next Parliament," Cecil cautioned. "You must not leave until then."

"Next summer, then," said Elizabeth. "We can meet . . . somewhere in the north. Perhaps Nottingham?"

"She will meet you anywhere, and gladly," said Maitland. He hoped he was right. "In July, then?"

"August. I can combine it with a progress."

Both wily Cecil and handsome Dudley looked surprised.

"The young Duke of Norfolk will have to provide the hospitality and entertainment, then," said Dudley. "Who else is up there? The Earl of Northumberland, the Earl of Westmoreland . . . but they are so unpractised."

"Therefore more resourceful and resilient," said Cecil.

There was amiable chuckling all around. Elizabeth motioned to one of her ladies, and soon a servitor appeared with a bowl of crystal, a plate of flat bread, and glasses of fresh cider.

"The autumn has been generous," said Elizabeth. She took a glass and sipped from it.

Maitland realized with horror that the interview was at an end, and he had not yet received an answer to his main business.

"This blackberry comfit is made from berries brought me by my dear Robert," said Elizabeth, indicating the contents of the crystal bowl. She smiled at him.

Maitland helped himself to the bread and comfit only after Cecil and Dudley had partaken. He made sure to eat slowly and give no hint of haste. At length he wiped his mouth with his linen handkerchief.

"Most gracious Queen, to continue on the topic of such interest to us all: my mistress will gladly sign the Treaty of Edinburgh if it is amended to recognize her now as your successor to the throne—failing your own issue, that is."

Elizabeth turned and stared at him. There was nothing soft or dainty about her face now; her mouth grew so tight and small it looked like an old scar.

"What! Think you I could love my own winding sheet?" she finally said, in a low hiss. "The moment I name Mary Stuart my heir, I should be forced to hate her, as every time I looked at her"—she glared at the miniature— "I would be seeing deep into my grave."

"So must everyone think who makes a will," Dudley said lightly. "Yet lawyers tell us we must. Sure, 'tis unpleasant to read those too-explicit phrases: 'upon the moment of my death,' 'within ten days of my death,' 'my body shall be embalmed with,' yet we shudder and sign, because not to do so is . . . irresponsible."

"Robert!" she snapped. "Do you say—do you *imply*—that I am irresponsible toward my throne and my people?"

"To refuse to marry and refuse to name an heir . . . yes, it is irresponsible!"

"Ah!" Elizabeth cried in exasperation.

She must truly love him, thought Maitland. No one else could dare speak to her in such a manner. Yet it is needful. Perhaps . . . thank God for Dudley?

"Robert!" She laughed and caressed his hair.

Maitland was shocked.

"You know that cannot be," she said fondly. Then, quickly, she was as imperious as before. "The moment I name my heir," she said seriously to Maitland, "I lose control. *Plures adorat solem orientem quam occidentem.* Most people are ever prone to worship the rising rather than the setting sun. The heir becomes the focus of all the unfulfilled dreams of the people. I saw it in my sister's reign, when *I* was the heir. Let me explain something to you."

She drew Maitland off into an alcove of the chamber, where there was a window seat, well furnished with cushions. She sat, and indicated that he was to do likewise.

"A future ruler is a dream," she said. "A present ruler is the waking world. Children dream of apples in December, and cry when they awaken and have none. Just so subjects will dream of what a prince will give them when he comes into his inheritance, and cry when they find it is but a lost dream. For I tell you this: there is no prince living, or who ever lived, including Solomon, who is rich enough to satisfy the cupidity of the people. So subjects always long for the future prince, and never love the present one according to his deserts. Unless the present one is their only hope."

How well she understands the ugliness of human nature, thought Maitland. Yet if she refuses to marry, she will eventually undo her people. For no one lives forever to be anyone's only hope.

"I see," he said.

"However, if at this moment I were *forced* to choose an heir, I should choose Mary Stuart above all others," she said unexpectedly. "I prefer not to choose, but if I were *forced* to . . ." She arched her thin, pale eyebrows.

"Are you willing to commit that to paper? I fear my mistress will ask me to repeat it so often my brain will wear out."

"It looks healthy enough to bear a few repetitions," said Elizabeth, smiling. The smile changed her face and made her look mysterious and fetching. Even her sharp, dark eyes seemed sympathetic rather than interrogating. "And no, I will not put it in writing. Your Queen must trust your memory and my intentions. Besides, soon enough she will be able to ask me face to face. Just a few months! In the meantime, tell her I will send her a portrait soon, and I give her this diamond friendship ring."

She pulled a ring off her finger. It was a double ring, made in two intertwined parts: two hands clasped two diamonds in the middle, which together formed a heart. She separated the two parts and gave one to Maitland.

"This is an English custom," she explained. "If the Queen of Scots would be my heir, she must begin to understand English customs. We give a diamond ring that fits a mate. It can be returned to the giver in time of distress, to presume upon the friendship. When the two halves are fitted together again, then I am obligated to come to her aid."

"She will be deeply honoured," said Maitland, examining the ring.

"Tell her not to presume upon it, nor to return it to me for a trifle, like Master Knox," said Elizabeth, laughing and rising. The interview was at an end.

VIII

Mary felt her hat fly off as she galloped through the forest of Falkland on this last day of October. It lifted and spun like one of the leaves falling lazily, landing—who knew where? At the same time her hair came loose and streamed out behind her, like an untidy schoolgirl's. Panting and laughing, she kept on riding, not slowing to let the rest of her party catch up.

The French were, she knew, comparing this forest to the ones at Chambord and Fontainebleau, and she did not want to stop and let them make snide remarks to her about Falkland. This was *her* forest, and a forest that her father had loved, and by now the Frenchmen—her uncles the Marquis d'Elboeuf, the Duc d'Aumale, and the Grand Prior François, as well as the writers Brantôme and Chastelard who had accompanied them—seemed like intruders. Or rather, people she had to pretend in front of. And she disliked always having to defend Scotland to them. The unkind thoughts she herself harboured she kept to herself, for the courtiers would magnify them and report them gleefully to Catherine de Médicis.

She caught herself using the word *gleefully* and felt ashamed. That is my own interpretation, she thought. I cannot know how they really feel. But I know I will be relieved when they return to France.

Now she reined in her horse on an open knoll and let the others catch up to her. The great forest of Falkland, beneath the Lomond Hills, spread out golden on all sides of her. Down in the hollow the hounds were baying—had they cornered something? She and her party had already taken a roe and several hares and had no need of more today. Besides, the sun was halfway down the sky, and they had all been warned that they should be back at the palace well before dark on this night of all nights.

"Hallowe'en," Mary Beaton's father had intoned ominously.

When Mary showed no recognition of the word, he had shaken his head. "The worst night of the year for God-fearing men . . . it's the beginning of the dark time of year, and the devil and witches celebrate. Stay indoors."

The French had shrugged their shoulders and laughed.

But Mary Beaton had whispered to her mistress. "My aunt is a witch. Lady Janet Beaton—she bewitched Bothwell and took him for a lover, and she a married woman twenty years older, with seven children! Now she's old, but doesn't look it. She has the face of a young maiden."

"Is he still—are they . . . ?" asked Mary. Bothwell! A witch's lover . . . It made him, suddenly, an object of curiosity.

"I do not know. I imagine they must meet at least occasionally for old times' sake. A spell of witchcraft cannot always be broken."

Mary Fleming had overheard the exchange and, tossing her head, looked scornful. "Mr. Maitland says all that is nonsense, and is used only to frighten superstitious, simple people and bend them to one's will."

"Oh, Mr. Maitland?" said Beaton. "Aren't you formal about him?"

Flamina looked embarrassed—something that happened rarely. She had found herself drawn to him, and liked to believe that he was attracted to her, as most men were.

"I heard he was an atheist," Beaton persisted. "That he said God was a bogey of the nursery."

"No one is an atheist!" said Flamina. "What a vile thing to say about him!"

Maitland. Atheist or no, he was an able diplomat. Mary was anxious for Maitland's return, probably more eager than Flamina, for politics could be as exciting as love.

Now young René, Marquis d'Elboeuf, came up to her, his horse all in a lather.

"By the Virgin! What are you doing?" he said. "Must you ride like the— what do they call it here?—the banshee?"

Chastelard galloped up, clutching her hat. "Here, Madam. I had to climb down a ravine to rescue it." He handed it to her, his eyes accusing.

"Make a verse about it, Chastelard," said René. "Tell of your undying love for the *cruelle princesse.*"

Chastelard did not smile.

"Let us return," said Mary. "It grows late." She replaced the hat on her head and nodded her thanks to Chastelard. He continued staring at her. What did he expect—a reward?

The sun was bathing the voluptuously rounded gatehouse towers of the palace in dying red light when the hunting party trotted into the courtyard.

"Have we time for a game of tennis?" asked the Duc d'Aumale, hopping off his horse.

"It will be dark in less than an hour," said Lord James. "Have you not had enough playtime and exercise for one day?" He himself was anxious to get to his desk, piled high with papers; and he had secret correspondence to get off to Cecil.

"*Mais oui*, but it is such a fair court!"

Lake a gang of children, the Guises and the poets dashed across the lawn to the stone-walled *jeu quarré* tennis court. It resembled a large, high-roofed black box with a net stretched across the middle.

"It seems our father was not to be outdone by his uncle," said James to Mary. "I have seen Henry VIII's famous tennis court at Hampton Court, and this is better."

"Ah." Mary watched as the four Frenchmen threw off their riding cloaks and tossed their hats on the ground to begin playing. Little René gathered up the leaves that were lying on the black polished floor.

"Perhaps I will learn to play!" she called to them.

"Women do not play tennis!" cried Brantôme.

"My Marys and I will practice in private here, behind the high walls," said Mary with a laugh.

"Then you will be as scandalous as Master Knox makes you out to be," said Mary Seton, standing quietly beside her.

"Good!" said Mary.

"Have a care, dear sister," said Lord James. "Do not provoke Knox. Remember the Scripture: 'Abstain from all appearance of evil.' "

"So tennis is evil? Fie!"

"A woman cannot play tennis unless she dresses herself in men's clothes, and that is an abomination unto the Lord."

Mary burst out laughing.

"Deuteronomy twenty-two, five," intoned Lord James. "And I pray that the sound of your laughter at the Scripture does not carry beyond these walls."

"Why, how could it? Unless someone reported it? See, the laughter has already gone, carried away on the wind."

Lord James sighed. "I leave you to this amusement. I have work to do." He glanced up at the sky, laced with purple clouds in hovering shapes. "Do not linger here much longer."

A sudden rising wind soon brought an end to the game, swirling masses of leaves through the windows of the court in a vortex. Laughing and tired, the young people made their way into the palace, glad to be indoors, to have a supper of rich white soup and "friar's fish": red trout with lemons, anchovies and Rhenish wine. They sprawled in front of the great fireplace in the Queen's privy chamber and ate, washing down their food with French wine.

Soon the men decided to go to the Duc d'Aumale's chambers to play cards and backgammon, and the women were left alone, dreaming before the fire.

Mary looked at her Marys, a great feeling of protectiveness and affection sweeping over her. They sat on their stools around the fire, their heads

171

bent, each one dreaming her own, enclosed dream. Mary Seton, tall, self-possessed, the oldest of the four—of what was she dreaming? Seton had a certain seriousness of purpose that caused the others to call her "the duenna," and that kept men from being attracted to her.

Mary Fleming was restlessly moving her head. La Flamina, with her fiery temperament and flamboyant looks. She had tumbling red-brown hair, and her vitality was so marked it gave life even to colourless people she associated with.

Mary Beaton, with her golden colouring, like Midas' daughter . . . she reminded Mary of a marigold, an unshowy but very beautiful flower.

Mary Livingston was beginning to peel an apple, cutting off its skin in one long, winding strip. A little plump, with less spectacular looks than Fleming and Beaton, Lusty had an easygoing warmth that was alluringly disarming. She took the peel and threw it over her left shoulder, then jumped up to look at it, walking all around it. Finally she shrugged, looking disappointed.

"Whatever are you doing?" asked Mary, her voice the first sound to rise above the snapping of the logs in the fireplace and the rising wind outside.

"Telling my fortune. 'Tis an old Hallowe'en custom in Falkirk, where my family is from. If you throw an apple peel over your left shoulder, it reveals the initial of your future husband."

"Well, what does it say?" asked Fleming, jumping up.

"Nothing. It just lies there in a corkscrew."

"Here! Let me try!" Fleming grabbed an apple from the bowl by the fireside, and began peeling it.

"You do it," said Seton, handing Mary a large apple and a knife.

Mary stared at the apple as if it were the one offered Eve by the serpent. Then, slowly, she took the knife and began to peel a strip. When it was long enough, she gingerly tossed it over her shoulder and forced herself to go look at it.

To her relief, it also spelled nothing; nothing recognizable. It lay at crazy angles.

"Nothing." She started to pick it up.

"Wait!" Fleming got down on her knees and inspected it. "It could be an *H*."

"No, never." There were no *H*s in any of the candidates who had been paraded before her—on paper—for her hand: Don Carlos, Prince Erik of Sweden, Archduke Charles of Austria, Charles IX of France . . .

"Clearly, there is no one," said Mary, feeling relief.

"But there will be," said Flamina.

"It is not yet a year since François . . ." Mary's voice trailed off.

"You are only eighteen," said Beaton. "You must not pass your life alone."

"All the men I might marry—or rather, the children—are not appealing," replied Mary.

"We will not marry until you do!" cried Lusty. "We hereby vow. Do we not?" She stood and looked around the circle at the others. One by one they stood up, and clasped hands.

"I vow not to marry until my mistress is wed," said Beaton.

"I vow to stay unwed until my sovereign has taken a husband," said Flamina.

"I vow to keep myself only to her until that day," Seton finished.

"Ah, that is a touching but perhaps a foolish vow," said Mary. "I would not keep you from happiness."

"We will not be happy until you are." They all embraced her.

She had to smile at the brave sacrifice they had made—in advance.

"It is easy to give up something you do not yet possess," she told them. "When it is a real person, then I fear you will regret this vow. As for me, at this time, I have no wish to marry."

A great wave of loneliness swept over her at the implications of that decision. I wish there were someone . . . but not a stranger, like those men on the list . . . a companion, someone like me, not someone who shares nothing of my soul, my background, my language. . . . The Marys are lucky—just such a person is waiting for them, somewhere, whereas with me, it is all politics.

"Perhaps someone will appear who will change your mind. Overnight!" cried the impulsive Flamina. "These things happen."

"Yes, in stories," said Mary. "Not for queens, who must make arranged marriages."

"But this man, perhaps, he would spirit you away—"

A man not arranged with her councillors, a man whom she had chosen, because she wanted him, liked him—! "Get thee behind me, Satan," she said.

"What?" asked Beaton.

"I am thinking out loud." Mary smiled.

"About Satan? They say he's abroad this night, but—"

Mary laughed. "Then perhaps it is time to bid one another good night."

They gathered up their needlework and stood up.

Mary was still up, reading, near midnight when she heard the sound of someone's arrival in the courtyard, and then the voice of Maitland in the guardroom below. Quickly throwing on a mantle, she stepped out of her rooms and descended the stairs.

Maitland looked up at her with surprise. "Your Majesty." He threw off the hood of his mud-spattered cloak, and a guard closed the door behind him, shutting out the wind. A clump of leaves blew in and scudded across the floor.

"Pray come and tell me what has happened," she said. "Unless you are too weary. But I will order refreshments—how long have you ridden?"

"From London it is four days' journey without rest," he said. He climbed the stairs, and she could see the effort it required for him to lift each leg.

173

"Come, sit." She motioned to him to take the widest chair, heaped with cushions. She had her servitors add more logs to the fire and bring him a bowl of the leftover soup.

"My mother's favourite," she said. "It is made with veal mixed with tender fowl and rosemary . . . truly restorative."

Maitland was much too polite to gulp it down as he would have wished, but she waited until he was finished to begin questioning him.

"It is over?" she asked.

"Yes. I met with the Queen, and presented all our concerns." He paused. "The answer is no. She will not name you her successor."

"But—" Mary was so disappointed that she could not frame the sentence. Finally, she said, "What exact reasons did she give, when I was prepared to sign the modified treaty in return?"

"Some nonsense about naming a successor forcing her to look into her own coffin. Then some hardheaded political observations about how a successor always becomes the focus for discontented subjects in a realm. For whatever her reasons—a personal quirk, political caution—she declines to clarify the succession."

"Oh." She felt helpless and thwarted. How could Elizabeth ignore the claims of blood and custom?

"However, she said if she were *forced* to name a successor, there was none whose claims would come before yours."

"What does that mean?"

"Nothing. It is just Elizabeth-talk, for which she is already becoming renowned. She herself calls it her 'answer-answerless.' "

"Oh!" Mary's frustration was quickly turning to anger.

"She suggested a meeting between you, and also sends you this." Maitland opened his pouch and brought forth a box, which he handed her.

She took it and wrenched it open, breaking one of the clasps.

Inside was a velvet pouch, and she could feel something hard within it. She shook it out, and a ring tumbled out—it had a hand clasping a diamond.

"It is a friendship ring, Your Majesty," said Maitland. "It comes apart, and Elizabeth has retained the other half. It is to be returned to her if ever you are in distress. It obligates her to come to your aid."

"How nice." Since she would never need to use it, it was a meaningless little diplomatic bauble. She put the ring down. Then, on second thought, she slid it onto her finger, where she could see it and brood on it.

Maitland looked stuporous.

"You may go to bed," said Mary. "I apologize for keeping you from it. This could have waited until morning."

After Maitland had gone and she lay in her bed, she could hear the howling of the wind and the rattling of the tree branches on this haunted night.

They say the spirits are walking abroad, she thought. And nearby is the room where my father died, where he turned his face to the wall in despair.

Are you here, Father? If you are, help me with this difficult land you have left to me! If it is true that the dead have wisdom, impart it to me!

But her dreams were trifling and senseless, and in the morning she felt herself no wiser.

IX

The summons had come at last. John Knox, who had enjoyed the triumph of having Edinburgh to himself after his followers had been moved to defend themselves against the moral pollution of the mass, knew the day would come when the Queen must return. He had been informed that she wished to speak with him then. But in the meantime the cowardly, timorous child had run away, travelling around the realm, as if to get up her courage to speak to him.

Now she had returned, and a specific summons for his audience with her had been delivered. He had reread it several times, feeling privileged to be chosen as the Lord's instrument to confront her and show her her errors.

He could hardly wait until the prescribed hour to go to the palace. When it was within a quarter-hour of the time—he possessed an accurate clock made in his beloved Geneva, that had stood on his desk in that happy place—he set out, walking briskly down the smooth, sloping Canongate, nodding at the nobles he encountered near their town houses on either side. He strode in through the great gateway at Abbey Strand, passing into the area that still constituted sanctuary for debtors and lawbreakers—another Papist folly!—and gazed at the Frenchified round towers and the formal entrance to the palace. In there, then, the contest would take place. He prayed for strength and the right words.

From her audience chamber—the largest room in her suite of royal apartments—Mary saw Knox standing in the courtyard. He was tall and thin, and the morning sun made him cast a long shadow. He looked like the gnomon on a sundial, she thought. Then the gnomon moved, and came toward the palace doors.

Now the time was here. She would actually look this man in the face, this man who had been her mother's greatest adversary and was now hers. For so long he had seemed a demon, almost a mythological creature like the Gorgon or the manticore, that it seemed impossible that he should be mounting the stairs to her presence this very instant.

She took her place on a chair—not a throne—with her cloth of estate over her head, arranged her skirts, and waited. Her brother, Lord James, would serve as witness to the proceedings; two guards stood at either end of the chamber. A lack of sleep the night before had quickened all her senses, rather than dulling them. They seemed to quiver with readiness as she waited for his appearance. But his footsteps on the great stair outside the chamber were soft, and so she did not hear him until the door swung open and he stood upon the threshold.

"Master John Knox, pastor of the High Kirk of St. Giles, framer of the First Book of Discipline of the Congregation," announced the guard, so warmly it was obvious he was a follower.

Knox stepped into the chamber and with one motion swept his flat cap off his head and came to the very foot of her chair. "Your Majesty," he said, staring directly into her eyes. "Lord James, brother in Christ." He nodded to James, then turned his hard gaze back on Mary.

His eyes were dark brown, and were capable of staring for a long time without blinking. His face was not unkind, thought Mary. He had level eyebrows, a well-proportioned straight nose, and well-formed lips. In fact, there was nothing remarkable about his face, except that it was so ordinary; only his excessively long, flowing beard made him appear different from any middle-aged courtier. That and his severe, dark clothes: the uniform of the Reformers.

For his part, he was grudgingly forced to acknowledge her beauty. His scrutiny revealed that the portraits he had seen had duplicated her features—large, hooded, amber-coloured eyes, long, straight nose, small, curved mouth—without catching her allure. Perhaps it was the colouring, the skin tone, or the posture, or her slenderness, or perhaps . . .

"Master Knox, we sent for you because we have been troubled by your doings for some time."

The voice. Her voice was as beguiling as a sea siren's: sweet and rich and caressing. It aroused a longing to hear more words.

"You have been a rebel against our late mother the Regent, causing her great grief and sorrow; and you have written words that say a woman should not be queen. That is treason, as I *am* your Queen and sovereign, by God's grace!" Let him answer that! She was no longer afraid of him. He was just a man.

"So you have not forgotten your Scots," he said, with grudging surprise. "I feared Lord James would have to translate my words into French."

"I continued to hear Scots while I was in France. You forget, sir, that my ladies were with me, as well as certain Scotsmen from my court." If he thought he could make asides to James that she could not follow, he was sorely mistaken.

"But as for *The First Blast of the Trumpet*"—his voice changed from conversational to his pulpit tone—"for that is what I assume you refer to—indeed it specified that a woman ruler is an abomination and an aberration, but God permits such to exist for His own purposes. If the people are content to live under a woman, I will not rebel. Indeed, Madam, I am as content to live under you as Saint Paul was to live under Nero."

So she was a Nero? How could he make such a statement? "I am no tyrant, sir, as well you know! I have issued a proclamation respecting your religion, saying that no changes are to made in the religion of the country as I found it when I returned to Scotland. Have you not read it?"

Knox snorted. "Your cousin the Queen Elizabeth of England issued the exact same proclamation when she first took the throne. But within half a year she and Parliament changed the religion to the one *she* practised . . . in this case, a sort of halfway thing between the Catholics and the Reformed Kirk. So such proclamations mean nothing; they are but a cover to the ruler's true intentions, which become plain soon enough."

Mary drew herself up on her chair. "Good sir, you know that God commands subjects to obey their rulers in all things, therefore if they profess another religion than that of their sovereign, how can this be sanctioned by God?" Indeed this had troubled her, as she had no intention of changing her faith, and thought others should be accorded the same privilege.

Knox smiled. Now he had her out in the open; she had betrayed her ultimate design. "Dear Madam, you err! As Christ said to the Pharisees, you know not the Scriptures! What if Moses had submitted and followed the religion of Pharaoh? What if Daniel had embraced the faith of Nebuchadnezzar? What if—God forbid!—the Christians had obeyed the Roman emperors and returned to worshipping Jupiter and Apollo? No, good Madam! They were bound to obey, but not in matters of conscience."

He was becoming excited; his dark face was taking on a glow. But he was omitting an important point, she thought. "None of these people—not Moses, not Daniel, not the Christian martyrs—raised the sword against their princes," she said slowly. "And that is the true issue."

He continued to look directly into her eyes as he said, "God had not given them the power or the means."

James started a bit, and Mary felt her heart pounding.

You knew he felt this way, she told herself. Why, then, are you surprised that he openly professes it?

"So you think, then," she said, "that if the subjects have the power, they may allowably resist their rulers?"

"Indeed, if the rulers exceed their bounds, then by all means they should be resisted, and by power, if necessary." His beard jerked up and down as his mouth moved.

She stared at him.

"After all," he continued, "it is a commandment to honour one's father and mother, and the duty to the ruler follows in that wise. It is of the same case. But if a father should fall into a frenzy, or become mad, so that he should try to do violence upon his children, are not the children bound to arise, restrain the father, and take away his weapons—in order to *prevent* him from dishonouring himself by killing his children? Do you think God will be displeased with them for preventing their father from committing a great wickedness? It is even so, Madam, with rulers who would murder their subjects, who are children of God. Their blind zeal is but a very mad frenzy. Therefore to take the sword from them, to bind their hands, and to cast them into prison, until they be brought to a more sober mind, is no disobedience against rulers, but true obedience, because it agrees with the will of God."

Take the sword from them . . . bind their hands . . . cast them into prison . . . was this his plan for her? No matter what she did, was deposition and imprisonment her ultimate destination, should Knox have his way?

She was not aware that many moments had passed, until James said, "What has offended you, Madam?"

She brought herself back to the matter at hand. "Well, then, I perceive that my subjects shall obey you and not me, and shall do as they please, and not what I command. And so must I be subject to them, and not they to me." She appealed to Knox, standing before her: "Answer this charge."

"God forbid," he said, "that ever I take it upon me to set subjects at liberty to do what pleases them. But my desire is that both rulers and subjects obey God. And your duty is to be a foster mother to His Kirk, and a nurse to His people."

So she was to sponsor his Reformed Kirk?

"It is not the church I will nourish," she said. "I will defend the Church of Rome, for it is, I think, the true Church of God."

"Your will, Madam, is no reason," he said, in a booming voice that could be heard beyond the chambers by all the eavesdroppers and even out in the forecourt, as the windows were open. "Neither does your thought make that Roman harlot to be the true and immaculate spouse of Jesus Christ. Why, the Jews at the time of the crucifixion of Christ had not perverted the law of Moses as far as the Church of Rome has that of the Apostles!"

He did not frighten or convince her. His booming voice, his narrowed eyes were simply a device he used, as some men rode horses; she could perceive that well enough. "My conscience holds it not so," she replied quietly. She knew what she knew, and knew it from the heart.

"Conscience, Madam, requires knowledge. And I fear that right knowledge you have not." He lifted his head like a great stag.

"But I have both heard and read, concerning the matter." And prayed, she thought.

"So, Madam, did the people who crucified Jesus. They had read both the law and the prophets, but they had interpreted it after their own manner. Have you ever heard anyone teach besides the official churchmen permitted by the Pope and his Cardinals?"

Without waiting for her reply—for he knew it already—he said, "The ignorant Papist cannot patiently reason, and the crafty Papist will never submit to a hearing to be judged. For they know they cannot sustain any argument, except by the fire and sword of repression, and by setting up their own laws."

She felt weary of him. He could not understand her at all: not her feelings nor her position nor her calling. All he wanted was to have a Scriptural-quote duel, and stun her with his memory, no doubt prodigious. There was

178

higher knowledge than that, mystical knowledge and knowledge of the heart; but it was beyond words, by its very nature.

He was blathering on with another long Scriptural analogy.

"You are over-knowledgeable for me," she said. "But were my teachers here, they would be well able to dispute with you." We have pedantic exhibitionists, too, she thought.

"Madam! Would to God the learnedest Papist in Europe, he whom you would believe absolutely, were here. When he was convinced of the truth, then you would follow!"

This was nonsense. Imagine the Abbess Renée being converted by Master Knox! Or her Uncle Cardinal!

Smiling at Knox, she stood up. The interview was over.

Next time you stir up my subjects to disobedience and disorder, I may banish you, she thought. I am not afraid of you; you are just a man, she kept repeating to herself. She felt a great wave of relief pass through her. It was over.

Late that night, although his energy was low—for such a confrontation and opportunity to witness drained him mightily—he felt it obligatory to write his impression of the Queen of Scots:

> If there be not in her a proud mind, a crafty wit, and an indurate heart against God and His truth, my judgement faileth me. In communication with her, I espied such craft as I have not found in such age.

This report must be dispatched immediately to all his spiritual and political colleagues, especially to his brethren in the English court.

X

Mary watched as the light outside the windows of the Chapel Royal deepened into the murky sapphire hue that marked the early winter dusk. Here in Scotland it began darkening by three o'clock in the afternoon in December, and torches had to be lit in the courtyard at Holyrood. They winked in the blue gloom as the fireflies had in summer.

The memorial requiem mass for François was to begin at four o'clock. It was exactly a year since his death, an unbelievable year. Would François be startled at the changes in her if he could see her now? *Were* there any changes?

She was still wearing her mourning of black Florence serge, but she had provided her Marys and her French household with black velvet for the second mourning period. Glancing down the row of those around her, she saw that they had already had their garments made and were wearing them for the first time. Her gentlemen and domestic servants wore black cloth and mourning grey.

She looked around the chapel to see others filing in for the mass. None of the Lords would be there, of course, except the Earl of Huntly; their tender consciences would not permit it. But the two newly posted ambassadors from Savoy and France would attend, and her entire household, and her one remaining Guise relative, the Marquis d'Elboeuf.

Bishop Leslie of Ross, one of the few Catholic clergymen still in Scotland, entered in his black vestments, preceded by two tall lads bearing enormous candles in rimmed silver holders. He proceeded slowly to the altar while the sound of the dirge rose, softly and delicately, in the chapel.

Sound of agony! Sound that captured, somehow, her feelings of lost yesterdays, empty todays, lonely tomorrows, stretching out like a long corridor, a candle sconce for each year, and she walking alone down that corridor, leaving François farther and farther behind. Sound that embodied her own words in her poem, the words *yearning and regret*. Fragile, aching, the music touched her where no loud trumpets could have reached her.

I am proof against that, she thought. Strident noise, public eulogies, ceremonial clothes . . . they do not touch me. But this . . .

Just then a matchless voice, breathtaking in its purity, rose from the whispered lightness of the rest, rose in deep, rich, dark splendour, and both embodied all her grief and assuaged it.

He knows. He understands. He feels it, too.

The ecstasy of knowing that someone else had touched those depths was like a wild gift to her.

Thank You, God! she cried within her soul. Thank You for sending him, whoever he is. Perhaps he is not even real, but an angel.

She looked carefully around through her tears to see if others heard him, too. She did not know whether she was disappointed or relieved to see the rapture on everyone's face as they listened to the mysterious voice.

Afterwards, Mary had planned a formal reception to mark the end of the year's obsequies. Although her antechamber was hung with black, the fire burned brightly and the tables were furnished with the most elaborate "funeral meats" her French cooks could devise. There were rolls of roast swan sprinkled with gold dust, fish swimming in aspic seas, and—in one concession to simplicity—François's favourite, smoked boar from Chambord.

The Ambassador of Savoy, Conte di Moretta, was talking to the Earl of Huntly at one end of the room. The Conte's robes were that lovely blue that seemed to be found only in warm lands. She was very pleased that at last ambassadors were coming back to her realm. An English ambassador,

Thomas Randolph, had also taken up residence—although he, as a Protestant, was of course not present today. But the French ambassador, de Foix, was munching on some dainty and listening in on Moretta and Huntly.

Standing in between them was—a dwarf? Mary started as she saw an exceptionally ugly man, as swarthy as an ape, cocking his head and engaging in conversation with the two men. He barely came up to their shoulders.

She made her way over to them, and she could hear a most strange sound: two languages being spoken simultaneously, then repeated back separately. The Italian was coming from Moretta, and the French from de Foix; the little ape-man would shut his eyes and twist up his face, then repeat back the words to each speaker. The effort was telling on him; sweat was rolling off his face despite the chill in the chamber. Moretta and de Foix would then redouble their efforts, speaking faster and in longer sentences. The little man looked as if he would burst.

"Stop torturing him!" said Mary with a laugh. But of course it was a command, and they had to stop immediately.

"Oh, he thrives on this," Moretta assured her. "This is my secretary, David Riccio di Pancaliere. He speaks several languages, he *claims* all perfectly. He says he can even separate them out if they come in by different ears. So we were just testing him out. He's as good as his word." Moretta took a long sip of his spiced wine.

"My sovereign lady!" Riccio fell to his knees and took her hand, kissing it with reverence. His large eyes were shining.

Mary bade him rise. As he stood, she saw that he was not a dwarf, nor was there anything amiss with his limbs, he was just very short. "Your skills are impressive," she said. "Where did you learn?"

"I was secretary to Monsignor the Archbishop of Turin for a spell, until *he*"—he winked at Moretta—"stole me."

"He was content to be stolen," said Moretta. "You enjoyed the posting at Nice, did you not?"

"Ah, yes! The sea, the warmth—"

At the word *warmth*, everyone laughed. Just the word evoked longings.

"You were from Pancalieri in Piedmont?" asked Mary. "How came you, then, to the household of the Archbishop of Turin?"

"My father was a musician, and it was actually as a musician that I entered his household; I was employed to play the lute and sing in his choir. But because of my command of the idioms of French and Italian, and my ability to write in elegant Tuscan—"

"Plus your modesty!" Moretta broke in.

Mary could not help laughing, but Riccio blushed.

"He hasn't given up his music entirely, he still likes to slip off and sing at masses, he's a bass, surprising, isn't it, in one so tiny you'd think he'd be a soprano!"

Guffaw, guffaw.

It was him. He was the singer.

Mary felt her heart pounding. That beauty in sound, that deep knowledge of life and pain that he must have—otherwise his singing would be only a voice, and it was so much more than that, it was aching experience itself—to be wedded to such an earthly body! Was God absurd? Or merely being fair, saying, "These gifts and only these for one person; no one shall have all?"

"I—am deeply grateful that you sang today," said Mary, looking into his dark, shining eyes, and all laughter ceased. "And I would be grateful if you could sing in my masses from now on." She attempted to banish the tremble of excitement from her voice. "I am weary of having my priests and mass attacked. Perhaps if I have a chorister who is under diplomatic protection . . ."

Moretta tried not to look inconvenienced at losing Riccio's valuable secretarial services. "Of course, Your Majesty. I present him to you with pleasure."

❦

Gone were the black hangings, and even Mary had laid aside her mourning—as she now permitted herself to do on ceremonial occasions—in honour of the Christmas festivities in her quarters. Fir branches decorated the walls, and satin ribbons were entwined within them. Down the long chamber ran the table, set for the high feast. In the back of the chamber, the musicians were practising, and the singers rehearsing. Riccio, attired in garnet-coloured satin, had taken his place among them with ease. Mary could hear his distinctive voice even when it blended with others.

This would be a curious, walled-in Christmas, confined only to the royal quarters. The Reformed Kirk did not celebrate it or allow it to be celebrated, and thus Christmas would stop at the doorsill of the Queen's outermost chamber.

But, oh! Within all would be light—to drive back the oppressive night that seemed to last twenty hours—and warmth to rout the creeping chill that seeped in everywhere. And clear, soaring music to change the ordinary into beauty. And most scandalous of all, there would be dancing to that music, and there would be a puppet show from Italy—courtesy of Moretta—and games and . . . everything that offended the Reformers. Well, they were not invited.

Riccio had tried to tell her that perhaps that was not wise, but she had brushed him off. After all, he was a foreigner and could not understand the peculiar ways here.

"If you do not invite them, it will appear as if you were hiding something naughty from them," he said.

"Since they consider everything that gives comfort, cheer, or beauty 'naughty,' then I suppose that is what I am doing," she replied.

"Perhaps it would be better to invite them and have them refuse," said Riccio. "That way they will not be slighted, but will feel they are slighting you."

182

"I do not care for them to feel they are slighting me! What astonishing advice!"

"Very well." He sighed. "Forgive me, Madam." He bowed low.

No, there would be no Lords here tonight, although the English ambassador, Thomas Randolph, not being officially a member of the Kirk, had been invited. Christmas was still celebrated in splendour in his own country, and he longed to do homage to it here. That was what he had said, but the truth (if Mary had any eyes) was that he had developed an attraction for Mary Beaton and wished to have an opportunity to flirt with her.

The banquet was properly riotous. Gallons of wine—the finest from Bordeaux—flowed, and the number of geese alone was enough to warn Rome of enemy approach.

Mary herself drank little, but allowed herself to take pride in the fact that, four months after her arrival, she was so well settled. Her furniture and belongings had finally arrived from France, and seeing these old friends of her bedchambers and privy chambers had been comforting. Several beds, bedecked with hangings of red silk, crimson velvet, and white velvet, were now set up in Holyrood. Small couches, stools, seats, and folding chairs provided places for guests to sit, and her personal belongings made her feel that at last this alien place was home. Her harp and lute, her pictures, her embroidery, her globes of the heavens and earth, her maps and charts, her extensive library, had come to keep her company.

Up and down the table were the people she loved: the Marys, dressed now in holiday colours (by her royal permission), Father Mamerot (why should he not sit openly in company?), Madame Rallay, Bourgoing the physician, Bastian Pages, master of revels and head of her French staff. Other honoured guests brought a smile to her face: Moretta, with his high spirits; de Foix; Thomas Randolph, the serious English ambassador who kept glancing at Beaton. There were other members of her household, often related to the Marys, like Lord George Seton, and John Beaton, an attendant in her privy chamber. Some of the younger courtiers had managed to get themselves invited—those who were not keen on the deprivations of the Kirk. There were still young people in Scotland who wished to sing and dance, like John Sempill, son of one of the Reformers, who had been following Lusty about for several weeks.

After the banquet tables were cleared away, Moretta begged patience while the stage was set up for his puppet show. Everyone sought a place to sit down so as best to see this novelty—little dolls that could be made to dance and walk.

The play involved a great deal of hitting and yelling and lost objects. The puppeteer skillfully hid himself and did an admirable job of providing voices for all his characters. The play was carefully nonpolitical.

Then a deep voice said, "I will do a play as well! Put out the candles, leaving only three large ones some twelve feet from the curtain."

Mary saw Riccio detaching himself from the musicians and making his way over to a place before the tiny stage curtain. What was he about? Did Moretta know?

The servants obeyed, and one by one the candles were put out. The only source of light was the candles before the curtain. Faces turned toward Riccio looked as though they were all wearing half-masks.

He flourished his fingers, weaving them in and out of each other. "Now, I wish you to look straight ahead. Do not look at me."

On the curtain ahead were shadows that looked amazingly like Lord James and Maitland. Mary heard Flamina gasp.

"My dear Lord James," said a voice exactly like Maitland's, "have you been invited to John Knox's feast?" The profile bobbed up and down.

"I did not know he ever feasted." The imitation of Lord James was perfect—the nasal "I did not *know*" had been captured.

"He made a most delicious Scripture pudding. He took leaves from Deuteronomy, and layered them with Geneva cheese, and baked the whole until it was as dried out as an aged nun's privy parts."

"Sounds wonderful!" said Lord James.

The room exploded with laughter.

Next the Pope came on stage—they could recognize his Papal hat. The Pope fulminated against Elizabeth of England, who also came on stage and let loose a volley of obscene oaths.

Riccio's mastery of the shadows and his uncanny vocal imitations were what impressed Mary, not the clumsy political jokes.

At the dance that followed, Mary's change into satin breeches, with her Marys doing likewise as they had in France, excited little comment. Riccio had stolen the evening.

The next day he presented her with a gift. He looked somewhat embarrassed, and indeed, Mary did not know what to say to him. He had not done anything wrong, but his performance had been so unexpected.

She opened the box, and inside was a ruby brooch of a tortoise.

"Please take it with my humble apologies for last evening. I perhaps overstepped my bounds. I am, after all, newly in your service by your most gracious kindness—"

He did not mean a word of the rote apology. "I forgive you. But I would prefer that you think before you speak so freely in public. Although your skill has much to commend it." She lifted the tortoise out of the box to show that she accepted his offering.

"The tortoise is the symbol of long life, which I wish you. But since it carries its house about on its back, it also symbolizes safety. What better gift for a Queen?"

❦

Mary was sitting near the fire, laboriously pulling her needle in and out. Her fingers were cold and she could scarcely feel to hold the cloth. Madame

Rallay was kneeling before her, adjusting the flannel over the silver *chaufrettes*, footwarmers from France, that she was putting under Mary's feet.

The snows had come to Edinburgh, falling gently and coating everything with a cold blanket. January was a long tunnel of blue bleakness, although the snow made it prettier. Around her the Marys were also sewing: they were all making bedcovers, and they had been teasing each other about who would lie under the bedcovers with them.

Flamina's bedcover was crimson, and she was embroidering a pattern of knights and unicorns on it.

"Oh, will it be Mr. Maitland who lies under it?" giggled Lusty. "Or snores under it. He's so *old*, he probably wheezes at night and shivers and snorts."

"He is not old, he is only thirty-three."

"More than a decade older than you," said Seton. Her own bedcover was of violet and grey silk, with leaves and flowers of cloth-of-silver. "Now, John Sempill is the right age, he's young, stupid enough to fall in love devotedly—"

Madame Rallay adjusted Mary's skirts daintily over the *chaufrettes*, so that the heat wafted up from them all around her legs. Mary continued sewing, hoping the warmth in her legs would somehow benefit her fingers. Her own bedcover was tawny satin, and she was embroidering her initials on it.

A decade older . . . will I have to wed someone a decade older, or younger? wondered Mary. I care not to think about it. But the Lords are beginning to talk about it, to suggest candidates. Why are they so anxious for it?

Beaton was carefully measuring out gold and violet silk threads to use on her own white velvet covers.

"Randolph is even older!" said Flamina suddenly. "If you were to wed him, people would think he was his children's grandfather!"

"No, he isn't!" said Beaton, as heatedly as her languid nature would allow. "I am sure he is not forty."

"Ah, my girls, look for love in whatever shape it comes, and do not disdain it if it is lowly," said Madame Rallay.

Just then a message was brought to Mary. Melville was seeking audience.

"What about *him*?" Beaton giggled. "Does anyone here have a fancy for him?"

They all shook their heads and burst out laughing just as the unfortunate Melville made his entrance.

"Your Majesty . . ." He looked distressed. "You had told me I should call on you whenever . . ."

"Oh, you may speak freely here. These are my sisters, and Madame Rallay here is my mother." Mary gladly put down her needlework—she was tired of it—and waited for her scolding.

"The Christmas revels—" he began.

"Yes, I realize what you will say," she said contritely. "I thank you for calling it to my attention."

"We understand that you would wish to celebrate the holiday, but it was

185

the other . . . the dancing in breeches, the kissing and flirting, and the insulting shadow-show put on by that impudent Papist agent—"

"What do you mean," asked Mary, "Papist agent?"

"Well, he was employed by the Archbishop of Turin, wasn't he?"

"What of it? Archbishops everywhere keep large staffs."

"They think that he must be a Papal agent."

"Who is 'they'?" demanded Mary.

"The Lords . . . Ruthven and Lindsay and Morton."

"But not Lord James and Maitland. Of course not, they are too intelligent, even if he did make fun of them in his skit. Very well, Melville. Your criticisms are well taken." She signed. *Abstain from all appearance of evil* is to be my lot. "But it *was* fun."

He nodded. "I wish I could have been there," he said wistfully.

XI

M ary had spread out one of her large maps of Scotland for Riccio to study.

"You are so insistent to know where all things are located, what lands lie next to what, who owns what—here, you may see for yourself!"

Outside, the snow was still gently falling, falling in the opalescent haze of a February afternoon. It had been a lazy, enclosed, wintery Sunday. Mass had been celebrated as usual, with Riccio singing, and then there had been a large midday meal, following which everyone had drifted back into the Queen's chamber to read, play cards, and daydream beside the fire. Her lutenists and viola players entertained for an hour, and Mary truly thought this the sort of Sabbath the Creator had had in mind when He commanded rest upon the seventh day.

But then Riccio, with his ever-busy mind, which never took a Sabbath, began asking questions. "Lord Bothwell, where are his lands?" "How far north are the Earl of Huntly's lands?" At length she had taken down one of her scrolls—now that her library was all unpacked—and bidden him study the geography of Scotland.

Now his dark head was bent over the part of the map showing the Lothian region. "Crichton. Is that where the wedding took place? Is that in the midst of the Bothwell territory?"

Last month, Bothwell's sister Janet had married one of Mary's half brothers, Lord John Stewart. Mary herself had attended the ceremony, and even spent the night in the castle. She had been pleased with the match, for

Lord John, happy and free-spirited as a child, had turned into a wild young man. She hoped that marriage would calm him down.

"Yes. His ancestral lands lie in that region."

"Why is he so reckless?" Riccio asked bluntly. He had never seen Bothwell, who had been employed in the Borders and did not come to court. Mary had invited him to come at the time of François's requiem, but he had returned the mourning cloth she had sent and said he could not be there, without giving a reason.

"Do you refer to the escapade with Alison Craig?" asked Mary.

"What else?"

"Ah, they were young—"

"Perhaps the Marquis d'Elboeuf was, but Lord John and Bothwell were not."

Mary laughed. "Men will be men."

"From what I understand, it was not men being men, but a deliberate insult against the Hamilton family. To try to visit Hamilton's mistress—"

The Hamiltons. Next in line to the throne. Although merely tepidly Protestant, they had withheld their allegiance to Mary until several months after her return, only sheepishly making their way down to Edinburgh around Christmastime. There were really two Hamiltons to be reckoned with: the father, Duke of Châtelherault, who was timid but hardly evil, and his son, "young Arran," who was reputedly unstable in his wits. No wonder Queen Elizabeth had rejected his suit!

Bothwell had a long-standing family quarrel with the Hamiltons, as Mary understood it, one of those typically Scottish feuds that was handed down over the generations.

"It was a combination of men being men and trying to embarrass young Arran," Mary explained. "Arran makes himself out to be as holy as John Knox, yet he's availed himself of a married woman. So Bothwell and my brother and my uncle set out to show the world what he was about."

"Enjoying themselves in the process," said Riccio.

"Well, that is all over now," said Mary. "The Hamiltons came out to seek revenge, but John Knox reconciled the parties." Poor Bothwell—to be lectured to by John Knox! It was a worse punishment than an honest sword-thrust.

Bothwell had seemed in high enough spirits at his sister's wedding since then, proud to be able to provide a festivity that included his Borderers' bounty for a feast—eighteen hundred wild does and roes, rabbits, partridges, plovers, moorfowl, wild geese, wild duck and drake, and even hedgehog—and afterwards, celebratory sport down in the bracken-grown meadow by the River Tyne.

Riccio stabbed his finger at a large section of the map showing a region of Scotland that was shaped like a bulge on the upper right side. "This section—it is the lands of the Earl of Huntly?" he asked.

"Yes. The Gordons control that land," said Mary. She would like to see it, to go beyond the nearby lands she had visited.

Just then Madame Rallay told her that Lord James wished to see her.

On the Sabbath? Mary hastily rolled up the map and told Riccio to retire to the outer chamber. But before he could leave, James entered the room. Riccio scurried out, almost running between his legs. James stared after him in distaste. Then he turned to Mary, and she could see that he was genuinely disturbed.

"Forgive me," he said, "for coming to you today. But there has been such disturbing news. . . ." He shook his head and then closed his eyes as if trying to gain control of himself. Finally, after several deep breaths, he said, "A plot has been revealed! Bothwell has urged young Arran to kidnap you and take you as a prisoner to Dumbarton Castle, there to—to—" Lord James choked.

Mary burst out laughing, a frightened laugh. Then she said, "How do you know this?"

"Arran confessed it to John Knox! And then he wrote it to Randolph, the English ambassador."

"But . . . where is he now?"

"He and Bothwell have been taken into custody," said Lord James. "Arran is being held at his father's castle, and Bothwell is under house arrest at Crichton."

"Then there is no danger?" Mary felt herself relax.

"Not for now. But they must be examined before the Privy Council," said Lord James.

Why was he so excited, if the danger was past? Mary said, "Of course." Poor James was still clenching his jaw. "Dear brother, pray sit down, take some refreshment. We can talk. We have little opportunity these days, there is so much state business." She rang her little handbell and Madame Rallay appeared. "Have some cakes and drinks brought in," she told her. "And ask my musicians—"

"No! No music!" said James quickly.

How foolish of her. Of course, no music on the Sabbath for him. "No music," Mary agreed.

James took a seat on one of her little ebony chairs and stuck his hands out before the fire. "You are right, dear sister. We need some time together, apart from the council and other duties." He sighed. "How like you to remember that."

"Soon you are to be a married man, and then your wife can remember it," she said. "You need someone to look after you, James."

Lord James was to be married in only two weeks, to Lady Agnes Keith. "Yes, it is about time," he finally said. "I am almost thirty."

"One by one the bachelors fall," said Mary. "First Lord John, now you. Next Bothwell or Argyll or Arran?"

"Next it should be you." James was looking at her with concern. Just then she noticed that he was wearing a miniature pinned to his doublet, of a man whose mouth was like his own.

"Who is that?" she asked, pointing at it.

He started and tried to cover it up, as if he had not realized he was wearing it. "Why, it is—the King, our father!" He acted embarrassed.

"It is a fine study," she said. There was something vaguely familiar about it. She compared the faces and realized how much fleshier and broader her brother's was than the King's. Her own was closer to the King's shape.

"Will you not consider marriage, dear sister?"

"You should wait until you have sampled it yourself before you urge it on others," she replied. Why was he so persistent?

"But seriously, have you given any thought to it? I know that at one time you were thinking of Don Carlos of Spain—"

"I have no appetite for children," she said.

Just then Madame Rallay entered, setting down a tray of heated, frothy milk caudle, and some tarts made with orange rind. The conversation was suspended.

"But his domains—"

"I do not care to go to Spain," she said.

"What of the Archduke Charles of Austria?"

She burst out giggling. "They say he has an enormous head!"

"Well, you seem not to mind weird-looking people. Riccio is in your chambers enough, enjoying your company!" Lord James said indignantly.

"He is in my outer chambers, not my inner." Mary could not stop herself laughing, although she knew it annoyed James.

"There is King Erik of Sweden," he went on.

"He is writing love letters to Queen Elizabeth just now. When she has rejected him, then I will consider him."

"Dear sister, what *will* satisfy you? 'It is not right for man to be alone—' "

"Always Scripture! Can you not speak your own mind unaided?" She laughed. "Will you create an 'help meet for me,' then? Make him spring full-formed from my forehead, as Minerva came from Zeus—"

"You are so silly, sister!" But he said it kindly. "How do you imagine this fanciful mate to be?"

"Tall, like me. I've hardly met a man my height, it would be a delightful novelty. Writes poetry. Sings. Rides. Loves me." She was enjoying making him up.

"Of what complexion?"

"I care not."

"Is he athletic?"

"Oh, yes!"

"Learned?"

"Oh, yes!"

"Of royal blood?"

"But of course!"

"Handsome?"

189

"It goes without saying."

"My dear sister, I fear you will never find him."

"Perhaps that is why nuns become the brides of Christ. There is no one on earth like that."

"That way is not permitted you."

"Yes." She had known that, at St. Pierre's. "My mate, I fear, will be altogether of this earth." She watched James sipping his drink. Some of the milk clung to his lips. "Now, as to this business with Bothwell and Arran . . ."

⬧

Mary took her place at the head of the Privy Council. Already waiting, looking as if they were to attend a funeral, were all six of the inner circle: Lord James, Maitland, Morton, Huntly, Kirkcaldy, Erskine. The seventh, Lord Bothwell, was to be brought in to answer the charges hurled at him by the noblest blood of the land, young Arran.

"You may bring in the men," Mary told the guards, and within a moment or two, from separate doors, Bothwell and Arran entered, stopped, and glared at one another.

"Come closer, and let us hear what you have to say," said Mary in a loud voice.

Arran, distrust showing in his eyes, edged near to the chair of state.

He would have been handsome, but his face had that bloated, drained look of someone who has been ill. His colouring was bad; he was flushed where he should have been pale, and blanched where he should have been flushed.

Bothwell walked forward as though he were so disgusted he could barely stand to be in the same room as everyone else—including the Queen. She noticed that he wore his riding clothes; he had not seen fit to put on the proud attire that she had seen him in at the wedding.

"James Hamilton, Earl of Arran, explain yourself to us and to the council here present," Mary said.

Arran pointed a shaking finger at Bothwell. "He's a traitor! He tried to lead me into treason! He wanted me to waylay you, to kill Lord James and Maitland, to take you captive—"

"He's stark raving mad," said Bothwell calmly. "This is all his sick fancy. You know he takes it of his mother; she has been mad for years."

Mary saw Morton start as if he had been bitten. He ran a pudgy hand through his wiry red hair. Then she remembered: Morton's wife was the sister of Arran's mother, and they said *she* was insane, too, that Morton kept her locked up while he pursued other women. . . .

"Mad? Mad?" cried Arran. "No, I'm not mad! He whispered it in my ear, he thought no one would ever know!"

"I tell you he's mad," said Bothwell. He did not seem afraid for his life,

190

his station, or his reputation. He merely stood calmly, as if he were a long-suffering victim.

"Alas, I must verify that," said Kirkcaldy. The young soldier stood up, obviously hating what he had to do. "He had escaped from confinement at his father's home and came to me, half naked, in the middle of the night. Then the spell came upon him, and he cried out about witches and devils attacking him. Then he—" Kirkcaldy stopped, ashamed. "He imagined himself to be the Queen's husband and in bed with her."

There were sharp intakes of breath all around, except for Bothwell, who let out a hoot of laughter.

"Isn't she? Isn't she?" Arran cried plaintively, and ran toward Mary. A guard jumped into action and grabbed him.

"Take him to Edinburgh Castle," Lord James said decisively, before Mary could say anything.

"Yes," she said. "*I* order that he be taken there."

When the guards had led Arran away, Bothwell said, "I am free to go?" Every muscle in his body showed that he was already moving in his mind.

"No," said Lord James. "There are yet questions we need to ask you. Arran may be mad, but who is to say that something you said was not the basis of it? Even a madman needs seeds planted in his mind. Now, what was it you advocated?"

Bothwell was astonished. "Nothing! I advocated nothing!"

"Why were you in touch with Randolph?" Maitland suddenly asked.

Mary watched Maitland as he stared intently at Bothwell. His genial demeanour had been replaced by something from the Inquisition.

"Perhaps you have been in league with the English," Erskine suggested.

Bothwell looked incredulous. "You must know that I am proud of the fact that I have never been in league with any foreign power."

"Proud? But 'Pride goeth before destruction, and a haughty spirit before a fall,' " Lord James intoned. "Perhaps your very pride has drawn you into sin!"

"I am sure that, being a man, I am a sinner, but in a general, rather than a particular, sense," said Bothwell. His manner had changed a little, Mary noticed. He now seemed more truculent and ready for combat. "Try me, then, in a court of law. If no fault be found in me, acquit me and let me go."

"But we cannot acquit you," said Maitland.

"What do you mean?" Mary demanded. "Of course he is entitled to a trial!"

"But not an acquittal," Maitland said smoothly. "Do you not understand? An acquittal of Bothwell would then convict Arran of false accusation, making him a traitor deserving of death. Arran is the next blood to the throne; it would not be seemly. It would make of us a laughingstock among nations."

"Let me go!" roared Bothwell. If he had had a sword, Mary knew he would have drawn it. Guards immediately grabbed his arms and pinned them behind his back.

"Then we shall not try him," said Mary slowly. "For now I remember the maxim of Livy: *Hominem improbum non accusari tutius est, quam absolvi.* That is, not to try someone suspected of something is better policy than to acquit him."

"There is a letter just arrived from Queen Elizabeth pleading for him," said Lord James. "How did she know of all this, if he had not been in league with Randolph?"

Had Bothwell been all the deceitful things he had so stoutly claimed not to be? Mary felt a great, flooding disappointment.

"I have been good to you," she finally said to Bothwell. "And is this how you repay me?"

"Is *what* how I repay you? Lord James is twisting the facts, poisoning your mind to discredit me!"

"I pray you, remove to Edinburgh Castle. Your temper is growing as distracted as Arran's," Mary said. She would question him later, in private, away from this tribunal.

"You are faithless, like all monarchs!" cried Bothwell. "To think I was so deceived in you!"

"Obey the Queen!" Lord James had risen and he roared out the order. The guards hustled Bothwell from the room.

"I well see there is no justice here!" said Huntly, gathering up his papers and following in Bothwell's wake.

XII

Maitland pulled his cap down more tightly over his ears, and wrapped the end of his mantle over his head. The March wind, coming off the sea here at St. Andrews, was piercing. And to think they would have to stay out here for hours! And all for an ostensible religious ceremony. Not for the first time, Maitland wondered why the Lord required His followers to be uncomfortable, to torture themselves in His name. Assuming He did require it, that is . . .

"Knox will be here soon," said Lord James. The chill made his face look pinched.

"Good," muttered Maitland, all the while thinking, *Bad.* Knox would complicate things. But then, he was needed to give colour to their reason

192

for being there: to honour the anniversary of the martyrdom of George Wishart.

"Isn't that similar to celebrating the saints' days?" Maitland had asked innocently, trying to keep the sarcasm from his voice.

Morton had shrugged. He did not care to complicate his mind with any such technicalities. "Just be there," he had said.

And so Maitland was there, along with Erskine, Lindsay, Ruthven, and Kirkcaldy of Grange, pacing before the walls of the castle, helping to pile on the wood for the bonfire they would light—none too soon—and watching to see if Archbishop Hamilton was inside the castle. Hamilton, a bastard member of the clan, had remained a Catholic, although he was said to be "everything by turns and nothing long." He had taken over Cardinal Beaton's old post, and might even now be watching them.

Kirkcaldy pointed up to the walls of the castle. The whistling wind all but drowned out his words, as the castle was situated almost overhanging the sea. "To think we held out there for a year!" Pride was plain in him.

"Was not the captivity a brutal punishment?" Maitland asked. Kirkcaldy had been one of those taken away by the French, although his high birth meant that he was merely imprisoned, rather than becoming a galley slave like Knox.

"Captivity is bitter," said Kirkcaldy. "Yes, it is."

Erskine walked over to them, bundled up so that he resembled an upright bear. "Knox is here," he said.

Maitland saw the Reformer, still on horseback, gesturing to Lord James. But Knox dismounted and came over to them, his cloak, heavy as it was, lifted behind him by the ocean wind. He was rubbing his gloveless hands together, his Bible tucked under one arm.

"Praise be to the Lord it is not raining, or snowing!" he cried.

Maitland was touched by the way he found something to praise even in the weather. And he was right, it was not raining or snowing, even if it was blowing up a gale.

"It was here, at this very spot, where the blessed George Wishart took his stand against the forces of evil!" said Knox. "It was here that our faith received its blessing."

"Tell us about it," said Lord James, like a child. "We did not see it."

"Ah! That was a day!"

Knox became so excited that his cloak encumbered his movements, and so he threw it off jubilantly.

Maitland thought he saw movement in one of the castle windows. Was the Archbishop even now calling for harquebusiers to attack them? Knox had his back to the castle, defiantly.

"And let us never forget the difference between the English martyrs and the Scottish. The English go to the stake whispering prayers. But when our own Patrick Hamilton, who was martyred almost twenty years before Wishart, was suffering for hours in the flames, and the Prior approached him and asked him if he repented, he turned and, through the very smoke and flames, called the Prior an emissary of Satan, and warned that he, Hamilton, would indict him before God. And when in England Bishop Gardiner burned the faithful, he was safe in his bed. But Cardinal Beaton—we Scots didn't let *him* rest so!"

Now would come the injunction to attack Mary in the same way, Maitland thought wearily, and braced himself for it. But to his surprise, Knox's voice faltered with tears, and he simply said, "Let us remember our brother Wishart."

He gave the signal for the fire to be lighted. Morton stepped forward with a torch and touched it to the waiting logs. They were cold and wet, and so at first nothing came forth but clouds of smoke. Maitland choked on it, as the wind blew it straight in his face, and shuddered to think what it would be to be tied up there, blanketed with smoke. . . .

He lifted his eyes out to the sea, dark and dull now, reflecting the season. Few ships were out this time of year, but soon the commerce would pick up again, messages would be flying back and forth, and his official duties would increase.

The fire had caught now, and it crackled and struggled to break free from its wood prison. It glowed through the sticks as if they were bars of a cell. Then at once the fire burst out and roared upward, shooting off showers of sparks in its escape.

"Everyone pray, according to his own conscience," said Knox, barely audible above the blast of the fire and the shout of the waves. "See how He accepts our offerings?"

My offering, thought Maitland. What is it? A questioning mind that tries to keep itself unclouded, like a glass of pure water? That is all I have to offer in service to Scotland.

As the fire died down, the men were still standing, heads bowed. The heat from the fire had bathed the sides of them facing the flames, and for a little while the cold had been beaten back. But then Maitland felt it taking hold of his toes once more, just as Lord James was saying, "You are welcome to come back to my quarters here."

All of them gladly trooped the short distance between the castle and the Abbey of St. Andrews, thankful to leave the salty wind, and the watching eyes of Archbishop Hamilton, behind.

Lord James's possession of the Abbey of St. Andrews was an anomaly; he had been granted it under the old system, the system of abuses so criticized by the Reformers. He should have surrendered it, thought Maitland, but of course he has no intention of rectifying *that* particular excess of the old Church. Now, of the Seven Deadly Sins, I do believe that Brother James is most beset with avarice. . . .

Lord James's home, the Prior's lodging, was spacious and well appointed, although the truly luxurious furnishings of the Prior had doubtless been discreetly removed. Lord James welcomed them all, offered them food and drink, and then waited for most of them to leave, so that the remaining four could get down to business: the Queen's business.

They were seated now around the fireplace, which burned brightly in its grate: Lord James, Maitland, Erskine, and Morton.

"We called her home, and she came," said Lord James. "You were all there, you all signed the paper inviting her. And I daresay we are—satisfied with the outcome?"

"Well enough," said Erskine, his thin voice enthusiastic. "She has been better than we had dared to hope."

"Do you mean religiously?" asked Lord James.

"Yes, certainly. Although she herself has not converted—and shows no likelihood of it—she has been content to allow our faith to stand unmolested."

"And she and Knox have reached a standoff," said Morton slowly. He licked his lips; they were badly chapped.

"Bothwell is gone," said Lord James. "He'll not trouble us any longer. He's always trouble, because he's unpredictable. And the Hamiltons are discredited now; the poor old man had to surrender Dumbarton Castle to the Queen."

"That takes care of nearly everyone who might cross us," said Maitland. "The next in line to the throne—rendered impotent. The loyal-to-the-crown Borderer with the strong sword arm—locked up."

"But there's still one," said Morton. "One big one, who is not of our persuasion."

"George Gordon, fourth Earl of Huntly," said Lord James. "The Chancellor of the Realm. And a Catholic."

"A militant one, too," said Erskine. "He's always urging the Queen to set up the mass again."

"If we are fortunate, then the Cock o' the North, as he likes to call himself, will crow once too often and offend the Queen. You saw how he stamped out of the Privy Council at the Bothwell verdict?"

"Please! There was no trial, so there could be no verdict!" Maitland objected.

"Oh. Yes, of course. But if he refuses to attend Council meetings, then who knows where it may lead?"

"If he could be crushed, then all opposition to the Congregation would vanish."

"First he would have to rebel," said Maitland.

"Perhaps he will," said Lord James. "Perhaps he will."

XIII

he spring came, but only after a seemingly interminable winter that dragged out its footsteps in a trail of snow, ice, dankness and darkness, of winds that dashed the North Sea against the rocks of the coast. When the first eerily clear, light days came, people burst outdoors. The light seemed to expand to fill the entire twenty-four hours, and an otherworldly energy flowed into everyone.

Mary had welcomed the spring, feeling that she was being rewarded for her difficult first few months in Scotland. She had not questioned her decision to return, but only her ability to do what she felt called to do. Things had not gone as she had hoped and planned.

Before she had actually arrived, she would have found it difficult to understand how the Kirk pervaded even the most personal actions; now she understood only too well, having felt its grip all around her.

Religion! It was supposed to provide comfort and order in life. Now the news was that even in France it had turned destructive. Her own uncle the Duc de Guise had opened fire on a gathering of Huguenots at Vassy, and twelve hundred had been massacred. Both Catholics and Protestants then armed themselves, and the war was on.

The last of her high-ranking French entourage had returned to France, leaving only the household staff she needed for embroidery, cooking, and her wardrobe. She missed Brantôme, but for the rest, it had been a relief to see them go.

The removal of Bothwell had greatly disturbed her; she had relied on him more than she had realized. The fall of the House of Hamilton, although it had enriched her by one magnificent fortress, was not a thing to be welcomed.

It was now the turn of the Earl of Huntly to be out of sorts. She understood how he felt, being so outnumbered by the Protestants, but that was all the more reason to stand at his post. Instead, he seemed to be absenting himself more and more. And now one of his sons had been involved in an unseemly brawl and was locked up.

These brawls! Why were there so many of them? The forces of Bothwell and Hamilton that had almost come to blows over that fracas with the Craig woman . . . the roistering of Lord John . . . and now this John Gordon business, with a street fight between Gordon and Lord Ogilvie in which Ogilvie had been severely wounded.

Thus the three men whom Mary had counted on to help balance the obvious power of the Lords of the Congregation had failed her or, worse, turned against her. And after she had tried so hard to be conciliatory!

No one treated Queen Elizabeth thus! She kept all the men in line, and no one dared to take liberties or presume. How did she manage to control her large, masculine court?

Mary felt tired. She did not know the answer, only that she was obviously doing something wrong. Perhaps she would have to marry; perhaps there would be no other way to assert her dominance over male courtiers.

Mary was anxious to meet the fabled Queen Elizabeth and see if she could discern the reasons for her mastery of those who served her.

The only one I control is Riccio! she thought sadly.

The meeting between the two Queens would take place at Nottingham in only six weeks. Already the passport and safe conduct for Mary's journey into England had been received, and Bastian Pages, the revels-master, had written and produced the masque to be performed: the punishment of False Report and Discord by Jupiter at the request of Prudence and Temperance. Mary had duly dispatched a new portrait of herself to Elizabeth and received one in exchange.

Now she twisted the "friendship ring" and watched the sun splinter into different colours inside the diamond as she stood on the links at St. Andrews, playing golf with Flamina, Beaton, Maitland, Randolph, and Riccio. Normally she enjoyed it; she loved being near the sea cliffs, where the grass grew tufted and sweet. The sea was piercingly blue and the air bracing, and her senses appreciated that in itself.

"Take aim! Take aim!" cried Riccio, as Mary Fleming prepared to strike her ball with the special crooked stick used in golf.

"Silence, you foreigner!" said Maitland. He pretended to be joking, but his contempt for the alien who could not seem to understand the rules of golf was obvious. One must maintain silence during a swing, but this inane monkey chattered on regardless.

Thack! Flamina's horn-edged club knocked the leather ball but a little way; it wobbled toward the hole but stopped far short.

Riccio then stepped forward to his own ball and hit it, playing out of turn. The fact that he managed to get it into the hole made the affront worse.

"Can you not control him, Your Majesty?" Randolph asked in a silky tone.

"Riccio, I pray you, mind your courtesy," she said sharply.

The Italian spun on his heel, his satin doublet making a shiny blue blur. He bowed deeply.

Mary took her turn, swinging her club quickly. The ball flew over a hillock and disappeared. Riccio rushed off to sight it. Fleming and Beaton began to giggle, but Randolph and Maitland were not amused.

She looked over at Maitland, who was stroking his neat brown beard. Lately he and James had been most insistent in discussing the advantages of a marriage to Don Carlos of Spain for her. Perhaps she would have to consider it, if—

Just then she caught sight of a rider galloping across the sandy hills and then slowing as he saw them at play. He dismounted and led his horse over, then allowed him to nibble on the thick, moist grass.

"Melville!" She was delighted; undoubtedly Melville, one of her most sophisticated courtiers and the one in charge of the meeting with Elizabeth, brought news of just that.

"Forgive the interruption," he said. "But—"

He held out a letter, and suddenly Mary saw that his usually jovial face was solemn. She opened the letter and quickly knew why.

"It is—she—cancels the meeting," Mary finally said. She felt as though a large bull had squared off and kicked her straight in the stomach; she actually lost her breath.

"It is, then, as the special messenger indicated," said Melville, shaking his head.

Maitland and Randolph dropped their clubs and came running, alarm written all over their faces.

"She says she . . . cannot meet with me while the Huguenots are being killed in France by an army led by the Guises," Mary said slowly.

"Yes, I see. As the champion of the Protestants, she cannot be seen to meet with a Catholic sovereign at this point," said Randolph.

"But Elizabeth is not religious!" Mary burst out.

"No, she is making the *appearance* of religion the reason," Maitland explained patiently.

"Appearance is the important thing, not the reality," Melville chimed in, as if he were tutoring a backward child.

"No! It is not!" cried Mary. "It should not be!"

The three courtiers and diplomats shrugged, embarrassed.

"It is politics," said Maitland.

With a cry, Mary ran from the links.

Melville sighed. "It is a pity," he finally said. "Inconvenient timing. Very bad luck for us. And, oh, yes—Huntly's son has escaped from jail in Edinburgh and fled north. Tell her as soon as you can," he asked Maitland. "I will ride on and inform Lord James at St. Andrews. The Congregation will have to assemble its forces to meet the Cock o' the North." He stared after Mary's retreating form. "The Queen has a war on her hands."

❧

Refusing to call it a war, and trying to put a good face on the cancelled meeting with Queen Elizabeth, Mary merely announced to her people that she had long wished to travel to the northern regions of her realm, and only the projected meeting in England had stood in her way. Since it was only August, there was ample time to convert the southern progress into a northern one, and therefore she would set out for Aberdeen and Inverness straightway. She insisted on giving it every appearance of a true hunting and hawking progress to the wilds, bringing her Marys with her, as well as ambassador Randolph. If Lord James saw fit to have a few extra soldiers along, well, it was only to help clear roads and assist with the transport wagons. She even announced that she intended to visit the Earl of Huntly in his castle at Strathbogie, giving him the opportunity to stop his aberrant behavior before it was too late. As for his son, Sir John Gordon, he should give himself up to authorities in Aberdeen forthwith.

The journey had started well enough, and they made their way up to Perth and then, to avoid the mountains, stayed on the more rolling countryside on the way to Aberdeen, where the Gordons held their power. There was indeed good hawking near Glamis in the golden autumn afternoons, and Mary could not help relaxing and even taking pleasure in the flirtations between Randolph and Beaton, and the more restrained courting of Maitland and Flamina. Flamina had not lost interest in him, for all that he seemed to Mary to be staid and too controlled for the likes of her.

Mary was gratified to see a large number of Catholic wayside shrines still standing; the farther away from Edinburgh they went, the looser was the grip of the Kirk. The little hand-painted shrines, draped with garlands of wildflowers and heather, seemed to be at the crossroads to reassure her.

Upon reaching Aberdeen, a fair-sized town on the eastern seacoast, Mary made a point of visiting Scotland's newest university, founded only about sixty years before. "England has only two universities, whereas we have three," said the Chancellor proudly. Mary inspected the library and made a resolution to bequeath some of her own books to increase the collection of this young university.

Having established her presence in the area, and given the Huntlys time to come to her, Mary at last issued her order that Sir John Gordon give himself up to the authorities, if not in Aberdeen, then at Stirling. Still no one appeared, except Lady Huntly with a large retinue of attendants, who begged her to be merciful to both her husband and son.

But the wife could not substitute; where was Huntly?

"Dear Queen," said Lady Huntly, "he feels punished for his zeal for the Catholic faith. For you have ignored his suggestions—"

"Yes, his suggestions were rash and went against common sense," said Mary. "Just as his failure to come and present himself to me does now. He thus appears a petulant, unstable rebel."

"He looks for you to come to our castle at Strathbogie," she said.

"He looks in vain unless he comes to me first," said Mary. "And you may tell him—" She hesitated. Should she do it now? Yes, why not? She looked over at Lord James, standing beside her, attired in his forest-green velvet, looking, she thought, most noble.

"Lord James," she stated, "you have been administering the rights and revenues of the earlship of Mar."

He nodded, his hooded eyes—so like those of James V in portraits—looking guarded.

"These belong, by tradition and ancient right, to the Erskine family. And of course you already have the abbotship of St. Andrews. It is not needful that you hold the title to Earl of Mar as well."

199

His face betrayed no emotion; it was as unmoving as one of the carved wooden heads at Stirling—the ones which had so frightened her as a child.

"But as you are a man of great authority as well as integrity, and Scotland seeks to reward her loyal sons, I hereby proclaim you Earl of Moray, the stewardship of which the Earl of Huntly has forfeited by his treason."

A smile broke over James's broad face. "Thank you," he said.

Lady Huntly looked as though she had been slapped. "Madam," she said quietly, "we have administered those lands faithfully for many years."

"Yes, you helped yourself to the revenues without holding the title," said Mary. "Did you think to continue this forever? Or did you delude yourself into thinking that I was not aware of it?"

"Madam, please—"

" 'Tis done," said Mary. "And lest you lose more, tell your husband to change his ways."

It began raining that night, and the weather turned foul. Maitland told her that this corner of Scotland, protruding out into the North Sea, could be one of the coldest spots in the realm when the winds blew from Russia, and now she found that out for herself. They plodded on, through desolate tracks of moor and moss, the hawking and hunting forgotten. Word reached Mary that Sir John Gordon had decided against surrendering at Aberdeen, and was now tracking them, following their movements with a thousand horsemen, watching them from the cover of the forests that dripped with the perpetual rain.

When they passed into the vicinity of Strathbogie, news was brought to Mary that Sir John and his father planned to fall on them as they slept in his castle, kill Maitland and Lord James, and abduct her. Then the father would force her to marry his son, who was known as the handsomest man in Scotland. The fact that Sir John already had a wife did not seem to matter to their wild plans.

"Sir John purports himself to be in love with you," said the young messenger.

"Sir John is in love with himself and his power," said Mary. "But he is not as powerful as he imagines." She turned to Lord James. "We will not sleep there tonight!"

James looked at the dreary, raining vista. Already it was growing dark. "There's the castle of Balquhain ahead," he said. "Let us try to reach it."

The darkness was just closing in as they reached the castle at the sloping foot of the dark mountain of Bennachie. They could feel the watching eyes of Sir John and his men, waiting and biding their time. As Mary settled herself in her hard bed, she could hear cries from the mountains that sounded like wolves.

The next morning found them, still wary, picking their way through mossy groves, cankered old pines, and brambles. Overhead, in the brief respites between rains, Mary could see buzzards riding the air above them.

200

Late in the day the royal party halted before the swollen waters of the River Spey, which foamed and rushed over its banks.

"Can we ford here?" asked Maitland. It looked as though the water would come up over their saddles.

"Aye!" Mary spurred her horse into the cold, turbulent water, which indeed rose almost to her saddle. But the swirling currents failed to suck them down, and her horse kept his footing on the weed-covered rocks. She splashed across, and soon the others followed, soaking their clothes and chilling themselves.

They came at last to Inverness, a town in the shadow of the highlands overlooking the Firth of Moray, the northern body of water that cut Scotland almost in half. Mary's weary party approached the royal castle there—a castle administered by Huntly as Sheriff of Inverness. To their shock, they were refused admittance.

"Treason!" cried Maitland with genuine surprise. "To refuse to admit the Queen to her own castle!"

They stood in the rain, looking up at the grey battlements running with water. The sky overhead was the same colour, looking as solid as a soldier's mantle.

Mary ordered her trumpeters to blow, and the sound brought out the curious in the countryside and the surrounding hills; to them she cried that she had been treacherously cast out. They rallied, with their swords, staves, scythes and clubs, and Huntly sent word to his deputy to admit the Queen's party, since the Highlanders were coming to her aid. But it was too late to appease: the Queen's forces, upon entering the castle, punished the castle's captain; he was hanged. Huntly was now duly warned.

While they waited for Huntly's obedience, Mary and her party met at last a company of Highlanders, for they took it upon themselves to keep watch in the fields, sleeping out with no protection at all. They were curious creatures, these men wearing furs and carrying claymores, dirks, and leather-covered shields. And although she knew they could not understand her, she exclaimed, "I am sorry I am not a man! I should like to know what life it is to lie all night in the fields, or to walk upon the causeway with a jack, a helmet, a Glasgow buckler, and a broadsword!"

Yes, to lie there all night, keeping alert for the enemy . . . she would revel in that!

Five days passed; no Huntly. Mary announced that they would turn back toward Aberdeen, mayhap to meet with him there. On the way they would stay with the Bishop of Moray, Patrick Hepburn, Bothwell's great-uncle—and a noted profligate.

"With *him*?" Lord James had looked disdainful. "Better to sleep out in the fields!"

Mary watched the sheeting rain outside the castle windows. "Better not," she said. "I think you can manage to guard your honour well enough from the Bishop's taint."

They set out from Inverness, escorted as far as the Spey by two thousand warriors of the Fraser clan, who had pledged loyalty to her. There had been word that she would be attacked there, but nothing happened, and she proceeded on to Spynie.

There, in the Bishop's palace, with its enormous defensive keep, old Patrick Hepburn welcomed them. He did not *look* like the lascivious gourmet he was supposed to be; he looked almost fatherly. But Mary had already heard the stories of his trysts with married women and his numerous bastards.

"Welcome, oh, most hearty welcome!" he was saying. His sandy-coloured hair—with flecks of white in it—was in disarray. From his bedsport? "I have been most distressed to hear of the rebellion of the Earl of Huntly. Have you encountered him yet?"

"No, he hides himself from us," said Mary. "It seems he does not dare look us in the face."

"Ah! Then he must be the one man in ten thousand who does not wish to do so!" said the Bishop. His eyes still had their kindly look, but now it was more intense.

Now I see what there is about him, thought Mary. Unhappy wives find understanding with the good Bishop, and compliments when they have had none for years. . . .

I myself have had a round dozen women, and seven of them were other men's wives. So the uncle was supposed to have said in a "married woman as a mistress" bragging contest. But what a pity that so many wives were neglected by their men that they were forced to seek the lovemaking of a priest! The shame was on the husbands, thought Mary.

"It is less my face I wish him to see than my foot. He should kneel before me," said Mary.

"As I do!" said the Bishop, kneeling with a flourish.

She could not help smiling at him. The old reprobate was indeed charming.

What was it like for Bothwell to have spent part of his childhood with such a man? Was that why Bothwell was reputed to have so many women? Had he learned it from his great-uncle, the way other boys learned a trade like carpentry? There had been Arran's mistress, numerous lowborn women from kitchens and households of Edinburgh, and a Norwegian mistress from whom he had borrowed money and then abandoned on the Continent— so she had been told by Lord James. But then, Lord James did not like him. But Mary Beaton herself had said that Bothwell and her aunt Janet had been lovers when Bothwell was little more than a boy, and Janet twenty years older.

What did the uncle do—take women and pass them on to his protégé? Or did Bothwell simply stand and watch, and learn . . . ?

The Bishop was making noises of discomfort. She had forgotten him, still kneeling on his elderly knees!

"Oh, please rise!" she said.

With a grunt, he stood up. His backbone crackled. He attempted to smile. "Come, consider this your home. . . ."

He presented them a banquet worthy of Tiberius in all respects. It was toward the drowsy end of the evening that the Bishop sought her out. No one was listening; for once, Maitland and Lord James seemed to be less than alert.

"You know young Arran is insane," said the Bishop. "His testimony should not be used to keep my nephew in prison any longer. He has been loyal to you. That one of Your Majesty's most devoted knights should be so dishonoured! Why should Huntly then be obedient, if this is to be his reward?"

Mary could not help wondering herself. The episode had disturbed her greatly, and she had not yet had the opportunity to question Bothwell. "Bothwell," she finally said, "should do what he is able to do."

"He already has," said his uncle. "Grown tired of waiting for royal justice, he has acted as a true Hepburn. Bothwell has escaped from Edinburgh Castle." The Bishop said this as proudly as a father whose son has won honours at the university.

Escape? From Edinburgh Castle? "That is impossible!" she said.

"Not so, not so." Again the pride in his voice. "He broke one of the stanchions in his window, squeezed himself out, and climbed down the very face of the castle rock."

"Where is he now?"

"He's at the Hermitage in the Borders. An old friend, Janet Beaton, has brought him provisions."

Janet Beaton! The witch-mistress!

"And—this may interest Your Majesty—Lord Gordon, Huntly's oldest son, has sought him out to beg his help for his father's rebellion. He assumes Bothwell will have reason enough to turn against you now."

Oh, God! Mary felt her heart rising up into her throat. "And?"

The Bishop paused, his merry eyes searching hers. He knew how to tease, too—the tormentor! "Bothwell said no. He plans to leave Scotland entirely. He has no use for what he sees here."

"And go where?"

The Bishop shrugged. "I know not. Wherever the first ship is sailing, I assume."

"The Lord High Admiral of Scotland, stealing away on a foreign ship?"

"You must needs find another for the post, for it is now vacant."

Leaving Spynie, Mary's party made its way back toward Aberdeen. As they passed beyond Findlater Castle on the sea, Sir John Gordon at last came out in the open and attacked some of Mary's men after the main body of the party had moved on. Thus, when they reached Aberdeen, Lord James said, "We need reinforcements. Let us send to Edinburgh for a hundred or so harquebusiers, and additional commanders like Kirkcaldy and Lord Lindsay with a thousand men apiece."

So it had come to this! Mary reluctantly wrote out the orders, and summoned Huntly to come and meet with her. He sent messengers back that he dared not come without his soldiers; she replied that he dared not come *with* them. He therefore declined to come at all.

"He hides in his house at Strathbogie by day, and sleeps elsewhere at night," Mary's scouts told her. "In that way he thinks he can avoid capture."

"Then we must surprise him by day. A small force, under the command of Kirkcaldy, should be able to sneak up on him."

Kirkcaldy set out at dawn with a dozen men in order to reach Strathbogie by noon, but the sentries saw him and gave alarm. Huntly rushed out the back, barefoot and without his sword, jumped over a wall and seized a horse, and rode away, still free.

"So he goes to join his son," said Lord James. "He proclaims himself at last."

"We do not know that he has gone to join Sir John," Mary argued.

"His flight is evidence of his guilt," James insisted. "The time for holding back is past."

At the market cross, Huntly and his son were proclaimed traitors by three blasts of the hunting horn. "They are to be hunted down like wolves, thieves, and foreigners, for any citizen to capture or expel!" cried the herald.

Huntly took to the wild mountains of Badenoch, hiding from the royal forces. No one could have followed him there, where ancient, drooping trees and slippery, moss-covered stones provided a secret sanctuary. But his wife—who consulted with "tame" witches—persuaded him that he should leave his mountain fastness and meet the Queen's troops in open battle. The witches had assured her, she told him, that by nightfall he would be in Tolbooth at Aberdeen without any wound in his body. He boldly marched toward Aberdeen, proclaiming that he would capture Mary and marry her to whomsoever he chose.

Then he took up his position on a hill above the field of Corrichie, some fifteen miles west of the city. The Queen's troops faced him across the field, blooming now in full purple heather.

Lord James, Lord Lindsay, and Kirkcaldy of Grange led the royal troops. They looked stern and completely unafraid as they sat listening to Maitland exhorting the soldiers, "Remember your duty to your sovereign lady, and have no fear of the multitudes before you!"

Mary would not ride with them herself, but she felt her heart pounding. Oh, to be a man today! Her commanders had fought before, and Kirkcaldy was already an experienced soldier, but how would Lord James fare?

Across the field, Mary could see the glint of Huntly's gaudy pink-and-gilt armour. Completely certain of victory, he advertised his presence insolently. The Cock o' the North, portly rooster that he was, already strutted like a victor.

The horn sounded, and Mary watched the men gallop away. She had almost twenty-five hundred men in her service—how many did Huntly have?

Maitland looked grim as he watched, and Mary saw the look on Flamina's face as she watched him. Not until then did Mary realize how deeply she must care for him. And Lord James, newly married . . . what of his wife?

Thank God I have no husband or sweetheart out there upon the field, Mary thought. But then . . . I also have no one to welcome back and rejoice with.

A strange loneliness swept over her as she watched the forces charging. She felt utterly and completely alone, with a deep, personal solitariness.

There was a sound of firearms. Kirkcaldy's harquebusiers were firing into the Earl's men on the hill, killing them in numbers, forcing the rest of them down from the heights and into a bog at the foot of the hill.

Mary felt herself scarcely able to breathe. The sound of the guns, and the wailing shrieks of the dying men, were hideous and sickening.

The noise of the fighting rose, and clouds of dust hung over the opposing armies. Mary could see that Huntly's men were trapped in the bog, falling and unable to escape from Lord James and Lindsay, who were closing in.

James, like an avenging angel, fell on the Gordons, hacking his way through the ranks to the Earl and two of his sons, seventeen-year-old Adam as well as Sir John.

Where had James learned to fight like that? Mary was astonished.

"Lord James is a fine commander," she said to Maitland. "And Kirkcaldy—he is a genius of a soldier."

Huntly was forced to surrender, then was trussed up and set upon a horse to be brought before the Queen. But he suddenly pitched off the horse and fell to the ground—dead of apoplexy.

His heavy corpse was conveyed from the battlefield on a makeshift litter of fishing baskets, and taken to Aberdeen. That night his body indeed lay on the cold stones at the Tolbooth, clad in a cammoise doublet and grey Highland hose, without a single mark on it.

After being paraded like a criminal through the streets of Aberdeen, Sir John was to be executed in the marketplace. It was deemed necessary that Mary attend and witness it.

"Else it will be said you encouraged his affections," said Lord James sternly.

From the scaffold errected in front of Mary's lodging, Sir John looked up at Mary, seated in a chair of state at an open window.

"Your presence, fair Queen, solaces me, as I am about to suffer for love of you!" he cried.

Mary gripped the chair arms and tried to keep her eyes open, but without seeing, as the handsome youth was forced to open his collar and lay his head upon the block. Just before doing so, he knelt and raised his eyes toward hers in a silent plea. The headsman's assistant pushed his head down roughly and the headsman raised the axe.

He struck, and wounded Sir John, missing the neck. The indignant spectators groaned aloud, and Mary screamed with the horror of it. Outside, the headsman finished his grisly business, and Sir John's head rolled lop-sidedly on the scaffold boards.

Before returning to Edinburgh, Mary pardoned both Lord Gordon, who had been in the south, and seventeen-year-old Adam Gordon, taken with his father and brother. There was to be no more killing.

XIV

The box placed before her was ornamented with a ruff of finest lace, secured with a Spanish comb. Mary took it up and shook it gently. Flamina had given it to her, and was having trouble keeping from laughing.

"Shall I open it now?" asked Mary.

"No! We have others!" Lusty handed her a basket tied with violet ribbons, and Riccio stepped forward with a paper package shaped like a crown.

"And this." Seton gave her a box secured with a lock, bound all round with brass fittings.

"Enough!" said Mary, as one of them slid off her lap and onto the floor. "This is enough for anyone's birthday."

"But a twentieth birthday is special," said Madame Rallay. "And you cannot refuse to accept them." She placed a small bundle wrapped in silk in her mistress's hands.

Already piled on a small table were the gifts from her household staff, Lord Seton, Bastian Pages, Bourgoing, and Balthazzar.

"Now, Riccio, sing as she opens them," said Beaton. "Sing something *appropriate.*"

They all laughed.

"Why, what is this? Such mirth, and I ignorant of its cause? Or am I the cause of it?" asked Mary.

"In a manner of speaking," said Riccio. "Or, rather, your situation is the cause."

"What situation?" Mary was puzzled.

"Open them! Open them, and you will not need to ask!"

Mary took the first box, the one with the ruff and the comb, and began unwrapping it. As she did so, Riccio strummed his ebony-and-ivory-inlaid lute and began playing a Spanish melody. He got down on his knees, singing, "Oh, most noble Queen, accept my suit! I, lonely Don Carlos, only need you to set me free from the lowering brow of my father, King Philip, and the snorts of the bulls!"

Mary took out a bar of fatted-oil soap with a tag that read, "When you add me to your bath, let thoughts of me waft into your nostrils." Mary lifted it and smelled it; the heavy scent of jasmine and gardenia leapt out as if they had been contained too long.

"It truly is from Spain," said Flamina.

Riccio's music reached a crescendo.

"Spanish music is so . . . insistent," said Mary. "Unlike the Spanish in their courting. Alas, Don Carlos does not seem as eager as you portray him." She laughed; she was not at all eager for Don Carlos either. She undid the silk bundle from Madame Rallay; inside was a slender bottle with a carved glass stopper. She removed it and sniffed, and felt herself transported back to France. It was the blend of flowers from Provence that Catherine de Médicis's perfumiers had made; Mary had first been allowed to wear it when she was twelve.

She closed her eyes and inhaled deeply. She could almost hear the sound of the voices at Fontainebleau, little childish voices of Charles, Claude, Elisabeth. . . .

Riccio was now playing a French *chanson*, the tune so sweet and finely balanced. His fingers plucked the strings as lightly as a breeze.

"I have loved you always," said the attached note. "Charles IX."

"It is always good to return to happy memories," said Mary. "But I fear that little Charles woos in vain."

Even as she was opening the crown-shaped box, Riccio had switched to a mournful-sounding folk tune. The gift box was made so that the top would flip off, and inside were imitation jewels, surrounding a round bottle with its own little crown on top. The note read, "I shall make you the Queen of ice and snow and nights of love that last twenty-four hours. Yours eternally, Erik XIV, King of Sweden." Mary twisted off the cap and sniffed it cautiously—would it smell like wolves and wilderness? But the unguent inside had a clean smell, like birches.

"King Erik is indeed persuasive," she said. Everyone in the circle was laughing now.

"Another, another!" cried Lusty, handing her the brass-bound box. Now Riccio raced over to the virginal and began playing a dancing, lively tune. Mary opened this one and pulled out a gold-encrusted flagon that winked even in the low light in her chamber. "Though my head is oversize, my heart is even bigger, and my Catholic chapel is larger yet," the card read. "Be my bride, and sample all three. Yours to command, His Highness Archduke Charles of Austria."

Mary opened the flagon and was almost overcome with the powerful scent of rose and carnation mixed. It filled the air and seemed to envelop her.

"Oh! His suit is strong!"

Last was the basket; Mary untied the ribbons and found an ornamented box inside. It was filled with powder that had the most delicate scent of

207

lavender. She had always loved lavender, but had only known the French variety. This was different, smelling both sweeter and lighter. The card read, "Do not overlook your humble English cousin, who is shy like this flower of the field, but will endure for more than a season, to perfume your bed or trample underfoot if it please you."

"Whoever is that?" asked Mary. "It is not signed."

Riccio was playing "Greensleeves" on his lute, and no one owned up to the package.

"My humble English cousin?" asked Mary. "This lavender comes from the area of Norfolk, I know, but the Duke of Norfolk is married, is he not? And he is not my cousin, he is Queen Elizabeth's . . . although I suppose that makes him a sort of cousin-in-law." She looked at all the faces; would no one confess?

Humble English cousin . . . English cousin . . . the Earl of Lennox's son, Henry Stuart? He was some three years younger than she, she knew. Once that had made him a child, but now that she herself was twenty, that was no longer true. At seventeen, men went to war as soldiers, and ruled as kings without regents. She wondered if Henry Stuart was that sort.

"Henry, Lord Darnley?" she asked.

"Yea!" Riccio leapt up and ran into the adjoining chamber, then reentered, tottering on stilts. Everyone laughed. "I am so tall, I make myself dizzy!" he cried.

"Is my cousin really so tall?" asked Mary. She really knew very little about him. His father, Matthew Stuart, who was related to the French Stuarts, had been banished from Scotland when she was only two years old, and had lived in England ever since.

"Very tall, like Goliath!" Riccio assured her.

Just then Lord James and Maitland entered the chamber, also bearing gifts. They both stared at Riccio as he hung there in the air, looking down at them.

"You are now one of her ladies-in-waiting?" asked Lord James, disbelief flooding his voice. "You live with the ladies?"

Maitland had a look on his face like someone who has just seen an embarrassing object where it ought not to be—an expensive gift in a trash bucket, a dog turd on a clergyman's shoe sole.

"No, indeed not!" he said, hopping down.

"You are here so *much*," said Maitland.

That evening, Mary asked that a hot bath be prepared for her, so that she could enjoy all the fragrances she had been given.

"I will soak in water scented with the Spanish soap, will rub my toes with the birch unguent, dust myself with the lavender, put the roses on my neck, and sprinkle my handkerchiefs with the flowers of Provence," Mary told Lusty.

"And make Holyrood reek like a harem," said Lusty.

As Mary lay in the scented water—so laboriously hauled up to fill her tub—she let herself relax. The fragrance was delicate and soothing, and she stretched out her legs and tilted back her head.

It had been very amusing today. Very clever of her loved ones to think of those presents and play that game. But . . .

She splashed water on her face and felt the warm rivulets run down her cheeks.

It was not really a game.

I realize now I must marry, she thought. Part of me wants to marry; I am tired of being alone, I long to have a companion. And after the Huntly rebellion, I lost my last ally against all the convinced Protestants. I have no one to support me, should I wish to do anything contrary to their wishes. Perhaps a foreign prince would not be unwise. The might of Spain would serve as warning to any overzealous lords here. But I would be just as lonely, for Don Carlos would remain in Spain except for short visits.

Charles IX is hopeless. The Archduke is a distinct possibility. King Erik of Sweden? The same problem as Don Carlos. If I have a husband, I want him with me. One does not marry to escape loneliness and then continue to live alone.

Henry, Lord Darnley? If he is already a man, then perhaps. He is not an English subject, but he also has royal blood. He is the last male in the Tudor line, Elizabeth's cousin as well as mine. Perhaps this match would please her, and induce her to soften about the succession. I would like to marry to please her as well as myself, if such a thing is possible.

"Madam." Madame Rallay was standing beside her, holding a letter. "This is for you."

Mary opened it, and found a poem in gushing, overexcited French, praising her beauty, wisdom, and majesty.

"What *is* this?" she asked.

"The poet Chastelard," replied Madame Rallay. "He has unexpectedly returned to your court, and wishes to pay homage."

Annoyance tugged at her. She had been glad to see the tiresome man gone—and now he was back?

"Another time," she said.

The sleek oil from the fatted bar of soap was coating her skin, making her feel as slippery as a fish. Emerging from the tub, she allowed Madame Rallay to blot her with a soft towel and dust her with the lavender powder. A box was waiting on the stool just beside her bath-screen. She opened it and found an embroidered silk stole, a gift from Lord James. She put it on, draping it over her robe, enjoying the luscious smoothness next to her neck.

She was surprised, as she entered her bedchamber, to find Riccio there. He stared at the stole.

"It is beautiful!" he said. "Yellow silk of such a vibrant shade . . . I did not realize there were dyes that could duplicate the colour of marigolds. And the embroidery—pure gold thread?"

She nodded, and undid her hair, which fell down about her shoulders. "A gift from Lord James," she said.

Riccio's bulging eyes bulged even wider. "Oh, my. Well, it is only fitting that he pay tribute with such an expensive gift. After all, you have made him very rich. The earldom of Moray . . . such extensive lands!"

"Yes."

"Almost the most extensive in Scotland."

"For a newcomer, you seem to have learned quickly who owns what."

"A hobby, most gracious Majesty."

"I fail to see how concerning yourself with others' possessions can be called a hobby."

"A study, then, if you will. A study of power. Power interests me. I wish to put my knowledge, such as it is, at your service always."

"I thank you."

"I would not give Lord James any more lands or honours, Your Majesty. Too much land can result in too much power."

"That is for me to decide."

Just as she was finishing the sentence, the door opened quietly and Lord James stuck his head in, nodding it in respect.

"I am pleased you like my gift, dearest sister," he said. But he was looking at Riccio.

The warm May sun hit the cages and crates, making the animals within them whine and begin to stir. Half the court had come out to see the opening of the Queen's imports, and now they only awaited the gardeners and keepers to arrive with their pry-bars and saws. The Queen and her ladies were standing about, laughing and letting their spirits enjoy the fine day. Mary noticed John Sempill, one of those young courtiers whose dancing had caused John Knox to lecture his father about its evils, keeping close by Lusty's side. Ambassador Randolph likewise hovered near Beaton. Ah, spring!

Although Mary still wore a lighter version of mourning, it was difficult to feel sad on such a day, when all the world was rejoicing. Overhead the trees had unmasked their leaves just a few days earlier, and they seemed to expand before the Queen's eyes. If the leaves were the size of a ducat in the morning, they would be the size of a bowl by evening. Flowers were springing up, undeterred by having to push their way through the remains of last year's. Flowers had no memory, although they evoked it in others.

"Ah!" Mary was delighted to see the workmen and gardeners coming. They strode down the path, carrying their shovels and pushing their wheelbarrows, whistling as they walked.

"Gentlemen!" she said. "Before you in these crates are plants I have sent for from the gardens of France. There are Persian lilacs—"

"They won't grow here," said one workman quickly.

"Too cold," said another.

"We can try planting them on a slope that faces south, and protecting them a bit," said Mary. "And here are rose gallica, the red rose which blooms so profusely, and moonflowers which climb up trellises and open only at night—"

The gardeners said, "It will take manure!"

"I am sure there is no shortage of that from the royal stables," said Mary. "And here, I have sent for sycamore trees." She pointed to the tallest crates. "I do hope they grow here! The sound of the wind in them is one of the loveliest sounds on earth."

The men grunted.

Just then several strong young men approached, dressed in studded leather with gloves and leather caps. They carried whips and clubs. Leading them was an older man with a pistol, the menagerie-master whom Mary had appointed.

"Where are the beasts?" asked the man.

Mary pointed toward the cages with bars and air holes. "There."

"What is the variety you have?"

"Two lionesses, a bear cub, a wolf, and a porcupine."

"Lionesses!" The men looked interested. "Adult ones?"

"No, but more than cubs," said Mary. "At least that was what I was told."

The men approached the cages carefully. "Where will you want these beasts?"

"In a menagerie here at Holyrood," she said. "Later I will send for animals for the one at Stirling."

One thing at a time, she thought. One step at a time. Slowly years of neglect are reversed. The flower beds we laid out last year have thrived with the native varieties. And the menagerie had to be rebuilt before animals could be brought; a lioness cannot wait long in a cage!

The Marys were laughing and examining the plant stocks the gardeners were unpacking. Some of them looked dead in their straw wrappings. But that could be deceiving. The French roses, for instance . . .

At the thought of France, a darkness seemed to flit across the clear, joyous day. Things were no longer light and happy in France. The wars of religion had wrought much sorrow. The Duc de Guise, her beloved uncle, had been assassinated by a Huguenot, shot in the back. All the leaders of both sides had been either killed or captured: Antony of Navarre killed in battle, Conde of Navarre and Constable Montmorency captured, before a treaty of sorts was signed.

Chastelard, the poet attached to Montmorency's son, had reappeared in Scotland, some thought now on a political mission of some sort. But the fool—the stupid pawn! Mary felt wretched remembering his strange behaviour, hiding under her bed, claiming to be overcome with love—it had ended with his execution. But Lord James had assured her it had meant to end with hers. The poet had gone to his death quoting Ronsard and saluting his love for her, "the most cruel princess in the world."

211

A spring of killing. Mary prayed that it would be over now, that the demon of violence had been purged. But she would have to wear mourning even longer now, in honour of her uncle.

Behind her and on the paths of the still-bare garden, Lord James and Maitland were looking critically at the gathering.

"More French nonsense," muttered Lord James. "Crates of such things. I hope she is paying for it out of her French dower revenues, and not from crown money."

"I am pleased that she labours to improve her home, all the more if she does it at her own expense," replied Maitland. "Soon she may bring a husband to share all of it." Seeing Lord James frown, Maitland continued smoothly, "Clearly our Queen must marry. That is the *natural* order of things. But whom? He should be royal. He should, ideally, be Catholic to please her, but lukewarm in the practice of it to suit her subjects. It is difficult."

"The ideal candidate, then," said Morton, who had been standing by and listening, "would be an irreligious Catholic who would consent to having his son raised Protestant. He should be of royal or noble blood. He should be of sound mind and body. And, preferably, he should be a foreigner—"

"Quite so," said Maitland.

"And why is that?" persisted Morton.

"So that Scotland is raised into the ranks of the highest councils of Europe, her prestige increased—" began Lord James.

"No one is listening but us," said Morton. "Save that bull's pizzle for the simpleminded. It's so that she will marry her prince and sail off for Europe to his court, never to return to Scotland. Then we, the Lords of the Congregation, can rule as we are meant to do. All in the name of little James or Robert or Malcolm or whatever she names him."

"Ignacio or Pierre or Ludwig, more like," said Maitland.

"So negotiations are under way with Don Carlos, Charles IX, and the Archduke Charles?" asked Morton.

Lord James smiled and shrugged. "The mails are slow after the long winter. And the Queen has not shown herself to be exactly consumed with interest in the entire issue."

"That puzzles me. She seems to inspire passion in men but have none of her own," said Morton. "That John Gordon episode. And then the scandal with the French poet last month." He shook his head. "Both of them died for their obsession with her."

Maitland shook his head. "Strange business."

"Poor little poet. He was someone's dupe—someone who wanted to dishonour the Queen of Scots. An agent of some sort," said Morton. "Sent from France."

"Whoever sent him knew the Queen well. She is not circumspect; she is too free and familiar with everyone. She encouraged him, unknowingly perhaps, but danced with him, hung on his neck," Lord James remembered. It had been coquettishly disgusting.

"As she does with that Riccio fellow." Morton frowned with the impropriety of it all.

"Indeed. Precisely." Lord James nodded. "It is not seemly. And of late I believe she has been confiding things of a political nature to him, and seeking his advice."

Morton raised one eyebrow. "Then you should look to it, men, or you will find yourselves without a position." He looked at Lord James and Maitland. "I am Chancellor now, in Huntly's place. But the little Italian may soon be the master of all of us."

"Nonsense!" cried Maitland.

"Is it? How often have you conferred with the Queen in private since the Chastelard affair?"

Lord James shrugged. "I see no change. She has been upset, naturally, and—"

"And sought solace from her faithful lute player. Yes. Understandable." Morton snorted; *he* understood all too well. Sins of the flesh.

"She is unhappy about the continuing religious wars in France," said Lord James. "The death of her uncle the Duc de Guise. Orleans, where François died, desecrated by killings and destruction. The forest where they hunted, now filled with soldiers and artillery . . . it grieves her."

"France is past," snapped Morton.

The cries of astonishment and excitement as the lion cages were opened drew their attention.

"You must admit she has brought graceful ways to Scotland," said Maitland.

"Scottish lions," said Lord James. "They are our emblem. They mean power as well as grace."

"If it is power she wants," said Maitland thoughtfully, "then she should try to please Elizabeth by marrying to suit her."

જી

A year later, still unmarried, Mary lay prostrate in bed—alone. She had been struck down by a virulent fever, fierce aches in her back and legs, and chills that shook her so badly that she was mounded under heaps of covers, even though it was once again May and quite warm. She called for a fire to be lit in the chamber, and Madame Rallay and Bourgoing obeyed, even though it made those two indefatigable caretakers sweat profusely. Mary's teeth were chattering; her lungs were on fire and she coughed in spasms, but nothing came up.

It had come upon her quite suddenly, while she was going over dispatches with Riccio—promoted now to secretary in charge of her French correspondence, which was most of it. A quick stabbing pain in her head, a feeling of heat, of dizziness . . .

"I must stop for a moment," she had said, and made her way unsteadily to her bedchamber. "I will rest here, just for a while. . . ."

When Riccio peeked in an hour later, he found her asleep, but groaning. He put his hand to her forehead and found it hot; he summoned Bourgoing.

During the next few hours she had worsened, baffling Bourgoing, until he had suddenly said, "I know what it is! It is 'the New Acquaintance'— so called because it is so catching it makes many new acquaintances! I have heard of it, but never seen it myself."

"Do you mean *la influenza?*" asked Riccio. "The ailment that comes from the influence of the stars?"

"Is that what causes it? I had heard it was prevalent in Italy; I have been told it is making its way north—"

"Now, pray, don't blame Italy!" said Riccio with a laugh. "And don't blame me—I didn't bring it!"

"Of course I won't blame you!" said Bourgoing. "What an absurd thing to say. Do you think everything centers on you?"

"It is not I who think it, but others. It is Riccio who is blamed for everything these days—the high price of grain, the drought, the Queen's disinterest in Robert Dudley."

"You exaggerate," said Bourgoing. But the Italian had a point.

"No, it is *they*, the Lords, who exaggerate. They greatly exaggerate my influence—my *influenza*, ha, ha—with the Queen."

Mary gave a groan and both men were instantly beside her. "Riccio, I am sorry . . . cannot finish the letters now . . . you do it . . . routine. . . ." Her eyes were closing again.

Riccio sighed. "And they are routine," he assured Bourgoing. "A sympathy letter to Catherine de Médicis on the fifth anniversary of her widowhood, an inquiry to Her Majesty's ambassador to Paris, Archbishop Beaton. Such things are all I attend to."

Mary could hear them talking, but it was as if she were a great distance away, and the voices were echoing in the well of her head. Her head throbbed with the pulse in her temples; she felt so weak that she could barely lift her hand to tug at the covers, and her body was one giant ache. She slept, whirled away, but not into normal sleep. Dreams of huge dimension seized her, and thoughts began to run like stampeding animals through her mind.

Dudley. Robert Dudley, Elizabeth's favourite . . . shall I take him, as she says? She wants me to marry him, her own subject, and hints that if I do so, then she will recognize me as her chosen successor.

But will she? What if I were to marry him, only to have her decline to name me after all?

Why, then, I'd be in bed with Master Robert. Lord of the Horse, Robin of Cumnor Place, Cumnor Place, broke her face, tripped on her lace, fell in haste. . . .

"Drink something!" A bowl was being forced between her lips, and she could feel liquid spilling down over her chin. Nothing was going down.

In bed with Robert, Robert, Robert . . . shall I?

She lay ill for five days, sweating, coughing, and floating in and out of consciousness. Then, abruptly, she began to feel better. She could feel the illness ebbing in her, giving up its grip. She struggled to sit up, but found that the exertion was more than she could bear. Instantly, Madame Rallay was beside her.

"Oh, my lamb, my dearest! Do not struggle! Are you better? Are you hungry?"

"Nay," said Bourgoing, staying her hand. "First liquid, then food." He held open her eyelids and examined the inside linings, then had her open her mouth so he could look in. "Food will be too rough on this throat; it will remain tender for many days."

"Uhhh—" Mary attempted to speak for the first time since she had succumbed to the complete grip of the illness. Her throat felt unused, and the voice that issued from it was not her normal one.

"Don't try to talk!" scolded Madame Rallay. "Now here, have this soup—"

By the next day she was sitting up in bed. Seton had come to brush and arrange her hair, combing through the tangles earned in the days tossing on a sweat-soaked pillow, and she felt presentable, attired in a bed-mantle.

Her first visitor was Maitland. He came into the room, neatly dressed as always, his thinning hair combed so that it did not look quite so thin. She expected him to look around furtively for Flamina (why else had he combed his hair that way?) but he did not; he seemed genuinely concerned only for Mary herself. "Thank God!" he said. "Although we knew you were healthy, and the New Acquaintance prefers her victims feeble, still, when a Queen is ill, it is a dangerous thing." He smiled, and extended his hand. In it was a just-opened, deep red rose. The scent was as rich as incense. "The first blossom from your imported roses, planted last year. Is it not a sign?"

She took the rose and held it carefully. Indeed it seemed to be. The roses were blooming; the transplants were thriving. "Thank you, dear Maitland."

The next day she insisted on getting up and calling for her Marys to help her dress, although she was still shaky on her feet. But when Beaton brought out her favourite spring-weight gown of pearl grey, she found that it was too big. She had lost a great deal of weight in the short time of her illness.

"We'll have new ones made, then," said Mary. The prospect of new gowns was not displeasing.

Balthazzar took out his tape measure and slid it around her waist, and chest, and even her upper arms, and shook his head. "Yes, you are much thinner. I could take in the other gowns. But I think it would be better, since, as you recover, you will regain your weight and strength, if we simply made two or three new ones for now. Is it time—is Your Majesty ready to wear colours again?"

"No, I will keep to grey, black, white, and violet."

"Dearest Madam, if you are entertaining the suits of candidates for your hand," said Seton, "then would not something gayer be more in keeping?"

"I will know when it is time, Seton," Mary said quietly.

Late that afternoon Lord James arrived, bearing a letter that had come direct from Queen Elizabeth. He could barely restrain his curiosity as Mary broke open the seals and laboriously read the letter. She had always loved the beautiful signature:

"She asks that I allow the Earl of Lennox to return to Scotland and inspect his forfeited estates," she said.

"That traitor!" said James. "He who sold himself like a mercenary to Henry VIII, to deliver Dumbarton Castle to the English! Well he deserved to lose his lands and titles!" James's voice rose in disgust. "And all out of spite because our royal father did not adopt him as his heir. He did not have to, after you were born. So you see, he's been your enemy since your birth, and doubtless still wishes you ill."

"It was a long time ago," she said. "If he now wishes to do penance, be forgiven—"

"Once a traitor, always a traitor. You are too softhearted, sister!"

"A good ruler must be merciful," she insisted.

"A good ruler must look to his own safety before showing mercy."

Her eyes returned to the letter, ignoring his comment. "And so I will show mercy," she said, "though some mistake it for weakness. I will pardon the Earl of Lennox and restore him to his estates, as Elizabeth has requested me to do. It was twenty years ago that he turned and worked against his king. Twenty years . . . may not a sin be expiated after twenty years? How long must someone be forced to pay for a youthful mistake, a folly?"

"*This* is folly!" said Lord James, flatly. "One folly does not wipe out another. It only compounds the folly. One folly bred to another gives birth to disaster."

"She does not mention Robert Dudley in this letter," said Mary, trying to change the subject. Lord James looked so unhappy.

"And if she did?" he asked. "What would you say?"

"Why, I would say . . . that I would like to have a look at him, see what all the fuss is about."

In spite of himself, Lord James laughed. "I have seen him."

"And?"

"He's . . . fetching, considering his low origins. Or rather, perhaps he

216

is fetching *because* of his low origins. Some women like that sort. Queen Elizabeth herself, so it seems."

After he left the Queen's quarters, Lord James hurried away to find Maitland. He almost forced him into a small chamber, hustling him in and locking the door behind them. "Queen Elizabeth wants the Earl of Lennox given leave to return. And *our* Queen is like to do it! Her illness has made her lightheaded. Stop her! She listens more to you than to me; she thinks you have less vested interest in things."

"I cannot stop her. When she sets her mind on something, she is as stubborn as Elizabeth herself. The more I tried to argue against it, the more she would strain to do it."

"Then pretend you are in favour of it! Oh, Maitland! If that man returns, everything changes. He will assert his claim to being heir to the throne, he'll bring that son of his in his wake—"

"The pretty Lord Darnley?" Maitland mused. "And use him to dazzle the Queen? Oh, Jesu!"

"The two of them would be formidable, and undo all our good work. They care nothing for Scotland, that's plain, but only for advancing themselves. Why, their family motto shows it: *Avant Darnley! Jamais d'arrière!* Forward Darnley! Never retreat! Stop her, Maitland, stop her!"

"I tell you, I am powerless." And he was beginning to feel powerless, too. His legs were weak, and he had a pounding headache. "Pray let me sit down just a moment—"

Maitland took to his bed that evening. The New Acquaintance, notoriously catching, had found a new friend. The secretary's kindness in being the first to visit his Queen and bring her a rose had earned him this reward. Consequently he was unable to discuss Lennox with her, and by the time he recovered, word had been sent to London granting Queen Elizabeth's request.

XV

adame Rallay had surprised Mary when she casually said, "I have been studying the stars, and great changes—some good, some not, all of great magnitude—are pending."

"Studying the stars? How do you come by that?" she asked sharply. She looked over at her lifelong servant and thought, Are there surprises in every person?

"At the French court, you know, Catherine de Médicis had her astrologers and fortune-tellers. Do you not remember? She was quite dependent on them." Madame Rallay paused. "Well, there were many hours, especially when we were at Chaumont, when time hung heavy. I used to talk to Ruggieri—you remember him, the one in the tower?"

Yes, Mary did remember. She had climbed up there, although it had been forbidden. There had been a mirror that he used to foretell the future. "Yes, a little," she said.

"He taught me the rudiments of the science."

"But it is forbidden!" said Mary. She looked carefully at Madame Rallay, who was now almost sixty. "You know Christians must not engage in fortune-telling! And you are of an age where people might suspect you of being a witch! For shame, Madame!"

"But astrologers are not witches," Madame Rallay said. "They hold respectable positions in society. Why, Queen Elizabeth selected her Coronation Day on the advice of astrologers. And if it weren't a science, and didn't reveal the future, why would it be forbidden to consult them concerning a king's health?" The old lady was eminently sensible. "It was a good skill to acquire, like darning hose or being able to dry herbs for medicines." She paused. "However, it would be best if you did not mention this to Father Mamerot."

Mary sighed. "Very well, then. What do you see?"

"I am no expert, so all I have been able to read is that there are major changes in the heavens."

"I do not need the stars to tell me that!" said Mary, with a laugh. "First of all, there are always major changes afoot *somewhere*. And second, there are two in my own life: I have sent Melville to talk with Queen Elizabeth about her proposed husband for me, Robert Dudley. And I have also sent notice that the Earl of Lennox shall be allowed to return to Scotland."

Both of these things had caused her much concern. She was puzzled by Queen Elizabeth's offering her own favourite, Robert Dudley, as a husband. Did she really mean it? If so, why? Mary had almost laughed at it, it had seemed so ridiculous. Robert Dudley's own father and grandfather had been executed for treason, and the family's lineage before that was obscure. Dudley was described as coming from "a tribe of traitors." Everything in the offer smacked of insult, except for one thing: although the whole world snickered at Robert Dudley and looked down upon him, it seemed that Elizabeth herself loved him above all others and considered him her dearest friend. Whatever the rest of the world thought, in offering him to Mary, Elizabeth was making a sacrifice herself.

The match with Don Carlos had come to nothing; Philip himself had withdrawn the offer and it seemed that Don Carlos was mad and had been locked up. Erik of Sweden had sent love letters but little else, and the Archduke Charles had suddenly been rediscovered by Elizabeth. Round and round it went.

Mary turned and said to Madame Rallay, "Come, brush my new clothes. They are almost ready for the ceremony and must please you, since they are in colours. You know I will allow myself to wear colours for state occasions."

She called for Balthazzar and asked him to bring her gown. "Indeed it is almost ready, Your Majesty. And the coat of cloth-of-silver—!" He rolled his eyes.

Mary was now dressed for the elaborate ceremony that was part of the reception of the Earl of Lennox back into Scottish society. She sat in state in her presence chamber at Holyrood, waiting for him to make the final part of his journey down the Canongate. At this very moment he was being officially pardoned at the Mercat Cross by the Lord Lyon King of Arms, heraldic representative of the Crown, and his outlawry was being rescinded. The wand of peace would be delivered to his representative, and then he would come here. . . .

Matthew Stewart, or Stuart. What do I know of him, really? she thought, as she waited. I know he's a second cousin, being descended from James II. I know there is a French branch of his family that spells its name Stuart, just as mine was spelt that way there. It dates back to the Hundred Years War, when Sir John Stewart of Darnley was one of the commanders of a Scottish force that helped the French in their struggles against the English. John Stewart turned into John Stuart, Sieur d'Aubigny, and his family is still there.

I know Matthew himself spent many years in France in his youth and even fought with François I in his Italian wars. He came back to Scotland briefly, joined the pro-English group, and was therefore declared a traitor and expelled. He went south to England and married Lady Margaret Douglas, my father's half sister, and has been at the English court ever since.

She could hear the sound of the crowd outside. Lennox must be approaching. Swiftly she continued to review exactly what she knew of him. The Lennox Stuarts were the hereditary enemies of the Hamiltons, because both claimed to be the most direct descendant of James II, and therefore the next natural heir to the throne after the monarch's children.

My father favoured Lennox's claim, she remembered. He promised, if he had no child of his own, to recognize Lennox as his heir to the crown. But then I was born, and Lennox turned traitor and was banished. . . .

The trumpets were announcing his arrival. Mary could hear the footsteps as his large company mounted the stairs, and then the doors swung slowly open and the guard proclaimed, "Matthew Stuart, Earl of Lennox, petitions to be admitted."

Standing in the midst of a retinue of some forty gentlemen, a middle-aged man was looking steadily across at her.

"You may enter."

As he approached, she thought of his strange background, and how he would seem foreign to most of her nobles. But for this very reason, she expected him to contribute something to court, as he had a breadth of outlook and experience few local lords could match.

"Welcome," Mary said, rising from her throne and allowing him to embrace her and bestow a kiss of homage. "As my cousin, as the husband of my dear father's sister, I render you all affection and respect."

He bowed low again, his bejewelled back looking like that of a patterned tortoise. Then he straightened and smiled.

He had once been handsome, that much was evident. His round face still bore traces of boyish appeal, and his eyes were kindly.

Mary smiled at him. "We are pleased that you return to us, and pray that you find your estates in good order," she said. His hereditary estates were in the midwestern area of Scotland, near Glasgow, and before he could pass by to inspect them, he must be formally pardoned and received by the Queen and the nobles.

"Your Majesty is too gracious," he said.

"Another ale!" The serving girl called out to the tapster, and Melville gave her a conspiratorial smile. She smiled back, a long, slow smile, and he wondered what—if anything—it betokened?

She brought him the refilled leather mug and he paid. Probably nothing, he thought. It betokens nothing and it is just as well. I must needs keep my breeches on and my purse guarded. But it is sweet to imagine all the unknown things that could pass with an unknown woman.

"Where are ye comin' from?" the man seated on the bench next to him asked suddenly. His voice was unpleasantly pitched.

"Edinburgh," replied Melville. He had to raise his voice to be heard above the clatter in the dining room of the inn. "I'm on my way to London."

"To see the Queen?" bellowed the man, then broke out singing, "Pussycat, pussycat, where have you been? I've been to London to look at the Queen!" His fellow diners stared at him with distaste.

"No," Melville lied. How surprised they would be if he were truthful.

"How long have you been on the road?" asked the man.

"Five days. I stopped first at Berwick, then at Newcastle."

The man whistled and a bubble of pork fat flew from his lips, from the meat pie he was eating. "You move swiftly. Another day should see you in London. Or St. Albans at least."

"I hope so. What condition will I find the road in?"

"I've heard that the road to London is dry and well travelled just now," said the serving girl, mysteriously reappearing just at Melville's left shoulder. "A group from London was here last night. They stopped early as they liked our sign."

Indeed it had been the sign, beautifully painted, that had caught Melville's eye: The Jolly Tortoise. A finely rendered tortoise with black and yellow markings danced in a field of strawberries. It promised an inn with clean linens and a good table.

"So did I," he said. "But I must then leave early tomorrow."

He was just as happy to rest, eat, and drink before the next stage of his journey. Once he arrived in London he would find scant rest; indeed, he would have to guard every word he spoke, his mission was so double-sided.

His sovereign mistress Queen Mary had sent him publicly to pursue the Dudley offer while evaluating Elizabeth's sincerity, and at the same time secretly to approach the Lady Lennox and ascertain exactly what sort of man Lord Darnley had grown into. The Earl of Lennox was anxious that his son follow him to Scotland to inspect his estates, but Darnley needed Elizabeth's permission and a passport to do so.

Ordinarily, Melville would have looked forward to a lengthy visit at the English court—a visit long enough to permit him to have another pair of boots made at his favorite cobbler's, to pass civilized evenings of conversation and entertainment with Cecil and the Duke of Norfolk, to meet with the Imperial and French ambassadors. He had been honoured to be selected and elevated to the rank of trusted envoy. (Or was it merely that Maitland was ill? he wondered.) But being charged with a mission that involved deceiving Elizabeth was not a palatable thing. She, the great deceiver, did not take kindly to others playing her own game; worse yet, she could quickly spot it in others.

"I cannot eat but little meat
My stomach is not good. . . ."

The company began singing, and the loud voices and flushed faces generated a happy heat of their own. Melville enjoyed it, and his own anonymity.

Queen Elizabeth looked at him sharply as he approached her in the garden at Westminster, where she was taking her customary early-morning walk.

"Mr. Melville," she said, "are you come to me about the succession or about my Lord Robert Dudley?" No hint of surprise to see him, no opening pleasantries.

"Both, Your Majesty," he replied directly.

She laughed. "Welcome, then." She gestured round at her garden behind its walls. The dampness of the river nearby made everything green. She touched a branch of a thick, gnarled pear tree and then plucked off a fruit for him.

"This is a butter pear tree. My father told me his fruiterer had brought it over from Germany. Certainly it is very old. The pears from it are as sweet as honey."

Melville nodded gravely. What was he supposed to do with the pear? It was a soft, juicy one and would make a mess in his hand if he tried to eat

221

it now out of politeness. In fact it was so soft it was beginning to ooze on his hand.

Elizabeth laughed. "Henry VII used to feed overripe fruit to his pet monkey. You may throw yours down for the birds and squirrels."

Melville felt foolish as he wiped off his hands with his stiff lace handkerchief. "I bring heartfelt greetings from the Queen my mistress, your good sister and cousin," he said.

Elizabeth raised her eyebrows. "And what answer does she make of the proposition of marriage offered by Mr. Randolph? That is, to Lord Robert Dudley?"

She would give him no grace period, then, but would go straight for it. Melville replied, "She awaits a conference between her ministers and yours, great Queen; I mean most like between the Lord James and Maitland on her side and my Lord of Bedford and Lord Dudley on yours."

"Oh!" Elizabeth stopped walking and planted her feet firmly. Her nostrils flared. "So you make small account of my Lord Dudley—you name him last! Well, sir, before you return to Scotland you shall see him made a far greater earl than that of Bedford. Yes!"

Melville merely nodded. "How fortunate."

The morning light, still gentle and golden, lit up Elizabeth's face. Melville saw her, for a brief moment, as the girl in the tavern, as a lady of a modest house, as a merchant's daughter. Her golden red hair, her fine white skin, above all the intelligence and person in the dark eyes, made her a woman a man would be drawn to, were she placed in ordinary life.

"I esteem Lord Robert as a brother," she was saying in her pleasing voice, "and as my dearest friend. We have a bond between us, stronger than that of husband and wife . . . and I would be happy to be his wife, were I minded to marry. But I am determined to end my life in virginity."

He almost believed her when she said it.

"But I offer him to my sister Queen in all sincerity, as he is the person next to myself I may trust—and *would* trust—with the succession."

"Does this mean, then, that should my lady the Queen of Scots marry him, you would declare her—or rather, them—your successor?"

"Have I not said?" She jerked her head and began walking again, leaving the row of fruit trees and pacing the bricked paths of the open garden, where sweet williams and periwinkles formed a border.

"Have we your word on this? The solemn word of a prince?"

"Have I not said?" she repeated. "And now I ask you—for I cannot command you, being not your sovereign—to keep company with Lord Robert. I shall command *him.*" She gave a wicked smile. "You shall come to know him, and thereby can persuade your mistress the Queen as to his virtues."

Queen Elizabeth later sent word that she would have Mr. Melville attend her at dinner at Whitehall Palace, and stay for an entertainment in the banqueting hall, and she would have him conveyed in the royal barge, with its twenty oarsmen.

He was barely settled on a cloth-of-gold bolster inside the cabin and expecting a pleasant journey on the river—something one could not experience in Scotland, which had neither navigable rivers nor a royal barge—when someone appeared in the doorway and then, ducking his head, descended the steps into the cabin.

Dudley.

He was so fashionably dressed, with his full, stiff sleeves and shoulder wings of yellow brocade, he looked like a fashion apparition, a ghost from a Parisian tailor's den.

"Good day," he said to Melville, looking around at the otherwise empty cabin. "I see she means us to be alone." He laughed. "Sometimes my Queen is complex, sometimes simple." He turned around so that Melville could view his costume. "Does this pass muster? I understand the Queen of Scots is very fashionable and sends regularly to Paris for patterns and material."

Melville laughed, too. Then he looked carefully at Dudley and concluded a woman could look far without doing better. And evidently he had humour and humility.

"Very smart, my Lord."

"And what will you tell your mistress?" Dudley seated himself nearby on a cushioned bench. He looked directly at Melville, but smiled.

"That you are pretty on the eyes," he replied.

Dudley made a disparaging sound. "Good sir, we are alone. My Queen arranged it and I thank her for it, for such an opportunity is rare. Let me use it to assure you I have no pretensions of marrying so far above myself. It would be an insult to the Queen of Scots, as well I know. I am not worthy to wipe her shoes!"

Melville felt the boat moving as the rowers took her out into the mainstream of the river. But the lurching was within himself, not the boat. What was this all about? Was nothing certain or honest here?

"That is a strange utterance, coming from you," he finally said.

"It is all Cecil's doing! My secret enemy. He means me to offend both Queens and be utterly out of favour, leaving all power at court to him. For if I seem to desire the marriage, I offend my Queen by unfaithfulness and yours by presumption; and if I seem not obedient to it then I likewise offend mine by disobedience and yours by insult. So either way, I am discredited and dispossessed of my Queen's favour." He slumped miserably on his seat.

Melville almost felt sorry for this proud man, reduced to a woman's pawn by circumstance. He was like a sacrificial bull to their ambitions.

"I think neither Queen will require anything of you," was all he could say.

"Pray beg your Queen's pardon for my seeming presumption," insisted Dudley.

Several days later the sacrificial bull was led to kneel at Westminster before his Queen, and the peers in their Parliament robes, and to be made Earl of Leicester—a title last borne by Henry V and hitherto reserved for princes alone. It was all very solemn, until Elizabeth leaned forward and, in fastening his robes of estate, let her hand caress and tickle his neck.

De Seurre, the French ambassador, looked at Melville and made a cynical face.

As the party turned to process out, Elizabeth stopped to speak to Melville and the ambassador.

"How like you the new Earl of Leicester?" she asked eagerly, brightly.

Ahead of her, Lord Robert was walking straight and proud in his new embroidered cape with its fur trimmings, and before him Henry Lord Darnley was bearing the sword of honour.

"He is a happy servant who has a mistress who can discern and reward good service and worthiness," Melville replied. To leap from simple "Sir Dudley" to a royal earlship was a head-spinning elevation.

"Yet you like better yonder long lad," said Elizabeth, pointing toward Darnley.

She knew! She had found out his secret mission! What spy—how—? Or was she simply so devious herself it was impossible to fool her?

"No woman of any spirit would make choice of such a man, who resembles a woman, not a man! He is lady-faced, and has no beard," said Melville stoutly.

"Indeed," Elizabeth said, smiling sweetly. "Yet he carries the sword well, being as supple and strong as a blade himself."

XVI

nd then what did she do?" Mary asked. She and Melville were closeted in the tiny chamber off her bedroom in Holyrood.

"She made no further reference to 'yonder long lad'—and he *is* 'long,' Your Majesty. So I cannot know what she knows, or has surmised. I believe I was unobserved when I visited the Countess of Lennox, but I am not certain. I am relatively sure that my conversation there could not have been overheard." He sighed. The entire time in England had been strained, and even the boots were not made to his satisfaction.

Mary took a blackberry tartlet from a platter and offered Melville one.

He declined. She took her time chewing before asking, "Is he taller than I?"

She stood up, her loose gown falling in thick columns from her waist.

"I believe so. And I must say he is handsome. Of course I twisted that when she asked what I thought of him, so that it seemed to be a flaw rather than a gift. As first prince of the blood at court, he led the ceremonies, and made a pretty showing."

"Hmmm." She smiled. "And spoke well, you say?" She returned to her seat and leaned back in the chair. Could it be possible . . . just possible . . . that this cousin of hers, who looked so right on paper, could also be personally attractive to her?

"More than well. Exquisitely. I had occasion to speak to him at length several times."

"And what did you speak of?" She had begun twirling a thick strand of hair around her finger.

"Nothing, really." He could not remember. It had been insubstantial— the weather, popular tunes, court gossip. "Lord Dudley was also well spoken," he added as an afterthought. "He is an interesting man."

"Could you see what captured Elizabeth's fancy in him?"

Yes. Yes, he could. "It is difficult to understand any woman's fancy, let alone a queen's. A queen's heart is unfathomable," replied the diplomat. "And particularly *this* Queen's. Let me tell you what she did: she tried to make me disloyal to you!"

"No! How?" Mary's eyes sparkled with excitement. She left off playing with her hair and stared at Melville.

At that moment he coolly analyzed her features, the ones Elizabeth had interrogated him about. Her hair was undoubtedly one of her best attributes, shiny, thick, curly, and of a luxuriant red-brown. But her pink and white colouring and her slanting, luminous, amber-coloured eyes were so striking they created an impression of fragile vitality—if such a paradox made sense, he thought. The life was there, the high spirits, the *joie de vivre*, but the physical body delicate. She suggested fleeting joys and elegiac pleasures; she made a man want to hold her right now, today, in this moment.

He tried to shut out such disrespectful thoughts toward the woman who was his earthly sovereign.

"She flirted with me," he said.

"How?"

"She put on different gowns and asked me to judge which of them was most flattering."

Mary burst out laughing. "And which did you choose?"

"The Italian. She has a wardrobe of gowns from every country, and she wore one day the English, the next the French, and so on. But the Italian flattered her most, as it allowed her to show her hair wearing a caul and bonnet."

"And what is her hair like?"

"Ah, now you sound like her! Her hair is more reddish than yellow, and curls naturally. But she asked about yours, and which colour of hair is preferable, and who had the fairest?"

"No!" Mary cried. "Surely she must have toyed with you?"

"Indeed, she was in complete earnest. She demanded me to declare which was the fairest."

"And?"

"I said that the fairest of both was not your worst faults. Then," he lamented, "she asked me to declare outright which of you was the fairest. That was simple. I said you were the fairest Queen in Scotland and she in England. But she was not satisfied with that. She pressed me further. At length I said that each of you was the fairest ladies in your countries, but that her complexion was paler, although your colouring was lovely."

"And did that satisfy her?"

"Indeed no. For next she asked who was taller, and when I proclaimed you to be of greater height, she replied, 'Then she is too tall, for I myself am exactly the right height.' "

Mary burst out laughing.

"And she went on from there. She began to inquire about how you passed your time, your interests. I replied that you had just returned from Highland hunting, and that you often read histories, and sometimes amused yourself in playing the lute and the virginals. Then she turned on me—Madam, she has a riveting eye, like a bird of prey—and asked if you played well. 'Reasonably well, for a queen,' I replied."

Mary made a face. "Traitor!"

"I thought it would disabuse her of the notion that she must excel in all she does. But no! For she next arranged for me to 'accidentally' overhear her playing. She affected to be embarrassed to be heard, but it was no such thing. Then she inquired, once again, who played better, yourself or her? I must confess, Your Majesty, I gave her the praise, just out of weariness with this game."

"Ah! Double traitor then!"

"But it did not end, no. It went on, as she detained me two extra days so that I might see her dance, and compare your skills. She queried me as to who danced better, my Queen or herself? I answered that Your Majesty danced not so high or disposedly as she did—and 'twas true, for she forgets all modesty in dancing and leaps about like a man. But, God be thanked, she took it as a compliment and let me depart at long last."

"How peculiar! She seems to have the same curiosity about me that I do about Lord Darnley or Lord Robert," Mary said.

"She did and said other odd things. She took me up to her private chamber and showed me portraits of you and Lord Robert. She kissed your portrait and then said she would send either Lord Robert or a great ruby as a token to you."

"But as to Darnley—do you think she will grant him the necessary passport?" Suddenly she knew she would be immensely disappointed if she could not see Darnley in person.

"There is an even chance of it. Particularly if you seem warm to the match with the new Earl of Leicester."

"Then, good Melville, write my tender cousin the Queen that I am deeply disappointed that you have returned without the portrait of Lord Robert, and disappointed that Leicester himself sent no token to me. Tell her I await it. Then tell her how pleased I was to grant her request about the Earl of Lennox, and mention that the father would like the son to be able to see the estates—just to *see* them, which he never has. In the meantime I will send a handsome present."

Melville sighed. This seemed like a tennis match that would go on and on. Serve, volley, serve . . . "Yes, Your Majesty."

After Melville had left, Mary sat looking out the window for a long time. On paper, as she had said, this cousin looked so promising. He was not a foreigner, he was of royal blood and also had a claim to the English throne, and had spent time in France. He was even tall! He sounded too good to be true.

If I had made him up, I would have included all these features, Mary thought. Even to his being Catholic . . .

❧

In the cold December days just before her twenty-second birthday, Mary opened Parliament at the Tolbooth. She had convened it expressly for the purpose of restoring the Earl of Lennox to his honours and estates, and she marched slowly up the Canongate from Holyrood in procession, with Lord James bearing the crown, as the Hamiltons—who should have done so—refused to participate in the restoration rites for their political enemy. The Earl of Atholl bore the sceptre and the Earl of Crawford the sword of state.

Once inside the dark building, Mary stood and addressed the Three Estates of the Realm as to her purpose in forgiving the Earl of Lennox. Then Maitland rose and gave a second address.

"Dear countrymen," he said, "you know full well the noble descent of Matthew Stuart, and his further affinity with the Queen by way of his marriage to her aunt. Our Queen, with her tender heart, does not wish to see any noble house come to ruin; she wishes the ancient blood to continue to be revered. In the three years that Her Majesty has governed us, we have had proof of her frank and magnanimous dealings, and many notable examples of her clemency. We have been most fortunate. . . ."

Afterwards, at the banquet at Holyrood in which Lennox was feasted, Maitland had the opportunity to seek out Lord James, who had been glaring at him all day.

"Not only did you not prevent this, you had to laud it!" he hissed.

"I was powerless to prevent it," said Maitland. "You know that."

Riccio and his musicians had left off playing, and the men had to turn to general conversation until the instruments could once again provide a background to cover their voices.

When the strains of "Adieu, O Desire of Delight" were struck up, Lord James said, "Now we can expect the worst! I have heard that she exhibits great curiosity about this Darnley, her cousin. Next he will be here, following his father's trail like a puppy."

"It could be worse. At least Darnley is Elizabeth's subject, and not a foreigner."

"No, it could not be worse, if she takes a fancy to him! A whole party will be created; the Lennox Stuarts will reign supreme. And there will be no place for anyone else." Lord James looked grim. "At least not for this generation."

"Darnley is a boy. He might prove easy to rule. Once he is here, he may suit our purposes exactly." Maitland sighed. "One must look for opportunities," he said. "One must always look for opportunities."

The music had risen louder, and Mary and Melville were dancing a galliard alone on the floor. Soon Lusty and John Sempill had joined them, the dancing becoming more vigorous and abandoned. Now even Randolph and Beaton were making their way toward the others.

"I have heard reports about this 'boy,' " said Lord James. "When he was in France, away from his mother—who rules him in all things—I heard he was not so well behaved. He has a taste for wine, too much of it, and pranks."

"So he's silly and rebels against his mother. What lad does not?" said Maitland. "Did *you* never do anything you would not want your mother to know? I'll warrant even John Knox did."

XVII

Henry, Lord Darnley, sat as straight as he could in the saddle and craned his neck. They were approaching the border of Scotland; soon he would be able to see his native land for the first time. The remains of the Roman wall had been left behind at Newcastle. He had looked forward to seeing it—had even composed a poem in advance about it, a fine one too—but the wall had proved disappointing, just a moss-covered mound wrapped in mist. Perhaps once it had been mighty, had served as some sort of barrier, but now it could not stop even a grazing flock of sheep from passing to and fro. Nonetheless he whispered the refrain from his poem as he and his five attendants passed through the gap:

"Hold fast thy guarded mission,
Though the fates assail thee;
Thou hast the charge that we would wish on
To stand, to keep, and not to flee."

From the time he was a child he had heard stories of the fabled wall, built to keep the barbarians at bay. Now the wall lay engulfed in civilisation, and barbarism had been pushed farther north—north to Scotland, where he was going, although farther north than Edinburgh and Glasgow and Stirling.

There had been jolly times on the road since he had left court—stopping at inns to sport, and even drink too much. With each flagon he had toasted his mother, who customarily oversaw every morsel he ate, every costume he wore, every letter he wrote.

"Here's to you, Mother dear, Mother most watchful, Mother most grave," he cried that first day out, lifting his tankard. Then he giggled and rattled off, "Mother most pure, Mother most chaste, Mother inviolate, Mother undefiled, Mother most amiable, Mother most admirable, Mother of good counsel, Mirror of Wisdom, cause of our joy—well, that's true, she arranged all this. And now, I'm a young man going off to seek his fortune. Spiritual vessel, singular vessel of devotion, Mystical Rose"—he laughed uproariously at the image of his stout mother as a mystical rose—"Gate of Heaven, Morning Star—"

"Watch your tongue, you sotten puppy!" cried a burly man seated nearby. "If you insult the Virgin once more—"

"Insult the Virgin?" asked Darnley. "I am speaking of my mother, *my* blessed mother, not *the* Blessed Mother."

"You're perverting the Litany to the Virgin, and we don't take kindly to it. Be warned." He raised a bushy, tangled eyebrow, and the eye that stared out was like a marble.

"Aye." Darnley returned to his beer. The freedom, the freedom from *her* had quite gone to his head. It was that, rather than the liquor.

To be free of her at last! Of her meddling and lecturing and conniving and counselling. Our Lady of Constant Counsel. He giggled, and the man next to him gave another baleful stare.

Even as he had been standing in his bedchamber trying to remember if he had packed what was needful, she had come in and brushed his hair.

"Like a shining crown of gold," she had said dreamily. "Make sure when you wash it you rinse it with chamomile water to keep its colour."

"Mother!" He had clapped his hat on in disgust.

"They say *she* is partial to golden hair," she said.

"I heard she preferred black hair," he said, just to argue.

"No, I have it on the best authority—"

"Bah!" He fastened his cloak sooner than he had planned to, in order to leave. The open road beckoned, the high road to freedom. What mattered what waited in Scotland? Its most compelling charm lay in the fact that his mother was forbidden to enter. He could go where she could not follow.

As a result, he had not thought enough about Scotland itself; it had been an escape rather than an entity or reality in itself. And now that reality was lurking just a few miles away, and he felt ignorant and unprepared.

Why did I not read more about it, study more? he bewailed as they approached Berwick and the border.

Because *she* assailed me so constantly I had no leisure or privacy, he answered himself. But it was no comfort.

They passed through Berwick, the border city that had once been Scottish but had been won by the English in 1482 and remained in their hands. The Earl of Bedford, watchdog for the area, greeted them ceremonially and then escorted them to the very border itself, where the Lord James and Maitland and a company of horsemen received them.

"In the name of Her Majesty Queen Mary, we bid you welcome to Scotland," said Lord James.

His speech was perfect London English, and Darnley was disappointed.

"You sound like Englishmen," he said.

"I' th' name o' Her Majesty the Queen, we bid ye welcome tae Scotland," said James. "*Ken* ye this better?"

Darnley laughed. "They are almost two separate tongues, then."

"*Twa leids*," confirmed James.

And I have not learned it! thought Darnley with a grey feeling. They will be able to talk, and I not understand.

"I will learn," he promised. "For it is the language of my family."

"Ye are tae bide i' Holyrood for a space," said James. "An' tak yer ease at Edinburgh. Yer faither is at Dunkeld, but will soon join ye. The Queen, she is at Wemyss Castle."

It sounded like Dutch to Darnley, and it quickened his unease.

"Slowly, sir, slowly. I am but little learned in Scots as yet," he said.

"Ye'd best *leir* quickly, then," James advised, and his voice was cold.

XVIII

ary shivered even in her woollen undergarments that were supposed to keep the cold at bay. They were woven of fine light wool and were close-fitting, so they would not show under regular clothes.

She had had them made up in France, and if they proved satisfactory, she planned to order a trunkful both for herself and her Marys. But they offered scant protection against the peculiar, seeping wet chill of this February, which did not produce honest ice and snow, but white mists and creeping damp that left fingers stiff and made one shiver continually.

Throwing on her thickest mantle, fastening her beaver-fur hat, and pulling on her gloves, she decided to walk about the garden. Fight fire with fire, cold with cold, she thought. If I go outside, properly dressed, it may feel warmer than staying inside the cold stone rooms of Wemyss Castle. And walking will stir my sluggish blood.

She descended the spiral stone staircase of the corner turret of the old castle, and pushed open the thick iron-and-oak door into the garden. It was deserted in this dead time of year, its hedges bare, its flowerbeds covered in straw and burlap. Frost lay on the mounds of mulch and made a coating on the statuary. Cupid with his arrow, poised on one chubby foot, had ice on his rounded buttocks.

And tomorrow is Valentine's Day, thought Mary. Poor cold lad, you'd best cover yourself.

Strange how we forget that Cupid grew up to be a handsome god. He was as beautiful as a male Venus, and Psyche fell in love with him at one glance. Instead we cling to the dimpled child instead of the man. Why is that, I wonder?

She smiled as she thought of the little celebration she had planned for her company—Valentine choosing in the traditional manner, games, tokens. The Marys would enjoy it, particularly Mary Livingston, whose suitor John Sempill was close to hand. They would marry soon, all of them. And it was time. They were all in their twenties and had already waited long enough out of deference to their mistress.

It is good that we are here out of eyesight—and spy-sight—of Knox, she thought. Wemyss Castle is not a place he'll come, nor any of his fellows, for all it's just across the firth from Edinburgh. He has become more vociferous of late, more demanding.

She turned down the avenue of cypresses that formed a double row in the centre of the garden. The tall, sloping green trees kept a watch over the rest of the garden, almost bidding it be silent. And silent it was; no birds sang, no noise was heard, except the chafing of the water on the rocks far below. The dash and slither of the cold sea made an icy, mournful sucking sound as it pounded and withdrew, pounded and withdrew.

Mary walked to the border of the garden, which looked down at the Firth of Forth from the very edge of the cliff. A small wall had been built along the edge to prevent accidents. But it was only waist high and a person could leap over it easily. Or be pushed.

She pulled her mantle closer and lifted its hood to cover even her hat, for the wind was fierce. It blew in from the North Sea, whipping through the funnel made by the firth with its cliffs, and kept blowing, past Linlithgow and all the way to Stirling, perhaps, where it would die down, trapped in the rising inland hills.

The sky was grey and blanketed the sun. Across the firth the hills rose gently toward Edinburgh, but the fog and mist obscured it and Mary could not see the city. Even as she watched, the fog rolled in from the North Sea, almost as if it were boiling, and it climbed up the cliffs and snaked its way into the garden, obediently following the open gravel paths, getting obstructed in the brown leafless hedges, and muffling the statue of Cupid, wrapping him in a cloudy mantle. The garden turned into a smoky sea, with just a few landmarks sticking up to provide orientation: the cypresses, the top of the sundial, the tallest topiary sculptures.

I shall be swallowed up, thought Mary, as she saw that even the tower door was now invisible. She turned to grope her way back, but suddenly she saw a movement, the only one that had occurred in the garden the entire time. Something moved in the white mist—moved, then stopped. There was a gleam of metal. But no sound; no sound at all.

She made her way in that direction, keeping to the gravel path, then following a wide one that went to the very cliff-edge of the garden, where the movement had fluttered.

The gleam of metal came again, then a clanking sound: metal against metal.

Standing on the path, looking out toward the water, was a tall man, swathed in a dark cape. His head was covered, and there was a long sword hanging from his belt. He grasped its hilt and it clanked against something metal in his costume, making a low thick sound.

He seemed taller than a mortal man, and his black cloak did not seem to move with the wind; it hung as if sculpted in stone. He did not move, either, except for his hand on his sword, and the collar of his mantle obscured his features.

She came closer, and still he did not move, and made no sound. Beyond him there was a stirring, and through the mist a pale horse's head appeared, with eyes the colour of fallen leaves. She approached the man and touched his arm. He turned and looked at her.

He was pale and his eyes were as cold as the mist and blue-tinged. His lips were full but looked bloodless, and there was no colour in his cheeks. He was ageless, his face unlined as in youth, but somehow graven with all the knowledge of mortality.

She gave a little cry; he blinked and looked uncomfortable.

"I beg your pardon for frightening you," he said. A smile loosened his lips and his face changed. "I was frightened myself, and waiting here to pluck up my courage."

His horse curled back its lip and moved; the fog drifted away for a moment like smoke and revealed a pale animal with an elaborate saddle.

"What was the deed that required so much courage?" Mary asked. This young knight seemed an apparition from antiquity, perhaps even from King

232

Arthur's time. He fingered his sword—a great bejewelled one—with long white fingers.

"To present myself to a fair Queen," he said.

"And why should that affright you so?"

"She did not send for me; I came hither on my father's orders. He told me he could not leave Dunkeld for a week at least, and therefore I must go alone to present myself to her. But to presume—to just arrive—nay, it sounded better when I was far away."

"Why—you are Henry, Lord Darnley," she finally said.

He turned even paler as she threw back her hood.

"O Holy Mother! It is you! You are she! You are—oh forgive me, triple fool that I am!" He grabbed her gloved hand in his white ungloved one and began kissing it.

"Dear cousin," she said, embarrassed by his embarrassment, "I have long looked for your coming." She extracted her hand from his cold bony one. "Fret not. Is this not better than a public meeting? An exchange of civilities under the eye of all our entourages? We were both drawn here, to this dead deserted garden, for a reason . . . belike the same reason."

"Yes. A wish for solitude, for reflection, for privacy." A look of happiness sent colour into his face and at once roses bloomed in what had been a winter visage.

"Which is in scant supply for either of us," she said. "One must take it whenever possible." She motioned to him. "Will you come in now?"

"In a moment. Must we join others so soon? And be engulfed by them?"

She understood exactly what he meant, even though all the people here with her at Wemyss were of her choosing, and the people who made her feel most under scutiny were missing: Lord James and Maitland and even the kindly Erskine and Melville.

"If you wish." She smiled at him, seemingly lightly, but actually she was measuring his height and revelling in the fact that his eyes looked down on hers—something few eyes had ever done. She was used to the fact that she was taller than almost everyone, did not consciously think of it, it was so incorporated into her being, as a person on land does not think of how he balances—until he goes to sea.

"Can we see Edinburgh from here?" he asked.

"On a clear day," she said, leading him toward the lookout at the edge of the garden. "But today the mists obscure it."

Great clouds were blowing along the water, writhing and twirling. Every few seconds a quick glimpse of the land across the water showed itself.

"Almost directly across is Leith," she said.

"Edinburgh's port," he said, like a bright schoolboy. He had obviously memorized it. "And far to the left, at the tip of the landmass, is Tantallon Castle. Where my uncle the Earl of Morton welcomed my father."

"He seemed gladdened to be allowed back into Scotland."

"Oh, to come home is a joy beyond words. Is that not what Heaven is?

'Tis said we are not at home upon this earth, being only strangers and aliens cast out, but eventually we return home—if we are privileged to do so. Just so it is a second joy to return to our earthly home, when we have been cast out. It is probably the greatest happiness we are afforded in this life." His face was shining.

"But you were not cast out," she finally said. "You have never been in Scotland before. You were born in England; you are an English subject and even first prince of the blood there."

"But Scotland is my ancestral home."

"But what can that mean, precisely? It cannot inform your memories, your sensibilities. Such things must be grasped on site; they cannot be passed on like a mysterious vapour."

"Ah! You cannot understand," he said forlornly. "I only know that I *feel* Scottish, that there is something in me that always leapt at the word 'Scottish,' that thrilled when I would discover that a poem was written by a Scot or a valiant deed at arms was done by a Scot abroad or that a hitherto seemingly ordinary person had some Scots blood. At once he would seem different, elevated. Nay, I cannot explain it."

"I understand." And she did. "I felt the same when I returned to Scotland. But alas, I found that although the French considered me Scots, the Scots considered me French. I have all the feelings you described, but no one would ever ascribe them to me. Even now they consider me 'foreign,' using religion as an excuse to do so. How absurd are the subterfuges we employ— Scotland was Catholic for a thousand years. She has been Protestant for barely five. Who then is the better Scot, the more traditional Scot, the truer Scot?"

"Yes! Yes!" he said. "It is the same in England. Our ancestral religion is suddenly pronounced traitorous. Yet Edward the Confessor and Henry V professed and defended it. How then can they still be praised as heroes?"

"By holding two contradictory creeds in their heads at the same time. 'Tis most fashionable."

They both laughed.

"Our mutual great-grandfather, Henry VII—how simple his world was," she said. "One faith. Only Europe to take into account. No Protestants. No New World. No Russia or Turks. He had only the Yorkists and Lancastrians to settle. We have Protestants, preachers, heathens, heresies, the common people and their representatives, John Knox—"

"We?"

"Yes," she said calmly. "We."

Henry, Lord Darnley, was warmly welcomed into the castle where the Queen had withdrawn to have a retreat of sorts. It had a holiday air, a feeling of shoes being replaced by soft slippers and jewel-stiffened bodices by soft wrappers. Mary often took these retreats, staying in merchants' houses and dispensing with her servants and even the trappings of a queen, as a person will shed his clothes to take a restorative medicinal bath in the curative springs.

The Marys were in holiday spirits, as they treasured these times they had their mistress away from protocol and strictures. Then they could pretend to be—and could even be, for a precious space—simple maidens together. The nineteen-year-old Darnley entered into their midst easily, himself fleeing from duties and the future, playful and at ease.

On Valentine's Day there was a private celebration: an old-fashioned drawing of names for Valentines, singing and dancing. The Great Hall—although it was not a great hall but a small one—of Wemyss Castle was prepared for the event. Red ribbons were threaded in and out of the wall sconces, and the floor was cleared. Musicians were sent for from Dunfermline, as the castle lacked cittern and viol players, and music was selected.

The ancient legend was that birds chose their mates on this day, and so must humans. Accordingly two Valentine's baskets were festooned and all the men's names put in one and all the women's in the other. The company was to draw names and pair themselves. Accident and nature would assure the correct pairing.

But human needs intervened. Mary miraculously drew Darnley's name, and Mary Livingston, John Sempill's. Mary Beaton and Mary Fleming, their suitors being too much a part of the government to be present at this retreat, had to content themselves with the sackbut player and the master of the castle.

Darnley slowly unrolled the name he had drawn from the decorated basket. It said, "Mary Stuart," not "the Queen."

"Do I dare?" he asked.

"Shall I be left matchless on this day?" Mary laughed. " 'Twould be an insult." She turned toward him. "Well met, Valentine."

She looked at his handsome face. He was like a knight from a dream, so straight, so tall, so intelligent, so golden.

They danced. He danced exquisitely. Then he insisted on playing his lute, and to the astonishment of all, he was expert. Even Riccio, hugging the corner and sitting out the Valentine's festivity, nodded in approval. When all was over, Darnley sat before the fire and sang. His voice, a silky tenor, trod each note with surety and passion.

> *"What harvest half so sweet is,*
> *As still to reap the kisses grown ripe in sowing?*
> *Kiss then, my harvest Queen,*
> *Full garners heaping:*
> *Kisses ripest when they are green*
> *Want only reaping."*

Mary, lounging at his feet, was caught in the golden net he cast. Within that net, all was youth, beauty, understanding—a homecoming in her alien land.

At the end of the celebration, when the weary company betook themselves to their chambers, Darnley motioned to Mary, whose eyes were nodding from the spiced wine and the warmth of the fire. "I have a gift for you," he said. "Come see."

Behind the arras there was a bulge, and Darnley went behind it and pulled something out. It was an elaborate birdcage, made all of wicker and painted with delicate gold patterns.

"It is a pair of songbirds," he said. "Chaffinches, captured before the weather grew cold. A hen and her mate."

When she looked puzzled, he said, "Valentine's Day is when birds choose their mates, is that not so? Thus it seemed a fitting present for me to make to you, my Valentine." He knelt and presented it to her.

She peered at the birds. "Will they sing?"

"It is only the male who sings," said Darnley. "As I do when I am with you." He grasped her hand.

"You sing extraordinarily well," she said, extracting her hand.

"Will you be my Valentine?" he said.

"I am that already," she said. "We drew names."

"I mean—beyond tonight."

He seemed sculpted out of a maiden's secret dream, and he had appeared at exactly the moment when her yearning was at its highest pitch.

"I—I do not know," she replied.

"Oh, tell me that I may hope!" he cried, grabbing her hand again and covering it with kisses. His head was a gleam of gold as he bent over her hand.

"As I may," she said. "As I hope for—" What did she hope for? So many things. But at that moment, that someday she could kiss his hair, his lips . . ."—happiness."

"Let me make you happy!" he murmured. She slipped her hand out of his and cupped his jaw in both her hands. She bent to kiss him, and as her lips touched his he rose and stood taller and taller, until her head tilted far back. His lips were like sweet jelly, and she wanted to roll on them, crush them, bite and taste them.

"Ah. Mary," he breathed, and clasped her to him. His body was lean but hard, slender, and trembling slightly beneath his thick velvet. "I wish to say something we can remember always, but only 'Mary' comes to my lips," he said. He kissed her in many ways: lightly, like a schoolboy; hungrily, like a woman-starved soldier; slowly, like a sated man savouring the last morsel of honeycomb.

"So much for poetry," she finally said, pulling away to catch her breath. "It is never to hand when we need it." She attempted to laugh, but he put his fingers to her lips.

"Sssh," he said. "We do not need it. We need no poetry." He kissed her again. "You have not answered me. Will you be my Valentine?"

"Yes," she said. "Yes, yes."

236

Mary returned to Edinburgh a week later, and Darnley followed. There he was reunited with his father and formally welcomed by Lord James and all the Lords of the Congregation. James held a large banquet at Holyrood for Darnley and Lennox to meet Randolph and all the Scots noblemen present in Edinburgh. Mary laughingly sent word that she felt excluded, to which her brother sent back word that it was her own palace and she was free to do as she wished. Whereupon she invited the entire company to come to the royal apartments at the end of the evening. They did, crowding into the audience room and overflowing into her bedroom, where they drank more wine and used up all the cherry logs in her log basket, which she had been saving to burn some special evening, as she was very fond of their scent. Riccio and Darnley led the singing, their bass and tenor voices twining round each other.

> *"I wish I were where Helen lies,*
> *Night and day on me she cries;*
> *O that I were where Helen lies,*
> *On fair Kirconnel lea!*
>
> *"O Helen fair, beyond compare!*
> *I'll mak a garland o' thy hair,*
> *Shall bind my heart for evermair,*
> *Until the day I die!"*

Mary was lost in a reverie induced by their voices when she became aware of Mary Livingston and John Sempill holding hands next to her. Even their arms were intertwined and for the first time in years she did not feel lonely and excluded at the sight of lovers holding hands.

Darnley was singing just to her; he lifted his eyes and looked straight at her. Almost imperceptibly he tightened his lips, and at once she was awash in a surge of memories and desire.

His kisses. From those first kisses on Valentine's Day, to all the kisses he had given her during their private meetings at Wemyss, each seemed different. Each seemed to touch her in a different place, as though there were invisible threads between the lips and all the secret places in the body, and each place trembled in a separate way. And once each place had been touched, it hungered for further touching.

Why did no one tell me of this hunger? she thought.

"Your Majesty," said Mary Livingston. "I—we—" She leaned close and whispered, "John has asked me to be his wife. And I have told him I wish to be."

"Oh!" Mary said. "Why—you will be the first—the first of my Marys to wed. Yes, of course—I release you from your vow. With all my heart."

Livingston kissed her mistress gently on the cheek. "Thank you, kind Queen."

"And I insist you be married here at court. It will be the first wedding festivity at Holyrood. Oh, Lusty! This is the beginning—the beginning of happy times, weddings, and love, and births . . . for all of us."

They were married on Shrove Tuesday, in a Protestant ceremony, and afterward there was a banquet and dancing at Holyrood. Mary had combined the masquing and elegance of a Shrovetide ball in France with the grandeur of a wedding feast. By the light of thousands of candles, silver-masked dancers moved in stately measure to the sweet music of psaltery, archlutes, and recorders.

Mary, dressed in a gown of silver tissue with a ruff of lace-edged lawn and a mask of white and black feathers with diamond-studded streamers, danced with a variety of fantastical partners: a knight from King Arthur's court, with antique armour, which limited his dancing ability (his voice betrayed him as Melville); a green and yellow cockatoo whose headdress was three feet tall (Randolph); St. Giles Cathedral, complete with crown-shaped spire (the portly Earl of Morton); Julius Caesar (Lord James), with woollen hose and sturdy boots peeking out from under his toga; a Highland chieftain, whose sword clanked and dragged across the floor (the French ambassador). Then Darnley, dressed as Goliath because of his height if not his breadth, took her in his arms.

"Queen of mystery," he said. "From across the hall I could see you, glittering in black and white."

"Colours that are no colours," she murmured.

"Because you have no colours?"

"Because they are mourning colours."

"You are not in mourning."

"Not formally. But my late lord—"

"Your 'late lord,' as you style him, is gone for four years. Convention does not demand mourning of such length."

"Convention does not know the heart," she maintained.

"The heart is a living thing, and yours, surely, is above all a living, and loving, thing."

He held her close to him, and his scanty costume pressed his bare flesh against her silver gown.

"Will you love again, Madam? Nay, I know it. You have, you do, you will. But publicly, will you lay aside your mourning? I am well aware that mourning carries its own voluptuous beguilements—the cocooning, the reveries, the delicious recitations of memories and guilts. Also the feeling of accomplishment: I've loved, I loved well, it's done."

"How dare you?" She pushed him away.

"Because I love you." He grabbed her, fending off the hovering solicitations of the Earl of Argyll nearby, awaiting his chance in his dolphin's costume. "I love you, I love you, I feel I cannot live without you. And to see you pouring your love, your present, your future, offering it all to someone who is gone and cannot partake—nay, it breaks my heart! Though I may well be unworthy, offer it to someone more worthy; that I can applaud. But do not take the fairest flower of all the earth, and lay it in a tomb!"

Tears trickled down his cheeks, and she gently wiped them away with her handkerchief. "Why, Henry," she said, so surprised she was at a loss for words.

"We go so soon to our own tombs," he cried. "Do you not see that? To keep company at one out of season is an abomination." He stopped dancing and clasped her hand. "Marry me, Mary. I would ask that of you if you were Mary the chambermaid and I Henry the groom. Let us cheat the tomb while we can, for we cannot cheat it long. But for now there are sweet-scented fires and verse from Ronsard, Bordeaux wine in Venetian goblets, and masks with peacock feathers. There are even diamonds on the ribbons and a Riccio to sing for us. Be my wife, Mary, and I promise you we will revel in all the beautiful things, the brief things, that earth offers us. Together we will romp as if we were in the Elysian Fields, along with Helen and Paris, Antony and Cleopatra . . . oh, they will envy us, the happiest mortals on earth."

" 'Happiness' and 'mortal' are not two words that can be linked," Mary replied. She began dancing again, to distract attention from them.

"Not permanently, no, but ah! what a flare they can make upon this earth whilst they blaze."

"And extinguish themselves shortly thereafter."

"Why, you are afraid! You are a coward—this great daughter of the Stewarts, so brave in battle, so willing to risk shipwreck and bullets—you are afraid of this! To snatch happiness, if only for a moment, from the gods—"

" 'The gods'? Are you not a Christian, a Catholic? Who are these pagan gods you invoke?"

"Fate, Madam. For we all have a destiny, Christian or no, and creed has little to do with it whilst we live. Only afterwards . . . but why talk we of 'afterwards'? Be mine now, upon this earth, in the palace, in my bed—" He kissed her as they danced, bending her head back, until her mask fell off.

"Yes, I will," she murmured. She retrieved her mask. "But I pray you"— they resumed dancing—"it must be our secret, for now. Powerful people will try to prevent it. Not fate, but certain people."

"I will slay them," he said.

"In this court there are many little Davids with accurate little slingshots," she said. "Dear Goliath—let us keep our secret from them for our own safety, for now."

"Then you will be my wife?" he whispered.

"And you will be my king," she said softly, and he smiled in disbelief.

A hulking black bear made his way toward them, recognizable through his costume as Lord Ruthven.

"Here comes the jawbone of an ass," said Darnley, laughing wildly. "Keeping to the Biblical theme."

The black bear came slouching up to them, growling. He lifted up a furry paw—accurate in its details even to the claws neatly sewn on each footpad—and raked at the air.

Mary backed away; what was he doing?

The bear took a swipe at Darnley, and a guttural, "Go back to your dam, you jackal," issued from the muzzle. Darnley looked alarmed; the beast was uncomfortably real.

"Why, how now, is it not Lord Ruthven?" he said, his voice unusually high.

"It matters not who I am; it only matters that you return from whence you came, and right speedily." The bear made another swat at him, and this time the claws caught on his costume.

Mary said, "I command you to cease this provocation, whoever you are!" But she knew it was Lord Ruthven: his topaz-coloured eyes were showing through the costume's eyeholes. Those eyes . . . she remembered hearing that he was a warlock with supernatural powers, and thinking, Yes, he had those eyes, yellow like the Devil's. . . .

Abruptly the bear turned and shuffled off.

§

John Knox shook his head as he let himself picture the masked wedding ball at Holyrood, with all its Whore-of-Babylon associations: Shrovetide, the annual Catholic excuse for overindulgence; men and women dressed in immodest costumes; lascivious dancing. Regardless of James Stewart's assurances, the Catholics were regaining a foothold in the kingdom. Not only had the Protestant lords grown lax in their vigilance against the Papacy—as shown by a certain disinclination of late to attend Knox's sermons at St. Giles—but the Lennox Stuarts had crept back into the land and even into the graces of the Queen. A foreigner, a slick, deformed Italian Papist spy, Riccio, now had insinuated himself into service as the Queen's secretary for French affairs, and trotted after her everywhere, like a lapdog, panting and wagging his devilish tail.

Knox felt tired. I am fifty-one years old now, and no end of this battle in sight, he thought. For a while it was going so well, and You were at my right hand, O Lord. But now my arms grow weary, and they droop, and the battle begins to turn. Pray You, send someone to hold them up when I falter. Send me an Aaron and a Hur.

He shuffled over to his work desk. He did not feel like writing, he felt like lying down. But he flung off this lassitude and pulled his thick journal toward him.

March 5, 1565: It is well known that shame-hasted marriage betwixt John Sempill, called the Dancer, and Mary Livingston, surnamed the Lusty . . .

He sighed.

What bruit the Marys and the rest of the dancers of the Court had, the ballads of this time do witness, which we for modesty's sake omit.

Why were people always so attracted to cavortings? Why so many ballads of lust and violence, and so few of God's love?

In the meantime, there is nothing in the court but banqueting, balling, and dancing, and other such pleasures as are meet to provoke the disordered appetite; and all for the entertainment of the Queen's cousin from England, the Lord Darnley, to whom she shows all the expressions imaginable of love and kindness.

Darnley. Knox slumped back in his chair and remembered the blank-faced lad who had come to St. Giles only once, in tow with the Lord James. He had sat in the area reserved for royalty and nobility, had come dressed in choice robes and furs, and had left before the sermon—on tithing—was over.

Wherefore had he come? He was a Catholic—at least his mother was a notable one. Out of genuine desire for the Gospel? At first Knox had thought, had hoped, so. The Holy Spirit called forth from strange quarters. But looking at Darnley's altogether innocent and empty face, his dusky eyes that held no depths or intellectual searching, he had realized it was either a completely spontaneous and meaningless accompaniment of the Lord James, or else it was a calculated political gesture, meant to disarm his Prostestant critics. The Lord Darnley was not a seeker after the truth.

But then, who was? And among them, who would stay the course?

Knox pushed his bound journal out of the way and laid his head on his arms. He was so tired.

❧

James Melville strode into the audience chamber of the Queen with a certain amount of confidence. In the very beginning she had asked him, after all, to act this part, to be her private monitor. He had, at first, been puzzled and reluctant to accept this strange position, which, as she made clear, consisted of pointing out to her her errors made from ignorance of local custom and manners. He had assured her that her natural judgement and her experience in the French court would suffice, but she had demurred.

"I have committed many errors, upon no evil meaning, for lack of the admonition of loving friends," she had said. "As I know, courtiers flatter princes, and will never tell them the truth, because they are afraid to lose their favour. But you—you will not be so. And you will never lose my favour. Unless you go and kiss Master Knox during one of his sermons! So pray restrain yourself!"

Now Melville must exercise this heavy duty. For the Queen, of late—

"James Melville, pray enter."

A guard gestured him into the audience chamber. He stood and waited.

"Dear Melville!" Mary came forward, emerging from her private chamber, her arms extended.

"Your Majesty."

She smiled and took her seat in her chair of estate, with its royal canopy. Yet she settled on it like a woman merely entertaining a friend.

"Good Melville, thank you for coming to me." She continued to smile, and he saw that the smile was different, coming from something happy deep within, something self-sustaining.

"My most beloved Queen, you asked me to come to you when I perceived anything that might hinder your standing with your people. Of late—of late—"

"You are so agitated, dear James." She stepped down from the chair of estate and seated herself next to him. She had put on a heavy perfume and it was cloying. "Now, what is it?"

He wanted to wave his hand to waft away the perfume. It smelt like dying violets.

"Your servant, Riccio," he said.

"What of him?"

"He has become, of late—so people perceive—more prominent than ever. They see and hear of him everywhere. For your own sake, and his, I must advise you to keep him more in the background."

"I do not know what you mean." She stiffened beside him.

"The common people perceive he is a spy, a Papist spy. They are using that deadly word to describe him, a word that bodes ill to a Stewart: *favourite*." He managed to make the word sound like a curse. He took a breath and went on. "The royal Stewarts are a great dynasty. Their courage and beauty and devotion to their people is unparalleled. Yet they have a fatal flaw: they choose lowborn favourites. James III, with his favourite, Robert Cochrane, the architect of the Great Hall at Stirling, incurred the hatred of his nobles. And, begging your royal pardon, your own father's devotion to his favourite, Oliver Sinclair, was in large part responsible for the failure at Solway Moss. The nobles would not follow him."

She said quietly, "And they think David Riccio is my Oliver Sinclair?"

"I fear it, Madam."

"But he merely attends to my foreign correspondence."

"That is not how it is perceived."

"I am closeted with him only to give him instructions!"

"Again, that is not how it is perceived."

"Ohhh!" She stood up and clenched her fists. "Is every hour I spend to be scrutinized? What matter what hours I confer with him?" She began pacing the room.

"It is not just the common people. As you spend more time closeted with him, conferring with him, those who have served as your principal advisers are increasingly shoved aside. They view this with alarm. Madam, this is no secret. You have long known that your own councillors harbour ill will toward him."

"Oh. You mean, of course, the Lord James and Maitland."

"There are others as well," he said quietly.

"Oh! I am so tired of being misunderstood!" She stood still for a moment, as though she would calm an inner sea. Then she spoke. "It grieves me that people have misperceptions. Truly, Riccio is only—"

"You need not convince me, Your Majesty. It is they whom you must convince, the great nameless *they* who populate the land and plague all rulers who do not suit them. And in England, your sister Queen is sending ever more strident messages about your lack of interest in her 'dear Robin.' "

"But not to me. Never directly to me."

"Reportedly she has at last declared her intentions about 'dear Robin' and the succession." He was pleased to see the curiosity on her face, but it was an oddly impersonal curiosity, as if the outcome did not concern her. Suddenly he noticed her unusual amount of jewellery, and the fact that her gown was scarlet. She was out of mourning. "Spies reveal news at least a week earlier than the official couriers, but it is not always accurate. Nonetheless, as a first reading it is instructive."

"Well?"

"She has said that although it would please her greatly if you would take her beloved and most highly esteemed Earl of Leicester as a consort, she feels herself unable to declare a successor until she herself is either married or has decided never to marry."

"Ohhh!" Mary exhaled a long low sigh. "So in the end she declares nothing. Thank God I did not marry him!" She walked over to the window that overlooked the forecourt, as if something of great interest was below. "So I am free to do as I like! I need not consider her at all. Nay, I shall not! Nay, I would not! What a fool I have been even to entertain the idea!"

"No, no, it was politically expedient to consult her. But as I told you when I returned from her court, I perceived neither plain dealing nor upright meaning in her, but only great dissimulation, envious rivalry, and fear."

"Hmmmm." She smiled as though all that were welcome news. "Envious rivalry, you say? Well, I care not."

Indeed she did seem careless of what she had so eagerly sought earlier and for so long: recognition by Elizabeth, approval by Elizabeth.

"One plays a better game that way," Melville conceded. "It can be a winning tactic."

"Hmmm." She continued looking out the window, and he realized she was awaiting something—or someone.

"Marriage seems to be in the air, though it is scarcely spring yet." Lumps and mounds of snow lay everywhere, piled against gateways and plugging up the drainage channel in the High Street. "The first of the Marys has wed, and John Knox enjoys his honeymoon just up the street," said Melville.

"John Knox!" She laughed. "And with my distant kinswoman, too!" She laughed even harder, so tears began to stream down her face. "His little Stewart is only seventeen! Someone my age is too old for the fifty-year-old widower, I see! His first wife must have died of a surfeit of Scripture-pudding, and now his new one must perform the duties of Abishag and lie on his feet to warm them—and the angels only know what else!"

"Your Majesty!"

She gave a wild laugh. Then she turned back to the window and continued to keep watch.

Melville took his leave, backing out of the audience chamber. The high doors were closed behind him, and he turned and descended the wide staircase leading to the ground floor. He emerged into the forecourt, with each cobblestone a little island in the March slush, and began treading his way carefully across it. What had come over the Queen? She seemed possessed, not herself.

Riding through the gateway was Lord Darnley, on his big pale horse. He was flipping an hourglass.

"Now Master Knox will have to trim his sermons!" he cried. "I have switched it for one with less sand, by the pulpit at St. Giles." He grinned and spread his black cloak like a magician.

From her window, Melville saw the Queen waving at Darnley.

XIX

Mary and Darnley kept to themselves, in front of all the others, as they trotted along the road leading from Edinburgh to Stirling. It was a bracing March day, clear and haunting, with winds that seemed to have raided winter's larder and found it empty, triumphantly proclaiming an early spring. Already the hawking and hunting would be good at Stirling, and even if they were not, Mary felt that she must escape the confines of Edinburgh.

Edinburgh—where Knox all but reigned, where the houses huddled darkly together like gossiping women, where her spirit felt stifled. The Lords of the Congregation were the true lords of Edinburgh, and their hands were heavy upon it.

But outside, away in the countryside, ah! what space, what colours, what clean wild wind. Stirling lay some thirty-seven miles to the northwest of Edinburgh, if one followed the Firth of Forth until it became just the River Forth. As the river became shallower, it turned silver, and reflected the March sky with all its shades of grey-blue and racing clouds. The land around it was just shedding its mole-coloured winter coat, and an iridescent shade of green was already visible in certain lights.

"The hawks will be waiting?" asked Darnley. "I had a wonderful falcon in England, but I had to leave her."

"These are from the Orkneys. You will be pleased with them." She turned around in the saddle and saw the rest of the party a hundred yards back, all strung out in a brightly coloured line: the three Marys, Riccio, Melville, and the Lord James. The servants, musicians, churchmen, and chamberlains had gone on ahead to prepare the royal quarters.

"Will they obey me?" he asked.

"Of course. Will they not recognize a true prince?" She leaned across her saddle and kissed him.

Ah . . . his kisses . . . We must be married soon, she thought, or I shall surely fall into sin. I think of him and his body even in my sleep, when I am supposed to be resting.

"How much farther?" Darnley was asking.

"It is not far until we reach Stirling Bridge. Where—"

"Where Wallace defeated the English in 1297. Pray do not give me another history lesson. Just because you have felt obligated to memorize every fact about Scottish history, pray do not bore me with it."

His flip words annoyed her. And what of his speech about feeling Scottish? "It is *your* history too, or so you claimed. And if you are to be King—"

"King of the present, not of the past."

"Still, you should learn the rudiments of Scottish history," she said.

"Ah, you sound like a schoolteacher." He frowned and put on a begging aspect. " 'Tis true you are three years older and a queen, but I am loath to be your pupil."

"What would you be, then?"

"Your husband, your lover, your lord, your friend."

"All these . . . can one person be all?"

"In an ideal world. Which we will make."

They approached Stirling Castle, rearing two hundred and fifty feet from the plain like a gigantic mushroom. The sides of the cliff served up the castle like an offering. It was massive, grey, an apparition from Camelot. There were battlements, bastions, portcullises, and cannon; there were royal apartments, a ceremonial great hall, a lady's lookout bower, formal knot gardens, a royal park for the breeding of deer, and jousting grounds: a self-contained dream world of knighthood.

"I spent my childhood here before I left Scotland," Mary told Darnley. "It was not safe for me to be anywhere else. King Henry VIII's soldiers were invading our land and trying to kidnap me."

"You had to take refuge here? You could not live anywhere else?" He sounded incredulous.

"Yes. I was born at Linlithgow, the palace we passed on our way here. But within a few months I was brought here, to Stirling. I was crowned Queen here, in the Chapel Royal, when I was only nine months old."

"Which, I take it, you cannot remember."

"No. Of course not."

"What a pity. To be crowned a queen, and not remember it." He frowned.

"We stayed here all the time, my mother and I, and the Marys. And some of my half brothers and sisters . . . James was here, and Robert and John Stewart, and Jean Stewart. And while we played, and rode our ponies, and had our lessons, Henry VIII was destroying our land. At one point the English came within six miles of Stirling, and so my mother and I fled to a little island in the Lake of Menteith."

"How boring."

"No, it was lovely. There was a monastery there, and—" And it was a special time, a private time I cannot describe, even to you. I am not sure it all really happened as I remember it.

"Monks!" He made a face. "But *then* what happened?"

Could he really not know? "Henry VIII died, but it was no release for us. His successor, Edward VI, let them continue plaguing us. His foremost general, Edward Seymour, led troops right up near Edinburgh. There was a big battle, the Battle of Pinkie Clough, and the Scots lost. Then my mother and everyone knew that the Scots could not withstand England on their own. We had to sell ourselves to France." How ugly that sounded. She had never recited all these things out loud before, had never heard their ominous, leaden inevitability. "So I was promised as a bride to the Dauphin, in exchange for French protection. The French King sent a royal ship for me. And so I went to France. And there I grew up, married the Dauphin—"

"And ended up back in Scotland," he finished. "Thirteen years later."

"But the whole world changed in those thirteen years. Two new rulers for England—"

"And a new one for Scotland. The Reformed Kirk," said Darnley. "It rules with a heavy hand."

"Aye." Its hand was sometimes heavier than she felt she could bear. "But its hand lies mainly in Edinburgh. Here we are free of it."

"Yes. Except for—" he jerked his head toward the Lord James, far in the rear. "Why ever did you bring him along?"

"He wished to come. And he works hard. 'Yet the labourer is worthy of his hire.' "

Darnley made a face. "I do not like Bible quotes, even in jest."

They passed through the outer defences and over a ramp leading to the gatehouse with its huge, drumlike towers guarding the entrance to the castle, and attained the height of the rock. The wind tore at them. Mary Fleming's hat blew off and tumbled quickly across the paved stones before being sucked out over the battlements and disappearing.

"Oh!" she cried, astonished at the speed with which it happened.

"Gone to grace some townsman's wife," said Lord James. "An act of charity."

Mary assigned Darnley to the King's apartments, which caused the entire company to whisper, as she had known it would. But she could not help herself. Why should she place him in the crowded west wing of the royal apartments, when the gracious and well appointed King's apartments stood empty?

Stirling boasted a fine set of double apartments for the Queen and King, with adjoining bedchambers. James V had built the facilities only two years before his death, and he had been proud of all the fashionable features: the series of three chambers in increasing degrees of privacy, leading to the conjoined bedchambers in the eastern wing, the private closets off each bedchamber, with work quarters and bathrooms, the high ceilings in the King's Presence Chamber, decorated with carved roundels. The view from the Queen's apartments showed all of the countryside out beyond the castle, and let in the morning light.

Marie de Guise had kept the King's apartments shuttered and silent, and had let no one pass into them. It was her way of mourning. Mary remembered that she had once ventured into them and received a scolding all out of proportion to her offense. The rooms had been dark and filled with dust, and the big carved heads on the ceiling had looked like monsters. She had not wanted ever to go there again, but had harboured a secret fear that her father's ghost or skeleton was there. But upon her return to Scotland, she had ordered the King's apartments opened, aired, and painted, and today they were sumptuous and inviting.

They settled into their assigned quarters. Mary ran through hers, finding all in order, and hesitantly knocked on Darnley's connecting door. He flung it open.

"No spies," he whispered, taking her in his arms. "Is it not a miracle?"

Alone, after dinner, the royal party having said its good nights, Darnley felt safe when he closed his door. He looked around the room, with its gilded furnishings and its high bed with elaborately embroidered hangings and valances fringed in gold. This was the King's room, and he, Henry, Lord Darnley, was soon to *be* King. King of Scotland. *That* for Queen Elizabeth and her mouldy old court!

He sat quietly for a few moments, listening for any noise. Had everyone truly settled down for the night? Mary was not likely to come seeking him; she had looked almost apologetic as she told him how tired she was. Still, he waited. Then he got up and made his way across the chamber to open his travelling bag. Inside was something he wanted very much.

He felt around his other personal belongings, his ledger, his writing materials, his medicines which his mother had packed for him ("Never be without them!" she had said sternly) for his coughs and rheums, his sleeping mask to combat his insomnia, until he found it, gurgling as sweetly as a babe in its swaddling clothes. He drew it forth: it was a flask of whisky, the legendary drink up here. Oh, how he had longed to try it! Now he had managed to obtain a bottle from the accommodating Earl of Atholl.

Eagerly he twisted off its cap and took a giant swallow of it. It was so much stronger than the wine he was used to that he felt as if a fist had smashed into his chest, and he coughed. He could not believe a liquid could have such strength; even poison would be gentler, he thought.

Neither was he prepared for the fact that the whisky seemed to race from his stomach into his brain. It felt as if he had poured it directly into his head.

I might as well have poured it into my ear, he thought. The idea struck him as extremely funny. He took another large gulp. This one did not burn so much as it went down.

Your fellow has already left a path, he thought. His head was starting to feel as if it were lifting off his shoulders, and he was getting that lovely feeling he got from nothing else. It was a feeling he looked forward to, a feeling of peace and being where no one could touch him, where he did not have to answer to anyone. His mother faded as if he had left her behind in another room, as he had. This room was his private room, the spinning one in his head that he sought as often as he could.

He did not know how long he sat there or how much he drank. He only knew that he was hearing knocking. Someone was intruding! He shook his head to clear it; to his disappointment the thick, muffling feeling had begun to thin out and he no longer felt as if he were floating.

"A moment." He stood up and fastened his doublet. "A moment." He stumbled across the room and flung open the door.

Who was it? He could barely see in the dim light.

"I beg your pardon for disturbing you," a voice was saying. "And evidently I *have* disturbed you."

Lord James! Darnley clutched at his doublet. It was buttoned wrong. "Not at all," he said, wondering if he sounded normal. He listened to the tone of his own voice. "Pray come in."

He turned and expected James to follow. But from the doorway he heard him say, "I see you are in no condition to talk." The door slammed.

The next morning was Sunday, and in the freedom of her own castle, Mary ordered mass to be said in the Chapel Royal. As it was already the fourth Sunday of Lent, a time allowed for brief relaxation of the Lenten rigours, rose-coloured vestments were worn instead of purple, and there was a celebratory air to the service. The Catholics in the group attended, while the

Protestants stayed in their quarters, either sleeping or reading Scripture. Mary did not know and would never presume to inquire.

As was customary, a dinner would follow in the Great Hall, and then they would go hawking. The day was fine and clear, and promised good riding if the ground was not too muddy from recent rains. But before Mary and her group had reached the entrance of the Great Hall, they encountered the Lord James and all his party saddling up.

"We are not yet ready for the hawking," said Mary. "The falconers will not be prepared. Pray you, wait a bit."

"We are not interested in hawking," said James. "We feel these Popish ceremonies in the Chapel Royal to be insufferable. We cannot remain here."

"You were not even present, so how can you have found them 'insufferable,' brother? Perhaps you ought to have attended. There were words spoken that might have comforted you. And when you say 'we,' do you mean yourself in the royal sense? If not, whom do you mean?"

James straightened in the saddle. "I mean myself and my attendants. Of course I do not mean the royal we."

"I see." She paused a long while. "I am grieved to see that you cannot remain," she finally said. "Within these walls we played as children and came to know each other. In that sense they are sacred. Must you part from me now?"

She went over to him and, touching his saddle, laid her hands upon it and looked up at him. From that angle, his chin looked as heavy and immovable as the outer defenceworks of the castle.

"You drive me away," he said, jerking the reins of the horse and wheeling around, so that she lost her grip on the saddle and almost fell. "You and your folly. The mass is the least of it."

His words made no sense.

"The people you choose to love," he finally said, urging his horse forward. The animal trotted off toward the guard towers.

With so few to dine, Mary abruptly ordered the dinner to be served in the Queen's Presence Chamber instead of the Great Hall. The reduced company was presented with dishes of smothered rabbit, capon in lemon sauce, boiled onions, and sweet cubes of jellied milk. Sunlight streamed into the room, filling it with light.

"The Lord James and some others have departed," Mary announced. "Alas, they could not stay. Methinks it is an April Fool, this being April first, and they having no cause of displeasure. Nonetheless we will eat, hawk, and hunt as planned. They will doubtless rejoin us on the morrow."

A wide grin spread across Riccio's face. "Then let us propose a toast for their safe journey to . . . wherever it may be," he said, raising his goblet. The thin April sunshine caught the rubies and sapphires along its rim.

Afterwards, as they were making their way across the upper courtyard toward the palace, Mary turned to Darnley and said, "Now we will have

249

until dark to hawk. All is prepared." She had meant to turn back to speak to the others, but the frown on Darnley's face stopped her.

"I do not feel well," he said. "My head hurts."

In walking across the courtyard, Darnley's head throbbed with each jarring step, and by the time he reached the palace, only a short distance away, it had increased to such a pitch that he had to hold his head in his hands. He rushed into his bedroom and fell on his gigantic bed, groaning. Taylor, his servant, pulled off his boots and undressed him. By evening he was delirious.

"It is the ague," said Bourgoing, Mary's physician from childhood, and a friend as well. "In someone of his age, it is not of concern. He will sweat and dream and toss and sleep. When he awakens, he will remember nothing. It is us, the watchers, who will be tired."

Darnley lay fevered for several days and then, abruptly, the fever departed. He sat up and ordered his favourite soup, sorrel with figs, and the cooks had to stir round to locate a recipe for it. The musicians came and played in his chambers, and Mary visited him, pleased to find him well. But before morning he felt worse, and could retain no food.

Mary sent Bourgoing to him straightway, and the French physician at length emerged from the chambers shaking his head.

"Measles," he said. "The Lord Darnley has taken measles, in the footsteps of the ague."

Darnley lay in the great royal bed in a trough of sweat. He was drowning in water that seemed to come both from within and without him. He was oozing, and surrounded by an oozing bog. He did not feel the *valets de chambre* lift him and change the linen and fluff the mattress and place him once again on dry cloth. His fever mounted higher and all he felt was a hot buzz in his head, and intensely rendered images behind his closed eyelids. Then there would come a soft assurance, a presence. It seemed familiar. But he could not know. Who was it?

"Monsieur Bourgoing, he does not know me," said Mary, weary after having kept vigil all night by Darnley's bedside.

"He knows you in his dreams," the physician said. "But you must rest. Why do you persist in this vigil?"

"I do not know. Perhaps because it is the first vigil I am honoured to be given . . . since the King. King François."

"Sickbeds are not an honour, but a cross."

"I love Darnley!" she burst out. "Pray tell me he will not die!"

Bourgoing looked surprised. "A young man will not die of measles. Unless he harbours some other debilitation, like syphilis, or is unusually weak."

Darnley lay hacking and coughing, each cough racking his thin body and searing his already raw throat. Inside his mouth were white eruptions, and all the tissue was red and swollen around them, making it impossible to eat, although he kept vomiting from his withered and empty stomach. Each time the muscles contracted, it felt like bleeding paper being ripped asunder. His eyes were so sensitive to light that all the windows had to be shaded, and no candle could burn near his bed, lest it cause him stabbing pain.

In the darkness Mary sat by him, watching over him like a delicate Egyptian goddess standing guard over a Pharaoh's tomb. Whenever she reached out to touch him, his skin was dry and felt as hot as one of the *chaufrettes,* the silver footwarmers she used here in the winter. François had never been as hot as this. Could someone be this hot and live?

Mary would look at his shrunken body—he had lost so much weight— and feel him slipping away from her, and she prayed for hours, sitting on a stool beside him. In the dim light he already seemed to be in a sepulchre, and his pale face and draped body to be that of a tomb effigy carved in alabaster.

She could not lose him; she could not lose to death a second time.

If I could take your place, she thought, lie down in this spot, and wrestle with the abhorred shade when he steals into the chamber, thinking to have an easy victory. I'd grab and twist his bony fingers, break them off, hear them snap, see the pieces fall on the floor.

Darnley groaned and rolled over.

No, he shall not have you! Death will have to meet and overpower me here, disarm your gatekeeper. He is no match for me, she promised, wiping his brow in cool, violet-scented water.

On the sixth day Darnley broke out in red spots on his face and neck. The spots spread rapidly to the other parts of his body, and his temperature fell. His eyes fluttered open and he saw Mary for the first time.

"How . . . long have you been here?" His voice was a croak.

"Through the whole illness," she said

He smiled a crooked smile. "How long have I been ill?"

"Since Sunday mass on Laetare Sunday. Tomorrow is Passion Sunday."

He shrugged. "I know not these terms."

A good Catholic should. "Almost two weeks."

He rolled his eyes—still bloodshot. "So long."

"A short time for two severe illnesses. A weaker man could not have recovered."

"I will never recover," he whispered. He raised his hand, so thin it looked like a translucent web. "I can barely lift it."

Mary took his hand in hers, and hers was the thicker and stronger. She twined the fingers together. "Together we are strong," she said. "Nothing can separate us."

❧

"Is she still closeted with him?" asked Knox, drawing aside the Lord James after the Sunday service at St. Giles. He had preached on life in the midst of death, and death in the midst of life: a thorny concept of joy and resignation. It had gone confusingly well.

"So they say." James nodded and smiled at the other worshippers filing out, particularly the Lords of the Congregation, who had all dutifully attended this windy April day. Now they would walk down the Canongate, enjoying the brisk air and swirling their mantles, on their way home to their Sunday dinners. "Young Darnley took the measles on the heels of the ague and almost left this world. An ignominious end to an ignominious boy." James smiled and lifted his hand. "Good day, my lady." Jean, Countess of Argyll, nodded. "He is altogether insufferable."

"How so?" Knox spread his hands in greeting. "My Lord of the Byres." He bowed to Lord Lindsay.

"He is vain, empty-headed, arrogant, and touchy. Oh, and he dislikes the Bible."

"Indeed?"

"Yes. I overheard him say as much on the way to Stirling."

The church was emptying out, and Knox returned to the pulpit to gather his notes and close the Bible there. He pointed to the hourglass on its stand before the pulpit.

"He stole the hourglass and replaced it with this half-hour glass," he said. "That is the level of his ingenuity. As if I cannot turn it twice."

James shook his head. "Precisely."

"The hourglass he took was one Calvin had given me," said Knox. "It was unkind of him to take it. There cannot be another." Calvin had died a few months earlier.

"He plays these childish pranks," said James. "He is but a spoiled baby, a mother's boy. And his mother will be wild with excitement when she learns that the Queen has fallen in love with him. Why, Darnley's mother has been scheming for him since he was born. You know she was even sent to the Tower once for being a bit too eager to advance his 'royal claims.' Now her dreams are fulfilled." Lord James paused. "And I think he may have a tendency to depravity."

"He is not old enough for that. Thoughtlessness and selfishness are the first steps on that road. But 'tis a long walk until one reaches depravity." Knox ran his hand over the Bible and then reverently draped its satin cover over it.

"He is farther along it than one would imagine," said James.

"Come home with me," said Knox, putting his hand on James's shoulder. "Dine with me this Sabbath."

"And so you left after that first mass, the one with all the pink vestments?" asked Knox, as they sat in his parlour after the meal of stuffed cod and turnips and cabbage. Knox's new wife, Margaret Stewart, a distant cousin of both Lord James and the Queen, had withdrawn to leave them alone after bringing in a plate of figs and a pitcher of claret. She was pretty and amiable, but little given to chatter.

"Yes. Being safely out of Edinburgh, she was giving full rein to the Popish ceremonies. There was incense, chanting"—he saw Knox's eyebrows rising—"I could hear it clear across the courtyard! So I spoke my objections and left. For the rest, they are still there."

"Riccio, too?"

"Need you ask?"

"She has sent Maitland to Elizabeth to ask her blessings on the marriage. Oh—you did not know?" Knox slowly stirred the sugar into his red wine.

"No. I did not."

"He left a week ago. What will you do when this marriage comes about? What will Scotland do, with such a king?" He sipped the wine, then abruptly banged the goblet down. "We do not deserve this! Nay, we've earned the right to a decent king! It is not to be borne! And we won't bear it!"

"You have just answered your own question. I fear Henry, Lord Darnley, cannot have long life amongst us. And as for his not being depraved—what else can you say of someone who shuts himself up in his room and drinks? I saw him!"

"Drinking alone? You are sure of this?" Knox's eyes were boring into James's.

"Indeed. He recked of whisky, his doublet was undone and rumpled, and he could scarcely talk. And all the while the Queen was dreaming sweet dreams about him in her chamber, no doubt!"

Knox hated to imagine it. "A pity."

James nodded. "Most of the time, she is with him. She lived there during his illness, so I heard. Her continual presence in his bedchamber night and day gives scandal."

"She remains there even after he has recovered?" Knox shook his head. "The shame of it! It is the scandal of David and Bathsheba!" He paused. "Speaking of David, which brings to mind swords, did you hear that Bothwell has left France, where he has been ever since he escaped from Edinburgh Castle, and is even now on his way back to Scotland?" Once again Knox's news made Lord James start.

"That is all we need!" he cried. "I thought we were rid of him forever!"

"He's a good enough Protestant," said Knox, watching James's face.

"He's not good for anything, except brawling, whoring, and ambushing."

"And keeping order in the Borders," Knox reminded him.

"Yes, I grant that." James leaned back in his chair and hooked one arm over its back. "Let us keep him there, then. Rounding up and hanging those who steal sheep and reive by the full moon."

⁂

They brought in the May in the early dawn, Mary and her Marys, Riccio and Darnley. They left Stirling Castle just as the sky was lightening in the windows in Darnley's bedchamber, which lay in the eastern range of the

253

palace. The air was as chill and calm as an icy lake, and it seemed impossible that warm weather would ever come again. But Maypoles were being decorated in the villages as people prepared to honour spring to force her arrival. Robin Hood and Maid Marian, forbidden in Edinburgh by the Kirk, would strut and play openly all day in the country, and lead the games of skill. A waning half moon was fading out against the growing light and soon would be setting, old and outworn.

"To the forest, to cut the branches," said Mary, touching spurs to her horse's flanks. She hoped some early buds would be out, lest they return with only bare sticks. She pulled her grey mantle closer about her.

But there were many birch and rowan trees, vines of eglantine, and hedges of hawthorn that had already opened their leaf buds and showed miniature, sticky, translucent little leaves, shining on the branches like dew. And in the meadows, violets and snowdrops were blooming. Mary stopped and let her horse nibble the tender new grass while she picked the little flowers and wove a chaplet with them.

"Here, let me," said Darnley, taking it from her. He placed it on her head, admiring the way the little starry wildflowers became her. "No amethysts or diamonds could be fairer," he said. "No Queen of the May could ever be more beautiful than you, wearing the flowers of the meadow." He leaned over and kissed her. "This moment is privileged," he said in a hushed tone. "I am happier than I have ever been." He looked around the meadow, watched the light on the dew, saw a small dun rabbit waiting for him to move. "Stay, moment. Never change or leave." He looked into her eyes.

"How solemn you are," she said, smiling. She moved her left hand and brushed a lock of hair behind her ear. The rabbit started and bounded away.

"Now you have ruined it," he said. "The perfect moment. It is gone."

"Only statues cannot move," she finally said. "And things move around them, and moss grows on them, and ice covers them, and at last they themselves move—topple over or crumble. There's no help for it, I fear." She took a small vine of myrtle she had cut; its bright periwinkle flowers glowed against the shiny dark oval leaves. "Here's a crown for you," she said, twining it around his head. "Now you are King of the May, king of the perfect moment."

> "To the Queen:
> Be governor both good and gracious;
> Be loyal and lovesome to thy lieges all;
> Be large of freedom and of nothing
>   desirous;
> Be just to the pure for anything may befall;
> Be firm of faith and constant as a
>   wall. . . ."

he recited. "I wrote it for you. There is more."

"I am touched," she said. "Pray walk with me and recite the rest. But not if it is dolorous. I will hear only happy things today."

When the company returned from the Maying, wearing their garlands and playing the horn and tabor, they festooned the Great Hall with the flowering branches and held the holiday feast. Afterwards they went their ways to their chambers to rest; they had been up for many hours.

Mary was looking forward to a short sleep and then, perhaps, a surreptitious visit to Darnley. They would tease and romp in the royal bed, while Riccio stood guard at the door. She wanted to lie in his arms and watch the birds flying and wheeling in the sky outside, to turn her head and marvel at his perfect profile.

The day had warmed considerably and she had opened her mantle at the neck. As she walked along she sang to herself:

> "As Robin Hood in the forest stood
> All under the greenwood tree
> There was he aware of a brave young man,
> As fine as fine might be.
>
> "And when he came bold Robin before,
> Robin asked him courteously,
> O hast thou any money—"

"Your Majesty!" The voice rang out over the courtyard stones. A tall, red-haired man, dressed for travelling, walked toward her.

"Nicholas Throckmorton!" she exclaimed. The young English ambassador had served in France when she was Queen there. "How delightful to see you again!"

He smiled and kissed her hand. "More beautiful here than even you were in France," he said. "Your native land agrees with you. The air, the food, the water—all seem to enhance you."

"But those were magic days in France," she said. Just looking at him brought them back. Exactly so had they stood and talked in Paris, at Chenonceau, at Chambord.

"Yes. Before the present troubles. It all seems so far away."

"But . . . why have you come?" Suddenly it seemed very odd to see him there.

"Queen Elizabeth sent me. With personal instructions and messages."

"Tell me!"

He looked around. "What—here?" He had envisioned an audience, a meal, pleasant conversation first to stave off the official business.

"Yes!" Before he could answer, she grabbed his hands and squeezed them with surprising strength. She looked as eager as a child going to bed the night before a holiday. "What does she say? Is she pleased? I know this match with Lord Darnley is exactly what she had in mind when she suggested I marry an English subject. She sent him up here, but she could not have foretold how I would have loved him! Oh, I know she rejoices with me. Will she attend the wedding? Will she travel to Scotland?"

Throckmorton cleared his throat to steer himself in this sea of words. "Good Madam . . . Your Majesty . . . the Queen forbids the marriage. She orders Lord Darnley and his father, the Earl, to return to England under pain of treason. She has committed the Countess of Lennox to the Tower for promoting the marriage. She absolutely forbids it."

"Wh—what?"

"The Queen is in a rage."

Mary shook her head in stunned bewilderment. "She says I must have her approval to wed, but there will never be a man to meet her approval. No foreigners, no Catholics, no English subjects, no lowborn men, no kings . . . well, then. I see that I shall never please her, and therefore I must please myself. As I shall, and marry the Lord Darnley."

"He can never return to England if you do."

"Poor Darnley! First he is forbidden to return to Scotland, and now he will be forbidden to return to England. Strange, when he himself has done no harm to either country." She stood looking at him, her eyes bright and hard. Behind her stretched the valley of the Forth, and, as it was a clear day, Edinburgh was just visible by the smoke from its chimneys far to the east.

"Unfortunately he is more than just a person who can do right or wrong. He is a symbol of many things," said Throckmorton.

"I do not love the symbol, but the man!" Mary cried.

"Yes. But you yourself are a symbol, as is my Queen. Be reasonable. It is one of the facts of life with which all monarchs must contend, a parameter like the net in tennis or the conventions of rhyme in poetry."

"I know myself to be royal; I never forget my royal blood."

"Then show yourself to be royal in your thinking as well as your blood. Think, think what marriage means, for a queen! You choose not only a husband for yourself but a king for your people. It cannot be undone, being once done."

"I know that; I keep faith with my promises. You may tell your Queen that she has long beguiled me with fair speeches, and then deceived me in the end as to her intentions with me. Therefore I cannot trust her now. On what grounds does she object? She herself suggested I marry someone of her realm. My Lord Darnley is the only one of suitable rank who is unmarried. The offer of the Earl of Leicester . . . why, I would not remind her of it, it was such an embarrassment for all concerned."

"I believe she was in earnest, Your Majesty."

"All the more embarrassing. I will graciously forget it."

She turned from him and walked quickly to the royal apartments. Once within, she marched down the gallery with its busts and statues and then through her own apartments—the guard hall with helmeted guards standing at attention, the presence chamber with its throne and cloth of estate, and then finally the bedchamber. Two of the Marys, dozing on their pallets, scarcely blinked as she passed through. Carefully she pushed down on the door handle connecting her bedroom with Darnley's, and swung the door open.

He was lying on the great bed, partially undressed, resting and covered with a fur. She approached the bed as quietly as possible and stood looking at him a moment. In the corner, Riccio stirred. He, too, had lain down after the early morning and the heavy meal. Mary tiptoed over to Riccio and touched his shoulder. He sat bolt upright.

"Good Riccio," she whispered, "you have a Catholic chapel in your quarters, have you not?"

He knitted his brow. "Indeed. I fitted it up myself. It is small—just an altar, and the candles, and of course the Sacrament, reserved—"

"Is anyone there? In your quarters?"

"No. I am alone there." He shook his head as if to clear it.

"And your confessor? Is he nearby?"

"Unless he has gone into the town of Stirling, as he sometimes does when he has no duties."

"Go to your quarters. Make the chapel ready. Find your confessor—and if not, I will bring mine. Lord Darnley and I will come there in less than an hour to plight our secret troth, binding before the eyes of God. Then nothing can separate us, and I will not be swayed or tempted by their arguments. Go!"

She turned to Darnley, still sleeping in the bed. His light-lashed eyes were closed, and he clutched his pillow lovingly.

Soon he can clutch me in the night instead of a pillow, she thought. And nobody can fault us or cry foul on us.

"Henry," she said, stroking his forehead.

He opened his eyes, and as always, his immense grey-blue eyes took away her breath.

"Dear Henry, rise up. For I have an adventure for you, a game. We will outwit them, outwit them all."

"Outwit whom?" He wrestled with the covers and fought himself free of them.

"All of them!" Her voice was fierce. "The Lords of the Congregation, and Knox, and Elizabeth, and—"

"Well, that is everyone, is it not?" He groaned. "Is anyone in *favour* of our marriage? Besides you and me?"

"The Earl of Morton—"

"Because my mother relinquished certain lands to him. And?"

"Riccio."

"A servant."

"I expect the King of France—"

"A child."

"And Philip of Spain—"

"Who hardly matters *here*."

"And the Pope—"

"Even less."

"Others will come in time to love you. As I do!"

"It seems I threaten or insult everyone's pride. How odd, as I have all the correct blood, the proper breeding and manners . . . there can be no *objective* reason. Therefore they must dislike my *person.*" He set his lips and looked angry. "Something about *me*, something about my speech, my bearing—"

"They are fools! Come, my dear lord—rise up and come away with me, where we'll confound them all!"

They stood before the Italian priest, Riccio's own from his father's estates near Turin. He had the rounded olive face and the shiny dark eyes Mary imagined everyone in Italy to have. She had her own fantasies of that land: it was a place where everyone was interested in art, everyone was Catholic, there were many flowers, and nights were warm and invited people to come outdoors. Somehow it was fitting that, in her own grasp for pleasure, she should employ an Italian to implement it.

Riccio's little altar, graced with some artwork from Tuscany, and twined silver candlesticks, had a lace-trimmed linen upon it. Riccio stood solemnly to one side as Mary and Darnley clasped hands and went through the betrothal and contract ceremony as prescribed by Holy Mother Church. The ceremony was binding, and recognized them as having made a vow before God to wed—a vow from which only formal legal procedures could release them.

"I, Mary, Queen of Scotland, Queen of France, Sovereign Lady of the Isles, do solemnly promise to take you, Henry, Lord Darnley, as my husband according to the rites and dictates of the most holy Catholic Church." She looked at the tall young man standing beside her, and his face was pale.

"I, Henry, Lord Darnley, do solemnly promise to take you, Mary, Queen of Scotland, Queen of France, and Sovereign Lady of the Isles, as my wife according to the rites and dictates of the most holy Catholic Church. And thereto I plight you my troth." He took off a ring from his smallest finger, and slid it on Mary's fourth finger.

"Kiss her," said the priest, and Darnley did.

"Ah, for a feast!" said Riccio. "If things were as they should be—"

"We have just finished a large dinner," said Mary. "Everyone sleeps. We will steal away in private, and that is better than any ceremonial feast." She took Darnley's hand. "Let us hope no one sees us crossing the upper courtyard. And Riccio—we release you from any duties tonight!" She laughed and lifted his cap.

Together she and Darnley rushed across the courtyard. It was growing dark now, and lights were showing in the windows.

"How now!" cried Robert Stewart, as he saw them.

Usually Mary liked her brother, but tonight the playful, empty-headed man was unwelcome.

"Well met, brother!" she said quickly. "I trust you had good Maying!"

"Aye, aye!" He reeled around, so quickly did Mary and Darnley pass. He was clearly tippling.

"Quick, inside!" Mary pulled Darnley into the guardroom, then through the presence room and finally into his bedchamber. She slid the bolt into the door. Then she slumped against it.

Darnley was standing in the middle of the chamber, where she had all but flung him.

How thin his legs are! she suddenly, oddly, thought. He has been truly ill.

"Dear husband," she said, savouring the word. "For so I may now truly call you." She walked over to him, so pale and unsteady.

"Wife." He took her in his arms, but he seemed carved in wood.

"What, are you fearful? You ought rather to rejoice. We have taken our lives and our loves in our own hands. Nothing can separate us now." She embraced him.

"We are bound forever?"

"Yes. That is what the ceremony did." Mary led him to the bed. "It made us one."

She made him lie down, and he stretched out on the great bed. "We have no servitors tonight," she said. "No one to undress us, no silly ceremonies of being observed in bed and toasted." She leaned forward and kissed him. "We are alone. It is only us. We have been given the most precious gift of all: privacy. No one will intrude on us."

She pulled off his doublet, easing each arm out of it. "I will be your valet," she whispered.

Darnley soon lay naked, sprawled out across the great royal bed. Mary could not help staring at him. She had never seen a naked man before, not a full-grown man. How was it possible their bodies could be, truly, so different?

She removed her own clothes, slowly. Off came the headdress, then the entire gown, then the stiffening material that held out her gown at an alluring angle. At last she was in her petticoat and undergarments of satin with lace trim.

Darnley took her in his arms. "Is all this truly mine?" he whispered.

"Aye, my lord, my love . . ."

"Your husband, your friend," he murmured, framing her face in his hands. "Pray I may be worthy."

He kissed her and drew her down into his warmed nest of covers. She felt the ever-present vigil against danger melt away.

The bed formed a little world for them: the covers a tent, the feather mattress a safe encampment. Darnley took her in his arms, and the last of her clothing was slowly removed. His fingers were unaccustomed to the fastenings, but his very difficulty and bafflement inflamed her desire. When the final shred of covering was gone, she felt she could exist no longer as a separate being from him.

"Oh, Henry," she murmured, feeling his body all along hers in its full length. "You make me more than I am."

"That is impossible. You can never be more—oh, oh—" he cried out.

She felt that nothing could ever bind her to him enough, that she wanted to merge totally with him, yet remain separate only so that she could continue to give to him, minister to him.

They came together in the only way possible to assuage that feeling, to both tame and release it. They were both virgins, and yet the act was completely natural to them.

"Oh, Henry," she cried, holding his sweat-soaked head against her breast. "Oh, my husband!"

She was wife at last.

In the middle of the night, before it grew light, she awoke. Darnley was sleeping beside her, breathing lightly. It was so odd to wake up and find another person beside her . . . would she grow used to it?

No, never, she thought. It will always remain a miracle to me. And he . . . She looked over at him, trying to see him in the dark. He murmured and moved. She touched his shoulder and whispered that she must return to her room before the Marys awoke.

She slid slowly out from under the bedcovers and felt her feet touch the cold stone floor. She rearranged the furs and sheets and made her way toward the connecting door. Carefully she opened the door and crept into her room. The Marys were still asleep, although she knew they had noticed she had not returned earlier. Still, she often stayed up very late, conferring with Riccio or even playing cards until two. They were accustomed to that.

It must be three or four now. She tiptoed over to her bed and climbed into it. She was naked, and her clothes were still in Darnley's room. How would she hide this from them? They always helped her dress, bringing her warmed undergarments to her and folding her nightgown to put it away.

The nightgowns were in the elmwood chest on the far side of the room. Could she find her way over there in the dark and extract one silently? Cautiously she crept out of bed, feeling her way toward it. She felt the silk carpet under her feet and knew when she was halfway there. There was a heavy chair to be avoided.

At last she reached the chest and lifted its lid, bidding it be silent. It obeyed. She pulled out the top gown, knowing it by feel to be the rose-coloured wool one lined with satin. She had had it since before François's death, although she had not worn it often since, as it seemed too bright and luxurious for her in her widowhood.

I'm no longer a widow, she thought suddenly, but a bride. I'm no longer a virgin, but a wife.

She climbed back into bed and slid beneath the covers, feeling altogether a different creature from the one who had last slept there. Her body was hot and dirty and stuck to the fine silk lining of the gown.

She had never felt vaguely unclean before, except after a hard day of riding, and even that was a different sort of grime and odour, although there was a similarity.

Ding-ding-ding-ding. The little clock struck the hour. So early. So late.

But I am safely back, and no one knows. It is my secret, mine and Darnley's.

The sun streamed in the windows and the clock was sriking *ding-ding-ding-ding-ding-ding-ding-ding-ding* when she awoke. Her eyelids were sticky and her body was stiff, and there was an aching rawness between her legs.

The Marys were dressed and bustling around the room. One of them—Flamina—was winding the clock, another was cleaning her jewellery with a soft cloth and paste of gum araganet and alabaster. The Great Harry lay like a child's trinket awaiting its turn.

Mary asked for a bath, and the warmed, perfumed water was brought up straightway and poured into the large tin bathing tub placed near the fireplace. Behind the screen she allowed her robe to be removed, and then quickly stepped into the tub. She had a horror that prints from Darnley's hands would be visible on her body, that his lip-prints would show on her skin. Would the warm water bring them out? She slid down farther.

"Your Majesty, shall I add the oil of sandalwood we got from the gypsies to the water?" called Flamina over the screen.

Would it blot out that strange odour she had carried with her from Darnley's bed to her own and thence into the tub?

"Yes, please."

Flamina stepped around the screen and took the flask of oil and poured it in a long thin stream into the water. It spread out in little droplets on the surface and floated like miniature opals there. She sniffed the stopper. "Exquisite. It reminds me of something eastern. Myrrh. Or Balm of Gilead, whatever that may be. I have always imagined it to be languid and rich, like this."

"Thank you." Mary splashed the scented water over her shoulders.

"You kept late hours last night."

"Yes. I—I could not sleep. And I needed to speak with Riccio about the arrangements for the—the ceremony for the revival of the Order of the Thistle, which I mean to hold soon."

"The Order of the Thistle?"

"Yes. It is—it is—the ancient chivalric order of Scotland, like unto the Order of the Garter in England and the Order of St. Michael in France. It has not met since my father's death, and only a few knights are left." Nervously she splashed more water over her shoulders.

"But you cannot revive it, as you are a woman," said Fleming. "Women cannot be knights and wear the golden spurs."

"I will appoint a substitute," said Mary. "I am the sovereign of the Order. And it is needful that Scotland restore herself to her former glory and dignity." She looked at Fleming. "You may leave me now."

Leave me, leave me, let me alone, to think of what has happened, of my husband, my secret. . . .

The oil of sandalwood gave off delicate fumes, enveloping her, filling her nostrils.

XX

Darnley thought he heard a knock on his door. On the door of the King's quarters! *His* quarters. Why did so many people keep interrupting him? He could have no peace! He hid his whisky bottle under his mantle, which was lying in a heap where he had discarded it. He was halfway across the room when he decided to return and have another fortifying sip. He had learned, now, how to swallow this stinging stuff, quickly, so that it did not burn his mouth.

He tugged on his sleeves to make sure they covered his wrists and then flung open the door. To his surprise, standing outside was James Hamilton, the old Duke of Châtelherault. The white-haired, broad-faced old man looked as though he had come on a mission that was distasteful to him; his repugnance of Darnley was written all over him.

"What do you want?" Darnley sneered. This was his enemy, his father's enemy, the man who *dared* oppose their claims to be next heirs in line for the throne. Well, now he'd see! Darnley would be sitting on that throne, the throne they had coveted. And my child will be King, he thought. To his surprise he found he had said the words out loud.

"I beg your pardon?" said the Duke. "Did I hear you correctly?" He looked at Darnley and then smelled the whisky. Pointedly he looked at the sun, which had not been up very long. "I have come to discuss the long-standing differences between our houses, in hopes of reaching an understanding. Will you not do me the honour to invite me in?"

"No," said Darnley. "No, I will not. When does one invite a foe to step over his threshold?"

"But I come not as a foe." Châtelherault's voice was rising.

"Never as a friend!" cried Darnley. "You tried to betray the Queen, and set your crazy son on her! The Earl of Arran, he fain would have kidnapped her—"

At the sound of his son's name, the Duke stiffened. "Do not insult my family!"

"He's still crazy, is he not? Locked up in your house, as befits a madman."

"I came to speak peacefully, but I see there can be no peace with such an ass as you!"

"When I am well, I will knock your pate! Be thankful I have not yet recovered my strength!"

"Fool! Fool of a boy!" The Duke turned his back and walked away.

Messengers were sent out all over Scotland to summon certain men to Stirling to attend the ceremony of the Order of the Thistle, to be held at Her Majesty's pleasure.

Lord James, in Edinburgh, decided that he had urgent business in the city that would, alas, prevent his coming thither to Stirling.

William Maitland of Lethington, already departed for France to seek the approval of the King and Queen Regent for the marriage of Queen Mary and Lord Darnley, was not there to receive the summons.

James Melville made ready for the journey, puzzled as to the wherefore of the ceremony.

Erskine, Morton, Ruthven, Lindsay, Argyll, and Kirkcaldy of Grange accepted and began choosing their wardrobes.

Paul de Foix, the French ambassador, had been assigned quarters.

John Knox had not been invited.

James Hepburn, Earl of Bothwell, secretly returned without royal permission to his ancestral home in Liddesdale, did not even hear about it.

Into the Chapel Royal, now hung with royal banners and the green and white banners of the Order (hastily sewn up to be ready for the ceremony), Mary Queen of Scots came in procession, her head held high and her gait majestic. Around her shoulders was the gold chain of the Order, enamelled with thistles and sprigs of rue, last worn by her father in 1540. Around her ankles were the golden spurs of knighthood, and she wore a dark green velvet mantle the colour of an ancient forest.

The fourteen men to be dubbed Knights Companion of the Order were awaiting her, standing at attention. They had fasted and kept vigil all night as custom demanded. Now she, with her attendants, took her place in front of the altar.

The Lord Lyon King of Arms strode forward and puffed out his chest.

"Now you, as worthy knights, chosen by your sovereign to attend her in this noble and ancient order, must come one by one and swear allegiance to your Queen, and to the Order of the Thistle as well, bearing in mind its motto: *Nemo me impune lacessit.*" He gestured toward the banner, with the cross of Saint Andrew and the satin thistle superimposed. " 'No one harms me with impunity.' "

The trumpeters blew two blasts on their silver horns.

Mary now raised her hands, and the long sleeves of her garment hung heavy, almost to her knees.

"My good people, loyal nobles. As a woman, I am unable to perform the ceremony, for I myself am not a knight. Therefore it is my pleasure to exercise the ancient prerogative of *choosing my knight* to carry out the duties of an office restricted to men and forbidden to women."

Everyone stood even straighter, waiting.

"Henry Stuart, Lord Darnley, come forth." Her voice rang loud in the high-ceilinged chapel.

From one of the back stalls a movement: a tall, blue-velvet-clad figure emerged from the shadows and walked down the center aisle. He took his place before her. For a long moment he and the Queen stood close, eye to eye. Everyone in the chapel was aware of the look that passed between them: a look of desire and purpose. Then he knelt on the footstool in front of her, his new-soled boots showing shiny leather faces toward his audience.

"Take your oath," she commanded him.

"I shall defend the Christian faith with all my power," he said in a loud voice. "I shall be leal and true to my Sovereign Lady, the Queen of Scotland, and her successors.

"I shall use and exercise myself in the office of chivalry.

"I shall do diligence whenever I hear there are murderers, robbers, or masterful thieves who oppress the people, and bring them to the laws to the utmost of my power.

"I shall never fly from my Queen, master, or fellow in dishonour in time of need.

"I shall fortify, maintain, and defend the noble Order of Knight of which I am ready to receive the horse, arms, and knightly habiliment, according to my power.

"I shall never bear treason about in my heart against our Sovereign Lady the Queen, but shall discover the same to her. So help me God, the holy Evangel, by my own hand, and by God Himself."

"Amen," said Mary. She bent down and lifted her gown, unbuckling the golden spurs. Then she held them up and passed them to the knight standing before her. She cupped his hands as she gave them to him.

"Fasten them on," she said. She took the sword that had belonged to her father and then touched his neck lightly on each side.

"I dub thee Sir Henry."

He stood back up, his spurs clicking on his slender ankles.

"I create you Lord of Ardmanach, a baron and a peer of Parliament."

He inclined his head slightly.

"And last, for now, I do name you to be Earl of Ross."

The inaudible gasp from the nobles present was louder than any audible one. Earl of Ross was a royal title, to be borne only by a Scottish prince.

He knelt on the footstool once more.

"I shall be true and leal to my Sovereign Lady, Queen of Scotland, maintain and defend Her Highness's body, realm, lieges, and laws, to the utmost of my power. So help me God, the holy Evangel, and mine own hand."

She bid him rise, then motioned to a servitor, who brought out a belt and a sword upon a velvet pillow.

"The belt of your title," she said, fastening it about him.

"Now, my Lord of Ross, I request you do my office, wearing the spurs of knighthood, and invest the candidates for knighthood in the Order."

Passing out of the chapel into the May sunshine, she saw Throckmorton standing anxiously to one side, near the passage to the Great Hall, where the ceremonial tables were already laid.

"Your face is long," she said, coming to him.

"The Earl of Ross is a royal title," said Throckmorton.

"The Lord Darnley has royal blood, has he not?" she replied.

"More to the point, in spite of the noble declarations of loyalty he has made, to accept a Scottish title and nomination to the Scottish Parliament is to repudiate his allegiance to his own country, England, and his own sovereign, Elizabeth. In swearing fealty to you, he has betrayed his own Queen."

"How so? I have not called upon him to repudiate her."

"A man can have only one sovereign, Your Majesty. And he who changes his master so easily today can change again tomorrow. Beware." Throckmorton sounded sad—whether at her ignorance or at her implied duplicity she could not tell. It stung her.

"Your mistress changes her behaviour to suit her clothes; each day she professes something different, promises something different, takes back what she says!" replied Mary.

"But her courtiers and knights never waver in their loyalty to her. She has not known the sting of false servants and councilmen," said Throckmorton. "And this Darnley, having once turned his coat, is like to turn it again. I—"

"I have not yet created him Duke of Albany, the highest title of all. I await the word of Queen Elizabeth before proceeding further. I wish to show her respect and give her the opportunity to bless this marriage after all," Mary said. "You see how reasonable I am and do remain. For the moment. Good day." She lifted her head and, catching up her green velvet mantle, turned to go into the hall for the feast.

Mary sat on a stool, holding an ivory-backed mirror in her hand. In its dull reflection—even aided with light from the open window of her privy chamber—she could not see her own features sharply. She looked closely at her eyes, searching their depths. But all she saw was the searching within them.

Was she different? She felt different, and wondered if it was visible. Poets spoke of love showing in the eyes, changing the features. But then, she strove to remain unchanged in outward appearance.

She looked at her ears, hanging with heavy earrings: a gift from Darnley. They had sapphires and diamonds and an elaborate metaphorical message about families and heirs and hopes and destiny.

"But we have no need of symbolism," he had said, bending his fair head down and kissing her breasts. "Symbolism is a poor cousin for what is at hand."

Then he had . . .

Remembering it, Mary felt herself blushing, just as Flamina pushed open the door and advanced toward her with a letter.

"It is from France," she said, handing it to her mistress.

It was heavy, and Mary recognized the seal of the Cardinal upon it. Thank Heaven! It was he, her uncle the Cardinal, whose advice and opinion she most sought in these perilous waters. She had waited weeks for his reply.

"Thank you," she said, taking the letter and breaking open its thick, brittle orange wax seal.

"Dearest niece and sister in Christ"—

Yes, yes.

"We are apprised of the situation with the Lord Darnley, a prince of royal blood and one whom we had the opportunity to observe at leisure during his sojourns in France at various times. We are well aware of his lineage, his niceness of person, and his general commendations."

She closed her eyes and clasped the letter to her bosom. Oh, thank you, dear Lord.

At length she commenced reading again.

"My child, if it were not for my deep love of you and my concern as your uncle and shepherd in Christ, I would not speak. But I must. Without giving particulars (for there were a hundred of them, observed over time when he abided here without the restraining hand of a parent), I must tell you that in my opinion he is *un gentil hutaudeau*, a highborn quarrelsome coxcomb, a weakling who is propped up and held aloof only by the valour of his ancestors and the resultant titles in recognition. But these were bestowed by long-ago sovereigns upon long-dead ancestors. It is for the living to reevaluate, and alas, the living scion of the House of Darnley is not worthy of you. Pray, spare yourself—"

She uttered a groan and crumpled the paper.

Uncle. *Et tu?*

Why does no one see him as I do? she cried out in private anguish.

A letter was delivered from the Duke of Châtelherault, complaining of the dishonour the Earl of Ross had done him in threatening to knock him about the pate for an imagined slight.

"Such a challenge is hardly to be ignored, except when one bears in mind the issuer of it," he had written. "Then it is best reported to a higher authority."

The Duke and Darnley's father were old political foes, thought Mary, and of course the Duke would oppose any elevation of the Lennox Stuarts. But had Darnley actually threatened to "knock his pate as soon as he be well enough," as the Duke claimed?

And why did he not tell me of this? Mary asked herself.

266

Throckmorton had enjoyed the fire in the dining room at the inn in Stirling, and dreaded going up to his solitary room. The singing was still hearty in the common room; in fact the verses were just becoming scurrilous, albeit in Scots it was difficult to follow. But if he drank any more, his head would ring in the morrow. Reluctantly he paid his reckoning and made his way up the steep steps to his cold but well-appointed room. Sighing—for his inclination was to go straightway to bed—he forced himself to put his candle down and sit before his work desk. He must write to Cecil and Elizabeth.

"The Lord Darnley," he wrote, his pen reluctantly forming each word—oh, how he wanted to sleep!—"received the honours specified, after my last audience a few days earlier, the creation of the Duke of Albany only excepted—the conferring of which honour the Queen did promise to defer till she might hear how Your Majesty would accept the proceedings and answer to my legation."

He filled his cheeks with air and slowly blew it out.

"Nevertheless, I do find this Queen so captivated by love or cunning, or rather, to say truly, by boasting and folly, that she is not able to keep promise with herself, and therefore not able to keep promise with Your Majesty in these matters."

Now to the crux of it.

"This Queen is so far passed in this matter with my Lord Darnley that it is irrevocable, and no place left to dissolve the same, unless by violence."

XXI

Mary smoothed down her doublet and turned her foot this way and that, studying the way her leg looked in the wine-coloured trunk-hose.

"Do you think this looks like a man's leg?" she asked Darnley, standing beside her in her chamber. "Or is it too slender?"

Darnley stuck out his own for comparison, and it was nearly as slim as hers.

"Certainly not. 'Tis a most masculine and fine leg," he replied. "Come, you dally overlong. I think you are afraid to do as your father did, for all your suggestion of it."

"When my father went abroad in disguise, it was as Goodman Ballengeich, not Goodwoman Ballengeich. This is a more extreme change." She fingered the knot of hair underneath her velvet cap. She was afraid it would come tumbling down if the fastenings came loose: the cap was too small to contain it.

"You make a fine man," he said. "You are too tall to pass for any woman but yourself. Now Queen Elizabeth, though lower in stature, must needs disguise herself as a woman every day. She is by nature a man, so her gowns and jewels are called upon to disguise the fact and let her rule as a queen— for she can hardly be a king."

Mary nudged him, then spun round and kissed him. "You are wicked. But is this true?"

"There is talk amongst her launder-women that her courses are not as normal women's," he said. "In truth, they do not talk but as they are paid to talk," he admitted.

"Paid people will swear to anything," she said. "It is when people must pay themselves for what they say that one can believe them."

Darnley made a gesture of impatience. "Come, my Queen. You make a perfect man. The night grows older, even as we do." He took her hand. "Let us go!"

Together they descended the little winding staircase connecting Mary's bedroom with Darnley's at Holyrood Palace; then they traversed his suite of rooms to emerge into the wide forecourt of the palace.

Past the flaming torches in the forecourt they ran, hand in hand, and over the drawbridge and past the great gates separating the Palace from the Canongate leading up to the Edinburgh city wall.

It was a fine July evening, and light still lingered in the sky even at ten o'clock. The Canongate would be full of people strolling up and down, and attending to late business, so they went around by the Horse Wynd, the nearest side street to the palace gates, walked for a bit on the Cowgate, the great street parallel to Canongate, and then cut back through by way of Blackfriars Wynd. This way no one could know they had come from Holyrood Palace. The wynds were silent and dark and afforded private passage.

"I love Edinburgh," Darnley whispered as they stopped to catch their breath. "It is so secret, so tantalizing. All these side streets, branching off the main one, the tall buildings, the deserted closes—so different from London. A man may come and go here, unlike Stirling. I am glad we left Stirling."

Together they emerged from Blackfriars Wynd and began walking up the Canongate. So many people were abroad it seemed like a holiday fair.

"Good evening," said one man, touching his cap.

"Good evening," Darnley replied, touching his. Mary imitated him.

"Good evening," boomed another voice, belonging to a rotund merchant making his way purposefully toward the Netherbow gate. They followed him and passed through the great wall of Edinburgh and its city gate, and emerged on the other side of the High Street. Almost immediately to their right stood Knox's house. A light showed from its deepest quarters, but the work room, over the sidewalk, was dark.

"Knox sleeps," said Darnley, pointing upward.

"Knox never sleeps," said Mary. "Except with his young wife."

"Think you he does what we do?"

Mary blushed. "Nay. I doubt it."

"So do I, wife." Darnley took her hand and kissed it. "Do you know, even at this hour I am planning for the later one when I may come to you in the dark?"

"Aye. I also." It was true.

Darnley reached down and began feeling the cobblestones in the gutter. He found a loosened one and drew back his arm to throw it, aiming at the window.

"Stop it!" Mary restrained his arm. "What are you about?"

"Knox is against our marriage." He twisted his hand to free it. "He shall need to replace his windowpanes."

"No." Mary dashed the stone from his hand. "His windowpane is not his mind. And he blames every obstruction and petty annoyance on me; pray do not give him true cause."

Darnley sighed and turned away from the window. "I would love to knock his pate."

"That seems to be a favourite phrase of yours," said Mary. "You have said it to the old Duke of Châtelherault, to—"

A crowd fresh from the tavern jounced past them, still singing:

> *"Drink up your liquor and turn your cup over*
> *Over an' over an' over*
> *The liquor's drink'd up 'n the cup is turned over.*
> *I've bin to Glasgow and I've bin to Dover. . . ."*

"He needs it. His pate is addled to begin with."

They passed the town house of the Earl of Morton.

"It is not your place to knock pates. That is for apprentices on their holiday." Would even Robert Dudley have threatened to knock pates on a London street? "Not for princes."

Darnley made a disagreeable sound but kept walking up the street. "All right, then," he muttered.

Now that they were in Edinburgh proper, the street became even broader, became, in a way, the meeting place of the citizens. In the widened area near St. Giles Cathedral squatted the immense Tolbooth, a combination Council House and gaol. Right below it was the Tron—the public weighing beam—and the old Mercat Cross. Here the citizens of Edinburgh had their daylight needs met—from worship of God to enacting legislation to having their wool weighed—and at night they tended to gather there as well. The area was fairly well lit by torches and provided the requisite milling area for large groups.

As they approached the Tron, Darnley ran toward it, jumping onto its weighing bucket. It sank and hit the ground with a thud.

"How much does the young gentleman weigh?" called a strong, sure voice from the steps of the Mercat Cross. "What is he worth?"

"A golden crown," replied Mary, forgetting that her voice was at variance with her costume.

She pulled Darnley out of the bucket. "And I shall give you one," she whispered, taking his hand. She drew him over to the Mercat Cross, with its huge, waist-high circular base. People were sitting all around on it, their legs dangling.

"From this place, where all royal proclamations are read, I shall have you proclaimed King the day of our wedding," she promised him, whispering in his ear.

"And what does this fine young gentleman do?" asked the voice, now almost beside them.

Mary looked up to see him perched on the rim of the pedestal base. He was dark and had a well-trimmed beard and longish hair. Suddenly behind him she saw the pale faces of prisoners staring out of their windows in the Tolbooth. She nudged Darnley to reply; she dared not speak herself.

"I am cousin to the *valet de chambre* of the Lord Darnley, visiting at Holyrood Palace," he said. "My duties are light—mostly looking and listening, truth be told. And this"—he indicated Mary—"is my younger brother."

"Height must run in your family, then. And at an early age, for you've got your growth before your voice."

Observant man. They would have to be careful, but that was the higher sport.

"Aye. I am but fifteen," Mary said boldly. "I am so weary of waiting."

"All will come in time, lad," the man assured her.

"And what, if I may be so bold as to ask, is your trade?" asked Darnley.

"I am a printer. I work yonder"—he pointed at a doorway across the street somewhere—"at Bassandyne's. We printed five different books last year, and sold nearly all." There was unmistakable pride in his voice.

"There is little to do in the long dark winter here except read," said Darnley. "Little wonder your business flourishes."

No, no, Darnley, thought Mary. Do not say that. Say how well chosen his books must be.

"What do you know of winters here?" said the man. "You haven't spent one."

"We came in February."

"In the middle of February. And to a hunting palace. You've no notion of what we do here in Scotland in the 'long dark tunnel'—the short days from November to January—do you? And in England, where you come from, there's frippery and concerts and such like, so I hear. But *I* don't pretend to understand England, never having been there myself." He drew himself up as a model to be emulated.

"How do you know exactly the time we came?" Mary asked.

"Everyone does. We follow everything concerning our Queen. We know when she comes and when she goes, who visits her and when, whom she eats with, what she wears, what songs she and the deformed little Italian sing, and on which night."

This stranger knew all about her, and she did not even know his name!

"But how true is your information?" Mary could not help asking.

"That depends on the informant," the man replied. "Some are, of course, more reliable than others."

Who are your informers? Mary could see that Darnley was on the verge of asking, and she stayed him with a look. Nothing would warn the man quicker.

"This information you have just recited is, for example, false. The Italian is not deformed. I know, for I have spent time with him," Mary said.

"Not deformed? But I was told—and from an absolutely reliable source—that he was hunchbacked and had protruding eyes like a bullfrog's!" The man was obviously disappointed.

"No," said Mary, laughing. "He is of low stature but otherwise normally shaped in all respects. But tell me—what have you heard about the Queen's marriage?"

The man now laughed. "Shall I tell you, and you of Lord Darnley's household?"

"Why not?" said Darnley. "I've no liking for my master's master; I'm simply here for a change of scene. I think he's a . . . oh, I know not."

"A simpleton," said the man. "An *ambitious* simpleton. And the Queen so taken with him. Still, she must wed, and there is no one else available. 'Tis my opinion that whatever suitor had come in person, she would have swooned over him. Only Lord Darnley came; the other fools fiddled with ambassadors and letters—hardly very enticing. *If* she had seen the Lord Dudley—pardon me, the Earl of Leicester—in person, now that might have been different. But the Earl, being another ambitious man, sticks close to his own Queen. Ah, well. She's a good woman and deserves a turn in the bed, and an heir." The man moved his legs and swung them down. "I'm going to Ainslie's Tavern," he announced. "Come with me."

Mary and Darnley scrambled after him, their hearts beating wildly. This was fifty times better than eavesdropping.

As they were crossing the street, a horse and rider made their way down past them. People uncovered their heads and called, "Blessings, Lord Moray." The person acknowledged them freely and then moved majestically on.

Lord James! How easily and naturally he accepts the homage of the people in the street, thought Mary.

"The Earl of Moray," explained the man. "You have most likely not met him, as he has not frequented court since your master's arrival. He's the King's bastard and the foremost man in Scotland."

How simply the man said it: *the foremost man in Scotland.*

"How so?" Mary asked.

They were standing in front of the tavern now, but she clutched the man's doublet and wanted an answer before they entered the noisy room.

"He alone spans the time before the Protestant Kirk, going back to the old Queen's time. He's the one man we have had to run things through all the troubles during the war against the French, the time when we had neither queen, but only John Knox, and during the first years of the young Queen's return. He has held Scotland in the palm of his hand, and treated her tenderly. 'Tis a pity—and an ill omen—that he has withdrawn from the Queen's council and, indeed, from the entire government."

"Where did you hear that?" Darnley demanded.

"Everyone knows," said the man. " 'Tis no secret." He looked longingly toward the tavern, where loud noises and the smell of beer and bread puffed out each time the door opened.

"But what will happen to the Earl?" asked Mary, her hand still on his doublet.

"He will either grow stronger and overthrow the Queen and her chosen, or he will wane in strength and fade away. The people will decide."

Mary let go of him, her fingers releasing their hold. "And it is of no matter to you which one?" she asked.

"Not really. As long as my printing press is undisturbed. Moray seems a good man, the Queen is a good woman—nay, let the people decide." He shrugged. "Come." He gestured toward the tavern.

"Nay. I have little thirst," said Mary. The heat and noise from the tavern were repulsive. Who would choose to go in there, when he might remain outside and have clean air and see the stars?

"Suit yourself." The man turned in.

Mary walked rapidly away, up toward the dark bulk of the castle ramparts. Once they were away from the Tron and the Mercat Cross, there were few people abroad.

Lord James. He had a following, and common people saw him as her equal. She had not fully understood this.

"The printer is only one man," said Darnley. "His opinions are his own," he insisted. "He does not speak for everyone else."

But his words sounded hollow.

The Lord James had indeed withdrawn in protest against her forthcoming marriage, and was gathering his forces. Everyone on her own island was against it: Queen Elizabeth, Lord James, most of the Lords of the Congregation. She had forced the Lords to sign a document in Convention approving of the marriage, but the paper was worthless, and she knew it. From France, Charles IX and Catherine de Médicis had approved, as had Philip II and the Pope. But what weight did that carry? In the arena of the outside world, a great deal. But this was of most immediate concern in the Scottish and English world, and that was the stage she now walked upon. The boards were shaking, and did not feel at all steady under her feet.

Did she need permission from her own people to wed? And if so, how to get it? What about Knox? He had been preaching against it, booming out in his sermons about the dangers of letting two Papists wed. But if his mind could be changed?

She looked back down the street at St. Giles, its prickly crown spire, partly blocked by the square Tolbooth, curving over the roofs. Every Sunday in there, hundreds of people hear his sermons, she thought. If only I could harness them! They would have more influence than a thousand proclamations. Knox cannot be entirely stubborn and blind; surely he is open to common sense and political considerations. An heir for Scotland—without an heir, we are lost. And I'd permit him to be instructed in the Protestant faith as well as my own, so he could be wise and understand all his subjects. . . . Yes, I can offer that promise to Knox.

Knox it must be, then. I must endure Knox once more, and speak with him.

❦

John Knox looked out the window. What was all that commotion? There were people milling about, and someone had drawn back his hand to throw a stone aiming at his—Knox's—window. Hooligans! There had been so many of them of late, roaming the streets of Edinburgh, yelling, carousing, causing destruction. It was the influence of the Queen, and all those filthy Papists she had brought with her—or, more correctly, revived. For the latent Papists had been brought out again, as a rain will renew dried and scorched grass.

And if she succeeded in marrying that English Papist, Darnley, it would only worsen.

That is why it is my duty to speak out against it at all times, he thought. It may yet be preventable.

The man's hand was down; the stone had not been thrown. His companion had restrained him, and now they were passing on. Knox sighed. That saved him the trouble of having to replace whatever little panes would have been shattered. Any time spent on such things, necessary and trivial as they were, took time away from the true things in his life.

"John, are you coming to bed?" The sweet voice called from the back bedroom, drifting down, and he heard it above the raucous noises of the night outside, as a greyhound can discern his master's voice above a thousand others.

Margaret, his new wife. He gripped the iron window latches as if that would steel him, quiet his heart that had leapt up at the sound of her voice.

He had loved Marjory well, the mother of his sons, and had wept for weeks after her death. God had removed his helpmate, and there were moments when he begrudged God her presence and even begrudged Marjory her place sitting beside Jesus in supreme bliss. All the rebellious earthly thoughts came to possess him: I needed her more than You did. Why did You take her? You have so many; I only one.

And, blasphemous final feeling: God is like that rich ruler Nathan described to David: he required the poor man with only one ewe to surrender it for his feast, when he had large flocks of his own. At length he had, after much praying and weeping, been able to surrender her into God's keeping and say—and mean it—the Lord has given, and the Lord has taken away: blessed be the name of the Lord.

As he had finally rested in the Lord's will, Margaret had come into his life.

Margaret Stewart, the daughter of Lord Ochiltree, one of the foremost Protestant lords. She had royal blood, being descended from James II, and in the ordinary scheme of things would have been far above his station—he, the son of a Haddington merchant. But as "there is neither bond, nor free, there is neither male nor female, for ye are all one in Christ Jesus," so the humble man and the daughter of nobility could mingle in marriage with the blessing of the new Kirk.

And Margaret had wanted him, had been more eager for the match than he.

I felt a desire for bachelorhood once more, but the Lord had other plans, he thought.

"John!" Her voice was more insistent.

"I come," he said. He turned from the window in the darkened room and made his way through the rooms and up the narrow staircase.

His feet were reluctant—why? Was it that he lacked energy for what he knew would be required of him? Or was it that he hated to see that other side of him arise, that no amount of energy could tamp down?

He walked down the narrow connecting hallway until he reached the bedroom with its great double bed. Margaret lay in it, the covers up around her chin.

"At last," she said.

Knox removed his everyday doublet, a dark brown leather one, and sat on a stool to take off his shoes and hose. He kept trying to think how tired he was, but already his lower body was tingling. Deliberately he pulled off each shoe with great effort, stressing to himself his weariness. The shoes dropped heavily on the bare wooden floor.

He went to his chest and pulled out his coarse linen nightshirt, unironed and rough. He slid it down over his shoulders, almost enjoying its unpleasant rasp on his skin.

He could delay no longer. Slowly he walked to the bed and pulled back the covers in a decisive military manner. It was more convincing to him than to her.

He lay rigidly in bed on his back, half dreading and half aching for them to come together as man and wife. He clutched the covers; his long brown beard lay neatly on the blanket outside, like a horse's tail that had been combed straight.

"John . . ." his wife whispered, moving closer to him. She slid over and was now right next to him.

She reached out and touched his hair, smoothing it carefully, running her fingers beneath it to his scalp, caressing it. Again he felt his groin tingle.

She raised herself on her elbows and then turned her face to his and kissed him. Her lips first pressed themselves on his, then forced them to part. She had a small, moist tongue which she wriggled into his mouth, past his tight, chapped lips and guardian teeth. At first, as always, his reaction was to withdraw his tongue to keep it safe. Then something—not himself, never himself—let it loose and it began to entwine and probe with hers.

She was now half on top of him and her breasts felt like filled wineskins, jostling and squashing this way and that. He almost expected to hear fluid sloshing in them. It was comical, amusing. Why then did his pole, his manhood, start to throb and expand?

Could he command it to lie quiescent? He tried, by sternly ordering it to do so. The he tried to ridicule everything that was causing it excitement. *A woman's breasts: big bags like a cow's udder. A kiss: two sets of lips pressed together, like a wine press. The tongues: two slugs crawling slowly over each other, leaving a trail of slime. And soon, a crevice and a protuberance fitting together with a lot of heaving and thrusting, like a donkey with too wide a burden caught between two posts—straining and pulling and groaning.*

At the picture of the donkey straining, he grew even more excited. He was now as large and erect as any donkey, and he was on fire to relieve himself.

He rolled Margaret onto her back, where she lay, an entire body of obedience and sensual opportunity.

"Take off that shift," he whispered, and she sat up in bed and slowly removed it. First one arm, then the other.

I should have just pushed it up, he thought. His member was starting to twitch on its own; it would not be long now. I cannot just let it happen by itself like a sixteen-year-old apprentice, he thought. The embarrassment of it, the shame. His member stirred again and a wave of heat passed down it.

O God!

The shift was gone at last, and now there was no time for him to remove his own. He pulled it up and quickly positioned himself between her legs, nudging them far apart with his knees. Then, aligned properly, he thrust at her soft inner self. He felt himself go in and sink all the way, so their bodies were rubbing at the groin. It amazed him: he had felt as large as an oak tree and as long as a village Maypole.

Delicious, agonizing pleasure was sweeping over him. She was squeezing in some miraculous way to increase that pleasure, moving as if she were seeking something of her own. His pole shuddered and spurted, but did not lose its hardness and shape, and she continued to move against it. Did she not know it was over?

"Thank you, dear wife," he whispered in her ear, beneath her sweat-soaked hair.

"Ohhh," she murmured, but she did not stop moving; indeed, she seemed driven, twisting this way and that, pulling and pushing. Like the stuck donkey.

Then she gave a loud cry and began jerking spasmodically. He felt her insides contracting in waves, felt something caressing his member inside her, stroking like a piece of velvet. The waves came and went and felt infinitely tender, then they died away.

"Oh, John," she breathed, as if she had just run up a flight of stairs. Her hands fell away from his neck.

What had happened? Knox felt frightened. He rolled off her and tried to put his arms around her, talk to her, but she was either asleep or unconscious.

Pray God she is unharmed, he thought. This must never happen again. Oh, Margaret—I cannot bear to lose you. God will be jealous and snatch you away, too.

❧

John Knox—his member now small and obedient beneath his breeches, so that it had ceased to exist for him except to perform its excretory function—made ready for his audience with the Queen. Margaret Knox, discreetly dressed in the dark clothes of a respectable wife and entirely subdued, helped him with the final adjustments to his wardrobe.

"Your collar should lie flat," she said, patting it down. "I put starch in it, and I pray I put enough."

"It is adequate." He pulled away. He was nervous, although he knew he should not be. He had had many interviews before this; and the Holy Spirit would tell him what to speak, would direct his words.

The Queen had summoned him to Holyrood. It was not the first time, and it would not be the last. It meant his ministry was effective, that his words were hitting home.

No one kicks a dead dog, he repeated to himself with satisfaction. Close on its heels came, *The dogs bark, but the caravan passes on.* That was less satisfactory.

"The hour is come," he said, straightening his collar for the last time. Outside, a throng of his followers and well-wishers were waiting for him, and would escort him as far as the palace gates. He descended the stairs in grave dignity and was greeted first by Margaret's father, Lord Ochiltree.

"Come, brother, we will walk with you." He gestured toward the large group. "For if God be with you, who can be against you?"

They set out, moving down the Canongate, keeping company with their leader. When he reached the Holyrood Palace gates, he turned to them and bade them farewell.

"Now must needs I face this pagan ruler alone, like Daniel in the lion's den," he said.

"Aye, but you are the lion!" cried someone. "Show her your teeth!"

He strode across the forecourt and was soon being ushered into the broad entrance hall and from thence up the now-familiar wide staircase and then into the adjoining audience chamber. The Queen was already there, seated on her throne with the embroidered cloth of estate in gold and violet behind it.

She was all bedecked in the red and yellow Scottish colours, as if she meant to appeal to his love for his country. Her hair was smoothed back and her face shiny; it had just had an anointing of almond oil—imported from France, he guessed. She was smiling and obviously happy.

Why, she's no prettier than my Margaret, he thought in genuine surprise. Suddenly she was diminished in his eyes.

"Master Knox," said John Erskine, "I have been chosen by Her Majesty to be present, to answer questions and witness what passes between you."

Erskine: a mild and kind man, and a staunch Protestant, recently named Earl of Mar by the Queen. The absence of Lord James was blatant and more to be felt than if he had been present, thought Knox.

Knox bowed slightly and awaited the Queen's words.

"Dear Master Knox," she said, her voice smooth and offensively pleasant, "I must congratulate you on your recent marriage and wish you happiness." She smiled as if she had just offered him an estate.

"I am sure you did not call me here for that," he replied.

"I wish no unkindness to pass between us," she said, still smiling, as if she had not heard his rebuff. "Whatever there has been in the past, I know that we are different now, that we have learned much since our early days." Still she smiled that inane smile.

"Every day I learn in the Lord. It is not the same thing as general learning, by which even a child, and a dull one, increases in knowledge day by day, with little effort on his part. I can detect no changes in you, Madam, not since you first landed here in the ugly fog that surrounded you four years ago."

"You have not seen me in person," she persisted. "Now, perchance, when we talk, you will see changes, willingness to accommodate."

Was that clumsy hint supposed to tantalize him? "Of what do you wish to speak, Madam?"

"Of the future of Scotland, in that I am sure you share my anxiety that an heir be provided."

"God will provide," Knox said stiffly. So that was it.

"God cannot provide by himself without provoking scandal," she replied sweetly. "I cannot bring forth a child without a husband. It would not be seemly."

"An unseemly husband is even worse," he said. "And the man—nay, I cannot even call him a man, he is a debauched child—you propose to take to yourself is an insult even to you! You must not even think of it!" He raised his voice so that it could be heard through the windows and doors. He had trained his voice to carry great distances.

"So it is true!" she said, still infuriatingly, falsely, pretending a sweet mood. "You have been preaching against my intended marriage to the Lord Darnley."

"I do not deny it. Is that what you expected me to do?"

"You must desist in this obstruction." She kept her voice even and reasonable.

"Never." He glared at her.

"Master Knox!" she cried out suddenly, her voice shrill and not at all the soft, pleasing tone she had adopted until then. "Never has a ruler been treated as you have seen fit to treat me! I have borne with your rude words, both against myself and my family, and my faith. I have even sought your counsel and advice, only to be spurned. But this preaching against my marriage—I cannot permit it to continue! You must stop at once. I command you to do so!" She burst into tears, and an attendant rushed over with a handkerchief.

Knox shifted back and forth from foot to foot as he patiently waited for her to regain control of herself. Stupid, vapourish girl!

"Outside of my preaching, there is nothing in me to offend others. And when I preach, I am not master of myself, but must obey Him who commands me to speak plain, and to flatter no flesh upon this earth," he finally said.

"But what have you to do with my marriage?" she cried. "The Lords have given their permission."

"If the Lords consent that you take a pagan husband, they in effect renounce Christ, banish His truth from them, betray the freedom of this realm. And"—he felt these words come from somewhere outside himself—"perchance in the end this choice will do small comfort to yourself." He had suddenly felt a weight of sin, suffering, and ugliness pressing upon him.

"What have you to do with my marriage?" she repeated. "And what are you within this commonwealth?"

"A subject born within the same, Madam," he said dryly. "And albeit I be neither earl, lord, nor baron within it, yet has God made me—however abject I may be in your eyes—a profitable member of the same." He drew himself up to stand as thin and tall as possible, as though an invisible wire were attached to the top of his head, suspending him. "I am as bound as any member of the nobility to speak out, if I see something harmful approaching."

Mary began to weep again. Erskine mounted the platform of her throne and said, "Do not be distressed, lovely Queen—you who are so beautiful, and merciful, and held in such esteem by all the princes of Europe—"

But she continued crying, until Knox's acerbic voice cut in. "Madam, I never delighted in the weeping of any of God's creatures; yea, I can scarcely well abide the tears of my own boys whom my own hand corrects; much less can I rejoice in Your Majesty's weeping. But seeing that in truth I have offered you no just occasion to be offended, but have spoken the truth, as my calling craves of me, I must sustain Your Majesty's tears rather than I dare hurt my conscience, or betray my country through my silence."

It was hopeless. Sorrow at the realization made her cry out, "Master Knox, leave this chamber!"

Bowing, he submitted to her request and backed out. The high doors of the chamber were opened for him and he found himself standing in the stair landing that served as antechamber just beyond. A bank of pretty young court girls were sitting on a window seat, each wearing a different coloured bright dress. The summer light made them glow, and their healthy complexions were ruddy.

"O fair ladies!" he found himself compelled to say, calling them to attention. His voice was light and merry, as if he would banter and dally with them.

"How pleasing this life of yours would be if it could abide, and in the end you could pass to Heaven with all this gay gear!" He shook a finger at them. They reminded him of flowers in a garden border: beautiful and simple and perishable.

"But fie upon that knave Death, who will come whether you will or not! And when he has arrested you, the foul worms shall be busy with this flesh, be it ever so fair and so tender!" He flicked a finger underneath one girl's chin, felt the soft melting flesh surrounding the eternal jawbone underneath. "And the weak soul, I fear, will be too feeble to carry anything with it— gold, ornaments, tassels, pearls, or gems."

Abruptly he turned and left them to their common doom, the doom no one ever thinks is real.

Not me, they all secretly think. Not me. And all the while they sit secure, perched on their tree branches, Death is sawing at the base of the tree, he thought, satisfied that he had disturbed them.

They will think about it at least three minutes, he thought sourly, clumping down the steps.

Human frailty. What could one man do against it, its self-serving lies, pleasure-blindness, and powerful desires?

XXII

wo weeks later, on July twenty-ninth, Knox rode through the main street of St. Andrews, making for the old Abbey, where the Lord James was Commendator. Earlier in the day Knox had preached the Sunday sermon in the parish church, fulfilling the vow to do so that he had made in the galleys.

How long ago that was—almost twenty years! The sea sparkled in the bright midsummer sun, the surface glittering like a million tiny fish scales. Out on the promontory the ruined church of St. Andrews had stood like a broken sand castle. O those days, those days, the first fruits of the rising against the Cardinal and the corrupt church of Satan! That was when we first struck terror in their hearts, showed them we were the marching army of the Lord!

The memory of the men storming the castle and surprising the Cardinal in his bed with his whore warmed him. And after he had been stabbed in retaliation for his cruel burning of Wishart, his body was hung from the very ramparts where he had smiled as Wishart burned.

The Cardinal and his whore . . . why was it that those who practised the religion of Rome seemed either to keep whores—if male—or be ones themselves if female?

But we purged St. Andrews, and today it is the foremost seat of the Reformed Kirk: our showpiece.

It was a pleasant town on its rocky cliffs overlooking the North Sea, with its broad streets, gracious town houses, and colleges. The town was filled with scholars and their students at St. Mary's College, St. Salvator's College, or St. Leonard's College. Ironically, St. Leonard's, founded in 1512 to train recruits for the Church of Rome, had become a hotbed of reformers.

This is our little Geneva, Knox thought, with pride. And I myself came of age here—I myself first stepped forward upon that long road I am still treading.

He urged his horse to break into a trot. He had been glad enough to leave Edinburgh, leave behind the mess and turmoil. The Queen had had the banns called for her marriage to Lord Darnley the Sunday before, and his palace informants told him she meant it to take place soon. There would not be three weeks of banns, as her own—supposedly cherished—Church required.

Perhaps she is with child, Knox thought. That would explain the haste.

He came upon the Abbey, with its high grey stone walls and gatehouse. There were no guards, as the Abbey no longer guarded secret treasures inaccessible to the public. He rode freely into the enclosure, seeking the Lord James's house. It was formerly the Prior's dwelling, a well-appointed stone house, somewhat apart from the grouping of other ecclesiastical buildings.

The Lord James had sent him an urgent and uncharacteristically beseeching message to come to him in this crisis of the Queen's impending marriage. Knox was pleased to acquiesce, and also pleased that the Lord James was not yet so haughty as he had been depicted by his enemies. He still had need of him, Knox.

Knox approached the Prior's quarters, and even as he did so a servant appeared to take his horse.

"The Lord James?" Knox asked.

"Within, good Master Knox," the boy replied, indicating the main entrance.

Knox strode in, past the ancient carvings of saints and entwined fruits framing the entranceway, and into the darkened antechamber. He announced himself to the guard—little more than a lad—and waited.

The heavy oak door at the far end of the antechamber creaked and swayed. It was warped, and the upper part would not let go of the door frame. At last it flew open. Lord James emerged.

"My dear brother in Christ," he said, moving forward and embracing Knox. "I thank you that you have come." He drew him after himself through the warped door, then through a series of rooms until at last they were in a spacious gathering hall, with windows overlooking a garden now exuberantly blooming. The hollyhocks swayed in the slight breeze, and their stalks were as big as a girl's wrist.

The Lord James looked agitated; his brow was furrowed and his eyes seemed to be looking not at what was in front of him but at something he could not see. He kept snorting as if to clear his nostrils, but he did not have an ague or a cold. His nose must be raw, Knox thought.

"What passes in Edinburgh?" he finally asked. Then he gave an almost inaudible snort.

Knox tried to remember how long ago the Lord James had left the city. "The Queen is to marry Lord Darnley. The banns were called last Sunday. All goes forward. She will proclaim him Duke of Albany and—this is certain—King before long."

"She cannot do that on her own authority!" cried James. "Parliament must approve and bestow the Crown Matrimonial, as they did with that miserable François."

"True. But she can still 'name' him King, whatever that means."

"It means nothing. It is a title that is granted as a courtesy, and will expire at her death. If she dies, he cannot remain King, but will revert to just plain Lord Darnley."

Knox was uninterested in the eventualities. Why was Lord James so concerned with them? He studied his face as he continued talking.

"Has my absence caused stir or comment?" he asked. "I withdrew from her Council and refused to sanction the marriage. Then I left Edinburgh."

"Your absence has indeed been noted, but what it betokens I know not. That depends on what it means. What exactly does it mean? If you are at liberty to reveal?"

James pulled out a heavy carved wooden chair, a legacy from the last Prior, who had been despoiled of all this by the Reformers. He sat down in it as if he were under oath.

"I mean to fight."

"In what way? And to what purpose?"

James looked surprised. "This marriage means a Catholic child; a Catholic child means a Catholic King. We cannot permit this. The Reformation will be utterly undone. I am surprised—nay, shocked—that you would ask."

"And who will fight with you?" Knox wanted particulars, not vague statements.

"The Hamiltons. They hate Darnley, ever since he insulted their leader, Kirkcaldy of Grange. Lord Ochiltree, your wife's father, and their kin."

"Not enough," Knox said.

"Others may join; there are many fence-sitters who may see their way clear to us."

"Fence-sitters by definition go either way. So you've only the Hamiltons?"

"The Douglases are kin to Darnley's mother, and hence cannot lend themselves to the enterprise. Argyll is a possibility, for all that his wife is the Queen's bastard sister. He would bring many with him."

"The Erskines?"

"Hard to say. They've a personal attachment to the Queen, but they are committed to the Reformed Kirk. Lord Ruthven, the Lindsays . . . we can count on them, I believe. Possibly Glencairn."

"And on the other side?"

James opened a silver reliquary that had once housed Saint Medard's teeth—the patron saint of those with toothache—and drew out a paper.

"The son of George Gordon, the late Earl of Huntly, himself George, remains locked up and can do nothing for either side. The Setons, the Beatons, the Livingstons, the Flemings, the Maxwells, the Earl of Atholl—all will support the Queen. But they are lesser figures. Only Atholl is an earl."

"But added to the entire Douglas and Stewart families, they make quite a weight. And then there's the Earl of Bothwell, traditionally loyal to the crown. He has sneaked back into Scotland and may be looking to win favour with the Queen." Knox shifted in his chair. These massive carved seats were works of art, but decidedly uncomfortable. "Now, God forgive me, but I must ask: there is one name that can assure our success, and you have not mentioned it. Where stands the Queen of England on this?"

"She has been discreetly silent."

"As always."

"But I believe she favours our cause and will support us, if not with troops, most certainly with money."

"On what do you base this belief?"

"She has reacted vehemently to the Darnley marriage. She does not want a Catholic king in Scotland."

"Perhaps not. But"—now here was the crux of the matter, the one question that above all must be answered—"what else can you offer her? Have you another ruler more suitable to her tastes?"

James sighed. He opened his lips as if to speak, then closed them.

So he sees himself as king, thought Knox. But at least he has the good sense not to blurt it out. Or perhaps not even to speak the words to himself.

"The Lord will provide," James finally said.

"The Lord can only make the same selection as the rest of us. I see no other alternative to the Queen. She is the last remaining royal Stewart. Now, if the idea of royal blood is dispensed with altogether, many interesting possibilities arise. Directed by the Holy Spirit, we could elect a ruler. As the Vatican claims the Popes are elected." He laughed dryly.

"Aye. Perhaps." James gave a tentative smile.

So that's the route he foresees, Knox thought.

"But the English Queen will never permit this," Knox pointed out. "For she herself must, perforce, honour the concept of royal blood being somehow different from all other blood. Without that, she herself has no claim to the throne. Her title was not based on unchallenged legitimacy, nor on Parliamentary permission, but on the magic of royal blood. She'll not support your rebels."

"I have royal blood, too! As much royal blood as Queen Elizabeth!" cried James. "Both our fathers were kings, both our mothers commoners!"

"With this difference: Elizabeth's father married her mother and had her crowned Queen."

"Then he repudiated her and executed her!"

"Nonetheless, a form of ceremony was gone through. The Pope does not recognize it as legal, but that has become her glory." Knox had a sudden thought. "You *do* have enough royal blood that, were you to win in this attempt to unseat the Queen, it could be conveniently recognized. But"—he glared at James with his bright brown eyes—"first you must win."

A few hours earlier, whilst Knox was still in bed at the merchant's house at St. Andrews who had offered him hospitality prior to preaching his sermon, Mary had arisen and put on a great mourning gown of black with a wide mourning hood—the gown she had worn to the memorial mass ending her forty days of deep mourning for François. She had worn it many times since then, and each time she had felt that in so doing she was coming back to François and saying, "I have not left you, and I never will." Now, on her wedding morning, she felt compelled to wear it for the last time, to have François present at the marriage, to give his blessing and release her. Only François could give her away.

At six o'clock in the morning, the Earl of Lennox and the Earl of Atholl came to escort her, one on either side, to the chapel at Holyrood. She came slowly down the long aisle, where the priest was waiting, and then Darnley stepped forward and took his place by her side.

Quickly the final banns were read, and quickly they repeated their wedding vows to one another. Darnley took a triple ring with a diamond in the middle and side rings of red enamelled gold, and at the words, "With this ring I thee wed," he slid it on her finger.

"I now pronounce Henry, Duke of Albany, Earl of Ross, and Mary, Sovereign Lady of Scots and the Isles by the grace of God, to be man and wife indeed," said the priest. The sound echoed throughout the chapel.

"*Te Deum laudemus!*" Riccio exclaimed. "It is done and cannot now be broken!"

Mary and Darnley turned to him and embraced him as the only confidant for their secret betrothal.

Mary allowed herself to be escorted back to her chambers, there to lay aside the mourning clothes, never to resume them. The Marys pulled out the pins and, with solemn respect, helped her to disrobe. They laid the mourning cloak out on the bed and folded it almost tenderly, putting sweet herbs along its length. Mary leaned forward and kissed it before allowing it to be closed in an embroidered satin bag.

Mary Seton saw the tears in her eyes and, drawing her aside, away from the gay chatter, embraced her. "You honour François by your tears of loyalty and remembrance. But, my lady, he died in the flower of youth, leaving you to grow older without him. The young you will always be his wife. But you are a different woman now and that part of you, the part that has arisen since, is not disloyal to love the Lord Darnley."

"Think you this is so?" whispered Mary.

"Lady, I know it." She reached out her hand and wiped away one small tear on Mary's cheek. "Now go to your new lord and husband with gladness."

Mary clasped her hands and then let them go. "I am both more happy and more sad than I have ever been. Is it possible?" she murmured.

"Yes. I can see it is so. But, pray you, the Lord Darnley must not see your tears." Seton wiped away the next gathering of them. "Your bridal gown awaits!"

Fleming and Beaton were bringing out the scarlet gown, embroidered with pearls and gold thread. It was stiff with richness.

Mary allowed herself to be fastened into it and then put on her finest jewellery: her black pearls and the Great Harry, and huge pearl earrings from the oceans beyond India. The Marys brushed her hair and then fitted a pearl-encrusted satin cap upon her head. The rich hair spilled out behind it.

There was dancing and a formal dinner, followed by trumpets and the distribution of largesse in the courtyard, then a supper. Mary and Darnley twined round one another in the stately dances played on the slide trumpets, recorders, and violas. Darnley never took his eyes from hers, staring at her as at a goddess or an apparition throughout the long day.

At length, after the formal dinner, three separate dances, the supper, the trumpets, the largesse, Mary and Darnley took their leave of the company, making their way to her apartments and finally to her bedchamber.

There were no attendants, by her command. When they shut the doors they were completely alone.

Candles burned in all the sconces, and a large candelabrum of French workmanship stood on her work desk with ten white tapers. She came to him and embraced him. She had meant to say something, but there were no words worthy, no words to express her feelings both of final sorrow and of the release from it, the finding of her new treasure.

One by one they blew out the candles, one by one they removed their bejewelled clothes until they lay together in the great royal bed, smooth young flesh seeking its own.

"You have made me King," he finally murmured, the first words he had spoken since entering the chamber.

"King indeed; King of everything," she whispered.

"This bed is my realm, your body my land," he said. "Let Christopher Columbus and Francisco de Coronado go to America; you are my new-found land and I seek to explore it all."

Outside in the streets of Edinburgh, the citizens were causing a tumult about the marriage, and some near the Mercat Cross stepped aside as the royal herald approached the Cross, then mounted its base and unrolled his parchment. Two trumpeters blew a fanfare as he read the Queen's proclamation that her beloved husband Henry, Lord Darnley, Duke of Albany, was henceforth to be styled and honored as Henry, King of Scotland, by her own wishes.

No one cheered.

A week later, another proclamation was read at the same site, this time at high noon. Three blasts of the royal horn followed, officially declaring the Lord James Stewart, Earl of Moray, an outlaw and rebel traitor to the Queen.

XXIII

"And is my armour ready, my love?" Darnley was waiting anxiously in his bedchamber at Holyrood as Mary sought him out in his quarters. She had had an unpleasant discussion with Lord Seton; not that Seton himself was unpleasant, but the topic was: the rebellion of her brother Lord James, and the refusal of him and his compatriots to appear at her summons.

"I had no choice, did I?" she kept asking her faithful Master of the Household. "I had to call for men and arms to support me. Now I must take the field against him."

Lord Seton shook his head. "It is a tragedy."

"This is the second rebellion against me by a subject!" Mary could hardly believe her own words. "First Huntly, now Lord James. And after all I have done for him!"

"It is *because* of all you have done for him," Riccio's voice piped up.

Lord Seton looked up in surprise. "I thought we were alone," he said pointedly.

Riccio emerged from the little side room. So that was where he had been hiding!

"Forgive me, I could not help overhearing," Riccio said. "I was addressing some correspondence in the turret room. But, my dear Queen, as I said, it was precisely because of all you had done for him. You gave him vast tracts of land, elevated the bastard to be the greatest in the land. Is not the rest predictable?"

"No," she snapped. "I despise ingratitude! It is the one failing I cannot tolerate!"

"He had no incentive to follow you any longer. Withholding favours would have been a surer method of ensuring his loyalty."

"I am his Queen, by divine right of royal blood!"

Riccio shook his head pityingly. "I think his own portion of royal blood is speaking more loudly to him."

"I will be revenged upon him!" she cried, leaving the room and rushing to Darnley's quarters. Now there was Darnley, waiting, eager for his armour.

"I—I know not." She had forgotten about his armour, which was to be gilt and was being hastily made up for him by local blacksmiths by welding other pieces together, and coating them with gold.

"Oh." He looked so disappointed. Then he brightened and said, "What will *you* wear?"

"I shall just borrow some men's half-armour. And as I shall wear it under my clothes, it is not important that it be ornamented—or even fit very well."

She allowed herself to admire Darnley in his setting. He had overseen the furnishing of his apartments, and had paid particular attention to his bed. Only the finest velvet hangings were selected, and on them were embroidered his own familial crest and lineage.

"Do you know what my mother has on her bed hangings?" he had said, holding Mary dreamily one afternoon after a tender interval of lovemaking. He had begun to laugh. "She has images of saints pinned to them! Only pinned—that way she can ch-ch-change them according to the s-s-season!" He was laughing so hard he could hardly finish the sentence. "My mother. I shall always think of her that way."

"I should like to meet your mother," said Mary. Darnley talked about her a great deal.

"No, you wouldn't. She's a harridan."

Now Darnley was standing, fingering the hangings on his own bed. "I am tired of the purple," he said. "Perhaps I shall change to gold."

He had only had the purple for a month! "I am afraid all such expenditures will have to wait," she said. "In order to pay for the troops to march against

Lord James, I must pledge my jewellery. Five thousand men are costly to maintain in the field."

Darnley dropped the bed curtain. "Thank you for my armour!" he said. "I had no idea that it would be such a sacrifice."

She smiled at him. "Consider it a wedding gift," she said grimly.

Mary had issued a call to arms for able-bodied men, asking them to muster at Edinburgh with fifteen days' provisions. Five thousand had come to follow her banner, with the Earl of Morton leading the advance guard, and the Earl of Lennox commanding the rear guard. Riding with Mary in the midst of the host were Darnley, the Marys, the lords who were still loyal, and Riccio. Just before leaving, she had released Lord George Gordon from prison, where he had languished since his father's rebellion, and restored him to his hereditary title as Earl of Huntly.

It was Lord James who benefited from Huntly's rebellion, she thought. It was Lord James who reaped the reward of his fall. Now, at least, the son will always be the enemy of his father's enemy. And the enemy of my enemy is my ally.

The rebels, under Lord James, had gathered at Ayr, on the west coast of Scotland. He was not alone; the Duke of Châtelherault was with him, as an hereditary enemy of the Lennoxes, and so was Kirkcaldy of Grange. That hurt Mary as well as surprised her; she had always thought Kirkcaldy loyal and clear-headed. The Earl of Argyll was also on their side. Reports were that they had only about twelve hundred men, but were expecting northern troops from the Earl of Argyll to join them shortly.

"We will engage them in battle before their reinforcements come!" Mary cried. "On to Ayr!" She and her troops streamed out of Edinburgh, banners flying, in late August. The days were golden and hazy, and it was easy to pretend they were just on a progress through the countryside, enjoying the mellow warmth and seeing the farmers bringing in their harvest. But under her scarlet and gold embroidered riding dress was the light armour she had felt called to wear, and under her hood and veil she wore a steel helmet. She carried pistols, thrust into her waistband, to have instantly to hand.

Behind in Edinburgh she had left Erskine in command of the castle, and had told Randolph that if he attempted to aid the rebels with money from England—for Lord James had attempted to put a religious colour on his insurrection by painting it as a matter of Protestant conscience outraged at the wedding of two Catholics—she would have his house surrounded by guards.

They marched westward, through Linlithgow and Stirling and thence on to Glasgow. The weather held, still giving their venture a holiday air.

To Mary's surprise, the rebels did not stand to fight them, but instead attempted to slip past them and take advantage of her absence in Edinburgh. Wheeling the troops around, Mary's forces retraced their own steps back toward Stirling. But suddenly a violent storm hit; water spilled from the heavens like Noah's downpour, swelling the small streams to raging forces.

The rain was coming down so hard that it ran into their mouths and left them gasping for air. When they reached the banks of the usually small stream called the Carron, some of the men were swept away and drowned in what was now a mighty river.

"Let us stop! Let us stop and wait here!" cried Darnley. The rain was running off his helmet like a veil, and his hair straggled out from beneath it.

"Nay!" cried Mary. "We cannot! We must press on!" She looked at the churning, muddy waters of the rampaging stream, and crossed herself. "God have mercy on the souls of the lost." Then she urged her horse forward, praying that she not be swept away. Her horse, a strong swimmer, made the other bank safely. Behind her, Darnley was following, his arms clutching his horse's neck.

The rebels entered Edinburgh just ahead of the storm, but could not take the city. There was no sympathy for their cause; the townspeople did not rally to them, and Erskine, loyal to the crown, fired on them from the castle, so they were forced to flee. This time they retreated back in the direction of Stirling, then went south to Dumfries, where they waited forlornly for English aid.

Mary's army stopped at last, and tents were pitched in the field. She was excited beyond measure; word had just been brought to her of the rebels' flight. She stood in the door of the tent, holding its flap, watching the sunset that was now staining the waters of the subsiding Carron.

"I wished for this," she murmured. "I wished to see what it was to be a man, and wear armour, and lie out in the fields all night. They say you should be careful what you wish for, that it will surely come to you."

"And do you like being a man?" asked Darnley, who was stretched out on the camp bed.

"In some ways."

"Fighting is such fun!" cried Darnley. "I have enjoyed it immensely."

"We have done no fighting as yet," said Mary. "All we have done is ride and chase the rebels."

"Indeed, we should call it the Chaseabout Raid. Lord James and his men have kept out of our way," said Darnley. "He will flee across the Border by tomorrow. Unless Bothwell intercepts him."

"Aye. Bothwell rules the Borders. But I did not charge him with tripping the rebels." ·

"Why ever not?"

"I am testing him. He reentered Scotland without permission, still technically under arrest. He has yet to come seek an audience. So I am curious whether he will now come actively to our aid, or look the other way. He may perhaps be bitter at his mistreatment at my hands. Again, it was directed by Lord James!" With a sickening realization, she saw that many of her actions had been urged on, prompted and promoted, by Lord James, actions that had driven men away from her and left her isolated—and in his hands.

"Never mind about that," said Darnley. "Come here!"

Puzzled at the tone in his voice, she ignored it. "Look at the river," she said. "The Carron . . . but to the poor men swept away, it proved to be Charon himself."

"I said come here!" Darnley was smacking the camp bed. "And close the tent flap!"

Mary went over to him, where he was lying full length, a strange look on his face. As she came near him, and bent over, he grabbed her and pulled her on top of him. His fingers were digging into her neck.

"So you want to know what it is to be a man?" His voice was rough. "Very well, then. You be the man. Take me. Take me against my will."

Mary felt an unfamiliar sensation of fear. He was, suddenly, different. His eyes held a cold, staring look. "Nay, what a foolish thought!" She tried to pull herself away, but he held her fast. There was surprising strength in his grip. "Pray, release me."

"No." He stuck his face up into hers. "Then if you won't play my game, I'll punish you!" With astonishing speed, he flipped her on her back and began pulling at her clothes.

"Henry, no!" What had come over him? He smashed his lips down on hers, causing her to bite her lip, and she could smell an odd but not unknown odour. What was it? It was something she had tasted before.

He was ripping at her underclothing, exposing her. "Don't move!" he was hissing in her ear. "Don't move! I command you!"

Instead of obeying, she tried to throw him off. He clamped his hand down over her mouth and breathed, "You must not defy or disobey your husband! You know that you are to be submissive to my will!"

"Mmmm—mmmm—" she kept trying to speak. What was happening to him? Then, suddenly, she recognized the smell. It was whisky. He was drunk. She almost laughed with relief. That was all it was.

"Hush!" he said. He was biting her shoulder; his free hand was still ripping at her clothes. Like a madman, he held her a victim while he satisfied his desire.

Outside she could hear the sound of a soldier's horn being blown, announcing that it was time for camp supper. It seemed very far away.

✿

John Knox, left behind in Edinburgh, wrote his description of the failed rebellion and said, "Albeit the most part waxed weary, yet the Queen's courage increased manlike, so much so that she was ever with the foremost."

Yes, he had to admit it: the Queen had matchless courage. And the rebellion had come to nothing. Lord James and his compatriots had had to flee into England and take sanctuary there.

I warned him, thought Knox. I warned him there were not enough sure men on his side. The fence-sitters came down on the wrong side of the fence.

Back in Edinburgh, Mary gratefully took possession of Holyrood again. Entering the palace, she was struck with the thought that only a short while ago the rebels had come there, hoping to enjoy it. Never had it seemed more precious to her.

Late that night, she knelt in front of the ivory crucifix from St. Pierre and spoke softly to it.

"Dear Lord," she whispered, "thank You for delivering my kingdom." But inside there was a deep sadness. She could not help but remember her high hopes, her trembling expectation when she had first received the summons to return to her land, before this very cross.

"I have tried, in all ways, to be a wise ruler. I have sought Your guidance. Yet some nobles have been dissatisfied, and rewarded my efforts with treason." That was the truth of it, and it hurt, even if they had been thwarted.

"Please help me!" she blurted out in a louder voice. There had been more disturbing episodes with Darnley, violence followed by unctuousness, and she was frightened. At times he seemed to change into a person she did not recognize.

And he showed no interest in helping her with the aftermath of the rebellion, the justice to be administered, the rewards given. It was as if he had no part or concern in the country at all, although he kept begging to be granted the Crown Matrimonial. Sometimes, when he was being rough, he would say, "No wonder I will not sign the papers or attend the Council meetings, when you withhold my rightful title! Do it, and then I will!" Her answer was always the same: "Show yourself worthy first."

A sound! Someone had come into the room! Mary froze, afraid it was Darnley. But a gentle hand was placed on her shoulder, and she heard Mary Seton's soft voice saying, "I will pray with you." She knelt down beside her mistress and kept absolutely still. Not until Mary rose did Seton stand as well, rising in that beautiful motion that gave grace to all she did.

"It sorrows me to see your heart so troubled," said Seton.

"There is nothing that He"—she nodded toward the crucifix—"cannot cure."

Seton took her hand and led her to a chair. She sat opposite her and took both hands in hers. "I thought that marriage would bring you happiness," she said.

"So did I," said Mary. "And I cannot say I am unhappy. I have some happy news. I think I am with child."

"That *is* happy news! And what does Lord Darnley say?"

"I have not had the—opportunity to tell him."

"I see." Seton waited to see if Mary would say anything else. Then she said, "I am sorry about Lord James. I know it grieves you in many ways. Betrayal is worst when it comes from those who have reason to love us."

Yes. That was it. He was no ordinary rebel. "He deluded himself that he would receive support from Queen Elizabeth," Mary finally said. "But when he got to England, all he got from her was a public scolding. He was humiliated before the foreign ambassadors." She laughed. "I was pleased to know that Elizabeth could be counted on to support *me* during a crisis. My sister sovereign has proved my good sister indeed!"

❦

"Does it not please you, what happened to the rebels when they were granted audience with the English Queen?" asked Riccio, looking up from the correspondence he was transcribing. Mary had been dictating a formal reprisal of it to her uncle the Cardinal, full of balanced, carefully chosen phrases. Riccio sensed a withholding, a distance from the Cardinal. But then, the world had become a hostile place for her since her marriage, full of people who disapproved of her choice. Riccio suspected—though he had no proof—that the Cardinal was one.

"Ah—my brother!" Her face grew sad. "To have lost his loyalty . . . nay, I cannot lose what I never had. But I was so deceived in him!"

"Then what you have lost is your innocence, not a brother."

"Aye. But I shall miss him. Miss what he was to me, miss him as a person."

"You have a husband now. That should take the place of any brother."

"They are not the same." She was withdrawing again; it was the word *husband* that had done it. "A husband is a new grafting, a brother an old one."

"Yet a husband is supposed eventually to be the strongest bond there is."

"It takes time." She turned again to a letter. "Shall we continue?" she said brightly.

Riccio put aside the writing materials. He was tired. It was tedious work to make each letter perfect, to space the words correctly on the page so they were visually attractive and worthy of the personage to whom they were addressed. The ink smeared easily, and the smoother the paper, the more difficult it was to keep the writing even.

"Now," said Mary. "Would you care to be present at the forthcoming interview with Lord Bothwell, or do you wish to retire? I do not expressly need your services."

Could he take her at her word? Interviews could be quite boring.

Just then Darnley appeared. He looked peevish. That decided Riccio.

"I believe I shall take my leave, dear Queen," he said, rising and kissing her hand—and then, impulsively, her cheek. He turned from the writing desk and left the room.

Darnley glowered after him, then turned on Mary.

"You favour him above prudence," he said, pouting. "Servants should not kiss queens."

"Indeed they should not," she agreed, to placate him. "But he is more like a brother than a servant."

Still Darnley frowned. "I would think you have had enough of brothers," he finally said.

His words caused an actual physical pain to pass through her. *Enough of brothers . . . not enough of a brother . . .*

"He was once a good brother," she finally said. "I will cherish that memory."

"You are charitable." Darnley sniffed. "Do you mean to be so to the Earl of Bothwell?"

"Indeed. I must confess I admire his audacity. My justice was unjust, in that I took the Earl of Arran's word against him—words since proven to emanate from the mouth of an insane man. Did he stand still for them, wait patiently in prison? No, he escaped."

"And returned to Scotland without permission. Is that something to admire? Why is his disobedience more commendable than that of the Lord James? Because he did not see fit to raise an army against me, but rather to aid me?"

"Yes." Darnley frowned again. "And now you wish to give him the Lieutenancy of the Borders in preference to my father."

"And wherefore not? Bothwell is a native of that area. He knows it well, knows every man in it. He knows the intricate braid of loyalty and history, entwined in so complicated a pattern we can never make it out. Your father"—she had never come to like him—"being from a different area of the country, could never do suchlike. Loyalties are very local."

"Bothwell did little enough," Darnley persisted.

"He did not need to. The rebels fled forthwith."

"Ummmm."

Mary went over to him, threw her arms around him. "Do not begrudge him his recognition. We need him. We have lost so many others! Lord James gone, and Kirkcaldy—a very brave soldier! The very ones who fought for me against Huntly turned against me. They were the foremost soldiers in the realm!"

"The Earl of Bothwell," the guard announced.

"Pray admit him." Mary looked at Darnley, warning him. Darnley retired to a far corner, seating himself with an injured air and crossing his arms. He was so in shadow that no one would have seen him.

Into the room walked James Hepburn, his hat tucked under his arm. He came forward with purposeful steps, then knelt. All Mary could see was the top of his reddish-haired head. Then he raised his face and looked at her.

"Most gracious Queen," he said, "it has been four years since last I saw you. Many things have happened during those years to change us into different creatures. Yet I affirm—and I am no flatterer—that your beauty has greatly increased, along with your power and reputation. You are now a true Queen. Scotland is fortunate."

"Pray rise," she said.

"Indeed." He stood up, and she motioned him to her.

He walked, as stocky, muscular men do, with a sort of energetic purposefulness. He was thirty years old now, and whatever deprivations he had suffered in prison had been more than made up at the tables of France afterward. He radiated compact strength and self-sufficiency.

"Lord Bothwell, you entered Scotland without our royal permission," she stated.

He smiled. "I beg forgiveness, Your Majesty. I had a yearning to return, and you were immersed in other concerns." He raised his eyebrow. "I sought to spare you another administrative task—that of signing my papers."

She could not help laughing. "Nay, you are incorrigible! That was not your true reason."

He made a little gesture of humour.

"But whatever your reason, once here, you proved loyal to us in the recent rebellion. We are grateful for that, and return you to your former appointment as Lieutenant of the Borders, and commend you for your vigilance in securing the Borders for us when they were, of late, threatened."

"No one came *my* way," he said. "The rebels slipped across the border to Carlisle on the far western side, away from my jurisdiction. Oh, they've since migrated to the eastern side. I hear they now lie at Newcastle, sustained by an insultingly paltry subsidy from Queen Elizabeth."

Mary felt herself start. So Elizabeth *was* supporting them, despite her haughty words to the contrary!

"Newcastle," he continued, "is a dreary town with a stout castle. And those ruins of the wall nearby: poets and scholars make much of them. Perhaps the Lord James can amuse himself with them. He can sit amongst the moss-covered, tumbledown mounds and speculate on the passing of time and of queens." He paused and cocked his head. "Elizabeth publicly ordered him from her realm as a traitor. Yet there he remains and even receives support from her."

Was that a question? "Then things truly are not what they seem," Mary finally said.

"I could not agree more," Bothwell answered.

"Yet who *is* to be trusted?" A thin voice issued from the corner: Darnley's.

"Until I know who speaks, I dare not say," said Bothwell, with a smile. "It might prove too dangerous."

"The King speaks." The slender voice came again.

"Ah." Never had Bothwell's voice sounded richer and thicker. "Then must needs I say, trust only those who love your liege lady and Queen as devotedly as you do. Although she is beautiful, kind, clever, and trustworthy, there are those who dislike her for all those virtues, and would work her harm. 'Tis a mistake to assume a good ruler will be beloved. Her very virtues can inspire envy and hatred among lesser men."

"The rebels are considerably lessened men now," said Mary. "For they will forfeit all their lands and titles as soon as Parliament meets. No more Earl of Moray. He overreached himself."

"A dangerous thing, Your Majesty." Bothwell sounded amused. "A good lesson for us all."

"Then don't overreach yourself with this lieutenancy she's given you!" shrieked Darnley, suddenly standing up.

"I wouldn't think of it," said Bothwell earnestly. "I'm content with what Her Majesty sees fit to give me."

After Bothwell had taken his leave, with assurances of loyalty, Mary turned to Darnley.

"You need not be so harsh," she said, sinking down in a chair.

"I do not trust him," was Darnley's cold answer.

"He has done nothing to merit distrust, unlike all the others. I had to expel Ambassador Randolph for his part in encouraging the rebels. Morton remains here, but I know he dallied with my brother and keeps up a constant correspondence with him for all that he led *my* troops and is Chancellor of the realm. It is true that Argyll did not openly support the rebels by bringing his promised troops, nor did he flee with them, yet he has forfeited my trust, for he betrayed both sides."

"Do you, then, hold loyalty so dear?"

"Above all else. Once someone has betrayed me, or even looked on and not lifted a voice or sword to halt the traitors, he is forever lost to me."

"A sad thing, passing sad, to be lost to you," Darnley said, kissing her hand. His beautiful, long-lashed eyes were closed.

Now she would tell him. Now, when he was being sweet.

"Henry, we have a joyful event before us. We are expecting an heir . . . see, even now he makes me tired. But I can rest. For the next seven months there will be quietness and pleasure—a perfect climate for the baby."

Darnley's face was flooded with happiness. "A baby! Oh, Mary, my love! A baby, our baby!"

She felt relief, although she had not known how uncertain she was of his response. Of late, his response was so unpredictable.

Darnley hugged her. "I am eager for the birth, and proud to be the father of your child. The father of a king—that is what I will be! An undisputed king. *He'll* not need to get Parliament's approval for his title, nor rely on his wife to procure it for him!"

"Oh, leave this. You worry it like a dog a bone."

"You order me to leave you? Very well!" He turned and rushed toward the door.

"I did not order *you* to leave me, but to leave the subject—"

The arras flapped as he slammed the door of the chamber behind him. It was a familiar sound, and a familiar sight.

Mary left the audience chamber and made her way into her bedchamber. She was tired, and moved slowly. So far the pregnancy had made itself felt mainly by causing her to feel drowsy all the time and draining her of energy. She had not suffered any of the nausea or fainting Bourgoing had predicted. She still carried on all her duties, which, in the aftermath of the Chaseabout Raid, had turned from battlefield action to political decisions. It was tiring.

Of late, confined by physical lassitude, she had enjoyed needlework, particularly designing emblematic panels. At first it had been something merely to keep her hands busy and keep idleness at bay, but gradually it had grown into a challenging mental exercise and, beyond that, into an easeful escape, an escape into a world where all was ordered according to some arcane pattern. At present she was working on a panel that depicted herself and Darnley in symbolic form. It showed a land tortoise climbing up the base of a crowned palm tree. He was the tortoise, she the tree. When the Marys had asked her what it signified, she refused to tell. That was the virtue of emblematic panels: they could mean anything.

She sank down into the sitting-chair that had been padded with a quilt and positioned in front of the window, and took up her sewing box. The design expressed her growing unease about Darnley—*was* he a land tortoise seeking only to climb to a higher position through marriage? He harped and harped on the Crown Matrimonial . . . why had not Parliament granted it? Why was she so cruel as not to call Parliament and demand it?

In the meantime he paid scant heed to his kingly duties; he was never there to sign documents, so a stamp facsimile of his signature had had to be made. He was always hawking, or riding, or . . .

She pulled out a thick strand of tawny silk and began separating the threads. She threaded the correct number through her needle, holding it up to the light.

. . . going out at night. Where did he go? She used to descend the winding staircase to his room after supper, hoping to see him alone, only to find him gone, no matter how foul the weather. When she questioned him about it, he would refuse to answer. Sometimes, very late at night, she would hear a commotion in the courtyard as he would demand to be let back through the gatehouse. His voice would be loud and slurred. Even during the day the odour of wine was sometimes about him.

She began filling in the yellow spots on the design of the tortoise's shell. Pull the thread through, pull the thread out, pull the thread through . . . it was so soothing.

She was lonely, more lonely than she had ever been, because the one person she should have been able to talk to, she could not.

I married to escape loneliness, she thought, and instead I have found it in a most terrible form.

And the realm had not quieted with the end of the Chaseabout Raid. There was still discontent; she could sense it in the silences about her, in the sullen low spirits that seemed to pervade Edinburgh. Darnley was heartily disliked; and now there were times when she, too, disliked him. It had begun with his cruelty in the tent, during the aptly named Chaseabout Raid.

This time last year he had not even arrived in Scotland, she thought. Then he came and I loved him. Is it really over in so short a space? Can love be so fleeting?

After the baby comes, things will be different. Yes, they will, they must be.

But in the meantime . . . I miss Lord James, she thought with surprise. Miss his presence, and what I *thought* he was.

No more of that! she told herself sternly. What prince would have so little pride as to miss a traitor?

XXIV

Darnley made his way along the back alleys running parallel to the Canongate, his mantle muffling most of his face, walking hunched over so he would not look quite so tall. He had got away again, escaped from the stifling Holyrood to where he could breathe in peace. It was an easy enough matter to disappear in the darkness of Edinburgh once the sun went down. The good men of the Kirk were all indoors—reading their Bibles, most like!—but Edinburgh offered more than just what the Kirk sanctioned. In the wynds and closes there were taverns to drink in and houses where other comforts were available.

Of the latter he had only recently begun to sample, in a timid, hesitant fashion. The truth was, he felt guilty about it. He was, after all, married. Why should he need to do this? But the things he wished to do disgusted him, and obviously they would disgust his wife as well. It was better to pay directly for it, to buy it from someone who considered his ideas tame, or at the most merely routine.

And as for the drinking—it was relaxing to go to an establishment where that was the endorsed activity, rather than something that one was always fighting to get a bit more of. Servers were so slow at banquets! (Although the wine was the finest.) And in his chambers there were always the valets, Taylor and Anthony Standen, who looked at him if he poured out an extra dram or two. He *knew* they were keeping count in their heads.

Darnley pushed open the door of the Monk's Arse Tavern—the one with the sign showing a monk lifting his robes to display his naked buttocks. It was a small, dark establishment just off Blackfriars Wynd, and Darnley found it perfect for his purposes: it was popular enough that he did not stand out, but not overly crowded at this time of night. He looked for a place on a bench and signaled to the serving woman before even sitting down.

"Well! Good evening, Your Majesty!"

Darnley jumped. Who had recognized him? His eyes raked the room and then he saw the muscular bulk of Archibald Douglas sprawled across one of the benches. Archibald lifted a mug and saluted him.

Damn! Now he would have to go and sit with his distant relative. He shivered a little; the saturnine, sarcastic Archibald was rumoured to be a murderer, or for hire by murderers.

"Well met, cousin," said Darnley weakly, sinking down beside him. He saw the bulging thigh of Archibald only inches from him on the bench; Archibald did not move it, as politeness decreed.

"I did not know the Queen's husband favoured such places," said Archibald. "What a happy surprise." He took a long drink from his mug, and when he was finished, Darnley saw tiny droplets of ale glistening on the beard-hairs around the man's mouth.

"Everyone likes a change," said Darnley. "And their ale suits my taste." Indeed it did. Of late he had had to forgo his whisky. Not only was it difficult to obtain, after the disturbances with the Earl of Argyll and his estates up north, but whisky upset his stomach and gave him pounding headaches. He had had to switch to ale and wine.

"What else suits your taste?" asked Archibald, and Darnley froze. Did he know about the visits to the houses? "I liked the flavour of the Earl of Argyll's whisky, but that's hard to come by these days."

"Aye." Archibald grunted and took another drink.

Darnley's drink had arrived and he took a big gulp. He had been waiting hours for this.

Together they drank several mugs. After the first three, Darnley began to get the release he sought. It took three big mugs of ale to equal the effect of one small vial of whisky, but once it was obtained, it was the same sensation. He did not even mind Archibald now; indeed, he felt a certain camaraderie with his kinsman. The candles in the room seemed to glow as beautifully as horn lanterns, amber and soothing. The wooden panelling on the walls seemed to be as rich and rare as ebony. And suddenly a picture of Mary flashed into his mind, Mary with her hair down, in her nightgown, in his bed . . . with her white feet, like a marble statue's, peeking out from under the covers. . . . Those feet . . . sometimes they met over the small of his back when her long legs encircled him. . . .

"Is the Queen busy tonight?" Archibald was saying.

"No." He did not know if she was busy or not; he only knew that he felt called to the ale and the women upstairs in the little house a few doors down, where he could drown his fantasies without questions or shame, and so he had gone out.

"Then she is not with her secretary?" Archibald looked surprised.

"I know not."

"Ah."

The word hung in the air like a hummingbird.

"What do you mean?" Darnley was forced to ask.

"I mean, it is unusual for her not to be with him—with the strange little man with his strange little tastes."

Darnley burst out laughing. "I have been friends with Riccio for some time, and there is nothing strange about his tastes." Indeed, the Italian had good taste, in clothes, food, wine, books . . . most of the things the Kirk deemed sinful.

"Then why does the Queen indulge herself with him?" Archibald asked, as if he were genuinely puzzled.

"I don't know what you mean."

"Of course, you would say that. I beg your pardon, then. If it is with your permission . . ." Archibald shrugged.

Was he implying—did he *dare* to imply—that he, Darnley, was an acquiescing husband? That he stood by while the Italian secretary pleasured his wife? "Such insult is not to be borne!" cried Darnley, leaping up and grabbing for his sword.

Archibald stood up, too, and the mass of the man seemed to grow and fill the tavern. "I meant no insult," he said. "I was merely trying, as your kinsman, to warn you and tell you of danger. It was my *loyalty* that made me speak." He looked properly sincere.

Darnley, who was too drunk even to manage to extract his sword, sat back down. His head was spinning. "You lie. It is not true—" he muttered. Where had Archibald gone? The man had left. Darnley called for another ale.

He slumped back against the wall, and closed his eyes. He would not go to the women tonight. No, he would go to his wife. To the Queen. Was there any reason why she should not give him what he desired? To hell with the women. And to hell with Riccio!

Darnley allowed himself to picture the imaginary scene that always aroused him. He wanted Mary to kiss and lick his feet, then lick his legs, slowly, inching bit by bit toward his groin, and wrap his legs in her hair. She would do this by touching his feet with her forehead, and then part her hair in two and envelop his legs, making a tent as she licked her way up to his privates. The thought of the smooth, sleek hair, the warm tongue . . .

Suddenly he was so excited he could barely stand it. He fumbled in his purse for money to pay for his ale, and staggered out into the night, hardly able to walk because of his painful erection.

Mary had just asked Mary Seton to bring her the elderflower-water to smooth over her shoulders and neck. It was late, and she looked forward to bed. These days she seemed to need more sleep, and, she had to admit it, she was pampering herself. The delicate scent of the elderflowers seemed to induce sleep, and she liked to close her eyes and imagine herself lying in a summer meadow of flowers.

"Thank you, dear Seton," she said, taking the thin glass bottle. The liquid in it was a pale tint of pink. She poured a little out in the palm of her hand and rubbed it slowly over her neck, feeling it easing her, relaxing her muscles.

"Shall I return later for our rosary?" asked Seton. They had often recited the rosary together just before bedtime, but since Mary had married, that had been interrupted. Lately, with Darnley away in the evenings, they had resumed the habit.

"Yes," said Mary.

Alone in the bedchamber, she took her time in applying the lotion, then read some of du Bellay's poetry.

> Si notre vie est moins qu'une journée
> En l'éternel, si l'an qui fait le tour—
> Chasse nos jours sans espoir de retour . . .

> If here our life be briefer than a day
> In Time Eternal, if the circling year
> Drive on our days, never to
>   reappear . . .

The door swung open, and Darnley stood there, hanging on the doorframe.

"So you are alone!" he said. His voice was loud and accusing. He stepped in and banged the door behind him.

"Yes, for a little while. Soon I expect—" She closed her book, and rose to greet him.

"Oh, so you expect a guest? Well, dismiss him!"

"Him?"

"You know who I mean!" Darnley lurched toward her.

Not again! Not drunk again! Mary felt her heart sink, and at the same time she was enraged. Her elderflower-water ritual, her quiet moment, the little circle of beauty and refinement she had created, privately, was now to be smashed. "No, I do not." She backed away.

"Come here! Do not back away from me!" He grabbed her and pressed himself against her. She could feel his arousal, and it was as much an assault as Lord James's rebellion. He started tearing at her clothes, but he was so drunk all he could do was paw at her.

"Down here! On your knees, and serve me!" He grabbed at her head and tried to push it down toward his feet. She pulled back and slapped him, hard, across the face.

"Sober yourself, you drunken bully!" she cried. "How dare you come into my chambers like this?"

"Your chambers, your chambers?" he said, in a wavering, singsong voice. "What is this 'yours' and 'mine'? Are we not one flesh? Is not a husband made one with his wife? Come, and be one with me!" He jumped forward and tried to tackle her, but she easily sidestepped him.

It was all she could do not to kick him as he lay there on the floor. She was trembling. She backed up and, walking to the door of her chamber, called her guards.

"Remove the King," she said with a flat voice. "Take him to his own chambers. Call his valets to attend to him."

When Darnley was gone, dragged away, she was overtaken with a violent fit of shaking.

When he drank, her husband was a monster. And he was getting worse; the times were coming closer together now. She would have to keep her door locked from now on. She walked over to it, still shaking, and turned the big iron key in its latch.

XXV

Darnley had tried the inner door to Mary's bedchamber, and it was bolted. Until then, he had not even entertained Archibald Douglas's suggestion that there was anything amiss. Indeed, it was to prove Douglas's sly innuendo wrong that he had mounted the spiral stairs between their rooms and walked softly across the landing and grasped— ever so gently—the door handle. Pulling the door snugly toward its frame to muffle sound, he had turned the handle and then pushed. No motion. It was bolted from the inside. It had never been bolted before.

He put his ear up against the thick wood; there was no keyhole to look through. He heard the voices plain and clear: hers and his. Mary's and Riccio's.

Feeling physically ill, he slumped against the door. He was betrayed.

Or was he? Could it not have an innocent explanation?

But why the locked door, then?

No. There was no explanation other than the one Douglas had hinted to him.

Riccio. Riccio was Mary's lover.

Darnley would have laughed, had not the insult to himself been so great. The Italian was old—at least fifty!—and a head shorter than Mary. He was ugly, and of low birth.

But that made it all the more personally degrading.

If she had chosen Maitland, smooth and sophisticated and highly intelligent . . . well, then . . . or Bothwell, with all his bed-training and knowledge of how to please a woman *that* way . . . or even de Foix, the French ambassador, with his European *savoir-faire* and his background of intrigue . . . any one of whom I might say, "He has this and I have not" . . . But Riccio!

He turned and descended the steps, so stunned he was almost surprised he could still put one foot in front of the other. He reentered his bedchamber and flung himself facedown on the great bed. The bed that Mary used to visit. But she came no more. . . .

Tears blurred his eyes as scenes from their former trysts insisted on playing in his mind, as vividly as any Dutch painter might depict them. How she had sought him out . . . the things she had said. . . .

Were they all lies? Was she saying the same things to Riccio at this very moment, directly above him?

He beat his fists against the feather mattress. The thought of Mary in the embrace of another man tortured him.

You must face it, he told himself sternly. The truth is the truth. She amused herself with you, used you to get herself with child so she could provide an heir with royal blood for the throne, and now she has no further use for you. She promised you the Crown Matrimonial; now she says that is impossible, that you must sign papers and attend Council meetings to earn it. But that is just an excuse. The truth, the truth . . . the truth is you've served your purpose. Now you are expendable. The truth is she loves you no more.

At that realization a pain akin to a sword wound went through him. But it was as nothing compared to its brother-thought: perhaps she never did, and all your memories and treasured words are but untruths. Even that which you thought you had, you never had.

Maybe the child is Riccio's. . . .

He wept, squashing his pillow. He wept until he felt limp and almost dead.

He must have fallen asleep, for when he opened his eyes they were crusted shut by dried tears. He groaned. Why was he fully dressed? There was something ugly, something unpleasant, crouching just outside his consciousness . . . what was it? It was as hulking and silent as a great hayrick casting a shadow on new-reaped fields. Suddenly it rushed upon him with a cry of triumph.

Your wife has deserted you. Furthermore, your wife never loved you.

He lifted his head. The palace was silent. Riccio must have long since departed from the rooms above.

But there were places in Edinburgh that never slept. Little places behind even the wynds, with doors unmarked and plain.

Suddenly he felt overwhelmingly lusty and desirous of a woman. All women were alike in the dark, he had heard it claimed. And it was so! Yes, it was!

He swung his legs over the side of the bed. His new woollen tights pulled pleasingly over his knees.

Why, I need not even attire myself, he thought. I am prepared already.

His feet touched the floor and he padded quietly to the lit candle flickering on his writing desk.

I think I will invite Riccio to join me, he thought. Perhaps he will say something to allay all this. Perhaps there is some explanation. Perhaps it is not true. . . .

Perhaps it is not true. At that thought, his heart leapt up.

He took his candle and made his way along the gallery to the rooms of Riccio. He knocked softly.

There was a stirring within, a shuffling. Surely Mary was not in there with him?

I am the King, he told himself. I may enter where I will. He turned the handle—this one was unlocked—and strode in.

Riccio sat up in bed, gasping.

Robbers, thought Darnley. He thinks I am a robber. What a jest—*he* is the robber!

"Good Lord D—Your Majesty—what troubles you?" Riccio sputtered.

Darnley thrust the candle directly in his face. It was lined and weary. The hair was lank and greasy. That made it all the worse.

"Nothing troubles me," he said lightly. "I have a mind to sample some rather unorthodox offerings in certain quarters of Edinburgh, and I thought a companion would be a jolly thing."

"Oh." Riccio lay back on his pillows. He looked exhausted. An old man should not involve himself in what he was evidently involving himself. "I must beg to excuse myself," he finally said.

"Nay, that you must *not!*" said Darnley, yanking on the neck of his nightshirt. "You *must* accompany me. I refuse to go alone! And I am, after all, your King!"

Riccio roused himself and left the bed. Even in his embroidered nightshirt he was a comical—under ordinary circumstances—sight. Now he was just disgusting.

"You must excuse me for a moment," he said, retiring to a screened alcove to dress.

Was his member red and raw from its recent employment? As he tucked it away, did he pat it and relive each moment?

"I am ready," he finally said, emerging.

"Good," Darnley replied.

They set out silently, Darnley pulling the sleep-clumsy Riccio along the palace corridor and then out into the fresh air. He stumbled on the cobblestones and Darnley jerked him up.

"Wake up!" he hissed. "You must be alert for what will follow!"

So Riccio was exhausted from all his lovemaking? What clearer proof?

Darnley knew a side gate that led them out, avoiding the guards and their torches. It took them around the south side of the palace, and then along dark alleyways and narrow wynds where moonlight never penetrated. All was dark; there were no lanterns left burning, and no lamps still flickering inside any rooms as they passed. It was the very deepest, stillest time of night, with no sound except for the scurrying of rodents disturbed at their passage.

The stone houses seemed to radiate the cold, and soon Darnley was shivering even inside his wool mantle.

"Turn here," he told Riccio, and around a corner the faint sound of voices could be heard. And then he was knocking softly on a door, and it was opened by a woman who had obviously been already awake. Yet the room behind her was too dimly lighted for honest work.

"I seek Letitia," Darnley said. Now his voice was thick with excitement.

The woman looked at Darnley. Suddenly she realized who he was: the King. She reached out and stroked his cheek.

"So fine a skin," she said in a low voice. "I will give you to no other but me." She led him into a small bedroom, after instructing someone else to take Riccio. There was nothing in the room but a gigantic bed.

"Come." She pulled him after her, drawing him up into the bed as if by suction. She lay down and held out her arms to him.

She seemed eager to touch him, kiss him. If her desire was feigned, it was impossible to detect. It seemed more real than anything his mother had offered him in childhood or Mary had offered him in marriage.

And it was true . . . *all women were the same in the dark.* . . . She felt the same as his wife. . . .

Afterward, she did not pull away or talk of politics or duties. Instead, she fondled him. To what purpose? He could not understand it. Then she whispered, "I think our pleasure could be increased ninefold if it were widened to be threefold."

"Do you mean—?"

"Wait and see," she said, rising expertly. She rang a bell, and a servant appeared at the door. She whispered something and the door closed.

"Now," she said, handing him a huge goblet of wine. "Refresh yourself."

Soon the door creaked open. Riccio looked in.

"Is this not an unusual dish?" the woman whispered. "Do with him what you will."

"Ah, Riccio, my friend," murmured Darnley. "Pray join me." His voice was slurred with the wine.

Hesitantly, Riccio approached the bed.

"We are eager for you," Darnley said.

Riccio looked sick. Obediently he climbed up into the bed.

The woman began deftly removing his clothes. When she got to the breeches, she nodded to Darnley.

Darnley unlaced the front of them carefully, drawing each thong out of its eyelet in a long, slow motion. The V-shaped opening grew wider. Underneath lay an undergarment of silk. Darnley slid off the breeches. The silken drawers yet remained.

Under there . . . under there . . . he thought, lies that which my Queen prefers to mine. He whisked them off and then stared: the member was

303

completely hidden under a bush of wiry hair that called to mind the brooms of peasant women. Nothing was stirring there.

"I just finished," said Riccio apologetically.

"That is no matter," the madam said. "That part of you we require is virgin yet. At least, so far this evening." She motioned for him to roll over. He looked frightened.

"It is nothing to be feared," she assured him, caressing his buttocks as he obeyed and turned on his stomach. She spread the sides of his muscular buttocks. "Nay, do not tense up. Then it *will* be painful."

She turned to Darnley. "Is it not alluring? So rounded, so perfectly sculpted . . . it will feel different, of course. But just as beer tastes different from wine. They both afford a buzz in the head, and many a man drinks both and feels the better for it. . . . There, now . . . I can tell the thought excites you."

She gave a knowing glance at his privates, where his member was stirring again, like a man who has been knocked about the head and then, after some grovelling, regains his feet.

Yes, it excited him, but not for the reasons she thought. It excited him to think of violating the man who had stolen his wife, of forcing him to do acts that were obscene to him, of humiliating him. . . .

"Yes. It does," he murmured.

"But there's more to it than that you should take your pleasure directly of him," she said. "I too have desires, and if I lie a certain way they can be fulfilled. Everyone wants a change, and you and I have already tried one thing. So I think I will require of Master Davie—that is your name, is it not?—that he perform the most difficult role. He must thrust even while being thrust into. From you, sweet prince, I shall only require a supple and loving tongue. But first I must see you settled one upon another."

Smiling, she arranged Darnley over Riccio, and then, upon a signal, pushed Darnley down.

Darnley felt the hatred and fear from Riccio, but that made the pleasure all the more intense. He wanted to abuse him, to tear his insides, to shame him. When he heard Riccio stifle a cry of pain, he felt victory. The little Italian went rigid.

"I told you, relax," said the woman.

"Ahhh—" Riccio's voice was edged with pain.

Darnley felt Riccio will himself to relax, but it made little difference. They were not made to fit together.

All the better, thought Darnley.

He cruelly punished the little man, using him as roughly and meanly as he could. He could feel the pain he was inflicting, even as he worked mechanically to bring pleasure to the woman with his mouth. She gave groans and grindings of pleasure, but Riccio was silent.

Darnley continued to work Riccio long after the woman had pulled away in satisfaction. Evidently Riccio had managed to perform his duty there, for she lay limp, with a half-smile on her face. But his stubby little fingers were grasping the pillow and his jaw was clenched as Darnley went farther and farther inside his body.

"For Jesus' sake, stop," he finally begged.

"Nay, I have had scant pleasure yet," Darnley insisted, thrusting harder. Riccio cried out.

Then Darnley felt a spasm coming over him, but it was different from anything else he had ever experienced. It was one quarter pure hatred, one quarter curiosity, one quarter revenge and only one quarter physical. He cried out in triumph, a high, shrill shriek. Then he collapsed on Riccio.

Only as he separated from him did he see the bright blood on himself.

So that was what was so slippery, he thought. It was not the oil of passion . . . but of course, that would be impossible.

Riccio was crying.

"You didn't like it?" the woman was saying, sounding surprised. "Some men actually prefer it. I am sorry . . . but there is salve that will help ease the pain. . . . "

Riccio flung himself off the bed, gathered up his clothes. The red on his buttocks made a comical sight.

"You are evil," he said to Darnley. "You will regret this day."

"Oh, is it day?" sneered Darnley. "I thought it was night."

The woman lifted the curtain at the window and peeked out. "Daybreak. The changing between day and night."

Riccio left.

XXVI

ary started to ask Beaton to bring her her hooded fur mantle, but stopped. The notes of the song Riccio was playing were so sweet she wanted to finish hearing the piece. And she had no desire to hurry to the merchant's house where she would be dining.

She stood at the window of the small supper room in her suite at Holyrood and looked out at the lights up and down the Canongate. The layer of ice on the stones made them reflect like a mirror.

I must be careful with my footing, she thought.

The pregnancy, now in its fifth month, was beginning to affect her sense of balance.

The song ended. The time had come.

"Thank you, dear Riccio," she said, turning to him.

He smiled. "I have two others, which I will play next time," he said.

"Beaton, my mantle," she said wearily.

The girl fetched it from the wardrobe and brought it to her mistress.

"You must send to France for the cloth for your wedding gown," Mary scolded her. "Already you give the tailors little enough time. Remember, choose what you like; it is my gift."

Mary Beaton smiled, but it was a stiff little smile. Was she still smarting from the failure of her romance with that meddling English ambassador, Randolph? The romance had come to an abrupt end when Mary had had to expel him from the country for his encouragement of Lord James's rebellion. Since then, she had been courted by one of her own countrymen.

"Alexander Ogilvy is a lucky man," the Queen assured Beaton. Indeed, Mary thought, he is straightforward and honest and will never betray her.

Riccio scrambled from his seat and walked with Mary the length of her apartments and then down the broad stairs. When they were out of earshot of Beaton, he whispered, "Ogilvy does not *feel* lucky." He paused, but could not wait for her to ask why. "He loves another—Lady Jean Gordon. But a more powerful lord has claimed her. To be young and in love and powerless is a sad state."

"Who has claimed her?" Mary asked, as she swept down the stairs, her velvet gown trailing obediently on the steps behind her.

"Lord Bothwell. They're to wed next month." Riccio rolled his eyes and delighted in being able to astound the Queen. "There's no love there— just property. That's the pity of it."

"Bothwell! Does he—does he marry her against her will?"

"Indeed. But her family has sold her."

For an odd instant she wondered what it would feel like to be taken, married against your will. Would you resist or submit?

Bothwell! Imagine having to give yourself to him. . . . He would be rough and demanding. He would crush you. He would use you like a horse.

But he would never smell of strange odours and come to you demanding abominable gestures, created from sick fancies.

The memory of Darnley's behaviour was painful to her. He had lately turned the marriage bed into a field of scurrility and seaminess. He—

"My dearest." Darnley was standing at the foot of the stairs, attired in the finest velvet breeches and jewelled cape. His face was as beautiful as ever and his smile was like a curve of ivory. But she shuddered as he took her hand. He glanced at Riccio to dismiss him, but the Italian had turned away already.

"And what has my fair Queen wrought today?" he asked lightly.

"Many dispatches needed to be read," she said. Earlier it would have been a hint or a command, but she no longer wished him to involve himself in those matters.

"And?"

There is something ugly brewing, she thought. "There is a great deal of correspondence passing between Edinburgh and London," she said cautiously. "As if there were pressing business of some sort. Cecil writes to the

Scottish rebels at Newcastle almost daily, and also to Knox. And I—" She stopped. She had no desire to tell Darnley of her suspicions. He might blab.

"Yes, my love?" He leaned over to her and kissed her.

The odour of wine was on him. So he had been drinking already. Yet it was not apparent in his demeanour.

"Why do you drink so much?" she asked sadly.

"I don't know what you are talking about," he said, turning away.

They made their way in silence up the Canongate and then through Netherbowport into Edinburgh proper. The merchant, Donald Muir, was an importer of wines from Bordeaux and La Rochelle in exchange for wool and the skins of goats, sheep, and rabbits. He was not wealthy, but was well-to-do and an important councilman of the city. Mary enjoyed the merchants and their gatherings as a welcome escape from the stifling atmosphere of palace functions, and always accepted their invitations.

"Welcome, welcome!" Muir was gesturing enthusiastically from his door as he saw the torches accompanying the royal couple.

Inside his house it was snug and exuded an air of having all things in hand. The table was laid with pewter and glass, and an array of spices— ginger, pepper, cloves—allowed the diners to adjust the taste of any dish to suit themselves. The company was carefully selected: another merchant, who dealt in Baltic trade, particularly hemp and iron; a theological student from St. Andrews; a physician from the University at Aberdeen who had made an investigative study of the plague; a lawyer who specialized in wills and inheritance; an English bookseller with a shop in Edinburgh; and a quiet young man who claimed to be a scholastic mathematician. All these men, and their wives, proved to be lively talkers, and Mary loved hearing them. Their work was as exotic to her as a trip up the rivers in South America.

The mathematician . . . he spent hours doing figures, but not for practical reasons like finding a sum!

The physician . . . he had written a treatise pointing a finger at garbage, flies, and rats as a cause of the mysterious plague, after careful observation during one severe outbreak.

I would sooner peer into an erupting volcano, she thought. This serious, quiet-voiced man must be very brave.

"But what has garbage to do with it?" Darnley was suddenly heard to say. "There's garbage everywhere—piles and piles of manure, shit, piss—" He pronounced each word loudly and let it carry down to the end of the table. The company fell silent before his rising voice. "Yet there's not plague everywhere!" He nodded to the servitor to refill his wineglass and bolted it down immediately, then stuck it out again for more wine. "Good honest filth has never yet made man ill!"

"Your Majesty," the physician said carefully, "as I stated in my thesis, *A Short Description of the Pest,* the plague must have broken out initially. Then all these things exacerbate it. It does not originate in filth, but is incubated in it."

"Bah! Like all scholars, you raise more questions than you answer! But can you hawk, eh?" He laughed loudly. "That's the measure of a man, not studying manure!"

The host attempted to lead the conversation elsewhere. "I understand that the Low Countries are growing increasingly restive under the hand of Spain. They are unable to stomach the Inquisition."

"Who could?" the theology student suddenly said. "It is an abomination, an affront to God! And I hope our good Calvinist brothers persuade William the Silent to be silent no longer, but to—"

"I said, can you hawk?" yelled Darnley. "You, knave, answer me!" He stood up and glared at the physician. "See, he insults me!" he screamed. "He refuses to answer!"

"Henry, no!" cried Mary, rising clumsily. She put out her hand to touch his shoulder, but Darnley swatted it away.

"We'll fight, then!" Darnley grabbed at the place where his sword usually was, then reeled around. He was completely drunk. He crashed against the table and then careened against a cupboard.

"Stop this!" Mary commanded. She was shamed beyond embarrassment. He looked possessed.

"So you betray me! It is as they said, then!" He turned once, twice, as if trying to right himself. "Farewell!" He rushed toward the door, wrenched it open, and stumbled down the steps. They heard him lose his footing and fall, then emit a string of curses.

"Our King," said the theology student bitterly.

Mary felt deep shame. The host attempted to quiet the people and have them take their places once more at the table, but Mary turned away. Taking her mantle, she motioned away the attendants who would accompany her.

"Nay. I would go alone."

"Your Majesty, it is not safe—"

"Leave me! It is safe enough. Thank you, good Sir Muir. Your kindness will not be forgotten." She went quickly down the steps and began walking back down the High Street, toward Holyrood.

Why am I hurrying back there? she asked herself. To be with Darnley? He's not there—he'll be off to whatever dark places he seeks at night. I care not.

The night was cold and calming. She had been sweating and shaking, but now the rush of frigid air was a relief. She passed John Knox's house and saw the candles burning in his study, and all at once she felt a rush of envy for him and for the life he had. He had children, a loving wife, loyal friends, and a clear calling. He must rise up in the morning eager to begin, and lie down at night feeling satisfied. All because he had a clear call, and answered it.

She slowed her steps as she approached Holyrood. There was no need of hurry. There was nothing in there for her, as there was in Knox's little house for him.

XXVII

Bothwell stood preening himself before the mirror. He did not like the little hat he was going to wear for his wedding, but the gold doublet of ribbed silk with puffed sleeves and short cape of tawny velvet were of fine workmanship and would doubtless impress his bride. The narrow lace ruff, buttoned tight around his tanned throat with little gold studs, felt uncomfortable. But it was too late now to have it reworked. After he was married—

Married. He was going to be married. And it was a fine bargain he had worked out, pleasing to all. The Queen had written in the marriage contract that it met "with her advice and express counsel." From the Queen's point of view, it united two loyalists from two different regions, the Highlands and the Borders; from his point of view, it shored up his shaky finances; and from Lady Jean Gordon's, it brought her family out from under the shadow of her father's rebellion four years past. Now, in the wake of his loyalty during the Chaseabout Raid, her brother George was restored to the earldom of Huntly and she was considered an eligible woman.

Not that she was exactly to his taste. Her age was suitable—she was just twenty. Her looks were passable, even attractive, if one liked sandy hair and broad features. But her manner! It was so grave, so preeminently sensible, so boring. Worst of all, she was highly intelligent. If she had merely had the first three characteristics without the fourth, he would have had *carte blanche* to do as he pleased. As it was, she might prove an irksome watchdog. He would have to disabuse her of the notion that he could be hampered.

Now his grooms were come into the chamber, ready to escort him to the Protestant Kirk of the Canongate. The Queen had wanted them to be married in the Chapel Royal by Catholic rites. But he had refused, for all that his bride came from a Catholic family. He would decide where the ceremony would be, and not be the guest of the Queen.

Then she had insisted that she and Darnley—he could not refer to him as "the King," even in his own mind—would provide a banquet afterward at Holyrood. Again he refused, choosing instead to have it at Kinloch House, the home of a rich burgher. In addition, she gave cloth-of-silver and white taffeta from her own cupboard to the Lady Jean for her wedding dress, and his bride accepted, to his displeasure.

"She wants to wed us, dress us, and feed us," he had grumbled. "As if we were indigents or infants."

"Is not the Queen to be nourisher and mother to her people?" Jean had said. "Doubtless she takes pleasure in it. And she may feel she needs to make amends for the execution of my brother John."

"Bah. If he died for love of her, is that *her* doing? Men fall in love and do foolish things. Why should she feel obliged to recompense us?"

"And why should we feel obliged to refuse? The material she offers is worth many pieces of gold. We must take what fate, guilt, and circumstance offer us; the same partners will rob us of plenty in times to come."

He had turned away. Her practicality smacked of opportunism.

Ah, his bride!

The groomsmen surrounded him, hailed him. In a buoyant body, they conveyed him to the Kirk, where she would be waiting for him.

Mary sat calmly in the royal box at the Kirk: a royal box that had never seen a Stewart until this day.

What would the Pope think? she wondered. If he could see me now, gracing a Protestant wedding . . .

She glanced over at Darnley, sitting beside her. He was sober and, as always when in that state, ingratiating and innocent.

The church was crowded; there was scarcely an extra seat. Since the Reformed Kirk did not allow music, the buzz of voices filled the sanctuary. Now the Bishop of Galloway, the Lady Jean's uncle, made his way down the aisle, wearing the modest attire of the Reformers. He took his place at the front of the church.

At a signal, the guests began reciting a Psalm, and then Bothwell appeared from the right, flanked by an attendant. He stood quietly in front of the Bishop.

The Psalm changed to a canticle of joy, and then the Lady Jean, heavily veiled in gossamer so that her cloth-of-silver gown shimmered like opal, made her way down the long aisle to join Lord Bothwell.

Mary could not hear their voices as they recited their vows. She saw Bothwell take Lady Jean's hand, then put a ring upon it. She saw him kiss her, lifting her face-veil to reveal her features. She heard the Bishop announce in ringing tones, "They are man and wife together." Then they turned and, facing the congregation, marched out. Bothwell was grinning. Lady Jean looked pleased.

In the large hall of Kinloch House, the company waited for the Queen and King to make their appearance before starting the festivities. The musicians were playing discreetly, delicately, and the banquet tables were laid with fine linen and glittering with crystal and gold. At the head table, ornate carved chairs were reserved for the bridal couple and the royal couple.

As Mary and Darnley passed through the doorway, Bothwell bowed and his new Countess curtsied.

"Felicitations," said Darnley, taking their hands. "Felicitations, and may Hymen bless you and your hearth."

"Hmmm." Embarrassed, Bothwell nodded curtly.

Mary led the way to the waiting table, moving gracefully through the throng of her subjects.

The larger, more ornate chair was hers, and she did not offer it to Darnley. He pretended not to notice. Seated on Mary's right was Bothwell, and on her left was Lady Bothwell. Next to her was her brother, the new Earl of Huntly, blond and handsome. The rest of the company quickly seated themselves and the servitors began bringing out the streams of dishes—some delicacies from the Strathbogie region, seat of the Gordons, and some from the area of Liddesdale, Bothwell's stronghold. Mary, whose appetite had waned during her pregnancy, took small helpings of salmon pie and powsowdie. The latter looked most unappetizing, a mixture of sheep's head and mutton flank, but tasted surprisingly good.

"I was brought up on this," said Bothwell, motioning to the server to bring him more. "It is nursery food, in truth, something Border mothers give their bairns to serve as supper. But I always loved it."

"In France we had cinnamon broth with stewed Normandy apples," she said, remembering with a stab of sweet longing those happy evenings in the royal nursery with François and Elisabeth and Claude. "I miss their apples."

"You'll have to send for them, then. They should survive a sea journey well enough." He took a great gulp of wine. "Still longing for France," he said matter-of-factly.

"No, that I do not."

"True, you've no reason to long for France when you surround yourself with Frenchmen, speak French, sing in French, write in French, sew with French threads, read French books, and have a French cook to prepare proper French dishes. And, oh yes, your confessor, that Dominican, what's his name?—and your physician, Bourgoing. Didn't I warn you long ago?"

"You make it sound as though I have committed a crime!" She glared at him, sitting there so smugly, so much at home. "Can I help it if"—*the Scottish foods, physicians, and books are so inferior,* she almost said, but stopped herself—"if . . . if I was brought up there and I, too, formed childish preferences? I am trying to learn of Scottish things—"

"With that Italian, Riccio?" He drank some more wine and plunged his knife into a hunk of venison on his plate and then transferred it to his mouth. He deftly ran his tongue over the sharp blade to clean it. She watched, expecting to see a thin line of red spring up along the broad tongue. But he went on talking as if nothing had happened. "Everyone detests him."

"Their hatred baffles me," she said. "He has done nothing."

"He has displaced your Scottish councillors. People think he is a Papal agent. Some even whisper that you are his lover." He repeated the venison, knife, and tongue feat.

"How absurd." But she remembered Melville's warning months ago. She looked down at Riccio, seated at a lower table. He was smiling and gesturing. Suddenly she had to admit it: from a distance he *did* look like a frog.

"It offends me that he is here today," said Bothwell. "Why did you bring him?" His voice was rough.

"He is of my household; he is a friend."

"Yet you are not providing the feast, but good burgher Kinloch." He jerked his head toward the lean, blue-eyed merchant of Baltic trading. "Did you assume an Edinburgh tradesman would want to feed a foreigner?" He glared at her. "You underestimate their hatred of him. You underestimate their dislike of your consort and your marriage. You underestimate the weakness of your position. You underestimate—"

"You overestimate my mercy and tolerance!" she snapped. "For a subject to use such licence in speaking to me, no, it is not to be borne! You are impudent, sir, and above your station, and for all it's your wedding day, your mouth is an unruly knave!" She turned to Lady Jean, who had been talking to Darnley. "I wish you much joy in this rash, overbold talker!"

"I could say the same to you," said Bothwell, his words in the ear of her turned head, "for you've just described your own husband."

She started to retort, to leave the table, when she realized that no one else had heard him, and that indeed, Lady Jean was attempting to answer her hasty words.

"Your Majesty, he's a soldier and speaks as he would to his troops," she said in a quiet voice. "If I must choose one or the other, I prefer a rough-spoken soldier to a smooth-spoken courtier." She glanced subtly at Darnley, who was smiling blankly, and the point was made.

"I hope his wooing proves more gentle than his manners," said Mary, looking at the placid, self-possessed young bride. Bothwell's quick, rough amours were well known. She had even been told—by Riccio—that Bothwell's embraces were so crude he often posted someone as a lookout while he had his way in a corner with a wench, then buttoned his breeches and departed five minutes later. Poor Lady Bothwell!

"We will be honeymooning at Seton," she said, interrupting Mary's vivid picture of Bothwell hunched in a corner indulging his lusts.

"I wish you joy," Mary managed to say.

"We anticipate it," she said. "Thank you."

"Indeed we are longing for it," Bothwell added in a low voice.

The banquet went on until late afternoon, and then was followed by a ball—for all that Bothwell professed himself a Knoxian, thought Mary. Indeed, the Protestants seemed to savour the entire experience much more than they ought, and the musicians played so long and so enthusiastically, she wondered where they had obtained their musical scores. From forbidden France?

By dancing with him and talking with him, Mary managed to keep Darnley away from the wine servers, and indeed he was quiet and polite for most of the evening, occasionally speaking at length with the Earl of Morton and several of his Douglas clansmen, then breaking off with a smile for another dance.

On their slow and stately passage back down the High Street toward Holyrood afterwards, they passed the dark, hulking Tolbooth.

"Do you still plan to pass the Bill of Attainder against Lord James and all his men when Parliament meets next month?" he suddenly said.

"You once pointed out that he had far too much land," Mary replied. "Now he shall have none. Yes, the Lord James and all his supporters, now hiding in England, shall forfeit their land for their treason. I am surprised that you ask. Why is that?" She was suddenly suspicious.

"No reason. Only that—perhaps it is unwise, perhaps there might be some other way—"

"There is no other way, Darnley."

As she got into bed that night, she wondered what approach Bothwell would make—might at that very moment *be* making—to his new wife in the bridal bed. She hated to think about it. Poor Lady Bothwell!

XXVIII

The winter seemed to be a whining dog, sinking its teeth into human bones and gnawing, refusing to let go, worrying and teasing its victim. Some days the sky would lighten and a hint of warm air, seemingly from Italy somewhere, would spread out over the land. Courtiers would be able to play tennis and practise archery. Then the leaden pall of cloud would clap shut overhead once more, and the light, singing air of the south would vanish, squeezed into nothingness by the abrupt grip of Arctic air.

The variations in temperature, the lack of exercise, and the confinement indoors made Mary weak and listless. Although it was Lent, she was given special permission to eat meat to help her regain her strength.

The second Saturday in March—when flowers would already be blooming at Chenonceau—great mounds of ice lay in the courtyard at Holyrood, their surfaces granular from the repeated thawings and refreezings. Little ice nuggets sparkled like diamonds in the grey crust.

Mary stood at the window looking out. This inactivity is driving me mad, she thought. I cannot ride or hawk because of the child. At least Riccio and Darnley have been able to play tennis.

"Did you play in your shirt yesterday, David?" she asked Riccio, who today was wearing heavy velvet.

313

"Indeed. It was warm enough," he replied. "And Lord Darnley took off his shirt."

Was she mistaken, or did he shudder slightly?

"But he soon began to shiver," he said. His face was turned away, and she could not see his expression.

"Tonight it is back to winter pastimes," she sighed. "We will have a small supper here in my apartments. But there will be meat for all my guests; that should be a treat. Anthony Standen to sing with you. Perhaps even a fortune-teller, for fun."

"Damiot the fortune-teller came to me yesterday," he said suddenly. "He told me to 'beware the Bastard.' But the Bastard is in England."

"Do you mean Elizabeth?" she asked with a laugh.

"No. Lord James."

"England is full of bastards. See how we thought of different ones? But Scotland is also full of bastards. Two of them shall dine with us tonight: my sister Jean and brother Robert. Need you beware of them?"

"I suppose one cannot be too careful."

"I shall make them lay their weapons down, then, before entering the chamber!" She laughed.

The little birds Darnley had given her twittered in their cage.

Twilight fell, and in Mary's chambers the three remaining Marys lighted the candles and helped Riccio and Bourgoing the physician and John Beaton, a relative of Mary Beaton's who served in the household, to lay the little table in the tiny supper room. It was warmer than the main bedroom and the curtains could effectively shut out more drafts. As Mary Fleming sang and Riccio played on his lute, it seemed to Mary that there was an inordinate amount of noise out in the courtyard—low rumbling sounds and muffled voices. But when she looked out the window, her eyes could discern nothing, as twilight is the most difficult light to see in. Some moving shapes were down below, but not in any great numbers.

Her sister and brother, Jean and Robert, came in, their arms full of oranges and figs.

"A special treat!" they said. "All the way from the south of France. A merchant on Murray's Close had just received them!" They put the basket down and selected some for the platters. "Very un-Lenten!"

"There's meat," said Bourgoing, with a wink. "As her physician, I prescribed it."

"What of the rest of us?" Jean teased. "Do we all have bodily infirmities calling for meat?"

"I would vouch for it, Madam," he said solemnly.

"Ah, let us sit—here comes Arthur Erskine, my captain of the guard!" said Mary. "That is our full company for tonight. And Standen, a page of my husband's."

"Eight people in this rabbit-sized room," said Jean, shaking her head. "You have need of a large private dining room, dear Queen."

"We can squeeze in here," Mary insisted.

They wiggled and pushed their way in, and were eventually all seated, although as they ate they continually bumped elbows and jostled. Still, the wine lightened their spirits and made it all seem a joyful game, like an indoor picnic.

"To the end of Lent," said Arthur, raising his cup. "May it come soon."

They laughed and drank.

"Is it my fancy, or does this Lent already seem to have gone on long past forty days?" asked John Beaton. "Never have I felt one drag as this one. And March is such a *loooong* month."

"I hate March," said Lord Robert. "It is my most unfavourite—"

There was a rustle at the door, and Mary looked over to see Darnley standing there. He said nothing, he just stared.

"My Lord," she said, trying to keep the surprise out of her voice, "have you supped already? Pray join us." Darnley never came to her chamber anymore, and never dined with her. The private spiral staircase linking their rooms went unused.

"I have eaten," he said. "But I will join you." He slid in and put his arm around her waist, bending down to kiss her.

"Riccio, slide over and make space for my Lord," said Mary.

But she saw the shock on Riccio's face and turned to see what he saw: standing in the doorway was Lord Ruthven, his face the colour of old bedsheets and his eyes as red as Hell.

A ghost! She gasped and clapped her hand over her mouth to stifle a scream. Ruthven had been reported on his deathbed several days before, wasting away from an unknown disease; now, in death, he had come here. The flickering fire played over his bloodless features and rimmed his bony eye sockets. It rippled and reflected on metal glimmering beneath his white nightshirt. Armour. Did a ghost wear armour? As he moved slightly, it clanked.

"How now, my good Lord Ruthven, how come you here? Are you quite recovered?" she said, trying to keep her voice from trembling. He was reputed a warlock—perhaps this whole apparition was straight from Hell.

"I have, indeed, been very ill, but I find myself well enough to come here for your good." His eyes stared, their amber-coloured irises almost blending into the jaundiced whites.

"What good can you do me?" she asked, her voice shaking in spite of herself. "You come not in the fashion of one who means well."

"I am come for that poltroon, Riccio," he said with slow, rasping words. He raised his arm, slowly and stiffly, then pointed right at him. "Come forth from the Queen's privy chamber, where you have tarried overlong!" His voice grew louder.

"Why, what wrong has he done?" Mary saw Ruthven reach for his dagger. "If he has done anything amiss, let him answer before Parliament!" She rose to shield him, but suddenly Ruthven nodded to Darnley.

315

"Take your wife to you! Hold her!" he barked, and Darnley, still standing behind her, grabbed her shoulders and pinned her into her chair.

"What do you know of this?" she cried.

Riccio jumped up and sought a way out of the chamber. But Ruthven blocked the way. Frantically, Riccio pressed himself against the window recess, the farthest possible from Ruthven, but still only ten feet away. Ruthven lunged forward, but Anthony Standen and Arthur Erskine held him back.

"Lay not hands on me, for I will not be handled!" Ruthven cried, brandishing his dagger. He kicked the table and it upended, hitting Mary's pregnant belly; the platters and food went flying, and the one candelabrum fell to the floor and broke, while Jean grabbed the other one and held it aloft, providing eerie lighting for the melee.

More men appeared at the doorway, followers of Ruthven, tumbling from out of the private staircase—they had come from Darnley's quarters, then—yelling and crying for blood. Then, from the outer quarters, up the main staircase, came the cry, "A Douglas! A Douglas!" and eighty of the Earl of Morton's men poured in, overpowering the royal guards and stampeding through the presence chamber and then into the bedchamber.

One of them swung a rope, yelling, "Hang him! Hang the little spy!"

"Traitors and villains!" screamed Mary, recognizing the telltale bright orange hair of the Earl of Morton and, at his side, Lord Lindsay of the Byres.

Riccio crawled across the floor and hid behind Mary's skirts, clutching and crying, "Justice, justice! Save my life, Madam! Save my life, for God's dear sake!"

Then the great barrel-shaped form of George Douglas "the Postulate," Darnley's bastard uncle, was upon Mary, and, swiftly and savagely, he swung his fighting arm over her shoulder in a wide arc and stabbed Riccio. The dagger made a dull *thwunk!* as it sank in up to its hilt, and blood splattered out all over the back of Mary's dress.

Riccio sagged, and she felt his hands dragging at her skirt, almost ripping it from its fastenings at her waist. He made no sound but a dull, gurgling groan. She turned slightly and saw the dagger sticking out of his side, and just then Darnley grabbed her again and held her, whilst one of Ruthven's men put a cocked pistol against her side and another held one to her breast.

"Fire," she said, "if you respect not the royal infant in my womb." She spoke as one in a dream. She could feel the cold iron through her dress, and yet she was oddly unafraid, as also in a dream.

Darnley deflected the pistol, but continued holding her fast as a prisoner.

Around her Riccio was now crawling and rolling, and men were falling on him. Mary then suddenly felt a rapier thrust near her breast, but Anthony parried it aside using a torch as a weapon.

They mean to kill me, too, she thought, but then Darnley pried Riccio's fingers loose from her gown, and the assassins dragged Riccio out of the little room. The birdcage was knocked over, and the chaffinches escaped, swooping about the room like bats. Mary could see Riccio grab on to the bedpost in the bedroom, only to have his fingers clubbed with the stock of a harquebus. Then the mob fell on him and he disappeared like a hare beneath a pack of hounds howling with bloodlust. There was a frenzy of movement as the men swung and stabbed, their arms rising and falling in deadly thuds, and then screams: the men had cut each other in their ecstasy of killing.

George Douglas grabbed Darnley's dagger and ran after the mob, arm raised to strike, yelling, "This is the blow of the King!"

There was more thudding and yelling, then cheering, and finally the voices were echoing from the great staircase, from whence came a mighty crash.

A few minutes passed before one of Darnley's valets came into the supper room from the outer chamber.

"Where is Riccio?" she asked. Her voice was hoarse and her throat so dry she could hardly speak.

"Madam, it is useless to speak of Riccio, for he is dead," he sneered. Then he laughed a braying laugh.

Mary Beaton came in, trembling. She had been in the bedroom the entire time, hiding beneath the bed. "I have seen him, I have seen him! He is mangled, dear lady, cut in collops! And—they kept saying it was all by the King's orders!" She pointed at Darnley.

"Ah, traitor, and son of a traitor!" said Mary softly, looking at Darnley's arm around her. "Now do I know thee."

"No traitor!" he cried. "For it is you who betrayed me with Riccio, offering me the greatest outrage a wife can to a husband! You never have come to my chamber, nor given yourself to me as my wife, since he has crept so into your favour. You saw me only if *he* were present, you locked me out of your chamber—"

"Because you were stinking, and drunk, and—repulsive to me!" she said.

He let out a cry like a wounded animal.

"I shall never be your wife nor lie with you nor rest content till I give you as wounded a heart as I have now!" She turned to Jean. "I beg you, go see what has happened, where they have taken him."

Jean ventured out and returned within a few minutes.

"It is as they said, Madam. Riccio is indeed dead, stabbed all over, and with his"—she nodded to Darnley—"dagger left in him. They flung his corpse down the grand staircase, where it landed on his very own trunk, the trunk he himself brought from Italy. Then the night porter stripped him. He lies there, naked and bruised and covered in blood. The porter counted fifty-six wounds on his body."

Mary felt hot tears trickling down her cheeks, and a knot in her throat so she could scarcely breathe. "No more tears," she whispered. "I will think upon revenge."

Ruthven suddenly appeared in the doorway, sagging and wheezing. He dragged himself to a chair and, with scrabbling fingers, hunted for a cup and a wine flagon among the scattered vessels. His sleeves were bloody, and his hands smeared with red.

"So this is your infirmity," said Mary coldly.

A great noise arose in the courtyard, and the Earl of Morton came panting in. "There's fighting out there between my men and the palace servants, led by Bothwell and Huntly." He sounded mildly annoyed, like a man who has had an extra errand forced on him.

"I'll go!" said Darnley eagerly.

"Nay, I'll go. *You* stay here," said Ruthven, rising to his feet.

"There's almost two hundred of us," said Morton. "And the gates are locked. But if the townspeople—"

"We'll placate them," said the pistol-wielding henchmen of Ruthven, who had reappeared at the door, like cats returning from a kill licking their whiskers. One of them, Andrew Kerr of Fawdonside, waved his gun like a bouquet of flowers.

Morton—the Lord Chancellor of Scotland—a common murderer. Mary glared at him, at his smug face and neat black attire. One of the original Lords of the Congregation. One of Knox's men.

"Why have you done this?" she asked. "Did you mean to kill me, too? To what end? Who would rule instead? Elizabeth? My Lord Darnley? No one kills for an empty throne."

"Be silent, Madam!" said Morton. Why was this woman interrogating him? She was supposed to be in shock, miscarrying, or reduced to quivering silence. He clapped his hand on his sword and rushed outside to command his forces.

Mary went to the window and watched as the Douglas men, expert fighters, gave no quarter to the small band of Bothwell's retainers and those of the new Earl of Huntly, allied with her serving men and kitchen workers armed with spits, cleavers, and mallets. They were driven back, as the Earl of Morton joined the Douglases and gave them heart. His bright red hair peeked out from under his helmet, making him easily visible.

"So," she finally said to Darnley, "you win. What is it you want? You must want it badly, to murder and cause such mayhem."

"The Crown Matrimonial," he said without hesitation.

"Do you not realize that such an insurrection weakens the crown? It gives nobles the idea that they can threaten kings and queens with death and make and unmake them at will."

"You would not have given it to me otherwise."

"So you turn her subjects against your own wife? And you wonder that I do not love you."

I hate him, she thought. He has betrayed me and was even willing to have me murdered. He wants the Crown Matrimonial. Perhaps that is all he ever wanted, perhaps that is the only reason he sought me, married me—

The pain was so great it felt like a labour pain.

No more of that, no grieving, not for something that never was, she told herself. They mean to depose me in some manner, rule for me. Darnley will be their figurehead. He is weak, and they can use him. After my child is born, they will set him up as King and depose Darnley in turn. I must escape from them. I must escape.

Darnley still loves me. They mean to use his weakness, but I can use it better.

"Ah, if only we could be happy again," she said as if to herself.

He heard it and leaned over to her, gingerly putting his hands on her shoulders. She did not flinch or pull away, but seemed to lean toward him. Or was it his imagination?

"I would give anything," he said, "if—"

Just then a mob of Edinburgh citizens, led by the Provost, stormed the palace gates, yelling and threatening to invade the palace itself. Flaring torches indicated the size of the crowd: it was at least five hundred. They had heard of a tumult, they shouted, an attack on the Queen's person. Let her show herself and tell them the truth.

The alarm bell of the city was ringing loudly.

Rescue! Mary jumped up and flung open the window, but Kerr pulled her forcibly back and, caresssing his dagger, said, "If you utter one word, I shall cut you in little pieces and feed you to the carrion crows."

Darnley looked on helplessly as Kerr nodded to him and shoved him toward the open window. "Get rid of them!"

The pitiful coward! Was he made of blancmange? No wonder his complexion was so creamy! She hated the cheeks she once had marvelled over.

"Good citizens!" he cried. "Thank you for your loyalty and concern! But there is no need for alarm! The Queen is quite well, safe, and resting. The Italian secretary is dead, punished for having been discovered to be a Papist spy in an intrigue with the King of Spain. Thus perish all the Queen's, and Scotland's, enemies!" His voice rose gleefully.

The people, reassured, turned away and began trudging back up the Canongate, their staves and pitchforks and pikes lowered.

"Well spoken," said Kerr. "Of course they would believe their *King*. They will learn to trust and obey you, Your Majesty."

With Kerr here I can do nothing, Mary thought. She turned a beseeching and submissive look toward Darnley.

I can do nothing until we are alone, she thought. I must get him alone!

She sank back into the chair and allowed herself to slump. Kerr turned and looked at her.

Even my slightest movement is noticed, she thought.

Silence had fallen in the courtyard outside. Silence reigned in her quarters. Where had everyone gone?

"Mary? Mary Beaton?" she called.

"All gone." George Douglas stood in the doorway, his thick arms braced against each doorpost, as if he would tumble them down, like Samson in the temple. His hands were dark with blood. "They are—how shall I put it?—dismissed, *Your Majesty*." He managed to make the title sound like an

319

insult. "And we"—he nodded to Darnley and Kerr—"think it best you should retire now. After all, it is late."

"Not so late, to have accomplished so much," said Mary. "It was seven o'clock when we sat down at the supper table. And it is now—"

"Half past nine," said Darnley.

"Only two and a half hours. And half past nine is yet early."

"For you, yes!" said Darnley. "For you are—were—wont to stay up until two with Signor Davie!"

"Riccio is already abed, fast asleep," sneered Douglas. "His slumbers cannot be interrupted. And now we deem it proper that you should retire also."

"Where are my women? I must needs have attendants."

"They are—detained."

"Is there no one to keep me company on this foul night?" she cried. "My husband—"

"Nay, not your husband," said Douglas firmly. "We have need of him. There is much to discuss."

"Pray do not leave me alone in this chamber, here—" She stood up and pointed to the places on the floor where blackening globs of blood lay like scabs. "Have mercy!" She commanded her voice to tremble piteously, and it obeyed, when all the while anger was raging in her veins.

"There is one, perhaps, available," ventured Darnley. "Old lady Huntly, dowager of the Earl."

Douglas raised his eyebrows. "Clever. Very clever. Yes, the old lady, made a widow by the Queen. She can be trusted. Go find her."

He orders the "King" about like a servant. And indeed, he will soon be their servant, thought Mary.

She waited, while Darnley left the chambers. She became aware of a dull pain that came and went within her abdomen.

O Blessed Mother, do not let me lose the child! It is too early yet; he cannot survive.

The pains rose and then subsided by the time Darnley returned with Lady Huntly.

"Your servant, Your Majesty," she said, bowing. She looked nervously about the room, smoothing her skirts. The disarray, the blood, was everywhere.

"Put the Queen to bed," Douglas ordered. "Permit no one to enter or leave. If anything untoward happens, I shall be stationed just outside, on the landing of the great staircase. Come!" he motioned to Darnley. They left the chamber, Darnley casting one backward look.

As soon as the doors were closed and a moment or two of silence had followed, Lady Huntly whispered, "What has happened?"

"My secretary Riccio has been slain, and in my presence, by an armed faction of lords. But there is more to it than that. It has to do with the exiled lords, with the coming censure of them in Parliament, with the King's ambition, with even a threat to the throne and my own life. I do

320

not understand all the threads of it yet, but in time the pattern will emerge and clarify itself. I only know that they threatened my very life, and only God saved me tonight."

"Holy Mother of God," said Lady Huntly, crossing herself.

Mary's pain stirred itself again.

"I must rest," said Mary. "Perhaps it is best that I lie down." She started to stand up, but felt dizzy.

"Stay seated, Your Majesty," said Lady Huntly. She knelt and removed Mary's shoes, then came behind her and unbuttoned her gown. "Raise your arms," she said, and slid the dress off. As she took it to the little wardrobe room, Mary saw the spray of blood across the yellow satin.

Lady Huntly found the chest where the sleeping attire was stored, and brought out a pearl grey woollen garment. Mary stood up, suddenly feeling tremulous, and retired behind the screen, where with clumsy fingers and heavy hands she removed her underclothes and put on the gown.

Lady Huntly was waiting for her on the other side, and with a gentle touch she guided Mary toward the bed. She had already turned the covers back.

"You—an earl's wife, a great lady—how do you know how to perform these duties?"

"I am a woman, Your Majesty, and you are a woman in distress and with child. One does not need training. Now, where is your rosary?"

Mary pointed in the direction of her chest, and the little box of ivory atop it. Lady Huntly brought it to her and put it in her hands. As if Mary were a child, she folded her fingers over it.

"When I draw the curtains, then you should pray to Our Lady. She will help you. She understands." Lady Huntly's plump face was as calm as a July evening that promised only stillness and rest.

Could this woman be truly so kind? Was this a trick? Would she stab her in the night?

"Your lord perished because of me," Mary said.

"He perished of an apoplexy," Lady Huntly said. "I think in that way God was signalling His displeasure with those who rebel against their sovereign."

"Your son, John—"

"Love was never meant to lead to treason, Your Majesty. Saint Paul says, 'Love is long suffering and kind,' and Saint John says, 'He who says he loves God and hates his brother is a liar.' No, it was not for love that my son perished, but for lust and rebellion."

Could she truly feel this way? Was it safe to trust her?

"You are good, Queen Mary. You have showered my eldest son George with honours, and restored him to the Huntly estates. We are entirely loyal."

So this remarkable woman was so able to bend her natural affection to God's commands that she had become an ally?

"I believe I can serve you. I can perhaps carry messages from the chamber.

They do not suspect me. The Earl of Bothwell and my son, the young Earl, await your command. They managed to escape from Holyrood after the clash in the courtyard with the Douglases, and can be counted on to be at the ready with horsemen and troops should you so desire." She laughed. "They had to escape through Bothwell's window and out through the den of wild animals Your Majesty keeps here. Lord Bothwell got a nip in his breeches from the lioness."

Mary giggled.

"Now rest, Your Majesty, and talk to our Blessed Mother. She awaits you." She closed the curtains resolutely.

Mary lay in the darkness. She heard the soft rustle of Lady Huntly's gown as she crossed the room. Then she heard her find the little truckle bed and pull it out, and lie down upon it. In a few minutes she heard the gentle snoring.

Assassins do not snore, she thought. So she means what she said. She is loyal, in spite of my having bereaved her of her husband and a son. . . . How strange are the ways of God. How demanding, and how heavy . . .

Holy Mary, Mother of God, pray for us, now and at the hour of our death . . .

Is my death nigh?

Only if I allow it.

Hail Mary, full of grace. Blessed art thou—

What are their plans?

—amongst women and blessed—

Will they imprison me? Who is the leader of this insurrection? Morton? It is not Darnley or Douglas. They have not the brains. Maitland? Knox? Surely a clergyman would not . . . Lord James? He was not here. But messengers . . .

I must escape. It is all very well that Bothwell and Huntly stand ready on the outside. But it is a long way to the outside. I must make my way there. Those hundred yards to the outskirts of the palace are as long as the distance to Muscovy. Darnley, my husband. I must win him to my side. I must. He alone can act as surety for me.

He still loves me. It was his vanity that was betrayed, not his love. I can win him to my will.

A sudden picture, so vivid it seemed to have come from Hell, flashed across her mind: Riccio, his blood settling, his open eyes staring, his limbs stiff and cold. Where did he lie, even now? *Abed, fast asleep,* the evil Douglas had said.

Let him at least be laid in a grave, she prayed. They are not above feeding him to beasts.

But if the beasts had been satisfied, they would not have nipped at Bothwell. . . .

Her head spun suddenly, and she was carried off in sleep. The rosary fell from her fingers.

She dreamed of her rubies in the Great Harry turning to globules of blood and oozing out and soaking into her bodice. She dreamed of being locked in a turret and seeing a knight outside waiting to rescue her, but his visor was down and she could not see him—as Henri II's visor had been down during the fatal tournament. She dreamed of Riccio, playing for her on his ebony lute, and his voice was so sweet she sat upright and awoke.

"I must have him play that again," she murmured, drawing aside her bed curtains and seeing a dull grey light coming into her chamber.

Then she saw the blood on the floor.

"No!" she cried. He had been so alive, so alive and singing, only just now. . . .

She lay back down in her bed.

Riccio is dead and I am a prisoner, she thought. I even have a turret here. But there is no knight outside. Only Darnley to rescue me, and first I must convince him. It is not the same as the dream.

Beside her on the floor, Lady Huntly was sleeping, a smile on her face.

Your troubles are over, Mary thought. How long did it take before you could sleep soundly again? It has been more than three years since your lord died.

Where will I be in three years?

Where I will be in three years is where I put myself. It all lies in my own hands.

She was dressed and waiting when Darnley appeared at her chamber. She had chosen a dress she knew he liked, a greenish blue with lace at the neck, and had pulled only part of her hair back. She wore no jewellery.

Darnley had clearly not slept.

Good, thought Mary.

He smiled when he saw her, but it was a hesitant smile. He crossed the room and took her hands in his.

"Ah, my Mary," he cried. He looked into her eyes.

"Good my lord," she said, "you appear troubled, and well should you." She wanted to take her hands away, but to do so would reveal her revulsion. Instead she indicated that they should take their places on the bench near one window.

Once seated, she turned to him, willing her eyes to be wide open and show nothing but concern for him.

Else I am doomed, she thought.

"Dear husband, I am distraught when I think what danger you are in," she began. "I know not what their plans are for me. . . ." She hesitated, to allow him to tell her. But he was silent. "But the fact that I am an anointed queen will stay, or at least slow, their hands. I fear it will prove not so for you."

Darnley's pale face grew ghostly. The planes of his countenance looked lumpy.

"They are murderers," she continued. "And not just ordinary murderers, but torturers. Else why slay David in my presence? They could have set on him whilst you played tennis, or attacked him at night when he was alone. Nay, you must question why they chose to dispatch him as they did. 'Twas not a simple killing, but a strike of terror." She looked deeply into Darnley's eyes. "These are twisted and desperate men. They used you . . . did you sign a bond?"

"Yes," he admitted miserably.

"They have it in their keeping?"

"Yes."

"Ah! Then they have what they wanted: the King's signature on the murder bond, the King's dagger in their victim. Now they can dispose of you," she said lightly.

As she had expected, he stiffened beside her.

"Yes, dispose of you. You don't imagine they will let *you* be a figurehead ruler, when they can have *him* instead?" She grasped her belly. "However acquiescent you are, a baby is more acquiescent. No, you have served your purpose."

She ceased talking to allow this to sink in.

"And what mean they to do with me?" she asked, telling her voice to sound unconcerned, as if she knew already.

"To transport you to Stirling tomorrow, or the next day."

"And then?"

"To allow the birth to take place there."

"And then?"

"I know not." He hung his head, showing that he knew all too well.

"Ah." She allowed silence to fill the room. "Are we to be separated, then?"

He shrugged. They had not told him.

"For if we are separated, we are doomed. Together we can outwit them and escape the deaths they have planned for us."

At the word *deaths*, he started.

"Henry"—she had not called him that except in their most intimate shared moments—"they have shown they respect neither our royal persons nor our sacred rank. They have attempted to divide us, knowing that together we can withstand them. They have succeeded in the first part of their plan: to frighten us and make us their prisoners. But the rest of their plan, to divide us and then kill us, is long from fulfillment. It depends on your helping them, until they no longer need you. But if we could escape—"

"It is impossible," he said. "There are guards everywhere. All your people have fled."

"All *our* people," she said, taking his long bony hand in hers and squeezing it. "But they trust you. If they thought you would act as my guard—"

"They would never dismiss all the guards."

"Is there no way to persuade them to vacate the palace? Suppose I promised them a pardon?"

"They would never believe you."

"But if you convinced them?"

He shook his head.

I have not convinced *you*, she thought. Natural coward that you are, you need something more to move you.

"Ah, Henry," she said, leaning over to kiss him. It was the first time she had kissed him on the lips in months, and she could feel them tremble under hers. He sighed and put his arm around her.

Now I will have to lead him to the bed, she thought wearily. Lady Huntly was nowhere to be seen in the chamber, having gone to take the messages to Bothwell and her son.

Obediently he followed her, and once in bed he threw off his clothes with great enthusiasm and drew the bed curtains like a boy playing at forts-and-soldiers. He ignored her stomach and instead gushed words of appreciation and adoration. Tears came to his eyes before he lost himself in action.

"Ah, my Mary," he wept.

In her presence chamber, Mary stood demurely as the Earl of Morton eyed her. Could he know?

"The Lord James, Earl of Moray, is back in Scotland," he said.

"And I did not call him," she stated.

"Parliament is dissolved by proclamation of the King." Morton shot a look at Darnley, who smiled back brightly.

He dissembles well, thought Mary. But then, I knew that.

"So there will be no attainders passed against the rebel lords of the Chaseabout Raid. How convenient." She opened her hands and gestured, palms upward. "It is good the King is so magnanimous. For it was against *him* they rebelled, it was *his* person they evidently could not stomach. It is indeed kingly to overlook this failing."

"Madam, will you meet with your brother? Will you receive him?" asked Morton. He smoothed his bushy orange beard.

Why does he not trim it? Mary thought irrelevantly. It is so unruly, so wiry and repulsive. It looks like a place where mites live.

"Yes. I must, so it seems."

"He will come this afternoon, then," said Morton. Was there a smirk hidden in the beard? He nodded curtly, commandingly, and Darnley followed him out of the room.

Do not revert, cried Mary silently. Blessed Mother, do not let him revert back to *them*. She started shaking all over.

"Madam, take this soothing drink," said Lady Huntly, pressing a glass into her hands. "And when you have done, there is this cheer: I have gotten your messages out. Both men await your next instructions with troops and horses."

"I pray it is not all in vain. The next part of my task involves many other people, and can so easily go awry," sighed Mary, sipping the frothy drink. "It frightens me, it is so delicately balanced. Like my clock." She indicated the little clock she had had in her chambers since childhood, the one that had struck the hours when the Cardinal came to tell her that the date of her marriage to François had been finally fixed. These days it struck erratically, and no clockmaster had been able to correct it.

"My brother is the next part of my task . . . my staged reconciliation with him. Oh, but his hand was present last night . . . he struck the fifty-seventh blow. Beware the Bastard, they said. . . ."

She ran her hands over her own arms nervously, but hated touching herself; she felt ugly and violated from having let Darnley take her, as if her skin were contaminated. Quickly she turned her head to look outside. The fickle March weather had turned again, and it was warm and sunny. Piercingly blue skies arched over the palace grounds, and the grass under the winter mat was showing emerald green. The windows were open, and a bee bumped against the leaded panes and then flew in.

Wherever did he come from? Mary wondered. It is too early for bees. Could he have been waiting, biding his time, all winter?

Like the Lord James?

How bold of him to return. Who had summoned him? Or was he in such close contact with the rebels that he himself monitored the murder and knew when to return?

The bumblebee flew from wall to wall in the chamber, seeking a flower. He meandered along the tapestry, buzzing.

There are no flowers in March, Mary thought. Bee, you seek betimes. Therefore you will die. Like all of us who guess wrong.

A sharp rap on the chamber doors, followed by an unfamiliar soldier's announcement: "The Lord James Stewart, Earl of Moray."

Mary rose and clasped her hands in an imitation of serenity.

Into the chamber came Lord James, his eyes warm, an expression of tenderness, concern, and apology on his face. He came toward her humbly, beseechingly, like a little boy testing his parents' mercy for some childish prank.

She felt herself responding to what she wished were true, rather than what she knew to be true.

"Oh, James!" she said. "If only you had been here, none of this would have come to pass!" She held out her arms and embraced him. "It is so good to have you back!"

Neither of them mentioned the reason he had been away from Scotland.

"A sorry business," he murmured, holding her. "And now, alas, we must do all we can to heal the rift that has come upon Scotland."

Now he will dictate to me, she thought. He will pronounce the terms of the traitors.

"You will have to pardon everyone," he said, as if he had just thought of it. "Those who fled with me and those who rose against Riccio. All these parties must be reconciled so that we can start all over."

She kept her face buried against his chest so he could not see her expression.

"We will gather in your chamber later today," he said, and she could feel the words rumbling from his deep chest, as well as hear them. "Morton, and Ruthven—"

"Not Ruthven!" she cried.

"—and Maitland and myself," he continued calmly.

"Is Maitland a traitor as well?" she said, pulling away. "I knew full well he was envious of Riccio and felt slighted, but I presumed he was too civilized to dabble in murder."

James smiled his false, remorseful-little-boy smile. "The civilized feel hate and passion just as other men," he said. "Queen Elizabeth and her minister Cecil are not above murder and plots—why not Maitland? Besides, why is it 'treason' to kill a foreigner?"

Yes, why not Maitland? Why not John Knox, for that matter? she thought. "And when may I expect you?" she asked, keeping any hint of expression from her voice.

"Later this afternoon. First we must gather at Morton's house."

❧

Morton's house lay conveniently near Holyrood, in a close with its own stable and a private courtyard. It had a large enough solar on the first floor to accommodate all the conspirators, and as the afternoon wore on, they filed in and stood talking pleasantly as if this were a joyous occasion, a betrothal celebration, perhaps. Ruthven shuffled to a chair and propped his feet up on a stool, but the killing seemed to have enlivened him; he did not look nearly as sickly as he had the previous evening. Lord James, attired in fresh clothes he had miraculously found at the ready at Morton's house, now exuded an air of calm majesty. Maitland, who had been absent from Edinburgh, seemed reinvigorated by his timely sojourn in the country. Only Lord Lindsay of the Byres was as unhealthy looking as ever, his lips cracked and broken, his eyes with black circles. A number of lesser members of the party milled about: Lord Sempill, Patrick Bellenden, James Makgill, Kerr of Fawdonside, and several Douglases.

"We meet with the Queen before supper," said Morton, holding up his hands for attention. "Just a few of us. She'll sign a pardon for us . . . for *all* of us, absent and present. And then, when once we have that paper exonerating us, we shall keep the Queen in custody. Who shall reign, you may ask? Why, we have a king—King Henry!"

"Shall the Queen be kept in captivity all the days of her life?" asked Lindsay. Spittle flew from his lips, and he dried them with the back of his hand. "I know of no such instance in history. Not in the monarch's own country. 'Tis true James I was an English prisoner for many years, but—"

"Let her be taken to Stirling, and there fall ill and fail to recover." The clear, smooth voice of Lord James spoke.

"Impossible! She would have her own physicians, her own cooks," objected Ruthven.

"Cooks and physicians can be bribed," James persisted.

"Not French ones!" This time Lindsay spat deliberately.

Lord James rocked on his heels, a smirk on his face. "So I see no one disagrees with my suggestion, but only with the plausibility of its success?"

"I am not sure I understand entirely what your suggestion is," Maitland protested.

Lord James laughed. "Now that your innocence is on record, may I ask if you would agree, in principle, that the reign of Queen Mary has been an experiment which has failed? A Catholic Queen who has been unable to control her Protestant country, and who has proven herself weak and in need of a man's guidance? But in her folly and lack of discernment, she has chosen unworthy men like Riccio to lean on, alas."

"Yes. I would agree," Maitland admitted.

"Good. Then I trust that you, like all of us, would welcome better days."

Mary opened all her coffers, searching for the white face-paint she had kept from a masque in France. At the time she had packed it up, she had berated herself for the sentimentality of keeping it. But it had been the last masque in which François had danced. To leave it behind seemed a betrayal. I will throw it away later, she had promised herself. When I am ready.

She found it in the bottom of the largest oaken coffer, buried beneath exercise books from her tutoring days with the French schoolmaster, outgrown riding habits, and her first communion dress of white satin and lace.

She pulled it out and found the coloured clay within the pot to be dried and hard. But she went to her pitcher of washing water and added a few drops to the material, mixed it, and almost cried with relief and gratitude when she saw the hard material turn to liquid.

Expertly she dabbed it on her face—first in little dots on her nose, cheeks, chin, and forehead, then she spread it out over her skin. Instantly her complexion grew ashen. She added a bit to her lips, then smiled in satisfaction. She looked ill.

The four men stood before her, dressed in their best: brocaded doublets, shining with gold thread, linen collars edged with lace trim, rich capes lined with fur. Morton, Ruthven, Maitland, and the Lord James. They held their hats in their hands, but there was no hint of subservience in their manner. Their eyes—deep brown, cat's-iris yellow, grey, and hazel—met hers boldly. By her side, Darnley stood stiffly. Pray God he does not falter! she thought. She did not dare to smile at him or even look at him, lest it advertise their complicity. The morning in bed was now eight hours old, and his body memory was likely to prove faulty. Blessed Virgin, help me! she cried silently.

"Your Majesty, my beloved sister," James began, stepping forward slightly. He smiled his sweet-little-boy smile. "We are all rebels to some degree," he said, "in that we have all failed to give complete, unthinking obedience to our anointed Queen. We confess it." He jerked his head toward his comrades, who nodded for him to continue. "Just so we are all rebels in the same manner toward God. But that does not mean we have joined the ranks of God's enemies, nor of yours. Nor does it mean that, having seen— or believed—Your Majesty to be misled or fallen under the influence of evil councillors, we were wrong to stand against them. Just so the prophets were constrained to do in ancient Israel."

He stopped, realizing that the evil influence over whom he had rebelled was standing just a few feet away.

"Your Majesty"—he bowed to Darnley—"I was wrong to have resisted you and attempted to block your marriage. Forgive me; I was blind."

Darnley smiled nervously. He noticed Mary's long, graceful fingers moving, fingering a brooch on her bodice. It was a ruby tortoise. With a start he remembered it had been given her by Riccio. *For safety.*

"You rebelled, and caused us to lead an army against you!" he said. But then he got a warm memory of putting on his gilded half-armour and riding out in the yellow September sunlight.

"Yes, to our shame!" said James. "But I have paid for it. I have endured exile in England, and a rating by the Queen there—"

"Our sister Elizabeth does not encourage rebels," said Mary.

"Indeed not." James laughed and then they all joined in.

"Tell me, brother, what it is you want," Mary said in a gentle voice.

The smile faded from James's face. "An unqualified and complete pardon. For all the rebels, of whatever cause." He gestured toward the three men. "We have all gone astray, like the sinners we are. And what does Scripture say? 'There is none that doeth good, no, not one.' But the quality of a ruler, as of God, is to have mercy. 'I have no pleasure in the death of the wicked, but that the wicked turn from his way and live.'"

"And what would I receive in exchange for this pardon?" she asked. "Besides the spiritual blessings, of course."

"A united Scotland," said James quickly. "There have been troubles, misgivings . . . as in the early stage of a marriage, we have been learning to live together, learning one another's habits—"

"Like treason?"

"That word—"

"Is an ugly word. It describes an ugly thing," she insisted.

All four of the men fell to the floor. Their knees hitting the smooth wood made thumping noises, only slightly muffled by their thick hose.

"Forgive us," they cried. "Look not on our sins, but on thy great mercy. Let us start anew—let us make this our true wedding day!"

Ruthven's knee was right over the clotted blood from Riccio's murder. When he shifted his weight, Mary heard a slight crunch as he ground the crust of it under him.

May he stain his fancy breeches with an everlasting stain! she thought.

"You are right," she said softly. "We must put the past behind us. It does Scotland scant good for her rulers and councillors to be at odds. I will draw up a pardon for you all, and present it to Parliament."

"We have a draft of one ourselves," said Ruthven, moving. His knee was indeed stained, and the place where he had ground the crust by kneeling had a depression in it. Mary felt truly sick.

She took the paper and pretended to study it. "This looks complete," she said. "We will have it copied, and subscribe my—and my husband the King's—royal signatures to it." She paused. Now was the moment.

"I feel faint," she whispered, leaning up against Darnley. Alarmed, he took her in his arms. She sagged, and clutched her belly.

"Pains . . . " she murmured.

"Midwife!" cried Darnley.

"No . . . no midwife," said Mary. "The pains will pass, if I may but lie down. Please!" She gestured toward her bedroom.

The four men rose. Darnley and the Queen were making their way toward the bedchamber. They entered, and the door shut behind them. In a few moments, Darnley reemerged.

"She is resting," he said. "The strain—pray the child does not come betimes."

"The paper—" said Lord James.

"It is on her desk. She will sign it in a few hours, when she is recovered. Never fear. It will be ready by morning, even if I have to sign it by forging her signature." He winked at them. "And now, my lords, you may retire."

"And leave her unguarded?" growled Ruthven. "Nay, never. This may all be a trick. Never forget that she was trained in the court of France, where lies and dissembling are a way of life."

"Just as violence and murder are here?" Darnley said. Seeing Ruthven glaring at him, he smiled. "No court has special training in duplicity. The Queen my wife is ill. But she has given her word to sign the pardon, and as she is a true prince, she will stand surety to it. I pray you, dismiss the guards and go to your homes. You must needs be tired, and it is now the second night since the . . . incident." He gestured toward Mary's closed bedroom door. "She needs no guards now. She lies on a sickbed, a weak woman. All her attendants are gone, her few supporters like Bothwell and Huntly far away . . . and besides, I will guard her. I will stand surety for her!"

"Then on your head, and on that of your posterity, may the vengeance fall if aught goes amiss!" Mary heard the rough voice of Ruthven even through the door of her room.

Then she heard more talking, and finally footsteps and quiet. The bedroom door creaked open and Darnley stuck his head in. He looked whiter than Mary, even without the aid of makeup.

"He cursed me!" he said, shaken.

"Did you expect blessings?" said Mary, sitting up quickly. "He is an evil man, and he has nothing but evil to give. Are they gone?"

Darnley sighed. "Yes. I promised them they would have the pardon by morning. But what if they return? We'd best flee now!"

Mary got up out of bed. She felt both very strong and very weak. The baby stirred and turned as if to reassure her he was safe.

"No," she said. "Doubtless they have left guards to test us for that very thing. It is still early; it is not even fully dark. We must undress and pretend to go to bed. Then, at about two o'clock, we will escape. I will come to your chamber and then we will make our way through the postern gate and through the graveyard to where our rescuers will be waiting with horses."

"You have arranged—?" His face was incredulous.

"Everything," she said.

Now would this fool leave so she could remove the white clay from her face? It stung and burned.

She lay in bed, in her sleeping attire, so fully did she play her part. She knew exactly where her riding garments were and how to get to them in an instant. In the meantime there were all those hours to get through, when she would have to lie still but fully alert.

There was no fear in her; only anger filled her veins, and the deep, aching desire for revenge. She wanted to raise an axe and split Ruthven's skull open, see him fall twitching to the ground.

There would be occasion for that, once she escaped . . . escaped. . . .

Mary crept down the little spiral staircase connecting her bedroom with Darnley's, feeling her way carefully. There were twenty-five steps, winding to the left, and she leaned that way. Once in Darnley's bedchamber, she sought his bed by memory, as there was no light burning. It had been a long time since she had sought that bed, but it was easy to find in the small room.

Darnley was sleeping. Like a child he was breathing lightly, and like a child he was hard to awaken.

"Come," she whispered. "Now."

Obediently he put his hand in hers and let himself be led out through his presence chamber and thence through a gallery to a staircase, where they descended into the cellars, cold, moist, and empty. The palace was silent, and no guards were posted before Darnley's door as they had been at hers.

They *did* trust him, she thought. Or they are simply careless.

"Not much farther," she whispered. The long passageway, lined with sacks of last year's apples, old cabbages, barrels of salt fish, and casks of wine, smelled like the memory of a winter meal.

"There is a door . . . at the end of the wine casks . . . yes." She reached out and touched the rough wood. Pray God it was not locked!

It had a wooden latch, easily lifted. The door creaked open, and fresh cold air with the smell of spring earth flooded in.

"Come!" There were three steps up to ground level, and then they stood outside, free.

After the utter darkness of the food cellar it seemed as light as day to them, and they could see the headstones and mounds of graves all around them. The wind rustled the bare branches of an ash tree overhead.

"They wait for us on the other side of the Abbey burial grounds, where Holyrood properly ends," said Mary. "Now come—but bend over, weave between the headstones so no one can see us moving. There must be guards outside the palace."

She let go his hand and lowered her head, moving in a crouching position from tombstone to tombstone. The Blessed Mother be thanked, there was no bright moon tonight. They would be darkness moving within darkness.

Suddenly Mary's foot sank in soft dirt and she pitched forward, her hands buried in soil.

A fresh grave.

She almost shrieked, as she felt something hard not very far beneath the surface. She crawled away and sat panting, her heart racing.

"Riccio," she whispered.

"Oh, Davie," mumbled Darnley, running his hands over the makeshift mound. "Every day of my life I shall regret this . . . I have been miserably cheated!"

The poltroon was about to cry!

"A bigger one than he shall sleep nearby ere a twelvemonth has passed," Mary said in the softest voice she possessed.

"What?" asked Darnley. His voice quivered.

"I said we must go on. We are halfway there." Mary got to her knees and pulled Darnley's hand. He stepped on Riccio's grave as he made for the next headstone.

Headstone, mound, headstone, little mound, monument . . . it was like a huge chessboard, and they the moving pieces.

A horse snorted some thirty yards away. A guard? A rescuer? Mary waited for the sound to come again. There was a slight movement at the end of the graveyard, where the rescuers were supposed to be waiting.

It must be they! It has to be! Mary thought. And the only way to know is to get so close to them I am lost if it is not.

Slowly she picked her way closer, creeping forward foot by foot. Now she could hear voices, whispering, that mingled with the call of the owls and the scurrying small rodents in the dark.

"—past three—" She caught just those two words.

"gallop—" And in the saying of that word she recognized Bothwell's voice.

She stood up and ran the last twenty yards. The horses started and the men drew their swords.

"Bothwell!" she whispered, but a loud whisper. "All is well!"

And then she was being lifted over the fence by arms that felt like elm, and Bothwell's voice was saying, "Thank God and all the demons!"

There were Arthur Erskine and Lord Stewart of Traquair, Mary's equerry and the captain of the guard, and Bastian Pages, Mary's servant. Not enough horses.

"You will ride pillion with me," said Erskine, and Mary was lifted—again by Bothwell—up and settled there behind Erskine's saddle.

"To Seton House," said Bothwell. "Two hundred men await us there. When the guards change at daybreak at Holyrood, we'll be miles away!" He sounded both disgusted and amused at the same time. "Can you ride so far, Your Majesty?" he suddenly said to Mary.

"Why, I must," she replied. "And that's an end to it."

He nodded curtly, but she saw a flash of his teeth in a quick grin. "Come, away!"

Erskine's horse leapt forward, and Mary had to cling to stay on. Her large belly made it difficult for her to reach her arms around Erskine, and she felt herself in danger of slipping. Sensing her unbalance, Erskine slowed his horse.

"Come, faster!" cried Darnley, pulling alongside them. The wind touched them with long cold fingers as it streamed past. "We are being followed, I am sure of it!" He leaned over and whipped her horse.

"I can go no faster without endangering the child," said Mary. The sound of their horses' hooves punctuated every word.

"It is no matter; if it dies we can make another!" he yelled.

"Then leave me and save yourself," said Mary, and he did.

He is beyond even hating, thought Mary. Beyond pity, beyond any human consideration.

Bothwell shot her a look, but she refused to be pitied or disdained, and she hated him for having overheard. She turned her head and looked straight ahead, as if she could see all the way to Seton. The bouncing and thudding of the horses' hooves reverberated through her belly.

Poor baby, she thought. Blessed Mother, protect him.

She looked behind her into the dark. No one seemed to be following.

The night was still completely black, and as they galloped toward the Forth and Seton House, they had to trust the horses' instincts to avoid dips and loose ground on the uneven terrain. Low-hanging branches were a constant hazard, and the riders had to keep ducking to avoid them; nonetheless they were often sideswiped or whipped across the face in the darkness.

It was twelve miles to Seton House, and by the time they reached the gatehouse, Mary's fingers were stiff from clutching Erskine's clothing, and she was chilled through and through. But as they clattered into the courtyard, she saw the flare of torches, heard and smelled a great company of horses, and knew that a contingent of loyal riders awaited her. She was safe.

Erskine's horse stopped. Bothwell lifted her down, and Lord George Seton—Mary Seton's brother—and the new Earl of Huntly came forward.

"Welcome, Your Majesty!" cried Seton. "Thank God you are safe! We all await your command."

She looked around. On her feet after the long ride, she felt a little dizzy, but exuberant. "It is not safe here," she said. "It is too near yet to Edinburgh. We must make for some truly fast fortress."

"Dunbar," said Bothwell decisively. "It's guarded on three sides by the sea, and as near impregnable as any stronghold can be. It's another thirteen miles to the coast. Can you—"

"Of course I can ride! And on my own, too! Bring me a horse." Did he think she would need to be carried in a litter?

He looked doubtful, but nodded to Lord Seton. "Bring the Queen a fleet palfrey," he said. Lord Seton looked surprised to be given orders in his own home.

"Away!" cried Mary, after she was mounted. Two hundred men lifted their torches, shouted, and followed her.

In the three hours it took to reach Dunbar, the sky began to lighten, and as they approached the grey, boxy fortress it was lit from the ocean side by the rising sun, surrounded by an aureole of fire. A chorus of seagulls sang their entrance.

"Who goes there?" called the watch from the crenellated battlements.

"The Queen!" called Mary. "Open in my name!"

Once inside, Mary, Bothwell, and Seton ascertained that the keeper, Simon Preston, the Provost of Edinburgh, was absent. Whose side was he on? In spite of his timely appearance leading the citizens to the gates of Holyrood, had he known about the Riccio plot in advance? Why had he allowed himself to be dismissed so easily by Darnley's lies? Where was he now?

No matter, thought Mary. He was scant aid to me in my hour of need, and settled for the easy way out. Therefore he is keeper here no longer. Such a fortress belongs in the hands of someone I can trust. Bothwell. Yes, he has surely earned it.

The cry of the gulls outside the windows sounded like the shrieks of hungry children.

"I pray you," she said to a servant, "bring me two dozen eggs, some butter, some cheese, some ale, and an iron skillet. And light the fire in this fireplace." She turned to the leaders and said, "Gentlemen, I shall make you breakfast!"

As they sat at a small table eating what Lord Seton called "eggs à la Reine d'Ecosse," "cheese Royale," and "Her Majesty's ale," Mary announced that henceforth Bothwell would serve as Dunbar's keeper, and in the same breath asked the men to raise an army of loyal soldiers to march on Edinburgh with them.

"However many you believe are needed," she said, "to chase the rebels out." She looked to Bothwell as the most experienced soldier.

"We'll get the Scotts, and that's all the fighters you'll need," he said with a laugh. "Aye, they'll be loyal, and—"

"We'll put out a call to *all* Scotland," Huntly corrected. His clear blue eyes were steady and cool.

"And what do you suppose my lords of Morton, Ruthven, and Lindsay are having for breakfast?" Mary asked suddenly, passing a second bowl of eggs. She grinned.

"They are eating crow, as the saying goes," said Lord Seton. "And not served as prettily, I warrant."

"Is there pen and ink here?" she said. "I must needs write immediately to Charles IX in France and Elizabeth in England! They must be informed!"

XXIX

The sun came up gilded in a bank of clouds.

"Rain today," muttered Bothwell, taking only one glance of the sky. The wind was chilled, and outside the castle windows the sea looked thick from cold.

Darnley was huddled in front of the fire in the hall, shivering. "What are we to do?" he asked.

"I'll send out the call for my Borderers," said Bothwell. "As soon as they come, we'll march back to Edinburgh in strength."

"And drive the rebels out!" cried Mary. She looked at both men; Bothwell was clearly exhausted, but Darnley looked worse. "Drive them right into England, or wherever they want to run and hide!"

"Aye!" Bothwell almost shouted.

The evil, cold-blooded murderers . . . and the foremost among them was sitting right here, in front of the fire. Mary ran her hand over her stomach, gently, as if afraid that only one more touch could kill the baby.

And after you are born, I shall have my revenge, she thought, looking at Darnley out of the corner of her eye. No, I'll not ever be wife to *you* again, traitor!

* * *

By that afternoon, word reached Mary that other lords, made bold by her courage and Bothwell's strategy, were coming to Dunbar to offer themselves and their men in her service.

Bothwell entered the room where she was sitting and reading the dispatch.

"Do you not ever sleep?" he asked, staring. "Do you not need your rest for . . . for the child?"

"The child will be a true Stewart, and be most at home in action and high deeds," she said, repressing a sigh of exhaustion. "But look—the earls of Atholl, Sutherland, and Crawford, and the lords, brothers of my Marys, Fleming, Seton, and Livingston—are coming to Dunbar. We have prevailed!"

"Not yet," said Bothwell. "There has been no fighting yet."

At last Mary allowed herself to rest, stretched out on one of the beds in the old quarters. She had been awake now for how many hours—forty? She was not sure. Everything blended together, from the moment she had alighted on the plan of escaping at night, to the ride through the countryside. . . . She was abruptly, heavily weary. She slept.

When she awoke, it was to a new feeling: a cold, certain fear. It was only now that she could see all the events together and realize how precarious her situation was. She was utterly surrounded by traitors and murderers. Her innermost guarding circle had turned out to be a dangerous circle of enemies rather than safety. And these were the powerful nobles, the ones with intelligence and many men-at-arms.

I always knew Knox was my enemy, she thought. To his credit, he proclaimed himself so from the beginning. And whatever he preached, he never wielded a dagger himself. I could invite him to my chamber without fear of being stabbed.

But Ruthven . . . Morton . . . Douglas . . . the foremost names in Scotland! And then there is my brother, Lord James, the highest in the land . . . how quickly he appeared on the scene! He must have directed the whole plan from England. For one thing is certain—this was planned. It was not done on sudden impulse. It took place on the day before Parliament was to punish the rebels from the Chaseabout Raid.

She found herself shaking. She pulled a fur over herself.

It is with the cold, she told herself. It is not from fear.

Outside the wind was moaning, and she could see rain falling in a steady pelting from the skies.

Whom can I trust? Is Bothwell the only loyal lord in the land? He has never abandoned the crown, and supported my mother against her enemies. . . .

"I wish I had my armour."

Mary heard a familiar, revolting voice nearby: Darnley's. Wearily she turned her head and beheld him, standing forlornly in the middle of the sparse stone chamber. This was a chamber for rough warriors, not perfumed courtiers.

"I left the armour behind in Edinburgh. How can I ride out with the troops without armour?" he was whining.

That was all he had enjoyed about the Chaseabout Raid: wearing his armour.

"Borrow some from Bothwell," she replied.

Darnley threw back his head and laughed, a braying, high-pitched, unpleasant sound. It echoed in a peculiar way off the uneven stones in the chamber. "It wouldn't fit. I'm taller," he said disdainfully.

"I meant from the military stores here," she said, equally disdainfully. "This is a royal arsenal and supplies of armour, artillery, and gunpowder are stored here."

"Oh, yes." He looked around vaguely. "Well, I shall see to it."

She sat up. "Has anyone arrived yet?"

"Atholl is already here, with a thousand men. And some of Bothwell's troopers—"

"Aye, the Scotts have arrived." Bothwell stood in the doorway, his blocky form almost filling it up. "I came to tell you."

"With how many men?" asked Mary. She arose from the bed.

"Several hundred. And they sent word that the Robsons and Taits are on their way, and with some of their best men: Crack-spear and Cleave-the-crune—you can guess how they got their names!"

Mary laughed. "They can cleave as many crowns as they wish, and with my blessings!"

"What a disgusting celebration of violence!" said Darnley.

"The names are very descriptive," said Bothwell. "There's Curst Eckie, Ill Will Armstrong, Buggerback Elliot, and Bangtail Armstrong. Perhaps if you went to the Borders, they'd find the proper name for you as well."

Darnley turned and left the room, his back stiff.

"Yes," said Mary. "They could call *him* Craven Henry." She shuddered. Now that he had left the room, she felt as if an ugly spirit had departed.

"Are you rested?" Bothwell asked. "You should make sure that you are."

"What will we do now?" she asked. She was ready to do whatever he said.

"We wait. And when enough men have come to Dunbar, then it is time for us to march upon those miscreants."

❧

Within three days, four thousand men had gathered at Dunbar, and the news of this travelled quickly back to Edinburgh. Bothwell and Mary decided that the time had come to leave Dunbar and march west; Bothwell led out his Borderers and Mary four companies of professional infantry. Altogether they enlisted the support of seven earls and four lords, and more joined them as they marched. Darnley managed to ride in front of the forces of Lord Seton as if he were commanding them.

As they neared Edinburgh the crowds thickened, cheering them. Just outside the city, Archbishop Hamilton, in the name of his clan, welcomed them. The people of Edinburgh streamed out, escorting them back into the city; Bothwell fired his field guns.

"Soldiers!" he cried. "You are to be billeted in the city!"

There was no resistance, no fighting. The field guns turned out to be merely a salute, not an opening salvo. The traitors had fled the city, and were even then on their way south to cross the border.

Mary entered the city, deserted by her enemies, to the ringing sound of cheers, at the head of eight thousand men-at-arms. The city was hers; the victory was hers.

By the next day she and her Council—excluding Darnley, who did not show any interest in attending—promptly attended to the work of punishing the offenders and setting the government on its feet again. All those who had not actually been present at the murder, but were indirectly involved, were ordered to keep away from court; this included Argyll, Boyd, Maitland, and Rothes and Kirkcaldy, still in England from the last rebellion. Morton, Lindsay, Ruthven, and the Douglases were all outlawed, both they and their partisans.

And what was to be done with Darnley? He had to be kept by Mary's side, to vouch for the legitimacy of their child. A solution was found: He would swear his innocence before the Council, and this declaration, clearing him, would be published and posted. And so Darnley, his face shining and guileless, swore that he had had nothing to do with the conspiracy, and had "never counselled, commanded, consented, assisted, nor approved of the same."

Afterwards he went out drinking at a tavern directly across from the Market Cross, where his signed declaration was posted.

"Good, good, good!" he kept muttering, lifting his mug in a salute to it.

XXX

he very sound of Darnley's knife clinking against his platter grated on Mary's nerves. She hated everything connected with him, any reminder that he even existed; the noises he made as he chewed his meat, as he swallowed his wine, all were repulsive to her. She forced herself to look at him, commanded herself to smile. He smiled back, the simpleton. Could he not tell how false her expression was?

Not much longer now, she thought. He must be flattered and mollified in order to acknowledge the child as his own and put the final lie to the Riccio slanders. Have I not done everything possible to placate him: issued a proclamation that he was entirely innocent of the killing, kept him by my side . . . everything except admit him to my bed, and in that I have had the excuse that the physicians forbid it—thank God!

Darnley was still smiling at her, cocking his head to one side like a dog. "Shall we walk upon the ramparts, my love?" he asked.

She willed herself to stand up and nod. She even took his hand and together they walked slowly from the chamber out into Edinburgh Castle yard.

The thin May sunshine had no power to warm them, and Mary sent a servitor to bring her a cloak. Fastening it about her shoulders gave her an excuse to let go Darnley's hand. As they left the protection of the inner courtyard walls, the raw spring wind, fresh from the Forth, hit them. Darnley laughed with glee, like a child. He rushed over to the walls of the fortress, while Mary followed him at a more sedate pace.

"Look there! Look there!" he said, pointing to the patterns the wind was making on the surface of the Nor'Loch, at the foot of the castle rock. The long thin lake, where the bodies of plague victims were tossed, sparkled today in the sunshine, its blue-grey colour a reflection of the sky.

"Yes, yes," she said, trying to keep the irritation from her voice.

What a child, she thought. And I thought him a man, and pledged fealty to him, and put him on a throne. This time last year . . . no, I'll not think of that. It's too painful.

The harsh sound of laughter carried across the courtyard, followed by the ring of nailed boots. Bothwell and his brother-in-law Huntly were deep in conversation as they headed down toward the Long Stairs and the gateway, their cloaks flying out behind them.

Wait! Mary almost called, and raised her hand to signal them. Then she dropped it. They had disappeared around the wall.

"As to the godparents, I think my father—" Darnley was saying.

"No!" said Mary. "No, not your father!" She distrusted him; she suspected he, too, had been involved with the Riccio murderers. "I had thought that we should ask rulers of other countries to be godparents. After all, this child will be monarch of Scotland, and possibly England as well. It is fitting that this be recognized from the start."

Darnley sighed. "Who, then?" he said.

"I hoped to ask Charles IX of France, and the Duke of Savoy, and Queen Elizabeth."

"Queen Elizabeth?" screamed Darnley, so loud that the soldiers keeping watch on the walls turned around. "What, when she forbade our marriage? No, no, no!"

339

"But this is the way to win her, don't you see?" Mary tried to keep her voice low and reasonable. "Queen Elizabeth loves children, and if she has bound herself in vows to ours, she will look on it with favour later—"

"Never! The insult was too great! Never, never, never!"

"I intend to ask her, and I am the Queen," said Mary firmly.

Darnley ignored her, in one of his sudden changes of mood. He turned and looked out at the loch again. Suddenly his voice was quiet. "Do you think it's true what they say, that witches float? That's how they tried them here, so I heard."

Mary shuddered. "I hope never to see such a trial. The poor wretches are hauled out of the waters and then burnt at the stake."

Witches, she thought, and all sorts of evil seem to surround me. My mother died within these walls, and I may follow her.

Her thoughts were so heavy she felt pulled downward toward the glistening surface of the loch.

"My love!" Darnley was holding her, with surprising strength. His face was pale and he looked alarmed. He turned her away from the height and led her back across the courtyard.

Why was he holding her protectively? She tried to shrug him off.

"You almost fell," he said. "You swayed forward, and had I not caught you—" He was trembling.

Holy Virgin! She herself began to shake. Did I faint, then?

"You must lie down," he was saying. "I shall see you to your chamber."

She lay on the royal bed, resting her cheek against the tawny satin bedcovers, the ones she had embroidered with the Marys when they were all unmarried. They had laughed and sung and teased one another about their future mates, making wishes about the beds these satins would cover.

Now I lie on it and know all too well what my huband turned out to be, Mary thought. If I could never lie in this bed, or any other, with him—it would be all I would ask. Are Livingston and Beaton happy? Beaton married just a month ago, and seemed content with her fate. Flamina still writes to banished Maitland, even though she knows he was involved with the murder. Seton . . . she shows no interest in sweethearts.

"*Ma Reine*, they said you fainted up on the ramparts." A small woman was suddenly standing beside her. A familiar smell of sweet lemon balm soothed Mary.

"Madame Rallay." Her presence was more comforting than any satin bedcovers. "I fear I did. Yet it is most unlike me. And I am feeling much better now. And no, I do not need to partake of any of your calvados and frothed-cream concoctions!" That had been Madame Rallay's cure-all for her since the days in France.

"I have already ordered it, and you must drink it!" said the Frenchwoman sternly.

Mary knew better than to argue. But she suddenly knew what she wanted, and it was not a posset. She clasped Madame Rallay's hand. "I will drink it, I promise. But after I have had it, I pray you send for my confessor. I need to see him. It is time."

Mary was sitting on a bench in the shuttered room, awaiting Father Roche Mamerot. She found herself shaking. Death: it was all around her, and lying on the bed she had suddenly felt its presence, waiting for her as it had for her mother. Childbirth was dangerous, and she could well die. Die . . . and go to Hell for her sins.

"My child." The old Dominican, who had come with her from France and had grown elderly as her sins had progressed from refusing to share her toys with the other children in the royal playroom, to unsettling desires for vanity and luxury, to adult failings, greeted her kindly. He had always been a good confessor, stressing God's mercy rather than His wrath.

"Bless me, Father, for I've sinned, sinned, sinned—" She grabbed his hand and covered it with kisses, closing her eyes to try to stop the tears.

"There, my child, the sacrament is meant to ease hearts too burdened. . . ." He tried to extricate his hand, but she clung to it, weeping. "What is it that troubles you so?"

"I have committed sins of commission, the sins of pride and anger! I have failed to practise charity! I have—"

"People do not weep over 'failing to practise charity.'" His voice was gentle, almost teasing. "Such abstracts do not wound the soul, producing the pain of repentance that I see here. What is it you have done?"

"I hate him! I hate my husband! I hate him in my heart! Is that not evil? I wish he would die . . . I wish he were dead . . . I despise him!" She buried her face in her hands and wept stormily. "I cannot bear his presence! He feels repulsive to me! Father, what can I do?"

"You must, unfortunately, overcome this aversion. He is your husband, and in the eyes of God you are one flesh. You know it is your duty—"

"I cannot! I cannot!"

"Humanly you cannot, but with God's help—"

"Nooo," she moaned, holding her side and bending over. She looked as if she had been kicked.

"You say no because you cannot bear to submit yourself, not because you doubt that God has the power to help you." He looked stricken himself. "And there can be no absolution without a sincere attempt to change, I fear to say."

"I am afraid, Father, I am afraid that if I die, Darnley and his father will rule, and that they will kill the baby—such dreadful, nightmarish thoughts torment me! How can I go to the bed of a man I believe wants me dead?"

"Is there—do you have desire or lustful thoughts about any other man?" He had to ask.

"No. No, I never think of such a thing. I tell you, Father, you know that I came to this marriage a virgin, and that before that I had never even given much attention to that part of life . . . even though others seem to think about it, sing about it, and gossip about it endlessly. I was as much a Virgin Queen as my cousin. Would to God I were again! No, there are no such thoughts!"

He studied her tear-stained face. "I believe you. You should be thankful that the Devil has not seen fit to torture you in that respect. It would only compound the suffering you now experience." He sighed. "I do not wish you to face childbirth with any sins on your soul. Your feelings are understandable. But do you have the strength to try to overcome them? All God asks is the willingness. He requires no promises beyond that, and He certainly does not require actual success."

"Yes. If you say I must. And you have been the guardian of my soul for many years," she said in a whisper.

"Then make an Act of Contrition, so that I may absolve you," he said.

Mary bowed her head. "O my God! I am heartily sorry for all my sins; and I detest them above all things because they displease Thee, who are infinitely good and amiable, and subject me to the rigours of Thy justice; and I firmly resolve, with the help of Thy grace, to do penance for them, and never more to offend Thee. Amen."

"Then I forgive you in the name of the Father, the Son, and the Holy Ghost," said Father Mamerot. "And for your penance, you must set this matter straight as soon as you are able." He glanced at her stomach. "And may God grant you a safe childbed."

❧

The labour pains began a month later, on a June evening. Until then, Mary had anxiously asked the matrons, "How will I *know* if it is truly labour?" and they had all answered, "You will know. You will know." And now she understood why they had all been so certain.

It hurt. It hurt from the very beginning. She had been told that it could start gently, but the very first pain was like a thin-bladed knife going through her, passing sideways from her back to her belly. Neither had they paused, once they had truly begun. Women had told her of being able to do needlework, of enjoying music-making in the early stages, but Mary could not stand up. She felt as though she were fighting an enemy inside herself, one that could best her and overpower her at any moment.

Lying in the great bed in Edinburgh Castle, clinging to knotted bedsheets, she tried hard not to scream. Everything the midwife told her to do, she did—lie this way, grasp this thing, smell this handkerchief soaked in water of wallflower—for the woman *must* be privy to secrets that would help. But nothing helped, and the pains grew more and more intense, until she felt that if she had a dagger to hand she would have killed herself at that moment.

"Take my hand!" commanded Lady Atholl. "Squeeze it hard!"

Mary obeyed, although she did not have the strength to squeeze it as hard as she would have liked.

"My sister lies in childbed herself at this very hour," the woman whispered. "Yes, within this castle. Now that I have your handclasp, I can go to her and take your pain with me. She will bear the pain!" The woman—almost as heavy as the pregnant ones herself—heaved herself up from the bedside.

"No!" cried Mary. "No, I do not wish that." She reached out to try to restrain her.

"Hush." The midwife gently pushed Mary back down. "Let the witch go. Do not keep her by your bedside."

Witch? Was the woman a witch? "Lady Atholl—" she began, but a ripping pain cut her words off. Her abdomen felt as if it were being torn with searing irons, yet the huge mass within it—it had ceased to feel like a baby—did not move. What were all these pains accomplishing? They seemed to dash and writhe around the immobile creature like waves beating against a stone.

"Help me! Help me!" she cried, but she knew no one would. They could not reach up inside her and pull the child out. "Ooooh!"

Suddenly the pains seemed to break open, like sunlight streaming through a break in the clouds, parting to show an instant without feeling. Then they returned, full force.

"Push! Push! It is time!"

And now the pains were something to bear down upon, something that had a beginning, a core, and an end. And in the sheet of pain that was her belly, she felt a movement.

"Make ready! Make ready!" the midwife cried. Her assistant rushed over to the foot of the bed with a wrapping sheet and heated water.

The midwife was panting and sweating as if she were working in front of an oven. She bent and her sinewy arms strained.

"It's here! It's here! Oh!" she cried. "*He* is here! He! It's a prince, a prince!"

"A prince!" all the attendants murmured, stopping to stare.

"The work is not over!" bellowed the midwife.

Mary heard the cry, "a prince," and felt infinite relief. But—was he whole?

There was scurrying and movement where she could not see, then the midwife held up a slippery, gleaming blue baby. A caul covered his head, and was stripped away by the midwife; it was gossamer-thin. Mucus dripped off him. A slap on his wet buttocks, then a wail, mewling, tremulous.

"God be thanked!" cried the midwife. She thrust him into the arms of one attendant. "Clean him!" She herself set about to attend Mary.

As Mary lay there, her body still laced with pain, she heard the baby whimpering softly, heard the women exclaiming over him. He was perfectly formed, then. Thank the Blessed Mother!

They slid clean linen under her, wiped her sweat away with warm scented towels, and gave her a fresh gown. A dry pillow was substituted for her soaked one, and then the wrapped baby was put in her arms.

He looked so . . . so *old*! was her first thought. His eyes, with pouches under them, looked sombre. And his skin was wrinkled.

"All newborns are ugly, Your Grace," said the midwife. "Even Helen of Troy, I warrant."

So the child was unusually ugly—otherwise why would the midwife try to assure her? But Mary did not care if his features were ugly, she was so relieved to have him safely in her arms.

And—his complexion was fair, his hair downy golden. His puckered little eyelids opened, showing bright blue eyes.

Now no one can say he is Riccio's son! thought Mary, with infinite relief. Until that instant she had not been aware how much she had worried that the dark side of the Stewart blood would come out. James III, they said, had been so dark he looked foreign. But this child was fair, like Darnley.

This child, James Charles . . . she could call him that now; he could be named. James for her father, and Charles for her distant ancestor Charlemagne. May this child inherit a great kingdom, she prayed.

"Shall we call in the King? And the court?" asked the midwife.

"Aye."

One of the attendants flung open the chamber doors and announced the event to the guard, who shouted with joy and then called another guard to run and proclaim the news to the castle.

In a few moments the entire room shook as all the castle's cannon fired a salute to the new prince.

"Preserve the caul," said Mary, suddenly remembering what she had seen.

"Aye, of course," said the midwife indignantly. "Do you think we do not know our business? A caul must be preserved—else the good luck that comes with it will be lost. Here in Scotland it means this wee one will have the gift of second sight, and be free from the powers of sorcerers and fairies. A good thing for a King to have up here."

It would be more useful to be protected against traitors than fairies, thought Mary, especially here in Scotland. There are more of the former than of the latter.

Little James Charles stirred in his sumptuous state cradle covered with ten yards of velvet. "Is the King coming?" asked Mary. There was still that to be got through.

Just then Darnley and his groom of the chamber, Anthony Standen, appeared in the doorway.

"Oh, my heart rejoices!" cried Darnley, hurrying to her side. "My darling!"

Lord Erskine, commander of Edinburgh Castle, and other members of the court followed him into the chamber, and began filling the room.

"Please, my lady, the Prince," said Mary, nodding toward the cradle. The midwife reached toward the cradle and lifted the infant out, and placed him gently in Mary's waiting arms. Mary pushed back the coverings and showed the child's face to Darnley.

"My Lord," Mary said, "God has given you and me a son whose paternity is of none but you." She placed the baby in Darnley's arms. Then, raising her voice so everyone in the chamber could hear, she said, "My Lord, here

I protest before God, and as I shall answer Him at the great day of judgement, this is your son, and no other man's son; and I am desirous that all here, both ladies and men, bear witness. For he is so much your own son I fear it may be the worse for him hereafter."

A moment of stillness. Would Darnley accept the child and thereby confirm her claim?

Darnley looked at the child's face a long time and then, kissing his cheek, placed him back in Mary's arms, and then kissed Mary.

"This is the Prince who I hope shall first unite the two kingdoms of England and Scotland," she said in a clear, triumphant voice. The baby squirmed and wrinkled his already wrinkled face.

"Why, Madam!" exclaimed Standen. "Shall he succeed before Your Majesty and his father?"

"Alas," said Mary, unable to stop herself, "his father is broken to me."

"Sweet Madam!" Darnley's voice rose like a cat whose tail has been nipped in a door. "Is this your promise to forgive and forget all?"

"I have forgiven all, but I can never forget. What if Kerr's pistol had shot?" Her voice began to shake. "What would have become of him and me both? Or what estate would *you* have been in? God only knows, but we may suspect."

"Madam!" answered Darnley. "All these things are past."

"Then let them go," she murmured, speaking to herself. "Let them go."

Outside, the news spread through Edinburgh. Throngs convened at St. Giles for a solemn act of thanksgiving for the safety of the Queen and the birth of an heir, and the first of celebratory bonfires were lit on Arthur's Seat and Calton Hill. From there five hundred beacons throughout Scotland blazed forth the news: Scotland has a Prince!

The Prince had been born at ten in the morning of June nineteenth, 1566. By noon James Melville had left Edinburgh en route to London to announce the infant's arrival to his godmother, Queen Elizabeth.

XXXI

In the early dawn, Mary stood shivering slightly as she waited on the dock at Leith. It was chilly here at this hour, even though it was July. But her shaking was due not only to the cool breezes blowing in from the Forth, but from nervousness. Was *he* following? She kept looking back toward the road to Edinburgh, expecting any moment to see a group of horsemen descending. She would recognize Darnley from any distance.

She had planned this escape to Alloa, not secretly perhaps, but she had not told Darnley. Seven weeks had passed since the birth of the little James Charles, and at last her physicians and court etiquette had released her from her literal confinement in Edinburgh Castle. But what they had released her to was the duty to return to Darnley's bed—or let him return to hers. And Darnley had been eagerly waiting, he had made it all too plain.

She shuddered. The thought of it was now worse than ever, since she had been spared it for so long. It was like an abominable habit that, once broken, cannot be resumed without utter debasement and revulsion. Perhaps this retreat would give her the strength, or the courage, to submit, or else the final resolution to flee from his embraces forever.

John Erskine, the Earl of Mar, had offered her his castle on the north shore of the Forth, near Stirling. She would sleep, read, stroll in the fields, gather midsummer flowers to make chains and potpourris, daydream. And pray—pray for direction. She felt so lost, just when she should feel most triumphant.

She glanced over at Lady Reres, a relative of Beaton's, who was rocking little James gently. She was acting as the baby's wet nurse, and her great bulk seemed to provide him with comfort in itself. Mary was going to be entrusting him to Erskine soon, for that family was traditional keeper of the royal children, as his father had been hers. But until the day when she must be parted from him, she kept the baby in her own room, listening to his every whimper and sigh, studying his features for family likenesses.

No sign of Darnley. But also, no sign of the ship Bothwell had promised to have waiting for her if she came to the docks before sunrise. Mary turned to Madame Rallay and began to murmur under her breath.

"He will come, Madam. That is not your worry," Madame Rallay said.

"Can I trust no one?" Mary burst out. If Bothwell was not to be relied on, who was? He alone had not accepted bribes or turned coat on her, Protestant though he was. He had seen her through the Riccio horror.

Two rough-looking men came toward them; one had a beard so bushy and streaked with red it looked false. The other man was thin and dressed so lightly Mary wondered if he had any blood, or whether he had hardened himself by sleeping out in the snow; she had heard of such people.

"Yer Maj'sty?" said the false-bearded one. He swept off his hat. "Yer ship awaits, on th' other dock. I'm the captain. Captain William Blackadder, at yer service."

Black Adder. Never was a man better named, Mary thought. He looked like a blackguard, poisonous as a snake.

"Lord Bothwell sent me," he said stubbornly, as if it should not be necessary to add this.

"Indeed I did." Bothwell's head poked up from a piling, where he had climbed up the iron rungs. He clambered up on the dock and gave Black-adder a shove. "Is the leak plugged?" he asked, then, seeing the look on Mary's face, he laughed. "I jest," he said. "Truth is, Blackadder's ship is quite seaworthy. A pirate's must be, if he is to ply his trade."

Laughing, Bothwell gestured toward Mary and her ladies. "Come. The ship is ready, the sailors await, and the tide swells." He looked around pointedly. "I see I did not need to procure such a large vessel."

"Others may come afterwards. Perhaps by land," said Mary.

"Do we await the King?" Bothwell asked bluntly.

"No."

"Then let us depart."

He led the way across two wharves to where a well-trimmed ship was tied up. It was called the *Defiance,* and it had brown sails. Suddenly Mary remembered hearing that name . . . it *had* been a pirate vessel!

Bothwell strode up the gangplank, the captain following. The sailors, dressed in dark homespun, greeted him with affection and respect. They merely glowered at Blackadder.

With Bothwell commanding, his voice carrying clear and far over the water and the creaking of the ropes as the sails were maneuvered, the ship cast off, seemingly effortlessly. The shore receded as they made for the mid-channel of the Forth. Was that a movement on the road? Was Darnley arriving, but too late?

Then he'll follow me on land, she thought, miserably. Is there no escape from him, no respite, even for a few days? His behaviour never improves, it only worsens. . . .

Bothwell, having turned over the sailing to Blackadder, came and stood beside her at the railing. "I will be at my other duties soon," he said. "I mean the ones on land."

"It is hard for you to be responsible for two such different realms," she said. "It is as if we asked a sea serpent to hunt in the jungle as well as at sea."

He laughed. "I could be compared to worse things than a serpent, so I'll hold my peace. The Borders need discipline and a heavy hand just now. Ever since Lord James got tangled up in the first rebellion, there's been little order down there. I am afraid, in plain language, that they have got quite out of hand. I can administer my own justice, but the truth is, they need the royal presence. You should come on a progress there, and hold courts of justice to try the worst criminals, and then hang them on the spot. They understand nothing else. There have been no hangings there in years. Just blood-feuds and murders."

"Do you truly think I should go there?"

Now the sun had risen and was making a glittering path on the waters. She pushed back her hood and let the wind touch her hair. The chill was leaving the air.

"Aye. They need to know they have a queen. At present they feel they have to answer to no one but the head of their clan. They answer to me, somewhat—or rather, to my sword arm. But they should feel *your* presence, and now they do not. I'll round them up, if you will judge them."

"And hang them? You'd have me do that?"

"It's the only way to get their attention." He laughed again.

"It would earn their hatred, not their respect," she objected.

"In the Borders, they are the same thing. Besides, once they had seen you, they might become your liege men. They're a sentimental lot. Courtly, in a strange way. You might win them over."

"With smiles and fair words? Or hangings and beatings?"

"You could try both and see which is more effective."

She could not tell whether he was serious or not. "I will come, after you have rounded up the bandits, murderers, and thieves."

"A fine assignment. I'd best be about it, then, whilst you take the cool summer breezes and forest paths at Alloa." He turned from the railing and waved a signal to one of the seamen.

"Perhaps you should stay at Alloa a few days yourself. We could confer— I wish you would tell me about the Borders!" she burst out. "You know more than anyone else, and I need to learn!"

"You could never understand about the Borders," he said. "It is impossible for an outsider ever to understand."

"I cannot stomach that any longer!" she cried. "Calling me an outsider has been everyone's excuse to exclude me from everything! 'You cannot understand Scotland, you're a Frenchwoman!' " she mimicked perfectly. " 'You cannot understand the Scriptures, you're a Catholic!' 'You cannot understand warfare, you're a woman!' 'You cannot be trusted to rule, you're a daughter!' Well, I can tell you that an outsider can learn more than anyone born to the thing—whatever that thing is!"

He looked as though her words had blown him back an inch or two. "Well spoken. So you do understand. I too am an outsider in some ways. You speak the truth. We will have to talk more. Another time. When you visit the Borders to try my malefactors!"

❧

It was a week before Darnley came to Alloa. Until then, Mary was able to luxuriate in the freedom that came from being away from him—a freedom she had taken for granted before she knew him, but this was different.

She was sitting out in the castle forecourt, just watching the birds flying overhead, the hawks circling in the dappled blue sky, when Lord Erskine came out.

"A messenger has told me—the King has been seen leaving Edinburgh this morning. I imagine we can expect him here tonight." As befitted the game everyone was playing about "the King," he made no faces, had no meaningful expression in his words. His long face—mournful-looking under normal circumstances—did not look less mournful now.

"Oh. I see. Thank you for telling me."

Mary tried to read something else in Erskine's face. She had known him so long—his father had been one of her childhood guardians, and he himself had attended her at court since the beginning. But he was also Lord James's uncle, and an early member of the Lords of the Congregation. In some ways all the contradictions and mysteries of Scotland were contained in this one inscrutable man. If I could understand him, thought Mary, I could understand everything here.

"Shall I make his quarters ready adjoining yours, Your Majesty?"

"No. I prefer that he have separate quarters."

"As you wish." Erskine gave a little bow of obedience. "I am so happy you have come here!" he burst out.

"I am happy, too," she said.

And she was. The fresh air, the quiet, the rest and sleep, had been completely restorative. And Erskine, who would become the guardian and keeper of her most precious possession, the baby Prince, had had an opportunity to hold the baby, to play with him and watch him, as if he were any ordinary child.

"I greatly appreciate your bringing the Prince to me now, privately, so that I can come to know him. Rest assured I will guard him and cherish him," Erskine said.

"Promise me that you will protect him!" Mary suddenly said. "Promise me that no matter what happens, no matter what turmoil or fighting or disruption, you will not surrender him into anyone else's hands—not the English, nor the French, nor—nor anyone who might claim possession of the throne."

"It is my hereditary duty and privilege to be able to promise this," he assured her. "But are you so troubled—"

"Yes!" She grasped his hand. She should not be talking to Erskine, she should not confide her thoughts to anyone, she knew that, but the words seemed to come of themselves. "Everything is murky, since Riccio was murdered. Even the Chaseabout Raid was different—Lord James and the others openly declared themselves enemies, and an honest confrontation occurred. It was a manly manner of treason, so to speak."

I must not say anything against Lord James, this man is his uncle and undoubtedly loyal to him, she thought. But he seems so kindly, so sympathetic. . . . That has been the problem all along here in Scotland for me. I cannot read what is.

"But this killing, and secret bonds, and bribe money—" She shuddered. "I fear it is not over yet, that some monstrous thing is yet unfinished." There, she had given voice to her deepest fears. "It hangs over me like a cloud, and I feel choked and enveloped in it!"

Erskine's face was full of concern. "My dearest Queen—you must rest assured that all that is over and we can look forward to a glorious clear future here in Scotland, now that the Prince is here." He looked over at the baby, sleeping in his little cradle out in the sun.

And when you get possession of him, then what? The plan is not complete yet, but soon. . . . Mary, stop these thoughts, they are evil and come straight from hell to torment you.

Erskine's gentle eyes were probing hers.

But kind eyes can hide evil intent. Look at Darnley! Who has more glistening, innocent eyes?

All this has murdered my trust and confidence in anything beyond myself. Even God! Why was He so powerless to stop it?

"Your face is troubled," said Erskine. "I beg you to rest your cares and worries."

Darnley came on the morrow, riding up on his white horse and looking as splendid as Lancelot. Mary pretended to be pleased to see him, but as soon as he got her alone, he grabbed her arm.

"Why did you run away?" he cried. "And with Bothwell!"

"I did not 'run away,' " she said stoutly. "I only came here to rest and restore myself. All Bothwell did was to provide the ship—as was his duty! He went straight to the Borders after that."

"Aye, where he has been busy rounding up reivers, so I heard," said Darnley sarcastically.

"What does that mean?"

"Nothing." Darnley crossed his arms and stood like a soldier on duty.

"I have been thinking about the baptism," said Mary. "Pray, come and let us talk about it." She took his hand—limp and sweating, she noticed—and led him to a sunny spot in the solar. "Henry, would it not be a wonderful thing if the baptism was an occasion of great ceremony and importance? The Prince has the highest-ranking godparents. Why, Queen Elizabeth is sending a gold font that weighs two stone!"

"She hates our son! You know what it's reported she said when first she heard of his birth? She groaned and said, 'The Queen of Scots is lighter of a fair son, and I am but a barren stock!' Now she seeks to cover her true feelings beneath this costly gift. Ha!" sneered Darnley.

"Forget that gossip. Think only of how this is an opportunity to throw Scotland open to the inspection of the world, after the recent . . . troubles. We could show everyone how beautiful and civilized our country is. It would help trade, it would boost our importance in the political arena."

"What exactly are you thinking of?" His voice was cautious.

"A grand ceremony, like the kind they have in France. With fireworks, and a week of celebrations . . . jousting, and maybe even a bullfight!"

He frowned. "But it would be expensive," he finally said. "How would we pay for it?"

She hated his use of the word *we*, but forced herself to ignore it. "I will go to the Exchequer House and review all the finances, and, if necessary, raise the money by taxes."

"How will the Lords agree to that? Unless the ceremony is Protestant?"

"I know not. But we shall see."

Darnley then moved over to her and took her in his arms. He kissed her, and she felt as if she would faint from revulsion. His arms tightened around her, and he tried to lead her into the adjoining chamber where he assumed her bed was.

"Nay, not now—it is noontime, the ladies are about."

"Fie on the ladies! You're the Queen. Turn the key and lock them out!" he jerked her toward the door.

"No, Henry, I dare not offend—"

"To hell with you!" He flung her away. "I am leaving! I see I am not received in your chambers!"

That night the first of the Bothwell dreams came. She dreamed only that he was riding with her, as he had that night to Dunbar. It was dark and rainy; she could almost feel the wet on her cheeks. When she awoke she rubbed them, surprised that they were not streaked with raindrops. She was embarrassed, as if he would know that she had dreamed about him.

But that made her think of him intermittently during the day. She wondered how he was faring in the Borders. Darnley's remark was what had put it into her mind, she decided. Bothwell had not stressed the danger in his task, but it had to involve risks. Perhaps risks were what propelled him.

What did she know about him, really? She had arrested him after that fracas and accusation by his enemy, a Hamilton—who had turned out to be insane. On such flimsy evidence she had had Bothwell imprisoned, from which he had quickly escaped, so that for most of her reign he had not even been in the country. He was therefore a mystery to her, unlike the other nobles, whom she had come to know all too well.

He's a nobleman, she thought, but he's different from the rest. I know that his father divorced his mother when Bothwell was nine, and that Bothwell was sent away to his great-uncle's in Spynie. The "Bishop" had a host of bastards and specialized in trysts with married women. So Bothwell observed all that when he was growing up . . . that must be where he learned about women. But where did he learn his fighting? And his seamanship? Because by the time he got his inheritance at twenty-one he was already known as a hero in the Borders and had a command at sea. I know he fought in support of my mother. . . .

I know so little about him, really! And yet he seems to have become my true right arm.

That night, after she had been asleep several hours, and dreamed forgettable dreams, he visited her again. She dreamed that he was holding her, kissing her. In the dream they did not speak. He merely reached for her, putting his powerful hand on the back of her head, putting pressure on her skull. He had burrowed his fingers all the way through her hair, touching her scalp. His broad face had no expression at all; it was blank. His eyes, green-brown as an October day, did not blink.

In the dream he was wearing a rough homespun shirt, such as country

351

people wore. It was the colour of barley bread, with little nubbly imperfections in it, open at the throat, showing his collarbones.

With his other hand he held her tightly against him. He kissed her, and he ground his mouth against hers so roughly it erased all immediate sensation in her lips except pressure. She felt his body pressing against hers, as if he were a knife and she a whetstone. The pressure of his fingers on her head and her back was intense and forcing. She could feel this so acutely that she knew it was real.

Then, as dreams do, abruptly Bothwell faded like a ghost in the morning light, melting and floating away. Mary awoke to find her gown up above her waist and her hair twisted around her neck. She was drenched with sweat from the heavy covers, and fought free of them. Then she lay on her mattress and let the cool breeze from the window flow over her, until she began to shiver.

XXXII

Mary was at Traquair House, a mellow old estate in the valley of the Tweed, in the Borders, that had once been a royal hunting lodge. Now it was the ancestral home of yet another Stewart cousin, John Stewart, fourth Laird of Traquair, who was the captain of Mary's guard and had helped in her escape from Holyrood. He had invited the royal party to come and spend a week hunting in the forests surrounding the house, which abounded in game, both large and small. There had been, at one time or another, wildcats, wolves, bears, and boars, as well as stags and elk in the woods.

She had brought Darnley, knowing how he loved hunting and hawking. Trying to force herself to endure his company, she hoped that this would be a safe way to do so. He would spend his time outdoors, in the company of others she had brought—Bothwell, Mary Seton, and her French secretary, Claud Nau. Afterwards he would be too tired to be demanding. And if he were—well, it had to be faced.

To further distract him, Mary had insisted on bringing baby James, in tow with his fat wet nurse, Lady Reres. That should also occupy Darnley—so she hoped.

Seeing Bothwell again somewhat embarrassed her, after the dreams. She felt ashamed of them, as if he knew about them. He would find them demeaning. But in person he now seemed different, and she was glad she could see that the dream-Bothwell was only a creation of her own mind.

This one was more affable, shorter, and had peeling skin from the sunburn he had gotten from his long hours of riding.

"I've had great success in the Borders the last month," he had told her. "Of course, the glorious full moon we had in July helped."

"How so?" she had asked, curious.

"Why, the moon is the goddess of all cattle thieves," he said. "The Scotts even have as a motto, 'There'll be moonlight again.' And so there was. As the moon rose so huge for three successive nights, it allowed me to bag an entire band that were just in full raid, so to speak. They await your justice in the autumn. You are coming, are you not?"

"Yes. I promised." She smiled at him. "I am pleased you could come a bit north to join us for *this* type of hunting. Tell me—where have you been riding?"

"Oh, we chased the Kerrs around the countryside. Ran them through the wastes of Liddesdale and Eskdale, splashed through the waters running all through the Borders. But now my men can carry on for a bit on their own. I needed to attend to some other business, so it's just as well I have a few days off duty." He had smiled, and suddenly she remembered that Lady Reres was a sister of that old mistress of Bothwell's—what was her name? Janet Beaton, the one who still looked like a young girl, even at fifty. Witchcraft. They said she was a witch. Did he have "business" with that family still?

"A fine pack of hounds," Bothwell was saying.

Sir John's master of the hounds was bringing out his hunting dogs, fallow hounds and buckhounds. They were straining at their leashes.

"Oh, you'll go, my boys, you'll go," said Sir John tenderly, stooping down to let them crowd round him and lick him. "Hello, Jethro, how's the paw? Quite better?"

Mary looked up at the sky, where dark clouds raced across, making fleeting shadows on the ground.

"It will not rain," Bothwell assured her. "That is the way clouds behave here. They run free, like the outlaws."

"I am grateful that there are fewer outlaws since you took over as Lieutenant of the Borders," she said.

"Oh, there are just as many of them, and half are waiting for your judgement. The Elliots still cause great trouble."

Sir John, mounted on his hunting bay, led them out the gates and toward the hunting forest. Mary rode abreast of Bothwell, her velvet bonnet with its feather perched on her elaborate mound of hair, her back straight as a board. She leaned over to continue talking to him as they trotted along the path.

"Someday you must tell me more about the different Border families. I wish to know; I have heard, for example, that the Kerrs are left-handed and that their stairs spiral to the right instead of to the left so they can use their sword arms unhindered. Is that true?"

"Aye," said Bothwell. "Not all of them are left-handed, but a large number are, 'tis true. In the Borders they call all left-handed people 'ker-handed,' 'car-handed,' or 'corry-fisted.' "

"Is it also true that here in the Borders a male child's hand is held back from the christening so it remains unhallowed and free to murder?"

Bothwell threw back his head and laughed so loudly the other four turned around.

"No. That is a tale," he finally said. "Good Christians can murder as well as anyone else, 'tis no hindrance. Why, Lord Ruthven, who just expired across the border in Newcastle, beheld an angel choir on his deathbed, did he not?"

"So they say," Mary replied. "But I would not like to answer for his whereabouts now."

Sir John sounded his hunting horn, and the hounds were unleashed. "From here on in, the forest grows denser. Let us not become separated. Two stags were sighted a mile or so from here a fortnight ago." Raising his arm, he led them single file.

The trees grew closer and closer together, a mixed forest of oak, birch, and pine, and overhead the branches began to mesh and weave together to form a roof. They fell silent. Up ahead they could hear the scampering of the hounds through the underbrush.

But after an hour, no game had been sighted, not even a hare. Suddenly they came upon the remains of a great stag, stretched out in a small clearing. Evidence of a campfire was nearby.

"Poachers," said Sir John, shaking his head. "That they could be so bold—could come so near the estate!"

They passed the stag, already picked clean by carrion crows, and continued riding. A mile or so farther on they saw two more deer, likewise slaughtered. Sir John pulled his mount to a halt and just stared.

"It seems your game wardens are blind, incompetent, or bribed," said Darnley in a haughty tone. "And obviously, *Lieutenant,* your writ does not run here." He glared at Bothwell.

"Come, let us try a bit farther," said Sir John. He attempted to keep his voice calm.

But within five miles they found four more poached deer, and no live ones.

"I am leaving," said Darnley, wheeling his horse around. "Clearly we would do better at hawking on the moor."

Before Mary could stop him, he was trotting off.

"He will get lost," she said to Sir John. She was embarrassed, like a mother having to make sure her headstrong five-year-old does not come to harm.

"I will attend him," said Sir John with a knowing smile, turning back. Seton and Nau followed him. "Lord Bothwell knows his way." In a moment they had disappeared from view in the dark, narrow forest path.

"I agree with Lord Darnley for once," Bothwell said. "There is no point in hunting today. Poachers have been bold here. There is nothing left for us." He blew on a small whistle he carried. Sir John's huntmaster answered it with a call of his own and Bothwell then blew several notes, instructing him to bring the hounds back to the kennels.

As they emerged from the forest, Bothwell said, "I've no mind to return to Traquair House, nor am I in the mood for hawking. Tell them I've gone toward Ettrickbridge on business that will occupy me the rest of the day." He reined in his horse to change direction, and saluted her. "You know the rest of the way; you can see the house from here."

"Let me go with you!" she suddenly said. "I would rather ride than hawk."

"I have business to attend to as well. Personal business."

"I will not hinder you."

"Very well." He touched his horse's flanks with his spurs and set out south, away from the Tweed River and toward the Yarrow, skirting Minch Moor.

The hills were not high, but they were wide and rounded and swelling, like a nursing mother's breasts. One after another they rose, all covered with short, bushy heather, gorse, and moss, and spotted with grey stones. Overhead the sky was a dappled dome of white and grey and blue.

Bothwell rode as fast as possible on the stretches where it was fairly level, but going up and downhill he had to slacken his pace. Seeing him in this setting, where he seemed to belong as much as the lichen-covered stones and the native hawks soaring overhead, it was hard for Mary to remember that he had spent time abroad and had a fashionable wardrobe at his disposal.

He rode ahead of her, not looking back, confident that she did not need watching. They were traversing landscape that was a green-grey-brown, strewn with rocks, the rounded bare hill tops encircling them, the wind moaning softly as it combed through the stiff dead gorse. Little streams of clear water, called burns, flashed in the intermittent sunshine as they tumbled down the mossy banks, rushing into the black pools below.

As they descended one of the hills and approached a clump of trees bordering a burn, Mary realized that she was hungry. They must have been riding for hours, but she had not kept track of the time. Looking up at the sky, she saw a bright spot through the clouds that told her it must already be midafternoon. For hours she had not thought of anything but the overwhelming landscape around her. Everything else, including thoughts of Darnley, had been blotted out in the majesty of the skies and hills, and the clean wind blowing through them.

Abruptly Bothwell stopped, and dismounted. "Are you not hungry?" he asked, as if he had read her mind.

"Aye," she admitted, dismounting.

"You have the endurance of a soldier," he said admiringly. "Of course I had heard of your tirelessness in the Chaseabout Raid. And I saw it myself right after the Riccio murder. But anger can act as a powerful spur. Today you were not angry. It was a truer test."

"You were testing me?"

"Only as I test all things, to see what they are made of. I cannot help myself." He smiled, as though confessing a secret fault. Then he led his horse over to the burn, and let it drink the clear brown water.

"Why is it brown?" she asked.

"Because of the soil and peat it flows through," he said, cupping a handful of it. "But look. It is absolutely clear, and clean. The brown is not dirt or mud. Drink it."

She bent her head down and sipped the water until her lips rested on Bothwell's palm. The cold water was slightly flavoured, with a tingling freshness.

"It is better than wine," she finally said.

"Aye." He wiped his hands on his breeches.

They sat on a boulder by the side of the burn and shared Bothwell's food: hard cheese, smoked meat, and heavy barley bread. Around them the hills watched, naked and silent.

"How can anyone find his way about?" Mary finally asked. "It all looks the same—vast and tractless."

"That is why only a native can enforce law here," he said, chewing his bread. "Your brother the Lord James, as an outsider, could not. Nor, begging your pardon, could your royal father, King James V."

At the mention of those names, she was suddenly transported back to court and its old concerns.

"Let us not speak of these things," said Bothwell, again reading her mind. "You wanted to know more of the Borders, so let us speak of the code of honour here. It is: never betray anyone to the law, offer hospitality to all, and never break a promise. That is all. Only three things. And they vow thus, 'I swear by Heaven above me, Hell beneath me, by my part of Paradise, by all that God made in six days and seven nights, and by God himself.' " He leaned his head on his arm. "Is it not simple?"

"You are fortunate to belong to a world that you understand," she said. She pulled herself back further from him, in a way that only she was aware of.

"I understand it, but my true place in Scotland and in my own home was disrupted when I was still only a boy. My father divorced my mother and I was sent away; and just before that, I saw my father betray George Wishart, so that he was burnt at the stake. My father lied to him, right in my presence, swearing he'd be safe. Then he arrested him and turned him over to his enemies. You can see why I have no use for liars, why I hate them so." He bent down and carefully folded the cloth his food had been wrapped in.

"Ah." She sighed and twirled a piece of spongy moss in her fingers. "Fortunate is he who knows his own world and is allowed to live in it."

"We often find that we must choose our own world, decide for ourselves where our home will be, then hack out a place for ourselves. Come." He gathered up his horse's reins. "I have a bit more to patrol, then a visit to pay."

Patrol? Had he been doing that all along? He had not seemed particularly worried or watchful.

"The area seems empty and quiet," he said, again reading her thoughts. "We are not in the territory that sees much activity. But I wanted to make sure."

Over more swelling hills they rode, as the sun sank lower. There seemed to be no place where a man could hide, save behind the occasional drystone dividing walls running over the hills. But as the mists began to rise gently from the low-lying areas, she was not so sure. The mists, thin at first, quickly thickened as the sun sank behind the hills.

At length they came to a cottage made of stone with a thatched roof, nestled in one of the folds between the hills. Bothwell dismounted and tied his horse up outside, then motioned to her to do likewise and follow him. He knocked on the door and a man, past middle age but still sturdy, opened it a crack. He stared for a moment at Bothwell, then called someone from within. Then the door creaked all the way open.

Mary stepped inside the low-ceilinged, one-room dwelling. A peat fire smouldered in the middle of the floor, where an iron pot was suspended over it, with a soup or brew bubbling. Several little dogs with long, silky hair began to bark.

The couple, dressed in frayed wool garments, were gesturing to Bothwell and offering him the only seat they had: a three-legged stool. He started to defer to Mary, but with a look she forbade him to reveal her identity.

"Bless ye, Earl, bless ye," the woman was saying, opening a leather pouch with coins which Bothwell had handed her.

"A man's life is worth more," Bothwell said. "But it is not given to mortal man to repay in kind. This is the best I can do."

"He was but a lad, not important in your forces," said the father. "And it was almost a year ago."

"What is a year?" asked Bothwell. "Do you miss him any less?"

"No," admitted the mother.

"Did I not promise?" said Bothwell. "I gave my word I would not forget your sacrifice. But your Rob was hard to find. I had to make many inquiries; forgive my delay in reaching you."

"But to bring this in person . . . we now wish to give you something as well, if we can," said the woman.

"You already have."

"I mean something to remember us by—to remember him. He'd want it—"

The bare little room offered nothing. Then Bothwell's eye fell on the dogs. "What sort of dogs are those? They seem to be all hair."

"They're Skye terriers, very loyal and fierce, they're one-man dogs. Good hunters, too, you'd be surprised, they don't look it. We'll be having pups soon."

"That is what I would like," said Bothwell decisively. "Two—one for myself, one for my mother. A male and a female, so we can make more of them!" His voice rose, and Mary realized that he genuinely wanted them, and genuinely knew and loved dogs. Another unsuspected thing about him. "I'll collect them later, then."

"Is this your wife, Lady Bothwell?" the man suddenly asked, eying Mary. He was ready to be deferential.

"No." Bothwell gave an amused smile that was barely visible in the dim light. "She merely rides with me this day."

"Is the Countess with child? I pray you may have an heir."

"No. She is not. But I thank you for your prayers."

The woman thrust an earthenware cup of the broth at Mary, and she took a sip. It was mainly water, with only the faintest trace of kale and beremeal. How did these people survive? She nodded in appreciation, and drank it all. It provided warmth in the stomach, but no nourishment.

After drinking his soup, Bothwell took his leave. "The debt is still mine," he said, after they thanked him again for the gold.

The moon was just rising as they set out across the moors and hills for Traquair. Behind them there was still a faint glow of sunset, while the moon shone with a fuzzy, shrouded light ahead of them. The mists were creeping higher on the hills.

Suddenly Mary was very tired, and wondered how she could remain alert for the journey back, which would necessarily be much slower in the dark and swirling mists. But at the same time she felt detached from her tired body and wished the ride to go on and never end. She wanted to ride behind Bothwell over the dangerous terrain forever, to stop intermittently and have him continue to surprise her with her own desire to be with him, hear him speak, look at him.

But he rode on ahead of her, not slowing or looking back.

He does not want it to last, she thought. He does not care to linger with me, as I do with him.

Desire so fierce and startling swept through her that she was first stunned, then bewildered. It was unlike anything she had ever experienced, or even prepared for: a strange mixture of yearning for possession, awe, and an actual physical ache that the words *hunger* and *longing* were inadequate to describe. At the same time she felt protective of him, as though she already possessed him, had always possessed him, even before she knew him. As though he had been reserved for her, set aside.

If only he would turn around, look at me! she thought. She willed him to. He did not.

By the time they reached Traquair House it was so late that the moon, muffled in clouds, was almost directly overhead. The mists had enveloped the house, and only the torches and the candlelit windows guided them to the courtyard.

"Ah, I'm tired," Bothwell sighed, swinging down off his horse and handing the reins to a stableboy. He strode quickly toward the front entrance, not waiting for her.

His tone is so offhanded, so dismissive, she thought. Yet if I commanded him to stop, he would have to obey.

"Wait," she finally said, coming toward him. "Do not rush away." Did she keep her voice free from command or complaint? She came up to him and looked at him while trying not to seem to do so. What was his expression? In the poor light she could not tell.

"This ride meant a great deal to me," she said, moving with him up the front steps. He gave a deprecating little laugh. "I would know more about the Borders," she insisted. "Will you take me again?"

"If you wish it, I will arrange it. Next time we can take some of my troops, and you can meet my allies. You would like Sore John and Archie Fire-the-Braes—"

No! Not others! she screamed to herself. I am sick of others, of always being in someone's company. I want to be alone, alone with you. . . .

"No, I think I would be reticent to ask the questions I need to in front of others."

"Whatever you wish." He turned at the door and made for his chambers.

"Will you not sup with us?" she asked.

"I will eat in my own chambers," he answered, over his shoulder, as he disappeared down a passageway.

"And so will you," said Darnley, who had suddenly appeared around the corner. "The rest of us dined hours ago." He looked her up and down, then shrugged. "I was concerned. I thought you might have met with an accident."

"With Bothwell?" she quickly said. "He knows the land and the people hereabouts so well there was no danger of that."

"Oh?" For a moment Darnley's eyes flickered, but the question died away. "I am happy you are safe, that is all," he said. "Come, my dear." He draped his arm over her shoulder and led her up the stairs to their chamber.

The stone balustrade slid under her hand as she leaned against it to keep herself as far away from Darnley as possible. She shrank from his touch. They had not lain together as man and wife since that time after Riccio's death when she had used that as a means to win him to her side. Then she had been so deep in shock she had felt like a dead person herself, and had not felt anything. But since then it seemed that every nerve in her body had become highly sensitive, and could not tolerate his touch. She had fled from him, had managed so far to be always out of reach. Now she was cornered and could not escape.

She had steeled herself to this, after her confession to Father Mamerot, knowing it must come, coming finally to view it as a test of her ability to sacrifice. She had even presented Darnley with a gift of a magnificent canopied bed, with violet damask curtains, violet-brown velvet hangings with ciphers and flowers sewn with gold and silk, and fitted with sheets of

Holland linen, as if that would somehow serve to be mother of desire in herself.

And now—now he was at her side, eager and pressing. And after Bothwell . . . when all she wanted was to be alone and think of Bothwell . . .

But as she thought of Bothwell, a strange excitement came upon her, and she shook.

"Are you chilled, my love?" said Darnley, feeling her shudder. "It was foolish of you to ride on the moors at night! Dangerous, and foolish!"

He kicked the chamber door open, and it reverberated on its hinges and slapped against the panelled wall.

"I am so tired," she began, as a prelude to what she hoped would be a miraculous reprieve for one more night.

"I know, and I want to soothe you," he said tenderly, closing the door and taking her in his arms.

There would be no reprieve.

"I fear I must rest, I feel almost faint," she persisted.

"Here, lie down. Let me wait on you," he said, leading her to the bed. She climbed into it and lay down, stretched out full length. Above her the embroidered hangings with the armourial bears of Traquair looked down in merciless amusement.

Darnley began to massage her feet, rubbing them as if they were the feet of a saint. He kissed them reverently, and it was all she could do not to jerk them away, or kick him.

Oh, I cannot, I cannot, she thought. I cannot bear it!

Perhaps you should look on it as your punishment for the thoughts of Bothwell. Fitting that it is tonight you must pay the price. Coveting your neighbour's husband. For he's married, and it was you yourself who provided the wedding gown for his bride.

"Ah, now I see you smiling," said Darnley. "Would you forgive me, my love, I must—absent myself for a moment." He slid off the bed and made for the garderobe to relieve himself. Mary quickly removed her clothes— she did not want him to do it—and put on a thick, woollen-lined night dress that buttoned up around her neck. She took the pins from her hair and loosened it herself. She bent her head forward and shook it, feeling strangely aroused by the thick luxury of her own hair. What if it tumbled down around Bothwell's face as he lay on his back? What was Lady Bothwell's hair like, in bed?

"If you could see your face," Darnley murmured.

She opened her eyes to see him standing across the room from her, awestruck. His slender young body was outlined in the moonlight, his arms motionless at his side.

She looked at him, objectively, remembering when his ivory slenderness had appealed to her. But it had been an aesthetic response, the same feeling one feels looking at an exquisite carving, she suddenly realized. It has nothing to do with—it is nothing like—

As a beautiful object, he appealed to her. But only as an object, perfect in its workmanship.

It is what I must do, it is my duty, and my punishment for all I have done that is wrong . . . now I must atone, she thought. And I am not even allowed to choose my own atonement. I would far rather fast a month or walk barefoot to Rome. But instead I am commanded to do *this*.

He clasped her to him with a gasp. "I thought never to feel your arms round me again," he cried. "O God, I love you past idolatry!"

He climbed up into the bed with her.

"When you presented me with the bed at Holyrood, with its beautiful curtains and hangings, in my favourite violet-brown . . . I hoped . . . but I did not dare to believe . . . that I was forgiven and that you wished to be wife to me again. Then you did not come. . . ."

"Hush, Henry," she said, smoothing his hair. He had started to cry. Not this. Not a long talk, with the lovemaking postponed. No, she could not bear it. If it did not happen tonight, she could not promise herself that she could bring herself to the brink again. She must arouse him to the act and leave this mewling behind.

She pulled his face up to hers and began kissing him. His tears stopped. He began to kiss her hungrily, biting her lower lip and taking it into his own mouth.

She felt his slender, almost bony body pressing hers. There was no strength in it, just need. In pity and charity, she unbuttoned her own gown and let him feel her naked flesh against his. He shivered and began to cry. Quickly she ran her hands over his back and kissed his bony shoulders. This crying could not continue.

"Mary—wife—you may have heard that I have gone where I should not in Edinburgh, sought out women—I was wrong—I shall not sin again—"

"Hush," she repeated. As if she cared whether he sinned with whores or not!

But I am supposed to care, she cried to herself. I should care that my husband does wrong. . . .

But her inner voice was almost drowned out by the insistent noises of Darnley's desires. He was lying on her, trembling and indecisive as to whether to worship her or ravish her. She kissed him with every verisimilitude of passion to try to push him to the physical act. She could stand it now.

He responded like the twenty-one-year-old he was, blood surging. She lay back and allowed him to make love to her, willing herself to think of something else . . . of the hawks soaring overhead today, of the black pool of water between the boulders where she and Bothwell had stopped today. . . .

At the thought of him, all her muscles tensed and gave Darnley a jolt. He cried out, interrupted, but she soothed him. He subsided.

Think of the sky, so blue beneath all those chasing clouds . . . think of the cottage, a hut, really . . . those people . . . they looked so much older than they probably were . . . will they give Bothwell the dogs? The dogs were odd-looking, but they said they were hunters . . . how can they run with all that long hair . . . ?

Darnley cried out and clutched her. Was it over, then? She kissed his forehead. It was beaded with sweat. Yes, he was done.

Thank God, and all the saints, especially the virgin ones! I got through it! she almost wept to herself.

"Mary, Mary," he was murmuring. "Ah, my Mary!"

"Sleep now," she said. "Sleep here beside me."

Contented, he curled up and fell instantly asleep on her shoulder.

In a few moments she slid out from under him and reached for her gown that was lying on the floor. Drawing it over herself, she made her way over to the window and looked out over the grounds. The clouds had parted and broken up. They lay in opalescent clumps all across the sky.

Not far away, the River Tweed sparkled as it ran past in the full moonlight. If she had been nearer it, she could have heard the murmur and tumble of its shallow waters over the rocks. What was the rhyme that Bothwell had taught her about the Tweed?

> *Tweed said to Till—*
> *What gars you run so still?*
> *Till said to Tweed—*
> *Though you run with speed*
> *And I run slow,*
> *Where you drown one man, I drown two.*

So the Tweed was dangerous, though it might look tame here, near the house. They had dined on salmon and trout from its cold waters on many evenings, and it had seemed a benign river.

The moon shone in the courtyard, touching each of the rounded cobblestones with light. The trees dipped and swayed slightly in the wind, waving their fat August leaves like fans.

The entire house was dark. Even Bothwell's rooms, which she had made a point of noting.

The next morning they all gathered on the stone forecourt, where Sir John had set out chairs and tables. The sun was already dappling the leaves and promising fine weather for another day; the pale, drained moon was just setting in the west.

"Pray help yourself," said Sir John in a jovial tone, as the servitors passed the heated ale in small tankards, and plates with eggs in mustard sauce and cold mutton.

Bothwell took a platter and sat down easily. He threw one arm over the back of his chair and drank some ale, his throat rising and falling as he did so, then he ran his tongue over his lips and set the tankard down.

"You had a long ride yesterday," said Sir John, as if it were not a question.

"Indeed," Bothwell replied, chewing his mutton and swallowing it before answering. He smiled, showing white, even teeth. "In distance not so great, but in time, what with the steep and winding paths, many hours. But I saw what I needed to see." He picked up the tankard again.

As did I, thought Mary.

Her feelings for him had not gone away; indeed they had intensified, as if by magic, in the hours when she had not seen him. The interlude with Darnley had not affected them.

In France, her tutor had once taught her that to truly fix an image in the mind, to fasten it down completely so that it remained forever captive and vivid, she should carefully name each aspect of the thing to herself, as though she were describing it to a blind person.

"For, *ma petite*, such is the fickleness of the human mind that it soon lets go of whatever it sees; if you would keep it, you must tack it down with words." She had tried it and found that it worked on flowers, rooms, faces, ceremonies.

Now, when she wanted to keep Bothwell forever as he was at this moment, sitting near the entrance to an old hunting lodge on this fine August day, in his thirty-first year, she began silently to name his features.

Behind him are the soft, cream-coloured walls, and they have ivy growing part of the way up them, above the rectangular windows. The sun is hitting the walls, but Bothwell is still shaded by the long shadows of the trees guarding the house.

His head is round and rather large for his body. His hair is almost red but not quite; it has enough brown in it to soften it. It is cropped short like a soldier's, and his ears show. They are beautifully shaped ears, and they hug his head. He has wide earlobes.

His skin is taut and tanned and clean-shaven, and his jawbone shows prominently. His lips are wide and curved, and faintly pink.

His neck is thick and sun-browned like his face, and his shoulders are broad. He is wearing a rust-coloured leather hunting shirt, but even though the sleeves are full I can see the muscles which make his arms so large. His hands are big, with blunt fingers and no rings.

She looked farther down at his muscular legs, well outlined in his riding breeches, and at his sturdy wide feet in their low-heeled boots.

Then she looked back up at his eyes.

There is a scar above his left eye from the fight he had with Cockburn of Ormiston. But he has no other injury and even has long eyelashes. His eyes are a green-brown, the colour of winter moss.

"Is there something amiss?" Bothwell was speaking to her. "You are staring at me as if there were an insect crawling on me."

"There was one," said Mary, horribly embarrassed, "but he flew away. He was on your—your—"

Everyone laughed, and Mary blushed.

"So that is why your eyes were riveted to his—his *what?*" said Darnley snidely.

"Nothing," snapped Mary.

"Well, well," said Sir John hastily, "what is your pleasure today? Shall we try to hunt in the Ettrick Forest, and hope the poachers have not been there first? I am mortified about what happened yesterday."

"I fear I must depart," said Bothwell. "This is a pleasant interlude, but duty, in the form of the Elliots, is calling. They are by no means broken yet, and time grows short." He stood up and took one last draught of the ale. "I mean to have them all at our mercy by October."

"Then shall we hunt together?" Darnley asked Mary. "That is, if you think you can sit a saddle after last night."

"She is a fine horsewoman; the ride yesterday did not even begin to test her limits," said Bothwell.

"No, I mean after our ride in the bed last night," said Darnley, almost cackling with pride.

Mary gasped in hideous embarrassment. Not at Darnley's repulsive bragging, but—and this realization embarrassed her even more—in shame that Bothwell should know that she had given herself to Darnley, in this very hunting lodge, a few rooms away. She hated him knowing.

"Come, perhaps you are with child!" yelled Darnley. "And, good people"—he winked lasciviously at Sir John and Bothwell—"ought we not to work a mare when she is in foal? Come, let us ride, and ride, and ride!" He laughed and reeled around and around, spilling out the contents of his tankard.

"Drunk!" cried Mary, shocked at the revelation. "It's true, then, what they told me, your drinking has become worse, your constant, foulmouthed drunkenness! It is only nine in the morning, and how many of these have you had?" She kicked the tankard and sent it rolling down the cobblestones and onto the grass. "You drunken, stupid fool! You'll never touch me again!" She slapped him on the face so hard it sent him spinning around even faster. His legs tangled and he fell in a heap.

The servitors, hovering near the steps, froze in position.

Suddenly she felt strong, wide hands on her shoulders and a commanding voice in one ear. Bothwell was bent so close to her his lips almost touched her cheek. "Quiet. Let him lie there. Do not demean yourself." He let her go and stepped back.

"Sir John, I must take my leave." He looked disdainfully at Darnley, sprawled out on the ground. "May I suggest fresh cider or perhaps milk with your future breakfasts, Your Majesty? Good day." He turned and walked across the forecourt and into the house to collect his belongings and make a speedy retreat.

Once he was gone, Mary threw her head in her lap and began to sob. She was more miserable than she had ever believed it possible to be. Then she wiped away her tears and commanded herself to cease crying.

She left Darnley still lying in a huddle on the ground, shaking and whining.

I will leave here, too, she thought. I will take the little Prince and bring him directly to Stirling and give him into the care of the Erskines.

Within her chamber, she lifted the sleeping infant from his elaborately carved rocking cradle, a gift of her host. It was of dark wood, lined with padded velvet. The two-month-old baby, his face now filled out and his plump cheeks flushed, stirred and opened his deep blue eyes.

A rush of fierce love and pride shook her as she looked down at him. It was all worth it, then, so that this child could have been created? Hearing his breathing, holding his warm body, the answer felt like yes.

"Dress him for travelling," she told Lady Reres. "And pack all his things." She turned to Sir John, who had followed her. "It is necessary that he be transferred to the safety of Stirling Castle, as I once was," she said. "It is customary for the heir to the throne. And it is almost the appointed time . . . what matter a few weeks one way or the other? Gather your men and make me an escort within the hour."

"Your Majesty, do not do this in haste or anger—"

They could hear Darnley stumbling into the hall and then climbing the stairs toward them.

"And lock *him* up!" she cried.

Sir John looked in genuine pain. "Your Majesty, I am not allowed to lay hands on him. He is the *King* . . . have you forgotten?"

"Yea, wife, have you forgotten?" Darnley's slurred voice sounded from the doorway.

Mary clutched the baby more tightly.

"I have not forgotten that I granted you the title of King. But you have not been anointed or crowned, or recognized by Parliament. Nor will you ever be! Now"—she raised her voice and called for the chamber guards— "I give orders, as the only anointed sovereign in the realm, that you restrain the Earl of Ross and Duke of Albany here. Confine him to his chambers until he recovers from his temper-fit. Should he become violent, bind him."

The guards looked to Sir John, to Darnley, and then back again to Mary, then reluctantly stepped forward and grabbed Darnley's arms. He attempted to throw them off, but could not.

"I go to convey the baby Prince to his nursery in Stirling, where he will be raised in safety. When you recover, you may follow," she said to Darnley. "Take him away," she ordered the guards.

"You will pay for this!" snarled Darnley. "You will go to join your beloved Riccio, and there will not be anything left to bury! No need for you any longer—you've produced the Prince! No need—no need—your life is worth nothing. . . . " His voice died away as he was dragged down the hall.

"The feeble, unimaginative threats of a coward," said Mary, pretending to a disregard she did not feel.

"I beg you, be vigilant. A coward is the deadliest enemy there can be," said Sir John, alarmed.

Mary hugged the baby one more time before handing him to the nurse. "A coward is dangerous only if he has accomplices," she said. "And there is no one now who would intrigue with him, after he once betrayed them all." She sighed and smoothed her skirts nervously. "And if I were removed, before he had title to the Crown Matrimonial, he would no longer be husband to a Queen, but just a—a male dowager!" She began to laugh in jerky little gasps. "He would have to go about in a white veil!"

Just then she heard a clatter of hoofbeats in the courtyard, and leaned out of the window to see Bothwell astride his chestnut horse. His reddish hair glinted in the sun, and he wheeled his horse about, looking up at her window.

"Fare thee well," he said. "I shall see thee in Jedburgh." He stared at her, as if he had watched everything that had just happened.

"God keep thee," she said, feeling her strength departing with him. Slowly she waved at him, and he saluted her and turned away.

I used *thee,* she suddenly realized. I have not used *thee* except to my mother and my child and my once-husband.

And he used it to me.

❧

"You have my heart," Mary said to Lord and Lady Erskine, handing them the bundled baby that was the surety for Scotland's independence. As he left her hands, she felt a pain almost as great as when he was born.

Poor women do not have to leave their bairns, she thought. Nor does John Knox have to surrender his sons into the keeping of another family.

"We will guard him as our own," said Erskine. He nodded to the formally dressed chamber attendants, and a plump matron stepped forward and took the baby. James cooed and reached out a hand to her face.

"She will replace Lady Reres after a fortnight or so," said Erskine.

No, no, I cannot bear it! screamed Mary to herself.

Now you know how your own mother felt, she thought.

"Come, you must know that he will always be yours," said Erskine. "You may come here and spend as much time with him as you wish. You will select his tutors and consult with them about his readings and schoolwork."

But I will not be here to see him struggle with his lessons and learn his games. I will only be shown them after they are practised and perfect. I will not comfort him the first time someone hurts him with words, or answer his odd, unexpected questions. . . .

"Socrates' gaoler said, 'Try to bear lightly what needs must be,' " said Erskine.

XXXIII

Mary returned to Edinburgh after a few days spent with the Erskines at Stirling, seeing Prince James settled. Then she rode slowly back to her capital. She tried to think of the baptism, to plan for it. It would be glorious, and throw Scotland open to the world. For a few brief days the French would come, and see what had become of their erstwhile Queen, after leaving their realm. She would take pride in welcoming them. And Elizabeth? Would Elizabeth actually come?

But planning for a fête, no matter how magnificent, could not still her anxious heart. The happenings at Traquair had shattered the platform upon which all else was erected: the finality of her marriage to Darnley, her need to honour it, to forgive and endure him, to consider herself dead to anything else. Her sudden preoccupation with Bothwell so profoundly disturbed her that she thought about it continually, as a problem to be solved. She analyzed it constantly, seeking some explanation for it. The logical ones she found were that in her detestation of her husband she had imagined qualities in Bothwell to distract her from the dreadful truth that she was afraid to confront about Darnley. Or that he simply appealed to her memory of her uncle François, Duc de Guise, the great warrior Le Balafre, complete to the scar on the face. As a child she had thought him the ideal man; now she saw his shadow in Bothwell. Or that, because he had rescued her from Holyrood after Riccio's murder, she had confused gratitude with attraction. There was a simple explanation for it, she was sure, one that, in explaining it, would nullify it, render it harmless.

As soon as she returned to Holyrood, Darnley fled from Traquair House into the countryside to go hawking. She was relieved that she did not have to see him, but knew that eventually he would have to be fetched back. Oh, would this never end? What was the answer?

It was time to call back the lords who had been punished by being sent away from court, particularly Maitland. All must be tranquil for the great public ceremony; when the noble foreign guests arrived, they must not find half the court in banishment. Maitland returned, along with Argyll. Lord James and they were all reconciled with Mary.

Things are back as they were, she thought. At least on the surface.

John Knox had taken refuge in Ayrshire in western Scotland, and was not present to plague her with sermons or threaten her about the baptism, which she hoped would be according to Catholic rites. She needed to settle that with the Lords of the Congregation.

Accordingly, at one small Privy Council meeting, Mary brought it up to Lord James, when he inquired as to who would officiate at the ceremony.

367

"I had thought . . . Archbishop Hamilton," she said quietly.

There was a moment of deep silence. Then Lord James said, "A Catholic?"

"Yes."

"The people will not permit—" began Maitland.

"The people must have expected it! The Prince's mother is Catholic, and his father"—painful subject—"comes of a Catholic family!" she said.

"But he is the heir to the throne of a Protestant country," said Lord James.

"Do you expect me to have John Knox perform the baptism?" she cried. "I realize his country will be Protestant. Why do you think I am content to have Lord Erskine train him—Lord Erskine, a good Protestant? I *want* my son to understand that faith. But for his baptism—nay, it cannot hurt him either way, and it will help *my* conscience. A Catholic baptism is no bar to becoming a Protestant later—as every one of you can attest, as well as John Knox!"

"So you are willing to entertain the idea that he may choose freely to be Protestant, once he reaches the age of reason?" asked Lord James cautiously.

"Yes, of course. None of us can have our faith chosen for us by our parents; if our faith means anything, we must choose it for ourselves. But no one can choose from ignorance. One must know something in order to be free to choose *or* reject it."

Maitland smiled. "She makes perfect sense, and a good case. I say let the ceremony be Catholic if the Queen wishes."

"Very well," said Lord James grudgingly. "Now, as to the costs—what is your plan? I know nothing of such ceremonies; we never have them in Scotland now."

"Since the Prince has godparents from three countries, each will send an ambassade of at least fifty persons; and then there will be the banquets, the fireworks—I cannot reckon now exactly how much. But I will look at the books kept in the Exchequer House and see how much the treasury can allow. I will do this immediately, so that if a tax is necessary—"

"Oh, the people won't stand for a tax," said Lord James quickly.

"If a tax is necessary," she continued evenly, "I am prepared to make concessions that the people may find acceptable. Or even welcome."

Within the week she moved to the Exchequer House, a dwelling on the Cowgate—the street that ran parallel to High Street—ostensibly to avail herself of the account books at all times, in reality to do both that and have privacy. She found that she could think best in small rooms without the protocol of palace life, not to mention the watchful eyes of the court.

She took her secretary, Claud Nau, who was so good with figures and had a working knowledge of the expenses of such a celebration, and Madame Rallay, and in a few days Lady Reres joined her, having been replaced at Stirling. She brought news of Prince James and all his nursery arrangements.

368

Mary soon discovered that she enjoyed going over the books of both the government and her household. She found the old ones, going back to her mother's reign, and delighted when she saw the first entry for herself— "white taffeta for the princess's baptism." Sometimes she would call Lord James or Maitland to consult over an entry, to explain notations in abbreviation, but mostly she liked to puzzle over them herself, leaving the books open to the area in question. She would thus be able to work on them continually as she pleased, without worrying about losing her place in them.

Her initial understanding, however, was correct: the crown had very little money, not enough to finance the celebrations on the scale she wished. Very well, then, there must be a tax.

"We are a poor realm, sister," said Lord James. "You have only to compare your coronation with that of Queen Elizabeth's to understand that. So the only way is a tax." Clearly he thought the baptism an extravagance, and a foolish one.

"It will not help us if the world perceives us as a poor realm," she said. "If we hide it and make a goodly show, it will stand us in good stead later."

"What of—the King?" asked Lord James. "Will he behave himself and attend? There is no point in borrowing money, and putting on a show, only to betray to the world what we have as a King. I know he objected to asking Queen Elizabeth."

"He'll come, he'll come," said Mary, with an assurance she did not feel.

The weather turned nasty—cold, rainy, and dark. Mary was loath to leave the Exchequer House, which had become her retreat from the world, and now she was trapped inside it. She retired to her private chamber and read in a comfortable chair before a fire, revelling in the few hours of complete privacy and lack of outside demands. The rain dashed against the windows.

She looked out and saw women hurriedly taking in bedding that they had been airing in the adjoining courtyard. When the house servant brought up more logs for the fire, she pointed out the dwelling attached to the courtyard and asked, "Whose house is that?"

"David Chalmers, Madam," he said. "Lord Bothwell's servant."

"A fine house for a servant!" she said, surprised.

"Oh, he's more than just a servant—he's a companion, a friend who serves him. Yes, Chalmers lives here most of the year."

Mary stood gazing down at the house. Had Bothwell bought it for him? How generous he was with his friends, then! The house was four storeys. She saw lights being lit, and that enabled her to see into the rooms, which seemed to be well furnished.

Bothwell. She had had no further news of him than that he was busy in the Borders, as she had ordered him to be.

Sighing, she returned to her book. The candle was guttering in the strong wind that managed to create a draft in the room. She would go to bed soon. One of the happy things about her stay here was that she made her own hours, in deference to nothing but herself.

She yawned. Perhaps it was time for bed now. Yes, she would call Madame Rallay, put on her night attire—

There was a soft knock on the door.

"Enter," she said.

Bothwell stepped in.

She was too surprised to act surprised. It was impossible that he be here. He was here. She stared at him. "This is not Jedburgh," she said, matter-of-factly.

"No."

Only then did she look around. There was no one with him. No one had showed him to her room. "How did you—"

"I came to Edinburgh on the sly, I fear. No one knows I'm here. I am staying next door, at Chalmers's. Lady Reres kindly allowed me in, through the back door. The courtyards are adjoining."

"Lady Reres?" she said. "Why—yes, of course, you are old friends. . . ." Just so she must have let Bothwell in to see her sister Janet many times. Suddenly she was not glad to see him, she wished he would go away, back where he belonged, the Borders, or confine himself to her dreams. "What do you wish?"

"To talk to you," he said. "May I sit down?"

Only then did she see that he was splattered with rain. "Of course. What did you wish to see me about? Do you have a particular problem with the prisoners, or the date we had set for the justice court?"

"No. No, all is well there. But—"

"Pray sit closer to the fire. But what?" Now she was beginning to get used to him, to realize he was not an apparition after all.

"There is trouble here, I fear. Where is Darnley?"

"Hawking somewhere. I know not."

"You should have him followed at all times. Word has reached me that he has been plotting, sending and receiving secret letters from Europe, yes, even from the Pope! And that he plans to flee the realm. He has a boat in readiness—"

"Good!" she cried. "Let him flee the realm! Let him sail to Mexico, and dwell on top of one of their pyramids! I care not!"

"Perhaps you care not for his person," said Bothwell, choosing his words carefully, "but he is more than a person. He is a symbol, capable of being exploited by others. He can be 'Catholic,' or 'last male Tudor,' or 'heir-apparent' . . . what you will. After all, those are some of the reasons you sought to marry him. For what he symbolized. Is that not true?" His voice was gentle.

Miserably, she nodded. "It was partly my foolish desire to please Elizabeth, and place myself in the line of the English succession. Elizabeth had said she desired me to marry an English subject rather than a foreign prince. And there was Darnley, with his dose of royal English blood. And he *was* pretty, and tried so hard to please . . . and I thought I loved him, he was different then, or he seemed different. . . ." She felt herself close to tears.

370

She did not mind saying these things; Bothwell had already seen them for himself first hand.

"Poor Queen," said Bothwell. "You only sought to please."

"Yes!" cried Mary. "I was taught that if I tried to think of others, tried to please, then I would be rewarded! And when I came here to Scotland, I tried so hard to please! But the more I tried, the more I vexed people— ah!" She threw up her hands and gave a choked laugh. "Remember how we talked, that day on the moors, about having a place where one belongs? Since then I have come to see that I never have, not really. You are fortunate. You have a home in the Borders and a home on your ships. The ships appeal to me."

"Yes, I know you love sailing; I heard how on your way to France you were the only one who wasn't seasick, or frightened of the storms. The sea has proved a country to many a countryless man. You should have been a sailor."

"Where have you sailed?" she asked. "Have you been to the far north? Have you been to the little isles in the west, the Hebrides?"

"Aye, I've sailed there. The seas around them are rough, and when you arrive, you feel you have made a true pilgrimage. They are truly other-worldly—of a world we do not, cannot, know. The bitter isolation . . . what drove the monks there, what kept them there in their little stone cells?"

"Ah! How I long to go! If only you could take me!"

He leaned back in his chair and smiled. "There is no reason why I cannot. Someday." He paused, then gave her a level stare. "If you survive your husband's plotting and treasons."

"I already have." But she hated to have it named. *Treason.*

"He is not done yet. I pray you, watch him. Set spies on him. Do not underestimate him."

Bothwell had not heard Darnley's threats at Traquair. If he had, he would have been even more alarmed.

"Very well," she said. "I must trust you, and heed your advice."

"Never underestimate such a man," Bothwell insisted.

"And you came all the way here to warn me of that?"

"Yes. Don't you think it is important? You seem very unconcerned about your own safety. Let me remind you of a soldier's maxim: never let down your guard, never assume the serpent is incapable of striking."

Gradually the attraction to him was creeping back. At first, stunned at seeing him, she had not felt it. She had been relieved that it was gone, like a person who finds a treasure with an elaborate set of instructions to go with it, burdening it. This feeling for Bothwell would be at best demanding, at worse bankrupting. Better to have found that it vanished of its own accord before any damage was done.

But it was here again, as strong a presence as the man himself. She felt convinced that he could see it, it was that palpable. At the same time she prayed that he would go away without any further ado.

She stood up. He stood up, following her example. She heard herself saying something about how kind it was for him to have come, how she appreciated it. Would he like any refreshments? My, how late it is, good night, I look forward to Jedburgh. . . . Was he following her to the door, whence she was leading him? She dared not look back.

His hand touched her shoulder, and she turned immediately in a way that meant his arm was around her. She was only six inches from him, facing him. He did not drop his arm, but brought up the other one to encircle her. He held her to him, gently. There was nothing in the touch but solicitation and kindness.

He feels sorry for me, as he did for those people in the cottage. . . . His touch is like that of a brother, only my brother's is cold. . . . He must be happily married, and sees me as—what did he say?—Poor Queen. His looks, his hands, all are brotherly . . . I know how looks and hands are when there is desire . . . I've seen and felt it enough when I did not want it . . . Chastelard, Gordon, Arran, now Darnley. . . .

Never had she wanted something so badly; never had she felt so rejected.

She lifted her face to look at him, and he kissed her.

She had been mistaken. There was desire there, great desire. His kiss was nothing like the one in the dream. It was lingering and sensual. She felt him breathing gently, easily, against her. It felt natural to be held by him, to be kissing him, without thought or hesitation. She loved the feel of his lips; they were smooth and promised intimacy at all levels, of which this was only a beginning.

All she felt was the lips, and the promise of them. . . .

Bothwell had pulled away. "No!" he said. "No, forgive me!"

She wanted to draw him back, but she could not allow herself to. He looked ashamed and confused. "There is nothing to forgive," she finally said.

"It will not happen again," he said, stepping far enough away that she was out of reach. "I can promise you that, if only you will forgive me this one lapse, this one presumption."

"There is nothing to forgive!" she insisted. "Pray, do not run away. The rain has become worse—" Outside they could hear the rattling of the rain on the roof.

"I must go!" he said, reaching for the door. "Remember what I told you about Lord Darnley!" He was out the door and gone in an instant.

Darnley! His last words were of *Darnley!*

With a storm of weeping, she threw herself on the bed. The sound of the rain drowned out her sobs, so that no one came to inquire about her.

XXXIV

After Bothwell returned to the Borders, he busied himself attacking his hereditary enemies, the Kerrs. In addition, he took an entire band of Armstrongs of Liddesdale; they were now imprisoned in the huge fortress of Hermitage Castle, and would be tried, and probably executed, when the Queen came to Jedburgh.

After three successful weeks in the field he returned to Crichton Castle, where Lady Bothwell awaited him. He was strangely eager to tell her of his exploits, perhaps because he wished to show her *his* part of Scotland was as dangerous and exciting as her beloved Highlands, and that *her* husband was more to be feared in the field than any Gordon.

He found her seated on a giant cushion before the fire in an upstairs chamber, drinking a goblet of wine and engaged in needlework. She scarcely looked up when he came in, which incensed him. She was always so calm, so self-possessed. It was all one to her whether he came or not, whether he had been hurt or not. He wanted to say something, just to see if she would pay attention to him, but stopped himself. He turned on his heel and walked out, just as she looked up at him with her pale, bulging eyes. As she saw him leaving the room, she smiled and went back to her needlework.

Bothwell found himself standing on the upper landing of the staircase, staring down two flights of stairs. He descended angrily, intent on returning to the stables, when he caught sight of Bessie Crawford, one of Lady Bothwell's young serving women, ascending with a tray. She tossed her head and seemed to be talking to herself. She was almost opposite Bothwell before she saw him and stopped talking, embarrassed.

"Pray continue your conversation with yourself," he said. "I enjoy eaves-dropping."

"Oh! Sire! I—I did not realize you had returned! Why was it not—not announced?" she stammered.

"I have spent the past three weeks sneaking up on people. It is a difficult habit to break." He lifted the covers of the dishes. Stewed hare. Scones. Cheese. He popped a wedge of cheese in his mouth, then followed it with a scone, waiting for the girl to protest on behalf of her mistress. "It can be gratifying to be a thief," he said. "Especially if one is truly hungry."

"I fear the Countess will be disappointed," said Bessie. "Now I must return to the kitchen to replenish the tray."

"Aye." Bothwell turned with her and followed her down the steps. She kept glancing over her shoulder to see where he was, and a smile crept over her face.

Across the passageway they went, then into the kitchen, where only one cook was languidly stirring a pot, and French Paris, one of Bothwell's serving men, was baiting some mousetraps with scraps.

Bessie put down her tray and asked the cook to refill it, while Bothwell whispered some instructions to Paris. Then he took Bessie's arm and firmly led her toward the door of the attached kitchen tower. In an instant they were in the small room that served as a pantry, and Bothwell closed the door and leaned against it, his arms crossed. "Paris will see we are not disturbed."

Bessie was staring at him, her little face white. But she did not back away when he reached for her. Christ! He needed a woman! He ached at the need of it.

He pulled her stiff little body toward him. She was bony, except that she had big breasts. He bent to kiss her, expecting her to turn her head and squeal, making soft little noises of protest, which would soon die away. He knew she was no virgin; Paris had had her, as well as the cook.

Sure enough, she bowed her head for a moment, allowing him to kiss her ear and her neck, before turning back to him. The obligatory demurring now over, she kissed him passionately and allowed him to feel her body. Without his even asking, she undid her bodice, and murmured, "Now you may do what you like," offering her melon-like breasts to him as if they were on a platter.

He was not much interested in kissing her pallid face or availing himself of the breasts; he wanted to relieve himself in only one way. She lay back on the floor and pulled up her skirts for him, accommodatingly. Now he knew the stories that Paris and the cook had told him were true. Quickly he undid his breeches and climbed on her, ashamed of the perfunctoriness of it, but needing to do it and get it over with. The sooner he was able to mount her, the sooner he would end this burning, throbbing call of his body, which was tormenting him—no thanks to his wife!

"Ah," she whispered softly as she felt him on her, probing her, then she gave the expected squeal when he entered her. "Oh, my Lord Bothwell, my Lord, my Lord . . ." Her voice was rising and he managed to put a hand across her mouth to silence her. But he was engulfed in gratifying himself and stopped heeding the noise; he thought he was going to explode if this exquisite teasing and torment of his body did not end. Thrusting and stabbing, he felt as if he were trying to skewer her from the inside, and then the long-sought relief flooded him and he groaned with joy.

But it had happened so quickly he was not even out of breath. And as soon as the waves of sensation subsided, he rolled away from her. It was over.

"That felt good," he said, lightly, reaching for his breeches. Bessie was still lying there, looking at him forlornly. He reached over and pulled her skirt down, covering her.

"Will you be wanting me again, Sire?" she asked sweetly.

He was taken by surprise. "Why, possibly," he said.

"I will be honoured to do it again," she said.

"Why?" he asked, curious.

"You know how to do it so well," she said matter-of-factly, "even when you are in such a hurry. I would like to see how you do it when you have more time."

He threw back his head and laughed. "I will do my best to satisfy your curiosity."

XXXV

Bothwell was up betimes. There was thumping and noise from the dungeon in the Hermitage; it was filled with Armstrongs he had captured the day before. He rolled off his camp bed and rubbed the muscles of his back and then felt his sword arm to see if it was stiff or sore. It had better not be; he had a mighty lot of work to do this day.

No, there was no tenderness there. He flexed his arm and made a fist. What a fine day yesterday had been, bringing in the lairds of Mangerton and Whitehaugh, the thieving bastards. Their peel-towers hadn't saved them. And now they could bloody well rot in there and wait for their trial when the Queen came.

When the Queen came. Oh, yes, he'd have more outlaws for her. It was going to be another fine day today. He knew it.

He crossed the damp stone floor in his bare feet and, stripping off his shirt, plunged his hands into the stone basin of water in the corner. He washed his face and then splashed his shoulders, shivering as the frigid water hit his flesh.

It builds character, he snorted to himself.

A trickle of dampness made little sounds as it ran down the walls. Even the inner walls had a sheen of moss here in the Hermitage.

Bothwell reached for his riding clothes—his linen shirt, his quilted outerwear coat of leather sewn with horn for added protection, his leather boots and breeches—pulling them on slowly as if he were not cold. Then he picked up his dag—his horse-pistol—his sword, and his dagger, and was ready to face the Queen's enemies. The Queen . . .

He and his men, a force of about a hundred troops, gathered just outside the colossal arched front wall of the fortress, which soared up like the portal of a cathedral, but seemed as dark and sinister as the gates of Hell. The barking of the scent hounds, lean black beasts, was fearsome as Cerberus.

"Ah, my men!" cried Bothwell. "We have another fine day of hunting!" Actually it was grey and misting, but that had nothing to do with the matter. "The Elliots! The Elliots! We'll attack the peel-tower of Jock o' the Park!"

The men were thunderously silent. Jock o' the Park was one of the most notorious and ruthless outlaws. And he had never yet been taken, or beaten.

Bothwell laughed as loud as he could, but the thick, insensate stones of the citadel soaked it up and it sounded weak.

"So you remember the verse?

> *"They leave not spindle, spoon nor spit,*
> *Bed, bolster, blanket, shirt nor sheet;*
> *Jock o' the Park*
> *Rapes chest and ark.*
> *For all such work,*
> *He is right meet."*

"Come now, won't he be a bonny prize?" Bothwell raised his sword and waved it over his head.

"Aye! Aye!" The men raised theirs, and then they all clattered over the rough planks that bridged the moat and galloped down alongside the burn, splashing through it and onto dry ground. They followed the burn as it flowed toward another, Liddelwater, where the two waters coming together formed the Park: home territory of the Elliots.

The countryside was in mottled autumn splendour, with purple streaks of heather on the steeper hills and russet and orange bracken and reeds near the trickling water. Patches of velvet-green grass spread out next to withered wastes of brown gorse on the hills, and glowed unexpectedly bright beneath fallen leaves and old yellow cattails. The sky was a pale pearl grey.

They passed thick rectangular peel-towers spread out along the heather-speckled braes of the burn, revelling in their own powerful horses and the misty day.

The mighty peel-tower of Jock o' the Park loomed up ahead, arrogantly sitting on a pasture at the confluence of the waters—a spot known to both the Scots wardens and the English as the very cockpit of the Borders, where the writ of neither side ran.

Bothwell gave spurs to his horse and raced ahead of the others to surprise Jock and keep him from escaping. But there were enough people about to see the lone armed rider approaching and warn their master, so before Bothwell reined in his horse and shouted at the tower, "I arrest you in the name of the Queen," Jock was already galloping away across the burn-bed and toward the hills.

Bothwell spotted him and debated whether to await the arrival of his own men to give chase. No, by then Jock would be out of sight. Quickly he turned his mount and lit out across the fields, galloping over the new-reaped stubble and between the upright sheaves, then into the thicker entangled broom as he followed Jock into the wilder reaches of the hills. Jock was climbing upward, leaving the watered valley; he had a mountain hideout he was making for, then.

I cannot let him out of sight, thought Bothwell, urging his horse forward.

The distance was closing: three hundred yards, two hundred yards, one hundred, fifty—and then Bothwell could see Jock looking over his shoulder, could even see the colours of the plaiding in his riding-mantle. The man was grinning.

"Halt!" cried Bothwell, reaching into his belt and pulling out his pistol. He fired it once up into the air, making the mountain fastness reverberate.

Jock reined in his horse, and kept that menacing, smug grin.

"You'd best keep your distance, *Lieutenant, Queen's Man*," he said, disdain dripping from every word.

"I'm my own man," said Bothwell. "And Keeper of Liddesdale. If you refuse to obey my summons, let us see who is the better man. I command you not only on my authority as officer—for what's an office but a bestowal and a title, and oft it ill fits the man it is hung upon—but as man to man. Single combat."

All the time he was speaking, he threaded his way closer to Jock until he was only twenty or thirty feet from him, in the little green clearing where he had stopped. Then, in one motion, he dismounted and unsheathed his great two-handed sword.

Jock eyed him curiously for a moment, then likewise dismounted. Carefully he took out his own sword and approached Bothwell.

"You are from another time," he said softly. "Do you see yourself as one of King Arthur's knights? Single combat!" He laughed roughly. "Or is there a sin you wish to expiate? No matter—I will help you punish yourself." He rushed at Bothwell brandishing the great sword. Bothwell barely had time to duck and recover his own balance.

He spun his sword arm out and his sword whizzed by Jock like a whirling blade, snagging his plaid. Jock pulled back, then took aim again, parrying for Bothwell's shoulder. The tip of his blade touched the padded leather and nicked it, but Bothwell did not flinch. Instead he lunged forward, startling Jock, pressing the edge of his sword against Jock's chest. Jock stumbled and then fell backward, dropping his sword. Bothwell covered him and forced him onto his back, making him helpless. He laid his own sword with meticulous care across Jock's neck, where the Adam's apple bobbed up and down.

"Now," Bothwell whispered, as if there were others who might be listening, "do you surrender?"

Jock, who still looked more surprised then frightened, said, "Yea." But had he understood what he was saying? Or was it just a trick?

"Will my life be safe?" Jock asked. "Will you guarantee my safety?"

"You must stand trial when the Queen comes to hold her justice court," Bothwell said. "But if the hearing clears you, I shall accept it and stand content. You shall go free."

"The Queen!" said Jock. "What does she know?"

"She knows of mercy. Too much for her own good, the good of the realm, and her own safety, perhaps. But in her mercy lies your safety."

"I accept it, then."

"Very well." Bothwell slowly took away his sword and released Jock from the hard grip in which he had held him.

The outlaw stood up as if his dignity had been trampled, and brushed himself off.

"You must return with me," said Bothwell. "I shall not do you the dishonour of binding you, for your word must suffice."

He sheathed his sword and walked back to his well-trained horse, who had been patiently waiting through all the scuffle. When he swung up into the saddle, he turned and saw that Jock had mounted and was galloping away, fleeing.

A liar. A man who betrayed his own word.

Calmly Bothwell took out his pistol and shot Jock, knocking him out of the saddle. The outlaw was lifted up with the impact of the blast and then, clutching wildly at his horse's mane, tumbled down beneath his hooves. The horse kept running, but Jock lay in a hollow, his legs sticking out of the heather and bracken. One foot was twitching and jerking.

"A man who breaks his word is lower than an animal," said Bothwell, riding over to the plaided huddle.

There was no sound, and the movement had ceased. He must be dead, or dying.

Cautiously Bothwell dismounted and made his way over to the heap, alert for any movement. But there was nothing but the abnormal quiet of eternal stillness.

Closer now, he could see blood staining the green and red plaid; it was hard to distinguish the new red from the red in the pattern.

The fool. Why did he not return with me? The Queen would have pardoned him, most like. She's yet to order an execu—

With a shrieking yell, Jock rose up swinging his sword and hit Bothwell in the arm, knocking him over a mossy, slippery stump, exposing him belly-up like a beast to be slaughtered. A further slash to the underside, tearing through the padded leather and ripping into his entrails . . .

A red tide of anger and shock and revenge took possession of Bothwell, running just before the pain, and he grabbed his own short, sharp dagger in his right hand, wrenching it out of its belt.

The face of Jock was right up in his own, grinning its death's-head grin, breathing its foul breath directly in his nostrils. Then with all his strength, a tiny second ahead of his own incapacitation, Bothwell plunged his dagger into Jock's chest, piercing through the cloth and deep inside, then pulled it out and managed to thrust it into a second spot. The grin faded from Jock's face, drained away like a water-bag emptying, and blood gushed from his mouth and spilled into Bothwell's face, blinding him. He felt Jock rolling off him, tried to stab him again and found only air, then suddenly a blinding, slicing force crashed across his head. Lights exploded inside his eye sockets, sending showers of sparks, different coloured and shaped ones, cascading like the fall of sparks from a blacksmith's hammer forging metal.

All sound dimmed, feeling receded, and only taste remained: the rusty, hot taste of blood pouring down his throat, drowning him, choking him, rising in a tide to carry him away, down a black, swirling chute.

There was no air. Bothwell's lungs were filling with blood, and he had no strength even to turn over to drain them. Blood gurgled and overflowed out of his mouth, like one of the thousand trickling burns, making its own well of crimson liquid, submerging his face.

XXXVI

ord Lieutenant Bothwell is dead," said the soldier, standing before Mary. He was tired and dirty from the twenty-five-mile ride from the Hermitage, so near the English border, to Melrose, where Mary was on the first stage of her journey to Jedburgh.

When the Queen did not speak, the man went on, "He was killed by Jock o' the Park, an Elliot. He rode on ahead of us, giving chase to Jock, and caught up with him out of our sight. By the time we got there, he was lying in his own blood, dead."

Dead? Bothwell, dead? No, it was impossible, unthinkable. He could not die. She heard herself saying to the man, "You must be weary. Pray refresh yourself," and nodded to the only servant in the room.

I should summon Lord James and Maitland, she thought. No, not yet. Not yet.

She seated herself gracefully and waited, hands folded, while the messenger—one of Bothwell's men, perhaps one he had spoken of earlier—drank two goblets of fresh-pressed cider.

I will see thee in Jedburgh.

Now, never.

"They took his body back to the Hermitage. I came directly here," said the man.

Body.

"Is he . . . has he been buried yet?"

Had they just given him a soldier's burial, shovelled him in? Or was there to be formal interment in a family vault somewhere? Bothwell would have preferred the former, she somehow knew.

"I did not go with them back to the Hermitage. I do not know what they have done with the corpse. Oh, I beg your pardon, I did not mean to offend you. If you have instructions—"

Corpse.

"I assume . . . Lady Bothwell's wishes should be followed." She had almost forgotten about Lady Bothwell. "Yes, you should go directly to his . . . widow, and inform her straightway. She must not hear it from others."

Dead. Quite, quite dead?

"How did he . . . in what manner was he mortally injured?"

"He was badly cut in the face and belly, and his left arm was both slashed open and broken, evidently from the force of the attack with a two-handed sword. But we'll never know from Jock. We found him dead a half-mile away, shot in the thigh and stabbed twice in the chest. Bothwell got him," he said proudly. "He just crawled away to die. He was slumped over a mossy stump, his blood still warm. Of course, so was Bothwell's," he added.

These details suddenly made it true. The broken arm, the warm blood—

"O God!" She burst into tears, and impulsively embraced the young soldier. He had seen him, had come directly from his side. There was blood on his sleeve—Bothwell's? She clutched at the spot. It was black and had a hard sheen to it.

She swallowed hard and pulled herself away. "Pray call my councilmen," she said to the attendant.

"What is it, dearest sister?" asked Lord James, as he entered the room a few moments later. He was all solicitation and hard eyes.

"Yes, what is it?" echoed Maitland, close on his heels.

Bothwell is gone and once again I am in your hands, with nowhere else to turn, she thought.

Now his loss, simply as a military and political ally, as he had started out, dropped like a weight into the net of despair where her love for him as a man already lay dead.

She held her head high and gestured to the messenger. "He will tell you." She did not trust herself to speak; and besides, she wanted to hear it again. Oddly enough, she wanted to hear it over and over.

The lad—he was little more than that—cleared his throat. "Lord Bothwell has been killed in a fray with Jock o' the Park. 'Little Jock,' they called him. Because he was so big." He laughed nervously.

Lord James and Maitland shot looks at each other.

"God grant him rest," said Lord James mechanically.

"What now?" asked the practical Maitland.

"We must proceed to Jedburgh as we had announced," Mary heard her calm voice saying. "The outlaws and reivers our loyal Lieutenant has arrested must not go free because of his death. That would be a mockery to his memory."

"Tomorrow, then, we proceed?"

"Yes."

She turned to the messenger. One was supposed to hate the bringer of bad news, she thought, but I never want to let him out of my sight. He is my last link to the living Bothwell. She looked again at his bloody sleeve. "Pray stay with us until morning."

There was no sleep for her that night. She was afraid she would dream of him again; nay, she knew it. And the anguish of having him alive in her dreams would only intensify her despair upon awakening again. It was better to stay awake, held in the very hand of pain, then to swerve from it and make it worse.

But lying awake was horrible, too. She felt his presence in the room, and feared to open her eyes, lest she would behold an apparition, all bloody and mutilated.

"I fear you, Lord Bothwell," she whispered, "and in doing so I know I wrong you, for you have never wished me harm. But you are another now, different . . . forgive me, I fear death and its changes, even to those I love. . . ."

With the dawn, the presence seemed gradually to fade.

The ride to Jedburgh should have been soothing, for there was beauty in the yellow October sunlight and in the lingering warm touch of the parting summer. They rode past the ruined Abbey of Melrose, its skeletal arches pointing toward the sky like slender ribs.

All dies, and is ruined by violence, Mary thought. The monks came here when Scotland was still wild and beyond the edge of civilization, and built their church, stone by laborious stone. But English violence destroyed it in a day; and if they had left it untouched, Knox's violence would have done their work for them. Bothwell tried to bring order to the Borders, but has been killed by an outlaw.

It seemed, on that golden day, that darkness, chaos, and disorder would always prevail, that sunset would always come early. The pale ribs of the ruined Abbey testified to that.

They were to lodge in a fortified stone house, a "bastel house," in Jedburgh, rented from the Kerr family. Jedburgh itself was a pleasant enough town, considering where it lay. It had been attacked numerous times by the English and had always picked itself up from the dust, like a village wrestler, set itself in order, and begun again.

There were three large rooms on the first floor of the three-storey house, with two on the next floor. The opposite-turning spiral staircase between the floors entertained them, they were so used to the normal kind. That night, lying in the cold, straight bed, Mary slept, and dreamed no dreams. There was no longer anything to dream of. She awoke thankful that the night had been blank, like being put in a locked black box.

* * *

The Court of Justice was to begin on the morrow. One by one the criminals would be brought forward, bound with rope or chain, before her for sentencing.

"Hang them," Bothwell had said.

Maitland had cautioned about the shortage of gallows and hangmen and advised mass drownings as more economical. "They are just as dead with water as with rope," Maitland had said.

"You are too merciful," Lord James had said, raising one eyebrow. "Just make sure there are executions."

૨

She sat in a high-backed chair with a cloth of estate over her head: a makeshift throne. The first person to be brought in was the notorious Willie Kerr, the father-in-law murderer.

"William Kerr, Laird of Cessford, you have been accused of killing your wife's father in the most heinous way, smiting off his head and arms by the axe. In addition to violating your marital duty and the Fourth Commandment—to honour one's father and mother—you have violated your spiritual duty, for the man was an abbot as well, and had even baptized your sons," recited the secretary, reading off the accusation matter-of-factly. "Judgement and sentence now rest with your sovereign Queen."

The man looked so ordinary. His shock of brown-and-grey hair stood up as if in fear, and his lined face was resigned, as it had been resigned to border reiving, warfare, burnings. . . .

"Mercy, Your Majesty!" he cried, flinging himself to his knees. "I sinned, I committed murder, but I repent! And my wife . . . she hated her father, he beat her and misused her, until she was so in fear of him she trembled at the sound of his voice, or even upon hearing his name. And besides— what business does an abbot have fathering children?" He stood up and his spine grew straighter and straighter. "He was a sinner, and I punished him! He was a stain on the Church! Do you wonder why John Knox and his mob have prevailed? It is because the Church has been besmirched by such as the Abbot!"

The man spoke true. The Church of Scotland had been undone, not by the greed of the King, as in England, but by the greed and ineptitude of its own leaders here. Cardinal Beaton, this Abbot of Kelso . . .

"I but struck a blow for honesty and justice, Your Majesty!" he cried. "Honesty in place of hypocrisy, abuse, and cruelty! And I stand ready to die for it! My death will not have been in vain."

"You shall not die," Mary said. "For you speak true."

She heard Maitland and Lord James snort with disgust.

Mary retired at midday to take some nourishment. Ten prisoners had been brought before her, and she had listened to their pleas. Not one had been sentenced to death.

382

Lord James and Maitland were so disapproving they withdrew into their own chambers and would not eat with her, although if she commanded them, they would have obeyed.

How can I sentence anyone to die who upholds his conscience? Mary asked herself. Kerr was right in what he said about the Abbot. But he was wrong to take the punishment into his own hands. It is hard to refrain; God is very slow to act, if we leave it to Him, as we are told to do.

She began picking at her platter of roasted partridge and cabbage. She had no appetite, not since the news from the Borders.

A knock on the door.

"Enter," she said.

A burly man, so heavy that his own flesh warmed him and therefore he had no need of mantles or capes, came in.

"I am one of Lord Bothwell's men," he stated. "There is glorious news! The Earl lives!"

"What?" Mary stood up, shaking.

"The Earl lives! We brought him back in a cart, all bloody and cold . . . so cold, the blood on his wounds had congealed, and he seemed not to breathe. But before we reached the Hermitage, he stirred. His wounds were not mortal." He threw up his hands. "And today he opened his eyes and inquired whether Your Majesty had been informed of his death. When we said yes, he ordered me to go immediately to tell you he lived. He seemed to care for nothing else. At least, not first."

"He lives?" The man must be imagining it.

"Aye. He lives and mends, on the hour."

"Is he—himself?"

The man laughed. "Indeed. He joked about Jock and was delighted he had not escaped. 'Ah, there's something to be said for the lowly dagger,' he said. 'When pistols and swords fail you, it's nice to lay hold of a dagger in your belt.' "

"Then he must be allowed to take his own time to mend. We shall come when the justice court is over."

For nine days she stayed at Jedburgh, administering justice. Daily she received bulletins about the progress of Bothwell. He had his arm in a sling. He ate three full meals. He went out in the forecourt of the Hermitage and talked to his men. He directed them on their raids.

At last all the malefactors had been paraded before her for sentencing, and she had not condemned anyone to death. Lord James and Maitland were clearly worried about her decisions, and kept insisting that only violence could cure violence.

"A fire is used to put out a fire," said Maitland. "These men understand nothing else. Your mercy is misplaced."

"You did not hesitate to avail yourselves of it," she said pointedly. "Why should the standards be different at court?"

"There is a difference between political disagreements and just plain pillage and murder," said Lord James.

"Riccio's murder was bloodier than what happened to the Abbot of Kelso. I see no niceties of difference, for all that the King's dagger had jewels in its handle." She did not wish to continue this conversation. "You have my leave to depart on the morrow. For myself, I will go to the Hermitage. There is much business to discuss with Lord Bothwell, if he is able."

"It is nigh thirty miles away," said Lord James. "You must start out early." He again raised that questioning eyebrow. "So you mean to ride over sixty miles in one day?"

"Why ever not?"

"Even in your flight to Dunbar, which was marvelled over, you only went twenty-five. And now sixty, just to cheer a sick man?"

"I go not to nurse him, but to receive and give reports!"

"Of course," said Lord James. "Then we shall accompany you. That is, if you will allow us to."

The dawn came up fair, but with an icy edge to it. They were in the saddle just as the sun was breaking over the tips of trees that were fast shedding their leaves.

Mary could hardly wait to be on her way. She wheeled her horse round in the cold air and said, "Let us depart, then. Our guide will take us by the shortest route!"

Out through the town's main street, past yet another ruined abbey, they trotted, until, reaching the open fields, they could gallop. The sheaves of grain glowed with frost, like ghostly sentinels, and the fields were silver. Alongside the fields were orchards, half harvested now. Ladders leaned against the trees, and baskets were scattered about on the ground.

But farther on, the tidy fields and orchards were replaced first by thickets and then by vast ranges of dun-coloured hills, with trickles of water cascading down their steep, mossy banks. A few white butterflies danced in the purple and brown heather and bracken, and hawks soared overhead in the huge skies, but the area felt abandoned and godless.

"Bog!" cried their guide, pointing to an area of thick reeds and grass that looked deceptively like everything around it. They skirted it.

By now the sun had risen almost to mid-sky and the temperatures were pleasant. They had been riding almost six hours.

"There!" he cried, pointing to a grey bulk on a rise two or three miles away.

Even at that distance it seemed big, and as they approached, it loomed larger and larger until it seemed like a portal to an ancient city. The grey fortress seemed to grow until it blotted out the sky and eclipsed the sun.

They approached the plank bridge that functioned as a drawbridge over the moat, but the sentries had been alerted to their coming as soon as they had been sighted at the crest of the hill. The portcullis was raised, and the guards ran to tell their master.

"Come, he lies in here," said one soldier, leading them past dank rooms where Mary could actually hear water dripping, and into one vaulted chamber where a crackling fire in a cavernous fireplace tried to keep the damp and dark at bay. Smoke filled the room, but it had a pleasant scent.

Lying mounded under furs and wool blankets, with a boy seated on a stool by his bed, Bothwell slept. As Mary approached him, she felt such trepidation her legs and arms grew chilled. But why? She knew he lived. She could see the top of his reddish hair, then, as she drew closer, his rounded face, with the eyes tightly closed. Instead of his usual tan, his face was pale and the colour of pear-flesh. She felt chilled all the way through at the vision. He looked like a corpse.

Then he stirred. One eye opened, then the other. He did not look pleased, or surprised, or comforted, to see her. The attendant brought over a short, flat board to help prop him up, as Bothwell began pulling off the covers with one hand and trying to use it as a lever to raise himself.

"Pray do not strain yourself," said the boy, sliding the board underneath his back and then stuffing blankets behind it.

Bothwell grunted and lowered his head until the boy was finished. Then he looked up and said, "Welcome, Your Majesty. My Lord James, Earl of Moray. Maitland." He ran his uninjured hand over his hair.

The movement, so telling of Bothwell, moved Mary in a way that words never could. She was flooded with delirious joy at seeing this little gesture, knowing that it described everything about him, everything that she loved.

Yes, loved. At the same time that word, which seemed to speak itself in her mind, sent a sickening feeling of doom through her.

Yes, I love him, but there can be nothing but shame and sorrow in it, and no good fate, she thought. In my very happiness lies embedded my woe; they cannot be separated.

And had I not known this, I perhaps could have gone on as I was, as Darnley's wife, wrestling with the ugly aftermath of his perfidy, and the deep antagonism of the Lords toward me, she thought. The lean diet of dullness, details, and depression could have been borne as a penance for my earlier ignorance in Scotland, when I first came, and even for the unthinking pleasures of my days in France when, idle and young, I passed what seemed to be perpetual summer. But now . . . I cannot go on . . . not as I was. Yet what I shall become, I fear to discover.

"We heard you were dead," Mary said quietly.

"Then I trust this is a happy surprise," he said. His voice, weak at first, became stronger.

"No surprise," said Mary. "We were relieved to hear by the next day that you were only injured, but not mortally."

"He woke up in the cart," said the bedside boy. "There we were, transporting the bloody corpse in this cart that was lurching and thumping and getting stuck every ten yards, when suddenly he groaned and moved. Well," he said with a gleeful laugh, "we ran! Have *you* ever had a corpse come back to life? It was only when we heard him cursing we knew it was no ghost."

"Cannot ghosts curse?" asked Bothwell. "I should imagine those are their first words. After all, who wants to be dead?"

Mary saw that his left hand was heavily bandaged, and that the bandage wrapping his head was soaked through with bloody fluid.

"My belly is the worst," he said, flinging off the covers with his good, strong right hand. His entire abdomen was so bandaged it looked like a padded jack, the quilted leather coat Borderers wore. "The wound runs lengthwise almost six inches. He got me when I was rounded over a log, asking to be carved like a pheasant. Ah, well. At least he's dead. Thus perish all the Queen's enemies," he said lightly. "*He* didn't wake up in the cart, did he?"

Maitland smiled at him. "No. And you will soon be well and fighting more enemies."

"Alas that the Queen has so many," Bothwell said carefully. "And the justice courts at Jedburgh? The session is completed?"

"Indeed," said Lord James. "We certainly would not have left betimes."

"Certainly. And . . . ?"

"Sentences were passed," said Maitland. "There were no executions."

"What of Kerr?" Bothwell's voice rose in disbelief.

"The Queen only fined him," said Lord James. "It seems she was touched by his tale of the Abbot's personal shortcomings. 'Twas not the way our royal father, James V, handled these criminals. I fear this womanish approach renders your wounds acquired in useless service. If Jock o' the Park yet lived, doubtless he'd have a sad tale to win a stay of execution, as well. Perhaps his son had the melancholy, or his hog choked on an acorn. How grievous!"

Bothwell was glaring at Mary. She shot a look at Lord James, commanding him to silence.

"If there are reports of your raids and of the other activities in the Borders, we shall take them back to Jedburgh and study them," she said as loftily as she could manage. "I have brought records of our proceedings for you to read. We will remain in Jedburgh during the month of October. When you are able to travel, we request that you come by litter to us there."

"By litter!" he cried. "Only pregnant women and invalids travel by litter!"

"I shall send one for you within ten days," she insisted. "And you will use it—by my command."

It was already midafternoon, and past time to be on their way. Mary had been loath to leave, but clutching the reports, she realized it was time. Darkness would overtake them on their way back.

The sun had come out, temporarily brightening the scenery, turning ochre into marigold yellow on the hills, dull deep purple into vibrant violet, sedge into bright brown. But that was short-lived, and before they had journeyed over three hills the sun vanished, all the colours dimmed, and mists began to creep up from the bogs, reaching long fingers toward the high places.

Mary was tired—nay, exhausted. Suddenly the prospect of the thirty-mile journey in the saddle seemed as daunting and impossible as going all the way to Jerusalem. Darkness was coming fast in the October afternoon, and their guide would have difficulty recognizing landmarks. Yet they dared not go faster, for the terrain was too uneven and dangerous.

Darkness caught them still fifteen miles from Jedburgh, in the midst of a vast waste that skirted peat bogs and was littered with boulders and scrub.

"The Devil's tract," muttered Lord James.

"Watch your footing!" cried the guide. "Keep in single file. I will dismount and lead." He held out a torch before him, testing each step.

The wind rose and penetrated their cloaks. It began to rain, a drumming, icy rain.

They would be out all night, Mary thought. Perhaps they should halt, erect some sort of shelter. Perhaps that would be safer. Perhaps—

Suddenly she lurched to the left as her horse foundered and his entire right side sank in a mire. The horse emitted a distressed cry, and the others stopped.

"What's that?" cried Maitland.

The horse, attempting to extricate himself, churned in the marsh. Mary was thrown off and landed in a cold, oozing slush laced with brambles. Her feet sank instantly, and she could feel no bottom. She instinctively flung her arms over the saddle and hung on. The horse was almost swimming in the mire.

"The Queen!" yelled the guide. "Stop! Help!"

He rushed over to her, thrusting his torch toward the commotion. The horse was neighing and frantically kicking the thick, slimy water.

"Climb on the saddle and over his back!" said Lord James. "The left side is safe! Come!"

Mary hauled herself up, the weight of her soaked skirts pulling her backwards. With one hand she clung to the saddle, and extended the other to her brother. He pulled her with such force she thought her arm would be wrenched off. She landed on top of him in a heap.

"There, there." The guide was calming Mary's horse and fishing for the reins. "Quiet, quiet." Gradually the animal stopped struggling. "Now." He carefully guided him toward the dry path, until the searching hooves found it. Then, with a loud sucking noise, spewing rotting vegetation and stinking water, the horse came out of the bog.

Mary, shaking with the cold, insisted on remounting him rather than switching horses with one of the men. And for another four hours she stumbled along, so exhausted and debilitated she could later remember nothing but the cold, the silence, the pelting rain, and the single flaring torch, leading on.

It was past midnight when they finally arrived back at the house at Jedburgh, but Mary did not know. Her teeth were chattering and she had to be carried into the house. When Madame Rallay removed her wet clothes she found her flesh to be colder then the cloth.

Warmth—in the form of hot wrapped bricks placed in the bed, a fire in the chamber, furs heaped on the bed—failed to revive her. She never opened her eyes but became delirious and then, by the following evening, unable to speak or, seemingly, to hear. First her legs, then her arms, became paralyzed.

"She is dying!" cried Bourgoing, in a panic.

"Of a fall in a bog?" asked Lord James, incredulous.

"A healthy twenty-three-year-old person does not collapse and die for no reason!" insisted Maitland.

"Her father the King did, after Solway Moss, and he was barely thirty," said the physician. "Royal blood is different. After a mental shock, the body can collapse."

"Bah! What mental shock?" said Lord James. "And *I* do not do such."

"Only half your blood is royal," the physician said pointedly.

"She is sinking!" Madame Rallay's voice rose in alarm. "Pray send for her confessor!"

Far away, Mary heard the soft voice of Father Mamerot, begging her to relieve her conscience of its sins and so enter Paradise. But she could not speak.

And how can I confess a sin that has not yet happened, but is more real than any of the rest?

"Speak!" he was begging her. But she could not.

"Her feet grow cold!" cried Bourgoing, and Mary was touched at the anguish in his voice.

He cares for me, she thought in gratitude.

But none of that seemed to matter, and she felt herself being lifted away, growing farther from them. Her only feeling was of deep sadness to leave Bothwell, and then that too faded, as something paltry and unsustaining. What she was being drawn to was so powerful it drowned out everything else.

She could suddenly see herself lying on the bed, could see Bourgoing frantically uncovering her and binding her limbs until they were all wrapped in white—a half-ghost. An assistant physician was applying hot oil, and she saw the gleam of the glass. It seemed amusing. Now Bourgoing was beating on her feet, slapping them rapidly, but she could not feel it. She was not there in that absurdly wrapped weak body.

She saw Madame Rallay, face twisted with grief, opening the windows to let her spirit pass. And she was drawn there, inexorably it seemed.

Maitland was wringing his hands in genuine consternation. And Lord James? His head was bent over the table in the back of the room, and he was writing something. It was difficult to see. She came closer, hovering just over him. A little chest was open.

He was inventorying her jewels!

She was dead, and this was his reaction!

A jolt of anger flew through her, and suddenly there was feeling in her lips. Bourgoing was forcing some wine down her throat, and it stung her cracked lips. It choked her. She was violently ill, instantaneously, and vomited onto the covers and floor.

The vomit dripped off her lips and she could taste it, and was sick again. She coughed and choked and was wracked with pain, imprisoned once again in her body.

"She lives!" cried Bourgoing, and dimly Mary heard Lord James scrambling from the jewel table over to her.

"Yes," he said coolly. "I do believe the Queen will live. The Lord be praised!"

XXXVII

or days Mary lay in the bed in that upper room of the Kerr's fortified house, trying hard to recover. She obediently drank the thinned gruel Bourgoing spooned between her lips, and gradually it was replaced by thicker gruel and then by eggs and bread pudding, and finally by stewed young chicken meat. She went from lying in bed to being able to sit at a small table and eat her food. But then she would have to lie back down.

And as she lay there, horrible thoughts would grip her. She would recover, but for what? Darnley? He had not even wanted to preside at the justice courts, for all he coveted the title of King. And now he was unreachable, off hawking somewhere in the west of Scotland. Had they even told him of her illness? Had he cared?

Thinking of him and her great folly in having bound herself to him, she would have paroxysms of anger and grief.

Yet there is the child, she would remind herself. It was my duty to provide an heir, the best one possible for our throne and later, perhaps, for the English one, and I did that.

If there were only the bad marriage, the marriage that is now no marriage, I could endure that. That is a Queen's duty. But there is more . . . the torture of Bothwell.

I became ill when I realized that the thing I most desired carried the promise of my own destruction, that if I could drink that potion, which I feel I must drink in order to live, than I betray everything I once was.

Oh, wretched, wretched Queen! she cried silently.

The leaves were swirling down, lazy spinning yellow wheels, the day Bothwell was brought to Jedburgh. She was sitting up at her little table, eating bread pudding with raisins, when she saw the single line of riders approaching, a great litter slung between two horses. Bothwell lay in it, his left arm still bound, his middle still thick with bandages. But his face—ah, his face!— was merry, and had colour. He was smiling, and she thought she heard him laugh.

They settled him on the floor directly below hers. She could hear the scraping and thudding as furniture was brought in and rearranged. If she strained, she believed she heard his voice. But the nature of a fortified house was to have thick stone walls and heavy floors, and true sound was muffled.

She would imagine him lying directly beneath her, and it charged each footstep she took, as she pictured him hearing it in his chamber.

On the fifth day after his arrival, she invited him to dine with her on her floor. He had no trouble negotiating the steps—his legs had not been injured—and emerged looking rather robust, considering his recent experience.

"I am gratified to see you mend so quickly," she said.

"A soldier cannot afford to take very long," he answered. "After the first week, the wounds have healed quickly. And you—you were taken suddenly, gravely ill!"

She had forgotten she had not spoken to him since; he had undoubtedly heard it from others. "Yes. I was thrown in the mire in the dark, and afterwards . . . I fell victim to a mysterious collapse."

But you know what it was, do you not? she thought. It seemed to her as if he could surely read her mind, as if he had been present with her every second since she rode away from the Hermitage that afternoon. But that was a foolish fancy.

"I am grieved to hear it." He was looking at her, taking in her new frailty.

"It is past now." She saw his look and wondered if she still looked ill. "I have been reading your reports. . . . Is it true that . . . ?"

For the rest of the dinner she attempted to discuss the Borders with him, and his duties there. "It is said here, in this patent, that your post carries the power to allow you to ride against rebels, attack them with fire and sword, besiege and overthrow houses held against you. It even says you can command assistance from neighbours, under pain of death, and direct letters in my name."

"Yes, Madam."

"Have you?"

"Have I what?"

"Directed letters in my name?"

"No, never. I would not hide behind your skirts, so to speak."

Darnley arrived, almost two weeks from the time she had been taken ill. She had seen his white horse approaching, seen his blue feathered hat from above, and been able to prepare herself. She drew on her robe and her velvet slippers and attempted to arrange her hair.

The door creaked open and Darnley poked his head in. His hat was cocked so that it was the feather she saw first, protruding into the room. Then his head followed.

"Oh, my love," he said, rushing to her side. He reached down to kiss her, and she turned her face so it was a cheek kiss.

Had he forgotten that the last time he had seen her he had threatened her life? How could he forget—or expect her to?

"I heard you were mortally ill!" he said.

"Yet continued hawking," she said matter-of-factly.

"Nay! I did not! I only heard two days ago! Someone kept the news from me! Someone—and there are many—who wish us ill!"

"You are chief amongst them. You play into their hands with your sulking, your statements against me, your withdrawals."

Yet could I bear it if he were underfoot, constantly attendant on me? she asked herself.

"If you would only listen to me . . ." he began, pacing. "Yet even here, I see, there is no place provided for me to stay! Lord Bothwell occupies my quarters! He keeps state there—"

"He recuperates. He almost lost his life in the defence of the realm." *While you were hawking.*

"He has no rights to the King's quarters!"

"They are not 'the King's quarters.' And am I obliged to keep chambers empty for you? They waited, Sire, whilst I alone sat for the justice court. They sat empty, as did your chair of estate, screaming, 'No King here, no King!' It is less conspicuous to have them filled. It calls less attention to your negligence!"

He glared at her. "I see I am not welcome here!"

"You are always welcome, when you are not drinking or in a rage," she said wearily. "But your arrival now is a bit after the fact."

He looked at her, his eyes searching hers. He wanted some confirmation of his importance to her, she realized. The same as I want from Bothwell. But I cannot give it.

"Adieu, then!" he said, flinging open the door and making for the stairs.

From the window she watched him gallop away, the muscular rump of his horse rounded and perfect.

He always had good taste in horses, she thought. She felt limp and weak, and climbed back into bed.

She had recovered, Bothwell had recovered, and it was early November. Time to leave this strange place of wounding and illness.

They set out, the entire company, riding eastward. Before her illness, Mary had meant to show herself to the people in this eastern march. It was the tamest of the three "marches," or districts, lining the border, each with its English counterpart on the other side. It was the corridor by which invaders always came up to Scotland, for the land was flatter and held fewer bogs.

At Kelso a company of a thousand horsemen joined them, under the command of the warden of the East March, Lord Home, to give ceremony to their passage. They made their way to the sea, but before turning northward Mary stopped and looked south. England lay spread out like a soft green blanket beyond the glittering River Tweed.

Maitland was riding beside her as she murmured, "England."

He edged closer and she became aware of his presence.

"I have never seen England," she said. "I imagined one could see the border, that it would be a tangible thing. Instead, one country just shades into another. They are not so different after all."

"Make no mistake, Your Majesty," he said. "They are quite different. And as for a border one can see, there once was one: the old Roman wall. But it is farther south. So the English can congratulate themselves that they succeeded in extending their borders and encroaching on our territory."

"It looks so beguiling, so harmless," she said, staring at it. Prince James would rule there one day, she knew.

"Like a snake underneath a green leaf," said Bothwell, suddenly beside her. His voice was as strong and sure as ever. "Believe me, danger lurks there, however beguiling it may appear."

She cast a last look at it. "Someday the realms may be one, and this border no more than a memory."

"Not in your lifetime, it goes without saying," said Bothwell.

She winced to hear him speak of her death so offhandedly.

They turned north now, and the cavalcade made its showy progress toward Edinburgh through Eyemouth, Coldingham, Dunbar, and Tantallon Castle. Mary wore the costumes she had brought for such an occasion, and put on the embroidered taffeta hats with their coloured feathers, the Highland mantles lined with satin, the riding habits trimmed in gold braid and ornamented with pearls and topaz. She waved and smiled to ever-greater crowds who gathered along the main road.

But she was still weak, and at the invitation of the Laird of Craigmillar Castle, and the urging of Bourgoing, she agreed to stop two miles short of Edinburgh and spend further time recuperating at the castle, a stone bastion situated on high ground, with a distant view of the sea.

XXXVIII

othwell slammed his fist into the straw-stuffed calf's skin as hard as he was able. He felt the pain hit his belly, travelling along the exact lines of his wound, and spread even into his good arm. Gritting his teeth, he pulled back his fist to do it again. He would do it as many times as necessary to build his strength back up. It hurt less today than it had yesterday. Being even temporarily crippled was a horrible experience, and he intended to stay that way as short a time as possible.

The stuffed calf's skin had been his idea, whereas the hot compresses and stretching had been the Queen's physician's recommendation—that affable Frenchman. Yet he seemed to know medicine well, Bothwell had to admit.

"Good day." The chamber door opened and Bourgoing entered. He nodded toward the stuffed skin, tied between two chests in this dry but cold and barren chamber in Craigmillar Castle. "I have already sent for the heated oil and water," he announced. "It is time to change the bandages." He patted a thick bundle of clean white linens under his arm.

Bothwell lowered his arm, which was aching. He was glad for an excuse to rest. Obediently he peeled off his shirt and waited, shivering, for Bourgoing's ministrations.

The French physician deftly removed the stained bandages and felt gently along the scabbed ridge of the great belly wound. "Mmm . . . mmm . . ." was all he said. He massaged unguent into the reddened skin. "This was an enormous wound. You will have a formidable scar."

"I await the day when the scab turns into a scar. I do not mind scars."

Bourgoing poked one of Bothwell's chest muscles and was surprised to find his finger could barely press it down. The man surely had muscles of iron, or as near iron as flesh could get. He murmured in admiration, "You will soon be out fighting again."

"Good. It is my charge and livelihood." Bothwell put his shirt back on.

"This evening you should apply the warm compresses," Bourgoing said.

"It will be a task for French Paris," said Bothwell. "You need not take your time for a valet's task." He grinned at the physician, reading his thoughts. "I promise to follow your instructions," he said.

When Bourgoing had left the grey, dull chamber, Bothwell turned again to the punching-skin. He pounded it with his fist, imagining it to be an enemy. Imagining it to be his greatest undoing, his lust for the Queen.

No intelligent man is undone by lust, he told himself.

Whap! His fist struck the skin.

That is for students and apprentices and old fools. An intelligent man harnesses his lust, brings it under subjugation, like an unruly horse. Or he even lets it serve him and bring him fortune . . . if another's lust proves his or her undoing.

Whap!

The business with the Queen . . .

He flinched as he remembered that shameful weakness on his part when he had kissed her at the Exchequer House. She had been alone, and he had always found her bonny . . . but it was a foolish thing to have done. Had he amended it sufficiently? Why did he feel as though it was still unsettled, or hanging over them? Yet to mention it again, to try to re-apologize, would be to emphasize it, give it new life.

Whap! That was what was so much better about encounters in the field—no ambiguity. Just fighting, the simpler the better. The best was single combat to settle an issue. But no one wanted to do that anymore. They preferred this business with "bonds" and assassinations. . . .

Now pain began to tear through him. His left arm felt as though it were on fire.

"So perish all the Queen's enemies," said a flat voice behind him. The Lord James stood in the doorway, his head cocked appreciatively, his gloves held in one flat palm.

Bothwell grunted and sat down heavily on a stool. "It grieves me to know she has so many enemies," he said. He gestured to the other stool and James sat. Bothwell picked up his wine flagon and poured out two cups without asking James if he wanted any.

James took one. "Yet she does. In many places." He took a sip of the wine.

Silence hung between them, with only the sound of the wind outside catching in the great stone windows.

"My sister—the Queen—" James finally continued, "at last regrets her marriage with her cousin, the Lord Darnley. She admits this openly. She has received a letter just today that makes her weep. 'How to be free of him,' she said, 'I see no escape.' And 'Would that I had died at Jedburgh!' "

" 'Will no one rid me of this meddling priest?' " Bothwell leaned back and threw one of his arms across the back of the chair. It smarted.

"The Queen would give anything to be free of the young fool and proud tyrant."

"Anything except give a direct order for achieving this freedom. 'Tis a prerogative of royalty to suggest the deed and then make others take the blame." He shot a look at Lord James, the craftiest man in Scotland. Only once had James come out in the open, in the Chaseabout Raid, and been severely trounced. It was not a mistake he would make again. He had taken care to hide all traces of himself in the Riccio affair. If he thought he could engineer a removal of Darnley in like fashion, using Bothwell as cat's-paw, he was mistaken.

"What do you want from me?" asked Bothwell bluntly.

"Only that you use your brains to devise some way that she can shed

him. There is annulment, divorce, censure by Parliament, trial for treason—
he did hold her prisoner and dissolve Parliament on his own usurped authority—mishap on the way to imprisonment. . . . Your own parents were
divorced. Perhaps you can persuade her to—"

"No. That was a different case."

"We mean to approach her and discuss all this. Maitland, Argyll, your
wife's brother Huntly, and myself. We need you to join us. She needs our
help."

Bothwell grunted again and took another draught.

"This is not treason! We mean to sign a bond and pledge to obey only
the Queen. Darnley has forfeited all rights—"

"To live?" A bond always had do with death, eventually.

"To be her husband, and to bear the title of King, even in courtesy."

The five men stood before Mary, their faces shining with nervousness and
sincerity. Mary herself, more slender than ever after her illness, stood very
white and still, looking from one face to another.

"Your Majesty, we are gathered here out of love and concern for you, as
loyal subjects," Lord James began.

Mary looked dreadful, Bothwell thought. Her face showed all the strain
of her situation and the demand of her recent illness. The colour of her
skin was gone, replaced by the dull sameness of chalky paste. Her voice
was weak and sounded resigned.

"Shall we sit?" she asked, and Bothwell realized she did not have the
strength to stand for any length of time.

She and the five men took their places in a circle of chairs near the
fireplace, which housed a good fire. The heat felt good. Craigmillar was a
very drafty castle, and its thick stone walls seemed to hold in the chill.

Lord James flipped up his cloak and sat down carefully. Just as carefully
he opened his mouth and spoke.

"We here"—he gestured to the others—"wish to help you in your dilemma. The Lord Darnley has proved unworthy of the high position to
which he was called, and for the sake of Scotland some remedy must be
found."

"Divorce," said Maitland, "would seem to be the solution. Certainly
there are grounds. His—"

"My faith does not permit divorce," said Mary in a small voice. "And
nothing must be undertaken that would prejudice my son the Prince's royal
rights."

"My own mother and father were divorced," said Bothwell. "Yet it did
not hinder my rights to succeed to my father's titles at his death." He felt
duty-bound to speak.

"Titles are not the same as a throne. And perhaps even a throne in
another realm as well," said Mary pointedly.

"An annulment is certainly a possibility," said Maitland. "The close
relationship—half first cousins—would raise questions. And—"

"No! An annulment is worse than a divorce! An annulment means a marriage never legally existed, and the offspring are left in no clear state!" Mary spoke in a surprisingly loud, clear voice.

Maitland looked abashed.

"There can be no prejudice, no impediments, to his title! Else all was sacrificed in vain! And think not to have some evil befall him, as did Riccio! No, although such things happen regularly here in Scotland, I will not have my conscience stained, nor my honour blotted, with such a crime! For I must face God and be able to look Him directly in His face!"

"Aye, aye," said Argyll soothingly. "Then perhaps he should be arrested and tried for treason by Parliament. The other conspirators in your servant's death were condemned and banished, while the head of the conspiracy and mischief went unpunished."

"Everything will be done aboveboard, lawfully, all approved by Parliament," said Maitland. "And although the Lord James is as devout a Protestant as Your Grace is a Catholic, he will put his fingers in front of his eyes and look the other way. That we promise you."

"I cannot stain my conscience!" she kept repeating, hysterically. "I cannot, I cannot—"

Bothwell dared not look at her.

"Leave it all to us," Lord James said smoothly.

XXXIX

Madame Rallay carefully placed the calvados-and-cream posset before her mistress as she sat at her little inlaid desk, not working, just staring off into space.

"Happy birthday, my dear Queen," she whispered.

Mary looked up and smiled in a preoccupied way. "Thank you," she said. Then she actually noticed what had been placed before her, and a genuine smile broke over her face. "You remembered," she said, touched.

"Indeed, yes, Madam. How could I forget?"

"I am four and twenty today. Yesterday was the Lord Darnley's birthday, and he is twenty-one. Yet we are not celebrating together, and although— or perhaps because—he is so young, dissoluteness has him in its grip. I fear he will never be delivered from it."

"You must stop brooding," said Madame Rallay. "If ever you hope to recover your spirits, you must stop thinking on these unpleasant things. Now, as to the baptism—when do the godparents arrive?"

Mary smiled. "Once again Elizabeth declines to meet me. Evidently she is not very curious to see me. She sends the Earl of Bedford, governor of Berwick, with her christening gift, a huge gold font. But of course everything is political—for the Earl, being a staunch Protestant, cannot actually attend, so he himself has to choose a proxy—a proxy for a proxy!" She could not help laughing.

"And the French?" Madame Rallay looked on approvingly as Mary drank the posset.

"The Count de Brienne will represent Charles IX; he is travelling from France. And dear Monsieur du Croc, the regular French ambassador, will have to stand in for the Duke of Savoy's own proxy, Moretta, who seems to tarry overlong in Paris." She could not help feeling slighted; even the glittering ceremony she had planned, and the accompanying honours, seemed not sufficient to lure people north. She hated the implied slight to her country, even though she herself had imported French people and trappings to this land. Still, that was different. . . .

"He will be sorry to have missed it, when he hears it described."

"I am having three contingents of the Lords, each wearing a different colour, to serve in the ceremony. The Lord James and his men will be in green, Huntly and his in red, and Bothwell and his in blue."

"The colour of loyalty."

"He has been loyal. And I need to speak with him. Pray, tell Nau to summon him."

"Indeed, Madam. And are you finished with the posset? I shall have the glass taken away."

Bothwell came straightway. She saw immediately that he was walking briskly, and complimented him on his recovery.

"It was partially thanks to your fine physician, Bourgoing," he admitted. "He babied me, made me treat myself like a French whore, almost, with stinking perfumes, hot cloths—but I enjoyed it. I trust you are recovering likewise."

"My wounds are not as treatable as yours," she said.

"I presume we speak now of the Lord Darnley?"

"Yes," she said, bowing her head in shame at referring to her husband as a wound. "What have you . . . decided? What is to be the plan? I left it all in Lord James's hands. I have not even received any letters from Darnley since the one at Craigmillar."

"I know not to what you refer, save the Lord James said you had received one that made you weep."

"In it Lord Darnley threatened not to attend the baptism at all. He said that since the foreign ambassadors would not address him as King, especially the English one, he declined to attend. Of course it will throw doubt on the Prince's legitimacy, when his father does not attend! Oh, Bothwell, what am I to do?" As soon as she said it, she regretted it. She did not want to make him uncomfortable, or make him feel she thought of him as anything other than a councillor whose advice was sometimes necessary. She did not want to chase him away—no, not when just being in his presence was her most treasured thing in all the world. He must not be allowed to know or even sense that—or he would go away. She knew it. She had known it after the kiss at Exchequer House. This was all she would have, all she should have; and it must suffice.

Bothwell looked perplexed. "You have no choice but to proceed as ever. Write him and try to persuade him to attend. But do not beg, or he will take pleasure in rejecting your plea. As for what we have decided to do . . . nothing, for the present. All must be suspended until after the ceremony. It would not do to have a fracas or a scandal or an . . . accident to the Prince's father while the foreign dignitaries are gathered here."

"There may not be as many foreign dignitaries as I had hoped," she admitted. "They seem to be avoiding Scotland."

Bothwell exploded. "Then they're fools! And I am weary of Scotland being slighted! They know not what they do! Why, this country—"

His outburst gave her the first happy feeling she had had in days. "Your loyalty is touching," she said. "And that is why I selected blue as the colour you and your men should wear for the baptism and afterwards. You are to serve at the banquet, presenting the ceremonial dishes to me."

"I am to act as a *servant?*"

"Not as a servant, it is an honour—"

"To present dishes, flourishing trays about?"

"You know it is ceremonial only! The Lord James is to act as cupbearer, and he actually has to kneel to present it."

"That should be a new experience for him. He's out of practice at kneeling and humility."

"And Huntly is to act as carver."

"My brother-in-law is a passable butcher, true. Not good with his head or anything too complicated, but he wields a dagger well enough, like a true Highlander."

"Will you do it?" she asked in a small voice.

"Do what?"

"Wear the blue and act as server."

He laughed. "Of course. Did you think I would refuse?"

"I didn't know. I know that stubborn conscience of yours."

"But I must tell you that I will remain outside the chapel for the actual ceremony."

"Keeping the Earl of Bedford company?"

"Yes. After all, good manners require us to be solicitous of our guests, does it not?"

"I thought it also required a guest to be polite to his host."

"Unless it interferes with his conscience," said Bothwell solemnly.

At length Darnley arrived at Stirling, and took immediately to his quarters, speaking to no one. His father, the Earl of Lennox, did not come at all.

Mary was forced to seek her husband out, as she did not want to disturb him by the gesture of asking him to come to her—although, in any normal circumstances, nothing would be meant by it.

She found Darnley sitting in a window seat, gazing out over the green far below the castle, a pout on his pretty face. He looked up to see her.

"So. You've come. What a surprise," he said. He turned away and pointed below. "What's all that down there?"

She came and stood beside him. "It's the fireworks display." Would that please or excite him? "It is taking almost six weeks to set up, it's so elaborate. There are going to be ground displays and explosions in the air, turning the winter sky white like midsummer."

"How much did it cost?"

"Too much." She smiled. "But is it not a privilege to have our son's baptism so memorable?"

"Memorable for whom? The Prince will not remember it. And the French ambassadors will have seen others, and better, in France. And I shan't see it!"

"Why?" She felt anger taking her over, even though she fought against it. "It will be impossible to avoid seeing the sky lit up, unless you are dead drunk. Do you plan to be drunk, disgracing yourself?"

"If I please, I will!" he yelled. He jumped up off the window seat, went over to his table, where a large—and already half empty—bottle of wine stood opened, and poured himself out a huge goblet of it. Then he bolted it down. "I told you not to ask Queen Elizabeth to be godmother! But no, you disobeyed me! You always disobey me, for all your marriage vows!" He poured out another goblet.

"Henry, please, I beg you." She never used "Henry" except in their calmest, closest moments. She hoped it would appeal to him. "Let us try to make this a happy occasion."

He made a face at her. Suddenly she noticed, as he was standing in the direct morning light streaming in the window, that his face had little red streaks all over it. "We'll see," he said grandly. "It depends on how you treat me. Treat me with honour, then perhaps. But if you ignore me for all those others, well . . ." He hunched his shoulders and turned his back.

The ambassadors and their suites began to arrive. The English contingent alone had eighty persons, and the two French ambassadors brought nearly as many. All the lords gathered, none stayed away: Lord James, Maitland, Kirkcaldy of Grange, the Earls of Argyll, Huntly, Atholl, Mar, Eglinton; the Lords Sempill, Seton, and Fleming, Sir James Melville. Darnley stayed secluded in his quarters, although reports reached Mary's ears that from time to time he wandered down into the town of Stirling to drink at a tavern. In any case, he declined to attend any of the receptions for the arriving dignitaries.

From the moment the festivities began, she entered into such a nervous frame of mind that she felt almost inebriated herself. She was in a heightened state of sensitivity; she talked and listened to what was going on immediately around her, but at the same time her ears seemed to hear other sounds from other rooms. There was another stirring, another whole set of activities taking place simultaneously, and she strained to overhear them.

Bothwell she was unable to speak with privately, and Lord James and Maitland seemed to be observing her very closely.

The baptism was to take place in the early winter dusk of December seventeenth. At precisely four o'clock, in the fading daylight, the Prince was borne from his royal chambers by his godparents, and taken in slow procession between a double row of courtiers holding flaming torches, across the courtyard to the Chapel Royal. The Catholic nobles followed, bearing the accoutrements for the ceremony: the Earl of Atholl carried a long, slender christening-taper of virgin wax, the Earl of Eglinton carried the salt, and Lord Sempill bore the chrism. The Bishop of Ross held the laver and basin. Behind them came the English contingent, the Earl of Bedford holding the great gold font, followed by the French and then the three nobles with retinues—Bothwell, Huntly, and Lord James.

The procession was met at the door of the chapel by Archbishop Hamilton and the bishops of Dunkeld and Dunblane, and then it proceeded slowly to the altar, where the great font was placed with all solemnity upon its waiting stand and filled with holy water. The baby was totally immersed in it and given the baptismal names of James and Charles. At the naming, the heralds proclaimed his name three times to the sound of trumpets, both inside the chapel and outside, where Bothwell, Argyll, Lord James, and the Earl of Bedford waited, along with a great crowd of onlookers. The silver trumpet tones rang out, cutting the air with their clear, perfect edge.

At the conclusion of the ceremony, the organ rang out and a choir burst into song, and the newly christened baby was conveyed back to his chambers.

Mary felt only relief. It was over. It had happened, in accordance with Catholic ritual, as she had hoped it would. No horrible event had occurred to prevent it.

The rest of the company then paraded back across the courtyard through the row of flaming torches to the great hall, where a banquet awaited.

Long ceremonial tables were set, with the Queen to be sitting at the middle of the highest one, the French ambassador on her right hand, the English on her left. Monsieur du Croc, representing the Duke of Savoy, took his place at the farthest end. Darnley's place remained empty.

The heralds, macers, and trumpeters preceded the three Masters of the Household, then came Lord Seton and the Earl of Argyll, each bearing a white wand of ceremony; they were followed by the entire company of guests, all holding white torches, so that the whole hall was lighted and glowing. As the lords and ladies took their places, servants stepped forward to take the torches, and remained standing all through the banquet, holding the flambeaux aloft.

The sounds of the banquet rose as the hall grew warmer and wine goblets were refilled. The musicians had to play louder, and still were difficult to hear over the din. From up and down the candlelit tables people were laughing and there seemed to be no constraints, no bitterness.

Mary's servers came forward to do their duty: the Earl of Huntly, her carver, cut thin slices of boar meat and venison with his exquisitely sharp-honed knife; Lord James, the cupbearer, knelt beside her when offering her a jewelled goblet filled with sweet dark wine. And Bothwell, her server, presented her with each dish after it had been paraded around the hall in its ceremonial trappings. His wide chest, gleaming in the blue costume she had required him to wear, was a bright background for the silver platters he carried.

As she helped herself to various dishes, he made remarks in a low voice that only she could hear—"This looks a trifle dried out"; "This smells like dog meat"—and she could hardly keep from laughing out loud.

Down near du Croc was seated Lady Bothwell, wearing a beautiful head-dress with a circlet of pearls.

Lady Bothwell, his wife. After the banquet was over, they would retire together. Then, sometime later, the candles would be quenched, and they would be alone together in a bed, in the wing of the palace where all the guests were staying. They would have to be quiet, else their neighbours would hear. But Bothwell would know how to keep silent, and—

"I am told this trout comes from Lochleven, where it abounds," Bothwell was standing beside her, with the decorated platter of poached trout. "It has a most delicate white flesh. Like a boiled nun's wimple," he whispered.

During the rest of the banquet, she tried to ignore Darnley's thunderously empty place. She thought the ambassadors would comment on it and interpret it, but no one alluded to it. Perhaps the fact that he actually was in the castle sufficed to endorse the baptism. She was stunned that his presence counted for so little, but heartened, too. He now had no hold over her; there was nothing he could withhold or threaten her with.

The second course was brought in, the dainty sweet dishes, wheeled in on a moving stage attended by a band of musicians. Ahead of them ran a group of actors costumed as satyrs, clearing a way for the wagon, twirling their tails. The Earl of Bedford and his assistant, a young courtier named Sir Christopher Hatton, purported to be shocked. "Is this what happens to us if we partake of your banquet?" asked Hatton. "Shall we grow tails?"

As she laughed and answered Sir Christopher, she noticed Lord James and Bothwell talking earnestly in the back of the hall, next to one of the fireplaces. It surprised her; what would be of such mutual concern to them?

After the banquet, and the elaborate masque designed by Bastian Pages, her French master of the household, it was very late. The Lords and their ladies, the entire company, left the hall and went yawning to bed.

Mary walked slowly over to the ramparts of the castle, and stood looking down over the river below, as the guests reeled one by one to their quarters. It was cold, standing there, but she felt a bit lightheaded from the heat of the fires, the wine, the music, the continual need to attend to conversation and make a suitable reply. The black sky with its hard, bright stars was silent and restorative. A brisk wind was blowing from the hills, and there was a smell of snow in the air. Tomorrow, perhaps, it would come, blanketing the countryside in snow. But the ceremony was over. It was over. Now it could snow all it liked.

She breathed slowly, letting the cold air soothe her lungs. Gradually the sound of footsteps on the paving stones ceased around her and she stood alone.

She was loath to return to her apartments and relive the entire ceremony with Seton and Flamina, her only remaining Marys. They had looked radiant, and would relish discussing each detail. But she was tired of it; she wanted to put it away and not think of it again for a long, long time. It was over. Excitement, which had flooded and sustained her, was now draining away, and all she felt was overwhelming relief, and exhaustion.

Barely visible against the dark, moonless sky she saw the ancient private chapel of the castle. It sat there, isolated and self-contained, looking almost like a child's playhouse. She had never been inside.

I was always too busy, she thought, or not alone. And when I was small, my mother would not let me go there.

She made her way over to it.

I must ask for the key, so that I may explore it in the light, she thought.

She touched the heavy entry door and took hold of the iron ring, and pushed. To her surprise the door groaned and then opened. It had not been locked.

She looked in. It was completely dark inside, and yet it was a friendly, sheltering darkness. But she returned to the Great Hall, only a short distance away, and snatched a candlestick from one of the tables, then returned to the chapel. Cautiously pushing her way inside, she held the candle aloft.

The chapel was even smaller inside than it appeared from the outside, as it was divided into two parts, with an arch separating the two sections. An altar stood in the inmost section, near a small window. In the outer section, chairs and tables were stored, candle stands, blankets, boxes.

They were using this ancient chapel, sacred to Scotland's history, as a storage bin! The Reformers . . . Lord Erskine, the earnest Protestant, who commanded Stirling, had done this. Or given permission for it to be done.

For an instant despair flooded her.

This is what your country has come to, she thought. The ancient chapel, turned into a musty place to hold furniture. What sort of men do this? They recognize nothing as holy; they either destroy or desecrate everything in their paths.

Forgive us, our noble ancestors, she prayed silently. Forgive us, your unworthy descendants, that we do not hold things dear. We have turned into savages.

So engrossed was she in trying to communicate with the long-dead Scots that she did not hear the door creak until it was already halfway open. Her heart stopped, half in fear, half in anger that someone should intrude now, of all times.

She swung around and held the candle aloft. The door continued opening, and Bothwell stepped in.

Her first wild, disordered thought was, He does not belong here! Not here, with my Catholic history! Then her heart leapt up and silenced her mind.

XL

As he actually stepped inside the chapel, he had wondered if he should proceed. Obviously the Queen wanted to be alone. And God knew she had earned it, after the interminable strain of that ceremony and the suspense about Darnley and what he might do to ruin it.

The entire day had gone surprisingly well, Bothwell thought. And the Queen had not shown herself to be anything but perfectly in command of everything about her, regardless of how she felt inside. For that, Bothwell truly admired her. Yes, she had earned the right to be alone for a few moments—something rare and precious for royalty.

But after what Lord James had told him, it was imperative that she know. Royalty could never afford to be ignorant, and remain in control. She must be told.

And so he had followed her, watching as she stood for long moments at the ramparts, reluctant to intrude. But when she entered the chapel, then he knew he must.

Now she whirled around, glaring at him.

"Forgive me," he said. "I saw you enter. I was seeking an opportunity to speak with you alone." He closed the door softly.

He could not tell from her expression whether she was angry or not. But he must proceed. "Lord James told me this evening that there was another, uninvited guest at Stirling," he said.

"Yes, I noticed that you were deep in conversation. Whom has he seen?"

"Archibald Douglas."

403

"O God!" She gave a cry of distress and jerked her hand. The candle in it went out. "That cutthroat cousin of Morton's! Is the whole band of them like that? Why is he here?"

"It seems that he has in mind—or expectation—that you will recall his noble cousin from his banishment."

"Never!"

"He wishes to plead for him. It seems he has already spoken with the Earl of Bedford, and also with Lord James."

"And?"

"They both believe you should recall him, but for different reasons." He moved closer to her in the dark, to speak more quietly. "Queen Elizabeth wishes the rebels to return home. She has told Bedford as much already. Perhaps she is tired of feeding all seventy-odd of them. Bedford had instructions to discuss all this with you before departing. Lord James wishes him back because he thinks he may be of some . . . help in dealing with Darnley."

"And why would that be?"

"Darnley is afraid of him. If Morton returned to Scotland, with your permission, it would signal better than anything else what low esteem Darnley is held in here; it would frighten him into behaving himself. Such a man as . . . your husband can only be controlled by greed or fear."

"And you think until now greed has prevailed? That perhaps all his actions have been motivated by greed—including marrying the Queen?"

"Madam, I did not say that." He moved closer; it was odd to stand in the darkness and converse with a presence that was only a voice.

"But you meant it! Yes, you think he only married me out of greed! That he cared not for me, and has shown it ever since the ring went on my finger and his titles were proclaimed at Market Cross when he was in the bridal bed!"

"Madam, I do not judge such things." Bothwell felt her presence so close to him that he dared not move.

"You think that! I know you do!"

"If he did, then he was a fool! But we know he is a fool!" Bothwell reached out and put his arms around her. "To have all this, and spurn it!" he said. "Oh, he's a fool!" With no thought at all for what he was doing, he suddenly kissed her. Her lips were as soft as a white lily petal.

He kept kissing her; he felt her stir in his arms. He held her tightly against him, pressed her entire body against his. Then all at once he became one ignited candle of desire, ignited and glowing along his entire length. He felt his body pulsating. There was magic in her, compelling mastery of desire. He kissed her yet again, and felt their bodies press together, longing to merge.

She had a husband, only a stone's throw away in the royal apartments. Even now, his wife awaited.

"No," he heard himself saying. Or had he actually said it? It would be double adultery, plus violating the Queen's person: treason. All she had to do was scream for her guards.

But she would not. He knew that. She was brave and headstrong and not afraid of desire. She bested him in that; for all his adventures, he had never had to risk anything for them. He had pursued desire only when it was easy, never when it was compelling or dangerous.

Desire washed over him and drowned his thoughts. They fell to their knees in the open space behind the altar.

"Block the door," she said. He had expected her to demur about the altar and the holy place. He rose to his feet and, feeling in the dark, jerked a heavy chair over against the door.

"No lights—no sound," he whispered. "No one would think to enter."

She gave a low, sweet laugh that inflamed his already throbbing body.

"I am alone," she said. "I cannot believe it. I am never alone. This little chapel . . . so old . . . it makes me shiver. . . . Scotland was at the end of the world once . . . sometimes it still feels like it." Her breath, and voice, were coming in little gasps. "I want you to take me, take me away, to the far side of the earth—all those places you sail to, the places you've known—the Indies—"

"Hush! You are mad!" He stopped her mouth by kissing her. Her mouth opened under his, trembling.

It was as cold as a tomb in the little chapel. Outside the wind had picked up, and there was a soft, fluttering noise as snowflakes hit the two little windows. The chapel would be blanketed with snow, covering them.

He must lay her down. The stones were icy cold and uneven. He fumbled with his cloak, finding the catch, and removed it to spread it on the floor.

"Lie here," he whispered. The altar was only a few inches away; he brushed it with his shoulder as he quickly undid his laces and removed his lower garments. Naked on his lower body, he could not keep from kissing her. He let his lips search out the hollows of her neck, her soft ears, her cheeks. She was almost crying with desire and response.

He put his hand under her dress. It was too cold for them to remove most of their garments. He felt her feet, how chilled they were, and ran his hands slowly up her leg, encased in a knitted stocking. Her leg was long and firm. Carefully he peeled the stocking down, caressing her leg. She moaned softly and seemed almost to go limp. He let his hand brush against the soft secret part of her, but took it away. This was to be their only time together, as it must be, so he would not hurry it on and have it end so soon.

He raised himself up and inched across her gown, crushing the velvet and brocade. He kissed her at the waistband and felt the flesh beneath it shrink back and then expand. He kissed her ribs, then her breasts, swollen—he knew—just under the velvet he was staining with the moisture from his mouth as he kissed it. Beneath it, even through two layers of cloth, he could feel her nipples hardening and standing erect. Now his whole body tightened and he was so excited he felt himself about to burst.

"Call your guards, punish me," he whispered. "Nay, you are too merciful, you would never do so. . . ."

In answer she kissed him, first brushing his lips with her tongue, tracing all the dips and swells of it, then opening her mouth and tasting him. She reached down and managed to remove her silken drawers, pulling them off over her shoeless feet, and then sank back onto her back, with him between her legs. Two layers of clothing, her gown and petticoat, separated his nakedness from hers. Now she was running her hands over his bare muscular buttocks, trying to press his skin directly against hers, as if somehow that would burn the intervening cloth away.

"I melt . . . I cannot bear this." Her voice was choked and far away. "End my torture."

Slowly and almost solemnly, he pulled himself away from her and, sitting back on his heels, lifted away the voluminous cloth of her skirts. The warmth and smell of her naked flesh, her secret parts, was unmistakable. The time was here; it could be delayed no longer.

He lowered himself toward her, holding her, positioning himself on his knees. He was trembling. His knees were shaking. The injured arm, in its bandage, was clumsy. His abdomen, with its fresh and tender scar, felt ripples of heat throbbing within. He was going to die if he did not end this.

Her legs encircled him, drew him in. They were long and slender and met, locked, over the small of his back. He felt himself enter her, slide down through her dark, open, and waiting passage of self. But there was still something held back; she was almost a virgin in her hesitant movements, her unsureness. It was more delicious than anything he had ever tasted or experienced, this virgin ripeness. Suddenly he was afraid he would explode, would disintegrate and give her no pleasure at all in the suddenness of it.

"Oh, my dearest love," she was whispering, moving against him. As her body moved, her head moved with it, making her voice fade in and out, next to his ear, then farther away.

This was wrong, wrong, wrong. . . . Part of him recoiled in sudden fear. This was not safe in any way . . . it was worse than an ambush on the moors, it screamed out its folly and danger. . . . Then a wave of the purest pleasure he had ever experienced kindled in him and spread upward, engulfing his whole being. He was on fire.

She was crying out, clutching his back, tearing his doublet. He could hear the pearls popping off, could hear them striking even the stones beyond his spread cloak. Her back was arching and her legs had started jerking. She was about to scream. Quickly he covered her mouth with his own to stifle it. Her body had gone wild, convulsing spasmodically. Then suddenly his own began to explode, and he felt the stores of his long-hoarded passion breaking forth, flooding her, swamping himself.

She was shaking and shuddering, clawing at his velvet-padded shoulder. She tore her mouth away, gasping.

And then, suddenly, all that passed away and they were merely lying on the floor in a cold little chapel. Mary reached out her arm and touched the base of the altar. She steadied herself and her breathing slowed. Embarrassed, she coughed.

She struggled to sit up, to regain some control. Her hand flailed out, searching for her discarded clothing. Her other hand, shaking, pushed back her sweat-soaked hair from her cheeks. Her breathing was still ragged.

Bothwell's thoughts were racing: What have I done? What will happen? He had trouble bringing his mind into focus when his body had not returned to normal; his heart was still pounding. He took Mary's hand, doubled it in his own against his chest. "Please have no regrets," he finally said. "I promise never to speak of it, nor remind you of it in any way. But you must know that I will treasure this forever—as a memory, not as a presumption of any power or favours."

She did not answer, but bowed her head and continued to try to dress herself. Quite suddenly he was touched with love for her.

He dressed himself. He did not wish this time to end. She stood up and, picking up his cloak, handed it silently to him. He took it and slung it over one shoulder.

"We are married to others," he whispered, finally.

"I know that well," she answered, her voice quiet in the dark. "I love you, Lord Bothwell. I have long dreamed of you, and in such a manner. I think I was seeing it before it happened, that in some way my mind snatched pictures from the future. So I have lived with this a long time."

"What is it you have lived with?"

"With what has happened."

"But what *has* happened? What can it mean for us, married as we are, and you a reigning Queen?"

"That I do not know. Only that I love you." Without waiting for his reply, she removed the barricading chair and pulled the door open. The blast of the wind, wet with snow, slapped him.

The door closed. She was gone. He did not even hear her footfalls on the stones outside, so soft were her shoes.

He smoothed out his cloak and draped it around his shoulders. He ran his hands over his hair and put his hat on. Then he, too, opened the door and made his way across the upper courtyard and to the lighted quarters of the guest apartments. Pray God there was no one dicing or singing in the outer chambers, no one who would beckon to him.

But it was very late. How long had they been in the chapel? Surely it had not been long, although it had seemed so at the time, the timeless time. Everyone seemed to have gone to bed.

He entered his own apartments. The servants had also retired. In his own bedroom, Lady Bothwell was sitting up, writing by candlelight. She was still dressed, and nodded to him with a bland smile.

"It was pleasant, was it not?" she asked sweetly.

"Aye." Hurriedly he undressed himself behind a screen and, in sleeping attire, made for the bed. He settled himself, and when his wife came to bed, he pretended to be fast asleep.

The next morning he awakened early, if he could claim to have slept at all. It had been a strange night of Mary's continual presence in his mind and heart and even, it seemed, in his body: his wounds had been stretched by the exertions and now they ached. The contortions on the floor had left him with scraped knees and a crick in his neck—lest he should fool himself into believing that nothing had happened.

It had happened. And suddenly he was gripped with fear about what would or could or might happen next.

Beside him his wife stirred, sighed, and then rolled over. Her sleeping form offered him a sort of comfort—the only physical comfort she had ever offered. But that was only because she did not know. If she ever did . . . this was not the same as Bessie Crawford. No, this was . . . what? Treason? Not exactly, since it was the Queen's desire as well. And the King was not a real King, so cuckolding him was not treason, either, as the English Parliament had made it a treason to cuckold Henry VIII.

Henry VIII, the Queen's great-uncle. The lusty old goat with his lusty she-goat of a sister—that blood ran in the Queen's veins, and what was not Tudor was Stewart, which was never icy. The Queen's blood was so hot last night it would have bubbled had it been spilt on those chapel stones. . . .

The memory of it excited him, much to his shame. Dwelling on love-making like a country girl was embarrassing. Better to think about what it meant, and what it could lead to: trouble. Immense trouble, beside which Jock o' the Park and his two-handed sword was nothing.

To be the Queen's lover was to risk getting her with child. There were time-honoured provisions for a King's bastard, but it was significant that there was none for a Queen's.

To be the Queen's lover was to risk the twisted wrath of her strange, unpredictable husband.

To be the Queen's lover was to risk making enemies of all the other men, the councillors, who were not. They would see him as a male Diane de Poitiers, a threat to them and their power.

To be the Queen's lover would be to discredit her to her religious enemies, the Knoxian common people, who would be scandalized and possibly try to have her removed from the throne. They called her "whore" already, as the Roman "whore of Babylon," but this was different. There was nothing the Bible-patting congregation of the faithful hated worse than the sins of the flesh.

He actually shivered, hearing their shrill cries in his mind. He had seen the glee with which the proper citizens of Edinburgh ducked scolds, gossips, and adulteresses, pelted them with fruit, and had them whipped and even branded. And if they knew the Catholic Queen had rolled naked on the floor of a chapel with one of her married courtiers—

He felt sick. He lurched up from the bed so suddenly he awakened his wife Jean, as he grabbed for the *vase de nuit* to vomit into. The sight and smell of what was already in there completed the task and he heaved everything up from his stomach.

Jean murmured something solicitous and climbed out of bed to get him a towel to wipe his face. She dabbed it in water and then tenderly cleaned off his face.

"You look dreadful," she said, examining his reddened face and bloodshot eyes. "You must have eaten something tainted."

"Aye." He got up off his knees and made his way shakily over to the table, where a bottle of wine was kept. Anything to chase that vile taste from his mouth.

"I pray you, return to sleep," he said. "It is too early to be up." He sloshed the wine around in his mouth and then swallowed it. He wanted to sleep, too. Now perhaps he could.

As he crawled back into bed and pulled the covers over himself in the chill of the early dawn, the small amount of wine in his empty stomach gave him a strange soothing feeling.

There was one last thing: to be the Queen's lover—to be *this* Queen's lover—was to live in Paradise. She was the woman he had long ago dreamed of possessing—beautiful, passionate, perfectly fitted to him in the dark. In those few moments she had proved able to match and answer all his desires, unspoken and untouched until now.

At midmorning, several hours after his second arising, Bothwell had a visitor: the Lord James.

"May I?" asked James. "I trust I am not disturbing you?"

"No, not at all," Bothwell forced himself to answer in a hearty fashion. His stomach still felt queasy, but he had satisfied himself that he looked well enough, and had taken exceptional pains in his dressing and toilet. "I was only waiting until time to go to the bullfight in the royal park."

"Yes, there are a mighty lot of festivities!" sneered Lord James, and in his clenched mouth Bothwell saw all ascetics. "May I?" he repeated.

Bothwell waved him in, then took him back to an inner chamber where they would not be disturbed. "It must be urgent business that brings you here, directly, to me this early. What is it?" Bothwell hated delays and circumvention.

"A blunt fellow, as everyone agrees," said James. "Regarding the business with Morton and the other murderers—are you going to speak to the Queen? I think you can persuade her." He looked directly into Bothwell's eyes with the cruel level gaze of a hawk.

Did he suspect?

"Why me? You are her brother, and have always been her chief minister."

"Oh, stop the flattery. Since your injury in the heroic antics down in the Borders, and your heartrending escape from death, your word is law with the Queen. Anything you ask, she'll grant." He continued looking at him, with a look halfway between a glare and a stare. "Your sword wounds have brought you much credit."

"But why would *I* want the Riccio murderers back? And for that matter, why would you?"

"Morton was a good man in many ways." Lord James chose his words carefully and took his time in selecting them. "Darnley double-crossed him. He knows Darnley better than you or I or even the Queen does. Some say you only come truly to know a man after he betrays you." James paused. "Since our talk at Craigmillar, I have been at deep pains pondering how we might keep our word to the Queen to free her from Darnley. I have come to believe that Morton will know the best way."

Yes. Murder him. So that is the plan, thought Bothwell. That is what is to be done? We let his most deadly enemy back into Scotland, a kinsman who has been betrayed by him, and who has already murdered once. . . . Bothwell felt queasy again. What if they find out my secret, how will they use that?

"Will you speak to the Queen soon?" Lord James was saying. "Of course the rest of the councillors will urge it as well, but if you add *your* voice to ours and Queen Elizabeth's—"

"I said I would, didn't I? If you advise it."

"Oh, I *do* advise it."

"Very well. I'll do it as soon as an opportunity presents itself." Bothwell felt as though a great pit were opening up under him. Murder and adultery and treason, all at once, were difficult to get used to in only a few short hours. He smiled wanly.

"Good." Lord James stood up. There were to be no pleasantries about the weather, the ceremonies, or the distinguished visitors, then. Just right to the point: the murder. "I do believe you could persuade the Queen to do anything these days. Even signing her own death warrant."

He knew!

"I am only joking," said Lord James, raising his eyebrows. "I must say, you look a bit ill. Perhaps you should avoid the bullfight. Too much blood. But *do* speak to her today, if possible."

❧

The expensive, week-long festivities were to come to a tumultuous close with an elaborately staged battle to capture a make-believe castle erected near the King's Knot. It was in the best tradition of France, for a Castle of Love to be stormed by lovesick knights, and defended by *cruelles dames sans merci*. For six weeks John Chisholm, a Scotsman who had studied this art in France, had laboured to construct it, and rumour was there was to be a spectacular finale. All were requested to attend, as it had been hideously expensive to bring into being.

Bothwell—who, far from seeking out the Queen to speak with her, had studiously avoided her—had attired himself in his best clothes, selecting the wine-coloured doublet with topaz stones outlining the gold-braided design, and puffed satin breeches over his silken hose. A velvet cap with feather completed the ceremonial costume of the most powerful lord in the land.

He joined the throngs streaming out of the castle gates to descend to the grounds where the spectacle would be staged. Just then French Paris tugged at his cloak.

"A message for you," he said. "I don't know who brought it; it was thrown into the room all wrapped up, and covered with wax."

Bothwell drew back from the jostling, overdressed crowd to break the seal and read it.

I pray you, come now to my private chamber.

That was all. He wadded it up and stuffed it into his waistband. Then he melted away from the chattering crowd.

The Queen's apartments were deserted. He opened the outer door, the one leading directly to the public rooms; there were no guards in the anteroom. Then he entered the ceremonial public chambers with their smooth paved floors, their silent tapestries of classical deeds and loves and labours, meant to give weight and formality to proceedings. No one there. The throne, carved and gilded, stood empty underneath its canopy. He passed through the three outer chambers and entered the private ones. The Marys, the servers, all were gone. The cushions lay dozing like rotund cats in the coming gloom. Only one candle stand had been lit, and the feeble light showed poorly against the bloody red of the sunset through the western window panes.

The inner chamber—which was it? There was a small door near the tapestry of Hercules' labours—this one the cleansing of the Augean stables—and it was slightly ajar.

She was in there, he knew it. Now he must see her. He stretched out his arm and knocked on the door. Let what would happen, happen. He felt no fear. He had put that behind him.

XLI

ary heard the soft knock on the door. She had been waiting for it, sitting rigidly in her chair; now she did not want to rise and greet him. The knocking came again, more insistent.

She wanted to see him; she could not bear to see him. Until she actually saw him again, the memory of that night in the chapel would remain exactly as it was: perfect and glorious and completely free, free of all examination and soul-searching and apologies and promises, a godly surprise and gift.

I wish I might never see him again; I wish I had died that night, died the second I got back to my bed, she thought.

She had hurried across the courtyard in the falling snow, soaking her shoes. Her feet would have been numb, perhaps had been numb, but she had not noticed. She had rushed into her own private chamber, not even speaking to Madame Rallay or Mary Seton, and closed the door. Then she had lain down, completely happy, and spent the night in reverie.

The next few days, with all their festivities, had passed for her as if she were in a trance. She saw Darnley passing down the steep path into town, probably to drink, but it mattered not. She even glimpsed Archibald Douglas skulking across the courtyard. She entertained Sir Christopher Hatton and thought, idly, how attractive he was, and wondered if Elizabeth fancied him. Every day she passed by the chapel and would incline her head toward it, giving it reverence, thinking it the holiest site she had ever visited.

She did not see Bothwell, although she kept seeing his wife. Suddenly Lady Bothwell seemed to be everywhere, as if she had multiplied during that night. Mary could not help studying her carefully, trying to see exactly what she wore. When her dress was green, was it because Bothwell was especially fond of the colour? Did she dress to please him?

At first she had been relieved that she did not see him. Then, gradually, she came to believe that he was avoiding her. The time was drawing near when all the guests would be departing. Embarrassing as it was, she would have to summon him. For it would be unthinkable for them to part without a word, although deep inside she would have preferred that. She could not bear it if he said something to soil even the memory.

He had other women, had had other women. In the past few days she had found out more about them, as if to torture and punish herself. It seemed he had been married twice before, in a manner of speaking: he had been "handfast" to Janet Beaton, and had lived in common-law marriage with the Norwegian woman. Neither of these was binding, of course, but what did they mean to him?

The knock was loud and demanding now. Mary rose and opened the door.

Even so, she was not prepared for the impact of seeing him again, after dwelling so intensely in her own memories. He stood there, completely real and impatient to be admitted.

"Come in," she said faintly, stepping aside.

He almost jumped in the door and closed it. "You left me standing there so long I was sure someone would see me!" he said. He looked annoyed.

Already this was different from anything she had imagined. The real Bothwell was disconcerting.

"I took care that no one should be here," she said. "They are all going to watch the castle-storming."

"If it truly costs a king's ransom, which they say it does, then we must go to watch it too. We will both be questioned about it, and we must witness it."

A *king's ransom.*

"We will. In a moment. Separately, of course." She paused. "What did you mean, a king's ransom?"

"It is merely an expression."

"One that is very appropriate, I fear."

"Mary—I trust I may call you that, here in private—please. Do not begin that."

She turned and indicated to him that he should take a seat on one of the huge cushions before the fire. He did so, and she sat opposite him, arranging her skirts so they completely covered the cushion, clasping her knees with her arms.

"I know not what you mean," she finally said. Nearby the fire crackled and spat.

"I mean, discussing your husband and what is to be done, and what we are to do, and so on. Mary, what happened, happened. But I cannot go on with it. You may laugh or call me coward, but I cannot take a married woman as a lover."

"So it is not my crown that intimidates you, but my wedding ring?"

"Yes." He smiled. "I am ashamed to admit it, it makes me sound like a Puritan, but that is one thing my moral code will not permit me. Last week I outraged my own code, but in passion. If I repeat it, it cannot be held to be in passion, but in cold decision, so to speak."

"Do you realize that is why I love you?" she said. "For those very same inconvenient principles? They are what make you who you are, and the man I love."

"Mary, please, stop this! Can we not go away and forget? I will still serve you as loyally as ever. But I would prefer not ever to be alone with you again. It is not safe."

He was looking at her with a level gaze. The wound on his face was turning into a scar, and soon would be just a memory. He wanted the night in the chapel to turn into a scar as well, she thought.

413

"So you will have it that we never meet again, except in necessary circumstances, under the eye of others," she said softly. "You will suppress what happened, attempt to forget it, and, in time, succeed."

"Yes." He did not turn his eyes away.

"I do not want to forget it," she said.

"If you choose to dwell on it, I cannot prevent that."

"Oh, Bothwell, I love you! I cannot let you go, send you back down the steep path from Stirling, and off to the Borders again! I cannot pretend!"

"You must. If you cannot mask what happened, then you doom us both!" His voice rose in alarm.

"Do you not care for me?" she heard herself asking, hating herself for letting the words escape her. It was begging; she was as much a beggar as the crowds even now gathering around the gate at the foot of the castle path, begging for alms and scraps from the banquets.

He rose from the cushion, clearly so uncomfortable that he wished to bolt away from her presence; at least that was what she thought. She rose with him. To her utter confoundment, he put his arms around her and held her to him.

"Yes, I care for you. I have cared for you ever since I first saw you, a little girl in France." He held her tightly, but there was no passion in it, just affection.

"You saw me in France?" she asked, her voice small and astonished. "How?"

"I saw you many times, passing by in your carriage. Did I never tell you I was in France when you were still a child there?"

"No, never. I did not know. What were you doing there?"

"Studying. I was at the Scots' College, the one by the Sorbonne. I lived in a room just near the Phillippe Auguste wall. And I would see you passing by in your carriage to the Louvre, or along the rue Ste.-Antoine to the jousts, and I would stand still and look, and I thought you the most beautiful, entrancing child I had ever seen. You made me proud to be a Scot! I would point you out to all my friends, saying, 'She is from Scotland; you can see what beautiful girls we have.' You were so much prettier than the Valois princesses!" His mouth was quite close to her ear; she could feel his warm breath on her skin.

"You saw me then?" she kept asking.

"I watched for you. I even went to some of those wretched jousts, just so I could see you. And there you would be, surrounded by the Guises and the Valois, shining above them all. I thought you were . . . an angel." He laughed as if it were a sad lost treasure.

"You were not there when—the King was killed?"

"No. I came back to Scotland by the time I was twenty-one, when I came into my inheritance. That was before your marriage." Now his lips were very close to her ear; he was almost kissing it.

"I love you; do not desert me," she said, burying her face in his shoulder. She kissed his neck, and felt him shiver.

414

He kissed her ear, as she wanted him to; she turned her face to his and sought his lips. He did not hesitate, but kissed her with a passion all the fiercer for having been fought against.

"Love me and share my fortunes," she whispered. "I cannot leave you."

"We cannot be together, but we cannot be apart," he said. "This is an exquisite torture." He let her go. "I know not what to do, where to go, even how to exist like this."

"You said your code would not permit it. I understand that . . . I honour it. At the same time I cannot bear it."

"But I cannot even live up to it!" His face was filled with anguish. "And what happens to a man when he cannot live up to his own code? Does love compensate or reward him? I do not know. No one in Scotland has ever done such things for love; we have no tradition of great lovers. There are no Scottish Tristans and Isoldes, no Lancelots and Guineveres, no Parises and Helens, no Antonys and Cleopatras."

"Then we will be the first. I shall be proud to be."

"To act like pagans?" He sank to his knees and stared at the Turkish carpet before the fire. "The infidels make objects of great beauty," he said. "Even their carved swords are engraved and studded with precious stones. The tiles of their mosques and dwellings are traced in patterns and fired to preserve them." He looked up at her. "The world is wide, my lady."

She knelt down beside him. "Nay. It is very narrow. It is only here, in this chamber, where we are."

"Our tragedy is that it is not. Surrounding this little chamber is Scotland, and it is not very forgiving of its sinners. In order to reach the wider world, we must flee through Scotland, where we will be stoned and treated as criminals. Is that what you wish?"

"No. But I believe that somehow we can avoid that. The fates will be kind, Bothwell. They have to be."

"All lovers think that. But it is not fate we must contend with, but people. Fate is nothing but the sum total of what other people do."

It was now fully dark in the chamber. The castle entertainment would be beginning soon.

"Mary," he said, "if we are to survive in this world of people and harness them to serve as our 'fate,' we must be cold-blooded with everyone save ourselves. Have you given any further thought to what I suggested? Morton and Lindsay and the other exiles? Will you call them back?"

"Yes. If you advise it," she said. "But I will never allow the three worst ones back!" she cried. "Not the foul George Douglas the Postulate, who stabbed Riccio over my shoulder, nor Patrick Bellenden, who aimed his rapier at my breast, nor Andrew Kerr of Fawdonside, who tried to fire a pistol into my side. I shall never permit them entry into Scotland. No, never!"

"As you decree," he said. "Your mercy is great."

Just then a popping sound reached them. She ran toward the window. "The castle!" she cried. "It is exploding! Oh, look!"

He came over to the window and watched as the walls of the mock castle on the green below, glowing yellow in the light of internal fires, began to collapse. Fiery balls flew from the ramparts and exploded on impact, sending up clouds of sparks. Then, suddenly, the structure blew up, sending cartwheels of fire and colour out into the night.

XLII

Darnley paced the spacious floor of his sumptuously appointed room, walking nervously from one end to the other. Every so often he glanced up at the ceiling with its carved roundels almost lost in the deepening shadows.

There they are, he thought. The things that Lord James frightened her with when she was a child. Oh, she told me all about it . . . when she enjoyed talking to me. Yes, there was a time—and not so long ago, either—when she would spend hours telling me about herself, her childhood, her secrets.

And now she won't even come near me, let alone talk to me!

Anger ripped through him and he stopped at a table in the middle of the room to pour himself a tall goblet of wine. Maybe this would make him feel better. God, he felt terrible—his joints ached and he had a perpetual headache. But did *she* ever come to inquire after his health? No!

Not even when I sent word I would not be attending the baptism, he thought. If anything should have piqued her curiosity, or alarmed her, that should have. But she went right ahead entertaining the English and French and the churchmen and God knows who else. Here at Stirling, where we were secretly married! She even ordered my silver plate removed to use at the banquet.

The bitch!

He smacked his palm down as hard as he could on the tabletop. It reverberated up into his head and intensified the throbbing there. He felt sweaty. He ran his hand over his forehead and was horrified to feel tight little bumps all across it. With a yelp he snatched his hand away, and went scurrying for his hand mirror. Extracting it out of its embroidered case, he held it up anxiously and peered at his face. Strange granular lumps were sprinkled not only across his forehead, but also on his cheeks.

They looked horribly familiar. He had seen such blemishes on the faces of some of the women at the brothel . . . but never anyone that he himself had trafficked with. And there had been that irritation on his privates, but it had healed over. . . .

Even as his thoughts raced frantically, he had a stab of fear in his inmost gut.

Syphilis. I may have syphilis!

White-hot anger tore through him.

No! I don't deserve it! *She* does!

Perhaps he had given it to her? A chortling sense of relief waved through him.

But no. They had not been together for months.

He sank down on his stool, stunned. He was astounded to find that his first thought was, Now we shall *never* be together again! He felt all the loss of the world in that realization.

I love her! Why does she not love me?

He burst into tears, and started sobbing into his hands.

Why did she turn against me? For Riccio? But I begged her to forgive me, and I led her to safety. . . . Because of my drinking? But I only did it because of my torment over her! And the same with the whores!

No . . . it's because of *him*! Because of Bothwell! The way she rushed to him at the Hermitage . . . the way she looks at him, I've seen that look!

He saw a reddish glare coming from far below, and went over to the window to see. Far below, like a red flower on the carpet of snow, was the castle, its thin paper-and-plaster walls glowing from within like a lantern. Around the structure, a dark stain of milling people surrounded it. Oh, yes, it was that stupid fireworks castle that she had wasted so much money on—she cared more about that than about *him*!

There were cheers as the flames leapt higher, and the knights within fought back with fire-spears. Then, suddenly, the knights were running out of the castle, waving their banners and yelling. The castle began to bloom like an evil yellow flower, and then it flew apart, huge chunks of burning material borne upward with swirls of fire. The crack of an explosion blew a volcano of debris up into the sky like a giant cannon.

I want to die, Darnley thought. I want her to die. If we cannot be together, then I want us to die in each other's arms, and then I'll know no one else can ever have her, and I'll die happy.

Another explosion rent the air.

Gunpowder will do it. It would take more to explode a house, but it could be a small house, it needn't be a palace. . . .

And then she would die, die, die, the cruel Queen. . . .

"And you'll be mine forever," he whispered, watching the flames buckling the flimsy structure.

XLIII

The ambassadors left Stirling; gradually the other entourages said their good-byes as well. During the week or so before they departed, Mary revelled in the secret meetings she would arrange with Bothwell, whispering instructions under the very noses of her eminent guests.

Meet me in the Privy Chamber . . . in the empty rooms left by the Earl of Atholl . . . in the tower chamber, the one that looks out over the King's Knot. . . .

And he would be there, waiting, hungry for her, seemingly forgetting his misgivings. In the cold places they could only embrace, and kiss, and talk. But in the warmed chambers, before the beds had been taken away— and the servants always allowed time for the bedding to air—they could strip away all that separated them from one another, and delight in their own nakedness. Mary would unbind her hair and let it serve as her only mantle, and Bothwell would stroke and kiss it, caressing it as if it had feeling. She would lie back, hanging her head off the side of the bed, exposing the sweet arch of her long neck with its transparent alabaster skin, and he could see the blood pulsing there. Her whole body was slender and seemed, in certain lights, to be a statue come to life.

"You are the goddess Ronsard proclaimed you," he would murmur, "but he could only see you thus in his poetic imagination—I hope!"

She would laugh. "I was swathed in white then."

"You are swathed in white now, in your exquisite skin."

Inhibitions seemed to have left him, along with his moral scruples.

But they could never meet enough; the difficulty of arrangements, the need for watchfulness, the constant scrutiny prevented it. So to lie together in a real bed, in a room with a fire, became a rare and much-sought prize.

And there was always Lady Bothwell to be appeased, Lady Bothwell asking questions, Lady Bothwell growing restless and eager to depart.

On Christmas Day, Mary called together the remaining lords: Lord James, Maitland, Argyll, Huntly, and Erskine. She unrolled her pardon for the exiles and read it slowly.

"They are all to return, under my forgiveness," she said. "You must welcome your brothers back, and let us pray that this is an end to all discord and strife."

That night Darnley, mounted on his favourite white horse, slipped away from Stirling Castle and made straight for Glasgow and his father's bailiwick.

XLIV

The sun was sinking on Twelfth Night when Mary stood to one side as Mary Fleming, her flamboyant Flamina, was wedded to Maitland. The ceremony did not take place in the Chapel Royal, as there were not enough guests to fill it, but in the Queen's Privy Chamber. Maitland looked at her possessively. He had waited patiently for almost five years, had waded through the problems of the age difference, and weathered all the political upheavals that brought him now closer, now further, from the Queen he claimed to serve.

As for Flamina, Mary looked at her with tenderness. She hoped she would be happy with the Chameleon, as he had been called by his political enemies.

May he never change his feelings for her, as he seems to change his alliances, Mary thought. Let him find in his bride the one thing he can be loyal to.

"Now that Darnley is gone, we are free of him. Come to my inmost chamber tonight," Mary whispered to Bothwell as she brushed past him during the dancing afterwards. She felt giddy with the sudden freedom.

Bothwell frowned and shook his head almost imperceptibly.

"Too dangerous," he murmured later, when he could insert it into a brief gap between two innocuous sentences spoken in front of the beaming Maitland. Lady Jean stood beside her husband, looking at him with her wide, perceptive eyes. She was fingering her wedding ring.

Pointedly?

"We wish you all the joy possible," she said in her low, drowsy voice. "Marriage is full of the unexpected, but it wears brighter and brighter as time goes on, like a gold ring." She displayed her ring with obvious pride.

"Let us dance," said Bothwell. "I learned this one in France."

"Ah, France. You must take me sometime. . . ." Mary could not hear the rest of the sentence, as Bothwell led his wife away into the midst of the dancers, but she could see the Countess smiling and touching Bothwell's shoulder, and could see him smile at her.

A pain pierced through her. How could it hurt so much, when she knew he loved *her*? And how could it be that she could not see him alone tonight?

She felt suffocated by the music, the torches, the celebrants, and wanted to run from the chamber and sit and wait for Bothwell to come to her later.

But instead she had to smile and dance and drink goblets of sweet wine, and kiss Mary Fleming and tease her about the wedding night.

"Your Stewart blood will see you through. Passion runs in your veins," she assured her.

Was it a blessing or a curse, this passionate blood?

"At last I can turn it loose," said Flamina. "And with the Church's blessing!"

Bothwell later sent word to her, and while his wife was out hunting the next morning they made quick, impassioned love in his quarters. Afterwards he told her that it was time they, too, departed. His wife was questioning their long stay and was impatient to return to her own favourite castle of Crichton, which she was in the process of furnishing.

"And she seems anxious to write our wills," said Bothwell, "and settle our inheritance."

"But you don't sleep with her!" cried Mary. "So how can an inheritance for her heirs be of concern to her?"

"Well, there are brothers, family—"

"You don't sleep with her!"

"Mary, be reasonable—"

"No! You promised! You mustn't—"

"I never promised *that*! I promised to love you always—"

"And sleep with your wife?" she shrieked.

"Quiet!" commanded Bothwell. "Do you want the entire castle to hear you? How can I not sleep with her? Do you think she would continue unsuspecting if I did not?"

"So, she craves your lovemaking and cannot be deprived of it! The proper Lady Jean Gordon—"

"Stop it! You sound like an ordinary, tiresome, demanding mistress, not like a Queen. I will not stand for it! I've had my fill of such women— whiny, jealous, clingy. . . ." He attempted to kiss her.

The thought of him naked with his wife was so repugnant to her she turned away.

"Do not be ordinary," he said. "It is a Queen I want."

"Must you go?"

"Yes. I must."

"When?"

"After a week or so, when the weather turns. You know January fourteenth, St. Hilary's Day, is by custom the coldest day of the year. The Ice Saint, they call Hilary. So I'll wait for his day to pass. Then I shall go."

But by the fourteenth of January, Mary had more anguish than just Bothwell's departure. The word had come from Glasgow, where Darnley had returned to his father, that Darnley was very ill with syphilis. And she herself felt ill, but of a different cause: she was pregnant.

She must tell Bothwell before he departed! By making discreet inquiries as to his whereabouts, she ascertained that he was in the stables, overseeing the packing of his horses. He was to journey forty miles in the cold weather,

420

and equipment was important. He would not think of setting out without horse blankets, tools, candles, and extra food, and he did not trust the stablehands to secure them properly.

Making an excuse that she wanted to see how her favourite white palfrey, Ladysmith, was faring after a bout with a mysterious swollen knee, Mary slipped out to the stables. She, with her love of horses, often went there, and so did not arouse any curiosity from the stablehands.

Bothwell was inspecting his horse's hooves, his brow furrowed. He looked up and saw her, and an expression of displeasure came over his face. It changed quickly to anger.

"Do you *want* to expose us to unnecessary suspicion? We said our farewells. Now go!" He glanced at the stablehands, busy in the stalls. So far they had not looked up. "Yes, Your Majesty, I will see if there is any word from Moretta. The last message I received in Edinburgh was that he has only just left Paris." He raised his voice slightly as he said this. "Pity he had to miss the ceremony itself."

"Bothwell!" She clutched his sleeve. "I cannot commit this to writing!" She leaned over and whispered in his ear, "I fear I am with child. So I must go to Darnley in Glasgow."

"No! He is diseased! You must not, must not—"

"I will not give myself to him, but what the world will see is that we have come together. What happens in our private moments cannot be proved—or disproved."

"It is dangerous there!"

A nearby stablehand turned his head and gave them a sly smile.

"I told you, I shall not give myself to him," she whispered.

"Glasgow itself is dangerous. It is filled with the Lennox Stewarts, and Lennox himself is lurking."

"Lennox is ill."

"He *pretends* to be ill. I cannot let you go there alone. I have—there are—rumours that both father and son are planning some monstrous action against you. Lennox signalled his intentions by absenting himself from the baptism. I have heard—"

"I have no choice!" Could he not see that?

"Rid yourself of it! Janet Beaton has remedies—"

"Your old mistress? That reputed witch? The remedy might prove worse than the condition itself!" Her voice was rising again.

"Keep your voice down!" he hissed. "I hear you well enough! Very well, then. But these remedies work."

"I'll not dabble in witchcraft."

" 'Tis not witchcraft, but simple country medicine." He looked around quickly.

She did not answer.

"You must not go Glasgow! Mary, I beg you—"

"Unless you have some true information of which I am ignorant—which I now command you to tell me—then I must."

He shrugged and shook his head. "Only rumours. But, Mary, there were similar rumours flying about before Riccio was murdered. Even Cecil heard them in London. Darnley wants the crown. He was promised it by the Riccio conspirators for his part in the plot. Now he knows you seek ways to be free of him. He must do something quickly, while he is still legally bound to you."

"I distrust him. But I will be on my guard." She reached out toward him, but stopped herself. She must not touch him. "I cannot believe that he would actually harm my person."

"I pray you are right."

"Farewell. I shall write you from Glasgow, reporting all his words, so that *if* anything happens, there will be proof—and he shall never come by the crown."

"I shall await your letters. And—God be with you."

XLV

A few days later Bothwell jounced along the rutted, icy path between Crichton Castle—where he had left his wife directing workmen to carve new oak panelling for the hall—and Whittingham, a Douglas stronghold fifteen miles away. January was a miserable time to travel even a short distance, but Mary's situation made it imperative. Immediately after her visit and "reconciliation" with Darnley, Mary must be rendered a widow. It was as simple as that.

It was true, what he had told her. There were rumours about that Darnley and his father planned some sort of coup against Mary that would result in their seizing the crown—in the little Prince's name, of course. But when it was planned, what exactly was to take place, and who were the conspirators, he did not know.

If only my spies were as well paid as Cecil's, he lamented as he pulled his wrap more tightly around his neck. Then I would know everything.

But then it matters not what the weak, mewling fool has planned, if I act first.

He had a sinking feeling. Good clean outdoor fighting, that he relished. But this plotting, this underhanded, inherently cowardly way of dealing with enemies, sat ill on him.

My entanglement with the Queen has led me into this, he thought. It has transformed me into a masquer, as false as everyone else at court. I hate it. And now with this child, I cannot just end it.

The great stone tower of Whittingham poked out from above the dull brown branches of the sleeping forest at the foot of the Lammermuir Hills. Bothwell trotted into the courtyard and was relieved of his horse by a shivering attendant. Awaiting him inside were the Earl of Morton, Maitland, and Archibald Douglas, Morton's all-purpose henchman: cutthroat, forger, and bully.

"Ah!" They turned to greet him, offer him a goblet of heated ale.

"Promptness is a virtue," said Archibald Douglas. "Now the meeting may begin."

Unlike a court ceremony, this was to have no niceties, no exchange of pleasantries, although Bothwell could not resist saying, "Well, Mr. Secretary Maitland, I see even a honeymoon does not keep you away from your necessary duties—like planning assassinations."

"Close your mouth!" Morton stepped forward. "We will confer outside."

Bothwell tapped the moist grey stones. "Even the walls have ears, eh?" He drank some more of the heated ale. He would have wished for a few more moments before the fire, so his numbed fingers and toes could at least begin to tingle.

"Your lack of originality disappoints me," said Maitland.

"As does your lack of lust for your new bride. But duty calls." Bothwell finished the ale and put the cup down. He pulled his hat lower on his ears.

Outside, the chill seemed to hover just above the ground.

"By the yew," said Archibald, pointing to a gigantic tree standing alone about a hundred feet from the house, surrounded by bracken and lichen-covered boulders. Carefully they made their way across the field, feet slipping on the stones and getting snow inside their boots.

Under its sheltering, low-hanging limbs, the tree seemed like a tent shielding them from the wind.

Morton settled himself on one of the flatter boulders, spreading his cloak underneath him. "You laugh," he said sternly to Bothwell. "But there are spies *everywhere*. And it is imperative we not be overheard."

Maitland the bridegroom spoke first. "The problem is simple, gentlemen. The Queen regrets her marriage with Lord Darnley. *We* regret her marriage. There is no one who does *not* regret the marriage, except Darnley himself and his proud father. It is time that the marriage is ended in the time-honoured way: till death us do part. Having just heard that vow myself, it inspired me."

"Yes," Bothwell said. "Divorce, annulments . . . they leave too many unsettled questions."

"And they don't punish the offender!" Morton snarled. "He betrayed us over the Riccio affair—turned on his own clan, the Douglases! It is not to be borne! I had many months to brood upon it while I was exiled, first to England, then Flanders, then back again to England." His dark eyes were glistening.

"So you'll strike the first blow?" said Archibald. "Keep up the family tradition, and use Bell-the-Cat's great sword. It's been in your keeping for a reason."

Morton fingered his bushy red beard. "I dare not," he finally said.

"What?" Bothwell was incredulous. "What did we bring you back for, then?"

"That is just it," he said gruffly. "I have just received a royal pardon for one murder. I dare not commit another so soon."

The wind rose and rattled the tree branches against each other. Everyone glared at Morton, until he finally cried, "I despise him, and I would gladly strike not only the first blow but all the rest—if the Queen would commission me."

"She *has* commissioned you. She has commissioned all of us," said Maitland. "At Craigmillar, we discussed it and her only condition was that it must not blot her honour."

"But 'it' was left undefined," admitted Bothwell. "She stated she wanted her freedom; when she said 'it,' that was what she meant."

"Do it, and she'll thank you for it afterwards," said Archibald.

"Not without her express command," said Morton stubbornly. "In writing."

"She'll give it," said Archibald.

"Then *you* procure it," said Morton.

"That I will," Archibald said indignantly. "And right speedily."

"But how will we do it?" persisted Maitland. "We should settle on a plan right now, since"—he nodded mockingly toward Archibald—"we are protected so effectively against eavesdroppers."

"Stab him in the fields," said Bothwell. "He is a fool for hawking, even in foul weather. It would be easy to lure him out into the wilds. And then—"

"We would have to murder his attendants—Standen, Taylor. . . ."

"You have overlooked the fact that the Lord Darnley knows you hate him and would therefore be suspicious of invitations from you to go riding far afield," said Maitland smoothly.

Morton's face fell. "True. But murder within a palace is difficult. Too many people about. Look what happened with Riccio."

"We can ambush him as he passes from one palace to another," Archibald suggested. "Then it could be blamed on outlaws and brigands."

"Hmmm . . . yes," said Maitland. "But it would depend on how large a party he was travelling with."

"We could ambush him on the way to his eternal hawking," said Bothwell. "That would have the advantage of a smaller party and a remote location."

"Someone would have to inform us of his movements. That means someone very close to him would have to be brought into the conspiracy," said Maitland.

"Sir James Balfour is known to keep company with him," said Archibald. "And he's corruptible."

"But he might betray *us* to *him*," Bothwell objected.

"Poison?" asked Maitland. "There is always that old standby."

"Again, there is the problem of needing someone close to him to administer it," Morton pointed out.

"Not if it is given at a public affair, a banquet."

"Perhaps the simplest way is best," Maitland said briskly. "Arrest him for treason in the name of the Queen, and when he resists, kill him. In self-defence, of course."

"Get the commission," said Morton to Archibald. "For I will be sorely disappointed if I cannot avenge my own betrayal."

XLVI

Mary stood looking at Archibald Douglas, the swarthy murderer who should have belonged to the Black Douglases instead of the Red ones. He had requested a private interview with her, and she had granted it on the eve of her departure to Glasgow. But when he whispered his request in her ear, she could scarcely believe it.

"No!" she cried. "No! I will not even listen to such a wicked suggestion! Get you from my sight!"

Permission to kill Darnley? She, of all people, wanted Darnley kept alive. Dead men beget no children.

She had even hurriedly dispatched Bourgoing to Glasgow to treat him, lest he might succumb to his disease before she could reach him and spend one night behind closed doors with him.

Evidently agitated, Bothwell had rushed to Edinburgh and now was insisting that he and Huntly would accompany her partway to Glasgow. Delighted to see him on any excuse, she was touched that he was so concerned. She arranged to spend the one night en route at Callendar House, the home of Mary Livingston's family. That way she was assured of safety and also of an opportunity to see Lusty again. Although Lusty came back to court regularly, bringing her little son, they had had few private moments together in the past two years.

The late-January day was comparatively mild as they set off, leaving Edinburgh behind. Even so, the route was mired and blocked with fallen trees and mounds of ice, so their pace was slow. Bothwell led the way, riding out proudly, his alert eyes searching the road on either side for anything amiss. She loved to watch him ride. His reddish hair gleamed sleekly in the low-slanting sunlight.

I wonder if the child will have his reddish hair? she thought, and instantly a feeling half of guilt and half of excitement flooded her. The child. She carried his child!

She had felt ill this morning, and so the ride would have been unendurable, except that it meant she could spend it in *his* company, and she cherished the queasiness as proof of the child's existence.

Bothwell had tried to indicate that he had information for her, but as yet they had had no opportunity to communicate. Five hundred horsemen with glittering steel armaments surrounded them and stretched out for almost a mile behind them, a long, shining dragon's tail.

They reached Callendar House, near Falkirk, by late afternoon; it had taken all day to travel twenty-five miles. As the sun was setting behind the stone tower, bathing its rough walls in pink, Mary was grateful to dismount and come into the open door where Lord Livingston, his wife, and her dear Lusty stood waiting for her. She rushed to them and embraced them, her friends for so many years.

Mary Livingston, round-faced, buxom, with her simple life . . . it agreed with her, evidently. She looked healthier than any women at court.

That night there were French songs—which Bothwell knew well, since he spoke perfect French—reminiscences, and guarded talk. No one indicated that anything was other than perfectly and boringly in order.

On the stairs going up to their rooms, Bothwell was able to lean over and whisper, "Double your care. I now know that Lennox has some scheme in hand with the Continent. Secret money has been sent from the Pope, and a Jesuit has arrived here."

"But *I* am Catholic!" she whispered back. "Why would the Pope plot against *me*? Your information is, must be, incorrect."

"No! I agree, on the surface it is confusing. But—"

Lord Livingston came up beside them, effusively describing their quarters whilst simultaneously apologizing for them.

". . . I fear they may prove too small, forgive me. But the new hangings on the bed, just in from Paris, I persuade myself that they will please you—"

"Indeed, yes, I am sure," said Mary. She had begun to feel ill again, and wanted nothing more than to lie down with a basin nearby. And she needed to finish hearing what Bothwell had to say.

But he was firmly escorted to another wing of the house and there was no opportunity.

As Mary stretched out on the bed, closing her eyes to rest and quell her stomach, Mary Livingston came to bid her a good night's rest. She lingered for a moment at the foot of the bed, and at the sight of that loved and familiar face, Mary felt profoundly comforted. She longed to be able to confide in Lusty, but even as she was tempted to do so, the utter impossibility of it showed her the great gulf now separating her from her former life. She could not tell Lusty, or anyone who had known her earlier. There was no one in whom she dared confide now, except Bothwell.

She was completely alone without him.

Early the next morning they parted, Bothwell to return to Edinburgh and thence back to Crichton, Mary to continue the remaining twenty-five miles to Glasgow. Lord Livingston took Bothwell's place accompanying her.

As they made their way carefully over the winter landscape, penetrating deeper and deeper into the hostile Lennox Stewart territory, Mary was aware of a feeling of disquietude. The western part of Scotland had different loyalties and its own strongmen.

Along the way they skirted the high earthworks that were the remains of the second Roman wall, called the Antonine, now completely overgrown. Mary felt a great sadness remembering that Darnley had once been interested in the traces of the old Romans. He had once been interested in many things—or so she had thought.

Outside of Glasgow they were met by Thomas Crawford, a servant of Lennox's. He was there to call to Mary's attention—lest any should miss the insult—that his master was not present to welcome her.

The poltroon! Was he cowering in his chamber in Glasgow Castle, chewing on his nails? Or was he merely mocking her?

She could not hide the contempt in her voice as she said, "There exists no medicine against fear."

"My Lord has no fear in himself, but only of the cold and unkind words you have spoken to his son," Crawford bristled.

What a disagreeable, proud fellow this Crawford was—like master, like servant. "Have you any further commission?" she asked.

"No," he admitted.

"Then hold your peace," she ordered, and signalled her party to go around him and continue the journey into Glasgow.

The little village, spread out on the banks of the River Clyde, looked innocent and inviting as they approached it. In the centre of the town were a castle, a cathedral, and an adjoining Archbishop's Palace, empty since Archbishop Beaton had taken up permanent residence in Paris when Knox and his followers had prevailed seven years ago. It was to this pretty little cluster of buildings that the Queen made her way just as the setting sun was turning the waters of the Clyde crimson.

XLVII

Darnley was fidgeting with his pen. He had been seized suddenly with the desire to write poetry, as he was lying in bed ruminating on Mary's cruelty in contrast to his own pure and intense longing. He had roused himself from his sweat-soaked, foul sheets, and left his bed to sit shakily at his little table. Anthony Standen, his servant, had been instantly at his side, ready to coax him back into bed, but instead had been ordered to bring him pen and ink. He complied; Anthony had learned to obey always, immediately and unquestioningly. It was one of the things Darnley liked best about him.

Now Darnley, clad in his nightshirt with furs draped round his shoulders, slumped over the table and eyed his verse.

"Sweet—what rhymes?—tweet? 'In pursuit of their sweet, they tweet . . .'? No. Meat? 'To adore her is my meat'? Heat? Ah . . ."

He stared off into space and let the words sort themselves out in his mind, arrange themselves into the proper rows, like soldiers. How wonderful it was to have this poetic faculty.

"Ah . . . here it comes." He sat straight up and let the words pour down his arm.

> Though I think in pain,
> In passing to and fro,
> I labour all in vain;
> For so have many more
> That have not served so
> In pursuit of their sweet.
> The nearer the fire I go,
> The greater is my heat.

Perfect! And already the next verse leapt fully formed out of his mind.

> The turtledove for her mate
> More sorrow may not endure
> Than I do for her sake
> Even her which has in cure
> My heart. . . .

The pain. The pain was so wrenching he could not have borne it, except that he knew it would be ending soon. That gave him great comfort; to know that he had the power to bring about his own delivery and surcease

428

of his pain. And that he and Mary would be together forever. In the chronicles of history their names would always be mentioned in one breath.

I will make us immortal, he thought. What higher gift can a lover offer?

"Sire, Sir James Balfour is here," Standen announced.

Now the last verse would have to wait. He hoped he would not forget it. The last line was to be 'Farewell, I say no more'. But now to the means.

Darnley adjusted the taffeta mask in front of his face and clapped a hat on to hide the patches where his hair had fallen out.

"Enter," he said, holding his head up proudly on his thin neck. He drew his robes about him.

Balfour came in and tried to keep his repulsion from being visible. He was a middle-aged man whose skin had a peculiar paperlike quality and was stretched tight over all the planes of his face, looking almost shiny. He kept his hair shorter than did most men; his eyes were so light they gave an immediate impression of being just hard, milky marbles with no colour at all.

"I am honoured to be summoned, Your Majesty. In what way may I be of service?" he said, kneeling.

Darnley had helped him receive his appointment as secretary of the Council the previous autumn, despite his reputation as "the worst scoundrel in Scotland," earned the hard way over formidable competition: the murder of Cardinal Beaton; the plundering of ecclesiastical property; betrayals and blasphemy. Balfour had been willing to serve him—until someone else might pay a higher price. So far no one had.

"If—just suppose—I wished someone to die in an explosion . . . would it be technically possible? I know cannon explode, and the flimsy castle erected for that express purpose on the green at Stirling was blown up, but if one wished to rig a chamber . . ." Darnley's voice was quivering. What if it were not possible? He would be so disappointed! He caught his breath and waited.

"That is an inexact science, Your Majesty. Powder varies in its strength, and often becomes damp in our climate and fails to light at all. You would do better to arrange it in Italy!" He laughed, a dry, humourless laugh, as hard as the planes in his face.

"Unfortunately that is not an alternative." How dare this man laugh at him? He was as bad as all the rest. "If it must be brought about in Scotland, how would one go about it?"

Balfour breathed through his mouth to avoid the foul smell of Darnley's breath; it smelled like a peat bog with a rotting corpse in its midst. "In order to achieve an explosion, the powder must be tightly packed and contained. For a small explosion, a barrel would suffice. But to demolish a stone chamber . . . ah, that would require mining underneath." He saw Darnley's mouth clamp in anger. "Or using a house that has a low crypt or vault already beneath it."

"Do you know of such a house?"

"Why—yes." Balfour grinned. "My brother Robert has exactly such a dwelling—the old Provost's house at Kirk O'Field. But it is a rather costly dwelling, and he, of course, would have to be recompensed." He crossed his arms. "It would be an expensive killing. Why not just use a dagger? Much more economical. Quieter. Cleaner."

"I don't want it to be quiet or clean. I want it to be spectacular!" he cried.

"I see. Of course, the advantage to an explosion is that many people can be killed simultaneously, so perhaps if you look at it that way it is not so expensive. And it obliterates all clues. And it certainly makes a statement. Everyone will know it was intended and no accident."

"Exactly," breathed Darnley.

Balfour winced at the odour.

"Can you arrange this?" asked Darnley.

"Indeed. But, even at the risk of displeasing Your Majesty, I must know whom you intend to kill."

"Why?"

Balfour said curtly, "Because even I have principles. I will not kill just anyone. There are some my conscience will not permit."

"Oh?" The man was a liar. He had no conscience; he was only afraid he himself might be the intended victim. "Come closer, then. I will speak it only into your ear."

Holding his breath, Balfour put his head near Darnley's.

"The Queen," Darnley whispered.

Balfour started, and Darnley saw it.

"Speak now," said Darnley. "Can you see your way clear to it, or no?"

Balfour slid his eyes sideways and grinned. "Aye. I can undertake the task." And what might it be worth to others to try to prevent it? he wondered. Perhaps I shall become a very rich man!

"Good," said Darnley. "You make me very happy."

XLVIII

Mary and her party reached the courtyard, dismounted, and made ready to enter the castle itself. Huntly, Livingston, and their retainers had found quarters in town, and the Hamiltons likewise. Attendants with flaming torches led their horses away. Suddenly in the twilight Mary caught sight of Sir James Balfour leaving by way of a smaller door to one side of the castle. He was forced to pass through a far corner of the courtyard to the stables, and though he kept his cloak pulled partly across his face, his distinctive colourless eyes betrayed his identity to Mary.

Why was he here? The erstwhile henchman of Knox, the Cardinal's murderer, was now supposed to be in Bothwell's pocket. So Bothwell had told her. Bothwell had not mentioned his being in Glasgow. Obviously Bothwell had not known.

Mary nodded to him and he perfunctorily acknowledged her. The very furtiveness of the gesture disturbed her.

Bothwell warned me, she thought. He said there was danger, of what sort he was not sure. But certainly there are things here we do not know. . . . I am deep in my enemies' territory. Here my husband and his father are kings indeed.

She made her way slowly up the stairs inside the castle, holding her skirts. What awaited? Darnley's nursing would require several rooms, all connected, to administer all the necessary medicine and treatments.

Smoking torches lit the dark, narrow, tunnellike passageway, throwing uneven shadows on the bald stone, unrelieved by any tapestries. It was like a corridor in a nightmare, murky, cold, beckoning. She almost expected the sconces to move, like ghostly hands.

Why were there no guards here? Mary quietly turned the handle of the first door she came to. Inside was only a pallet and a table with stoppered jars, opaque bottles, and open bowls of dried herbs. The odour of marjoram and angelica permeated the chamber.

The next room revealed a bed of royal dimensions, hung with blue velvet embroidered valances, topped with a tasseled canopy, and even a prie-dieu before a crucifix. But this room, like the one before, was empty. Nonetheless Mary entered it and passed through it to the next, where she heard the low murmur of voices and even the sound of a lute.

Darnley was bent over the lute, singing to himself. She recognized him only by his voice, for the creature she saw was almost bald and covered with livid purple sores, and his hands were skeletal. A death's-head plucked the strings of the lute, and sang,

> "O ye highlands and ye lowlands,
> O where have you been?
> They have slain the Earl o' Moray,
> And laid him on the green."

Darnley tilted his head back and closed his eyes, making him look truly like a skull.

> "He was a brave gallant
> And he rode at the ring
> And the bonny Earl o' Moray
> He might have been a king."

"A bastard will never be king," she said loudly.

Darnley snapped open his eyes and stared at her. "So you've come," he stated, but it was an accusation, not a welcome. Now it was too late for him to hide his face behind the taffeta mask. No matter—let her see him as he was!

"As you see." She tried not to stare at him, but the transformation was so startling she had to struggle not to. His flesh had melted from his always-delicate bones, so that he looked like one of those grotesque, sticklike figures swinging from gibbets, only his skin was not black and rotted, it was translucent and rotted, dotted with scabs and patches of purple. The bald head made him look preternaturally old.

"Bourgoing has helped me," he said, laying aside the lute. "You should have seen me earlier!" His eyes narrowed. "Come, dear wife, and kiss me!"

She forced herself to smile and made her way closer to him. He looked even worse close up. Some of the sores were still oozing. She found an unblemished place near his left eye, and lightly touched her lips to it.

"Thank you," he murmured. "Already I feel the healing begin."

His breath stank, with a distinctive odour unlike anything she had ever smelled before. It *festered*; there was no other word for it.

I cannot go through with this, she thought. No, not for anything can I allow myself to be shut up with him, to spend the night in that room. I will have to bring him back with me to Edinburgh, keep him close at hand, and then, one night when he is healed. . . .

Or will he ever *be* healed? What if this sickness is permanent, or mortal? What if he only gets worse? What if this is my only chance to spend the night with him?

Then I will have to endure my later shame, for I cannot—

"You stare, dear wife. Does the sight of me disgust you?"

This is what sin looks like, she thought. His happens to be visible on his face, that is all. Mine and Bothwell's is as yet invisible. But all sin is as ugly as this, could we but see it.

"No. I pity you." And it was true, she did. As when François had lain ill so many times, and as when Darnley himself had had the severe attack of measles, she was moved. "I would you could be instantly healed. It pains me to see you in such discomfort."

Anthony Standen, Darnley's handsome young English attendant, seemed to materialize out of the shadows in the corner of the room. Darnley scowled at him.

"Bring me some heated towels," he demanded in a querulous voice. "My face needs dabbing."

Standen left the chamber.

"Are you pained? It is your unkindness to me that has made me ill," he said. "It is because of your cruelty that I am as you see me." He glared at her and then slowly, accusingly, ran his hand over his bald pate. "God knows how I am punished for making a god of you and for having no other thought but of you!"

She stepped as far away from him as politeness would allow. "I fail to see

432

how I have treated you cruelly, nor have I ever in any way wished you to treat me as a god."

"You are cruel when you refuse to accept my repentance, to reconcile with me." He attempted to rise, but his weakened legs would not support him. They shook with the effort. "Oh, you say I repent and then fail again. But I am young! Am I not permitted the failing of youth? Why do you expect so much of me?" He glared at her. "You have forgiven others of your subjects who have transgressed—traitors like Morton and Lord James. Yes, to *them* you are merciful!"

He looked so innocent and helpless. But he was full of lies; possibly he lied so much that even he could not remember his lies and therefore felt himself honest.

"What of the rumours that have reached various members of the Council that you have a ship at the ready to convey you from Scotland? And there is a Mr. Hiegate who has revealed that you are plotting to seize me and crown the Prince. A Glasgow man, Walker, reported it to me." Mary attacked him back.

"I'll pluck his ears from his head!" cried Darnley. "He is a liar! There is no plot—except the one by members of *your* Council. Yes, I have heard about the plan to put me in prison and slay me if I resist. The Provost of Glasgow has revealed it to me! But then," he admitted with a cloying tone, "it was also reported that you refused to sign the request when they presented it to you."

Someone at Craigmillar had betrayed her! Or was it an eavesdropper, and not one of the five conspirators? She felt cold, and very vulnerable.

"Thus," he was saying softly, "I would never believe that you, who are after all my own flesh in God's eyes, would do me any evil."

His flesh . . . his rotten flesh . . . one flesh . . . but can I say the same of him, that he would never harm me?

Standen returned, carrying a tray of heated wet towels. He began applying them gently to Darnley's neck and face, wiping away the crusts from his sores. Darnley looked contented, like a cat being stroked.

"I will take to my bed," he finally told Standen, and the groom pulled him to his feet and then helped him to walk, trembling, into the bedroom. Darnley fell to his knees on the prie-dieu and looked longingly at the crucifix. Then he allowed himself to be ushered into bed. Shaking with the exertion, he managed to crawl beneath the covers. His spindly legs showed for an instant, like a stork's legs, before being covered.

"I desire nothing more in this life than we might reconcile, and live again as man and wife," he said, after Standen had left the chamber. "And if that should not be, if I knew it would never come about, I will never rise from this bed; no, never again!"

"It is what I wish, too," she said, in the most pleasant and persuasive tone at her command. "I came to see you for just this reason. But first you must be purged of your illness; and it is best you return with me to Craigmillar

433

Castle for treatment. It is healthier than low-lying Holyrood, and yet near enough that I can attend on you every day. And the chambers are such that the series of medicinal baths you must undergo can be easily administered."

"I cannot travel."

"I brought a litter to convey you."

"Are you, then, so anxious that I should recover and we be reunited?" He sounded touched. "Do you truly wish this?"

She nodded.

"Ah, then! I shall persuade myself that it is true; for were it otherwise, greater inconvenience might come to us than you are aware of." He sighed, and drew up his covers.

"We are both tired," she said, relieved that the encounter was over for the night. She turned to go.

"Stay here! Don't go!"

"Nay, I must sleep elsewhere, away from the sick-chamber. The Archbishop's Palace is only a hundred yards away. I shall come back early, I promise—"

His hand darted out with the speed of a striking snake and grabbed her wrist.

"No! You must not leave! You will not return—"

"I promise I shall!" She tried to unwrap his bony fingers.

"Is Bothwell here?"

Her blood stopped. "No, of course not!" She pulled her wrist away.

"Pretend this is the Hermitage, then, and the Archbishop's Palace is Jedburgh, and I doubt not that you shall return speedily enough in the morning," he muttered. Then his tone suddenly changed. "Oh, I am so happy to see you I could almost *die* of gladness!"

Finally settled alone in her inmost chamber as the guest of the permanently absent Archbishop, she slipped out of bed. Mary Seton, her only attendant—Madame Rallay was too old to make this wintertime journey—had dutifully prayed with her and then withdrawn, leaving her, as she thought, to sleep.

But sleep? No, this was not a night for sleep. Seeing Darnley like that, reduced to a mere manifestation of illness, was shocking. Even in this chamber, the strange mantle of evil that seemed to blanket Glasgow Castle lay heavy in the room. Mary Seton, earnest, pious woman that she was, might not have even sensed the aura. Perhaps one had already to be acquainted with evil to perceive it.

Mary pulled out some sheets of paper, which she had managed to hide with her personal effects, although they were not of the best quality. Quietly she smoothed one out and then placed a candlestick at one corner to light it and hold it down.

She took her pen and began to write. No salutation, no date, no address. She must not identify either herself or the receiver.

Being gone from the place where I had left my heart, it may easily be judged what my countenance was, considering what the body is without the heart. . . .

It had been so hard to leave him and ride away to do this repugnant and difficult task. It was because of their love, and their sin, that she was forced into it. . . .

But would I undo it? she asked herself. Would I erase every embrace, make every kiss not to have happened? No. I did not start to live until then, and to obliterate my joy would be to die.

Bothwell . . . She imagined him holding her, now, bending his head down to kiss her breasts, she laying her cheek against the sleek hair growing so closely on his head. . . . Her body ached to hold him, receive him.

She was trembling. The candle flame moved in the cold draft from the walls.

She must communicate what had happened today.

Four miles from Glasgow a gentleman of the Earl of Lennox came and made his commendations and excuses unto me. . . .

She wrote of her arrival in Glasgow, of the lairds who had greeted her and, more ominously, of the ones who had stayed away.

She recounted Darnley's answers to the rumours of his own plot, his counteraccusations of her plot to have him imprisoned and then killed, and his entire conversation regarding her estrangement from him and his desire to be forgiven and reconciled. The candle burned down and splashed wax on the paper. She replaced it with a fresh one.

The King asked me many questions, about whether I had taken French Paris, and Gilbert Curle as my secretary. I wonder who has told him so much—even of the coming marriage of Bastian, my French master of the household?

He became angry when I spoke to him of Walker and said that he would pluck his ears from his head, and that he lies; for I asked him earlier what cause he had to complain of some of the Lords and to threaten them. He denied it, and said he would rather lose his life than do me the least displeasure. As for the other, he would at least sell his life dear enough.

Perhaps Bothwell would understand this. It was good that it be recorded.

He has told me all on the bishop's behalf and Sutherland's, touching the matter that you had warned me about. Now to make him trust me I must pretend toward him; and therefore when he desired me to promise that when he should be well we should make but one bed I told him, feigning to believe his fair promise, that if he did not change his mind, I was contented. But to keep it secret, for the Lords feared that if we came together, he might take revenge on them.

"I am glad that you talked to me of the Lords," he said. "I hope that you wish to live a happy life with me from now on. For if it is not so, it could be that greater inconvenience should come to us both than you expect."

Those were his words. What had they meant? Perhaps Bothwell would know.

He would not let me go, but would have me watch with him. I made as though I thought all to be true and that I would think upon it, and have excused myself from sitting up with him this night, for he said that he does not sleep well. You have never heard him speak better or more humbly; and if I had not proof that his heart is changeable like wax, and that mine is already hard as a diamond, I would take pity on him. But fear not, I shall not fail of my purpose nor be untrue to you.

Darnley was touching, Darnley was a picture of contrition—but Darnley was a liar and a murderer.

I shall not be deceived in him, she thought, no matter how pitiable he is.

She felt as though there were some other presence in the chamber. She turned her head and looked into the shadows, but there was nothing. Just a feeling.

But I am now a liar, too, she thought. He has contaminated me and begun to make me like himself. One flesh . . . he called me his own flesh.

I do here a work that I hate much. You would laugh to see me lie so well, or at least to dissemble so well, mixing truth with untruths.

He said that there be some persons who commit secret faults and fear not to have them spoken of loudly, and that there is talk of both great and small. And even touching the Lady Reres, he said, "God grant that she serve to your honour," and that none should have occasion to think that my own power was not in myself.

Were these words meaningful, or just Darnley-babble? No one knew about her meetings with Bothwell—did they? Darnley was testing her. But if he thought this could drive her to confess, he did not know her.

I have told him that he must be purged and that it could not be done here. I told him that I myself would convey him to Craigmillar, so the physicians and I might cure him without being far from my son.

My son. I must be careful not to call him "our son" or "the Prince" lest the letter fall into enemy hands.

Excuse it if I write badly; I am ill at ease, and yet happy to write to you when others are asleep, seeing that I cannot do what I most desire, that is to lie between your arms, my dear life, whom I beseech God to preserve from all ill.

A love letter—this was turning into a love letter. How many love letters had Bothwell received? She knew he kept the most florid ones in a strongbox covered with studs and locked up. She would give him a silver one to hold hers, and make him destroy the others.

The others. She hated thinking of them, and knew there were many more she would never even know about. Janet Beaton, the witch-woman of Branxton, still supernaturally beautiful past the age of fifty; Anna Thrond-sen, the Norwegian admiral's daughter, who had followed him back to Scotland and skulked about for years in the country. Had she gone back to Norway now? There was an illegitimate son, William Hepburn, who was Bothwell's heir. But who was his mother?

And Lady Bothwell, Jean Gordon? She had not loved Bothwell when they married, but now? He had slept with her, had undoubtedly kissed *her* breasts, and she, too, had rested her cheek against his hair.

O saints! Jealousy transforms all my cherished private memories into a Hell if they be not truly private.

He will have to divorce her. And when the Lords and Parliament free me—for they will find a legal way—then we can marry.

> We are bound to two unworthy mates. The devil sunder us and God knit us together for ever the most faithful couple that ever he did knit together.

She looked at the words, horrified, and crossed out "devil" and wrote "the good year." How had she called on the devil?

She pushed the paper away. Why was she writing these things? She felt possessed.

There is evil here, I can almost feel it, she thought.

She wiped her sweating, but cold, palms on her gown.

Almost by itself her hand took up the pen and continued writing.

> I am weary, yet I cannot forbear scribbling as long as there is any paper. Cursed be this pox-marked person who vexes me! He is not much disfigured, but he is in a bad state. I have been almost slain with his breath, even though I sat no nearer him than the foot of his bed.
>
> To be short, I have learned that he is very suspicious, but nonetheless trusts me, and will go anywhere upon my word.
>
> Alas! I never deceived anybody, but you are the cause thereof. You make me dissemble so much that I am afraid with horror, and you make me almost play the part of a traitor.

But Bothwell had never wanted her to go through with this. He had rather she rid herself of the child. To him it was the simple, straightforward solution to a physical problem.

Bothwell. He was primarily a soldier and he himself was sinking in the bog of intrigue, as her white horse had sunk in the mire returning to Jedburgh. He was as much out of his element as she was. They were both in great danger.

> Now if to please you, my dear life, I spare neither honour, conscience, nor hazard, nor greatness. . . .

Then *she* was making a god of Bothwell, even as Darnley had made one of her. Yes, she was infected with his sin; she had caught the soul-sickness.

> I should never be weary in writing to you, yet I will end, after kissing your hands. Burn this letter, for it is dangerous, neither is there anything well said in it, for I think of nothing but upon grief. . . .

The sky was growing light; the yellow candlelight made the paper look smudged and dirty. She folded it up, and got it ready to give to French Paris, Bothwell's trusted messenger. She had never felt more alone.

XLIX

he little party made its way slowly across the cold, barren landscape. Lord Livingston, who had been patiently waiting in Glasgow for the last ten days, led the way. Mary and her attendants rode directly behind, and Darnley, stretched out in Mary's own litter, which was slung between two horses, was conveyed as gently as possible over the rough road. The litter was covered, so no wind could tear at his healing face. But he kept his taffeta mask on as a double protection from curious eyes and unkind weather.

He had improved greatly, although it would be months until the eruptions faded completely—so he was told. He was still weak, and unsure how he would endure the journey. But travelling this way, swaying gently as they descended or climbed the hills, was lulling, and he felt like a baby as he drifted in and out of sleep.

Mary was relieved to be out of the alien and vaguely threatening Lennox territory. Her time in Glasgow had been both tedious and ghastly, for it seemed always to be night there, and her hours followed no normal sequence. She took upon herself the rhythm of Darnley's sickroom, which remade the world in its own distorted image. Now the great empty sky, the sunrise and sunset, were welcome demarcations of unyielding normalcy. She felt she could not breathe deeply enough of the stinging sharp air, as though her lungs were still full of sickroom odours.

Strange, but her queasiness had disappeared once she had been confronted with the truly repulsive sight of Darnley's syphilis, and assaulted by the mortal smell of decay. It was as if she could not afford to let her body be weak in any way.

She had not heard from Bothwell, but then it was not necessary. She had done her best to inform him of whatever political statements she had been able to coax Darnley into making, but none of them seemed particularly alarming. Whatever mischief Darnley might have planned for later, he would be less effective now that he was separated from his father, and his father's men. There was no one in Edinburgh for him to plot *with*; none of the lords trusted him, or wanted to have any dealings with him.

A huge raven, its broad back gleaming iridescent, flew from tree to barren tree ahead of them and waited for them to pass, cocking its head. Then it would flap its heavy wings and skim through the air to the next tree. It never cawed, but just looked at them balefully.

They travelled in easy stages, stopping even between Callendar House and Edinburgh at Linlithgow. Bothwell was to meet them the next morning and ceremoniously escort them the rest of the way.

It is nearly over! thought Mary, not with joy but with profound relief. Knowing that she would soon be back in Bothwell's territory, she felt safe once more.

But the next morning, as Darnley walked a little unsteadily to his litter, he motioned to Mary. She left her horse, which she was just preparing to mount, and came over to him.

"I have decided against Craigmillar," he said. The words seemed unhuman, emanating from a mask.

"But I have installed the baths for you there," she protested. "The physicians have already moved into their quarters, and set up their apothecary's tables and weights. You know you cannot go to Holyrood—it is low-lying and damp. Nor can you go to Edinburgh Castle—it is cold and windy. There is no place else suitable." She tried to keep the irritation from her voice. If she irritated him, he would be all the more stubborn.

"I wish to go to Kirk O'Field," he announced.

"Where?"

"Kirk O'Field. I am told that the air is good there, and that Lord Borthwick, whose life had been despaired of, recently stayed there, and made a full recovery."

"But the arrangements have already been made."

"Then unmake them," he said grandly, drawing aside the curtain of his litter. "I wish us to lodge at Kirk O'Field."

" 'Us'? But I cannot stay with you until you have completed your course of treatment!"

"I request merely that you stay in the same house. It need not be the same room. All I want is for us to be under the same roof! That is all I ask! Can you not grant me that?"

"But, Darnley—"

"It is such a *little* request! And it is the last I shall pester you with!"

He sounded so unhappy, desperately pleading.

"Very well," she said.

Outside Edinburgh, on the Linlithgow Road, Bothwell and his men were waiting for her, sitting their horses as straight and still as if it were summertime, with no need to shiver or begrudge the time.

A great wash of excitement and relief surged through her. His dear face, his strength, were near once again. It seemed a long time since she had parted from him, instead of only a week. As she drew up beside him and he saluted her, she said, "We go not to Craigmillar, but to Kirk O'Field."

Bothwell's surprise registered on his face. "To the church?"

"Nay, to the dwelling where Lord Borthwick recuperated. The King wishes to take his treatments there."

"But—"

Mary shook her head. "The King insists."

When they reached Edinburgh, they passed through a gate in the town wall and then made their way along the High Street for only a short way. Near St. Giles they turned down Blackfriars Wynd, a side street that went directly south, dropping down as it crossed the wide Cowgate, and then rising again as it approached the ecclesiastical buildings on a hill almost outside the town wall. Indeed, some of them did lie outside the wall, for they had been built to stand in open fields—hence the name. In olden days there had been three imposing religious foundations all in a six-hundred-yard row along the hilltop: Blackfriars monastery, the church of Kirk O'Field, and a Franciscan monastery. The Reformation and Henry VIII's marauding armies had not treated them kindly. Blackfriars, which had once had a stately church and a sumptuous guest house for noble visitors, was now in ruins; the Franciscans had not fared better. Kirk O'Field, which had served as a *Collegium Sacerdotum*, a training school for priests, had retained its quadrangle of buildings, but these had passed into secular hands. Robert Balfour had taken over the Provost's house, and the Duke of Châtelherault, head of the Hamiltons, had moved into what used to be the hospital and guest house.

The royal party entered the quadrangle, with its old covered well in the centre, and the horses drawing Darnley's litter came to a halt. Reaching out a thin white hand, he drew back the curtains and then stuck his feet out. Sir Anthony Standen was instantly beside him, helping him alight.

Darnley turned around, looking over the buildings. The large building, belonging to the Duke, was not for his use. The Balfour buildings—for there were three of them, all attached—directly across from the Duke's, were the designated ones.

Sure enough, Robert Balfour emerged from the newest looking of the dwellings.

"Welcome, Your Highnesses," he said, bowing. He had light eyes like his brother, but was much more fleshy. "All is prepared. It is a great honour, yea, great—"

Indeed, the entire adjoining house, with its connecting long chamber, was in readiness. In the old Provost's house, the upper chamber had been aired and fresh rushes laid down. A dais had been constructed at the far end of the great chamber. Fires were blazing in all the fireplaces, and the chill had been thoroughly driven away.

Mary put out her hand and felt the stone walls. They were quite dry. It took several days, at this time of year, to dry them out. And building a dais fifteen feet wide took time and required carpenters.

They knew long beforehand to prepare for our coming, she thought. But it was only this morning that Darnley had suddenly announced that he wished to come here.

Announced it? Announced what had already been decided and arranged?

She felt a prickling and tingling in her scalp underneath her jewelled cap.

What is happening? Who knew we were coming? Why does Darnley really wish to stay here?

She glanced behind her at her husband, always tall and thin, but now almost wraithlike. Is he planning another murder? Who is it he wishes to kill now?

Me?

No, he loves me, like a love-slave.

Bothwell? He seems suspicious of him, but he must know that Bothwell is the only one of the lords never to have entered into an intrigue against us. Lord James? Maitland? Yes, he hates them, but he is alone in his hatred. Lord James and Maitland do not stand as helpless foreigners, like poor Riccio. . . .

A wave of contempt swept over her. Who was so poor in Scotland that he could not find allies and fellow conspirators? Only this weak, depraved, muddleheaded creature! Let him plan his plans—they would be as inept as he was!

"We must send for furniture," Mary said, looking at Darnley. "I had already ordered many pieces to be transported to Craigmillar. Now from Holyrood we will bring your bed, the one with the violet-brown hangings and silver and gold embroidery which I gave you as a recent gift; tapestries for these walls, which are already so dry we need not worry about harming the needlework . . . the seven-piece set called *The Hunting of Coneys*. And, of course, for the garderobe, your *chaise perchée*, for when you need to . . ."

She could not see Darnley's face behind the taffeta mask. Was he angry? Embarrassed?

". . . relieve yourself of the flux which troubles you so," she said loudly.

She hoped he was embarrassed. Let everyone picture him perched on the rim of the velvet-covered privy, making foul smells and noises. Oh, that would confirm his royalty in everyone's imagination!

He turned away, and she instantly felt bad. He was a fool, a whining, selfish child who was evidently planning more mischief. But to descend to the level of mocking his infirmity and making comments in public about his bowels was inexcusable.

"I will also send for all the medicines, and for the bathtub for your treatment," she said quickly. "And if there be a suitable place for me, I shall sleep here as well."

Still Darnley kept his arms crossed and looked down at the floor, sulkily.

"Naturally there is a place for you," said Robert Balfour smoothly. "It is directly beneath His Majesty's. May I show it to you?"

They turned and walked the forty feet back across the long chamber. In the connecting passage they had to ascend by two or three steps, as the two buildings were on slightly different ground levels.

Balfour led the way down from the stone-slab landing at the top of the spiral staircase, and around and out into a set of rooms identical to Darnley's: an antechamber connected to a larger bedroom.

Even here a fire burned, and sweet rushes mixed with herbs made the room smell like a faded June meadow.

"It seems you are either very wealthy, heating and scenting empty rooms, or else very meticulous, in that you dislike leaving anything undone," Mary said to Balfour. She watched him carefully.

"I confess to a certain extravagance," he said. "It is a failing of mine."

No it isn't, Mary was tempted to say, but something held her back, an instinctive caution. The fur on his doublet was frayed and he wore no jewels or gold. Extravagance was not his natural vice.

He has been told to prepare all this, and ready a chamber for me, to make it as inviting as possible, she thought. On whose orders?

Suddenly the isolated location, the small quarters—which would permit few guards—seemed an ominous choice.

She saw Balfour looking at her.

If anyone seeks my life as they sought Riccio's, they will surely fail, she thought. I have Bothwell to see I come to no harm.

"This chamber will be most suitable," she finally said.

As soon as she reasonably could, she left Kirk O'Field and went to Holyrood, ostensibly to select the furniture and accoutrements to be sent to the convalescent house.

It should have felt welcoming, but the same atmosphere of wrongness hung over it as over Kirk O'Field. Her own apartments seemed filled with ghosts: Riccio's, Ruthven's, and nameless ones that nonetheless had a presence. It had never been purged of its evil.

Why, that is because Bothwell and I have never been together here, she realized.

But the thought of making love in the chamber where Riccio had been slain was abhorrent.

She contrived to linger long enough that she might have an opportunity to speak, however briefly, with Bothwell. Her valets were busy laying a fire: even the royal apartments did not, as a rule, have fires blazing until their occupants arrived.

Those fires . . . the careful preparations . . . it was inordinately disturbing.

Bothwell appeared in the doorway, and her heart leapt.

'Tis true, what Diane de Poitiers once told me, she thought with surprise. To love someone is to catch your breath whenever he walks into a room.

His brow was furrowed and he looked distracted. She forgot her own troubling thoughts in her anxiety to soothe him. He was glancing around, annoyed, at the chamber attendants. Their presence prevented him from speaking, but to send them away would assure their suspicions.

So she said, "Is it not odd how the King took a sudden whim to lodge at Kirk O'Field? I cannot imagine why. It will make his treatment more difficult, but he insists."

The attendants were fanning the fire, which was having trouble catching. Clouds of smoke poured out into the chamber; they had not made sure the chimney was clear. There was a scrambling and hissing as some animal nesting inside was smoked out. Bothwell looked at them in disdain.

"Will you be joining him?" he asked in a matter-of-fact voice.

"I will visit with him, but I do not wish to impede the doctors. His treatment, after all, is the most important thing. There is a large reception chamber there," she added, "with a dais already fitted at one end. Perhaps, as he improves, some of the members of court can visit with him there. Yes, I must have his chair of estate sent down. He will need it to receive callers."

Bothwell glanced at the attendants, still on their knees, nursing the fire. He rolled his eyes. "I wish him a speedy recovery," he finally said. Bowing, he took his leave.

Wait! she wanted to say. *Wait.* I must talk to you about what is happening.

But it was hopeless. She would have to wait for a more private time.

❧

For the next few days, Darnley was kept in strict seclusion while the physicians put him through a course of treatment that included hot baths with salt and goat-fat ointment, broth with dried red peppers and mulberries, and applications of dressings of oil of roses and camphor to fade his lesions and prevent scarring. Between the treatments, which were administered every four hours, he was supposed to lie in bed and sleep. But in truth, it required so long to fill the tub with the hot water that half the time Darnley was kept awake by the attendants dumping their buckets of water into the tub and replacing the door that served as a lid to keep the heat in.

Since he knew they were watching him the whole time, he made sure he was engaged in edifying activities. He sang various Psalms and studied the Bible, and kept a rosary conspicuously by his bedside. He wanted to make sure that his last week was remembered for its piety and goodness. He wrote letters to his father, who had been so concerned about his safety, reassuring him and extolling the Queen's reconciliation with him.

> My Lord, I have thought to write unto you by this bearer of my good health, I thank God. Which is the sooner come to, through the good treatment of such as hath this good while concealed her good will, I mean of my love, the Queen. Which I assure you hath all this while and yet doth, use herself like a natural and loving wife, I hope yet that God will lighten our hearts with joy that have so long been afflicted with trouble. As I in this letter do write unto your Lordship, so I trust this bearer can certify to you the like. Thus thanking Almighty God of our good hap, I commit your Lordship unto His Protection.
> From Edinburgh the i. of February, your loving and obedient son,
>
> HENRY, REX

Yes. God would lighten their hearts with joy. Soon they would be together in His sight and transported from this vale of afflictions.

But when would these treatments be mitigated so that the Queen could spend the night? Otherwise it was not possible to carry out his plan. And if not here, then where?

After four days of this regimen, the doctors pronounced themselves astounded and gratified by his progress. The baths would be reduced to two: one upon arising and one upon retiring. The dressings would be discontinued, except only a light application of salve on the eruptions, and he could return to regular food.

"And Your Majesty may have visitors," they said, "after the morning bath. Only"—the physicians looked at each other—"we recommend that, before granting audience to anyone, Your Majesty rub his teeth with these dried rosemary twigs, and then gargle with this lavender water."

Darnley frowned. So his breath was *that* foul? It was due to his lack of eating real food, that was all. He snatched the twigs. "Very well."

One of the doctors handed him a little mirror. "It is no longer necessary to wear the mask," he said.

Darnley inspected his face. The livid purple had subsided, but his face was still blotched with pink round spots.

"This salve contains white clay. It will help to hide the marks." The doctor dabbed a bit on Darnley's face.

Darnley smiled. The result was astonishing. He could barely see the spot.

"And so for Your Majesty's hair, you can wear hats until it has quite grown in again."

The physicians were pleased with their expertise. The King could now be seen in public again—until his next attack, which was bound to come, and would prove fatal.

The reception chamber was thronged with courtiers, eager to pay their respects—or get a glimpse of the ailing King to satisfy their own curiosity and report their findings to their masters in France and England. The Lord James, Bothwell, Maitland, Huntly, Argyll, Mar, and Kirkcaldy of Grange all crowded round the double-seated chair of estate, covered with red and yellow taffeta, where Darnley and Mary sat together. The Balfour brothers came, as did John Stewart of Traquair. Philibert du Croc, the French ambassador, and Moretta, the slow-moving Savoyan who had arrived at last, were alert to every word.

The fires blazed, the musicians played, and there was superficial talk about the weather and the season. Lent was to start next week, and in other countries carnival was under way, but here in Scotland it was to be confined to just one Catholic celebration: the wedding of two of the Queen's household, the Frenchman Bastian Pages and his Scottish sweetheart, Margaret Carwood. After the ceremony on Sunday, a wedding masque at Holyrood would require costumes and games and disguises. Knox, after all, was in England and could not interfere.

Mary, as always, watched Bothwell as he moved easily in and out of the crowd, his broad shoulders creating their own space. She could pick his voice out from the babble of all the others.

God knows how I am punished for making my god of you and for having no other thought but of you.

How stupid it had sounded when Darnley said it to her; how different it was to feel it herself.

Was this idolatry?

Thou shalt have no other gods before me, for I the Lord thy God am a jealous God.

The thought of God taking vengeance and destroying her idol, Bothwell, as He had the Baals of Israel, terrified her. Suddenly he looked very vulnerable standing there, in spite of the strength of his body.

It is wrong to love him so, she thought. But how can I stop?

She glanced over at Darnley, who was laughing in a high-pitched, feeble voice. He seemed to sense her attention, and slid his glance toward her. Hesitantly he reached for her hand.

"Pray stay with me tonight. It would comfort me to know you are under the same roof." He squeezed her hand, but there was no strength in the grip.

Mary made ready to sleep. She had found the little bedroom—it was only about twelve by sixteen feet—strangely appealing. It reminded her of the room she had had at St.-Pierre, when she had visited her aunt Renée, the night the letter had come from Lord James and the others, bidding her to return.

She stood looking out the window at the enclosed yard of the quadrangle. A light snow had fallen, covering the ground in white. Across the way, about a hundred feet, was the imposing house of the Duke of Châtelherault, with many candles burning in the night.

The Hamiltons keep late hours, she thought. She blew out her own candle and settled herself under the covers. Purposely, she had dismissed her ladies. Tonight she would have no attendants, no witnesses. She and her lawful husband, King Henry, Lord Darnley, were alone under the same roof, except for his servants sleeping in the antechamber. If she later claimed he had visited her in her bed that night, there would be no one to contradict her. No one could prove it untrue.

She sighed. She was safe. She had delivered herself from the shame of bearing a bastard.

And as for delivery from the yoke of marriage to Darnley . . . she did not need the machinations of the courtiers and the help of Parliament after all. Darnley would not live long; the marks of death were on him for all to see, in spite of all the physicians had done. It was so horribly apparent that he was doomed, and it made the hearty well-wishing and compliments given him that day seem brutal and obscene. Everyone knew that syphilis disappeared for a time before its final attack.

Directly below her, she heard the noise of the cooks closing up the kitchen for the night, heard their tired voices trail off. Then the house was quiet.

She slept, then heard someone moving on the spiral stair outside her room. Not Darnley! Surely he would not really come? She sat upright, cold waves of fear running through her. She held her breath.

But no—they were ascending, not descending. Someone was going up to Darnley's quarters. Someone had to see him in the middle of the night. The physicians?

Yes. That must be it. The physicians.

She let out a breath of relief and lay back down. Now she heard the footsteps above her, heard a slight bump, but could hear no voices. They were speaking in whispers, lest the attendants be disturbed. She closed her eyes. Her only responsibility was to obtain the best physicians for her husband, not to monitor the treatment or the conversations. She could safely leave it in their hands.

❧

Darnley was sitting up in bed, his eyes shining unnaturally bright in the light of the single tall candle by his bedside, as the Balfours approached.

"We waited until three o'clock," James Balfour whispered. "Even the candles at Hamilton House are out. The Queen sleeps, and she has no ladies in her antechamber. We are completely unobserved." He took his place beside Darnley, and his brother stood on the other side of the bed.

"I am now determined to proceed with my plan," said Darnley in his lowest speaking voice. "As of tonight, I know that the Queen will pass the night here if I beg her. Before, I was not sure. And when I was undergoing extensive treatment—"

"For which we are so thankful you have responded so well," said Robert unctuously.

"We thank you," said Darnley. "Now as to the plan . . . ?"

"I would suggest that, if Your Highness is indeed resolved to carry it out, I obtain the requisite amount of gunpowder and store it in the cellar of your house, Robert." James glanced at his brother. "Then, when it is all collected, we can transfer it directly to the vaults beneath the long chamber. We can dig a small tunnel for the purpose and be assured of complete secrecy."

"The long chamber!" cried Robert. "You wish to destroy the long chamber?"

"Sssh. You will be recompensed by His Majesty," James hissed. "We do not 'wish' to destroy the chamber; we would, in fact, *prefer* to destroy the old house, where we are now. But two things prevent it. The kitchens occupy the ground floor, and the cooks and servants there might detect our activity just beneath them. And the ground slopes steeply here, so that the vaults are much higher beneath the old house than beneath the long reception hall. It would take twice or even three times the amount of gunpowder, for the powder must be tightly packed to achieve any force when it explodes. So you see, don't you, why we must sacrifice the long chamber? I know you are fond of it, but—"

"How much powder will it take?" Darnley's eyes glittered.

"Several thousand pounds, even for the long chamber," said James. "But I have means of obtaining it quickly."

"Without suspicion?" asked Robert sarcastically.

James smiled. "What do you take me for? Of course, without suspicion."

"Do it all tomorrow, then, and do your digging," said Darnley. "Tomorrow is Thursday. On Friday night I shall beg the Queen to be so kind as to stay here again with her ailing, melancholy husband. Then, at about this time— no, about five o'clock —the powder can be lit. I will order my horses to be saddled and waiting for me at that hour. Then, as the powder train takes a long time to burn, tell me just as it is lighted."

"The Queen seems most kind to you, Sire," said Robert.

"Seems, Robert, seems. But things are not always as they seem. There is no doubt that both Scotland and all the court and her subjects would be better off without her. For Scotland cannot have a Papist for its ruler, since it has chosen to be under the Reformed faith. If she lives, she will surely raise the Prince to be a Papist as well. The baptism was proof of that. And my refusing to attend was my statement about it. As for the court, have not most of the nobles already rebelled against her at one time or another? All except Bothwell. And even her subjects, though they know it not, deserve more than a sovereign who rides about looking pretty but has not the will to administer justice, and is so concerned with her rights to the English throne that she values the one she occupies but scantily. Does not

Scotland deserve a ruler who reveres its native throne, rather than belittling it?" He paused. The recital of reasons had taken away his breath. He hoped they were convincing.

"Still," Robert demurred, "to assassinate a ruler is a grievous sin."

"You assassinated a cardinal," Darnley reminded him. "And now let me summon Anthony Standen, my attendant, whom I trust absolutely. He must aid us in these plans."

The Balfours murmured their grave misgivings about including anyone else. But Darnley insisted on rousing Anthony and informing him of the plot. Because he was still sleep-befuddled, he did not at first question the idea or its execution.

"He has strong shoulders, and can help you dig and carry the powder," Darnley insisted.

"Begging your pardon, have you considered leaving clues to point to someone else?" Standen asked, waking up at last. "For, its being your own house, the finger of suspicion will surely point at you."

The lad was clever. "Hmmm—we might throw the blame on Lord James—or on Bothwell—with a few carefully arranged articles. An empty barrel. Or perhaps someone could impersonate them passing through the streets. I must think on it. Thank you, lad." James nodded gravely.

After they had slipped silently away in their velvet slippers, Darnley blew out his candle and lay back down. But his heart was pounding as if he had just run a race.

It was to happen.

He was so excited he was almost shaking.

For an instant he thought of doing just what he had convinced his dupes he meant to do: blow up the Queen and escape himself.

But no. If he made a miraculous, timely escape, everyone would know he had done it, and then he would be hounded and executed anyway. Better to die this way, by his own hand and in his own time. With *her.*

He had broken out in a sweat. He imagined the force of the explosion, of being thrown from his bed, of vanishing in an incandescent flash.

It was a death by fire, then, but as far removed from the slow, ugly death at the stake as a fiery Arabian stallion, trained to race, was from a hobbling old donkey. One was a marvel of nature, awe-inspiring in its power, the other a poor, paltry, failing thing.

Death by fire. It was a fitting way for an adulteress to die—prescribed by law, even. And she was an adulteress. Any lingering doubts had been removed that afternoon when he saw her gazing on Bothwell. The look in her eyes had been unmistakable.

And as for his own death—he felt a strange, almost erotic power in planning it and knowing he could achieve it in exactly the manner he wished. He felt like God. God might have planned for him to die of syphilis, or be murdered by the Lords like Riccio. But he had outwitted God. He would not settle for the donkey of God's choosing, but mount the Arabian steed and ride to a thrilling death.

A certain Edinburgh merchant accepted sixty pounds from Sir James Balfour in exchange for enormous quantities of powder on Thursday, February sixth. He was told it was needed for the royal arsenal—which, strictly speaking, was true. Later that day the Balfour brothers and Standen transported it to Kirk O'Field. But there was so much of it that even by nightfall only half of it had reached the cellars of Robert's house. In the dark they began digging the tunnel, but managed to complete only half of it by daybreak.

They laboured all that morning bringing more powder, but the merchant ran out. He himself awaited further supplies on Saturday, he assured them.

After the Queen had retired to her quarters that Friday night, they had to tell Darnley that all was not prepared. They were met with a string of curses.

"It was a greater undertaking than we expected," said James. "But by Saturday night —"

"Damn your lying soul to the blackest depths of hell!" Darnley snarled.

James Balfour felt anger rising in his tired body. They had laboured for a day and a half already, going without an entire night's sleep. Suddenly he doubted Darnley's promise of a reward. Darnley was ungrateful for all their efforts, and oblivious of the risks they were taking—for him. No wonder everyone hated him.

"Sire, we have done our best and will fulfill the task as we promised," he finally said. "It is only a day or two delay."

"You don't understand, you thick-skulled ape! This is the last night the Queen stays here! My course of treatment is over! We are to move to Holyrood tomorrow. I am cured," he said sarcastically.

"Then have a relapse," said James with equal sarcasm. "Surely you can manage that in order to extend your stay until Monday."

"The Queen will go to the wedding at Holyrood on Sunday. There will be festivities in the evening—"

"Bull piddle. You can prevail on her to return to Kirk O'Field afterward. After all, her life depends on it." He chuckled with a grating sound.

"This is all your fault. . . ." Darnley continued.

James Balfour stood there as Darnley called him every insulting name he had heard in France and England as well as Scotland. The abuse bounced off him, for he had long been inured to the power of name-calling. He even smiled at the foolish boy, blathering away, totally unaware that the illusory power of words was no match for the true power of information.

Surely Scotland would prove more grateful for the efforts, and knowledge, of Sir James Balfour. Scotland was aweary of Darnley.

He kept smiling until Darnley ran out of breath.

☙

Bothwell put his feet up on a footstool and warmed them before the hearty fire in the quarters he had been assigned at Holyrood. He liked the room;

it was on the south side and looked out over the palace gardens and park toward Arthur's Seat. He also liked the status the room assignment implied.

Now he had a little leisure to read Sextus Julius's *Stratagems and Subtleties of War* and escape into the military campaigns of ancient Rome. How different they were from the swooping attacks in the Border hills.

How would I have fared in these campaigns? he asked himself. Marching, with rows of men, forming the *testudo*, making a tortoise shell of shields when approaching enemy fire—

There was a soft knock at the door.

Bothwell heaved himself up to answer it; French Paris was out searching the merchants' stalls for Bothwell's costume for the coming masque, and he was alone.

James Balfour stood on the threshold, an expectant grin on his face. "May I?" he asked, stepping inside without waiting for an answer.

"Evidently," said Bothwell.

Immediately he sensed this was no ordinary visit. Balfour looked eerily excited.

"What is it?" asked Bothwell.

Balfour peeled off his mantle and gloves and threw them arrogantly on the little table where Bothwell's military book rested.

"I have information that may be the most valuable you have ever purchased," he said grandly.

"Oh?" Bothwell tried to sound calm, but he knew it was the missing part of the Darnley plot he had been seeking. Balfour had sniffed it out; like the vermin he was, he had managed to listen from holes and obscure vantage points. "How does a hundred pounds sound?"

Balfour laughed. "Absurdly low. Where is your much-vaunted sense of chivalry? Is that all the Queen's life is worth to you? Ah, there are others who will pay more to ensure it succeeds." He made a patently false move to retrieve his mantle. Bothwell grabbed him so hard the two bones in his lower arm grated against each other.

"Tell me," he breathed.

"Let go of my arm."

Bothwell dropped it. "Name your price, then. I haven't time to bargain like a fishwife."

"Or a soldier of fortune?" Balfour shook his arm. Suddenly he was suspicious. "Why do you care?" This was more than a soldier's or an adventurer's eye to the main chance.

"I have always been loyal to the crown," Bothwell replied smoothly. "Now tell me your price, and your information."

"A thousand pounds," said Balfour. "In French crowns, so as not to reveal its source."

"Done." He would get the money.

"May I have your signature on this?" Balfour produced a piece of paper to serve as a promissory note, and Bothwell hastily signed it.

After Balfour had slowly, deliberately folded the paper and concealed it

450

on his person, he insisted on pouring himself some wine and sipping it before saying, "The King intends to murder the Queen."

He had paid a thousand pounds for a rumour? A rumour he already knew? Bothwell flushed with anger. "The King could not manage to do so. No one will trust him or serve as his sword arm. The Queen's servants are all loyal," he said.

"Gunpowder is loyal to whoever lights it, and it lies obedient and waiting."

"Where?" Bothwell felt jolted.

"In the vaults beneath the house at Kirk O'Field. The plot is that the Queen will spend the night there on Sunday and be killed in an explosion."

"And the King?"

"He will light the powder and escape."

"How do you know this?"

He laughed a dry little laugh. "I have put the powder there myself. It took a day and a half."

"So you were paid to put it there, and now you'll be paid to take it away?"

"Indeed. My hourly labour fee is impressive, is it not?"

"You mined your own brother's house?" Bothwell was stunned.

"With his permission."

"So he is party to the plot. Who else is?"

"No one. As everyone knows, the King is so unpopular no one would plot with him."

Relief flooded Bothwell. The rumours had hinted at a widespread plot.

Balfour was smiling. "In truth, I have run out of powder. I bought all there was in Edinburgh, but it is not tightly packed enough yet. Another five hundred or thousand pounds is required."

"Leave me to remove it," said Bothwell. "I can dispose of it easily in the royal stores at Dunbar. Then no one can trace it. And doubtless your good brother Robert will be pleased to have his building spared." He attempted to smile at Balfour. "And the King will not know his plan has been discovered and dismantled?"

"No."

Balfour's promises were more worthless than lies. The only way to secure his cooperation was to deceive him.

"Leave it for now. You need rest after your exertions," said Bothwell. "You did right to come to me. Doubtless there will be further rewards, high offices granted from the crown. . . ." He ushered Balfour toward the door. "I will need house keys in order to remove the powder," he said.

"Here." Balfour dropped them in his hand: a thick iron ring with massive long keys. They weighed like a stone.

"Good evening," said Balfour. "Do not exhaust yourself. It is heavy work." He laughed again.

After he left, Bothwell sank down on a bench. He could hardly think, he could only feel. He had to sit and let his blood calm down.

Darnley had provided his own death warrant. All he, Bothwell, had to do was blow Darnley up before he knew what was happening.

I will bring the extra powder from Dunbar. French Paris and my kinsmen will help carry it and place it. Sunday night as he sleeps, we will light it and blow him up. People will think he blew himself up by mistake. The crime will punish the criminal, and that will be the end of it.

Mary will be free. And we can marry.

Instead of exultation, the word "marry" seemed like a manacle, dragging him to some unknown doom.

He reached for his military book and held it like a talisman.

I am a soldier, not a statesman. I only wanted to possess her body, not her crown. And there is something else besides. . . .

Those who love her seem to die untimely or unnatural deaths. François. Chastelard. John Gordon. Riccio. Now Darnley.

He shook his head. Womanish speculations and tremblings. He had a task before him, and if he did not carry it out, Mary would die.

Against his will he admired Darnley's ingenuity in harnessing alchemy to do his work when no man would set his hand to it.

"But to prevail requires more than ingenuity," he said softly. "It also requires courage, timing, and luck."

Be lucky, Bothwell, he thought fiercely. Be lucky now, just this once in your life, and you need never be lucky again.

❧

Mary was confused. Bothwell had not come to the reception chamber to pay court to Darnley in the past two days, and had sent her no private messages. French Paris was curiously absent too, and although Mary tried to involve herself in the spirit of the coming wedding festivity for Bastian and Margaret, the feeling of evil that seemed to be holding its breath did not abate when the bride and groom both chose black as the colour of their wedding attire.

Only two more days until Darnley would leave Kirk O'Field. He had obstinately refused to move until after the wedding, and had declined to attend the ceremony.

He does it to annoy me, she thought. But he cannot imagine how precious even an extra day of freedom from him is!

For on Monday he would move back to Holyrood, expecting to be received back into her bed. She felt a rush of revulsion in even thinking of it.

And Bothwell—how can I see him privately? Will I *ever* be able to see him, have the luxury of an evening alone with him, a quiet supper, a night in bed in which we make love and sleep and wake to make love again in the dark? It must be possible—it has to be.

Why could my father have his mistresses and enjoy them openly, and I am compelled to hide myself, like any serving wench?

In a gush of resentment she hated her father.

And my grandfather! she thought bitterly. He took Bothwell's grand-mother to his bed; 'twas no secret. And we, the grandchildren, cannot do likewise because I am a Queen and not a King. What James IV could do, I cannot.

He could not have burned as I do!

Her desire for Bothwell, her love for him, made her sway on her feet. *Hold me, kiss me, touch me*—

"Your Grace, pray sit down. You are unsteady."

In acute embarrassment, Mary turned to see Lord James standing behind her.

The proper Lord James, representation and embodiment of her father's kingly prerogative, whisked a stool toward her. Averting her eyes, acutely aware of the blood throbbing in her cheeks, she sat down.

"I must beg your pardon for intruding, but I wished to obtain leave to absent myself from Edinburgh." He seemed so deferential, as if he never had done anything without her approval and permission. "My wife needs me at St. Andrews."

Too preoccupied with covering her tumultuous thoughts, she merely said, "I prefer that you remain another day to attend the marriage festivities. Then you may go."

"No, I must not tarry!" He sounded alarmed. "My wife has had a mis-carriage, and the physicians fear the onset of childbed fever. It is imperative I go immediately!"

"Very well. When will you return?"

"When it is safe to do so."

❧

Bothwell patted the last of the wall of powder tenderly. It was done. What a backbreaking task. He stank with sweat, and the exertion had shown him that his injuries had not completely healed. His belly in particular pained him whenever he contracted the muscles.

But it was done.

And just in time. Lord James, as was his wont, had scurried away from Edinburgh. If anyone wanted the sure sign of an impending political murder, all they had to do was note the whereabouts of the Lord James. He was never on the scene.

To throw the stone without seeming to move the hand: that was his motto.

For Lord James and all the rest wanted Darnley removed. But in the end only Bothwell would stand to the task.

It is fitting, he thought. It is I who am the Queen's lover, and it is my child within her. My responsibility is personal, theirs merely political.

Now everything had moved into that most difficult of phases, waiting. Waiting for the long Sunday to pass; waiting for the wedding ceremony, the banquet, Mary's farewell to Darnley, her departure for Holyrood.

Archibald Douglas and his men were to surround the house to prevent

Darnley from escaping. French Paris would light the train of powder, although he, Bothwell, would like to have the honour. But it might not prove possible.

❧

The wedding, held in the Catholic Chapel Royal at Holyrood, had gone well. In spite of the desperate unhappiness of her own marriage, Mary had an innate optimism when she saw others taking their vows.

Bothwell was there, despite his Protestant scruples, and during the ceremony she stared at his back, unable to look away, wondering why even his back seemed distinctive and different from all other backs.

Everyone went on to a banquet celebrating the nuptials, and then a smaller group attended a formal dinner party celebrating the departure of Moretta, who had only just arrived, so it seemed, to represent the Duke of Savoy. He had missed the baptism by more than a month. Bothwell was seated far down at the opposite end of the table. Mary watched him without seeming to do so; watched him even as she made sprightly conversation with the earls of Argyll and Huntly.

"So late, perhaps he can stand as godfather to your next child," said Argyll with a wink.

"Indeed, yes—"

"His christening gift is magnificent. The jewels in the handle of the fan—"

Bothwell was gripping his wineglass with his powerful fingers. She could not see them shake at that distance.

The meal being over, she realized that there were several hours left before the carnival masque at Holyrood and the formal "putting the bride and groom to bed" ceremony. Laughing, she stood up and said, "Come, let us go to Kirk O'Field and cheer the King. He would appreciate your company, I know."

And I would appreciate being spared being alone with him, she thought.

In the descending gloom of the February afternoon, they made their way down the frosted cobblestones of the Blackfriars Wynd, led by torches to the precincts of Kirk O'Field. Their laughter rang out, their cloaks of scarlet, tawny, and violet showing bright against the grey stone houses and the light frosting of snow underfoot.

Inside the house, Darnley was waiting. Mary expected him to be sulking and hostile, but he was attired in sumptuous, jewel-encrusted robes and was animatedly hopping about. He had even provided musicians and hundreds of candles. Proudly he clapped a feathered mask on, and pointed his skinny legs, attired in silver hose.

"Welcome! Welcome!" he was saying.

Was he drunk? Had he spent the entire afternoon drinking? But no—his gait lacked the unsteadiness, and his words were not slurred.

"My lord!" said Mary, in surprise. She allowed him to take her hand and lead her in a dance.

The lords and guests stood watching, then cheered. Darnley bowed.

"Come, again!" he said, pulling her.

"Oh, my lord, you tire me," she said.

His cheeks were strangely flushed. Had he a fever?

"Drink! Dance! Enjoy yourselves!" he commanded, gesturing to the entire chamber.

"Ah, my Mary, you are so beautiful," he whispered. "So beautiful I wish you were not made of flesh but of marble, so you could endure forever." He took her hand and kissed it tenderly.

"Dice! We must play!" Darnley suddenly turned to the company. "Here, on this table! I have set everything up!"

It had grown late, but once the darkness had settled, all the subsequent hours had run together. There was no way of knowing whether it was seven o'clock or nine o'clock, and their full stomachs gave no hungry signals.

Mary had been engrossed in a game of Primero when suddenly Bothwell leaned toward her and whispered, "Have you forgotten your promise to return to Holyrood for the masque?"

"It is early yet," she replied, studying her cards. She had been winning.

"No," he said. "It is late, past ten. French Paris has just brought me word that they are waiting; they are holding up the performance."

"Oh!" And she would have to change her clothes, too. How tiresome. She was not in the mood any longer for the carnival; the long walk back to Holyrood in the cold, and then the costume, and then . . .

If there were any choice in the matter, she would not go, and continue playing cards in the comfort of this house, and then sleep in the little stone chamber again. But she could not fail to complete her duty toward her servants. Wearily she rose.

She caught Darnley's attention and put her hand gently on his brocaded shoulder.

"I must return to Holyrood," she said. "So I must bid you goodnight."

"But you must return!" He threw his dice down. "You must promise to come back and sleep here!" His voice was shrill and querulous.

"Alas, I am already weary. To travel back here in the deepest part of the night—"

"Then don't go!" He clutched at her.

She patted his hand. "I must. It is one of the obligations I feel I must fulfill. Margaret and Bastian are two of my dearest—"

"I am your *husband!*"

Bothwell's head jerked around.

"Yes, I know. But tomorrow you will be leaving this dwelling. It is only a few more hours."

"Please! Grant me this wish!"

"Henry," she said in her sweetest tone, "do not be unreasonable. It is not advisable. It is safer and healthier if we both sleep normal hours tonight. You are just recuperating. Look"—she removed a ring from her finger and put it on his—"here is a token—"

"Mary!" He was on the verge of tears.

She had to get away now, or he would prevent her. And the bride and groom would be hurt. Why was he so selfish?

She almost laughed. I ask that question as if he were normal and this is the first peculiar thing he has ever done, she thought.

"If I can, I will return," she said. "But please do not remain awake waiting."

Quickly the lords and ladies put on their mantles and hoods and passed out into the night.

Looking back, Mary saw Darnley standing, pressing his hands against the glass in the window of the chamber.

She was indeed very tired, and the masque, with its requisite participation, had sapped her strength. The child was starting to affect her and drain her. Or perhaps it had been the odd, tearful demands of Darnley, and having to extricate herself from him. Ordinarily she enjoyed such festivities, but this time she just wanted them to end so she could go to bed. Even the sight of Bothwell in his black and silver carnival costume did not stir her.

After the "putting to bed" had been duly enacted, and the rest of the party had returned to the hall for further dancing, Bothwell and Sir John Stewart of Traquair approached her.

"Let us draw apart," said Sir John. His face was white and he looked shaken. Quickly she looked at Bothwell, but his expression was completely different: grim and determined.

"Why, what is it?"

The two men took her by the elbows and steered her to an empty corner.

"Do not even consider returning to Kirk O'Field," said Bothwell. "I heard your words to the . . . King."

"In truth, I am too tired."

Bothwell nodded to Traquair. "Tell her."

"No. You told me. You know more."

"The King intends to murder you tonight if you return to the house," he said.

"How?" Her voice was small.

"Gunpowder."

"What?"

"He has prepared the cellars, packed them tight. It has taken many days. Now his mysterious choice of Kirk O'Field is made clear."

She was so stunned she could not speak. His entreaties that she return . . .

"We want your permission to arrest him," Traquair said gently. "He is a traitor."

She began to weep wildly. The perfidy, the gloating cold-bloodedness of it, was beyond her comprehension. It was demonic.

I shall be leal and true to my Sovereign Lady, the Queen of Scotland. I shall never bear treason about in my heart against our Sovereign Lady the Queen, but shall discover the same to her. So help me God.

"He has broken his vows," she whispered.

Bothwell shot a look at Traquair. What an irrelevant thing to say.

"When he became a Knight of the Thistle, he swore—"

"Have we your permission to take him?" insisted Bothwell. "We must act under your orders. He is a traitor."

Already Bothwell was turning away to do it, but she reached out for him. "Do not harm him," she said.

"If he resists arrest, I cannot speak for his safety," he shot back. "He is dangerous, and must be treated as such." He shot a look at Traquair. "Escort the Queen to bed. I will await you outside."

❧

But once he reached the stairs, he took them two at a time in order to get to Kirk O'Field way ahead of Traquair. The fuse was waiting. There would be no "arrest." But let Mary think there was.

The way Darnley had touched her and hung on her . . . it nauseated him. The traitor—the vile, unnatural traitor!

Running through the back streets of Edinburgh and making his way to Kirk O'Field through the old monastery garden, he felt the cold air biting into his lungs. He slowed a bit; it was dark, with no moon to guide his footsteps. He was gasping for breath and making too much noise.

Now he was at the house. No candles were burning. Darnley and his servants had retired.

Waiting in the south garden were Archibald Douglas and his men, hooded and swathed. Their breaths rose in little streams, like smoking chimneys. They were cold but dared not stamp their feet and move about.

French Paris, William Powrie, John Hay, and John Hepburn were waiting for him on the east side of the house. The powder train lay like a snake on the ground, barely visible.

No one had a torch, so Bothwell demanded a flint and struck it several times before he succeeded in lighting a small wick. Then, ceremoniously, he bent down and touched the wick to the powder. Slowly it glowed and caught. Bothwell watched as the smoke and the red glow began creeping toward the house.

"Remember, you are the one who actually lit it," said Paris. His voice was shaking.

"Gentlemen, it was my pleasure," Bothwell replied. "Indeed, it was my privilege to preside at this unparalleled occasion."

"Run!" said Paris.

But Bothwell stood rooted, staring at the glow as it ate its way toward its goal.

457

Darnley was dreaming: dreaming of himself whole and strong and well, a knight storming the walls of Jerusalem, slaying the infidel. He looked over to his right, seeing through the slit in his helmet his commander, Richard the Lionheart. Only suddenly, he *became* Richard, took on all his courage and might. . . .

Abruptly he awoke. Disappointment flooded him as the shreds of the dream melted away. He could not hold them. . . .

And there was something else besides . . . something sad, something bad. . . .

Mary had got away. He had failed.

He had waited up until one, hoping. He had made his entreaties so pleadingly; she might relent and come back. She was impulsive and kind-hearted. If Bothwell had not prevented her, that is. . . .

Never had he felt more powerful and yet more balked and thwarted. The plan had been *perfect*; Balfour and Standen had executed it according to his exact wishes.

Executed it. He chuckled at the words. Then he began to cry.

I could still kill myself, he thought. But without *her* here, it isn't right. And could I bear to hover unseen, a ghost, and watch Bothwell enjoying her afterwards?

Perhaps that way I could take my revenge.

But no. I am more powerful in the flesh than I would ever be in death.

Anger fluctuated with misery as he lay rigid in bed. The house was so silent it seemed already like a tomb. A stone sepulchre, dark, cold, still . . . The sleeping forms of his attendants looked like effigies in a church, stretched out in stone, sleeping for eternity.

He began to drift off in sleep again, when suddenly a faint noise came to him. A scurrying, a scuffling.

Rats! He felt himself shiver, and pulled up the covers tighter. He hated rats; he had never been able to accustom himself to their constant presence no matter how well furnished the dwelling.

Scrape.

It was a big one. O dear God, don't let him come out in the middle of the room!

A murmur. Human voices. Outside. Then that scuffling movement. But it, too, was outside.

He held his breath to hear more clearly. But there was nothing. His head began to spin from lack of air. He breathed out, then in.

A smell of burning. But not ordinary burning. It was not a wood fire, or a candle, or straw. It was—

Gunpowder! Someone had lit the powder!

With pure terror, he bolted out of bed and ran to the east window.

There was movement there. Men. How many he couldn't see. It was almost completely dark.

But there was a small spot of light, moving.

The powder train!

For an agonizing long instant he stood, shaking. His bare feet and legs were like ice. He was wearing only a thin nightgown.

But there was no time to dress. Even as he watched, the spark was coming closer. And he knew how many thousands of pounds of gunpowder were waiting to explode, and what would happen if it did.

He rushed for the enclosed balcony that opened off the sleeping chamber. He could climb out and drop down onto the town wall directly beneath it, then escape across the old orchard to open fields. The standing town wall would act as a shield to protect him from the greatest force of the explosion.

He stumbled over William Taylor's bed and woke him.

"Uhhh—" groaned the attendant.

"We must escape!" shrieked Darnley, but fear made his voice a whisper. He rushed to the side of the balcony and began climbing over it and out the window.

"My lord, wait. I will get warm clothes, and a rope, and a chair for the descent. I beg you, wait!" Taylor determinedly began gathering up the items he deemed necessary, not understanding the need for frantic haste.

Darnley could not wait. He hung by his fingers to the window ledge. The bitter cold made his legs numb, so he had no feeling in his bare feet as he let go and attempted to land on top of the wall. He stumbled and lost his balance, tumbling over and falling, unhurt, on the frozen ground beneath.

He was safe! The dark house still stood, and the wall stood sentinel in between. He heard Taylor trying to follow with all the apparatus of the chair and rope and garments; he was making a frightful lot of noise.

Darnley began to run barefoot across the orchard ground, gasping for breath. His sweat felt as if it were freezing on his skin, encasing him in cold.

Suddenly he ran smack into something. A tree. No. A man.

"Halt!" said the man in a deep, familiar voice. Others surrounded him. There was a company of them.

A rough, gloved hand grabbed Darnley's shoulder and someone else pinned both his arms behind him and held him immobile against a broad, battle-padded chest. The man reared back and Darnley was lifted off the ground, his numb feet kicking helplessly.

"You must not hope to escape," said the familiar voice, as if explaining something very simple. "You must pay your debt."

"What debt?" squeaked Darnley.

"The unforgivable debt of betraying your kinsmen. He who betrays his clan and kin is not fit to live."

Archibald Douglas!

459

Thank God, it was not Bothwell.

"Oh, cousin," whined Darnley, "do not commit the worse crime of murdering your own blood. Then blood shall call to blood and yours be spilt in revenge."

There was a soft laughter. Douglas stuck his face up in Darnley's.

"You *are* simple, cousin. Why, 'tis not we who will bear the blame. 'Tis Bothwell." He put his massive hands around Darnley's slender neck.

"No! No! Please, please have mercy on me! Ah, kinsman, in the name of He who had mercy on all the world, spare me!"

Douglas kept on squeezing, smiling all the while. He could feel the neck contracting and heard the wheezing. Darnley twisted and bucked, but the nameless man behind him held him fast, legs dangling.

Darnley struggled so long that Douglas's hands began to ache.

"He's a long time dying," he said matter-of-factly. "Who would have thought he had any strength left in him?"

Just then Taylor came clumping up, hugging the chair. The company of men turned toward him, leaving Douglas and his partner holding the long pale form of Darnley suspended.

"Another one," said Douglas. "Kill him."

Taylor dropped the chair and ran in the opposite direction, but three Douglases chased him, caught him, and strangled him.

"A good night's work," said Archibald Douglas. "Lay them out."

They placed the bodies beneath one of the pear trees of the old orchard, then arranged the articles Taylor had been carrying, like offerings to their fierce clan gods.

Bothwell had been standing at a safe distance a long time, and nothing had happened. Had the fuse gone out?

"I will go check the powder train," he whispered to Paris.

"No!" The page clung to Bothwell's waist. "Do not go close to look! It is too dangerous!"

Bothwell shook him off and walked quickly back toward the house. Suddenly a massive crack and force deafened him and threw him to the ground. He felt searing heat on his right side and looked out from under his arm to see an explosion beyond his imagination. The house was actually rising up from its foundations, the very stones separating—he could see the vivid red between the straight black lines of the cut stones—and raining outward. He scrambled to his feet and ran as fast as he could, debris thudding all around him. Just one of the stones would have the effect of a direct hit from a cannonball.

At last, far out of range of the deadly hail, he watched in macabre fascination as the house destroyed itself. The power of gunpowder was stupefying. It could have destroyed a hundred people, five hundred. . . .

All this to dispatch one man. But it would take this much to make sure he was truly dead. Evil was difficult to kill.

Another great explosion tore the fabric of the entire structure, and a pillar of fire shot out the top and into the dark night sky.

What if Mary had been in there, as Darnley had planned?

Feeling dazed, he made his way back to Holyrood, hugging the back streets and skirting the tumbledown portions of the wall. He had to tell Mary what had happened, had to see her to dispel the horrible vision he had had of her inside the conflagration.

People had rushed out into the streets, shrieking and pointing. Pulling his cloak over his face, he made his way through them. It was too dark for anyone to identify him, but his innate caution was operating even in his shaken state.

He reached the postern door of Holyrood in his wing of the palace. He turned to go to Mary's apartments, but it was too late. The passageways were filled with gibbering servants and guards. He could not risk seeing her privately. Quickly he made his way to his own room, stripped off his clothes, and dived into his bed. The clothes had not lost their body heat before there was a knock on the door. One of the palace guards rushed in.

"What is the matter?" asked Bothwell, rubbing his eyes.

"The King's house is blown up, and I think the King is killed!"

"Fie! Treason!" cried Bothwell, bolting out of bed, and grabbing his clothes.

The Earl of Huntly, blond hair tousled, came running in, followed by the earls of Argyll and Atholl.

"We must go to the Queen!" said Bothwell, pulling on his last boot.

They streamed out into the passageway and rushed toward Mary's apartments. The entire antechamber was filled with frightened servants.

"A noise like twenty cannon!" cried Mary Seton, clutching at Bothwell's sleeve. "Oh, sir, what was it?"

"How the devil should I know?" he snapped, pushing her aside. Did people suspect him already?

"Treason! They are coming for us!" wailed one of the French pages.

"Be a man, then!" said Bothwell. "Stand and fight!"

The Queen's inner door stood open, and she was standing just within, clad only in her sleeping gown, her hair loose and tangled. She turned a puzzled, imploring look at him.

"There has been an ungodly noise, like thunder and guns," she said. "What terrible thing has happened? Has there been an attack?"

Bothwell took a deep breath. It was he she was asking, not anyone else in the room.

"No. A horrible accident. The King is dead. Killed by an explosion in his house," he said.

"Dead?" She looked uncomprehending.

"Dead," he said, fixing his eyes on hers.

"Do we know that?" said Huntly. "All we know is there has been an explosion. We don't know the extent of the damage, or if anyone survived. Why do you say that?" he challenged Bothwell.

"Unless he was well beyond the vicinity of the dwelling—unlikely at this hour and in his condition—he had no chance." I made sure of that, he thought. When I have to kill, I make sure it is carried out. But I do not relish it—unlike the rest of you.

Mary slumped against Madame Rallay—in shock or relief?

"Go," she said softly. "Go and see what has happened."

"Aye." With pleasure, he thought.

Motioning to the others, he left the chamber.

❧

Mary stood watching from her window as Bothwell and the men made their way across the courtyard and up the Canongate. Smoke was still visible far to the left, marking the place where Kirk O'Field had stood. Outside, in the streets, was a tumult.

Darnley was dead. How had it really happened? Had the powder accidentally gone off, or had it been deliberately lit? What had Darnley said when Bothwell apprehended him?

"Your Majesty."

She turned and saw Sir John Stewart of Traquair standing behind her.

"Tell me what happened," she said weakly, waving the others away and drawing him aside. "You were there."

"No, Your Majesty, I was not." He looked saddened and embarrassed. "Bothwell left me behind here to protect you in case Darnley had sent assassins after you. So I did not see what happened. I only know . . . they are saying that Bothwell and his men are the ones who did it. He—or rather, someone *claiming* to be him and his friends—were seen passing up and down the High Street through Edinburgh, carrying the powder. Tonight."

"But he was with us all night!"

"I know. But whoever wishes the people to think otherwise staged the actors well."

Mary was shaking. It was not only she or Darnley who was to be a victim tonight, then. It was Bothwell as well. Someone else had discovered Darnley's plot and the gunpowder and had decided to use it to eliminate both Darnley and Bothwell together.

Who? Lord James?

But then he would want to eliminate me next.

Does he? Where is he now? He said St. Andrews, but—

She collapsed in shock.

*　　*　　*

She awoke and saw that daylight had come, filling her chamber with murky light. She tried to move and felt a great heaviness and pain in her belly. There were thick cloths and oozing stickiness under her.

Someone was dabbing her face. The warm, scented water felt soothing.

"You have had a heavy onset of your monthly courses," said Madame Ralley, close to her ear. "There was much blood, clots, and other matter. But it is over now, and there should be no further pain. Should I call Bourgoing?"

"No." He must not know. Had Madame Rallay guessed? But it must not be a matter of record.

The child was gone. Or had there ever been one? Perhaps all the symptoms had been due to strain, and there had never been a child at all.

She began to laugh, hysterically. I needn't have gone to Glasgow, she thought wildly.

"Sssh. Stop!" said Madame Rallay. She jerked her head toward the door. "They will think you are laughing about his death. They will think you are not unhappy about it. Then they may wonder if you know more about it then you should."

Indeed I do, she thought. I know he meant to kill *me*.

An hour later she was up and dressed and had taken some nourishment. She had to be ready for whatever news Bothwell brought.

"Madam," he said, when at midmorning he, along with others of the lords, stood in her chamber, "it is passing strange, what we found."

"In the hot, smoking stones, the crushed and cooked bodies of his chamber valets were found," said Huntly. "And there was not a stone left standing; the house was totally demolished. It lies in a heap, smouldering and steaming."

"But the King was not there." Bothwell's voice rose. "No, not anywhere in the house. It was five o'clock this morning before we finally found him, eighty feet away."

"Untouched by the fire," said Huntly.

"But dead," said Bothwell. "Very dead. Naked, too, at least below the waist. There he lay, his privy parts exposed to the carrion crows, his legs hard-frozen. Beside him lay his valet, Taylor. And on the ground all sorts of things: a rope, a dagger, a chair, furred jackets. . . ."

"No wound?" Mary asked.

"No wound, no cut, no bruise, no burn. Just dead," said Bothwell. "Mysteriously dead."

"We had him carried into a nearby house and decently covered. Even now he is being conveyed here, where you may behold his body," said Huntly.

"And we will accompany you," said Maitland, who had appeared at her side unannounced.

She did not feel able to walk even beyond her chambers, but she knew if she demurred, it would be taken as a clear sign of guilt. The room was filling up with people, all with bright, curious, accusing eyes. They were all looking at her—all except Bothwell. Alone of all people, she wanted him to look at her, to sustain her. But he was purposely looking elsewhere.

"Very well," she said, offering her arms to Huntly on one side and George Seton on the other. She moved stiffly out of the room.

A sheet of nothingness had enveloped her. Darnley was dead. She was delivered from him. Her great folly of tying herself to him was exploded along with the house. But the unnaturalness of the death meant that it was more than just a simple fact, an unalloyed deliverance.

Why could he not have just died of his disease? she thought wildly. Why this? It is his legacy to leave mystery and guilt. He sought to kill me; now he will be exonerated, and trouble me even from beyond the grave.

Ahead of her down the staircase trod Bothwell and Maitland. Where were they going? Where was Darnley to be brought?

They ushered her into a windowless chamber on the ground floor. Ordinarily it was used to store benches, trestles, and stools; as they entered, servants were carrying these out. At the far end of the room a makeshift bier had been set up, using two of the trestles and wide planks. A pair of workmen were hastily hanging black drapes on the wall behind.

"A seat for Her Majesty," Bothwell barked. His voice was rough and terse.

Gratefully, Mary sank down on the cushioned chair they brought. She felt faint and tremulous.

The doors at the end of the chamber flew open, and standing motionless, six men-at-arms held a litter aloft. It looked, for one bizarre moment, like one of the elaborate dishes served as part of the entertainment at formal banquets. Just so the costumed servitors had stood, proudly bearing sugar castles or gilded swans or forests made of pastries to guests.

Even the reclining figure on the litter looked made of sugar icing, so white was it. The golden hair looked like gilt, the rest all white: the nightgown and the features, drained of blood.

"Proceed," said Maitland, and the men stepped forward smartly, looking to neither the left nor the right. Darnley's sharp profile passed before Mary's eyes.

It was true. He was dead.

Yet, instead of feeling elation, or relief, she was flooded with horror. The sight of him dead was grotesque and terrifying. The young should not lie so still, nor be bloodless.

Slowly she stood, and pushing away the helping arms of the courtiers, she made her way to the bier where the litter had been set down. Tall candles flanked his head and feet.

The sight of the waxen face pulled her to it with a mighty power, almost commanding her to its side.

How motionless he lay! The utter, deep stillness of death, beyond even that of granite or jewels, seemed to pervade her living breast. She halted her breathing as if to breathe in his company were an aberration.

His eyes were closed, and they had spoken true: there was no mark on him. But he did not look alive; those who said "the dead but sleep" had never gazed on a newly dead person.

Stretched out in death, he was suddenly once again the shining, naïve boy she had met in the garden at Wemyss. The boy who had not completely died, but had peeped out occasionally from the drunken, weak bully. Some part of that earlier knight had survived. Until now. Now they were extinguished together, the innocence and the guilt. The lover who had tried to kill her.

Do not forget that, she thought. He planned to look upon *you* laid out on this bier. Only no—you would have been burnt beyond recognition.

Now in the pale flickering light the darker splotches of his disease showed up against the blanched skin.

Now they would never heal, she thought. It would have distressed him.

The lords were staring at her, their eyes riveted on her, trying to read her face. Suddenly she felt more open to inspection than Darnley.

In that moment the full force of what was happening burst in on her. *I am on display here, not Darnley!*

Even in death you seek to harm me! She thought. Her revulsion as she gazed at Darnley's face passed over her features and was duly noted by those present.

A letter was drafted in Mary's name by the lords to send to France later that day. Dully, not reading it carefully, Mary signed it.

> . . . if God in His mercy had not preserved us, as we trust, to the end
> that we may take a rigorous vengeance of that mysterious deed, which
> ere it should remain unpunished we had rather lose life and all. The
> matter is so horrible and strange, as we believe the like was never heard
> of in any country. . . .

Elizabeth. Elizabeth must be told.

At the thought of the English Queen, Mary shrank. Elizabeth, with her spies and ambassadors and inquisitive mind, would probe into it and attempt to twist it to her own advantage in some way. Yet if Elizabeth were *not* informed promptly, she would manage to use that as well to her advantage.

I have not the strength to compose a letter, thought Mary. I will dispatch Melville and trust him to satisfy her questions.

Night. Night at last—although it had felt like night all day—and she could sink into sleep, or attempt to. She asked Madame Rallay to light all the candles. Suddenly she was afraid that Darnley's pale, angry ghost would come up the stairs and slip into her room as he had the night of Riccio's murder. Yet at the same time she wanted to be alone, to face him. She ordered the puzzled Madame to sleep out in the antechamber.

She lay still and cold in the room. The palace was quiet, but it was not a tranquil quiet, rather the pause before a plunge into more horrors.

She could not think. It was better not to think. She closed her eyes. And then she heard the sounds: footsteps on the stairs. Quiet treading. Upward.

I am ready, she thought. I will not flinch from you, Darnley, no matter in what form you appear.

Yet she was shaking as if she lay naked outdoors in the February cold, as he had.

The door swung open silently on oiled hinges. The candlelight, gentle as it was, could not penetrate the darkness inside the stair landing. A hand grasped the door to keep it from banging against the stone and making a noise.

Short, powerful fingers. A wide hand.

Bothwell stepped into the room. His movement, his blocky body screamed *safety!* to her before she consciously recognized his face.

Stifling a cry of gladness, she exhaled in a great sob. Swiftly, soundlessly, he was beside her, half leaping onto the bed. He grabbed both her hands and kissed them roughly, his warm breath almost painful against her skin.

"O God," he breathed in her ear, pulling her up and against him, kneeling on the quivering mattress.

Frantically they sought one another's lips, both intending to talk, to explain, but unable to do anything other than kiss. At the touch of his lips, Mary felt all desire satisfied, all longing quenched. Bothwell was here.

He was tearing at the frilled neck of her gown, hungrily kissing her neck, biting and sucking on her smooth skin.

She tilted her head back and let his lips travel down her throat and between her breasts. With one hand she touched the top of his head. His hair was cold; unlike his fevered skin, it took on the temperature of the room.

He had started to caress her legs, to lift her gown. His breath was coming in short gasps. But she was strangely calm, unaroused. She put out a hand and stayed his.

"I am no longer with child," she said, as softly as possible, leaning over to his ear. "Sometime in the night, everything . . . everything . . . It is gone."

Abruptly he stopped his caresses. "Then . . . it was all for nothing."

His words puzzled her.

"All . . . for nothing," he repeated. He shook his head, and let go of her.

"No, not for—"

"You do not understand." He drew in a long, slow breath.

"Then you must tell me, explain it all. Why was there an explosion? What happened when you tried to arrest him? Oh, it has been so dreadful not to know, after you went forth on Sunday night!"

He rolled over, lying fully clothed beside her on the bed. "There was no arrest. As I approached the house with my men, he thought it was you returning. He lit the fuse and escaped. It was his intention that you would enter the house and be blown to pieces. The fuse was lit some ten minutes before your perceived arrival."

"But he was killed. Killed as he ran away." She had to know. "Did *you* kill him?"

"No," he answered. "No, I did not see him or touch him. Until the dawn when, along with the others, I discovered the body."

"Who, then?" Thank God and all the saints. Bothwell was not a murderer.

"I know not. There were many who would gladly have killed him, should opportunity have presented itself." He ran his hands through his hair. "And now those same people will seek to blame us, to destroy us." His voice was low and guarded.

"Who?"

"I know not. That is the agony of it. Everyone speaks fair and hides his true visage. We are in great danger." He paused. "Do you not realize that we are now bound forever because of that dead boy on his bier? There was murder done, Mary. It is a mystery, this murder, but it is a mystery that will swirl us away to destruction. We must cling together to survive."

He took her hands and put them around himself. "Hang on to me," he commanded. "Put your arms around me, and whatever happens, do not let go."

She could feel his hard body pressing against hers; in his clenched knotted muscles and long, hard bones seemed to lie safety from all danger. The very scars on his body were like badges of power. But as she rested her head on his tensed shoulder, she could feel that beneath the steel-hard muscles lay ordinary flesh and all-too-breakable bones.

L

Mary ordered the court into mourning, providing them with the requisite black cloth to be sewn into the costumes. A week after his death, Darnley was entombed with royal honours and a Catholic funeral in Holyrood, next to the vault of James V.

Watching the casket being borne to the altar and hearing the chanting, Mary felt nothing but relief that his unhappy life was over, then stabs of guilt that she could summon so little pity. But he had died as if by his own hand, attempting to kill others. And innocent people had perished in the explosion.

The court had been stunned, creeping about quietly until it became clear that the plot had perished with the man, that there was no further danger. Ashamed that this seemed to confirm the rest of the world's opinion that Scotland was a barbarous country, inhabited by savages where atrocious deeds were everyday occurrences, a murmuring arose—low at first, then rising. *Punish the villains.* No one seemed to believe that Mary had been in any danger, or that anyone but Darnley had been the target of the crime. In death Darnley acquired the majesty and importance he had lacked in life. Regicide had been committed! The King had been slain!

A barrel had been found by the ruins of the house, proof that the powder had been brought hastily from someplace—Holyrood? Men had walked the streets boldly that night, declaring themselves "friends of my Lord Bothwell's," so it was said. Black Ormiston, a henchman of Bothwell's, had been seen close to the fateful house just after the explosion.

Mary and her Council offered a reward of two thousand pounds for information about the perpetrators of the crime, although she knew none would be found. None except Darnley, and that must remain secret. She wished to protect his name, for his little son's sake, and knew Bothwell would never reveal the truth. Besides him, who would know? Whoever had helped to place the powder there originally? Yes, those accomplices would know. . . . An investigation was opened the day after the explosion by a committee of lords meeting at the Tolbooth.

The choking closeness of the mourning chamber at Edinburgh Castle was oppressive to Mary. Black drapes shrouded the walls, and fat beeswax candles burned serenely on their stands. She felt as though she were entombed herself. The continual companionship of death, where the spectre seemed as real as the hunched figure of Madame Rallay or the veiled face of Mary Seton, kneeling on the prie-dieu, was intensely disturbing. She even had horrible dreams in which she and Bothwell were dead, clutching each other in skeletal forms.

Bourgoing was alarmed at her agitated, morbid state of mind. He ordered her to leave the chamber as soon as Darnley's funeral was over, and seek the healthful open air of a site near the sea. Time and again he had found that being near water could help restore distracted spirits.

Mary Seton's brother George offered his castle on the Forth, and on February sixteenth, Mary left the mourning chamber with relief, riding out slowly from Edinburgh in the mists and drawing her black hooded mantle around her.

The day Mary left Edinburgh, a placard appeared, set up near the Tolbooth.

The most foul murder of our King!

Perpetrated by the Scurvy Sir James Balfour,
the Filthy Earl Bothwell, and the Witch
Janet Beaton. The Queen, knowing of it,
in the power of the Witch, and assenting thereto.

French Paris angrily ripped it down and carried it to Bothwell, but not before most of Edinburgh had seen it.

Two days later, another appeared in the same spot.

The Abominable Earl of Bothwell

Hath Killed Our King.

Underneath was a drawing of the baby Prince James, hands clasped in prayer, imploring:

Judge and avenge my cause, O Lord.

Again Paris took it down and destroyed it.

That night, a crier roamed the streets, his plaintive voice wailing, "The mighty Earl of Bothwell hath killed the King."

When good citizens looked out their windows in the dark dead of night, they could not see the crier. But they heard his voice echoing, "The Earl of Bothwell . . . the Earl of Bothwell is the murderer . . . murderer . . . murderer. . . ."

On March first appeared a placard with a drawing of Mary, stripped naked to the waist, with a mermaid's tail, bearing the initials *MR*. Underneath her was the crest of the Earl of Bothwell, surrounded by a circle of bristling daggers.

A mermaid was a siren, a Circe, a prostitute.

The whore and her dagger-man were adulterous murderers, the placard said without using words.

Mary sat on a bench, looking out at the glittering water of the Forth. The day was surprisingly mild for March, the sun was shining and there was an odour of promise in the air: brisk and stirring, as green as the reeds standing like sentinels along the banks of the water. She was wrapped in her great mourning cloak, staring off into the distance.

Lord George Seton, a gentle man, came up behind her. Gingerly he touched her shoulder, and she turned and looked at him.

"A letter," he said. "From Queen Elizabeth."

The messenger had brought it first to Edinburgh, then wearily come farther, to Seton House.

"Is the bearer still here?" she asked, reluctant to break open the seal.

"Even now he is taking refreshment."

"I would reward him for his pains." She did not want to open the letter.

"He will tarry here for a time, perhaps even sleep here."

"Good. Do not let him depart without my knowledge."

"No, Your Majesty."

Discreetly he withdrew.

She took the letter, heavily sealed. She dreaded to read it. Slowly she broke the stiff encrusted seal and began to read:

Madam,

My ears have been so astounded and my heart so frightened to hear of the horrible and abominable murder of your husband and my cousin, that I have scarcely spirit to write: yet I cannot conceal that I grieve more for you than for him. I should not do the office of a faithful cousin and friend, if I did not urge you to preserve your honour, rather than look through your fingers at revenge on those who have done you the pleasure, as most people say. I counsel you to take this matter to heart, that you may show the world what a noble princess and loyal woman you are. I write thus vehemently not that I doubt you, but for my affection toward you.

Mary let the letter rest on her lap. It partially refolded itself of its own accord.

How can I take revenge on the person who has perpetrated the crime? He has taken revenge on himself, she thought. And for my child's sake, I cannot reveal it!

The Virgin Queen could never, would never, understand such twisted and murky matters.

Suddenly she grabbed the taunting, simplistic letter and crumpled it. She wished to comply; in any other country and in any other situation she could. But this place, this place that seemed nothing but a series of plots and secrets and killings . . . perhaps Darnley had been normal in England. He had seemed normal enough when he first came to Scotland. But something happened once he got here. What was it? If Elizabeth had known him when he was normal, then she could have no comprehension of what had really happened, what he had become. Nor could she grasp the magnitude of the crime.

A soft shuffling of feet behind her. She turned to see the messenger. Yes, she had asked him to wait. But she could hardly tell him what she had been thinking. Quickly she hid the wadded letter and hoped he had not seen it.

"I thank my good sister and cousin for her kindness and honest advice," she said, choosing her words carefully. "She is wise and counsels well. I am fortunate to have such a friend in this time of misfortune." She lifted her hand and displayed the "Elizabeth ring" which she still wore. "I intend to do all that she suggests, and more besides."

The messenger bowed. "Is there any special message you wish me to deliver into Her Majesty's ear?"

"Only that I hope and pray she will continue my good sister and friend," said Mary.

She returned to Edinburgh, to the placards and the restive people. Darnley had not quieted with his entombment, but seemed to have taken on a new and stronger presence than before. The citizens of the city seemed to wait eagerly until nightfall, when they could be entertained by the placards and the ghostly crier, who eluded all attempts to capture him. Mary could hear his wails, "Bothwell . . . Bothwell . . . Bothwell killed the King!" echoing on the Canongate.

Suddenly an underling of James Balfour's was captured and killed, and Balfour himself fled the city.

"It was rumoured that he was murdered because he knew too much about the first murder," said Lord James to Mary. He had just returned from St. Andrews. "Now the question is, who murdered him? Balfour? Why did you not arrest him?"

"Why should I have arrested him?" asked Mary. "On what grounds?"

"On suspicion of murder! The placards name him!"

"Oh, the placards," she said with disdain. "Shall we now conduct justice by allowing anyone too cowardly to accuse in daylight to accuse anonymously under cover of darkness? That would be shameful! Above all, we must try to act according to law. It is time the sun of civilization began to shine here and dispel the mists where assassins lurk."

"The placard was introduced from France," said Lord James. "It is one of those new fashions you seem to like well enough in clothes and music." He paused. "And what of Bothwell?"

"What of him?"

Lord James made a disparaging sound. He fingered his smooth beard and looked right into her eyes. "You know what of him." Again he waited. "He is named in the placards. The crier calls his name. There are witnesses that he was about the night of the murder, seen with his men, carrying barrels of powder right through the city—"

"The placards! The crier! If they called 'Lord James Stewart, Earl of Moray,' would you be so eager to believe them?"

"It would never be possible to name me in any such manner."

"No, you are much too proper ever to put your hand directly to any deed! But you look through your fingers at the deeds of others, which may be worse. Is that not what you agreed to do at Craigmillar Castle, 'look through your fingers'?"

"I know not whereof you speak."

His words chilled her. He was not to be held accountable for his previous promises or commitments, then; indeed, he disavowed them. And how could anyone prove otherwise? He was a liar, for all his religious cant. And dangerous—more dangerous than any hot-blooded dagger-wielder.

471

She needed to sit down. She felt weaker and more drained than after childbirth, or even after the Jedburgh illness. "Do you not, then?" she said wearily.

"And there is the most damaging thing of all on the placards," he continued, sticking his face up in hers. "I note that you do not even allude to it. The allegation that you and the Earl of Bothwell are lovers."

A bolt of fear went through her. So it was to be pursued, after all, not dismissed as calumny.

"I found the drawing of you half-naked to be an insult to the royal honour," he said. "Strange that you did not protest it or seem offended."

"I did not see it," she said weakly.

"Would you like to? I have it with me."

He was merciless. He was daring her to look at it, hoping to break her.

"If you wish. I prefer not to look at obscene drawings."

Triumphantly he ducked out the door of the little chamber and reemerged carrying the placard. In spite of herself, she gasped.

It was large, covering almost a yard square. The colours were loud and the drawing flagrantly bold. On the top portion of the placard was a mermaid, naked to the waist, as James had said. She had long hair and wore a crown. In her right hand was what appeared to be a long-stemmed flower of some sort; in her left, a scroll. Lest anyone miss the point, the mermaid was flanked with the letters MR.

Beneath her was a hare—the family crest of the Hepburns, with the letters of JH—for James Hepburn—surrounded by a bristling circle of swords.

"Isn't it pretty?" said James.

"What is that thing in her hand?" Mary asked.

"Is that all you have to say?" James stepped back and held up the placard. " 'What is that thing in her hand?' Good God! A better question might be, 'Is this man in your bed?' "

"How dare you?" she cried. "You are questioning me as if I were a criminal or a suspect!"

"Evidently you are," he said dryly. "Or this placard would not have appeared. Now tell me, if you hope to have any help in clearing this matter— is it true? Is the Earl of Bothwell your lover? Did he kill the King?"

"No!"

"No to both questions, or only to one? Which one?"

"The Earl did not kill the King. And he is not my lover!"

"Who did kill the King, then?"

"I do not know."

"Aren't you at least curious? If you did not—and I believe you—then you would not want a person running free who has no hesitation to commit regicide. He could strike again."

"It may not have been 'regicide,' but only an accident. The King left the house—"

"Mary, for all the love that has been between us, for the love of our father, I beg you to pursue the murderer. Do not make the mistake of assuming this will be like the murder of Riccio—dropped and forgotten. It will not. This time everything must be brought to light." He dropped the placard on the floor.

He looked tortured, and his demeanour, she could see now, was tired and strained. There had been love between them, once, before Darnley had come along. And James had been right about Darnley; he was most likely right in this matter also.

"The Earl of Lennox is demanding an investigation as well," she admitted. "But where can I begin in an investigation? No one will be truthful!"

"You will have to rely on the advice of Secretary Maitland," said James. "Do not rely on Bothwell. He is an angry man, full of spleen. His only answer to the placards has been to surround himself with fifty cutthroats and swagger about the streets saying he will wash his hands in the blood of anyone who dares accuse him to his face. Do not allow him to direct anything. Maitland—"

"What about you? Can you not help me?"

"Certainly, but one reason I wished to see you today was to ask a passport to travel on the Continent for a few weeks."

"Now?"

"I have business—"

"Evidently your wife is quickly recovered!"

So Lord James meant to absent himself again. That meant he foresaw some impending nasty event. He would absent himself, then return afterwards. To what?

"I refuse the passport," she said. Let him stay here; she needed him. If he truly cared so much about Scotland—

"Now you sound as arbitrary and petty as your cousin Elizabeth. Remember how she refused you a passport?"

"This is not the same!"

"Perhaps not. But I could serve Scotland better abroad. I would be glad to undertake a mission to France, to speak directly with them there. I will not be gone long."

He was wheedling like a pedlar. Next he would offer to bring her some sewing silks and patterns from Paris.

"I know you love the gold threads which are not available here, and the covered buttons—"

She burst out laughing.

"I beg your pardon!" he said, stiffly.

He wanted badly to be gone. He knew something. Perhaps it would be better if he were gone. She and Bothwell could be freer to act. The thought of James watching them, analyzing every glance between them, was frightening.

"Very well," she said. "You may go. But I wish you to stop and confer

473

with Queen Elizabeth on the way. And," she said with a smile, "I would love it if you could procure some garnet buttons for me!" They were notoriously expensive and hard to find.

❧

Mary was desperate to see Bothwell. But he had deliberately stayed away from her; all eyes were on her as she went through the motions of mourning. Until March twenty-second, the fortieth day after Darnley's death, she was required to keep to the mourning chamber as much as possible.

But, with the tumult outside in the streets, with the flood of diplomatic correspondence, with the need to attend to the urgent requests of the Earl of Lennox, she was at least able to meet with her councillors, of which, of course, Bothwell was one of the leaders.

When, on an evening in early March, he at last stood before her without either Maitland, Argyll, or his brother-in-law Huntly, she felt it had been a long time, almost another lifetime, since he had come to her bedroom at Holyrood. His reddish hair stood out startlingly against the black of the draped walls, a jolt of life in a chamber of death. He stood awkwardly, looking at her.

Wordlessly she put her arms around him and kissed him. Now just to touch him seemed shocking. They had forbidden themselves even to look in each other's eyes while others were present; and others had been continuously present.

"Bothwell, Bothwell . . ." she was murmuring. She felt his body next to hers, and it was the first time she had felt any strength sustaining her during this whole ordeal. She had been standing completely alone.

Gently he pulled her arms off his neck. "We cannot. Not tonight."

But she must have him, or she would die! She wanted to be held by him, to touch his body, his naked flesh, to lie with him and take him into herself until she ceased to feel anything but raw pleasure. She clasped him to her and kissed him. He must change his mind. She would make him.

"No." He failed to respond, and she had no choice but to release him. "Have you not seen the placards, heard the accusations? They know."

"They do not."

"Yes, they do. Our only hope is to behave so openly and properly that the idea will wither of its own accord. And my wife has been ill—"

"Your wife? What has her illness to do with the matter?" Suddenly she had an ugly suspicion. "She is not pregnant?"

"No. But, Mary, my love, at this moment we need all the support and sympathy we can muster. You must be the grieving widow and I the solicitous husband. We cannot afford to alienate the Earl of Huntly, your Chancellor and my wife's brother."

"Nor I the Earl of Lennox, my husband's father," she said dully. She sat down on the padded bench. "He demands an inquiry, and a trial."

"And so he should." Bothwell carefully pulled up a chair and sat on it, keeping a good ten feet between them. Someone might "accidentally" intrude at any moment.

"I wrote him and asked how I could bring anyone to trial, so many were named in the placards. There was Janet Beaton, your old lover . . ."

He laughed, a soft, sweet laugh.

"—Black John Spens, whoever he is."

"A henchman of Balfour's."

"Balfour himself, several French members of my household. But do you know who he said he wanted tried?"

Bothwell shook his head, lowering it and placing his hands on either side of it.

"You. He wanted you tried."

Bothwell looked up at her from between his hands. "And?"

"I agreed. What else could I do? I tried to tie it to a Parliament, but he would have justice right away, the soonest legally possible. On April twelfth you are to be accused of the crime and tried before a jury."

He burst out laughing. "And who are to be my jurors?"

"Your peers. The earls of Argyll, Huntly, Arran, and Cassillis. Lords Lindsay and Sempill. Bellenden, Balnaves, Makgill, and Pitcairn of Dunfermline."

"Both of our brothers-in-law to sit in judgement?" He was incredulous. "And how does this help to clear our names? I can tell you this, if they dare to pronounce me guilty, I will do the same for them!"

"What do you mean?"

"I only meant . . . there is much yet we do not know. Who strangled the King? It was not I. But you know and I know it took more than one man, acting under orders of a sick one, to bring enough powder into the crypt of the old Provost's house to demolish it. And we also know that someone has gone to great lengths to leave false evidence connecting me to the deed. They carefully left a barrel outside the door, to look as if it was carried there and then abandoned when it would not fit through the doorway. But the truth is the barrel was so large—as indeed it had to be not to fit through a normal doorway—that had it been full of powder it never could have been transported, even by the strongest mule. No, it was conveyed empty, by whoever it was that paraded about proclaiming my name all that evening. Someone carefully planned to incriminate me. And it was not Darnley. It was someone else, someone—or even several someones— whose aim is to destroy all three of us. Darnley was to die in the explosion; you and I were to be blamed for it. I would be removed from power and you would be—what?—driven from your throne? It would be unthinkable, until they had the baby Prince to crown in your stead."

Suddenly it was not just Bothwell's idle speculation. Suddenly she was very afraid.

"And these men—whoever they may be—how will we know? How can we protect ourselves against them?"

"We will know, eventually. And the only way to protect ourselves is to yield them nothing, to say nothing, to keep our own secrets."

She rubbed her hands. They were icy cold. "What is the date?" she finally said, in a faint voice.

"March eighth," he replied.

"Tomorrow it will be a year since Riccio was slain. The nightmare has been going on for a year."

"Do not even allow yourself to wonder how much longer it must go on. However long, we must go on longer. We must outlast it."

He took both his hands and smoothed her hair along the sides of her face, lightly, gently. "We have many enemies, but that we have always known. Some of them are special to you, some are special to me. And when we become one, perhaps yet a third party of enemies will come into being. But it matters not."

"You cannot bury a proposal of marriage in the midst of so many other words," she said. "Surely it deserves a solemn space of its own."

Bothwell stepped back from her again, and took both her hands in his. They were cool and slender. "Like fleurs-de-lys," he said, kissing them one at a time. "My most gracious sovereign lady, will you leave behind the fleurs-de-lys on your old mantles, your memories of the Loire, your French confessor? Will you take my life for your own, and be my wife? I can offer you the songs of the Borders, I can take you sailing on the seas as far north as the Orkneys and the Shetlands and Norway, I can let you chase bandits with me, sleep in the field."

"I would leave everything for you but my religion," she said. "Do not ask that. But, oh! I would go to the ends of the world with you in a white petticoat, I care not what else I would lose."

"Sssh. Speak not of losing. If we act quickly, there will be no losing." At last he kissed her, and her mouth opened under his like a flower. "I was wrong to think there should be delay. Delay will only make it worse. We must be brave and bold."

"My demon lover," she said, touching the side of his face as if it were a delicate and rare ivory. "How beautiful you are."

He laughed harshly. No one, not even his mother, had ever called him beautiful. "My dear Mary," he breathed, "well I know I am not beautiful, nor even handsome. But I do love you, past madness I think. For I must be mad to be doing this." He bent his head and kissed each of her breasts, swelling up and over her gown. He kissed them slowly and let his lips and tongue linger on them. "Leave the particulars to me," he murmured. "Trust me, and I will see to it that no one can condemn you for marrying me. Let the blame fall entirely on me."

They made their way to the bed, and climbed into it. He noticed, idly, that she had put scented, smooth sheets on it, and that the pillows were fresh and plumped up. He sank into them. Then he reached out his arms to her and enfolded her. Her delicate, shell-like ear was by his mouth. He put his lips to it. "Trust me," he repeated, and the words sounded distorted in her ear. "We will be husband and wife. There can be no turning back now."

Sighing, he rolled over and, lying on top of her, let himself feel the delicious contours of her yielding body. Each time he made love to her, she was different. What would she be like tonight?

Almost as if she read his thoughts, she rolled over on him and began to unlace his shirt. She ran her hands over his chest and then laid her head down on it. Her thick and lusciously scented hair tumbled over his chest and felt like velvet. "I am your lover, your slave, to command as you will. Tell me what to do, and I will do it."

Languidly he began giving directions, just to test her. "Kiss my neck . . . the hollow in my collarbone . . . the scar on my belly . . ." Her lips traced the raised thread of the wound that the sword of Jock o' the Park had made; her lips, soft and yielding on that tender, sensitive flesh, excited him beyond any touching he had ever received. It was all he could do to stifle a groan of pleasure. He preferred noiseless lovemaking, but he heard sounds, moans and inarticulate cries, coming from his own throat as she explored his body with her sweet lips. He was drowning in pleasure. He gave himself up to it and let her be the master of him for the time.

Later he would revive, would brush her sweat-soaked hair until it was smooth and her scalp was tingling, would splash cooling rosewater on her breasts and rub it in, and then, lying side by side, hold her in a tight embrace and show her how to lock their bodies together when neither was on top, neither was master, both were equal. Calmer now, able to look at her face and listen to her breathing, he was determined to give her the highest amount of pleasure she was capable of receiving. She twisted and moaned and cried, and finally wept, and that made him happy.

They fell asleep like two children in one another's arms.

Later they signed a private marriage contract, to bind themselves. She gave Bothwell some rich old church vestments, three embroidered priest's robes, and ordered him to have them made up into new clothes to be worn at his trial. She also presented him with Darnley's favourite horse, and insisted he ride it to his trial.

"You are innocent, and we must shout your innocence to the world!" she said. "No shrinking, no apologies."

"Spoken like a true Borderer," said Bothwell, in stunned admiration.

But too many Borderers had ended up swinging from ropes for their audacity, that he knew well.

LI

othwell stretched himself in bed. There was no sleep that night, nor did he want there to be. He savoured the hours alone to think, and make his plans. The darkness provided a luxurious blanket for him that shut out the swirl of other people. He was to be surrounded by others all day. It was April twelfth—the day of his trial.

He welcomed it. Get it over with. Nothing could be proved against him, for the simple reason that no one except Lennox wanted too close an inquiry into it. He held in his possession in a locked silver box the bond the lords had signed, agreeing to rid Scotland of Darnley as their King. Conveniently vague language, but then bonds never said the word *murder*. Riccio's bond had not contained the word, either.

Morton had given the paper to him—Morton, who had held back from active involvement, acting only by deputy. But on the bond were the incriminating names: Maitland, Argyll, Huntly, Morton, Douglas, Lord James. The very judges of the trial, the leaders of the Privy Council. No, they hardly wanted to stir up Darnley's wretched ghost. Let it lie.

By all rights, Darnley himself should be on trial. He had meant to murder his wife, the Queen.

The Queen . . . the Queen must remarry. They would start a campaign to find a new husband for her, with the dreary round of French ambassadors and envoys from Spain and perhaps even Robert Dudley again, on Elizabeth's part. But it could not be. She loved him, Bothwell. There could be no turning back, for their liaison would come to light eventually in any case. He and the Queen would have to wed. There was no alternative, even had he not loved her.

"God save the Queen!" he murmured, tossing in bed. Now it will be up to me to find a way to make it possible, he thought. Some way that will make it appear we are doing it for Scotland's good, rather than for our own desires.

I am weary. Tired of fighting. But just this last battle, and it is over.

Red was sending faint streaks up the windowpane like a skeletal hand. Dawn had arrived.

Outside, by the palace gates, a great crowd had already gathered by six o'clock. Making his way through to the very front was the provost marshal of Berwick, carrying Queen Elizabeth's letter. He could not gain entrance, and could barely attract the attention of a guard.

"I pray you, I bring an official and urgent letter from Her Majesty Queen Elizabeth to Queen Mary," he said.

The guard scowled at him. "I cannot take the letter. Her Majesty is still asleep."

By nine o'clock, the crowd had swelled so that the entire street, from the gates of the palace to the Tolbooth, where the trial would take place, was jammed with people. The April day was soft and warm, with a clear sky and wispy, racing clouds. Windows were open in the tall stone houses, and as many people as were on the street were above and looking out, leaning elbows on the windowsills and breathing deeply of the rich, sweet air.

The provost saw Maitland making his way over to him. "The Earl of Bothwell has been told that you have a letter from the Queen of England to deliver. But he thinks it impossible that our Queen can read it until tonight. She is still sleeping." Maitland did not offer to take the letter or invite him into the palace grounds.

Amazed, the provost saw a great company of men assembling in the forecourt, mounted on horseback, followed by hundreds of soldiers with harquebuses—Bothwell's men. Then Bothwell himself rode out, wearing golden clothes and mounted on a huge charger. Darnley's horse!

Around him the people were muttering, "There's his horse, the dead boy's horse, and Bothwell in the saddle."

"Where else does he ride where the boy used to?" Loud shouts of laughter.

"Anywhere he pleases, and as often as he pleases!"

"And as long as he pleases the Queen, the ride continues."

Now there were howls of laughter.

"Look! There she is! The whore!"

The provost looked up to see Mary waving languidly from her tower window to Bothwell. He turned in the saddle and gave her a smart salute. Then he threw his head back and laughed, a great roaring laugh.

So this is how she sleeps, thought the provost. And refuses to receive the Queen of England's letter, while she fawns on her lover.

Bothwell was now riding just past him, glorious and powerful in the saddle. Around him his harquebusiers formed a living hedge, bristling with weaponry.

None of the warmth of the April day had seeped into the cold stone Tolbooth, where Bothwell now took his place to defend himself. Seated on benches were fifteen of the judges in this trial, with the Earl of Argyll presiding and the Justice-Clerk Bellenden recording and ordering procedure. The entire Scottish court was present, with three notable exceptions: the Queen herself, Lord James Stewart, and the Earl of Lennox.

The Earl had sent two representatives, Crawford and Cunningham. Cunningham read a paper from Lennox, stating that "His Lordship was unable to attend on account of the shortness of the notice, and because he was in fear of his life, being denied liberty to bring such a following as he considered needful for his defence. Therefore he required the trial to be put off for forty days, or for such time as he might require to bring sufficient proofs

479

of his charge against the murderers, whom he required to have committed to prison till such time as he should be prepared to convict them."

Bothwell gave a disdainful laugh. "First he requests the trial, insists it must be before Parliament meets. Now he pleads an excuse for not being present, and asks that the 'murderers'—unnamed plural—be locked up until he pleases to confront them with 'evidence.' Has any more preposterous demand ever been received in a court of law?" His mocking voice made everyone laugh.

"Perhaps everyone accused of any crime should be locked up on the whim of one man, just in case he might feel moved to bring evidence against them sometime? Fie, gentlemen! 'Tis the Earl of Lennox who should be locked up—for feeblemindedness!"

He turned round slowly, looking at all the rows of men staring back at him. Their different-coloured cloaks made splotches against the opaque brown of the wooden banks of seats.

"But nonetheless, although the Earl is not here and there is no one to charge me formally with anything, I shall be pleased to answer any questions you wish to address to me. For above all, I wish to be cleared of this crime."

From ten o'clock until seven in the evening, the assembled company discussed the "terrible crime," but it seemed that no one could provide any answers. No one knew who had done it, why it had been done, how many people were involved, or even whom the plot had aimed at. Bothwell was unable to enlighten them. At length, tired and hungry, the Earl of Argyll called a halt to the proceedings.

"You are acquitted," he pronounced. "There has been no accusation, and no evidence produced against you. You are free to go."

"Thank you, my lords and friends, for your patience," said Bothwell. "I know you must be hungry. I therefore insist you join me, as my guests, for supper at Ainslie's Tavern, as soon as you can gather up your things. God be praised!" He gave an expansive gesture of thanks and flung his mantle over his shoulder.

The tavern was a large one, with several connected rooms. In the one farthest back, a long table was set up, using a board over trestles, to seat the company that Lord Bothwell had brought with him. Ainslie, the owner, was anxious to accommodate the great Earl who seemed to rule the city. He strode in as if he were just on his way to a delightful, inconsequential meeting somewhere else.

"I wish to quench everyone's thirst," said Bothwell, "with the finest wines you have, as much as they can drink. For those who prefer ale, I am pleased to allow them their heart's content of that as well. And after dinner, bring whisky." He saw the look on Ainslie's face. "Cost is of no consequence," he assured him. "And the food—I wish lamb and beef, the most delicate, of course. White bread." He nodded at the guests filing in. "Take your places, my friends."

Warily they sat down, while Ainslie and his helpers lit candles in the middle of the table. The glow grew until most of the faces were quite visible from Bothwell's end of the table. Morton, with his hard shiny eyes, was seated nearest, and Argyll on the other side. The rest of them—Huntly with his blond good looks, serious Seton, Cassillis, Sutherland, Rothes, Glencairn, Caithness, Boyd, Sinclair, Sempill, Oliphant, Ogilvy, Ross, Herries, Hume—gazed expectantly at him. Others, at the farthest end of the table, waited.

"My friends, do not look so glum," said Bothwell, standing up. "This night is my night of freedom from the ugly spectre of suspicion and lies. I thank you for making it possible for my name, the name of James Hepburn, which has never been disloyal or judged traitorous, to clear itself so that I and my descendants may live in pride." He raised his glass. "Drink, I pray you. Drink to justice. Drink to honour. Drink to courage."

He sat back down. He was exhausted. The night of no sleep, of the war of nerves about the coming trial, began to catch up with him. He felt as if he were falling, collapsing, folding inward upon himself. He willed himself to swell up again with strength. There was much left to do.

He ate ravenously when the beef and bread were put before him. It was all he could do not to tear it with his teeth. He noticed that the others, reluctant at first, were now joining in, and he could hear the clink of the knives on the pewter platters. Individual knives—each man ate with his own dagger. Then he saw Ainslie bringing out more flagons of wine and ale and removing the empties. Good. They must drink deep tonight.

Flagon after flagon made its way to the table, and the noise at the table grew loud. The men were even laughing. They relaxed; they let their knives rest on the platters, and with full bellies they leaned back and let their heads begin to swim.

" 'Twas good tonight," ventured Huntly, who rarely pronounced an opinion. "Now let us hope the ghosts can rest."

"Aye," said Morton, spilling some wine on his beard, where it vanished into the brush, "Scotland is full of ghosts, and let them keep one another company. Riccio and the King can play tennis again together now. Haw, haw!"

"God rest their souls." Bothwell hoped he sounded pious enough. Then he nodded to Ainslie.

Eight stoneware bottles of Highland whisky from the Gordon estates were brought out. "Now let us partake of the finest whisky in Scotland," said Bothwell. He nodded toward his brother-in-law Huntly, who turned pink with pride.

The caps were ripped off and the bottles passed around. The smoky brown liquid burned in their throats and then made straight for their heads.

Bothwell did not partake, although he raised his glass and appeared to sip. Neither had he drunk the wine. He waited.

When all the company had drunk for another half hour and were smiling at him warmly, he stood up.

Softly he said, "Gentlemen, friends, and companions, I wish to enlist your help. I know there may be those abroad—ignorant fools who do not understand Scotland, who have never tasted our whisky nor eaten our bread—who will mock us and imply that we are not capable of justice or self-governance. They will question the proceedings today, casting aspersions on *all* our honours. It is to avoid this, to protect us all, that I ask you to sign this document."

He unfolded it. He had composed it painstakingly in the early dawn, gambling with it for the highest stakes he had ever attempted.

"Let me read it to you.

> "We under-subscribed, understanding that, although the noble and mighty Lord James, Earl of Bothwell, being not only bruited and calumniated by placards and otherwise slandered by his evil wishers and private enemies, as act and party of the heinous murder of the King the Queen's Majesty's late husband, but also by special letters sent to her Highness craved and desired by the Earl of Lennox to be tried of the said murder: he being examined and tried by certain noblemen his peers and other barons of good reputation is found innocent and guiltless of the said odious crime, and acquitted.

> "Therefore oblige us, and each one of us upon our honour, faith, and troth in our bodies, that in case any manner of persons shall insist further to the slander and calumniation of the said Earl of Bothwell as participant of the said heinous murder, whereof ordinary justice hath acquitted him, we ourselves, our kin, friends, servants, and all, shall take part with him to the defence and maintenance of his quarrel, against anyone presuming anything in word or deed to his dishonour, reproach, or infamy."

The men nodded. Should he just circulate the paper now and have them sign it? The light was poor enough, and they were drunk enough, that they might not even see the second, startling, part. But no. Unless they knew what they had signed, it was worthless to him. Besides, he had built his reputation on being open and blunt.

"I thank you," he said. "And there is yet another part of the paper, touching that which is of course in everyone's minds in these sad days. The Queen has been bereft of a husband in the flower of her youth, with only one child to offer for the succession. Foreigners will try, once again, to gain control of our land through this our misfortune."

There was nothing for it now but to plunge in. "Therefore, if you will:

> "In moreover weighing and considering the time and present and how the Queen's Majesty our Sovereign is now destitute of husband, in which solitary state the common weal of this our native country may not permit her Highness to remain and endure, but at some time her Highness may be inclined to yield to marriage; therefore, in case the affectionate and faithful service of the said Earl Bothwell done to her Majesty from time to time and his other good qualities and behaviour may move her Majesty to humble herself (as preferring one of her own

born subjects unto all foreign princes) to take to husband the said Earl Bothwell, every one of us undersubscribed permit the said marriage to be solemnized at such time as it shall please her Majesty to think it convenient and as soon as the laws will allow it to be done."

The men were muttering and moving. Bothwell could hear murmurs of anger and alarm up and down the table. At the same time, the unmistakable sound of the two hundred soldiers he had posted around the tavern penetrated into the room. He held his words so that the soldiers could be plainly heard above all else. The men quieted; they looked desperate and trapped. Bothwell cleared his throat and continued in a quiet, calm tone.

"But in case any would presume, directly or indirectly, openly or under whatsoever colour or pretence, to hold back or disturb the said marriage, we shall hold the hinderers and disturbers and adversaries thereof as common enemies and evil wishers and will take part and fortify the said Earl to the marriage. We shall bestow our lives and goods against all that oppose. As we shall answer to God and upon our honour and fidelity, should we not maintain this, we are never to have an honest reputation or credit in our time, but be accounted faithless traitors, in witness of which we have subscribed our hands as follows."

There was a swift shadowing movement as someone slipped away.

"Come back!" Bothwell ordered, in such an imperious tone that the rest of the company grew even more restive. He had not meant to speak so; it had just happened.

"Good my lord," Huntly was saying, with a stricken face. He would have to be well paid off for letting his sister be divorced. "How can you shame me so in public?"

Chairs were being pushed back, and men were standing up.

"You are not free to go," said Bothwell. "You must not leave." Outside the soldiers were noisily marching, as he had ordered them to. "I must insist you sign the paper first." This was going badly. But what other way could he have presented it?

He pushed the paper toward Morton and thrust the pen in his hand. The great thick head bent down over the paper and he scratched his name. He silently passed it to Sempill next to him.

Bothwell stood at the end of the table, watching intently. Suddenly it occurred to him that they might tear the paper up. The men waiting their turn were glaring at him, while the soldiers' boots scraped loudly on the cobblestones outside.

It seemed to him that he stood at least five hours before the paper, smudged with signatures, made its way back to him. He glanced at it to make sure they had not altered it or crossed out any phrases, and had signed their true names, not "Johnnie Armstrong" or "William Wallace" or "Judas."

"Thank you, my friends and allies," he said lamely. "You may go now. Please make your way with care." Some of them were doubtless so filled with whisky they might fall and break their necks. Yet they had seemed quickly sober when they had been confronted with the paper.

It had been a mistake. He never should have done it. Now he had made enemies out of them all. And embarrassed himself for his bullying, brutish behaviour.

But it was done. He clutched the paper in his hand and made his way out of the deserted room. By the time he reached the front door of the tavern, he saw that all the men had already dispersed. The news would be all over Edinburgh by morning and Scotland by the third morning and England by the fifth. He would have to act quickly. He dismissed his soldiers, promising them extra pay for the night's duty.

Extra pay for the soldiers, the cost of the dinner and wines, paying off Huntly—it was an expensive venture. But if all went well, it would be money well spent.

You must spend money to make money, his greedy old uncle the Bishop had taught him once upon a time.

The night was still and warm. Its very friendliness caused him to slow his footsteps as he made his way back to Holyrood. Linger a little while, the air seemed to be saying. Do not hurry through me, but breathe me in. Take deep breaths, let me fill you. And he did, turning slowly around, letting his mantle trail on the stones.

The sky was clear, and the moon so bright he could see even the few wispy little clouds that floated like an afterthought in the blackness. Life was sweet, hanging there for the taking, begging to be noticed as one walked along.

He sighed, and stopped turning. Down in the hollow at the foot of the long slope was the palace, painted silver-blue by the moonlight.

And there is even a princess in the tower, he thought. Waiting to be rescued, now that the dragon Darnley is slain. He gave such a roaring laugh that other passersby turned their heads.

He made his way to the royal apartments, down the now-familiar hallways and stairs and turnings. She was waiting for him in the inmost room. As she rose and came toward him, he had an instant of feeling that this was all just a story after all, the princess in distress—even, perhaps, the Circe who changed her lovers into animals and destroyed them. The shame of the scene in the tavern flooded him. What had he been driven to?

Then she was beside him, the light and dark of her face and hair close to him, the honey of her breath against his skin. She whispered, "Are you safe?" And in the sound of those three words, husky and aching, he forgot about the men in the tavern and their hate.

The trial. She meant the trial. "Yes. I am acquitted." He found himself whispering, too, why he did not know.

She kissed him, slowly. He allowed himself to savour it, linger over it just a little longer than he usually did. But he had no wish to proceed further; he was content, now, just to hold her.

Taking his lips away, he said, "The Earl of Lennox never appeared. He wished me to be detained until such time as he might gather his evidence. I insisted on the trial proceeding. But as no one could present any charge against me, nor produce any evidence, in the end I was pronounced not guilty and acquitted."

Her soft lips were on his neck, but he stepped away and found that he needed to keep his distance for now.

"It is nearly midnight. Did the trial go on so long?"

"No. The most important business took place afterward." He brought out the paper and gave it to her.

She took it over to a small table where a candle was burning, and held it close.

"Take care lest it burn!" he said with alarm. He had not purchased it with so high a price to his own honour just to see it lost through carelessness.

She read it, squinting at it in the poor light, bending forward so that her hair got in the way. Impatiently she brushed it aside. At length she turned to him.

"Unbelievable," she said. "How did you dare?" He could not tell whether she was appalled or admiring.

"In truth, I do not know," he admitted. "It had to be done. And now 'tis done, and there's an end to it."

"No. Not an end," she said. "If only it *were* ended! And your brother-in-law signed it?"

"Not willingly. And he will tell my wife." Shame flooded him again, that Jean would have to hear it from her brother. "The men did not wish to sign. I filled them with whisky and threatened them with my soldiers. I did not wish it to be that way. I had hoped they would be more amenable."

She laughed. "Sometimes you seem so innocent," she said. "While you were at the trial, a letter came from Queen Elizabeth, more or less threatening me. She calls my honour into question." She thrust the letter at him. Wearily he read the important part:

> For the love of God, Madame, use such sincerity and prudence in this matter, which touches you so nearly, that all the world may feel justified in believing you innocent of so enormous a crime, which, if you were not, would be good cause for degrading you from the rank of princess, and bringing upon you the scorn of the vulgar. Sooner than that this should befall you, I would wish you an honourable grave, rather than a dishonoured life.

She snatched the letter back. "And we are not safe even now," she continued. "Something much more distressing than the letter from Elizabeth has come." She handed him a large creamy envelope. "It is from my ambassador to France."

But alas, Madame, this day over all Europe there is no subject so frequently discussed as that of your Majesty and of the present state of your realm, which is for the most part interpreted sinisterly. I fear this to be only the beginning and first act of the tragedy, and all to run from evil to worse. I did thank the Ambassador of Spain on your behalf of the warning he had given you, although it came too late. He has yet desired me to remind your Majesty that he is informed by the same source that there is yet some notable enterprise against you, wherewith he wishes you to beware in time. I write this far with great regret, by reason I can come no ways to the knowledge of any particulars of his master.

Bothwell's eyes flicked over the letter. "Whoever it is, it must be the same party who so carefully set up the false clues of the barrel and the party of men parading about the streets shouting my name. And directs the placards, and the mysterious crier."

"So it is a party, not just one man?"

"I am the only man who acts alone. Everyone else acts in a party." He was aware that it sounded like boasting when he said it, but that it was true, and to his own manifest danger. In Scotland, it seemed, the man who walked alone did not walk long.

"Fie on all this!" He put the letter down, where it rested on top of the one from Elizabeth. "We are surrounded by dangerous enemies. But we must be stronger than they."

He looked tired, and, though he would have been shamed if he had known it, warily afraid. She wished to protect him, to do everything in her power to spare him the coming ordeal. But at the same time she wished to lie in his arms, even though it was the most dangerous thing she could do to him.

"Come to my bed," she suddenly said. "It is my command."

With an indescribable look—of relief? disbelief? reluctance?—he bowed his head in compliance.

"Take off your clothes," she said, "and quickly. All of them."

Again he complied, and stood before her naked. But she did not stand and gaze at him, but pulled him into her bed, where she had quickly undressed and covered herself.

"I am not sure I can make love on command," he demurred.

"I am quite sure you can," she said, touching him. "I know that we need this in order to be strong enough to face the next tests."

"You make it into a sacrament," he said.

"To me it is," she said.

"Mary," he said, holding her later, "do you trust me?"

"With my life," she murmured, her lips against his neck, her voice drowsy.

"Then you must trust me to bring about that which we most want, in my own fashion. Whatever I do, do not question me or, for a moment, lose faith in me."

"I told you, I trust you with my life."

LII

Mary walked slowly in procession from the closing of Parliament. Ahead of her, with stately pace, walked the Earl of Argyll bearing the crown, Bothwell bearing the sceptre; behind her was Huntly bearing the sword of state. She was aware of the hostile eyes of the people lining the street. Never before had she experienced this; always there had been nothing but adoration in the eyes of her common subjects. Only John Knox had ever caused such looks to be directed at her, and it was horrible to encounter him multiplied a thousand times, as it were. She smiled, hoping to elicit smiles in return. There were some, and one woman called, "God bless you, if you are indeed innocent of the King's death." It sent a chill through her.

If you are innocent of the King's death. How could they think otherwise? Do they turn on me so soon, and for no evidence? She shuddered.

Bothwell's straight back ahead of her comforted her. Yet he was only one man, and they were so many.

Already they were calling the Parliament "the cleansing of Bothwell," although it was no such thing. He had been confirmed in his office as Lord High Admiral and Lieutenant of the Borders, and granted complete authority over Dunbar Castle in recognition of his "great and manifold service," but others had been recognized as well: Huntly had been formally restored to his titles and estates, as had Morton and Lord James. All the old traitors had been forgiven and restored. It was a new beginning, at least on paper.

Bothwell had given no indication of his plan. She had not seen him alone since the night of his trial.

It would be a relief to be able to leave Edinburgh. She planned to go to Stirling and see her child, to see for herself how Erskine and his wife were raising him. Had they left up the painting of the Virgin over his cradle, or had that been taken down and replaced by a Bible text? Oh, Mary, Mary, she told herself. You are tired and think ill of everything around you. Weariness has dulled your sense of discernment and shaded even the bright things. You badly need the open air of Stirling, and to hold your baby.

Baby James seemed to have absorbed her malaise, for he whined and twisted when she picked him up. He had grown heavy; Lady Erskine said he had already tripled his weight, and had outgrown all the clothes that had come with him.

"But he's a long babe," she said, "and will never be fat!"

James started slapping Mary's face. She turned her head slightly to deflect him, but he kept on. It hurt, and it also hurt her feelings, although she knew it should not have.

"What toys does he especially like?" Mary asked, turning her head back the other way.

"He has a set of boxes that fit one inside the other," she answered. "He likes to put them together. And Peter here, the carpenter, he made him a box that has different-shaped holes in it, and then little blocks that fit the holes; there are round ones and square ones and star-shaped ones, and he likes to put them in there. He is most solemn when he does it."

Just then James yanked on her hair. "Does he like to play outdoors? It is a lovely day today. Would he like to see the swans on the pond down below?" She handed him back to Lady Erskine.

"He has never seen them," she said. "Let us take him down there."

Lord Erskine suddenly came into the room. His elongated face broke into a smile. "Such a bonny prince," he said. "It is our great honour to be entrusted with his safety." James gurgled and reached out a plump hand to Erskine, causing Mary a stab of pain.

My son, my son, she thought, already I am a stranger to you.

They went out into the courtyard of the palace, where the keen fresh winds of April were sweeping through and whistling around the corners. The watery, melting-snow smell and the whisking noise slammed into her, and suddenly it was April of two years ago, when Darnley lay ill here at Stirling and she had been overcome with love for him, and defiant of the Lords and Elizabeth. . . .

They descended the long, sloping pathway to the castle grounds so far below, where the white peacocks strolled and the swans, back from wherever they went in the winter, floated on the waters of the ornamental ponds. Lord Erskine carried James, and the baby squealed and laughed as he bounced along. At length he put him down on the soft new grass, where he crawled away, his little bonnet bobbing up and down.

"Your Majesty, you look weary," said Erskine solicitously. "I trust I may speak freely to you, as a friend as well as a subject? We have known each other for so long, and I have seen you in so many conditions—even one hour after the birth of the Prince."

"I feel weary," she admitted. "But I hope to rest soon. If such a thing is permitted to rulers."

Erskine was looking at her with deep concern. "The past two years have been so difficult, one cannot help but feel that they are part of a divine plan."

Not that. "Knox is away," she said with a smile. "Pray, let us rest from such speculations. I am content, as you know"—here was the difficult subject—"to have the Prince instructed in the Reformed Faith. To be ignorant of his subjects' faith would be a great gap for him."

"Then why do not you study it?" he asked bluntly.

"Those who would teach me have been vindictive," she said. "Knox and his foul words and curses do not entice me to come closer."

"That is a great pity," admitted Erskine. "For he is a man of the country, and surely he has heard the common saying, 'You catch more flies with honey than with vinegar.' He proclaims the sweetness of the Gospel, but he makes it sour."

She smiled. " 'Tis no matter. Oh, look, the Prince is trying to stand!"

Lady Erskine held up James's arms and let him walk a few steps. "He pulls himself up and walks if he has support," she said. "The next time you see him, he will be walking alone."

"The next time you see him," said Erskine, "he will be a right proper young Prince!"

The way back promised to give Mary and her accompanying party a pleasant ride in the countryside. Spring was now well advanced, and as Mary, Melville, Huntly, and Maitland made their way slowly along the soft path through meadows and woodland, she felt her spirits lifting. The breeze, turned warm since only the day before, was now lulling, and everywhere the birds were talking to each other, chattering, bickering, wooing, warning. Their active, energetic movements, hopping and jumping from limb to limb, stirred Mary's sluggish mood.

"The birds are rejoicing," she said, turning her head to speak to Maitland. "They are like little children let out of a lesson."

Maitland gave a wan smile. "Yes, Your Majesty," he said, with no joy at all in his voice.

Poor Flamina! thought Mary. He has only been married four months, and already he turns a deaf ear to spring? Perhaps he *is* too old for her, after all.

Behind him Huntly plodded along, his face equally glum. Usually Huntly had a smile and a rather lighthearted air about him; that was what made him a good companion, despite his limited mental powers. But he was clearly unhappy today.

The sun rose higher, shining through the mist of green on the tree limbs that had been bare only a week earlier. Back in the deeper parts of the woods, the green was barely discernible in the shade, but little spots of white from the earliest woodflowers were winking at them. And everywhere was the sound of the rushing, gurgling, and dripping of water released from the long lock of winter.

"Shall we stop and rest?" asked Mary.

"I do not see any suitable place," said Maitland. "Everything here is muddy."

And indeed their horses' hooves made sucking noises as they trotted along the path.

"The first high spot we find, then," said Mary, trying to keep her voice cheerful. In spite of her worry and suspense about her situation, she was enjoying the music of the songbirds—the robins, thrushes, and woodlarks—and even the deeper calls of the blackbirds and the raucous cries of the rooks. It was an exuberant chorus that spoke more loudly of life than anything composed for the organ in a church building. Overhead the silent hawks were soaring in the immense blue sky.

They began to climb up and away from the stream that flashed in its rocky channelled maze, swollen with spring water. A hillock, surrounded by hawthorn and sweetbriar hedges in white bloom, and carpeted with bright new grass, seemed to be waiting just for them.

"How magnificent!" said Mary, as she saw over the rim of the hill, and beheld the flowering meadow spread out before her. "It looks like a tapestry!"

Now Maitland allowed himself a smile. "Ah, now you are praising art! For you are saying that the artists do such a fine job that it seems nature copies them, rather than the other way around."

They dismounted, and the rest of the party followed suit. On all sides of the hill there were blooming woodlands and tangled underbrush; as Mary looked in one direction, she caught a flash of white that meant a deer hidden in the shadows, watching them warily before bolting away.

"Come, walk with me!" she said to her three councillors, but Maitland and Huntly had already drawn apart and were beyond reach of anything but a shout. Only Melville heard her and obeyed.

Melville, too, looked unhappy. All of them unhappy beneath this smiling, tender April sun! Surely God must think His creatures deaf, blind, and ungrateful, thought Mary. Just then she saw a family of hedgehogs scurrying for safety at their approach, and she laughed out loud.

"The hedgehog needn't be so timid," she said. "Although I suppose he hasn't the defences of his more formidable cousin, the porcupine. Have you ever seen a porcupine? I am minded to do an embroidery—"

"Your Majesty," said Melville, "I think—again, forgive me, I am only doing my duty—that you have weightier matters to concern yourself with than porcupine embroideries." He stopped walking and looked at her forlornly.

"Dear Melville," she finally said. "You have been with me through so much. So, once again, you see fit to warn me? My behaviour is giving offence?"

"Yes, Your Majesty. It is Bothwell. You must divorce yourself from him."

No, she thought. It is not divorce I need, but a marriage. "I am not married to him," she said.

"No, nor must you ever be. He is not worthy, and it would compromise you to take such a man. When he forced the Lords to sign that pitiful petition, it showed just how desperate his case is. It was laughable, pathetic."

"But they signed it."

"Only by force. Your Majesty, has he . . . attempted to act on it? The strange thing about it was, it was a licence to woo! He was saying '*if* I should convince her to accept me.' But heaven must put that thought far from your mind! You must be deaf to his entreaties, like Ulysses to the sirens. Put wax in your ears and lash yourself to the mast, if necessary!"

"Ah, Melville. You have my good at heart," she finally said.

All the while she was thinking, What *is* he going to plan? What can he *possibly* plan to overcome such opposition? *Trust me,* he had said. But how?

She rode along, a sprig of lily-of-the-valley from the meadow tucked in her bodice, its sweet scent keeping her company. Her party seemed to be in slightly better spirits after their stop. Perhaps they had needed a rest, or perhaps it was only that the scurrying of life and busyness, like the hedgehogs, was proving impossible to resist.

Suddenly there was a crashing in the brush ahead, round the bend where the bridge over the little Almond River awaited them. A great company of horsemen were there—hundreds of them.

"Why, what is this?" cried Mary, reining her horse back. Soldiers. She could see the glint of the sun on their metal helmets. No! Not another Scottish attack or rebellion. Even as she fought to master her reeling horse, she felt her heart begin to pound and that familiar extraordinary energy flooding into her veins. It was the same as that which had come to her when she pursued Lord James in the Chaseabout Raid, as that when she fled through the graveyard with Darnley; it was beginning to feel like a friend she could count on to appear in times of danger.

"What is this?" she cried. "Who blocks our way?" Now filled with courage, she spurred her horse and galloped forward, around the bend. Before her was an army. And at its head, Bothwell.

He sat his horse like a wooden effigy, huge and immobile. His visor was down and she could not see his eyes; there was only a long, thin slit like a corpse's mouth, rounded at the corners.

"What is this?" she repeated. She stopped just before Bothwell, this odd Bothwell whose face was invisible.

"Your Majesty," he said, "there is danger in Edinburgh. I and my men, my loyal Border troops, are here to escort you to safety. We will go to Dunbar Castle." He reached out with a quick, darting movement and grabbed her horse's bridle. "I pray you, do not resist."

"Who is in arms against us?" she demanded. Was it Morton, or the Lennox Stewarts, or some Knoxians?

"I cannot say at this moment. It is all confusion. Come." He turned his horse and began to lead hers away. "You as well," he told the three courtiers.

Concerned for them, Mary turned to assure them. But Maitland and Huntly did not look worried or even surprised; only Melville did. Shocked, she realized that once again there had been a plot to which she was not privy. They had already known about it. That was why Maitland paid no attention to the blooming countryside; his attention was on the blooming plot. And Huntly—it was not to his liking, so he wore a frown, but he had agreed to it nonetheless. Dear God! Was *this* Bothwell's solution to their dilemma?

"If there is indeed an uprising, then send one of your men back to Edinburgh to raise the alarm," said Mary.

"As you like," said Bothwell, jerking his head toward Lord Borthwick in his party. "Go, my good man. In the meantime, we must hurry."

They passed by Edinburgh, where a cannon volley was fired at them, but missed. They skirted the city and continued heading due east, toward Dunbar and the sea. Suddenly the blooming hedges, green glades, and foaming spring waters became invisible, and Mary saw nothing but the swarms of soldiers ahead of her. Bothwell did not speak again, but led her ever onward, like an emissary from some dreadful undiscovered region charged with bringing back a captive.

Why did he not speak to her? She swallowed hard as the first rush of excitement drained away, deserted her veins, and left her uneasy and confused.

The sun set behind them, and torches were lit as they passed through the little Lothian villages of Dalkeith and Haddington—Knox's home town—and skirted the estate of Maitland. Had he wished, he surely could have bolted at that point. But no—he was paid to continue on the journey; no clearer proof was needed of his complicity.

She began to smell the sea, and by midnight they came to Dunbar Castle. For an instant, as she rode into the courtyard and heard the cries of the gulls just beyond, hovering over the sea, she felt a leaping joy, for it was just so that she had ridden to safety after the Riccio murder. But only for an instant. This time was entirely different.

Bothwell rode out into the middle of his milling soldiers. "I have eight hundred men here, all loyal to my command," he shouted. "Do not attempt to test my word, for I assure you they will obey me and slay anyone who tries to escape, regardless of who he is."

There were murmurs and shouts, but only amongst the small train of Mary's retainers.

"Do not attempt to fight," Mary told them. "You can see that he has hundreds of men, and you are less than thirty. We must submit." She did not want any show of bravery that would result in bloodshed. They were hopelessly outnumbered.

Bothwell rose in his stirrups and cried in ringing tones, "The Lords of Scotland have signed a bond allowing me to marry the Queen, and to account anyone who attempts to prevent it as a faithless traitor." He waved a piece of paper in the air. It was barely visible in the red flaring torchlight. "But I know there are those who will attempt to prevent it! Now I will marry the Queen, no matter who objects—yea, whether she herself agrees or not!"

There was a shocked silence. Bothwell jumped down off his horse and came over to Mary and pulled her down into his arms. He held her so tightly she could scarcely breathe.

"I have her, and I will make it so that she is mine, indisputably mine. Seek not to interfere, or I will make a corpse of you!"

He picked her up and carried her through the yawning entranceway to the inner fortress. She was trembling and stunned. He marched through the courtyard and into the keep, then, still not halting his pace, up the stairs to the uppermost floor. Releasing her, he slammed the thick wooden door behind him and bolted it with a beam as big as a gangplank. Outside she could hear a tumult rising.

"No one can break in here," he said, as if reading her thoughts. "We are safe."

Inside the square room, its ancient walls made only of irregular, unfinished stone, three torches flickered from their wall sockets. One of the three windows was open, on the sea side, and a loud wind was rushing in, almost drowning out his words.

"Safe?" She stared at him, at the rough, leather-clad warrior standing before her. She had thought she knew him. Now he looked like one of the Northmen carved on old stones she had seen depicting the Viking invasions. "You must be mad. Why have you done this?"

"So that I have a thousand witnesses that I kidnapped the Queen and lay with her against her will. I could have done with a bit more protesting on your part, for the sake of convincing skeptics." He was smiling as if he had just done an ordinary thing.

"How do we dare do this? No one will believe us!" His sheer audacity was astounding.

"Seeing is believing," he said. "That's what they claim. Now a thousand people have seen. And I will keep you locked up here long enough to make it credible."

"That you . . . dishonoured me?" Her voice was shaky. He was asking her to endure that shame, just for him.

"Yes. You know that in Scottish law there is only one way to repair that particular dishonour. Marriage."

Shame flooded her, but at the same time, his daring and straightforwardness were compelling. "But they will hate you for doing this! You've degraded *yourself*, and there's no repair for that. Oh, Bothwell! How could you resort to this? I cannot bear it for you to have hurt yourself so!"

"I love you, and in order to have you, I have sacrificed my—"

"Your honour!"

"No, my reputation. It is not the same thing. Sometimes you must sacrifice your reputation to maintain a deeper form of honour."

"Oh, Bothwell!" She threw herself in his arms, anguished over what he had done to himself.

He bent down to kiss her. She touched his lips hesitantly, so shaken and confused that she scarcely knew how to respond. She wanted to protect him, save him. She was touched at his immense sacrifice, stunned by his sheer audacity. Once she touched him, she wanted never to stop. Outside the noises were rising; she could hear shouting and the beginnings of a fight.

"They are coming for us," she whispered.

"No one can break in here," he repeated.

They clung together while they heard more shouting, and footsteps climbing inside the tower. Then something metal—a sword? a shield?—struck the door with a resounding thud.

"Are you in there?" said a thick voice. "Surrender the Queen's person!"

" 'Tis only Borthwick," said Bothwell. "He does not mean it." He was kissing her shoulders, and pressing her body against his as they stood trembling together in the middle of the chamber.

"Surrender the Queen's person!" Borthwick was yelling again—so loudly that it would surely carry far out into the courtyard where Melville, Maitland, and Huntly could testify that they had heard it.

"Never!" Bothwell roared back, making sure it would carry just as far out of the window. "Even now, if you could rescue her, it would be too late!"

He picked Mary up and carried her across the room to a pallet that lay against the outer wall, and laid her down gently. He sat back on his heels and began slowly, carefully, unfastening her gown. He took his time, as if they were alone together in a secluded glen.

Outside the door, Borthwick kept on banging. Pulling the fur covers over them, Bothwell held Mary tightly against him.

Mary felt Bothwell's strong body on hers, and they made surprisingly prolonged, tender love as Borthwick's shouts and bangings reverberated through the door, punctuating their pleasure.

It was quiet. Borthwick had left, and evidently the courtyard had emptied out. There was no sound at all but the sea far beneath them, echoing up into the chamber. They lay naked together under the furs, their shoulders cold where they were exposed to the air. Bothwell was sleeping, a heavy, still sleep.

Mary saw the shadows jumping on the walls. The torches had almost burned out. She closed her eyes and tried to sleep. But she was oddly excited.

Now we are truly married, she thought.

And she realized that until now she had never been truly married, for neither of her husbands had ever had to sacrifice anything for her. That was marriage's true consummation.

So this is my bridal bed. A pallet with wolf-fur covering, in a windy tower room in a castle keep. And it is more a bridal bed than the one in the King's quarters at Stirling, or the one in Paris where—O saints! Where nine years ago today I was married to François! She thought tenderly of that childish bedtime with François, while Bothwell lay heavily by her side. *Childhood is past and now at last I am full grown.*

* * *

There was no sleep for her that night. The torches burned out, and slowly a purplish blue light crept into the room. She lay still and watched as it grew brighter and brighter, and she knew when the sun came over the horizon, for it reflected in shimmering light on the ceiling from the restless sea below.

She could see the room better now. It was perfectly square, and the walls were of crude, large blocks of roughly dressed stone. This was the very earliest part of the castle, built hundreds of years ago. The furniture was simple: a table made of a plank, wooden benches, stools, and two studded trunks. There was no bed, only this pallet. Swords and shields hung on the walls.

Turning her head, she watched Bothwell sleeping. He had pillowed his head on his folded hands, as if he were praying. She could see the scar on his forehead so clearly; it remained white when the rest of his face was darkened by the sun and wind. They were bound together now, their fates one and the same. It was what she had wanted, and had even commissioned him to do. Why, then, was she so filled with foreboding?

Silently she rose and made her way over to the window. The stone floor under her bare feet was cold and clammy. As she approached the window, she was surprised at the force of the sucking wind; it drew her hair out the window like a pennant. Down below, the sea was crashing on the dark, jagged rocks, sending spurts of spray up into the air, where they hung for a moment like the veil of an infidel dancer before falling away in the air. A flock of gulls dove and darted, and their cries were plaintive and raw.

Bothwell touched her, pressed his naked front against her back. He had risen so silently she had not heard a single sound.

"Good morning, my love," he whispered against her ear. He encircled her with his arms. "How do you like my stronghold? You gave it to me."

"I had no idea what it would be used for when I did." He was touching her neck. She could not decide whether she wished him to or not, just then. Then she could tell that he was becoming aroused. She turned to face him.

"You are insatiable, my good Earl," she finally said. "You are worse than the famous black ram of Yarrow."

"Is there a ballad to the ram? There should be. There is a Border ballad for everything, it seems. . . ." He delicately kissed her eyelids, shutting them. Then he knelt down and buried his face against her thighs, pressing himself up against the slender columns, revelling in the touch of them. Softly he kissed the seam between them, then the insides of them, and finally, when he could feel the muscles begin to quiver, he brought her back to the pallet.

"May I change my clothes?" asked Mary, later. "Or am I to remain without even my toiletries and underclothing?"

Bothwell rolled over and propped his head on his elbow. He grinned.

495

"Of course you may have your belongings brought up. I apologize. I also apologize for these quarters. I know they are somewhat . . . er . . . lacking. But I also knew what we most wanted was privacy. The newer portions of the castle are quite comfortable, but unfortunately open to all."

"Do you mean to keep the councillors prisoner here as well?"

"No, they are free to go as soon as they have heard you consent to marry me, and can act as witnesses. That is part of our agreement."

Suddenly she had a chilling thought. They might acquiesce to the marriage just so she could be made to share Bothwell's odium. And then be driven from the throne. *And there is yet some notable enterprise against you.* The Archbishop had written that a month ago.

"But you are still married," she pointed out.

"Huntly has agreed to allow his sister to be divorced."

So that was why Huntly had looked so sullen. "And what of . . . of . . . Jean?"

"She will cooperate."

"Does she not care?"

"I know not," he admitted.

How could he know so little of his wife's feelings? "I see."

"Mary." He reached out his hand and touched her cheek gently. His intent greenish eyes looked directly into hers. "I have not been a good man to everyone in my life; some of it is not my fault, but I shoulder the blame for it all. Perhaps my marriage could have been better, had my bride wished to marry me. She did not; her brother sold her as he is selling her now. The man she wished to marry was promised to someone else. It was hard for her. But she made it hard for me, as well. Arranged marriages take a toll. Sometimes I think the hardest way to earn money is to marry it."

He looked so earnest. "But what of the Danish woman, or whatever she was?" she heard herself asking, hating herself for it.

"What of her? She was boring. I could not bear to think of spending a lifetime listening to her bad poetry." He laughed. "She was a Norwegian admiral's daughter, and I met her in Copenhagen. She was dark, which is unusual for a Norwegian, and so she fancied herself to have a hot Latin temperament. She even had a Spanish costume which she affected to wear and thought herself most fetching, when in truth it was silly."

"Nonetheless you lived with her."

"Her father, who had seven daughters, was most anxious to marry them off, and promised a dowry of forty thousand silver talers." He sighed. "I told you, it is the most difficult way to earn money. I know."

"So you took the money and then left her."

"No. There was no money, as it turned out. Now who was the deceiver, and who the deceived?"

"Pray send for my clothes," she suddenly said. "And I wish something to eat." She pulled the fur cover up around her shoulders.

"As you command," he said, rising and going to the door. He hoisted the great bar that bolted it off its brackets, and pulled the door open. She was surprised to see that the door itself was at least five inches thick. He stuck his head out and muttered something; evidently there was a guard on the landing.

Bothwell only had time to put on his breeches and pull his shirt on over his rumpled hair before three servitors entered the room, carrying trays of food and her bundles of clothes. They were finely dressed, their liveries new and embroidered with the Hepburn crest. Obsequiously they bowed and put their burdens down. Bothwell bolted the door after them. Then he began to hum as he uncovered the dishes and arranged them on the table. He was even smoothing out a white linen cloth.

"I did not know what you would like," he said. "But I have here herring and oysters and grouse and pigeon." He whisked the covers off more platters and bowls. "And here are oatcakes and Ayrshire cheese, and rowan and apple jelly, and—"

"Stop!" she said, laughing at his eager face. He would make a good father, becoming like a child himself at times. "Being kidnapped has made me hungry, but not that hungry." She pulled up a bench and took one of the wooden platters and began to select food.

"I would have thought it was something else that had made you hungry," he said, looking at her with a guarded tenderness.

"All that hunger has been quenched," she said, spearing a piece of smoked fish with a wooden skewer and tasting it. "But perhaps it is the sea air that has made me so hungry."

"Perhaps. When I am at sea, I do find myself oddly hungry." He picked up the largest chunk of meat on the serving platter.

"Tell me about your voyages," she said.

"I learned to sail as a child," he said, chewing. "I think I was not more than eight or nine when I took my first little voyage. It was in the North Sea, off the coast of Spynie. I was living with my uncle, the Bishop—the one you met—and my cousins there, his bastards, were at home on the sea like a rider on a horse. I loved to sail out, to chart a course and see how near I could come to it. I sailed to the Orkneys when I was twelve." He smiled at the memory of it.

"What are the Orkneys like?" she asked, eating more of the oatcakes than she wanted to. She was very hungry after all. "I have always wanted to see them."

"I told you, marry me and I will take you there. They are cold, but clean, like an eagle. They seem almost to soar. They are incorruptible. My ancestor was Earl of Orkney. I assume it is in my blood to love it." He poured a large amount of wine into his goblet and diluted it with water.

"How long ago was that? Why is your family no longer there?"

"Long, long ago. In 1397 my ancestor received the title. And then, later, my family was forced to sell the earldom to James III."

"I will make you Duke of Orkney and Lord of Shetland," she said impulsively.

"But not King," he said.

"No."

"It is better thus. I am content that my sons be princes; I am a field soldier and a sea captain first and foremost."

A flood of relief washed through her; the unspoken worry had been answered. This would be no repeat of Darnley. Ironically, this man, better suited to wear a crown, would not hanker after it.

Days passed in the tower, and they turned day into night and night into day, sleeping when they pleased, eating whenever they liked, making love, lying and talking. They created their own rhythm and fashioned the hours to their own desires, and the sun rising and setting had little to do with it. It seemed like a dream, and each did things that surprised the other. Mary astounded him with her knowledge of weaponry and ability in cards; he surprised her by his love of poetry and music.

"I know you like to think I spent all my time fighting in the Borders or sailing off the coast, but the truth, which it pleases you to forget, is that I was educated in all the classics. I even brought some here to show you." He pointed toward a small pile of books, proud like a boy. "I wanted you to see some of my library."

She went over to them and picked one up, turning its pages idly. "Virgil. And look—Aelian on *The Order of Battle*. A military book! I think I have more need of that than poetry."

"The ideal life supplies them both. Like life in the Borders. There is much poetry in the Borders, beautiful ballads that ring with fine phrases like 'The wind doth blow today, my love, and a few small drops of rain; / I never had but one true love, in cold grave she was lain,' and 'You crave one kiss of my clay-cold lips, but my breath smells earthy strong; / If you have one kiss of my clay-cold lips your time will not be long.' Then it goes on to say, ' 'Tis down in yonder garden green, Love, where we used to walk, / The finest flower that ere was seen is withered to a stalk.' "

He reached for his lute. "I should have given it its music. It is missing half a life without its music." He touched the strings and the rounded sweet notes came forth. " 'The stalk is withered dry, my love, so will our hearts decay; / So make yourself content, my love, till God calls you away." His rich voice trailed off.

She felt herself shivering. "Think you they will make a ballad about us?"

"They already have," he said, shaking his head. "These things spring into life before the events are even over."

"Sing it." She both did and did not want to hear it.

"As you command. It is not very flattering. It is about me." He plucked the lute.

> "Woe worth thee, woe worth thee, false Scotland!
> For thou hast ever wrought by a slight;
> For the worthiest prince that ever was born,
> You hanged under a cloud by night."

"You notice how the Lord Darnley has now become 'the worthiest prince that ever was born,' " he said. "Thus do ballads make their own truth.

"The Queen of France a letter wrote,
And sealed it with heart and ring,
And bade him come Scotland within
And she would marry him and crown him King.

"There was an Italian in the place,
Was as well beloved as ever was he,
Lord David was his name,
Chamberlain unto the Queen was he.

"For if the King had risen forth of his place,
He would have sat him down in the chair,
And though it beseemed him not so well,
Although the King had been present there.

"Some lords in Scotland waxed wondrous wroth,
And quarrelled with him for the nonce;
I shall tell you how it befell;
Twelve daggers were in him all at once.

"When the Queen saw the chamberlain was
          slain,
For him her cheeks she did wet,
And made a vow for a twelvemonth and a day
The King and she would not come in one sheet.

"Then some of the lords of Scotland waxed wroth
And made their vow vehemently,
'For death of the Queen's chamberlain
The King himself shall die.'

"They strewed his chamber over with gunpowder,
And laid green rushes in his way
For the traitors thought that night
The worthy King for to betray.

"To bed the worthy King made him bound,
To take his rest, that was his desire;
He was no sooner cast on sleep,
But his chamber was on blazing fire.

"Up he leaped, and a glass window broke,
He had thirty feet for to fall.
Lord Bothwell kept a privy watch
Underneath his castle wall.

'What have we here?' said Lord Bothwell,
'Answer me, now I do call.'

" *'King Henry the Eighth my uncle was,*
Some pity show for his sweet sake!
Ah, Lord Bothwell, I know thee well;
Some pity on me I pray thee take!'

" *'I'll pity thee as much,' he said,*
'And as much favour I'll show to thee
As thou had on the Queen's chamberlain
That day thou deemest him to die.'

"Through halls and towers this King they led,
Through castles and towers that were high,
Through an arbour into an orchard
And there hanged him in a pear tree."

"That's a lie! It's all lies!" she cried.

"Of course it's lies, and mixed up ones at that. First the King is worthy, then the lords want to kill him for killing the Italian, then he's worthy again, then the lords want to blow him up . . . some imagination. Darnley changes character every other verse."

"But you are made to be the murderer," she said slowly. "And they knew I banished Darnley from my bed. Truth twists itself round lies and makes a braid. It is not all lies after all." She found herself shaken. "Do you think all this is finished yet, or will there be more twists and additions to the story?"

"Once we are married, we will be stronger than all their plots and lies."

She looked down at her finger, gleaming with an enamelled ring. Slowly she pulled it off and handed it to Bothwell. "This is your betrothal ring," she said.

He took it and looked at it, puzzled. "This is covered with bones and tears," he said. "Black enamel and gold. Is it a fitting betrothal ring?"

"It is what I have with me now. In taking it, you pledge to share my fortunes as they come, unexpected and perhaps woeful."

He kissed her and slid the ring on his smallest finger.

LIII

hey rode slowly back toward Edinburgh, torn from their secret life in the tower—only ten precious days!—ready to face whatever lay ahead. Huntly, Maitland, and Melville had been released days earlier, and the divorce had already been set in motion. There were to be two divorces, a Protestant one and a Catholic one, just to cover any future objections from any camp. The Protestant one was to be based on Bothwell's adultery with Bessie Crawford, and the Catholic one on the blood relationship between Jean and her husband; four generations earlier an Earl of Bothwell had married the daughter of an Earl of Huntly. The banns were to be cried as soon as possible by the pastor of Giles High Kirk; luckily Knox was still in England and they would have to deal only with his substitute.

As they passed through the little villages, curious people lined the paths, but they stared silently. No one cried, "God bless that sweet face!"

They are inspecting me to see if my clothes are torn or if I look anguished, Mary thought. If I were covered with bruises, that would content them.

But her defiance grew more and more shaky as she rode nearer Edinburgh. The eyes of the people were not cruel, just puzzled . . . and betrayed. They could not understand what was happening. She felt as if she had indeed betrayed them, for they were obviously frightened and insecure.

Ahead of her, Bothwell was riding placidly along. She could see Edinburgh on the horizon, could spot Arthur's Seat rising up, dazzlingly green with the new May grass. Now Bothwell was slowing, waiting for her to catch up.

He looked down the road. "I do not see anyone," he said. "But I think it best that we do not enter the city by the Netherbow Port. Let us come in as close to the Castle as possible, and make for it straightway." His voice did not sound very confident.

"So we should stay in the Castle?" she asked.

"Aye. I have appointed Balfour its captain, to secure it for us."

"Balfour? Whatever for?" She distrusted that skull's face.

"For past services he has rendered," said Bothwell. "Come."

They could see the ruins of the buildings at Kirk O'Field as they skirted the southern side of the town walls. Nothing had been cleaned up, and stones lay in heaps, with single ones flung far outside the wall. On their right was the orchard where Darnley's body had been discovered. Mary turned her head away as they passed.

Once inside, by way of the West Port, they found the streets oddly empty.

Although a few people were there to stare at them, they hurriedly made their way up to the castle gates and scurried to safety behind its walls.

In the royal apartments, they found Maitland waiting for them. He was sunk in agitated melancholy, leaning crossed arms on a table and staring at nothing. He jumped up when they entered the room.

Bothwell threw his gloves on the table with no ceremony. Mary asked Maitland how he was.

"All is confusion and disarray," he said glumly. He looked at her as if he hated her for putting him through this, for demeaning himself so on such a task. Poor bridegroom!

"The divorce hearings?" asked Bothwell, without giving Mary a chance to say anything.

Maitland rolled his eyes. "Shameful. They have dragged out every detail about your . . . doings with Mistress Crawford. Your wife questioned the man you had posted as a lookout. He even told about the time you . . ." He stopped, embarrassed. Mary turned away.

"Has it been granted?" asked Bothwell. "That's all I care to know."

"Your wife—"

"So she is still my wife!"

"No, your former wife, she demands that you grant her Crichton Castle, or she will not free you."

"I grant it," said Mary, in a small voice.

"It is mine," said Bothwell.

"All properties are ultimately mine," Mary insisted.

"You are wrong," he said. "It is in my purview. Yes, I will grant it. I will pay any price! Oh, what a hardheaded woman of business—this is the second time I have had to pay a fine over Bessie. The first, when she learned of it, was that I give her the lands of Nether Hailes and its castle. Now Crichton. I have paid such a high price for her favours, Bessie might as well have been Salome." He sounded angry. "Well, what else? Has that churchman cried the banns?"

"No," said Maitland. "He refuses to."

"What? Bring him here!"

"And Morton, Argyll, and Atholl have met at Stirling. Others were summoned."

"Who?" Bothwell slammed his fist down on the table and yelled. "Who?"

"My Lord, I know not, I swear it. I only know that after the meeting Atholl galloped north, and Argyll west, and Morton to Fife."

"To gather an army," muttered Bothwell. "So soon. Get that preacher in here!"

The Reverend John Craig stood before Bothwell and the Queen. They had at least changed into fresh clothes, and Mary had taken her place upon her throne under the canopy of state, to lend weight and authority to the proceedings.

Craig was a thin, balding man with sharp features. He looked remarkably like Knox, or what Knox would have looked like had he been clean-shaven. Fleetingly Mary wondered if it was a requirement for all Reformed ministers to have that look: lean, small-eyed, pale, straight-spined.

"Why have you not announced our forthcoming marriage?" Mary asked in her gentlest tone. "We requested you to do so straightway."

Craig shot looks back and forth between Bothwell and Mary. He shifted on his feet. Finally he said, "So it is true! I did not believe it!" and the disdain in his voice could not have been greater had he beheld the Witches' Sabbat in full orgy. "Will you sign a paper to that effect, releasing me from responsibility in looking away from sin?"

"Yes," snapped Bothwell.

"What sin?" inquired Mary. She could see Bothwell glowering at her for pursuing it.

"What sin? You dare to ask what sin?" The preacher was incredulous. "The kidnapping and ravishing of the Queen, not to mention common adultery, collusion between yourself and your wife, and suspicion of murder of the King."

"Do you mean me? Suspicion of murder?" inquired Bothwell.

" 'You are the man!' as Nathan said to King David. But you are worse than King David. He only committed adultery with Bathsheba and killed her husband—only!—whereas you have kidnapped, raped, and degraded your own sovereign, in addition to killing her husband and committing adultery with a maidservant."

Bothwell gave out a roar and reached for his sword.

Mary rose from her chair and grabbed his arm. "Never! Do not strike him!" She turned to Craig. "Doubtless your master, Mr. Knox, will rejoice at all this. Truly there has been sorrow in Scotland, but I mean for there to be a new beginning. It is my royal request that the marriage be performed. And I will appear at a meeting of Parliament to give all the reasons for it, and I pray the people will be content."

"Never!" said Craig. "It has gone too far. They cannot stomach any more! As God is my witness, they will abhor and detest this approaching marriage as much as I do!"

Mary stood in the Tolbooth, in the same spot where Bothwell had stood only a month earlier. All the eyes gazing down at her were either hostile or blank. The Lord Chancellor, Huntly, was both. All the Lords of Session who were still in Edinburgh were there, but a suspiciously large number of seats were empty. Various Kirk dignitaries, in sad-coloured clothes, lined the walls.

"I am minded," she said, "to make you privy to my thoughts concerning the Lord Bothwell. I was very angry when he interrupted my journey, and took me to Dunbar against my will. But when, in spite of my sending for aid, none was forthcoming, and his behaviour toward me gentle and good, by and by I came to listen to his words and to entertain his suit. His proposal of marriage was an honest one, and one that had been already approved by the Lords and barons. He showed me the signatures. And so, keeping also in mind his former loyal services toward the crown, I agreed to become his wife."

Not a single smile, nor even a hint of one, lightened any face. They sat in judgement of her, looking down smugly.

"And thus, I am content and forgive him, and all others with him for his actions during those ten days. I ask that you do likewise, my good people." She lifted her hands in supplication, although the law was that only her royal pardon was required.

Her steps were heavy as she made her way back to the royal apartments. She had heard the derisive comment, "So the laws of Scotland, which pardon rape if the woman later acquiesces, is now used to blanket over murder as well? She perverts even the law for her lusts!" It was a Reformed minister, naturally. He looked away, embarrassed, when he realized she had heard him.

But even in her own apartment she found no security. Her dear French confessor, the Dominican friar that Lord James had scowled at, was waiting.

"Your Grace," he said, "I must ask leave to return to France. I can no longer stay."

"Oh, good Father Mamerot! You have been with me always, do not leave me now!" she cried.

"I must. My superior has so ordered me. I cannot stay." He looked genuinely pained, as if he were about to cry. He held out his arms and encircled her shoulders.

"Your superior? But I am the Queen." Her voice was small and muffled.

"The Pope, Madam. The Pope," he said. "The Holy Father . . . the Holy Father orders me to separate myself from you until such time as you amend your life. He himself says that he will have no further communication with you until then. He says that you are damned!"

Mary gave a cry and fell to the floor.

❧

So early in the morning it was still night, about four o'clock, Bothwell took her hand and led her to the old chapel at Holyrood, where they were married by a Protestant minister. No priest would have anything to do with the rites, nor would any upstanding minister of the Kirk, so Bothwell had prevailed upon the Bishop of Orkney, a man known to turn his coat to line his purse, to conduct it.

The pliable Earl of Huntly was there, as well as the faithful lords Livingston and Fleming, and a few other lower-ranking noblemen. There was no procession, no music, no beautiful costumes. Mary was forced to endure a sermon about Bothwell's repentance of his earlier evil life. When she said the vows, she kept feeling that they were not real.

This man is not a true priest; he has no authority. These rites are not binding.

"Will you take this man, the Duke of Orkney and Lord of Shetland, to be your husband? Will you love him, honour him, keep him, in sickness and in health, keeping yourself only unto him, as long as ye both shall live?" the Bishop intoned.

"Yes, I will," she said, but her voice was faint; only Bothwell and the clergyman could hear it.

It was so dark in the chapel she could not even see Bothwell's face. All this seemed like some mysterious rite, as if she were entering the underworld. She half expected to see Cerberus, the three-headed dog that guarded Hades, bark beside her. And Bothwell turn into Pluto, the god of the shades, of death. . . .

He was taking her hand, slipping a ring onto it. His fingers were cool.

"I now pronounce that they are man and wife together," the Bishop was saying. Bothwell squeezed her hand. Still she could not see his face.

"What God has joined together, let no man put asunder," the Bishop warned. Bothwell turned to her.

Do not touch me, else I can never leave your side, can never come up to the green earth again, but must wander forever in the silent darkness and flickering firelakes of Hades. . . . Her heart was pounding in fear.

He bent down and kissed her, sealing her as his.

LIV

ary ran her hands over the glistening gold font. She loved the feel of gold, its lustre, its glow that was unlike any other metal. It never felt as cold as steel or iron; there was some warmth stored away in the heart of gold, she could swear it. Perhaps that was the true source of its magic.

The jewels—sapphires, rubies, emeralds, and pearls—winked on its rim. They formed a pattern like a vine, a vine that grew only precious stones. The workmanship was exquisite. Had it been made in England? Or had it come from Italy or France?

Sighing, she poured some perfumed water into it and then dropped a few petals from the blooming branch of apple tree that Madame Rallay had brought in. Pear had once been her favourite, but no, not pear, never pear again. . . .

She swirled her fingers in the water, watching the petals bob and circle. This font, the gift of Queen Elizabeth for the baptism . . . was it only five months ago? She had been shocked by Elizabeth's generosity, touched. It meant that Elizabeth felt herself to be truly the prince's godmother.

She did not want to give it up.

Bothwell had told her of the desperate need for funds to pay their soldiers, who must protect them against any uprisings. The treasury was empty. Her money from France had quit coming, dried up, for all that it had been promised her in perpetuity. There were ways of getting around that. Delays. Papers. Lawyers. Exchanges of property.

"And you gave away so many crown lands," he had said. "You were *so* generous. The Lord James owns tracts half the size of the Highlands."

"You benefited from my generosity," she had reminded him.

"Aye. But now, I fear, comes the hard part. You will have to pawn your jewels. And that font—it's precious gold!"

"I cannot," she had said. "It means so much. It is more than just a font, it is a bond between Elizabeth and me."

He had looked sadly at her. "Mary, all it can be to us now is thirty-three ounces of gold, which we desperately need."

She could hear his voice again in her mind. But she tilted the font and drained the water out into a basin, then wiped it dry with a linen cloth. She touched the font again, lovingly.

No. She would not give it up. Once it was gone, it was gone forever. And later, when all was calm, she would bitterly regret it. She folded its velvet covering back over it, and was returning it to its box when Bothwell flung open the door without knocking first.

"Where is it? You promised to have it delivered to the goldsmith this morning. He has had his fire at full smelting heat for two hours!"

"I have changed my mind. I will pay the smith for his coal, but I wish to keep the font."

"Pay him with what? That is the point, you cannot even pay for a goldsmith's coals! Now, give me that!" He wrenched it out of her hands.

"Return it to me! I command you!"

"Ha!" he laughed, tucking it under his arm.

"I am the Queen!" she screamed.

"Not without soldiers, you are not," he answered. "And there will be no soldiers without the gold to pay them. Now . . . is this bauble worth your throne?"

"Bothwell . . ." She could see beyond him, beyond the five thousand gold pieces the font was expected to yield. "Can a throne be retained for five thousand gold coins?"

"It is a lot more than thirty pieces of silver, and look what they bought."

❦

Never had the capital looked lovelier, thought Knox, as he approached it on horseback. June was always the time when no city on earth—excepting possibly Geneva—was more appealing; more delicately hued, more vibrant. It had been March when he had left, the month in which the city was at its annual worst, and so it had been easy to leave behind. But now . . . ah, he was glad to be home. And glad to answer the call. His country needed him once again; at last the wheel had turned and it seemed that the Lord would prevail against the wicked Jezebel who had tormented them too long.

When I called her that, everyone thought I was cruel. The Lords said, "Oh, Master Knox, you are so unkind. What harm a few dances? What harm a private mass or two? What harm the cards and the music?" But I saw what they did not. It was my privilege and sorrow as a prophet. They act as though I *liked* what I saw! I said I saw dolour and sorrow and heaviness—and I did grieve at the vision, not rejoice.

But human weakness is God's opportunity. I know that out of this will be born something according to His will. If only we have the courage to reach out and seize it!

Out of chaos can come order. And chaos is here in Scotland once again, as I foretold. The strongman Bothwell is being crowned with honours for his evil ways. Even now the Queen has made him Lord of Shetland! Yet the Psalmist says, "Arise, thou Judge of the World, and reward the proud after their deserving. Lord, how long shall the ungodly, how long shall the ungodly triumph? Wilt thou have any thing to do with the throne of wickedness, which imagineth mischief as a law?" And the faithful Lords of the Congregation are even now gathering, ready to throw off the oppression of the evil pair!

His house was waiting, swept clean and tidied by one of the faithful Lords, one of the few remaining in the city. It felt good to reenter it, like putting on a favourite shirt that has been cleaned and made ready. There was much work to do. He would, of course, have to consult with John Craig—that brave man!—and gird his loins for the coming battle. There were sermons to be preached, hearts to be strengthened—swords to be sharpened. The hour had come.

"And tell me, when you refused to announce the banns, what did they say?" Knox asked John Craig. They were strolling in the little garden in back of Knox's house. It had not been kept up or planted this spring and so its little paths were overgrown with weeds. But the irises and poppies were springing up anyway, poking their slender heads up above the weeds.

"Bothwell threatened me," he said. "He grabbed his sword, but *she* stopped him. He is a blustering, loud-voiced thug."

"I know," said Knox. "But he was not always that way. Strange to say, I have known him since his boyhood; in fact, my family were vassals of the Hepburns. It is his father, that traitor, who abandoned him and taught him the meaning of perfidy and made him into the hard man you see today. As

507

a boy, he was kind and spirited and imaginative. He did not deserve the father he had." Knox sniffed. "Nor the wife he is getting!"

"I tried to stop that," said Craig. "But of course they found someone else to marry them."

Knox stopped walking and grabbed Craig's collar. "Think you that the people are ready? Can they be toppled?"

"I have no doubt of it, sir."

"Ah. Then I am indeed come home."

That Sunday, at St. Giles, Knox walked stiffly to the pulpit. He had felt old, weakened, lately. His joints had developed rheumatism, his eyes were rheumy, and he had even noticed a disconcerting inability to distinguish certain sounds. He hated to keep asking people to repeat themselves, so he had begun guessing what they were saying, filling in the missing word for himself. He was, after all, fifty-two years old. But now, with a task to do, God had renewed his strength. It was just as Isaiah said, "They that wait upon the Lord shall renew their strength; they shall mount up with wings as eagles; they shall run, and not be weary." With a feeling of physical well-being which he had not experienced in years, he mounted the steep steps to the pulpit; he felt as if he could almost take them two at a time.

The cathedral was filled, with crowds in every corner, and standing behind every pillar. They stood in the niches where lately saints' statues had stood, and turned their faces to him. He looked out at them and gave silent thanks. Now, Lord, empower my tongue! he prayed.

Gripping the sides of the pulpit, he began. "Dear brothers and sisters, it is with great thanksgiving that I stand here again before you. Since I have last stood here, on that grievous Sunday in March a few days before the slaying of the Queen's wicked servant, that Riccio, there has been more blood spilled in heinous crime. At last the Lord has called me back, even at the peril of my own life. But so must it be. I take as my text today the first book of Samuel, chapter fifteen, verse thirty-five, and chapter sixteen, verse one:

> "And the Lord repented that he had made Saul king of Israel. And the Lord said unto Samuel, How long wilt thou mourn for Saul, seeing I have rejected him from reigning over Israel? fill thine horn with oil, and go, I will send thee to Jesse the Bethlehemite: for I have provided me a king among his sons."

Knox cleared his throat. Oh, it was so glorious to be restored to power, if only to preach this sermon.

"Now this very thing has happened in our land. God has utterly rejected and cast down the woman on the throne, because she has sinned and turned to abomination. God has provided us with another king, the Prince James.

In His goodness he has done this, allowing the harlot Queen to live long enough to provide an heir for the throne. In His mercy, he will not abandon us to the horror of civil war and fighting for the throne, but has given us his blessing in this Prince, who is a goodly child, for all his Romish baptism, and is being brought up and instructed by the Lord Erskine, a faithful member of the Elect."

He sighed and looked over at the hourglass: it was the one that the hateful Darnley had replaced after stealing the one from Calvin.

I should have taken it back before he died, thought Knox. Now no one will ever know where it has gone. A sense of loss pervaded him.

There was still plenty of sand left in it. Perhaps he would not even use up all his allotted time. He felt that he had already said what he came to say. He could harangue the crowd about Mary and Bothwell, but the important thing was to move ahead to the coronation of James. Still, it would not hurt to remind the people of why this was indeed necessary.

"I remember the day she came to Scotland—do you? There was foul mist everywhere, a warning from Heaven—it wrapped her up like one of her French cloaks, clung on her like one of her French poets, kissed her cheeks freely like one of her courtiers and foreign spies. . . ." He was warming up now.

"And then, in the filth of her lusts, she seduced a married man, and lay with him, and together they planned to murder her husband, which was done with an explosion, and then a pretend-divorce was secured, against the law of man and the church, that they might the better indulge themselves in their sin. Are we to stand for this? Are we to allow our nation to be so degraded and mocked in the councils of the world? No one would permit such a ruler, would obey or honour such a ruler, who is nothing but a whore!"

The people stared back at him and began moving around.

"Yes, I said a *whore*! There is no other word! Unless you prefer harlot, Messalina, hussy, bawd, adulteress! Or perhaps you prefer murderess? I say that *whore* in her *whoredom* should not be allowed to live. Burn the whore! Burn the whore!"

The people began shouting. Was it in protest or agreement?

"Burn the whore . . . burn the whore. . . ." It was in agreement.

"The law of the land calls for the burning of women who murder their husbands. And in the Scripture, Deuteronomy twenty-two, verse twenty-two: 'If a man is found sleeping with another man's wife, both the man who slept with her and the woman must die. You must purge the evil from Israel.'

"And this man, the Earl of Bothwell, the Scripture says of him, in Exodus twenty-one, verse sixteen: 'Anyone who kidnaps another and either sells him or still has him when he is caught shall surely be put to death.'

"Malachi, chapter four, verse one: 'Behold the day cometh, that shall burn as an oven; and all the proud, yea, and all that do wickedly, shall be stubble.'

"Sin upon sin, abomination upon abomination—they must die!" yelled Knox. "Let the dogs lick her blood, as they licked that of the evil Ahab, and consumed Jezebel!"

"They must die," echoed the people, their voices swelling and filling the dark nave.

As he fought his way through the surging crowd afterwards, Maitland plucked at his cloak.

"The Lords of the Congregation are waiting at Stirling," he whispered, covering his face. "They have an army."

Knox stared at him. "And you, sir?"

"I am with them. I will join them as soon as I may escape."

"Do not delay, lest you be numbered with the Queen and burnt along with her." So the Queen's secretary was scurrying away, like vermin from a house on fire. "Where are they now?"

Maitland laughed nervously. "At a regatta in Leith, celebrating their marriage."

Knox permitted himself a painful laugh.

LV

he waters sparkled, glittering under the ships dotting the surface of the Firth of Forth, where Bothwell had assembled the fleet of Scotland: galleons, carracks, and merchantmen. The vessels were yare and scrubbed, and the flagship was draped with garlands of flowers, ropes as thick as a man's wrist that looped around the rails and over the figurehead on the prow. The sails were white: a bridal ship for that day.

"You are mad to have spent the money," said Mary, but she was pleased nonetheless.

"It was not right for our marriage to pass uncelebrated," said Bothwell, "or unmarked by any ceremony or whimsy. Above all things, a wedding demands some gesture of happy extravagance." He looked at the sizable crowd gathered on the shore, staring out at the flotilla bobbing on the water. "We cannot deny them a chance to share our happiness with us."

The man was amazing: such steely calm in the midst of the hatred and coming storm. Was he heroically brave, or did he just not understand?

"Nor can we deny ourselves," he said. "For if we do not rejoice, who will rejoice with us? And wherefore was it done at all, then?"

He understood.

"Ah, Bothwell," she said. "I do not know if I can follow you through the fire in the way which will make you proud."

"I have watched you go through other fires," he finally said. "What do you think made me love you?"

Was that why he had loved her? It was confusing. Why would a man love a woman because she acted like a man at times? "They look so calm," she said, indicating the crowds. "There is no indication that they are hostile or will turn on us."

"They came out for the show, the food, the fine weather, an excuse to leave their work. If anything is free, a crowd will always gather. So it has always been and will always be. It means nothing. No, this show was for *us*, for you and me. So we can have something to remember always."

She shuddered. "When will it come, this blow? We have sold everything we can to pay soldiers. We have comported ourselves so circumspectly that even eighty-year-olds would find us dull company. Yet the Lords have not returned from wherever they are hiding!"

"The strong strike openly, the weak have to lie in wait. It is hard now to tell just how strong they are. We have Edinburgh Castle under our command, and Dunbar, and I can raise my Borderers. Then there are the countless numbers who will be loyal to you personally and follow your royal Stuart banner."

"I wonder if they are countless, or all too easily counted?" she said. Once the countryside had been filled with her supporters. But now . . .

The ships were coming into a formation, sailing abreast to show their seamanship. Bothwell was a worthy High Admiral; he had trained his fleet well in the years he had had it under his command.

"Is there any sight more lovely than a ship with its sails filled?" he said, in the tone he used only when touched by beauty. " 'There be three things which are too wonderful for me, yea, four which I know not: the way of an eagle in the air; the way of a serpent on the rock; the way of a ship in the midst of the sea.' "

"And what is the fourth? You said four."

"The poet said four. The fourth is 'the way of a man with a maid.' " He looked at her with that steady gaze that she loved so much, that sustained her like bread. "It is Scripture, believe it or not."

"You Reformers all know Scripture," she said, enviously.

"Knox is back." Bothwell let the words sit there.

She waited.

"He is preaching today."

So it was to come, then. Soon. If not today, tomorrow. Or the day after.

He reached out and took her hand and, raising it slowly to his mouth, kissed it. Then he held it tightly and kept it entwined in his, by his side.

Holyrood was oddly quiet and seemed almost deserted, although there were the usual retainers, servants, and guards about. But the throngs of courtiers, envoys, secretaries, and all their relatives were missing.

"Do you remember those tales about empty, enchanted palaces?" she asked. "There was always some treasure or sleeping princess there. I used to wonder what it would be like to stumble into one—whether there would be cobwebs or whether it should be miraculously clean—"

"You dream too much. This princess cannot sleep, at least not now, or she will wake to find herself with no palace at all." He was striding down the echoing halls into the royal apartments. At the door the guards gave him a slight nod, but otherwise seemed somnolent.

The light was fading, but no candles or torches had been lit. Cursing under his breath, Bothwell lit one and brought it over to the window ledge. He looked up and down the Canongate, which was also oddly empty.

"I feel uneasy," he said. "I think it is time we summoned the Lords and commanded them to leave Stirling and appear before us. And we should begin to gather an army."

"Already?"

"It is late. We should have done it two weeks ago. I hope it is not *too* late."

Mary shivered. But as much as she hated war, she had no doubt as to the outcome. Bothwell had never lost a battle, and his generalship was the foremost in the land. Lord James, a respectable soldier himself, was not in Scotland and could not be used by either side. Who else did the Lords have? Morton and Home and Lindsay—none of them particularly noteworthy or battle-tested. Kirkcaldy of Grange, who was a good fighter but surely no match for Bothwell.

Beside her, Bothwell made a sad, low sound. "This is the first time a new soldier will be fighting in the field. It will make military history. In later ages students will say, 'Ah, in Scotland a new player came to fight,' just as we now study siege-machines and the catapult and the harquebus. It is *the people*—it is Knox's hordes, who now have a voice and a presence the equal of Kirkcaldy of Grange or even Elizabeth of England. *The people,*" he said, and his voice was tired and bitter. "With all their pitchforks and fervour and bad breath, as mutable as the clouds on a summer's day, but stronger than a granite boulder rolling down a hill—and just as mindless. They will flatten and crush anything in their path."

"Then we can jump out of their way. They will be easy enough to see and dodge."

He laughed. "Now that's the royal spirit I love." He put his arms round her. "Write the summons calling our men to arms. Let us amass our own boulder."

* * *

A proclamation summoned earls, barons, knights, freeholders, landed men, and substantial yeomen to report with arms and fifteen days' provisions to the Queen and her dearest husband on June fifteenth at Melrose, in the Borders. The reason given was disorder in Liddesdale, that most untamed and dangerous tract.

At the same time, the Queen summoned the Lords of the Congregation to Edinburgh. None appeared, but from the safety of Stirling they issued an announcement that the men were being summoned to Melrose to over-throw the laws of the land and even to kidnap the baby Prince.

Mary was forced to issue a denial, saying, "As for her dearest son, of whom shall Her Majesty be careful if she neglect him that is so dear to her, on whose good success her special joy consists and without whom Her Majesty could not think herself in good estate but comfortless all her life?"

Then silence fell over Scotland—silence, except for John Knox's preach-ing about the Jezebel and her Ahab.

A week passed, a week of quiet that was not a true quiet but a waiting for action. Mary and Bothwell lived in the royal apartments at Holyrood like ghosts, or the last man and woman on earth.

"This should feel like Eden, like Adam and Eve," he commented one night as they finished their solitary meal. "But there is a great difference in being the first and in being the last. One is filled with hope, the other with dread or remorse." He wiped his full lips with the linen napkin. The fare had been pleasing: a creamy soup with oysters, a delicate fish from Linlithgow loch, which had been stocked by Marie de Guise and could be found nowhere else in Scotland, the most tender leaves of dandelion and cress in a salad, and finally a custard with raisins and walnuts. A light Rhenish wine had tasted good with the meal, and Bothwell poured himself another goblet of it, although he swirled it around and looked at it in a melancholy fashion before taking a drink. Finally he rose and put his napkin down.

"Gather your clothing and what jewels you have left. We must leave Edinburgh," he suddenly said. "They mean to surprise us here. Oh, they will answer the summons to come, but not in the manner you called them. They are on the march now; I can feel it."

"Then let us retreat to Edinburgh Castle. Balfour is holding it secure for us."

"No. Let us go to the Borders, gather our army, and then return. There is no sense in being bottled up in Edinburgh Castle with no army; they would simply have us trapped. We will go first to Borthwick Castle, and then on to the Hermitage."

On June sixth, the Queen and Bothwell left Edinburgh, but in an orderly, almost leisurely manner. Twelve trunks of Mary's goods were transported,

513

including a silver basin and kettle, and before vacating Holyrood they summoned Maitland and told him to follow. He demurred; he said he would join them later.

"He'll join us in Hell," said Bothwell, as they rode away. "That's another one gone." He drew himself up straighter.

Borthwick was only twelve miles south of Edinburgh, a huge, golden stone fortress with twin towers, rearing up out of a grassy mound. Crichton Castle, where Jean now lived, was visible from the tops of the towers. Bothwell took Mary up the narrow winding stairs, where they had to duck their heads to ascend, up to the flat, fortified roof, and they stood on it together in the warm June twilight. All around them the shadows lay long and undulating on the land. To the north and west the fields were green, and the setting sun made the furrows of the fields look like teeth in a comb. To the east and south the moors stretched out, dun and grey and moss green: the Fala Moor and the Moorfoot hills, wrinkled and weathered.

"It's worth fighting for," said Bothwell. "Do whatever you must to keep it. If you are forced to, you must choose it over me."

"It will not come to that." The setting sun outlined his face, his beloved profile. Behind him glowed the fields and land. There could be no choosing.

"It well could." He turned and took her hands in his. "I will fight to the best of my ability, but there are always surprises. The gods like to surprise us." Seeing the look on her face, he said, "Since I studied Roman military books, when I think of campaigns, I become a pagan. I think of Jupiter, Apollo, Mars—and all the tricks they like to play on mortals, never more so than on the battlefield."

"And who are you, then, in your imagination? Marc Antony, Caesar, Octavian?" She could see him amongst them, holding his own in bravery and strategy and strength.

"None of them. The mortals in the play change; only the gods are always the same characters. I am no one but myself."

Maitland gave the safety signal and the Lords of the Congregation streamed into Edinburgh: Morton, Home, Atholl, Glencairn, Lindsay, the young son of Ruthven. Lord Erskine left the baby Prince behind at Stirling and joined them. Even the notorious Kerr of Cessford, who had been kindly treated by Mary at the justice court, joined the insurgent Lords.

Maitland approached Balfour at Edinburgh Castle with an offer: join them and be forgiven any part in the murder of Darnley, which was too widely rumoured to be hidden much longer. He agreed. Together he and Maitland hammered out an agreement, setting forth the Lords' side of the story, and stating:

Sir James Balfour of Pittindrech, knight, clerk of our Sovereign's register, and keeper of the Castle of Edinburgh, tendering the Queen's Majesty's most dangerous state, and the peril that may come to the commonweal, has, upon the like zeal with us, faithfully promised, and by the tenour hereof promises, to aid and assist us, or any part of us that shall enterprise and put order to the premises of the Castle of Edinburgh, for furthering of our enterprises devised and to be devised. Providing always that he may be so required as his honour be safe at our first coming into the town of Edinburgh.

Therefore we make a covenant to support, maintain, and hold him harmless for all his former deeds, and to advance and prefer him to all honour and profit, and especially to maintain and continue him in the keeping of the Castle of Edinburgh.

The following day, June twelfth, the Lords put out their own proclamation, having it called from the Mercat Cross. They stated that they were determined to "enterprise the delivery of the Queen's most noble person from the captivity and restraint in which she has been now for a long time held by the murderer of her husband, who has usurped the government of her realm; to deliver her forth from captivity and prison, and to punish Bothwell both for the cruel murder of the late King Henry, and the ravishing and detention of the Queen."

Men flocked to the Lords' grisly standard—a banner showing the dead Darnley stretched out under a tree with little Prince James praying "Judge and avenge my cause, O Lord"—and by nightfall they had added a thousand to their side. Lord Home and Morton, with a force of cavalry, decided to make a night march to Borthwick and surprise Bothwell in the dark, cutting him off before he could reach the Borders. Under torchlight they streamed out of the city, twelve hundred strong.

Bothwell lay in the dark, not sleeping. Mary was by his side in the massive, worm-eaten wooden bed in the uppermost chamber in the tower. She lay quietly, and by her breathing he knew she slept. But he was unable to; although the sounds outside were the soothing ones of early summer—the whisking of tree branches, the hooting of owls, and, from far away, the sound of farmers carousing in a roadside tavern—the night seemed dangerous.

He heard the army when it was still far down the road, heard that unmistakable sound of marching men, and scrambled out of bed. Quickly he pulled on his breeches and peered out the window. Nothing was visible yet. He returned to the bed and woke Mary.

"They are coming," he said quietly. She was instantly awake.

"Where?"

"I hear them down the road. It sounds like a large company."

She, too, jumped out of bed and went to the window. She could see the winking of their torches, now visible. There were a great many of them.

"Get dressed," said Bothwell. "And I will tell you what we must do. They want to trap me here. They will surround the tower. Hold them off. I will escape from the postern gate."

His voice was crisp and calm. Although her head was clear, jolted awake by fright, she had trouble grasping what he was saying.

"Do not let them know I have gone. I will go to Black Castle; it is only two miles away, at Cakermuir. But it is hidden in the moor and small, and they will likely not know where to find it. I will wait for you there. When they leave, you can join me."

The torches were coming closer. "What if they do not leave? What if they capture me?"

"They won't. They cannot storm this castle. Lord Borthwick will hold it. It is impregnable except against cannon, and they do not have cannon."

"How do you know?"

"They are moving too fast." Quickly he threw on his mantle. "I must be gone. Do not let them know I have escaped until twenty-four hours have passed. Then tell them, or you will never be able to leave the castle yourself." He grabbed her and pressed her against him for a moment. Then, letting her go, he made for the stairs.

She heard his footsteps on the stone, growing ever fainter, and then saw a figure galloping away from the south gate, toward the moors. Darkness swallowed him up.

God keep you, she prayed. But already there were noises in the courtyard; she heard voices rising as the castle guards argued and then gave way. She climbed the stairs to the top of the tower and looked down at the sea of men in dark cloaks surrounding the tower, like oily water.

"There she is!" one of them screamed, and a shout rose. "Come down! Surrender that butcher you call your husband; surrender him to justice!"

"The justice of the people!" yelled someone.

"Who leads you?" called Mary. "Who is it who dares to besiege and molest his Queen?" Surely no one would dare admit to it. This was just a mob.

"I am the one," said Lord Home. "I speak for all the Lords of the Congregation. We are not ashamed. It is you who should be ashamed! You have been made a plaything of that vile and perverted Lord Bothwell, who aims to take the throne entirely. Surrender him! Surrender him to justice!"

Lord Home! She had ridden with him, eaten with him!

"And I, the Earl of Morton," said a familiar voice. "I am constrained to take up arms in defence of my country. All who love Scotland must do so! We cannot sit by and watch that foul fiend, that murderer, that warlock, rape everything around him!"

"King-killer!" someone screamed.

"Filthy abominator of persons!"

"Sodomite!"

"Nay, it is not so!" called Mary. "The Earl of Bothwell, alone of all the nobles in the land, has never been disloyal to the crown, nor taken bribes, nor entered into a murder bond. He is innocent! It is you who have done all the things you accuse him of!"

"None of us has kidnapped, nor raped, nor murdered the King!"

"He was declared innocent of all those crimes! You yourselves declared him innocent of the murder of the King, and in marrying him, I forgave him for any crime against my person. But if Bothwell did not murder the King, who did? It is you who have the King's blood on your hands!" she cried.

"Prove it!" yelled Morton. "You cannot! And if you do not abandon Bothwell, you will be admitting that you are guilty along with him. As Knox says!"

"Knox!" she shouted. "That ruthless inciter to disorder and murder! That wicked slanderer, who knows so well how to destroy by false accusation, but has no idea of how to build anything. Yes, he has broken the Ninth Commandment: thou shalt not bear false witness. And broken it again and again, for he revels in rabble-rousing; what matter if his words are lies? By the time anyone knows that, by the time anyone can investigate, he has destroyed another innocent victim."

She could hear the sound of horses' hooves; these men were well equipped.

"Jezebel!" some yelled.

"Whore!"

"Burn the whore!"

She fled from the rooftop and retreated to her room. All through the night she heard their yells and curses, and the useless thud of their guns against the thick stone walls of the castle. But never the fateful sound of cannon. Bothwell was right; they had no cannon. They could not take the castle.

They remained there all day, and by the light she could make out many familiar faces, and for the first time, the force of what was happening struck her. These were people she had known since childhood, people whose loyalty she had always taken for granted, men like the kindly stablemaster at Stirling, the merchant in the High Street who supplied the palace with sugar, even the barrelmaker who had a commission to make the beer barrels for Holyrood. Ordinary people had turned against her. This was different from the fickle Lords, grasping, greedy and calculating from birth.

"Let the coward appear!" they were yelling. Then, at last, someone figured out the obvious.

"He must not be here! He is never shy to show himself! He must have got away!"

Infuriated, they began throwing stones at the castle and firing. But they showed no signs of leaving. They wanted to capture a prey; they would not be cheated.

She would have to escape, herself. Their numbers had thinned, and they were concentrated now entirely in the front; the back of the tower stood unguarded, although the main entrance, opening into the courtyard, was closely watched.

Slowly she went over to Bothwell's trunk and opened it. She pulled out his dark brown leather breeches and his hose; farther down were his shirts and coats. She took off her gown and stockings and, leaving on only her underclothing, she pulled on a pair of his hose. They were rough and scratchy. Then, with trembling fingers, she drew on a wide linen shirt, buttoning it down the front. The leather breeches went on easily and were the most comfortable item of clothing. Boots. She would need boots. Her own would do, which was good, because their feet were not the same size. She twisted her hair and put it up in a knot on top of her head, then took one of Bothwell's hats from the wall peg where it hung, and pulled it down low. Did she look like a man? There was no mirror in the room for her to check. In any case, she looked less like a woman than she had ten minutes earlier.

She would have to escape from the window. There was no way out by the stairs. She looked out and was dismayed to see that the chamber was at least fifty feet off the ground. Perhaps there was another room, nearer the ground, that could serve. Silently she tiptoed down the stairs, and at the first landing she came to the banquet hall. Its empty spaces seemed to breathe, and she darted her eyes round, searching all the dark corners. But there was no movement.

She stole over to the window. This one was only about thirty feet, still too much of a drop. She returned to her room and dragged the bedsheets off the old bed. Again in the banqueting hall, she tied one end to a massive chair by the window, praying it would not topple over when it was jerked. Then she flung the other end out the window, noticing with satisfaction that it dangled about twenty feet from the ground. Gritting her teeth, she clasped the rope of sheet and began to lower herself bit by bit, steadying herself by her arm muscles so that she would not lose control. A foot at a time she went downward, her legs wrapped around the sheet and her arms aching. At last she reached the end and then she slid as far down as possible and hung, dangling, for a moment before she let go and fell the remaining twelve feet. She hit the ground hard and rolled over, tucking her legs under her. Trembling, she stood up. She was uninjured.

She could hear the noises just around the tower. She scrambled across the back lawn and then climbed the low wall at the rear. Beyond that was the grassy mound, and beyond that, the moor. But it was pitch dark.

She stood still and listened, hearing a horse breathing somewhere nearby. She took a step in what she perceived was the correct direction, stopped and listened again. Little by little she found her way to a small, sturdy horse, bridled and wearing a man's saddle.

Dear God, she thought, how did he come to be here? Did You put him here? For I know that even if Bothwell thought of it, he could not have placed him here. Unless thoughts have power to create.

She leapt into the saddle; it was not far to leap, as the horse was so small. She had no idea of where to ride, but headed for where she perceived the moor to be. The horse was sure-footed and seemed to know his way.

Soon the sounds of the clamouring men faded away, blocked by the rising hills. There were other sounds: small creatures that lived on the moor, the calls of night birds, the soft padding of the horse's hooves as it stepped on the moss, the scratch of thorny bushes they skirted. Soon her eyes became accustomed to the dark that was not entirely dark, because the ground was pulsating with the soft glow from thousands of glowworms. They provided an eerie fairy light, and made her feel she was dreaming all this.

She climbed hills and went down into small glens, passed swamps where strange, foul odours hung in the air, but there was no sign of any castle. As the dawn came up, she saw that she was utterly lost in a wild district of moor and moss and thorny brakes. Her head was swimming, and she at last stopped the horse—a thin nag, she could now see—and sat down by the edge of a bog. The frogs were calling, and crows sat on the branches of the twisted trees and cocked their heads at her as if they found her a curious sight. She sank her head down on her lifted knees and wondered what to do next.

She sat for half an hour, half napping, when suddenly she heard sounds. She leapt to her feet and climbed into the saddle. The horse perked up his ears. She wished she had a pistol with her, or even a dagger. If it was the Lords, she would have no defence. Why had she not remembered to take a weapon?

Over the rise rode Bothwell, accompanied by some twenty men. He galloped over to her, careless of the uneven terrain.

"Thank God!" he cried. "When you did not come—"

"You neglected to tell me where Black Castle was," she said. "I had no idea in what direction it lay. When you said it was at Cakermuir, I assumed it must be on the moor somewhere, but—"

"You make a fine soldier boy," he said admiringly. "And I see you have ridden using a man's saddle."

"What was I supposed to do? Return to the stables and request another saddle? It was a miracle there was any horse there, let alone with a saddle."

"Where was he?"

"Near the postern gate."

"Lord Borthwick may have left him there for you." He jerked the reins of his horse. "How bad is it?"

"They are still surrounding the castle. I sent two messengers with a summons to Huntly, but I do not know if they got through."

"Probably not. There were over a thousand of them. Come, let us proceed on to Dunbar. We will go the long southern way over the Fala Moor. From there we will summon Huntly and the Hamiltons." Only then did he smile. "My knight," he said. "I think you have well earned your spurs. How did you get out?"

"I knotted a bedsheet and let myself down out of the banquet hall window."

He laughed. "There is no prison that can hold us, so it seems. No prison yet constructed. Heart of my heart, bone of my bone, spirit of my spirit, we cannot be held."

The way to Dunbar, over the moors, seemed to take an eternity. As Mary rode along behind him, she felt as if this were all familiar, had been rehearsed; the sight of Bothwell bobbing along ahead, the sucking noise of the wind as it travelled across the flattened heather and low, thorny bushes, the smell of the wet bogs and mires all around.

Of course, she thought. I have done this before. It was on just such a ride that I first began to love him. Or began to know that I loved him. Only eight months ago.

She could not help smiling a tired, crooked smile. It had been a very full eight months; no man could ever have lived a fuller eight months. But now she was tired. She wished to live quietly and even have a chance to become bored.

But not yet. First there were the rebels to be put down. But she would prevail, as she had all the other times.

This is the fourth rebellion against me, after Huntly's initial one, she thought. There was Lord James's Chaseabout Raid, and the Riccio murder, and the Darnley murder. If I made a chart, which Lords would show up as being a party to all four? The Earl of Morton, that red-haired bear of covetousness and piety; the Earl of Argyll, who is little credit to any side, as he does so little; Kirkcaldy of Grange, who kissed my hand when I landed but is a spy for the English. Those three for certain. Maitland and Lord James are too clever, they've never been caught outright in any except the Chaseabout Rebellion. Lord James especially leaves others to do his secret and foul business.

Why did they all hate me so much and wish to plague my rule? Have I ever done anything to earn their hatred? I gave the Protestants control and never attempted in any way to thwart them. I gave these lords estates and honours. I kept Scotland out of war, and refused to aid the Pope in his attempt to win Scotland back by putting heretics to death. I do not know what else I could have done, or what else could be required of me. I used my own dower money to pay for many of the crown's expenses, rather than ask the people for taxes.

Is it all due to John Knox? Did he set his goal to drive me from the throne? But even he cannot do that. He must obey his Scripture, which is that an anointed ruler cannot be harmed.

She sighed and urged her horse along. She was so tired that she felt she might topple over against the horse's neck at any moment. The sun was still high overhead. They had a long way to go, and once there, there were plans to be made and, most likely, battles to be fought. Their men would be gathering at Melrose, and supposedly the Hamiltons and the Gordons would be bringing reinforcements. They would be able to fashion together a formidable royal army of at least five thousand or perhaps even ten thousand.

The day would be theirs. But it would be a long day.

When at length they reached Dunbar, and saw the mighty walls of the castle rearing up, it felt like home to her. Dunbar, where Bothwell always took her at moments of peril, and where they always emerged victorious.

LVI

hey stumbled into the courtyard, and then Bothwell seemed to revive. He dismounted and posted his guards around the entrances and approaches, and seemed in no particular hurry to eat or make his way to his quarters. Mary stayed in the saddle, waiting for him to finish his instructions, aching to get down, eat, collapse. His clothes were uncomfortable on her now, tight in all the wrong places and baggy where she wished they were tight. At length Bothwell indicated that they should go into the castle. This time they went into the newer wing, which had been built within living memory and boasted large windows, window seats, wooden panelling, and ceiling decorations.

"As my wife I welcome you to the lord's quarters," he said. "As a captive, you were housed accordingly." He ushered her into a comfortable chamber with a marble fireplace, and winked at her. "Although I do not know if a boy in such soiled clothing should be allowed in here."

"A soiled boy!" She looked down at her torn, mud-smeared legs.

He reached out and unpinned her hair. "When you look like a boy, then I treat you as one."

"Your clothes have served me well," she said. "But now I wish I could discard them."

"Then do."

"I have no others!" She laughed. "I left everything behind at Borthwick." Suddenly she had an ominous thought. She had fled and left everything behind: her papers, her jewels, her personal belongings. They were now all in the hands of the rebels. "Our things! They have our things!"

"Not for long," he said. "And it will take them a while to find them. But . . ." His face changed as realization crept over him. "My papers! My personal papers! My deeds and my property titles, and my—my—" His voice was rising in panic. "I still have your letters!" he blurted out.

"What letters?"

"The ones you wrote from Glasgow, and the poems—"

She clapped her hands over her mouth. "I instructed you to burn them! In the selfsame letters I told you! How could you? How could you have kept them?" Her stomach was churning, as she tried to remember exactly what she had said in them. There was the description of Darnley when he was sick, that whole threatening trip to Glasgow, the ominous Balfour, the fear of her intimacy with Bothwell being discovered, the necessity of bringing Darnley back to Edinburgh. She felt nauseated.

"I know not," he admitted. "I think, because I wished to have something of you to remember if ever we parted, to convince myself that it had really happened. I was sure that you would leave me, that you were just toying with me. I never thought you loved me as I now know you do."

"The moment we return to Edinburgh, they must be destroyed! Do you hear? O God! If they are found—where do you have them?"

"In that silver box you gave me. The one from France. It is in my quarters in Edinburgh Castle."

She groaned. Not even locked up! And in a container that advertised the presence of something precious inside! O God, what had she done? Had she hanged herself with her own pen? And him—to have kept them! This man who was so intelligent, who excelled in outthinking his opponents, who was a master of strategy—to have made the blunder of a village oaf! "O God," she kept repeating. She could only pray they would not be found. God, be merciful! Spare us!

"We must defeat them swiftly," said Bothwell, in his old confident voice. "They must be run out of Edinburgh. We must strike as soon as possible."

She jumped up and paced the chamber. Her hunger and fatigue were gone, replaced by nervous shaking.

When a substantial supper was brought in to them and set down on the table, Bothwell had to order her to sit down and eat. "You are exhausted and half-starved," he said. "You must keep your strength up for the coming battle." Like a stern father, he lifted the lid over the bowl of jugged hare, uncovered the dish of turnips, and broke pieces of bread for her.

After she had eaten, at least the lightheadedness left her, although her limbs felt heavy. "What do we do?" she asked.

"Sleep," he said, draining his goblet. "Don't you think we've earned it?"

"I meant tomorrow."

"I will tell you tomorrow," he said. "When you are better able to listen and understand. Now we must sleep." He picked up a candle in the now-dark chamber and gestured to her to follow him into the adjoining one.

A beautifully carved bed awaited them, with fresh linens and covers of the finest virgin wool. On a little inlaid table, a silver vase of roses gave off a deep scent. The windows were open, and they could hear the roar of the sea outside.

"Oh," she said, leaning against the bed. Bothwell pulled off her boots and then, as if he were undressing a child, he lifted the little coat over her head and unbuttoned his own shirt, removing it from her. He pulled off the breeches and the hose.

"What will I sleep in?" she asked, her voice slurred with tiredness.

"Nothing," he said. "No one will see you but me. And in the morning I will borrow some woman's clothes for you." He picked her up and settled her in the bed, then climbed in himself, drawing the covers over them.

She put her head on his shoulder, feeling as if she had been drugged. Bothwell was here. She need have no fear. No fear, no fear . . . He stood between her and all misfortune.

Morning found them wide awake long before the sun was up. Gone was Bothwell's calmness of the day before; he seemed in an agitated hurry to get dressed and begin receiving information about their resources. He quickly threw open the windows to let in the breeze and left her alone while he went into the outer chambers to confer with his people. She lay in bed, naked, feeling a prisoner inside the covers. During the time he was gone, she had time to think about the circumstances. The Lords—where were they now? Were they still surrounding Borthwick? Exactly who had joined them? And, more crucial, who could be counted on to support the royal side? Was there *anyone* left in Scotland whose loyalty to the crown was unalloyed? And again, the tearing thought: Why has it come to this? And its forbidden brother: What if we lose? What will become of us?

I must think of this. To whom would I turn for help to be restored to the throne? For I would not meekly submit and go quietly into exile, retiring to a convent like—who was it? A deposed king of some sort, a discarded queen. Was it Joan of Valois? I cannot think . . . I would go to France. Yes, France. They would help restore me. They would send a force, an army. But then they would have to fight England—would they be willing to risk that? My family, the Guises, do not have the power they once did in the land, and Catherine de Médicis is cautious and self-seeking. The little King Charles IX, for all that he's seventeen now, is completely ruled by his mother. He would have no say-so at all.

Philip of Spain? He is even more calculating and slow-moving than Catherine de Médicis, and fancies himself the champion of the Church; now that the Pope has condemned me, he would never lift a finger or a sword or a harquebus to restore me. No, not Spain.

The Scandinavian countries . . . Bothwell has connections there, he has performed naval services for Sweden. But they are Protestants and would never restore a Catholic monarch to a throne. Even a disgraced one!

She started to laugh, nervously. The Catholics would take the Pope's condemnation seriously and for that reason refuse to restore her, while the Protestants would consider it a family squabble and still regard her as a Catholic and therefore an enemy.

There might be no help at all outside of Scotland. This might be final.

England? There was always England, Scotland's traditional enemy, but now things had changed. James was Elizabeth's godson, and so far—although she might not formally admit it—heir to her throne. And Elizabeth was her own close kinswoman and one who took royal prerogatives seriously. She, who feared uprisings and rebels, could hardly countenance a group of traitorous Lords taking control in Scotland. And she had given Mary the ring, which meant—

"I have clothes," said Bothwell, stepping into the room, his arms full of material that was black and red. "I borrowed these from a tradesman's wife." He held them up. "They will doubtless be a little short, for there are few ladies in the land as tall as you."

"I do not care," she said. "I am just grateful to stop being a boy for today." Quickly she got out of bed and retreated behind a silk-embroidered screen by an alcove to dress. While she did so, she could hear Bothwell talking to himself and pacing.

The petticoat and skirt, in black and red, came only just below her knees. There was a bodice, a white ruff for her neck, and some ribbons to tie up the sleeves. Cautiously she stepped out from behind the screen. The skirt, hitting against her knees, felt strange.

Bothwell burst into laughter. "You look like a milkmaid."

"Wearing a skirt this short makes me feel halfway naked," she said. "Will anyone follow a Queen who looks like this?"

Bothwell gestured to the breakfast tray of ale, cheese, strawberries, and bread. He was eating standing up. "On horseback you will look regal enough." He paused between bites. "I have sent French Paris south to Melrose to bring back my troopers, however many have gathered by now."

She sat down and poured herself some ale, then ate three of the little wild strawberries. "It is only June fourteenth, and barely has morning broken," she said. "They were not required to be there until tomorrow."

"We can possibly wait. It depends on how many others we can count on to join us, and who has joined the Lords. Of course, the best thing we could hope for is that our forces come together before theirs."

Just then Geordie Dalgleish, Bothwell's personal servant and tailor, entered the room. "You wish to speak to me?" he asked. He was an ungraceful, large-featured fellow. But he spoke with a delicate voice, all at odds with his appearance.

"Yes. I need to know what has become of Huntly and the force of Hamiltons. They were supposedly coming from the north and west with their army. But they do not arrive. At the same time, Atholl and Glencairn were on the march with their Highlanders for the Lords, coming in the same direction. Have they met on their way? Why this delay?"

"Aye. I will go to Edinburgh," he said.

"When you go, tell Balfour I command him to fire on the rebels if they try to take refuge in Edinburgh," said Mary suddenly. "We must retain Edinburgh for ourselves, and Balfour must carry out his duty as captain of the castle."

After he was gone, Mary said, "It will be all right."

He shot her a look of gratitude. "You have a stout and kingly courage," he said. "Let it not fail in the hours before us." He motioned to the tray of food. "Eat. We may not get another meal before battle."

She felt alarm. "So soon? It might be so soon?"

"That depends on the reports we receive."

French Paris returned with a force of about a thousand Borderers, far below the number Bothwell had expected. Geordie Dalgleish came soon after with a confusing report: Huntly and the Hamiltons had indeed reached Edinburgh, but they had stopped there and were arguing with each other about which route to take to Dunbar. Another servant, William Powrie, reported that on the road between Dunbar and Edinburgh, Lord Seton and Lord Borthwick were preparing to join them. While Bothwell was going over these reports, there was a knock. Edmund Hay, Bothwell's attorney in Edinburgh, stood waiting just outside the door.

"Why, what is it?" asked Bothwell. "Surely you do not have papers for me to sign about property and suchlike? You lawyers are a devoted lot— always business as usual. Even funerals provide much of it."

Hay, who was sweating profusely, began to fan himself. "Forgive me. It is hot, unseasonably hot."

Indeed it was, Mary suddenly noticed. Until then, she had not even been aware of the hot puffs of air coming in the windows.

"Yes, what is it? You have worked up a sweat in coming," said Bothwell.

"I bring an important, private message from Balfour in Edinburgh Castle. It is this: The rebels will not stand their ground in Edinburgh, where they are now starting to mass, if they know the Castle will open fire on them. But they are pouring in so rapidly, and soon their numbers will be so great, that if the royal army lingers longer at Dunbar, Lord Balfour will be forced to come to terms with them. Therefore he begs you to delay no longer, but to strike out immediately and attack them forthwith, before they grow stronger."

"Is this even so? Have the Highlanders arrived yet for the Lords?"

"No, Your Grace."

"Ah!" He turned to Mary. "Then indeed we must strike. The fates have delivered them into our hands!"

Balfour sat on the ramparts of Edinburgh Castle, enjoying the wind. Usually it was uncomfortable to stand there, as the wind was always cool, as if it had been chilled against ice and then released. But today it felt refreshing; the heat was oppressive down in the city. Beside him, Morton sat sweating in his heavy black clothes, the ones he always wore because he imagined they gave his bulk dignity and made him look sombre and pious.

"Do you think it will work?" Morton was saying. "Do you think Hay will convince them?"

"I imagine so. Bothwell will trust his own lawyer. After all—why would he lie?"

Both men burst into laughter.

"They will be lured away from Dunbar and brought back here. We, our forces, will stand between them and any from the west and north who might wish, belatedly, to join them. Before the battle, Atholl and Glencairn will have arrived with their Highlanders for us. In the meantime, let us call all good citizens to be ready to march out at three hours' notice to give battle," said Morton.

"Let me word it," said Balfour. "I do enjoy composing things."

A notice calling "all who would not be esteemed parties to the aforesaid crimes and treasons to join the Lords in taking up arms" was read out at Mercat Cross. It stated that "all who will not take part in this righteous and loyal enterprise must quit Edinburgh within four hours."

❦

By noon, the royal forces left Dunbar and began marching westward. In addition to the Borderers, they had two hundred harquebusiers and sixty cavalrymen. Bothwell had ordered the three brass field guns from Dunbar to be taken with them. Along the way, attracted by the fluttering red and yellow royal standard, six hundred more horsemen joined, along with villagers and peasants armed only with farm implements. By the time they reached Haddington, they had a following of almost two thousand. Just beyond Haddington, at Gladsmuir, Mary halted and had a proclamation read.

"A number of conspirators, under pretext of preserving the Prince, although he is in their keeping, have shown their latent malice. With intent to dethrone the Queen, that they might rule all things at their pleasure, they have taken up arms against their anointed ruler. Therefore very necessity compels the Queen to likewise take up arms, and place her hopes in the help of all faithful subjects, who will be rewarded with the lands and possessions of the rebels according to the merit of each man."

The crowds grew larger and the ranks of the royal army swelled, but not with professional fighters. As they approached Edinburgh, the sun was setting and the mob, hungry and dusty, needed to stop.

Bothwell looked at their ranks. "I am satisfied," he said. "We can halt here. Seton House is not far away. Let us overnight there. Then, before it even grows light, we will march on to Edinburgh and overwhelm them by surprise."

❦

Kirkcaldy of Grange, who fancied himself a handsome knight, in spite of his balding head and lined face, was enjoying drawing plans for the coming battle. Should his cavalry flank and then charge into the centre of the royal forces, killing and trampling and causing a stampede? Or should he aim directly for Bothwell, ignoring the lesser men, as warriors of old did? Which would demoralize the Queen more? Humming, he drew another plan. If he divided the cavalry . . .

Someone drew aside the curtain. Annoyed, Grange looked up, already scowling. It was a nephew of one of the Setons.

"Yes?" he barked. He hid the wooden soldiers he had been maneuvering and covered up the plans.

"They are at Seton House. Lord Seton has joined them, giving them forces of almost three thousand. The body of the army is camped around Seton. They plan to move out early tomorrow morning, by five if possible, to take Edinburgh by surprise," he said.

"How do I know this is true?" Grange asked. "You could be lying to mislead us."

"I cannot prove it. But Ruthven will vouch for my loyalty to the Congregation. And Lindsay."

"Very well. I will send for them."

Grange did, and they identified the man as Peter Simmons, who had never trafficked with the royalists and had joined the Congregation years earlier, but who lived near Seton.

So Bothwell thought to surprise them. Well, he would be the one to be surprised. Grange gave the orders for the army of the Lords to march from Edinburgh at two in the morning and meet the enemy while it was still dark and before they could even group themselves in the confusion.

⟨℈⟩

In the room set aside for Mary, since she was a frequent visitor to Seton House over the past six years, Bothwell and Mary took their rest. It had been a relief to join forces with Lord Seton, and to see Mary Seton once more. She had not been with Mary in weeks. The other Marys had long since scattered, but Mary Seton was still a faithful attendant.

She had gasped when she first saw Mary. "Oh, Your Majesty, you are so changed!" she blurted out.

"Much has happened to change me," Mary answered. Ordinarily she would have probed to know exactly what Seton had meant, but now she was beyond caring. She was hot, dirty, and hungry. They had not eaten since that morning, and Bothwell was concerned because he had no provisions for his troops.

"That is why we must fight tomorrow. I cannot sustain them in the field, and a hungry army cannot fight," he said wearily. He flopped into bed, barely able to move.

Mary climbed in next to him. He was lying on his side, with his back turned to her. She attempted to lay her head on his shoulder and rub his neck, which was gritty with road dirt. He sighed, with a sigh that had a note of despair in it.

527

"Sleep," she said, kissing his cheek gently. "This time tomorrow night, it will all be decided."

He did not respond. Was he asleep? She tried to see his face. His eyes were closed.

"It will all be over, and our life can truly begin," she said.

Still no response.

She turned over on her back and lay looking up at the ceiling that she had seen so many times before. Seton House had always been a refuge for her, a place where she could act as young as she truly was, where no hateful spy lurked to twist every natural action of hers into something sinister and menacing. Here she had played golf and archery and walked along the sea wall, had sung and talked to Mary Seton and her brother, had been convalescent and stunned after the murder of Darnley. The Setons had let her sit for hours in a chair staring out to sea and not intruded on her private thoughts, but always let her know they would not be betrayed if she chose to share them.

I have had good friends here in Scotland, she thought. But they have been like an alternating pattern making up the fabric of life: friend, traitor, friend, traitor . . . it does not make a material one wraps around oneself for comfort. The traitors and their daggers prick the skin.

Bothwell gave a strange cry and turned over violently. He was muttering to himself. A flood of feeling beyond gratitude or even love washed over her. He was her life, a gift by which all others could be measured.

He was thrashing around, and swung his arm down on the covers.

"Hush," she said, taking him in her arms. "You are troubled with bad dreams." She kissed his forehead, which was sweaty. He groaned and shook himself partially awake.

"Banish these night ghosts," she said. "You are not a man to be affrighted by spirits."

"*Nei, vi kom i fjor,*" he said in a clear voice.

"What is this? What language is this?" she said, shaking him.

"*Jeg venter penger fra—*" he muttered, but he opened his eyes. "I dreamed of Norway—or possibly it was Denmark, I know not. I was a pirate, only I was becalmed, my vessel was in a harbour and I could not get free, could not sail away."

"How do you know it was Norway, or Denmark?"

"The way the houses looked, on a steep mountain. And the smell, a smell of the sea that is peculiar to that coast." He shuddered.

"It is good that you could be so far away in your mind. And as for the sea—it is the smell that is coming in this window."

"Yes." His voice was trailing off again, and he drifted away in sleep.

In the intense darkness later on, when the true dividing line between day and night was drawn, he stirred and took her in his arms. The wind had fallen, and even the sea seemed to be holding its breath between tides. She woke up to feel him holding her, feel his private need of her before the hour of reckoning. Never had his touch felt more immediate, more pressing. Gladly she turned to him in the secrecy of the darkness, exulting in his hands and body and soul.

Dawn came up. It stole into the room, lighting it gradually and relentlessly. Bothwell groaned and sat up. "It is late." He swung his feet over the side of the bed and shook his head groggily. "Pray it is not too late!"

She got out of bed, and strained her eyes to see the little watch she had left on the table. In the smudgy light it was hard to read. "Nay," she said. "It is but four o'clock."

"Late, late," he was muttering. He pulled on his clothes and kept on shaking his head to clear it.

By five, they were on the march toward Edinburgh, the thirty-five hundred men tramping along the path, with the few mounted riders and the field artillery bumping on their wheeled carriers alongside. With Mary rode Mary Seton, who had insisted on accompanying her. Bothwell rode with his troops, who seemed tired even after the night's rest. They had eaten little and had no prospects of finding food en route.

Bothwell planned to march directly into Edinburgh and fight the rebels there, with Balfour firing on them from above to drive them out. The castle, in royal hands, was the bulwark that assured the royal success, as it had after the Riccio murder.

But as they approached the city, he suddenly saw, to his horror, that the rebels had taken command of a hill outside the walls and were already waiting for them there. They were positioned on the slope, so that any soldier charging uphill would be a ready target.

"Betrayed!" he said. "Someone has betrayed our plans to them, so they anticipated our early march." He reined his horse and spurred over to Mary. "They knew our plans," he said. "Someone told them our movements, and now they have dug in and are blocking our way."

She felt a stab of surprise, followed by anger and disgust. "Is there no one we can trust?" Who could it have been? There were no other commanders in their ranks, only Bothwell. It must have been a regular soldier, one of the common people who had hitherto always been loyal.

"Evidently not," he said. "Now we must take up position on the opposite hill." He pointed to the rising ground on the other side of the little stream that ran between the two hills. "Do you know what this ground is? The Lords have chosen it well, since they are so fond of allegories and omens."

"It is . . . it is Musselburgh. Pinkie Clough," she said slowly.

"The site of the battle that made it necessary to send you to France as a child," he said. "I remember it well. I was twelve at the time, and itching to see a real battle. I looked on, but I did no fighting. Oh, had things gone differently, who can say where we would be at this very instant? Cecil was there, on the English side, and he narrowly missed being hit by a cannonball. If he had been killed, rather than the man next to him, history would be different. Old man Huntly was captured and transported back to England—'twas most likely there that he learned to be a traitor after he took the English gold. The English mowed us down—ten thousand fell on this very hillside."

The early sunshine was slanting across the dewy green meadows, creating an iridescent sheen. The rebels were sitting calmly, eating their breakfast.

"Black Saturday," she said.

"Aye. And because we could not withstand the English, we had to sell ourselves to France. And you were part of the bargain." He waved his arm across the field. "And had you not gone to France—"

"This is pointless. Had anyone not done anything he has done, his life would be different," she said. "Had you not come to Exchequer House, we would not be standing here today, called to fight. So let us fight, because we did come to the Exchequer House, though not by design." She lifted her chin. "Whether by purpose or design, I accept all that I have done, and all I will ever do."

A slow grin spread over his face, and for the first time that morning his features relaxed. "Then let us fight, and fate decide the rest." He saluted her, and fell back to his men.

Mary and Mary Seton took up their position at the foot of the far hill, behind the front lines. Bothwell positioned his troops all the way up to the summit of the hill, with his brass field guns studded halfway up to fire on anyone rushing the hill. The two hundred harquebusiers were stationed near the foot of the hill, the six hundred horsemen scattered throughout the ranks, the thousand Borderers guarding the flanks and front lines, and the other two thousand poorly armed, untrained villagers covering the rest of the ground.

A royal standard was planted near where Mary watched, and its red and yellow lion flapped in the parching wind blowing toward the water only a short distance away. The rest of the troops fought under the cross of St. Andrew.

Bothwell rode back to her, a changed man. He was crisp and almost quivering with energy. He pointed over to the rebels, staring at them across the two hundred yards' distance. "Now here's the sum of it," he said, sounding almost gloating. "Our numbers are evenly matched—although they have more trained cavalry and better weapons. But there are too many leaders. They will never get their orders straight."

She looked across at the groups of soldiers, each wearing livery of a different colour. But her heart grew heavy as she saw that the Highlanders had arrived, and were drawn up under the earls of Atholl and Glencairn. And there seemed to be thousands of horsemen.

"The earls of Morton and Home command the cavalry," he said. "The same ones that besieged us at Borthwick."

"Erskine," she said sadly, pointing to him. She recognized him even at this distance. "My son's keeper. So even he has turned against me."

"Not turned against you. He was always against you."

The hurt was very great. He had been a friend, someone she had known since childhood.

" 'Even my close friend, whom I trusted, he who shared my bread, has lifted up his heel against me,' " she said.

"In Scotland, that is just about everyone," he replied. "Look, over there are the young Lord Ruthven, son of the warlock, and Lord Lindsay. Riccio's murderers have reassembled. But aside from Kirkcaldy of Grange, there is not a notable or seasoned commander amongst them. Lord James would be the one to fear."

"Perhaps he *is* here."

"No. I have it on good authority that he is in Normandy, waiting for a signal. He will not cross until he deems it safe—which I intend to be never. I hope he likes eating French tripe à la Caen, for he may be eating it the rest of his life!"

"That banner!" she cried, seeing the ugly white satin banner with the figures of Darnley and the baby James and his prayer of "Judge and avenge my cause, O Lord."

"Pay it no mind. It is there merely to take your heart out of the battle. After it's over, I'll cut it up and use it for horse trappings."

"Where is Huntly?" she cried. "And Hamilton, with his men? Why do they not come?"

"Our best tactic would be to delay the fighting in hopes that they will come and reinforce us," he said. "But it is difficult to delay too long. The men may, in hunger and boredom, desert."

"Desert?"

"It is a possibility," Bothwell said. "After all, the bulk of our army are not trained soldiers but merely villagers who happened to fall in with us on the march. They may drift away, and we could hardly even call it desertion."

The difficulty of the position now became clear. Their armies were evenly matched in numbers, but the royal army lacked weapons, food, and dedication. It would melt in the hot sun, and might even collapse in the fighting. Inaction was deadly, but action was a gamble as well.

"I will work the men south, searching for ground advantage," Bothwell said, squinting over at the rebel troops.

Mary could see movement there. Evidently they were doing the same thing.

As Bothwell rode off, Mary found herself trembling. Her horse snorted and pawed the ground.

"Waiting is torture," she said to Mary Seton, who was sitting her horse so gravely she looked desolate. "Of all the things I am ever asked to do, I find waiting to be the most difficult."

"It goes against your nature," Seton said. "Oh, Your Majesty, why have you—"

"Stop. Do not say another word," Mary commanded. "It is a question you have no right to ask."

She turned back to watch the men on the other side. Some of them were splashing cold water on their faces, filling their helmets and drinking. The heat of the day was rising, but her men could not get close enough to approach the little stream that offered relief. Suddenly she was very shaken. The heat, itself unseasonable, seemed to be an enemy who had joined the rebels' ranks.

The sun rose higher, and no one moved. Both armies looked at each other, but as each commanded a hill, neither side wanted to be at a disadvantage in attempting to charge the other. From the direction of Edinburgh no column of dust rose to show Huntly or Hamilton on his way.

Bothwell rode up to her. He was sweating in his leather clothing and metal helmet. "No one stirs," he said disdainfully. "A battle in which no one moves!" The only motion was the rising columns of heat, now ascending in wavy lines toward the sky.

"They want us to charge," she said. "Do not give them what they want."

He looked at her in amusement. "I believe you might make a good general. Do you, then, command me to stay still?"

"No. I trust your judgement. As for myself, I would ride out into them now, shooting my pistols."

"Look!" said Bothwell. "Someone has broken ranks."

Coming down off the hill were some fifty horsemen surrounding a rider. The body of them splashed across the little stream and made their way determinedly toward the royal standard.

"Fire on them!" cried Mary. "Do not let them come within range of us!"

"Nay, they have a white flag. They wish to talk." Bothwell spurred his horse and gave orders for some of his mounted soldiers to meet them. About thirty rode out and formed an escort for the rider and his men.

"Philibert du Croc!" gasped Mary. It was the French ambassador, the little man who had refused to attend her marriage.

"Your Majesty," he said, saluting her. With her leave, he dismounted and came to her. He bowed and kissed her hand, bending his round, fluffy-haired head. Then he straightened and smiled.

"Alas! My good lady, what anguish it would cause your mother-in-law and the King of France to see you in such trouble!" he said. "And the Lords of the Congregation, who have sent me, assure you that they are your very humble and obedient servants."

Mary felt a jarring laugh escape her. "Is this how they show it, then?"

"Madam," he whispered, "they say that if you will withdraw yourself from the wretch who holds you captive, they will recognize you as their sovereign, and serve you on their knees as the humblest and most obedient of subjects."

"The wretch, they call him!" Now her laughter rang out. "It was they who signed a petition urging me to marry him, it was they who pronounced him innocent of any crime, and now they turn on him! But if they are willing to acknowledge their duty, and request *my* pardon, I will forgive them, and receive them with open arms."

Bothwell came up and shouldered his way over to them. He held out his hand to du Croc, who refused to take it.

"So!" said Bothwell, in a loud voice that carried up the hill. "What are the Lords about? What do they want?"

Du Croc cleared his throat and spoke loudly himself. "I have just come from speaking with them, and they assure me that they are very humble subjects and servants of the Queen." He edged up to Bothwell and added in a very low voice, "But they are your mortal foes."

Bothwell looked at him scornfully. "They gave me many assurances," he said, his voice ringing out. "What harm have I ever done them? I never wished to displease any, but have sought to gratify them all. They only speak as they do because they envy my favour." He turned around once, twice, revolving slowly, lifting up his head and speaking to the multitude, but also to Mary personally. "But Fortune is free to any who can win her— and there is not a man of them"—he pointed toward the hillside—"who but wishes himself in my place!" He took Mary's hand.

Du Croc was staring.

"For the love of God," said Bothwell suddenly, "and to put the Queen out of pain, and to spare the blood that will flow otherwise, let the Lords select a man and I will fight him in single combat. Let that decide the day. For my cause is so just I am sure God will decide in my favour!"

"His quarrel is mine!" said Mary fiercely.

A body of men began to advance from the Lords, making their way across the brook, spears at the ready.

"Look!" said Bothwell. "They approach! Now, if you wish to model yourself on the man who attempted to mediate between Scipio and Hannibal when the armies were about to engage, remember that he took up a post of observation, where he could see the bravest pastime he had ever beheld. If you wish to do the same, I can promise you a fight well fought!"

Du Croc shook his head. "I have no wish to gaze on carnage. But you are a great captain, speaking with such confidence when you cannot be sure of your men. I will convey your request for combat to the Lords." The old ambassador turned away and, mounting his horse, rode slowly back over to the other side.

When he did not return, Bothwell mounted his war-horse and rode down to the stream.

"I challenge someone of worthy rank to meet me in single combat!" he cried. He rode up and down, his horse prancing nervously. At length Mary could see someone come forward. It was James Murray of Purdovis.

Bothwell returned to camp and called for his armour. The metal was hot to the touch, and he was panting before he had even finished being strapped into it. Rivulets of sweat ran down his face.

"Murray of Purdovis is not worthy!" she said. "You must not fight him. It must be someone of your rank!"

"There is no one of my rank," he said. "The only other duke of Scotland is the feeble old Châtelherault, who was exiled to France after the Chase-about Raid. And, titles aside, there is no title of equal honour as that of the Queen's husband."

A second challenge was issued, and this time the Lords put forward the Earl of Morton as their champion.

"Yes! Run him through, like the traitor he is, and see if he even has any blood!" she said.

Bothwell took out a water bottle and drained it. He had now been wearing his armour for over an hour, and it was past four o'clock. Almost twelve hours of tension and readiness had passed, but nothing had happened. He had had nothing to eat all day. He did not feel weak, but in some ways this seemed like a dream.

In the other camp, they could see that it was not Morton putting on armour, but Lindsay. Morton had delegated his duty to a younger man. Now he was bending and belting on a sword. It must be the sacred "Bell-the-Cat" sword of yore, which Morton had endowed with almost magical qualities.

"Oh, let him come!" cried Bothwell, raising his arms to heaven in a plea for action. But from the other camp, no movement. Bothwell took Mary's hand and kissed it.

"I go," he said.

She wanted to hang on to it, to prevent him, but he was so grimly determined it would have been impossible. She watched him descend the hill and go to the appointed place, with thousands of men looking on. But Lindsay did not come out to meet him.

Suddenly she saw the Lords starting to advance, marching forward sternly and resolutely under their gleaming banner. The sun was low in the sky; the day was drawing to a close. Kirkcaldy of Grange, his armour glinting, now led a charge of cavalry in a flanking movement, coming up around the royal troops like an embrace.

The royal army broke and melted. The ranks had been thinning all afternoon, as the weary, hungry men had grown tired of waiting. Now they began to scramble away. Kirkcaldy yelled and put spurs to his horse, raising his sword.

Bothwell turned and galloped back to his men, giving quick orders. Then he rode to Mary.

"It is too late," he said. "We have lost the day. We waited too long, for reinforcements that never came." He smiled a wavering smile. "Thus it ends. For today."

"God! No! No!" She clutched at his smooth, metal-encased arm. She tried to look in his eyes and see what he really wanted her to do, but the shadow cast by the helmet covered them. "Is there nothing you can do?"

"I cannot win with the troops I now have. Let us retreat to Dunbar!"

"There will be a massacre!" cried Mary, as she saw the attacking army charging up the hill. "Stop!" she shouted, galloping into the midst of what remained of her army. "Stop!" The rebel soldiers halted in obedience. "You may tell your commanders that I will speak with them, and discuss terms," she said. Her voice was clear and strong.

Bothwell rode up beside her. "Do not trust them. Let us retreat. It is our only wise course of action. We can regroup there."

"No. They say they are loyal to me. They will not harm us."

"They will kill me, and they will do something bad to you as well."

"They have my son as a hostage," she said.

"That is a pity, but it is no reason to let yourself be taken captive as well!"

They looked over to where they could see a knot of men on the other side talking.

"Now! Let us escape now!" His voice was rising in frustration. "Can you not understand?"

"It is better to pretend for a while and win them back," she said.

"These men are not Darnley, and they are not in love with you. They hate you. This is not Riccio all over again. Mary, my love, if you are mistaken, you will lose everything. Can you take that chance? Can you trust their words, knowing that they have lied to you ever since you set foot in Scotland, and hated you in their hearts? Run now, while you still have the chance. Never voluntarily surrender your freedom. Never!"

A band of men was coming up the hill, led by Kirkcaldy of Grange. He had taken off his helmet, but was still wearing his other armour. Mary stood her ground and awaited him.

"Most gracious sovereign," he said, bowing. "I protest our loyalty to you, and you alone. We wish to serve you, but only if you are a free creature, no longer in thrall to the Earl of Bothwell."

She did not allow him to kiss her hand, but drew herself up and clasped her two hands together. "What assurances of safety can you give me for my husband the Earl?" she asked.

"None," he answered. "They are determined to kill him if they can get him."

"Ah," she said. "Those who ate with him, who toasted him, who approved his advancement . . . I must insist on his safety."

"Then, sir," he said, turning to Bothwell, "you had best leave now. I can guarantee a safe conduct only until you are off the field. But if you leave now, you can be well on your way to Dunbar before the Queen joins the Lords."

Bothwell snorted in disdain. "The Battle of Carberry Hill, where not a shot was fired," he said. "And this is your victory?"

"We have the Queen, sir. Now whether you will stay or not is your affair."

"Save yourself!" said Mary.

"Save *yourself*," said Bothwell. "If you go with them, you are lost."

"Liar!" said Kirkcaldy. "Do not seek to persuade the Queen against her own astute judgement."

"A word in private with my wife, if you allow," said Bothwell.

He drew Mary aside. "Mary, I cannot live with myself if, as your husband and protector, I abandon you to these traitors."

She looked at him. He was exhausted from the last week, from the escape from Borthwick, the hasty preparations at Dunbar, the attempt to raise an army, the long march to Carberry Hill. He had been roasted like an animal inside his armour while he waited in vain for someone to accept his challenge to combat, had waited, nerves on edge, all day to direct the battle that had never come. Her heart seemed to tear itself in looking at him, having gone through this ordeal for her.

"I cannot live with myself if harm should come to you," she finally answered. "They will kill you. I cannot let that happen. I must accept their terms and surrender myself into their hands, for they will not harm me. They will not harm their anointed ruler."

"Oh, you are so blind!" he cried.

"I love you," she said. "I cannot live without you. But we must part for now, till the danger is past. Then, when I have won them again to my side, I will send for you. Keep yourself safe until then, I beg you. I must know that you are waiting for me."

He put out his arms and embraced her. "If they seek to declare me an outlaw or condemn me for the Darnley murder, use this." He slipped a piece of paper into her sweating hand. "It is the bond they signed at Craigmillar. They are all guilty. This paper will convict them, if it comes to it. Guard it well. It proves their villainy."

She clung to him, clutching his wide shoulders and burying her face in his neck. "My life, my love, my lord, I cannot, I cannot—" She began kissing him frantically.

Slowly he disengaged her arms. "The armies stand ready to kill, unless we end this." He kissed her once, firmly and sadly. "Farewell, wife. Remember that you are my loyal wife, as you promised before God."

"What, do you doubt me?" She was hurt, and wanted to call him back, hold him again, kiss him until he was warm with her. "Bothwell—"

He was already a few yards away, nodding toward Kirkcaldy in a mocking manner. "Allow me to mount my horse," he was saying.

Mary rushed over to him and embraced him, surprising him and almost causing him to lose his balance. "My dear heart, I will never forsake you nor stop loving you, and will wait for you forever!"

He looked at her, as if he would imprint the image forever in his mind. "Nothing can part us," he finally said. "I love you, wife of my heart." Then he stepped away again, and quickly mounted his horse. With a quick farewell gesture, he gathered the reins and put spurs to his mount, and galloped away with three of his servants. Mary watched, refusing to move, until he disappeared from sight on the road to Dunbar.

LVII

ary stood watching the empty road for a moment, as if to seal him in safety. Then she turned back to Kirkcaldy, who was standing in mock deference with his helmet tucked under one arm.

"My Lord of Grange," she said, "I render myself to you upon the conditions you set forth to me in the name of the Lords." She extended her hand to him; he knelt and kissed it. Then he rose and helped her to mount her horse, which had been led over to them. He remounted his black charger and preceded her down the hill, around the shiny, useless field cannon. As she descended, she passed the puzzled, tired faces of her forces, and tried to reassure them by smiling and giving them encouraging words as she dismissed them and thanked them.

Her horse splashed across the little stream, and suddenly she was facing the hostile faces of the other army. The men glared at her and even began to mutter in tones that showed disparagement.

Kirkcaldy escorted her to Morton, who was standing, arms crossed, waiting. As she dismounted and walked through the men, she was aware of them staring and tittering at her short, borrowed dress, all stained and dusty now. She kept her head high and her eyes on the glowering Morton. Next to him was the Earl of Atholl, and Ruthven and Lindsay. Fleetingly she noticed that the young Ruthven looked like a warlock, too, although a handsomer, tawny version.

"My lords," she said, "I am come to you, not out of any fear I had of my life, nor yet doubting of the victory, if matters had come to the worst, but to save the spilling of Christian blood; and therefore have I come to you, trusting in your promises that you will respect me, and give me the obedience due to your native Queen and lawful sovereign."

Morton stepped forward, moving in his clumsy, shuffling gait. He bent his knee. "Here, Madam, is the place where Your Grace should be, and here we are ready to defend and obey you as loyally as ever the nobles of this realm did your ancestors."

"Burn her! Burn the murderess!" yelled some of the men standing nearby. "Kill her, she is not worthy to live!"

Mary's blood ran cold. These were not faceless crowds, but men who were so close they could see her face, could step forward and kill her themselves. And what were they calling her? Murderess? Did they truly think that? She pressed the paper Bothwell had given her closer to her bosom. What names were on it? In privacy she would see. But the hatred of the men, the viciousness of their tone . . .

"What is your purpose?" she asked Morton, letting the words ring out. "If it be my blood you desire, take it. I am here to offer it. You need wait no longer, and it is not necessary to seek the Earl of Bothwell to exact revenge." She stood there, daring them to take her and bind her. She was also daring the soldiers to come forward and stab her.

When no one moved, she realized they still hesitated to proceed against her person, and a desperate plan came to her. The Hamiltons . . . there seemed to be movement on the road. Were they on their way?

"Good my lords, let me go and meet the Hamilton party, thanking them for their efforts on my behalf, and dismissing them."

A sneer spread over Lord Lindsay's face. "Such royal courtesy is not necessary," he said.

"I wish it," she answered. To her dismay, no one overrode Lindsay or said he had no authority to pronounce what she could or could not do. She tried to turn and remount her horse, but the young Ruthven grabbed her arms.

"No," he said firmly. "You will go nowhere but where we say."

He had laid hands on her! She besought the others by looking at them, but they did not interfere. Ruthven forcibly turned her back in the direction she had been standing.

Then Atholl and Morton advanced with the banner of Darnley and stood on either side of her. "How is this, my lord Morton?" she asked, trying to keep her voice steady and scornful, free of distress. "I am told that all this"—she pointed toward the army—"was done in order to get justice against the King's murderers. I am also told that you are chief among them." She was sure his name was first on the list hidden on her person.

He merely tossed his head and said, "Come, Madam. The day grows late." Ruthven then turned her around again and made her mount her horse. Then, slowly, they began the ride back to Edinburgh.

Ahead of her rode Atholl and Morton with the banner held between them like an arch, which she was forced to ride beneath. On either side of her were two thugs, a Master Drumlanrig and the notorious Kerr of Fawdonside, who had threatened to shoot her during Riccio's murder. The fact that he had been banished from Scotland for it did not trouble the Lords, who evidently welcomed him in their midst.

As they rode along, Kerr leaned over and began whispering, "Murderess!" She did not even attempt to answer, knowing he was a murderer himself. When she ignored him, he spoke louder. "Adulteress!" She kept her eyes straight ahead. "Whore!" He raised his voice to a shout. "Whore! Slut! Rolling in Bothwell's bed, with your husband and his wife looking on! Slut! Taking on stableboys and grooms and guards to satisfy your lust!"

"Bothwell took them, too! The world knows he's a sodomite!" Drumlanrig joined in.

She willed herself not to listen to these obscene, and silly, accusations. They were like schoolboys trying to think of new dirty words. *Catamite. Necromancer. Onanite.*

Her lack of response infuriated them, and they began shouting, "Whore! Murderess!" The soldiers marching along took up the cry, adding, "Burn her! Kill her! She is not worthy to live!"

The sound of their voices—hungry, yearning, strident—struck fear into her. They were like eager dogs straining at the leash, wanting to leap at a throat. They were a killing mob.

Ahead of her, Morton and Atholl plodded along, making no attempt to quiet the soldiers, tacitly encouraging it. Only Kirkcaldy held up his sword menacingly to keep them at bay. Now they were approaching Edinburgh, and townspeople were coming out to meet them, lining the road in curiosity. It was dark, but torches were lighted and the people could see them well enough as they passed.

Their faces, upturned, were hostile. "Adulteress!" they screamed, and this time the voices were those of women.

Women! Not coarse soldiers, paid to echo their commanders' ideas, but ordinary women in the town. They hated her!

"Adulteress!" they screamed. "Burn the whore!"

The cavalcade made its way through the city gate and turned up the High Street. Now the crowds were thick, and every window was full of spectators. A yell of derision rang out from the roof of one house, followed by a sickening splat as a chamber pot was emptied. It barely missed Mary, landing on the cobblestones right in front of her. Some of the excrement flew up and spattered her horse and her bare legs.

"Whore!" The crowd, excited now, rushed forward and leering mouths screamed curses. Spit flew through the air, and she could feel its spray on her legs, hands, cheeks. Her horse was startled and jumped and almost threw her off. She did not want to land among them; they would tear her limb from limb.

They would kill their own Queen with their bare hands.

She was so shaken she did not notice that they were stopping halfway up the street.

"Off!" said Morton. "You will be safer here!" He yanked her arm and quickly she was pulled into a fortified house that was next to the Tolbooth. She recognized it as the Black Turnpike, where criminals awaiting trial were often put when the Tolbooth was full.

The Lords poured into the house and then slammed the door, shutting out the jeering, violent mob. Even Morton looked relieved to be away from them, although he did not usually show emotion. He took off his wide-brimmed hat, the one he was never without, and fanned himself. His face was flushed and, along with his red hair, made him look like something combustible.

"Well," he said. "We will dine here, courtesy of the Provost, whose house this is." He did not ask her to join them, nor would she have.

"I will return to Holyrood when the mob disperses," she said. Holyrood— it was only ten days since she and Bothwell had left it. "In the meantime, fetch me Mary Seton to attend me."

Ruthven laughed. "You will not return to Holyrood. You will remain in our company. And as for your Mary Seton, she has been left behind at Carberry Hill to fend for herself."

"What, am I a prisoner? I shall return to Holyrood, and who shall gainsay me?" She looked from one face to another.

"It is not safe," Morton finally said. "Listen to them outside!"

"Yes, I hear them. I hear what you have whipped them up to!"

"Nay, Madam, that I have not. They speak of their own accord; were it not for us, they would break in here and take you."

"Ohh!" She turned and mounted the stairs to get away from them, so smugly gathered in the entrance room.

Upstairs there was a bedroom already made ready for her. So they had planned this all along. She sank down on the bed and lay full length, staring up at the ceiling. Her heart was beating like a drum; she could feel it. Her legs dangled out from under the short dress.

Burn her, kill her, drown her. The words floated up from the street below, filled with a milling mob.

She could not think. She could hardly even feel. For so long her body had had to move, jump, fight, ride, almost with no direction from her brain or heart. There had been no time to bring the two together as she and Bothwell had dodged and run to keep ahead of events.

Bothwell. He was gone, safe at Dunbar by now. Her heart went out to him, hoping he was asleep in a secure bed. He would find a way to rally the royal supporters and oust these rebels. All was not lost. There were still the Hamiltons, Huntly and his Gordons, the Borderers.

But the people. Those looks. Their hatred . . .

Her head was swirling. She was ravenously hungry, but nauseated at the same time. The bed seemed to revolve around the room.

Shaking, she rose and went to the window. On the street down below stretched the offensive Darnley banner. As soon as they glimpsed her, the people, excited, began yelling. Just then she saw Maitland hurrying toward the house.

"Good Maitland!" she called, and stretched her arms out the window.

The mob, inflamed, began to chant. Maitland pulled his hat down over his eyes and pretended he had not heard or seen her. He disappeared from sight.

She reeled back toward the bed and flung herself on it. Again the room spun. Just then the door flew open—with no polite knock—and she looked up to see two enormous guards station themselves in the room and stand there with crossed arms. They did not greet her or ask permission.

I am a prisoner, she thought. Bothwell was right.

She ached to be with him. With the soldiers there, she would not even be permitted the comfort of tears. She rolled over on her stomach and felt the hidden paper crinkle slightly under her weight. It was all she had of Bothwell, for now. That and the child she suspected she was carrying, which she had not told him about, else he would have insisted on staying with her.

There was only nightmarish rest that night, with the red glow from the hundreds of torches outside lighting up the walls of the room, with soldiers breathing heavily and shuffling nearby, with her own aching stomach. Earlier she had heard the Lords all feasting in the downstairs room, then they had dispersed. But escape was impossible. Every time she turned over, the soldiers jumped to attention.

The hours passed slowly, and she felt dizzier and dizzier. Ghosts floated into the room: Riccio's form passed by her, and Darnley's, trailing faint laughter. A man who looked like the portraits of her father, and the laughing Duc de Guise. François came, too, dragging a dead pony—or maybe it was only the skin of one.

Who would have suspected I know so many dead people? she wondered. So many dead people . . . and traitors, and other ugly things . . . She wept silently, overcome by all the heaviness surrounding her, the weight of it, dragging her down into cold, oily depths where she could not breathe.

Was it morning? Was that what the sunlight meant? Where were the soldiers? She pulled herself out of bed and dragged herself over to the window. The sunlight, glancing off the slate tiles of the roof right under her window, hurt her eyes.

The crowd was still there. At the sight of her, a tumult rose. She flung her arms out the window and called to them.

"Help me! Help me! Oh, good people, deliver me!" The agony of seeing them was unbearable. She tore at her bodice and ripped it open. Her hair, tangled and unbound, hung down out the window.

"Ooooohhh," the spectators gasped. She looked like an apparition, a madwoman.

"Either slay me yourselves, or deliver me from the cruelty of the false traitors who have me in captivity!" she cried.

The mob murmured, and some began to cry, "Save her! Save her!" Then another part of the mob unfurled the Darnley banner again, flaunting it before her. Another part cried, "Away with that!" and rushed the banner, trying to tear it off its poles.

"Help me! Help me!" she shrieked, in a ghostly voice.

The Edinburgh alarm was sounded, calling all citizens to arms.

Rough hands grabbed her shoulders and forced her back in. It was Morton.

"So the second the soldiers go down to eat, you raise the alarm!" he said, staring at her.

For a moment she did not understand. Then, suddenly, she saw that her entire bodice was open, revealing her breasts completely to his searching eyes. How had this happened? How had the bodice been torn open?

"And you wonder that the people call you whore!" The disgust was dripping from his voice. "When you show yourself naked to their eyes. Expect no deference due a Queen, then!" He was gloating.

Then his eye spotted a piece of paper lying on the floor. "What's this?" he said eagerly.

The paper! The paper had fallen out of her bodice! When she had torn the bodice in her frenzy, she had forgotten the paper. But then, she had forgotten everything. She leapt to retrieve it, throwing herself on the floor and covering it before Morton could get it.

"Give it to me," he ordered.

She found herself staring at the tip of his boot. He moved it back as if to kick her full in the face. But she did not budge.

"Give it to me!" he said, bending down and lifting her up. She crumpled the paper and clutched it in the innermost part of her fist. He grabbed the first and tried to pry the fingers open.

"It is my paper, my royal property, and I forbid you to take it or even look at it," she said.

He laughed. "How royal. How full of presence. But that is all over now. Give it to me."

That is all over now. What did he mean?

"No."

He took her fist in both his hands and put enormous pressure on it, as if he were crushing a walnut shell. She could feel the bones in her hand start to give way. He meant to cripple her! It was her right hand, the one she wrote with—

"There!" He pried her fingers open and extracted the paper, torn now and almost illegible.

Mockingly he unfolded it and read it. "This is not worth losing the use of your hand over," he said lightly. "There's nothing here of any import."

"Save that you and others signed a bond to murder my husband!"

"Did we? Who says so? Bothwell? How like him, to forge a bond. He is full of false bonds, like the one he forced everyone to sign at Ainslie's Tavern—with a little persuasion from wine and two hundred soldiers!" Slowly, deliberately, he tore up the paper and let the little pieces flutter to the floor. "I think it is time you had some nourishment. Lack of food has turned your wits. I will send up a tray. And then the secretary Maitland wishes to speak with you."

After he was gone, Mary fell to her knees and gathered up the scraps of paper. Perhaps later she could put them together. Most important, she could read it, so she herself would know the truth.

Ashamed, she sought to cover her exposed breasts. Why had she ripped her clothes? She did not even remember doing so. *Was* she losing her wits?

In a few moments a tray appeared, along with a soldier. She had draped a sheet over herself, and ate slowly of the fruit and bread on the plate. She had no appetite, but if she had truly become so disoriented she had ripped her clothes, then she needed nourishment. Afterwards she lay down and attempted to rest.

She looked up to see Maitland standing at the foot of her bed. The soldiers were gone. So was the tray. She felt groggy. Somehow she must have slept. She struggled to sit up.

"Good Secretary," she said, "I see that today you recognize me."

He chose to ignore the gibe. "I am sorry to intrude on your sleep. But the Lords have required me to ask of you whether you will leave Bothwell. If you do, they are prepared to reinstate you to authority."

"Reinstate me?" she asked. "Have I been deprived of it? Legally, I mean. But you can tell them no. I will never leave the Earl of Bothwell, my wedded husband."

Maitland looked pained. "My dear Madam. I have known you so long, and through my wife, who has known you since childhood, I feel I have known you always. Please, I beg you, see him as he is. Since the divorce from his first wife was obtained under collusion, it is undoubtedly illegal— or could be proved to be so. You need not cling to him any longer. You can be delivered. You are safe now."

Safe! With the howling mob outside, and in complete custody and sub-jugation to the predatory Lords? She could not help giving a gentle, de-spairing laugh.

"No," she said. "He is my husband, and I will never leave him. I would gladly be set adrift in a boat with him, to go wherever the winds take us, to try our fortune."

He looked pained. "It is as I feared, then. You must face the truth about him. I tell you, he wrote letters to his first wife, telling her he but regarded you as his concubine." When she did not respond, he added, "He paid her visits at Crichton Castle and continued to visit her bed."

She laughed outright. "That is a lie!"

"So you will not leave him?"

"Never. And should you wish a practical reason to take back to that council of jackals who call themselves the Lords, tell them I am with child and will never consent to allow that child to be labelled bastard—like the Lord James!"

The mob was still howling outside. Maitland looked at her sadly. "Then I fear, due to the anger of the people, we will have to protect you from their wrath. And should you fail to recover your wits and strength, it may prove necessary to alleviate the heavy burden you carry. I see the crown has proven too weighty for that slender neck."

That evening they staged a ceremonial transfer to Holyrood for her. Morton and Atholl escorted her on either side, with a guard of three hundred footsoldiers. Behind them marched the Lords and another twelve hundred soldiers. All deference was shown to Her Majesty, and the crowds were satisfied. During the day they had gradually swung over to sympathy for her, and now they were clamouring for her release or rescue. Seeing her treated in a respectful manner, and walking in freedom to her own palace, they dispersed and went home to their own houses.

Once inside Holyrood, Mary was at last reunited with her women: Mary Seton, Mary Livingston Sempill, who had come to be with her, Madame Rallay, and two newer but no less faithful ladies who had replaced the departed Marys: Jane Kennedy and Marie Courcelles. They took her upstairs to her own room and helped her change clothes. Dinner was served, and at last Mary had an appetite and could eat among friends without fear.

❧

In the middle of the night they roused her. "Get ready," they said, and it was not the voices of her women, but the voices of Lord Lindsay and Lord Ruthven.

"Why, what is this?" She clutched the covers about herself.

"We have a journey to make. Get dressed."

She looked round. The women were nowhere to be seen. "Where? Why?"

"We are not at liberty to divulge."

"Very well." She climbed out of bed. "Will you permit me the privacy to dress?"

They nodded and faded away, or so it seemed.

This seemed like a dream. Or something that had already happened once, long ago. She had been awakened and told to get ready, that she was being taken to a secret place. . . .

Quickly she put on her sturdiest clothes and selected her riding boots. There was a coarse riding cloak, rust-coloured, and that she would need. Yes, it all *was* like something that had already happened. . . . Her women . . . she must speak to them, must leave a message with them. She had a note ready to take to Bothwell, telling him briefly what had happened and assuring him of her loyalty.

"Let us go," said Ruthven's voice from the door.

"I come," she said.

As she passed out through the outer chamber, she stopped. There were her women, having been ordered to wait there. She made her way to them, and Ruthven did not attempt to stop her.

"Take a message to Balfour at the castle," she told Mary Seton. "Tell him no matter where I am taken, to keep faith with me, and not to surrender the castle into the hands of the Lords. I will get word to him later. And to Bothwell at Dunbar." She thrust a paper into their hands. There was no envelope. She did not care if they read it. She loved Bothwell, and there was no shameful secret in that.

"Come." Lindsay's voice was impatient. Lindsay: the proud young lord who had dared even to think he could fight her husband in single combat.

Squeezing Madame Rallay's hands in farewell, she turned and made her way to the door.

Once they had descended the steps and reached the courtyard, they nudged her to turn to the back of the palace. It was the same place where she had crouched and crawled to hide herself when she had escaped from these very men, or their fathers, when Riccio had been slain. Then Bothwell and Huntly had been waiting for her, but now there was no one.

"Mount up," ordered Lindsay, the older and rougher of the two. He jerked the bridle of an unfamiliar horse and led him over to her, and forced her to climb into the saddle. Then he swung himself up onto his own mount, and motioned to the young Ruthven. A band of men-at-arms appeared, seemingly out of nowhere, and then, at a signal, they all trotted off.

They went down the road toward the water, and then, instead of going to Leith, turned left and descended to Queensferry. At the wharf a vessel was waiting for them; they and their horses were taken abroad quickly. The crossing was made with little difficulty, and when they alighted at the other side, Mary expected that they would take the road to Stirling. She had assumed that they would hustle her to Stirling, that great fortress which could also serve them as headquarters. So she was surprised when they rode straight for Dunfermline, and did not stop.

They clattered through the little town in the darkness, and emerged on the other side, then out into the open country. In the soft summer air— it was still warm, even now—she could hear the nightingales singing in the woods. They came to Blairadam Forest and Lindsay led the way through; he seemed to know it well. Here in the shrouded darkness there were other sounds: the sharp cries of the owls, the snarl of a polecat, the whining of a wild dog somewhere in the underbrush who resented being disturbed.

By the time they emerged on the other side of the forest, the east was growing light, with a pearly white glow. Mary saw, swimmingly outlined against the light, the shape of Benarty Hill and, to her left, the dark Lomond Hills. She heard the sound of geese honking, and suddenly she knew where she was and where she was going: to Lochleven Castle.

Of course! It was a strong castle on an island in the midst of a deep and often storm-tossed loch; but most important, it was held by the mother of Lord James and her considerable brood of nonroyal offspring. Lady Douglas had seven daughters and three sons besides her beloved Lord James. Lindsay was married to a Douglas daughter, and the elder Ruthven's first wife had been a Douglas. Her imprisonment would be a family affair in a stout family prison, with all the gaolers loyal to each other.

She could see the broad flat surface of the loch now, bearded round its edges with reeds and cattails, and she could hear the geese who nested within them. She had come here on other occasions; she and Darnley had stayed here just after they were married, and had gone hunting in the surrounding countryside, returning at night by rowboat to their island retreat. Then it had seemed dreamy, perfect, remote—a lover's dream come true. She even furnished her own rooms here with her royal accoutrements.

A bitter laugh escaped her, and Ruthven jerked his head around to see what she found so amusing.

My suite is just waiting for me, she thought. The bride's dream retreat has now turned into a gaoler's dream.

They swung a lantern back and forth three times, and a light answered them from the island, about a mile away. They boarded the small rowboat and two of Lindsay's retainers did the rowing, their thick-muscled arms making it look easy. It took them very little time to make the crossing, and Sir William, Lord James's half brother and keeper of the castle, was waiting for them at the landing. As the prow of the little boat pushed through the weeds, startled birds flew up. The water lapped up almost to the foot of the thick, high walls surrounding the castle.

"Welcome," the wheezing Sir William said, bowing. He was a sickly man, Mary remembered, always having to send for medicines for his chest and perpetual cough. Although he was very nearly the same age as Lord James, he had none of his stolid robustness. That was supplied by his redoubtable mother, the Lady Douglas, who was also standing there.

Mary had known her earlier, and although the lady had always been polite and had tried to make Mary's stay at Lockleven comfortable, there had always been the jostling between them inherent in two women, both beautiful, one of whom was in her prime, and the other past it. Now the lady was smiling and welcoming Lindsay, her son-in-law.

"We have a warrant for her incarceration," said Lindsay loudly. "Signed by Morton, who is acting as head of the Lords in the absence of Lord James."

Sir William took the paper in a shaky hand and held it out to read it in the dim light. He then folded it and was about to put it away when Mary said, "May I have it read? I am entitled to know what it contains."

"Oh . . . yes. It says, 'The said Lord William Douglas is to reserve her within Lochleven and keep Her Majesty surely within. So shall she be detained and kept from harm until she agree to part herself from her pretended husband the Earl of Bothwell, the evil ravisher and cruel murderer who seeks to oppress and destroy that innocent infant the Prince as he had done his father, and so, by tyranny and cruel deeds, at last to usurp the royal crown and supreme government of this realm.' "

She laughed. "You yourselves have the Prince safe in Stirling Castle, and as for cruel murderers—why, my lords Lindsay and Ruthven, I saw the knives in your hands when Riccio was killed. I forgave you and Morton for that crime, as I recall, when you were at my mercy."

Ruthven stepped forward and took her elbow. "Enough of this. That was before your wits were turned by the potions of the Earl of Bothwell."

Again she laughed, but this time desperately.

"You see?" said Ruthven. "We must get her to a resting place."

"Yes, yes," said Sir William, leading the way.

As they entered through the fortified gate, Mary saw that she was not being taken to her customary quarters in the square tower, but was being paraded across the green inner courtyard to a circular tower diagonally across from it, which was built into the southeast corner. Lady Douglas unlocked the thick wooden door and gestured that they should enter.

It was dark and musty within. Only the plainest furniture was in the ground-floor room: a rough table, three stools, two old-fashioned candles in huge, wrought-iron holders.

"The bed is upstairs," said Lady Douglas.

Mary pulled herself slowly up the spiral staircase by holding on to a rope. Sure enough, an ascetic single bed was shoved into one corner. The light was poor, and there were not even any rushes on the floor. Behind her, Lady Douglas held up a candle.

"Is this the way you honour guests?" Mary asked, but her voice was soft. Where were her hangings, her ebony sofa? Stolen, most like. This little tower room was more roughly furnished than the one in Dunbar Castle where Bothwell had taken her. And then it had been different, altogether different, for *he* was there, and where he was, she was cared for.

Lady Douglas looked away, embarrassed. Another person suddenly joined them in the room, emerging from the stairwell. It was a young man of about Mary's own age, with enormous blue eyes framed with spiky black lashes.

"They say you may send for two of your own lady attendants," he said. "And a physician or secretary."

"This is Geordie, my youngest son," said Lady Douglas.

One of them. Another enemy. But he was handsome, with his wavy dark hair and ruddy complexion. How different all the members of this family looked.

Mary felt great relief. "Then tell them I would like Mary Seton and"— not Mary Livingston Sempill, she had family duties—"and Jane Kennedy, and Claud Nau, my secretary."

"With gladness, Your Majesty," he said in a lilting voice. Was he mocking her? She was too tired and heartsick to care.

She sank down on the little bed and put her feet up. Everything seemed to spin, with the centre beam of the ceiling the still point of a great turning wheel. Outside, the water was lapping against the stones of the tower and she could smell its dank odour. The ground-floor room would be mouldy and damp. A fit place for a prisoner. Like being at sea.

At sea . . . at sea with Bothwell . . . She fell into a deep sleep.

LVIII

Bothwell sat in his room at Dunbar, his head in his hands. It was the middle of the night. He should have been fast asleep on this, the night on which he was more tired than he had ever been in his life. But he was so tortured he could not allow himself to lie down.

He had failed. He had lost the battle without a blow ever having been struck. It was the one possibility he had never considered. He had been ready to die, but not to limp away like this. And Mary—what must she think? Oh, she was quick-witted and brave, and would not be intimidated. But now she was among enemies, with no one likely to be susceptible to her special pleading or even a bribe. Would they honour their word? He knew them well, and he knew the answer to that.

There would be no possibility of a bribe, because the Lords were now in control of everything. Mary would have to have their permission even to take possession of her own belongings. Only if the people rose up and demanded her release . . . But no, the people were dead against her, whipped up by Knox and his like. Knox was demanding her death, saying that even that was not severe enough, that she should be eaten by dogs, like Jezebel. The gentle, sweet Knox, showing everyone the deep love of God.

What had happened to Huntly and Hamilton? Why had they not arrived?

I can rally the forces if I move quickly, he thought. There are still many who are loyal to the Queen. Then we can storm Edinburgh and take her back.

Edinburgh. They are in possession of everything there, except the castle. Balfour still holds it for us.

I need my personal belongings from my apartments there; my titles and deeds and the patent creating me Duke of Orkney and Lord of Shetland; the marriage contract, all my plate and jewels. . . .

He poured himself out a goblet of wine, and bolted it. Instead of making him feel better, it muddied his thoughts. For an instant fear went through him, but then it disappeared. He sent for Geordie Dalgleish, and instructed him to go to Edinburgh Castle and retrieve the papers and personal effects from his old quarters.

❦

Morton was allowing his beard to be trimmed. He had let it grow rather bushy, and his mistress was complaining about it. She liked to twine her fingers in it, but said it was like a thorny hedge now. Women! They were so opinionated about such things, so quick to criticize. But if it made her happy and more willing to indulge him in bed, it was a fair enough trade.

The barber, snipping away under his chin, was attempting to question him without being obvious. " 'Tis a fair day, my lord, is it not? June so hot this year, and your having to fight under this sun. The battle—oh, I'm told it wasn't a battle at all, just a staring-down. And the Queen—they were most unkind to her on the road back to Edinburgh. I am told she had to go past Kirk O'Field. Most distressing. She *was* distressed, I know."

"Do you?" asked Morton. "Did you see her?"

"No. I was not there," he admitted.

"Ah," said Morton, pretending he did not recognize the man's question.

The barber tilted up Morton's chin and began to shave it delicately where the hairs always got caught in his collar. It would feel good to be rid of them. Morton relaxed.

"Is the Queen . . . ?"

"Safe. And resting," Morton assured him cryptically.

Little curls of red hair lay all around them on the floor. The man produced a broom and pan and swept it up. "Lest witches get hold of it!" he attempted to joke.

Morton did not smile. There were altogether too many witches about, and one could not be too careful. Why had the man said that? Was he working for one?

"The bottom of the Nor'Loch is lined with witches," he said pointedly.

The man was whisking off the towel he had draped around Morton's shoulders. "There," he said, fluffing up the shortened, thinned beard. "How do you like it?"

Morton ran his fingers through it. "It feels light. Just right for summer." He dug into his purse and gave the man his customary payment. He was eager for him to be gone along with his questions.

Best not to have too many questions just now. Not until things sorted themselves out. It had all happened so quickly that they needed time to think.

Morton returned to his room to select his clothes for this sunny, fine day. He usually wore black, but today he felt like something in a bright colour. But no—he had purged his wardrobe of all the yellows and reds and purples when he became a Lord of the Congregation. Today, though, he wished he had retained just one or two items, for the rare June day when the spirits were soaring and one wished to feel young and free.

He did have a secret scarlet nightshirt that he wore when he and Mistress Cullen met, when her husband the Captain was away. . . . At the thought of Mistress Cullen he felt excited. At the same time he laughed to himself. It had been so much fun to be morally outraged by Bothwell and the Queen's adultery and to demand that they be punished for it.

The Captain was becoming a nuisance. He was home too much. Perhaps it was time the Lords of the Congregation gave him an assignment out of

549

town. Or perhaps it was even possible that the Captain was a traitor and therefore not fit to live.

Morton pulled out an embroidered topcoat that had little scarlet flowers on it, albeit on a dull, earth-coloured background. He pulled it on, noting with satisfaction that his beard now only grazed the starched ruff.

There was a sudden knock on the door. "Lord Morton!" an excited voice called, and Archibald Douglas stepped in. His eyes were glittering. "There's been a find! A real find, for us. . . . Bothwell's servant has been caught by Balfour breaking into Bothwell's rooms in the Castle. He escaped, but we caught up with him."

"And? Who was it?"

"Geordie Dalgleish, his tailor. He came to get Bothwell's clothes, so he said. But the night in 'little ease' in the Tolbooth changed his mind. Or perhaps it was the sight of the Spanish collar . . . or the iron boots . . . or maybe it was the Scavenger's Daughter. . . ."

Archibald was growing dreamy-eyed; he was a delighter in cruelty and enjoyed the ingenuity of torture instruments, each one attuned to a different faculty or limb.

"And?" Morton prodded.

Archibald snapped out of his reverie. "He took us to a little house on the Potterow outside the walls and there gave us this!" Archibald produced an ornate silver casket, with entwined initial Fs on it. He set it down reverently.

"Why, what's this?" said Morton, bending to examine the lock-box.

"Something very precious to the Lord Bothwell, evidently. Also stored in another box were the royal patents creating him Duke, and his various land grants and inheritances from his father. I think it must be valuable, else he would not have risked his servant's life to obtain it."

"He did not know he was risking his life," said Morton. "Remember, he does not know the Lord Balfour has gone over to us. Undoubtedly he assumed that Dalgleish could come and go unhindered." Morton turned the box upside down. He could hear some contents, which sounded like papers, thump inside. There were no jewels, then, or he would have heard them clink.

"Smash it open!" said Archibald.

"No," said Morton. "Perhaps it would be wiser to have a little ceremony in which we broke open the lock in front of witnesses and recorded the contents. Our own witnesses, of course. Go and tell the Lords to assemble here as soon as possible."

While he was waiting, Morton took the silver casket and put it on a marble table on the first floor. He paced the room, looking anxiously out the window. The crowds of the day before were gone, and Edinburgh looked normal. Removing the Queen had been the correct thing to do. Now she could not be touched, either by the mob or by her warrior rescuer, Bothwell. There she could stay until they had decided what to do, and until the Lord James returned to help them decide. Bothwell would have to be executed speedily in order to shut his mouth. Even though the paper with the names he so stupidly gave the Queen had been destroyed, he carried in his head enough information about the King's murderers to undermine the Lords' position of innocent outrage.

Morton paced up and down the room. He loved his town house, loved everything about it, from the way the sun slanted into the upper rooms to the inlaid wood pattern of the hall downstairs. He had surely been blessed.

That afternoon, eleven of the Lords of the Congregation gathered around his marble table. There was Maitland, of course, and three earls: the earls of Atholl, of Mar, and of Glencairn. The Lords Home, Sempill—father of Lusty's husband—and Sanquhar looked on, along with the Master of Graham and the Laird of Tullibarden, and Andrew Douglas. The silver strongbox sat gleaming like a miniature trunk; it was even shaped like one.

Morton tried several keys that he had obtained from an Edinburgh locksmith, but none opened the lock, as it appeared to be a foreign one. So he took up a hammer and file and broke open the box. He dented the lid slightly, but that did not hinder his lifting it up to reveal a pile of folded papers and letters lying inside.

"Ah!" he said. "Documents. Let us see what they are!" Quickly he began unfolding them. His face fell with disappointment.

"A long French poem," he said. He laid it aside and took out another.

"A letter. In French. It pertains to . . . something about a servant." He put it aside, too.

"Now this . . ." It was yet another French letter. His eyes skimmed it. It was even duller than the other one, with classical allusions to Medea.

Love letters. His heart sank, and he felt like a fool for having summoned all the Lords to come and see a stack of love letters.

He picked up another. This one, also in French, mentioned the Earl of Lennox. It had to do with his retainers.

The next piece of paper proved to be a marriage contract. It was dated April fifth, 1567; in it Mary promised to marry Bothwell. Naturally it, too, was in French. Well, no wonder he had kept it. It was a legal document proving her intent.

"What was the date?" Maitland asked.

"April fifth," he replied, then it hit him. "Three weeks before the 'abduction.' This proves it was false! He and the Queen planned it! They were in collusion together!"

Eagerly he pulled out another letter. This time the phrases leapt out at him. " 'And thereupon hath preached unto me that it was a foolish enterprise, and that with mine honour I could never marry you, seeing that being married you did carry me away.' " He looked around at the other Lords.

He grabbed another letter out, a very long one, written on several sheets of paper. His face turned first white, then pink. He stammered with excitement.

"Oh! This letter—it is a strange nightmare, all feverish and full of fits and starts, but it—it proves—O Holy God—"

"Read it!" said Maitland.

"I cannot. It is too long! But you can each read it, taking care not to harm or smudge it. It says—oh, listen to this: 'Alas! I never deceived anybody, but I remit myself wholly to your will; and send me word what I shall do, and whatsoever happen to me, I will obey you. To be short, I have learned that he is suspicious, and yet he trusts my word.' "

Maitland snorted. "This means nothing. No names are mentioned. For that matter, is it addressed, dated, or signed?"

"No," Morton admitted.

"If you were writing an adulterous love letter, would you sign it?" asked the Earl of Atholl with a smirk.

"No," said Morton, who had written many. "But there is more. The King is mentioned. 'The King sent for Joachim and asked him, why I did not lodge nigh to him.' "

"Altogether too vague," said Erskine. "It could refer to anything. It could be written by a servant, for that matter."

"Not this!" Morton said triumphantly. " 'But now to make him trust me I must feign something unto him; and therefore when he desired me to promise that when he should be well we should make but one bed I told him feigning to believe his fair promises, that if he did not change his mind between this time and that, I was contented.' "

"So?" argued Erskine. "This only proves it was written by the Queen, then."

"And why was she writing such things to Bothwell? Here is why: 'I am glad to write unto you when other folk be asleep, seeing that I cannot do as they do, according to my desire, that is between your arms my dear life whom I beseech God to preserve from all ill.' "

"So they were lovers, and she seems to regard God as some sort of celestial procurer," said Glencairn. "Amusing, but everyone suspected as much."

"*Suspected* and *proved* are not the same thing! This proves they were lovers before Darnley's death! And that she went to Glasgow with secret motives. That was why she brought him back. It was a plan!"

"It does seem to tend that way," admitted Atholl. He held out his hand to receive one of the documents.

The Lords spent the rest of the afternoon perusing the letters, quoting suitable phrases with great glee, as if they had discovered hidden treasures.

" 'Being gone from the place where I had left my heart, it may be easily judged what my countenance was. . . .' "

" 'But fear not but the place shall continue till death.' "

" 'Now if to please you, my dear life, I spare neither honour, conscience, nor hazard, nor greatness, take it in good part, and not according to the interpretation of your false brother-in-law, to whom I pray you, give no credit against the most faithful lover that ever you had or shall have.' "

The men tittered. "It sounds like a lovesick child," said Lord Home. "But then, Bothwell seemed to inspire such passion in the female breast. How do we know all of these are from the Queen? He had many conquests, and it would have been like him to have kept all the letters and gloated over them. Or left them out to make whoever it was of the moment jealous. I suspect that was their real function."

"Well, whatever their original function for the Earl, they'll serve quite another for us. With these, gentlemen, we can justify keeping the Queen in captivity."

"Oh, listen to this! It cannot be the Queen who wrote this one, it's too servile and whiny: 'God forgive you and give you, my only friend, the good luck and prosperity that your humble and faithful lover doth wish unto you, who hopes shortly to be another thing to you, for the reward of my pains. I have not made one word, and it is very late, although I should never be weary in writing to you, yet I will end, after kissing of your hands.' It was probably that Norwegian woman who followed him here and hung about, neglected," said Erskine. He laughed.

"Gentlemen, I think it is of greatest importance that we let the world know about this shocking proof, and in the Queen's own handwriting, of the plot between her and Bothwell to murder the innocent King," said Morton sternly. "Are we agreed?"

All the men nodded solemnly.

After the main party of them had left, Maitland and Archibald lingered on. Maitland put his arm around Morton's neck familiarly. "Let us not forget that it is we who planned the King's death, or at least were considering it. It would be easy to forget, and thereby confuse our stories and our evidence."

"We may have signed that paper, and we may have met at Whittingham, but the truth is we didn't kill the King," Morton insisted stubbornly.

"Well, then," said Maitland, "I wonder who did? I mean, *really?*"

ॐ

The Lords marched in solemn procession down the Canongate, their singing hearts at variance with their long faces. They were going to the royal apartments at Holyrood to cleanse them, clear them out. The Queen's reign was over.

There were six of them: Maitland, Morton, Erskine, Atholl, Glencairn, and Douglas. Word had spread, and soon a crowd fell in behind them, hoping for some spoils or at least a diversion this bright June day. Since the Kirk had banished May Day revels, Robin Hood, and the riotous fairs accompanying holy days, the populace had been hungry for high jinks.

The Lords left the crowd behind when they entered the palace itself, but encouraged them to remain in the courtyard. Once inside, the Lords ascended the grand staircase and began happily honouring various sites of violence or humiliation, creating a Protestant Stations of the Cross. "Look, here's the trunk where Riccio's body lay after it was stripped." "Here's the landing where they threw him down." "Here's the room where John Knox made the Queen cry." "Here's where he admonished the silly Marys on their vanity." "This is where Riccio was first stabbed." "And look, here's the staircase where Darnley came up!"

The three rooms that had been Mary's private domain stood empty, with everything still in its place. There was the supper table ("the one that got overthrown and hit the Queen's belly") in the little room, polished and bare except for two candlesticks. Her bed was made, its green and yellow silk cover with its green silk fringe hanging neatly down to the floor. Her little desk, inlaid with ivory and mother-of-pearl, held a locked writing cabinet and an ivory box for pens and ink. There was also a silver box with a green velvet cover resting to one side. Everything had been precisely arranged and they knew, before even looking, that the contents of the box would be in order and held with scarlet ribbon.

Against one wall was a crucifix with a kneeler under it, flanked by two candles. A small framed painting of the Virgin was nearby.

Large studded trunks were against another wall, locked. And there were two smaller cabinets, painted with flowers and birds, with a mirror lying atop one.

The men looked around silently. Habit made them want to speak softly, to give honour, to watch how they stood and held their hats. Mary's presence filled the room; for a moment it seemed impossible that she was not there. Then the fact that she was not rushed over them, and it seemed bizarre and unnatural.

All this was theirs, to do with as they would.

All this.

Glencairn was the first to take action. He grabbed the little writing cabinet, the one with the story of Cupid and Psyche painted on it, and twisted its handles. When it did not open, he lifted it over his head and smashed it on the floor.

"It's French!" he said. "Something the French whore would have brought with her!"

Maitland grimaced. "It is not necessary to destroy it."

"Let's see what's in it!" Glencairn bent down and tried to pull out the drawers. When they still refused to open, he kicked it with his studded boots and splintered the delicate wood. "Ah!" He emptied it. A pile of papers and letters fell out.

"French dung!" he cried. "Look, they're all in French!"

"Yes, Glencairn. That is customary when writing to the French," said Maitland. "Most people can read French," he added pointedly, knowing Glencairn could not. He picked up the letters and skimmed them.

"This one is a copy of one written to Catherine de Médicis—this is to her goddaughter, little Marie d'Elboeuf—this is to her aunt the Abbess—"

Glencairn was pulling out other papers. "Now here it is—her ciphers!

Look at them!" His voice rose in genuine amazement. "There must be sixty codes here!"

Maitland grabbed a handful. "So that's what Riccio did. Translate all these. A boring, tedious job. No wonder she missed him. There wasn't anyone else patient enough to do it. I certainly wasn't. We didn't use all these when I was still principal secretary."

"What I want to know is, why is it necessary to use codes at all?" growled Morton. "I mean, only spies and people who are involved in underhanded things need to resort to codes." He shuffled around the room, a look of distaste on his face, stopping to finger the tapestries and the velvet covering of one table. This embroidery might go well in his hall.

"She ought to have used codes in the letters to Bothwell!" crowed Glencairn. "Where were they when she needed them?"

"Oh, passion put them out of her head," laughed Atholl. "Can you imagine writing about 'my heart, my blood, my soul, my care, you promised we should be together all night at our leisure' and having to think, 'let's see, I substitute 2 for *y*, and *a* for *r*, and so on."

The men howled with laughter, and Atholl fell on the bed. He grabbed a pillow and embraced it passionately. Then he rolled over on top of it and began thrusting at it, while crying in falsetto, "Oh, my Lord Bothwell, oh, oh, stop, stop, oh, oh, don't stop. . . ."

"Where do you suppose it first happened?" asked Erskine suddenly. "Was it here?"

"This chamber has had a surfeit of evil, so perhaps it was," said Maitland. "I cannot help but think that it was a doomed day that she ever set foot in it. Almost as if it dragged her down into evil, instigated it."

Morton folded a tapestry neatly and put it down to take away later. "Oh, come now. You can't imply that if she had just used Falkland Palace or Edinburgh Castle for her main residence, things would have been different?"

"I know not what I imply. I only know there is something overwhelming about the events that have happened in here." Maitland turned to the window, the one overlooking the courtyard. The people were still out there, hoping for excitement of some sort. "This is where she listened to the music the people played for her when first she arrived." He shook his head. "It seems that she *tried.*"

"Lust undid her," said Morton righteously.

"It is not that simple." Maitland glared at him. "A marriage ceremony turned the lust into legal wedlock. If lust alone could bring a person down, there's not a one of us that wouldn't also be imprisoned in Lochleven."

"Only the Lord James would still be free!" said Mar, trying to regain the lightheartedness that Maitland was ruining.

"Not even Knox would escape," chimed in Atholl. "He wears out his young wife, so I hear. And when he was courting, he dandied himself up like a French whore himself!"

"Look!" Morton was prying open the locked drawers of the painted chests, and extracting jewel chests, also locked. He broke the locks and dumped the contents out on the velvet table cover.

They were all there: her personal jewellery, her watches and rings and brooches and necklaces; her heirlooms, the Great Harry and the rope of black pearls. In reverent awe, Morton looped the pearls over his paw-like hands, holding them up. They were so long he had to spread his arms out as far as they could go to stretch them out to their full length.

"I remember her wearing these. God, how she treasured them!" said Erskine.

"And now they are ours. Or, rather, Scotland's," said Morton, licking his lips. "Think of the money they will fetch."

Suddenly Maitland had an idea. "I know one person who likes pearls even more than our own Queen," he said. "The Queen of England! I'll warrant she will pay well for them. We must offer them to her!"

"Break open this one!" cried Douglas, jerking the velvet cover off the curved silver box. Eagerly Morton took his hammer and chisel to it. The top sprang open.

Little silk-wrapped packets were inside. Morton had trouble handling things that small. Finally he managed to unwind the silk on one and out tumbled a miniature. It fell on the floor and shattered before he could catch it. Annoyed, he picked up the pieces and tried to fit them together. "It appears to be a miniature of François," he said.

The rest of them proved to be miniatures of her French family, of Darnley, and of Elizabeth. The ones of Darnley and Elizabeth were greeted with embarrassed silence.

"Why would she keep these?" asked Glencairn.

"She is crafty," said Morton. "You notice there isn't one of Bothwell." He pocketed the miniatures and returned to the jewel table.

While Morton was gloating over the jewels, the rest of them systematically emptied the drawers and trunks. Then Glencairn rolled his eyes.

"The Papist chapel!" he suddenly cried. "It must be destroyed!"

"Yes!" cried Douglas. "The heart and soul of her affront, the Papist chapel! The one that we tried to destroy that first Sunday!" Together they rushed out of the apartments and ran down the gallery, hunting for the chapel.

They rounded a corner and there it was, its doors open, not even pretending to be anything else, not even having the modesty to hide itself, but instead, flaunting itself like the Whore of Babylon! With a yell, the two men tore into it, ripping down the hangings, overturning the altar, opening the tabernacle where the sacred hosts were kept, and scattering them all over the floor. Then Glencairn had an idea. Scooping up handfuls of them, he tossed them out the window to the waiting crowd. They surged forward, cheering, catching the sacred bread, pelting each other with it.

"Get rid of this abomination!" cried Douglas, kicking at the carved wood of the altar base. Glencairn was yanking down the ivory carvings, smashing the saint statues, and breaking the stained glass. In a few minutes the entire chapel was nothing but debris.

"Knox would be proud!" Douglas said. "He always said, 'Cut down the tree, else the birds will return to nest in the branches again.' This tree is down!"

The other four men were awaiting them back at the door of the apartments, their arms laden with embroideries, jewels, plate, paintings, hangings. "Take what you wish, and let us go," they told the chapel-smashers.

In the midst of Maitland's bundle of spoils lay the ivory crucifix from the wall. He meant to send it to Mary at Lochleven. It was an old one, from France, and doubtless had some personal meaning for her.

"Morton, you mean to send the Queen her miniatures, do you not?" he said. "They are worth nothing, and I cannot imagine that you will derive any pleasure from contemplating the likeness of the Lord Darnley."

Morton glared at him. Next he would want him to give up the ruby tortoise—if he had seen him pocket it. "Of course," he said indignantly.

LIX

It seemed there was no awakening for Mary. The sea-dreams of Bothwell blended into other dreams, dreams of Stirling Castle and a man who was half Lord James and half Darnley, dreams of the fierce wind there and pony races from long ago. Lord Lindsay's wife kept watch over her until her attendants arrived two days later, rowed across the choppy waters of the lake and carrying bundles of clothes and prayer books and medicines.

"She has been like this since her arrival," said Lady Lindsay softly, showing them the Queen, still lying in bed. "She has not eaten or roused herself." She sounded genuinely concerned.

Mary Seton made her way over to the bedside and stood silently looking down at her mistress, whom she had seen in so many circumstances and over so many years. She saw how white and almost bloodless the Queen's face was, how still she was lying. She seemed to be in a state deeper than sleep.

Seton knelt down beside the bed and took Mary's hand in hers. It was cold. She squeezed it and tried to bring some warmth into it. She brushed back the tangled hair and massaged her temples.

"Your Majesty," she whispered close to her ear. "We are come to help you."

Mary gave no indication that she heard her, and her eyes stayed tightly closed.

"It is so damp in here," said Seton, "and it feels so cold, even though outside in the sun it is warm. Can we have a fire, please?"

Lady Lindsay nodded. "And you may have any food you wish; we have offered broth and bread and soup, but she has refused to eat. My mother says it is because she has made a vow not to touch food until she be reunited with her husband, but that is fanciful. She *has* called his name in her sleep, but she has not eaten because she is ill. When they brought her here, she had not lived normally for days, and it had taken its toll."

Lady Lindsay left the chamber to ask about the wood, and Seton turned to Jane Kennedy and Claud Nau. "Perhaps it is merciful that she cannot hear or think for now. She has heard too much already."

The faithful attendants kept the fire burning to keep the chill at bay, and dutifully offered their mistress food every few hours when she seemed to be awakening. In the meantime they paced the quarters, unpacking the few things they had brought, trying to make the chamber as comforting as possible. Seton hung up the crucifix which Maitland had quietly given her to take along.

Days passed, days in which news from the outside flew over the waters of the loch like the wheeling water fowl. The Lords had taken one of Bothwell's servants in the act of recovering some of Bothwell's treasure and papers; the bold warrior had sent him straight into the nest of his enemies, like a gull diving for fish. The papers were incriminating, especially to the Queen. Meanwhile, Bothwell was still at liberty—at least the Lords had kept their promise to the Queen not to harm him—and trying to raise another army to rescue the Queen. He had gone to the Borders, and to the west, talking to the Hamiltons and others.

Then, suddenly, the Lords put a thousand-crown price on his head, at the instigation of Knox and the Kirk, who declared it shameful that the scoundrel was allowed to roam unpunished. A few days later they issued a call for him to appear at the Tolbooth on July twenty-second to answer to the threefold charge of murdering the King, kidnapping the Queen, and forcing her into unlawful marriage with him, or be branded an outlaw and forfeit of all titles and property. By that time he had quitted Dunbar and journeyed north, still attempting to raise troops.

The French evidenced interest in obtaining custody of the baby Prince, as did the English, both claiming to be acting on their duties as the child's godparents.

All these things were whispered in the little tower room, out of earshot of the Queen. No communication from Bothwell succeeded in penetrating the stout defences around his captive wife.

When Mary finally swam up into consciousness, she saw the familiar crucifix on the wall, floating there against the grey stone. It seemed to reach out and tell her she was safe and at home. She closed her eyes again and drifted, waiting to sink back into that place where she had come to belong. But now she did not sink down, but only floated near the surface; it was as if the depths did not want to take her back. She could hear voices, not the wavering voices in dreams, but real voices: hushed, tender, insistent.

"I think the boat is returning. . . ."

"We must get this cloth mended. . . ." A soft woman's voice.

"The letter said there may be an envoy from London." An accented man's voice.

The voices were familiar, but none of them was *his* voice; he was not nearby. There was no one else she wanted to talk to. She kept her eyes shut and lay still, praying to be taken back down into those cushiony velvet depths where there were no demands, no passage of time, no recognition.

"Her breathing has changed," said a voice. The person was standing right over her. The next thing Mary knew, her head was being propped up with an extra pillow, and other excited voices surrounded her.

"The colour! Her colour has come back!"

They were bending her neck forward to put another pillow under it, and it hurt. Her whole neck was tender and aching. She groaned.

Immediately there were hands dabbing her face with wet cloths, and someone started rubbing her wrists. It was so unpleasant she could not help opening her eyes. The light stung them.

"She is awake!" cried Mary Seton. "Oh, Your Majesty! No, don't shut your eyes, I beg you! No, no!"

It took all Mary's strength just to keep them open. She attempted to smile at Seton, but her mouth would not obey.

Next Claud Nau was bending down to her. "Oh, thank God and all the saints!" he cried. He was motioning frantically and saying, "Soup! Soup!"

In a few moments they had pulled her to a sitting position in bed and Seton was spooning soup into her mouth. It tasted foul, and almost made her gag. She had to force herself to swallow it.

Exhausted by the effort, she lay back down and closed her eyes again and slept, but this time it was a different sleep, and when she awoke a few hours later, she struggled to sit up by herself.

Again she was given soup, and this time she swallowed it without difficulty, and drank some watered wine. A night's sleep followed, and by the next morning she knew that the way back into her dream retreat had somehow been barred to her. She awoke normally and called for Seton in a voice that was croaky with disuse. Seton was instantly by her side.

"I feel so weak," Mary said, holding up one hand. She could see how thin her arm looked, and it ached with the effort of holding itself up. Even speaking seemed to demand some superhuman strength.

"You have lain without food, almost without moving, for two weeks," said Seton.

"Two weeks? I am still at Lochleven?"

"Yes, my lady, where did you think you were?"

"I knew not." She began to weep. "But I thought it was a friendly place."

"You have friends here," Seton assured her.

"But I am still a prisoner, am I not?" Her voice was a whisper.

"Yes. You are."

It all came rushing back like a black tide. "The Lords . . . Bothwell. What of Bothwell?"

The attendants looked at each other. Finally Seton said, "There is no word of Bothwell, my lady."

"No word . . . no letter . . .?"

"None that has reached here. We are closely guarded."

"Ah." Mary's voice was a soft sigh. "It is no use, then."

In a few days Mary left her bed, dressed herself, ate normal meals. But she performed all these actions like someone in a trance. Her face was masklike and her eyes were not animated. She sat for hours without speaking, and did not attempt to write letters or win concessions from her gaolers. She prayed in front of the crucifix, silently, and once asked, in a listless voice, how it had come to be there. Seton told her that Maitland had obtained it for her; she did not describe the destruction of the chapel that went with it, and Mary evidenced no curiosity about it.

Once Nau pulled up a chair and, taking her hands in his, told her as gently as possible about the rumours that Lord James had been called home, and that her enemies had some sort of evidence against her that might compel her to abdicate.

"Abdicate?" she murmured. "Give up my throne? So Bothwell was right. That has been their intention all along."

"Your Majesty, can you recall anything that was in Bothwell's possession that might serve that purpose to the Lords?" he prompted.

"Yes," she said with a twisted smile. "I wrote him love letters, which I asked him to destroy. But he kept them. I assume they will use those in some manner, taking out certain phrases and putting their own interpretation on them. But I care not," she said. "I care not."

"Will you in no wise consider leaving Bothwell and consenting to a divorce? They still claim they will restore you to the throne if you do. Bothwell's case is hopeless now; he is discredited and soon will be declared an outlaw. But you can still save yourself, and your throne."

"Never!" she said, with more vehemence than anything she had uttered since coming out of her slumber days earlier. "Never! I carry his child, and I will never allow that child to be branded bastard, dishonouring all three of us."

"Bothwell's star is fallen," Nau insisted.

"All the more reason that I, as his wife, should remain loyal. And so I shall, until death."

She felt dead already, enveloped in this mantle of lassitude and profound sadness. It was a mantle she could not remove, and no amount of sleep or wholesome food seemed to dislodge it. Waking or sleeping it weighed on her, sometimes with pain and other times with the more frightening absence of all feeling.

I have nothing, she thought. I have been Queen for four and twenty years, but if I died in my sleep this very night, there would be nothing to write of me in the chronicles. I was Queen of France for a year and a half, but when François died, all that passed away, and today France remembers me not. I have reigned directly here in Scotland for six years now, and although there has been no foreign war, the nobles never made peace amongst themselves. My whole reign has been a series of plots, followed by my pardons. My marriages have all failed in one way or another. I have not succeeded in being recognized by Elizabeth as her successor. The Catholics abroad have turned against me because I was not severe enough with the heretics in Scotland, the heretics in Scotland hate me because I am a Catholic at all.

I have failed.

Once in this melancholy recitation, she poured out her heart to the crucifix, but it seemed as unresponsive and stony as the Lords. She remembered how it had graced the wall of the Abbey of St.-Pierre, and how she had prayed before it when she had taken retreat with her aunt and had decided that her destiny lay in Scotland.

The abbey. It had been so sweet, so tempting, and she had wanted to stay there forever. But no—she had believed that she was being called to Scotland, that God wanted her to do her duty there.

God. I have failed God, too, she thought miserably. I flattered myself that I had a spiritual life. Instead I have lived in a manner to give the people reason to call me whore and even to suspect me of murder.

The crucifix offered her no mercy as it hung on the wall, its Jesus staring at her with cold eyes.

She was allowed to walk about the scant grounds on the island, always with a guard. The castle itself occupied most of the land above water, except for a little enclosed garden. She would stand at the very edge of the low garden wall and look out at the water, across to the little town of Kinross. They said William Wallace had swum the distance, clad in leather, with his sword bound upon his neck. But she was not a swimmer, and had no hopes of ever escaping that way. Idly she wondered if the loch froze in winter, but assumed it did not, else the island would never have served so effectively as a prison. Even the idea of walking across seemed beyond her at that point. Everything seemed beyond her, and she took no pleasure in the dancing butterflies in the water reeds, nor in the shiny iridescent green of the tops of the mallards' heads, nor of the bobbing baby ducks following their mothers.

"The waterlilies will soon open their flowers," said Lord Ruthven, who was her keeper that day.

"I care not," she said, and it was true. Let them open, spread themselves open to the sun, emit the perfume of Cleopatra—it mattered not. They might as well be slimy, festering weeds.

"I was told you like flowers," he said.

"Who told you that?" she answered. "Your sainted father?"

"Mary Seton told me." He smiled at her.

He was trying to be charming. He must want something. How unfortunate for him that it was useless. Even nature could no longer charm her.

"Mary Seton would never talk to you of my likes and dislikes." She sighed. Even this much conversation was wearisome.

"That is where you are wrong. She is anxious to talk about you. We wish you to recover."

Mary reached in her little cloth purse and drew out some bread crumbs and tossed them to the ducks. They came swimming over slowly to investigate, making low sounds that were more gurgles than quacks. Then they began snapping at the food, rustling their feathers and flicking their tails.

"I see." My heart will never recover, she thought. It will remain numb, without desire and without pleasure and without will.

"When you are yourself, you are a Queen indeed," he said.

She looked at him. What an odd thing for him to say. He kept his eyes downcast, as if he did not want her to look into them. He had long lashes that caught the sunlight, and his eyebrows were the exact same colour. His hair was a darker, richer shade. His looks were actually rather winsome.

"A Queen to be deposed," she said. "I have been told you—the Lords— wish me to abdicate."

"Some of them do," he said. "But if you were free—"

She laughed gently. "Ah! If I were free!"

What would I do if I were free? she thought. I fear I would not have the strength to do anything. I have played my strength out. There is nothing left for me but a convent or to be an invalid. It is all I am fit for now. The world seems to me as unappetizing as a platter of pig's offal.

"I could make you free," he was whispering, standing altogether too close.

"What?"

"I have it in my power to set you free. All you have to do is yield yourself to me." He lifted his eyes and looked directly into hers.

He was not jesting. Mother of God, he meant it! Before she could stop herself, she burst out laughing.

"Hush!" he cried, alarmed. He shot a look toward the castle walls in fear that someone had heard. She was still laughing. "Is it that amusing? You can come to my bed; there are no guards in *my* quarters. I want you."

They must truly believe her to be a whore. That this man would expect her to give herself to him, when she was married, pregnant . . . At that moment she realized she had fallen even lower than she had imagined, even in her most despairing moments.

"I am married," she finally said.

"What of it?" he answered. "You were married when you took Bothwell to your bed."

She drew back her hand and slapped him across his smooth cheek. "You are steeped in filth!"

"We have the proof about you and Bothwell. How you took up with him while you were married, how you got him to rid you of your husband!"

"Lies! I never—"

Ruthven smiled, the smile of a victor. "I can promise you pleasure," he said. "And afterwards, freedom."

"The promise of a confederate Lord means nothing. For I surrendered to you all on a promise of being obeyed and served, and instead you have imprisoned me."

"Never trust a group of people. But this is different—an agreement between you and me. A private pact." His voice was smooth near her ear.

She stood, steeped in shame. This is my nadir, she thought. It is more degrading than even signing an abdication would be. It is more humiliating than the ride through Edinburgh, with the people spitting at me. Those moments are a public tragedy, but they are grand as well. This is little, squalid, nasty, and—what did he say?—private.

He took her silence for consideration of his offer. "I said I want you. You fire my blood. I want to taste such heights of pleasure that I will not die ordinary."

"If it were in my power," she finally said, "you would certainly not die ordinary."

"Then you grant me my wish?" he gasped. "I cannot express my joy at your answer!" He tried to grab her hand and kiss it.

"Alas, although I would see to it that your death was not that of an ordinary criminal, but of a felon and traitor, I have no power to carry it out. I can only imagine it, and see you in my mind being gutted and quartered."

He leapt away in fury at his misunderstanding. "Then, if you're fool enough to reject my offer, to turn my love to hate, you can rot here! And you will!" He took her head and turned it in his hands, hands that were strong and unhesitant. "Look out there across the lake. The waters are deep and cold. Before long there will be an unfortunate accident when you try to escape, as you are known to have a habit of doing. Or else you will be taken away to a fortress deep in the Highlands and held there the rest of your life. A living death, I believe it's called by the poetically minded."

"Did they choose you because they wished to subject me to lewd propositions? It would be beneath the integrity of any of the others, who are hardly notable for their integrity."

He took her arm and twisted it, turning her around. "It is time for you to return to your tower. You have between here and there to change your mind. After that it will be too late." He marched her toward the outer castle wall. "Do not imagine that Bothwell can ever come for you again, or that your child will ever be in the succession. If that is why you have said no to my offer, I suggest you think again."

"That is not why," she said. "Were there no Bothwell, and no child, my answer would be the same. You flatter yourself to think otherwise."

"If you think there will be other offers, or better ones, you flatter *yourself*, my lady."

"Thank God there will be no others!" she said. "For the insult is so great I could not endure it twice."

Once back in her little room, she did not dare tell Seton or anyone else of what had just passed between her and Ruthven. It would make the shame even greater if anyone knew. The mute crucifix stared down at her as she silently ate her meal, a meal that was tasteless to her. All food was tasteless to her now.

After dinner she tried to sew. They had brought some of her needlework from Holyrood, along with the threads and frames. But her eyes were tired, and she had trouble focusing. Everything in the pattern reminded her of the humiliating incident. The lion's mane in the panel she was embroidering was the colour of Ruthven's hair, and the green of the background was like the green of the ducks' feathers.

It took all her effort to pull the needle up through the thick canvas that had the pattern drawn on it. This lethargy, this weakness, made her feel very old.

It was while she was drawing out a particularly long brown thread that she felt a sharp twinge in her lower abdomen. It came and went swiftly. But a few minutes later another came, and this one rippled across her belly, taking its time before it, too, disappeared. Before Mary Seton had finished the last verse of the song she had begun at the first stab of pain, a third one had come. This time she recognized it as a horrible, familiar visitor. It was a labour pain.

"No!" she cried, standing up and dropping her sewing. She touched her belly as if expecting to discover something.

Mary Seton stopped playing and looked up.

"I fear—" Mary sat back down. "No, perhaps it is not. Has the fish we had for supper disturbed your stomach?"

Seton shook her head.

Just then Mary felt the pain again. "It is the child!" she cried. "Send for the doctor!" Seeing the look on Seton's face, she said, "There must be one here, for the Douglases! I care not who he is, as long as he is knowledgeable about childbirth! Oh!" She got up and staggered up the stairs to her bedroom.

Throwing herself down on the narrow bed, she waited, holding her breath, willing the pains to stop. Suddenly all her debilitating languor had disappeared and she knew there was still one thing she wanted, and cared about, passionately: Bothwell's child. She must not lose it!

The castle physician, veteran of many births at Lochleven, came quickly. He made her undress and felt her stomach for tenderness.

"Oh, please, save my child!" she begged, crying. They were the first tears she had shed on the island.

He rummaged in a box he had brought, muttering to himself. "A mixture of strong wine and thornapple and English nightshade may work. But it is dangerous, because it is hard to give the proper dose. Too low, and it will not help; too high, and you will be poisoned."

"I will take the chance," she said.

He took out two small bottles and sent for some strong wine. Then, working on the little table in the center of the room, he carefully measured the plants and stirred them into a goblet of rough red French wine. Mary watched him swirl the contents around and hold it up against the candle. While she watched, two more pains came and went.

He diluted the mixture a little and then brought it to her. She drank it; it was bitter and sharp.

"Now close your eyes," he said. "Try to remain as still and calm as possible."

She could hear him walking around the room, rearranging things and making ready. There would be no cradle; if the child was born, it could not survive. She recognized the soft slap of material being folded; these must be the linens they used to staunch blood and tend the wounds incurred in childbirth. There was the clink of copper pans being dried and set aside; one would hold warm water and the other would catch the spurts of blood that would come.

Dear God, she prayed, let none of these things be necessary. Let there be no blood and no birth and no need for bandages and water. I know I have failed you. I ask forgiveness. But do not fail me, do not abandon me. . . .

The potion took effect and made her feel drowsy and dizzy. But the pains continued unabated and ever more frequently. She heard the doctor saying, "Now we must make ready!" in an agitated, disappointed tone, and felt the cold rim of the copper basin being slid under her.

"Push!" he was saying, but she disobeyed him and, crying wildly, tried to hold back the form she felt trying to dislodge itself from within her. It was moving down, in spite of her strongest attempt to prevent it. She clenched her muscles as tightly as she could and shrieked with despair and supplication. But the birth process continued relentlessly, and the physician received a minute, bloody, slippery lump into his hands. It was quickly followed by a second one, as Mary twisted and wept.

"Twins!" he said, in surprise. The tiny things were so early they were never meant to live. He washed them off gently and saw that they were male. Then he wrapped them in soft flannel, just as Mary was calling out for them. Mary Seton was standing by her, holding her hand and attempting to quiet her.

"You know they were born betimes," he said, trying to make the harsh words as kind as possible.

"Let me see them!" she was crying.

"It is not advisable—" the doctor began, but Seton nodded.

"Let her see them. Nothing can hurt her more than what has already happened."

Reluctantly he brought over the little cloth where they lay and let her see them. She stared at them dumbly, then reached out a shaky hand and touched each one once. She closed her eyes and fell back on the pillow. The doctor took them away.

"You will bury them, will you not?" asked Seton. "Do not just destroy them, but give them an honourable burial."

The doctor nodded. "If you wish it." He glanced over at the Queen. "I fear it may take a long time for her to recover fully. Let her rest. And call me if there seems to be anything amiss."

The doctor had barely finished his bedside glass of wine before Seton came for him. "There is a lot of blood," she said. "It started suddenly, and now it won't stop." He hurried across the castle yard and back into the round tower. By the time he got there, the bed was soaked in blood, and more was gushing out. He worked as swiftly as he could, elevating her feet, packing the place from which the blood was issuing with clean cloths, and giving her a draught of dried yarrow and agrimony, again mixed with wine. But it was the middle of the night before the blood finally seemed to dry up at its source and the bubbling stream abated. By that time Mary was white and so debilitated she could barely move. He feared the drugs would overcome her in this weakened state and she would lapse into unconsciousness and possibly die.

By dawn she was slipping in and out of awareness, and her eyelids fluttered shut in spite of all her efforts to keep them open. The struggle seemed overwhelming and pointless. The babies were gone, Bothwell was gone . . . yet, strangely enough, she fought slipping over the edge of darkness, the soft, friendly darkness that beckoned. She wanted, at last and after all, to live.

LX

ary lay all the daylight hours, watching the sunlight move from one window to the next as the sun passed across the sky. Seton brought her soup and fine white bread and red wine to replace the blood she had lost. She lay as limp as a silk scarf draped over a chair, and felt as transparent.

My child—no, children—will never be, she thought. How odd to think of *children* rather than *child.* Boys. They would have been princes, and if they had had half of Bothwell's strength and courage, they would have shone in the annals of Scotland. Gone. And now . . . there may never be a child of ours, never ever, she thought, and grief, as sharp as the labour pains, pierced her.

Bothwell, Bothwell . . . where are you? I used to believe I could send my thoughts far away, and that you could hear them. But now I do not even know where you are.

I am completely and utterly alone. I have never been alone before. There has always been someone, a man, near me to rely on. My uncles in France. Lord James. Riccio. Then Bothwell. I always consulted them, let them guide me. I have never been at my own mercy, with only myself as a source of knowledge.

Had she not been so debilitated, that thought would have been more frightening, more revolutionary. But it only felt like a small part of the enormity of her losses.

The next day the physician pronounced himself pleased with her recovery. The hemorrhaging had ceased, and she had been able to take nourishment, although she showed no real appetite as yet.

"Keep giving her the wine, and see if you can add a little chopped meat to the soup," he told Seton, who had become the chief nurse. "And allow her complete rest—no disturbances."

Nau, who had been looking out the window, suddenly said, "That may be difficult. A boat is approaching, and it is not the laundry maids or the guards, or any of the household from the mainland." The Laird maintained a separate large manor house directly across from the island.

Jane Kennedy joined him at the window. She took pride in her ability to see long distances, saying she had been born with the eyes of a bird of prey. "It is Melville," she said. "And he has a glum look on. He's carrying a large leather pouch."

Mary groaned and made an effort to sit up. "We must admit him, when he comes. *If* he comes here. He may just speak to the Douglases and the other gaolers." Like the unspeakable Ruthven and the vicious, bloodthirsty Lindsay.

The boat landed and they saw Melville get out, then disappear inside the castle grounds. It was near sunset when the expected knock came on Mary's door down below. He was admitted and brought upstairs, where Mary was lying in bed, unable to rise.

She was unexpectedly glad to see him; in this nest of hatred he seemed like a true friend. "Dear Melville," she said, stretching out her hand.

He knelt and kissed it. "Your Majesty," he said, with pain in his voice, "I am distressed to see you in this state."

"Oh, the worst is over," she assured him. "I can only get better, as I am

567

doing hourly. I have had an untimely birth, and it was difficult. But my good doctor here assures me I will fully recover—my body, if not my heart."

"Your Majesty—may I possibly speak with you privately?" He looked around at the attendants.

"Why, yes." Mary watched as her attendants silently left the room and descended the spiral staircase to the public room below. Then she said, "Dear friend, what is it? You look anguished. Is it—is it truly that dreadful?" She drew her breath. "I am ready to hear it, no matter what it portends." And, surprisingly, she was.

"Your Majesty, I will be honest. I have been sent to persuade you to agree to allow young James to be crowned King."

She exhaled. "To abdicate, you mean? Speak it plain."

"Yes." The one word hung there. Then he added, "Let me explain—"

"Yes, there are always explanations. But history never remembers the explanations, no matter how mighty they may be. Only the bare fact stands out, undressed of explanations. But pray tell *me*. I wish to know." She put her hands under her thighs and pulled herself up to a sitting position. Pain shot through her.

He continued kneeling. "This is painful for me as well. I made the journey, as you requested, to England, and spoke directly with Elizabeth. She was outraged at your behaviour since the death of Darnley, and had written a strong letter about it. But when the Lords imprisoned you, it changed her mind. At once she was on your side; she said that no matter what you had done, your subjects had no right to imprison you or judge you, that they owed you obedience, and that only God could judge you. She was ready to send an army to help you. But then—"

"Ah. There is always a 'but then.' Pray rise, and take a seat. I fear this is uncomfortable enough in the telling, without wearing your knees out on the cold stone floor."

Stiffly he rose and brought a stool over to the bedside. He took a long time arranging his breeches and settling himself before continuing. He took a gulp of air and plunged in. "But then the Lords said they would kill you if any English army set foot in Scotland. They have you as a hostage. So Elizabeth was forced to desist, and sent Throckmorton north as ambassador to negotiate with the Lords and talk with you. The Lords refuse him permission to come to Lochleven. They have kept him waiting, dangling, but finally said he may not see you. But he has given me this letter from Elizabeth to give to you."

He fumbled with the scabbard of his sword, and pulled out a folded piece of paper from deep within it. "Here," he said. "I have concealed it here at peril of my own life."

She took it. Her eyes skimmed over it rapidly. Then she handed it back to Melville for him to read.

It is my most sisterly advice that you should not irritate those who have Your Majesty in their power, by refusing the only concession that could save your life. Nothing that is done under your present circumstances can be of any force once you have regained your freedom.

"But how am I to regain my freedom, as there is no one to liberate me? The English army cannot come, and Bothwell—what news of Bothwell? Where is he?" Her voice grew eager.

"Madam, my reports are that he has fled to his uncle the Bishop's at Spynie, but that Balfour, who has betrayed him—"

"Balfour has betrayed him?" she gasped. "When did this happen?"

"Why, he joined the Lords before the battle of Carberry Hill."

"Then his message to us—it was false, and meant to lure us back to Edinburgh! It was a trap!" It was not fate, then, that had done them in, but human villainy.

Melville did not know to what she was referring. "Balfour caught Bothwell's servant in the act of removing certain of Bothwell's papers and effects from the Castle. The Lords took possession of them . . . of your letters to Bothwell, which they claim incriminate you in the King's murder. And they destroyed the rest, the ones that Bothwell was keeping because they incriminate the Lords. Then Balfour's kin made trouble for Bothwell in Spynie, attempted to kill him. He killed *them* instead, but it drove him away. He has left the mainland now and is in the Orkneys, trying to raise a navy. He wants to be a pirate king and have a floating kingdom, so it seems, manned with buccaneers, traders, and soldiers of fortune. A novel concept. He claims that his title as Duke of Orkney, his ancestral rights, and his hereditary title of Admiral of Scotland grant him this privilege."

She smiled. Bothwell was on the sea, where he belonged. And perhaps he would succeed, would actually create a private naval hegemony of his own. He was so daring, imaginative. . . . The loss of his children hit her once again.

Seeing her smile, Melville said, "Kirkcaldy of Grange has sent ships after him to take him dead or alive. Bothwell has five ships with three hundred sailors, and Kirkcaldy eight ships, guns, and four hundred harquebusiers aboard. Their commission was 'to pursue the malefactors with fire, sword, and all other kind of hostility.' It will be a fight to the death, my lady."

It sent shivers through her. "It will be Kirkcaldy's," she said. Bothwell could not die.

"Do you not want to hear what the Lords have pronounced about *you?*" he asked gently. "They say you must resign the crown in order to save your life and honour. If you do not, they plan to charge you with three crimes, using the captured Bothwell letters as proof of them. They are . . ." He opened his bag and poked around in it, finally extracting a paper. "They are these: tyranny, for breach and violation of the common laws of the realm; the murder of the King; and incontinency with Bothwell *and others*, as proved by your own handwriting and sufficient witnesses."

"So they now paint me as a tyrant like Nero and an orgy-mistress like Messalina? Their imaginations eclipse even Rabelais's."

"You have friends," he said. He handed her a turquoise ring. "This is from the earls of Argyll and Huntly, and Hamilton. Maitland is a hidden ally. They support you, but now beg you to save yourself. The Lords of the Secret Council—as the inner circle of your enemies now call themselves— have determined to take your life, either secretly or by a mock trial among themselves. You must do as they say. Anything you sign under duress or in prison is not binding. You may repudiate it as soon as you are free. But to be free, you must be alive."

"Yes. I must be alive."

"Knox has proclaimed a week of fasting, and daily tells the people that if you are not killed, God will send a plague on Scotland. He pushes the Lords, and makes it easy for them to do this. Do not compel them to it."

"I cannot sign. I will die Queen of Scotland."

"Your Majesty, that is just how you will die."

"Then so be it." Her jaw was set.

Melville took her hand and wrung it. "I beg you, consider carefully!"

"I will not sign."

She had barely lain back down after Melville's departure when the door flew open. The crash of the wood against the wall startled her and she grabbed for her covers. Towering in the doorway was Lord Lindsay. He marched over to the bed.

"So you won't sign?" He was waving papers, *the* papers. "I say you'll sign, and sign now, and we'll have no more obstruction from you!" He flung the papers on the little table where the doctor had set out his medicines.

"Shall I set my hand to a deliberate falsehood, and, to gratify the ambition of my nobles, relinquish the office that God has given me, to my son, who is only a year old and incapable of governing the realm? No!"

"It is you who are incapable of governing the realm; even an infant would do better! Now, Madam, I can tell you this"—he grabbed her by the shoulder and yanked her up in bed—"that if you do not sign, you will be smothered between the mattress and these pillows, and then hung up from your bedpost. It will look as if you have killed yourself, so you cannot even have a Christian burial. Pity." Then he grabbed her hand and dragged her out of the bed. She fell heavily to the floor. He dragged her across it and heaved her up into the chair at the table.

He took out his dagger and ran his finger along its blade. Then he licked it, and delicately put its point right up against her left breast. "If you do not sign these documents yourself, I will sign them in your name, using your heart's blood. Yes, I'll just plunge this in and twist a little, dip the point of the pen into the hot red blood that bubbles out, sign 'Marie R.,' and then, when you're dead, cut you into pieces, and throw you in the loch to feed those famous Lochleven trout." He grinned. "I would like to do this, so I hope you will make it necessary."

His eyes were glittering as if with lust.

"No. I will not sign."

He let out a roar of anger and made a tiny X on her skin over her heart. "Come in here!" he yelled. "It is time!"

Melville, Ruthven, and the young George Douglas emerged from the stairwell where they had been waiting, along with the official notaries. Lindsay flicked the knife up and down in front of Mary's eyes.

"The whore won't sign!" he screamed. "But we'll make her sign, won't we?" He reached out and clutched Mary's arm, as if he were trying to break the bones. He tore the skin with his rough fingernails. With his other hand he shoved a pen in her hand, and, covering it with his, formed the words and scratched out *Marie R.* on each of three separate pieces of paper, none of which she was allowed to read.

"There!" He threw the pen down and picked up the papers and blew on them to dry the ink. "It is done!" Triumphantly he rolled them up.

"They lack the seals," she said in a faint voice.

"Those are easy enough to procure. But thank you for reminding me," he said, bowing mockingly. "*Your Majesty.* But no, it's no longer that. What are you now? Lady Bothwell?"

"I am your anointed Queen, and nothing can change that, nothing, nothing!"

"Soon there will be two anointed rulers in Scotland," he said. "If you can find suitable attire, perhaps we'll let you attend the coronation. Would you like that? You always enjoy fêtes, celebrations, don't you? You've wasted enough money on them. The ceremony will be Protestant, of course. So you see, you really did waste those thousands of pounds you spent on the Catholic baptism."

"There cannot be two anointed rulers, and you know it."

"Can't there? What about Saul and David? Saul did as bad a job as you, and so God himself directed that he be replaced, even while he still lived. You still live, but for how long?" Humming, he descended the stairs, the rolled papers tucked under his arm.

Melville followed with a downcast look, Ruthven could not meet her eyes, and George Douglas looked ashamed. The two notaries trailed after them.

❧

Nicholas Throckmorton had little to do in his quarters in Edinburgh. He had arrived almost a month ago, hastening north in the belief that the Lords would be swayed by Elizabeth's threats and promises, and eager to placate her. He had expected to be able to confer with Mary and to negotiate her release. Instead he had been forbidden to see her or even send her letters. The Lords were in no mood to be conciliatory, and they seemed indifferent to Elizabeth's wishes. When he had, in a moment of daring, told them that Elizabeth would punish them if they harmed even a hair of Mary's head, they had shrugged and said that would be regrettable, but that Scotland would survive any English pillaging, as it always had before.

He leaned his head on his hand. What could he do when there was nothing the Scots either feared or wanted from England? They seemed confidently self-sufficient, and politely but firmly rejected his meddling.

He took pen and ink and began another letter to Queen Elizabeth. Writing gave him the feeling that he was doing something, that he was not entirely useless to her. He wanted to capture the dangerous mood here, the almost reckless defiance of fate and custom.

The people were ridding themselves of a monarch on moral grounds. The common people did not ascribe to Elizabeth's neat theory that it was "not in God's ordinance the Prince and Sovereign to be in subjugation to them that by nature and law are subjected to her." They had come to the shocking conclusion that "the Queen hath no more liberty nor privilege to commit murder or adultery than any other private person, neither by God's law, nor by the laws of the realm." The sovereign was no longer above the law—not in Scotland.

The Lords were in complete control—they and the shrieking Knox. They had outlawed Bothwell, put a price on his head, and sent soldiers north to capture him. The Queen's adherents had no leader and were hopelessly disorganized and demoralized. They said they had succeeded in obtaining the Queen's abdication, that she had granted permission for the Prince's coronation and for a regency. They also said she had lost any hope of an heir by Bothwell.

> It is to be feared that this tragedy will end in the Queen's person, after the coronation, as it did begin in the person of David the Italian, and the Queen's husband. I believe I have preserved her life for this time, but for what continuance is uncertain . . .

he was writing, when he heard the heavy tread of footsteps on the stairs. He rose and flung open the door. Lord Lindsay and Maitland were standing there, about to knock. Others were behind them.

"You spare us the trouble, sir," said Lindsay, with a disarming smile. He waited, smugly, to be invited in.

"Pray enter," said Throckmorton, glad he had covered up the letter as a precaution.

"We have the honour to invite you to attend the coronation of the new King," said Glencairn. "It will be held at Stirling two days from now."

"So you have seen the Queen?" Throckmorton asked, deferring an answer.

"The late King's daughter, you mean, and the mother of the King?" asked Lindsay.

"Just as the Pope is also the Bishop of Rome, I suppose?" said Throckmorton. "I mean the fair lady imprisoned at Lochleven. What you style her does not affect what she *is*."

"Quite so." Lindsay laughed at some private joke. "She signed the papers, and we affixed the Privy Seal afterwards. Oh, the poor lady was so burdened with her cares she simply could not carry on. The loss of her dear Bothwell—" He exploded with laughter, making a noise like the hind end of a cow.

Maitland glared at him. "The exact wording of her statement is—" Maitland began, and pulled out a paper and read smoothly:

> "As after long and intolerable pains and labour taken by us since our arrival within our realm for government thereof, and keeping of the lieges of the same in quietness, we have not only been vexed in our spirit, body, and senses thereby, but also at length are altogether so vexed thereof, that our ability and strength of body is not able longer to endure the same. Therefore, and because nothing earthly can be more comfortable and happy to us in this earth than in our lifetime to see our dear son, the native Prince of this our realm, placed in the kingdom thereof, and the crown royal set on his head, we, of our own free will and special motion, have remitted and renounced the government, guiding, and governing of this our realm of Scotland, lieges, and subjects thereof, in favour of our said son."

Now Throckmorton would have laughed if it had not been unseemly. "The language does not sound like Her Majesty's," he finally said.

"You mean 'Her Grace,' " said Lindsay. "What better proof that she is no longer herself? However, she may be well enough to attend, as we assume you will."

"Who else will attend?" Throckmorton asked.

"Oh, all the lords of Scotland."

"Name them."

"We have not finished notifying everyone," said Maitland.

"Well, of the ones you *have* notified?"

"Morton, Atholl, Erskine, Glencairn, Lord Home, Ruthven, Sanquhar."

"Hardly the majority of the leading lords. What of Huntly, Argyll, Hamilton?"

Maitland coughed. "I have had trouble tendering the invitation to them, as they are not in this part of the country."

"Come, sir, your answer!" said Lindsay.

"My answer must be no. I represent the Queen of England, who is greatly displeased by these proceedings and will refuse to recognize James as King. My attending the ceremony would seem to condone it."

"You knew you would refuse; you just wanted us to read the names and the statements so you could report them back to your paymasters! Spy!" snarled Lindsay.

"What a charming manner. Is this how you persuaded the Queen to sign? If you treat the envoy of a neighbouring country thus, I can imagine how you treat someone at your mercy," said Throckmorton in his slow voice. He looked at Lindsay's half-lidded eyes. What an ugly man he was.

"Come. We have other men to speak to," said Maitland, tugging on

Lindsay's sleeve. He gave Throckmorton an apologetic smile. "Good day, sir."

Throckmorton closed the door quietly, then returned to his letter.

All here await the return of the Lord James, the designated Regent. The Lords of the Secret Council are of the mind that once he arrives, he will take the burden from their shoulders. The Queen's friends hope that her brother will be kind and free her once he is firmly in power. But no one truly knows his mind, nor how he will wear the diadem of the Regency. And I fear he may find it fits him so well that he will never willingly lay it down for his nephew.

On July twenty-ninth, 1567—exactly two years since the marriage of his parents—little James Stuart was carried in procession from his nursery at Stirling to be crowned King of Scots and Lord of the Isles. The scanty line of men—only four earls, seven barons, and one clergyman—made their way past the Chapel Royal at Stirling, where the Papist baptism had been performed, carrying the regalia into the Protestant kirk at the gates of the castle. A force of armed men guarded all approaches to the castle grounds.

John Knox was waiting inside. He had been hastily called to preach the sermon at this hasty ceremony, and he had hastened to accept. This was a wondrous moment, one he had often dreamed of, but had left in the Almighty's hands as to timing. The Catholic whore was gone, and never more would there be a coronation ceremony in the old rite. This was a glorious new beginning, and all because many years ago they had stepped out in faith.

Here they came, *his* Lords of the Congregation: the flaming-haired Earl of Morton, the long-faced Erskine, the handsome Ruthven. They bore the baby up to the altar, where his throne awaited, then gathered on the altar steps.

Lord Lindsay unrolled a declaration, and began to read it in loud, ringing tones.

" 'I swear in the presence of God and the Congregation here present that the Queen our Sovereign did resign, willingly and without compulsion, her royal estate and dignity to the Prince her son, and the government of the realm to the several persons named in her commission of regency.' "

The justice clerk, Sir John Bellenden, brought out a gigantic Bible and opened its pages. The Earl of Morton laid his pudgy left hand on it and, holding up his other hand, took the Coronation Oath in Prince James's name. The all-purpose Bishop of Orkney—the same who had married Mary and Bothwell when no one else would—anointed the Prince with the sacred oil. The Earl of Atholl stepped forward and put the crown on the baby's head.

Now it was time, time for his message. Knox mounted the pulpit slowly. His knees were quite stiff now, even in midsummer. He hoped he had been guided to choose the correct text.

"This day, as we welcome our first Protestant sovereign, is the day we have all prayed for. Surely God has preserved him for us, sheltering him amid all the havoc and turmoil in our land. Just so did he for his chosen people of Israel, keeping a king from David's line for them. For the story, as told in Second Chronicles, chapter twenty-two, is this:

"But when Athaliah the mother of Ahaziah saw that her son was dead, she arose and destroyed all the seed royal of the house of Judah.

"But the daughter of the King took Joash the King's son, and stole him from among the King's sons that were slain, and put him and his nurse in a bedchamber. So Joash was hidden from Athaliah, so that she slew him not.

"And he was hidden in the house of God six years, and Athaliah reigned over the land.

"And in the seventh year all the congregation made a covenant with the King in the house of God. And he said unto them, Behold the King's son shall reign, as the Lord hath said of the sons of David.

"Moreover, Jehoiada the priest delivered to the captains hundreds of spears, and bucklers, and shields, that had been King David's, and were in the house of God.

"And he set all the people, every man having his weapon in his hand, from the right side of the temple to the left side of the temple, along the altar and the temple, by the King round about. Then they brought out the King's son, and put upon him the crown, and gave him the testimony, and made him King. And Jehoiada and his sons anointed him, and said, God save the King. Now when Athaliah heard the noise of the people running and praising the King, she came to the people into the house of the Lord.

"And she looked, and behold, the King stood at his pillar at the entering in, and the princes and the trumpets by the King; and all the people of the land rejoiced, and sounded with trumpets, also the singers with instruments of music, and such as taught to sing praise. Then Athaliah rent her clothes, and said, Treason, treason!

"Then Jehoiada the priest brought out the captains of hundreds that were set over the host, and said to them, Have her forth of the ranges: and whoso followeth her, let him be slain with the sword. For the priest said, Slay her not in the house of the Lord. So they laid hands on her, and when she was come to the entering of the horse gate by the King's house, they slew her there.

"Then all the people went to the house of Baal, and broke it down, and broke his altars and his images in pieces, and slew the priest of Baal before the altars.

"And all the people of the land rejoiced: and the city was quiet, after they had slain Athaliah with the sword."

575

Knox took a deep breath. He hoped they had followed the lengthy reading, so apropos of the present events. They were all staring at him. The little King had fallen asleep on the throne.

"Now you, my good friends, are like the true priests of the temple, and the congregation that cleansed the land of the priests of Baal and of the wicked Queen. Here before you is your King, miraculously preserved, as was Joash. And as Joash, who, Scripture tells us, restored the temple, which had been defiled by Baal-worshipers, so this young King James will restore true worship here in our land." Knox paused and cleared his throat. "Athaliah—who was she?" Of course everyone should know. "She was the daughter of Jezebel! Yes, the wicked, wicked Jezebel. We, too, have a Jezebel in our land. And surely she should also be slain, so that we may also have quiet in the land! I say, let the dogs drink her blood!"

The members of the congregation were twitching in their seats. "Having come so far, we should not flinch before the last requirement. She should be slain, but not in the house of the Lord! And so I leave it to you to carry it out."

Knox noticed that Morton was frowning. The Lords had shown a curious reluctance to follow the thing to its logical conclusion. Jezebels and Athaliahs, no matter how pathetic and appealing they could seem when at one's mercy, would always rise to fight and take revenge unless they were utterly destroyed. How could he make them understand the pressing necessity of it?

"I appeal to you to spare not anyone if God commands otherwise. Remember that Abraham stood ready to sacrifice Isaac without question!"

After a concluding prayer, he stepped down from the pulpit. The peers approached the sleeping baby on his throne and, one by one, knelt and did homage. Then the titles of the High and Puissant Prince, James VI of Scotland and the Isles, were proclaimed at the doors of the chapel to the sound of trumpets.

❧

Mary sat at the window recess on the lower-floor room of her tower apartments. It was some eight feet off the ground, a great big belly of a window that protruded out from the tower. From where she sat, she could see across the loch to the other small islands, including the one with ruins of an old monastery on it. The trees were in full leaf and were rustling in the stiff breeze, teasing her with obscured vision.

She had sat thus for two days during the daylight hours, turning her back on the chamber and just staring out the window. It was as if by sitting very still she could keep her thoughts from straying back to the scene enacted in her bedroom. If she just did not move, but concentrated on emptying her mind of all thoughts, then she would feel no pain. It worked for bodily injuries, and she had those as well.

Every time the thought of Lindsay and the papers began to steal into her mind, she obliterated them. But still there were the reminders of the abrasions on her arm where he had grabbed her, and though she kept them covered with her shawl, they hurt.

I am still alive, she thought, feeling like a liar as she mouthed the words. But why did she feel dead?

Because, said her intellect briskly, you have lost a kingdom, a husband, and all your children—born and unborn, all in a short space of time. But the truth is you are not dead, only stunned.

Your words are but wearying words, she answered herself. You tire me and convince me not. I have no desire to do anything ever again but to sit here.

Believe me, you will rise from the chair and find there is still delight in the world, and that there is no such thing as a final battle.

She smiled at the lecturing of her sensible, worldly self. But it was no use. Tell that to Marc Antony after Actium, to Richard III after Bosworth Field, she answered. Some battles are final; in some cases we know it at the time, and in others not until much later. I have lost all, I tell you.

Bothwell still lives, and Lord James is returning, the Prince has not been crowned yet, and Elizabeth of England has shown herself your friend; she is the only ruler to have stepped forward for you in this dark hour. How can you say you have "lost all"? You yourself know that the papers you signed have no validity since they were signed under duress.

Yes, Bothwell still lives. . . . At that thought, her heart stirred a little. Perhaps there was hope. Where there's life, there's hope, tiresome people said. But there was truth in it.

What date was it? She had lost track of time since coming here. She and Bothwell had parted on June fifteenth, and they had brought her here late the next night, June sixteenth. And then she had lain ill for . . . how long?

"What date is it?" she asked, in a voice so soft Mary Seton could hardly hear her.

But at the slightest sound from her mistress, she flew across the room. "What?" she asked breathlessly. The Queen was talking!

"I asked if you knew what the date is," she said, her voice a whisper.

"Why—July twenty-ninth." Should she add the year?

July twenty-ninth. Her wedding day to Darnley. It seemed impossible that it had been only two years ago. Even her time in France seemed, somehow, nearer.

She nodded and patted Seton's arm. "The dancing leaves make a very intricate pattern," she said. "Perhaps you should sketch them, and we could make a tapestry based on it. See, the darker green of the oaks with their rounded edges, with the oval, thin lighter green of the birches would be most subtle and unusual."

"Aye. I will use the charcoal and a handkerchief." When she saw her mistress looking at her oddly, she said, "We are allowed no pens, inks, or papers."

"Ohh!" So they would keep her from writing anything, except her signature on an abdication! No letters at all? How could a queen not correspond with the world?

How could she make her plight known to anyone?

A sickening feeling came over her, like a hand tightening around her chest. To be deprived of the power of speech to those out of earshot . . . She felt like a mute, a helpless mute.

"I see," she finally said.

What difference did it make, anyway? She was dead, as good as in the tomb. This stone room was nothing but a sepulchre. Dead people did not write letters, and was she not among them? Had she not just said so?

But somehow it was different to have no choice, not to be *able* to write if she wished. It aroused in her a fierce, burning desire to do so. And Bothwell—unless she found a way to write, that meant she would never speak to him again, in any form whatsoever.

A bright sparkle caught her eye. It seemed to be leaping and quivering, and even as she watched it grew taller. A fire. Someone had lit a fire on the grounds near the boat landing.

The size of it continued to grow, until it gave off great rolling clouds of smoke and obscured her view of the loch. She heard people around it start laughing and cheering.

It was a bonfire. What was it for?

Then she heard the startling boom of the castle ordnance firing from the walls. The report was so loud that even the floor shook in her room. She jumped up in fright. Were they being attacked?

The cannon continued to fire, one after another, in a salute.

"Send for George Douglas," she told Mary Seton. "Ask him what this is." She could have asked her guards, but they were surly louts who would take pleasure in pretending not to understand the question. George had shown himself to be pleasant, and he alone, of everyone in the castle, never mocked her in any way. And he was a handsome young man, even if a trifle unworldly.

Quick as a garden snake, a thought passed through her mind: Perhaps George would bring me paper and ink. Immediately she felt ashamed. But the discovery of just how strict her imprisonment was, coupled with the realization that she had no way to affect it by any outside help, infuriated her. If they treat me thus, how can I be blamed if I use any weapon that comes to hand to help myself? They have taken everything else from me. Nothing remains but whatever sympathy I can excite in someone's heart. If I cannot write to my friends outside the castle, then I must create new friends inside it.

Interesting thoughts for a dead person, her intellect said with amusement. I told you you would rise from the chair, my lady.

George Douglas was standing in the doorway, looking awkward. He had beautiful colouring: very fair skin, eyes the colour of wild hyacinths, and thick, wavy black hair. That was good; she had an aversion to the red-haired Douglas type of colouring, but that was probably because it reminded her of Morton, who exemplified it.

"Yes?" he said.

"Master Douglas," she said, wrapping her shawl about her, "what is the reason for the firing of the cannon salute? And why have you lighted a bonfire?"

"I—I—Let my father tell you!" he blurted out, growing even paler. Before she could stop him, he bolted out the door, leaving her standing in the middle of the room, alone.

She waited, growing more uneasy. At length the Laird William Douglas entered, using a walking stick.

"Good sir," she said, trying to sound pleasant, "wherefore have you fired a cannon salute? And lit a bonfire?"

He blinked at her. What a weak, weedy little man. He seemed older than his thirty-four years, and made of flimsy stuff compared to his thickset half-brother, Lord James. It was as if James had usurped all the good building material from their mother's womb and left William with barely enough to constuct a human being.

William coughed and, taking out a handkerchief, honked into it. Then he put it away and, leaning on his cane, said, "We celebrate a glorious family event today. The fortunes of the Douglases have risen to the highest pitch. For we have a new King in Scotland, and my brother, the Lord James, will be Regent."

A cold shiver went through her, in spite of the warm July day. "Today?"

"Aye. Today, at Stirling, the Prince was crowned. Anointed, and crowned!"

"Today?"

"Not two hours ago, my lady."

"Ohhh!" It was like a physical blow to her, and she fell to her knees as if she had been struck. "Ohh! O heaven, take pity!" she cried, and great sobs shook her.

A few moments earlier, she had not known she had anything left yet to lose.

❧

The following days passed quietly. After six weeks in which event after event, each one more shocking and profoundly hurtful than the one before, had followed like toys strung on a rope pulled by a child, it seemed odd to have nothing happen. Mary wept some days, lay down and rested some days, walked some days, prayed some days, read some days. Gradually, without her being aware of it, the days sorted themselves out and she no longer lay awake all night and dozed all day. She knew what day it was, even down to the saint's day, although no priest was permitted her. She began working on the embroidery she and Seton designed. She began to enjoy her meals occasionally, and drank too much wine once in a while.

She wrote to Melville, asking him to deliver her some clothes that she had left behind at Holyrood.

They moved her to the square tower keep across the courtyard, into her old quarters, where she had stayed in happier days. Her tapestries, the series of ten depicting hunting scenes in green and yellow silk, were rehung, and the walls had been freshly plastered during the month she had been in the other tower. This one had wide fireplaces and even an eastern window that had been used as an oratory, a Catholic prayer niche, earlier. They brought out the original Madonna (stored away now that the family was firmly Protestant) for it, and she hung the crucifix nearby.

In some ways she missed the isolation of the round tower, because now she was annoyingly near the rest of the Douglas family, and they could watch her much more closely. She assumed that was why they had moved her here. On the other hand, she could watch them, study them, and get to know their habits and weaknesses; and she could see George Douglas many times in passing. She always contrived to look at him from underneath her downcast eyes. She caught him staring at her often. When she did, he would blush furiously.

George was a man who should have been born at least two hundred years earlier, or perhaps even served at King Arthur's court. He and Bothwell were the only men she had ever known who truly believed in settling things through trial by single combat. He and Bothwell . . . perhaps they were alike in many ways. Perhaps Bothwell had been like George when he was very young, before his father had taught him that the world was a nasty place and true knights did not fare well. Bothwell . . .

She would sit and dream of Bothwell, wondering where he was and what was happening. She gathered, from the guarded conversations of the Douglases, that Kirkcaldy had not encountered him yet in his pursuit north. Once she heard Lindsay talking about what they would do to him when they caught him, and even the Laird said, "You must not merchandise the bear's skin before you have caught the bear."

Ruthven suddenly disappeared from the island, removed from his position. Lindsay muttered about how he might have to do the same if it would manage to get him taken from this odious duty. But why Ruthven was gone she did not know. It was a pleasure not to have to encounter him any longer, although he had actually been surprisingly gentle with her since that horrible afternoon. Perhaps he had been ashamed after all, like a normal person.

She had managed to get George to bring her pen and ink, although she had not found anyone to carry letters for her. That would come in time, she thought. In the meantime it felt good to be able to write again; it made her feel stronger. She had noticed that George had a habit of supporting lost causes; monasteries, the crusades, Troy, Carthage, and Constantinople all excited him. Perhaps she was another lost cause in his mind, and therefore alluring.

The Lord James had arrived back in Scotland, so she heard. He had come through England, taking his time, conferring with Elizabeth and Cecil, and finally had reached Edinburgh. She knew that he would come to Lochleven, and she was grateful that she had had these two weeks to rest and be restored before encountering him. He must see that she was herself again: calm, in good health, clear-headed. When he realized that, he would have to make arrangements to alter what had been done by the Lords in his absence. He would not take the regency, but recommend that she be restored to power . . . if . . .

There was always an *if*. The *if* would be that she allow him to be her Cecil, her most senior adviser. That she would agree to. It seemed a small price to pay at this point. And had he not been that, in the beginning, before Darnley? He and she had governed well together. Those days seemed almost idyllic, when all they had had to worry about was the senior Huntly's revolt.

She almost laughed in remembering it. Why, there were no problems at all, none to speak of, for four years! My biggest problem was pestering Elizabeth to recognize me as her successor, and trying to decide whom to marry, which foreign prince to favour. And there was Knox, of course, but he was more like a buzzing fly, or a crocodile snapping at a distance. Oh, I did not know what a paradise I lived in then!

I will impress James with my regained health and sensibility; I will persuade him to liberate me and restore me to my throne, with him at my side as a reward.

❧

It was Assumption Day, August fifteenth. Every Assumption Day as long as Mary could remember, she had marked the day in some way, and in France it had been a day of celebration. Now, on Lochleven, without any way to observe it formally, she knelt before the Virgin in the embrasure in the misty dawn. She did not speak to the Blessed Mother, even in her mind, but just let the peace of the presence wash over her. She had prayed herself out of words, and now wished to rest in silence. She still did not feel able to meet the gaze of the eyes on the crucifix.

She could hear the lapping of the water near the castle wall, could hear the deep rumbling croaks of the frogs. They called all night, in a chorus to remind her that all creatures had their amours. She had found them soothing, although her companions—a daughter and granddaughter of Lady Douglas—who had been posted in her bedroom complained of the noise.

The ladies slept on, snoring quietly. Her own attendants were forced to sleep on the floor above, adjoining Nau in his quarters.

A little privacy, here, in the pearl-blue dawn, was all Mary could hope for. Day and night she was attended. The privacy, the privilege of being able to kneel unobserved, was like a gentle soothing of aloe-balm.

A few moments later, after listening to make sure the women were still asleep, she drew out the paper on which, whenever she had the rare chance, she was composing a letter to Bothwell. How he would get it she did not know, but when the opportunity to send it suddenly came, the letter would have to be already written. With a silence that she had taught herself well, she wrote quickly.

> My dearest heart, my soul, it is now almost two months since I have beheld your face, a thing I never thought I could have sustained. My misery is beyond what I once thought it was in the human soul to endure. Without you, I have lost the best part of myself, but my constant fear for your safety has turned ordinary yearning and fierce desire and regret into fearsome torture. They speak of you in the vilest manner, and torment me by withholding what they know of your whereabouts and state. . . .

A groan and a stirring from the other room sent Mary quickly back to the prie-dieu. When Euphemia Douglas emerged from the bedroom, rubbing her eyes, she saw the Queen of Scots on her knees, hands folded, eyes closed in adoration.

The rest of the day passed as all the days there passed: occupied in minute, harmless, inconsequential actions. Mary strolled by the water's edge—accompanied by her gaolers—played at archery, and even danced a bit when the castle fiddler played "The Bride of Loch Lomond" on the castle green. In the shade of an oak, she and her two ladies sat and played cards, and invited the garrison soldiers to join them. Some of the friendlier ones did, and they sat on the grass and played Triumph as the shadows grew long.

The company of the castle always ate separately from Mary, who was served in her apartments, and as suppertime drew near, Mary ended the card game and prepared to return to the tower. Just then she saw a boat full of people making its way toward the western landing stage.

"Jane! Who is that?" she asked.

Jane Kennedy shaded her eyes and looked hard. " 'Tis Lindsay," she finally said, and Mary shuddered. It had been pleasant without him these past few days, when he had gone to Edinburgh for more directions from his masters. "And Morton. I recognize his red hair."

Morton! Then this was a delegation of some sort. What could they want now? She had given them everything. Except . . . her life.

"And Lord James!" Jane clutched her sleeve. "And Atholl, sitting in the rear."

Lord James! He had come at last—but with Morton and Atholl. What did this mean?

Mary walked down to the castle gate and waited for it to open. She wished she had had an opportunity to have her hair combed and rearranged. Without her wigs she felt altogether too much like an ordinary woman and not enough like a queen. Only wigs made it possible to have huge mounds of hair that cried out for a crown.

The gates swung open with a creak and the four men strode in, Lord James leading. He saw her at once, but no hint of a smile softened his stony face. Instead he nodded jerkily, like a puppet whose strings are stiff. "Your Grace," he said.

"Welcome, Your Grace," someone else was saying, but it was addressed to James, not to her. Never before had she heard him addressed thus; it was a title for the children of kings and of high-ranking prelates.

"Thank you," he said, accepting the honorific. "You look well," he finally said to Mary, staring at her like a little boy who suddenly finds a snake in his path.

"And you," she said. "Your sojourn on the Continent must have agreed with you." She did not mean the words to sound sarcastic, but they did. What had struck her was how rested and preserved he looked. He had absented himself during all the crucial moments of terror, and it showed.

Morton, Atholl, and Lindsay came up and flanked him, as if daring her to charge at them. They looked almost afraid of her.

"Come," said Mary. "I look forward to speaking with you, dear brother." She turned and led him toward the tower, and then up the stairs. To her dismay, the other three came along and stood there in the main room with James. She cast him imploring looks, but he ignored them and made no effort to dismiss the other men. Lindsay had his usual sneer on, and Morton was repulsive to her. She could not bear to look upon him. Atholl was a cipher.

"My dear sister," Lord James said, clearing his throat. "I see here that you are well cared for." He glanced around the chamber.

"Well cared for? I have barely any clothes, nor is there any appointment for me as queen—no canopy of estate, nor even a cloth of estate."

He gazed at her steadily, still no hint of a smile, still with the peculiar immobility that made him seem waxlike. "I will have clothes sent," he said. "And as for keeping of a queen's estate—there is no longer any need of that."

"If it is indeed possible for me to resign my office, as you"—she glared at Lindsay—"claim, then there is no longer any reason to keep me a prisoner. If it is as a queen that I am being held prisoner, then I should be allowed the appurtenances of a queen. You cannot have it both ways."

"This is a most troublesome case," said James. "Although you have resigned your crown, there are superstitious people who may be confused."

"I am sure you are not among them, nor are your mother and family."

The more she talked, the more remote he grew, until she felt that he had died abroad and been replaced by a facsimile made of some Italian stone that was the colour of flesh and could pass, except under close inspection, for a human being. Was the real Lord James lying dead of fever in Venice, while this clever copy was sent north to Scotland?

Lord James. She tried to remember exactly what he had been like as a child. Had he laughed, sung, bent? When had this creeping coldness stolen into him and taken away all the warmth?

". . . and thus we will take our leave," he was saying, as the kitchen maids were entering with her food.

"No!" she said. "Please eat supper with me, brother."

"Nay. I dine with the Lords in the main dining hall."

"I remember when you served me on bended knee, handing my napkin to me," she said quietly. "You did not consider that beneath you. And now you will not even sit with me."

He turned to the Lords. "May I have permission to remain?" he asked. Only when they nodded did he allow himself to sit.

The door clanged shut. The Lords were gone. She could hear their heavy footsteps descending the stone steps. Now James could speak freely.

"Yes?" he said, colder than the waters of the loch, turning his grey eyes on her.

"James!" she said. "Why do you speak so artificially to me? This is not you, but some impostor. Unless the other James was the impostor until now."

"How dare you speak of impostors!" he snapped, throwing his hat on the floor. At once his face rearranged itself into the lines and planes of a living person. "You, who have raised the art of dissembling to the highest pitch! You, who deceive everyone!"

His fury was strange to behold. "Dear James—" She touched his arm, and he shook it off in revulsion.

"You wanted me alone, so you could bend me to your will. You overestimate your charms. I am proof against them, Madam! When we were children, and you were that pretty, laughing little girl, riding your ponies and playing at hide-and-seek, then I loved you. But France changed you; you came back here steeped in the art of lying and deception. Knox was right about you! He said, after that first interview, 'such craft I have not found in one so young, no, and if there be not in her a proud mind and crafty wit, my judgement faileth me.' But I could not see it; I was blind."

Mary was shocked at his twisting of the truth. "No, you were not blind, just greedy. As long as you could be my chief minister, you cared not if I were a Caligula! You were always ambitious, James, and eager to wear a crown. It was *I* who was blind."

Hold your tongue, she told herself. This is no way to ingratiate yourself with him, or win his confidence. He is your only hope of being restored to liberty.

". . . George," he was saying.

"What?"

"I said you are as serpentlike as ever. You have been attempting to make my brother George fall in love with you, so that you can escape, and you so thoroughly inflamed Lord Ruthven that he has had to be removed from office!"

"What? Is that what he said?"

"He said nothing. It was his looks and the way he acted, like a lovesick duck—"

"Let me tell you what really happened with the noble Lord Ruthven!"

"I will not hear your lies! Doubtless you will attempt to make a satyr of him, to say you gave him no encouragement. But nothing you say carries any weight any longer. Not now that the letters have come to light!"

"I do not understand."

"The letters you wrote Lord Bothwell, in which you revealed that you were lovers and that you went to Glasgow to bring your husband back to Edinburgh so Bothwell could kill him." James was pacing the chamber, his voice rising.

"I will be honest with you," she said. "I did love Lord Bothwell, and I did go to Glasgow to see my husband, for private reasons of my own. But Bothwell did not want me to go; he tried to prevent me from it. He did not want me to go near the King, because he was diseased. But I insisted. And, not to besmirch the dead, but it was the King who brought *me* to Kirk O'Field to be murdered. The choice of site was his, and it was he who packed it with gunpowder. I was grieved that he died by his own method. But I would be as false as you claim if I pretended I wished to have been in his place, however much others may have wished it."

"You have dishonoured our father's house," said James, ignoring what she had just said. "Your actions since the murder have cast shame on you yourself, on your throne, and on all Scotland. An honest person would have caused the murder to be investigated, and would have hidden nothing."

"If I had investigated it too closely, many of the Lords would have been made uncomfortable. For they are implicated as well. I know there was a bond signed to murder the King. Bothwell showed it to me. It had your name on it, and Morton's, and Argyll's, and Huntly's, and Maitland's—all the fine Lords of the Secret Council."

"Where is it? Does Bothwell have it?" he asked sharply.

"Bothwell gave it to me when we parted. Lord Morton tore it up."

"Ah." James smiled.

"But the guilty ones know who they are! And—"

"And therefore they are not safe as long as you live," said James smoothly. "They will seek your death. Indeed they already seek it."

She gasped.

"But I will not permit it," he said. "As long as I am Regent I can make that a condition of my office. Should anyone else become Regent . . ." He left the phrase dangling, threatening.

"And will the noble Lords obey you? There is an old Scottish saying, 'He who will not keep faith where it is due will not keep it where it is not due.' I am the King's true daughter and an anointed queen; you are his baseborn son. If they rebelled against me—"

"Madam, I will not make your mistakes!"

"No, but you will make others. And now the people are apt to be less and less forgiving of mistakes, like a finicky woman who finds she must reject a dish unless it is perfect, even though she started out able to stomach ordinary food well enough." He looked uneasy. Now was the time to press her point. "It is not too late. Things can be restored. I have learned much, and neither will I make those mistakes again. Together we can—"

He looked at her, incredulous. "Do you not understand? The people call for your death. It is all we can do to hold them back; that is why you are here, surrounded and protected by water. I can guarantee your life, but not your liberty. And if you were restored, what of Bothwell? No one will tolerate him, and yet you will not leave him. No, there is no hope. It is over for you."

"James!" She threw herself, sobbing, against his chest. It was hard and unyielding. "I am not yet five and twenty—"

His arms hung down, heavy, by his side. He did not attempt to embrace her or comfort her.

"James, what of Bothwell?" she said, between sobs.

"Always Bothwell!" He pushed her away. "You continue to crave the poison that has killed you. Very well, then—it may please you to know that I have sent a fleet of ships to take him where he is hiding in the Orkneys. The officers aboard have been given jurisdiction to hold a court then and there. What that means, dear sister, is that he will be tried and executed on the spot. Then they'll send his head, arms, and legs back here—as they have sent back the heads and limbs of his men they've already caught. Dalgleish, Powrie, Hay, and Hepburn are decorating the gates of Leith, Haddington, and Jedburgh—or rather, certain parts of them are."

She glared at him. "So they were silenced before they could implicate the Lords. I suppose that is the purpose of the faraway trial of Bothwell, as well."

"You are finally becoming politically astute," he said. "Pity it comes too late."

"May I remind you of what even your brother the Laird has said? He said you cannot merchandise for the bear's skin before you have the bear."

James smiled. "I know nothing of bears, but Bothwell's flagship is called the *Pelican*, and we will make him disgorge the fish in his bill, never fear."

LXI

othwell looked out across the sparkling waters of Bressay Sound, where his little fleet lay at anchor. He had eight ships at his command; five had been his as Admiral of Scotland, and another had been on its way to Lord James laden with food and armaments when he and his men had boarded her in Cromarty Firth and taken her. The fact that it had been bound for St. Andrews to succour the Lord James and his men made its despoiling all the more delightful. The Admiral had struck the first blow in their personal battle.

Next Bothwell had sighted a trading ship and taken out a lease on her. The last ship he had acquired was a fine two-masted vessel armed with guns, the *Pelican,* which he had leased from a Hanseatic merchant at a trading station at the far south of Shetland. He had seen her lading fish as he passed by from the Orkneys, and she had caught his eye.

He had had to make a hurried retreat from the Orkneys. Things had not gone according to plan there. Although he was Duke of Orkney and the descendant of the first Earl of Orkney, one of the Balfour brothers was sheriff of the islands and held the royal castles of Kirkwall and Noltland. When Gilbert Balfour fired on him and refused to admit him to the castle, he suddenly knew why Balfour in Edinburgh had sent that urgent message the night of June fourteenth, urging him to leave Dunbar. The Balfours had secretly gone over to the Lords long before Carberry Hill, then. At the same moment, as he gave orders for the ships to sail on, to the Shetlands, he realized what this meant for Geordie Dalgleish, whom he had confidently sent to the castle to retrieve his papers and goods. He had sent him straight into the viper's nest.

The ships ploughed on through the churning, choppy seas. This far north it was always cold, and often there were mists on the waters. The northernmost Orkneys were fifty miles north of the tip of Scotland and the Shetlands began sixty miles north of that.

Bothwell was disappointed and alarmed to be driven off the Orkneys. Aside from the fact that he had always had a fondness for the islands, for the varied landscape and the people who spoke a strange tongue called Norn, and who took as their past kings Vikings like Earl Thorfinn the Mighty, he felt as if he were being swept out to sea and away from Scotland.

He had had little luck in his attempts to raise troops to free the Queen. At first he had moved about freely enough, and several lords, like the Hamiltons at Linlithgow and Fleming at Dumbarton, and the ever-changing Argyll and Boyd, had pledged themselves to the royal cause. But when he went north to Strathbogie to consult with Huntly, his former brother-in-law had shown his true colours. He had turned against Bothwell when Jean Gordon had returned home and spoken ill of him. Huntly was no longer an amiable ally, but the outraged brother of a betrayed sister.

Even in his uncle the Bishop's palace at Spynie in the far north, his enemies had managed to turn things against him. The Bishop's bastard sons formed a plot to assassinate him, and although he had killed them instead, obviously he could not remain. It was there he had first formed the idea of concentrating his power upon the sea, since it seemed there was no safe footing for him on the mainland, in spite of the upwards of fifty names he had secured for the Queen's cause, including those of Seton, Livingston, Kerr, Ormiston, and Langdon.

With the return of Knox, the abdication of the Queen, the Queen's strict imprisonment, and finally his own outlawry, the scales had begun to tip and more and more people deserted the royal cause and made their own peace with the Lords. His servants John Blackadder and John Hepburn of Bolton, whom he had sent south to Dunbar with letters to his friends, were both captured, tortured, and executed. The Lords, in outlawing him, forbade anybody of every estate and degree to "supply the Earl in their houses, or to support him with men, armour, horse, ships, boats or other furnishing by sea or land" on pain of being judged "plain partakers with him in the horrible murder."

Still he had his eight ships and a company of good fighting men, and the Shetlands lay ahead as a base. If that did not work, there was always Sweden or Denmark or France. He could make for them over the open sea.

The Shetlands had welcomed him, and their overlord, Oliver Sinclair, had honoured him as a kinsman, as Bothwell's mother was Lady Agnes Sinclair. It seemed that the sad news about him had not penetrated this far north, and in any case the people liked to think themselves not obliged to follow decrees from Edinburgh. Both the Shetlands and the Orkneys had been Norwegian until 1468, when they were given to Scotland as part of a dowry for the wife of James III, and they had never felt very Scottish. Here, too, they spoke Norn, and on both sets of islands the old longhouses of the Vikings remained. The people here were taller than those on the mainland, and more of them had blue eyes. They were intensely involved with the sea.

Bothwell had been able to anchor his ships and allow his men to roam the island, stocking up on food and water and fitting the vessels for either a fight or a long voyage. His own trusted messengers were able to slip through to the south and bring him both some coveted and hurtful documents: the proclamation naming him Duke of Orkney and Lord of the Shetlands, the commission issued by the Lords to hunt him down, the proclamation branding him an outlaw—and a letter from Mary.

He had descended into his cabin and shut the door before opening the letter. His fingers were trembling; he could hardly believe she had managed to write a letter and smuggle it out, and that it had found its way into his hands all the way here. It seemed almost like an apparition, one of those false sights conjured up by dark spirits to fool people and lead them to doom. *Her* handwriting, something so commonplace before, and now so precious . . . He broke the seal.

> My dearest heart, my soul, it is now almost two months since I have beheld your face, a thing I never thought I could have sustained. My misery is beyond . . .

The Lords had completely betrayed her. They had broken all their promises made at Carberry Hill, as he had told her they would.

Mary, Mary! he cried to himself. I should have truly kidnapped you then, and taken you to Dunbar.

He continued reading, devouring every detail of her life under lock and key at Lochleven. It sounded so dreary, so soul-deadening. There was no one there to sustain her, except Mary Seton and some others of her old household, and the island seemed escape-proof—not that any place is truly escape-proof, he reminded himself. And she must have some sympathetic supporter there somewhere, or else the letter could never have got out. Who could it be? She did not say, as was wise.

He ached to hold her, just to speak with her, even if through bars.

We do not deserve this! he thought. For me to be hunted like a wolf, and her to be locked up like the insane Earl of Arran. I am indeed to be hunted like a wolf; that is what the proclamation of outlawry says. Very well, then—they shall see that this wolf has long fangs. I will tear their flesh.

He folded the letter, but did not put it in his locked leather pouch with the other documents, for he knew he would reread it many times before he would finally allow himself to put it away. His heart felt heavier than his two-handed sword. He tried to tell himself that they were still strongly bound, but truly he wondered if he would ever see her again.

Heaving himself up from the cramped, ill-lighted cabin, he went up on deck. The *Pelican* had only two masts and was not a warship, but at least she carried guns in case of pirate attacks. These were not expensive brass guns, but the cheaper iron, and included port pieces, slings, fowlers, and hailshot pieces, in addition to handguns and harquebuses that he himself had provided for the soldiers to use.

The *Pelican* rocked gently on the swells of the water where she lay at anchor. Today, late in August, the waters were still relatively calm. That could change at any moment, and the rocks and shoals were always treacherous, even in summer. There were more than a hundred islands in the Shetland archipelago, and many of them were nothing but sharp, dark rocks hungry for a ship to gash open. He was thankful he had been able to procure a number of local sailors who knew their native waters so well.

The big canvas sails were furled and tied with their intricate pattern of ropes, awaiting a chance to open and fill with the wind. But for now, barrels of fresh water were being filled and brought aboard, and the men were out all over the main island, exercising themselves and trying to find food. Not that there was an abundance of it on this rocky, barren island; unlike the Orkneys, there was little land suitable for farming here, and the people lived mainly by fishing.

If a man had a mind to wander, this empty, stark land would speak to him. Bothwell found its very harshness stirring, and for the first few days he had walked out under the sky, which seemed enormous, listening to the sea, watching the birds that nested in the rocky cliffs rearing up, ragged and black, from the sea. He liked the solitude, after being too much among men. Sometimes he would get a glimpse of a band of dark little wild ponies, but they always kept their distance, as if they, too, had had all they wished of man and his ways. The wind whistled about his ears, and Bothwell, who hated hats, understood why the Shetlanders wore those close-fitted wool caps.

Bothwell glanced up at the sun. It must be nearly noon, and time for him to keep his appointment to take his midday meal with his cousin Sinclair in his manor house on shore. He enjoyed the man, enjoyed talking of their ancestral rascals, enjoyed hearing about the way life was lived in the islands. Every day his cousin would have a suggestion about a sight that might interest Bothwell: a peculiar, ancient, round stone dwelling; St. Ninian's Isle, with the remains of the holy monk's dwelling; a beach with basking seals.

Today promised to be no different. As he settled himself down at table, ready enough to taste some wine, Sinclair, who delighted in offering rare imports, was smiling at him.

"Good cousin," he said, lifting the flagon to pour out some bright wine, "I have today some strong sweet wine from Cyprus." He tasted it and nodded. "It has taken a long time to get here, but has not spoiled. The Venetians in their galleys can bring it quickly."

Bothwell sipped it and looked out across the water to his ships. Four were anchored here, and four in a harbour on the other side of the island. The sun had shone in cloudless splendour today, and its brilliance on the water was breathtaking. Each ship seemed etched against the intense blue of the sea and sky, a dark, rich blue that made the skies elsewhere seem weak or diluted.

"Thinking of your captains and men?" asked Sinclair.

"Aye. I was wondering what they were doing this morning. I hope they have not caused trouble in town. I have kept the sailors on board; they are generally the worst."

Sinclair laughed. "One can understand why the galley-rowers are kept chained."

"Aye." He got a warm feeling, thinking of the Balfours having served in the galleys years ago. The double-dealing traitors. They were liars and betrayers from far back.

The servants were just bringing out the mackerel and oysters when Bothwell suddenly caught sight of something out of the corner of his eye, moving on the water. Instantly he put down his knife and went to the window.

Eight ships, moving fast toward his, lying at anchor. Quickly he jumped up and shaded his eyes for a clearer view.

"Why, what is it?" asked Sinclair.

"They have come," Bothwell said. "My men!" He suddenly realized his horrible predicament. "The soldiers are all ashore! There is no one to fight!" Throwing down his napkin, he raced out of the house. Sinclair followed.

They stopped at the top of a cliff overlooking the harbour. The ships of the Lords were closing in, when suddenly all four of Bothwell's ships in the harbour hoisted sail, cut their cables, and fled.

"They decided not to wait to be boarded," said Bothwell, approvingly. "But the full complement of men is still ashore!"

As they watched, the chase began. Bothwell could see the biggest ship of the Lords, the *Unicorn*, pursuing hotly. Clearly it felt itself to be the leader, the one meant to run him to ground. It had to be manned by Kirkcaldy and his archenemy, William Murray of Tullibardine—the man who had started the placard campaign against him. Grange, that lying, foul, false bastard! And Tullibardine, in the pay of the Lords to frame him for the murder!

Would I were aboard, he thought, I'd welcome a grapple with you and make sure I cut your throats, no matter what.

As it was, he had to watch helplessly from shore as the ships ran north out of Bressay Sound.

One of his ships was slow. They had nicknamed it *Tortoise*, for it always lagged behind and was incapable of matching the others in speed. Now the *Unicorn* marked it out for a victim and was following it closely, catching up with every second.

The captain of the *Tortoise* managed to keep just ahead. Then, suddenly, it looked as if he had lost control; as Bothwell watched, the *Tortoise* was driven into an area where the waters became milky with foam from hidden rocks. It steered directly for the breakers, in a brave, seemingly suicidal gesture. Then the ship, which only grazed her keel on the rocks, shot up and out through the cresting foam into deeper waters.

Too late to alter course, the bulky *Unicorn* followed in its wake, and from his lookout point Bothwell saw the vessel shudder and strike. She was stuck on the rocks, and lurched to one side. Dozens of sailors and soldiers were flung overboard, falling like little pieces of dust. A boat was let down, and quickly it was jammed with people. Someone jumped from the *Unicorn*'s deck into the boat, causing it to spin around and almost sink. Then, even while Bothwell and Sinclair were watching, the *Unicorn* sank in the roiling waters. Bothwell gave a hoot of delight.

"He did it on purpose," said Sinclair. "The captain of that ungainly ship knew her draught and knew the water around the rocks, down to an inch, I'll warrant." He laughed. "What a feat of seamanship!"

The rest of the pursuing fleet had to stop and rescue their fellows, and Bothwell's ships disappeared from sight over the horizon.

"They will anchor at Unst," said Sinclair, "and wait for you there. That is the northernmost island. Gather your men and head north. Here, I will give you horses." He clapped Bothwell on the back. "Pity our meal was interrupted. I see you won't have time to see the seals today."

Bothwell mounted hurriedly and clattered down into the town. He knew where to find the most part of his men, and they would have to borrow horses to get across the island in time. Already the *Unicorn*'s boat was making its way to shore, and Kirkcaldy would start searching. He must have realized that Bothwell had not been aboard the *Tortoise*.

Bothwell found some hundred men in the town, and as he was supreme lord of the isle and had the authority, he commandeered nearly all the horses in the town. They were brought out, sturdy, woolly beasts, and even a number of pet ponies. Anything that had four legs and could carry a man would do, even mules and donkeys.

"To the north!" cried Bothwell, rallying the men, and hastily they set out, making for the interior of the island. They rode as fast as they could on the uneven terrain, passing over the wrinkled green landscape strewn with boulders. They rode hard for twenty miles under that strange, huge, cloudless sky until they ran out of mainland. Then, abruptly, the land ended, and they found themselves staring out across two miles of open water separating them from the next island, Yell.

Where were the boats Sinclair had promised? Bothwell dismounted and clambered down to the shore. He saw fishing boats, and gestured to them. Slowly—agonizingly slowly—they rowed closer.

"We need to cross!" he yelled, indicating his party. The fishing boats just sat there. Then one of them rowed away, around a headland.

Bothwell felt his pulse racing. How would they manage to cross? The sea was too turbulent even to think of swimming in it, and the distance was too great, even if the water had not been numbingly cold. Neither the horses nor the men could survive it. He felt oddly concerned about the borrowed horses.

Damn! Were they to be caught here, like the fish in the nets being hauled aboard the boats? Kirkcaldy must be hot on their trail.

The fishing boat reappeared, and with it six larger boats. As they slowly came nearer, Bothwell gave silent thanks.

"We'll take you for a fee," the captain of one of the boats said. He named an outrageous one. Bothwell argued a moment, hoping to strike a better deal, or at least not leave the impression here that he was an absolute fool, but he kept glancing over his shoulder. Kirkcaldy might come up over the rise at any moment.

"Done," said Bothwell. "Now let's load!"

The men were herded onto one kind of boat, and the flatter, heavier boats agreed to take the horses. But only a few could be ferried across at a time. It took three crossings to get everyone onto the shore of Yell.

"Let us go!" cried Bothwell, touching spurs to his horse, and they set off north again, across land so forlorn it looked as if even God had forgotten it. Black rocks, brown bare soil, a sheen of green from moss and bracken— and the wind, like a creature itself: a howling, whistling, tearing wind that had ice in its mouth. Now, in the late afternoon, white, puffy clouds appeared and raced across the sky, demonstrating the speed of that wind.

They rode twelve miles along that cold, rocky desert, and then they came to another strait, Bluemull Sound. This one was much less wide than Yell Sound, and although Bothwell thought of risking a swim across, five boats were nearby and willing to ferry them across—again for a high fee.

They stepped ashore on the rock-strewn beach of Unst. Night was falling, but they did not dare to light fires for fear of betraying their whereabouts to Kirkcaldy. They huddled on the beach and tried to sleep, covering themselves with their cloaks. The wind was so fierce that it tore right through the material, and the crashing of the sea on the rocks kept them awake. When dawn came up, they shook the sand and pebbles off their cloaks and prepared to scour the island.

By midmorning they had found the ships, anchored in a sheltered bay. Bothwell signalled by flapping a cloak, and soon a boat was on its way.

"Thank God!" said both Bothwell and the men in the boat.

"Quick thinking," said Bothwell to the captain of the *Tortoise*, once he was safely aboard. "As fine a display of seamanship as ever I've seen. I watched from shore."

"When I saw that fat ship, I said to myself, 'She deserves to be wrecked,'" said the captain. "That bishop they had aboard, the one who's supposed to try you and pronounce sentence—it was he who jumped and almost missed the boat. I wish he'd sunk like his ship."

"I wish it as much as you—nay, more, for that turncoat churchman is the very one who married me to the Queen. What a vile betrayer," said Bothwell. "The rest of the ships stayed behind; they were hard put to rescue all the men and try to regroup."

"They'll be here before long," said the captain. "I would say we have only a few hours' head start. What do you aim to do?"

"Why, fight, of course," said Bothwell. "What else?"

"They have more men and more ships."

"Then they will be cocky. If you think I mean to flee without a fight, or if that is what you wish, I release you now. I will not have the fainthearted on my side; and you have already struck a mighty blow for us. You may in all good conscience be excused."

"Nay. I'll stay," he said. "But we have only a few hours to prepare."

"So be it."

Bothwell counted the men and realized a large contingent was still on the mainland. He dispatched his treasure vessel, the one carrying his plate, jewels, armour, and personal belongings, to sail back to the western side of the island, to Scalloway, to collect the men left behind.

It was early the next morning when the first of the enemy ships came over the horizon. There was so much mist that they had come fairly close before Bothwell or his captains were able to spot them.

"Enemy! Enemy! Alarm!" cried the sailors. The cannon were loaded, and the soldiers manned the decks, standing shoulder to shoulder with their harquebuses. Torches soaked in pitch to set aflame and throw onto the ships in close fighting were at the ready, as were longbows and grappling hooks if it came to boarding and hand-to-hand fighting.

They cut the anchor cables and started out of the bay, to avoid being bottled up or run aground. The whistling wind filled the sails the second they were unfurled, and the captains steered for open water.

The seven ships of the Lords followed, and began firing their long-range brass cannon. But they were still at too great a distance, and the cannonballs fell harmlessly into the water.

The *Tortoise*, true to its name, fell behind its fellows, and soon was boarded by Kirkcaldy's men. Bothwell was down to two ships now, and he wished the captain of the *Tortoise* had elected not to fight. He hoped that Kirkcaldy would be merciful, but mercy did not seem to be a leading trait of the Lords.

Cannon fire was hitting their ships, tearing through the sails and riddling them with holes, and thudding into the wooden sides. Bothwell gave the orders to reply, and the guns of the *Pelican* roared in answer, striking the sides and deck of the *Primrose*, the *James*, and the *Robert*, raining down on the heads of the hands on deck. The four smaller ships hung back out of range, like reticent maidens.

A fireball landed on the deck, expanding up into a sphere of pure flame. The soldiers fled, but some had their clothing set afire, and had to roll on the deck or be doused with water. In the confusion they left off firing, and the *Primrose*, with Tullibardine aboard—Bothwell could see him manning the deck—was able to approach closer and let loose with the close-range guns. A rain of gunshot fell on them, scattering Bothwell's men and once again disrupting their defence.

Bothwell rushed to one of the cannon and loaded and fired it himself. He aimed right at the waterline of Tullibardine's ship, hoping to sink it, but the hole that appeared in the side was above the water.

The fight continued, all the time working its way farther and farther out to sea. The shoreline grew hazy and disappeared. The ships fought on, volleys of cannonballs landing on deck, blasting holes in the vessels. The sails were aflame on the *Robert*, and it lost control of its steering and revolved around and around like a wheel in the water.

Then there was a gruesome splintering sound as a cannonball hit the *Pelican*'s mainmast and tore it away. Like a stately tree being felled, the tall timber toppled slowly, majestically to the deck, tangled in its stays and rigging. Only one mast remained now.

Tullibardine started closing in. His sailors were standing by with grappling hooks.

"Surrender!" Tullibardine yelled. "Surrender, Bothwell, you pirate, you murderer!"

"I'll see you in Hell first!" he answered, firing on Tullibardine with a harquebus. The ball ripped through Tullibardine's hat and sent it flying.

"Damn!" screamed Bothwell. Another three inches and it would have been Tullibardine's brains flying instead.

A chorus of gunfire sounded, and eight of Bothwell's men fell.

Bothwell fired again. "Don't give up the cannon!" he yelled, but the men were falling back under the rain of fire.

"I've got you!" yelled Tullibardine, aiming at Bothwell, but he was so excited he missed widely.

The sky darkened, as if a squid had suddenly released a huge cloud of ink. The sun disappeared, and in its place came a howling wind from the southwest. The blast was so strong that the *Pelican* heeled over and several sailors fell overboard. So did the *Primrose,* and the fact that the enemy ship had its full complement of sails intact actually hindered it, as the wind took control of its sails. It almost capsized, and heeled so far over that water rushed into the hole Bothwell had shot in its side. Rain poured down from above as if a giant's cauldron had been tipped over on them.

The ships began to run before the wind, Bothwell's vessel, lighter and more maneuverable, outdistancing Tullibardine's. Bothwell's second ship was not far behind, and the ships raced northward. Tullibardine pursued for sixty miles into the open sea before he turned back.

Bothwell could hardly keep his footing on the slippery deck of the lurching boat, and the waves on either side looked like hills. He clung to the railing and watched as tons of water washed over the deck. The hills rose and fell. They were ominous, dark, pulling him into them. They looked horribly familiar; they were the hills of Hell where the Demon Lover was pulled to his doom in the Border song he knew so well and had sung to Mary. *Those are the hills of Hell, my love, where thou and I must go.* They were taking him home. Still he grasped the rail and told the captain, "Steer on!" and they shot in and out of the hungry waves all night long.

In the dark, the roaring of the sea and the pitching of the ship—sometimes her decks were almost perpendicular—made them feel that they were indeed being tipped down into the maws of hell. The sailors, fighting to control the sails on the one mast left, could believe the stories of the giant *kraken* that old Norwegian seamen swore infested these waters—a huge, tentacled beast that would suddenly rear up and devour a ship, masts and all. The icy arms of the sea that flung themselves over the deck, lashing them in the face, felt like the slimy arms of the monster.

The one remaining mast creaked and groaned, straining at its base. The helmsman and his assistant fought the rudder, which bucked like a mule and could barely be controlled. Rudders often broke—and they had no spare on board. The men wept and prayed, remembering all their sins and begging for another chance. There was no sight of the second ship, and no way to tell whether it was following or had been blown off course, or even sunk . . . or perhaps had been devoured by the *kraken.*

The storm raged all night and half the next day, gradually abating by sunset. As the giant waves fell, and they could once again see over the troughs, night fell again, so that they were unable to get their bearings. Judging from the stars, they had been steering—or had been blown—north-northeast.

As the skies lightened in the next dawn, Bothwell sighted land at a distance. It was shrouded in mist and bluish white, and very high indeed. Mountains, capped by snow, came almost down to the water.

"Norway," he breathed. Yes, it had to be.

Suddenly he remembered that odd dream he had had about Norway, in which he had actually spoken Norwegian. An omen? It made him shudder, but at the same time it made the Norwegian coast seem a friendly, beckoning place. I have already been here, in my dreams, he thought. So I have nothing to fear.

The captain came over to him on unsteady legs. He draped himself over the rail, his arms limp.

"Thirty-six hours of battle," he said. "I hope never to endure its like again." His voice was a whisper.

"Where are we?" asked Bothwell. "Can you determine it when the sun comes out?"

"Aye," he said. "The astrolabe will tell us exactly how far we've come. But I know this is Norway; no other place has these mountains. It is not Iceland or Denmark. The tip of the Shetlands is a good two hundred miles from the Norwegian coast, so I imagine we've put our enemies far behind. Look!" He pointed out to starboard, at the bobbing shape of another boat. "Our other ship is with us! God has brought us both safely through!"

"Thanks be to Him," said Bothwell. He looked at the strewn deck, burnt from the fire, pocked with holes, littered with frayed ropes and pieces of torn canvas. Overturned barrels and debris lay everywhere. The mast was crooked, but still held. "We will have to refit ourselves in port. But what of that? We are free! We have won!" He embraced the captain. "We are free!"

LXII

Mary stood by the water landing, waiting for George Douglas to return. She knew it gave him pleasure to see her there, enveloped in one of her hooded mantles, and it gave her a reason to stand by the water's edge without causing her guards alarm. She liked to watch the water, with its surface rippled by the rising winds, its colour changing as it reflected the intermittent clouds and sunshine. Some days, now that it was well into autumn, the entire lake was a swirl of mist, like a dream disappearing into a dream.

Gradually her guards had grown more lax, but she was still not allowed beyond the castle walls by herself. They allowed her to stand at the boat landing only because they could watch her from the main gate.

The routine was unyielding. Soldiers—there were some sixty of them in the island garrison—guarded the walls and the single entrance gate. The only time they deserted their posts was during the brief supper hour, when they all went into the hall to eat. Then the gate was locked, and the keys placed by Sir William's plate while he dined. Thus they were never out of sight.

Mary and her party were still housed in the square tower, and two of the Douglas ladies would sleep in the quarters with them. As far as they knew, Mary did not write or receive letters, and her only source of news was what Lord James permitted them to tell her. In truth, young George, outraged at their treatment of her, acted as her liaison with the world. To be safe, she wrote very few letters, but he kept her abreast of the news from Edinburgh and beyond.

Dear George! Sometimes she thought he must have been provided by fate, because there was no other explanation for him. He was everything she had imagined Darnley to be—brave, honest, innocent. Now he was her only consolation, bringing her news, treating her as someone worthy of love and respect, when all the world had branded her whore and murderess, and condemned her without a trial.

She tried to tread a fine line between showing George that she deeply appreciated him, and encouraging his affections. She now knew so much more than she had before; Bothwell had taught her about her own desires, and in their new existence it was hard to keep them hidden. She was no longer the virgin who had danced merrily with Chastelard and then been bewildered by his response; the careless queen who liked to lean against people, whispering secrets, warming herself; the nonchalant woman who could sit up late at night alone with Riccio and think nothing of it. Then her body had been an innocuous thing, something neutral and easy to disregard; now it seemed a dangerous creature of its own that could speak without her knowledge, and say things to others she did not wish to say, and without her permission. Perhaps it had spoken all along, and others had heard it, although she had been deaf to it herself.

At night she often lay awake, reliving times when she had lain in Bothwell's arms, trying to recall every detail. It made her hot and achy, and frantic that she could not remember things exactly. She had dreams in which he came to her, dreams in which their times together were recreated in minute, explosive detail. She would awaken in wonder, her heart racing, her body shiny with sweat, and sit up gasping. Then she would hear the snoring of the Douglas women, smell the water of the loch, and weep with disappointment.

As her health recovered, Bothwell grew stronger in her mind rather than fading away as her enemies assumed he would. She never mentioned him to them, partly because she did not want to desecrate his name by exposing it to them, but also to mislead them. If they thought she had given him up, then perhaps they might be less likely to persecute him.

But where was he? She had heard nothing since Lord James had taunted her with the squadron of ships he had sent to capture Bothwell in the Orkneys. Where, where, where, was he?

For a while in her dreams he stormed the walls of the castle and rowed her away. But for a good time now she had realized that she would have to manage her own escape, and then go to him. Hence, George Douglas: her only dim hope of escape. Yet she did care for him and his safety, and did not want to bring trouble down on his head as well. Already his family was watching him closely, after Lord James's warning.

The boat was approaching; she could see it bobbing on the water. George had gone to Edinburgh at the behest of his father to confer with his august older brother, the Regent. She hoped he had been able to linger long enough to talk to the French or English ambassador.

The boat tied up at the dock, and Mary allowed herself to wait before greeting George; the soldiers were watching and would notice any eagerness or friendliness on her part, or his. So he merely nodded at her and whispered, "By the oak," as he passed by on his way toward the gate. He would dutifully report everything to his parents, indulge in a lengthy visit with them, drink wine, and only later be able to see her. "The oak" was the huge tree just outside the round tower, and technically outside the walls. The guards did not care, as there was so little ground there and no boat landing, so that it was impossible to escape.

It was twilight before George strolled toward the gate and, with Mary by his side, said grandly to the guard, "It is all right, Jock," and walked out. They made their way slowly round the castle, staying close to the walls— for the water was within ten feet of them—until they finally reached the large boulder that lay at the foot of the oak. The water touched its foot, but they could sit on its rounded hump and be sheltered by the heavy branches of the tree, now covered with yellowing leaves that fell crisply.

"Now, George, tell me quickly!" she said. "Is the Lord James well?" I wish he were not, she thought, but I must not stretch George's loyalty, for they are brothers.

He turned his open smile on her. "Aye. He thrives on the Regency."

"He has coveted it long enough," she said, before she could stop herself. "Undoubtedly he has rehearsed it many a day."

"In truth, things are quiet. The city is recovering; so are all the Lords. I have heard they plan to call a Parliament in December to publish their reasons. But for now, no one stirs. Even Knox has fallen uncharacteristically silent."

"He wore himself out whipping up hysteria to drive me from my throne. Even rabble-rousers need rest." She looked over at George, at his clean young profile as he was staring out across the loch, his eyes narrowed. Oh, why could Darnley have not truly been like this? "But what of my son? What of James?"

"He slumbers on at Stirling, but from all reports is healthy and even beginning to talk."

"Alas, poor child!" she said. "I wonder what words they are teaching him?" *Mother, murderess,* and *adulteress* were probably high on their list, above *duck* and *stool* and *cheese.* Oh, if only— She stopped her thoughts, "Have the foreign governments recognized him as King?"

George shook his head. "Queen Elizabeth refuses to, much to Jamie's anger." He used the family's affectionate nickname for the stern Regent.

Mary laughed in glee. "He did not count on that!"

"Nay, and she's stubborn. The French hem and haw, but do not dress down Jamie the way the English Queen does. By God, she has courage!"

"Yes." Yes, she did. But she was so unpredictable. She had always supported the Lords, and yet now she refused to recognize them. Mary remembered the "Elizabeth ring," and wished she had it with her now. It was in Edinburgh, where she had left it behind in her flight.

"If I were to escape," she said idly, "what do you think she would do?" And what will *you* do to this suggestion? She almost held her breath waiting.

"Why, I think she would help you, and restore you to your throne," he said. He was looking directly into her eyes, so fiercely that she could not drop hers or look away. "But first, of course, you would have to be free. And that would be difficult. You would need a confidant, someone you could trust."

This was the moment. If she was wrong, that would end it. But if she was right, this was the time to speak.

"I believe I have that. Have I?"

He hesitated, as if steeling himself. "Yes," he finally said. "I will do what I can." Immediately he grasped her hand as if to caution her. "But I am only one person, and closely watched—and unproved in battle. I am no Bothwell—"

"There is only one Bothwell," she said, and her meaning was clear. She was so relieved and excited that George had declared himself on her side that she hated to open herself up to sorrow so soon on its heels, but she had to ask. "Is there—has there been any news of him?"

"Aye." The single word hung there, and it was as if the noise of the water rose up and became louder around them.

A dreadful, cold fear gripped her. "What?"

"He managed to escape from Grange and all Jamie's forces. There was a long sea battle, and just when it seemed he was doomed, a fierce storm blew up from the southwest. Now they say this is proof of his witchcraft, that he raised it by the black arts."

"And they truly believe that?"

"They fear him, so they comfort themselves by saying he is in league with the supernatural."

"So he has escaped?" That was all that mattered.

"For a time."

"What do you mean?"

"He was blown all the way to Norway, where he landed safely. But then, once there, he encountered difficulties with the authorities. They have taken him to Copenhagen as a prisoner."

"Oh!" she cried. "When? Why?"

"I know not why, but it was on the last day of September. And now that the Lord James knows of his whereabouts, he is busy trying to get him extradited, or else executed in Denmark. To his credit, King Frederick has refused both requests. But still he continues to hold him prisoner. It is my guess he wants some ransom for him."

She stifled a cry by stuffing her fist into her mouth. "O God! If only I had something! But everything has been taken from me—my jewels, my plate, even my clothes!" She had to think of something. "Do you think— if I appealed to the King—can you take a letter from me?"

"It would be known, dear lady. King Frederick would announce it. And then they would know who carried it, and remove me from the island."

She felt panic rising in her. "But I must help him!"

"There is no way you can," George said sadly.

"Is there no one to help him?" she cried. "No kind soul, whom I can repay?"

"Only the Queen of England or of France could do that, and neither would," George replied.

"There must be no torture greater than this," she finally said. "To be unable to aid the one you love, and just to sit by and watch him suffer."

"Aye," said George, looking at her.

❧

The leaves fell from the trees, leaving bare, twisted limbs, and the sedge and reeds withered. A little crust of ice, like a wispy bread, formed around the edges of the island, but as Mary had suspected, the loch itself did not freeze.

In the cold, nasty weather, the number of boats passing to and from the island were few in number. The laundresses made their weekly journey, collecting the soiled linens and delivering the clean, and fishermen brought in their catches, but all other business ceased. The Laird shuffled about with sad, rheumy eyes, coughing incessantly. Normally he vacated the island castle during the winter and lived in his manor house on the mainland, but because of his royal guest, he was now a prisoner here as well. Lady Douglas was solicitous of him, and gave Mary resentful looks.

You needn't look at me in blame, Madam, Mary thought. I would gladly free you—were I free myself.

She and her ladies worked on their embroidery in the dull candlelight, huddled in the tower room with a fire burning at all times. The days stretched on interminably, long pale days when nothing happened, when the most exciting thing was matching two shades of red exactly from two different threads.

Sometimes she and George were left alone before the fire, she sewing, he mending weapons and sharpening swords.

"Tell me a story, George," she would say, and he would smile and tell her of the voyages of Ulysses, or the fall of Troy. His face would grow dreamy and his voice thick and drowsy as the sleet beat against the windows and he recounted stories that had happened on dusty, windy plains, or on the high seas. Mary Seton and Nau would draw up a cushion and listen. George could tell stories the way Riccio could sing songs.

It helped the days to pass—dark, cold days with creeping damp and bitter mists. There was no word of Bothwell.

❧

It was March before they were able to work out a plan. Christmas had come and gone, a dreary Twelfth Night, with nothing to celebrate for Mary. The Lords had carried out their threat to publish the reasons for their behaviour. Throwing aside all pretence of having acted in order to "save" Mary from Bothwell (or, rather, from her own insane passion for him, depending on which official story they quoted), they now switched to branding her a murderess along with him. They announced the incriminating letters that they claimed proved her to have planned her husband's death and to have lured him back to Edinburgh on her lover Bothwell's instructions, acting as a decoy. Lord James, the conscientious Regent, sent a herald to Lochleven, in accordance with the ancient custom of Scotland that forfeitures and outlawry of any great peer be announced at a place where the sovereign was personally present, to read her the Act of Privy Council, and inform her that Lord Bothwell's estates were forfeit, Maitland and Morton having received part of them.

The gold and scarlet tabards were fluttering, and the lion-banner at the prow of the boat made a bright spot of colour in the dull greyness the day the herald arrived. He stood and read out:

> "That the cause of their taking up arms, and taking of the Queen's person upon the fifteenth day of June last past, and holding and detaining of the same within the house and place of Lochleven, and all things said and done by them since the tenth of February last, on which day the late King Henry, the Queen's lawful husband, was shamefully and horribly murdered, was all in the said Queen's own default, in as far as by divers her privy letters, written and subscribed by her own hand, and sent by her to James Earl of Bothwell, chief executer of the said horrible murder, as well before the committing thereof as after, and by her ungodly and dishonourable proceeding in a private marriage with him, it is most certain that she was privy part and parcel of the actual device and deed of the forementioned murder of the King her lawful

601

husband, committed by the said James Earl of Bothwell, his accomplices and partakers, and therefore justly deserves whatsoever has been attempted or shall be used toward her for the said cause."

Then, having fulfilled his official duty, he stepped back in the boat and was rowed away, leaving the castle inhabitants standing on the landing and staring after him.

Since then, in desperation, Mary had redoubled her efforts to find some way to escape, all the while trying to act like a placid, broken person—someone who did not bear watching too closely.

There was only George to try to arrange things, although a kinsman of some sort (could the Laird have his own bastard?), named Willie Douglas, might also be recruited. He seemed to come and go as he pleased, and the family still regarded him as a child, although he was almost fifteen.

The first plan George offered was that he would manage to organize a group of loyalists on shore who would seize the Laird's great boat when it was tied up at the manor house, row out to the castle, and storm it at night, aided by George from within the walls. Unfortunately, somehow the Laird got wind of a possible plot by unknown persons, and locked up the great boat. Next he proposed to lie in wait with his men—the same loyalists—in the ruins of the monastery on the deserted St. Serf's Island in the loch. Then Mary could prevail on the Laird to allow her to go hawking there; when they arrived, the Laird and his servants would be overpowered and Mary spirited away to freedom.

But this involved too many other people, and would require being rowed across the water twice: once to St. Serf's, and once to the mainland. At one point George thought it might be simpler just to board Mary up in a box and let it be transported innocently back to Kinross.

"Nay, that's foolish," little Willie objected. "It is always better to rely on your own two feet. Let the Queen walk out, in disguise. That is surer." He had a strange way of jerking his head when he spoke that made him appear stupid, which he was not.

"Yes," George had mused. "Perhaps she could change clothes with one of the servants. But how would she get out? The gates are always guarded, except when the soldiers are eating, between half past seven and nine at night, and then they are locked." George had found himself spending more and more time thinking of the Queen: of her low, intimate voice, of her slender, delicate hands. She was starting to invade his dreams as well, giving him things in them that he dared not think of in the daylight.

"She could jump from that oriel window in the round tower," said Willie. "It is only about eight feet from the ground."

But when Mary Seton tried it as an experiment, she injured her leg. There were boulders underneath the window, with crevices and gaping cracks that afforded no safe footing.

Then, as George was sitting on the landing dock one day in late February, he watched the boat with the laundresses approaching. They were making their weekly visit, and the vessel carried hampers of clean linen in the middle. Four boatmen rowed, straining at the oars in the choppy grey water.

The laundresses! There were three of them, and they wore shapeless dark mantles; their faces were plain and almost colourless. Underneath the mantles George could see their heavy, stained wooden clog-shoes. They looked monumental, dark, foreboding, like the Three Fates, as they trudged slowly up the path to the castle, balancing their hampers with great slow dignity. George found himself hurrying after them, compelled to glimpse their faces, to see if—oh, strange thought!—they actually resembled Clotho, Lachesis, and Atropos. Was there a Clotho there—she who spun the bright threads of youth? For she surely might hold the Queen's in her power.

The women turned and glared at him, and he felt foolish. Once again he had imbued an ordinary person or situation with mythic grandeur. He merely nodded at them and turned away.

But his heart was racing. This was the way! Mary could disguise herself and simply walk out with them, keeping her face hidden. That should be easy, as they were enveloped in those voluminous mantles. It would have to be arranged while it was still cold.

He bribed the laundresses, and the Three Fates took the money in an all-too-human fashion. On Mary's instructions, he sent messages to John Beaton, a relative of Mary Beaton's from a staunchly loyal family who had served Mary at Holyrood, to Lord Seton, and to the Laird of Riccarton, one of Bothwell's loyalists. They were to gather with men-at-arms in a mountain glen near Kinross and wait for the signal that the escape had been successful. Then they would make off for a Hamilton stronghold.

"All depends on your being able to walk unobserved that hundred feet from the tower, through the gate, and then to the boat," said George. "Make sure you evade my sisters."

The two youngest Douglas girls, aged fourteen and fifteen, had been assigned to "keep Mary company," and in rebellion against their parents had conceived a worship of her; as a result, they watched her every movement, to Mary's secret despair.

Mary laughed. "That will be the most difficult part. I have noticed them watching me even when they think I am asleep."

"I cannot blame them," said George.

She felt a tremor of warning pass through her. She did not dare look at him, lest she encourage him in his burgeoning affection. Yet she was touched—and flattered.

"It is tiring to be regarded as a goddess," she finally said. "It is not nearly as enjoyable as one would imagine." There, she thought. I have warned him.

"As the laundresses leave by three o'clock, I will try to distract my sisters or give them some task, like . . . like sorting the threads and darning, about that time," George said quickly, and then she knew it was now safe to look at him.

He was very handsome, so handsome he was known as "Pretty Geordie" to his family. She wondered why he did not already have a wife, or even a betrothed. Certainly he came from a wealthy family, high in standing, ambitious. He himself was well spoken, learned, and athletic. Was he religious? Saving himself for God? But no, the Protestants did not do that. Look at Knox!

"What are you smiling at?" He watched her as intently as his sisters.

"I was wondering if you had a secret desire to be a monk," she said teasingly.

"Do you mean, am I religious? Or do you mean, am I abstinent?"

He was so serious, as only the very young can be, she thought. She waited to answer. "Either," she finally said.

"I am not saving myself for religious reasons, if that is what you think." He sounded insulted. "Nor for any reason, other than that there has never been anyone worthy of my love." His intense blue eyes seemed to glow in his face, incandescent.

"Ah, then you *do* seek to worship," she said, smiling gently. "Beware of that in love."

"As I suppose you know only too well!" he said with hurt in his voice, then immediately fell to apologizing.

She stopped him. "Yes, as I know only too well," she said. "You have spoken true."

The day was fixed for March twenty-fifth. Mary prayed that a storm would not arise, or one of the girls take sick, or she herself take sick. Let nothing happen to spoil it! she begged God.

As if in answer to her prayer, March twenty-fifth was exactly the sort of day she desired: it was dull and overcast, so that people would not want to linger outside, and would grow drowsy and sleep in midday, but not so unpleasant that the laundresses would have to postpone their journey.

All day she had to force herself to walk slowly, eat slowly, seem to have no reason to hurry or step lightly. Of her own attendants, only Mary Seton was allowed to know. Time enough later for them to know if the plan worked; until then, she had learned, every person who knew had the potential to betray her inadvertently.

To be free! This time tomorrow, would she be riding, a free Queen, among her subjects? It was now two years since Riccio's murder, and since then she had been kept as someone's captive three times, not to mention the vague captivity of threats and murmurs and illness. Let this be the end of it!

They dined quietly at midday, and Mary forced herself to eat the boiled trout. She was weary of the Lochleven specialty, and associated it with her imprisonment. I will never eat trout again, she vowed, if only I am freed.

Under her bed was the shabby mantle that she was to wrap herself in, with a long scarf which she would pull across her face. As the dishes were being cleared away, George appeared at the doorway and called to his sisters.

"Arabella! Meggie! You are wanted in the sewing room!"

It was the signal! Reluctantly the girls rose and left the room, saying to Mary, "Remember, afterwards you promised to help us sketch the next part of our pattern."

Mary looked out the window and saw the three laundresses making their way toward the castle. She knew they took only about a half hour to deliver their goods and to collect next week's washing. She had to hide her hands to keep others from seeing them tremble. How could she endure the next fifteen minutes?

She excused herself and went and sat on her bed, clasping her hands to calm herself. She said a rosary, then recited several prayers in Latin. Then she knew it must be time. Dropping to her knees, she drew out the cloak and put it on. Then, as quietly as she could, she passed through the main room and down the stairs. She did not pause or give anyone a chance to notice her.

Out she went, from the base of the tower and then across the grass, dull brown and matted now. The soldiers were leaning against the wall, too bored to talk to each other. Some even slept, cradling their heads on their arms. Some were cleaning their guns.

The gate stood open. Two of the laundresses were already near the boat. What luck that the third was evidently lingering behind. Mary made her way to the boat, carrying her bundle of bedsheets. Quietly they took their places in the boat. Mary nodded slightly to the other two, but kept her face down and the hood well forward so that she was hidden. She pulled the scarf up to muffle her mouth.

Now the boatmen were ready to cast off. Where was the fourth woman? George must have paid her to stay behind—of course!—lest the men notice their extra passenger.

Achingly slowly, the men untied the boat and pushed off. There was one foot between them and the dock, then two, then three . . . then the gap of water widened, and they shot forward as the men rowed.

Free! Free! The hateful island was now fifty feet away, seventy. The walls of the castle grew smaller, dwarfed by the trees around them. The boat rocked and made its way across the water.

"Oh, look!" one of the men was saying. "Is this a new one?"

"Looky here!"

Mary kept her eyes on the bottom of the boat and hunched her shoulders, ignoring them.

"Let's see!" another voice said, and suddenly the boat lurched. One of the men had left off rowing and leaned forward, trying to pull off her scarf.

"I'll warrant she's a bonny one, maybe wants a man—" He tugged at her scarf. "Come here, sweeting, I just want to see!"

Mary jerked the scarf out of his hand and fumbled with it, trying to readjust it. In the wind, her fingers got entwined with it and she had to disentangle them.

Suddenly she heard a low, startled sound from the man.

"It's—you're not a washerwoman, look at those hands!" he cried, grabbing them. He turned them over and inspected them as if they were exotic jewels. "So white, and slender-fingered, and the skin is too soft, it's never been in water."

She started fighting with him to get her hands away, and stood up. The boat rocked madly. She pulled away from him, but as she did so, the wind ripped the hood from her face. The men stopped rowing and stared.

"Yes, I am the Queen!" she said. "And I command you to continue rowing. Row me to the shore!"

The men sat there. Finally one said, "Madam, we dare not."

"I am the Queen!" she cried. "You dare not disobey! Row, I tell you!"

"We may not," the same man said. "The Laird would punish us dreadfully, us and our families."

"I will reward you!"

"Madam, here is our home. We would not be in disgrace here." The man—clearly the boat's owner—turned to the other men. "Turn around," he said. "Return to the island."

"No! No!" Could she not stop them? Was there nothing she could do to persuade them? "Good sirs, please have pity on me! You are my only hope!"

"We have served the Laird and his family for generations, and we will do nothing to imperil him," the man insisted. "He has been good to us, and deserves our loyalty."

Mary burst into tears as the boat swung around and the island began growing bigger again. "Please, please!" she cried. She could not bear to return there.

"It is not our wish to cause you sorrow," said the man. "We will not reveal this to the Laird. No one shall ever know. When we land, go inside quietly and send out the woman left behind. We will pretend that she forgot something."

Mary watched as the boat approached the island and tied up once more. Rearing up in front of her was the ugly wall and its gate. Numbly she got out of the boat and walked slowly back into her prison. The yawning guards barely even looked up. It had indeed been a perfectly executed escape. That made it all the more painful.

As she was walking back across the green, wadding up her mantle so that it would not arouse questions, George came out of the attached building where the soldiers dined. He stopped stock-still and stared at her. His face grew even whiter than usual. She walked past him, ignoring him, the tears welling up in her eyes.

Making her way back into the privacy of her quarters, she flung herself down on the bed. She would pretend to be asleep; she could not bear to talk to anyone or try to keep her tears at bay. If she kept her face down in the pillow and let her hair fall over her face, she would have privacy for her sorrow.

Failed! She could scarcely credit it. Never had she failed in any of these escape attempts, and it had seemed natural that this one would be as successful as the rest. What had Bothwell said? *No prison can hold us.* And so it had seemed. Yet now he was in custody of the King of Denmark, and she was shut up on the island. Forever? Did they mean it to be forever? The Lords had not said anything to indicate their ultimate plans for her.

She was so stunned by the very nearness of the escape that she felt weak. Everyone was so loyal to the Laird. Only George dared cross him. But George required accomplices, and they were evidently not easily found. Who was it that had betrayed their earlier plan to steal his boat?

She was truly frightened now. What if she could not escape? What then?

"My dearest sovereign." George was kneeling near her bed. "What—what has happened?"

"Oh, George!" She sat up, throwing back her hair. "They saw my hands!" She held them out and he took one. "They knew I did no washing. Then they insisted on returning me here, even though I commanded them to row me to shore. It seems they are loyal to their Laird before their monarch."

"Ah." He sounded heartbroken. "And you were halfway there! I saw it." He kept caressing her hand. She took it away.

"Never have I felt more bereft."

"We will try again. There will have to be another plan. This time we will supply our own rowers."

She could not help laughing a little. "And who will that be? The men of the garrison?"

"I will find someone," he said stubbornly. "Perhaps your people—"

"George, I think I should give you something that can always serve as a signal between us, if perchance it becomes difficult for us to communicate, as well it may. It is a miracle there is no one here now." She unfastened one of her pearl earrings. "Earrings are easily lost, easily found, and if ever you return this to me, I will know it means 'I have received your message' or 'all is ready.' In short, it will stand for 'yes.'" She dropped it into his hand.

The next day, George was nowhere to be seen. Nor was he to be seen the next. At length, on the third day, she inquired of Lady Douglas about him.

"My son has been sent from the island, Madam, on account of his overfamiliarity with *you.* It has come to the attention of several persons that he has become—how shall I say it?—captive to the Stuart charm. I myself know how difficult it can be to resist." She smirked.

"How fortunate for Scotland that you did not," Mary said. "Else now, in her hour of need, there would be no Regent." Had she managed to keep the sarcasm out of her voice? But what of George? "But history does not repeat itself. I do not know to what you refer, in regards to George."

"He has fallen into a fantasy of love with you, and you have encouraged it," said Lady Douglas, "a fact that has greatly distressed his half brother, Lord James. However, as a mother I must think of *all* my children and their futures. . . ." She arched her eyebrow in her aging face and gave that smirk again. "I only want what is best for George," she said with mock humility.

"As do I, Lady Douglas. I am most fond of him"—she let the phrase dangle temptingly—"and find him most pleasant company. But I had no idea he might have entertained deeper feelings toward me. This bears some consideration, some reflection. . . . In the meantime, it is best that he not be here until a conclusion has been reached, some way found to . . . Hmmm . . . You are very wise!"

Lady Douglas smiled. The fortunes of the Douglases might rise higher yet.

March, with its ugly grey skies and constant fogs and rains, gave way to April. Mary and her household attempted to keep Lent, and in their dejected state of mind, it was easy for them to put away all merriment and wear long faces. Only Mary Seton knew about the failed escape attempt, but everyone knew about the banishment of George for his partiality to the Queen. It seemed that anyone suspected of showing interest or pity for Mary was to be removed. First Ruthven, now George.

Mary managed to get one letter out to France. She wrote to Catherine de Médicis:

> It is with extreme difficulty I have been able to send a faithful servant to explain the extent of my misery, and to beseech you to have compassion on me, inasmuch as Lord James the Regent has caused me to be told, in confidence, that the King your son is going to make peace with the French Huguenots, and one of the conditions of the treaty is that he shall not give me any help. This I cannot believe, for, next to God, I place my whole reliance on the King and you, as this bearer can tell you. I beg you to give credit to him as if it were myself, for I dare not write more, save to entreat God to have you in his holy care.
>
> From my prison this last of March.

The disciples of Calvin! First they had converted and ruined Scotland, and now they were attempting to do the same to France. In Scotland they were called the Kirk, in France the Huguenots. It was said that in France they numbered in the thousands, and were organized like an army. Wave after wave of violence had washed over France as the Catholic Church and the Huguenots fought for supremacy. It was the Huguenots who had killed the Duc de Guise and the Constable Montmorency, and had become powerful enough that Catherine de Médicis sought to find an accommodation with them.

Everywhere the battle lines were being drawn. The Dutch—also Protestants—were rebelling against Spanish rule. In Spain, the Inquisition sought to exterminate any Protestants hidden in their midst. The earlier, softer Reformers and the easygoing Catholicism they had sparred against were replaced by intransigents on both sides. The Council of Trent, which had ended only five years earlier, had belligerently concluded that there could be no accommodation with the Protestants. Everything the Protestants had questioned—confession to a priest, praying to the saints, the supremacy of the Pope—was embraced and declared to be absolutely necessary to salvation. A Catholic could not even attend a Protestant service without endangering his soul. The battlefield was open, the trumpets sounding. On the Protestant side, like players in a village football game, were the Scandinavian countries, England, Scotland, the Netherlands. On the Catholic, Italy, Portugal, and Spain. Split down the middle, Germany and France.

And to think it is my misfortune to be trapped thus, thought Mary. My fate depends on the actions of religious zealots—I, who have always practised toleration!

She would have laughed, had it not been so ironic and painful.

There had been no further word of Bothwell's fate. She knew that he had been transferred to Copenhagen. The Lords had attempted to convince King Frederick that Bothwell should be delivered up to justice, but Frederick had continued to hold Bothwell. For what reason? As far as she knew, no ransom had been asked, and no one had approached her representatives, like the Archbishop of Glasgow, her trusted ambassador in France, with any demands. Why could Bothwell not escape, or talk his way out? She had written a letter to King Frederick protesting against Bothwell's extradition, and managed to smuggle it out just before George had been banished. She had no way of knowing whether it had ever reached him. She also wrote to Bothwell, pouring out her pent-up feelings and bidding him to be of good cheer. Of her own troubles she said little, not wanting to cause him any more pain than he already had. She had even less idea of whether this letter ever reached its addressee.

George had told her there was a rumour that Bothwell had offered the Orkneys and Shetlands to Denmark in exchange for his freedom, and that Frederick had been interested, but that, in spite of Bothwell's titles to them, he realized the Lords would have to recognize the transfer. Perhaps that was what was detaining Bothwell—perhaps Frederick was going to offer them Bothwell's person in exchange for the islands.

In mid-April, just before Holy Week, Willie showed his ingenuity. He managed to bring Mary two precious letters. One was a copy of a letter Bothwell had written to Charles IX—so we are both throwing ourselves, begging, at his feet! thought Mary—and the other was just to her.

"They say his prison is not as bleak as yours," Willie whispered, when they were walking together in the little kitchen garden. Some of the soldiers had been put to work turning the soil to ready it for planting. "He's been moved to Malmö, in Sweden, to a castle there—the same room that housed Christian II of Denmark, a deposed tyrant. It is large and vaulted, so they say, and on a ground floor. They had to put extra bars on the windows in preparing it for Bothwell."

So they knew his skill at escaping! Her heart sank a little.

Willie passed her two papers, and she quickly hid them in her sleeve. The soldiers seemed to be busy digging, but they were undoubtedly watching closely. She would have to wait until she was in the garderobe to read them.

"I miss George," she said loudly enough to be heard.

"Yes," said Willie. "I have heard that he plans to go to France. He says he cannot make his fortune here, and if he is to be banished, he prefers to go abroad, as at least there are new sights there."

"Oh!" she gasped. To lose George, too! Then she saw Willie make a hint of a wink at her.

"His mother and father will be grieved," Willie said. "But that is how young men are."

That night she feigned stomach pains and a nausea that required her to spend an unusual amount of time in the garderobe of the tower. The hovering young girls were more solicitous of her health, and wanted to bring her cold compresses and stroke her forehead. Perhaps, she told them, but only after the most violent, purging stage of the attack was over. In the meantime, they should stay away, as it was an ugly sight.

In the dim light of her single candle, and while making false moans and retching noises, Mary unfolded the letters.

To His Most Christian Majesty Charles IX of France
Sire:
   I left Scotland to let the King of Denmark hear the great and manifest wrongs done to the Queen of Scotland, his near kinswoman, and to me in particular. Intending thereafter in all diligence to seek Your Majesty, I have been cast by a storm on the coast of Norway and thence have come to Denmark. Here I found Monsieur de Dancay, your ambassador, to whom I have made full discourse of my affairs, praying him to acquaint you by express messenger, which he has promised. Not doubting the performance of his promise, I entreat Your Majesty very humbly to have regard to the good will to do you service that I have shown all my life, in which course I intend to continue. May it please you to honour me with such an answer as you would give to one who has no hope in any but Your Majesty, save in God.
   Sire, I commit me very humbly to your good grace and pray Almighty God to grant you a happy and long life. From Copenhagen, the twelfth of November.

Your very humble and very obedient servant,
James, Duke of Orkney.

The twelfth of November past! Nothing had been done, no action taken by France. The letter, with its dignified appeal, had gained him nothing.

She emitted a long, low sound of suffering that was not feigned. The world was turning its back on them. And Frederick, she suddenly remembered, was one of Queen Elizabeth's erstwhile suitors. England would have his ear.

She opened the other letter with trembling hands.

> *My dearest wife—*
> I write this as you once wrote me, almost as if I am speaking to myself, not knowing if you will ever see it, but in writing to you it is the same as writing to myself. For we are one. I feel that more strongly now than ever; even more so than when we were together.
> So we are both in prison, being held against our wills. Yours is worse than mine, my beloved, for your gaolers are your enemies, whereas mine have nothing personal against me. In Bergen I was detained on local matters, and here I am held as a political pawn. I have hopes of being able eventually to convince them that they hold me to no purpose. No one will pay ransom for me, and I am of little political consequence now. My only use, which it grieves me to have failed, was to gain aid for you.
> If it ever, in any way, would be of service to you to stop being my wife, then avail yourself of that avenue. It may be all I can render to you. But know that it is a political gift I bestow on you, not something I will ever honour in my heart, where you will always be my wife.
> Be strong, and love me always, as I love you.
> —James.

She bent over the little stool in the room and gave herself up to a storm of weeping.

❧

Holy Week began with a rainy Palm Sunday. As they had no priest on the island, there was no way to celebrate the sacred days. Lady Douglas had suggested in a horrible inspiration that they invite John Knox to come and preach to them—a suggestion that fortunately was impossible, owing to Knox's indisposition.

So Mary had to provide for her own means of honouring the days. She had her devotionals and book of hours, and requested that her household keep silence during the morning and evening, and fast, and that those of her faith join her in prayer and meditation.

The island was now wearing a new sheen of green, so bright it was vibrant. Each branch of the trees was covered in a translucent green mist, each tree having its own different shade; when the sun shone through the bushes and trees early and late in the day, everything was bathed in the tender green glow.

The sad liturgy of betrayal, parting, torment, and death enveloped Mary.

Never had the events seemed so near, so ever-present. The spying Judas, who had lived with Jesus and known him intimately, betraying him for money: *Lord James*. The stalwart, brave, but in the end helpless Peter: *Bothwell.* The crowd, which had yelled "Hosanna!" and spread their cloaks, six days later crying for his crucifixion: *the Lords and the mob at Edinburgh, screaming, "give us Barabbas!" and "burn the whore!"* The religious leaders, who ought to have been the most just, planning the murder. Caiaphas, the high priest, who said it was expedient that one person should die for the people: *John Knox*. The Sanhedrin: *Lords of the Covenant*. The Roman officials, who were supposed to be unbiased, siding with the mob: *the French, the English.*

The parting with the disciples: Mary leaving Bothwell on that windy field of battle and watching him gallop off. *More I could tell you, but you could not bear it now. Now comes the prince of this world. . . . Are you come out, as against a thief, with swords and with staves to take me? What accusation do you bring against this man? If he were not a malefactor, we would not have delivered him up unto thee.*

Everyone scattered: *Behold the hour cometh, yea, is now come, that you should be scattered, every man to his own, and shall leave me alone.* The Hamiltons who never came, the Gordons who never came, the Borderers on Carberry Hill who melted away in the hot afternoon. Yes, her forces were scattered, in hiding, or had made their peace with the Lords.

Yet, in all the hours she spent praying, kneeling on the floor before the crucifix, she now knew what the cold eyes of that figure were telling her: *If he had not been a malefactor, we would not have delivered him up to you.* She was not innocent. She had loved Bothwell and taken him to her bed, and had wished in her heart to be delivered from Darnley. That someone had overheard that murmur deep within herself and carried it out must be her burden. The fact that Darnley had planned to murder her did not negate her own sin, for she had hated him in her heart long before that.

O dear Lord, she prayed, in the beginning of the week, have mercy on me and my sufferings. Deliver me from my enemies, and set me free. By the end of the week she simply said, O Lord, have mercy on me, a sinner.

❧

Easter came in a blaze of glory, a brilliant, sparkling day that rattled the tree branches and caused them to swoop and swing. From the west a warm wind, laden with promise of summer and softness yet to come, blew across the island. The Laird provided a feast in the hall, and the garrison soldiers stuck dandelions in their buttonholes and played handball on the green. The Douglas girls put on their perfumed gloves and ate more of the steamed almond pudding and candied violets in syrup at dinner than they should have. In the late afternoon the entire castle enjoyed the spring day, strolling, singing, playing games on the newly sprung grass. Lady Douglas and Mary took hands and did a dance together. Lord Lindsay's wife, heavily pregnant, sat on the grass with Mary Seton and applauded them. The wind lifted off her hat, and nimble Willie ran after it and retrieved it before it blew into the water.

April deepened and grew toward May. It had been a year since Bothwell had embarked on his daring gamble to make their marriage acceptable by abducting her to Dunbar. The very scents in the air, of lily of the valley, of hawthorn, brought it back to her so vividly that she dreamed of him night after night. In the dreams his presence was overlaid and imbued with another, heady feeling: freedom. They had ridden and loved and walked in freedom, and had not even known it, as fish are unaware of the water they swim in, but gasp and writhe when taken out of it.

She ached for freedom. To be able to go into a room without being guarded and watched. To be able to lie down without permission. To be able to change the faces she looked at and the view she saw day after day. Only in her dreams was she free, and then waking was painful.

The Laird's wife was brought to childbed and old Lady Douglas was in attendance, and suddenly Mary was guarded less than before. Just to have those eyes, that presence, removed, was like removing chains. The new mother and grandmother were, for a little while, staying in the round tower apartments.

Mary wrote to Queen Elizabeth, hoping that an opportunity would arise for the letter to be carried out. Willie would manage somehow.

Madame, my Good Sister—
    The length of my weary imprisonment, and the wrongs I have received from those on whom I have conferred so many benefits, are less annoying to me than not having it in my power to acquaint you with the realities of my calamities, and the injuries that have been done to me in various ways. It may please you to remember that you have told me several times "that, on receiving that ring you gave me, you would assist me in any time of trouble." You know that Lord James has seized all I have. Melville, to whom I have often sent secretly for this ring, as my most precious jewel, says that he dare not let me have it. Therefore I implore you to have compassion on your good sister and cousin, and believe that you have not a more affectionate relative in the world. You should also consider the importance of the example practised against me.
    I entreat you to be careful that no one knows that I have written to you, for it would cause me to be treated worse than I am now. They boast that their friends at your court inform them of all you say and do.
    God keep you from misfortunes, and grant me patience and His grace that I may one day recount my calumnies to yourself, when I will tell you more than I dare to write, which may prove of no small service to yourself.
    Your obliged and affectionate good sister and cousin,
                                                                    Mary R.
                                                From my prison at Lochleven.

She folded the letter and hid it inside her prayer book. So far they had not searched her devotional materials, as if anything Catholic were untouchable.

On the last day of April the weather played games all day. Mary awoke to a pelting rain, which seemed to soak into the very stones of the tower. She could hear the water dripping and oozing through cracks in the old walls. Outside, the ground could not absorb it all and pools of water studded the grassy courtyard. But by noon the clouds had fled, running across the sky like mythological maidens trailing their skirts with satyrs in pursuit, leaving blue skies behind.

The strengthening sun sparkled on the puddles and dripping leaves and, after an hour of warm mist, dried them up. After their drink, the flowers opened with vibrant colour and danced in the spring air.

The perfume, the warm mist, was sensuously intoxicating. No wonder they think witches come out tonight, Walpurgis Night, Mary thought. May Day and the night before—it's magic, and powerful. She had to smile at herself. Before I came to Scotland, she thought, I had never heard of Walpurgis. But now I have learned more about witches than I ever cared to know.

A boat was approaching. Everyone turned to see who it was, and Mary's heart leapt when she recognized George. He began waving, and the guards made ready to open the gates.

George! Something must be afoot! Trying not to let herself get too excited, Mary waited with the rest of the people as George emerged from the gateway. He did not look at her, but saluted his father warmly.

"George," said the Laird, "you look well, but you know you are—"

"My conscience would not let me depart for France without a formal leave-taking," he said. "I will not stay long. Where is my mother?"

"I will bring her. She will be pleased to see you."

George bowed and, seemingly just looking about to amuse himself in the meantime, caught Mary's eye. He nodded all but imperceptibly. Then he looked away.

Lady Douglas was hurrying toward her son, and then they embraced. Her arm about his shoulder, they walked off together across the green.

Was that a signal he had given her? Would they have no opportunity to speak? Mary decided to wait in the open and hope to see George as he was leaving.

But George was accompanied back to the boat by his parents, and all he could do was give a courtly bow in her direction.

That night, after supper, Willie was skulking about in the yard, kicking a ball and humming to himself. Mary descended from the stairway and walked casually over to him. His head was down and he was practising aiming at a specific stone at the base of the wall. Three out of four times he hit it.

"Very good," said Mary, quietly, and Willie looked up and grinned. He reached down and picked up the ball and tucked it under his arm. Together they walked over to the gate, which was still open in the twilight.

"Only a few minutes," warned one of the guards. "We leave for supper and lock the gates soon."

Willie and Mary made their way down to the water's edge. The setting sun had left the sky laced with garish pink clouds, which were reflected in the loch.

"No bonfires for the witches tonight," said Willie. "But they'll be blazing up in the Highlands, I've no doubt. We're too civilized down here." He laughed.

"Tomorrow is May Day," said Mary. "Do you—is it celebrated here?"

May Day with Darnley, gathering flowers. May Day with Bothwell, shut up in the tower at Dunbar. May Day in France, riding in the countryside, when I was first a widow. May Day seems always to be linked with turning points in my life.

"This year it will be," he said. "I am to be Abbot of Misrule. And everyone is to do exactly as I say. They are to follow me and obey my commands."

"Good evening," said a voice from near the boats, which were tied up nearby.

Mary jumped. She had not even been aware of anyone. But Willie had been. That must have been why his speech was so formal and distant. He replied, "Good evening, sir."

A soldier came toward them in the gathering twilight. "Just securing the boats," he said pointedly.

"Good," said Willie.

The man disappeared inside the gate.

"We flushed him out," said Willie quickly. "Good. Now we are alone, for two or three minutes. Now listen: all is in readiness for your escape. That is why George came. He is not going to France, but needed an excuse to be seen in the vicinity."

A creak from the gate. The soldiers were getting ready to close it. "Come inside!" someone called.

"We come," said Mary.

"During the May Day celebrations, I will steal the keys from the Laird during dinner. When I have them, I will signal to you. Be inside the tower and disguised, ready for flight. Do exactly what I say."

Even walking as slowly as possible, they were now approaching the gate. "I will disable their boats. We will escape in one boat. Bring no one with you. Tell no one. I will— Good evening, officer." He greeted the guard. "Sleep well, Your Majesty."

Mary lay awake in the dawn, hearing the birds begin to chatter even before it grew light. So this was the day. She dared not dwell on it, lest she grow so excited she somehow betray all the plans. Best not to think about it. But as she arose, she could not help glancing round the tower room and wondering if she had spent her last night in it. Pray God that I never waken in here again! she thought.

She readied her shabby clothes once again, hoping they did not retain the bad luck of the last failed attempt. The absence of the Douglas women made it so much easier to make ready. She gathered up a few of her things, putting them inconspicuously in a pile that, if opportunity afforded, she could scoop up and carry with her.

Now there was the day to get through. Never had an ordinary day seemed so long. There were the morning prayers she and her household always recited, followed by breakfast, then sewing, then walking outside.

Today there was bustling as the Great Hall was being readied for the feast, and decorations—coloured banners and sashes—were being hung on the walls and trees. Musicians practised out on the green in the sunshine, already drinking ale. Much ale had been provided, and the soldiers were helping themselves by noon. Mary prayed that it would last until the crucial time. How ironic if it ran out in time for the soldiers to sober up just as she tried to run away.

"Now follow me!" Willie was parading out in a multicoloured coat of satin, with a high conical hat like a magician's. He crawled on all fours, and the people following him had to do so as well. Then he jumped up and whirled, and they had to follow suit.

"You there!" He pointed to one of the soldiers on the wall. "Stand on your head."

"What?" The soldier looked around. "From here?"

"Indeed, if you dare!" said Willie. " 'Tis only ten feet to the ground. It won't crack your head open!"

The soldier—actually a boy not much older than Willie—gingerly attempted to obey, but he toppled over and had to clutch at the stones to keep from falling all the way to the ground.

"Ah, too bad! Now you must be punished!" said Willie, while everyone was laughing. "You shall carry Mistress Meggie about on your back until dinner time."

More people had joined the line behind Willie, following him about, laughing and shouting.

The game went on all afternoon, with Willie exhausting himself trying to think of tasks and rewards and punishments. Everyone got drunker, and miraculously, the ale did not run out. How had Willie paid for it all?

Mary dropped out of the line. Her side was hurting. She stood for a few moments with her arms clasped around her sides, hoping the pain would subside. She could not be sick now, no, she could not!

One of the castle servants, a young girl, came to Mary. She handed her the pearl earring. Mary just stared at it.

"Your Majesty, George Douglas sends this to you. He says one of the other servants found it and tried to sell it to him, but he recognized it as being yours and ordered it returned to you. Is it indeed yours?"

616

"Yes," said Mary. "I had lost it some time ago. Thank you."

The girl curtseyed and said, "My honour is to return it, Madam."

The signal! All was in order, then! Mary felt dizzy with excitement, and the pain vanished from her side.

"I am so tired from all this," she said. "I must needs rest before dinner." She made her way back to the tower apartment, which was—another miracle!—deserted. Quickly she put on her servant-skirt underneath her own, and changed her shoes. Then she lay down, trying to calm herself.

In an hour she emerged. The revellers were nowhere to be seen, but she could hear them. They seemed to have retired to the great hall, where they could drink and sing.

Lady Douglas was pacing in the courtyard. Mary's heart sank, and she would have withdrawn quickly back into her room, but she had been seen. So she had to smile and make her way over to Lady Douglas, hoping that her shoes would not show beneath her skirt.

"Happy May to you," said Lady Douglas. "Have you ever seen such foolishness?" Her voice was not lighthearted.

"For me, in this prison, any departure from routine is pleasant," said Mary.

"Prison. Yes. Arabella has been troubled by dreams about a great raven carrying you away, across the water. She dreamed that Willie had brought the raven."

Arabella! That foolish girl, who doted on her!

"She was most upset. It seems she would hate to lose you," said Lady Douglas.

"I am most fond of her," said Mary carefully. "And her dream is not like to come true. I am rather heavy for a raven to lift!" She gave what she hoped was a silly giggle.

"Perhaps a company of ravens would be employed. But, Madam, I beg you, remember my family. We would be ruined if you escaped. The Lords would think—what's that?" She pointed to a movement on the shore.

A company of horsemen! Mary could see them plainly near Kinross.

"Your family!" said Mary, answering her first statement and not her second. "You mean your darling the Lord James! Is he all you care about? You have ten other children! Why is it that only he occupies your heart? He is cruel, greedy, grasping—did you know that when I was on my death-bed, and he thought I could not see, he began to inventory my jewels? *That* is your favourite son! You see what you have given birth to!"

"Lord James is a deeply devout man who has Scotland's interests always at the forefront of his mind!" Lady Douglas's face darkened and she stopped looking at the shore. The horsemen disappeared.

"*He* has the Lord James at the forefront of *his* mind! And, Madam, think how it sits with your family's honour to be his puppets and servants!" She dared not let Lady Douglas look back at the shore; only baiting her about James would distract her enough to make her forget what she had just seen.

"How dare you speak that way?" Lady Douglas attacked like a mother tiger, listing all Mary's sins and shortcomings.

Mary listened and pretended to be shocked and hurt, all the while keeping her own face toward the shore to make sure that her antagonist could not look that way.

As was his custom, the Laird brought Mary's dinner to her in the tower, where she took her meals. Tonight was no exception, and the shuffling master of the island, wearing a paper cap Willie had clapped on him, and belching from the ale, set before her a springtime meal: roast lamb, spinach tart, baked butter pudding, and an astringent drink called "spring tonic": fresh green leaves of agrimony and the juice of wild cresses, blended in new ale.

"I trust this will be pleasing," he said.

"Indeed, I am sure it will." Mary smiled at him.

I will not be sorry to leave, she thought. But the Laird has always been kindly and harmless. It is difficult to reconcile this self-effacing, ineffectual man with a gaoler. *Is* Willie his bastard? What story lies behind that?

The Laird began to pace her room, as if he was loath to leave. He stood for a moment, contemplating the crucifix on the wall near her prayer-window with sad eyes. Suddenly he started as he saw something out the window.

"Ehh!" he said. "What's that stupid Willie doing?"

Mary rose and went to the window. Willie was bent down between two boats beached on the shore. He must be disabling them, as he had said he would. There was a hiatus in the celebration before he was expected in the great hall.

"That boy!" the Laird cried. "Always some foolishness!" He started to motion to a guard outside to investigate.

"Oh!" Mary put her hand up to her forehead and groaned. She swayed and fell to her knees.

Confused, the Laird bent down to her, abandoning the window. "What is it?"

"I feel so dizzy. It comes upon me sometimes like this!" She slumped against him. "I pray you, help me to my couch."

The Laird sighed and put his arm under her shoulder, and helped her to walk feebly to the couch. "There," he said, straightening up and looking back toward the window.

"Would you please be so kind?" she said in a small voice. "Sweet wine from Sicily or Cyprus helps me when I have these attacks. Would you happen to have—could you bring me—ooh, I will try not to faint!" She rolled her head from side to side.

Disgruntled, the Laird had to go fetch it himself, as there were no attendants. By the time he returned, Willie had gone from the boats.

* * *

At the May Day feast, the Laird insisted on being seated where he could have an unobstructed view out the window to the shore, just in case there was something amiss on the mainland. Willie was presiding over the table, pouring wine with abandon. Everyone was getting befuddled.

In front of the Laird, beside his plate, lay the keys to the gate and castle, as they did every night after the gates were locked. There were five of them, linked on a chain.

Willie was at his shoulder, a huge bottle of wine braced on his arm.

"Wine, sir?" he said.

"No—no more." Things were starting to fuzz. "Uh—what kind is that?"

"This is the Rhenish, sir. Best we have. Better than the stuff you were drinking earlier."

"Umm. All right." The Laird held up his goblet, and his hand swayed a bit.

"Oh, this is heavy! Pardon me!" Willie groaned and threw his napkin down on the table while he shouldered the bottle in a different way, as he poured the liquid out. It gurgled like a happy spring toad in love.

The Laird did not notice that when Willie picked up his discarded napkin, the keys disappeared.

Mary, watching anxiously at the window, saw Willie emerge from the hall and walk quickly across the green. He raised his hand and nodded.

Mary removed her own skirt, revealing the maid's skirt underneath, put on her servant's cloak, and descended. Her hood was raised.

"I have the keys," said Willie. "Hurry! But do not run."

They walked together briskly. Mary was sure that her dark, billowing cloak, so out of place on this May evening, was going to attract attention. Her heart was beating so hard she now felt truly faint.

Willie pulled the keys out of his sleeve and stuck one into the gate lock. It did not fit. He tried another. It seemed to fit, but then did not turn. Mary did not dare even look behind them to see if anyone was following, lest someone see her face.

Willie tried another, trying to keep his nervous hands steady. It slid in and then she heard the sound of the bolt releasing. Willie extracted the keys, then pulled the door open, only wide enough for them to slide through. Then he closed the gate as quietly as possible and locked it from the outside.

"There! Now *they* are prisoners!"

For a moment they hid in the shadow of the wall, to see if anyone was following. But all was silent. They stole over to one of the boats. Mary lay down on the bottom.

"The rest are disabled?" she whispered.

"Yes. I pegged them."

"I think the Laird may have seen you. But I tried to distract him."

Willie pushed the boat off, wading into the water up to his waist, then

619

climbed in. He grabbed the oars and began rowing. The boat cleared the weeds near the shore, and floated out into open water.

Willie's arm flashed as he flung the keys into the water. They hit some reeds and then sank with very little sound. "Let them dive for them!" he said.

Mary cautiously sat up. The shore was already being left behind. But she had been farther than this when the men had discovered her that other time. Impulsively she took the second set of oars and began rowing. Anything to get them farther away!

Willie laughed. "That is not necessary," he said.

"Oh, but it is!" she said. "I must participate in my own escape! I am not old, sick, or helpless—I have never felt stronger!" As she said it, she realized that the food and rest on Lochleven, forcibly imposed though they were, had restored her to her old level of energy and well-being. Once again she was the athletic, active Queen of the Chaseabout Raid. She pulled on the oars, straining against them.

Darkness was falling. There seemed to be a movement on the shore. Who was waiting? Was it George? She could hardly see in the blue-grey mist rising from the loch. She fumbled for the veil she had brought, the prearranged signal: she was to wave her white veil.

It fluttered in the air, its red tassels snapping. Up and down, up and down. George and his men saw it; and so did the Laird and the company in the castle, watching helplessly from behind the imprisoning walls. Suddenly she could hear angry shouting from the island.

They reached the landing at Kinross, and there was George, looking pale and intense. He held out his arms to her and she alighted. She draped the veil around his shoulders and said softly, "Thank you."

"Your servant, sir," said Willie, bowing mockingly.

"Who else is here?" Mary asked.

Crowding toward her was John Beaton, from the faithful Beaton family. He headed a company of about twenty horsemen. "Borrowed from the Laird's stables here on shore," he said. Everyone laughed. Young John Sempill, Mary Livingston's husband, was beside him.

"Lord Seton is waiting, hidden in the glen, with fifty men," said George. "And the Laird Hepburn of Riccarton with him."

Laird Riccarton! Bothwell's friend and kinsman!

"Let us leave, and quickly. Can you ride?"

"Of course!" Mary mounted a muscular horse brought over to her.

The party galloped off.

The night was balmy. Somehow it felt different on land than out on the island. The air, the scents, were different.

Free. I am free. The feeling was so odd she could barely understand it.

They met up with Lord Seton and his men, and Laird Riccarton, at a clearing just outside of town.

"Dear Lord Seton!" She was delirious to see all these people, friends instead of enemies. She had not been among friends in so long! They embraced.

Then the Laird of Riccarton. "Dear friend," she said. Just seeing him made Bothwell real again. "Please—get word to my husband that I am free! He must join me!"

"I will ride for the coast," he said, "and be there by morning. There are many ships to carry letters swiftly across the seas."

LXIII

Mary and her party galloped around Kinross and then took the road leading south. She was retracing the miserable route she had followed when she was taken, a prisoner, to Lochleven with Lindsay and Ruthven. Every turning of the path brought back a particular memory of that time of terror for her: the overhanging branch that she had hoped would knock Lindsay off his horse, the sharp turn where she had almost been thrown herself. Now they just seemed like perfectly ordinary features of any riding path, nothing she would even notice.

Ahead of her, Lord George Seton was keeping a good, steady pace. What a friend he was! Always he had been there at her most precarious moments, and had helped her in her escape from Holyrood as well. Back at Lochleven, they were probably questioning his sister. With a brother and sister so loyal to her, what a contrast to her own brother, Lord James!

"Are we to stop at Seton House?" she asked him, when they stopped on the road to refresh themselves with a little wine and bread.

"No," he said. "I think we should get farther than that. Lord Claud Hamilton is to meet us at Queensferry after we cross the Forth. From there we will rest at Niddry, my other castle." It was dark enough that he could not see her face, but he could guess at her puzzled look. "Your escape has been planned, and looked for. Many who had joined your brother's cause have had time to rethink themselves. The Regency has not pleased the nobles nearly as well as they'd hoped; now a number of them have decided to come back to you. The Hamiltons are out in force for you; the Earl of Argyll, unstable man, has come over to us. So have Eglinton and Cassillis. You always had the west of Scotland's loyalty, and the lords from there, Herries and Maxwell, are waiting in their territories."

So people were turning against Lord James! Now he had seen how easy it was to please people before you came to power, and how difficult afterwards. Even the best ruler was never more beloved than before he ascended the throne.

They continued their journey, and made the crossing of the Forth in several ferries provided for the purpose. At South Queensferry, Lord Hamilton and fifty of his kinsmen, armed and mounted, greeted them.

"Your Majesty!" said Lord Hamilton. "It is with great joy that I see you!" His men lifted their weapons in salute.

As they passed through little villages on their way to Niddry, the people came out and cheered her. There was nothing but sweet welcome; no spitting, no name-calling, no calls for her to be burnt. Had the people forgiven her? She had not heard such acclaim since before Darnley's death. Perhaps they had forgiven, perhaps even forgotten. If only their hatred of her had been forgotten!

It was midnight when they reached Niddry, Seton's castle that lay several miles south of the Forth. There they halted.

"Come, Your Majesty," said Lord Seton. They swept into the courtyard and then into the prepared apartments. "All is ready," he said, and Mary walked into a tidy, well-furnished room. It was no bigger than the one at Lochleven, but the freedom made it seem ten times larger.

"With all my heart I thank you," said Mary, touching his shoulder.

Inside her room, alone at last, she looked around, dazed. It had been a very long time since she had arisen in that tower chamber at Lochleven. And her prayer had been answered; she did not ever have to go to sleep in it again.

Too tired to do anything but remove her shabby shirt and bodice, and grateful that she was completely alone, she climbed into the bed and fell at once into a profound, deep sleep—the best she had had in ten months.

She awakened to a feeling that told her there had been a momentous happening, but for an instant she could not remember exactly what it was. This bed—it was unfamiliar. The room's dark corners failed to disclose its size. She got out of the high, carved bed and groped her way over to a window that showed the east light. She was overlooking land, land—no water. No island. Nothing but this gentle green surrounding her. Then it all rushed back upon her—she was free! This was Lord Seton's castle.

What hour was it? She had no clock, and by the faint light she surmised that dawn was not far away. It must be before five o'clock. No one would be up yet. She returned to bed and forced herself to wait.

Later, getting dressed—still alone, blessedly alone!—she heard sounds outside her window. Looking out, where earlier there had been only green, rolling landscape, she saw a huge company of men milling around. They were armed with pikes and staves, and just as she appeared, one of the leaders was sounding a bugle, another a bagpipe.

Excited beyond measure, she rushed from the room, her long hair uncombed and flying, and ran out into the courtyard. Lord Seton, following, tried to stop her, but she outran him and made her way to the crowd. As soon as they saw her, a hushed reverence fell over the men. Then someone shouted, "God bless the Queen!" and a thousand voices shouted, "Aye!"

Tears made all the colours and faces blend for a moment in her eyes. Shaking her head to clear her vision, she held out her arms to them. "My good people! I am indeed blessed to be back among you!"

At the sight of her, long hair flowing, and not properly dressed, they were swept with emotion. She was surely the most beautiful queen in the world, and how fortunate they were that she was *theirs*. Future generations would envy them; their sons and daughters would ask them to recount exactly how she had looked on this morning. "We'll die for you!" they cried.

"I would have no one die," she answered. "Let my brother surrender and step down. And now that you have shown your loyalty, he will do so. He cannot ignore the will of the people."

Oh, how easy it would have been, immured in Lochleven, to have believed that she was unloved and unwanted. Prison kept reality at bay—as her brother, Lord James, had counted on.

❧

Mary sat, dressed—again in borrowed clothes—at a table in conference with her nobles. They had left Niddry Castle after that first night and headed west, toward Dumbarton. The mighty fortress on the coast was the only one still in loyal hands; Lord Fleming, Mary's brother, held it. The other strongholds, and their arsenals—Stirling, Edinburgh, Dunbar—were at the disposal of Lord James. The west was still mainly Catholic and loyal, and it made sense, strategically, to head for that area. They hoped to pause and provide a rallying point for the other loyalists to join them. The Hamiltons, that vast clan with hereditary rights next to the Stewarts, had been angered by Lord James seizing the Regency and giving them no part in the spoils. They were now the center of the loyalists, and meant to turn the upstarts out of power. Their territory lay just south of Glasgow, and so it was to Castle Hamilton that Mary and her party repaired and made their headquarters. Here the royalists could gather, knowing that the safety of Dumbarton was only twelve miles away. From there in an emergency they could go anywhere, just as Mary had sailed for France when she was a child.

Now, seated at the very long, polished table were nine earls, nine bishops, eighteen lords, and many lairds of lesser rank. Mary stood up, a queen among her nobles once more.

"My Lords," she said, "I wish to solemnly repudiate my forced abdication, and for you to witness it. Then we will publish it. I do swear on my immortal soul, as I shall answer on the dreadful Day of Judgement, that my signature on the writs and instruments procured at Lochleven was got by violence and threats to my life. And for this I have witnesses: George Douglas and Melville." She nodded to those two, seated down near the end of the table.

"Indeed, it is true!" said George, his voice trembling. "Lord Lindsay threatened to kill her—to cut her up and feed her to the fish, he said!"

"I can attest to the fact that Her Majesty agreed to sign only after I assured her that the Queen of England advised her to do it to save her life, knowing that nothing obtained in those circumstances could be binding," Melville added. He had come straightway from Edinburgh as soon as he was summoned, bringing with him two things Mary desperately wanted: the Elizabeth ring, and her horses from her own stable.

"My Lords, I constitute us to have the legal standing of a Parliament, and it is necessary that we attend to pressing business." Mary nodded to the Archbishop of St. Andrews, clever John Hamilton. "The Archbishop and I have prepared a statement concerning the Regent which we wish you to ratify."

The Archbishop stood up and read out in a booming voice, " 'We do hereby declare that our false abdication, extorted under threat of our life, is utterly null and void, and that we are Mary, by the Grace of God, undoubted and righteous hereditary Queen of Scotland, succeeding thereto of the immoveable just line, being lawfully elected, crowned, invested and inaugurated thereto.' "

All the men at the table nodded and murmured.

Then the Archbishop went on to detail the crimes of the Lord James, branding him "that beastly traitor, a bastard begotten in shameful adultery," and describing all his party as "shameless butchers, hell-hounds, bloody tyrants, common murderers, and cutthroats, whom no prince, yea, not the barbarous Turk, for their perpetrated murders could pardon or spare."

The men laughed uneasily. The Queen, then, could never make peace with her brother. She had turned utterly against him; he had betrayed her once too often.

"Now my good Lords," she said, "I pray you give heed to what intelligence we have of our adversaries."

Lord Seton stood. "The Regent was in Glasgow, holding an assize, when the news reached him that Her Majesty had escaped a few days ago, and he was sore amazed!"

The company laughed.

"He was alone except for a bodyguard, and thought perhaps he should retreat back to Stirling, as this area is so partial to the Queen. But he has evidently decided that it is better to stand his ground rather than be seen to retreat. Consequently he has set up camp there and sent out summons for men. He calls for"—he unfolded a paper—"for the preservation of the King's person, and the establishing of quietness."

Mary laughed scornfully. "And how has his summons been answered?"

"Kirkcaldy is bringing harquebusiers from Edinburgh, and Erskine is bringing cannon from Stirling. And there's Morton and his pikemen, hurrying to fight."

"How many?"

"Thus far, about two thousand. When Lindsay and Ruthven and Glencairn come, there may be as many as three thousand."

"Ha!" The Earl of Argyll gave a scornful snort. "Why, my Highlanders alone are nearly two thousand. Add the Hamiltons, and—we'll have over five thousand!"

Suddenly she was gripped with a cold hand of fear. Her army was larger. But it had no leader. There was no Bothwell, no one comparable. Without Bothwell to counter them, Kirkcaldy and Lord James and Morton became formidable enemies. What was only good became, in the absence of excellence, excellence itself.

"And who will lead my army? Who will be my general?" Mary asked.

"I," said Argyll. "I have brought the largest number of men."

Hamilton glowered.

"My dearest Queen," said Lord Herries suddenly, "you should know that there are only two ways to restore you to your throne so that you are in power: either by a decree of Parliament, or by battle. It is your choice to make."

Mary looked up and down the table at the faces of her supporters: George Douglas's handsome features and tight-lipped commitment; the plain, honest face of Lord Seton; the calm bravery of Lord Livingston.

Bothwell's face was missing, and always would be. But the others had already sacrificed much of themselves, and would not fail her.

"By battle let us try it!" she said, and purpose and resolve flooded her, washing aside any lingering hesitation.

In the next few days, more men flocked to her standard; more than one hundred lesser lords brought their vassals, tenants, and domestic servants for her army. Huntly had surprisingly thrown in his lot with hers, and was bringing his troops down from the Highlands. But torrential rains had swollen the streams and made them impassable.

"I've no doubt the Lord James plans to strike before Huntly can arrive," said Mary to George. "But even without him, we are stronger."

"My father has joined *them*," said George. "Yesterday he brought his men."

"My, how efficient spies are," said Mary lightly, but in her heart she was disturbed. How was information passing so freely between the armies? Yet she knew George was to be trusted. "But I am grateful he is able to fight, if that makes sense."

"Yes," George muttered. The Laird had tried to stab himself to death after he had discovered the Queen's escape; he had felt the dishonour keenly. Yet his servants had prevented him, and now the impulse had passed. "I am spared that guilt . . . a part in my father's murder."

"There has been enough murder in Scotland," said Mary, twisting the Elizabeth ring. Just having it on her finger gave her security. *I have the means of escaping to France by sea, should it come to that, or to England* by land if all else fails, she thought. She wondered if Elizabeth had received her last letter, followed by the news of her escape. So far there had been no word from England.

"There is the problem of pay," George was saying. "The Lord James has all the coin and plate and jewels of the crown at his disposal, and we have nothing. How will we pay these troops?"

"With promises," she said. "For once I regain my throne—"

"They cannot eat on promises," said George.

"Then the food and munitions must be given as gifts," she answered. "Those who support me will have to extend charity, for now."

"You ask a high price," he said. "Not everyone will pay it."

"Not everyone, no. There are very few like you, George—willing to be at enmity with what they perceive as their own best interests, or with their own flesh and blood. Poor George—you are going against both your father and your older brother."

"I have no other choice," he said. "But others may."

"No other choice?" she asked.

"You know all too well what I mean. Pray do not ask me to say the words."

Mary sent a proclamation to James, encamped only a few miles away, announcing that she was repudiating her abdication and reclaiming her throne, and that she desired, in the name of mercy, to receive his acceptance of this and to reconcile him to obedience to her. His reply was to tear it up and put her messenger in chains.

On May thirteenth, only eleven days after Mary had fled from Lochleven, the battle was joined. Mary's forces had swelled to six thousand men, even without Huntly, whereas James's were only three thousand. Early in the morning her commander, Argyll, gave the orders to march westward, skirting Glasgow, and engage James at his stronghold at Burgh Muir.

Mary, accompanied by Willie Douglas and Mary Seton—whom the distraught Laird had allowed to follow her mistress—took up a position on a nearby hill that gave her a view of the surrounding countryside. She saw her army, with Lord Claud Hamilton and his clansmen forming the vanguard, marching toward the little town of Langside; Argyll, with the bulk of the troops, followed a distance behind.

Suddenly there was colour and movement; Lord James was approaching! She could not follow all the motions, but later it was revealed that James had mounted two men to a horse and transferred his entire army quickly to an ideal position just outside Langside rather than face her army on the flat plain. In a daring maneuver, Kirkcaldy stationed harquebusiers in the orchards and alleys around the main street of Langside, while Morton and James kept control of the main body of troops, stationed on Langside Hill.

The vanguard of Hamiltons now filed into Langside, their progress slowed by the problem of processing through the narrow main thoroughfare. Shots rang out; they were fired upon by hidden gunmen on all sides, and they fell in confusion, bodies heaping up on each other as they tried to escape. The harquebusiers picked them off as if they were target-shooting, and the men panicked.

Behind them the Highland troops of Argyll stopped in bewilderment, unable to enter the bottleneck of the town. They heard the gunfire and the screams, and turned to their commander for direction. Just then piercing yells rang out; Lord Herries was leading a charge up the hill after Lord James.

Then a wailing and lamenting rose and swelled. The Highlanders were turning, breaking ranks, running the other way!

Mary looked across at Langside Hill, where, to her horror, she saw a cradle resting under a spreading hedge, with the now-familiar banner of the kneeling Prince fluttering above it. The Lords had brought the baby James to this battlefield!

Anger and hatred filled her. How could they have risked his life so?

Perhaps they did not care if he perished; perhaps that was even their purpose. "We lost him in battle," they could sadly say, when placing the crown on the head of the bastard Lord James.

With a cry of vengeance, she spurred her own horse and galloped down the hill, waving her pistols.

"Fight them, fight the evil usurpers!" she cried, entering the melee. She was almost run down by fleeing Highlanders.

"Where is your chief?" she yelled, seeing Argyll's horse without a rider. But no one answered, they only rushed away. Then she saw a bundle lying at the horse's feet; the loyal horse was standing over him and preventing him from being trampled.

His attendant was kneeling down beside him, rubbing his master's face. "A fit of apoplexy," he said, his face stained with tears. "He was struck just as we began the attack."

Apoplexy! How could he have been struck now? Could not God have waited another hour, another two hours?

"Do You hate me?" she screamed at the heavens. Around her the dust was rising as the men fled. She turned to them and yelled, "Stand! Stand and fight! The day will be yours!"

A shower of arrows rained down on them, and the next in command echoed her cry. "Fight! Regroup!"

"Shut up, you've no authority!" cried one of the other men, one of his cousins.

The two men sat on their horses arguing while arrows fell on all sides of them.

"Coward and poltroon!" screamed one. "Leave him and follow me!"

"He's no training, just a student, a soft book-lover—"

"Shut up!"

A scramble, and Mary saw Lord Herries leading a second charge up Langside Hill. But with no strength or reinforcements behind him, he could not sustain it. Lord James drove him back.

Mary reined in her horse, and keeping her pistols at the ready, she fled through the side streets of Langside, almost hoping she would find a harquebusier hiding in the trees. By God, I'll shoot him! she thought. The main street was filled with bodies.

As she galloped back to her hill, she was met by Lord Livingston, George and Willie, and Lord Herries's son. "Come," they said. She realized they were escorting her off the field of battle. "It is not meet—"

"Not meet that I see firsthand what has happened? They will not fight!" she shrieked. "Argyll has fallen, and his Highlanders flee—"

As she reached the summit of the hill, she saw Morton's pikemen advancing on the few remaining Hamiltons emerging at the other end of the main street. Hand-to-hand combat ensued, and screams of terror, sounding all but inhuman, filled the air.

Lord Herries galloped up, his horse sweat-streaked. "The day is lost," he said. "We must flee!"

"Lost?"

"Aye. Quickly, lest you be taken again!" He jerked her bridle.

Taken again. Then it was all in vain. It was all over—and in less than an hour. A lifetime in an hour.

"Where can I, in honour, go?"

"Let us make for Dumbarton. There we can gather strength, send to France for help!" He motioned to her, and she followed him down the hill. Below were the flashing staves and daggers of Morton's men, finishing off their victims. "Do not look!"

But she did. She watched as the helpless men writhed and twitched and then died, crying out.

They were past the battlefield in only a few moments, and then they headed toward the water, and Dumbarton. They would have to gallop across the fields now being prepared for planting. But the army was not in pursuit. Far behind them were coming George and Willie.

Unexpectedly, two men rose up in the field, brandishing scythes and hoes.

"You'll not pass this way, whore!" they yelled, and started running toward Mary's horse, trying to swipe it with their blades. Her horse reared and flinched.

Their eyes were full of hatred, and they aimed and swooped like boys trying to make a goal in a schoolyard game. "Get her!" sneered one.

The Earl of Lennox's lands! Of course!

She wheeled her horse around and fled in the opposite direction. Dumbarton was cut off; they had no hopes of reaching it. They could not go through Glasgow, which was solidly for Lord James, nor get across the wide Firth of Clyde, nor pass over the waters where they were narrower, for they lay in Lennox's territory. Her enemies made a living fence around her only fortress.

She and Lord Herries, in doubling back, came abreast of Willie and George. "We cannot pass to Dumbarton," Mary said, panting.

"We must try to go south," said Herries. "It will be through the wild districts of the Galloway mountains and moors. But I know the passes, and our pursuers will not. You must be a native to know them, and thanks be to God, all our people in these parts are still loyal. Come. Can you undertake this journey?" He looked not only at Mary but at George, Willie, Lord Livingston, and his own son, who had now caught up with them.

"With God's help!" said Mary, and all the others nodded.

"Then let us go!" Herries touched spurs to his horse and led them away, across the fields and south.

He had spoken true: once the softness of the valley of the River Doon— in full flower now, white starry violets dotting the banks of the water, wild plum trees in full scented bloom—with its shepherds and flocks of sheep and newborn lambs fell away, they found themselves in untamed tracts of mountains, with rushing, foamy streams and rocky waterfalls. The landscape changed from the lush green of the watered flat valley to the brown-and-moss-and-heathery crags of the high country. The sky was enormous, and brooded over them with moody racing clouds that threw shadows in the dips and rises. By midafternoon the clouds had coalesced and turned black on their undersides, and a fine mist descended, settling around them, dampening them without actually raining. It made the footing all the more dangerous.

Even the flatter areas were fraught with danger, as bogs were concealed under the heather and sedge and looked safe. They followed the passes and paths of the Glenkens, the glen that surrounded the cold River Ken, which was rushing to empty itself into a ten-mile loch.

Mary saw all this, but did not see it. She had done these things before, and done them separately; there had been so many mad rides to safety in her lifetime, usually at night or with pursuers just behind. She had travelled over dangerous moors and passes on the rides in the Borders, and had even fallen into a bog. But all that had been different. Always there had been Bothwell, present in some fashion. And never had there been this sense of finality, of a last, desperate headlong dash. Always before she had had a destination: Inchmahome, Dunbar, the Hermitage, Kinross. Now she had no idea where to go, and anyplace she went was not a destination, but a refuge—and she a supplicant.

They rode along the west bank of the River Ken, riding slower now due to fatigue. Lord Herries said they were nearing the mouth of the big loch. The mist was turning to outright rain, and they plodded on. Suddenly Herries reined his horse to a stop and pointed across a smaller loch.

She stopped and tried to see, through the gloom and rain, what he was indicating. She could just barely make out the outline of a castle on the banks of the loch.

"Earlstoun Castle," said Herries. "It belonged to Lord Bothwell."

Belonged! Belonged! Not belongs . . .

"Perhaps we could ask for refuge there. I know not who keeps it now— perhaps it is still in the hands of his loyal servants."

Tears filled her eyes, but she angrily bade them begone. Bothwell had never mentioned this castle; it had not figured large in his affections. And perhaps, perhaps, it was his way of providing for her now, as he always had, in some magical way.

"Yes," she said. "Let us approach."

They skirted the shore of the loch and made their way to the old castle. There were no lights visible inside.

"This was a Sinclair castle," said Herries. "The mother of the Lord Bothwell."

But who inhabited it now? Bothwell's mother lived in Morham. As they came closer, they saw the courtyard was mired in mud and there were no people about.

They halted in the muddy courtyard and huddled together in the pelting rain. At length Lord Herries dismounted and, sloshing through the muck, made his way to the entrance steps. He shook the mud off his feet and climbed slowly up the steps. Before he had reached the door, Mary had dismounted and followed him, holding up her skirts. He awaited her at the door—a massive, pitted wooden one of old-fashioned workmanship. It must have dated from the time of Robert the Bruce.

She drew back her hand and knocked on the door. It made very little noise; the wet wood muffled the noise. She beat on it again, harder. They could hear it echoing inside. But there was no answering barking of dogs or cries of servants. It was only then that she realized how deeply silent the castle was: no sound of horses, no crowing of roosters, no lowing of cows. And no human voices.

The castle was deserted and locked fast.

Frantically she beat on the door. There must be someone there! There had to be!

This was *Bothwell's* castle, Bothwell, her protector. . . .

"Do not leave me at the mercy of my enemies!" she begged him.

Lord Herries looked at her in wonder. Then he understood. "Come, Your Majesty," he said, lifting her fallen hood up over her head. Her hair was drenched, and rivulets of water were running down her face.

"You must be here!" Mary laid her face against the door and whispered the words. But the dead castle kept its dark and silence.

Like a child, she began sobbing against the wet wood.

He is gone, and it is all over. Nothing but death and nothingness is inside, and outside, and all around me, forever and ever hereafter.

"Perhaps we can pitch a camp here, in the courtyard, if it would please you," he said.

She looked horrified. "No! Let us leave this place!" She rushed back down the steps and out across the courtyard, not caring that her skirts were trailing in the mud. She hurled herself back into the saddle. "Come, we ride!" she said.

George tried to catch her distracted, red eyes, but she looked past him and, like a demented person, urged her horse on in the darkness.

At the foot of the Ken Loch, after riding sixty miles from the scene of the battle, Mary at last slid off her horse and allowed the men to make a camp.

They rested a scant three hours before the sun was up, trying to shine through the continuing mist. They had no food with them, and the only drink they could take was the loch water, which was icy cold.

"We will follow the River Dee," said Herries, indicating the stream that flowed out of the Ken Loch, a meandering pathway of reeds and lilies.

They set out, not rested, but at least able to go forward. The banks of the Dee were placid and spongy as the heights and crags of the wild country receded behind them and they reached the valley of the Tarff.

At Tongland a small wooden bridge, built in the time of the Bruce, spanned the narrowest point of the river. They trotted across it, then Herries commanded them to stop.

"Destroy it!" he ordered the men. "That will delay any followers—for without doubt, we have them."

"Can we not spare this ancient relic?" asked Mary wearily. Was everything to be broken up, wrecked?

"No," said Herries.

George, Willie, and Livingston dismounted, and began hacking at it with their swords.

Dizzy, Mary wandered away. She could hear the thudding and splintering of wood, but it seemed like a dream. I must get something to eat, she thought, ashamed that she needed it before the others did.

Ahead of her in the fields was a small farmer's cottage, put together with dry stones and lit only by the tiniest of windows. Smoke was rising from the hole in the thatched roof. She walked slowly and a bit unsteadily toward the door and, leaning on the doorframe, asked in a faint voice, "Is there anyone within?" She could smell the fire.

An old woman, not unlike the one Bothwell had gone to see on the moors that long-ago day, shuffled to the doorway. She stared at Mary.

"Please—have you any food?" she asked.

"No," said the woman. Her voice was so cracked it sounded as if her throat was injured. "No, that I do not." She rubbed her own stomach, not unkindly.

"Nothing?" How could it be that some of her subjects had no food? She remembered the thin broth of those other people.

"Come in," said the woman. "You look dreadful." She motioned for Mary to follow her, and brought a stool to her. Mary sat down and looked around at the plain little room. The women opened a cupboard and began to mix something up, then dumped it into a kettle and stirred it over the smouldering fire for what seemed an eternity. Then at last she turned to Mary and handed her a bowl and spoon, and emptied the kettle into the bowl.

"Here," she said, bringing over a pitcher of milk.

Oatmeal. It was oatmeal. Mary poured some milk into it and took a bite. The milk was sour.

"It is all I have," said the woman.

Mary looked, and indeed there was nothing else in the cupboard but the little sack of oatmeal. She nodded gratefully and ate the entire bowl.

"Do you wish more?" asked the woman gently, even though it would completely deplete her supply.

Mary was stunned at her generosity. To this woman, she was only a stranger, and a sickly-looking one at that. "You have been good to share this much," she said. "I am grateful."

Just then Herries came up and burst into the cottage. "Your Majesty!" he said. "Why did you not tell us—" He stopped as the woman looked at him in horror.

"Yes," said Mary to her, "I am the Queen."

The woman muttered and almost crossed herself in shock.

"I am in the protection of these my good servants," said Mary. "But I can never have better servants than the ordinary people who live in my land, like you. You have done me a great service today, far greater than you can imagine. What would you like as a reward? Name it, it is yours."

"Nay—I seek no reward," she said.

"And that is precisely why you shall have it," she answered. "Please, tell me. And quickly. I cannot linger here."

"Why, I—I wish I owned this cottage, and its land!" she said. "Our family have been tenants for generations."

"Good Lord Herries, you are overlord here. May she have it?"

"Of course!" he said. "With all my heart I grant it."

When Mary rejoined her party by the site of the wrecked bridge, she suddenly was seized with a strange desire. "Give me your dagger," she ordered George. With a puzzled look he handed it to her.

She unbound her hair and spread it out over her shoulders. It came almost to her waist. "I pray you, cut it off," she said. She handed the dagger back to him. "I cannot do it myself."

"No, Your Majesty! You must not!" said Willie.

"I wish it done," she said. "Do as I say."

"But—why?" George's voice trembled with pain.

"We are pursued. I now know that I can possibly hide myself among the people, but only if I do not look like the Queen. I can do nothing about my height, but this hair—"

"Your hair is beautiful! You must not destroy it!" insisted George.

"Why is this hair any better than this bridge? The bridge cannot grow again, and the hair can. I command you—cut it!"

632

Sadly George obeyed, hacking off the thick waving mantle that was one of her greatest attributes of beauty. She took the shorn hair and placed it underneath the broken boards and wood of the bridge, covering it carefully. With an oddly resigned look, she climbed back into the saddle.

See all our offerings, she thought. *See our most precious things sacrificed.*

"We will ride for Terregles, my home," said Herries. "But we must, I fear, take a roundabout way, to avoid the Morton strongholds of Castle Douglas and Threave Castle."

"That is of no matter," said Mary, and she meant it. Without looking back, she turned eastward.

They slept in the fields that night, and then resumed their travel by daylight. However, they were arousing too much curiosity among the farmers and villagers in this more settled area. They decided to rest by day and travel only by night.

Terregles House, near Dumfries, proved hospitable, and at last they were within doors in the Herries stronghold and able to eat. Herries ascertained that the countryside was indeed filled with pursuers, and also received the intelligence that the Archbishop of St. Andrews and other survivors of the royal forces had made their way to Dundrennan Abbey, farther south, on the Solway Firth.

"It will be safe to go there," he said. "My son is Commendator of the Abbey. Let us rest here, and then join the others."

"Yes," said Mary. "And whatever their news, I must bear it."

They approached Dundrennan on the misty morning of May fifteenth—a year to the day from Mary's marriage to Bothwell. The ancient Cistercian monastery, unlike its brother abbeys in the eastern Borders, was intact. No marauding English armies had come this way, and the arched cloisters and beautiful sanctuary slumbered undisturbed in the lush green valley.

Mary felt safe here in the embrace of the past. But unlike her aunt Renée's convent, where she had sought solace in another troubled time, this was but a religious relic. There were no monks here now: the monastery had been secularized, and was in the possession of Lord Herries. Upon bestowing it upon him, the Lords had ordered Herries to demolish the cloisters and church, but he had refused, for reasons of his own. Whatever they were, Mary was grateful for them.

They were welcomed by Lord Herries's son Edward, and soon were sitting at a substantial dinner. The fugitives ate quickly, leaving not a single morsel untouched. Simple lamb stew and bread pudding seemed miraculous to them.

Afterwards, the others who had gathered sought them out. Lord Claud Hamilton related the bitter news: there were more than one hundred dead, mainly Hamiltons, who had taken the worst of the assault in the ambush in the streets of Langside. More than three hundred of the Queen's men had been taken prisoner, including Lord Seton, who was dangerously wounded as well.

George Seton! Mary could hardly believe that the brave Seton had been taken. "Oh, my fortunes have run with blood," she finally said.

The Laird of Lochinvar had come, and it was from him that she was forced, once again, to borrow clothes. Lord Boyd, who had escaped the carnage, had found his way to Dundrennan, as had Lord Fleming, leaving Dumbarton Castle securely in the hands of his next in command. She fell, weeping quietly, into Fleming's arms. It was a sorrowful gathering of exiles and broken spirits.

"This afternoon we will hold a council," said Mary. "In the old chapter house. Everyone must attend, not just the lords."

The light was slanting in through the windows, with their delicately wrought stone mouldings, oramented with fleurs-de-lys and leaves, illuminating a chamber of exceptional beauty. It was here, in the chapter house, that the monks had been required to assemble every day for a reading of a portion of their rules, and the Abbot's seat was just under the central window, with carved wall-seats for the rest of the monks. Sitting in those wall-seats were now about twenty-five of Mary's people. Mary sat in the Abbot's seat.

So we are gathered here, she thought, the last vestiges of my power and position—driven right to the very shores of Scotland, and dressed in rags.

Yet she had never been prouder of any people, nor felt as beloved as she did in this little company, this last faithful band of followers.

"My dear people," she said, "I am aggrieved at what happened at Langside, I mourn those who have fallen, and I am grateful that God in His mercy has spared you and brought you here. But now I must consult with you. What shall now be done? What advice would you give me? Speak frankly."

Lord Herries was the first to stand and speak. "Dearest sovereign, this battle is not decisive. You must bide your time and gather strength to fight again. I myself can promise you that you will be safe under my protection here in this district for at least another forty days. That should allow us time to regroup and add the Gordons to our forces."

Lord Claud Hamilton now stood. "I must only add that you should retire to a stronger fortress. One that could possibly withstand a siege. Otherwise, I agree with Lord Herries."

Mary was aware of eyes fastened on her from all around the wall. They were staring at her short hair. She ran her hand through it, disliking the feel of the bristles. She was probably very ugly. She had not even looked in a mirror. "How can I remain in this countryside, when it is so hard to know who is loyal?" she asked.

Lord Livingston spoke up. "Your Majesty, it would be better to go to France. There you could gather your forces in peace. You have estates and the income of queen dowager in France, you have relatives there, you are still the sister-in-law of the King, who has always been fond of you."

"Never!" cried Mary. "I cannot return as a landless fugitive to the land where I once reigned as Queen! The shame is too great!"

"But, Your Majesty," said George, "you love the French countryside, the language, the people. You would recover your spirits quickly, and—"

"Say no more! I will not hear of it!"

The faces staring at her were truly shocked. France had been a constant in any scheme, an ultimate safeguard and refuge taken for granted. A few of the men had already looked ahead to make arrangements for going there with the Queen, just in case.

"Then—what else can there be?" asked George in a soft voice. "You will not stay, nor will you go. Yet you must do one."

"I shall go to England," she said. "That is the answer."

"Your Majesty, no!" cried Herries. "No, on no account! Why would you even think of such a thing?"

"I am astounded that none of *you* has ever thought of it. It is so obvious. England is the only country that has supported me during my imprisonment. Elizabeth threatened the Lords, and it was only that, I believe, that spared my life. She has refused to recognize the government of the Regent, or to call James King. She is my true kinswoman by blood, and bound to me with ties of honour."

"It is not safe to go to England!" said Livingston. "Have you forgotten that James I was held a prisoner there for twenty-five years? Have you forgotten that your own father did not deem it safe to go? The English cannot be trusted!"

"Elizabeth is not Edward I or Henry VIII. She is a woman, like myself, once wrongly imprisoned herself. She has shown herself to be my friend in my season of woe. I must trust to the deep conviction I have, which assures me this is the right course of action."

"Begging your pardon, Your Majesty, but you once said the same words about choosing to marry the Lord Darnley! Feelings are not facts!" blurted out Lord Fleming.

"I am touched by your concern, but I must decide, ultimately, for myself."

"Then we must beg you to sign a paper absolving us of responsibility for this decision, and stating that we advised against it!" cried George.

"Why, if you wish it," she said, surprised. "There is another thing that perhaps is hard to explain. England and Scotland—the truth is, one day they will be joined under the rule of my son James. I know it, and Elizabeth knows it. It is not as if we were such different countries anymore."

Mary was watching the sunset on the waters of the Solway Firth, which divided Scotland from England in a broad wedge that narrowed and narrowed and finally came together about forty miles to the east, right near the place where her father's army had met such demoralizing defeat at Solway Moss.

It was that which killed him, so they say, thought Mary. Well, I will not cross there. I will go by water. Arrival by water has always brought me fortune.

She seemed to be able to see land far across the water. "Is that England?" she asked Lord Herries, who was standing beside her on the rise overlooking the waters.

"No. Today you cannot see her. It must be exceptionally clear to do so. We are separated by about twenty miles of open water at this point. I think what you are seeing are purple clouds."

"Oh." She was disappointed. "Dear Lord Herries, will you please write the necessary letter to whomever? What official or lord has command of that area?"

"Lowther is deputy governor of Carlisle; it is to him that I must write, then." His voice was heavy. "The Duke of Norfolk is the foremost northern peer, but there are lesser ones, like the earls of Northumberland and Westmoreland, who are very pro-Catholic and will no doubt receive you gladly."

"You sound so sad," she said. "Pray do not be so. I have received guidance; I know what I do is right."

The sun had gone now, and the water was a rich burgundy colour. Beside them, the rushing stream of the Abbey Burn tumbled past, making its way down to the Firth.

"Sometimes evil spirits mislead us," he said. "Satan can assume a pleasing shape, can appear as an angel of light. I take that to mean that he has the power to trick us into believing our impulses are divinely rather than demonically inspired."

"I go in the name of peace," said Mary. "Surely you cannot call peace to be anything the devil desires."

Herries shook his head. "I do not claim to know as much about the devil as some folks, but I do believe he is out and amongst us more than he is recognized."

"Please write the letter before morning," said Mary firmly.

Now, after more arguments and pleadings from her company, she was alone at last, walking in the deserted Abbey church. She had had her way, and they had dutifully retired to sleep and left her to pace and keep her own counsel. The great stone columns in the silent nave were like man-made trees, their arches soaring upward to be lost in darkness. There was a mouldy, damp smell like moss. The Abbey, like all the still-standing old ecclesiastical buildings in Scotland, was in poor repair. Parts of the wall had given way, and there were leaks. She could tell by the water stains and the faint sweet smell of wet stone.

A half moon was shining, giving just enough light to make fuzzy outlines of the altar, the niches, the mouldering wooden screen that had once divided the monks' end of the church from the lay brothers'. Cistercians. White monks. It seemed to her she could almost see their ghostly shapes gliding between the aisles and columns. Shades, summoned up from some faerie realm. From a time before all these religious wars and hatreds.

Oh, gentle monks . . . She wished she could reach out to them, but she knew they would vanish. They were not real, of course, she knew that.

It is only my distracted, overtired senses that make me see forms in the moonlight. If I truly had the gift of the "sight," then I would see more than that, I would be able to predict the future, whereas it is dark and veiled from me.

She went out the south door and entered the cloisters, the arched stone arcades where the monks had walked during bad weather. The moonlight coated the grass court and turned it silver. Each arched section threw sharp black shadows across the silvered ground, making a stark pattern like the black and white tiles at Chenonceau.

Chenonceau. So many ghosts tonight!

From the arcade openings she could see the monks' graveyard beyond the church, their simple tombstones standing up like the mysterious circles of stone in northern Scotland and Brittany, circles where supposedly magic rites had been practised by vanished people.

Racing clouds covered the moon briefly, then passed on. Ghostly galleons. Bothwell used to call them ghostly galleons, she remembered. He said they were the spirits of seamen doomed to ride the skies for all eternity, always blown before the wind.

Bothwell, always a sailor, first and foremost a man of the sea.

I cannot see water without thinking of you, she thought. Perhaps that is why I want to go to England by water—as if you were a water-god and could favour me. Oh, my husband, where are you now? A year ago tonight it was our wedding night.

In the moonlight she could see the feathery white of the Abbey orchard in bloom. The rows of trees were like slim young girls attired in lace, waiting to dance. There was a sea of delicate, distant fragrance rising from them, a fragrance like youth, not overpowering but dizzy with sweet promise. The dead monks slumbered on.

Where are you? she wondered with a piercing sorrow. Can you see the moon tonight that I see?

Should I go to England? You are the only one whose opinion I wish to know. You are the only one who can stop me. If it is true that souls can speak across land and sea, speak to me tonight, and tell me what you would have me do. Speak to me in a dream, or in my thoughts, and I will obey. Speak, beloved husband.

She dipped her pen in the ink and began the letter.

Dundrennan, May 15, 1568

To the high and mighty Prince, Elizabeth—
You are not ignorant, my dearest sister, of great part of my misfortunes, but these which induce me to write at present, have happened too recently yet to have reached your ears. I must therefore acquaint you as briefly as I can, that some of my subjects whom I most confided in, and had raised to the highest pitch of honour, have taken up arms against me, and treated me with the utmost indignity. By unexpected

637

means, the Almighty Disposer of all things delivered me from the cruel imprisonment I underwent.

But I have since lost a battle, in which most of those who preserved their loyal integrity fell before my eyes. I am now forced out of my kingdom, and driven to such straits that, next to God, I have no hope but in your goodness. I beseech you therefore, my dearest sister, that I may be conducted to your presence, that I may acquaint you with all my affairs.

In the meantime, I beseech God to grant you all heavenly benedictions, and to me patience and consolation, which last I hope and pray to obtain by your means.

To remind you of the reasons I have to depend on England, I send back to its Queen this token, the jewel of her promised friendship and assistance.

Your affectionate sister,
M.R.

Lingeringly she removed the diamond friendship ring from her finger. It was time to send it. Time to redeem its promise.

The sun was coming up as Mary at last sealed the letter. She had received no messages, no impressions in her sleep. Bothwell had not visited her. Her dreams had been inconsequential and hard even to remember. She had prayed about the decision, but at last it had become clear that she must proceed.

It was the destiny of England and Scotland to be united under her son, James, and this would help cement it, and lay to rest the bad feelings and suspicions about her own intentions toward the crown. When Elizabeth received her, it would be tantamount to recognizing James as her successor.

I can rest in safety in England and receive my people there conveniently. Going to England will also prove to Elizabeth that I have no wish to bring foreigners like the French onto our soil. I have chosen England above them.

She dispatched the letter to go along with the one to Lowther. They would take several days to reach their destination, and then an unknown time after that before a reply was received. Mary stood on the little pier at the foot of the Abbey Burn, from which the monks of old had traded with England and Ireland, and watched the boat making its way out into open water. Around her the pastures were filled with cattle and singing birds.

Suddenly she was seized with a desire not to wait. It came upon her so completely and so overwhelmingly that it felt like a supernatural message, one that had her in its grip.

Go now, it urged her. *Do not wait for a reply. Waiting is dangerous. Surprise is the best element. If you are already there, then they must give permission. After all, have you considered what you would do if they refused? You be the master. You decide where you will go, and let them adjust themselves to that decision. Your instinct has never failed you yet. Your instinct is to go. Go now.*

"When is the next tide?" she asked Herries calmly. Boats could only leave during high tide, as during low tide there were long, exposed mud flats.

"At three o'clock," he replied.

"Find me a boat," she said. "I wish to cross this afternoon."

Herries stared at her as if she were demented. "No!"

"It has come to me that this is the right thing to do. I know it. Obey me, for it must be so."

They walked, following the Abbey Burn as it gushed for two miles through a grove of ash and alder trees, making its way to the Solway. Everyone was silent, as if they were going to a funeral. Only Mary felt lighthearted and at ease.

Almost twenty people insisted on accompanying her, determined to protect her and share her fate: George and Willie, of course, but also Lord Livingston, Lord Fleming, Lord Claud Hamilton, Lord Boyd, and Lord Herries, with their attendants.

Lord Herries had procured a common fishing boat that was also used for transporting coal and lime across the Solway, and it awaited them at the pier. It was a shabby-looking vessel, stained and weatherbeaten. Mary saw it without comment, then turned to look once more across the fields and back up at the Abbey, silhouetted against the sky. Then, without lingering over her farewell look at Scotland, she stepped into the boat.

"Come!" She motioned to her party. They filed down the pier and got in, wordlessly. The boat was packed; it rode very low in the water.

Those staying behind stood forlornly on the shore and dock. Suddenly the Archbishop of St. Andrews waded into the water and grasped the sides of the boat.

"Don't go!" he said in a fierce voice. "Dear lady, I beg you! I implore you! This is folly! Misfortune awaits you!"

Mary laughed uneasily. She nudged the boatman to cast off. "Why, you will ruin your clothes!" she said.

The boat started to move, being pulled by the heavy surf at the confluence of the creek and the open water. The Archbishop hung on, and attempted to stop the boat's drift. But the current was stronger, and he was pulled by the boat.

"Stop! Stop, before it is too late!" His knuckles were white from grasping the wooden sides.

"Farewell, my dear Archbishop," said Mary. "I shall be back in Scotland soon, restored to my throne by my cousin. We shall meet again in a few weeks. Now, I pray you, do not ruin your garments!"

The Archbishop was now up to his chest in the water. "I care not for the garments!" he cried, but the boat was torn out of his grip, drifting seaward. Unable to swim, he stood in the cold current and watched it until it was out of sight, upon the Forth proper.

The sea, which could be dangerous in that area, today was calm and inviting. The winds were fair, and conjoined with the tide, escorting them toward England. All omens were favourable. Mary turned to look back once more at the receding shore of Scotland.

"To England let us go, and merrily!" she said, more loudly than was necessary.

It took four hours to make the crossing. At seven that evening, they came into the harbour of the little fishing village of Workington. As they beached the boat, Mary noticed how unusual the stones on the seashore were: they were all egg-shaped, of various sizes, and in a rainbow of colours, pale blue, cream, brownish pink. She kept staring at them, as if this proved that England was indeed very different from Scotland. As she climbed out of the boat and alighted, she stumbled and fell on her hands and knees on the stones, seeing them very close up. She closed her fist around a handful of them.

" 'Tis not an omen of stumbling," said Herries loudly, "but that she comes to take possession of England."

There was an embarrassed silence. Fishermen had started to gather in curiosity.

"Nay, that is not so!" said Mary. "I do not come to take possession of England, but merely to be restored to what is rightfully mine in Scotland." How could Herries say such a thing? What if it was repeated to Elizabeth?

More and more people were gathering on the beach. It was a Sunday evening, and after a day of leisure, people were enjoying one of the first warm spring nights. It was imperative that they identify themselves.

"Where lives Sir Henry Curwen, lord of this town?" asked Herries. "I have brought hither from Scotland an heiress we hope to marry to his son. I pray you, direct me to his home, good people."

The fishermen spoke amongst themselves for a moment. "He lives at Workington Hall, to the east of town. Here, we will show you."

All the while Mary was looking around, expecting to see something unusual or symbolic of her decision. But it was an ordinary little fishing village with an ordinary pier. The spring evening was an ordinary evening. All the portents and warnings and implorings seemed terribly wasted on this moment.

England. I have crossed to England. This is English soil. It should feel to me the way it felt to Caesar crossing the Rubicon, she thought. But it feels like . . . nothing at all.

Sir Henry Curwen—who was an old acquaintance of Herries's—was in London, but his family welcomed the refugees. Once safely within the house, Mary revealed herself, and was relieved to find that the family, which was Catholic, almost trembled with admiration for her. She was warmly welcomed, fussed over, fed, and stared at. She asked Herries if there was any token she could give, and he had only an agate drinking cup he had brought from Dundrennan, but they received it as if it were a holy relic.

She had not been prepared for such idolization. Why were they treating her like a goddess? Of all the surprises she had received in the course of the last few weeks, this was one of the most unlooked for. But it buoyed her, making her feel that all would be well.

The change from whore to goddess was dizzying.

That night she asked for a paper and pen. The awestruck Lady Curwen brought her the finest creamy paper they had, and in addition insisted that she take a leatherbound book with blank pages.

"For you to use, and to remember us by. My cousin, who is a devoted son of the Church—*our* Church—cured and embossed the leather himself."

"I thank you."

"Oh, it is our pleasure, our delight! If only you could know—oh, if only Sir Henry were here! We are your greatest admirers!" She backed out of the room, her head bobbing like a ducking stool.

Mary had almost forgotten what it was to be admired in an unqualified manner. But now it seemed as unrelated to her real self as the curses had been. Both were directed at a symbol, and the person inside the symbol walked and breathed and slept as if in a suit of armour.

Now Elizabeth must be formally told of her arrival. She spread out the good paper gratefully. No more handkerchiefs and charcoal.

She began writing, slowly. She would explain it all to Elizabeth. She started as far back as Riccio, and in the telling, the letter grew and grew. She felt as if she were already before Elizabeth, that Elizabeth was actually hearing the words, as if by sympathetic magic.

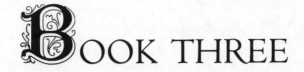

BOOK THREE

❧

Queen of Exile

1568-1587

I

Elizabeth was sitting before an open window at Greenwich, trying to do two things at once. Her councillors claimed she could actually do four—listen to one person talk, compose a letter, make plans, and speak herself. She encouraged them to think this, as it made her more formidable in their eyes; they were like little children who actually believed their mother had "eyes in the back of her head" and could see them stealing sugar. But today she was having difficulty doing even two things: looking out the window at her ships at anchor in the Thames, and composing a letter to her remarkable cousin, the Scots Queen. The breeze was gently blowing in, and the smell of the water was inviting. Only a queen would choose to be inside on a fine spring day like this. All normal people would be outside, savouring the delicate May warmth of the sun, smelling the new-turned earth. Well, after this letter was done . . . she would order the barge brought round, and she and Robert would go out on the river. They would trail their hands in the water and sing. Songs always sounded better outdoors—even banal lyrics seemed sweet and original.

She sighed. Now, as to this letter . . .

The Scots Queen had escaped from Lochleven! Another of her daring ventures, so it seemed. One could not help but admire her. She had courage and tenacity, and always seemed to find sympathizers, even among her gaolers. Curious, that. She made enemies of her councillors, and friends of her gaolers. But what did it mean, that Mary was at large? Could she oust the Regent? Would her son's anointing be undone? Thank God that, in her usual delaying manner, Elizabeth had "neglected" to recognize the new King. Hence she could afford to wait and see what developed.

They chide me for it, all of them—Cecil and Robert and Norfolk, she thought. For my caution and delay. But as often as not, it serves me as well as action.

Wind was filling the sails of the boats down below. Time to get on with it. She spread out the paper and began.

Madam,

I have just received your letter from Lochleven, but before its arrival came the news of your deliverance and timely escape. We must give thanks that God in His mercy has seen fit to hear your prayers. I rejoice at your freedom, and that subjects who seek to bind their true princes may be made to see, by this example, that heaven does not smile on it. It is to be regretted that your love for one who was an unworthy ruffian made you so careless of your state and honour and caused you to lose so many of your friends.

I, as your kinswoman and sister queen, will do all that lies in my power to restore you to your throne, but only if you will place yourself in my hands and not traffick with the French with an end to employing them on Scottish soil. Think not to toy with them in secret, my not knowing: those who have two strings to their bow may shoot stronger, but they rarely shoot straight.

Your assured cousin and sister,
Elizabeth R.

There. Did that put the warning strongly enough? The French must not set foot—or the embossed boot they so favoured—in Scotland. But the Lords would not just step aside meekly. There would be another civil war in Scotland.

She shuddered. Civil war in Scotland. Civil war in France. Now civil war was looming in the Netherlands as the Dutch rose up against Spain.

I will do anything to prevent civil war here in England, she thought. I will feint, and promise, and prevaricate, and threaten, and compromise, and sacrifice. There must not be civil war here. If posterity can give me no other credit, saying "there was peace in her land in her reign" will be enough for me.

Now she was free to go outside and take the air. She always felt oddly ill at ease when dealing with the Scots Queen, as if there were something she had overlooked. Now that unpleasant task was over—for the present.

Just as she was rising to go to the door, an urgent knocking came. It was a messenger, with two letters addressed in the same hand. He held them out apologetically.

She took them. One was lumpy, the other slim. She opened the lumpy one first. Out fell a ring bearing a heart-shaped diamond held by a hand. It was meant to fit together with another one. What was this?

The letter was from the Scots Queen. It was written at Dundrennan. Elizabeth sat back down and read it carefully. She exhaled to steady herself.

Mary was asking permission to seek sanctuary in England! She had met the Regent's forces in battle near Glasgow and had been utterly defeated. Now she was fleeing, and asked her sister Queen for refuge—on the strength of this diamond ring.

Elizabeth turned the ring around and stared at it. She could not even remember sending it to her. If she had, it was only a token, not to be taken seriously, like all the portraits and miniatures and other such things that royalty exchanged routinely. Surely . . . surely Mary had not put faith in it? No. No one could be that naïve. The Scots Queen was only playing a deep game.

She could not come here! It was unthinkable! Yet . . . if she went to France, that would be bad for England. She would stir up her French relatives to make trouble in Scotland. Spain . . . no, that was impossible. O God! Best to have her . . . where?

She tore open the second letter, and as her eyes flew over it, she actually felt the blood draining out of her face until it felt cold.

Mary was already here! That woman—she had not waited for a reply, but had just come ahead, in her own imperious way. Never thinking of me, and what position it puts me in! she thought angrily. How dare she? Hating herself for feeling only anger and no sympathy, she forced herself to reread the letter, this time slowly.

. . . My people seeing this, and moved by that extreme malice of my enemies, encountered them without order, so that, though they were twice their number, they were at so great a disadvantage, that God permitted them to be discomfited, and several taken and killed. The pursuit was immediately interrupted, in order to take me on my way to Dumbarton; they stationed people in every direction, either to kill or take me.

But God, in His infinite goodness, has preserved me, and I escaped to my Lord Herries's, who, as well as other gentlemen, have come with me into your country. I am assured that, hearing of the cruelty of my enemies, and how they have treated me, you will, conformably to your kind disposition and the confidence I have in you, not only receive for the safety of my life, but also aid and assist me in my just quarrel, and I shall solicit other princes to do the same.

I entreat you to send to fetch me as soon as you possibly can, for I am in a pitiable condition, not only for a queen, but for an ordinary woman. I have nothing in this world but what I had on my person when I made my escape, travelling across the country sixty miles the first day, and not having since ever ventured to proceed, except by night, as I hope to declare before you, if it pleases you to have pity, as I trust you will, upon my extreme misfortune; of which I will forbear complaining, in order not to importune you. I pray God that he may give to you a happy state of health and long life, and me patience, and that consolation which I expect to receive from you, to whom I present my humble commendations.

Your most faithful and affectionate good sister, and cousin, and escaped prisoner,

Mary R.

Where was she now? Elizabeth saw that the letter was written from Workington. That was a coastal town near Carlisle. Mary must have come by boat. Suddenly she could picture it: the dishevelled queen, a hasty council, not knowing which way to turn. . . . Like a person running naked

647

from a burning building out into the snow, there to perish from the cold. She must have taken leave of her senses. Or her courage and resourcefulness had failed her at last. Everyone had a limit—as the inventors of the rack and the iron maiden knew only too well. Mary had been living in a nightmare for so long it must have destroyed her reason.

I must send for her, thought Elizabeth. Yes, I must. Charity alone demands it. I must not add to her torment.

But of course I will first have to announce this extraordinary news to the Privy Council. They must be informed.

The Council did not enjoy being summoned to sit inside on this glorious May day. Occasionally a bee would fly in the window, buzz around in confusion, and eventually bump its way back out again. The councillors envied the bees. They had to sit, elaborately dressed, and stay as long as their mistress and sovereign demanded. And today she seemed agitated.

"My dear advisers," she began, glancing especially at Cecil, "a matter of great consequence has occurred on our northern border. Yea, I will not keep it from you: the Queen of Scots has fled into England." She waited to make sure they all comprehended. "She is even now at Carlisle, having been taken there in custody by the deputy governor, Sir Richard Lowther. She flings herself on our mercy, and desires to come to us."

The men looked around at each other as if the one sitting next to him would be privy to special insight. Only Cecil, Elizabeth's foremost adviser and councillor since the very beginning, stared straight ahead, impassive.

"She awaits an answer. Shall I send for her?" asked Elizabeth.

"Why does she wish to come?" asked Robert Dudley.

"To explain everything to me, so she says, so that I will be convinced of the righteousness of her cause and help her regain her throne."

"And what is your own, wise feeling about this?" asked Cecil. He fingered his forked beard.

"That I should send for her," said Elizabeth. "Poor lady, she is destitute."

"Ah," he said.

Elizabeth looked at the Duke of Norfolk. "And what say you, as the first peer of England, and premier estate holder in the land?"

The Duke, a thirty-year-old veteran of three marriages, looked startled. "I say—I say—that you must examine her carefully before admitting her to your presence. Do not look at her directly; let someone else do it. I have heard that she has the power to enchant and work others to her power."

Elizabeth laughed. "So we should send some victims north and see what becomes of them? Perhaps they should walk backwards in to see her, holding up a mirror! Do you wish to go?"

"N-no, Your Majesty." He swallowed hard, his Adam's apple rising pointedly in his long, narrow throat.

"If I sent for her, where should she be lodged?" asked Elizabeth. "Should I prepare a palace for her?"

"No, Your Majesty. That would be too generous. It would also be an implicit recognition of her as your chosen successor," said Robert Dudley.

"Oh. Then I should give her apartments within one of my own palaces?"

"That you should not!" said Sir Francis Knollys, Elizabeth's uncle-in-law and a leading Protestant. "She should not be granted access to your august presence until she has . . . shown herself worthy. I mean by that, that she has been acquitted of the crimes that drove her from her own country—and not by such blatant injustice as that mock trial the Earl of Bothwell went through. That trial was a shameful sham that merely confirmed his guilt!" His face was flushed with emotion and disgust.

"I must protest," said the Earl of Sussex, the Duke of Norfolk's brother-in-law and a man known to lean toward the Catholic faction. "Our most merciful Queen is not a judge. She herself has said she has no wish to make windows into men's souls."

Young Christopher Hatton, turning his handsome face toward his Queen, said, "I myself have seen the Scottish Queen, when I had the honour to represent our most glorious Majesty at the baptism in Edinburgh. I hereby declare to you that she is a most noble creature and must be treated with honour. Let us not prove as wicked as her lords in Scotland. We are *Englishmen*, and pride ourselves on our laws and justice, and our chivalry."

Elizabeth gave a sigh. "Ah, I know not what to do! My heart flies out to her in charity, while my Council bids me beware of the serpent!"

Cecil spoke at last. "It were perhaps best if you could detain her while you made arrangements for her safety. We know that there is no place for her at present. For her to go to France—and possibly reassert her claims to *your* throne, as she did once there already—is not wise. Likewise, Spain might resurrect those claims. Lastly, well we know that if she reenters Scotland she will be promptly executed. The only way she could return to Scotland—which is the only place for her—would be if she and the lords could come to some arrangement. Perhaps if you agreed to recognize the King in exchange for their permitting Mary to rule in name alongside him? But all these things would take time to arrange. . . ." He raised his hands in a gesture of delicate helplessness.

"Yes . . . ." Elizabeth thought silently about it for a moment. "Perhaps you, Knollys, should go to Carlisle, as my representative. I understand that the Earl of Northumberland has already hurried to her and attempted to whisk her away to Alnwick, his castle seat. Lowther and he nearly came to blows. The Catholics are already flocking to her, they say, bringing bouquets and obeisance . . . that region of the country has ever had a fondness for the old ways and the old religion. Yes, Knollys—you shall go to her, to my dear sister, and inform her that I cannot receive her in her present state."

Knollys looked discomfited. "But—but—have you nothing else, beyond that, to tell her? Am I then to allow her to go where she will?"

"Of course not!"

"But—if we cannot receive her, if we have nothing to offer, then she must seek her fortune elsewhere."

"But we *do* have something to offer her," said Cecil. "We will act as mediators, and insist the rebel lords justify themselves to us. If they can show no convincing proof that their actions were called for, then we shall restore Queen Mary." He nodded sagaciously.

"And if they bring forward proof?" Knollys persisted.

"Then we shall find some way to allow them to remain in power, provided Queen Mary can return to Scotland in safety."

"It shall be your task to convince Queen Mary that, regardless of the findings, she will be restored to her estate in Scotland," said Elizabeth.

"Will she be content with that? Or does she seek more? Perhaps she is just as glad to be quit of Scotland and on a larger stage where she can have a grander scope," said Walsingham, a saturnine young man who was Cecil's confidential lieutenant.

"I doubt that she has any such ambitions; they were most likely blown up at Kirk O'Field," said Elizabeth slowly.

"Ambitions do not die so easily," Walsingham insisted, "and soon Scotland may appear to her like a nightmare to which she would never return, whereas England will seem most meet for her appetites."

"We must not, then, serve to drive her to desperation. Knollys, you shall comfort her, and assure her of our loving concern for her. My only interest is to compose the differences between her and her subjects."

"When shall I depart?" asked Knollys, in resignation.

"Why, as soon as possible," Elizabeth replied. "Tomorrow. And be sure to take a mirror."

After the councillors filed from the room, Cecil stayed discreetly behind. As the one member of the Council who had already known about Mary's arrival, he had had time to prepare a memorandum on it. His memoranda, in which he always examined the pros and cons of any question in orderly form, were famous. Now he withdrew it from his bosom.

"Ah, my dear Cecil, I was waiting for this." Elizabeth took the paper. "Have you laboured over it long?"

"All night, Your Majesty. I must confess, this matter deeply troubles me."

"Your man Walsingham seems to fear the worst."

"He is . . . vigilant, Your Majesty."

"Oh, Cecil, what am I to do?" she burst out. "I have never been in such a quandary!"

Cecil could not help smiling. "You have indeed been in worse quandaries, in which your own life was at stake. Always you have acted with foresight and prudence; I have no doubt that you will do so in this instance. Always remember that there are two persons in one that you are faced with. There is Mary, an anointed queen who has been persecuted and driven from her throne, and who is now a crowned head without a pillow to lay it on. This woman has lost her husband, her son, her throne, her country. She is made of flesh and blood like you, and she shakes if she is chilled and becomes ill if she has no food. She inspires pity. The other

Mary is a political creature, the tool of the Catholics, who would not care if she were made of wood and spouted blood that was green, so long as she could function as their figurehead. This woman is your deadly enemy. She inspires respect and fear. To treat one with kindness and the other with wariness, when they both live together in one body, is an impossible task."

"Why did she have to come here?" cried Elizabeth.

"You should only be thankful that she is not in France," Cecil insisted. "You can use this for your own advantage."

"Oh, leave me!" said Elizabeth. "Leave me to study all your pros and cons!"

After he was gone, she opened the paper and stared at it. Cecil's neat handwriting covered the page.

PRO REGINA SCOTORUM:

1. That she has come willingly into England, trusting Queen Elizabeth's promises of help.
2. That she was unlawfully condemned, for her subjects seized and imprisoned her, charged her with her husband's murder, refused her permission to answer in person or by advocate in the Parliament which condemned her.
3. That she is a queen subject to none, and not bound by law to answer her subjects.
4. That she offers, in Elizabeth's presence, to acquit herself.

CON REGINA SCOTORUM:

1. That she procured her husband's murder, whom she had constituted King, and so he was a public person and her superior. Therefore her subjects were bound to search for and punish the offender.
2. She protected Bothwell, the chief murderer, and defended him to defeat justice.
3. She secured his acquittal by a legal technicality.
4. She procured his divorce from his lawful wife.
5. She feigned to be forcibly taken by him and then married him, increasing his power to a point that none of her nobles dared abide about her.
6. Bothwell detained her by force and yet when her nobles sought to deliver her she refused to dismiss him and helped him to escape.

It would seem that Her Majesty Queen Elizabeth can neither aid her, permit her to come to her presence, or restore her, or suffer her to depart before trial.

So there was to be a trial. There was no other way. Elizabeth felt as if all the peace in her kingdom, so carefully cultivated for ten years, was now in jeopardy. The Queen of Scots had come to sow dragon's teeth in her realm.

II

ary waited until Mary Seton had finally fallen asleep before she rose and went to the window. She stood, dreamily, looking out over the hills and dales of the gentle countryside around her. To think I fought so against coming here, she thought. I did not want to be moved from Carlisle; I even refused to go unless I was tied up. Everything was so confusing. Elizabeth's baffling behaviour—the way she kept Lord Herries waiting for two weeks before she even admitted him to her presence; the way she forbade Lord Fleming even to sail for France. Those ugly, worn-out clothes she sent for me—Knollys tried to pretend she had sent them for my maidservants. And her refusal to see me unless I was cleared of any suspicion of guilt in the murder—as if I would contaminate her. But since then I have come to understand that she means to restore me to my throne, but that in order to do so, she has to establish herself as an impartial party—else the Lords will not cooperate with her. How clever she is! She has got Lord James to agree to submit to a hearing.

A warm breeze, heavy with the scent of honeysuckle, blew into the window with little puffs. This Bolton Castle, located fifty miles deeper into England than the border city of Carlisle, had been her home since mid-July. It stood on a ridge in the western part of Yorkshire. Elizabeth had said it was necessary for Mary to move in order for her to be closer to her, Elizabeth. But she was still two hundred miles away from her. What good had it done?

Bolton itself was pleasantly situated—a very high castle that consisted of four towers joined together by curtain walls, making a square with an empty center. In this center was a cobbled courtyard with a heavily fortified gatehouse guarding it. Mary's suite of rooms—all four of them—was on the third, uppermost floor. The remarkable thing about Bolton was that the walls had flues running through them like a honeycomb, which carried heat from the fireplaces—not that this mattered in the summer. But in the winter . . . oh, but they would be gone by winter. She would not have an opportunity to compare this heating to the tiled room furnaces at Fontainebleau that she remembered from her childhood.

She leaned out the window and breathed deeply. She felt completely restored and calm, and her spirits were rising daily. She was eager to have her hearing, to be able at last to pour out the truth to someone who was not a Scot, but to whose arbitration the Scots would be submissive.

She tiptoed back across the room. They had given her a spacious suite of rooms, although they had had to borrow furniture from all the neighbours in order to furnish them properly. Even the smallest, the bedchamber, was large enough that a folding screen gave her privacy at one end; Mary Seton slept at the other. Seton and a large contingent of other followers had been allowed to join her; and Lady Douglas had sent all the possessions she had so hastily left behind. She had even included a kindly note with them. Well, Lady Douglas, as a king's ex-mistress, was used to the vicissitudes of fortune. She may have lost a prisoner, but her son George may have gained a royal wife, if fate decided to turn that way—Mary knew that was what she was thinking. She could not help but be amused at the adaptable old lady: a good loser, always looking ahead to the next hand.

Certain now that Seton slept and she would not disturb her, she crept into the adjoining day-chamber, which was a few steps lower down, lit a candle on her writing table, and took out the blank-paged journal that the Curwen family had presented her with. She found it such a novelty to be able to write whatever she wished, whenever she wished, that she had gone a little mad with it. She had never been surrounded only by friends before; everyone here was sharing her exile with her, at great personal cost to themselves, and would never use anything she wrote against her.

She had written poetry before, and had fancied herself to have a talent for it—so Brantôme had told her. In the delirium of her love for Bothwell, she had written poems to him, not very good ones, as she did not take the time to think of metaphors and similes, nor even of original wordings. But the essay, or the word-sketch, she had never attempted. Her letters—except for her love letters—were all political.

She opened the book. Its last entry was dated August first, 1568.

The countryside here—they call it Wensleydale—is soft and roll-ing, deep deep green, very different from Scotland. We are in the middle of the country, far from the sea, and there is no salt in the air. It is one of those places where the inhabitants can pass their whole lives unannoyed by any ruder intrusion. The cattle low, the milkmaids walk along the paths swinging their buckets at sunrise and sunset.

I am becoming more used to it now—my new "host," Lord Scrope, makes every effort to please me. Lady Scrope waits on me and whispers in my ear about the charms of her brother, the Duke of Norfolk. But he's been married three times already! Of course they could say the same of me. Strange how it always sounds worse when applied to someone else. Hear "three wives," and one's first thought is: I would not care to be the fourth! She hints—delicately, of course—that the Duke is in dire need of a wife, and that if I would consider it, Elizabeth would be pleased.

If Elizabeth would be so pleased, why must it be spoken of in whispers?

Now she smoothed out the page and wrote:

August 20, 1568. So many changes in three weeks! We are becoming settled. I write to Elizabeth and she responds. The Lords
have agreed to submit to the hearing! So soon I shall accuse Lord
James to his face, and Morton to his hideous red beard, and
Maitland . . . I shall speak loud and clear and tell the world just
what they are. I shall tell about the Craigmillar conference, in
which *they* suggested doing away with Darnley. Oh, to be able to
tell it at last! My breast is bursting with what I have to disclose!

I believe it is Cecil who has restrained Elizabeth from taking
my part more openly. The French ambassador in London and the
Spanish one as well keep me informed. I know more here than
ever I did in Scotland. Here there is no Lord James to intercept.
But it was better still in Carlisle. This place is so secluded; no one
ever passes through it. It is kept like a secret in this lush valley.

The Scrope family has always been sympathetic to the Catholic
cause. They took the part of the rebels in the Pilgrimage of
Grace against Henry VIII thirty years ago, and paid for it. On
my floor is an exquisite chapel, which the first Lord Scrope built
as a chantry where the monks could pray for the soul of Richard
II. Alas, no monks pray there now, so the soul of Richard II must
fend for itself in purgatory. But I go in there myself to pray, and
no one forbids me.

I am learning that so many of these families are partial to the
old religion; and after all, it is only ten years since all England
was Catholic. Memories are long. The great families of the North,
the earls of Northumberland and Westmoreland, are almost
openly Catholic. Northumberland has declared himself to be
sympathetic, and sent me several devotional articles of the faith.
And the Duke of Norfolk, for all that he is nominally Protestant,
had a Catholic wife and a son who leans that way. Here I am
among friends, though some dare declare it more openly than
others. The Earl of Northumberland has secretly sent me many
messages to the effect that he is my partisan and will stand by me
regardless, and that he can bring others to my side if necessary.

I am not as well guarded as I am sure Lord James would wish.
There is a garrison here, stationed in the southeast tower. But my
rooms, which face west, give out onto open countryside. I am
fifty feet up, but if I could be let down by a rope, I could escape,
if only I had horses. But if I tried to escape, it would look as
though I were trying to avoid the hearing. No, I am more powerful here, though I seem to be powerless—without even a horse
to my name. I must wait—the thing that is, above all, hardest for
me and against my nature, as it was against Bothwell's. We are
both being sorely tested, punished. . . .

I have heard that Bothwell was granted a hearing before King Frederick at New Year's, but was not released. He offered to cede the Orkneys and Shetlands back to Norway in exchange for his freedom, but it had the opposite effect: Frederick became more determined to keep him in custody and bargain with the Lords about the islands. Lord James declared that Bothwell was a convicted criminal in Scotland and should be extradited. Frederick bewailed the fact that transporting such a tricky and important state prisoner would require a squadron of ships which he could, alas, not spare at the moment. Lord James offered to send an executioner to Denmark, for Frederick's convenience. Frederick— who well must realize what a blackguard James is!—refused his kind offer. So Bothwell is safe, and from all reports quite comfortably housed in the governor's fortress at Malmö. Why can he not escape? I must get more particulars of his quarters. He must be closely guarded, for I have not received a letter in many months—since he came to Malmö, in fact. He *must* be strictly guarded, then . . . has he received any of my letters? The thought that he has not would be unbearable.

When I am restored to my throne—yes, then Frederick will set him free, and bring him home in a gilded warship, with reparations and apologies for such mistreatment! And it will all seem a bad dream, and we'll laugh together, late at night, about our prisons and how we endured them . . . Lochleven and Bergen and Carlisle and Copenhagen and Bolton and Malmö. Of course he's known my gaolers—he knows the Laird of Lochleven and Lady Douglas. But he doesn't know Sir Francis Knollys, Elizabeth's vice-chamberlain. That sweet, long-suffering gentleman. He dearly loves his Queen—and, I sense, not only because his wife is of Anne Boleyn's family and thus related to her. He *loves* the Queen in a way I have never seen before; not in France, not in Scotland. He reveres her, which is strange, since he is so much the older. I have attempted to make him joke about her, but although he tells many humorous stories about her, he never jokes about her—oh, it is very difficult to explain . . . exasperated humour without jokes.

And Lord Scrope: so proper. Rather stuffed, like a dish of capon stuffed with dates and oysters. His neck is peculiarly thick and round, so that when he turns his head he has to move his shoulders as well. Yet he's gentle, too. I have gentle keepers in a gentle country, compared to the beasts that call themselves men, hiding in their castles on the windy crags of Scotland.

Too many adjectives, she told herself, upon rereading the last sentence. But Scotland seemed to call for many, many adjectives. So she let it stay as it was.

September 8, 1568. The Nativity of the Blessed Virgin. I arose early and spent time in prayer in the chapel. I am not allowed a priest. When I asked for one, I was told, "There are no priests in England now." What a judgement they bring on themselves with that statement! Instead, Knollys has brought a Reformed clergyman to try to convert me. He "instructs" me daily in the Anglican religion; this pleases Knollys. I wish to please them, in whatever ways I can. Then I go and say my rosary and pray to Our Lady to forgive me.

There is more talk of Norfolk as a husband for me. I have been assured that many powerful people at court are in favour of this match—men like Robert Dudley, for example, and the earls of Arundel and Pembroke and Nicholas Throckmorton, my old friend the ambassador. They seem to feel that perhaps he can act as my permanent "keeper," an approved Englishman to keep me on a chain. (It is not unlike the earlier proposal of Elizabeth that I wed her darling Dudley. He is still unmarried, but evidently she does not wish to repeat the offer.) This way, they reason, I can be kept in reserve for the succession.

Why does no one remember that I am already married? And they call *me* disloyal and of shockingly short memory! Already there has been talk of marrying me to a Hamilton, to the newly widowed (for the third time—oh, how old we are becoming!) Philip of Spain, to George Douglas, to Norfolk, and then, today—oh, I almost burst into laughter—old Sir Francis Knollys offered his nephew, George Carey! If they truly think I am a murderess, then their own ambition and cynicism is shameful. Even Machiavelli would blush at such opportunism!

September 29, 1568. The Feast of Saint Michael and All Angels.

O! I can hardly hold this pen, and it was all I could do to wait until nightfall to be alone. During the dinner I wanted to scream at Knollys: *You knew all along.*

I am not to be allowed to appear at the hearing! I must speak only through representatives! And how can they truly speak my own words? They are not me. I had thought at long last to face my betrayers. But no! *They* will be allowed to come in person— and what persons! Lord James, Morton, Maitland, and the upstanding model of righteousness, Lord Lindsay! Yet I am to be detained here, forty miles away from York, where the hearings will be.

Elizabeth herself will not be there. She sends instead the Duke of Norfolk, Sir Ralph Sadler (my enemy from the cradle!), and the Earl of Sussex, Elizabeth's grand chamberlain, a Scots-hater if ever there was one. I have been told that *he* told Elizabeth that he had been taught by his grandfather never to trust any Scot or Frenchman. Of the three, only Norfolk does not see me as a villain.

And so I must find commissioners to act for me—as if anyone truly can!

But worse than that is the shocking news that Elizabeth is going to permit the Lords to submit the "casket letters" as evidence in the hearings. And yet they will not even allow me an opportunity to see them! I will have no idea exactly what they contain. Are they the letters and poems I wrote to Bothwell? Are they the letters, but copied over and tampered with? Or are they complete forgeries? How can I respond to them if I do not even know what their contents are?

I would recognize my own words, even if copied out in another hand and translated. Certainly the words, when taken out of context (or worse yet, put in a new context), might paint me as guilty. Yet I did *not* kill Darnley. There were many others who were involved, and who tried to incriminate Bothwell after the fact—the placards, the clue of the barrel, the impersonation of him in the streets of Edinburgh that night. It was the Lords themselves who did this—the very ones who now bring forward these letters.

O God, I am betrayed!

❧

The men filed solemnly into the chamber at York—by a strange coincidence, the very same one that had been refurbished by Henry VIII to receive James V at a projected meeting in 1541. The Scots King had avoided the meeting, for fear of being kidnapped; now his captive daughter's fate was to be determined there. They settled themselves on long benches and shuffled their papers, and tried to look grim and determined. But soon smiles were breaking out; these men had long known one another and were comfortable together.

"Sadler! How fares your daughter, the one who had a mind to marry a clergyman?" asked Lord James. Sadler had long been involved in Scottish affairs.

"Well, I thank you. And how is your dear wife? Ah, Lord Boyd!"

Much discussion ensued about the correct procedure, and what might be entered as evidence. Mary's commissioners presented a "book of complaints" for the Lord James's side. Lord James demurred about his evidence, and pulled the silver casket out and placed it reverently on the table. But he declined to open it, merely making Morton describe how it had come into their possession. It sat there, tantalizingly.

657

* * *

Late at night the English delegation was startled to hear a knock on their chamber doors. It was Maitland, who asked in a low voice if any of them would care to examine the letters from the casket—unofficially, of course? They all said yes, and Maitland brought them copies. The men huddled over them in the candlelight, reading them and clucking.

"There are most horrible and bloody," murmured Norfolk. "Foul and abominable!" He continued reading, avidly.

During the day, between a discussion of the legitimacy of Lord James's Regency and the hereditary rights of the Hamiltons, which had been set aside by it, Maitland plucked gently on Norfolk's sleeve and suggested that they ride for a bit. The autumn was at its golden best, fat and full in the fields.

"Yorkshire is a magnificent tract of country," said Maitland. He hoped that Norfolk would agree to ride with him. And more than that, he hoped he would listen to what he, Maitland, was about to propose.

Maitland realized it was time that the "casket letters" were put in their proper perspective, and he hoped there was a way to do it delicately, without calling his fellow Lords out-and-out liars. Which they were, of course. Maitland had come to know them all too well in the past two years, and what he had found out saddened him.

For all that I like to think of myself as hardened to the failings of people, I realize now I am more of an idealist than I thought. The Lords broke all their promises to the Queen, and showed themselves morally worse than she was, whatever her sins of the flesh. Isn't it held that Christ was more lenient with those sins than with the ones of pride and greed? he thought.

"Indeed, yes, and at this time of year it comes close to being friendly," said Norfolk. He looked eager to make the trip.

They rode out beyond the high walls of the city, and took their horses along the River Ouse, with a mind to go hawking. The weather—a gold and blue day—seemed perfect for such an outing. They let the birds go, little caring if they captured anything, just happy to watch them soar.

"How hard it must be for these birds to stay captive on their perches," said Maitland. He watched the Duke as he said it. But there was no hint of understanding on the Duke's blank face. The Duke was noted for being only somewhat more perceptive than the oxen of his farmers.

"Yes. They are difficult to train," he said, his thick lips moving slowly.

"Think how much more painful it is for a golden eagle to be taken from his skies and made a captive to man."

"Fortunately there are not many of them, as only a king can hunt with an eagle. The rest of us—even dukes—must make do with falcons or hawks. Even dukes like me, who have more territory than some kings!" He nodded. "I have over six hundred square miles in my possession, you know, and sometimes I feel more of a king there than a real king must feel."

The hawks had flown so far away now that they were just black specks on the brilliant blue sky. A breeze was rustling the leaves on the trees down by the riverbank, and they sounded like scribes gathering up papers.

"Perhaps you could be—" No, that was too blatant. "Dear Norfolk, as the greatest peer in England, doubtless you have spent much time in pondering the future of the country in which your ancestors have been so influential." Maitland coughed gently. "I myself have long had one vision—that England and Scotland be united. Not by the sword, as in time past tyrants tried to wield, but by peaceful means. It is so clear that a union of the crowns is in the best interests of both realms!"

"A united kingdom, stretching from Dover to the Shetlands—yes, it would be a strong country," the Duke agreed.

"Otherwise we cannot hope to hold our own. I tell you frankly, now that guns have rendered the longbow obsolete, we are at a severe disadvantage against France, with its larger land and population. As a small nation, we are vulnerable. My dream is to see us become as strong as possible."

A couple of hunters passed by on foot, their dogs scampering on ahead of them, splashing through the water. They removed their caps and nodded to Maitland and the Duke.

The Duke's eyes were wandering. He still had not taken the bait.

"Let me speak frankly again," Maitland persisted. "If you would marry the Queen of Scots, all these thorny questions would be settled."

"What thorny questions?"

"The succession. The reluctance of Queen Elizabeth to marry. The obvious incapacity of Queen Mary to rule Scotland alone. The scandal to the crown." He paused. "Shall I be completely specific? Queen Elizabeth is likely to have no heir; she is already thirty-five and shows no inclination to marry. The nearest Protestant successor was Catherine Grey, but she recently died. The English people will not have a Catholic queen, Mary Stuart or any other. But if she were married to an English Protestant, that would content them; it would, in effect, dilute her Catholicism. Do you see?"

"Yeeess," he finally said.

"Her child, James, is not Catholic and therefore could succeed. Or any children you would have together. The Lords of the Congregation will never let her rule in Scotland again; indeed, how could they? Her reign has proved nothing but tumult and upheavals, and if she were free, she would just send for Bothwell again, and the Lords cannot tolerate him. But, released in the custody of yourself—"

"But she is a murderess!" said Norfolk. "I have no wish to live with a murderess!"

"How do you know she is a murderess?"

"Because of those letters! They were foul, disgusting things! And in your indictment of her, the one prepared by Buchanan, you describe her abusing her body with Bothwell. No, I could never touch such a woman!"

"Ah, those letters . . ." Maitland laughed. "Lord Morton swears they were found as he described, but the truth is we have no way of knowing what exactly he found. He has had more than a year to prepare the contents of the casket. They are only as reliable as Morton is honest."

The Duke began to bite the inside of his lip. "Which is not very."

"An understatement. I know the casket contained other letters as well, ones that Morton did not see fit to show us at the time, but which were most likely love letters from that Throndsen woman."

"What Throndsen woman?"

Did Norfolk know nothing? thought Maitland.

"Bothwell's Norwegian mistress who, after being cast away, had what every discarded mistress in the world can only dream of: complete revenge," he explained.

"How? Did she give him syphilis?"

God, Norfolk was stupid! "Of course not," said Maitland carefully. "In that case her happiness would be blighted by the fact that she herself had the disease. No, the fates acted as her avenger. First the west wind blew Bothwell onto the coast of Norway, and then events so arranged themselves that Bothwell had to submit to an investigation by the Viceroy of Norway, Erik Rosenkrantz, in Bergen, before being permitted to proceed on his journey. And that official happened to be Anna Throndsen's cousin, and when the court asked anyone with a grievance or debt against Bothwell to come forward, why, just as Bothwell was thinking himself safe, in came Anna! In came Anna and out went his chance of freedom."

"My God!" Norfolk looked stunned.

"For the hearing with Anna delayed his departure long enough that other questions could be raised before he could slip away. He was sent to Denmark for further questioning. And now he's languishing in prison in Malmö, awaiting the Danish king's pleasure."

"So that's why Bothwell is in gaol! That's how they got him!"

"Fate, Norfolk, fate. His deeds pursued him and there was no escape. And thus Anna has injured him in Scandinavia and then again in Scotland. For Bothwell kept her letters against just such an occasion, doubtless as evidence to show how temperamental and demanding she was, in case there was ever any question of his treatment of her. Then they fell into the hands of his enemies, Morton and the rest. Make of that what you will."

"Ah."

"Just remember, all the casket letters have been copied several times over. The ones you saw are not the originals. Easy enough to weave in some phrases from the Throndsen woman, along with a few of Morton's ideas."

He paused for breath. He was not absolutely sure that was what had happened, but all evidence pointed that way. The phrasing in the letters the Lords chose to exhibit was too variable, the style blatantly changed from one paragraph to the next, and some expressions and feelings were incompatible with what Maitland knew of the Queen's temperament. She was passionate, she was impulsive, God knew she could become stormy and angry, but she never whined or whimpered, and she never debased herself.

Norfolk was looking confused. "But—"

"And even if the Queen was a murderess, it was with just cause," continued Maitland. "She had loved the Lord Darnley and heaped honours upon him, but he repaid her by unfaithfulness and public drunkenness. No woman of spirit should be expected meekly to endure that! Think you Queen Elizabeth would tolerate that for a moment?"

The Duke laughed. "No, indeed!"

"Think of it, Norfolk! Think of the duty you would render the two realms, and the peace of mind you would confer on your own Queen—and give longed-for freedom to the other one! And she would have a husband worthy of her noble self at last."

After her usual spare dinner, Elizabeth spent some time reading Roman history before summoning Cecil. She always found history soothing, reminding her that the best way to master present history was to be aware of what was happening, and always think carefully before acting.

She stretched her legs out before the aromatic fire, which was burning hot and silently, and lost herself in her reading. Only reluctantly did she finally put the book aside and call for Cecil.

Cecil came straightway and, smiling wanly at her, proffered a gift. "For New Year's, Your Majesty," he said.

"Ah, yes. The Year of Our Lord fifteen hundred and sixty-nine," she said. "Am I allowed to open it now? I am in need of something to lift my spirits. I fear they are sagging mightily."

"Oh, indeed you may. This is not the formal gift I shall present at the court ceremony, but something for your personal use." Cecil patted it. "I would be most pleased if you would open it."

"Thank you, then." She unwrapped it and found a long box with an envelope attached. "You have written verses," she said, with delighted surprise.

"Indeed, as everyone else at court does, I thought I would try."

Elizabeth skimmed them. "Well done. I believe you are becoming younger and younger. Only the young understand poetry. Now"—she opened the long box—"what's this? Ah—" She extracted a fan of exquisite workmanship. Its blades were carved in arabesque patterns, and the silk covering was painted with roses and lilies; about half the fan was pure lace. "Why, Cecil!" She was genuinely touched.

"I know you are fond of fans, and suffer in the heat."

She laughed outright. "But, Cecil—it is only December!"

"Well, we like to plan ahead."

"Indeed we do," said Elizabeth, and her smile faded. "I have heard rumours," she suddenly said. "Rumours about the earls of Westmoreland and Northumberland. That is why I added them to the commission, to see if they would betray themselves."

"What rumours?"

"That they are plotting with the Queen of Scots . . . for what, I am not sure. For more than just her escape, I fear. I believe it may be another Pilgrimage of Grace sort of venture. You know, the north has always clung to the old ways . . . it is very secretive and inward. The families of Northumberland and Westmoreland have been almost like monarchs safe in their domains. I pray it will not lead to treason. So the Queen of Scots is enticing them!"

"Your Majesty, I warned you, and Knollys warned you, that she is a danger. Knollys even said it would be impossible to hold her, and that she herself told him that if she were not set free, she would consider herself at liberty to take any means to free herself. She believed that after this commission you would restore her to her throne, and so she has waited patiently and made no overt moves. But you will not do that, will you? Let us speak honestly."

"Thump on the arras, Cecil, and check the windowsill," said Elizabeth. When he started to rise, she put out her arm and stopped him. "Nay, do not. Even if you found no one, I believe our words might still be overheard. I will not deliver my verdict in advance. But I can tell you that things have not gone as I had hoped. Things are not resolved by this conference. Lennox is still clamouring for vengeance, like a tiresome parrot. Knollys begs to be released from his duty, and so does Lord Scrope. There are rumours that the Duke of Norfolk is toying with whatever the two northern earls are planning. The Lord James fears to lose control of Scotland by his long absence."

"Well?"

"I have come to the reluctant conclusion that we must find a more . . . permanent situation for Mary. She must be placed out of danger."

"Her danger, or yours?"

"Both." Elizabeth smiled sweetly. "She must be moved away from the north. Bolton is too close to the earls of Northumberland and Westmoreland. And these makeshift arrangements must be improved upon. I will find someone who is willing to be her . . . long-term host. Someone who is rich enough to have many dwellings to choose from, and can house her in royal comfort. Someone who lives a fair distance from both London and the north. Someone who is married, and proof against her . . . charms. I almost said 'wiles'! Someone who is Protestant, and has no wistful leanings toward the old religion. Ah, where shall I find such a lord?"

"You impose many conditions. But doubtless one will suggest himself." He looked at her in consternation. "But, please, Your Majesty, can you not tell me—as your chief minister, as the one who must know your thinking in order to execute it—what are your true feelings about the Queen of Scots?"

Elizabeth thought for so long that Cecil assumed she meant not to reply. Finally she said, "I do not know." Her voice was soft. "Truly it depends on her behaviour from now on. I cannot pass judgement on what went before. It is too confused and contradictory, and most of it is compiled by her enemies. But now she has a clean slate. She can choose to live circumspectly and loyally, and in time . . . well, time brings in many revenges. Time can be her friend. Time, in this case, is probably the best friend she now has. But if she turns to false friends like Philip, and English traitors, then . . . that is her choice."

❦

On January tenth, 1569, Elizabeth gave her appraisal of the hearings. Cecil stood, and requested all the commissioners to stand while he read, " 'That forasmuch as there has been nothing deduced against the Regent and his government that might impair their honour and allegiances, so, on the other part, there had been nothing sufficient produced nor shown by them against their sovereign, whereby the Queen of England should conceive or take any evil opinion of the Queen her good sister, for anything she had yet seen.' "

The Lord James was free to return to Scotland, and even given a five-thousand-pound loan. Queen Mary was to remain in custody.

III

Mary jounced and jolted along as her horse made its way painfully over the rutted roads—if they could be called that—in the icy landscape between Bolton and Tutbury. Just after the conference ended, she had received an abrupt order from Queen Elizabeth: she and her household—reduced immediately to half its size—were to be transferred to the custody of the Earl and Countess of Shrewsbury, one hundred miles to the south. No promises, no explanations, no apologies. Just go.

Mary had resisted; she had refused to travel during this dangerously cold and severe winter. But it was to no avail. Her Majesty the Queen of England decreed that she must go, and go she must.

Now the journey was proving every bit as onerous as she had feared, and more so. The January winds were unrelenting, and they ripped across the landscape, already lying prostrate under heavy snowfalls. She had become ill after the first day's journey, but had been able to keep going. Lady Livingston had become so sick that they had had to leave her behind on one of their stops, this one at Rotherham. All along the way, Mary's heart was so heavy from the news about the conclusion of the conference that she had to force herself to look at the landscape.

After all, I may never get another chance. This is *England*, the land I wanted to see so badly that I insisted on coming, despite all the advice of my best friends, she thought. This is *Elizabeth*, my sister sovereign, who promised to help me in distress. She has helped me so much that she got me to agree to a hearing to allow my subjects to justify themselves to me so I could be restored to the throne, and as a result my so-called sins were aired in public but I was not allowed to defend myself—even though she stipulates that I must "clear" myself before she can condescend to see me. I must clear myself, but I am not allowed to speak! Ah, it is all so obvious! And so I am to be kept a prisoner while my brother returns merrily to Scotland, with English money in his pocket!

And why could she not free me as well? Because she means yet to help me, she says. O ye holy angels, have you ever heard such convoluted logic?

They were passing down through Yorkshire, following the course of the River Ure. This was the area trampled by the Pilgrimage of Grace, when forty thousand peasants had risen up to protest the religious changes; she could see exactly what they had protested, in the ruined ribs of the great Cistercian monastery, Fountains Abbey. Her little party made its way past the remains of the Abbey just at sunset. They showed stark and white like a skeleton on the already white landscape; this ruin was the handiwork of Henry VIII, the great spoiler and reformer.

The rebels had been in control here, briefly, before they were betrayed. Henry VIII had tricked them into laying down their arms and sending a leader to London. Then he killed him, thought Mary. Trusting a Tudor is most unwise—I know that now. Would I had known it earlier. I never thought to find Henry VIII in the bosom of a woman. The more fool I.

They spent a night in Ripon, then the next night in Wetherby. The next day they were to make their way to Pontefract Castle, at the southernmost extremity of Yorkshire. Daylight came late, and so they were not mounted and ready to set out until well after ten o'clock. Even so, a dull purplish grey light suffused everything and made it hard to see the cracks and sleek stretches of ice on the path. There were few other travellers, and it made England look as bleak and empty as stretches of the Scottish moors. Mary was deep in thought when a party of beggars hobbled out of a hedge by the side of the road and began crying for alms. They scrambled round the horses, squeaking like mice, holding up their babies, crying, "Food, alms, if you have mercy!" Their feet were bound in rags rather than boots or even shoes, and their hands were bare, black with dirt. They looked like witches.

I, too, am a beggar here, she thought with a shock. I had to borrow clothes; I was almost as naked as they when I arrived in England.

"A moment," she said, reining in her horse. She dug in her purse for some coins. Lord Scrope would be annoyed; let him be. "Pray you, wait." She turned and signaled to her guards. "Here." She pressed a coin into one man's rough hand. He kept hanging on to her saddle, and she attempted to detach him. "That is all I may spare," she said.

The man rubbed the coin and then bit on it. His teeth were surprisingly sound. He caught her eye and mouthed, "I am Hameling."

Hameling! One of the Earl of Northumberland's men. Of course! Now she recognized him.

"Move on here!" Lord Scrope was saying.

Quickly, Mary pulled an enamelled gold ring off her finger and gave it to him. "Bid the Earl remember his promise to help me," she said, pushing him away. "Get you gone now!" she said loudly.

As they plodded away, he winked at her.

Her heart was leaping with excitement as they made their way onward in the smudged winter day. She was not alone; she was not forgotten.

Pontefract Castle, with its gloomy associations of royal murder—it was there Richard II had been starved to death—reared up before them and then swallowed them up in the twilight. Within its walls dripping with cold, Mary tried to sleep. Her party, reduced now to only thirty persons, was huddled on makeshift beds.

Northumberland. Northumberland was sympathetic to her cause. That meant that his friend, Westmoreland, probably stood with him. Both those earls had been present—representing Elizabeth—at the conference. That they were unswayed by the prejudicial hearings was a miracle. And Westmoreland's wife was Norfolk's sister. A sturdy piece of cloth of family sympathies was being woven—a piece of cloth that might serve as her escape mantle. So thinking, she slept more soundly than she had in weeks.

They wound their way slowly down through Derbyshire, a small county that lay at the centre of England like the pit of a plum. Its hills were gentle and it appeared to have many streams and valleys; several forests covered faraway hills, making black patches against the white snow. It was reputed to be a very green, rich county, but of that Mary could see no evidence in this dead time of year. The Earl of Shrewsbury, her new "host," had most of his holdings here, and they passed near two of them: Wingfield Manor and Chatsworth. But, although these were new manors, the Queen had ordered them to take up residence at Tutbury Castle, farther south, at the very border of Derbyshire and Staffordshire.

Mary had asked about Tutbury, and had been told that it had a magnificent view over the surrounding fields beyond the River Dove, and had abundant game in its nearby Needwood Forest, which was also associated with Robin Hood. John of Gaunt had held his Court of Minstrels here, making the place, Scrope had assured her, "the very essence of Merrie England."

"Ah, yes, Merrie England," she had said. "Is that what I came to see? Indeed it is legendary—like the fashions of France and the wild country of Scotland." As a child she had wondered about King Arthur, Robin Hood, Richard the Lionheart, the longbow archers, and the Yule log and Merlin the magician. So now she was to be lodged in quarters that called all of that to mind. She was also curious about the Earl of Shrewsbury, and had managed to obtain only bits of information from the close-mouthed Lord

Scrope. The Earl was very wealthy. The Earl was newly married, but for the second time. His wife was almost as rich as he was, and eight years older. As part of the marriage negotiations, they had married their sons and daughters to one another, to keep the wealth in the family. The Earl was a Protestant, but was lax in prosecuting Catholics in his county. As a result, Derbyshire and neighbouring Lancastershire were well endowed with Catholic families.

"But what is he *like*?" Mary had asked.

"Colourless," Lord Scrope had finally admitted.

"What is his wife like?"

"Colourful. Besides her own colours, she's added the ones leeched from her three previous husbands."

They saw Tutbury on the horizon long before they reached it, as they approached the confluence of the rivers Trent and Dove. It bristled with towers and walls on a redstone cliff overlooking the banks of the Dove, and with the setting sun behind it, it looked like jagged dog's teeth. Mary shuddered the second she saw it. Merrie England? This was anything but merry; it was a prison.

A prison. I am a prisoner, she thought. A true prisoner, as bad as Lochleven.

For an instant she imagined turning suddenly and galloping away. I cannot meekly enter here! she thought. But then she knew there was nowhere to ride, no friendly subjects to hide and protect her. She was in the heart of enemy territory, where there could be no shelter for her. She did not even know her direction.

No, that is not the way, she told herself sternly. You will not ride out and hide in cottages and sleep on the ground, as you did in the flight after Langside. You have hopes among the nobles. Have you so soon forgotten Norfolk? And Northumberland? And even Philip of Spain? There is a good chance that he may invade here in response to Elizabeth's seizing of his gold ships that went astray. I am not alone. I am not alone. I am not alone!

They began their ascent to the castle, winding up a steep path. It was more than a hundred feet up to the top, and they had to pass over a wide dry moat, over a drawbridge, and through a formidable gatehouse—the only entrance to the castle. At length they emerged into the castle grounds; later Mary was told they were three acres in extent. Stout walls encircled three sides, and the fourth needed no walls, as it was a steep drop to the valley floor, a hundred feet below. Two watchtowers guarded the thick walls.

The ground was barren, and only a few torches were lighted, throwing eerie, leaping shadows on the frozen ground. Stiffly Lord Scrope dismounted and said, "I will announce our arrival." But by the tone of his voice, he betrayed his anxiety that Shrewsbury had not been waiting for them.

Mary and her attendants waited, patting their horses and assuring them they would soon be stabled. At length Scrope returned, bringing someone with him.

"Queen Mary," he said, "may I present George Talbot, the Earl of Shrewsbury?"

George. Always a lucky name for me, she thought. Pray that this may be so now. "I am pleased," said Mary.

Shrewsbury took her hand and kissed it. Only then did he look at her.

She saw a man of about forty, with a long, lugubrious face, thinning hair, and a greying beard. His eyes looked as though they had seen many defections and melancholias.

"My Countess and I welcome you," he said sadly.

Mary's household was to be lodged in the south range of buildings, which were two storeys. As she stepped over the threshold, the first impression she had was of an overwhelming odour of mould. It became more intense when she actually stood inside. The guardroom smelt and dripped like a grotto. A pervasive cold gripped her.

"Welcome, Your Majesty," said a low, powerful voice. A woman had emerged from the neighbouring chamber, and she approached Mary. "I am Bess, Countess of Shrewsbury."

Mary's first thought was that someone had taken Queen Elizabeth and rolled a millstone over her, flattening her out and broadening all her features. This woman looked like the Queen, with light reddish hair, a long thin nose, and tight little lips. But her face and person were square. Everything about her was square, from her head to her eyes to her shoulders and her hands and even, amazingly, her fingernails. Peeking out from under her heavy woollen gown were square shoes encasing square feet.

"I trust you will be comfortable here," she was saying. "We have sent for tapestries from Sheffield and furnishings from London. This place is in poor repair—very poor—we never stay here, and the Queen's information is sorely out of date!" She sounded as though she would like to box the Queen's stupid ears.

"I am sure I will be," Mary replied.

"Do not be so sure! It is most uncivilized! It was built over two hundred years ago and nothing done since. But," she said with a snort, "we do what we can!" She turned to her husband. "George, is there no word yet about the seven lined hangings with the story of Hercules? I sent for them last Monday. You said they would come from Wingfield. Well?"

"I have been told they are at Derby. One of the mules is lame."

"Your excuses are lame!" she bellowed. Then she said to Mary, "I will take you to your quarters, Madam."

❧

March 4, 1569. Tutbury Castle, Staffordshire. What have I done
to warrant such a punishment? This "castle" is not fit to house
Judas or Brutus, and yet I must endure it. It sits atop its cliff,
exposed to the elements; the winds rip across it and through the

flimsy south range of buildings where they have housed me. These quarters are even worse than they seemed when first I smelt them. The mould was delicate compared to the stench of the privies, which have nowhere to empty, and sit, festering, beneath us. Noxious vapours pervade every chamber. Wearing perfume to try to overcome it has only the effect that the perfume becomes mixed with the latrine odours and itself becomes repulsive.

They said Tutbury "overlooks the fields," but there are no fields below, only swamps and marshes. As they have thawed, the ice has released the deadly vapours from them as well, and the cruel wind blows them up here, to poison the outdoor air as the privies do the indoor air. My clothes reek of it, as if I had rolled in decaying slime.

This castle is so closely guarded, with its one steep path winding up from the little village behind it, and its gatehouse, that I have not been able to carry on any correspondence, besides with Elizabeth. Over and over I beg her to let me come and speak to her in person, or else to set me free to seek my fortune elsewhere. But her replies are evasive. O, how can I endure this?

I know nothing of what is happening in Scotland, or how my party is faring there. I know nothing of Bothwell's fate. I know nothing of what is happening on the Continent, of what my relatives in France are doing and whether Philip has responded to the English provocation. In short, I am kept in a dark dungeon!

I have established a code for Norfolk. The Spanish ambassador is "30." I am "40." Northumberland is "20" and Westmoreland is "10." I have had much ado to send any messages to any of them. They cannot send any in here, and I can only send them out when I let out my faithful Lord Herries or my recently arrived John Leslie, the Bishop of Ross, to take letters to Elizabeth. Then he can smuggle out messages to the others. But sometimes they are searched, and it is difficult to think of any hiding places that my adversaries have not already in mind. They say this Francis Walsingham, Cecil's deputy, is a spymaster and has spies of his own everywhere. Thus he knows all the tricks, and is most inventive himself. It is he who works behind the others like a shadow, and it is he, ultimately, whom I must outsmart every time I want to get a message out.

How amused Catherine de Médicis would be! She had such disdain for my attempts at games of intrigue, when I was a child in France. But even as a man with weak arms must learn to chop wood if he needs a fire, I have had to teach myself all these things, which I would rather not know.

Leslie says that things are moving, that Norfolk is being brought round. I must do something to strengthen his resolve! Of course I have no desire to marry him, but that is beside the point. I must be free in order to marry him, and once free, I will have a choice. I must put a petition to the Pope to dissolve my marriage to Bothwell, in order to seem sincere. Of course it is pointless, because I was not married to Bothwell by Catholic rites. But no matter—it will seem convincing. And it will give me an opportunity to write openly to Bothwell about it. Just to speak to him, if only on paper. . . .

There is now a priest in my household, going under the name of Sir John Morton and acting as a gentleman attendant. Shrewsbury is only too aware of it, but looks the other way, which is kind. With the departure of Knollys, they have stopped subjecting me to the Anglican priest. I am strengthened by the presence of Morton, and the opportunity to practise my own faith, however secretly.

I must stop now. My fingers ache. Since coming here, my joints have swollen and become stiff. My physician says it is rheumatism. But I am only twenty-six!

Mary put down her pen and capped the inkwell. The ink in it was thick with the cold. She then closed her book and wrapped it in the false cover she had devised for it that made it look like a ledger, and put it in the stack of other ledgers. As she stood and smoothed out her skirt, she was only too aware of the stiffness of her fingers.

She knelt for a moment before her crucifix—Lady Douglas had kindly sent it on from Lochleven—and prayed.

"Dear Heavenly Father," she whispered, "please have mercy on me, your child. You will not remain angry forever. In your holy Scriptures it says, 'He retaineth not His anger forever, because He delighteth in mercy.' I know You sometimes require suffering . . . is that what this is, rather than punishment and anger? I remember something the Cardinal said, long ago in France . . . about suffering as something required for its own sake. But I did not really hear it; I was young and happy. What was it? That suffering is to teach obedience, I think he said. Show me what I must do, then, and I will obey!"

She stood up and realized that her knees were also tender. The rheumatism was affecting them as well. A shiver of fear passed through her. Does God mean to afflict me in body as well as in spirit? she thought, with panic.

She left her room and made her way into the long chamber that served as both hall and great chamber, with a wainscot partition dividing the two. Each had its own fireplace, woefully inadequate for heating. Bess was already seated on a bench near the fire, a great woollen shawl around her shoulders. She looked up eagerly when Mary entered.

For three weeks now, Mary had been helping Bess design hangings and embroideries for her new mansion of Chatsworth. Bess had inherited it from her second husband, William Cavendish, the father of all her brood of children, and was building it with no help from her current husband, whom she always referred to, somewhat rudely, as "George." But Bess was childishly eager to consult with Mary about matters of taste, since Mary had lived in all the great châteaux of France, and seen firsthand the murals at Fontainebleau, the columns of marble at St.-Germain-en-Laye, the paintings by Primaticcio of Diane de Poitiers at Chenonceau, the secret cupboards at Blois. To her delight, Mary had sent for her books of embroidery patterns that were all the rage in France—or had been, in 1560. There was the *Devises Héroïques* by Claud Paradin, and *La Nature et Diversité des Poissons* by Pierre Belon. They contained suitable mottoes and fables, and woodcuts of animals which could be adapted for needlework. Bess did not read French well enough to understand the texts that went along with them, and relied on Mary to do so.

Now Bess held up the square of canvas she was working on. "I have begun the broken mirror!" she said gleefully.

Mary smiled. She was surprised at how fast Bess had progressed; she worked as furiously on this as she did on everything else, driving like a mad charioteer.

"Excellent!" said Mary. "It will be a fitting tribute to Sir William."

"Ah! If only he could see it!" Bess sighed, running her square fingers over it.

"But he does, Madame," said Mary. "He sees from Heaven."

"Hmmm . . . yes, that of course, but—" Bess bent back over the panel that she and Mary had designed in memory of Sir William, the bequeather of Chatsworth. In spite of the fact that his widow had allowed herself to be consoled by two husbands since, the panel showed mourning in full force. Tears rained down onto quicklime, encircled by the motto *Tears Witness That the Quenched Flame Lives*—in Latin, of course, to lend it dignity. Around this a border of mourning symbols encircled the device: a glove, symbol of fidelity, cut in two; broken intertwined cords; a cracked mirror; three (to account for Bess's three widowhoods) broken wedding rings; a snapped chain.

"He will look down from Heaven and be proud," said Mary. She opened her basket and extracted her own work. It looked innocent enough—a ghostly hand descended from the sky with a pruning hook, lopping off branches of a tree, with the motto *Virtue Flourishes by Wounding* curling around it. Mary had told Bess that it was to reflect her own growing belief that she was being chastened, to grow through suffering. It had her cipher, which incorporated her initials and those of François. Thus they had sighed and spoken in soft tones of their beloved departed husbands, darting their needles in and out of the canvas like fireflies.

But Mary was making the panel to be sewn into a pillow for Norfolk. The symbols were meant to convey a different message to him and rouse him to action: the unfruitful branch was Elizabeth, while the one which would bear fruit was herself—and him. How she would get it to him she did not know. But somehow she would manage.

After an hour Bess suddenly remembered she had to speak to "George" about the provender for the horses, and she stuffed her sewing into her basket and left. Mary dutifully kept sewing, eyes downcast, until she was sure Bess had indeed left. Then, as normally as possible, she stood up—her knees were aching still—and sent one of her servants to bring George Douglas to her. Her mind was made up.

George came straightway, and he looked relieved. He had had scant opportunity to be alone with her since coming to Tutbury. She smiled at him and mounted the step to sit in her chair under her cloth of estate.

"So you will be Queen in state today, and I must stand at your feet?" he said.

"I must sit under my cloth of estate, else day by day I shall forget what I am, and think myself only a poor prisoner."

"You have as your device on the cloth, *En Ma Fin Est Ma Commencement*. I have long wondered why you chose 'In My End Is My Beginning.' This is not your end, surely . . . or do you see it that way?"

He was so devoted, so singleminded. "No, indeed I do not. The phoenix rising from the ashes is pictured upon the cloth—now do you understand?"

"Yes."

George had remained with her all these months, and was obviously intent on remaining with her until "the end." She knew that he desired her, yet at the same time worshipped her. And there had been times when she was tempted by him, tempted by his male beauty and her own enforced celibacy, and she had thought, What else do I have to reward him with? and What harm would it do for me to take some little pleasure in this prison to which I am consigned? It would be an act of charity and mercy. But regard for him had stopped her. If he had been less noble, less pure—if he had been more like the opportunistic Ruthven, or even the practical Maitland . . . But then she would have had no desire for him at all. His very decency and purity was his attraction.

"George, I need your help," she said. "God knows I have waited and hoped to be released, but my imprisonment shows no end. I must send someone to France, to speak to my relatives the Guises, and to see about my estates. I am entitled to my income as dowager queen, but since my flight from Scotland, nothing has been forthcoming. I need someone I can trust. Will you go?"

"I do not wish to leave you!" he said.

This was going to be difficult. "You have served me so well. Now you see that I need further help. This is no different from procuring the horses and men to secure my escape from Kinross. It is just farther, that is all. You can help raise troops in France. Your work for me is not yet done."

"If the sea is between us, I cannot help fight for you myself. There are no men at arms in your retinue here."

Oh, he was so handsome; no wonder they called him "Pretty Geordie." She had seen Shrewsbury's servants of both sexes eyeing him. She motioned to him to come up beside her.

671

"Dear George," she said, "then I see I must command you. It is good that I am seated under my cloth of estate." She reached up and, taking his face in her hands, drew his face toward hers. She kissed him once, lingeringly, on the lips.

He trembled and drew back.

"That is my command," she whispered. "That you go on my mission. And if, while there, you find a Frenchwoman who suits your fancy, then I beg you, conclude an honourable marriage with her. You have lost your fortunes in following mine; now I send you to France to repair them as best as possible."

"I want no one else!" he blurted out. "There can never be anyone else!"

"Then you lay a burden of guilt on me that is unfair. You know I am married, and for you deliberately to forgo any chance for happiness and a family because of a married woman is cruel—to me. To me, whom you say you love!"

"So if I love you, I must marry someone else?" he said. "Strange love!"

"As you grow older, you will discover stranger still. France will be good for you; you will become educated in love there." She wanted to say, *I do not mean any of this; let us just find joy in one another's arms. It may be all either of us will ever have.*

"Perverted love!" he snorted. "Love in which a king wears his mistress's colours and publicly shames his queen!"

She laughed gently. "Most like, then, you prefer the burning, pure love of a king like Henry VIII? A love that would brook no other!"

George's icy blue eyes were riveted on her. "Indeed. At least he was honest!"

"Is honesty, then, the trait you prize above all others?"

He was nodding earnestly.

Ah, then go, she thought. Oh, George. I shall miss you—you take my youth with you. My knight of honesty.

After he was gone, she sat disconsolately. Her intrigues and ciphers and embroideries seemed, suddenly, to have lost their appeal. It was all so much work.

It would be so much easier to be completely honest, she thought. They say the wages of sin is death. But the wages of honesty will be a lifetime of imprisonment. Because other people are not honest. Fight fire with fire. Or die. All my attempts to act with mercy and justice were betrayed in Scotland and have brought me to this place.

❦

May 15, 1569. This ominous anniversary: two years since Bothwell and I became husband and wife; one year since the battle of Langside. Tomorrow I will have been in England a year—and yet to see Elizabeth!

George has been active on my behalf in France, and I have hopes of receiving an income once again. Without money I can do nothing, not even pay my servants, but exist on an allowance from Elizabeth.

In Scotland—oh, the sorrow of it, the perfidy!—Borthwick and Rothes have gone over to Lord James. There remains to me only Dumbarton Castle and scattered nobles who refuse to bow the knee to my brother.

Philip of Spain has retaliated against Elizabeth's hostile policy by seizing all the English ships and goods in the Netherlands, and so Elizabeth in turn has arrested all the Spaniards in England. This means that the Spanish ambassador is under house arrest in London, and, from my point of view, makes it all the more difficult to get and receive messages. A certain Florentine banker, Roberto Ridolfi, has served to deliver letters between the ambassador and Leslie, for me.

The French have proved less helpful than I had hoped, because Elizabeth has been negotiating with them to marry Charles IX—who is seventeen years younger than she! Is there no limit to her posturing? Next she will go after little Henri, or even the baby, who is twenty-two years younger!

The word is that the north is stirring, and my hopes of rescue are not without foundation. Now, ye spirits of war, infuse them to action!

Norfolk and I have at last found a safe channel of communication. I have sent him the pillow, which proclaims my message. He has sent me a diamond, which I wear around my neck, hidden under my clothes, as I promised him. I write him letters and even sign them, "Your own, faithful unto death."

God forgive me.

IV

The horses halted in front of the huge studded doors of Durham Cathedral. Westmoreland turned and shouted, "Dismount! We will not ride into the house of God like barbarians!"

Behind him three hundred men climbed down, their saddles creaking. Northumberland clasped his arm and said, "This is the day we have long awaited, brother!" His eyes were shining.

Together they each took hold of one bronze door pull—each as large as a serving platter—and hauled the doors open. Before them the long nave stretched, beckoning. Morning light was streaming in through the window over the altar. Like a mighty and silent forest, the massive stone pillars made a tunnel to that light. They were thick sentinels, standing guard as they had for hundreds of years.

"Reverently, my friends!" called Westmoreland. He turned his face toward that light and marched toward it, his army behind him. He and Northumberland walked down the aisle, over three hundred feet long.

Where the high altar had been, now was only a bare communion table. Rising high behind it was the delicate, cream-coloured, wrought stone altar screen, its niches empty, like blind eye sockets.

"Dry your tears, my Blessed Lady," cried Northumberland. "We will restore your sight!" He stood at one side of the communion table, and Westmoreland took the other. "Heave!" he ordered, and together they tipped the table over. It fell heavily, its wide feet sticking up like a tumbled child's. "Now!" he directed the men. "Chop it!"

With wild cries, the north-country men dashed toward it, swords raised, and began hacking at it. The thuds of their swords and hatchets resounded dully in the stone emptiness of the cathedral.

"And here's this abomination, the Protestant Bible, and the Book of Common Prayer! Gather them up, my lads, wherever you find them, take them outside, and burn them!" cried Northumberland. "Let us cleanse this place!"

"And when you're done, we'll rededicate it, and have a mass!" said Westmoreland. "Father Wright here will gladly officiate!" He twisted his fingers into the shoulder of a captive priest. "But not just for us! Let us bring in the townspeople! Yea, round them up!"

In front of a makeshift altar, Father Wright raised the host and celebrated the first mass there in ten years, to a packed cathedral. People fell to their knees, asking to be absolved of their sin of tolerating heresy, and local Anglican priests joined them, praying for forgiveness in going against their consciences. Incense rose, banned rosary beads clicked, and the sound of sung Latin carried sweetly in the air.

"And let us pray for our Holy Father, the Pope, and for all his Church, and for our Sovereign Lady, Mary Stuart of Scotland, France, and England," concluded Northumberland. "God bless her and bring her to reign over us!"

"Amen!" cried the people.

❦

Elizabeth grabbed Robert Dudley's shoulders the second he stepped into her privy chamber at Windsor. Her sudden attack almost caused him to lose his balance.

"What news? Where are they now?" she barked.

"Madam, the last news I received, they had celebrated mass in Durham Cathedral, after turning out the Protestant fittings. They built a big bonfire in front of the cathedral and threw the offending things into it. Northumberland and Westmoreland whipped the townsmen into a fury by telling them that the bishop's wife there had taken the ancient baptismal font and used it for a sink in her kitchen, and used monks' tombstones to pave the floor of her town house." He brushed off his shoulders where she had injured the velvet.

"How many are they?"

"In Durham, about three hundred."

"Pish!" she said. "Three hundred!"

"But altogether, perhaps a thousand on foot, poorly armed—you know, with pitchforks and shovels—and then another fifteen hundred, mounted, armed and dangerous. There is another group in Hartlepool, you know."

"Twenty-five hundred, then." Her voice was sharp. "And Sussex is awaiting reinforcements. He dare not rely on local people; we are unsure of their loyalty. Hunsdon must march north with his troops."

"I am ready to march!" he said.

"Yes, I know, Robin. But I want you here with me, in this—this prison!" She gestured round the room. "I hate being forced to retreat here to Windsor, like a coward! Hiding behind stone walls!"

"You are no coward, but have the heart of a lion."

"Yes, Robin. I know that, and you know that, but do *they* know that? Does *she* know that?" She looked around, her eyes narrowing. "How close have they come to Tutbury?"

"The farthest south they managed to get was Tadcaster. They did not cross the River Ouse. That was still seventy miles north of Tutbury. Now they are back up at Durham, a hundred and thirty miles north. They have retreated."

"I want her moved farther south!" she snapped. "They mustn't lay hands on her!"

"My dearest lady, there is no chance of that! You needn't be so concerned." He tried to catch her eyes and make her smile.

"They mean to rescue her! It was part of their plan!" Her mouth was so tightly clamped, no smile could be coaxed out of it. "Do not attempt to tell me what to do!"

"No, Madam. Never." He inclined his head in acquiescence.

"They issued a proclamation from Durham as they marched through the first time, saying they meant to determine 'to whom of mere right the true succession of the crown appertaineth.' Do not belittle it! Of course they mean to free her!"

"Their support is melting away. They did not find large numbers joining them as they tried to march south; it seems the Catholics are better Englishmen than they are Catholics, at least south of the Ouse. You need have no worry on that account."

"And what about the Spanish? Walsingham has discovered that they tried to arrange with Philip's general in the Netherlands, that brute Alva, to bring his troops over." She gave him a nervous, triumphant look.

"Yes, and the rebels even captured Hartlepool to give him a landing place. But he has done nothing. And will not. He is an intelligent, crafty man who does not conjure up support and sympathy where none exists." He tried to take her hands once more. "The Spanish are a phantom threat."

She snorted. "With ten thousand men sitting in the Netherlands, just on our doorstep?"

"There is water between us."

"Ah, yes. Water. The English Channel." She sighed and tried to smile. "Perhaps you are right, Robert. I tremble over nothing. After all, Norfolk is safe in the Tower."

Robert laughed. "Mary's plighted knight. Some showing—he cowered in his house on his estates. May all your enemies have such bold champions!"

Elizabeth shook her head. "To think my enemies are my cousins!"

❧

The rebels waited in vain for their ranks to swell with perturbed Catholics. But the English Catholics were curiously inert; they stood and watched, but did nothing. Lord Dacre, Norfolk's son-in-law, led an attack on Elizabeth's troops under Lord Hunsdon, but was soundly defeated. As winter closed in, the rebels fled northward, beyond the old Roman wall and then up into Scotland to the wilds of Liddesdale.

The Lord James, eager to have an opportunity to impress Elizabeth, hunted them down and tried to round them up. But the old Border tradition of harbouring fugitives made it difficult to find them, and he succeeded only in capturing the Earl of Northumberland. The Earl of Westmoreland and Northumberland's wife, who was more warlike than the men, escaped abroad to the Netherlands. Left behind to face Elizabeth's wrath were the citizens of Northumbria and Yorkshire, who had nowhere to flee.

They were executed by the hundreds in their towns and villages to the cry of "Thus perish all the Queen's enemies!" and left hanging from gibbets as a warning. A thousand corpses swung in the icy winds of January, creaking in their chains, seeming to whisper, "Betrayed . . . we were betrayed," from their fleshless mouths.

❧

March 15, 1570. It is all over. Northumberland and Westmoreland rose and attempted to raise the people to proclaim the old religion, but they were cruelly put down. I had foolish hopes of being rescued, and waited every day to see if this was my day of deliverance. But no. There is no deliverance.

Today Shrewsbury came to see me, his long face even longer.

He said, almost in a whisper, "There is sad news. Your brother is dead."

"My brother?" I said. Did he mean the Lord James? Surely he did, not knowing of my other brothers. And yet—surely not.

"He was shot in Linlithgow," said Shrewsbury. "It seems that some enemy of his, a Hamilton loyalist, waited in an upstairs room overlooking the main street, and shot the Regent as he was riding through."

"James—dead?" I felt a terrible tremor pass through me. James was the one who was always safe, the one who directed killings. If James could be assassinated, then—

"He died within a few hours," said Shrewsbury. "There was no hope." He paused. "It is a sad day for Scotland."

"Always killings! Will they never stop?" I cried. "And who rules now?"

Suddenly I realized that all things had changed in that instant in Scotland. Who *would* rule?

"Queen Elizabeth is attempting to persuade them to elect the Earl of Lennox as Regent in Lord James's place."

Lennox! That was unlikely. "That will take much persuasion," I said.

"And the other sad news—although perhaps it is not sad for *you!*—is that the Pope has issued a bull formally excommunicating Queen Elizabeth. Evidently the stupid, ill-informed man thinks it will help the English Catholics, put heart into them to make another attempt on Elizabeth's throne!" With a snort of disgust, he handed me a paper. "Read it for yourself!"

I looked at *Regnans in Excelsis*. It deprived that "servant of wickedness" of her pretended title to the throne of England and absolved all her Catholic subjects from their allegiance to her:

"Peers, subjects, and people of the said kingdom, and all others upon what terms soever bound unto her, are freed from their oath and all manner of duty, fidelity, and obedience. We direct these people, commanding moreover and enjoining all and every, the nobles, subjects, people and others whatsoever that they shall not once dare to obey her or any of her laws, directions, or commands, binding under the same curse those who do anything to the contrary."

"This is not wise," is all I cautiously allowed myself to say. And indeed it is not. I realize that His Holiness Pius V is anxious to draw the battle lines between the two religions, but he dwells already in the heavenly realm in his mind, and pays too little attention to earthly considerations. Had this bull been published before the Northern Rising, then it might have had some effect. Now all it will do is subject all Catholics to more hardship and suspicion. Years ago, his predecessor, Paul IV, declared Elizabeth a heretic and recognized me as the rightful occupant of the throne, but he did not so blatantly call upon her subjects to depose her. This is a slap in Elizabeth's face; the other was just a gentle finger-shaking.

"Wisdom does not reside at Rome!" Shrewsbury said righteously.

After he left, I prayed before my crucifix a long while, praying for James—although I knew it was not a form of prayer he liked! But we must pray each in our own way. I closed my eyes and thought of my brother as he had been long ago, drawing a veil across the present.

"Eternal rest grant him," I asked.

But now that the shock is over, and I have had a few hours to recover, I cannot help wondering—is the way perhaps cleared now for my return to Scotland? Might the Lords now call me home? Without Lord James at their head, they might prove kinder. And perhaps they will discover, as they did before, that they need their Queen.

V

Mary held the reins as tightly as her stiff fingers would permit as she directed her horse to trot out of the gates of Chatsworth and onto the path leading to her next residence of incarceration, Sheffield Castle. During the Northern Rebellion, she had been moved thirty-five miles south from Tutbury to Coventry for safekeeping. After the flight of the earls and the collapse of their rebellion, she had then been hauled over fifty miles north again to one of Shrewsbury's mansions, Chatsworth. Now, in November of 1570, a year since the rebellion, she and her entourage were to be moved yet another fourteen miles to Sheffield, where the Earl had two residences: the castle and a manor house about a mile away. That way she could be transferred back and forth between the two whenever one of them needed cleaning.

Gradually her company had achieved some semblance of permanence. She had her physician Bourgoing, a surgeon, an apothecary, an embroiderer, her tailor Balthazzar, grooms of the chamber, ladies of the chamber like the faithful Mary Seton and Madame Rallay, with Jane Kennedy and Marie Courcelles to replace the lost Marys, and secretaries like Claud Nau, all under the supervision of John Beaton, her Master of the Household. She had her secret priest. She had Bastian Pages to provide whatever entertainment was possible under the circumstances. She had a kitchen staff of eight, a coachman, and three grooms of the stable. Unfortunately she was not allowed to travel anywhere. Some of her partisans, like Lord Boyd and Lord Claud Hamilton, had returned to Scotland, but she still had Willie Douglas, John Leslie, and the Livingstons.

She and the Shrewsburys were settling into the strange semi-friendship of the keeper and the hostage; they exchanged gifts and pleasantries, shared confidences and news of neutral personalities, became involved in the minutiae of each other's everyday lives. Bess and Mary worked together on the decorating and furnishing of Bess's estates, Mary even writing to France for patterns and embroidery thread, but Shrewsbury having to read the letters before sending them on. Mary had not succeeded in finding any partisans within Shrewsbury's household such as she had at Lochleven; the only stalwarts she had in her service were those she had brought herself.

They were watched, but nonetheless Mary had managed to find ways to get and receive correspondence. Norfolk had been released from the Tower and put under house arrest in the summer, having made a written oath to cease and desist from any communication with Mary or any marriage schemes. But he had immediately disobeyed, and once again secret letters between them were passing in packets of sewing silks and foodstuffs, written in orange juice that was invisible until it was held up to the heat of a flame.

But the failure of the native uprising in England meant that there could be no deliverance for her without outside help—either French or Spanish. All the rebels in England had been so harshly punished that for all intents and purposes there was no longer any local hope of deliverance. Therefore she had been forced to begin negotiations with the Spanish through a papal agent, the banker Roberto Ridolfi. The Pope's excommunication of Elizabeth and his bull depriving her of her throne had whipped Englishmen across the board into a frenzy of Pope-and-foreigner-hating. Ridolfi, who had originally come to England with Philip, and as something of a financial wonder child, had remained as a court adviser to the likes of Cecil himself, had been investigated by Walsingham after the Northern Uprising, but had passed muster. Still, the times were chancy for any foreign involvement.

In the meantime, her party in Scotland was dwindling. Dumbarton Castle, under Lord Fleming and the Hamiltons, still held out, and in a surprise move, a repentant Maitland—he was not called "the Chameleon" for nothing, Mary thought—had converted Kirkcaldy from the party of the Lords and they both had taken over Edinburgh Castle, which they were now, in an about-face, holding for Mary. But the assassination of Lord James had done nothing to facilitate Mary's return.

Oh, I thought perhaps they would relent, the Lords, she lamented. I thought that Lord James was my chief enemy in Scotland. But no, there are many lesser ones. And Elizabeth—Elizabeth convinced them to accept the Earl of Lennox as their Regent! She is determined to keep me pent up here—why?

Lennox as Regent. Fate would not be Fate if she did not hold surprises. But Lennox!

Sad as Mary was, there was one good aspect of it: for the first time, little James would be in the everyday company of a relative. The poor boy, four years old now, had been treated as an orphan by everyone. Pray that Lennox does not poison his grandson's mind against me, Mary thought. I know he cannot say good things of me, for he hates me, but if God will have mercy on me, He will restrain Lennox from mouthing evil about me.

Little James. She had sent him a gift of a pony and a little saddle, with a letter telling him how she loved him, but she had had no reply. Had he ever received her gift and letter? Would she ever know?

They plodded along in the mists of late November, along Baslow Edge and then across Totley Moor, where gold and green lay in interspersed patches. A patina of purple heather softened the colours and blended with the grey that was swirling everywhere. The sky was also grey, but comforting, like an encircling arm. It looked enough like the moors of Scotland to call the memories forth, but it was tamer, kinder. A man would not be able to ride far enough here to hide himself.

For her, the moors would always be that ride with Bothwell.

They descended into the sheltered valley of the river Don, which made a big, lazy loop, like a **U**. At the bottom of the **U** rose a hill, surmounted by the castle to which they were going; also on the bottom of the **U**, the much smaller River Sheaf joined the Don. The ground beside them flattened out, and Shrewsbury, trotting up beside Mary, pointed to one side.

" 'Tis the Assembly Green," he said. "Every Easter Tuesday I review the town militia here. And across the road is the archery field." A great flat brown ground lay torpid in the dead time of year.

"So archery is still practised here?" Mary asked. How outmoded, she thought, when it is guns and knives now that do all the damage. Guns from windows, and knives in the back. And poison in cups, of course. Archery: noble and old-fashioned.

"Of course!" Shrewsbury said with a laugh. "Are we not near Sherwood Forest? If all the rest of the world gives up the bow and arrow, we are duty-bound to preserve it here—or Robin Hood's ghost will haunt us."

"I fear it will become just a game for children, or a sport for young men."

"Never!" said Shrewsbury stoutly.

They went across a stone bridge with an old chapel on it; Mary saw that the chapel was now used to store wool. By the banks of the river she could see the ducking stool for gossips. Two signs of the Protestant religion: the minding of everyone's business, and the use of holy buildings for secular gain.

The party wound its way up the wagon road that led beside the castle's tournament grounds and the ramparts. At the top of the hill they turned and crossed the castle's drawbridge over the moat, entering the forbidding area between two bastion towers. The mist curled around them.

Mary felt her heart sinking. This was the most fortresslike of the places where she had been kept. Perhaps it was the combination of its location deep within England, its moat and hilltop site, its high walls and inner and outer baileys, but this place seemed like the iron fist of a fully armoured knight. The idea that she was anything but a prisoner could not be sustained; only a prisoner would be lodged in such a strongbox.

"Why, what a . . . fair residence," said Mary, faintly.

Her apartments were on the northeast side, which looked down on the wide loop of the Don and out over the castle orchards and the archery field, across to the hunting park where the manor was. Huge oaks dotted the hunting park, their trunks looking like barrels from this distance. The leaves were all off, and so Mary could glimpse the red brick of the manor house through the limbs of the trees.

The number of rooms was generous, and she could not complain of being cramped. Her own privy chamber was large, with two fireplaces and ceilings that were high enough that they allowed ample headroom even for tall people. She tried to personalize her surroundings with her tapestries and embroideries, and with miniatures of her relatives: her mother, François, Darnley, baby James, Catherine de Médicis, the Countess of Lennox, and Elizabeth. She set them up on a little table of sandalwood that had been sent down from Scotland.

There was no miniature of Bothwell; the only one in existence had been painted during his honeymoon with Lady Jean, and she retained it. Mary assumed it was flung in the bottom of an old box, if not destroyed, and her heart ached for it. Yet, much as she would have loved to have it, she could picture him so perfectly in her mind that she consoled herself with the thought that in some ways a painted image would only damage and dull the one in her imagination.

She had a little portable altar, and that she set up in an alcove in the privy chamber, grateful that she could do so openly.

She also had a globe and maps that had been sent down from Edinburgh, and she spent many hours studying them, flying away in her imagination to the lands that were just painted curves and lines. Paris was only a name and a spot of brown, no different on the map from Lyons or Calais; the magic did not lie on paper. She and her attendants played games naming cities and rivers, as if to torture themselves. Rome and the Tiber and Athens and Jerusalem . . . all the places they could never go. Or rather, that Mary could not: all the rest were free to leave; their imprisonment was voluntary.

Voluntary suffering was altogether different from involuntary, thought Mary. In one sense it was nobler, in that it need not be borne; but in another it was gentler, because the power of ending it lay within a person's will, not God's. It was an exercise in will, not in humility.

681

No one showed any inclination to leave her. She wished those who had other callings would pursue them before it was too late. Dear Mary Seton—was she to remain unmarried only because she had chosen this exile?

It is different with me, Mary thought. I have had marriage, and a child, and if I now must live celibate, it cannot be altered. But Mary Seton—who will there be for her? She is not likely to want an English Protestant, and there are no eligible men in my party of exiles. I do not want to be responsible for her loneliness—or is that part of my punishment, too?

December 5, 1570. Anniversary of the death of François. My punishment. Why does it go on and on? Soon I will be twenty-eight; I will have been in captivity almost four years. I will have spent half as long in bondage and punishment as my entire time in Scotland. And there is no end in sight. The days stretch out, in a long road of sameness, as far ahead as human eye can see. Who can rescue me?

I try to endure the suffering—the bodily, with the strange visitations of pain in my joints; the mental, with the responsibility for what has happened in Scotland and to my followers; the spiritual, with the guilt for my personal sins. I know, in my inmost being, that suffering is to purify the soul. Mine was very blemished and faulty. Bur for how long, O Lord? "And his lord was wroth, and delivered him to the tormentors, till he should pay all that was due unto him." I have paid, and I am paying, and I will pay. But for how long? Or is my punishment to last until I stop crying "How long?", counting the days, and beating my wings against the cage?

On Mary's birthday, December eighth, Shrewsbury and Bess sent the Earl's new ward up to Mary's apartments with a pastry castle to help her celebrate. One side of the castle was open, to show the rooms the pastry cook had constructed in painstaking detail. There were miniature chests holding little name tags, and inside there were gold coins for Mary's attendants. Bess had even painted facsimiles of some of the embroidery panels they had done together, and hung them on the pastry walls. They had sent up Shrewsbury's musicians to join the few that Mary had in her company, and soon lively dance tunes filled the dark December afternoon.

Mary was actually in a great deal of discomfort; her joints were especially swollen and red that day, and she was troubled with a recurring headache. But she had dressed in her best gown, and had Seton arrange her hair—grown back to shoulder length—with a wig.

"Alas, my lady," Seton had said, "your hair is not as thick and luxurious as it was before."

Hanging in the air was the rest of the sentence: . . . *and I fear it never will be, that that is another thing left behind in Scotland. A permanent sacrifice.*

"Then put on my wig, the one with the reddest tints," said Mary. "How fortunate I am to have you to help me! They say Elizabeth's real hair is never seen, that she always wears wigs."

Mary saw her own hair disappear underneath the wig, just as the diamond from Norfolk she always wore around her neck lay hidden beneath her clothing. Norfolk . . . her one chance of escape. She had not received word from him in some time; the castle was tightly guarded.

Shrewsbury and Bess had joined them briefly, offering gifts: an ivory box, a magnifying glass with an ebony handle. Shrewsbury had then introduced the boy who had brought up the pastry, and had stood, ever since, silently staring.

"This is my new ward, Anthony Babington," said Shrewsbury. "He comes of an old neighbouring family, and his father was my good friend. I would like you to allow him to serve as your page, if you would," he said. "I can think of no greater consolation for the loss of a father than to enter the household of a queen."

"And what say you?" asked Mary, looking at the boy. He was a slender boy, with very fair skin and black hair. He did not smile at all.

"It would please me," he said quietly. Still no smile.

"How old are you?" she asked.

"Eleven," he answered.

Eleven. That strange, secretive age between childhood and manhood. His almond-shaped eyes were downcast.

"Eleven . . . do you know Latin? Have you studied history?"

"A little." Now his lips were curving up in a slight smile.

"Very well, then. You will serve half the day and study the other half. We will try not to make the lessons too hard."

Shrewsbury shook his head. "They cannot prove too hard for him. He is a brilliant lad—at least in book-studies. Try him."

෪

New Year's Day, 1571. A new year . . . a blank page upon which, supposedly, I have the power to write my fate. Fate? Is Fate a woman in London? I continue to write to Queen Elizabeth, but it is a futile exercise. She blames me for the Northern Uprising and for the Bull of Excommunication. She has stopped writing to me in her own hand and uses a secretary.

Cecil was here in the autumn. I met the famous man himself, my adversary. He came to lay out certain proposals to me that might result in my being restored to my throne in Scotland. But they were so harsh it was obvious he had only come so that he could say he had tried, and I was unreasonable. One of them was that Prince James should come and be a hostage in England. The others were that I must at long last confirm the Treaty of Edinburgh, renounce my present title of succession to the English throne, and make no marriage without the permission of Elizabeth and the Scottish Lords.

He was a gentle man. I enjoyed meeting him. He seemed so thoughtful, so open-minded. I would even have been misled into believing that he liked me, except that I had been informed that he had tried to beg off the task of seeing me and had fallen into an opportune illness, and that he had referred to me as offering "sugared entertainments to draw men toward her." I did not offer him anything with sugar in it when he came to Sheffield, but I tried to behave toward him as I would wish to be behaved toward. He was going on to Buxton after leaving here, a place nearby that has thermal baths of healing; it seems he is troubled with gout. I would like to go there sometime myself, if my painful joints do not subside. But of course I am not allowed to go without written permission from Queen Elizabeth.

Nothing more has been said about my "clearing myself" to her; evidently that ploy has been consigned to the dust heap, which proves that it was never anything but a ploy, an excuse not to see me.

Why will she not see me? I mean the true reason. There can be no true reason. Charity and statecraft both would require that she do so. She has met with my rebel lords, who were not even related to her by blood, nor were they anointed rulers. She has met with pirates and blackguards, with defrocked priests and renegades, with known murderers like Lennox—he who murdered the little children who were his hostages in the wars of 1547, before there was peace between England and Scotland. My own Lord Herries, when he was only seven, was the only one he spared. They say he has terrible dreams and cannot bear to be left alone at night. Yet Elizabeth meets with him! And made him Regent of Scotland, while she leaves me to languish here in captivity!

She hates me. She has always hated me. There can be no other explanation. Lennox cries daily for my extradition and execution.

✿

March 15, 1571. At last, after so many months of ciphers and messengers and negotiations, all the plans are set. Ridolfi has succeeded in obtaining the Duke of Norfolk's signature on a letter consenting to become Catholic. This was necessary before either the Duke of Alva or Philip could be persuaded to lend their efforts to freeing me. They were, understandably, reluctant to be part of any plan to put a Protestant in line for the English throne, or for me to be married to a Protestant. Now Ridolfi will set sail and make for Brussels to present all this in person to Alva, before proceeding on to Rome and Spain. Bishop Leslie's servant, Charles Bailley, will meet him on the Continent and serve to deliver letters back to England, to me and Leslie and Norfolk. Now, God go with him!

Mary was finishing a letter to Norfolk, written with the precious orange juice. ". . . On that condition I took the diamond you sent by my Lord Boyd, which I shall wear unseen about my neck till I give it again to the owner of it and me both. I am bold with you, because you put all to my choice. Let me hear some comfortable answer. . . ."

Suddenly she was aware that someone was standing in a corner of the room, barely breathing. But she could feel the human presence. She pulled a plain piece of paper over her secret one.

"Who's there?" she asked.

"Only me," said the small, distinct voice of Anthony Babington. He stepped out of the shadows and walked over to her, his handsome, smooth face holding no expression at all. In all the weeks he had been a member of the household, she had never seen him smile. Stare, often; smile, never.

"Anthony, I did not know you were here. Have you duties just now?" The little boy was an odd presence; in some ways he seemed older than eleven, because he was so intense. So far he had no friends or playmates.

"Yes, I was to gather the green cloths from the tables, take them out and shake them."

"Then you may do so."

Anthony did not turn to his task, but instead came over to her desk and stood looking down at the paper.

I wish he would go away, Mary thought, so I can finish this letter. Soon the other members of the household will be back in this chamber; since they are not allowed to leave the castle, they never stay away long.

He persisted in looking at the desk, then finally said, "You are writing a secret letter." He pointed at the little cup of orange juice and said, "The smell gives it away."

Now he will tell Shrewsbury, thought Mary. How can I persuade him not to?

"I know something better than orange juice," he said. "Something I could show you."

"Why?" she asked, startled. "I do not need to write secret letters. I was only—practising. In case I did."

"Then you must practise with my method." He looked at her from underneath his hair, which made a dark awning across his forehead.

"No, because if Shrewsbury saw me doing such a thing, he would suspect me of something wicked. All secrets are considered wicked, you know." She smiled at him, trying to make this moment only a game, so he would forget it later. He was now dangerous to her.

"Then we shall be wicked together," he said, his lips curving upward in a hint of a smile. "The way is this—use alum. Orange juice and lemon juice have this disadvantage, that once they have been exposed to the heat, and read, the paper bearing them must be destroyed. Now alum will also be invisible, and only become readable when the paper or fabric is dampened and held up to the heat, but it will fade again when it dries. So you need not worry about destroying it. It allows more things to serve as message-carriers."

She stared at this knowledgeable little boy, but somehow such knowledge seemed devilish. "How do you know this?"

"As the good Shrewsbury said, I have book-learning," he replied. "But I have not told you all the recipe yet. There is more."

"And what do you want in return?"

"I want a rosary blessed by the Pope," he answered instantly. "I have heard you say that you have more than one. I would greatly desire one for myself."

So he was a Catholic! "If you promise me that you will treasure it, for there is no means of any others coming into this country," she said. Or he was posing as a Catholic, to gain her confidence. Or he was a heretic, who wanted to desecrate a holy object.

Or he dabbled in witchcraft, and wanted it for evil purposes. . . .

"You need have no fears," he said, as if reading her mind. He waited, and she realized he wanted the rosary immediately.

She made her way over to the coffer where she kept some of her personal goods and found a carved ivory rosary that the Holy Father had blessed. Drawing it out, she brought it over to him and placed it in his outstretched hand.

He studied it carefully, as if it were a rare jewel. Then he closed his fingers over it. "Very well, here's the rest of the recipe," he said quickly. "Dissolve the alum in a little clear water twenty-four hours before you wish to use it. You may write upon white paper, white linen, or white taffeta. The writing will be invisible until you wet the letter in a basin of water and hold it up to heat. Then the writing will appear white, and stay readable until the paper dries. You may make a little cut or nick to indicate which material or paper has such writing. This way you can reread the letter if necessary."

"Have you tried this?"

"Many times," he said.

"Where can I obtain alum? The request for lemons is easier to explain."

"I can bring some. They let *me* out of the castle, as I am a native, and only a child." He grinned, and looked very impish.

Charles Bailley stepped off the ship from Flanders and onto the dock at Dover. The spring winds were blowing his clothes, and he had to clutch hard at his chest, to secure the pouch he was carrying under his shirt. The docks were swarming with people, and high above he could see the castle and tiny people looking down at the ships coming into the port.

He hurried toward the staging area where he could set out on the road to London, when suddenly he felt arms grabbing him and pulling him off the path.

"That's the one!" someone said.

"Search him!" Hands were thrust into his shirt, and the pouch wrested open. A fistful of letters was extracted.

"No!" He tried to snatch them back. "Who are you? By what right—?"

"Orders of Walsingham," one of them said. "Walsingham. You've heard of him? Cecil? Have you heard of *him*?"

"By what right—?"

"The Queen of England! Have you heard of *her*?"

VI

"So now we have them?" asked Elizabeth. "All of them?"

Francis Walsingham indicated the papers on the table that ran the length of his chamber. They were neatly arranged, and each bore a tag underneath. "Start *here*, Your Majesty," he said, gently steering her to the left. "The earliest are here."

The first tag was dated October 1568.

"You see that she was already writing to the Spanish ambassador such provocative things as 'Tell your master if he will help me I shall be Queen of England in three months and mass shall be said all over the country,' " said Walsingham. "That was during the hearings!"

Elizabeth picked up the letter and read it. "Yes, I see." Her voice was grim. "My dear cousin. And she sent me needlework as a New Year's gift shortly thereafter. Of course I, above all people, realize that prisoners will say and promise many things to anyone."

Walsingham shot a look at her. Wasted sympathy! "Next, the marriage contract with Norfolk." He indicated a paper labeled August 1569.

"Hmm." Elizabeth studied it. "So this is what a marriage contract looks like! Pray God I never have to sign one! Ah, poor dear Charles IX. I was forced to reject his proposal. Now they say he has already wed. So short a time—how can one believe the protestations of love? But here, Norfolk and Mary—!" She dropped the thing as if it were a snake. "My dear cousins both."

"Now, Madam. Here are the letters from November of 1569, the communications with Northumberland and Westmoreland. And now, our coup: these letters of Bailley's."

"And what, precisely, is the business with Bailley?" Elizabeth never forgot a name, but his connection with the Queen of Scots was most important.

"He was recruited to carry messages from the Continent back to Mary and Norfolk. Ridolfi—you remember that banker, Ridolfi?—was their agent in the plot; he was to seek aid from Philip for the purpose of invading England, deposing you, and freeing Mary. Now these letters, oh"—his voice rose an octave in excitement—"give us the link we need! Bailley is a servant of Leslie's, who is Mary's principal adviser. But some letters are in cipher, and are addressed to '30' and '40.' I assume they are noblemen here. Never fear, we will find out. I have taken the liberty of arresting Leslie. I trust you do not object."

Elizabeth felt herself on the verge of trembling. The mysterious lords "30" and "40" . . . who could they be? Who were the traitors?

Am I completely surrounded by traitors? Whom can I be sure of? she wondered.

Bailley gritted his teeth as they led him down the steep, dank spiral stair into the dungeon of the White Tower, the oldest part of the Tower of London. The upper reaches of the White Tower had a banqueting hall and a fair stone chapel where kings and queens had lain in state; but in the bowels of the earth there was a room that had never seen daylight or a happy human moment. The odour of wetness and vermin was overwhelming as he stepped over the threshold. The flickering torches in wall sockets showed every wall to be lined with torture instruments: Skeffington's Gyves, casicaws, manacles, fetters, and bilboes. In the middle of the room stood an enormous rack.

"No!" cried Bailley. "No!" He tried to twist away. "I have committed no crime, you have no right—!"

"Still harping on your rights?" said the warder. "It is not your rights that are in question here, but your knowledge. Pray share that knowledge with us, and you'll never know the rack."

Bailley stared at the legendary machine in fascinated horror. It was a rectangular frame of wood about six feet long, resting on legs some three feet high. The legs were secured by being sunk into holes in the floor. At the head and foot of the frame were two rollers, that could be wound by turning handles. Dangling from the ends of the rollers were four ropes, one for each limb of the torture victim.

"No!" Bailley was shoved onto the ground and held on his back in the middle of the frame while two of the guards tied his ankles and wrists to the machine. Then they stood back and began winding the winches, lifting Bailley up and stretching him until, like a sheet, he was suspended over the frame. His joints gave a few sighs and pops as his weight settled.

"This is a healthy stretching," said one of the men. "It can almost feel good. Now you can truthfully say you have been on the rack. But to avoid any discomfort, it would be well to tell us . . . everything. But we will wait for our superior to explain. Ah . . . here is our esteemed rackmaster."

A well-dressed man appeared at the entrance to the chamber and stepped smartly over to the rack. The perfume of his gloves struck Bailley as an obscene part of the torture.

"My friend, I see you have made the acquaintance of a device of which we are all justly proud here in the Tower," he said silkily. "The finest oak frame, the length of it, the *fixedness* of it—there is none like it in the land. Those portable devices"—he made a gesture of dismissal—"if one has no space, of course, can serve, after a fashion. Yet Her Majesty has graciously provided such quarters as required to give the rack its full potential."

Bailley kept staring at this man. How did one become a rackmaster? Was it a talent that started in boyhood, being particularly adept at dismembering live frogs, at drowning kittens and docking puppies' tails?

"Let me explain how it works," the rackmaster was saying. "We will tighten the winches, and at each half-turn you will be lengthened. Why, we can make you a foot longer than God did!" He laughed loudly, slapping his thigh. "But the joints protest. They do not want to be stretched, stubborn things! They rip and tear out of their sockets—it is always a surprise to learn which can be more stubborn, the mind at withholding information, or the sinews in clinging to their bones. That is what makes this work anything but routine." He paused. "This is your last chance. Tell us everything: the extent of the conspiracy, everything the Spanish and the Pope said, the ciphers and codes."

"No."

The rackmaster nodded and four guards—one at each corner—began winding the winches. Bailley's body jerked upward and quivered as he was held perfectly horizontal and the roller was secured at that tautness by ratchets and iron stops. Then the winches were turned another half-turn, and his shoulders groaned. There was a jolt as one became dislocated. His body sagged downward, but the slack was quickly taken up by another turn of the winch.

He screamed. His shoulder was on fire, and pain was searing through his chest.

"Now, then. The information."

Bailley was choking and babbling. Suddenly his hip ligaments tore. He fainted.

"Throw water on him," said the rackmaster with disgust. "This one is hardly worth torturing, he's so soft!"

John Leslie, the Bishop of Ross, was shoved into the room. He stared at the stretched form of Bailley lying on the rack.

"We'll have cleared it soon enough," said the rackmaster. "You will not have to wait long!" He nodded to the guards, and they began unfastening the ropes. Bailley dropped to the ground with a thud. They dragged him off; Leslie noticed the abnormal angles of his ankles. The body bumped and jounced as two of the guards hauled him across the floor and out of the room.

"I'll talk, I'll talk! No, don't touch me!" wept Leslie. "What do you want to know? The letters? I'll tell you! The Queen of Scots? She's wicked, she doesn't deserve the noble Duke of Norfolk for a husband. She poisoned the French King François, she murdered Darnley, and as for Bothwell—she tried to murder him too! Yes, she led him out to the field at Carberry Hill so he could be killed!" Leslie fell cowering on the ground in a heap, his hands up to ward off imaginary blows.

"See what a stouthearted servant the Queen of Scots has," sneered the rackmaster. "May she always be served by such." He looked at the shuddering Leslie and shook his head. "He is not worthy of our noble instrument!"

❧

"More information?" asked Elizabeth wearily, as Walsingham hurried in to her privy chamber, papers clutched under his arm. "I am not sure I wish to know any more. But no, ignorance is always worse than pain. Pray proceed!" Her head was aching; she had been feeling ill for the past three days. She was sure it was bad carp that she had eaten on the previous Friday.

"You will rejoice at this news, Your Majesty," said Walsingham. "Dumbarton Castle has fallen! A surprise attack on it has taken the stronghold for the Lords! Only Lord Fleming escaped, by scrambling down the rock and making his getaway. But all the rest are prisoners . . . with the exception of Archbishop Hamilton. They hanged him in his priestly robes."

"Who dared?" asked Elizabeth. "Was there no trial?"

"It was the Earl of Lennox who ordered the execution. He now claims that the Archbishop murdered his son Darnley."

"When he came to the hearings, he swore it was Bothwell. He cannot have it both ways! Oh, what is the truth up there? *Is* there any regard for truth?" She was close to tears.

"Your Majesty," said Walsingham, "I thought you would be pleased."

"Pleased? With more murders and lies up there? You fool!" She threw her fan at him. She hated the fan anyway; it was Spanish.

Walsingham ducked. "We work very hard for you," he said self-righteously. "Is it our fault that the world is a foul and disloyal place? Leslie has betrayed his Queen, and told us the extent of the plots. Now we have stumbled on another link: Norfolk has been sending money to the Queen's party in Scotland. It is French money, crowns and francs, direct from her dower allowance."

"Well, what of it?" Elizabeth snapped. "How do you expect her to spend her money? Aiding the Earl of Lennox?" She poured some water from a pitcher into a shallow bowl and dipped her handkerchief into it, then applied it to her temples.

"I care not how she spends her money, but these servants of Norfolk who were carrying the gold have betrayed him as well!"

Elizabeth sank down into her chair. "Tell me, pray, of something besides betrayal. Is there no loyalty anywhere?" She felt even sicker.

"Only to you," he said. "Cecil and I, Robert Dudley, Hatton, Sussex— we are all loyal! And we have discovered the few who are not. Are you ready? The '40' in the codes was the Queen of Scots herself, and '30' was the Spanish ambassador. And if you doubt this, the correspondence re- covered from Dumbarton reveals the extent of Mary's dealings with Alva, the Pope, and Spain."

"What of Norfolk?" she asked faintly.

"He had ordered his servants to destroy all his secret letters from Mary, but they hid them instead, and brought us to them. They were hidden under floor mats, and the ciphers were in the roof tiles. The Duke," he pronounced slowly, "is guilty of treason."

"Is there to be a trial here?" she asked. "Or am I expected to act like the Scots and proceed without one?"

"In England there is always a trial," Walsingham said proudly.

"Even if the verdict is known in advance," said Elizabeth. "I remember reading an account of the trial of an abbot: 'he was taken away to be tried and executed.' Let us not follow that example. Let us truly examine the evidence before pronouncing."

Walsingham looked at her, puzzled. "So it can be dragged out as long as possible?"

❧

The wet and sleeting May was unseasonable even for Scotland. There had been ice and snow even in April, and flowers did not appear until May, when they were promptly frozen, some of them still in the bud. Each side took it as an evil omen for the other: the King's Men, as the Regent's party was now called, said that as long as the land was divided, the skies would weep; the Queen's Men said that the very Heaven shielded its face from the sight of traitors.

With the fall of Dumbarton Castle, the King's Men could now turn their full attention to the stronghold of Edinburgh Castle, still held by Maitland and Kirkcaldy of Grange. The foremost fortress commanded the capital and held the regalia, the principal store of ordnance, and the register house of the records of the kingdom. Day after day the Queen's Men fired cannon balls down on the town, and when the Lords attempted to hold a Parliament in the Canongate, they had to crawl about on their hands and knees to avoid the cannon fire. Their enemies dismissed the gathering—which tried to pass forfeits against men still loyal to Mary—as the "Creeping Parliament," from the men's posture.

In control of Edinburgh, Mary's supporters held their own Parliament the following month, in the Tolbooth, the traditional meeting place. The regalia from the castle was brought down to give weight to the proceedings, but the Parliament was less well attended than the "Creeping" one just held. The Hamiltons, Huntly, and Lord Herries were there, but in the summer—a chilly one like the spring—Cassillis, Eglinton, and the hitherto loyal Boyd went over to the Lords.

In August, Regent Lennox called a Parliament at Stirling.

The Great Hall was readied for the occasion. Although there was little money in the treasury, Lennox ordered all that could be done for show and a few pence. The floors were scrubbed, the fireplaces cleaned, the benches oiled. Flowers, gathered from the fields, were strung in ropes and festooned over the walls and draped around the doorways. An imitation set of regalia was made, and new robes were hastily sewn up for the five-year-old King James.

On the day that he was vested in his ermine and velvet, the boy looked at his grandfather and said solemnly, "I will open the proceedings." His voice was low and he spoke in a dull monotone.

Lennox nodded. He stole a scrutinizing look as the boy stood admiring the mock crown. The child had a head too big for his body and sad, baggy eyes. He did not resemble either his gold-and-ivory father or his sparkling, elegant mother. Truth to tell, he did not even resemble the swarthy little Riccio. Where had he come from? He was like a changeling. But no matter; the title of King would suffice to cover all his shortcomings.

Trumpets sounded as the crown, sceptre, and sword were borne into the hall on three separate velvet pillows, followed by the sombre, measured steps of little James, then of his grandfather. James mounted his throne and Lennox took his place below him. The Lords and burgesses seated themselves, after a blessing was read by the ailing Knox in a shaky voice.

Suddenly James, looking upward to a small opening in the ceiling, said loudly, "This Parliament has got a hole in it!"

The assembly, including Knox, were struck with fear. The child was prophesying!

" 'Out of the mouths of babes and sucklings hast thou ordained strength,' " whispered Knox.

Kirkcaldy and his men were approaching the rocky cliffs of Stirling. They rode silently, their guns and swords at the ready. So these Lords meant to have a Parliament using imitation regalia? Did they think themselves safe here? Did they vainly imagine that the only place where they would have to assume undignified postures was within the scope of cannon fire from Edinburgh Castle? How foolish! Their enemies had arms, legs, and horses, and were not confined to Edinburgh.

They climbed the path winding up to the castle walls, and a Queen's sympathizer let them in the postern gate, as previously arranged. The men fanned out, keeping a careful watch. The upper courtyard was deserted; the Parliament was still sitting, evidently.

The sound of the horses' hooves penetrated into the Great Hall. The men inside rose from their seats. They flung open the doors and ventured out, nervously looking this way and that.

"Get them!" called Kirkcaldy, with a whoop. "Avenge the Hamiltons!" He swooped down on one terrified laird and was chasing him when he caught sight of Eglinton emerging from the hall. "Old friend!" he yelled. "Rejoin us!" He grabbed the man and dangled him from the side of his horse. Eglinton writhed and tried to twist free.

Kirkcaldy's men were chasing the Parliamentarians like a farmer chasing chickens across a barnyard. Then from the building emerged both Lennox and the little King.

"Stop!" cried Lennox. "I command you to surrender!"

A Captain Calder, one of Kirkcaldy's regular soldiers, turned in the saddle and fired at Lennox. The Regent fell, gasping. Blood flew and sprayed the King.

Kirkcaldy dropped Eglinton and cried, "Retreat! Retreat!" and galloped toward the escape gate. His men followed, leaving bodies strewn on the ground and Lennox gasping, tearing at his bloodied doublet.

Lennox died in a few hours. Before allowing himself to be taken inside, he had inquired about the King. "Is he safe?" he had whispered. When Knox had nodded, then Lennox said softly, "If the babe be well, all is well."

❧

John Erskine, the Earl of Mar, was appointed new Regent; once again, no one suggested restoring Mary to the throne. The King's Men continued to rule the country in the name of James, and to batter away at Edinburgh Castle, where Maitland and Kirkcaldy were still ensconced. While deploring the violence and instability, the English government continued negotiations to have the Earl of Northumberland delivered to them for justice's sake. The Earl's wife, writing from the Netherlands, offered a bribe for his safety, but the English outbid her for two thousand pounds, and the Earl was delivered up from Lochleven and handed over to the English.

All the evidence about the Ridolfi Plot and Norfolk's involvement was complete by late autumn of 1571. The Spanish ambassador, Don Gerau de Spes, the truculent crusader for Catholic insurrection, was expelled from England. The fussing Spaniard was escorted to Dover and forced to embark.

Norfolk's trial opened in January 1572. He admitted knowledge of the conspiracy but denied involvement in it, and claimed that he had never attempted to harness his considerable resources for any domestic uprising. But he was unable to produce any proof of his innocence that could counterbalance the proofs of his plotting—the letters, the codes, the gold, the breaking of his solemn signed oath to have no dealings with Mary. He was found guilty of high treason and condemned to a traitor's death.

In such a case, a royal warrant was also required before the execution could be carried out. Elizabeth must put her signature and seal on the order.

At length she signed an order that the Duke would be executed on Tower Hill on Monday, February tenth, in company with two other traitors, Berney and Mather.

Elizabeth was pacing in her chamber. It was late Sunday night, February ninth. Outside the wind was howling, louder than the crackling of the fire in her chamber. She had removed all her rings and was massaging her fingers. Her wig was off, and she would nervously run her hands through her hair every few minutes. Her hair was long and still thick and healthy, but she had a full wardrobe of wigs in elaborate styles. She never, however, wore hair of any colour but red.

Tomorrow . . . tomorrow the Duke would die. And she must wait to hear of how his head had fallen, just as her father had waited . . . no, it was too dreadful.

No beheadings until now. No treason in high ranks until now. *My cousin's blood. And they will say, She is her father's daughter after all. Blood will out. Next it will be . . . whom?*

Elizabeth stood looking out the window. She was at Richmond, and she could see the river flowing past, dimly lighted by the half moon. The night was passing, Norfolk's last upon earth. His last moonlight, his last bedtime . . . The river was flowing past the Tower, too, and he could see and hear it as well. This same water would be passing the Duke in an hour or so.

Must it be so? Must he die? Once his head was off, there was no putting it back on.

She could not help but smile at the idea. If only it were possible to reattach a head, to say, "Oh, we change our minds, pray live after all." But the only time to do that was before the deed.

She was trembling.

As if I were the one being executed. And well I know what it is to wait in the Tower.

Suddenly she called for a page, and directed him to bring Cecil to her immediately.

Cecil, still suffering the aftereffects of his latest debilitating attack of gout, made his way painfully into Elizabeth's privy chamber. He was forced to lean on a stick, but his greatest concern and worry was what he would face with his Queen.

He saw her standing in the middle of the room, her hands clasped demurely. Without her wig and makeup she looked very young, as she had when first she had come to the throne. "Madam," he said, bowing as low as he could.

"Thank you for coming at midnight, dear Cecil. I trust your wife was not too inconvenienced."

"She is accustomed to it, Madam."

Elizabeth laughed. "One of the disadvantages of your office. I trust becoming Lady Burghley will make up for it." She whirled around, her mood changing in a second. "Oh, Cecil, I mislike this execution!"

He had feared that was it. "It is most unfortunate," he agreed.

"He is my cousin! His grandfather and my grandmother were brother and sister!"

"Yes, it is most unfortunate," Cecil repeated. What did she expect him to say?

"Remember the Bible—how Cain was punished for spilling the blood of Abel. 'The voice of thy brother's blood crieth unto me from the ground. And now art thou cursed from the earth, which hath opened her mouth to receive thy brother's blood from thy hand.' What if God punishes me? I can bear it of myself—but I am more than myself, and I fear he will punish the realm through me. And I—I, who have taken England for my husband and child as well—will not bring misfortune on my land."

Cecil sighed. "Cain slew Abel through anger and malice. This is an entirely different situation. Twenty-six peers of the realm—including myself—have examined the evidence and concluded that he is a traitor and dangerous to the realm. Far from bringing disaster on the land if you execute him, danger will result if you do not."

Elizabeth was scratching her arms, leaving long thin white marks on them. "But he is of my own blood!"

"It is unfortunate," Cecil could only repeat. He paused.

"Justice must be done," Elizabeth finally said. "He has been found guilty."

"Yes, Your Majesty."

"To balk justice is injustice."

"Yes, Your Majesty."

"Yet mercy is a higher virtue than justice."

"In God, yes."

"Am I not God's anointed on earth? Should I not look heavenward for a model of my behaviour, rather than to the peers of the realm?" she asked.

"Madam, this looking heavenward can be a highway to tyranny. When a ruler begins to disregard the laws of his land in favour of heavenly guidance, he often tramples the most basic justice underfoot. Stick with the paths of the law, and you cannot be led astray into tyranny."

"You are right," she said, sitting down abruptly in a chair. "And I am in danger from all these plots! My cousin did not hesitate to traffick with my sworn enemies! He regarded my life lightly, so it seems. His head wished to feel the weight of a crown. Well, it shall feel the edge of a sword instead!" She slapped the edge of her hand down on the chair arm.

"Yes, Your Majesty." Cecil bowed. Relief flooded him.

"But not tomorrow," she said. "Stay the execution. I promise it is merely postponed, not cancelled."

The crowds were milling around the newly erected scaffold on Tower Hill, the mound just outside the walls of the Tower where public executions were held. There had been no executions in London in Elizabeth's reign, and the old scaffold had rotted from disuse. The people had started coming at dawn, staking out a good position to see the killings. It promised to be a good show, as the blue-black clouds had parted and revealed a pallid sky behind them. There would be no rain or snow, the plague of a winter execution.

On the new scaffold was the venerable block from the old one, hallowed by the chops that had severed the heads of Thomas More, Cromwell, Anne Boleyn's lovers, and Henry Howard himself, the Duke's own father. It had two depressions in it, for the shoulders on one side and the chin on the other, with a strait in between where the neck could lie flat and exposed to the axe.

A thick mat of fresh straw was spread all over the platform, and cloths to cover the headless bodies were at the ready. Separate cloths were provided to catch the heads as they fell forward. The cloths matched so that when the parts were gathered up for burial, the correct head would accompany the body . . . that is, if the heads were not required to be displayed on London Bridge.

The actual sentence was the one of hanging first, then disembowelling, drawing and quartering, followed by beheading. But doubtless the Duke would only be beheaded, while the other two would endure the entire sentence.

The crowd cheered when Kenelm Berney, a young man who had plotted to kill Cecil, was brought out. He made the usual farewells and prayers, and was strung up and hanged until he was dead—thus being mercifully spared suffering when the rest of the sentence was carried out to the letter.

Within fifteen minutes his remains had been removed, the straw changed, and his partner, Edmund Mather, led out. He, too, suffered a quick death.

Now the crowd hushed, awaiting the Duke. This was what they had come for; the two ordinary traitors were just a prelude, an appetizer. The highest lord in the land was to have his head cut off! Why, it had been so long since such a sight—once common enough—had been available. Some children had never even seen it, and had to make do with their elders' reminiscences: "The buzzards swooped down on Sir Francis Weston"; "More made a joke about his beard, begging the headsman not to cut it, for it had done no treason"; "Henry Howard had an unusual amount of blood in him; it kept flowing for ten minutes, and ruined the headsman's shoes." Now they would see it for themselves, and be able to tell their own children.

Someone was coming forward, wearing the Queen's livery. He was going to read off the sentence, and then the Duke would be brought out, wearing gorgeous apparel. The people got even more excited.

"It is the wish of Her Majesty the Queen that the execution of the Duke of Norfolk not take place today," the messenger announced.

The crowd groaned. Some of them cursed.

The execution was moved to the last day of February, at six o'clock in the morning. At four o'clock, Elizabeth recalled the warrant.

&

Elizabeth lay in her bed, so ill she thought she was dreaming when the faces of Robert Dudley and Cecil appeared before her eyes. She had lain thus for several days, and the realm was paralyzed with fright. What if she died? What would happen to them? The Duke of Norfolk yet lived, as did the Queen of Scots. Would Spanish troops arrive to put Mary on the throne? There was no successor to the throne named. Without Elizabeth they were lost. All that stood between them and chaos was the life of an unmarried thirty-eight-year-old woman.

"You must rally," whispered Dudley. "I myself will feed you, like a father with his babe."

He and Cecil looked at each other. If she lived—provisions would have to be made. She could evade them no longer.

Elizabeth maintained that her life had never been in danger, that she had only suffered from tainted fish that she had eaten. True, she had had a fever and violent stomach pains and vomiting, but that was only normal in such cases. Her body was purging itself from the poison of the fish.

The Council was adamant: she must call a Parliament to deal with the grave issues of the day. She could not continue to take all upon her own shoulders—her fragile shoulders.

With grumbling acquiescence, she sent out writs for a new Parliament in late March.

&

In April, while the new members of Parliament were making ready to come to London, Elizabeth made a treaty with the French. Her erstwhile suitor Charles IX had now married elsewhere, but Elizabeth pretended to be interested in the next son, Henri, who was eighteen years younger than she.

The negotiations for this treaty had been going on for some months, the French always insisting that Mary be included in any provisions. But on the day that the English envoy was taking leave of the French King, letters arrived from the French ambassador in London confirming Mary's part in the Ridolfi Plot.

Charles, the king, exploded with anger and disgust. "Ah, the poor fool will never cease until she loses her head. I meant to help, but if she will not be helped, I can do nothing more." He waved his jewelled fingers. His spaniels trotted forward eagerly, expecting a sweet.

"Yes, my love," said Catherine de Médicis. "It is most sad."

Charles took a long sip of his sugar water from a stemmed Venetian goblet. He sighed. "Dear Mr. Ambassador, this treaty will doubtless be of great benefit to both our countries. Let us leave the Queen of Scots out of it entirely, and reword its provisions to be a defensive treaty between our two realms. If either of us is attacked—by *anyone*—we will come to one another's aid." He reached down and nuzzled the top of a dog's head. The animal flung himself on his back and wiggled on the rug. Another dog whined.

"Do you permit the Queen of Scots to receive gifts?" he asked the ambassador. "I could send her some puppies. Perhaps that would console her."

VII

ary opened the basket eagerly. She could hear the sounds of the puppies inside, and could feel the warmth from their little bodies. She peered in.

Curled up in the warm lined basket were three black-and-tan puppies, toy spaniels. Just seeing them took her back to France, where the royal family had had so many of this type. Her brother-in-law, King Charles, had sent them.

Carefully she lifted them out one by one and handed them to Mary Seton, Lady Livingston, and Anthony Babington. "Come see!" she called to Madame Rallay; the old woman put aside her sewing and shuffled over. She could hardly stand straight now.

"Do you remember?" Mary asked softly. "These must be the grandchildren of the dogs that roamed our chambers at Chambord and Blois."

Madame Rallay, who was almost seventy now, smiled. "Oh, indeed. I think I see a bit of Sleepy in them." Sleepy had been a lethargic but prolific bitch. "It was kind of Charles to send them. Now the birds will have company."

"My menagerie grows." Mary took the letter from the French ambassador that had accompanied the puppies. She waited until she was at her desk to open it. Letters were a source of power to her now—her only power. Sitting at her desk, scribbling letter after letter to anyone she could think of—the Pope, Philip, Charles, Catherine de Médicis, the ambassadors, the Scottish Lords, Elizabeth, Cecil, Knollys—she felt less helpless and alone. The words, flowing off her pen, felt mighty. She did not want to imagine that once they left her hands they could be disregarded or ignored.

The fine paper was a pleasure to open—so much better than the mean stuff she was forced to use. The French always had such beauty around themselves. And the seal—such a good quality of wax, brittle and shiny. She unfolded the page with pleasure.

Her smile faded as she read the ambassador's words. She reread them slowly.

"The French have abandoned me," she finally whispered, more to herself than to anyone else.

"What is it?" asked Willie Douglas.

Wordlessly, she handed the letter to him.

"So the French have made a treaty with the English, in which you and your rights are not even mentioned," he finally said.

"I have been discarded. My former country deems me and my troubles as something they wish to slough off," she said in wonder.

The French. Her adopted country, the country of her mother, of her favourite language, her sensibilities, her dress, her memories. Her mother's kinsmen. All gone. No help from there.

She felt as though she had been kicked. France, her treasured past and the place she had stated she wished to be buried, did not want her.

What if I had gone there instead of England? For four years I have tormented myself with making the wrong decision, imagining that a safe haven awaited me there, she thought. But no—it is no safer than England.

She began to weep stormily, putting her head down on her arms. Anthony and Madame Rallay tried to comfort her, but the truth allowed her no comfort. They left her in privacy.

In the outer chamber, Willie shook his head and murmured to Mary Seton, "This is a heavy blow. She had always counted on France as a last resort. This, on top of the betrayal and defamation of Bishop Leslie, may break her spirit."

When Mary's eyes cleared, she reread the letter. Only then did she note where the treaty had been signed: at the Château of Blois.

She laughed bitterly. She had always loved the octagonal staircase there; she had dreamed of it often since leaving. Someday I will stand on it again, she had vowed.

Shrewsbury returned from his duty of presiding over Norfolk's trial and announced that owing to Elizabeth's extreme displeasure with her cousin the Queen of Scots, she was to reduce her suite of attendants immediately. She was to choose the ones to remain, and the rest must depart from

Sheffield. Sorrowfully, Mary drew up the list. She could not be without Mary Seton, or Willie, or her priest, or Madame Rallay, or Bastian Pages and his wife, Margaret Carwood. Those serving her had been Scots, French, and local English people. The orders were that she should retain only sixteen of them.

Shrewsbury had returned in a weakened condition. Mary guessed that he had been chided for allowing plots to flourish under his roof and not providing strict enough guard over her. Bess now shot her venomous looks, blaming her for her husband's condition. The sewing ceased.

But Mary's secret channel of correspondence had not been detected, and she was able to continue writing letters. When she had first heard of Norfolk's sentence, she had taken to her bed in grief and guilt. But when his execution was halted by royal reprieve twice, she began to wonder how Elizabeth thought. Why did she hesitate?

After Elizabeth's illness, another warrant was issued for Norfolk's execution, and again it was halted. Shrewsbury wordlessly gave Mary a copy of Elizabeth's command.

> Methinks that I am more beholden to the hinder part of my head than will dare trust the forward side of the same, and therefore send the lieutenant the order to defer this execution till they hear further. The causes that move me to this are not now to be expressed, lest an irrevocable deed be in the meanwhile committed. Your most loving sovereign,
>
> Elizabeth R.

It was endorsed by Cecil "11 April 1572, the Q. Majesty, with her own hand, for staying of the execution of the D.N. Received at 2 in the morning."

Did this mean that Elizabeth was incapable of proceeding with an execution? Mary suddenly realized this might be the case. And it would not be surprising.

She was safe. Norfolk was safe. Nothing could touch them after all. Elizabeth was an impotent victor.

Mary's spirits rose as spring came to Sheffield. Her rheumatism improved with the warmer weather, and it was impossible not to respond to the greening of the earth, the flowers that sprang up around all the paths. There was talk of transferring to Sheffield Manor so that the Castle could be cleaned. The manor, situated in the hunting park, was a welcome summer abode. And security was looser there; it was more difficult to guard.

Anthony had proved adept at smuggling out letters; people did not suspect a boy, and one whose family had long been friends with the Shrewsburys. He amused himself devising new codes, and experimenting with hollowed-out corks and waterproof packets to be inserted in bottles. One of his triumphs was suggesting that black paper could be used to hide messages in a dark privy house; it was not a place where people were apt to linger or look closely.

Mary gathered her skirts and took her private book—hidden in a sewing basket—outside at Sheffield Manor to what she called the Bower. It was a sitting area with lilacs surrounding it, and a turf bench. She arranged her skirts and looked up at the tightly budded branches; the lilacs would not be out for another fortnight. But when they bloomed, what a fragrance!

At her feet the three puppies tumbled and played, happy to be outside. She had named them Soulagement, Douleur, and Souci: comfort, sorrow, and care. They were lively animals, with Douleur being the least sorrowful.

"I named you Douleur because you were nearly all black," said Mary, stroking his ears. "But you have a happy nature." The puppy wagged his tail and began chewing on her sleeve.

"Pray do not chew," she said. "My clothes are not easily replaced."

She took out her pen, set the inkwell on a rock where she thought the puppies could not reach it, opened the leaves of her book, and began writing.

May 8, the year of grace 1572. Month of Our Lady. All around me I see the tightly bound leaves ready to unfurl. They have been as tightly bound as I, and have endured the winter, the ice and dark. But I am still bound, and see no summer for me.

It is five years now since my marriage to Bothwell, almost five years since we parted. I have not received any word from him in a great long while. I believe he is still being held in Malmö; I have written to his mother, old Lady Bothwell, in hopes she has had some word that I have not. I pray for him daily, nay, many times daily, and dream of him often. The dreams are of a faded image now, no longer the white-hot heat that used to come to me in the night. But still alive, still very much alive, no ghost. I try sending my thoughts to him, believing that they somehow pass over the seas and through the stone walls. I know he understands about my attempts to make an honourable escape by means of a promise of marriage.

I reach out to my throat and touch the diamond that Norfolk gave me; I believed it was my passport to freedom. Now it seems nothing more than a reminder of despair. Pray God Elizabeth continues to spare him. Evidently she shrinks before spilling blood. That is such a novelty to me—has my experience in Scotland tainted me that much? There no blood was sacred, and everyone had a dagger ready to plunge into the man seated next to him at dinner. Even the men of God bay for blood there. Blood is all they understand.

Without a doubt, I am safer here. They do not assassinate in this land. The only suspected murder is that of Amy Robsart, and that was to clear the way for a marriage. Of course I guard routinely, as all persons do, against poison. But it is more a precaution than anything else. I always plunge the unicorn horn, a powerful antidote against poison, into my food and drink before tasting them.

I consider myself in mourning, and dress accordingly. I wear only black, relieved by white veils and lace. I am in mourning for my lost throne, my lost husband, my lost freedom. They try to have me dress in colours again, but I will not. Let them see me and be reminded of what they have done to me. Let them face themselves.

I spend an hour a day in prayer, and have prayers in my household twice a day. Not everyone serving me is Catholic, and the prayers must be acceptable to the Protestants as well; I try to select ones that will speak to us all.

As for my own private prayer—what a strange journey that has been! I try to keep my appointment with my Lord, so that He cannot reproach me with "Could ye not watch with Me one hour?" But as the months have passed, I found that it is a land of valleys and rifts. There have been four stages through which I have passed. The first was when, my heart so heavy, my mind stunned, my body exhausted, I would keep a formal appointment. Sitting before the crucifix, I would recite prayers, words. The rosary. The Pater Noster. Devotions from my book of hours. God was a distant, fearful personage I would limit to certain areas of my life. I kept my hand on the door and would only open it a little way.

Each stage has had its crisis, and the crisis here was that after many months this became boring. The appointment with God was so routine and dull that I began to dread it. Gradually I dared to push the door open wider, to become more honest with Him, to tell Him my feelings, even my anger and hatred toward Him. I shared my heart, and my prayers became more simple. Sometimes I was even silent, and just felt His faint presence. For an instant I would actually enter the room.

Then sinful thoughts, distractions would flash through my mind, and I would have to use words again to bring me back to the Presence. And the Presence, increasingly sweet, was something I desired.

But along with the sweetness was purity, and in the presence of that purity I began to feel stained. I longed for the love of God—it had become increasingly necessary, increasingly sustaining—but the more I longed for it, the less I felt I deserved it. I became mired in a recital of my own sins and guilts. I remembered not only the actual deeds I had done, but all the things left undone or half done: the things I had failed to value, the people I had failed to comfort or help, the opportunities passed by, the waste I had strewn about me, the gifts I had trampled underfoot.

Every good thought or intention I had ever had and failed to act on came back to haunt me. The letter I meant to write to a soldier's widow, and forgot until too late; the flowers I had meant to have cut and sent to the chamber where the cook lay ill; the time I had promised to pray for someone and had not. Even the blue skies I had failed to pause for a moment and appreciate.

I was human, but I believed that God expected more than that of me. I compounded my sin by assuming that God wished me to be perfect, and that I had failed. During that time, I had to catalogue all my shortcomings and accept each one of them, hating myself in the process. But one day, miraculously, it stopped. I could stand before God as a human being. I crept all the way into the room and sat silently, immersed in the Presence. It was God who had opened the door and beckoned me closer.

I sat silently, day after day. It was like sitting in a rainbow. I was drenched in His love, awestruck by it. I scarcely dared to breathe, or even move, because I was so afraid it would disappear—this feeling. I was like a lover, hurrying into the mystical Presence, just as I used to run to Bothwell. And waiting for me, always, was the heart of God, and a seat for me in it.

And then, one day, He was not there. I crept to my accustomed place and waited, but He did not come. I was abandoned. The door was closed and locked.

Had it all been a hoax? Was it only my intense longing, my loneliness, my imagination, that had created it? That was the cruellest feeling of all, the greatest betrayal I had ever faced.

Everyone noticed my sadness. But I could tell no one. They assumed it was because of bad news from Scotland, no news from Scotland, the onset of my rheumatism, the perfidy of Elizabeth. But those things could all be borne if I had my Lover; without Him, all was dark. I had come to depend on Him, and in such a short time. At length I told my confessor, thinking he would be scandalized or puzzled. But no; he was familar with it. He told me that I must put aside my guilt at feeling perhaps I had driven Him away, and simply wait. Wait for the return.

The weeks were long. But at length He did return, but in a different form. He was no longer a lover whom I met secretly, but diffused all about me, like the deep spring air. For a time everything seemed bathed in the Presence, like the fiery rays of a sunset. Then gradually they faded, and I found myself—back to formal prayers.

Once again I must ascend the ladder, hoping for that glorious vision at the top.

Will I ever be free? Is God keeping me here, a prisoner in this world, to purge me for the next? It is true I have had many sins, although the ones that seemed largest now seem smaller, while the smaller loom larger. I can no longer tell which ones require the most penance, which are the most offensive to God.

She closed her eyes, and breathed deeply. She felt herself to be at the bottom of a long shaft, with the eye of God focused on her.

VIII

The Parliamentarians assembled in London; the elected commoners went to their accustomed meeting place of St. Stephens Chapel at Westminster Palace, and the Lords to a hall at the south end of the palace. This Parliament was very Protestant, containing a number of members who belonged to that wing of the Anglican Church now called Puritan. They came, eager to settle the question of the Queen of Scots, the plotting Papist spider in their midst.

The Speaker of the House, Mr. Bell, addressed the problem in his opening speech. "There is an error which we have noted: that there is a person in the land whom no law can touch." Member after member rose and spoke his mind about this default.

"A general impunity to commit treason was never permitted to any," cried Thomas Norton.

"Shall we say our law is not able to provide for this mischief? We might then say it is defective in the highest degree!"

Mr. Peter Wentworth, a fiery Puritan, called Mary "the most notorious whore in all the world." Mr. St. Leger chimed in with "the monstrous and huge dragon and mass of the earth, the Queen of Scots."

Another old Puritan, his voice trembling, stood and let loose. "If I should term her the daughter of sedition, the mother of rebellion, the nurse of impiety, the handmaid of iniquity, the sister of unshamefastness; or if I should tell you that which you know already—that she is Scottish of nation, French of education, Papist of profession, a Guisan of blood, a Spaniard in practice, a libertine in life: so yet this were nothing near to describe her, whose villainy hath stained the earth and infected the air. To destroy her would be one of the fairest riddances that ever church of God had." He waved his arms wildly.

"Yea, hear ye her crimes: assuming the arms and title of Queen of England. Arranging a marriage with the Duke of Norfolk without the Queen's knowledge. Raising a rebellion in the north. Seeking foreign aid from the Pope, the Spaniards, and others, by Ridolfi, in order to invade England. Procuring the Pope's bull to depose Queen Elizabeth," another added.

"Let us cut off her head and make no more ado about it!" said Richard Gallys, a member from New Windsor.

"Yes!"

A joint committee of the two houses of Parliament visited Elizabeth with their suggestion: that Mary be executed or, at the very least, excluded from the succession, and a bill passed to try her for treason if any other plots were formulated in her name.

But Elizabeth refused utterly. "Shall I put to death the bird that, to escape the hawk, has fled to my feet for protection? Honour and conscience forbid!"

The Parliamentarians then presented her with a third demand: that she proceed with the execution of the Duke of Norfolk.

☙

Elizabeth was spending the mid-May afternoon walking through the gardens at Hampton Court, seeing the new-blooming primroses, columbine, and roses, and examining the strawberry beds where her favourite berries came from. Christopher Hatton had mentioned that he would like to lease the estate of the Bishop of Ely at Holborn because—one reason, at least—of the delectable strawberries there.

"Then I could smother you with baskets of them," he said.

"Please! The juice stains," said Elizabeth. "The Bishop is most reluctant to agree, so I hear. But perhaps I shall speak with him myself." She smiled at Hatton and he all but swooned.

Elizabeth had transferred to Hampton Court a few days earlier; now more members of court arrived by twilight, coming up in lighted boats, making stars on the water, laughing and singing. The night air was soft and they strolled toward the courtyards, in no particular hurry to arrive in their quarters. Moths, drawn to their lanterns, flitted with silent wings about them.

Only Cecil limped up the pathway with urgency, thumping along with his stick. There was something he must show his Queen, something that might induce her to act at last.

"We have recovered this from the correspondence of the Queen of Scots," he said, extending a piece of paper to her in privacy. "It is a letter to the Duke of Alva—Philip's general! Oh, it was in cipher, but we have broken the cipher."

Elizabeth took it, feeling a terrible dread. She held her magnifying glass over it, and read:

> . . . and to my most beloved brother Philip, I adjure him to send ships
> to Scotland to take possession of the prince my son, and bring him to

safety. I am closely guarded here in England, and yet I still number many as my friends and allies. There is yet a strong party in my favour, and lords who favour my cause, of whom, although certain ones are prisoners, the Queen of England would not dare touch their lives.

"So!" she said. "Mary thinks I 'dare' not touch Norfolk!" She threw down the letter and kicked it. "Does she not realize it is only through my mercy that he lives, that I fear no one? Am I not the daughter of a king, and have a king's courage? And have I not spared her out of my own courage?" she screamed.

Cecil put up his finger to his mouth. "Quiet, Your Majesty. *Her* spies may be about. Yes, she is bold, and overconfident. The people scream for her execution, and who protects her? You! Yet she does not appreciate it, evidently. Now let me remind you that the Duke of Norfolk has been duly tried and condemned. If you do not allow the sentence to be carried out, the rest of the realm will think as *she* does: that you *dare* not. Then they will see you as weak, vacillating, helpless, like Richard II. And then what? Rebellion, sedition, all the things you hope to avoid! For the love of peace, dear sovereign, you must carry through the sentence."

Elizabeth shook her head. "I will not be pushed into anything my conscience mislikes so."

"If you hope to save *her*, then you must yield on Norfolk. It is as simple as that." His gout was paining him, and he longed to sit and rest his leg. "It is one or the other. Which do you choose?"

"Neither!"

"Then read this letter from Knox. It will most like decide your mind. He urges the execution of all, but particularly her. He says"—Cecil extracted the paper and read it slowly— " 'if you chop not at the root, the branches that appear to be broken will bud again.' She is like a very hardy tree, that can spring up again and again, no matter how it is trimmed back. No matter how closely you have her guarded, no matter how you seek to frighten her, she will always be blooming with fresh treasons and mischiefs in this land. Or rather, inciting others to do so."

"There must be a way to stop her, short of killing her!"

"Nay, Madam. Hear again what Knox has written: 'Apply the axe to the root of the evil. Until the Scottish Queen is dead, neither the English Queen's crown nor her life can be in security.' "

"Knox is redundant." She shivered. "I thought he was mortally ill."

"He, too, is resilient."

Just then there was a knock on the chamber door. A basket was delivered, with a note to Gloriana, fair Goddess. Elizabeth opened it, saying, "I trow this is not from Knox!"

It was from Hatton.

Dearest, fairest goddess, I send you these to put upon your palate. You yourself are sweeter, richer, and they shall draw from your essence to themselves. Ah! I faint with the thought!

706

She handed the note to Cecil, who read it with raised brows. He did not dare laugh at it. The Queen had noticeably brightened.

It was a basket of strawberries, both the red and white varieties, including some of the tiny woodland type. Hatton must have ventured out in the late afternoon to find them. Elizabeth tasted one and smiled. "These are excellent," she said, offering them to Cecil.

They sat silently eating them. Then Elizabeth said, "I will recognize James VI as King. And I will allow the execution to proceed."

"Of both?"

"The Scottish Queen has not been tried and found guilty," Elizabeth said quietly.

"Which is precisely why Parliament wants a provision that she be brought to trial if any other plots come about. She must be made to account for her actions! If not this time, then the next."

"You are sure there will be a next time?"

"As of my life." Cecil sighed and stretched out his swollen, gouty leg. "You heard what Charles IX said: the poor fool will never stop plotting until she loses her head. It bespeaks a lack of intelligence to continue, but prisoners must sometimes do insane things in order to stay sane and give order to their days, which are otherwise meaningless. What has she to do from morning to night? Sew? Pray? Read?"

"What else had the monks to do?" snapped Elizabeth.

"The monks chose their station, and felt they had a vocation for it. Mary has no vocation for being a prisoner—all her actions in trying to escape show that."

"She had no vocation for being a monarch, either. That was evident from the moment she returned to Scotland to rule. Poor thing—does she have a vocation at all?"

"Many talents, many gifts, but perhaps no vocation," agreed Cecil. "But the omens this year—the comet that appeared—everyone agrees that some catastrophe may occur in England. It is, most like, some treason to overthrow you! It is only May—"

"A comet!"

"Remember the comet in 1066, that foretold the Norman invasion. Do not scoff!"

"You sound like an old country woman, Cecil. For shame! Nay, I have decided what to do to stop the Scottish Queen. I will allow the casket letters to be published. All that trash she wrote to her lover, Bothwell—let the whole world see it and judge her! Along with it, Buchanan's *A Detection of the Doings of the Queen of Scotland*. Then no one will want to elevate her. Until now the letters have been privately circulated, and only in England and Scotland. But now—let French and Latin translations be published, too, so the common people in every land can know what she is! The common people: Knox's new-found weapon. Well, others can use it as well!"

"Your Majesty! That is brilliant!" Cecil smiled for the first time since

707

coming into the chamber. "But are you sure? It is still a gamble. In your own way, you are more daring than even she is. She has nothing to lose, having already lost all. You have much to lose, if by ignoring the sound advice and warnings of your people and Council, you let the Bosom Serpent live—and she strikes!"

Elizabeth laughed. "The Bosom Serpent! Walsingham is clever with words." She opened her windows wide and looked out. "I see no comet."

"Then you are firm? Your mind is quite made up?"

"Yes. I dare fate. *Jacta est alia*—the die is cast."

After Cecil had gone, and she had made ready for bed, she sat, dressed in her tawny silken robe, at her desk. She kept reaching her slender fingers into the little basket and eating strawberries. They were delicious, with a tang behind their sweetness.

Elizabeth was writing a poem. But it was no love poem, no paean to flowery May or Roman gods.

The Daughter of Debate

The doubt of future foes exiles my present joy,
And wit me warns to shun such snares as threaten mine annoy.
For falsehood now doth flow and subject faith doth ebb,
Which would not be, if reason ruled or wisdom weaved the web.
But clouds of toys untried do cloak aspiring minds,
Which turn to rain of late repent by course of changed winds.
The top of hope supposed the root of ruth will be,
And fruitless all their graffed guiles, as shortly ye shall see.
The dazzled eyes with pride, which great ambition blinds,
Shall be unsealed by worthy wights, whose foresight falsehood finds.
The daughter of debate, that eke discord doth sow,
Shall reap no gain where former rule hath taught still peace to grow.
No foreign banished wight shall anchor in this port;
Our realm it brooks no stranger's force, let them elsewhere resort.
Our rusty sword with rest shall first his edge employ
To poll their tops that seek such change and gape for joy.

Mary writes of love, of passion, in her poems, Elizabeth thought. I write of England.

She put the paper aside.

I feel the need to write, but I fear my poetry is as stiff as Cecil's leg. We are much alike, she thought. The soul of a poet is not always given the wings to fly.

❧

On June second, the Duke of Norfolk was led up the steps of the scaffold on Tower Hill. This time the people were not disappointed. After giving the requisite speech, mingling Christian resignation with farewells, he laid his head on the block. The headsman was in good form that morning, and got it off with only one chop.

❧

On August twenty-second, the Earl of Northumberland was likewise executed at York, after having been extradited from Scotland.

The same day, Catherine de Médicis's assassins attempted to kill the Huguenot leader, Admiral Coligny, in Paris, where large numbers of Huguenots had come for the wedding of Marguerite Valois and Henri of Navarre. The assassin missed, as the Admiral stooped to adjust his shoe, and only succeeded in shooting his arm. His fellow Huguenots cried, "The Admiral's arm will cost thirty thousand Catholic arms!"

Two days later, on St. Bartholomew's Day—the feast of the apostle who had been martyred by being skinned alive—the Catholics of Paris, under the leadership of the Guises, claiming fear of the Huguenot vow, martyred four thousand Huguenot men, women, and children in the streets. The Duc de Guise himself killed Admiral Coligny. The blood in the streets spread out in a red web between cobblestones.

In the provinces, another six thousand Huguenots were killed.

❧

Elizabeth received the French ambassador at Woodstock on September eighth, the day after her thirty-ninth birthday. She was dressed in mourning and had ordered her attendants to dress likewise. She had kept the ambassador waiting three days before granting him an audience—all to impress on him the gravity of the situation. Protestant subjects had been slaughtered, and she, a Protestant queen, was outraged.

Yet when she met with him, drawing him aside to speak privately with him, she was by no means as stern as her garments. She seemed willing to accept the official version of events and the King's pledge of continuing friendship with England. The Anglo-French Treaty of Blois would stand.

❧

Anti-Catholic feeling now swelled to hysteria in England. The cries for Mary's execution rose. Her family house, the Guises, had led the massacre.

IX

The October skies were brilliant over Scotland; in only two days it would be Hallowe'en, usually a dreary time, but this year it would be golden. Morton had always enjoyed All Hallows' Eve for all that he was supposed to be a faithful member of the Kirk. He motioned to Erskine to seat himself where he could have a view of the trees outside the window of Morton's mansion at Dalkeith.

Morton looked dispassionately at the Regent seated across from him. The long-faced Erskine could expect another twelve years of control in Scotland, until the Prince obtained his eighteenth birthday. There seemed to be no danger of Mary being restored to her throne; the Ridolfi Plot had turned Elizabeth against her. Now she sought to be delivered from her. Well, it would cost her even more than the Earl of Northumberland had—in gold.

"My dear Erskine, you are looking weak and sickly. Are you quite sure you have recovered from the ague?" asked Morton solicitously, pouring him some wine.

Erskine coughed. "Not entirely. And with winter coming—Stirling is so drafty." He hacked again.

"I should think you would be used to it by now. I thought it was well insulated."

"Nay, nothing can keep out that wind." He shuddered. "The only remedy is to keep to one's bed, under mounds of covers. However, our envoy to Denmark has sent some remarkable undergarments guaranteed to keep one warm—and they do, although they itch."

"Denmark. I am glad *something* has come out of it. I am disgusted with King Frederick! Why does he not surrender Bothwell to us?"

"We should stop the 'trial' business and just go straight to bribery," said Erskine. He was looking at the dish of pigeon breast with juniper and roast saddle of hare before him. He helped himself. They were dining alone.

Morton smiled. That was his opening. "Yes. But for that we need money. How desperate are you for it? Would you be willing to undertake an execution for it?"

"An assassination, you mean?" He was chewing slowly.

"No, a proper execution." Morton took a big drink of the French wine from Gascony. "The King's mother."

"Mary?" Erskine put down his fork and stared.

"The English are willing to deliver her up to our justice. It seems the clamour and turmoil of keeping her is wearing on their nerves. They—or rather Cecil—would pay us to take her back."

"How much?" Erskine's voice was reedy. "Perhaps it is a trick for her restoration."

He does not mean to do it, thought Morton. He has lost his nerve and become a worn-out creature.

"I do not know yet. The question is, would you agree?"

"I cannot answer." He shook his head. "Knox is sinking fast. He can no longer walk unsupported. What will we do when he leaves us?"

"Then make his last days happy. He has long urged us to it." Morton tried to keep the edge of distrust out of his voice. "We should proceed while the English are in the mood. Elizabeth has been hurt by her cousin's plotting. But, womanlike, she will change her mind soon enough."

"I cannot do it," said Erskine at length. "It is a monstrous crime, to slay one's anointed sovereign. I will not have it on my soul."

"Nor, so it seems, will Elizabeth. My, what cowards we have about us!"

He cannot stay Regent another twelve years, thought Morton. He will turn us all into timid girls and skirted eunuchs. Scotland needs strength at its helm, not quivering.

"You may call it what you will," insisted Erskine. "I could call some of our doings tyranny and sin."

This was alarming. "Are you planning to retire back to your family monastery of Inchmahome, Erskine? What is this turnabout?" asked Morton in a taunting tone.

"Just reflection. There has been too little of it amongst us."

"Very well, then. Forget the English suggestion. How fares the little King?" Morton was noticing how clear and unclouded the French wine was as the light shone through it from the window. A thought had come to him.

"A true scholar. Very quiet, diligent, and obedient. Nothing like either of his parents, unless he is keeping his true nature hidden. He has a pet monkey," he suddenly remembered. "He calls it his 'little infidel' and lets it cling to him. A sailor brought it to him as a pet. It is the only thing he ever shows affection for."

"His mother tried to send him a pony, but we did not permit it," Morton remembered. "I trust he still hates her?"

"Yes, Buchanan has seen to that."

"Good. Else he might try to 'rescue' her someday."

"No chance of that," said Erskine. "I imagine that he will come to guard his throne carefully and not wish to move over and make room for another. All this hating of her was probably unnecessary." He looked mournfully at Morton.

He has changed! thought Morton. He is veering off on a new course. For the next twelve years? No!

They talked about general matters: gossip about Elizabeth's new favourite, Hatton; a translation of Caesar's *Commentaries* just printed in England; the fact that Ivan the Terrible of Russia had protested the brutality of the

Massacre of St. Bartholomew's. Drake had just set off on a marauding voyage to the Spanish Main, with Elizabeth's blessing. A Royal Exchange building had been opened in London, and it was said to be glittering. At the Battle of Lepanto, the forces of Philip had routed the forces of the Turk under Ali Pasha in an heroic sea fight. Suleiman's navy had been destroyed, and ten thousand Christian galley slaves set free. Unfortunately this freed Philip to devote his entire energies to exterminating his other enemy: heretics.

"We live in exciting times," said Erskine. He looked down at the sweet that Morton had brought out himself and set before him. It was a pale mound with slivered almonds and cinnamon.

"Plain country fare," said Morton. "This is a curd cheese, with a lemony taste. Sometimes the taste can be refreshingly bitter. But that is as it is supposed to be. My cook tells me that the local people here eat it to gain strength for the winter."

They each took their spoons and tasted it, then proceeded to eat.

The taste was quite tangy, with lemon and something else, thought Erskine. Perhaps a bit of tansy.

He took his leave shortly thereafter for the forty-mile ride back to Stirling.

" 'Tis a glorious day, and I shall enjoy seeing the sunset," said Erskine. "I will stop after dark near Linlithgow."

By the time he reached it, he was stricken with stomach pains so severe that he had to be helped out of the saddle. He was taken to his usual inn, where, after a night of agony, he died—the second regent to expire in Linlithgow.

Morton immediately succeeded him.

❧

Just after Hallowtide, the weather abruptly changed, and gales swept through Scotland, bringing torrents of stinging, icy rain and high winds. The oceans were vexed and waves crashed against the coast and into the Firth of Forth, sending clouds of ocean spray high in the air. The few remaining leaves were stripped from the trees and carried far out over the water.

Knox, ailing badly, managed to ascend the pulpit of St. Giles on November ninth and preach to his successor the duties of a minister, but his voice was so weak that no one more than a few feet away could hear him. Then, shakily, he was helped down, and the whole congregation followed him as he limped painfully back to his house.

He had invited some friends to supper that night, and insisted on sitting with them at the supper table.

"Open the new hogshead of wine," he rasped to Margaret.

"Nay," one of the guests demurred. "That's over one hundred gallons, and we can't drink it all. Save it for a larger group."

Knox said calmly, "Please drink as freely as you wish, and do not hold back. I shall not live to finish it." He reached out and patted Margaret's hand.

712

After supper he took to his bed.

"I cannot read," he said to his wife. "I cannot hold my eyes upon the text. I pray you, please read to me from the seventeenth chapter of the Gospel of John. It was, you know, where first I cast my anchor."

"Wh-what do you mean?" She could not understand his leave-taking. He was not yet sixty, and his mysterious illness—the weakness and paralysis and coughing—did not seem to signal a particular disease.

"I mean these are the words that called me directly, and that seem to speak in the intimate voice of my Master."

"John, why do you not call the physician?" she cried.

"You may call him if you wish," he said gently. "I will not neglect the ordinary means of healing, but I know the Lord will soon put an end to my warfare. My trumpets all are blown. But others will be calling me home." Again he patted her hand. "Now read, I pray you."

" 'I have glorified Thee on earth: I have finished the work which Thou gavest me to do. I have manifested Thy name unto the men which Thou gavest me out of the world. I pray for them: While I was with them in the world, I kept them in Thy name: those that Thou gavest me I have kept, and none of them is lost, but the son of perdition.' "

He sighed and let his eyes seek the lighted window of his study that overlooked the High Street.

"So much vanity," he murmured. So many had passed beneath that window, going to and from Holyrood Palace. He could hear the shouts and cries of that day eleven years earlier when the Queen had made her ceremonial entrance to Edinburgh, and she had passed by, jewels on her bosom and grey cloak spread out across her horse's flanks.

"Son of perdition," he whispered. Yes, the son of perdition had been lost, he had not succeeded in saving her. She had gone down to ruin, in a trail of lovers and vice and murder. And it was not over yet. "Jezebel . . ." he sighed. "The dogs shall drink thy blood, as I prophesied."

"John, do not torment yourself with her memory," said Margaret. "Think of your children! Our little daughters—think of them, not of her!"

"I think of Scotland, dear wife, and all things concerning her."

Scotland was in peril. In spite of the flight of the evil Queen, in spite of the triumph of the Kirk, in spite of Elizabeth's recognition of James VI, the country seemed to be in the grip of lawlessness and disorder. Three regents had died in only four years, and there was no one able to enforce government decrees. Bothwell's strongmen were no longer at hand to control the Borders, where outlaws once again roamed freely. The clan hatreds—Hamiltons and Lennox Stewarts, Douglases and Gordons—raged on. Maitland and Kirkcaldy still held Edinburgh Castle and rained cannonballs down on helpless townsfolk, although the other lords loyal to the Queen—Argyll, Huntly, Hamilton—had retreated out of the city.

Martha, Margaret, and Elizabeth, his three little daughters, crowded round his bed. "Father!" said six-year-old Martha, pulling gently on his beard.

"You may cut it a bit if you wish," he said. They had had a game about his beard, with his daughter wishing to trim it. Sometimes he let her, but once she had botched it and left him to preach at St. Giles with a ragged beard flapping up and down. "You may even make it uneven."

"What is that?" asked Margaret, the four-year-old, pointing at a neat stack of boards along one wall.

"No, you mustn't!" said her mother to Knox.

"And why should I not tell her? 'Tis to be my coffin, dearest. I asked my friend Bannatyne to start preparing it."

Margaret the elder began weeping.

On the nineteenth, Morton came. The new Regent was stern and had aged much in the past few months. The violent red of his hair and beard had softened, and there were threads of white in them. His dark eyes were troubled, although he tried to hide it from Knox.

Knox remembered him as he was in the first days of the Covenant of the Lords of the Congregation. Morton had been a staunch supporter from the beginning, and had never wavered like so many others. He had been in the prime of life then, and was still flourishing. Now he had his reward: the highest power in Scotland.

"Leave us alone," Knox asked the others who were present, and they withdrew. Then Knox motioned to Morton to bend close. "Did you have any knowledge of the murder of Darnley?" he asked. "You must tell me the truth."

Morton hesitated. Did a lie to a prophet count as a heavier sin than a lie to another man? Did Knox have the power to forgive sins? Could he see through the lie? He had the gift of prophecy. "I—I knew that certain men wished to rid the world of him," he finally said. "But I refused to be a party to it. I am ashamed to say it was not because of pity for the King, but because of caution for myself. I had just been allowed to return to Scotland after the Riccio murder, and I dared not involve myself with another so soon."

Knox relaxed his grip on Morton's wrist. "You may then call the others back in."

Lord Boyd, David Lindsay, and the new minister of St. Giles returned to the bedside. Knox struggled to sit up, and Boyd placed a bolster behind him and helped him.

"I am troubled about the lords still in Edinburgh Castle that daily wreak havoc on the people in the streets of the city," he said in a wavering voice. "I make a dying request of you, that you go to Kirkcaldy in the castle and tell him, in my name, this: Unless he repents of his desertion of the Lords, he shall die miserably. For neither the craggy rock in which he miserably trusts, nor the carnal prudence of Maitland, whom he looks upon as a demigod, nor the assistance of foreigners, as he falsely flatters himself, shall deliver them. He will be spewed forth, not by the gate, but by the wall."

He suddenly sat bolt upright and his voice deepened. "For he shall be disgracefully dragged from his nest to punishment, and hung on a gallows in the face of the sun, unless he speedily amend his life, and flee to the mercy of God." His voice subsided. "The man's soul is dear to me, and I would not have it perish if I could save it."

"What of his companion, Maitland?" asked Morton.

"He is a godless man, I daresay even an atheist. I can hold out no hope for him." Knox slid back down in his bed, wheezing and choking.

On the evening of November twenty-fourth, the gales were tearing at the house. Knox was lying in bed, motionless, attended by his wife, his physician, and the friends to whom he had entrusted his family. Evening prayers were recited, and Knox stirred.

"Do you hear the prayers?" asked his physician.

"I would to God that you and all men heard them as I have heard them, and I praise God for that heavenly sound." Knox smiled, and died.

Morton led the Lords in mourning at the funeral two days later. Knox was buried in the new-built coffin in the yard of St. Giles, and as the coffin was being lowered, Morton said, "Here lies one who neither feared nor flattered any flesh."

In his will, Knox addressed the "Papists and the unthankful world," telling them that "because they will not admit me for an admonisher, I give them over to the judgement of Him who knows the hearts of all." The rest of his worldly goods were distributed to his family.

In February 1573, Morton was able to negotiate with Huntly and the Hamiltons one at a time, and they at last agreed to recognize James VI as King and Morton as Regent. Argyll followed suit. Only Maitland and Kirkcaldy, barricaded up in Edinburgh Castle, held out for Mary. It was six years since the death of Darnley, and one by one her supporters had fled, died, or gone over to the other side.

The Lords attacked the castle, but were beaten back. In April, English help arrived: ships anchored in Leith, and troops and ordnance under the command of Sir William Drury, Marshal of Berwick, trundled ashore. Among the cannon was one of the celebrated Seven Sisters captured by the English long ago in the Battle of Flodden, and now returned to Scotland in the hands of the enemy.

After an unsuccessful attempt at mining operations, the castle was bombarded from five positions night and day. The weakness of the castle was in its water supply, and the besiegers succeeded in blocking one with lime and wheat. But not until a massive assault on the David's Tower, with a resulting collapse of its wall, was the second well stopped. Still the castle fought on, until the English captured the outworks defending the gentler eastern approach to the castle.

Standing on the outworks, Drury shouted, "Surrender! If you do, all the defenders are free to depart in peace, except the leaders, Maitland and Kirkcaldy. I would speak with them!"

Kirkcaldy appeared on the rubble rimming the ramparts. "What terms do you offer?" he shouted.

"An honourable surrender. Give yourself up, and there will be no harm to your persons."

After several hours of shouting back and forth, Kirkcaldy agreed and tried to meet Drury, but was unable to pass through the castle gate because of the rubble from the bombardment. He was therefore let down over the wall by a rope.

"Knox prophesied that he would be spewed forth, not at the gate, but by the wall," whispered the onlookers.

Inside the castle, Maitland dragged himself over to the window and saw what was happening. Drury's men had seized Kirkcaldy and were roughly dragging him off, in spite of their promises.

"Liars to the end," he whispered. "There is no truth in them, in these 'men of God.' " He would have laughed, but he had no strength. The truth was that he had been smitten for the past few months with a creeping paralysis and had almost lost the use of his legs.

"May twenty-ninth. I must then say farewell to thee, world." He had prepared for this, and laboriously extracted a vial from his cabinet. "Forgive me, dearest wife." The fair Fleming! Their marriage had been little but a test of her forbearance and fidelity; it was a far cry from the life he had hoped to give her.

In the world that used to be, when it was all young, when there was singing and dancing, he thought, it was there I thought to take you and keep you. Not to this one—of murders and fleeing, and bodily failure.

Slowly he poured the contents of the vial out into a glass. He held his hand as steady as he could, fearful of spilling a precious drop. The liquid *venin de crapaud*, derived from the distilled body fluids of toads killed with arsenic, would bring death in a few hours.

He held out the glass, studying the contents. Death in a cup. The opposite of the ambrosia that mortals could drink on Mount Olympus and become immortal.

Why is it, he thought, that we can make ourselves a cup of death but not a cup of life?

He sat down in his chair and took deep breaths. Below he could hear yelling and marching. They would soon be breaking in. He had to do it.

He gripped the glass and shut his eyes.

You are delaying, he told himself. If you would be master of your fate, then drink it. If you wish them to be master of your fate, then do not.

He brought the glass to his lips and swallowed the bitter, viscous liquid. It burned all the way down his throat.

"Farewell, you men of God," he muttered. "Spare me from your gentle mercy. I prefer the kindness of poison—it is more trustworthy. Poison always keeps its promises."

Kirkcaldy was hanged by the market cross in the High Street. He had stood facing toward Holyrood, and his last sight was of the conical towers of that palace. But as he died, his body swung round, toward the afternoon sun behind the castle.

"As Knox foretold," the people murmured, "he was hanged in the face of the sun." They were hushed with fear.

There were no more Queen's Men in Scotland.

X

Bothwell watched as the sun threw longer and longer slants of light on the floor of his chamber. Soon it would be going down, leaving the sky, and a semblance of darkness would prevail. This time of year, it was never entirely dark, even at midnight. But the heavens would deepen into a rich plum-sapphire color, and would serve to cloak his activity.

Tonight he would escape.

The tides were right. The light would be right. And the guard would be almost nonexistent, for tonight was their beloved Midsummer Night festivity, when people caroused all night, lovers met in the woods, and the governor of the castle always gave a boisterous celebration, with unlimited wine and blaring trumpet music. Bothwell had now witnessed this annual activity for five years; this would be the sixth.

And there will not be a seventh! he vowed.

Every year he had noticed how lax the security became, and every year the celebrations seemed to grow more and more lavish. Bonfires blazed all along the shore, and the sound of the drunken townsfolk running in the narrow streets carried up into the castle. The entire town of Malmö went on a spree, and normality was suspended. For the next few days they were equally befuddled with the aftereffects of the wine.

They claim Midsummer Night is a night of enchantment, of magic, he thought. Let it make me invisible! The lovers go out to gather fernseed

717

on this night to confer invisibility on themselves; no one needs it more than I.

He had come to know his guards well: the thickset Sven, the lecherous Tor, and the conscientious Bjorn. Over the years he had learned Danish, and had been a pleasant and cooperative prisoner, until he had gained their confidence. Hours of listening to them discuss their women, religion, and ailments had made him well acquainted with their strengths and weaknesses.

The governor of the castle, Captain Kaas, was a bluff, plain fellow who did everything by the book. He kept the rooms for King Frederick always at the ready, with fresh linens and potpourris, but the King never came. Bothwell had never had his audience with him, and he knew now he never would. The King had forgotten him, as completely as if he were dead. As far as Frederick was concerned, he *was* dead; he was of absolutely no political value any longer. But being a thrifty sort, Frederick never relinquished anything, just in case. And so he kept Bothwell tight in his castle of Malmö.

In the beginning, Bothwell had had visitors and been kept informed of what was happening beyond the Øresund. But over the years the visits had ceased; he had had to rely on whatever the guards happened to hear in town, and so he only knew of the most striking events. He knew that Mary was still a prisoner, and that, just as he had never been granted audience with Frederick, she had never succeeded in seeing Elizabeth. He knew that Knox had died, and that the Queen's party in Scotland was a spent force. He knew that Elizabeth had been excommunicated, and the Lord James assassinated. He had heard of the Massacre of St. Bartholomew's. But the motives behind these things, the fine shadings of them, the diplomatic outcome of them, he did not know. King Charles IX not only never helped him, but never acknowledged his letter. The letters from Mary, few and far between, still came through once in a great while. In them she always beseeched him to be of good courage and know she was loyal.

When the guards went out to the adjoining courtyard to watch the lighting of the bonfire, that was when he would do it. His rooms were on the ground floor, and he had carefully loosened the back of the wooden "closet" on the sea-wall of his quarters. This gave out directly on the sea, and had been strengthened to prevent just what Bothwell now hoped to achieve. But he had had six years to work at it. He believed that he had adequate strength to force the boards now if he had only ten minutes or so. Then, to squeeze out, land safely near the ocean, and slip away over the rocks. Even that would be favourable tonight: it would be low tide, exposing them like stepping-stones for him to dash across. There would be small boats tied near the harbour, and they would not be guarded; a simple matter to take one.

And then what? Row out beyond the harbour, hide himself in a fishing village, then hire himself out as a hand on one of the larger merchant ships crossing the Baltic Sea to Germany. Thank God he knew Danish now, and could concoct a reasonable story about himself.

My ancestors had a Viking or two amongst them, he thought, up in the Shetlands. Pray I look enough like them to blend in with the Danes.

The sun duly went down, and as Bothwell's windows faced south, it remained light in his rooms a long time. He could hear the three sentry guards making impatient noises as they waited to be relieved. They looked forward eagerly to this night all year long. At last—it seemed four hours— the young soldier who was assigned to forgo his revelry that night arrived to relieve them. He had already done his drinking, as if in defiance of his superiors. Bothwell heard him sit down heavily, and then a few minutes later unmistakable snores came from the guardroom.

Swiftly, Bothwell went to the door of the closet. He had nothing to take with him; he had never been permitted to retain any weapons or money, and so there was nothing to gather up. He would survive on this flight only by his nerves and wits.

He loosened the nails—which he had pried out over many months, always being careful to replace them so they looked secure—opened the door partway, and slipped behind it. Now he would have to move as fast as humanly possible, lest the guard peek in the room and see no one there. The back boards, thick ones, had been nailed with heavy studs, but had loosened somewhat due to the salty air and sea spray. He threw his shoulder against them and prayed they would give way without making a loud noise.

His prayer was answered; one of the boards splintered quietly. He hit it again, and it and its nearest neighbour broke open. A gush of fresh air hit him. He kicked a third board and was elated to hear it give way. Now! The opening was wide enough. He wiggled through and found himself hanging about ten feet over mossy rocks. He cautiously climbed through and hung by his hands to drop down as silently as possible.

The rock underneath was as slick as if it had been covered in grease. Immediately his feet flew out from under him and he landed heavily on his back. Pain tore through him, and for a horrible instant he thought he could not move his legs. But feeling flooded back into them and he rolled over and made his way carefully, shaken, on all fours across the expanse of rocks. Fifteen feet or so farther out, the ocean was nibbling at the rocks, which were covered in long strands of seaweed.

The area he had to traverse was much longer than he had thought. But he had never had a view of it and had had to imagine it. He could never get to the harbour this way; it would take all night. Nervously he looked back up at the bulk of the castle, its bastions reflected in its moat. He thought he could see a red reflection of bonfire flames coming from the courtyard, but as yet there was no noise of alarm.

He would have to pass through the town in order to reach the main harbour. But in this twilit night of revelry, he would appear as just one more tippler. He saw the city wall on his right, just ahead; the gate was gaping open on this night, and people were gathered around it, listening to a fiddler who sang of trolls and witches. He edged toward them, slowing his pace.

They looked at him and smiled, and did not show that they saw anything unusual in him. He passed quickly through the gate, then walked along the old Västergatan. This was the heart of the old town; its streets were very narrow and dark, and that suited Bothwell's purpose. To his right he could hear loud shouting and music, and guessed that a bonfire might be there, in a main square, along with its crowds. Best to stay away from it; he had the Västergatan almost to himself, with only an occasional youth running down it in a hurry to get somewhere.

I'm in a hurry, too, Bothwell thought. But the last thing I can do is to show it.

He continued until he found a street that appeared to go down to the harbour, or where he guessed the harbour should be. He ran along it lightly, trying to imitate the way the others were running, carefree and happy. His spirits had risen so that his heart was pounding with exhilaration, and he had to exert all his willpower to keep his head and not dissolve in triumphant excitement. He had escaped! He had outsmarted them! Their escape-proof prison had been bested.

The harbour opened up before him, dark and inviting. The large boats of the Hansa merchants were tied up, everything in order as was their wont. It was tempting to stow away on one. He could perhaps hide down in the hold and wait. But all these ships would be searched, and even if he escaped notice the first time, the ship might not sail for days. No, he had best get as far away as possible before his escape was discovered.

On the far side of the harbour were the smaller boats: fishing craft, rowboats, coal transports. He would steal one of them and row out to sea, searching for a place to put in along the coast. He made his way over to them, wondering how they were secured and which would be the best to take. It would have to be large enough to afford him some protection; he could not hug the coast too closely, since he was unfamiliar with the shoals and rocks. But it should be the smallest possible to do the job, so he would not call attention to himself.

There was a small boat like a fishing craft beached on the far side of the harbour. In the purple, hazy light it looked to be in good repair and fairly new. He could smell the freshly oiled planks.

He made his way over to it and looked. It was barely tied up, and he was able to untie the knot easily. Throwing the line into the boat, he shoved off and leapt into it. Grabbing the oars, he began to row furiously. The boat rocked and began to move across the gentle waves.

"Thank God and all the saints!" he exploded. He felt the wood of the oars biting into his palms, and nothing had ever felt so good. It was real; he had done it.

Suddenly there was a movement in the boat, a scuffling. Rats! He shivered. He hated them, and any second now they would start scampering and racing with their horrid little feet all over his legs.

I should have whacked that canvas to get them out before I set out, he thought. But there was no time.

And now it was too late. Harbour rats were vicious; he hoped they would not attack him.

"What the hell?" A huge form rose up out of the canvas like a ghost. "God damn you!"

It was a man, an immense naked man. More stirring, and a woman sat up beside him, also naked. She screamed.

Lovers! He had interrupted their tryst. Why hadn't he seen their movement under the canvas? Because there wasn't any. They had lain still in hopes he would go away.

"I—I—" Bothwell stuttered, still grasping the oars.

"You dirty thief!" screamed the man. "It isn't your brother, Astrid! It's just a filthy thief!" He lunged at Bothwell, hands outstretched to grab his neck.

Bothwell dropped the oars and fought to get the man's hands off his neck. He had the strength of the devil, and he was furious, with all the outraged morality of a disturbed lover. "Please—stop—no—"

The woman, her long blond hair covering her shoulders and breasts, was beating on him, too, screaming at the top of her lungs. Together they toppled over, and then the man raised a wooden bucket to bash Bothwell's head. But he was struggling so fiercely in the midst of all the slippery naked flesh that the man was unable to hit him. Bothwell had a glimpse of a face that seemed to be all yellow beard and snarling teeth. The smell of human arousal was stronger than the smell of the sea as the couple tumbled over themselves, entwining Bothwell.

"Please—" Bothwell said, trying to pull himself free. "I meant no harm, I will pay for the boat—" Even as he said it, he realized he was doomed, as he had not a penny on him.

"This boat isn't ours. Do you think we'll be thieves with you?" cried the woman.

The huge man had taken the oars and was rowing back to the harbour. Obviously the most important thing to them was to return the boat and cover up their activity, and nothing would dissuade them. One of them was probably married, or else the woman was supposed to be a virgin.

"Wait—please. Can you help me find another boat?" Bothwell pleaded.

"What for? What honest man would want a boat to row out to sea on Midsummer Night?"

"I—wish to meet my lover, too," he said quickly. "Her father keeps her so strictly. But I know that tonight she will be allowed out. I am poor; her father does not approve of me. But I am saving to start a smithy—"

The man stared at him. "Where is this girl?"

"In the next village. In"—oh, God, a name!—"Klagshamn."

"He speaks strangely," said the woman. "He is a foreigner."

"Yes," said Bothwell. " 'Tis true, I came on one of the Hansa ships, a sailor from Lübeck. But I stayed here—"

"A German! No wonder her father does not approve!" The man nodded his massive, bearlike head slowly.

"But love knows no boundaries," said Bothwell. "You can understand that!"

"Perhaps your brother's tiny boat—"

"No, he would be furious!" said the woman.

The man continued rowing inexorably back toward the shore. There were ominous noises from the wharf.

Bothwell turned to see a party of men with flaming torches standing at the end of the wharf. Some wore soldiers' uniforms, and they had harquebuses.

"You may let me out here," said Bothwell, pointing to the shore as far from the wharf as possible. He tried not to let panic enter his voice.

"What are all those men?" asked the rower. He took the boat back to its original spot and beached it. Then he and his lover started hurriedly pulling on their clothes.

Attempting to be polite, Bothwell nodded to them and climbed over the side of the boat. "Farewell," he said.

He made his way quickly over the pebbles into the almost-darkness on the farthest possible side of the wharf. But he could hear the search party coming to the little boat; they were questioning the couple. Then the hue and cry was raised.

Bothwell began running, trying to keep his balance on the rocky shore. If he could just get into those marshy reeds a hundred yards ahead. The prospect of crouching in them for hours was horrible, but it was his only hope. He stumbled along, keeping his head down. Behind him he could hear his pursuers.

He reached the edge of the marsh and splashed out into it. He ducked his head and swam underwater until he thought his lungs would burst. The marsh was full of weeds and goo, and sucked him down. Gasping for breath, he surfaced in an area of cattails and lilypads.

But behind him he heard dogs following him into the water, dogs expert in flushing game. They sent up exultant howls as they found him.

"It seems our guest has found his rooms inadequate," said Captain Kaas. The sun was streaming in the windows of his quarters; it was midmorning. Bothwell had been marched across the courtyard and then into the governor's quarters of the castle. It was the first time he had been inside them, and from the little windows he could see the harbour where he had failed so miserably. The merchant ships with their tall masts were rocking gently, and beyond were the small boats, and beyond them, the marsh. They looked so innocent and beckoning in the June sunshine.

Bothwell knew better than to answer or to plead.

"Yes," continued Kaas. "We tried to make him comfortable, gave him airy quarters with braziers in winter . . . yet he was dissatisfied. He has repaid our hospitality with ingratitude, trying to leave us without permission. This would have resulted in severe punishment for us, his hosts." He cast a doleful look at Bothwell. "It seems he had no thought of us."

The captain then walked briskly over to his desk and wrote out some orders. "It is with great regret that I grant your wish to leave us. There is

722

another prison which will cause you to look back on us with fondness. But 'tis ever true, as the poets say, that we never prize a thing till 'tis past. So, in due time you will prize your days at Malmö and wish to recapture them. But that will not be possible." He nodded to the two guards. "You will accompany the prisoner across the sound to his new accommodations. A wagon will be necessary for transport across Zeeland."

"Where am I to be taken, sir?" asked Bothwell.

"To the state prison of Dragsholm," answered Kaas.

Both guards gasped.

The wagon trundled across the flat plain that stretched west of Copenhagen, the watery reaches of reclaimed land called Zeeland. Bothwell rode along in it, his hands bound and tied behind him. He had a leg iron that secured him to a bolt in the bottom of the wagon, but he could stand up and look around as the oxen trudged onward.

The sky seemed like a freshly washed sheet held up to dry: taut and stretched. Birds wheeled overhead, taunting Bothwell with their freedom to fly. He revelled in the open air and space around him, and watched the wind passing gently over the flat fields of grain, whispering warm secrets. It made him long so acutely for the lost fields of the Borders that he could feel tears trying to spring up in his eyes. To ride out along those fields again, to gallop free, to see his dogs . . . He wondered how many litters the people on the moor had raised by now. If he had had the opportunity, he would have improved the breed, trying to create the perfect terrier—an indestructible, loyal, fierce fighter, like the best of the Border men.

It was almost fifty miles across Zeeland to Dragsholm, and the cart would take several days to reach it. The driver and the two guards stopped at small inns for refreshment, and permitted Bothwell to come in, too, although he had to wear his leg-chain. To eat, they allowed his hands to be untied, but they would allow him no knife to cut his cheese or bread. Instead, they cut it for him, like a child.

To simply sit in an inn, to have a cool mug of beer, to eat a meal: Bothwell did all these with the wonderment of a child, as well. He had never appreciated the glory of the most ordinary things like these. And he had a feeling he would never behold them again.

He was unable to make anyone tell him anything about Dragsholm, other than that it was a state prison, on the water, with Frans Lauridson its keeper. A man named Olluf Neilson was his assistant. Neither man had a title, which meant that the King had chosen keepers who were common people and owed their loyalty only to him, Bothwell deduced. That did not bode well for him, a nobleman. Such men often hated peers.

They approached Dragsholm, which reared up like a ship over the sea of grainfields and woodlands on the landed side. With every jolt of the wagon, the high keep seemed to grow higher, and the grey, forbidding walls came into view. The little fortress was revealed at last.

The wagon halted before the heavily fortified gate, with its portcullis and guardhouse. The guards checked their papers and then laboriously pulled the doors open and let them rumble through.

There was a small, grassy courtyard and a bleak stone tower in one corner. They waited until a man walked smartly over to them and said something in Danish so rapidly that Bothwell could not follow. Papers were handed to him, and he read them carefully. Only when he was finished did he look up and observe Bothwell.

Their eyes locked. This man had narrow blue eyes and wrinkles at the corners of his eyelids. He looked as if he had spent a large portion of his time outdoors, perhaps even as a sailor. "Captain Lauridson," he said, nodding at Bothwell.

"The Earl of Bothwell," Bothwell answered.

More rapid Danish followed. Then Lauridson motioned to two soldiers standing guard at the door of the tower. They came quickly over, mounted the wagon, and, taking Bothwell by both arms, lifted him down. Then they marched him over to the door in the tower.

He had only time to notice that the walls were very thick, and glance up at the upstairs windows, before he had to step inside. It was cold and dark in there, despite the brightness of the day outside. But in a moment his eyes grew used to it. He could see light coming from the upper rooms. He prepared to climb the steps.

"No!" They took his arms and turned him round. A third man pulled the ring of a trap door in the floor; groaning, he opened up the heavy stone lid.

"Here!" One of the men thrust a torch down.

There was a dungeon room, completely without natural light, waiting. They lowered a ladder, and one of them descended. Then Bothwell was made to follow. The cold hit him like an icy hand. He looked about; there was a thick oak post in the middle of the room. The floor was dirt.

"Now," said one of the men, and they forced him over to the post. He fought as best he could with both hands tied behind him, but they quickly snapped a short chain bolted to the base of the post onto his leg iron. Thus shackled, he could only go halfway round the post, like a chained bear. They cut his hands free and stood back.

The ladder creaked as Captain Lauridson descended. He strode over and looked critically at Bothwell. "Now, my good friend, you may put any hope of escape from your mind. The last man who tried it hanged himself in despair after he was recaptured. He is buried right under the gallows."

He raised his torch and stuck it in a wall bracket. "I will leave this here so you may see your surroundings. It will burn another two hours. Look carefully while you still may." He nodded. "Good day, Your Grace."

The keeper and his guards climbed back up the ladder, and the stone door clanged shut from above. Bothwell was left alone in the dungeon, waiting for the darkness to swallow him up.

XI

The sound of the drumroll from the outer courtyard at its customary six o'clock did not wake Mary; she had been lying awake since the hour when, although it is still dark, night changes imperceptibly into morning. Her pain kept her awake, the rheumatism and swollen joints that were constant now, even in the summer.

But the drumroll meant that the rest of her household would now begin stirring. Mary Seton would sit up promptly as she always did, as alert as a soldier in the field, and rise from the bed where she always slept near her mistress. The little dogs would stir, eager to be fed and walked. In the connecting maze of rooms at Sheffield Manor, Mary's secretaries, her physician, her pages and valets and *femmes de chambre* would begin their unchanging round of duties: keeping a little court that went through all the motions and protocol of a real court, but which was invisible to the outside world. They performed their rituals and tasks to no audience but themselves, for the aim of Queen Elizabeth was that for all intents and purposes no one in the countryside should be aware of the presence of the Queen of Scots in their midst.

She was not allowed to go beyond the great octagonal towers that guarded the gates of the manor, and no one was allowed in to see her. So she kept state in isolation, a Queen with no audience to grant in her audience chamber, and with only her own presence in the presence chamber with its throne and cloth of estate. Male courts-in-exile had traditionally been busy places; but the only female court-in-exile in European history was a tomblike establishment, sealed shut.

Mary Seton was removing the covers on the bird cages, and immediately the turtledoves and barbary-fowl began cooing and chirping. Mary's aviary was growing: the Guises sent her tame birds, and Philip promised to send canaries and parrots, although he had not. Philip was slow to keep all promises. "If Death came from Spain, we should all live to a very great age," went a common saying. It was frustrating to continue to importune Philip, but she dared not cross him. Perhaps someday the canaries would come.

"Ah, Seton, good morning," said Mary, rising from the bed. Her knees throbbed and hurt as she put her weight on them.

Seton brought over two dresses for her to choose from: one was stark black, the other grey, trimmed with jet braids. Mary started to choose the black, but Seton said, "Oh, Your Majesty, 'tis a warm June day! Be a *little* lighthearted! Choose grey!"

Mary smiled and agreed. She never wore colours anymore; all her gowns were black, white, grey, or violet, the colours of mourning. She softened the costume with a long, filmy white veil that fell below her shoulders. But then she always added a heavy piece of religious jewellery: a huge gold rosary, an Agnus Dei of rock crystal engraved with the Passion.

If only Ronsard could now behold me, she thought. If only *anyone* could now behold me. I go through the motions of my life completely concealed from the eyes of the outside world. Would Ronsard even recognize me as I am now? He remembers the girl at the French court; the black-clad captive invalid is another person entirely. I do not even show my own hair anymore; as if it, too, were in mourning, it never grew thick again after I cut it. And now it is growing grey, although I am only thirty-two.

Ronsard had addressed a poem to Queen Elizabeth. It went:

> *Queen, you who imprison a Queen so rare,*
> *Soften your wrath and change your mind,*
> *The sun from its rising to its sinking to sleep*
> *Views no more barbarous act on this earth!*
> *People, your degenerate lack of will to fight*
> *Shames your forebears, Renauld, Lancelot, and Roland,*
> *Who with glad hearts took up ladies' wrongs*
> *And guarded them, and rescued them—where you, Frenchmen,*
> *Have not dared to look at or to touch your arms,*
> *To save from slavery such a lovely Queen!*

Elizabeth was angered at this poetic call to arms, and had Mary guarded more strictly than ever. But she need not have concerned herself about the French. Their treaty with her showed that they would never stir for Mary.

"I will wear the red-brown wig today," she told Seton, and seated herself to have her hair dressed. Seton was adept at pinning up Mary's hair—after carefully brushing it and massaging the scalp—and adjusting the wig, curling the strands of hair until it looked entirely natural. No one in the outer rooms knew the hair was not her own. Anthony Babington was always praising its lustrous beauty. If only it were hers!

Once it was, she thought. Once my hair was as beautiful as you believe it now is.

Anthony had remained her page, although he was fast approaching the age when he would be sent away. He was fifteen now, grown tall and staggeringly handsome with vivid black-and-white colouring. She and he had worked together on all manner of smuggling out messages: stuffing them into high-heeled slippers in place of hollowed-out cork, inserting them between layers of wood in trunks and coffers. They devised a method of sending messages in books, in which the invisible writing was only between the lines on every fourth page; the books so treated bore a green satin bookmark, and were included in a shipment of other books. Alum-treated cloth would always be an odd length, to mark it for the addressee. Anthony reveled in these games, for he saw himself as a knight helping a captive queen—as Ronsard had begged his laggard countrymen to do.

Anthony believed she would be rescued. Did she? Or was it merely something she felt duty-bound to keep trying, as if to give up entirely would be to wither into nothingness? Since the Parliament that had cried for her death, and caused the Duke of Norfolk to go to his, her life had been relatively quiet. In the three years since then, there had been no rescue attempts, no plots, no plans. The only thing that had become startlingly clear was that the only possible help would come from Spain. The native English sympathizers had not the strength to do it, as the Northern Rising had proved, and the French, awash in their religious wars, were drowning in their own blood.

And so she dutifully courted Philip as her rescuer, her hope. She had grieved for the Duke of Norfolk, although she had never met him. He had represented her one chance to make a respectable exit from her confinement, and with him perished her only English escape route. Now she was forced into what the English would call treason—dealing with the Spanish.

But letters were only letters, and so far nothing had happened to disturb the placid succession of days in Sheffield.

Abroad, death continued to cut down the Valois: Charles IX died of a wasting disease—some said of anguished remorse for the St. Bartholomew's Day Massacre—and was succeeded by Henri III. And Mary's uncle, the Cardinal of Lorraine, went to meet his Maker, trailing satins and silks and perfumes. Heaven—or Hell—would be a more refined place now.

The bell was ringing softly, calling the household to prayer. Mary and her attendants went out into the presence chamber, which was the largest room available to them, and waited while the rest of the forty-odd members came in. There was Bourgoing, the physician; Andrew Beaton, the brother of John, who had died since their exile; Bastian Pages; Claud Nau; Andrew Melville, her master of the household; Gourion, her surgeon; Gervois, her apothecary; Balthazzar, her old, infirm French tailor; Anthony Babington; and Willie Douglas, a grown man of twenty-two now. Her women—Seton, Jane Kennedy, Marie Courcelles, and old Madame Rallay—made a half-circle around her in front of the French priest, Camille de Préau, who was officially in the guise of an almoner and had replaced the English one.

Father de Préau swept in, the silver pin in his hat gleaming.

He looks the way we all used to, Mary thought. He does not look like a captive or an exile yet. But then, he is free to go.

She looked around at all her household. They are all free to go, she thought. Every person here can pack his bag, notify the Earl of Shrewsbury that he has decided to leave, and have the gates swing open for him. Only I cannot leave—I alone.

Father de Préau led the prayers in French. As some of the members of the household were Protestants, Mary always insisted that the readings and prayers be ones that they could participate in. Private mass and confessions would take place in her chamber at other times.

"Saint Paul says, in the second book of Corinthians, 'We are troubled on every side, yet not distressed; we are perplexed, but not in despair; persecuted, but not forsaken; cast down, but not destroyed. For our light affliction, which is but for a moment, worketh for us a far more exceeding and eternal weight of glory.' My friends, my brothers and sisters, take heart!" the priest enjoined them.

Mary felt the nagging voice that had been troubling her of late: Is all this to be rewarded? Or is that just a vain hope, something to make each day bearable? "For there is no work, nor device, nor knowledge, nor wisdom, in the grave, whither thou goest," the Scripture also says. If there is nothing hereafter, then I am a pitiable fool and suffering means nothing.

The prayers were over; now the household would go about its repetitious tasks until time for dinner at eleven o'clock. Shrewsbury's people dined then, too, and the gates were locked during that hour.

Mary and her ladies retired to her suite of rooms, there to work on their needlepoint. They embroidered ceaselessly, and there were now embroidered stools, bed hangings, pillows, and panels everywhere. Mary made gifts for Elizabeth—caps and petticoats—and sent her French relatives little mementoes. It was a way of reminding them of her existence.

Today she was working on an elaborate set of genealogical bed hangings to be sent to her son, James. On a field of rich emerald green, they traced her ancestry in France and Lorraine, showing Charlemagne and Saint Louis. James must be reminded of that side of his family and his glorious inheritance.

She picked up the gold thread that would be used to indicate shiny surfaces of shields, swords, helmets. James was almost ten now, and in the custody of the Earl of Morton. The poor child, she thought, he is as much a prisoner as I. With this difference: that every year that passes brings him closer to freedom, whereas my hope of it recedes. Some day he will be a grown man and can dismiss his warders and gaolers as he pleases.

Mary had written him and sent him gifts over the years, but never received a reply. Still she continued, never knowing what became of her missives. She had already written the letter that was to accompany this gift, labouring over the wording. She called him to be faithful to God and to remember his mother, "she who has borne you in her sides."

She sighed and rubbed her eyes. They were bothering her of late. She spent so many hours focusing on close work, sewing, reading, and writing, that she was straining them. She could feel the muscles in her forehead relax when she looked up.

I must stop squinting, she told herself.

She motioned to her little spaniels to come over to her, and they trotted quickly, their nails clicking on the smooth floor, their tongues hanging out. She had come to rely on them as children to amuse her. They alone seemed happy in this place.

"Yes, my dears," she said. "I believe there will be chicken at dinner, and possibly mutton. I will bring you some."

The bell signalled dinnertime, as it did every day, day after day after day. The ladies rose and went into the hall, where white cloths were spread over long tables. They never ate with Shrewsbury's retainers in the Great Hall; the two households must never mingle.

As always, there were sixteen dishes to prepare—seven meat, three vegetable, three soups, three sweet desserts. It never varied. Like sleepwalkers, they partook of the meal they had already partaken of so many times. Yesterday, today, tomorrow—it was all one.

Now I know what eternity is, Mary thought. Some wag once said, "Eternity is two people and a haunch of venison." But he has never had his forty people and sixteen perpetual dishes.

They rose. The men would attend to their tasks, stretching them out as long as possible to fill the hours. The coachmen would polish the coach wheels, still shiny from yesterday's polishing, since they had travelled nowhere. The apothecary would rearrange his bottles, moving the powdered mandrake root to the place where the tinctures of Solomon's seal and milkwort had stood. The *femmes de chambre* would air and brush the Queen's dresses, still fresh from yesterday's airing, and put them back in their proper places. They would refold all the clothes that were already perfectly folded. The grooms would take the Queen's three horses out for exercise—exercise she was not allowed to give them. The secretaries would stack the writing paper and trim the sealing wax. There were still at least ten hours to get through before they could sleep, to begin all over again the next morning.

As Mary walked slowly, painfully, back to her rooms, she wondered if she should sew this afternoon, or read a history. Or perhaps she could get permission to walk her little dogs in the inner courtyard. But her knees and ankles were bothering her so that even a short walk would be trying. And her head was aching.

"Madam," said Bourgoing, hobbling up beside her, "I notice your steps are especially slow today."

She looked at him with amusement. He had shrunk over the years, becoming stooped and gnomelike. His gout was far worse than hers.

"Your pains are worse than mine, friend," she said. "Yet I do admit, my legs ache today. Is it for this you preserved me from the scars of smallpox?" She made sure to laugh as she said it, so he would know she was teasing.

"Have you received *any* word from the Queen as to when you may go to Buxton?" he asked.

"Yes—when cherries ripen in January, and pigs dance the galliard," she replied.

"Surely she is not so cruel! Shrewsbury goes regularly!"

"Yes, but she says I may escape, and that even his new quarters there are not secure enough. It must be a stout prison to hold a woman crippled with gout and rheumatism, you know."

"Write to her again!" he said.

"I have written at least fifteen times on the subject. I have no new approach for the sixteenth time, I fear." Mary smiled. "I must content myself with your hot wax treatments. Truly, they do help."

Together they traversed the gallery where she had hung portraits of her Scottish ancestors, and were just on the verge of entering her private apartments when Anthony came running up.

"A messenger from Scotland!" he cried. He pointed down at the courtyard, where a dusty man, carrying a large covered basket, was talking to the guards. There was much gesturing. Finally the rider took out a letter and let the guard read it. Only after he and two others had read it was the man allowed to dismount and enter the building, escorted by yet another guard.

Mary stood and waited; the man and his companion made their way down the gallery toward her.

"Most gracious sovereign," the messenger said, kneeling and removing his hat. "I come from Lady Bothwell, your husband's mother. His—late mother."

Lady Bothwell! Mary had never met her, but she knew Bothwell had taken his stubborn courage from his mother, who had stood her ground after his father had so cravenly discarded her. As the Lady of Morham, she had held her head high and watched as her erstwhile spouse met an ignominious end, never gloating, but never shrinking, either. Bothwell had spoken often of her, and she knew he visited her.

The *late* Lady Bothwell, had he said?

"She has died?" asked Mary. "It grieves me to know." She gestured for him to follow her into her privy chamber.

Once inside, she asked him for the letter. He put down the basket and gave her the letter, apologizing for its having been opened.

"I saw the reason," Mary said. "All mail that comes openly to me is treated thus. That is why I—we"—she nodded at Anthony and Monsieur Nau, who had been waiting in the room—"maintain another line of communication . . . one that is, alas, often shut down."

She opened the letter herself and read.

My most *esteemed sovereign and daughter,*
My time on earth drawing to its close, it is meet that I set my worldly affairs in order. Thus it is that I am drawing up my will, and mean to bequeath my belongings to William Hepburn, my natural grandson, who has lived near me during his lifetime. My land I leave to my widowed daughter Janet. I tell you this so that, should you be able to communicate with my son James your husband, he will know.

Having lived so many years as I have, seeing much sorrow yet much of joy, I am ready to take my leave of it all in peace. I regret only a very few things, one of them being that I never saw you as my son's wife, you being spirited away so soon, and he following not long after.

It grieves my heart as a mother to know her son lies in prison across the seas, and separated from his wife. I wish to give you something of his, in a manner of speaking. As a boy he had an especial affinity for dogs, which I am proud to say he took from me. Some years ago he sent me two Skye terriers. They thrived, and these pups are their great-grand-pups. I am told that you are fond of little dogs and already have several pets, so I hope these will find a welcome home with you as a remembrance of him.

The Skye terrier, as you may suppose, I was told came originally from Skye. They will not grow very big, only some eight inches or so. As they grow up, their hair will get longer and longer until some say "you canna see the dog for the hair." But let not that fool you. They are no dandies like the curly-haired fops at French courts, but are strong, fearless trackers of game, can burrow, and swim in treacherous waters. They are one-person dogs and fiercely loyal. But one warning: if they are unsure of their master's love, they can fall into a melancholy.

I now take my leave of you and of this world, begging it to treat you well, and in lieu of my James, to take unto you these his "relicts."

Agnes Sinclair, Lady Bothwell of Morham

Mary felt her eyes clouding over with tears. The courage of the old lady, the sanguine acceptance of all . . . it was poignant. She quickly folded the letter and turned to the basket. These were the descendants of the dogs from the cottage on the moor!

"So you have carried pups all the way from Scotland," she said to the messenger. "It must have seemed a long journey!"

"Nay, they were no trouble," he said, unlatching the lid of the hinged basket and revealing three pups inside, all of different colours: black, cream, and grey. They began whining and squirming as soon as they saw the light.

"They are just lately weaned," he said. "Lady Bothwell died before she had meant them to be sent, but I took them anyway, before they could be lost in the confusion."

Mary lifted out the black one. "What peculiar ears! They are beginning to stick up like a sail!"

"Yes, in the mother they were spread out like two high sails atop her head, just perched there. Of course the hair will get longer."

"Is it really as long as she said?"

"It drags the ground, Your Majesty."

She remembered the ones in the house on the moor. Yes, they had had hair that looked like the caparisons of horses. She laughed. "They are welcome in our household. But they will have to make their peace with the French spaniels."

"French and Scots have ever had a strange marriage," said the messenger.

"Tell me—when and how did she die?"

"Of extreme old age, is the only ailment I know. She was always healthy, and then just slowly began to—fade. Like the colours of a gown left out to dry in the hot sun; everything grows fainter. Her skin got paler, her grip looser, her eyesight weaker . . . and her hearing became very bad. Even the barking of the dogs she couldn't hear! It took her longer to walk across a room, longer to wake up, and then, one day, she didn't wake up. It was very simple, like a ripe apple falling from a tree—or rather, an overripe apple giving up the ghost at last."

Mary crossed herself. "May God grant us such a comfortable death! An easy death—such a great gift! And did she know this was coming?"

"It would seem so, in the orderly way she took her leave of everything, even down to providing for the puppies."

An easy death . . . an orderly death . . . God must have loved her, thought Mary.

The afternoon passed slowly as Mary Seton, Jane, and Marie did their embroidery, sitting on their already embroidered stools around their mistress. In this series of panels—where, oh, where would they put them?—they were depicting animals, exotic ones. There was a toucan from America, a unicorn, a monkey, and a phoenix. Mary herself was working on a scarlet petticoat embroidered with silver flowers, which she planned to send to Elizabeth. It was a very ambitious work, involving an entire border of intricate flowers, stems, and leaves. Perhaps it would soften Elizabeth's heart.

How could she actually wear something made with my own hands and still not see me as a real, breathing person? Mary thought as she pulled the hard silver threads in and out.

The sun warmed the chamber, and even with the casement windows wide open, the women grew drowsy. Mary put aside her sewing and decided to read instead. She had marked her place in *Lancilot de Laik* just where Lancelot and Guinevere had become lovers. She was determined to get through it for the first time since Bothwell had entered her life. She had hated knowing that after the falling in love came the reckoning with King Arthur and then the sentence of burning. . . .

Burn the whore!

But they didn't burn me, she told herself, and Darnley was no kindly, noble King Arthur. . . .

She found herself fighting sleep by the late afternoon and lay down to rest. She knew she would fall asleep and hated to give in to it, for it meant she would be up late again. The cycle must somehow be broken, but there was no incentive to do so. The hours of captivity somehow seemed friendlier and softer late at night, playing cards and talking in low voices in the candlelight. It was easier to imagine she was up late at Fontainebleau or Holyrood, surrounded by her intimates after everyone else had gone to bed. . . . She slept, one arm across her eyes, and dreamed of Lancelot and his lake, and the Lady of the Lake and Arthur's sword, dripping with water, then with blood. She awoke with a gasp.

Just then she heard the drumroll again from the outer courtyard. The sound of evening; another day had dragged itself through and now was to be locked away. Another day to be recorded and its good and bad totted up, blemishes and brightnesses of souls to beam out for eternity. Some people had died today and were even now having to face a roll call of all their days—this day that seemed so very ordinary to her. *Be with us now and in the hour of our death.*

732

She forced herself to stand up, shake her head, clear it. It would soon be time for supper, with its reduced number of dishes and lessened ceremony. She had no appetite for it, but she must take her place at the table.

After dinner, the ladies retired back to their chamber. Mary took up *Lancelot* again until the household gathered for evening prayers.

Again they arranged themselves in the largest chamber and listened while the priest intoned Psalms.

" 'My God, my God, look upon me; why hast Thou forsaken me, and art so far from my health, and from the words of my complaint?' "

The light was fading in the chamber, and they all kept silent and then filed away back to their rooms.

There the women would read a bit, once again tidy their things, and then, yawning with the intense debilitation of having done nothing all day, take to their beds and try to sleep. Nau and Andrew Beaton would go over their books, making neat entries in the proper columns, then close them and put them away. Willie Douglas, Bastian Pages, Anthony, the coachmen, the grooms, and the ushers would gather in a corner of the gallery and play cards until late at night. Sometimes Mary and her women would join them.

But not tonight.

My heart is so strangely heavy tonight, she thought, as she prepared for bed. I do not wish to have any company.

She could hear sounds of the armed guards at their posts, keeping watch over the entrance to the royal apartments, as they did every night when the great outer gates were closed. Some of them were laughing and talking. Why shouldn't they? she thought. They were young and the night was warm and starry.

She lay down on the bed and lighted the single candle that was affixed to her headboard. She closed her eyes and prayed to be able to sleep, to let the hours pass unnoticed and uncounted.

In eight hours the morning drumroll sounded, and another day began.

❧

One day in high summer, the tedium was broken after dinner when the Earl of Shrewsbury paid a formal visit to Mary, being duly announced by her page.

"Ah! My dear Shrewsbury!" Mary greeted him with uplifted hands.

She and Shrewsbury had a unique relationship. On the one hand, it had all the cosiness of those living in close proximity, the camaraderie that springs up in spite of itself in enforced companionship. On the other, it had all the distrust of warden and prisoner, made more complex by yet another factor: in acting as her gaoler, Shrewsbury had doomed himself to a sort of house arrest himself, as he could never leave and go to court. So she, in a sense, was also his gaoler. Beyond that, there was always the unspoken knowledge that, in the twinkling of an eye, in the sudden onset of fever, in a dry cough that turned into something else, Elizabeth could die and Mary be Queen of England. It might be his sovereign that Shrewsbury was now facing.

"Madam, I bring good news." He held out a letter.

Mary saw the green wax of the official English seal. She ripped it open.

"She gives me permission to go to Buxton!" In her excitement, she almost hugged Shrewsbury.

"I know." He held up his letter. "I am pleased."

Mary said, "I am so grateful."

"We can leave next week," he said. "I will make sure that your quarters are in order. I—look forward to it, Your Majesty." With a shy smile, he bowed.

In her coach, bumping its way along the rutted excuse for roads, Mary looked eagerly out at the countryside as she was transported the twenty miles between Sheffield and Buxton. She was alone, except of course for Mary Seton and Shrewsbury, who was riding along ahead, greeting all the people who lined the road to glimpse their overlord.

He had ordered Mary to keep the shades drawn in the coach, not to stare out, and above all, not to make any gestures to the people. But she had rolled up one corner of the shades and peeked out. The closed coach was drawing almost as much attention as if she had been leaning out and waving.

"The Scots Queen!" they whispered, pointing. They stood on tiptoe and tried to catch a glimpse inside. "Has anyone seen her?" they asked. Little boys ran after the coach and tried to jump up on it, and had to be shoved off by the guards. Shrewsbury was met with cries of "Show her! Show your captive Queen!" He rode on, ignoring the calls, but dreading the stir that was going to be caused in Buxton.

Queen Elizabeth had given lengthy and detailed instructions, but what they amounted to was that Mary must be kept in strictest isolation. It could not be helped that she would have an opportunity to see others during her bathing times at the warm spring itself, but as for all the rest of the socializing—the walks, the games of bowling, the hawking—she was not to participate. There were to be no strangers coming and going from Buxton, Mary must give an hour's notice preparatory to leaving her rooms, and she was to have no visitors after nine at night.

Meanwhile, Queen Elizabeth herself would be on progress in the Midlands, and might—just *might*—come to Buxton herself. If she did, she would expect to find her instructions being followed to the letter.

Shrewsbury sighed. He did not know whether to hope she came, or hope she did not.

The warm springs of Buxton were held to cure an array of illnesses, from rickets to weak sinews, from ringworm to "hypochondriac winds," but were most known for the soothing of aching limbs. The waters here were not scalding hot, as were the ones at Bath, and so were more attractive to the infirm. They gushed from deep springs into a covered bath house with marble seats built all around the pool, so that the patients could sit and soak in the waters for two or three hours, while their clothes were being aired. In addition to this the cure-seekers were to drink the waters obtained from St. Anne's well, starting out with three pints a day and working their way up to eight pints; the various prescribed courses were fourteen days, twenty days, and forty days.

After leaving the waters, and dressing in his freshly aired clothes, the patient was expected to exercise. The stronger men could hawk, shoot, and bowl; sicklier men and all women must confine themselves to a gentle version of bowling that involved a board with slots.

Men at court like Cecil, who were unable to attend at that time, drank from barrels of Buxton water specially sent down for medicinal purposes. Dudley, too, was a devotee of the waters.

They arrived, and Mary was helped from the carriage into her quarters in the new four-storey hostelry that could accommodate thirty people, owned by Shrewsbury. In truth, Bess owned Buxton itself, and had established a schedule of fees to be collected from the patients; half was to be given to the poor, and the other half paid to the resident physician on duty there. There was a buzz of voices; the lodge was a busy place and a centre of activity. The buzz turned into silence as the Queen of Scots made her way through the common rooms and up to her apartments.

She was relieved to get to her rooms. She had hated the staring; for the first time she was hideously aware of how she must appear to others now: stooped, infirm, older than her years. It was a novel, unwelcome feeling. She had always taken her grace and allure for granted, until now, when it had abruptly vanished. Perhaps it would be better if she had not come.

First my reputation is ruined by the printing of the casket letters, then my faith is besmirched by the St. Bartholomew's Day massacre, next my cause is wrecked by the final fall of Edinburgh, and now even my last possession, my beauty, has been snatched away in the common mind, she thought. I do not mind losing it so much for myself, but as a spur to action. People are more likely to help a beautiful poor prisoner than an ugly poor prisoner. And . . . if ever I see Bothwell again, I do not want him to see me ugly.

She looked at her reflection in the glass of the windowpanes. From a distance, and in the wavering glass, she still looked fetching. But she knew that in the light of day, and close up, she was no such thing, at least not in the eyes of strangers.

Mary put on her white bathing robe and gingerly made her way to the edge of the pool. She stuck her foot in it, and found it to be pleasantly warm and caressing, so she eased herself down and took her place on the underwater bench. The waters lapped up around her shoulders; gentle steam rose and settled in a mist on her face. Her ankles and knees, so swollen in the mornings that sometimes she could hardly bend them to arise, now began to tingle and loosen in the warm, circulating streams. She extended her legs to flex the muscles, which often had spasms and became stiff. She sighed and put her head back.

There were only a few other bathers there that morning—an old woman with a skin affliction of some sort, a man who looked swollen with dropsy, and a thin boy who kept wheezing with asthma. They looked at her with eyes dulled with pain and did not seem to recognize in her anything but a fellow sufferer.

After her bathing, and her slow walk within her own quarters, and a light supper—for the regimen imposed a semi-fast—she was put to bed with two pigs' bladders filled with hot water, so that she might sweat. The heat had already proved therapeutic; her limbs had relaxed their tightness. And her headaches had ebbed away.

Shrewsbury stopped in to see her, but she begged him to excuse her for not leaving her bed.

"God forbid I should interrupt Your Majesty's treatment, for which we have journeyed here!" he said. "I see that you are smiling; are you in less pain?"

"Indeed I am. I do believe I may be cured here."

"Here is some news to lighten you further. I have just received word that Her Glorious Majesty Queen Elizabeth is nearby at Kenilworth, only some sixty miles away."

"Sixty miles!" Mary said. "The closest we have ever come!"

"You may come closer yet," he said. "She plans to journey afterward to Chartley Castle, only thirty-four miles from here. And then, perhaps—to Buxton itself."

"Here? Then I may, at last, meet her face to face?"

"It is possible, Your Majesty. Entirely possible."

Elizabeth! To meet her now—and in this condition!

"I pray it may be so," said Mary.

"It is in the hands of the gods—specifically the pagan ones Robert Dudley has summoned to meet him and his Queen at Kenilworth."

XII

 he Faerie Queen was passing through the outer courtyard of Kenilworth, beneath the azure-painted astronomical clock in Caesar's Tower, when delicate, angelic voices began to sing of her divine beauty. Elizabeth—attired in such stiff and shining brocade that she could not turn in the saddle, encased in an armour of cloth-of-gold, pearls, and precious stones, her head framed by a starched ruff that stuck up like a lacy sail—looked up to see a young boy, dressed as Cupid, suspended by a gold-painted rope over the clock's face. He was touching the hands, stopping the clock.

"For you, O Gloriana, fairest Virgin Queen, time shall stand by and cease to run, whilst you are here amongst us!" chorused the voices.

"You see, my beloved?" said Robert, riding beside her. "Even Time is your obedient and adoring subject."

She smiled and continued on her way in to her quarters. It was twilight, a drowsy summer twilight, and she had come at last to Kenilworth, dear Robert's monumental estate in Warwickshire, "the navel of England." She had given it to him, as was her prerogative to present it to her favourite, ten years earlier. But although she knew that he had enlarged it and made many alterations, she had never journeyed to see it. Now she was to be his guest—she and three hundred of her courtiers on progress with her—for the lengthy period of seventeen days. He had promised that she would leave the ordinary world behind and enter one that he had created especially for her.

"You will not be disappointed, my heart," he had said. "Only come and do me the honour of setting foot in my world!"

He had met her when she was still seven miles away, feasting her and her company in a golden tent so large it took seven carts to haul it away after it was dismantled. They had hunted, using bow and arrow, all the way to Kenilworth. Then, as Elizabeth had approached the artificial ornamental lake, a lighted "island" had floated up, and riding on it was a Nereid, who called, "I am the lady of this pleasant lake. Come, refresh yourself!"

A sibyl beside her, dressed in a floating white gown, prophesied, "Health, prosperity, and felicity to Your Majesty!"

And suddenly trumpeters of superhuman size, dressed in Arthurian costumes, blared out a fanfare from the ramparts.

"The legend is that this was one of King Arthur's castles," said Robert. "And so our lake must have a lady, too."

Guns blasted out a salute, and then Elizabeth passed over a temporary bridge, guarded by Hercules and other gods and goddesses stationed at each of the seven pillars: Jupiter, who promised due season and fair weather; Luna, who promised to shine nightly; Ceres, who promised the malt for beer; Bacchus, full cups everywhere; Aeolus, to hold up winds and keep back tempests; Mercury, the entertainment of poets and players, and Diana, good hunting. From the huge windows on the new addition, light flooded out and illuminated the outdoors, like a gigantic lantern.

Elizabeth turned to Robert as the clock hands were being stopped. "If only we could command it so!" she said.

"Believe it!" he urged.

But she could look over at him and see that he himself was touched by time. His youthful suppleness was being replaced by a certain hardening of his form; his face was often red, and his gorgeous red-brown hair was thinning and fading. *My Robert,* she thought. *If it were truly in my power, I would keep time's hands from holding you.*

They passed indoors, and Elizabeth was astounded at the gleaming wooden floors, the high ceilings, the huge gallery, a Turkey carpet at least fifty feet long with delicate blue background. Everywhere the eye could see, there was light; crystal candlesticks glittered by the hundreds.

"This is . . . truly enchanting," she finally said. She had never built any palaces herself, and so none of her royal dwellings were this modern, with the huge windows, wide staircases, and galleries the size of a London street.

"It was all built just in hopes that you might glorify it for one instant," he said.

And she knew that, in one sense, this was true.

It was the height of summer, July, with heat simmering on the horizon, and each leaf on the trees still and covered with dust. All of time did seem suspended, even the seasons themselves: summer trembling on its very apex, pausing just to breathe in and out before descending into autumn. Ripeness pervaded the air, the feeling of vegetation being at its prime, its greenest, its fattest, its heaviest.

Every day there were diversions and entertainments in the beguiling Country of Nowhere that Robert Dudley had created. There was dancing in the enclosed garden, an acre of fragrant flower beds, with obelisks, spheres, and a marble fountain with figures of Neptune and Thetis that squirted people roguishly. A classic temple abutted the garden, its pillars painted to look like precious stones, and a net enclosing it turned it into an aviary where exotic birds from Europe and Africa sang and preened.

There was hunting in the chase, of the hart and red deer. As they returned, they were met by Wodwose, a wild man of the forest, covered all over with leaves and moss, who uttered praises to the Queen.

There was a special play reenacting the raids of the Danes on East England hundreds of years earlier. There was one day devoted to "country pleasures," with a mock "bridal party," a morris dance, running at the quintain. There was a ferocious bear-baiting with thirteen bears and packs of mastiffs. One day was set aside for "queenly ceremony," in which five men were knighted and the Queen touched nine sufferers of the "king's evil" to cure them of their scrofula.

In the evenings there were banquets, including one that featured more than three hundred different dishes, followed by fireworks displays that not only lit up the skies but hit the waters of the lake without being extinguished, so that the waters glowed. There was a masque by Gascoigne, and an Italian contortionist who seemed to have no human backbone at all, but to be made only of cords.

The most stunning and elaborate event was a water pageant depicting "The Delivery of the Lady of the Lake," and involving a mermaid with a twelve-foot tail, and Triton and Arion, who rode to the rescue on an unusual dolphin: one that had a choir and orchestra inside. As Arion approached the Queen, mounted on horseback, he climbed to the very top of the dolphin's back and began to recite his piece.

"O fairest, O rarest," he cried. "O Goddess Divine!" Then there was a long pause. The mermaid made signals to him. But Arion just stood there, until at last he growled and ripped off his mask. "I am no Arion, not I, but just honest Harry Goldingham!" he said.

The Queen roared with laughter, and pronounced it her favourite entertainment.

The seventeen days were over, and the royal party was making preparations for leaving. Even the weather had obeyed their desires, and nothing rough or unpleasant had intruded, as Jupiter had promised.

Elizabeth's master of the household had already been sent ahead to Chartley, the home of the Earl and Countess of Essex.

"It will be the farthest north I have ever gone," said Elizabeth, "although it is still only a hundred and twenty miles from London."

"And where after Chartley?" asked Hatton. "Will you proceed even farther north?"

"Perhaps." There was Buxton, about thirty-five miles north of that. Buxton—where the thermal waters were. And Mary, the Queen of Scots.

I could go there, see her at last. It would not be the same as receiving her in London, at court. It could be impromptu, unrehearsed, just an afterthought in a packed itinerary. . . . If I saw her, perhaps at last the spell would be broken, and she would be just a woman to me, not a symbol.

I will sleep on it, she thought. And I will decide as I ride out tomorrow.

The next morning, as the party passed out across the bridge with its sad gods and goddesses bidding farewell, and as Cupid released the clock hands to start them moving again, Elizabeth looked out at the high towers of Kenilworth, and felt as if she were leaving Camelot.

Sylvanus, god of the woods, emerged from the rows of trees, and began reciting verse to express his unhappiness at losing them, promising to double the number of deer and make a continual spring in the gardens if only she would never leave. From an arbour of holly at the end of the avenue, a character proclaiming himself Deep Desire, a messenger from the Council Chamber of Heaven, begged them to stay.

Underneath his costume Elizabeth could see that he was a husky local man, probably a farmer or a smith. She remembered Harry Goldingham, and his red-faced embarrassment at playing Arion and forgetting his lines. Perhaps it was best not to gaze too closely on legends.

"I will not be going farther north," she suddenly said to Hatton.

She would not go to Buxton, no; Mary was better left ungazed upon.

XIII

S ten hated helping his grandfather make his rounds of chores in the courtyard of Dragsholm. They were all unpleasant: shovelling manure, feeding the mastiffs and mules, checking underneath the gallows for weasels and snakes. But his family had always been in charge of maintaining the courtyard, and someday he, too, would take over this task.

The smell of the nearby sea was especially strong this morning, with a brisk wind coming off the water. It was April, and the skies were piercingly blue. The land was awakening from its winter sleep, and the already plowed furrows gave off the characteristic odour of fresh-turned earth that promised so much. As he tramped around the courtyard, Sten was glad, at least, that he worked outdoors. How dreadful it would be never to go outside, to have to do all your work in a room, at a desk, like a schoolmaster or an engraver or a moneylender. Or not to do anything, but just *be* there . . .

"Grandfather, is this the morning we feed the prisoners?" he suddenly asked. That was the worst task of all. He hated shoving the wooden plates in under the doors and hearing the scuffling as someone reached for it.

"Yes, shortly we will do it. Tell the cook to ready the portions, cut the bread in chunks."

The prisoners got bread, ale, and the leftovers from the garrison mess.

An hour later Sten trudged along behind his grandfather, holding a stack of filled plates. Before each door—thick and heavily locked and bolted—there was a tiny slot just wide enough to allow a plate to pass through. "Food!" his grandfather would yell, and the old plate would be passed out and the new one shoved through. Sometimes they would hear muttering, and see the bony fingers on the rim of the plate, but they never saw any faces. There was a very small peephole in each door, so that they could check the whereabouts of the prisoner and never be taken by surprise should it become necessary to open the door, but they did not look in otherwise.

There was one prisoner, though, whom they had to behold. This one lived in the dungeon, and his plate had to be lowered by rope and then pushed with a pole over to where he could reach it. It was utterly dark down there, and the keepers also had to lower a lantern in order to see. The man, chained to a thick post, had gradually turned into an animal in the five years he had been there. Sten thought he remembered a time when the man was dressed in regular clothes and spoke normal words; but then, Sten had been only four or five years old himself then, and perhaps he was mistaken. Perhaps they were not real memories at all, but only portions of a story he had been told.

But now the man was stark raving mad, his grandfather said, and had long been so. He was all overgrown with hair, like an ape, and slobbered and growled and ground his teeth. Sometimes he howled, throwing back his head, but usually he was silent, restlessly walking to and fro in an endless half-circle around his post, the extent of the length of his chain. The base of it was steeped in his own filth, but he had worn a track in it with his feet. Back and forth, back and forth . . . Whenever the lid was lifted in the ceiling of his cell, and light came in, he would flinch and cover his eyes from the brightness. His eyes seemed to have become filmed and all but useless, but still he would stop and look upward at the light. He was naked; his original clothes had long since rotted and dropped off, and he had not seemed to understand how to put on the replacements that Sten's grandfather had brought. The clothes had lain in a heap near the man and eventually the rats made nests in them, before shredding them and carrying them off. His nakedness was not so obvious beneath all the hair and filth, but Sten always stared at his private parts, which were visible and still looked like a human's.

Now, this morning, Sten's grandfather tugged at the stone covering of the opening and got it up, while Sten lit the lantern and prepared to lower it. He let it down slowly, expecting a howl to come in response, as it usually did. But there was silence. Then he attached the rope to the plate and lowered it. He stuck his head through the opening to aim the pole at the plate, and saw the man slumped by the side of the post, unmoving. He rattled the pole against the plate to try to get his attention.

"Come on," said his grandfather, ready to close the door and go.

"No!" said Sten. "He does not move."

His grandfather grunted and took the pole. He maneuvered it so it could touch the man, but got no response. The man felt hard, like the post.

"I will have to go down. Get another guard," he told Sten.

When the guard arrived with a ladder, they carefully descended, armed with swords, staves, and guns. Gingerly they circled the man, then poked him again. He did not move. The two men stood for a moment. Sten could see neither of them wanted to come close, in case the man suddenly sprang up. Finally his grandfather sighed, and took the few steps over to him. He reached out his arm slowly, and at last touched the man's overgrown cheek.

"Dead," he said, snatching his hand away, as the man toppled over. "Dead, quite dead!"

"Why?" asked the other guard.

Sten's grandfather looked around the room and back at the post with its chain. "Of confinement," he finally said. "He lasted longer than anyone else has in here. But even the Earl of Bothwell could not survive forever."

Dead, the Earl of Bothwell was suddenly elevated to revered status befitting his rank. His ulcerated, hairy leg was unchained from its iron, and his stiff body was hoisted aloft, where he was bathed, shaved, his hair cut, and he was attired in the clothes of a gentleman, hastily purchased.

He was placed in a wide oak coffin, lying on a white satin pillow, wrapped in a fine linen cloth lined with green silk. His hands were neatly folded, and Sten's grandfather partook of the honoured custom of helping himself to the dead prisoner's jewellery. There was nothing, though, but a ring enamelled with bones and tears. The grandfather removed it anyway, forcing it over Bothwell's knuckles. He held it up and examined it.

"I was told this was the betrothal ring that the Queen of Scots gave him," he said. "If so, the promise came true."

"Don't keep it, Grandfather!" cried Sten. "Who would ever want to wear it?"

"Leaving it on him would give him an unquiet grave, I think, and it's time now that he be quiet and in peace." The grandfather put the ring on his own finger, and Sten shuddered.

"There now," said his grandfather, pulling up the shroud almost tenderly around Bothwell's shoulders.

The Earl looked, not at peace, but angry. His mouth was set in a grim straight line, and there was a faint diagonal scar on his forehead, the relic of some fight. Sten half expected him to rise up with a wail and a knife.

His grandfather finished fastening the shroud and then closed the coffin lid, nailing it down. The guards carried it across the courtyard and out of the castle precincts—the only time Bothwell had passed the gates. He was laid to rest in the nearest church, the Faarevejle chapel on the promontory where the seawater sprayed the whitewashed walls, and the tower served as a lighthouse. The prayers were intoned by a Reformed minister, as the coffin was slid into its vault. No inscription was left to mark the spot.

The next day, Lauridson filed his report in his official calendar, and sent notices to the Scottish and English governments. *The Earl of Bothwell, sometime husband of the Queen of Scots, is dead this April 14, 1578. May God have mercy on his soul.*

XIV

Mary was humming as she finished her midday meal and gathered up her sewing. It was May, mid-May, and it was one of the warmest, lushest seasons they had ever had. Every growing thing had burst forth at once, as if it had been stored up not only for months but for years: the baby leaves shot out of the branches like cannonshot, daffodils and irises erupted from the soil and exploded in flowers, and overnight the matted last-year's grass was overgrown with a velvety carpet of new grass so sweet the rabbits hopped about in it deliriously, stuffing themselves on the tender green shoots. Mary was unable to resist the overwhelming spirit of urgency in the season. She must sit outside today, and do homage to the gift of new life that God had bestowed.

Chatsworth always offered pleasant places to sit outside; Mary had taken her seat in the moated pleasure-house so often it had been renamed "Queen Mary's Bower" in token of her fondness for it. Today would be a perfect day to sit on her folding stool—embroidered, of course—and give herself over to the ethereal mildness of the air.

She made sure to take along her wide-brimmed hat. How good it was to pick it up again! During the long, pale winter, when she saw it hanging on its peg, it always seemed a forlorn survivor from another world, the only proof amid the ice and dark that there had ever been a summer.

Hope is a straw hat hanging beside a window covered with frost, she thought.

She had meant to go straight to her bower, but there were so many blooming shrubs and bushes on the grounds that she found herself drawn to them. The gooseberries were covered with little blossoms, the grapevines were flowering, and the honeysuckle was starred with its own creamy flowerlets that emitted a characteristic scent that, strong as it was, was impossible to recapture in a perfume.

Mary closed her eyes and made her way over to the honeysuckle bush by smell alone. It was so heady it seemed to suffuse her entire body when she breathed it in, as if it had the power to intoxicate by airborne magic.

It enveloped her, and she opened her eyes. She was right beside it. She reached out and pulled off one of the slender, trumpet-shaped blossoms and sucked on its broken stem. Sweetness of taste from the nectar mingled with the sweet scent and became one.

The bees had been drawn to it, too. She was astounded at the motion of so many bees changing places around each flower, making a drowsy hum. It was a soothing lullaby of spring.

She did not hear any footsteps until Shrewsbury was almost ten feet away. Her first thought was how sour, worn, and altogether out of place he looked against the brightness of the day. Human beings did not always fit the season as easily as animals, she thought.

"Good day, dear Shrewsbury," she said. She smiled and hoped to make him do likewise. But he just kept trudging forward, his mouth set.

He then looked intently at the honeysuckle bush, as if there were something hidden in there he sought. Mary could not help looking herself, but all she saw was a bright blue-and-black winged butterfly hovering and about to light.

"I have received some news that will sadden you," he finally began.

Suddenly she knew what it was and wanted to say *No, no, do not tell me that, I cannot bear it.* Instead she said nothing. The butterfly seemed to hang, motionless, above the bush.

"The Earl of Bothwell is dead," he said, with dull finality.

She saw him reach out to take her hands, to comfort and steady her, then withdraw them. It was not his prerogative to touch her.

"I received word this morning from Cecil. King Frederick had informed them as soon as he was notified by the authorities in the pri—at Dragsholm," he continued.

Everything seemed to pass under a great stilling hand. Everything stopped. Even though the butterfly's wings quivered and it swooped gently down and alighted at last, it seemed no real movement. It was nothing at all.

"How did he—die?" Mary asked.

I said these words before. I said, How did he . . . in what manner was he mortally injured? And the boy told me and I died then too. At Jedburgh, so many years ago. But he was not dead, he was not, and by some providence he was restored to me, restored and then our life together truly began. . . . Can there be two restorations? Or was the first only a dream as well?

"Peacefully, my lady. Peacefully in his sleep. When his guards brought his food, they found him stretched out on his bed, a smile on his face."

Thank God, thank God, thank God. . . . "Had he been ill?" she asked, in a small voice.

"Not that anyone knew, no."

"Is he . . . has he been buried yet?"

Those words, those words, the same questions, and now I must hear another answer, another answer. He must be sent here, here, where I can visit his tomb.

"Yes, he was buried in a little church near Dragsholm."

She gave a cry. He was gone, taken. She could have no part in his funeral, or even behold his tomb.

Shrewsbury could not help himself; he broke protocol and put his arms around her, holding her as she shook with sobs.

"Comfort yourself, my lady," he said. "He did not suffer. He was well treated, well fed and looked after. His quarters were near his beloved sea, and he is buried where he can hear its roar. He can hear the sea singing for eternity."

May 15, Anno Domini 1578. I sit here, holding the pen, staring at the paper, about to write the words, but not able to. To write them is to fix them and make them real. Not to write them is to have to carry them in my mind every second. If I write them, will it lift the burden? Or will it double it, the knowledge now being contained in two places?

Eleven years ago, this was my wedding day to my Lord Bothwell. We lived together as man and wife only one month. The rest of our marriage—ten years and eleven months—we have been separated, lying in different prisons, in different countries, held for no legal reason, save that we are who we are. We vowed to be faithful unto death, and now it has come, and we are sundered forever.

My lord and love and husband, James Hepburn, Earl of Both-well, is dead.

There. I have written it.

But it does not make me feel better, it lifts nothing.

Shrewsbury told me two days ago. He came and spoke to me himself. He was very gentle and I could see that it distressed him, but I am thankful he had the courage to do it. It is true; it has been confirmed by Denmark. He said Bothwell left no personal effects, and there was nothing he could bequeath me. He said he did not suffer, but died in his sleep.

How could Bothwell die in his sleep? I cannot imagine that he would be so meek; I always thought he would meet Death like a warrior. But Death is a sly knave and takes us unawares. He delights in cheating us of the end we have planned for ourselves. To warriors he imposes a sleep-drugged departure; to the trusting, a cup of poison or a knife in the back; to the robust, a wasting away; to the man of words, silence. Martyrs at the stake hope for brave words and a good example, but often they are robbed of it and perish ignominiously, or even recant and thereby refute their lives.

Bothwell is dead.

Can he see me now? Is he nearby, in this room, watching? Has his spirit, freed now from prison, flown here? O, would that it were true!

When Shrewsbury told me, I felt a creeping cold paralysis come over me, as if the very life in my own limbs was stopped. My teeth started chattering, even though it was a warm spring day. Death himself has an icy grip, fingers of icicles, hands of leaden cold, and I felt his presence around me and in me. I took to my bed, and lay there, staring, shaking.

It was as it had been at Jedburgh long ago, when my life was despaired of. Then I also lay cold and immobile, and worsening by the moment. Would that I had died at Jedburgh!

But instead God spared me for all this misery. I have only had a few happy moments since, and most of them with Bothwell. Now he is gone, and we shall never see each other again upon this earth.

Does he see me now? Will I see him again, when I am dead?

The shadowless sun of high noon lies over the land which I see from my window. Death seems most pitiless in the bright daylight. At dusk, at midnight—then, perhaps, I shall write more. I cannot bear it now.

The household sleeps, and I have the little candle over my bedstead lighted. I am writing in bed; a difficult thing to do, but I do not want to leave it. I feel safe only here in bed. The window is open and a cool wind steals in, touching me with a chill

certainty. Now Death is at home; this is his hour. I should welcome him, sing Ronsard's "Hymn to Death." If I welcome him,
will he be kind to me? Will he grant me the presence of my beloved, release him from his silent grip, and let him slip away to
my side?

Death is the cruelest gaoler. There is no bribing him, no persuading him, and he never softens. . . . O Death, please, just
one moment . . . I lost him once before to you, and you relinquished him into my keeping. Do so again!

I felt the presence of my husband in this room calling me, bidding me rise up from the bed and follow him. But when I felt it,
never was I more afraid. I told myself it was only Bothwell, Bothwell who would never harm me, but somehow Death might have
changed him into something else, and that I could not bear. And
so I waited, my knees drawn up, my arms around them, trying to
get either the courage to follow the calling or the sense that it
was all my imagination, and calm myself. But I could do neither.
He was here; he called; but I was frozen and could not move. I
saw nothing; there was no movement; the presence was speaking
directly to me, inside my own mind.

Bothwell, I failed you. Forgive me. I am mortal, and afraid.

She closed the book gently. She was frightened, badly frightened. Her
heart was pounding, even after writing the words in her journal. She had
thought it would calm her and it did, after a fashion. But the room and
its horrible darkness were oppressive, closed—like a tomb itself. She did
not want to stay in bed, where she would either lie rigid and sleepless all
night, or be haunted by nightmares.

She made her way slowly and carefully over to the chair by the fireplace
where Mary Seton usually kept a shawl to wrap around her shoulders. It
was indeed there, and she draped it around herself and made her way to
the doors of her outer chamber. Her bare feet made no sound on the floors,
which were not cold enough to warrant her returning to her bedside and
searching for her slippers. She decided to seek out the private chapel to
pray. There the dark would not seem so threatening.

As she entered an adjoining chamber, she was surprised to see a glow of
light from yet another connecting room, and to hear the faint sound of
men's voices. She had thought everyone was asleep. Were the guards bored
and restless on this warm spring night?

Above all, she did not wish them to see her; she wanted to be alone!
She tiptoed up to the doorway, planning to cross it stealthily, when she
heard the word: *Bothwell.*

She stopped as if a rock had been thrown at her. His name, his name
itself seemed to crash all around her. It was as if no one but she had
permission to use it.

How dare they? was her quick, angry response. She stood stunned.

746

"Been dead for days, they said," a familiar voice was saying.

"Who found him, anyway?"

"Some boy who changes the straw. They had him so isolated in that dungeon that nobody came near him normally." It was Babington—Anthony Babington's voice! "He had completely lost his wits, and lived chained up like an animal. But then, I suppose it was the dark that did it. Locked up in the dark for five years!"

"How do you know?"

"I have a friend who assists Cecil in his correspondence. It's being whispered about court to all concerned—everyone but Queen Mary. Poor lady, who would have added to her sorrows?" said Babington. "Shrewsbury pretended he died peacefully in a comfortable bed. 'Tis better that way."

"But what exactly *happened* to him?" the other voice persisted.

"I told you, they just found him dead! Sitting up and stiff! But he had gone mad long before that. They say"—the voice grew low and confidential, and Mary had to hold her breath in order to hear the words—"he used to struggle and dash himself against the restraining post. But that was in the beginning. In the end, he had been utterly and completely abandoned, and he sat still. They say he was all overgrown with hair and filth—"

Mary ran back to her chambers, clutching at her head as if that would drive out the pain and banish the words.

O my love, I cannot bear this knowledge. She wept as she ran, bowed by desolation. *I cannot, I cannot. Would that I had died in your stead! My love, my life, my soul!*

XV

July 15, Anno Domini 1579. Saint Swithin's Day. They have a belief here, that if it rains on Saint Swithin's Day, it will rain for forty days. It has something to do with there being a downpour when the saint's body was moved on that day against his wishes, back in the year 971. They have many charming beliefs like that here. Anthony Babington told me this morning about this one, when everyone awakened to driving rain.

When it rains here, it can rain in astonishing torrents. The heavens turn black, the skies rumble, and sheets of it come down, so much the earth cannot absorb it all. It fills the gulleys with swirling streams and turns the roads into mires. Here at Sheffield Manor, where we spend the summers, the sound of the rain on all the great oaks of the park sounds like spears rattling on Roman soldiers' shields.

Anthony came to bid me farewell. Another person leaves my life, a person I cared for. One by one they all leave. It is right that Anthony do so; he is a young man, ready now to go out into the world.

"I am going to London," he said. "I have come into my inheritance, as you know, and it is a tidy one. But I will never desert my principles, dear sovereign, nor abandon you or the True Faith. In fact, I look for a Catholic wife. It is time."

I looked at him; he was even more handsome than he had been as a boy, and any woman would find him an attractive match. His father being dead, he was much freer than most to make his own choice.

"I will miss you, Anthony," I could not help saying. The eternal voice of the left-behind. "But it comforts me to know you will be true to the Church. God knows, it is becoming more and more difficult."

"Yes, and more than that—I may be able to help actively," he said. "There are plans afoot . . ."

"Hush, Anthony," I said. "Do not mix yourself up in them. Not now." Live a little first, I meant, do not risk your life before you have tasted it.

He looked disappointed. If he had thought I would applaud his plans, he was wrong. It is becoming more and more dangerous to dabble in this. Since my arrival in England, things have become much more tense for the Catholics. Elizabeth evidently hoped that once the old priests died out, Catholicism would die along with them. But some stubborn exiles set up a Catholic seminary in Douai with the express purpose of training new priests; since 1575 these have been sneaking into England, and suddenly many of the secret Catholics who went obediently to Anglican services have stopped going, and young people are being reconverted. The renegade priests slip from house to house, saying mass, hearing confessions, preaching sermons. The old Catholic families, like Anthony's, have formed a secret network of houses where the priests can hide. There has even developed a profession of carpenters and masons who specialize in constructing ingenious hiding places for the priests. Like any forbidden thing, Catholicism now has become attractive for rebellious, adventurous youth. Oxford is particularly Catholic-leaning.

I know Anthony, and I know he is drawn to this, and probably sees himself as a leader of the persecuted English Catholics, hiding them, guiding them, giving them money. He is ambitious; he would want to be a ringleader, not a mere follower.

He glared at me. "I am going to study law," he finally said.

"Good, Anthony. That will stand you in good stead."

"The Jesuits are coming," he said. "That will change things. They will take charge, and there'll be no more of this cowardly sneaking and hiding. Oh, no! That's not their way."

"Anthony, I pray the Jesuits do *not* come," I told him. "The new Pope, Gregory XIII, has stirred up enough English patriotism with his ill-fated invasion of Ireland. That stupid, stupid plan—to oust the English! It has forever destroyed the defence of the priests that their work is not political, and made the English see them as evil foreign agents in the land."

"Pope Gregory at least retracted the bull excommunicating Elizabeth—*that* should have pleased them!" said Anthony.

"No, that made it worse!" I said. Anthony looked dumbfounded (perhaps his political sense was naïve after all), and so I explained, "In his *Explanatio*, he says that the bull is not binding 'except when public execution of the said bull shall become possible.' In other words, all Catholic subjects may *pretend* to obey until the army arrives to overthrow Elizabeth."

"So!" He looked disdainful.

"That means that when a Catholic swears loyalty, it now means nothing—other than that he is biding his time. The *Explanatio* has made us all dissimulating traitors."

"Not you!" he said. "How can a queen be a traitor?"

"I meant all Catholics. Anthony, be careful."

But he swept away with a smile and a laugh. He is young, and wants adventure.

I had meant to remind him about the execution of Cuthbert Mayne two years ago, and two other Catholic priests last year. These were the first martyrs to suffer death for religion under Elizabeth. I fear they will not be the last.

July 22, 1579. It is still raining, as it has been for the past seven days. The ground is so soaked that horses' hooves sink into it up to the fetlocks, so messages are slow coming and going.

I wished I had reminded Anthony of other things, like the increasingly militant stance of Philip. He has recently issued a proclamation blaming William of Orange for the disturbances in Christendom in general and in the Netherlands in particular, and has authorized his murder. First Lord James was murdered in Scotland, then Coligny in France, and now Philip calls for William's murder. It *does* make the Catholics into the assassins that Protestants fear. Two of their staunchest Reformist leaders *have* been murdered. Little wonder Elizabeth feels threatened, and that her subjects seek to protect her.

All this means for me is that I am increasingly viewed as the dangerous "Bosom Serpent" that Walsingham calls me, the enemy in their midst. But it is they who have insisted on *keeping* me in their midst, when I have begged and pleaded to be freed!

October 15, Anno Domini 1580. Is it possible it has been so long since I have written in this little book? When first I came to England, and was presented with it, I thought it would only last a year. But I find that most of my writing has been in the form of letter-writing, and when I am finished with that task, I have no desire to write anything more; my hands ache and are numb. These letters—how many of them have there been? Enough to fill several volumes, were they collected. And the sad thing, the amusing thing—depending on who you are—is that they all say the same thing. In all of them the prisoner cries for release, to anyone she feels will help. No stratagem is unemployed: there is begging, and appeal to sentimentality, appeal to justice, appeal to blood, appeal to charity; there are threats, both of the here-and-now and of the hereafter. There are wild promises and offers to perform any tasks. But in the end, the answer has always been no. And so perhaps I would have been better had I just recorded my own thoughts, for myself and posterity, than to pour such effort into crying to deaf ears.

But no. It was impossible to remain silent. For there was always the hope that this time, perhaps . . .

Gradually my memory of what it is *not* to be imprisoned faded. It has been thirteen years now since I was taken to Lochleven. They say I have lost touch with the world, which is changing rapidly, that I live in the past, among dead ideas and dead people. Perhaps that is true, although it seems to me that more and more I live in the realm of eternity, in the time that is yet to come. When I finally conquer my fear of Death, then there will be nothing more here to hold me. But now I have not conquered it; I still see him as a rude arresting officer who will hustle me away, as the English did, and take me away from the few things that I still hold dear.

Retribution. Recompense. Return. Is this what I suffer? When first the doors of the prison turned on me—and all the doors are alike, be they at Lochleven, at Carlisle, at Tutbury, Wingfield, Sheffield—I thought it was. But now the punishment, the retribution, the suffering, the effects of the failings, whatever you wish to call this, have extended so much longer than the thing itself. It seems all out of proportion, and so I must continue to wonder: Why?

Scotland sometimes seems like a dream to me; even now I find it confusing in retrospect. They say with distance all things become clear, but with distance Scotland has become even more unreal and misty. It was my crucible, and I failed there.

Scotland continues to exist, of course, and is still a dangerous place. Lately a new element has arisen, predictable, but one that has thrown the Lords into a panic. James is growing up; he is fourteen now, and has a mind of his own. He is not so easily ruled, and has taken his French cousin Esmé Stuart to his side, rebelling against his keepers. They say the Guises sent him over to "corrupt" James. Be that as it may, there was yet another revolt and plot, and the Earl of Morton was ousted as Regent and brought to trial. And for what? For Darnley's death.

Morton was executed on his favourite device, a beheading machine called "the Maiden," which works by releasing a suspended blade over the victim's head. It is called the Maiden because they say "although she lies down with many men, no one has yet got the best of her." It is said to be much cleaner and surer than a human headsman. And thus perished that vile man, my enemy.

Now that James is free of him, I may be able to approach him. All these years, they have prevented us from communicating. But surely now he will listen to his mother. I have a proposal to make, which may benefit us both.

June 11, Anno Domini 1582. I am now in my fortieth year—how chilling that sounds! I cannot be the first to be surprised to be suddenly "old", but when I was fifteen, twenty, and twenty-five, I thought youth would last forever.

Nicholas Hillard came to Sheffield recently to paint miniatures of Shrewbury and his family, and he painted one of me, too. I hated it. The woman he painted was like a distorted vision of the girl painted by Clouet long ago in France. She had the same features, but they had blurred and run, were softened like an overripe pear. I have often observed such pears lying on their platters. They still hold their shape, but they are soft enough that the bottoms are a little flattened where they are lying, and the skin is slightly swollen. These, incidentally, make the best eating, if one eats them just at that moment. The next day they are inevitably mushy and show spots.

To think that I am in that state! And yet, upon looking in my glass, I had to admit that the portrait was accurate, it captured all the features. It was even, truth to tell, a little flattering. My chin is fuller than he painted, and my nose sharper.

A woman of forty. She is seen as a simpering, silly thing, a witch, or else a lascivious man-eater, hungry for young male flesh. Bothwell's Janet Beaton was seen as such, and even the elegant Diane de Poitiers with young Henri II, both women being some twenty years older than their lovers. I have been reading Chaucer, and his Wife of Bath is a chortling, lip-smacking libertine who admits that she took on her twenty-year-old husband when she was forty, and "truly, as my husbands all told me, I had the silkiest *quoniam* that could be; I never could withdraw my Venus-chamber from a good fellow." I blush to write such, even though Chaucer did not.

I suppose, had I the inclinations of the Wife of Bath, there would have been Anthony Babington to hand, although to me he will always seem a child. But Anthony, although he did seem to admire me and find me pleasant, never looked at me in any improper way. And I have heard that after he went to London, he made a good marriage with a Catholic girl, and made quite a fashionable showing at court. Then, he took himself to France and, so I have been informed, has made contact with Thomas Morgan, my representative in Paris. He still yearns for adventure, I think, and I pray he does not himself become the prey of true adventurers and scoundrels.

But on this Wife-of-Bath business—there is the most astounding, pitiful, and comical courtship now proceeding between Elizabeth and little François, Catherine de Médicis's baby. There is a twenty-two-year age difference between them! François, who was only six years old when I left France, has come to England courting her, and, from all reports, she is smitten! It seems that he is the only one of her many suitors actually to have crossed the Channel and come in person to woo—and thus, although he is tiny, pockmarked, and of an hysterical disposition, she purports to find him charming. She calls him her "Frog" and wears a gold frog pin with emerald eyes, and hangs upon him and sighs.

Robert Dudley is not amused, but then he cannot afford to complain. He himself made a secret marriage, to Lord Knollys's daughter Lettice, and the Queen was furious when she was told—by the Frog's *aide*. Her faithful Robin had finally grown weary of waiting, after seventeen years, and deserted his post. Some say she pursues the French marriage only as a sort of revenge, others as a compensation. She is on the verge of being unable to bear children at all, and perhaps she snatches at this as her last chance. Certainly I doubt it is in a Wife-of-Bath manner that she wants him. But her Council and half the realm are suddenly unsure they want the Virgin Queen to desert her post as surely as Robert Dudley did his. For twenty-odd years they have hounded her to marry; now that she may, they are horrified.

And I? If she marries and has a child, then my son will be dislodged from the succession. But I cannot begrudge her marriage—although I myself would never marry again. I will die as Bothwell's widow, and that is what I wish.

And as for James, I have put forward a proposal that is being actively considered: that he and I rule together in a sanctioned Association. This would confirm his kingship, as well as procuring my liberty. I believe there is a real chance that it may be approved, and thus at last everyone shall be satisfied. My old enemies in Scotland are all dead: Lord James, Morton, Lennox, Knox. There now should be no hindrance to my return. Surely the English would be relieved to end their keeping of me!

For more and more it works against them to have me here. It has long outlived whatever purpose it had, and far from buying them safety, it provokes plots and unrest. I cannot help it that the situation between the Protestants and the Catholics has deteriorated so. But it has, and my presence here is dangerous for me and for them. I am powerless to prevent madmen from scheming and weaving their schemes around me. I am a hostage to my own partisans, and will be punished for their plans.

It happened: someone attempted to assassinate William of Orange, the Protestant leader of the Netherlands, in response to Philip's call. Luckily he lived, but now Elizabeth's life is feared for as well, for she is the other great Protestant leader. The cardinal secretary Como, papal secretary of state, said—in writing—that anyone assassinating Elizabeth would be doing a good deed. He said, "Since that guilty woman of England is the cause of so much injury to the Catholic faith, there is no doubt that whosoever sends her out of the world with pious intention of doing God service, not only does not sin but gains merit, especially having regard to the excommunication sentence passed on her by Pius V of holy memory." So the Holy See counsels murder—what would the Prince of Peace make of it?

In response, the English Parliament passed a series of vicious laws against Catholics: it became high treason to convert an Anglican to Catholicism; anyone saying or hearing mass was liable to a large fine and a year's imprisonment; a heavy fine was laid on anyone who failed to attend the Anglican services.

Yet the Jesuits continue to come to these shores, risking their lives for their faith, and mine as well. They have set up a secret press and pour out pamphlets and books; several hundred copies of one were even distributed at Oxford in the very church where a formal academic exercise was being held! They have recently reached the Sheffield area, and I had the supreme happiness of receiving one, a Father Samerie. Although he could not stay, it was a blessing to have him even for a day. Yet I fear for him, and for his fellows. May God protect them!

In this climate, there has been launched the "Holy Enterprise"—launched in words, that is. The "Holy Enterprise" is nothing more or less than the retaking of England for the Catholic faith. This time it is my relatives, the Guises, who mastermind it, along with Pope Gregory, Philip, and the English Catholic exiles. Their dream is to invade England with five thousand borrowed Spanish troops from the Netherlands, led by the young Duc de Guise, my nephew; they will then be joined by twenty thousand native English. They will liberate me, they say. And I, through my secret messenger Francis Throckmorton, Nicholas's nephew, have kept myself informed of all these plans. Who am I to gainsay them? They promise to liberate me. If my prison door is thrown wide open, shall I refuse to walk out? Shall I be like Saint Paul and stay in my chains? Nay, that I shall not. For Saint Paul was imprisoned for what he preached and what he believed, whereas I was imprisoned for no good reason—no earthly reason, that is. If it is for God's reason, then I submit. And if it is for God's reason, then no power on earth can break me out.

⟨⟩

August 15, 1584. The Feast of the Assumption of Our Lady. Yesterday I left Buxton, and I fear I shall never return. It was a feeling that came to me, a whisper that all would be changed soon—does that mean my death? I had taken the warm waters for six weeks, lying in them, letting them soothe my stiff limbs. I now know I will never be cured, but only find a temporary relief of symptoms. The entire day was built around taking the cure, and at night I would return to my chambers in Shrewsbury's hall and, rubbing my limbs with the oil of ripe olives, mixed with chamomile and rose-dew, I would feel them grow warm and limber. Then I could sleep peacefully. Mary Seton, who is always with me, now has the rheumatism as bad as I, and has been availing herself of the waters as well.

I would sit at the window, looking down at the empty street—empty because so few people are allowed to come while I am here, lest some spy or messenger slip through. For that reason alone, I cannot stay here long, as I cannot in good conscience keep the whole place for myself.

But last night as I was looking down, I suddenly was seized with an urge to write a farewell message on the glass; taking off the Duke of Norfolk's diamond from around my neck, I scratched *Buxtona, quae calida celebrisis nomine Lymphae, forte mihi post hac non adeunda, vale:* "Buxton, whose fame thy milk-warm waters tell, whom I, perchance, no more shall see, farewell." I have loved Buxton, but I can bid farewell. I have learned how to bid farewell to everything I hold dear or have enjoyed. Now, as I have told my English gaolers, there are only two things that can never be

754

taken from me: my royal blood and my Catholic faith, which are the true reasons I am imprisoned.

Coming through the countryside and back to Sheffield Manor, the beauty of the land in high summer was one of fulfillment and peace. I remembered how in France there were always processions through the countryside on Assumption Day, the image of Our Blessed Lady being borne through the fields of grain, riding like a ship in the summer harvest. But nothing of that sort any longer in England. As we passed through the extensive deer park that surrounds the manor—for it was originally a hunting lodge and summer residence—the shadows under the massive oaks seemed as cool and restorative as a deep well, beckoning us to stop and rest awhile. But of course that was not allowed. We must go straight through the high brick gatehouse and directly back into the apartments.

I was allowed to rest and my ladies to unpack our things before I was presented with the unwelcome and ominous news: William of Orange had been assassinated, shot down in his own house in Delft by a Burgundian agent of Philip's. "Shot at revoltingly close range," was the way Shrewsbury put it.

"It grieves me," I said.

"It does not grieve your relatives the Guises, nor the Pope, nor the Jesuits lurking about here, nor, of course, Philip of Spain. Your friends!"

"They are not my friends," I replied. And indeed I had faced the fact that they were not. All they had to give was words. I had begun to suspect that they had no real intention of helping me, that I was just a verbal pawn to be used in their game of international politics. Only they had the power—armies and men—to deliver me, but they never would, because they did not care. The ones who cared—fanatic loyalists, gentry families of ancient Catholic allegiance—had not the power to do it. And thus I would die here in England, in my tower, guarded by staunch Protestant dragons.

"Of course they are your friends! If they are not, why do you intrigue with them? The Throckmorton Plot—" Shrewsbury's sad eyes had begun to glow.

Yes. The Throckmorton Plot. That was what they were calling it, named after my agent who had been captured and tortured by Francis Walsingham. He had served as a messenger between me, the Spanish ambassador, and all the plotters in Europe who were planning the "Holy Enterprise."

"I was merely kept informed about it," I said. "I offered no advice, no support."

"You should have reported it to Queen Elizabeth! Your failure to do so means that you are a traitor! Have you heard of *misprision of treason*? It means to be aware of treason and fail to report it. It is a felony!" His voice was rising, and his gentle demeanour was changing. Of late, Shrewsbury had undergone a transformation; he was worn down and worn out, and weary of his thankless task in being appointed my Protestant guard-dragon. He also, understandably, felt betrayed that I had dared to "plot" right under his nose. It was a delicate matter.

"Dear friend, let us not quibble. This is but a reflection of a larger issue, one that loomed from the first moment I was illegally detained here. I told Sir Francis Knollys then, and I have continued to say it; 'If I shall be held here perforce, you may be sure, then, as a desperate person I will use any attempts that may serve my purpose either by myself or my friends.' It is the role of the prisoner to try to escape, and the role of the gaoler to try to prevent it. But within those prescribed courses of behaviour, we may still be honourable people."

"Honourable! To try to assassinate Elizabeth!"

"Nowhere has it been recommended to assassinate Elizabeth."

"That Somerfield man—"

"The Somerfield man was a madman," I said. "You mean the man who set out from Warwickshire to shoot the Queen and put her head on a pole, for 'she was a serpent and a viper'? Surely you know that all rulers live in fear of just such a person? We all tremble at the thought."

"I am sure you would tremble less than anyone should he have succeeded!" Shrewsbury's bearded chin thrust forward.

I was deeply offended at this, but tried not to show it. I, who had lost Riccio and Darnley to violent murder, could not stomach the thought. Murder was dreadful, whether by poison, bullets, knives, or blows—even if the end result was not undesirable. "You malign me," I finally said.

"You know, as well as anyone, what happens at the death of the monarch!" He was almost shouting now. "Do not play the innocent with me! All commissions expire along with her: the sheriffs, the councillors, the lords lieutenant, the judges, the magistrates, Parliament. The only authority is in the heir, the next in line. And here that would be you!"

"Then I would have to fear the assassin as well," I said. "For do you really think I would be allowed to ascend the throne? No."

"So you have thought about it!"

"Of course I have thought of it. Who has not? Elizabeth, in not naming her successor, gambles every day."

"Because there are plots against her?" Shrewsbury was gripping the subject like a mastiff.

"No, because every day that we live is a gift from God. We can be struck down—by natural causes—at any moment. Nothing is certain."

"What *is* certain is that assassination is quicker and surer than these lumbering 'invasion' plots that require such coordination and planning that they undo themselves. And require so many messengers and letters that they are inevitably discovered," he said smugly.

"Thanks to your Walsingham and his Tower rackmaster," I said. They had captured Throckmorton, seized his papers, and tortured and then executed him. The Spanish ambassador, who had been in the thick of the plot, was expelled by Elizabeth. There was now no Spanish ambassador in London, which meant that I had to rely on the French for all my correspondence.

"Yes, thanks to him! And thanks to him, you might be pleased to know, that Jesuit Creighton was taken by the Dutch on his ship to Scotland. Oh, he was laden with papers about the 'Holy Enterprise of England'—every pouch in his robes was bulging! He tore up the papers and threw them overboard. But guess what? The winds were in love with Elizabeth, and blew them right back on board, where our agents gathered them up! What do you make of that?"

"Only that the metaphors must have come true, then, and all nature stands in awe of the Faerie Queen, Gloriana."

"Do you dare to blaspheme our Queen?" He was sputtering.

"Elizabeth is but a mortal, and one cannot blaspheme a mortal," I said. "Poetry is not reality. I fear you, and all the English, are blurring the line between them. Call her Faerie Queen, Gloriana, Astraea, Cynthia, Britomart to your heart's content—she is first and foremost a politician, and not a goddess. Besides," I could not help saying, "is it not blasphemous of *you* to elevate her to become a pagan goddess, and make your own national cult of the Virgin?"

"Parliament is meeting soon, and we will then decide how best to protect her. It will not be a good occasion for you, that I can assure you."

"My friend," I said, "it has not been a good occasion for me since I stepped out of the boat at Workington, and stumbled and fell. I have never risen since to stand at my full height. And now"—I attempted to lighten the conversation—"I cannot stand straight, due to my rheumatism. Which is much improved, thanks to your kindness in letting me take the cure at Buxton."

He smiled wanly. It was a difficult position for him. We could never truly be friends.

Through all this, I still had one hope: the Association with James. There might still be an honourable exit for me from this purgatory. But if not . . . then I must endure it, for it is God's sovereign will. He, the sovereign over Elizabeth and me, the sister sovereigns, will prevail, regardless of our plots and plans and Walsinghams.

XVI

"So long as that devilish woman lives," said the thin dark man softly, "Her Majesty Queen Elizabeth cannot count on continuing in quiet possession of her crown, nor can we, her faithful servants, be sure of our own lives."

He held the miniature of Mary, Queen of Scots, aloft and showed it to his companion, as if holding up a talisman of awesome power.

"But, Sir Walsingham, our glorious mistress refuses to see the truth," replied the man, Walsingham's chief agent, Thomas Phelippes. Phelippes looked as if he were made of melting tallow: his hair and skin had a greasy glow, and his face was pitted all over with pock marks, as if he had come too close to a flame and started to melt.

Walsingham picked up another miniature, housed in an identical frame, and even by the same artist, Nicholas Hillard, and compared them side by side. "She sees the truth," he said. "But her motto is *Video et taceo*: 'I see and keep silent.' She has seen the truth ever since the wretched Ridolfi Plot, and that was fourteen years ago. Parliament called for Mary's death then, and Parliament was right. But the Queen would have none of it." He stared at the portraits intently. "There is a certain similarity between them, after all. Family resemblance."

Walsingham sighed and leaned back in his chair. He was seated in his London quarters, the navel of his far-flung system of espionage and security for Her Majesty's safety. They were austere but functional, like Walsingham himself.

"Wine?" asked Walsingham, in a manner that made it incumbent on Phelippes to refuse.

Phelippes looked around the room. His eyesight was poor for distance, as though he had worn out his eyes poring over books and deciphering codes for so many years. He could just dimly make out the neat rows of boxes lined up along the wall, each proudly wearing a label: Spain, France, Italy, Germany, Scotland, Netherlands, Byzantium, Africa. In each box were the reports filed by the agents in those countries, some fifty or so altogether. His master had even managed to place spies within the Paris embassy of the Queen of Scots herself, and for the past ten years he had had informers within her English household as well. The box with those dispatches was simply labeled "Serpent," his favourite nickname for her. Within England, Walsingham's agents and informers were everywhere: in the ports, in the London taverns, within the foreign embassies.

Framed above the rows of boxes was a motto: "A Most Subtle Searcher of Secrets." It was what his old master Cecil had called him, and he was prouder of that title than he was of the knighthood he had been given in 1577 for his spy work. Below it was another motto: "Knowledge is Never too Dear." He wished he could convince the Queen of that; as it was, in spite of his budget, he paid for much of the expenses out of his own pocket. Still, he did not begrudge it. Knowledge, and the Queen's safety, *were* never too dear.

"There is only one way to move the Queen to act," said Walsingham finally. "There must be proof, absolute proof, and in writing, of Mary Stuart's participation in a plot to assassinate Elizabeth. Then she could be tried, and once convicted—"

"But that is exactly what happened with the Duke of Norfolk," Phelippes reminded him. He brushed a lank strand of yellow hair off his greasy forehead. "And the Queen kept recalling the warrant. She agreed to his execution only in order to save the Queen of Scots. He was the sacrificial goat. But for whom would she make Mary the sacrificial goat? There is none she protects more."

"Only herself, Phelippes, only herself." Walsingham had put his palms together and was mumbling into them. "She will not sacrifice the Scots Queen until she does it as a last resort to protect her life or her throne. That is why it is incumbent on us to persuade her that this is indeed the case."

"I beg your pardon. I had trouble hearing you."

"I said"—Walsingham removed his hands—"that only if she is convinced that Mary means to murder her will Elizabeth steel herself to murder *her* first."

Phelippes grimaced. "Must you say 'murder'?"

"That is what an execution is—murder, dignified by rituals. Rather a civil version of the hated mass."

Phelippes blinked. Walsingham was preparing to launch into an attack on Catholicism, and must be diverted. Not that Phelippes did not agree with him, but he had heard it all before—many times. His master was obsessed with the subject. "The people tried to enact a means of ending the menace of the Queen of Scots, but Elizabeth once again protected her," he said, annoyance rising in his voice.

"Yes." Walsingham was sitting immobile, staring off into space, thinking deeply. "The Bond of Association that thousands of loyal Englishmen signed, promising to protect Elizabeth with their own lives, and to kill Mary forthwith if anyone even attempted to harm Elizabeth on her account—it was farsighted, assuming that if it were known that the Scots Queen would cease to exist along with Elizabeth, who would bother making plots on her behalf? Their motive would be removed in advance. But Elizabeth said no! And what was her reason? That no one should be punished for the sins of another!" He threw up his hands in disgust. "As if we were not all punished for the sins of another every day!"

"I can understand that, in that Elizabeth was herself at the mercy of others before she came to the throne. But that she would not even allow the Scots Queen to be removed from the succession! I cannot fathom it; surely she would never *want* Mary to succeed her? A Catholic, and a tainted plotter! So why not remove her?"

Walsingham shook his head. "I know not," he said softly. "I know not. She is a great mystery. She began to negotiate with the Scots after the Ridolfi Plot to send Mary back to Morton and have her meet her just deserts, but then changed her mind."

"And now poor Morton is gone that way himself. Well, Parliament will settle the issue when it meets. This time they are militant, and will attack both the Jesuit menace and Mary, never fear."

"Gradually it all becomes clear. The remaining traitor Catholic lords like Paget and Arundel have been smoked out. Paget has fled to Paris and joined the Scots Queen's partisans there." He gave a humourless laugh. "Once a traitor, double a traitor."

"What do you mean?" Phelippes asked. He found this exciting.

"Paget has come over to us," Walsingham answered. "He reports to me." He stood up and pulled open the drawer marked "Paris—Serpent" and extracted a paper. He handed it to Phelippes.

"This is in code," he objected.

"I thought there was no code you could not read. I thought you even dreamed in code!"

"This is an easy code, one used by children," Phelippes said. "I can undo it in my head."

"Then do so." Walsingham leaned back and watched him intently.

" 'I—watch all—dispatches and there is—nothing—now in the works. The Guises are hard—at work—plundering Mary's dower—estates. With— her uncle the Cardinal dead—there is none—to act on her—behalf.' " He handed the paper back to Walsingham with a proud flourish.

Walsingham smiled. "Very good! Very good! And so fast! You are indeed all my enemies claim you are. Now do not *you* go over to them! That would be a sore loss. Yes, as you see, the income of the Scots Queen has been sorely cut. The French are weary of supporting three dowager queens: the widows of Henri II, François II, and Charles IX. Catherine de Médicis complained, 'The Queen of Scotland holds the fairest rose of France,' and has swapped the rich dower lands of Touraine for inferior ones elsewhere. This has cut Mary's income in half, severely curtailing her ability to pay for her plotting, not to mention her ostentatious almsgiving here in England. The tide turns our way, Phelippes, it turns our way."

"Can we speak honestly?" asked Phelippes. "I hesitate to say what I think and wonder, even in my own thoughts."

"There should be no barrier between us. Between husband and wife, between lover and beloved, between mother and child, yes—but never between spymaster and his agent! Pray speak," said Walsingham. "I am true to mine own."

"Now that it can be assumed that Queen Elizabeth will have no heir of her body, since the French 'Frog' came to nothing . . . who will it be?"

"James of Scotland," said Walsingham. "He is Protestant, and shows himself eager to please Elizabeth, even to the extent of ignoring his mother's plight. Queen Elizabeth will be succeeded by King James."

"Or, as they sometimes say in the streets, King Elizabeth will be succeeded by Queen James," Phelippes giggled.

Walsingham stiffened. "Pray do not joke about Her Majesty! But as for James, yes, he shows that distressing Stuart predilection for taking male favourites." He winced. "At least that meddling French cousin has been run off. Another blow for the Guises. I told you, the tide is turning, turning, in our favour."

"Not if James agrees to rule jointly with his mother."

"He won't. He, like all true Stuarts, wants to sit on his throne alone. He has nothing to gain by allowing his mother to join him on it. She's only a nuisance to him, as she's a nuisance to Elizabeth, as she's a nuisance to everyone. There's no place for her any longer, Phelippes. And do you know what happens to something when there's no place for it any longer?" He jerked open one of the drawers and pulled out a letter. "This is outdated. Its contents are of no relevance." He tossed it out the window, where it landed in the street. Three horses in a row stepped on it and ground it into the mud. "That's what happens. It's very simple. We have to keep our drawers neat, Phelippes; we have to get rid of the useless."

He stood up and pulled open another drawer. "I keep things tidy. All these drawers have locks, and the keys—let me say that there is no way they can be duplicated. The locksmiths who made them are . . . unavailable. The windows have bars, and there is only one door into this chamber. I never leave it unlocked, never, even for an instant, any more than I would leave the lid off a cage with venomous serpents. A second of carelessness can cause a lifetime of regret. Do you understand me, Phelippes?"

"Yes."

"What I am saying is that everything here is precious, and secure. Now in this drawer lies an exhibit of how I shall render the Scots Queen to follow that scroll out into the street, there to be trampled under." He pulled the drawer out and set it on his table. Lifting its hinged lid—for it had a cover—he took out a high-heeled shoe, a bottle, a prayer book, and a length of material, and lined them up neatly.

"Several years ago, in 1575 to be exact, I had the good fortune to have the opportunity to threaten to torture a certain London stationer, Henry Cockyn. The mere threat was enough! He revealed to me all the secrets of the Queen of Scots' methods of communication. Silly things like these!" He held up the shoe and scratched at the middle of its heel. A round plug soon tumbled out, revealing a hollow chamber. "And this!" He pulled the cork out of the round bottle, revealing a similar hiding place. "This was a little trickier, because the contents had to be protected against the moisture of the wine." He patted the material. "This used the alum writing. As if to help me, she also wrote instructions to all her correspondents." He shook his head. "She took a certain delight in all this. I suppose it was like her needlework, and helped her pass the time creatively."

"Where did you get all this?" asked Phelippes.

"Here and there," said Walsingham. "The extent of her correspondence has been staggering. Naturally, the more of it there was, the more could be intercepted. The shoe is courtesy of the connection to Lady Northumberland around the time of the Northern Uprising. The material went under the protection of the French envoy, who thought he was sending a simple gift. The bottle was carried by a Jesuit posing as a merchant of Bordeaux wines entering Dover. And while Anthony Babington was still in her household, the codes bloomed like the daffodils on a spring hillside. Now he has left, and is just as busy fomenting plots in Paris, which are promptly reported by Paget."

"You will have to have a trunk to house these," said Phelippes.

"I think not. I have at last come to an understanding of how to destroy her," said Walsingham. "Are you familiar with the thirty-fifth Psalm? 'For they have privily laid their net to destroy me without a cause: yea, even without a cause have they made a pit for my soul. Let a sudden destruction come upon him unawares, and his net, that he hath laid privily, catch himself: that he may fall into his own mischief.' "

Walsingham waved his hand over the exhibit. "This is how we'll catch her. Her childish faith in such tricks will be the bait. It's very simple: we'll shut off her lines of communication. Then we'll reopen them with one *she* will believe is utterly secret. For that we'll employ all these devices: secret bottles, codes, and so on. Every line she receives and sends out will be monitored by us. Sooner or later a plot will come along, and when she agrees, in writing, to it—" He jerked his head sideways as if a noose had tightened on it.

"Shall the plot be false?"

"No need for that. A real one will do. Of course, since we will be aware of it from the beginning, it will be harmless." He began putting the objects back in their drawer. "The Throckmorton Plot was instrumental in revealing to us the extent of her freedom to send and receive letters. Shrewsbury has been far too lax. It is time that he was replaced by one of our own persuasion, and that she became truly imprisoned. She'll be locked up, like the princess in the tower her admirers always imagine, and there'll be no letters of any kind." He sighed. "Oh, how distraught she will be . . . and then how happy, when the 'secret' communication is opened!" He laughed for the first time that afternoon. "I daresay it will be the happiest day of her life—and of ours."

XVII

The two ladies stood on the roof of the Turret House, a little square tower built on the edge of the great manor hunting park, and looked out over the October countryside. The hunt was beginning; down below they could hear the baying of the hounds making their own peculiar sweet music, the music of autumn and the frosty chase. Shrewsbury had magnificent dogs, and today all his packs were ready. There were the long-legged coursing hounds, like the deerhounds and buckhounds, and the smaller hounds that tracked by scent, like the bassets and bloodhounds. Their voices blended and rose up, yearning to begin the hunt, as their masters tried to restrain them.

By Mary's feet, her own little terriers and spaniels were answering their larger cousins, scampering and crying out in high-pitched yelps.

"No, my dears, you cannot join them," said Mary, bending over and trying to soothe them. "You must stay here with us and merely look on. Why, you are so small they might mistake you for a hare and run you to ground." She picked up the Skye terrier and ran her hands over his smooth coat. "I know you have a keen sense of smell; the kennelmaster says you can follow a scent two hours old. But, my old friend, the truth is, I could not bear to lose you." She held him close to her; he was the only survivor from the litter that Lady Bothwell had sent her almost ten years ago. She had named him Armageddon because it seemed a long and comical name for the fierce little animal, and because whatever else Bothwell had been, he had been a warrior who had longed for the final battle. Of course they had shortened it to Geddon, which sounded innocent enough.

"Look! Shrewsbury is calling to us!" said Mary Seton, who was her mistress's companion on the roof. They leaned over the edge and looked down.

Shrewsbury, mounted on his hunting horse, was waving up at them. "We'll return after the hunt, and come up then," he called.

Mary waved back at him to show that she understood. Often the hunters came back to the tower lodge for refreshment after the hunt, and recounted their adventures. Shrewsbury had quite recently built the three-storey tower, a fashionable feature of hunting parks, and decorated it beautifully—fine plasterwork ceilings with flowers of France, England, and Scotland, the arms of the family over the fireplaces, and heraldic designs in the glass windows.

The party put spurs to their horses and galloped off, the bright sun gleaming on their horses' flanks, the excited hounds scampering ahead.

Mary Seton watched as her mistress looked yearningly out after them. There had been times when she had been allowed to go hunting, but exaggerated reports—some saying that she roamed far and wide—had reached the English Privy Council, and Shrewsbury had been reprimanded for carelessness, and the privilege withdrawn. Not that it mattered now; Mary was unable to ride these days owing to her health. There had even been days last summer when she had to be carried about in a litter, and her only outside activity was to sit placidly beside the duck pond. But Seton knew that still she was unable to hear the sound of the hounds baying, and watch them rushing off, without wanting to go, and forgetting the state she was now in. Her heart was still athletic and young, captured in an aging, immobile body.

As is mine, thought Seton. I, too, have stiff fingers and a spine that no longer wishes to bend and bear weight.

Mary was standing framed against the blazing reds and golds of the trees in the park, with the deep brilliant blue of the sky enfolding it all. Suddenly Seton remembered seeing this before . . . where?

"How well those colours become you," said Seton. "They are—jewel tones, like the ones Clouet used in painting you." Yes, that was where it had been.

"Clouet!" Mary said with a laugh. "In the days of long ago. You have the memory of a scholar." She sighed and gestured toward the park. The hunters were almost out of sight, but they could still hear the hounds. "These colours are more beautiful than any paints could ever be."

"Come, let us bring a bench over and sit."

Side by side they sat on a plump embroidered bench cushion, letting the sun warm them. They were both dressed in black, and the rays of sun soaked into their clothes and heated them.

Mary's profile was still clean and pleasing, and had changed little over the years. Seton had seen it before the bridge on Mary's nose formed, when she still had the upturned nose of childhood; had seen it bloom into beauty, carried aloft on the swanlike neck, in France; had watched it settle and set in adulthood; and, last, had seen it all but disappear behind the veils and headdresses the aging exile had affected. But today it was visible, kissed by the sun and still bonny.

I believe that a man would still love her, thought Seton, if there were any worthy of her. But she'll never meet any, no, never anymore.

"Do you remember the oak trees around Chambord?" asked Mary. "And how we would gather leaves about this time of year, and look for the biggest acorns to use for dolls' cups?"

Aye, in that time when all the world was young . . . "I could never forget."

"I wish we were back there."

"Do you wish we had never left?"

"No. Not that. But I wish I could be permitted to return. Well, I will be, someday."

How odd that Mary would say that with such certainty. "How do you know this?"

"Because it is in my will. I have requested to be buried in Reims, near my mother and my uncle. But I fear I will not be aware of the journey!"

How calmly she said it! "Do not speak thus!" cried Seton.

"And you will be there to receive me," continued Mary.

"What do you mean?" Seton was alarmed.

"I mean, dear Seton, dearest companion—I am sending you back to France, and before the winter."

"No! No! I will not leave you!"

Mary turned and looked at her. Her eyes were lined, and such sadness showed in their depths that Seton knew what was meant by the saying, "the soul is in the eyes."

"I am your Queen, am I not?" said Mary. "If I command it, then you will go."

Seton flung herself on her knees and clasped Mary's feet. "Then do not command me! Do not cast me away!"

Mary stroked Seton's shoulder. The material of the dress was warm from the sun. "I wish you to go to the Abbey of St.-Pierre. My old aunt Renée is still Abbess there, and she will take you in. Seton, Seton—you are almost as ill and crippled as I. I must release you from your duties. Why, you cannot even dress my hair anymore! Soon everyone will know that my hair is grey!"

"If you can stand to remain here, so can I," said Seton. "How could I go where you so long to go, and leave you behind?"

"Because in doing so, it will be as near as I ever come to going myself. And Seton—I will not be remaining here. I am being transferred to Tutbury. I cannot allow you to go there as well. My conscience would never permit it. Just think—to return to France . . . to see our old friends and relatives . . . to see your dear brother . . . ah, he has suffered, too!"

"Indeed." Lord Seton, after being captured and wounded at Langside, had gone into exile in France, where he was so poor he was reduced to driving a wagon.

"You cannot tell me you do not long to see him!"

"Not as much as I wish to remain with you."

"That is not your choice. I am ordering you to go, and to go before the winter comes and you are trapped." She took Seton's face in her hands and held it tenderly. "We have always been so close. You have been my true companion all my life, and even our mothers were companions—your mother came from France with mine, two Frenchwomen married to Scotsmen. Now you must carry my heart with you back to France, for if you go, I will feel that I have gone, as well."

Seton started crying, the tears making long, silent paths down her cheeks.

"Pray do not cry," said Mary. "I cannot stand that. All my life has been a parting until now, but this is the first time it has been by my own doing. When you are there, when you are safe and loved and cared for, then you will thank me. And I will have something to be proud of, some good that I have done someone." She sighed. "You know they are trying to prevent my even giving alms now? But it is of no matter. My income has dwindled to where I have almost no alms to give. France is different now from before. 'Now there arose up a new king over Egypt, which knew not Joseph.' All the leaders we knew have died, and control is in the hands of those who were only children when we were there. Little Henri is King! The other little Henri is Duc de Guise! They have no memories of me, nor I of them. My own mission there has deteriorated into a band of exiles, and there is no Frenchman of any note directing my affairs. That is why they are so badly handled, I fear. Also, time makes my claims there seem odd; it is over twenty years since I left."

"Just think—we left before the religious wars there," said Seton. "I fear France is a ravaged place now. No, even if I go back to France, I cannot go back to *our* France, the France we loved."

"It is gone forever." Geddon whined and pawed at Mary's gown. "What, are you sad, too? You are an aged and wise dog, dear one." She patted his head and pulled at his ears, which still amused her after all these years. "Pray give me some words of consolation." Geddon licked at her hand and shook his body.

"Dogs have more sense than to mourn and wallow in melancholy," said Seton. "Perhaps that is why we need dogs about us. Do they have dogs at the convent?"

"I believe so. They used to. Of course, that may have changed, too."

They watched the sun go down over the tops of the trees, sending out shafts of bronze light. A haze lay over the horizon, slumbering and golden. There was an intense peace about it, an urge to acceptance in the remaining hours of light. Mary took Seton's hand and held it tightly, and they sat silent and still.

In the glowing dusk, they heard the distant sound of the hounds, and knew the hunters were returning. They would be gathering at the foot of the tower, milling about, while they dismounted and the game was taken away to be dressed.

Mary stood up and watched as pinpricks of light came closer; torches had been lit. The company was singing, shouting, in spite of their weariness. Three deer carcasses were being borne on poles. The hounds were trotting along, their tongues hanging out.

"Your Majesty!"

Mary recognized Shrewsbury's voice, and so she called down, "Yes, good Lord Shrewsbury!"

"We will be having refreshments in the ground chamber," he called. "Pray have the fires lit and come and join us!"

"With pleasure," she said. Turning to Seton, she said, "It will take me an hour to descend, I fear. Here, let us go down together."

On the ground floor, the fire was already crackling, the ornate white plaster arms of Shrewsbury, with the greyhounds supporting his family shield, illuminated above the fireplace. Indeed, the ceiling of the room, with its exquisite hexagonal designs and intricate flowers twined one round the other, were emphasized by the shadows of the firelight. It reminded Mary a bit of France, of the great hunting châteaux there, only in miniature.

Shrewsbury had his hat off and was fanning himself. "Plenty warm in here," he was saying.

"Was the hunting good?" Mary asked.

He answered cautiously, as if he were afraid it was a veiled request. "Yes, we took both antlered deer and fallow deer," said Shrewsbury. "Ah!" He helped himself to a cup of steaming red wine, with roasted apples floating in the bowl. "The hounds did well, expecially the buckhounds and my special breed of 'Talbot hounds.' I understand your little terrier is good for badgers. He'll have to come along sometime." He looked around as if awaiting rescue.

"I fear he is too old now," said Mary. "He could not keep up—like his mistress."

One of Shrewsbury's sons was present, as well as some neighbouring gentry. They were, as always, staring at Mary, ready to remember every detail so they could report on it. Shrewsbury had been reprimanded for that, as well. The English Council had complained that he was showing off his famous captive. Well, it was almost over now, he thought with relief. Fifteen years of captivity for both of us, about to come to an end.

"Madam," he said in a low voice, keeping his wine cup up near his lips, "it is as I had heard. You are to be transferred from my keeping into that of another."

"Who?" That had been the mystery. Who would replace Shrewsbury? He would have to be noble, and wealthy, and politically trustworthy. Robert Dudley? Cecil?

"Sir Amyas Paulet," replied Shrewsbury.

"Who?" Mary had never heard of him.

"A worthy gentleman, and a good friend of Sir Francis Walsingham's."

"Is he—of the same religious persuasion?" Mary knew that Walsingham was of the church party increasingly known as Puritan—militant, strict Protestantism of a sort that the genial Martin Luther would have found uncomfortable. Puritans were the spiritual children of John Knox.

"Yes, and more so," said Shrewsbury, and Mary's heart sank.

After the hunters had departed and night had fallen, Mary and Seton made their way back to their rooms. The fires had already been lit, chasing the chill out as best they could. Dear old Father de Préau was waiting to say the nightly prayers that closed their day. The members of the household were gathered, and at the end of the prayers, Mary added, "And may God keep us when we are parted."

Afterwards several people came up to her, puzzled.

"I have just received word that I am to be transferred to a new . . . host. There is a possibility that they may request my household to be reduced. I do not know; I only ask that you keep this in mind so that if it comes, we are prepared," said Mary.

Before they could question her further, she withdrew into her private chamber. She did not wish to talk about it, or anything else, at the moment. The decision to send Seton away had drained her.

Quietly they made ready for bed, Seton helping her with gentle, practised hands, as she always did. Before retiring, Mary opened her little coffer with her miniatures, and took them out one by one, holding them up to the candle.

There was François, and one of her mother. There was Darnley, as he had been when first he came to Scotland, and all at once she remembered that meeting in the misty cold garden, and why she had loved him. There was Darnley's mother, whom Mary had never met. There was the flat face of Catherine de Médicis, and the baby face of the infant James. And then there was . . . Elizabeth.

A face I shall never see, she thought. Never in this lifetime. And yet . . . if I could just see her . . .

No more of that, she told herself. No more of that.

She wrapped up the miniatures and returned them to their little tomb. Slowly she stood up and made her way over to the crucifix hanging over the prie-dieu, flanked by two candle sconces. Laboriously she lowered herself down onto the kneeler and fastened her eyes on the old beloved object.

She remembered when she had first seen it, in that room at St.-Pierre, when she had knelt and agonized over whether to return to Scotland.

My heart was aching then, she thought. I thought all the pain in the world was contained in my loss of François. Little did I know that was just the beginning. And then my aunt Renée, she came in and spoke to me. And all seemed to be clear, and destined.

Mary looked over at Seton, sitting quietly and reading.

Yes, it is right that she go there. It is right that there is still some haven and protection I can offer my servants. Thank You, God, for sparing Aunt Renée! She is sixty-two years old now—please keep her in health and service to You for many more years.

She looked around the chamber, the chamber that had been home of sorts for almost fifteen years—longer than any other home. It had a consoling familiarity.

Why, I have been in Shrewsbury's keeping longer than the entire time I lived in France! she realized.

And now that is to end, as well. I am prepared for whatever is to be. But I fear that, in my life, all changes are for the worse.

XVIII

"I hate Tutbury!" said Claud Nau, her secretary, rubbing his hands vigorously to try to warm them.

"Of all my prisons, this is the worst," agreed Mary.

If they had wanted to make me as miserable as possible and hasten my death or complete crippling, they could not have chosen better, she thought. But I refuse to assume that is why they did it; I refuse to attribute such demonic insight to them. To *them*—or is it *her*?

"I cannot work in this cold," he said, putting down his pen.

The February winds were howling over the castle, elevated a hundred feet above the plain and exposed on all sides. This time Mary was housed in a flimsy wood and plaster building called "the lodge"; it had once served as a hunting lodge for nobles who came to Needwood Forest for recreation. But now there were actual gaps in the walls and holes in the windowpanes. Besides, it backed on the earthworks of the ramparts, so that no sun or air could enter on the long side, making everything so damp that no furniture placed there could avoid being covered with mould.

The castle yard was muddy, and the only semblance of a garden was a little fenced area near the stables, which resembled a pigsty; the stench of the privies that emptied just over the walls permeated the air; and fevers and pestilence rose with the vapours from the swampy, ill-drained marshes at the foot of the hill.

"Then leave off for today," said Mary. "I believe we are up to my escape from Langside. I need to recall the flight to Dundrennan in more detail, although I hate remembering it."

Together they left the tiny withdrawing chamber and went into the presence chamber, where Mary's throne consisted of a high-backed chair with splintered rungs underneath. There was never anyone to whom she could give audience, but the chair was there nonetheless. Perhaps there would be messengers from Elizabeth, from James, from the French ambassador. Perhaps they would come; someday they would come.

Just then the door was flung open and Sir Amyas Paulet strode in, the buckles clinking on his polished shoes. He stopped and glared at Mary, obviously displeased to see her there.

"Good day, Madam," he said shortly. He nodded to Nau. Then he stepped smartly over to the throne, and began yanking at her cloth of estate, the old green one with her cherished motto, *In My End Is My Beginning*. It fell down with a great *whoosh!* of noise, enveloping the throne like a tent.

"Stop! What are you doing?" Mary shrieked. She rushed over to him faster than she had been able to move since her arrival.

He cocked one eyebrow and gave her an icy glare. "Well, Madam, I see you can move right speedily when you like!" He began tugging at the cloth, wadding it up against his chest.

"Don't touch that!" she said. "Put it down! I command you!"

He stopped and gave a cutting laugh. "Command me? But you are not my sovereign. I owe you no allegience."

"True, you are not my subject, but the subjects of other sovereigns are adjured to treat all rulers with courtesy."

"And what rule book did that come from?" he sneered. "One of those outdated French chivalry books to which you are so devoted?"

"From the book of common human decency," she said. "By what right do you remove this symbol of my royalty?"

"It was never permitted to begin with, therefore I am correct to remove it," said Paulet. "There were no orders about it, and everything that is not expressly allowed is forbidden."

"No," said Nau suddenly. "You have it backwards. Everything that is not forbidden should be allowed."

"Be quiet, servant!" barked Paulet. "You yap like one of those annoying dogs of your mistress! Now, Madam, procure for me an order from Queen Elizabeth, and I'll restore this trumpery soon enough." He tucked it under his arm.

"How can I procure anything from Queen Elizabeth when I cannot write letters? You and your friend Walsingham have closed my channels to the outside world. I can neither send nor receive letters!" she cried. "Please, sir, do not destroy it! It belonged to my mother!"

"If you are prevented from writing letters, it is because you have written too many in the past," said Paulet. "Seditious letters, knavish letters, letters tending to the danger of Elizabeth and the realm of England. Plotting letters—*Popish* letters!" He spat on the carpetless, stained wooden floor. "You did nothing but sit with your pen, pouring out rubbish and incendiary garbage to your Catholic allies in Europe, inviting them to invade England! Nay, now restrict yourself to your memoirs with your nattering French secretary—that's all I'll permit!"

"But I should be allowed to write to the Queen. The lowest subject in the land has the right to write to the Queen," insisted Mary.

"Oh, so now you claim a subject's rights? Are you then saying that you are a subject?"

"No, of course not." How quick he was!

"Then you must bear with your own isolation and punishment."

"Punishment! Of what am I guilty?" she cried.

He shook his head in disgust. "Oh, Madam! You know full well!" He turned and walked out of the room. She had not given him leave to depart, but then he did not regard himself as under her control, but vice versa.

As the door slammed, Mary turned to Nau. "Have you ever beheld such insolence? Write it down, Nau, write it down, that someday others may know, and judge for themselves!"

He was shaking with anger. "An ordinary little man, not even a nobleman! And all pretence of your being a 'guest' departed with Shrewsbury; this man is clearly a gaoler. He guards you in a castle that is not his, he takes his orders not even from the Queen but from her principal secretary, following the rules Walsingham has laid down. And they are so strict!"

"Yes. Do you remember the day Paulet read them out to us? No mingling between the two households, my servants not to walk on the walls, the coachman not to go abroad without Paulet's guard, no laundresses, I am not to speak to any member of his household except in his presence, no mail to be sent or received except through the French embassy, and unless it passes through his hands first. He opens my letters and dares to hand them to me with the seals broken! The insolence, Nau, the insolence!"

"It is a new world, this world of the Elect of God," said Nau. "It makes tyrants out of little men."

Mary was still shaking. "My cloth of estate! My very emblem of royalty!"

"They cannot take away your royalty, Madam. That is why they fear seeing the symbols of it."

Mary and her reduced household had been in the grip of Sir Amyas Paulet for almost two months. Never had she envisoned such bleakness, not only from the surroundings and from her ill health, but from the smug spite of the Puritan keeper. She had no doubt that she had been given into his hands because he was seen to be proof against her persuasions. All her life she had been blessed with the ability to make people sympathetic toward her, once they had actually met her. Only Knox had actively disliked her, finding her annoying and tedious. Now it was as if Knox's spirit had come to dwell in another's body, for the same narrow-eyed distaste stared out from Paulet's face whenever he looked at her.

Old Madame Rallay had died within five weeks of their arrival; she had been almost eighty, and the cold and damp had proved too much for her. With sorrow Mary had seen her buried at the little priory church of St. Mary, just outside the walls of Tutbury. It had once been a Benedictine priory, founded as a thank offering by the first holder of Tutbury, back in the days just after William the Conqueror. But Henry VIII had put an end to the monks, and so the faithful old French Catholic servant had been laid to rest in an Anglican service, with the sanctimonious Paulet reciting Scripture. He had insisted on attending, his dark eyes darting this way and that, ever on the lookout for messengers or secret letters being passed.

But Mary had not been thinking of the wider world that day, but of the ever-shrinking personal world she inhabited.

One by one they all leave me, she thought. Soon I will stand completely alone on the stage.

Watching the plain wooden coffin being lowered, she gave silent thanks that she had sent Seton away, away from this hell of ice and cold, so like the ring of Hell in Dante's *Inferno*.

In March, Paulet paid a visit to her chamber. "Madam," he said stiffly, "it pains me to hear that once again you have set your mind on evading my rules. I refer specifically to that Popish habit you have of giving alms at Holy Week in accordance with your age. I was told that you have distributed woollen cloth to forty-two poor women and, as if that were not enough, to eighteen poor boys, in honor of James. As if James would indulge in such superstitious nonsense! Now, since you persist in the illusion that all that is not actually forbidden is allowed, let me add this to the list of forbidden things: *No more alms!*"

Mary replied, "Good sir, I am afflicted in both body and spirit, and I need the prayers of the poor."

"*Nonsense!*" he yelled. "Enough of this absurd reasoning! You attempt to win them over to your cause, to make yourself an object of loyalty and admiration. But you cannot fool me, however much you can fool a few simple people."

She felt tears stinging at the corners of her eyes, but did not allow them to show.

"I was coming to see you on other business, when this foolishness was reported to me. Now, as to the other—here are two communications that will interest you." He handed her two letters, already torn open. Then he stood there, intending to watch her reaction as she read them.

"You may go," she said. "I can read them without your help."

With a scowl, he turned and left.

She waited for him to be gone before she felt safe in reading them. The first was a report from the French ambassador.

My *dearest daughter,*

 This is to advise you of the measures recently adopted by Parliament, a Parliament dominated by the so-called Puritans and other staunch supporters of all things English. As you know, the Queen's privy councillors drew up a bond of loyalty pledging themselves to do or die for her, in the style of old King Arthur and his knights, and thousands of her subjects signed the bond.

 This was prompted by the threat of plots against her, and as a sort of hysterical reaction to the assassinations abroad. The Queen let it be known that she preferred it to be a spontaneous act of loyalty rather than a law *per se,* but Parliament insisted on making it a law. Thus a new law is on the books, the Act for the Queen's Safety. It empowers a panel of judges to investigate any plot or plotters and to punish them as they see fit.

 In addition, Parliament came down hard on the Jesuits. Any priest ordained since Elizabeth's accession has forty days to leave England, on pain of high treason. Any layman sheltering such priests is guilty of a felony.

 As if these events were not disturbing enough, yet another assassination plot surfaced—a Dr. William Parry, who claims to have been commissioned by your agent in Paris, Thomas Morgan, and the Pope, to kill Elizabeth. He had a letter from the Papal secretary, Cardinal Como, promising him an indulgence if he succeeded. He arrived armed with a bullet blessed by Rome to do the deed. As a result, my King has seen fit to imprison Thomas Morgan in the Bastille. And Parry is to pay the price of his treason at Tyburn, hanging, drawing and quartering, and so on—the entire bestial procedure. So angry were the citizens that they demanded a more extreme measure—as if anything could be worse! But Elizabeth said the usual methods would suffice.

It grieves me that I can only be the bearer of such unhappy tidings. May God be your comfort.

Mary laid the letter down. Her heart was pounding. She felt trapped in a new and subtle way now; she could be blamed by any madman pointing a finger at her and implicating her in these wild schemes. It seemed that assassination fever was sweeping the land.

Do I read this second letter? she thought. She remembered Paulet's expression of triumph. Both letters must somehow be to her misfortune. With trembling fingers she pulled out the second document and began reading.

To the Most High and Mighty Prince, Elizabeth:
It having been considered and examined at length, it has been concluded by us that the Association desired by our mother, in which we might rule jointly, is neither right nor desirable to us. Therefore we deem it to our pleasure that such Association should neither be granted nor spoken of hereafter.

James VI, by the grace of God King of Scotland.

Official copy certified by Wm. Cecil, Lord Burghley & Francis Walsingham, principal secretary. March 2, 1585.

Mary let out a moan and the paper dropped from her hand.

James repudiated her utterly, and had not even the courage or filial kindness to write directly to her himself. He was almost nineteen now—Darnley's age when she had met him, and his father's son indeed.

XIX

he sea wind was filled with stinging salt, and assaulted the leathery cheeks of Gilbert Gifford as he stood at the rail of the merchant ship plying the heaving sea between France and England. The ship rolled up and down, in and out of the troughs of waves, and few of the passengers were not seasick, but Gifford had always prided himself on having the stomach of a merman. He could eat food that was tainted, could drink beer that was spoiled, and never even have a rumble in his stomach. It was a blessing from God, thought the renegade Catholic.

Oh, there were so many blessings from God, he thought, counting them. There was, first and foremost, his heritage—an ancient and honourable Catholic family from Staffordshire. There were his relatives—his slippery brother George and his fiery uncle William, all active in the band of permanent exiles that had set up shop in Paris and lived in a fevered dream world of restoring England to the True Faith. Yes, a man should have a mission, no matter how farfetched.

He, Gilbert, had flirted with the True Faith all his life. What an ordeal, to feel called and yet not called! At length he had had himself ordained a deacon at Reims, after a trip to Rome. But the robes had not exactly fit. Meanwhile, his uncle William was embroiled in the nasty strife between the regular priests and the Jesuits, all wanting to save England. Gilbert had hied himself to Paris and offered his services to the "regular" priests there, all of whom were swarming around the Queen of Scots' little embassy like wasps around a sweet cake. It was a hive of conspiracy and grandiose plans. Quickly he had ingratiated himself with Thomas Morgan, the ambassador's cipher clerk, and Charles Paget, his assistant. Oh, it was a fine life, as it turned out; much more gratifying and exciting than praying and reading. And that was another blessing: to have found work he enjoyed.

And he did enjoy it. The ciphers. The whispers. The smuggled money. The danger. Poor old Morgan had run afoul of that. One of the assassins he had supported, a Dr. Parry, had been apprehended in England before he could kill Queen Elizabeth, and now Morgan was languishing in prison—the Bastille. But it was not an arduous imprisonment, and he carried on his plotting from there with little interruption. This plotting was something that got into a man's blood, evidently. Life was dull without it. Even Gilbert, in the heat of the moment, had been sworn into an assassination plot against Elizabeth with his uncle and a soldier appropriately named Savage. But it had fizzled out.

Thomas Morgan remained adamant that Mary Queen of Scots should be rescued, and England re-Catholicized. Now Gilbert was carrying letters from him to her, vouching for him as a trustworthy carrier and messenger, in an attempt to reopen her lines of communication. She had been held incommunicado for several months, ever since she had been transferred to her new overseer, Paulet. But there must be a way to get around him and his strictures. The Catholics in the area would have means, and Gilbert knew them from his boyhood, and was trusted by them.

It should be an exciting few months, until he tired of it. He was thankful he had not been ordained a full priest, now that it was treason for any priest to set foot in England. Yes, the war was heating up; even the tolerant Elizabeth had passed severe measures to protect the national religion.

Did he care if England became Catholic again? Honestly, in his soul? He asked himself that question, as he clung to the rail and rode the sea like a man on a bucking horse.

Well, it would be nice . . . . It would be fitting to return to the old way.

But do you *care*, truly? he asked himself. Does it matter to you if it's English or Latin that rises above the altar in a plainsong chant? More to the point, do you care if it's the Lord's Supper or the Eucharist? What do you think of it as?

I don't, he answered. But I like working for a cause; it's more exciting than mending shoes or tending the sick.

He could see the coastline of England ahead. It would not be long now.

The ship had docked at Rye, a small port in Sussex, avoiding Dover. The shoals were tricky here, and often there were sandbanks and hidden currents. But their landing was safe, and Gilbert gathered up his things and stepped ashore, feeling invigorated. He carried little, to avoid any suspicion or searching. Just the letters.

As he was making his way through the dock area, past the wharves and warehouses, he felt a hand on his shoulder.

"You have not passed through our inspection booth," a voice was saying, and Gilbert found himself staring into the face of one of the Queen's customs officers. "Come, sir!"

"I beg your pardon," said Gilbert smoothly, "I did not see any booth, nor did the captain instruct me to search for it, as I carry no goods. I am just a simple passenger."

"Passenger? On business?"

"No, just a native son returning to his home." He managed to sigh. "I have grown so homesick, and my mother—"

"Where were you abroad?"

There was no safe answer. The Netherlands harbored exiles, as did France. Rome was suspicious, as was Spain. "Paris," he finally said. Paris could be anything one wanted: school, service to the French court, culture, women, mercenaries.

"Where's your passport?"

Dutifully, Gilbert presented it. It was all in order; nothing was forged.

"Signed by Walsingham," the customs man said.

"But it does not say what his business is," said his associate. "How long have you been in Paris?" he queried Gilbert.

Before he could answer, they grabbed him and began searching him. They seized his pouch of personal goods. The letters had been hidden between layers of the leather. But their expert fingers felt the extra thickness, and a knife flashed in the dull afternoon light and slashed open the secret pocket.

"So!" They pulled out the documents. "Something to the Queen of Scots! I think you'd best tell your tale to Secretary Walsingham, friend."

*   *   *

Although it was only midafternoon, in the short December day Walsingham had already lit a candle on his desk and now he stared, unblinking, at Gilbert across from him. The light, yellow itself, made Walsingham's skin look even sallower than usual. He looked at his quarry with dark, shiny eyes, moving only them and not his head as he appraised him.

It had the desired effect. Gilbert grew nervous, and began to squirm.

Verily the man does look like a Spaniard, Gilbert thought. So dark and saturnine. And still. Utterly still, and waiting. They say Philip of Spain is the same way. Quiet, calm, always in control.

Why doesn't he *speak?* thought Gilbert.

Still Walsingham continued staring. He folded his hands like a man who deliberates upon everything. Outside, Gilbert could hear the cries of the London street vendors, calling about Christmas.

"So you are a spy for Morgan and the Queen of Scots," said Walsingham in a flat, even tone.

"No, not a spy! I was returning home to Staffordshire, and Morgan asked me to carry a simple letter!" He smiled what he hoped was a convincing, disarming smile. I'm just a simple country boy, he hoped to convey. I know nothing of these matters.

"Nonsense." Walsingham's voice was crisp. "You aren't returning home. You haven't been here in eight years, and you don't belong here now. You are a soldier of fortune, a man who has no real country anymore."

"No, I—"

"A modern man, a man above parochial strife. Who are you loyal to, Gilbert? The Catholic Church? Your family? I think not. I think you are loyal to only one thing: to Gilbert Gifford. Am I right?" He continued staring with those level eyes.

"Yes, of course I am loyal to myself, but not only to myself! To greater things as well!"

"Like the Queen of Scots?"

"I have no particular loyalty to her. I was only helping in a lowly way to reconnect her to the outside world," said Gilbert.

"Would it surprise you to know that I, too, am anxious to reconnect her to the outside world?" said Walsingham.

"Yes!" said Gilbert, with a laugh. "For you of all people want her gagged so she cannot foment any more plots. And it is by your orders that she *is* gagged."

"Yes, but now I find she is *too* effectively gagged. Do you understand me, Gilbert?"

"Yes . . . yes, I do."

"Now, you know what the penalty is for carrying letters such as you had, do you not? Death. Alas." Walsingham opened his hands in a gesture of helplessness. "Do you wish to die for that lady imprisoned at Tutbury? For you will."

"Unless?"

Walsingham gave his first smile of the interview. "So you would entertain an 'unless'?"

"Indeed, yes."

Just then someone knocked on the door and entered, bearing some fig cakes and candied fruit. "A Christmas gift, sir," he said, putting down the silver tray.

Walsingham fingered the sweets. "I love the Christmas foods, although I abhor the excesses of that pagan celebration," he said. He popped a piece of crystallized ginger in his mouth. "Here." He extended the tray to Gilbert.

Gilbert forced himself to take one and rolled it around in his dry mouth.

"Now, Gilbert, I wish you to join my ranks," said Walsingham. "Work with me. My agents are the finest. You could do work you would be proud of. I believe you have the capability. But your task would be simple: continue doing exactly what you were sent here to do. Deliver your letters. Make your contacts. Receive the messages. Only report it all to me. That's all. That's the only difference. Do you think you could agree to it?"

"Oh, yes!"

As if there were a choice between hanging and spying!

"And, Gilbert—if you attempt to deceive me, I shall know," he said. "And you will be deeply sorry, and wish you had taken your original punishment instead. A double traitor who attempts to betray on yet another level is a creature who will find no mercy from any quarter."

"Yes, sir."

"Stay within my call," said Walsingham. "Soon I will need you."

That night, Walsingham and Phelippes met after supper in the guarded inner room of Walsingham's house. Three doors in a row were locked after them. Then Walsingham wound up a contraption that consisted of wheels and cogs and gongs and sticks. When it was going, it made such a clamour of metal and dull thuds that any eavesdroppers would have had trouble discerning the low voices speaking in the background.

Phelippes had been restless with inactivity, and was eager for the meeting. He hoped this meant that some new venture was to be launched.

"We have a new agent, Phelippes," said his master. "I had the pleasure of welcoming him into our august company this afternoon. He is exactly what we have been searching for: someone whose credentials are impeccable and absolutely acceptable to the other side. He needs no made-up story to explain himself, because his own story is perfect: a man from a well-known local Catholic family, active in Catholic circles overseas, recommended by Thomas Morgan himself! And yet *his* Catholics are in opposition to the Jesuits here, giving him a perfect excuse to have dealings with our office."

"And his name?" asked Phelippes. He narrowed his already slitlike eyes as if he would sit in judgement.

"Gilbert Gifford." Walsingham paused to see if Phelippes would recognize the name. "Now the rest of the plan can be realized. It is time to reopen the post office of the Queen of Scots. She is being transferred from Tutbury to Chartley, and this will prove a change for the better—as far as her mail is concerned. We will be able to peep into her letters, by arranging for there to be a falsely secure transfer of them. As I said, Phelippes, she loves this 'secret message' business. So let us indulge her! Let her letters pass through . . . oh, let me see! What would be dramatic? A beer keg! Yes, let her put her secret messages in a waterproof package in a beer barrel. Chartley has no brewery of its own, so it will be necessary for a barrel to go back and forth from the nearest town."

"One letter at a time?" said Phelippes.

"Naturally. We do not want a flood, and the beer barrel will not permit a very large package to be hidden in it."

"But the brewer! What if he does not cooperate?"

"Phelippes! That is your job, to make sure he does!" Walsingham was looking sternly at him. "I find, generally, that between the threat of government displeasure, the promise of money, and the thrill engendered by this sort of thing, they never say no."

By New Year's Day, Phelippes was able to report that the brewer, who wished to go by the code name "the honest man," was with them.

"He looks like his own beer barrel," said Phelippes. "And you would hardly believe this, but his name is Bruno! As they say, 'a great big bear of a man.' He also has a bear's appetite for payment; he demanded more than you mentioned."

"And?" asked Walsingham.

"I paid it, of course. I had no choice."

Walsingham winced. Yes, he was right, of course, but bother! all this was so expensive, and he would never recoup his expenditure from the Queen. "Indeed, yes. Now that that is taken care of—by the way, did he take to the idea?"

Phelippes laughed—a braying sort of laugh—and nodded. "He is like most folk, longing to feel wicked in a safe sort of way. I gave him to understand that *he*, and he alone, was the only 'corrupt' man in the whole chain. The Queen of Scots' secretary, that Frenchman Nau, will give him the packets."

"And he will give them directly to Paulet, who will then give them to you. You will translate them, then return them to Paulet, who will then give them back to the brewer. *Then*, the brewer, Mr. Honest, will give them to the man he believes is the simple messenger to take them directly to the French embassy. However, that man will be our friend and new colleague, Gilbert Gifford. Gifford will once again give them to Paulet, who will give them to you."

"Why a second time? This will be time-consuming, and perhaps the delay will cause suspicions—" Phelippes was scowling, and all the pits on his pockmarked face shifted and elongated.

"To check on the brewer, to make sure he hasn't added anything or held anything back from Paulet. To make sure he isn't playing a double game. And the same thing in reverse when the letters come back, to check on Gilbert. One must always have a check on one's own corrupt agents to make sure their corruption has not run amok or been utilized by others."

Phelippes now relaxed his face. "That is why you are the master," he admitted. "No one can equal you in this game."

Walsingham permitted himself a momentary warm feeling. If only Elizabeth would show her approval thus! "I thank you. I do it all for Her Majesty. No knowledge is ever too dear. Now, later today I would like you to meet our Gilbert Gifford." He paused and got up to rewind the noise machine, which had run down. Turning back to Phelippes, he said, "He has been busy about London, ingratiating himself with the French at the embassy. The ambassador's secretary, Sieur de Cherelles, is a trusting soul, and Gilbert is convincing him of his ardent devotion to the Queen of Scots. He is giving Cherelles time to check on his references. Soon he will break the news to Cherelles about the secret post office, and offer to carry the letters that have been piling up at the French embassy for a year now. Cherelles will accept, and—*voilà!*—our links are complete. The road will open—the road down which the Scottish Queen, we hope, will gallop to her destruction."

XX

e are getting a Christmas present," Mary told her household, as they huddled around the fireplace in the main hall of the lodge at Tutbury.

"A book of annotated Scriptures from Sir Paulet?" said Jane Kennedy, with a giggle.

"No, underdrawers with embroidered admonitions on them," said Marie Courcelles, the high-spirited Frenchwoman who tried to fill Seton's place in Mary's heart.

"A privy stool with Queen Elizabeth's face on the bottom," said Willie Douglas.

"Willie!" cried Mary. "That is not funny!"

But everyone was screaming with laughter.

"We are going to be moved," she said, over the laughter. At once everyone cheered. "To Chartley Manor, an almost-new manor house not far away, belonging to the Earl of Essex."

"New!" Marie exclaimed. "New!"

"To what do we owe this?" asked Willie, ever suspicious.

"Perhaps to God's love and concern for us," said Mary. "Or perhaps just to pure luck. No one ever has all bad luck, you know. Even our luck has to change sometime."

"Chartley Manor will have down mattresses," said Marie, looking at the old stained mattress of foul, flattened, mildewed feathers on her mistress's bed.

"Chartley Manor will have huge glass windows to let in the sunlight," said Jane.

"Chartley Manor will be made of rose-red bricks that soak in the warmth and hold it long after the sun goes down," said Barbara Curle, a new attendant who had come and quickly fallen in love with, and married, Mary's Scottish secretary Curle. There had been a threadbare wedding in the drafty hall at Tutbury only two months earlier.

"Chartley Manor will have espaliered pear trees against those warm bricks," said Elizabeth Curle, sister to the secretary. "And a bower to sit and read in, where we can just lean back and lazily pick one of the pears."

"Chartley Manor seems to have inspired your imaginations," said Mary affectionately. "I can no longer even picture such luxuries." She glanced at the ugly, dark room with its one guttering, smoky candle. "But dreams are free."

Geddon came trotting over to her and stood, his ears pricked up as high as they would go.

"Did you hear me, Geddon?" she said. "We are going to a new home. A better place for your old bones. If a year in a dog's life equals seven of a human's, then you are . . . seventy-seven. Almost as old as old Madame Rallay, God rest her." Mary looked around at the birdcages, all covered now for the night. Not that it mattered, the days being almost as dark as the nights. So few of the birds had survived Tutbury; the drafts had killed them. And the Cardinal, who had sent them to her, gone now as well. No one was left in France who cared about the little things for her. Only the exiles and their eternal plotting.

To them I am not a woman who would like a pet bird, or some new silver embroidery thread, but only a symbol of Catholicism. Symbols don't need living, breathing things; they don't read or become lonely or need medicines. They exist on slogans—or so they think, Morgan and Paget and his like. For that is all they offer me for my comfort. Sometimes I would rather have a pair of turtledoves.

Early the next morning, Willie came bursting into the hall where they were filling their mugs with breakfast ale.

"Damn his black soul!" he cried, throwing down a smouldering box. Sparks and ashes flew out of it. "He was stuffing it in the furnace next to the wall!"

"Why, Willie, what is it?" Mary made her way over to the box, which was emitting puffs of smoke.

"It was from Mary Seton," he said. "They actually sent it through, from the French embassy. A fellow was here, a Nicholas de Cherelles, and he handed it right over to our friend Paulet. And while I was watching—for I had gone out to empty the chamberpots—that black-hearted wretch, that self-righteous ass, opened it, peeked inside, and then thrust it into the furnace!"

"What happened then? How was it rescued?"

"I ran up to him and shoved him. I grabbed it out and yelled. And do you know what he said, that clodpole with Scripture-books for a spine?" Willie twisted up his face and mimicked him perfectly. " 'This is full of abominable Papist trash!' "

"Yet he let you keep it," said Mary, surprised.

"I did not give him a chance to grab it back," Willie said. "He is probably coming after it now."

Mary and her ladies went to the smudged window and looked out at the courtyard. Paulet was indeed there, talking to two men, and nodding gravely. But he was not following Willie.

"That one's Cherelles, I heard him say his name," said Willie. "The other fellow—I don't know who he is."

Mary had bent down to the package and was pulling off its singed lid. Inside were rosaries, paintings of saints, holy medals, and silk badges marked *Agnus Dei*. There was no letter—or if there had been, it had been removed.

"I know Seton sent them," said Mary. "I remember the sisters making just such badges at St.-Pierre."

She would treasure the little devotional objects. But, oh! it would have meant so much to have heard directly from Seton how she was faring in France.

❧

Chartley Manor was indeed a stately house, built on a hill with a moat encircling it, and overlooking the surrounding countryside. An older castle was adjacent to it, its towers embellished with crosses proclaiming that the original owner had gone crusading in the Holy Land. In the summer, doubtless it would prove pleasant enough, but now it lay in the grip of snow and ice, and huge flocks of crows perched on the bare trees surrounding the house. They seemed to be holding their own Parliament, cawing and interrupting one another raucously. Mary shuddered as she had to pass beneath them.

Once settled, everyone—Paulet included—seemed to be in better spirits. The quarters, while not fulfilling the soaring dreams of Mary's attendants, were so much more spacious and comfortable that they seemed like paradise. Once again the dreary, calcified routine was put into effect, and Mary's days were ordered from sunrise to midnight. She trod them like a donkey harnessed to go round and round a waterwheel, always turning, but going nowhere.

She was sitting in her chair, one thoughtfully sent from Sheffield that she had always liked, as it had a rung where she could rest her feet above the cold floor, when Nau approached her. She sighed. It was time, then, for the daily business meeting. She would have preferred to go on reading. But deviating from the schedule upset the household, particularly its older members like Nau, Balthazzar the tailor, the physician, and the apothecary. So be it.

"Yes, Nau, I know it is time to continue with the memoirs."

He just stood and bit his lip. She saw that he was trembling.

"Why, what is it? Bad news? Is someone ill?"

"I can hardly relate this to you, I am so filled with joy," he whispered. "There is—he came this morning—a messenger. From Paris."

"Without the knowledge of Paulet?" She tried to keep her voice steady. Could it be, could it possibly be?

"Yes. He came, he said, to bring letters to Paulet from the French embassy. But he managed to signal to me—as if he knew me—"

"Perhaps you had been described to him?"

"It would have to be by our friends. No one at court has seen me. That is one advantage—perhaps the only one!—of being shut away from the world as we are. He said—he said—that a way had been arranged to get letters in and out, right under Paulet's nose. It seems our sympathizers have managed to bribe the brewer who brings the beer from Burton every week, to carry letters."

"It can't be true," said Mary. "Paulet has closed us up so tightly that nothing has got through."

"But it is! There is no such thing as a truly sealed dwelling. And this fellow—"

"What is his name?" asked Mary.

"Gilbert Gifford. He comes from a Catholic family nearby."

"How are we to reach him?" she asked.

"Through the brewer. I will transmit the letters to the brewer when he arrives. We must wait until the beer is stored in the cellar before approaching. Gifford himself will come but rarely; otherwise it will be too suspicious. He said to expect the first delivery next Saturday, January sixteenth. And have your letters ready to send. Only one or two, though, as the secret box in the beer barrel is of necessity small, to avoid detection."

She smiled with delight. "A waterproof box in a beer barrel! How ingenious!"

Her eyes were shining.

She did not dare to write any letters, lest it was a hoax and Paulet would swoop down upon her, search her rooms, and find them. But she waited, so anxiously that she was glad the nights were so long in the January cold, so that others could not see her nervously tossing and turning. She, who usually talked so freely, hugged this secret to herself, praying that it was true.

January sixteenth came, a cold, clear day. There would be no trouble in the cart making its journey from Burton-upon-Trent, twelve miles away. It was Saturday, and the routine was somewhat relaxed, in comparison with the rest of the week. The laundresses passed in and out—searched down to their shifts by Paulet's women—and the miller delivered his flour. Then Mary saw the cart, with its huge barrel, creaking up the entrance road. It lumbered across the drawbridge and finally stopped in the courtyard. The fat driver called for help, and soon three guards were struggling to hoist the barrel down. In the meantime, the empty one from the week before was being rolled out.

Mary clutched at Nau's sleeve. "Is it in there?" she whispered. "Is it really there?"

"We will have to wait, and send a page down to the cellar. It would not do for me to go, or even Willie."

She wished she still had her little clock, or even an hourglass. She had no way of setting a time to wait. "Let us count to a hundred," she said. "No, let us say a rosary!"

When the rosary had been recited, Nau peeked out the window and saw that the brewer's cart had gone. He called over one of the pages, the one who always helped him with his regular duties, and gave him the instructions. The boy nodded gravely, and was gone.

Mary went to her private corner—the one where she was never to be disturbed—and waited. She could not even pray; she tried to suspend her thoughts. Soon enough, Nau was wordlessly handing her a leather-wrapped package. She rose and, drawing him aside with her, unwrapped it.

Inside lay two letters.

Her heart was pounding, and she hardly dared open the first. But she did, and quickly.

My dearest sovereign lady and Queen,
    This is to vouchsafe the bearer, Mr. Gilbert Gifford, as someone in complete accord with our mission. You may safely confide in and employ the same, a deacon in our own Holy Mother Church, devoted to your cause. His uncle dwells within ten miles of Chartley.
                        Yours to command, in loving obedience,
                                    Thomas Morgan.

Mary gave a long sigh, almost like a cry. It had been so long!

She unfolded the second, and read it. It was from the French ambassador, and it merely affirmed the authenticity of the messenger, and said that twenty-one packets of letters were piled up in the French embassy—a year's worth of correspondence to be forwarded.

"This is from the French ambassador," said Mary, "proving that all is in order."

She handed it to Nau, and he read it quickly.

"All my mail! A year's worth!" she said.

During the next few days, she spent all her time writing four letters, three to France—to her agent Morgan, her ambassador Archbishop Beaton, and her nephew the Duc de Guise—and one to the French ambassador in London. In them she enclosed the new cipher code to be used for future communications. And to the French ambassador, she wrote assuring him that she had found Gifford a faithful messenger, as he had promised: "You may safely entrust all the letters that have been sent to you for me to this new and devoted agent, through whom you may henceforth safely communicate with me."

On the last day of February, the French ambassador turned over to Gilbert Gifford a sack containing the twenty-one packets of letters received from all over the world—from Morgan and Paget and Beaton in Paris; from Catholic political exiles and agents in the Netherlands; from Robert Parsons, the Jesuit mastermind, and Sir Francis Englefield in Spain; from the Duc de Guise and the Duke of Parma.

In March, they began appearing—their seals broken because they had had to be inserted into the small box—at Chartley, and Mary was able to read, for the first time, what had been happening in the outside world since the failure of the Throckmorton Plot.

She read how the Catholics had lost hope in the promises of Guise and his "Holy League," and had turned increasingly to Spain and the promise of using Spanish troops to effect an invasion of England. She read that hostile actions between England and Spain had already begun, with the Spanish seizing English shipping, and Elizabeth formally taking the Dutch rebels under her "protection."

"Why, Elizabeth has even sent troops over there!" Mary told Nau in disbelief. "And sent her beloved Earl of Leicester to command them!"

"Ah! With the English so occupied, now will be the time to escape, if ever!" he said. "If the Duke of Parma can just spare a few troops, effect a landing. . . ."

"Nau!" she said, clapping her hands to her mouth. "There is a new Pope! Look—Sixtus V! So many changes!"

"Yes, the world has rushed on, while we mouldered here," he answered grimly.

In late March the unexpected happened: Nicholas de Cherelles, the French ambassador's assistant, arrived at Chartley, bringing letters from the royal family in France, and asked to be allowed to deliver them personally to Mary. Paulet made a great show of frowning and complaining, opening the letters himself, and finally saying that it might be allowed, but only if he himself was present.

The young man was ushered into Mary's presence, where she was seated on her makeshift throne minus its canopy, and immediately fell to his knees.

"Oh, Madam," he said, "to behold your glorious visage is something all true knights long to do!" The words rushed out like a spring torrent.

"You need not garble your words, nor speak at such a gallop," said Paulet, "for I understand French well enough, having served Her Glorious Majesty Queen Elizabeth as ambassador there."

"It was an honour to have you, sir," said Cherelles.

"And how are His Majesty King Henri III and his royal mother?" asked Paulet.

"Fighting against their cousin Henri of Navarre, and the Duc de Guise," he replied. "They call it the War of the Three Henris."

"Always wars," said Mary. It saddened her. France had fought itself almost continuously since she had left. This Cherelles—a handsome, blond young man—probably had no memory of anything else.

He handed her the letters and she opened them, exclaiming how delighted she was to receive a letter, and thanking Paulet for allowing it. While she read, Paulet suddenly was called out, leaving them alone.

"Madam," whispered Cherelles, "my master the ambassador bids me ask you to please send him another copy of the cipher. He has lost his! Never fear, it was not stolen, merely an accident. His Excellency's dog—I see you have dogs also, so you will understand—made a . . . an accident of nature on it, rendering it illegible."

Mary began laughing. By her side, Geddon barked. "Yes, Geddon, we know what he means. Certainly. He shall have it forthwith."

Paulet stepped back into the room, muttering. Cherelles took his leave, and after he was gone, Paulet sniffed, "Henri III, so I hear, prefers women's clothes and men's company, and carries about little dogs in his bosom." He looked at her sadly, as if it were her fault.

XXI

alsingham reached across his desk and took a small stoppered medicine bottle, and, after removing the top, drank directly from it. The bitter taste of the physic—made with sorrel from Cecil's own medicinal garden—hurt his throat, but it was supposed to be good for those suffering from a "feeble stomach," and Walsingham's was decidedly feeble. He was minded to settle his stomach before Phelippes arrived.

Not only his stomach, but his leg was acting up these days. It always did, just before the full warmth of spring came. But now, in the luxury of blooming mid-May, he would soon be on the mend.

May. He had the casement windows open wide to let in the sweet, soft air. Petals were falling from the apple tree just outside. Why, it was on just such a May morning that Anne Boleyn had walked to the scaffold and paid the price for her treason. He had always thought that the date made it all the harder to die.

This time next year, will the Bosom Serpent still be alive? he thought. Or will she be going to her execution? Or—God forbid!—will we still be intercepting her letters and hoping for a means of undoing her?

Phelippes knocked, and Walsingham admitted him. After offering him some fresh mead, Walsingham reluctantly got up to close the windows. It was sad to have to shut out the May, but spies might rely on just such carelessness and human weakness as a wish to smell the spring.

He looked at the man with the peculiar narrow eyes, seated before him. He was pleased with him, and with the arrangements he had made.

"Today's letters, sir," said Phelippes, handing them over. "I think you'll find them of considerable interest."

"Hmmm." Walsingham took out his reading glasses and flipped the letter—or rather Phelippes's deciphered copy of it—open. "From Mary to her agent Paget—her agent and ours—and another to Mendoza, the Spanish ambassador." His eyebrows shot up as he read. "So. She has committed herself, in writing, to a plan for Philip to invade England on her behalf. She not only permits it, she strongly encourages it. She makes suggestions about how to go about it. How helpful. I am sure General Parma will treasure these instructions from her, with all her vast experience in battle."

"We've got her!" said Phelippes. "We've got her! When do we notify Elizabeth, and strike?"

"No, we haven't got her," said Walsingham.

"What?" Phelippes sounded disgusted. "Why do you hold back?"

"Because we need something more irrefutable than this. What does this tell us that we did not already know? That Mary is in complete sympathy with the enemies of England? That should an invasion come, she will side with them? Who did not know that?"

"But the evidence! And in writing!"

"It will never convince Elizabeth that Mary should be done away with. There is no invasion, so the entire thing is an exercise in words. Elizabeth will never consent to the removal of Mary on such a flimsy charge as a nonexistent invasion. Ah, Phelippes . . . it must be something more compelling." He sighed. "And, having set up such a perfect trap, we should never betray it unless we are absolutely sure we have what we want."

He fingered a leaf from a huge potted plant that was sitting on the floor. The leaves were long and floppy, like a hound's ears. "Do you know what this is?" he asked Phelippes. "Tobacco. I mind to plant it out at Barn Elms in the country. From the New World. One of the voyages I put a little into has brought back such exotica. Not that I would smoke it, not I . . ." His voice trailed off as he suffered a stomach pain. Some people said it was good for cramps. Well, perhaps . . .

"There's another letter, coming the other way, from Paget to Mary. The usual plotting and planning." Phelippes put it in front of Walsingham and looked bored.

Walsingham read it and, to Phelippes's surprise, seemed to take it seriously. "So that crazy priest, Ballard, is still running about," he said. "And has just returned from a conference with Paget. I am beginning to doubt Paget. He may not be ours after all; he has not reported this to *us*. So Ballard claims that the English Catholics are ready to rise on the instant that Spanish troops land? And Paget has put him in contact with Mendoza. And Ballard has been talking to John Savage, the soldier who swore to kill Elizabeth last summer. Ballard himself went to Rome two years ago, and possibly pledged himself to kill Elizabeth. What does this add up to, Phelippes?" Walsingham drummed his fingers on the desk. "Two plots to kill Elizabeth are joining forces, so it would seem. Where is Ballard now?"

"According to our agent Bernard Maude, he has just returned to England. He landed at Dover two days ago. He seems to have a passport that permits him to come and go as he will."

"And where has he gone?"

"To London. He's here now. I took the liberty of having him followed."

Walsingham leaned back and smiled. "Good, Phelippes. Good. Now perhaps, if we are very lucky, someone will inform the Scottish Queen about this Ballard-and-Savage plot, and she'll be foolhardy enough to join it."

"Sir, Ballard has a friend in London, an Anthony Babington—"

"Ah!" Walsingham sat bolt upright and smashed his fist against his palm. "Ah!"

Phelippes was puzzled. "Sir?"

"I have it here, I have it here—" Walsingham had jumped up and was yanking open the "Serpent—England" drawer. "Yes, yes, here it is!" He thrust the letter into Phelippes's hand.

"Oh, yes, that letter Paget wrote in late April suggesting that the Scots

Queen get in touch with Babington. He even sent a draft. You didn't send it on to Chartley?"

"No. I was waiting. Now I know why." He shook his head. "This is why. If Babington can be brought into the plot, and if Mary then somehow becomes involved in it—! Oh, it would be exactly what we have sought! This Babington, tell me what you know about him."

Phelippes cocked one eyebrow. "Sir, I am only a lowly decipherer, not actually an intelligence agent. I do not know much about him, other than that he lives in a fashionable part of London and has court connections. You must know about him; *you* tell *me*." He folded his arms and waited.

"Right gladly. I was just testing you. By the way, Phelippes, I am impressed with your work in this whole operation. And it was truly a stroke of genius to be bold enough to send the French secretary directly to Mary to obtain those ciphers, since we were having trouble with some of the letters. Boldness, boldness! How admirable!" He suddenly laid hold of a dispatch on his desk. "Here's more boldness, from one of our agents in the Netherlands. Now that's a spy's dream, to be there."

Phelippes took the lengthy dispatch and skimmed it. There was a lot of information about cannons and horses and stores of ammunition. Then followed a page of poetry. "Poetry?" he snorted. "Why should an agent send poetry?"

"Poetry can lead to interesting ideas, Phelippes. Do not despise it." He held out the paper and began quoting, " 'I hold the Fates bound fast in iron chains, and with my hand turn Fortune's wheel about.' Is that not what we do, or hope to do? Young Christopher Marlowe here writes about Tamburlaine, but of course he is really writing about Elizabeth and Philip."

"Why are all the soldiers poets these days, and all the poets soldiers? They should stick to one trade. What if spies thought themselves poets, and filed all their reports in blank verse?"

" 'And 'tis a pretty toy to be a poet,' Marlowe admits. You must learn to understand them, the way the young people think, if you are to use them. Now this Anthony Babington thinks himself a wit, and consorts with poetry-making courtiers like Chidiock Tichborne and Charles Tilney, all Catholics, of course. He comes from an old Catholic family and was once a page in Shrewsbury's household, where he formed a worshipful attachment to the Scottish Queen. He left six years ago, went to London, got married, joined Catholic secret societies, made the usual journeys back and forth to France to the plotters' nests. He has even, in the past, acted on her behalf, forwarding and delivering letters. The point is this, Phelippes: she *knows* him. Better yet, she *trusts* him. Now if he will just urge this plot on her . . ."

"Do you think he will entangle himself in Ballard's line?"

"Most likely. He is a firebrand, and six months ago was urging a foolish plot to 'kill all the councillors at once in Star Chamber.' Yes, he'll bite."

"And then *we'll* bite."

"Like the steel jaws of a trap, Phelippes." He leaned forward and took another draught of the medicine to ease his gnawing stomach pains. He felt as though a steel trap were inside *him*.

XXII

"Roses, roses for all!" Anthony Babington dipped his hand in the silver bowl and drew out a dozen roses, which he began passing around the table to his companions. He took a deep red one and stuck it behind his ear, getting it tangled in dark curls. "These are from my own garden, just gathered this dusk. Is there anything more intoxicating than roses in June?"

He felt intoxicated. Perhaps it was the lulling, perfumed air that had wrapped itself about him as he strolled, a basket of roses under his arm, to the tavern. Perhaps it was the intimate sounds he heard all about him on the London streets, as desires and secrets spilled out into the open after a winter of confinement. Perhaps it was the promise of a great adventure and service before him. Or perhaps it was just that it was June, and he was twenty-five, and rich.

"These wear a most delicate scent," said Charles Tilney. He shut his eyes and inhaled.

"As delicate as the scent of the Queen's perfumed gloves?" asked Babington. Tilney was at court as one of Elizabeth's gentlemen pensioners.

"Which queen?" asked Tilney. "Our *true* Queen, or the usurping competitor?"

"Hush!" said Babington, laughing. "There may be spies about! So let us refer to *her* as 'the UC,' for safety's sake." He flourished his wine goblet. The wine, fresh from France, was rosy red and tasted of the sun and soft rain. "Drink all you wish, it's my pleasure!" he said, passing the flagon around.

"The UC's gloves are most delicately perfumed. She cannot stand strong odours. As for our Queen, I cannot know," admitted Tilney.

"Well, I do! I can tell you, there's no creature quite like her," said Babington. "Her own aroma is like the fragrance of a dream." He sighed and closed his eyes, remembering.

Around him at the table were his best friends here in London, men as eager as he to try the great adventure: rescuing a captive queen. And more than that, putting her on the throne she deserved. Babington laughed softly and said, "I have something to show you. It is done!" He pulled a portrait out of a leather bag and stood back from the table, displaying it.

In it, the company—with Babington at the centre—had all been painted in their best attire. Above them, in bold letters, was *Hi mihi sunt comites, quos ipsa pericula dicunt:* "They are allied to me in a dangerous enterprise."

"Is it not a good likeness?" Babington asked.

"Indeed yes, but—" Chidiock Tichborne glanced over his shoulder at the crowded tavern. "Is it advisable to show it thus in public?"

"Why, man, what harm can it do? No one here will know what it means!"

"Let's sing the Cobbler's Song," said Tilney. "I'll begin: We cobblers lead a merry life, dan, dan, dan, dan, dan!"

"Void of all envy and of strife," sang the next man, Jerome Bellamy, "dan diddle dan."

"Our ease is great, our labour small," continued Robert Gage, "dan, dan, dan, dan."

"And yet our gains be much withal," cried John Travers, "dan diddle dan."

"Tell me more particulars," Tichborne whispered under cover of the chorus.

"On the way home," said Babington. "Oh, is it my turn? For merry pastime and joyful glee, dan, dan, dan, dan."

Late that night, when the tavern had almost emptied, Babington and his group at last drank their final round and then reeled out into the soft, beckoning dark. In threes and fours they went their ways, and Chidiock, who lived near Babington, walked with him back to his house. The streets were anything but empty; London never slept. And on a warm night like this, people were drawn outside like moths toward flickering candles. The two men walked purposefully, to avoid having to respond to any of the murmured remarks as they passed, and they kept their moneybags about their necks and inside their shirts. But the temptation was great to slow down and savour the delicious feeling of the night.

They passed down Bishopsgate Street, through a parish churchyard, and past a hospital for "distracted people," called St. Mary of Bethlehem.

"Sometimes I feel I could be put there," said Babington, glancing at the brick wall surrounding it.

"Why, are your wits unhinged?" asked Chidiock. "Sometimes you do talk wildly. Ever since I have known you, you have been nervous. But not illogical!"

"I do not know," said Babington, all jest gone from his voice. "Sometimes I get thoughts that pursue me, take hold of me, I don't know exactly where they come from. Then I say, 'Get thee behind me, Satan!' " He gave a weak laugh.

"Satan—now you sound like a Puritan. They are always talking about *him.*"

They had passed beyond the brick wall surrounding the hospital and now came to a traveller's inn, the Dolphin. Most of the patrons had gone to bed, but there was a faint noise from the attached tavern.

"I am very much aware of his presence," said Babington. "They say he can take a pleasing shape. Sometimes I hear his voice. . . ." He broke off as he saw Chidiock staring at him. "In my imagination, I mean."

Now they were passing a water conduit, and even at this late hour, people were clustered about, filling their jugs. The sound of the splashing water was playful and inviting. The men went over and, filling their hands with water, rubbed their faces and let the water drip down their necks.

"Do you think this venture is . . . of him?" Chidiock asked. "For I must admit, I am confused by my own feelings."

They walked on in silence, passing more traveller's inns, then merchant's houses, and came at last to Babington's beautiful house, with its pleasure garden and bowling alley. Suddenly they were aware that there were footsteps behind them that seemed to echo theirs, stopping when they did, hurrying when they did, and yet when they looked, there was no one there.

Babington ordered the gates of his house opened, and they entered the grounds. "Let's go to the garden!" said Babington. They could hear a clock somewhere striking two.

"It's so late," said Chidiock.

"Does it *feel* late?" asked Babington. Somehow, on this night, time seemed to be playing tricks. "Come! You can stay here tonight!"

Laughing, he ran toward the dark shapes of the cypress trees, and down the marble steps into the elaborate garden. Far down at one end, a fountain was splashing, like a mountain spring. Babington began running in circles, throwing his arms out and swooping up and down. Chidiock followed him, watching the silent marble statues of Greek gods and goddesses emerging from their little alcoves of yew, observing the antics of the two men. The moonlight was bright and friendly.

Chidiock caught Babington's arm. "Why?" he said. "Why do you want to do this? Look at what you have." He gestured down the long avenue of the garden and toward the magnificent house. "You are young, rich, have a lovely wife. Why do you not rest content? Why do you gamble it away? I cannot think that you are so religious. If you were, you would have gone to be a priest. You like this life too much. Why squander it?"

"It won't be squandered. You write too much poetry. You think always of loss and sorrow. That poem of yours—the one about dying young—"

"My 'Elegy'?" said Chidiock. " 'My youth is spent and yet I am not old, I saw the world and yet I was not seen; My thread is cut and yet it is not spun, And now I live, and now my life is done.' "

"Gloomy stuff," said Babington.

"You should think on it. Why are you doing it? Is it for *her*? Or is it for *him*?"

"For her, of course. You know I have always loved her." He held his breath and waited. It was absolutely still. "I have received a letter from her, herself, just yesterday. She bids know how I am, and so on. And at the same time, I have talked with Ballard, the priest. He is ready to perform the deed—

to dispatch the Usurping Competitor. He and six others. I assume you will want to be one of them? You can get near her person."

"One of *them*?" Chidiock's voice grew faint.

"I am going to reveal to her our plan. Without her blessing, it can only come to naught. But with her blessing it cannot fail!"

"I beg you, don't put it in writing!" cried Chidiock. "And as for her blessing—man, everything she touches seems to fail. Almost as if *she* and *he* were one!"

"You seek colouration for your cowardice! I'll find another to take your place!"

"Nay, I'll come, only . . ." he paused. "Please move with caution."

Alone in his spacious workroom, fashionably appointed with an inlaid Italian desk, ebony-trimmed chairs, gold candle sconces, and a marble bust of Marcus Aurelius, Anthony Babington sat down to write to his chosen sovereign. On the desk was an ivory Virgin, looking imploringly over at Marcus Aurelius. Anthony's grandfather had treasured this Virgin, and she was very old; family legend said she had been carved in thanksgiving for their family's having been spared the Black Death.

But now there's another Black Death stalking the land, Babington thought. The Black Death of heresy, or the loss of the soul. . . . He shook his head to clear it. He was tired; the wine and the late hour had finally caught up with him. But he must write the letter now, while he had privacy and complete quiet.

He lit a candle on his desk and sat for a moment watching how the light brought out the beauty of the delicate face of the Virgin. Such beauty, all trampled underfoot nowadays, desecrated . . . surely it must pain Christ and His Blessed Mother.

Yes, that is why I am doing this. That is why it *must* be done.

He spread out the fine-quality paper and began his letter to Mary, Queen of Scots, unjustly imprisoned, true Queen of England.

He set out the plans, as Ballard and Savage had described them. There would be an invasion from abroad, courtesy of the King of Spain, with sufficient force to ensure that it would be successful. These would be joined by all the loyal Catholics throughout the land, a mighty force. Elizabeth must be captured and assassinated, else all was pointless.

> *O mighty and virtuous Queen,*
> I salute you, to whom I have ever, as you know, been loyal. Now it is the determination of myself and my friends to effect, at the risk of our lives and fortunes, your deliverance from prison, and the dispatch of the Usurping Competitor. We await your approbation; when we have received it, immediately we will engage to succeed or die. I humbly beg your authorization to act in your royal name, and ask that you direct our proceedings.
> For the dispatch of the Usurper, from obedience to whom we are by the excommunication of her made free, there are six noble gentlemen,

all my private friends, who for the zeal they bear unto the Catholic
cause and Your Majesty's service will undertake that tragic execution. It
rests that according to their good deserts and Your Majesty's bounty
their heroic attempt may be honourably rewarded in them if they escape
alive, or given to their heirs. I ask that I may be able by Your Majesty's
authority to assure them of this promise.

Yes, he hoped that she would agree. This was indeed a solemn and risky
venture.

I myself, at the head of ten gentlemen, will take you from your
prison. We will be part of a larger force of at least a hundred men who
can forthwith overwhelm the garrison that holds you, and spirit you
away.
O my most dread sovereign, my liege lady, I can barely endure the
passage of days that must elapse until the moment, when, face to face,
I meet you and deliver you into freedom.

He sighed. It was true. Every moment between now and then seemed
wasted, foolish, worthless.
Outside it was growing faintly light. The June nights were short. He
could hear the slightly different sounds that distinguished early morning
from the dead, still hours of night. There was a rustling, a quickening.
Three houses away from his stood the dwelling of the ambassador representing Frederick II of Denmark. Remembering that caused a shadow to
pass over his joy. Bothwell. *Everything she touches seems to fail.* Or die.
But everything dies, he thought. To die in a noble cause is a privilege.
The blood of the martyrs is the seed of the Church.
Still, perhaps I should take the precaution of securing a passport for
leaving England. If the plot fails, it would certainly be nobler to flee to
safety and make other plots, than to be taken here like a rabbit in a trap.
Once the plot has failed, there is no point in dying for it.

XXIII

Walsingham walked slowly to his main office, the one where anyone
could walk in off the street and request a passport or import licence,
or any of the thousand and one legitimate concerns of Elizabeth's
loyal subjects. In this office, not far from his home, he had three assistants,
who were busy all the time. One entire room was devoted to storing the

records of these transactions; like everything Walsingham touched, it was methodical and neat. He was most proud of it; after all, Parliament had no permanent storage place for its records—imagine! he would think, when he saw Parliamentary clerks scurrying about with the books tucked under their arms, looking for a place to stash them safely.

Now, as he made his way through the London streets in high summer, he prayed that no outbreak of plague would strike, as it often did at this season. This was not the summer to be interrupted; no, not when they were so close to success. The ingredients were curdling together now, setting like a baked pudding. Only a little longer . . .

All around him, stenches rose from the garbage in the gutters. The hot July sun seemed to draw the very humours of decay and rottenness out into the air; no wonder the court left London in summer. Dead rats and discarded offal lay in iridescent gleams, crawling with flies. He turned his head away and walked faster, dodging a lumbering cart that squashed all the refuse under its wooden wheels, releasing even more odours.

He was grateful to reach his office, an island of cleanliness and order. His three clerks were already at their desks, and looked up respectfully. He nodded to them and retreated to his inner office.

He was reviewing the recent agreement with the Bordeaux shippers about maximum tonnage when there was a knock at the door, and it opened hesitantly.

"Yes?" said Walsingham, annoyed at having been interrupted. But the annoyance faded as he saw who it was. He struggled to keep his expression expressionless.

"Good morning, sir. I am Anthony Babington." A smooth, sculpted face was smiling at him, a face framed by dark curls and a fashionable hat.

"Yes?" Walsingham repeated. "What may I help you with?"

"Sir, I foresee a future need to travel abroad, and so I am applying for a passport in advance. Your assistants insisted I petition you directly."

"And this vague future need—what does it concern? Pray sit." He gestured toward his most comfortable chair.

"I often have business in France, sir, in Paris, as a matter of fact." Babington was staring blandly at him.

"What sort of business?"

"I am somewhat embarrassed to admit it, sir." He hung his head charmingly, and looked up from underneath his curls. His eyes were blue as Aegean skies. "But I am often at court, and dress is important to me. I also like to bring Her Majesty news of the fashions, and little trinkets of the sort she likes."

"Like what?"

"Oh, gloves, perfume, leather books of poetry."

"So you make the voyage to France just to acquire such things? Is this what the youth of England does now? Tell me—why are you not in the Netherlands, fighting with others of your generation? Sir Philip Sidney is there, Christopher Marlowe, young Essex—is that not a nobler calling than remaining at court, passing back and forth to France to procure womanish trinkets?" He surprised himself by his own outburst. "You are nothing but a lapdog, like the kind the Queen of Scots keeps under her skirts."

Babington shrugged. "It is not given to all men to be soldiers on the actual battlefield. We can fight in other arenas. Surely you, sir, are the best example of that." The blue eyes were looking directly into Walsingham's.

"I strongly urge you to consider my words," said Walsingham. But in this duel, of course I want you to disregard them. As you are compelled to do, you proud young fool.

"Sir, I stand by my original request for a passport."

"For what time?"

"Oh"—he looked around vaguely—"for the rest of the summer, and autumn."

"I see. Well, I am unable to grant your request at present. Reapply in two or three weeks, to agent Robert Poley."

Babington shrugged. "I think you should reconsider. Perhaps I can help you."

"In what way?"

"As you said, there are other battlefields. I could spy for you."

"In what way?"

"In any way you choose. I am Catholic, I am accepted there—"

Walsingham was shocked, and was shocked at his own shock. No one had surprised him in ten years.

"I have access to Morgan in the Bastille, and Paget and Beaton in the Queen of Scots' embassy in Paris. And Mendoza—"

"I already have agents there. What can you do that they cannot?"

Babington's face registered confusion. "I thought you would be delighted at my offer!"

"Come, come. All spies are not equal. Bumblers are worse than no spies at all, for they betray their presence. I will consider your offer, but you must write me a detailed plan of exactly how you would perform your duties. 'Many are called, but few are chosen.' You do not think my fifty-three agents throughout the world attained their position and my confidence by walking in off the street?" He laughed softly.

"Very well." Babington rose and clapped his hand to his sword. "You shall see!"

After he left, Walsingham found himself so stunned he could not concentrate on the tonnage report.

No, my friend, he thought. *You* shall see.

The day climbed toward its noon, the heat increased, and stillness descended upon the streets of the city. At length Walsingham rose and bid his secretaries good day; he was going to his other office. They locked up and went to the White Hart, three doors down, to have their midday meal; Walsingham went straight to his destination, ten minutes' walk away.

As he walked, avoiding the refuse, and holding up a pomander to guard his lungs from the repulsive odours, he was haunted by the strange visit. Why had Babington come? Was he driven to guilt, ready to confess? Or did he sense that his plot had been penetrated, and was testing Walsingham?

Was I the observer, or the observed? he wondered.

Or has he lost his nerve, and stands ready to betray his fellow plotters? Is he that unstable? Then we must work fast, before it all falls apart. He must want a passport so he can flee.

Those eyes . . . such odd eyes . . . so innocent looking . . . so misleading . . .

Walsingham shook his head. If only my faith did not prevent my completely embracing the philosophy of Machiavelli, he thought, it would all be so much easier. I could fabricate evidence and not be bothered with all this labour, nor in fathoming Babington's motives.

Sighing, he turned the key in his lock and entered his dark, quiet quarters. Stepping aside, he examined the fine dusting of Alexandrian sand he had sprinkled about the door to catch footprints. None. Then he went to the next door and checked the strand of hair from a horse's tail that he had affixed to the door and door jamb; it was unbroken. No one had entered.

He now checked the third, inner door, bending down to see if there were any handprints on the handle, which he had coated lightly with Arabian gum. None. He wiped it off with a handkerchief and let himself into his inner refuge.

All was awaiting him, and there was not an item in the entire room that did not in some way reflect his personality. He felt more completely himself in this room than in any other place on earth; at the same time, sometimes he felt imprisoned by it, as if all these drawers and their contents were his master, rather than the other way round, as if somewhere there was a large drawer with his own name on it, and it was within these dark and dreary confines that he operated.

He jerked open the window-covers to let in some light, then settled at his desk.

I most likely have calluses on my buttocks, he thought. If a young man came to me asking what is the most important trait to have for this line of work, I would say a large, flat bottom accustomed to immobility.

Babington . . . he made that visit to disturb me. Why, then, does it? I refuse to let the game pass from my hands to his . . .

A knock on the door.

"Enter," said Walsingham.

Phelippes poked his head around the door, grinning like a death's head. He waved a piece of paper like a handkerchief, then sauntered in. Walsingham could not help thinking he looked like a poor imitation of a coquette. "Here," he said, putting the paper on Walsingham's desk. "Here it is."

Walsingham took the letter and read it. As he did so, all weariness vanished and all nagging questions about the worth of his work evaporated. It was a long letter from Babington to the Queen of Scots, detailing the plans for the rescue of Mary and the assassination of Elizabeth. Babington! Walsingham drew in his breath and closed his eyes. "Yes. Here it is."

"Here is the original." Phelippes handed it reverently to Walsingham. "I myself will take it to Chartley; I will entrust it to no other messenger. The Honest Man is due to make his next beer delivery on Saturday, July ninth. That night she shall hold this in her very hands!"

"And, pray God, answer!"

"She will, never fear. Rashness is her leading personal trait. When has she ever hesitated to embrace a dangerous enterprise? Her earliest behaviour with Elizabeth was bold and insolent: sailing from France without a passport and daring her to capture her. She delivered a staged, emotional speech about it prior to boarding the ship. Do you remember those words? 'I am determined to adventure the matter, whatsoever shall come of it; I trust the wind will be so favourable as I shall not need to come on the coast of England; and if I do, the Queen your mistress shall have me in her hands to do her will of me. If she be so hardhearted as to desire my end, she may then do her pleasure and make sacrifice of me; peradventure that casualty might be better for me than to live.' Well, now—the winds did blow her to England, and what she said so flippantly twenty-five years ago is to happen. We should guard our words; they have a way of pursuing us."

"She has never guarded her words," said Walsingham. "It is the one constant we can count on." He stared at the letter in awe. "For twenty-five years she has evaded her fate. Now it catches her. Deliver it, and quickly. And, Phelippes—" He started to tell him about the Babington visit, but something stopped him.

"What, sir?"

"Nothing." He looked long and hard at the letter. "We await her very heart at the answer."

XXIV

Mary had left out the miniature of James, as if by some magic the infant in the picture could plead with the grown man in the letter. Could they really be the same person? James had just had his twentieth birthday. Twenty years since she had borne him that June day in Edinburgh Castle. Darnley had been there; Bothwell; Maitland . . . the roll of names was a melancholy toll. All dead, and dead because . . . why?

Only I am left, she thought. Only I remain on the stage. I, and Elizabeth. And James, grown now. Grown into a stranger. The presence that I told the Riccio murderers would avenge me has deserted and betrayed me, like all the rest.

Two days ago, on July sixth, James and Elizabeth had signed a treaty, called the Treaty of Berwick. They were now permanent allies, bound to assist and protect one another. James had been awarded—and rewarded—with an English pension. There was no mention of Mary in the treaty. As far as the two sovereigns were concerned, she did not exist. No need to take her into consideration in any of their negotiations or promises.

I am a dead woman to them, she thought. I have passed off the stage as surely as Darnley and Maitland. Once there would have been edgy accommodations with the French, guarantees of this and that. Now, nothing. Elizabeth can deal directly with James. James can deal directly with Elizabeth, with no fears of reprisals.

She took the miniature of the infant and kept staring at it, almost willing it to come to life. But the bland blue eyes looked back, unblinking.

My child, my child, she thought. Even my own child deserts my cause and sells himself to my enemy. He wants to reign as King; if I am Queen of Scotland, obviously he cannot be King. Like a true Stuart, he believes in his own absolute divine right to rule. I am an obstacle to that.

But above and beyond that was the aching feeling that the last of her family was gone, the very one who should have stayed when all the others had fled, deserted, or died. A son was supposed to be a mother's right hand to avenge her cause, her caretaker in old age, her consolation for wrongs suffered and pains endured. He was her dearest possession and achievement.

This makes my catalogue of losses complete, she thought. Lost father, mother, three husbands, kingdom, health . . . now my only child.

She looked over at her prie-dieu, with the old crucifix hanging above it. Paulet had allowed her to keep it, on specific orders from Elizabeth.

I should kneel down and pray, she thought. I should just submit all these sorrows to God and let Him console me, as He has promised to do.

But I don't want to! she thought. God cannot know how I feel! He may have created the universe, but He has never been a mother.

That afternoon, as she was walking stiffly toward the gardens, where she liked to sit and soak up the July sun—like an old failing cat, she thought—she caught sight of Paulet and a strange-looking companion. The man had greasy yellow hair and walked in a sidewise manner. Mary seated herself on a marble bench and drew out her sewing; she was working on a panel depicting turtledoves. The men were coming closer, and the stranger seemed to be staring at her. He refrained from actually pointing, but she could see that he was straining his eyes. Even from a distance, Mary could see that his complexion was horribly disfigured by pox scars, and she felt pity for him. There was no way to disguise such an affliction, and it was the most outstanding feature about his looks.

He and Paulet seemed to be deep in conversation, glancing repeatedly toward her. She hoped they would not come over; she could not bear to engage in one of Paulet's mocking exchanges today. She kept her head down in hopes they would go away.

When she looked up again, they were gone.

The shadows began to creep out from under the bushes, like shy animals that had to be coaxed forth. A breeze came up, fresh and hot. The warm weather had been beneficial to her rheumatic limbs; her physician, Bourgoing, had prescribed taking as much sunshine as possible, and was pleased with the results. Her knees and elbows now bent easily, and only her fingers still gave her pain.

"Soon you will be able to ride again," he had said.

"If I were permitted to," she had answered. "But as it is, it makes little difference to me."

"That could change at any moment," he had said, raising one eyebrow.

She was touched by his enthusiasm, misguided though it was. "Ah, my friend," she had answered, with a smile, "thank God for unfailing hope!"

In the twilight, she opened the little window in the alcove that served as her oratory and let the summer air in. She leaned on the windowsill and inhaled deeply. The sounds of the night were just beginning in the countryside spreading out all around the manor house. From the meadow pond, frogs were singing, one old bullfrog's bass thumping insistently underneath the chorus of higher voices. She had been told that lilies grew in the pond, wide waxy white ones, but she had never been allowed to walk there— even had she been able to.

Perhaps if I had been allowed to, I would have been able to, she thought. Which came first—the imprisonment or the crippling? I believe I could walk there tonight, even now. If I had someone to walk with me besides ghosts.

Ghost of Bothwell in the fields . . . If I thought you would be there, dearest love, she whispered, I would meet you, even as I am.

She did not know what she believed about ghosts. There were times when she felt Bothwell's presence with her as surely as if he were there in the flesh; there were other times when she told herself she was glad he could not see her as she now was. They could not both be true. Either he saw her as she was or he saw nothing.

More and more of late, she yearned for the moment when they would be reunited; in that state, she would not be crippled, nor broken-spirited, but quick and radiant, and bathed in joy. This vision had grown steadily until it had a reality at least as firm as the fields rustling now before her, stretching out all around her prison.

Lanterns were being lit and hung on the walls, and amid the great trees Mary could see the quick darting shadows of bats stabbing the air. Their flight was so different from any bird's, so fast and jerky. She had heard them rustling in the fat round towers of the old castle, where they slept away the days undisturbed, their odd odour permeating the air.

Outside, later, the moon would rise, reflecting in the pond; the night-ingales would start singing. She promised herself to come back to the window and watch.

Sometime, in the stillness of the absolute centre of the night, she awakened and kept her vigil at the window. The waning half moon had risen laggardly and was just beginning to appear above the treetops.

Even the moon grows old, she thought. Even the moon.

"My sweet mistress," whispered a voice in Mary's ear. She awakened to see Jane Kennedy bending over her, where she had fallen asleep, one arm trailing out the window. Where the moon had been, the burgeoning robust sun was already peeking above the horizon, its rays hazy golden. "You pray overmuch," she said, glancing accusingly at the little altar with its crucifix.

"Nay, not enough," said Mary.

"After breakfast, will you walk with me through the gardens?" asked Jane.

"Gladly," said Mary.

Attired in light gowns, the two went to the gardens by midmorning. There was no sign of Paulet or the ugly pockmarked man this time. Jane took her pens and inks and paper; of late she had amused herself by sketching flowers and birds. Mary took her own bound book, where she had continued intermittently to write her thoughts and compose verses over the years. Sometimes she would forget about it for months at a time, only to have a sudden need to write in it as she did today. A bond of silence was honoured between them: Jane would never ask her what she was writing, nor interrupt her.

The gardens at Chartley were laid out in the new fashion: long, straight reflecting canals, pagan gods and goddesses presiding over avenues of evergreens, marble fountains and trickling waterworks. At one end was a two-storeyed pleasure pavilion; in the centre was an artificial "mount" with stairs and a statue of Zeus on its summit, an imitation Mount Olympus. The young Robert Devereaux, Earl of Essex, had designed them, and the young Earl, from all reports, was the very mirror and incarnation of fashion.

It was odd, thought Mary, living in an unknown man's house when he was not there; rather like Psyche dwelling in the mysterious house of her unseen husband. Young Essex was just twenty-five; everyone whispered about him and predicted great things for him, saying, "He is young, he shows great promise . . ."

But when I was twenty-five, my reign was over; there were to be no more chances for me, and no one said, "She is young yet. . . ." No, I was judged and found wanting; having taken the throne before I was twenty, I was pulled off it at an age younger than the "wise virgin" Elizabeth was when she mounted it. If only I had been permitted to begin ruling at twenty-five, instead of ending then!

She looked up and down the dusty, drowsing clipped hedges of the garden, wearing their borders like the trim of a uniform. Essex's costume. Well, my lad, may you fare well, she thought. Delay your entrance into the world of court as long as possible. But youth will never wait, or it is not youth.

A faint breeze was blowing, bringing the sweet scent of fresh-scythed grass in the fields. Two white-winged butterflies played round and round each other, tumbling in the air. High above, bleached in the sky, was the remnant of the moon, so pale it was difficult to see now.

In a strange, whole flash of insight, Mary saw that the moon was herself, and the sun Elizabeth. *So my moonlit ghost fades out in the blaze of Elizabeth's daylight. I vanish in the brillance of her sky.*

"Shall we sit here?" Jane was saying, motioning to a bench in the shade of a cypress.

As if in a daze, Mary nodded and followed her. The daytime moon was blotted out by the branches of the overhanging tree.

Humming, Jane got out her pens and began earnestly sketching one of the magpies cackling on a hedge. Mary also drew out her book and sat staring blankly at its page. Then, slowly, she began to write.

> *What am I, alas, what purpose has my life?*
> *I nothing am, a corpse without a heart,*
> *A useless shade, a victim of sad strife,*
> *One who lives yet, and wishes to depart.*
> *My enemies, no envy hold for me:*
> *My spirit has no taste for greatness now.*
> *Sorrow consumes me in extreme degree,*
> *Your hatred shall be satisfied, I vow.*
> *And you, my friends, you who have held me dear,*
> *Reflect that I, lacking both health and fortune,*
> *Cannot aspire to any great deed here.*
> *Welcome, therefore, my ultimate misfortune;*
> *And pray that when affliction ends my story,*
> *Then I may have some share in Heaven's glory.*

She waited to see if any more words came, but there were none. Then she glanced over to see Jane gazing at her with a stricken look.

"Dear Queen, you look like a goddess of sorrow," she said. "It is wrong to be so sad on such a glorious, sunny day."

Glorious, sunny day . . . But that is why I am sad, my friend.

Mary smiled wanly.

"It is nearly time for the noon meal," said Jane. "Come, we must return." She spoke to the magpies. "You will have to wait for your portrait to be finished."

The courtyard of Chartley was bustling. It took Mary a moment to remember that it was Saturday, the day the brewer came.

Ordinarily she felt excited about it, but today she did not care. What difference, what letters he brought? What difference, what went on in

France, or Spain, or Scotland? She would sleep away the rest of her life here, sealed away, like the bats slumbering in their tower. It did not matter. None of it mattered.

She did not even talk to Nau about going down to the cellar. In a way she was tired of the teasing letters, the post, the secret messages. Children's games that were swept away each night by the adults, that is all they were. Something to keep the prisoner occupied.

After the dinner, in the hot part of the day, the ladies lay down. Mary was tired already, and the heat made her drowsy. She was sound asleep when Nau touched her gently. She awoke with a start.

"Sssh." He gestured round them. All the women were sleeping, lying still. "Your Majesty, it has come. Your summons to freedom," he whispered. "Arise, and read it."

Too late. It was too late. She closed her eyes and shook her head.

"I have just finished deciphering it. Please, read it quickly! Else it must wait until next week for an answer."

His voice was excited and trembling. As quietly as possible, she rose from the bed and tiptoed through the bedchamber and out into the audience chamber. Only then did she sit down on a window seat and read the letter, freshly written out in plain language by Nau.

It was from Anthony Babington. Dear Anthony. It was good of him to write.

But her eyes widened as she read.

A Spanish invasion. A small English army to rescue Mary, with Babington at its head. A smaller band of six unsuspected courtiers to assassinate Elizabeth at the same time.

> . . . who for the zeal they bear unto the Catholic cause and Your Majesty's service will undertake that tragic execution. It rests that according to their good deserts and Your Majesty's bounty their heroic attempt may be honourably rewarded in them if they escape alive, or given to their heirs. I ask that I may be able by Your Majesty's authority to assure them of this promise.

She felt a rush of fear and cold dread come upon her. What did he want from her? She reread the letter, this time seeing the words:

> We await your approbation; when we have received it, immediately we will engage to succeed or die. I humbly beg your authorization to act in your royal name, and ask that you direct our proceedings.

They wanted her to act as their general! But how could that be? She turned and looked at Nau, with bewilderment.

"Is it not what we have been waiting for?" he was whispering.

"Yes—no—I know not!" Mary felt close to tears.

"What answer shall I return to him?"

"I—that a longer answer will follow, that for now I merely acknowledge having received the plans." She held her head between her hands, as if she could squeeze wisdom and an answer out of it.

Nau bowed and went to his writing room to complete the task before the brewer left for the day. Even a paragraph took an hour or so, because it all had to be translated into code.

Mary was no longer sleepy, but shiveringly wide awake. What should she do? Always before, she had made it a policy never to entangle herself with any of these plots, purposely never to authorize anyone to act in her name. It was that which had saved her. In the Northern Uprising, the Ridolfi Plot, the Throckmorton Plot, she had communicated with the plotters but never acted as their commanding officer. Elizabeth knew that and appreciated it, if no one else did. But this one was different.

Anthony Babington was organizing it. Anthony, whom she had seen grow up, who had been her companion for years, and who was, evidently, more devoted to her than her own natural son! For her, Anthony was willing to risk his life. The appeal was personal, from a personal friend who wished to deliver her—after seeing firsthand what her conditions of captivity were. She was deeply touched.

And that he had been able to find Englishmen brave enough to "undertake that tragic execution" was extraordinary. Supposedly everyone was in love with their Faerie Queen. But these were not foreigners who had volunteered for the duty. "Six noble gentlemen, all my private friends"—what had the letter said?

Mary unfolded it and reread it carefully. The men were most likely young, with their whole futures before them, like Anthony himself. "Who for the zeal they bear unto the Catholic cause . . ." How had young ones even maintained loyalty to the old religion?

It is different with me, Mary thought. I was brought up Catholic, instructed in the faith when it was not only allowed but expected. I now must maintain the faith because I am a visible symbol of it. But for a young person to embrace it, at a time when it is outlawed! I blush to compare their faith with mine.

And that they do this in fear and with misgivings . . . "undertake that tragic execution." They see it as tragic, not good, not an adventure. And it would be tragic. Murder is always tragic, and those who maintain otherwise are lying to themselves. I am glad they would see it as tragic, otherwise they would be no better than the Lords in Scotland, who saw killing as a sport.

Of course I will not agree to it. I cannot. But if I did—what justification would I have?

She got up and began to walk about her chamber, nervously fingering her rosary.

To begin with, she told herself, I have been detained here illegally. I have tried every means, over the years, to gain my liberty. I begged Elizabeth for a private hearing, I asked to be heard by Parliament. I laid aside my royal prerogative and submitted to the degrading "York Hearings" when first I arrived. I tried to marry my way out of prison, only to have my betrothed executed. I have watched my sympathizers and co-religionists hounded out of the country, likewise imprisoned, even executed. Only then did I turn to foreign help, begging for relief from France and Spain. The French discarded me and the Spanish merely toy with me. If this time they are in earnest, then . . . ?

She sighed. Of course she would not do it. Of course she would not lend herself to this plot. But what if Anthony went ahead with it anyway, assuming that once the deed was done, she would bless it? Youth will not wait, or it is not youth, she reminded herself.

The list of Elizabeth's perfidies, when enumerated like that, was stunning. I came into this country to begin with because she promised to help me! thought Mary. How could I forget? But Elizabeth has hardened her heart against me, like Pharaoh. What was it Scripture said about Pharaoh?

Mary called for Father de Préau. He would know. Was there, perhaps, some spiritual principle here that she should follow? Perhaps assassinating Elizabeth would not even be a grave sin. What about the fact that the Pope's secretary had said, "Since that guilty woman of England is the cause of so much injury to the Catholic faith, there is no doubt that whosoever sends her out of the world with pious intention of doing God service, not only does not sin but gains merit, especially having regard to the excommunication sentence passed on her by Pius V of holy memory." What could he mean by that? Certainly Anthony's friends would be acting in "pious intention." He says it is for "the zeal they bear unto the Catholic cause."

Father de Préau had arrived. He looked curious to see what she had wanted, and surprised to see her pacing so rapidly.

"Ah, my dear, you must have improved. I have not seen you walking so vigorously in many months."

She stopped, shocked. She had not even noticed how fast she was moving. He was right. Then she realized why: she was excited, and strength was flowing back into her. "Yes, our prayers have been answered," was all she said. "Good Father, do you have the Scriptures that tell the story of Moses in Egypt?"

"Why—yes. Shall I fetch them?"

"Please." When he went to get them, she continued her thinking. Would this be a sin? Or was it merely a clever test?

"Here, Your Majesty," said Father de Préau, a bundle under his arm. "It is most inspiring that you wish to pursue this. So many never venture beyond the Gospels and Epistles. Now, as to Moses and Pharaoh . . . let me see. . . . " He put the volume down on a table and searched. "Here, in the Book of Exodus . . . yes. The Lord says, 'I have seen all that hath befallen you in Egypt. And I have said the word to bring you forth out of the affliction of Egypt. . . . But I know that the king of Egypt will not let you go, but by a mighty hand. But I shall harden his heart, and he will not hear you: and I will lay my hand upon Egypt and will bring my people out of the land of Egypt, by very great judgements.' Is that what you wished to know?"

"Yes. Read me about Pharaoh's heart being hardened."

"Hmmm. 'And Pharaoh's heart was hardened, so that neither this time would he let the people go.' 'And his heart was hardened, and the heart of his servants, and it was made exceeding hard.' 'And the Lord said to Moses: Pharaoh will not hear you.' "

"Yes!" said Mary. "It is all true! 'His heart was hardened, and the heart of his servants'—Cecil, Paulet, Shrewsbury!—'and it was made exceeding hard.' 'Pharaoh will not hear you.' I wrote her once, saying, 'Be not like the serpent that stoppeth his ears,' and begged her to hear me. But no!"

Father de Préau closed the Scriptures. "Please do not excite yourself. It is merely the old, old story of Moses—"

"It is more than that!" cried Mary. "More than that!"

And I will bring my people out, by a very great judgement. Great judgement indeed! she thought. But of course I will never agree to it. Never.

She was alone, before the crucifix. It was very late and the household was sleeping. Mary had insisted to her ladies that she wished to be completely alone for her devotions. Now she knelt in front of the crucifix that had seen her through so many decisions, and spoke softly to it.

"I offer You what has been offered to me," she whispered. "Young Anthony Babington wishes to free me from this prison, and he has found friends who are willing to risk their lives to achieve it. Just think—what bonds of kinship and blood have failed to call forth, this person is willing to undertake. Did You—is it possible that You sent him to begin with, to my very household? I know that You have the ordering of all things under Your mighty hand. He appeared in Shrewsbury's house as if he were sent. Yet I cannot believe it would be right for me to agree to such a scheme. You have said, in the very commandments, 'Thou shalt not kill.' "

She bent her head down and rested her forehead on her arms. "Help me," she prayed. But she no longer expected a direct answer, as she had long ago. She knew the crucifix, and God, and herself, so much better than that now.

Lying in bed, she tried to sleep. Idly she turned her wedding ring on her hand, the ring that Bothwell had put on her finger so very long ago. Bothwell . . . Would he let scruples stand between himself and freedom, when those holding him had sinned in doing so? She did not even have to answer the question. Bothwell would be ashamed of her for lying here so still, for meekly turning aside the offer, for obediently following Elizabeth's stingy dictates. Once I was as brave as he, she thought. What did he call me? "Heart of my heart, bone of my bone, spirit of my spirit, we cannot be held." Yes, he died in prison, but only because he had made a daring escape from another prison. Only the harshest dungeon could hold him, whereas I sit here in a chamber saying, "I dare not, I dare not!" Prison has robbed me of my courage.

She turned over, her heart heavy. Thinking of Bothwell and how she was betraying his memory of her was painful.

Perhaps I owe it to him, and to my loyal supporters, she thought wearily. James has abandoned me, but there are others who have not.

Suddenly she did not feel so old and outworn. She had not been entirely forgotten. Perhaps she was more than just a scarecrow wearing a crucifix, standing guard in a barren field.

She closed her eyes. She would not have to answer the letter for days. In the meantime . . .

The letter was waiting for her in the morning; indeed, it had not even waited until morning, but had invaded her consciousness even as she slept. She had dreamed of it, of its tantalizing words, of Anthony, grown now to manhood. Flashing images of England's proud young men like the Earl of Essex and Sir Philip Sidney, fighting in the Netherlands, were superimposed on another secret band of equally daring young men. Not everyone had answered Elizabeth's call to take up the Protestant banner; other battlefields still beckoned, commanding loyalty.

She found that the interval of sleep had given her a fierce longing for action—the first action that had been possible in years. Swept away were the hours and days of patient praying and resignation that had enveloped her so comfortably and felt so natural; resurrected was the old self that she had thought long dead.

Yet she knew the letter for what it was, a mirage and a temptation. Desperately she threw herself on her knees before the little altar and begged to be prevented from yielding to it. Never had she felt more acutely the two sides of her own nature: the spiritual, which sought to transcend the limitations of the earthly, and the natural, strong and vital and unable to die except when the heart actually stopped beating.

The letter was visible, folded neatly on her desk nearby. She could see it out of the corner of her eye. She focused more intently on the crucifix.

"So, as Saint Paul said, I find this law at work," she whispered, "when I want to do good, evil is right here with me. What a wretched woman I am! Who will rescue me from this body of death?"

She buried her face in the soft velvet of the prie-dieu.

Rescue me from this body of death.

That is what this letter is about. One way or another, it will rescue me from this body of death. My summons has come at last.

She found Nau's mood to have changed from enthusiasm to caution overnight.

"My friend," she said, strangely calm, possessed of an otherworldly resolution, "this is a timely offer. I am minded to give myself to it."

The little Frenchman, his pointed beard neatly combed, shook his head. His beard did not quiver, so oiled was it. "No, Madam, I have misgivings."

"Yesterday you were enthusiastic."

"But in the night, other thoughts came to me. All these plots have failed. This one is no different from the others."

"With this one exception: this one specifies the death of Elizabeth."

"Yes, and that is what gives me pause."

"In truth, all the others would have had to come to that," said Mary. "For Elizabeth would not be contented to retire to the country. Queens do not; I myself am all the example one needs of that. I do not wish her death, but I do wish my freedom. Pray take my answer, and take it now."

"Very well." Nau seated himself to take the dictation she would give in French, the language she always used best for expressing herself.

Mary stood beside him, and began reciting in a mechanical voice, " 'Dear Friend, with all my heart I give you leave to act in my name, and will endeavour to direct your proceedings. As to my rescue, there could be three means of it: the first, as I am taking the air on horseback on a plain between this place and Stafford, where few people are ordinarily met, some fifty or sixty men, well armed and mounted, might come and seize me. . . . The second is to come at midnight and set fire to the barns, stables, and out-buildings. . . . The third is that when the carts, which generally come very early in the morning, arrive here, you could join them in disguise. . . .' "

Her detailed plans tumbled forth without rehearsal, making her realize that she had been forming them, hidden from her vigilant conscience, for some time already. She was startled, almost frightened, by their complete-ness.

Nau was writing furiously. At length he said, "Perhaps, Madam, it were best not to be specific. Do not reply to their plans; ignore them, as you have similar ones in times past. What if it is a trap?"

"This may be my last chance; sooner or later Paulet will discover the secret post, or the brewer will decide to stop helping us," she said.

"But it is unwise to commit yourself in writing this way!" he protested.

"Pray continue," she said firmly. " 'When the troops have landed from Spain, affairs being thus prepared, and forces in readiness, both outside and inside the realm, then shall it be time to set the six gentlemen to work, taking order, upon the accomplishment of the said design, I may be suddenly transported out of this place.' "

She stopped and caught her breath. *Set the six gentlemen to work.* It sounded so businesslike, like carrying a litter. Or a coffin. Were there not always six pallbearers to a coffin?

Nau was clutching his sleeve. "My hand trembles to write it," he said.

"My heart trembles to think it," she answered. "But to continue. 'Now since there can be no certain day appointed for the accomplishment of the said gentlemen's design, so that others may be in readiness to take me from hence, I would that the said gentlemen had always about them, or at least at court, four stout men furnished with good and speedy horses, to come with all diligence as soon as the said design shall be accomplished, to inform all who have been appointed for my rescue, before my keeper can have knowledge of the execution of the said design, or time to fortify this house.' "

"Why do you keep saying 'said design'?" asked Nau, his voice trembling. "Do you think that will fool anyone? Or save yourself if our enemies read it?"

"I know not what else to call it. I will not say . . . the word," she said. "But I do not wish it to take place! Perhaps I can be rescued without it, and I must lay out those plans as well. Continue: 'Do not allow any English uprising to take place without the support of foreign help, neither stir without having first made sure I am safe, either taken from my prison, or safeguarded there by a good army. Otherwise the Queen would simply capture me again, incarcerating me in some hole from whence I should never come forth again. And she would persecute with the utmost extremity all who had assisted me in my escape, which I should regret much more than any ill that might befall me myself.' "

"Now you are confusing them," said Nau. "First you say Elizabeth must be killed first, then you say you must be rescued first. Which way will you have it?"

"The way fate will have it!" she said, about to scream with the torture of it. "Whatever way fate will go—I know not—her death or mine, or neither, or both—"

"Then, Madam, you are better off not replying at all, or returning a vague answer. This tells them nothing, but tells your enemies everything," he said sternly.

"I care not!" she burst out. "I care not! Let my enemies take me, I give them leave, only this must be ended, I cannot go on like this, a living death, my punishment is too great! Welcome, therefore, my ultimate misfortune!"

Nau rose. "I will send for Father de Préau. You are speaking now of suicide; it is a mortal sin to bring about your own death in despair."

Mary grabbed his arm. "I forbid you to go. I am not contemplating suicide, nor am I in despair. This is my last decision, the decision that ends all others for me, and thereby I embrace my fate. I embrace Fate like a lover. All my life, Fate has wished to be my lover, and tried to govern me. Now I turn to submit to his embraces."

"To reply to this letter is the utmost folly," he said.

"My friend, it is not folly, but a gamble. But it is a gamble I am willing to take, for, no matter what happens, I shall be the victor. If I am freed, then I shall rejoice. And if I am caught, tried, and executed, then I shall also be free, and shall rejoice. I will be no more a prisoner!"

"But, good Madam, your loyal supporters—"

"I owe this to my loyal supporters. They are willing to die for me; they are brave indeed. Shall I not be equally willing to die for them, and witness to the truth—the truth that I have been held here not because of what befell Darnley twenty years ago in Scotland, but because of my faith and my royal blood?"

"Do not give in to this temptation!" said Nau. "I beg you!"

She felt calm, delivered from fear. She knew this was what she must do, and she knew it in the part of herself that was beyond words or thinking. "Give the letter to Curle and have it ciphered. Make it ready to go out with the brewer next time." She burst into tears of relief.

XXV

The letter was taken by Nau to the page; the page took it down to the cellar and inserted it into the secret box on July sixteenth, the day the brewer was due to return. That afternoon the empty barrel was rolled out and put on the wagon, and driven out of sight of the castle. Then the brewer dismounted and retrieved the letter. Paulet and Phelippes were waiting nearby, and took it.

By nightfall Phelippes had deciphered it. He sat grinning. It was all over. He drew a gallows mark on the outside of his translation. Walsingham would appreciate the humour.

Suddenly he had an idea. It would be convenient to have the names of all the conspirators spelled out by the unfortunate Babington. An expert forger, he had no difficulty in adding a postscript to the original letter:

> I would be glad to know the names and qualities of the six gentlemen to accomplish the design, for it may be that, upon knowledge of the parties, I shall be able to give you some further advice necessary to be followed therein; as also, from time to time particularly how you proceed; and as soon as you may, for the same purpose, who be ready, and how far every one privy hereunto.

He handed it over to Arthur Gregory, his accomplice; Gregory was a genius at breaking open sealed letters and resealing them without trace.

Phelippes leaned back in his chair. Time to start rounding up the conspirators; they had served their purpose. They only had to wait for Babington to reply, and even that was not really necessary, just an extra touch.

Walsingham had known it would be difficult, but not this difficult. He had presented his evidence to the Queen, deferentially. He had expected her to be sad; he himself was depressed by his own success. Just once he wished that when he thought the worst of someone, he would be proved wrong. But it never worked that way.

Still, the Queen took it hard. She read and reread the letter, silently. She put it down and paced.

"Dearest sovereign," Walsingham finally said, "do we have your permission to arrest her?"

"No!" Elizabeth snapped.

"We must have access to her papers," insisted Walsingham. "She has stacks of them in her quarters at Chartley, zealously guarded. Now it is necessary, for your own safety, that we take them, so we know the extent of the plots."

Elizabeth kept scratching her neck, leaving red welts. "This letter . . . " she finally said, faintly. It had clearly disturbed her greatly. Her face looked as if it had been slapped: it showed shock and profound disillusionment. "This letter . . . I would she had never written it."

"She will soon feel the same way. But what was it Pilate said? 'What I have written, I have written.' It must stand as it is. And she must be arrested."

Elizabeth laughed, a thin little laugh. "How can a prisoner be arrested?"

"And formally charged with her crime," Walsingham insisted.

" 'At last,' she would say. 'After eighteen years, I am formally charged with something.' Perhaps that is why she did it. Perhaps—"

"There can be no excuses. Treason is treason. The law is the law."

"What I have written, I have written. Very well. Do it." Her voice was gruff.

After Walsingham had left, she sat for a long time, unmoving, hoping the pain would subside.

The extent of the pain was astounding. A ruler must come to accept walking with death every day, accept the hatred that would always come from a disgruntled few.

But my own flesh and blood, a woman like myself, also an anointed queen, to plan my murder! The words kept repeating themselves in her mind, marching proudly in succession like a parade of knights: . . . then shall it be time to set the six gentlemen to work, taking order, upon the accomplishment of the said design . . . . She shuddered, feeling the knife. Who were these courtiers? Who were these people who served, unsuspected, in her very presence?

And lest she misconstrue the reference, Walsingham had supplied the letter to which this was an answer, which was more explicit: . . . who for the zeal they bear unto the Catholic cause and Your Majesty's service will undertake that tragic execution. . . .

Thank you, Walsingham, she thought.

Yet at the same time she was deeply grateful for such a clever and faithful servant. What if he were working for the other side?

It has ever been my blessing that the Queen of Scots has never had a competent and loyal servant. Those that are competent have proved disloyal, and those that are loyal have proved incompetent.

She dreaded what was now to come, what must now come.

❦

On July twentieth, Gilbert Gifford crossed over to Europe, to avoid any questioning. Two weeks later, Ballard was arrested; at the news, Babington fled from his home into the depths of St. John's Wood. Hiding by day, he cut his hair, stained his face with walnut juice, and moved only by night in the forest. He had never obtained the precious passport, and had no hopes of leaving England. At length, hunger drove him to the house of another of the conspirators, Jerome Bellamy.

Walsingham's agents were waiting, and arrested him on the spot. The wild-eyed young man was dragged away, his face gaunt and gypsylike in its darkness.

"No! No!" he screamed. "Mercy!"

While Babington's wife waited in the gardens of their great house in the Barbicon, the rest of the little band of conspirators were rounded up and herded into captivity.

The plot was over, easily dismantled and quickly ended, gone like a sigh.

XXVI

With the dispatching of the letter, Mary felt a panic overtake her that quickly replaced her calmness. How could she have done it? She remembered all the reasons clearly, but now they receded before the one great fact: she had yielded to the temptation. And while it was true that if this came to light and she was punished, it would be less a punishment than a release from an afflicted existence, she was ashamed. Her only consolation came in the fact that undoubtedly the plot would come to nothing, as all the others had. Ironically, her body had responded stirringly to the prospect of battle: the swelling of her knees subsided; her spine straightened and her fingers tingled with newfound suppleness.

From out of the windows she watched as the thick, dull green of July fields turned to hints of gold in early August. Sometimes she trembled as she laid her head against the window frame and looked down the road and across the fields. She had no idea from what direction Babington's men

811

would come, or whether she would even see them approach. It did not matter; that was the mysterious thing. Her part in it was over, just by sending the reply. There were no daydreams about crossing to France to live out her days, no fantasies about seeing James face-to-face at last and coming to an understanding, undoing all the damage that had been done between them. She did not imagine visiting her mother's grave in Reims, or seeing her aunt Renée. The future was a blank, and did not concern her; for the first time in her life, she was free of both its menace and its promises. She had made her last decision.

Paulet had taken to looking at her quizzically, observing her movements as if he were inspecting a racehorse. He himself had not been well, and was limping slightly. Mary's servants reported that he had been seen walking in the fields, talking earnestly to someone from court, far out of earshot. Was she to be moved? Transferred to another keeper? It was all the same to her now.

On August eighth, Mary had just finished her morning prayers when Paulet himself appeared on her threshold. He was leaning on his stick, and his smile looked painted on.

"Madam," he rasped, "an invitation has been received from one of our neighbours, Sir Walter Aston, to hunt the deer in his estate at Tixall. Would you care to try it? I notice your health has improved mightily in the last month."

"Hunt?" she said. It had been so long since she had been hunting, and Paulet had never allowed her out beyond the grounds. "But, my friend, what of you? You seem as uncomfortable in your legs as I was of late."

He allowed himself a slight smile. Was this her celebrated charm—to notice and care about the little things around her? Even though he knew it was false, it was strangely warming. "I can manage well enough. Would you like it?"

"Oh, yes!"

"Then make yourself ready. You may take a few attendants with you. Who knows whom you might meet? I understand Sir Walter may join us; if not on the hunt itself, he will certainly entertain us at his home afterward."

"Is not Tixall a new mansion?"

"Indeed, yes. It is completed but recently, and is the most luxurious in the county, for comforts at least. Perhaps he will give us a tour, show us the new inventions he has installed. I have heard that there are some . . . sanitary arrangements . . . ahem . . . " His face grew red. "And he has had the house built facing south, most daring, what with the evil winds from that direction . . . nonetheless, he uses less wood and coal in winter for heating."

"I do look forward to seeing it, and thank him for the invitation," said Mary.

"Can you be ready to leave in an hour?" asked Paulet. "We can picnic in the fields for dinner." He bowed stiffly, and took his leave.

"Nau, Curle! Did you hear?" said Mary. "Would you care to join us? And Jane? Elizabeth?"

"Nay, we have work to do," said the women.

"So do we, but we can lay it aside," said the men.

"Your main work is done," said Mary to the secretaries. "Now you can take your ease. Come, let us make ready!"

She threw open her trunk and pulled out a green riding habit. She had never had an opportunity to wear it, since old Balthazzar had made it for her with shaking hands two years earlier. There was even a little feathered bonnet go to with it. They had designed it based on sketches that had come from France just before her letters had ceased, so it was not so terribly out of style.

Jane dressed her hair, putting on her best wig. She never went without her wigs, as her real hair had been kept short the better to enable the preferred treatment for headaches—medicinal poultices—to be administered.

"You look lovely," said Jane, studying Mary's face. The colour had come back into it, the lines softened, for no apparent reason. Nothing had happened, no easing of the conditions of confinement, and yet this noticeable change.

"Thank you." Mary wondered if they would be met by any of the neighbours, if not on the hunt itself, then at the reception at Tixall. It would be heaven, to see some new faces.

The day was hot and fair, and by ten o'clock they were riding out beyond the moat—Mary and her two secretaries and faithful physician. Not that she expected to be taken ill, but she was glad to be able to give him an outing, something pleasant in his long days of serving her.

The guard contingent was heavier than usual, but it was of no moment. They descended from the hill, leaving Chartley behind. Mary turned to look at it, able to see it in its setting for the first time. Her own quarters looked so tiny.

The hazy August air, the thick smell of heated earth, enveloped her like a mantle.

It is no wonder the pagans always had an earth goddess, she thought. Today even I feel her presence—mellow, swollen, kindly. I see her in the weighted grapevines and branches of the pear trees, bent with heavy fruit. I feel her radiant touch in the sun on my cheek; I smell her perfume in the flanks of these healthy horses; I hear her voice in the cries and calls of the half-grown birds now leaving their nests and learning to fly. In France they understood that to honour the classic gods was not to be unfaithful to the true ones; in France . . .

If I go to France . . . No, do not think of it.

The hunters halted and gathered in one spot preparatory to blowing the horn and loosing the hounds. Many knew this was her last opportunity to refasten her bonnet and take a drink from her riding-bottle.

Suddenly a company of horsemen appeared on the horizon, riding fast.

They must be chasing someone, was Mary's first thought. But I saw no one else on the road.

Then at once she realized: It was Babington! He had come for her!

But I am not ready, this is not the time, I wanted to hunt . . .

Fool! How ungrateful can you be?

She clutched her reins, preparing herself. Her heart was thudding. This was not supposed to happen, not really, it had all been a game of pretend. . . .

The men were approaching, and their speed was not slackening. Did they mean to run Paulet and the guards down? There was a flash, the glint of metal in the sun. The swords were out. She flinched, and turned her head away.

She heard the thunder of the hooves, then voices. She raised her eyes to see a thickset gentleman, dressed in an elaborate green-and-gold costume, dismounting. He saluted Paulet, who seemed unsurprised. Paulet then dismounted, and together they walked over to her.

"Sir Thomas Gorges, special emissary from Queen Elizabeth," announced Paulet in a high, nasal voice.

"Madam!" cried the green-and-gold envoy in ringing tones. "The Queen my mistress finds it very strange that you, contrary to the pact and engagement made between you, should have conspired against her and her State, a thing which she could not have believed had she not seen proofs of it with her own eyes and known it for certain." He glared at Mary.

"Sir, I know not what you mean, I have not—"

"A horrible conspiracy against the life of the Queen has been discovered, in which you have shared!" he cried. "As a result, I am to conduct you to Tixall. You are under arrest, Madam!"

Nau and Curle had ridden over, taking their place on either side of her.

"Away with them!" said Gorges. "They are under arrest, too! Take them to the Tower!"

Soldiers immediately surrounded the secretaries and dragged them away.

"Now, Madam, turn your horse toward Tixall!"

He nodded to one of the soldiers, who positioned his spear at Mary's horse.

"Master Paulet, you knew of this!" Mary cried. "It was for this you brought me here!"

The keeper just looked at her, and did not answer.

"I refuse to go! I refuse to go!" she cried. "You want only to search my rooms, and steal my possessions, and plant false evidence against me in my absence! You have no right, you know it is illegal! You Judas!"

"I am no Judas," he said with an injured air. "I know whom I serve: my Queen Elizabeth. I never pretended to be your friend, nor to serve you. Indeed, it would be impossible to do so, as you are my own Queen's enemy."

"No! It is not so!"

"Be quiet! Obey the orders, or I shall bind you and put you in a carriage and transport you to Tixall. For, make no mistake, that is where you are going!"

Gorges yanked on her horse's bridle. "Come!"

Surrounded by soldiers with bristling spears, Mary rode in silence along the road to Tixall. Only her physician remained by her side; Nau and Curle had been taken away.

Was she to be summarily executed? What was it this man had said? *You are under arrest.* But the Act for the Queen's Safety—what had it specified? That anyone who had been involved in a conspiracy against the Queen could be executed? Or was that the Bond? Yes, that was the Bond. The Act had softened it to the extent of saying the guilty parties must at least be examined before being executed.

But it did not say how official the "examination" must be. Perhaps just a few rough questions from Gorges, the "official emissary," would suffice for form's sake.

You have conspired . . . a horrible conspiracy . . . those were his words.

What was he talking about? Was it the Babington Plot, or something else entirely? Was it even a real plot, or merely a manufactured one for the government's purposes?

Her heart now seemed to have stopped beating, where just a few moments earlier it had raced so fast she had felt faint. Her hands were chilled, and all the warmth was gone from the summer afternoon.

You must be ready to die. It has come to this. Today is the day.

They reached the gatehouse of Tixall, a grey, three-storey decorated box on the edge of the hunting park. Four octagonal towers, capped by rounded roofs and stiff bronze pennants, guarded each corner of the building. Beneath its arched Italianate entrance they trotted, Mary still as cold as death as she passed into the shadow.

"Courage!" said Bourgoing, the physician. "Queen Elizabeth is dead. This is all only for our own protection, in case there are other assassins about."

"No," said Mary. "It is this Queen who is dead."

They pushed her into a room of the older portion of the manor house, and dragged Bourgoing away. The door slammed shut, and she was utterly alone. There was no attendant, no servant, not even a guard. One little room opened off the larger one, and there was no paper, no pen, no books. And for once she did not have her cross or rosary with her.

When darkness fell, a maidservant brought in one candle and placed it silently on a table. Then she left and locked the door behind her.

Mary sank down on a small chair, so drained she could hardly move.

Here it is, she thought. It has come to this at last.

I knew it would, she answered herself. And it is all right; it is acceptable.

I can bear it. Elizabeth still lives, and the plot came to nothing. God has been merciful; He has spared me from being a murderess. Now I will not have her death on my conscience. I failed in the test He had set me, but He held me back from calamity.

She crawled onto the bed and fell asleep, deeply relieved.

For seventeen days she remained at Tixall. In a few days they allowed two attendants to bring her a change of clothing. She asked to be allowed to write to Queen Elizabeth, but Paulet—who had stayed on at Tixall to guard her—refused.

During those seventeen days, she reviewed all her past life. There was nothing to read, no distractions, no conversation, and the long hours must be passed in thinking. When events were actually happening, there seemed to be no pattern to them. But seen in retrospect, a pattern emerged. Only at the end of a life could the pattern be discerned; only then was there a completed weaving to be seen. And hers was this: since the moment of her birth, she had been an inconvenient person, a person who did not fit in, who ruined other people's tidy patterns.

She had been born a girl when her father longed for a male heir, a princess when the realm longed for a prince.

She had French blood and a French upbringing, making her a stranger in the land she was given to rule and hateful to her own people.

She was a Catholic ruler in a Protestant land, the only one such in the world.

By sex, by upbringing, by religion, she was out of step with her own people. Yet those three things could not be repudiated; they *were* her very self.

She had tried to compensate for these shortcomings by marriage, but her marriages rendered her even more obnoxious to her own people. They would not tolerate a foreign prince, a Catholic, but the native sons she married instead were unacceptable. One was too weak, the other too strong.

She was peace-loving in a country where only ruthlessness and power were respected. She had pardoned rebels instead of executing them; after each plot she had allowed the traitors to creep back into Scotland and into favour. She thought it was Christian kindness; they saw it as weakness, and scorned her.

Lord James, Knox, Morton, Erskine, Darnley, Lennox . . . the list was endless. Those she had treated kindly had betrayed her.

What were the duties of the Messiah, and therefore of all Christian rulers? *To preach good news to the poor, to proclaim freedom for the prisoners and recovery of sight for the blind, to release the oppressed.* Yet it was I who was blind, it was I who ended up imprisoned.

After the final upheaval, it had become clear there was no place on earth that even wanted her. There was no rest for her, no haven. Her beloved France—the country for which she had suffered so in her own!—would not lift a finger for her. Elizabeth of England, her kinswoman, had found her too close in blood to dispose of, but too alien to welcome.

To think of it: no place on earth where I can find a home! she came to realize. Day after day she thought these melancholy thoughts, cataloguing her failures.

On the sixteenth day she arose, and it was all different. She had had one simple, revolutionary thought: My life is not over yet. By my death, I may redeem it.

From far away, from her childhood in France, her mighty uncle Guise's words returned to her.

"My child," he had said, touching her curls, "you possess the hereditary courage of your race. I think, when the time comes, you will well know how to die."

Know well how to die.

How did a person know well how to die? It was the one thing for which there could be no rehearsal.

But it was also the one time all the eyes of the world were upon you, if you died a public death. . . .

A public death! she prayed. Grant me a public death! That is all I ask. Grant me a public death, and leave me to arrange the rest in a manner pleasing to You, as an offering I hope You will accept. As a sacrifice to make up for my agreeing, only for a moment, to murder . . .

&

At the end of the seventeen days, they came to fetch Mary, to take her . . . where? Was she to be taken directly to the Tower? Had it not been that she would regret not bidding a personal farewell to all her faithful servants, she would have preferred it that way. Let it happen, and happen quickly, before her resolve faded.

As she passed underneath the long passageway in the jaunty gatehouse, she was greeted with crowds of beggars. They had heard she was held here, and had gathered waiting for her release; the Queen of Scots was reputed to be a generous almsgiver.

"Alms! Alms!" they cried, pushing forward. Mothers held up ragged babies and pointed at them; crippled men leaned on their sticks and extended clawlike hands.

"Ah, good people," she said, gazing on them. "I have no alms to give you, as I am a beggar now myself."

"Liar!" hissed Paulet in her ear. "Always misrepresenting yourself, and for the better. You are no beggar, but have rolls and rolls of money put away in your cabinets."

"It is money for my funeral expenses," said Mary.

"Then you are right to save it, for you shall need it," he said ominously. He prodded her into the waiting carriage with its shades rolled down.

When they returned to Chartley, Mary saw what had happened. Her quarters had been ransacked, all her private papers removed, and some of her personal possessions, which obviously could have no political value, taken: trinkets, a woollen shawl, even toys. The intruders had not even bothered to straighten up the mess, but left it contemptuously as it was. Doors hung open, discarded objects lay in piles around the cupboards and chests.

"The papers, letters, and ciphers were all boxed and sent to Queen Elizabeth," said Paulet.

"I wonder how Her Majesty will feel upon reading so many secret letters of support from her own loyal courtiers?" asked Mary.

Paulet glared and turned on his heel, leaving her alone.

Slowly she walked around the room. It no longer felt like her room, nor did she have any part in it. She was done with those concerns.

Hurry, she thought. Hurry, before the old cares and fears return! Now I know why Thomas More rejoiced when they took him to the Tower and he no longer had an escape. Until then, he could have bolted through the great wide gate and onto the broad path.

"You will face a trial," said Paulet. "It will be held elsewhere. Prepare yourself."

"When will it take place?" asked Mary.

"That I do not know. Nor where. The Privy Council wished you to be sent to the Tower, but the Queen refused. They are in the process of selecting a site."

"I see." It was hard for her to continue standing; her legs had reverted back to their infirmity. But she was determined to stand there as tall and straight as possible.

"Are you not curious to know what has happened to your fellow conspirators?" Paulet said. His distaste for her was now being flooded with curiosity about her strange demeanour.

"I do not know to what you refer," she maintained.

"Very good, very good, legally you must claim that. Clever. Your legs may be rotten, but your mind is sharp as ever. But I shall tell you anyway: Ballard and Babington and Tichborne and all fourteen of them were arrested, taken to the Tower, and tried. Found guilty, of course. People were in an uproar, and demanded a new form of death for them, one that was more cruel than the usual felon's execution. But our gracious Queen refused; she said the normal one, if carried out according to specifications, was enough." He watched her carefully for any signs of emotion. "So Ballard and Babington and five others were taken to St. Giles and drawn and quartered. This time the hangman did not let them hang until dead, but cut them down still alive and disemboweled them and castrated them."

Mary felt waves of revulsion and fear taking control of her. She swayed slightly on her feet and reached out to steady herself against a table.

"Their private parts were cut off and burnt—"

"Enough." She held out her hand. "It is a sin to revel in the sufferings of others, friend. So I must forbid you to speak further of it."

"I am not revelling in it!" he said indignantly. But he, like many others, had been disgusted by the Queen's command to execute the other half of the criminals as humanely as possible. Such squeamishness and misplaced charity did nothing to discourage further attempts at assassination.

"When you speak of mine, then, I hope your eyes have less shine in them."

XXVII

No warning was given. One night Mary said her evening prayers with her household, and the next morning her servants were locked in their rooms, while Sir Thomas Gorges and his henchman, Stallenge, arrived to conduct her away. They were armed with pistols, and treated her as if she were either a dangerous swordsman or a poisonous adder who might strike a mortal blow at any second. They posted guards at her servants' windows so that they could not even wave farewell.

Mary descended the stairway slowly, in spite of their attempts to rush her. She could not walk as fast as they imagined she could, but she refused to be carried.

Outside a carriage awaited, two bay horses swishing their tails briskly.

"Where am I to be taken?" she asked.

"To Fotheringhay Castle in Northamptonshire," replied Gorges.

Surrounding the carriage was an armed body of Protestant gentlemen of the country. Their spears and muskets shone in the friendly September sunlight.

"If a dove flew there, it would be seventy miles away," said Gorges. "But on the roads we have, it will be longer. Three or four days' journey."

"Will I be permitted to look out at the countryside?"

Gorges and Paulet laughed and looked at each other. "She wants to see the sights! Fancy that!" said Gorges. "Shall we also stop at the ancient monuments, and point them out to you? Yes, you may look out the windows. But at the slightest sign of waving to the people, or stirring up sympathy, the shades go down!"

The carriage rolled away down the long path leading from Chartley, whence the brewer had come labouring up with his wagon, onto the main road leading eastward. Chartley, with its rounded towers and large expanses of glass, diminished until it was just a speck on the horizon, no bigger than a stick.

The road took them through Needwood Forest and through Burton-upon-Trent—the very home of the fateful brewer—and then through Charnwood Forest and into the large, thriving town of Leicester.

Cardinal Wolsey was buried here, Mary knew. In the last month she had been reading extensively from English history. He, too, had been summoned by the monarch to come and stand trial for "treason"; he, too, had stayed at Wingfield Manor for a time. He had died among the monks at Leicester Abbey, possibly by his own hand, with the now-famous farewell, "Had I but served my God with half the zeal I served my king, He would not in mine age have left me naked to mine enemies."

She shuddered and crossed herself. There was yet time to make sure that those words, those doleful, tragic words, would not apply to her. There was yet a great service she could do for God.

Fotheringhay reared up from the uninspiring landscape. As they had travelled east, the rolling hills had disappeared and the surroundings had begun to take on a level appearance, although the meadows were pleasant enough. The gigantic, brooding pile was situated on the River Nene, and surrounded by two huge moats: the outer one was seventy-five feet wide, and the inner sixty-five. The road leading up to it had always been called Perryho Lane.

It sounded Latin to Mary, and a sad, appropriate phrase at that. "Perio," she whispered. "I perish."

The carriage rolled across the drawbridge and in through the massive north gateway, its only entrance. The very stones of the ancient fortress were grey and stained and seemed to emanate gloom.

High on each side of the courtyard the thick walls soared, almost shutting out the daylight. A castle had stood on this site since the days of the Conqueror, and it seemed to have gathered and concentrated all the foreboding doom of each age within itself. It was now exclusively a state prison. It had once belonged to David of Scotland, but had been lost to the Plantagenets, who had played out their own painful parts here. Richard Plantagenet, Earl of Cambridge, had been beheaded for conspiring against Henry V; Richard III had been born here; Edward Courtenay, Earl of Devonshire, had been imprisoned here. Henry VIII had tried to send Katherine of Aragon here, but she had refused.

Mary descended from the carriage, and found herself standing in the courtyard. She could see that there was a Great Hall, and also a chapel, along one side of the buildings. An octagonal tower stood in the northwest corner, and it was to this that she was led by a troop of armed men. There had been no formal greeting, no welcome from the castellan—whoever he was.

Up the stairs she laboured, stopping every fifth or sixth step. The old-fashioned stone stairwell was dark and the stones worn by countless feet passing over them, until the lip of each step dipped like a lily petal. At last she emerged onto a landing on the first floor.

"This tower is yours," said Gorges. "There are two chambers on this floor, two on the floor above."

She looked around the almost-bare room. It was only about sixteen feet across; the other "chamber" was nothing but a tiny closet.

"I thank you," she finally said. "Will my furnishings—what is left of them—be sent?"

"Aye, they're following."

When they left, with a clang of the door, Mary stood shivering in the middle of the room. This was the sort of place where political killings took place—and there had been so many of them in English history: the smothered little princes in the Tower, the gruesome murder of Edward II in Berkeley Castle by a red-hot poker, and Richard II's secret murder in Pontefract Castle. And who had murdered these kings? Other kings who had found them inconvenient, in the way.

Have they sent me here to be murdered? she cried silently to herself. O God, preserve me from a secret murder! For then I could not honour You in it, nor make a statement for posterity. Which is exactly what the English would wish to prevent. . . .

Shuddering, she sat down on a stool in the cold, dark room.

In a few days, a reduced suite of her servants joined her, and some of her furniture arrived. Her prie-dieu and portable altar and old ivory crucifix were set up to make a makeshift oratory. The remaining personal possessions, like the miniatures of her family, and treasured letters that had survived the rifling, came like friends to comfort her.

Her suite was quite small now: Jane Kennedy; Elizabeth and Barbara Curle; Gilles Mowbray; Andrew Melville, her master of the household; Bastian Pages and his wife; Willie Douglas; her old tailor Balthazzar; equally old Didier her porter; Dominique Bourgoing the physician; Jacques Gervais the apothecary; Pierre Gorion the surgeon; and Father de Préau. All her "outdoor people," her horsekeepers and carriage driver, had been dismissed. She was not to go outdoors ever again.

All these people were jammed into the octagonal tower rooms; some of her bolder servants managed to explore the rest of the castle and reported back that there were many empty staterooms along one entire side of the courtyard.

"Ah," said Mary, understanding the meaning. "Those are to house the men who are coming to judge me."

A week after her arrival, Paulet stepped into the room. He looked triumphant as he said, "Madam, your misdeeds are now to be punished. You will be interrogated by the lords of the land. I advise you, therefore, to confess your crime now and beg pardon before you are formally convicted by a court of law."

She looked at him, standing there so earnestly. She herself was seated, and did not rise. "You treat me like a child," she said, "who should confess to its parents and so avoid a spanking. I have nothing to confess."

His mouth dropped open and anger tore across his face. "Why, you—"

"As a sinner," she cut him off, "I am truly conscious of having often offended my Creator, and I beg Him to forgive me. But as Queen and sovereign, I am aware of no fault or offence for which I have to render account to anyone here below."

"Queen! Sovereign!" he sputtered.

"As therefore I could not offend, I do not wish for pardon; I do not seek it, nor would I accept it from anyone living."

He shook his head angrily. "Pride, Madam, pride! You drown in pride!"

After he had left, Jane said to her, "You will be made to pay for those words, I fear."

"What words I say now mean nothing. The Act for the Queen's Safety was framed to destroy me. It is true, they have no legal right to judge me or try me. But they hold my body, and will punish it regardless."

On October twelfth, a small deputation of lords, including Paulet again, visited Mary in her rooms. They came to announce what Mary already knew, simply by looking out her windows: that the commissioners had arrived at Fotheringhay, bolstered by a force of two thousand soldiers. There would be a trial, and Mary would have to answer to the charge of joining a conspiracy to hurt Elizabeth. She would be judged as "a person that shall or may pretend to the title to the Crown of this realm." The punishment was, first, to be deprived of her title to the English crown forever, and second, to be put to death.

"You know you have no legal right to try me," said Mary calmly. "As a sovereign Queen, there are no peers to sit in judgement of me but fellow monarchs. Are the stands to be filled with the kings and queens of the earth? If so, I welcome them. If not, I refuse to appear."

Paulet thrust a letter into her hands. "The Queen commands you to appear."

"The Queen cannot 'command' me. I am not her subject." Mary read the letter quickly and handed it back to Paulet. "I am not subject to the laws of England."

The Lord Chancellor, Thomas Bromley, snapped, "Yes, you are! You have lived under protection of them, and are therefore subject to them."

Mary could not help laughing quietly. "I came to England to seek Elizabeth's aid, and instead was put in prison. So I have not enjoyed either protection or benefit from these laws—nor have I understood from any man what manner of laws they were. They seem strange laws indeed."

"Your prerogative as a sovereign avails you nothing in the realm," replied

Cecil. "And if you fail to appear, it makes no difference! You will simply be judged *in absentia.*"

Mary had not anticipated that. "Is it even so?" she murmured. "Judged even if I do not appear? How you twist the laws! I have begged to be heard. For twenty years I have asked to speak to Elizabeth, and to answer questions before a free Parliament. But to appear before a closed, secret tribunal . . . what are *you* so afraid of others hearing?"

Cecil, who had dreaded her arguments and recalcitrance, now broke in. "Never fear, all your words will be heard throughout the land—and all your deeds made known. You will have cause to wish they had been kept secret!"

Sir Christopher Hatton suddenly spoke up. Mary saw how the once-handsome courtier had aged since he had come to Scotland for the baptism. The baptism . . . "If you do not appear, it will be thought that you are hiding shameful things. If you are innocent, you have nothing to fear. But by avoiding a trial, you stain your reputation with an eternal blot."

"I would rather die a thousand deaths than acknowledge myself subject to the authority of the Queen of England in any way, to the prejudice of regal majesty," answered Mary. "I cannot thus submit to the laws of the land without injury to myself, the King my son, and all other sovereign princes. I do not recognize the laws of England; I do not know or understand them. And as for a trial, I am alone, without counsel or representation. My papers and notes have all been taken from me, so I cannot even prepare my own defense, except from memory. *You* have all my papers to use against me, whereas I am denied them to defend myself."

"No treason trial permits counsel for the accused," said Bromley.

"Enough of this," said Cecil. "Hear the words which the Queen addresses directly to you. She foresaw just this arguing and resistance. 'You have planned in divers ways and manners to take my life and to ruin my kingdom by the shedding of blood.' "

Mary gasped. The words were blunt, rude, and addressed not from one sovereign to another, but from a master to his disobedient slave. "Was there no salutation?" she interrupted him to ask.

"No. No greeting, no titles."

The note of a master to a slave, indeed.

" 'I have never proceeded so harshly against you,' " Cecil continued. "On the contrary, I have maintained you and preserved your life with the same care which I use for myself.' "

Mary indicated the cramped, dark room. "Is this how she maintains herself?" she asked.

" 'These treasons will be proved to you, and all made manifest. Yet it is my will that you answer the nobles and peers of the kingdom, as if I myself were present. I therefore require, charge, and command that you make answer, for I have been informed of your arrogance,' " Cecil read. " 'Act candidly, and you will receive the greater favour from me.' " He held up the paper and slowly rotated it for all to see.

Mary looked around at all the faces forming a semicircle around her. "I am already forejudged, and condemned to die by this assembly here convened, yet I adjure you to look to your consciences and remember that the theatre of the world is wider than the realm of England!" she cried. "Remind your Queen of it!"

After they were gone, Mary motioned to Jane. "I pray you," she said, "bring me warm cloths for my head. I have a pounding pain in the forehead."

"Forgive me, but I could not help overhearing," she said.

Mary smiled. "You were meant to. I wish Elizabeth could have heard my very words rather than have them repeated to her in a twisted manner later."

"Their words were harsh."

"Yes, and they meant them. You know, Jane, that they will never permit me to live. I know this and am ready." She sighed as she bent her head back and Jane laid the soothing warm cloths across her forehead. "I only pray that my courage will not fail at the test. It is easy to be brave here in my own chambers; every man is a hero before his own private mirror."

"So you will appear?" Jane was rubbing the cloth methodically, sending the warmth deep inside Mary's skull.

"Yes. Not for legal reasons, but for higher ones. I need to speak at last; I will not go silently into their prepared grave for me." She gave a long, regretful sigh. "My courage has always been of the physical type—run, fight, ride. The kind that comes from pounding blood and anger. This requires courage of a different order. And, I beg you—whatever happens, when you leave this place, tell my story. Do not let my words and actions perish, or be snuffed out in this castle."

Jane shuddered. "I cannot bear to think of it! Yet you plan it all so calmly."

"For once in my life I must anticipate. I know it will be their aim to silence me, and I must counter that. I come from an ancient and honourable line of kings, and it is imperative that I die worthy of my blood."

Even if I have not always *lived* worthy of it, she added silently to herself.

The night before the opening of the trial, she spent an hour in prayer before sending for Father de Préau. When the old priest came, she took his hand and withdrew into one of the tiny closets for privacy.

"Bless me," she said. "Strengthen me for tomorrow!"

"I do," he said. "Remember not to worry about what you shall say or not say, that in the necessary moment it shall be given to you what to say. Believe that."

"I am frightened." Her hands were cold, and she knew she would not sleep that night. "Frightened that I will be made to betray myself, my faith, my royal blood. For those are the things of which I am found guilty, those are the things that affront them." She was shaking. "I will be all alone against the multitude of them."

"Not all alone," said the priest. "*He* will be there, right beside you."

"I wish I could actually lean against Him. I wish there were something solid there." She clasped her hands and dug the nails into her palms to steady herself with the pain. "Oh, Father, I have made such mistakes! Yet, in each choice I made, I made it in good faith, thinking it was for the best. I acted according to the knowledge I then had, which was limited. I saw that I should marry, and I loved Darnley, and he had royal blood to make him acceptable to my nobles. On paper, he was the perfect husband! but the things I did not know . . ."

"That is past," said de Préau firmly. "No human being is God, to see into another's heart, or into the future. Forgive yourself; God has. And never forget that out of that 'sin' came James, who will unite the two kingdoms someday. Leave these things to God."

Mary lay wide awake all that night, all the while fearing that her wits would be blunted by fatigue.

Sunlight, diluted but golden, poured through the tiny windows as Mary was being dressed on the morning of October fifteenth. She felt tremulous but no longer afraid; everything seemed already to have happened, and it would unfold before her in the trial chamber. She therefore had no fear of ruining what had already been written, but only curiosity to know what it was.

The trial was to take place in a chamber directly above the Great Hall. She found her legs to be unusually swollen and stiff on this morning of all mornings, much to her embarrassment. That meant she would have to lean on two people, using them as crutches—hardly a regal entrance. But that, too, was written. So she selected Melville and Bourgoing, and twined her arms about them so she could walk slowly into the chamber, passing between two files of armed halberdiers to the entrance of the judgement hall.

Stretching before her, seventy feet to the end of the chamber, sat her judges. Two long benches ran the length of the chamber, and in the middle, a smaller table with the law officers of the crown: an inner and an outer rectangle, crowded with men. She was the only woman in the room. As she entered, forty-four faces turned to stare at her. She counted them, slowly, deliberately, as if to steady herself.

One for each year of my life, she thought. Was it deliberate—or a wink from *Him*, reminding me of an order above all their arrangements?

Silence prevailed; the men were staring at her, gaping at the legendary Bosom Serpent. Few in England had actually seen her in all the years she had been among them; indeed, they were more likely to have seen a ghost.

Was this the *femme fatale*, the woman who had driven so many men to distraction, to their doom? Time had stilled her dangerous charms, had utterly disarmed her. They felt a twinge of disappointment, mixed with relief. The black-clad woman making her way through the door had a double chin and a thick waist.

At the near end of the chamber, a canopied throne presided over the gathering, on a small dais. Mary made her way to it before she was gently stopped and pointed to a chair below it.

Mary cast a despairing look at the empty throne. "I am a queen by birth, and my place should be there under the canopy!" she objected.

"That is Elizabeth's place," said the Lord Chancellor.

Elizabeth's place—mockingly empty. Her absence seemed more solid than the living presence of the judges.

Mary took her place in a velvet chair below the empty, lowering throne, settling herself gingerly.

She looked round. Here were the faces to go with the names she had heard for years. "So many councillors," she whispered to Melville, "and not one for me!"

The Lord Chancellor rose and read the accusation against her. She was to be tried for conspiring the destruction of Elizabeth's person and of the realm of England, and for the subversion of the national religion. She replied, as she had many times before, that she had been illegally detained in England, and that she had agreed to appear only to show that she was not guilty of the attempted murder of Elizabeth. She would answer only on that question, she said. She did not recognize the jurisdiction of the court over her, but came only to clear her good name.

The Lord Chancellor read, in Latin, the commission to try her; Mary protested that the new law had been enacted strictly to snare her.

Serjeant Gawdy, on behalf of the crown, now rose and accused her of attempting to kill Elizabeth, and of inviting foreign invasion of England; both were treason under the Act for the Queen's Safety, which was law, regardless of how newly enacted or for what reason. He then detailed the Babington Plot, accusing her of knowing about it, assenting to it, promising her assistance to the rebels, and showing them ways and means.

"I knew Babington as a page in Shrewsbury's household!" she replied. "But since he departed from thence, I have never held conference with him, written him, nor received letters, of that kind, from him; nor have I ever plotted, or entered into plots, for the destruction of your Queen." That was what he would want her to say; she owed him that loyalty. That was what one always said, one always denied and dared others to prove it.

"Babington confessed!" said Gawdy. "Yes, he eagerly confessed, thinking that somehow that would buy him a privilege. As if to confess to treason were to buy forgiveness!"

He confessed! thought Mary, with a sinking heart. He betrayed himself and his beliefs. She winced inwardly to picture him broken, with the kind of brokenness that was worse than death.

"He told us of the letters that passed between you; indeed, he kindly reconstructed one. And it happens that he was telling the truth—for we have a certified copy of the original letter!"

Mary felt faint. How had they got it? The secret post . . . how had it been breached?

Walsingham now spoke. "The business with the brewer was all our doing," he explained, looking directly at her.

So this was Walsingham: this sallow-faced, ruff-clad Puritan, the dark man who had been her adversary for so long. She stared at him, filled with shock and anger.

All their doing! she thought. From the beginning . . . to have taken the bait so unquestioningly . . . She felt sick.

Walsingham now read Babington's letter in its entirety, followed by her answer to it. She suddenly wondered if Babington had written the letter at all; maybe the whole letter was merely a Walsingham forgery.

"I—It may be that Babington wrote that letter; but let it be proved that I received it! And to prove that I have consented to any wicked design, it will be necessary to produce my own handwriting! It is an easy matter to counterfeit ciphers and characters!" she said. "Besides, if Babington confessed such things, why was he put to death, instead of being brought face-to-face with me as witness to convict me?" She looked round in distress. "I appeal to the statute enacted in the fifteenth year of Queen Elizabeth, which expressly provides that no one should be arraigned for intending the destruction of the sovereign's life but by the testimony and oath of two lawful witnesses, brought face-to-face before him."

Cecil said sarcastically, "I thought you were so ignorant of English law! You see, gentlemen, how much credence can be placed in her statements and disclaimers."

"Perhaps the Babington letter is a forgery!" she cried. "How do you know it was not tampered with? It has obviously passed through many hands! This is Walsingham's doing! He will stop at nothing to achieve my death!"

Eyes flashing, Walsingham rose. "I call God to witness," he said loudly, "that as a private person I have done nothing unbeseeming an honest man, nor, as I bear the place of a public man, have I done anything unworthy of my place. I confess that being very careful for the safety of the Queen and the realm, I have curiously searched out all the practices against the same. If Ballard or Babington had offered me his help in this matter, I should not have refused it; yea, I would have recompensed the pains they had taken. If I have practised anything with them, why did they not utter it to save their lives?"

"I speak only what I have been told, sir, that you are not above creating your own evidence!" said Mary. "You can see by that how dangerous it is to believe ill-wishers. I pray you not credit my slanderers any more than I credit yours."

The hearing went on, with the confessions of Nau and Curle read out. The secretaries had confirmed the text of the Babington letter.

"Then they were threatened with torture," Mary insisted.

On and on went the hearings, pausing only to take midday refreshment. Mary found herself thirsty and faint. Her composure was starting to slip, and she felt as if she were being attacked by a pack of wolves.

In the afternoon, more details were paraded out. Nau and Curle's statements were reexamined, then Cecil accused her of refusing to sign the Treaty of Edinburgh. Next the Parry Plot and Morgan's part in it was brought up, and Mary was questioned as to why she had paid Morgan a pension. She countered by asking why Elizabeth had given Lord James and the other Scottish rebels a pension.

Other accusations were thrown at her: her assumption of the arms and title of England in 1558, her declaring herself the sole legitimate descendant of Henry VII, her presumption in drawing up a pedigree proving herself a representative of the ancient British monarchs by descent from Edmund Ironside, her failure to reprove the Pope for naming her Queen of England—the commissioners not even waiting their turns, shouting that she was "guilty, guilty, guilty!" The sound rose to a babble, drowning out the cheerful crackling of the fire in the huge fireplace. The hearing broke up, dismissed by the Lord Chancellor until the morrow.

Mary was so drained she could scarcely walk unaided back to her quarters. But she was determined to stand erect while she was still in sight of the commissioners. When she reached her room, she had only the strength to say, "It is not finished," to the waiting attendants.

Lying on her bed, stretched out full length, she gradually stopped shaking. The hearing had gone on for almost eight hours. Their evidence was damning; it was clear that she was doomed.

Yet I believe I answered well and nimbly, she thought. Perhaps there will be some who will carry away a kindlier impression of me than they came with. Jesu, so many of them, and ones I had wished to see. And dear old Shrewsbury there. He scarcely said a word. . . . Hatton, grown so worn . . . Sir Ralph Sadler, who saw me naked when I was just a baby, inspecting me . . . who would ever have thought he would outlive me? All these gentlemen, what did they say they were? Nine earls, thirteen barons, six privy councillors . . .

The trial resumed the next morning. Mary again entered the room leaning on her servants' arms, and took her place in the crimson velvet chair. The forty-four faces appeared eager to resume; their colour was high and their voices loud. As she looked round the room, she was struck with a subtle difference between today and yesterday, but she could not immediately name it.

Now Mary rose and addressed the assembly. "Friends," she began. Then she saw how the use of that word unleashed a volley of head-shaking. "Judges," she amended it, "I came here voluntarily, out of regard for my own honour, to vindicate myself from the horrible imputation of having been a party to the hurt of Queen Elizabeth. But instead I have been attacked on many other issues; you have attempted to confuse me and lead away from the main charge. And as to the main accusation, you have produced no witnesses; neither have you produced any original writings, but only 'certified copies.' If you can condemn me by my own words or writing, I will submit. But I am sure you cannot produce any."

It is true I agreed to it, she thought, in a moment of weakness. But I refuse to be condemned on false or tampered evidence. God has mercifully seen to it there is no earthly evidence of my lapse. He is my shield and protection.

"Listen to how sure she is! It is not innocence speaking, but craft! She knows full well they do not exist because she systematically destroyed them—proving her wiliness!"

"Hear, hear!" seconded other voices.

The noise rose until it was a rumble. Suddenly she realized what was different about the men this day: they already wore their riding clothes, they were booted and spurred. They meant to end the hearing early enough to leave while it was yet daylight. The time was already set; it mattered not what she said.

"My crimes, for which I am really on trial here today," she continued, holding her head high, "consist of my birth, the injuries that have been inflicted on me, and my religion. Of the first I am justly proud, the second I can forgive, and the third has been my sole consolation and hope under all my afflictions. I am the last Catholic member of both royal houses of England and Scotland, and I would cheerfully give my best blood to procure relief for the suffering Catholics of the realm; but not even for their sake would I purchase it at the price of religious war and the blood of many others, having always been tender of the lives of God's meanest creatures."

"Yet he who is tender with foals and piglets is often cruel to his wife!" cried one man.

"And every murderer has a mother who stands at the gallows-foot, extolling his kindness to his relatives!" yelled another. " 'Not my Gregory! He always watered the flowers so faithfully!' "

Everyone screamed with laughter, and even Walsingham guffawed. Cecil struggled to maintain order.

Mary burst into tears, which just ignited them more. She had always hated bear-baiting, where the chained animal was attacked by waves of snarling dogs, their jaws dripping with red foam. She had refused to watch this so-called sport, remembering with pain her tame bear in France, so gentle and obedient. Now she felt as if she had been transformed into a bear herself, held fast to be slashed and killed. And they said Elizabeth greatly enjoyed bear-baiting, that it was one of her favourite pastimes. . . .

"Let us proceed," said Cecil. "Let us move on to the next charge, that of trafficking with England's enemies, inviting invasions by Spain." He nodded to Walsingham.

Walsingham rose. "There are numerous letters to prove this. She has written to her agents in Paris, to Mendoza the Spanish ambassador, to Philip himself, urging just such action." He opened a great pouch and let the letters fall out like a shower of leaves. One or two landed on the floor.

Mary commanded her chest to stop heaving, and stilled her own trembling by willpower. "I do not deny that I have longed for liberty and done my utmost to procure it. In this I acted from a very natural wish. When it was denied me by Queen Elizabeth, I turned to other countries," she said. "Yet I was not driven to this until I had been cruelly mocked by deceptive treaties, all my amicable offers slighted, and my health destroyed by rigorous imprisonment."

The room had at last grown silent.

"I have written to my friends, and solicited them to help me to escape from Elizabeth's miserable prisons, in which she has kept me now nearly nineteen years, till my health and hopes have been cruelly destroyed."

"Enough!" said Bromley, raising his hands. "It is not Queen Elizabeth who is on trial here today!"

"And, Madam," said Cecil, "when the last treaty was being negotiated for your liberty—the Association with your son the King—what was your response? Parry was sent here by your pensioner, Morgan, to murder our Queen!"

"No!" cried Mary. "I knew nothing of this! If Morgan did this wicked thing, he acted without my knowledge."

"Ha!" said Cecil. "We know you are in back of all these plots. Oh, you think to deceive us, but we know you for what you are! Daughter of sedition, indeed!"

Mary stared at him. "My lord," she finally said, "you are my enemy."

"Yea!" cried Cecil. "I am the enemy of all Queen Elizabeth's enemies."

She looked out at the faces of the men, flushed and agitated. Their spurs clinked as they shifted in their seats. Soon they would be out in the October air, riding south, laughing, stopping at taverns. They would imitate her and mock her, putting on little plays for the other patrons. Someone would wrap a black blanket around himself, drape a white veil over his head, and say, "I am an anointed Queen . . . " in a squeaky voice.

"I will speak only to a full Parliament, in the presence of the Queen and her Council," she said. "For I see that it is extreme folly to stand for judgement here, where all are so evidently and notoriously prejudiced against me." She stepped away from her chair. "I forgive you all," she said to the whole assembly. "My lords and gentlemen, I place my cause in the hands of God."

She turned and made her way slowly to the nearby door, the one through which she had entered. As she did so, she passed by a table of lawyers frantically taking notes. "May God keep me from having to do with you all again," she said with a smile.

Then, before Cecil or Bromley could stop her, she disappeared through the door.

Cecil rose and called for order.

"Gentlemen, gentlemen! You have heard all the proceedings. Our gracious Queen calls us to reassemble in London to pronounce sentence, ten days from now." He held aloft the scribbled instructions from Elizabeth. "You are free now to go!"

With a burst of energy, the men leapt up from their chairs and benches.

From her window, Mary saw the courtyard swarming with men, their bright mantles making a rich pattern against the dull stones. Soon they would swirl away, carrying their news throughout the countryside.

She lay down and shut her eyes. When she arose and looked out again, the courtyard was empty.

XXVIII

Walsingham dragged his sore leg as he walked alongside Cecil, who was also limping, because of a riding injury. The two men made their way painfully from the boat landing to the path leading up to Walsingham's country house, Barn Elms.

The weather had remained warm very late; although it was the end of November, neither man needed a mantle, and the sun was radiant on their shoulders. Behind them the Thames lapped at its banks, and there were still many boats plying the waters.

"My infirmity is caused by a fall," said Cecil. "To think that in attempting to speed my journeys, I have only succeeded in laming myself." His right leg was splinted and bandaged.

"Mine is caused by Her Majesty's stubbornness," said Walsingham. "Truly, I am at a loss as to how to proceed. My stomach churns, my knee swells, my leg bleeds. . . . " His voice rose in distress, and Cecil looked at him in alarm. Was he about to cry?

They passed the rows of tobacco plants that Walsingham had set out; they seemed to be thriving.

"She does not care!" Walsingham muttered. "She cares not for our hard work, our diligence, her own safety . . . it has all been for naught, Cecil, for naught! The Serpent will live."

Cecil put his arm around him. "Nay, nay. Progress is being made. The Serpent has been pronounced guilty by the commission, and both houses of Parliament have petitioned the Queen to proceed to the execution."

"But she refuses! She merely thanks them for their pains and says she cannot give an answer! She asks them to find some other way—she says that she would accept a personal apology from Mary—God knows, she cannot seem to do that which she needs to do for her own good!"

Cecil sighed. He looked over at a large boulder. "Come, let us sit here in the sunshine. It will do us good." He settled himself with a sigh, extending his hurt leg. "You must understand that she is in a terrible position. She has an abhorrence of being seen to shed blood. Perhaps she wishes to efface the ghost of her father. Perhaps in some corner of her mind she equates Mary with her own mother, Anne Boleyn. Both were brought up in France, both were accused of indiscretions, both convicted of seeking the death of the monarch. Yet Elizabeth and many others can never be sure of Boleyn's guilt; perhaps Elizabeth wishes to atone for it this way. Who can say?"

"Perhaps she is merely indecisive," snorted Walsingham. "Or cowardly."

"The Serpent used her trial as a showcase for her own eloquence and wit," said Cecil. "So, they say, did Anne Boleyn. But it availed them nothing. And as for Mary, even her supporters were forced to admit that the evidence against her was overwhelming. Still"—his voice trailed off— "she was most impressive."

"Now you sound as if you were in love with her!"

"Nay. I spoke true. I am the enemy of all Queen Elizabeth's enemies."

"I was disappointed in her. She was just a stout middle-aged woman mouthing pieties and platitudes, and oozing with self-pity." Walsingham winced as he massaged his leg. "Like Katherine of Aragon. No wonder Henry VIII shut her up in a tower. Those tedious, artificial speeches . . . " He shook his head. "Instead of exciting pity, they had the opposite effect. Disgust!"

"The Earl of Leicester is returning," said Cecil suddenly. "Perhaps the Queen will listen to him, when all else fails. He has been urging her to action, but letters are not so persuasive as a personal appeal."

"Meanwhile the Scottish and French ambassadors have already begun their agitating on her behalf, further eroding Her Majesty's resolve. And it does not help that the Serpent has embraced martyrdom and *wants* Elizabeth to have her publicly executed. In order to thwart her, Elizabeth may keep her alive! I think that filthy and wicked creature of Scotland has been ordained of God for our punishment! Oh, Cecil! What a thankless task we perform!"

Cecil shrugged. "Let her act out her pitiable martyrdom," he said. "The most wicked criminals have God on their lips at all times, for God is the only one who can stomach them."

"Oh, let Lord Leicester come soon!" Walsingham turned his sad eyes toward the heavens. "Work your magic on the Queen!"

Elizabeth stood before her mirror in the privacy of her chamber at Richmond. She was wearing only her chemise, and her bare feet stuck out from under its hem. Her wig was gone, and her natural hair had been released to fall over her shoulders. Shorn of all her earthly glorifications of jewellery, lace, brocades, padding, and cosmetics, she stared at what was left.

If she squinted, she could claim she had changed little since she first came to the throne: still slender, her natural hair still golden red, most of her teeth still with her. She was fifty-three now, and her childbearing years were over. Spared from motherhood, her body had retained its girlish lines and an unusual youthfulness. Yet she knew, too, that her last romance had passed with her fertility. There had been no more courtships after the one with the Frog.

I kept my virginity, and my virginity has kept me, she thought, gazing at herself. And I am thankful.

She drew her robe about her and twisted her hair up, fastening it with a silver clasp. She poured out a small portion of sweet Cyprus wine and took a sip. Her abstemiousness in eating and drinking had helped to preserve her health as well.

At my age, my father the King was marvellously fat, she thought. I remember someone said that three of the biggest men in the kingdom could fit into his doublet. I have now lived almost as long as he did; he died when he was fifty-five, and he had long called himself "the old man." But I do not feel like "the old woman"!

Death . . . I do not feel death near, not from natural causes, but . . .

She finished the wine and sat staring at the inlaid pattern of her desk. On the desk was a *memento mori*, a skull. And in her open prayer book was a page showing death grabbing innocent people: death as the artificer, whispering "No compass or art can cause me depart." Another motto was engraved on the tomb of a recumbent knight: "No one device, no art, no toil, could make us give death the foil." She shuddered and closed the book.

She ran her hands over her cheeks, feeling the pointed cheekbones just beneath the skin.

She had seldom felt so beset as in this, her fifty-third year. Her spinsterhood was now settled and unchangeable. Robert Dudley, her own Robert, Earl of Leicester, had now been remarried for seven years. For the past year his courtly presence had been denied her, as he had been away commanding the English forces in the Netherlands. She had been disappointed in his performance there, and in the revelation of the extent of his ambition. Yet she had missed him by her side in England.

The war in the Netherlands had been a ghastly mistake. The Treasury was beginning to run dry, in spite of her vigilant thrift. Little by little she was being drawn into the wider, all-out war of religion that she had so striven to avoid; relations with Spain were becoming more and more strained; soon open hostilities would break out. She was being forced into the role of universal champion of Protestantism—by circumstances.

And then there was the Queen of Scots business.

No one seemed to understand Elizabeth's dilemma, her quandary. No one was sympathetic to her reluctance to execute her royal cousin. She was completely alone.

In spite of Parliament, in spite of devoted servants like Cecil and Walsingham, in spite of thousands of loyal subjects who proclaim themselves ready to die for me, only I have the power to act, she thought. It is I who must sign the death warrant, and it is I who must bear the entire blame. In the eyes of the world I stand alone.

That is the true burden of kingship: ultimately, I must decide alone and bear the consequences, she thought. Until now I have been able to share that burden with my councillors and people; we have acted together in all things. But although they urge me to this, it is my decision and mine alone.

Is Mary guilty? Indeed, yes. It is not justice that brings her to the block this time; if justice had been served, she would have gone years ago. It is long overdue.

She unwrapped a miniature of the Queen of Scots that she had kept for years. It showed her young, as the fair, lucky ruler just mounting her throne in Scotland. Then, in the same paper, she drew out the diamond ring that Mary had sent her upon her arrival in England as a fugitive, claiming that it entitled her to Elizabeth's help. The little ring sparkled in the candlelight. Elizabeth turned it this way and that, as if she would see something in it this time that she had missed before.

This is just a toy, she thought. It is impossible to believe that this little thing has brought about such momentous results—that a queen may die because of this ring.

May die? Many have died already. It is neither dream nor toy, but a true *memento mori*.

The next morning, Elizabeth dressed in her most flattering colours—russet and gold—and fastened the black pearls of the Queen of Scots around her neck, to make her aware all day of Mary's presence. The Lords had sold them to her long ago, when Mary had first been swept from her throne. Beautiful things—they were not truly black, but a deep, opalescent purplish grey, their surfaces gleaming like grapes still on the vine under a late autumn sun. So much had Mary lost . . . Elizabeth's makeup was skilfully applied, to simulate the flush of youth, and her best wig, the one with the thickest, shiniest curls, was put on. Now the creature in the mirror was a heightened version of the pale, slight figure of the night before; now Gloriana shone forth in the sunlight in the dazzle of majesty.

Robert Dudley was coming, and she wanted to be as she always had been for him. Time must never intrude on them—nor wives, nor other courtiers. Lettice Knollys and Christopher Hatton and Walter Raleigh were only appendages to the two, forever one: Robert and Elizabeth.

She waited in her privy chamber. Outside there was attenuated sunshine, thin and cold. Now she heard the footfalls, and knew he was almost here.

"Robert!" She rose as he came into the room.

He was stout now, and red-faced, and losing his hair. But that was of no moment; it was not even seen; it was not really him, but just a jesting overlay. The real Robert was unchanging, as was the real Elizabeth, and they were always young and beautiful.

"My Queen!" He fell to his knees and kissed her hand. "Oh, now I am truly home!"

"Stand, my dear," she said, drawing him up. "Now I am safe again!"

They stood looking at each other for several long moments. Then Elizabeth waved him to a seat, offering him a drink of heated wine.

"My most beloved majesty," he said, "I fear you will not be safe until . . . you be moved to do what your people petition you to do."

"Have they sent you?" she asked sharply. "Cecil, and Walsingham? To try to persuade me?"

"No, they have not," he answered quietly. His brown eyes were full only of concern for her. "Walsingham lies sick in his home; he has spent himself in your service and now is grieved and fearful. But his part is over. However, Parliament has met and decided that you must proceed to carry out the sentence against the Queen of Scots."

"Must? Must?" she cried. "Who is Parliament to tell me what I 'must' do? Who rules here? The crown or Parliament?"

"The crown," he answered promptly. "Parliament has no power to carry out the sentence. If you do not publish the sentence, and put your signature to the death warrant, it cannot be carried out. She will live until you decide she must die. It is that simple."

"I know that!" she snapped. "Why do you think I am so tortured?"

"But," said Robert, "your genius as a ruler has rested in your being always in perfect accord and harmony with your people. You reflect them as still water does the clouds; together you have formed a seamless whole. You speak of being married to your people, and I above all, know how true that is. You are one flesh with them. And they are now certain, and resolved, that this danger to themselves and to you must be removed. If you disregard their wishes, you show that you take your safety and theirs lightly. They will not forgive that, nor forget it."

"Oooh." She crossed her arms over her stomach and bent over as if she had a pain. The pearls rubbed against her arms. "I know you are right," she finally said.

"You have asked Parliament to find another way. They have searched and declared that there is no other way. You called them to help you bear the burden—"

"No! I called them because—because it would satisfy the world better, because I wish even my enemies to know that I was just, and so they could never accuse me of tyranny or hasty actions!"

Robert laughed. "Hasty actions! No, you are certainly not guilty of that, never, in any way! Why, if you had to select a symbol of your reign, you could choose the tortoise: wise, cautious, slow-moving, peace-loving."

Elizabeth smiled now as well. She stroked the pearls, as if she would call forth some spirit to do her bidding. "And long-lived, I hope." The skull flitted through her mind.

"Not if Mary and her partisans have their way," said Robert. "And no man knows what tomorrow can bring."

No one device, no art, no toil, could make us give death the foil.

"If she should outlive you," continued Robert cautiously, "and sickly people sometimes live to a great age, then she might inherit your throne. Catholicism would be restored, and all your wisdom and compromise would be undone. You and your people are one, but she and those same people would be at odds, just as she and her people were in Scotland. And you know what happened there. Spare your people this possibility."

"Do you remember, Robert, what I said long ago?" she suddenly asked. "I said I was their anointed Queen, and I would never be constrained to do anything by force. Yet that is what has happened—that is why I hate it so!"

"I know not what you mean." His face was puzzled.

"First I was forced to allow Babington and the conspirators to be tried. Once they had been tried and found guilty, I was forced to have them executed. I hoped that that would satisfy the people, and spare Mary, as did the execution of Norfolk. But no! They made it clear that it was Mary's head they wanted, not the conspirators'. They would not be satisfied! They blamed her for ensnaring these poor young men. So then I was forced to allow Mary to be tried. Once she was tried, I was forced to call Parliament to try to mollify the foreign powers. And once Parliament was involved, it pressed most diligently for her execution. I have been led step by step; I have been constrained by force!"

"There are some things that even you must obey," said Robert. "Not Parliament itself, but the sentiment in back of it. The time for legal niceties and hesitation is past. The Queen of Scots must die."

She clenched her fists and beat them helplessly against her sides.

"If you fail to carry through," Robert went on, "then what becomes of the law of the land? It will be seen that no law has any force. We are a country of laws; we pride ourselves on our legal system. To evade it is to step back into barbarism."

"But to execute a crowned queen!" she cried. "Such a thing has never been done. What will happen?"

"What will happen if you do not?" he asked. "Pray, do not put more stock in the opinion of foreign powers than in that of your own people."

"What will France do? What will Scotland do?"

"The French will do nothing. They have long since ceased to care what happens to her. As for Scotland . . . James must, of necessity, make public noise about his mother. But in private, he will choose his own best interests, which are to remain on good terms with England. He enjoys his pension, and will not jeopardize the treaty he has just signed with you, with its implied understanding of his inheritance, for all the mothers in Christendom. And especially not that mother. You remember what he said when he was told she had been taken in the Babington Plot? 'Now she must drink the ale she has brewed.' No, he'll sit quietly."

"I have been informed that certain Scots nobles, including the ever-chivalrous George Douglas, have been urging him to invade England and free her."

"The Scots, who had to be prevented from executing her themselves—and by yourself at that—are hardly likely to hazard life and limb for her now. No, you are quite safe from that quarter."

"Oh, I would that it were over and done with!" she cried.

"Then end it," said Robert. "End it, most gracious Majesty."

Elizabeth suspended Parliament, and called for it to reassemble on February fifteenth. Two days afterward, on December fourth, she allowed the publication of the sentence to the sound of trumpets: Mary was found guilty of "being not only accessory and privy to the conspiracy but also an imaginer and compasser of Her Majesty's destruction." Church bells rang in London for twenty-four hours, bonfires blazed, and people drank and danced in the streets with wild celebration.

Elizabeth asked Cecil to draw up the death warrant, and dispatched a deputation of councillors to announce the verdict and sentence to Mary at Fotheringhay. Then she shut herself in her chambers for two days.

XXIX

Mary had just finished her midday meal, served quietly in the largest chamber of the octagonal tower, when Paulet appeared in the doorway.

"You have visitors," he said cryptically.

Before she had time to rise from the table or even wipe her lips with her napkin, a crowd of men stepped into the chamber. She did not recognize any of them; some of the faces looked familiar from the trial, but she did not know the names.

"I am Robert Beale, clerk of her Majesty's Privy Council," one man stepped forward and said. He was a healthy-looking man, robust without being portly.

Mary rose and left the table, with its remains of food and dirty dishes. She walked slowly to the other end of the chamber, where her throne would have been. Then she turned and faced them.

"Madam, we are sent here to announce to you the sentence: you are found guilty of conspiring against the life of Queen Elizabeth, and are condemned by the Parliament of this country to die," he said softly.

Mary just looked at him and said nothing.

Behind him the other men shifted from foot to foot.

"These gentlemen, all leading members of the Privy Council, lawyers of the crown, and other officials, are witnesses that we have indeed communicated this to you. The sentence has been proclaimed by heralds and published throughout the realm," Beale continued.

"Ah," said Mary.

"Now is the time to confess and ask forgiveness!" said Paulet, who had joined them.

"Confess? Ask forgiveness?" said Mary. "The trial and its sentence are illegal." The men began to murmur, and she went on quickly, "But it is no matter. I know the real reason I am to die, and I am humbly grateful for it. It is for my religion. What a privilege has thus been bestowed on me!"

"You may stop that right now!" said Beale. "It is a clever move to try to make yourself out to be a saint and a martyr, but the truth is you are neither, and are condemned to die for common plotting and treason against the Queen."

"I beseeched Him to accept the sorrows and persecutions I have suffered in both mind and body as some atonement for my sins, and I see He has answered my prayers!" Mary went on.

"You see, gentlemen, what I have had to endure," said Paulet. "Long, tedious speeches that have nothing to do with the matter at hand! It would be charitable to say her long imprisonment has robbed her of her good sense, but she has never had good common sense. She has indulged herself with fancies, surrounding herself with flatterers and foreigners even in Scotland, to the end that she has lived in her own little world all her life. So now she erects another little stage where she can act out a part: the sainted martyr, lifting her eyes to Heaven, clutching her rosary and mumbling Latin."

"Madam," Beale persisted, "if you would but confess to the Queen—"

"When is the sentence to be carried out?" Mary asked.

"That is in the hands of the Queen's Majesty," answered Beale.

"And it is to be a public execution?" she asked.

"Yes."

"You will not do me to death secretly, and rob me of that public death?" she asked Paulet.

"Madam!" he almost shouted. "I am a man of honour and a gentleman, and I would never dishonour myself by exercising such cruelty, or conducting myself like a Turk!"

"For which I am grateful," said Mary.

After the deputation left, Paulet reentered the chamber and went quickly upstairs to her bedchamber, carrying a bundle under his arm. She rose and followed him, but it took her some time to ascend the stairs. When she finally reached the upper room, her blood ran cold.

Paulet was decking her bed with black hangings.

"What are you doing?" she asked.

"This is to signify that you are, in the eyes of the law, already dead. These are your funeral trappings. The rest of the chamber will be hung with black as well." He busily continued attaching them.

"So my bed is to be my hearse," she said. "I am to lie in state?"

"As it were," he answered. "And think upon your everlasting destination." He stepped down off his stool and eyed his handiwork.

"And your billiard table is to be taken away," he said. "This is no time to waste in idle recreations."

"I have never used it since it has been there. I have had other occupations. Pray take it away and give us some more room."

He snorted with disdain and left.

Later that afternoon, Mary called together her people and made the announcement to them. She hoped no one would break out in lamentations or anger; that would make it all the harder.

"My friends, today I have received the sentence," she said. "We all know what that is. And Paulet has kindly decorated my chamber so that I will feel at all times as if I am in the valley of the shadow of death."

"When is it to be?" asked Jane Kennedy. Her eyes shone with tears, but her voice did not tremble. Mary was grateful for that.

"I do not know. Therefore I must make preparations now. I will need paper, and certain lists to be drawn up of my remaining property. I must write my farewell letters, and make my will."

At that, Elizabeth Curle gave a cry, and Willie Douglas moaned.

"I am happy, truly I am, for this will see an end to all my troubles," she insisted. "If you love me, you will rejoice with me. The captive is to go free at last! And when I am free, then you will be, too. Only help me to part from this world easily and with grace. That is your task, that is all I ask of you. Help me disrobe from this mantle of sorrow, and put on my heavenly robes."

Mary's hand was aching. The rheumatism was especially bad in her writing hand, as if to plague her. But she had completed her letters: one to Archbishop Beaton, her envoy in Paris, one to Mendoza, the Spanish ambassador who had been expelled from England on her account for the Throckmorton Plot, and now was posted to Paris. One to the Pope, her spiritual father. And one to Henri of Guise, the head of the Guise family now.

To Guise she had allowed herself to speculate on her execution.

I am now, by an unjust sentence, about to be put to such a death as no person of our family, much less of my rank, ever suffered. Yet I thank

839

God for it, being useless to the world and to the cause of His church in my present state. And though executioner never yet dipped his hand in our blood, be not ashamed thereof, my friend.

There was still the will to compose, and then the hardest letter of all—the obligatory one to Elizabeth.

Although she had been in a curious state of exaltation all day, it was ebbing away and all she felt now was weariness.

Do I have the strength to go on? she asked herself. I must; I may not be given the time to compose these later. And they must be done.

The will was only a listing of finances, trying to make provision for her servants, and requesting that she be buried in France, with her mother. She tried to remember all the small sums and holdings, but without her account books, she could not be sure. Nonetheless, she hoped that either the King of Spain, the King of France, or the Duc de Guise would, in charity, cover the small bequests.

Now the letter to Queen Elizabeth. She shut her eyes and prayed for the words to come to her. Then she slowly began to write. At first the words were mere formalities. Then she came to the heart of the matter.

> Now having been informed, on your part, of the sentence passed in the last session of your Parliament, and admonished by Lord Beale to prepare myself for the end of my long and weary pilgrimage, I prayed them to return my thanks to you for such agreeable intelligence, and to ask you to grant some things for the relief of my conscience.
>
> I will not accuse any person, but sincerely pardon every one, as I desire others, and, above all, God, to pardon me. And since I know that your heart, more than that of any other, ought to be touched by the honour or dishonour of your own blood, and of a Queen, the daughter of a king, I require you, Madam, for the sake of Jesus, that after my enemies have satisfied their black thirst for my innocent blood, you will permit my poor disconsolate servants to remove my corpse, that it may be buried in holy ground, with my ancestors in France, especially the late Queen my mother, since in Scotland the remains of the Kings my predecessors have been outraged, and the churches torn down and profaned.
>
> As I shall suffer in this country, I shall not be allowed a place near your ancestors, who are also mine, and persons of my religion think much of being interred in consecrated earth. I trust you will not refuse this last request I have preferred to you, and allow, at least, free sepulture to this body when the soul shall be separated from it, which never could obtain, while united, liberty to dwell in peace.
>
> Dreading the secret tyranny of some of those to whom you have abandoned me, I entreat you to prevent me from being dispatched secretly, without your knowledge, not from fear of the pain, which I am ready to suffer, but on account of the reports they would circulate after my death. It is therefore that I desire my servants to remain the witnesses and attestators of my end, my faith in my Saviour, and obedience to His church. This I require of you in the name of Jesus Christ in

respect to our consanguinity, for the sake of King Henry VII, your great-grandfather and mine, for the dignity we have both held, and for the sex to which we both belong.

Her hand was trembling. She hated to think of Elizabeth holding the letter and reading it. At the same time she knew she would be bereft if she ever knew for certain that Elizabeth would never see it. She continued.

> I beseech the God of mercy and justice to enlighten you with His holy Spirit, and to give me the grace to die in perfect charity, as I endeavour to do, pardoning my death to all those who have either caused or cooperated in it; and this will be my prayer to the end.
>
> Accuse me not of presumption if, leaving this world and preparing myself for a better, I remind you that you will have one day to give account of your charge, in like manner as those who preceded you in it, and that my blood and the misery of my country will be remembered, wherefore from the earliest dawn of our comprehension we ought to dispose our minds to make things temporal yield to those of eternity.
>
> Your sister and cousin wrongfully a prisoner,
> Marie Royne

There. It was done. Mary folded the paper and stood up. Her head was throbbing. She had written many, many pages. When she looked at the stack, she could scarcely believe it.

At her little altar the candle was still flickering. The dim yellow light bathed the face of the Virgin painted on wood, which had served as her chief devotional object since she had removed her ivory crucifix and fastened it on the wall where her royal canopy should have been. When Paulet had uneasily admitted that he had no right to take it down, she had assured him that she preferred the crucifix in any case.

Now, kneeling before the Virgin, she closed her eyes and felt herself flooded with a peace born of more than just completion of a task. She marvelled at how this could be, imagining having received the sentence of certain death at any other time or place in her life, when the blood ran strong and her attachment to the earth was fierce.

In France, when all her senses were drowning in beauty; in Scotland, when her pride and ambition were engaged with the challenge of ruling, and then, later, when her courage had to confront the danger of treason; in the arms of Bothwell, when desire and love possessed her and made her exult in every aspect of her earthly being . . . no, at none of these times would she have wanted to be called away from this world. At first it was a garden to her, then an arena, and then a bed of pleasure, and she had drunk deeply of it. Now it was a draught that she put aside, never to taste again.

Like a mystery, words were coming to her, words in Latin that she must write down, as if they had been given to her. She rose and returned to her writing desk.

O Domine Deus,
Speravi in Te;
O care mi Jesu
Nunc Libera me.
In dura catena,
In misera poena,
Desidero Te.
Languendo, gemendo,
Et genuflectendo,
Adoro, imploro,
Ut liberes me.

O Lord God,
I have hoped in Thee.
Beloved Jesus,
Now set me free.
In cruel chains,
In bitter pains,
I have longed for Thee.
Now languishing
In sorrow sore,
Upon my knees,
I Thee implore
That Thou wilt
Grant me liberty.

Liberty, liberty . . . loose my chains, she whispered to the still room. Everything was quiet. It was after midnight.

It is now December eighth, she thought. My birthday. My forty-fourth, and my last upon earth. The knowledge of that is a precious gift.

The next morning she sent for Balthazzar to come to her in her chamber. The old man, bent halfway over, moved painfully across the room, having scarcely enough strength to lift his feet. As a result, they made soft swishing sounds on the stone floor.

"My friend," said Mary, "today is my birthday, and I am minded to employ you once again, as I have for so many years."

Balthazzar's eyes were white and filmy. Yet he raised them to her and nodded. She could tell that he had wept during the night.

"You made my dress for my first communion. And my wedding dress when I married François. And you made the gown I wore to James's baptism. Now, do you think you could undertake the grandest gown of all?"

He shook his head. "I cannot see so well, and my hands shake so I cannot cut material straight."

"But others can do those tasks. I wish you to design the gown. You can still visualize a finished garment, can you not?"

"Yes. Better than ever."

"Then visualize this: I want a gown in which I become immortal. A gown in which I pass from nature into eternity. Can you see this?"

"Yes, Madam." He wiped his eyes. "In my mind, I see it."

"And what do you see?"

"A red gown. Crimson. The colour of martyrdom. A low neck, and a full skirt. Yes, I see it."

"Then measure me for it, faithful servant. And make it ready for me. Tell no one, except your assistants. It will be our secret. Until the day."

Balthazzar put his head in his hands and wept.

"Nay, my friend," said Mary. "I rejoice to go; when I went to my weddings, and to my ceremonies, it was but a shadow of this, a passing taste of this joy beyond all joys. I tell you a secret: I feel it already. Eternity has already begun for me, and it is bliss and peace beyond all description."

Mary's forty-fourth birthday came and went; Christmas came and went, a dreary little celebration. All except Mary were downcast and barely able to go through the motions of living, except for the few who were ragingly angry. Only Mary seemed to float in a protected world of her own, oblivious of the cold, the dark, the damp, the endless rumours that seeped even into the guarded tower. There were tales circulating all over the realm that Mary had escaped, that Spanish troops had landed in Wales, that there was a new northern uprising. There was even a new plot against Elizabeth, said to involve smearing her stirrups and saddle with poison.

Daily, Mary made ready for the official to arrive with the death warrant. She thought of him as being in a race against the secret murderer who could strike at any moment, robbing her of a death with any meaning at all. She was sure that he was somewhere within Fotheringhay, that self-appointed executioner.

But as the days passed and nothing happened, a dread began to take hold of her. It was possible that Elizabeth would decide to spare her, in her "mercy." Elizabeth could delay signing the warrant as she delayed everything else, until she had her wish and people stopped hounding her about it—as they had quit hounding her to get married. She confided these fears to her writing-book.

> December 29, Anno Domini 1586. I could be kept like this for another twenty years! In that way Elizabeth would not be seen to shed my blood. Another twenty years of locked rooms, of no letters, of illness and isolation. And the obligatory plotting. The outsiders would continue plotting and I would have to become involved. More codes, more messengers—O my Saviour, spare me from that living death! Do not condemn me to it!

> January 1, New Year's Day, Anno Domini 1587. Another year dawns. Paulet yesterday made a comment about wages for my servants. From his tone and statement, it sounded as if they

would be employed for the foreseeable future. O God, O most tender and compassionate Holy Mother, do not draw me out longer on the rack here! I cannot bear it, cannot bear it, cannot bear it. . . .

January 8, Anno Domini 1587. Yes, I can bear it. *I can do all things through Christ which strengtheneth me.* But God, I want more than just to endure. I want to offer You a gift by my death. I want to die in a way glorifying You, to atone for all the ways in which I have not glorified You by my life.

> *Reveal Your presence*
> *And let the vision of Your beauty kill me*
> *Behold, the malady*
> *Of love is incurable*
> *Except in Your presence and before Your face.*

That is what my fellow sufferer John of the Cross writes. O, to have the gift of such words! But I must not covet what You choose to give others. . . .

All is quiet here, nothing happens. Elizabeth has quite forgotten me, leaving me to wait . . . and wait. My bodily infirmities, that I had neglected—for why patch the roof of a building that is to be demolished?—will soon have to be attended to once again. Bourgoing needs to procure certain herbs for treatment.

O, I hate these small indignities! I should have no more need of herbs!

But forgive my rebellion, Lord.

XXX

lizabeth hated the New Year's celebration, with the usual exchange of gifts. Not that she did not receive some costly and unusual gifts— gold saltcellars made in the shape of galleons, jewelled beasts, emerald collars. But she did not want to see the year change from 1586 to 1587. Parliament was reconvening early in the year, and that meant she had less and less time to find a solution to the vexing problem of Mary Queen of Scots. She had to have solved it before facing Parliament.

January did nothing to help her resolve the dilemma. Everything that would nudge her toward executing Mary seemed to occur: there was another assassination plot, this time involving the French embassy. The people were daily becoming agitated as one sensational rumour after another swept the land, all having to do with the Spanish invading, or Mary escaping. Some said that London was on fire, and that the north had erupted in armed rebellion. There had even been some riots in London, with the people demanding that justice to the "Monstrous Dragon" be carried out.

But once done, it can never be undone, she muttered, pacing her room. And such a thing has never before been carried out: the judicial murder of an anointed sovereign. What will it open the door to? The people are forcing me to do it. Today they force me to execute Mary; tomorrow they may just execute a monarch directly on their own authority. They will not even need to persuade some other ruler to do it.

She shuddered, as a world where mob rule was the law of the land suddenly presented itself to her mind.

It will not happen tomorrow, or even the day after, she thought, but it will happen, and I will have caused it to happen.

Yet Robert is also right—what happens when the people have spoken, have acted in accordance with law and procedure, only to be ignored? Might their frustration lead them to the same place, and quicker?

In a flash, she felt a sudden burst of strength. Quickly she called for William Davison, the Secretary of State, and asked him to bring her the death warrant.

As she waited for him to return, she realized that this opportunity would never come again. The French were penned up in their embassy in disgrace, following the discovery of the plot, and could not intercede for Mary. The Scots had abandoned their pleas for her, and no rescuers had come forward. The special Scots envoy, far from pleading for their erstwhile queen, had whispered that "a dead woman biteth not." It was the season of foul weather, and the Spanish would never send a fleet north at this time. It was now; the time was now, it was fleeting, and such a constellation of events would never repeat themselves.

"Strike or be struck," Elizabeth repeated to herself over and over like a litany. "*Aut fer aut feri, ne feriare, feri.* I am a rogue and unfit for my office if I do not press forward."

Davison appeared promptly, with the death warrant—which had been drawn up several weeks earlier, when the sentence had first been proclaimed—in his hands. He placed it reverently in hers.

She read it slowly, while Davison stood before her.

Elizabeth, by the grace of God, Queen of England, France, and Ireland & c.
To our trusty and well-beloved cousins, George, Earl of Shewsbury, Henry, Earl of Kent, Henry, Earl of Derby, George, Earl of Cumberland, and Henry, Earl of Pembroke, greeting, & c.
Whereas, since the sentence given by you, and others of our Coun-

cil, against the Queen of Scots, Mary, daughter of James the Fifth, is well known, all Parliament did not only allow and approve the same sentence as just and honourable, but also with all humbleness require, solicit, and press us to direct such further execution against her Person, as they did adjudge her to have duly deserved. They added thereunto that the forbearing thereof was daily certain and undoubted danger, not only unto our own life, but also unto themselves, their posterity, and the public estate of this realm. Whereupon we did publish the sentence by our Proclamation, yet hitherto have forborn to give further satisfaction of said sentence.

And now, we do daily understand how the wisest, greatest, and best-loved of all subjects of inferior degrees, how greatly and deeply, from the bottom of their hearts, they are grieved and afflicted, with daily, yea, hourly fears of our life, if we should forbear the further final execution, as it is deserved, and neglect their general and continual requests, prayers, counsels, and advices, and thereupon, contrary to our natural disposition, being overcome with the evident weight of their counsels, and their daily intercessions, we have condescended to suffer justice to take place, and for the execution thereof to proceed.

We do will, and by Warrant hereby do authorize you, to repair to our castle of Fotheringhay, where the said Queen of Scots is in custody of our right trusty and faithful servant and councillor, Sir Amyas Paulet. Then, taking her into your charge, cause by your commandment execution to be done upon her person, in the presence of yourselves, and the aforesaid Sir Amyas Paulet, and of such other officers of justice as you shall command to attend upon you; and the same to be done in such manner and form, and at such time and place, and by such persons, as you think by your discretion convenient.

And these our Letters Patents, sealed with our Great Seal of England, shall be to you, and to all persons that shall be present, a full sufficient Warrant and discharge forever.

In witness whereof, we have caused these our Letters to be made Patents. Given at our manor of Greenwich, the first day of February, in the twenty-ninth year of our reign.

Elizabeth laid it on her desk and quickly signed it with her bold signature:

Elizabeth R.

Davison was staring at her.

"Well?" she snapped. "Take it to the Lord Chancellor Bromley for the Great Seal. Keep the matter secret. But you might be so kind as to stop at Sir Walsingham's home, where he lies sick abed. The grief of seeing this will go near to killing him outright."

But she did not smile as she said it, and Davison did not dare to, either.

She handed him the warrant, still with a stony face. "The execution should be kept as secret as possible, and take place at Fotheringhay." She paused, then said angrily, "Others who loved me might have spared me this burden! To have been brought to this pass before all the world! I would that some might take it upon themselves to prove their love and loyalty and save me from the censure of the world!"

"Dearest Queen, I—"

"Pray, join Walsingham in writing to Paulet. Urge him to find some way to shorten the life of that Queen, other than—" She pointed at the warrant.

Shaking with fear and excitement, Davison took the precious warrant and rushed to Walsingham's London house. He found him in bed, his swollen leg propped up on a pillow. But when the warrant was unrolled before his eyes, he sat up like a man seeing a holy vision.

"At last! Can it be?" He read it over and over.

"There is—something else," murmured Davison. "Her Majesty is loath to carry it out. She wishes to be relieved of the burden. In short, she wants Paulet to murder the Queen before she can reach the block."

Walsingham groaned. "Oh, no!"

"And we are commanded to write this 'suggestion' to Paulet."

"Oh, no!"

"Yes."

"So she herself is stooping to that for which the Queen of Scots is condemned to die!" cried Walsingham. "Oh, I am sick indeed!"

When Davison left Walsingham's house, he carried with him a second paper, addressed to Sir Amyas Paulet.

> After our hearty commendations, we find by speech lately uttered by Her Majesty that she doth note in you both a lack of that care and zeal of her service that she looketh for at your hands, in that you have not in all this time found some way to shorten the life of that Queen of Scots, considering the great peril Queen Elizabeth is subject to hourly as long as the Queen of Scots shall live.
>
> And therefore she taketh it most unkindly towards her, that men professing that love towards her that you do, should, for lack of the discharge of your duties, cast the burden on her, knowing as you do her indisposition to shed blood, especially of one of that sex and quality, and so near to her in blood as the said Queen is.

Davison hurried through the night to the Lord Chancellor Bromley's home, where he obtained the Great Seal of yellow wax. Then together they sought out Cecil, after dispatching the private letter to Fotheringhay.

The next morning, Cecil gathered with the rest of the Privy Councillors, still clutching the precious warrant. Davison described what the Queen had said; he had been called back to her side just that morning.

"She swore a great oath and said she wished to hear no more about it until it was done," he said. "She had told me to delay a bit having the Great Seal affixed. Then, in the next breath, she said she would it were over and done with." He shook his head in confusion.

"I know her well," said Cecil. "We must carry through the order. We must take it upon ourselves. If we all act in unison, the punishment cannot fall on one individual alone. But we must hurry, before she changes her mind! Beale, prepare yourself to leave London immediately for Fothering-hay!"

"Walsingham will procure the executioner," said Davison. "He considers it his duty."

The next morning, with Beale safely on his way, accompanied by the earls of Shrewsbury and Kent, Davison found himself called back yet again to Greenwich and Queen Elizabeth's side.

"Ah! My dear Davison!" she said sweetly. "I had the most peculiar and disturbing dream about you last night!"

"Yes?"

"I dreamed I was forced to run you through with a sword, for having caused the death of the Queen of Scots." She did not let her voice play with the words, but just said them straight.

"Madam, most gracious Queen—is it your will that the execution proceed?" he said faintly. He wondered where Beale was at that moment.

"God's breath and liver, yes!" she cried. "Yes, it is my will! I would that it were done!" Then she rounded him and said, "Is there any reply from Paulet?"

"Yes. I just received this as I was leaving."

She snatched the letter from him and tore it open. Her eyes took in the entire contents at a glance and she flung it to the floor. "Oh, these over-conscientious fools!" She stamped her foot. "God's angels in Hell! Read this!" She shoved it at him.

> Sirs, Walsingham and Davison:
>   Your letter of yesterday coming to my hands this present day at five in the afternoon, I would not fail according to your directions to return my answer with all possible speed, which I shall deliver unto you with great grief and bitterness of mind. I am so unhappy to have lived to see this unhappy day, in which I am directed by my most gracious sovereign to do an act which God and the law forbids. My good livings and life are at Her Majesty's disposal, and I am ready so to lose them tomorrow if it shall so please her, acknowledging that I hold them as of her mere and most gracious favour, and do not desire to enjoy them, but with her Highness' good liking. But God forbid that I should make so foul a shipwreck of my conscience, or leave so great a blot to my poor poster-ity, to shed blood without law or warrant.

"Oh, these tender fellows, who swore in the Bond to perform great deeds to protect me, but all they perform is words!" cried Elizabeth.

"Madam—I am sure that Paulet loves and honours you," said Davison.

"Oh, go!" she snapped. "It is time the matter were dispatched! Jesu! It is a shame it is not already done, seeing that I have done all that law and reason can require of me!"

Three carriages were bumping along the road to Fotheringhay: in one rode Beale, carrying the warrant with the Seal. He reached Fotheringhay in the evening of Sunday, February fifth, two days after he had left London, and only a few hours after Elizabeth had dismissed Davison for the last time. He went straight to the castle and sought out Paulet.

Close on his heels was a closed carriage in which a man dressed all in black velvet sat, a box discreetly tucked under his feet. This was a Mr. Simon Bull, professional executioner, and he carried his axe with him in the box. Walsingham's servant Digby accompanied him. When they arrived at Fotheringhay, they lodged in an inn, and waited for the summons. No neighbouring nobleman wanted to house them.

Farther back, a third carriage transported the Earl of Shrewsbury and the Earl of Kent to Fotheringhay. Their mission had been disguised under another commission to hear legal cases in Bedfordshire and Hertfordshire. The Queen's wishes that the execution should take place swiftly and secretly were to be carried out. Shrewsbury looked forlornly at the passing countryside and wished with all the force in his being that he were not involved in this grisly, tragic mission.

The Queen of Scots changed my life, he thought. Keeping her in custody for fourteen years steered my fortunes both at court and in my marriage. . . . I would it had never happened. But would I have been content never to have known her? Oh—had I not known her, yes. But now, never . . .

He felt tears pricking at the corners of his eyes. He was going to have to tell her what was to happen, and then he would have to witness it. He did not know if he could bear it.

XXXI

"What is all that howling?" asked Jane Kennedy. Outside the tower, voices were rising.

Mary gestured to her to look out the window. She herself found that movement was so painful that she tried to ration herself to only the most urgent tasks.

Jane pulled open the shutters and gave a gasp.

"It's a—a bright light in the heavens—" she cried. "No—a flame!" she shrieked, and drew back. "At the window!"

As Mary watched, flames seemed to encircle the window frame; little darts of fire shot into the room. Alarmed, she jumped up and went to the window.

The flames had withdrawn, seemingly sucked up into the air. Outside, on the ground, the guards were moaning and rubbing their eyes. The light had blinded them.

Then, suddenly, the flames struck again, withdrew, struck again, before finally fading away.

Mary clung to the windowsill, gasping for breath.

"It is here," she said. "This is a portent."

Below, people were milling. She heard the guards say, "Nowhere else—just here, under *her* windows . . ." They looked up, fear in their eyes. "It's *her*."

Mary closed the shutters, her hands shaking.

She lay on her bed, stiff and aching. Her body seemed to have undergone a rebellion: it did not want to rise.

When it was reasonably light, she called Bourgoing to her side. "Do you remember the herbs that helped me when I was so rigid in my knees? Do you think it is possible to get any more? I must regain my mobility. For when the summons for my death comes, I would not wish to be unable to rise from my bed. It might be construed as reluctance or fear!" Her voice was firm.

"I will ask Paulet, Madam," he said. "In the meantime, have your ladies massage your limbs, and put hot wet cloths on them."

After the midday meal, Bourgoing approached Paulet and confided to him their desperate state. "She can hardly bend her limbs. There are certain herbs that can help. Would it be possible—could you allow me to go into the fields to collect them?"

Paulet looked uncomfortable, and less sure of himself than usual. "Write down the names of the plants you require, and I will send someone out for them," he finally said.

"Gladly would I, but I know not the English names." Seeing Paulet's frown, he added, "I am not trying to be difficult. It is the truth, God help me."

Paulet wrinkled his face and bit his lips. "I will consult with Sir Drue Drury, my new associate here, and if he agrees, tomorrow you may go out with the apothecary."

"Outside the castle?" Bourgoing was surprised.

"Yes. Ask me again tomorrow, on Monday. Remind me, lest I forget."

When Bourgoing reported this back to Mary, she was puzzled. "No one has been allowed beyond the castle walls since we arrived," she said. "And to think, it is no ruse. Perhaps this proves that it is always best to be truthful." She laughed.

That evening, as the last prayers were being said, Willie Douglas waited and then whispered to her, "Someone has arived from the outside."

She continued with her prayers, but indicated to him to wait. When the few remaining servants were dismissed, she drew Willie aside.

"Ah, Willie, what did you see? Your eyes remain as sharp as ever."

"Someone whose arrival has created a great stir. Paulet and Drury met him in the courtyard, and whisked him in quickly, looking up continually to see if anyone was watching."

"Did you recognize him?"

"No. I have never seen him before."

The next afternoon, Bourgoing sought out Paulet about the herbs.

"Have I your permission to go, sir?" he asked brightly.

Paulet refused to meet his eyes. "Not at this time," he replied. "Peradventure the Queen will not need them."

". . . and so I am not allowed to go," said Bourgoing bitterly.

"I see, then, that I will have no need of the herbs. You may cease your searching for them," said Mary.

It was Monday, February sixth. Outside of the exchange between Paulet and Bourgoing, nothing unusual happened. Had the summons indeed come? Mary wondered. Perhaps the mysterious man was just on routine business. Fotheringhay was a building, and a building had many needs, especially in winter. There were leaking roofs, plugged-up chimneys, flooded stables. All these things have nothing to do with me, she told herself.

I will bide here forever, so it seems, she thought, lying on her bed, feigning sleep. Each day will melt into the next, and finally weeds and briars will smother the entire castle and we will be utterly forgotten . . . forever and ever.

Jesus saith unto him, If I will that he tarry til I come, what is that to thee?

If You wish me to wait and wait and wait, why, then, I must obey, she thought wearily.

The next day was gloomy, with swirling mists on the ground and a sun that showed only as a fuzzy grey light. With great difficulty, Mary rose and took her breakfast, then read quietly until time for the midday meal. It was a meagre one, as little was available this time of year: some limp carrots, musty cabbage, and dried fish. But she had little appetite.

I must lie down, she thought. I hate to give in to it, but I need to stretch out.

Slowly she rose and, and bracing the small of her back, felt the bumps of her backbone. They were tender and aching.

"Madam, there is someone here," said Willie, coming from the outer chamber. "Someone you know well."

"Who?" A sudden stab of fear gripped her.

"It is the Earl of Shrewsbury. He would fain speak with you."

"I was going to take my rest. I must lie down, I fear. But allow me to settle myself, and then admit him to my bedside."

Shrewsbury! What was he doing here? Surely not—no, Elizabeth would not require that of him—of either of them!

She arranged a coverlet over her swollen feet, and pushed a large pillow behind her head. "Pray, admit the Earl," she told Jane, and lay back and waited for the door to open.

Shrewsbury came in hesitantly. Behind him were two other men, as well as Paulet and Drury.

"Welcome, friend," she said. She was surprised at how very good it was to see him; she had missed him without being consciously aware of it.

He looked stricken; his eyes were puffy and streaked with dark rings.

"It grieves me to have come on this mission," he finally mumbled, "although it gives me great joy to see you."

Robert Beale now stepped up to the bed. "As you know, I am clerk of Her Majesty's Privy Council," he said softly. "I bring—" he opened a velvet pouch and extracted a square piece of parchment with the yellow Great Seal dangling from it.

There it was. The warrant. Mary had never imagined how it would actually feel to see it. It looked enormous, deadly. For an instant her courage drained away. This was real, not a story.

"The warrant for my execution," she said in a faint voice. "Fear not to read it to me. That soul is not worthy of the joys of Heaven forever, whose body cannot endure for a moment the stroke of the executioner."

Beale read the warrant, word for word.

Mary listened attentively. *Also with all humbleness require, solicit, and press us to direct such further execution against her Person . . . taking her into your charge, cause by your commandment execution to be done upon her person . . . as you think by your discretion convenient. . . .*

She bowed her head. "In the name of God, these tidings are welcome, and I bless and praise Him that the end to all my bitter sufferings is at hand." Her knee was throbbing. Now it was of no moment; soon it would be stopped forever. "When is it to be?" she asked.

"Tomorrow morning at eight o'clock," said Shrewsbury, his voice unsteady.

"Eight o'clock? This time tomorrow, I shall have been dead four hours already?" she cried. "That is not enough time to prepare!"

"Madam, it is two months since you were read the sentence," said Paulet. "You should have prepared already."

"I have no power to prolong the time. You must die tomorrow at the time we have named," said Shrewsbury apologetically.

"I will have to—there are my servants to be provided for, they who have sacrificed everything for my sake, and who, in losing me, will lose everything; my will to be written—I could not do it until the very last minute, as I knew not from day to day what money or possessions I would retain," she said. "I will need my papers and account books."

"That is not possible. They are still in London, whence they were taken from Chartley," said Paulet.

"Pray, restore my dear chaplain, Father de Préau. You have separated us for the last few weeks. Now I need him to help me in the preparations my church deems necessary before death."

"No, that cannot be allowed. It is against the law of the land, and our consciences. However, we will permit a Protestant chaplain to attend you," said Paulet.

"Nay, that avails me nothing!" she said. "I must die in the religion in which I have been baptized."

"Madam, your life would be the death of our religion, and your death will be its preservation!" burst out the Earl of Kent.

She smiled, as if he had given her a great gift. "Ah! I did not flatter myself that I was worthy of such a death, and I humbly receive it as a token that I am one of God's chosen servants at the last." Her joy transformed her face.

The men made ready to leave her bedside.

"Has the Queen sent any reply to my requests?" asked Mary. "Am I to be buried in France?"

"We do not know," said Shrewsbury. His voice quavered, and Paulet shot a look at him.

"Oh, sir!" cried Bourgoing, tears streaming down his face. "The humblest individual, nay, the greatest criminal, would have been granted a longer time to prepare for death! If you have no pity on this noble Queen, at least have some on us, her servants, who will be rendered destitute if she has no means of providing for us!"

"I have no power to prolong the time!" said Shrewsbury, leaving the chamber. The door slammed shut.

Jane Kennedy fell weeping on the bed.

Mary looked around at all her grieving servants. Suddenly she was strong again; she had work to do.

She touched Jane's head. "Up, Jane Kennedy!" she said in a loud voice. "Leave weeping, and be doing, for the time is short!"

She clapped her hands to get the attention of the others. "Did I not tell you, my children, that it would come to this? Blessed be God that it has come, and fear and sorrow are at an end. Weep not, neither lament, for it will avail nothing, but rejoice rather that you see me so near the end of my long troubles and afflictions!"

She swung herself out of bed and went to her desk, where she busied herself in dividing up her few remaining things, the little money she had left, and wrote the name of each recipient on little pieces of paper. She tried to account for every object, wishing she had more to give them than these trinkets.

"Bring supper early," she told Bourgoing. "I wish to eat my last meal and then attend to the truly important things."

The meal was served without ceremony, as her rod and her dais had been taken away, along with her priest. Everyone sat weeping, choking and unable to eat.

"Did you mark how they said I was to die for my religion?" said Mary. "Oh, glorious thought, that I should be chosen to die for such a cause!" She took a large cup and filled it with wine, and handed it to Bourgoing.

"Now I wish each of you to drink to me, and pledge to me for the last time," she said.

Bourgoing fell to his knees before her, and raising the cup, scarcely able to speak, he whispered, "God grant you peace."

Jane Kennedy followed him, likewise kneeling. "I will follow you even to the block, and I will never be unfaithful, nor forget you," she said. Her eyes were brimming, but she kept her voice steady. She passed the cup to Elizabeth Curle.

"I hereby swear to keep your name burnished bright before all men, and to carry on your cause until the end of my days," she said.

"I helped you to escape from Lochleven," said Willie Douglas, "and now I must stand by helplessly as you go to a worse fate you cannot escape."

"Ah, Willie, you are indeed a faithful servant. But remember, I am escaping from my troubles. The Queen my cousin does me a great benefit."

Old Balthazzar knelt. "I have it ready," he said. "The dress. Would that I had some other gift to offer."

"There is none I would so gladly accept," she said.

After all had passed before her, she took the cup herself and drank to them. "Farewell, my good friends all. If I have done you any wrong, pray forgive me."

The supper over, Mary took her place in a chair in the farther end of the room and asked Jane to bring her her few remaining jewels and treasures, so that she might assign them. One by one she held them up and examined them.

"These are the relics of my former splendour," she said. "And they will go out as my envoys from this place." She took a sapphire ring from her hand, having a large square-cut stone. "This is for my brave kinsman, Lord Claud Hamilton."

Other jewels were to go to the King and Queen of France, to Catherine de Médicis, and to the Guises. Bourgoing was given her velvet-bound music book. "Pray remember all our winter evenings, singing," she said.

"I will carry this gold rosary to the execution," Mary said. "But on the scaffold I will give it to you, Jane. I wish it to be delivered after my death to Anne Dacres, the faithful Catholic daughter-in-law of the Duke of Norfolk." She touched the diamond she still wore about her neck. "It is time this were taken off," she said. "I promised him to wear it until death. And now it has come." She handed it to Jane. "Likewise I will carry the Agnus Dei to the block, but afterwards I wish you to have it, Elizabeth. Do not let the—the executioner take it."

Elizabeth burst out crying again.

It was now past nine o'clock. There was still the will to be done. She hunched over the writing table and tried, from memory, to account for all contingencies. She appointed the Duc de Guise, Archbishop Beaton, Bishop Leslie, and du Ruisseau, the chancellor of her dowry in France, to be her executors. There were arrangements to be made for requiem masses for her soul, charitable bequests for poor children and priests at Reims, a contribution to the seminarians. Her women were to be allowed to take her coach and horses to London and sell them for passage back to their home countries.

She finished it and rolled it up. Her hand was aching. But there were yet other letters to be done. Since she could not make a confession in person to de Préau, she must do it on paper. Wearily she took up the pen in her stiff hand and tried to think, imagining herself speaking. In the deep shadows in the corners of the room, she could picture death himself standing by and watching her, leaning, skeletal arms crossed, empty skull staring.

> Dear Father in Christ,
> I beg you to keep vigil and prayer with me this night, my last on earth. I freely confess my sins, knowing that they are many. . . .

The hour approached midnight. She waited, hushed, to hear any sound of a chime formally dividing the days of February seventh and eighth, but there was nothing.

She took out another sheet of paper and began her last letter, to Henri III, King of France.

> 8 Feb. 1587.
> Royal brother, having by God's will, for my sins I think, thrown myself into the power of the Queen my cousin, at whose hands I have suffered much for almost twenty years, I have finally been condemned to death by her Estates. . . .
> I have not had time to give you a full account of everything that has happened, but if you will listen to my doctor and my other unfortunate servants, you will learn the truth and how, thanks be to God, I scorn death. . . .

She looked up uneasily, peering with all her power of sight into the dark corners. Did she really mean that? Best not to scorn him aforehand. . . .

She went on writing, pouring out her concerns to him about her servants and her burial. Would he help her in these things? She had to trust him. Finally she fumbled with a little velvet pouch and took out two unset jewels: one was an amethyst and the other a bloodstone.

> I have taken the liberty of sending you two precious stones, talismans against illness, trusting that you will enjoy good health and a long and happy life. Accept them from your loving sister-in-law, who, as she dies, bears witness of her warm feelings for you.

Wednesday, at two in the morning.
Your most loving and most true sister,

Marie R.

To the Most Christian King, my brother and old ally.

Two o'clock in the morning! The night was slipping away.

But what of it? she asked herself. It is hardly to be expected that I would spend it sleeping. I will be sleeping soon enough.

Was it too late to have her customary reading with her ladies? Yes, of course it was. Stiffly she stood, and made her way over to her bed. It was too late now even to undress. She would not wake anyone up to do it, and her own fingers were too swollen to do it herself. She lay down on her bed fully dressed, and closed her eyes. O God, give me courage! Let me not fail at the moment of death! she prayed. I failed You at the last test, but in Your mercy You have granted me another. Help me now!

She heard a rustling beside her, and looked up to see both Jane and Elizabeth standing by the bedside. They were both already dressed in mourning black.

"You are ready early," said Mary. But the sight of them attired for the event shook her deeply. "I am laggard. But even though it is late, I would like to end the day in the customary fashion. Jane, can you read aloud from my book of hours?"

"Indeed," she said, fetching it.

"Choose the life of a great sinner," said Mary.

Jane read over the table of contents. "Mary Magdalene?"

Mary shook her head.

"Saint Augustine?"

"No."

"The penitent thief on the cross?"

Mary sighed. "Yes. He was a great sinner, but not so great a sinner as I am. May my blessed Saviour, in memory of His passion, have mercy on me in the hour of death, as He had on him."

Mary lay back on the pillow and closed her eyes, waiting for the soothing voice of Jane to begin the story.

" 'The two thieves, condemned to be crucified beside Christ, mocked him. But at length one of them, moved by some divine grace, rebuked his companion. "Do you not fear God, seeing we are likewise condemned? We have deserved the death. But this man is innocent," he said. Then, turning to Christ, he said, "Lord, remember me when you come into your kingdom."

Christ looked at him and said, "Verily, verily, this day shalt thou be with me in paradise." ' "

Today . . . paradise . . . Will I be there in only a few hours? Mary wondered. Can it be true?

A muffled banging reached her ears. The scaffold was being erected in the Great Hall, across the courtyard.

" 'Now this experience of the thieves condenses and foreshortens the whole of human existence,' " Jane continued, bending closer so that Mary could hear her without her raising her voice. " 'It shows us the bare essentials of life and death, when there is no more time left. But these men had one unique quality, one experience no one else has had or can have. They were dying beside Jesus, who was also dying.' "

But I die alone, thought Mary. I will have no fellows on the scaffold.

" 'This is both a unique opportunity and a unique challenge—to see God dying and yet believe. And what was their response? The first thief gave a doubting, hedged "prove it and then I will believe." This is the normal human response; it is what the world trains us to do. It is a contemptible doctrine.' "

Yes, we all want proof, thought Mary. Does that make me so great a sinner if I doubt, even for a moment?

" 'The second thief said, "Lord," not "*if* thou art Lord." He had no time, and perhaps no ability, to understand intricacies of theology. He may not even have grasped what "paradise" meant. But the main thing was that he saw—and believed.

" 'Now what does this mean to us? Foreshortened and condensed though it be, the thieves and their few hours of life left on the cross are in essentials the same as you and I. We face the same death—slower, perhaps, but no less sure. We face the same eternal question. We face the same opportunity. We must ask ourselves, "Which thief am I?" ' "

Jane closed the book softly. Mary's mouth held a smile. The sound of the hammering continued relentlessly.

"Even in the hour of death, there can be salvation," said Mary. "It is never too late."

Outside the room there was suddenly the tramp of boots. The guards had been increased, lest the Queen make a last-minute escape.

The quiet time of the night was over; already it was filled with the sounds of the business at hand.

At six o'clock Mary gave up all pretence of rest. She rose from her bed, and instantly the women rose with her. No one had slept.

"I have two hours left of life," she said in wonderment. "It is a curious thing, to have no mortal illness, no unclouded mind, and yet to know my end is nigh. I have no gift of second sight or prophecy, and yet I behold my accident to come." She felt along her arm, so solid, so warm. Its immediate mortality was entirely artificial.

"Come, my women. Dress me as for a festival; ask Balthazzar for my special dress. For this is a celebratory ceremony to which I go."

While they readied her apparel, Mary stood quietly, paying attention to her breathing. The very air seemed heavy and to be savoured; the act of breathing became conscious. The breath of life. To breathe is to live. *And the Lord God breathed into his nostrils the breath of life, and man became a living soul.*

O Lord God, I must believe that I will continue to be a living soul even when the breath departs in two hours, she thought. I must—

"Here, my lady," said Elizabeth, holding the crimson gown. It was all of satin, with a plain skirt and bodice cut low in the back to accommodate the stroke of the axe. Lace trimmed the scooped neck in front. There were detachable sleeves as well.

"Thank you." Mary started to put it on, then had a wild thought. What if it did not fit? She had never tried it on.

But it did. It fit perfectly.

And then Jane brought her overdress of mourning black, satin with velvet trimmings and jet buttons. With tears in her eyes, she fastened the dress over the crimson one. Elizabeth brought Mary her finest wig and arranged it before putting on the headdress: a white cap with a peaked front, from which flowed a long, transparent white veil, edged in lace. It reached the ground, as had her bridal veil at her first marriage.

The women stepped back and looked at her. She already seemed remote, costumed for a far journey to a different land. The clothes had transformed her.

She picked up her two rosaries and fastened them about her waist, along with a cross; an Agnus Dei hung from her neck by a jewelled chain. Her movements were careful and dainty.

"I thank you," she said. "I wish to ask you one . . . other thing. On the scaffold, after the execution"—her words rushed together—"I will be incapable of attending to this body as modesty decrees. Please cover me; do not let me lie exposed."

The women nodded, silently.

"And now, let the rest of the household join us. I would speak to all of you one last time."

When they were all together, Mary embraced the women and gave the men her hand to kiss. She had meant to tell them about the will, about what they were to do afterwards, but she found that words were unnecessary and awkward. Instead she put the will, along with her farewell letters, into an open box and merely indicated it.

She could see sunshine coming through her windows. The air smelt a bit like spring; probably, down by the banks of the River Nene, snowdrops were already blooming.

The eighth of February, she thought. This day, this very day, at its close will be twenty years since last I saw Darnley, and on the next he died. In my end is my beginning. For truly my deepest woe began on that day, and today it comes to fruition.

Then, after taking a little bread and wine that Bourgoing brought her for strength, she turned away from them and went to the oratory to pray.

She had imagined that she would have words and words and words to say, but instead, there were very few. *Strengthen me. Thank You for this life.* Beside her, Geddon, also at the end of his days but clinging to life, thumped his balding tail. It was that everyday sound, the summation of all the everyday things she was leaving, that brought tears to her eyes.

"What odd things I will miss most," she whispered.

It was past eight o'clock when the High Sheriff knocked on the chamber door and was admitted. "Madam, the lords have sent me for you," he said.

Mary rose and turned to him. "Yes. Let us go."

Bourgoing suddenly rushed across the room to where her old ivory crucifix was hanging, and took it off the wall. "Carry it before her," he said, handing it to one of the stewards. Mary smiled; how could she have forgotten it?

Together the company left the apartments and descended the great oak staircase, passing the wicket gate that had served as the outer boundaries of Mary's world, beyond which she was never permitted to pass. Now she swept past it, supported by two of Paulet's men.

At the foot of the stairs, the Earl of Kent stopped her attendants. "No farther! You are not to enter the Great Hall." He glared at Mary. "You are to die alone, by the Queen's orders."

Mary's people began to cry and protest. Jane flung herself on the floor and clutched at Mary's gown.

Fingers clinging to my gown . . . Riccio! She disengaged Jane's grip and turned to Kent.

"Pray, sir, let them witness my end. I wish them to see how I endure it."

"No! They will doubtless weep and wail, and distract the headsman. And worse, they will dip their handkerchiefs in your blood, to make a holy relic of it. We know what your religion does with such trumperies!"

Mary shuddered. "My lord," she said, trying to keep her voice steady, "I will give my word, although I will be dead, that they will do none of these things." She turned to the Earl of Shrewsbury, who had hidden himself in the back. "I know the Queen has not given you such orders. She, a maiden Queen, would certainly allow me the dignity of being attended by my own women at my death."

Shrewsbury, Kent, Paulet, and Drury conferred, and at length told her she might select six persons to accompany her.

"Then I must have Jane and Elizabeth. Andrew Melville, my master of the household, and my physician, apothecary, and surgeon. Unless . . . you will permit my priest to come?"

"No priest!" bellowed the Earl of Kent.

"Very well," said Mary.

Before they could proceed farther, Melville threw himself on his knees and cried, "Woe is me! that it should be my lot to carry back such heavy tidings to Scotland that my gracious Queen and mistress has been beheaded in England."

"Weep not, Andrew, my good and faithful servant. I am Catholic, you Protestant; but as there is but one Christ, I charge you in His name to bear witness that I die firm to my religion, a true Scotswoman and a true French-woman. Commend me to my dearest and most sweet son. I give him my blessing on earth." She made the sign of the cross in the air.

"The time is wearing away apace!" growled the Earl of Kent. "Come!"

The procession—headed by the Sheriff and his men, then Paulet and

Drury, Shrewsbury, Kent, and Beale—made its way into the Great Hall. Mary followed, determined to walk unaided. She straightened her spine and held her head up, by sheer strength of will.

The chamber was very large, but all Mary could see was the execution platform. She had heard it abuilding; now she beheld it.

It was about twelve feet square, with railings. It was almost a yard high, too high for someone to mount without steps, and so a neat little pair of steps was provided. The platform was hung all around with black. There were objects on it: a chair, a table, a cushion, two stools . . . and the block.

She tried to keep her heart from racing. But there had been no preparation for this. In everything else, there was an analogy in normal life. But there had been no way of steeling herself for the very existence of this death-platform, no substitute to accustom herself to.

The crowd was staring at her, watching her to see if she trembled.

Another crowd, staring as she was brought back to Edinburgh. Lord Lindsay and Ruthven on either side, like Paulet and Drury . . .

Burn the whore!

Execute the traitor!

She looked straight ahead and focused on the black gathered hangings skirting the platform. She paused at the foot of the stairs. Paulet stood beside them and offered his hand.

"I thank you, sir," she said. "This is the last trouble I shall ever give you."

Shrewsbury, Kent, and Beale mounted the stairs; they indicated to her that she should be seated in the chair provided. She obeyed.

She became aware of two men dressed entirely in black. Then she saw the axe, lying on the floor. It was the kind used to chop wood! No sword for her. She gripped the arms of the chair.

Beale began to read the warrant for the execution to the room. Only then did Mary look out at the people. There were more than a hundred gathered, and they surrounded the platform on three sides.

"Now, Madam," said the Earl of Shrewsbury in a faint voice, "you see what you have to do."

"Do your duty," said Mary. She felt a great peace flooding her; she smiled.

Just then a portly churchman, in full vestments, leaned over the platform. "I am the Dean of Peterborough!" he said in ringing tones. "It is not too late to embrace the true faith! Yea, the Reformed Religion, which hath—"

Not this! She was taken aback; never had she expected this, at this time.

"Mr. Dean, trouble not yourself, nor me," said Mary, "for know that I am settled in the ancient Catholic and Roman faith, in defence whereof, by God's grace, I mind to spend my blood."

"Have a care over your soul, soon to be departing from out of your body! Change your opinion, and repent you of your former wickedness!" he cried.

"Good Mr. Dean," she said, "trouble not yourself anymore about this matter. I was born in this religion, have lived in this religion, and am resolved to die in this religion."

"Madam, even now, Madam, doth God Almighty open a door unto you; shut not this door by the hardness of your heart—"

His voice faded and was replaced by John Knox's: *Conscience requires knowledge, and I fear that right knowledge you have not. . . .*

Shrewsbury interrupted the Dean. "Madam, we will pray along with the Dean for you."

Mary smiled at him. "If you will pray for me, I thank you. But I will not join with you in your manner of prayer; I cannot, as we are not of the same religion."

Shrewsbury attempted to hush the Dean, but Kent urged him on. The Dean raised his arms and boomed out, "Open, we beseech thee, thine eyes of mercy, and behold this person appointed to death, whose eyes of understanding and spiritual light thou hast hitherto shut up—"

He was pronouncing a curse! Mary shut her ears to it and began to pray in Latin, letting the ancient words drown out his cruel pronouncements. She slid off the stool and onto her knees.

"Conserva me, Domine, quoniam speravi in Te. . . ."

Preserve me, O God, for in Thee have I put my trust. . . .

She prayed louder, until her words drowned out the Dean's ranting in her own ears. She heard him no more; she was bathed once more in the radiant peace she had come near to losing.

She stood, gripping the crucifix, and, holding it aloft, cried, "As Thy arms, O Christ, were extended on the cross, even so receive me, and blot out all my sins with Thy most precious blood." The crucifix seemed to shimmer, and behind it she could see the walls of the room at St.-Pierre. It was all one; time dissolved.

"Leave this trumpery!" The Earl of Kent attempted to wrest away the crucifix. But Mary folded it against her breast.

The Dean retreated; the two executioners now came forward and knelt in front of her. "Forgive us," they said.

She looked down at their strong forearms, thicker than her neck. "I forgive you and all the world with all my heart," she said. "For I hope this death will make an end to all my troubles."

They rose. "Shall we help you make ready?" they asked politely.

"Nay, I am not accustomed to such grooms," she answered, again with a smile. She turned and looked out at the crowd. "Nor to undressing before so great a company." She motioned to Jane and Elizabeth, who were kneeling at the foot of the platform. "I have need of you," she said.

The two women rose and mounted the platform, but as they approached, they burst into tears.

"Do not weep," she said. "I am very happy to leave this world. You ought to rejoice to see me die in so good a cause. Are you not ashamed to weep? Nay, if you do not stop these lamentations, I must send you away, for you know I promised you would not behave so."

As she spoke, she removed her crucifix and rosaries and handed them to Jane. The executioner tried to take them, but Mary reproved him.

Carefully, with trembling hands, Jane and Elizabeth unbuttoned the black gown and revealed the crimson one underneath. The crowd drew its breath. They brought her the sleeves and she attached them, so she was now a glare of crimson even down to her fingers. Jane removed her veil and headdress, setting them on the little stool.

Mary kissed her ivory crucifix good-bye, and laid it down alongside her other things on the stool, placing her book of hours with it. Then she took up the gold-bordered kerchief with which her eyes would be covered, and handed it silently to Jane.

Behind all the people she could see the leaping flames of the fire that burned in the fireplace in the cold room.

My last sight. Golden flames and black clothes. But there is no sight more worthy than any other, and none which completely satisfies the desire to continue looking.

Jane dissolved in tears and could not fasten the cloth.

Hurry, blank out the sight, do not prolong it!

But the shaking hands just trembled in front of Mary's eyes.

"Hush," said Mary. "I have promised for you. Weep not, but pray for me."

Mary had to help her fasten it; it tied behind the head, and a portion of it covered her hair as well, so it was as if she wore a turban.

Now she could see nothing. She heard them breathing beside her, then the sound of them being led away and down the stairs.

Someone helped her to kneel on a cushion, which she knew was by the block. She settled herself on it and then stretched out her hands, groping for the block. She felt its hard edge underneath the cloth covering. She stretched her neck out and put her chin in the hollow meant for it.

Why was everything so real, so hard? It was supposed to be dreamy and soft and swallowed up in a blaze of ecstasy. Instead there was this nubbly feel of cloth, these aching knees, the feel of the kerchief knot that hurt the back of her head. She swallowed and waited, holding herself still.

"In Te Domino confido, non confundar in aeternum . . ." she murmured, in a private whisper. In Thee, O Lord have I put my trust, let me never be put to confusion.

Something was touching her. A fat wide hand was steadying her, pressing on her back. She felt the sweat passing through her garment and outlining itself against the hand.

"In manus tuas . . ." Into Thy hands, O Lord, I commend my spirit.

She could hear her own voice. Everything was achingly acute.

Nothing is ever as I expected. But always deeper, harder, wilder, sweeter, grander . . . I come, Lord, regardless . . . help me!

* * *

Shrewsbury, the Earl Marshal, lowered his baton as a signal. The headsman raised his axe high, and brought it down with a smash. He saw with horror that in his nervousness he had missed, and only gashed the side of her skull. She groaned and said in the smallest of whispers, "Sweet Jesus." The spectators screamed. Quickly he raised the axe again and swung it with all his might. It bit through her neck, cutting her head almost free. Angry and ashamed, he used the edge of the axe like a saw to fray away the last ligaments. The head fell off and rolled away. The body flopped over on its back, the shoulders covered in blood, the neck still spurting.

"God save Queen Elizabeth!" cried the executioner, leaning down to pick up the head. He grabbed it by the kerchief and held it aloft. Suddenly part of it fell away; the head itself rolled away, and the executioner was left holding the wig and the kerchief.

The people gasped to see how grey Mary's hair was. The head lay looking at them, the lips moving.

"So perish all the Queen's enemies!" yelled Kent, straddling the fallen head.

"Yea! Such be the end of all the Gospel's enemies!" cried the Dean.

Shrewsbury turned his head away and wept.

The executioner now tried to pull up Mary's skirts to take her garters, which was his time-honoured prerogative. As his hands fumbled with the skirts, a mournful yelp arose, and from out of the crumpled material a little dog emerged. It was Geddon, who had followed his mistress out of her chambers and hidden himself within her voluminous skirts.

"What—" cried Bull, snatching his hand away.

Geddon rushed to the headless neck and circled it, confused. He sat down next to it and began to howl, a loud, drawn-out otherworldly howl. He rolled in the blood and guarded the body.

Jane and Elizabeth scrambled to the stairs. They had forgotten their vow to their mistress, and her body was being desecrated. But their way was blocked.

"No! You shall not go there!"

"We must attend upon her! We promised—"

"Your duties to her are at an end."

The Dean leapt up on the platform and grabbed Geddon. He pushed the dog's muzzle down into the pool of blood and tried to make him drink it. "Remember what Knox prophesied about the dogs drinking her blood!" he yelled. "Drink, you cur!"

But Geddon, with a howl, turned around and sank his teeth into the Dean's wrist.

"Cursed beast!" he cried, letting him go.

Paulet had taken Mary's head and displayed it on a velvet cushion before an open window for the people outside.

But nothing was as it should have been. The head no longer looked like Mary, but like an unfamiliar old woman. The Earl of Shrewsbury was weeping. Mary had not been afraid or broken on the scaffold, but serene

863

and happy. And suddenly the task of telling Queen Elizabeth that her great enemy had perished was not an enviable one.

Nothing was ever as expected.

They took away her crucifix and her writing-book, her bloodstained clothes, the block itself, and anything else that she had touched, and burnt them to ashes in a bonfire in the castle courtyard. There were to be no relics, no mementos. The earthly presence of the Queen of Scots was to be utterly effaced.

Nothing was ever as expected.

There remained still the body of the Queen herself, which would not vanish; the witnesses at the execution, who would recite all the facts to wider and wider audiences; the mementos she had already given away. There were all the places she had lived, the people she had known, the child she had borne—all now elevated and enlarged by the death she had just died. The more thorough the government in scrubbing the scaffold and throwing her kerchief in the fire, the more treasured all the remaining relics became. As the fire consumed her crimson gown, somewhere in the castle the mouldering hangings with her motto, *In My End Is My Beginning,* took on a new life and began to stir.

XXXII

doro, imploro, / Ut liberes me.
I Thee implore / That Thou wilt / Grant me liberty.
With her bodily liberty, the many Mary Stuarts that had been contained in one body, bundled together as it were, fled to their various domains, diverging into irreconcilable elements.

The beautiful, youthful spirit returned to France. It flew to Reims and saw at last its mother's grave, its beloved aunt, its bereft friend Mary Seton. It lingered in fondness at the wall where the ivory crucifix had originally hung. It flew, no bodily constraints now, but pure spirit, to Notre Dame and heard its own funeral eulogy.

There, in the darkness of the great cathedral where she had married in a blaze of earthly glory, her spirit heard an old priest—young then—speak of her and of those days.

"Many of us saw, in the place where we are now assembled, this Queen on the day of her bridal, arrayed in her regal trappings, so covered with

864

jewels that the sun himself shone not more brightly, so beautiful, so charming withal, as never woman was. These walls were then hung with cloth of gold and precious tapestries; every space was filled with thrones and seats, crowded with princes and princesses, who came from all parts to share in the rejoicings. The palace was overflowing with magnificence, spendid fêtes and masques; the streets with jousts and tourneys. In short, it seemed as if our age had succeeded that day in surpassing the pomp of all past centuries.

"A little time has flown on, and it is all vanished like a cloud. Who could have believed that such a change could have befallen her who appeared then so triumphant, and that we should have seen her a prisoner who had restored prisoners to liberty; in poverty, she who was accustomed to give so liberally to others; treated with contumely by those on whom she had conferred honours; and finally, the axe of the base executioner mangling the form of her who was doubly a queen; that form which honoured the nuptial bed of a sovereign of France falling dishonoured on a scaffold, and that beauty, which had been one of the wonders of the world, faded in a dreary prison, and at last effaced by a piteous death?"

He looked around the cathedral. "This place, where she was surrounded by splendour, is now hung with black for her. Instead of nuptial torches we have funeral tapers; in the place of songs of joy, we have sighs and groans; for clarions and hautboys, the tolling of the sad and dismal bell.

"It appears as if God had chosen to render her virtues more glorious by her afflictions. Others leave to their successors the care of building fair and splendid monuments to escape forgetfulness, but this Queen in dying exonerates you from that care, having by her death itself imprinted on the minds of men an image of constancy which should not be for this age alone, but for time and eternity."

The youthful spirit was touched, and then moved on.

The Monstrous Dragon and Threat to Protestantism flew to London and beheld Elizabeth at last. It saw her grief and shock when she was told of the execution, and knew in its new knowledge that Elizabeth's ministers had carried out the warrant on their own authority. But it mattered not. It watched the celebrations in London, understood the hatred, but was not touched by it.

The mother went to Scotland and saw James, a grown man, dressed all in black. She saw the courtiers, too. New ones, ones that were not there when she had ruled. And the old ones, the ones who had held sway and terror in her time, now quite vanished. But Holyrood was the same; Edinburgh Castle was the same.

She saw the Earl of Sinclair striding in in armour; heard James ask, peevishly, if he had not received the order to wear mourning for the Queen of Scotland; heard the Earl cry out, striking his armour, "This is the proper mourning for the Queen of Scotland!" and flourish his sword.

Scotland . . . it had not changed. But now she could love it.

Mary the daughter of Rome, the martyr to the faith, saw the proliferation of pamphlets, of accounts of her piety, of portraits and poems that circulated as soon as her attendants escaped from England and made their way to the Continent to tell their story of her last days. Her spirit was touched by the devotion of her fellow Catholics. But it did not recognize this staid, stern captive they had created.

There were two burials, two funerals. The first took place six months after her death, in the nearby Peterborough Cathedral. The service was Anglican, and conducted by the Dean. Her spirit was not vexed by it, only filled with compassion. Father de Préau walked along behind him, his cross prominently displayed. Elizabeth was chief mourner, but of course was not there in person. She sent a proxy, the Countess of Bedford. The day was very hot, the coffin enormously heavy. The spirit knew that they had encased her body in a thousand pounds of lead, as if they were afraid she would escape. They did not understand, in spite of all their prayers and religion.

Time, which was no time, passed, and the second funeral took place. The coffin made its way slowly to London on the orders of James, who was now King of England and Scotland. He wished to honour his mother, and lay her to rest (*they did not understand*) in the chapel of her great-grandfather, Henry VII. In the same chapel, under a structure and statue carved by the same sculptor, lay Elizabeth.

The spirit saw her own coffin passing only a few yards from Elizabeth's monument. They were to be separated by the nave of the chapel, held apart by the walls and carved stalls, never to gaze on one another's tombs.

Mary's elaborate monument, with a black-and-white marble canopy, had a white marble statue of her lying in state. It was beautiful as only earthly things could be.

And so the spirit liked to visit it and linger there. Some of those who came felt its presence, and soon they were talking of miracles and sainthood.

They did not understand.

It wearied the spirit to see how little they understood, that the presence of the spirit was not extraordinary, or even unusual; so that in time, little by little, the spirit lost its desire to roam abroad.

It found its resting place in God, who had always understood that all the Mary Stuarts were one, and created for eternity.

The exile had come home.
In my end is my beginning.

AUTHOR'S AFTERWORD

It has been said that "the Age of Kings"—Henry VIII, Francis I, and the Emperor Charles V—was followed by "the Age of Queens": Elizabeth I the Virgin Queen, Catherine de Médicis of France and Mary Queen of Scots. Certainly the second half of the sixteenth century saw an unusual number of female rulers, if one remembers that before Elizabeth I there reigned Mary I ("Bloody Mary") and before Mary Queen of Scots, her mother Marie de Guise served as Regent of Scotland. John Knox, in his *First Blast of the Trumpet Against the Monstrous Regiment of Women*, argued that it was unnatural to have a female as head of a realm. He was a sworn enemy of Mary Stuart, queen of his own country, seeming to dislike her personally as well as on principle.

Of these rulers, it is Mary Queen of Scots who seems most elusive today. Opinions of her varied violently in her own day, and four centuries have done very little to reconcile the opposing views. Was she the depraved Jezebel of Knox's imagination, steeped in lust and folly? Or was she the long-suffering, tolerant goddess of her partisans?

In order to try to answer these questions, I have had to build up a composite picture of Mary as a person, much as modern reconnaissance missions use computer-enhanced and overlapping photographs to map surfaces. I have not felt it necessary to exclude any material, for some things cancel each other out. Gradually a coherent picture does begin to emerge, of a woman who is warmhearted, loyal, brave, generous, and spirited, but also unable to read character, volatile, impulsive, and better at quick action than at sustained strategy. She was clever but not intellectually brilliant, had marked artistic and poetic talent, and evidently had a great deal of charm and the ability to fit into any setting, whether opulent as in France or simple, as in a merchant's house in St. Andrews. She was not especially fond of elaborate fashions and jewels, and had a boyish or warrior side to her. Later in life, a mystical side emerged.

No book about Mary Queen of Scots can escape the controversial questions of her life: 1. Was she really in love with James Hepburn, the Earl of Bothwell, her third husband? 2. Who wrote the Casket Letters? 3. Who planned Darnley's death? 4. Did Mary wish Elizabeth to be assassinated?

On the answers to these four questions hang one's verdict of her character.

It is my opinion that she indeed loved the Earl of Bothwell and married him of her own free will. Her actions toward that end are too determined for the truth to be otherwise, and I tend to believe that she made the famous declaration that she "would go to the end of the earth with him in a white petticoat." It is almost impossible to believe that their liaison did not begin before Darnley's death—but it may just be that I wish to grant her some happiness, however brief.

As for the Casket Letters, when all the texts have been analysed and re-analysed, the famous Second Casket Letter sounds so exactly like what a distracted women, deeply in love but tormented about her situation, would write, that I accept Mary as its author. That does not rule out the possibility that other letters, from other women (we know Bothwell had a romantic history), were added to Mary's, and even some outright forgery may have taken place. The tone of the letters varies widely, and some of them do not sound like Mary. Even in love, Mary was never petty (although she may have been jealous or angry), and certain of the letters sound catty and mean-spirited, which is out of character. None of the originals remains, and thus we can never know what tampering took place.

As for who killed Darnley, I have taken the position that although Mary longed to be free of him, she did not actually authorize the murder. There are different levels of knowing and at the deepest level she must have "known" in some way what had happened, but she was not a conscious murderess.

The question of Elizabeth is a thorny one. We know that Mary was involved in four major plots during her imprisonment in England, and although only the last one specifically called for Elizabeth's assassination, it must have been implicit in all the others. How else was Mary to become Queen, as her rescuers wished, unless Elizabeth were dead? But the question of whether someone who is wrongfully imprisoned has a moral right to attempt to escape by any means is one best left to the theologians and ethical and legal scholars. In real life, someone of Mary's impulsive and fiery spirit would have been untrue to her own character had she not tried to extricate herself. She had a history of spectacular escapes: from Holyrood Palace after the Riccio murder, from Borthwick Castle, from Lochleven. Old habits—especially successful ones—die hard. It was probably just this history that gave her hope and kept her from seeing that her situation was fundamentally different in England. She was never able to convert any of her gaolers into accomplices as she had in Scotland. They were all loyal to Elizabeth. I believe she focused on the "escape" aspect rather than the fate of Elizabeth, because it was her nature to look to physical action and not give deep thought to long-range consequences. By the time of the Babington Plot, she was probably too demoralized to think very clearly.

A few final notes: I took the liberty of blending a few characters to avoid confusion. There were actually two French physicians, Monsieur Lusgerie and Monsieur Bourgoing. But since Bourgoing was present at her execution and wrote an account of it, I simply made him her physician all the way through. There were also two Messieurs Naus, the brothers Jacques and Claud, both of whom served as her secretaries in sequence. And there were two Melville brothers, James and Robert, who served as Mary's ambassadors.

I have used Antonia Fraser's distinction between the Scottish Stewarts and the French branch of that family, the Stuarts. So when Mary marries Henry Stuart, Lord Darnley, the spelling changes. Also, when she lived in France, her name was spelled Stuart.

There are over two hundred characters in this novel mentioned by name, and all of them are historic, with the exception of two minor characters in the Scots Guard of archers in the French court, Patrick Scott and Rob MacDonald. Likewise, there are over sixty poems, songs, and letters quoted in the novel. All are geniune except Ronsard's *Hymn to the Moon*, Darnley's poem about Hadrian's Wall, Mary and Bothwell's letters to each other from gaol (although it is known that they wrote to each other, no letters have survived), the letter from the dying Lady Bothwell to Mary, and the specific wording of notes, from the French ambassador in regards to Gifford, from Sir Christopher Hatton to Elizabeth, and from Thomas Morgan to Mary. (Again, we know the notes existed.)

I could not help making a few affectionate comments about my ancestors, the Scott clan. (My father's first name is derived from his mother's maiden name.) I was gratified to find that they indeed stayed loyal to Mary to the end—and so I am just following in the family tradition.

If you would like to read more, and form your own composite picture of Mary, I can recommend the following biographies of Mary: the account in Agnes Strickland's *The Lives of the Queens of Scotland and English Princesses*, 8 volumes (Edinburgh and London: Wm. Blackwood and Sons, 1858), is invaluable for presenting the minutiae of Mary's life. This Victorian account holds Mary blameless and near-perfect. Moving into later times, T. F. Henderson in *Mary Queen of Scots, Her Environment and Tragedy*, 2 volumes (New York, Haskell House: 1969 [reprint of 1905 edition]), has a more balanced and critical view. However, the period of her stay in England is not well represented here; it is very short. The leading modern biography, Antonia Fraser's *Mary Queen of Scots* (New York: Delacorte, 1969), has been invaluable, and it covers every aspect of her life.

In addition, there is a new biography written for the four-hundred-year observance of her death, by Rosalind K. Marshall, *Queen of Scots* (London: HMSO, 1987). *Mary Stewart, Queen in Three Kingdoms*, edited by Michael Lynch (Oxford: Basil Blackwell Ltd., 1988), includes detailed scholarly essays on such subjects as Mary's library and her dowager estate income. There is a "psychobiography" by Stefan Zweig, *The Queen of Scots* (London: Cassell and Company, Ltd., 1935). Martin Hume wrote *The Love Affairs of Mary Queen of Scots* (London: Eveleigh Nash & Grayson, Ltd.). For an analysis of the different schools of thought about Mary's character, see Alastair Cherry, *Princes, Poets, and Patrons: The Stuarts of Scotland* (Edinburgh: HMSO, 1987).

If you are curious to know what Mary looked like, the Scottish National Portrait Gallery had an exhibition of authentic portraits and engravings, as well as the later historical paintings. The catalogue, *The Queen's Image*, by Helen Smailes and Duncan Thomson (Edinburgh: Scottish National Portrait Gallery, 1987), reproduces these and analyses them.

Another book put out in honour of the quadricentenary is David J. Breeze, *The Queen's Progress*, (London: HMSO, 1987), which depicts all the buildings associated with Mary. Also, David and Judy Steele's *Mary Stuart's Scotland* (New York: Harmony Books, 1987), shows the landscapes and people of Mary's environment.

Books about the Casket Letters and the Darnley murder abound. The earliest, Walter Goodall, *An Examination of the Letters said to be written by Mary Queen of Scots to James Earl of Bothwell, also, an Inquiry into the Murder of King Henry* (Edinburgh: T.&W. Ruddimans, 1754), painstakingly tries to construct a case absolving Mary. T. F. Henderson, *The Casket Letters and Mary Queen of Scots* (Edinburgh: Adam and Charles Black, 1890), is more even-handed. R. H. Mahon constructed a model of Kirk O'Field in an attempt to discover exactly what happened. It was he who first proposed the theory that Darnley himself had put the powder there. For every known detail of the event, Mahon's *The Tragedy of Kirk O'Field* (Cambridge, England: Cambridge University Press, 1930), is required reading.

Other books important for understanding her years in Scotland are: Robert Gore-Brown, *Lord Bothwell* (London: Collins, 1937); Frank A. Mumby, *The Fall of Mary Stuart* (London: Constable and Co., 1921); Jasper Ridley, *John Knox* (Oxford, England: Oxford University Press, 1968); John Knox, *History of the Reformation in Scotland* (New York: Philosophical Library, Inc., 1950); Martin A. Breslow, *The Political Writings of John Knox* (Washington, D.C.: Folger Books, 1985); Gordon Donaldson, *All the Queen's Men: Power and Politics in Mary Stewart's Scotland* (London: Batsford Academic and Educational Ltd., 1983); George MacDonald Fraser, *The Steel Bonnets* (London: Collins Harvill, 1989).

Once Mary gets to England, the cast of characters changes. See Conyers Read's *Mr. Secretary Cecil and Queen Elizabeth* (London: Jonathan Cape, 1955); *Lord Burghley and Queen Elizabeth* (Jonathan Cape, 1960); *Mr. Secretary Walsingham*, 3 volumes (Cambridge, Massachusetts: Archon Books, 1967 [reprint of 1925 edition]) to understand Mary's political adversaries. Read Alison Plowden's *Danger to Elizabeth* (London: Macmillan, 1973), and *Elizabeth Tudor and Mary Stewart, Two Queens in One Isle* (Barnes & Noble, 1984), to understand the stage upon which Mary and Elizabeth were placed by fate. Gordon Donaldson's *The First Trial of Mary Queen of Scots* (London: B. T. Batsford Ltd., 1969) examines the forerunner of the final trial eighteen years later. For a succinct and elegant biography of the Virgin Queen, see J. E. Neale, *Queen Elizabeth I* (London: Jonathan Cape, 1934), still the definitive one.

1. "Is there no Scots in me at all?" Mary asks her uncle when she is still in France. To what extent do you feel that Mary—who never knew her father and was brought up in France—was truly Scottish? How much does "blood" count?

2. What do you think of Mary's choice to go back to Scotland to take her place as queen there? How did both Scotland's needs and her own figure into that choice?

3. All of Mary's major decisions were impulsive—to go to Scotland, to marry Darnley and Bothwell, to flee to Elizabeth. She was a cool and quick thinker in physical crises, such as the Riccio murder and her own escapes—but not in politics, where she was unable to read character. Is it possible for someone like Mary to be an effective ruler?

4. Who was Mary's strongest adversary—Knox or Elizabeth? Short of converting, there was nothing that Mary could have done to placate Knox, but were there ways that she could have won Elizabeth?

5. Mary's reign has been described as "a series of plots and pardons." Do you see any rationale behind all of her plots, raids, and skullduggery?

6. Mary had a difficult time in Scotland from the moment she landed in a dense fog, and in some senses she never came out of that fog. What could she have done differently—when she first arrived, when deciding to marry, when dealing with the aftermath of Darnley's murder? At what point was it too late to salvage her reign? Is there any scenario that would have altered the end result?

A Reading Group Guide

St. Martin's Griffin

7. How do you view Mary's involvement with Bothwell? Do you find it foolhardy, or do you admire her for it?

8. Was Mary literally a *femme fatale*? "Those who love her seem to die untimely or unnatural deaths," Bothwell muses. Queen Elizabeth warned Norfolk to "take care of his pillow." What would you think if you were prospective bridegroom #4?

9. Elizabeth gained her crown at age twenty-five, while Mary lost hers at the same age. They also had vastly different childhoods: Elizabeth had to protect herself from the vicissitudes of plots at court, whereas Mary was in France, far removed from the turmoil in Scotland. In what ways did their upbringings—Mary's sheltered, Elizabeth's exposed—shape them as adults and as rulers?

10. It has been said of the Stuarts, "they did not know how to rule, but they knew how to die." Mary was the first Stuart to fail as a ruler but succeed in a glorious, memorable death scene. Did her death redeem her life? Was she a martyr to Catholicism, as she claimed, or largely playing a theatrical part?

St. Martin's
Griffin